HIGHGATE RISE

Anne Perry

FAWCETT COLUMBINE

New York

A Fawcett Columbine Book
Published by Ballantine Books
Copyright © 1991 by Anne Perry

All rights reserved under International and Pan-American Copyright
Conventions. Published in the United States by Ballantine Books,
a division of Random House, Inc., New York, and simultaneously in
Canada by Random House of Canada Limited, Toronto.

Perry, Anne.
Highgate rise / Anne Perry. — 1st ed.
p.   cm.
ISBN 0-449-90567-5
I. Title.
PR6066.E693H54   1991

823'.914—dc20

90-85131
CIP

Design by Holly Johnson

Manufactured in the United States of America

First Edition: May 1991
10   9   8   7   6   5   4   3   2   1

To Meg MacDonald, for her friendship
and her unfailing faith in me,
and
to Meg Davis, for her friendship
and her guidance and work.

HIGHGATE
RISE

CHAPTER

ONE

Inspector Thomas Pitt stared at the smoking ruins of the house, oblivious of the steady rain drenching him, plastering his hair over his forehead and running between his turned-up coat collar and his knitted muffler in a cold dribble down his back. He could still feel the heat coming from the mounds of blackened bricks. The water dripped from broken arches and sizzled where it hit the embers, rising in thin curls of steam.

Even from what was left of it he could see that it had been a gracious building, somebody's home, well constructed and elegant. Now there was little left but the servants' quarters.

Beside him Constable James Murdo shifted from one foot to the other. He was from the local Highgate station and he resented his superiors having called in a man from the city, even one with as high a reputation as Pitt's. They had hardly had a chance to deal with it themselves; there was no call to go sending for help this early—whatever the case proved to be. But his opinion had been ignored, and here was Pitt, scruffy, ill-clad apart from his boots, which were beautiful. His pockets bulged with nameless rubbish, his gloves were odd, and his face was smudged with soot and creased with sadness.

"Reckon it started almost midnight, sir," Murdo said, to show that his own force was efficient and had already done all that could be expected. "A Miss Dalton, elderly lady down on St. Alban's Road, saw it when she woke at about quarter past one. It was already burning fiercely and she raised the alarm, sent her maid to Colonel Anstruther's next door. He has one of those telephone instruments. And they were insured, so the fire brigade arrived about twenty minutes later, but there wasn't much they could do. By then all the main house was alight. They got water from the Highgate Ponds"—he waved his arm—"just across the fields there."

Pitt nodded, picturing the scene in his mind, the fear, the blistering heat driving the men backwards, the frightened horses, the canvas buckets passed from hand to hand, and the uselessness of it all. Everything would be shrouded in smoke and red with the glare as sheets of flame shot skywards and beams exploded with a roar, sending sparks high into the darkness. The stench of burning was still in the air, making the eyes smart and the back of the throat ache.

Unconsciously he wiped at a piece of smut on his cheek, and made it worse.

"And the body?" he asked.

Suddenly rivalry vanished as Murdo remembered the men stumbling out with the stretcher, white-faced. On it had been grotesque remains, burned so badly it was no longer even whole—and yet hideously, recognizably human. Murdo found his voice shaking as he replied.

"We believe it was Mrs. Shaw, sir; the wife of the local doctor, who owns the house. He's also the police surgeon, so we got a general practitioner from Hampstead, but he couldn't tell us much. But I don't think anyone could. Dr. Shaw's at a neighbor's now, a Mr. Amos Lindsay." He nodded up the Highgate Rise towards West Hill. "That house."

"Was he hurt?" Pitt asked, still looking at the ruins.

"No sir. He was out on a medical call. Woman giving birth— Dr. Shaw was there best part of the night. Only heard about this when he was on the way home."

"Servants?" Pitt turned away at last and looked at Murdo. "Seems as if that part of the house was the least affected."

"Yes sir; all the servants escaped, but the butler was very nastily burned and he's in hospital now; the St. Pancras Infirmary, just south of the cemetery. Cook's in a state of shock and being looked after by a relative over on the Seven Sisters Road. Housemaid's weeping all the time and says she should never 'ave left Dorset, and wants to go back. Maid of all work comes in by the day."

"But they are all accounted for, and none hurt except the butler?" Pitt persisted.

"That's right, sir. Fire was in the main house. The servants' wing was the last to catch, and the firemen got them all out." He shivered in spite of the smoldering wood and rubble in front of them and the mild September rain, easing now, and a watery afternoon sun catching the trees across the fields in Bishop's Wood. The wind was light and southerly, blowing up from the great city of London, where Kensington gardens were brilliant with flowers, nursemaids in starched aprons paraded their charges up and down the walks, bandsmen played stirring tunes. Carriages bowled along the Mall and fashionable ladies waved to each other and displayed the latest hats, and dashing ladies of less than perfect reputation cantered up Rotten Row in immaculate habits and made eyes at the gentlemen.

The Queen, dressed in black, still mourning the death of Prince Albert twenty-seven years ago, had secluded herself at Windsor.

And in the alleys of Whitechapel a madman disemboweled women, mutilated their faces and left their bodies grotesque and blood-drenched on the pavements—the popular press would soon call him Jack the Ripper.

Murdo hunched his shoulders and pulled his helmet a little straighter. "Just Mrs. Shaw that was killed, Inspector. And the fire seems, from what we can tell, to have started in at least four different places at once, and got a hold immediately, like the curtains had lamp oil on them." The muscles tightened in his young face. "You might spill oil on one curtain by accident, but not in four different rooms, and all of them catch alight at the same time and no one know about it. It has to be deliberate."

Pitt said nothing. It was because it was murder that he was standing here in the mangled garden beside this eager and resentful young constable with his fair skin soot-smudged and his eyes wide with shock and the pity of what he had seen.

"The question is," Murdo said quietly, "was it poor Mrs. Shaw they meant to kill—or was it the doctor?"

"There are a great many things we shall have to find out," Pitt answered grimly. "We'll begin with the fire chief."

"We've got his statement in the police station, sir. That's about half a mile back up the road." Murdo spoke a little stiffly, reminded of his own colleagues again.

Pitt followed him and in silence they walked. A few pale leaves fluttered along the pavement and a hansom cab rattled by. The houses were substantial. Respectable people with money lived here in considerable comfort on the west side of the road leading to the center of Highgate, with its public houses, solicitors' offices, shops, the water works, Pond Square, and the huge, elegant cemetery spreading to the southeast. Beyond the houses were fields on both sides, green and silent.

In the police station they welcomed Pitt civilly enough, but he knew from their tired faces and the way the juniors avoided his eyes that, like Murdo, they resented the necessity of having to call him in. All the forces in the London area were short staffed and all police leaves had been canceled to draft as many men as possible into the Whitechapel district to deal with the fearful murders which were shocking all London and making headlines across Europe.

The fire chief's report was all laid out waiting for him on the superintendent's desk, cleared for Pitt. He was gray-haired, quietly spoken and so civil that it accentuated rather than hid his resentment. He had a clean uniform on, but his face was pinched with weariness and there were burn blisters on his hands he had not had time to treat.

Pitt thanked him, making little of it so as not to draw attention to their sudden reversal of roles, and picked up the fire report. It was written in a neat, copperplate hand. The facts were simple, and only an elaboration of what Murdo had already told him. The fire had started simultaneously in four places, the curtains of the study, the library, the dining room and the withdrawing room, and had caught hold very swiftly, as if the fabric had been soaked in fuel oil. Like most others, the house was lit by gas, and as soon as the supply pipes had been reached they had exploded. The occupants would have had little chance of escape unless they had woken in the earliest stages and left through the servants' wing.

As it happened, Mrs. Clemency Shaw had probably been suffocated by smoke before she burned; and Dr. Stephen Shaw had been out on a medical emergency over a mile away. The servants had known nothing until the fire brigade bells had disturbed them and the firemen had set ladders at their windows to help them out.

It was nearly three o'clock and the rain had stopped when Pitt and Murdo knocked at the door of the neighbor immediately to the right of the burned house. It was opened less than a minute afterwards by the owner himself, a small man with a fine head of silver hair brushed back from his forehead in leonine waves. His expression was very earnest. There was a furrow of anxiety between his brows, and not a vestige of humor in the lines round his gentle, precise mouth.

"Good afternoon. Good afternoon," he said hastily. "You are the police. Yes, of course you are." Murdo's uniform made the observation unnecessary, although the man looked askance at Pitt. One did not recall the faces of police, as one did not of bus conductors, or drain cleaners, but lack of uniform was unexplained. He stood back and aside to make way for them readily.

"Come in. You want to know if I saw anything. Naturally. I cannot think how it happened. A most careful woman. Quite dreadful. Gas, I suppose. I have often thought perhaps we should not have abandoned candles. So much more agreeable." He turned around and led the way through the rather gloomy hall and into a large withdrawing room which over a space of years had been used more and more often as a study.

Pitt glanced around it with interest. It was highly individual and spoke much of the man. There were four large, very untidy bookshelves, obviously stocked for convenience and not ornament. There was no visual order, only that of frequent use. Paper folios were poked in next to leather-bound volumes, large books next to small. A gilt-framed and very romantic picture of Sir Galahad kneeling in holy vigil hung above the fireplace, and another opposite it of the Lady of Shallott drifting down the river with flowers in her hair. There was a fine model of a crusader on horseback on a round wooden table by the leather armchair, and open letters scattered on the desk. Three newspapers were piled precariously on the arm of the couch and clippings lay on the seats.

"Quinton Pascoe," their host said, introducing himself hastily. "But of course you know that. Here." He dived for the newspaper clippings and removed them to an open desk drawer, where they lay chaotically skewed. "Sit down, gentlemen. This is quite dreadful—quite dreadful. Mrs. Shaw was a very fine woman. A terrible loss. A tragedy."

Pitt sat down gingerly on the couch and ignored a crackle of newspaper behind the cushion. Murdo remained on his feet.

"Inspector Pitt—and Constable Murdo," he said, introducing them. "What time did you retire last night, Mr. Pascoe?"

Pascoe's eyebrows shot up, then he realized the point of the question.

"Oh—I see. A little before midnight. I am afraid I neither saw nor heard anything until the fire brigade bells disturbed me. Then, of course, there was the noise of the burning. Dreadful!" He shook his head, regarding Pitt apologetically. "I am afraid I sleep rather heavily. I feel a fearful guilt. Oh dear." He sniffed and blinked, turning his head towards the window and the wild, lush garden beyond, the tawny color of early autumn blooms still visible. "If I had retired a little later, even fifteen minutes, I might have seen the first flicker of flames, and raised the alarm." He screwed up his face as the vision became sharp in his mind. "I am so very sorry. Not much use being sorry, is there? Not now."

"Did you happen to look out at the street within the last half hour or so before you retired?" Pitt pressed him.

"I did not see the fire, Inspector," Pascoe said a trifle more sharply. "And for the life of me I cannot see the purpose in your repeatedly asking me. I mourn poor Mrs. Shaw. She was a very fine woman. But there is nothing any of us can do now, except—" He sniffed again and puckered his lips. "Except do what we can for poor Dr. Shaw—I suppose."

Murdo fidgeted almost imperceptibly and his eyes flickered to Pitt, and back again.

It would be common knowledge soon and Pitt could think of no advantage secrecy would give.

He leaned forward and the newspaper behind the cushion crackled again.

"The fire was not an accident, Mr. Pascoe. Of course the gas exploding will have made it worse, but it cannot have begun it. It started independently in several places at once. Apparently windows."

"Windows? What on earth do you mean? Windows don't burn, man! Just who are you?"

"Inspector Thomas Pitt, from the Bow Street station, sir."

"Bow Street?" Pascoe's white eyebrows rose in amazement. "But Bow Street is in London—miles from here. What is wrong with our local station?"

"Nothing," Pitt said, keeping his temper with difficulty. It was going to be hard enough to preserve amicable relations without comments like this in Murdo's hearing. "But the superintendent regards the matter as very grave, and wants to have it cleared up as rapidly as possible. The fire chief tells us that the fire started at the windows, as if the curtains were the first to catch alight, and heavy curtains burn very well, especially if soaked in candle oil or paraffin first."

"Oh my God!" Pascoe's face lost every shred of its color. "Are you saying someone set it intentionally—to kill— No!" He shook his head fiercely. "Rubbish! Absolute tommyrot! No one would murder Clemency Shaw. It must have been Dr. Shaw they were after. Where was he anyway? Why wasn't he at home? I could understand it if—" He stopped speaking and sat staring at the floor miserably.

"Did you see anyone, Mr. Pascoe?" Pitt repeated, watching his hunched figure. "A person walking, a coach or carriage, a light, anything at all."

"I—" He sighed. "I went for a walk in my garden before going upstairs. I had been working on a paper which had given me some trouble." He cleared his throat sharply, hesitated a moment, then his emotion got the better of him and the words poured out. "In rebuttal of a quite preposterous claim of Dalgetty's about Richard Coeur de Leon." His voice caressed the romance of the name. "You don't know John Dalgetty—why should you? He is an utterly irresponsible person, quite without self-control or a proper sense of the decencies." His expression crumpled with revulsion at such a thing. "Book reviewers have a duty, you know." His eyes fixed Pitt's. "We mold opinion. It matters what we sell to the public, and what we praise or condemn. But Dalgetty would rather allow all the values of chivalry and honor to be mocked or ignored, in the name of liberty, but in truth he means license." He jerked up and waved his hands expansively, wrists limp, to emphasize the very slackness he described. "He supported that fearful monograph of Amos Lindsay's on this new political philosophy. Fabians, they call themselves, but what he is writing amounts to anarchy—sheer chaos. Taking property away from the people who rightfully own it is theft, plain and simple, and people won't stand for it. There'll be blood in the streets if it gains any number of followers." His jaw tightened with the effort of controlling his anguish. "We'll see Englishmen fighting Englishmen on our own soil. But Lindsay wrote as if he thought there were some kind of natural justice in it: taking away people's private property and sharing it out with everyone, regardless of their diligence or honesty—or even of their ability to value it or preserve it." He stared at Pitt intensely. "Just think of the destruction. Think of the waste. And the monstrous injustice. Everything we've worked for and cherished—" His voice was high from the constriction of his throat by his emotions. "Everything we've inherited down the generations, all the beauty, the treasures of the past, and of course that fool Shaw was all for it too."

His hands had been clenched, his body tight, now suddenly he remembered that Pitt was a policeman who probably possessed nothing—and then he also remembered why Pitt was here. His shoulders slumped again. "I am sorry. I should not so criticize a man bereaved. It is shameful."

"You went for a walk . . ." Pitt prompted.

"Oh yes. My eyes were tired, and I wished to refresh myself, restore my inner well-being, my sense of proportion in things. I walked in my garden." He smiled benignly at the memory. "It was a most agreeable evening, a good moon, only shreds of cloud across it and a light wind from the south. Do you know I heard a nightingale sing? Quite splendid. Could reduce one to tears. Lovely. Lovely. I went to bed with a great peace within me." He blinked. "How dreadful. Not twenty yards away such wickedness, and a woman struggling for her life against impossible odds, and I quite oblivious."

Pitt looked at the imagination and the guilt in the man's face.

"It is possible, Mr. Pascoe, that even had you been awake all night, you would not have seen or heard anything until it was too late. Fire catches very quickly when it is set with intent; and Mrs. Shaw may have been killed in her sleep by the smoke without ever waking."

"Might she?" Pascoe's eyes opened wide. "Indeed? I do hope so. Poor creature. She was a fine woman, you know. Far too good for Shaw. An insensitive man, without ideals of a higher sort. Not that he isn't a good medical practitioner, and a gentleman," he added hastily. "But without the finer perceptions. He thinks it witty and progressive to make mock of people's values. Oh dear—one should not speak so ill of the bereaved, but truth will out. I profoundly regret that I cannot help you."

"May we question your resident servants, Mr. Pascoe?" Pitt asked only as a formality. He had every intention of questioning them whatever Pascoe said.

"Of course. Of course. But please try not to alarm them. Reasonable cooks are so extremely hard to get, especially in a bachelor household like mine. If they are any good they want to give dinner parties and such things—and I have little occasion, just a few literary colleagues now and then."

Pitt rose and Murdo stood to attention. "Thank you."

But neither the cook nor the manservant had seen anything at all, and the scullery maid and housemaid were twelve and fourteen, respectively, and too horrified to do anything but twist their aprons in their hands and deny even being awake. And considering that their duties required them to be up at five in the morning, Pitt had no difficulty in believing them.

Next they visited the house to the south. On this stretch of Highgate Rise the fields opposite fell away towards a path, which Murdo said was called Bromwich Walk, and led from the parsonage of St. Anne's Church to the south, parallel with the Rise, and ended in Highgate itself.

"Very accessible, sir," Murdo finished gloomily. "At that time o' the night a hundred people with pocketsful o' matches could have crept down here and no one would have seen them." He was beginning to think this whole exercise was a waste of time, and it showed in his frank face.

Pitt smiled dryly. "Don't you think they'd have bumped into each other, Constable?"

Murdo failed to see the point. He had been sarcastic. Could this inspector from Bow Street really be so unintelligent? He looked more carefully at the rather homely face with its long nose, slightly chipped front tooth and untidy hair; then saw the light in the eyes, and the humor and strength in the mouth. He changed his mind.

"In the dark," Pitt elaborated. "There might have been enough moon for Mr. Pascoe to gaze at, but a cloudy night, and no house lights—curtains drawn and lamps out by midnight."

"Oh." Murdo saw the purpose at last. "Whoever it was would have had to carry a lantern, and at that time of night even a match struck would show if anyone happened to be looking."

"Exactly." Pitt shrugged. "Not that a light helps us much, unless anyone also saw which way it came from. Let us try Mr. Alfred Lutterworth and his household."

It was a magnificent establishment, no expense spared, the last one on this stretch of the road, and twice the size of the others. Pitt followed his custom of knocking at the front door. He refused to go to the tradesmen's entrance as police and such other inferiors and undesirables were expected to. It was opened after a few moments by a very smart parlormaid in a gray stuff dress and crisp, lace-edged cap and apron. Her expression betrayed immediately that she knew Pitt should have been at the scullery door, even if he did not.

"Trade at the back," she said with a slight lift of her chin.

"I have called to see Mr. Lutterworth, not the butler," Pitt said tartly. "I imagine he receives his callers at the front?"

"He don't receive police at all." She was just as quick.

"He will today." Pitt stepped in and she was obliged to move back or stand nose-to-chest with him. Murdo was both horrified and struck with admiration. "I am sure he will wish to help discover who murdered Mrs. Shaw last night." Pitt removed his hat.

The parlormaid went almost as white as her apron and Pitt was lucky she did not faint. Her waist was so tiny her stays must have been tight enough to choke a less determined spirit.

"Oh Lor'!" She recovered herself with an effort. "I thought it were an accident."

"I am afraid not." Pitt followed up his rather clumsy beginning as best he could. He should be past allowing his pride to be stung by a maid by now. "Did you happen to look out of your window around midnight and perhaps see a moving light, or hear anything unusual?"

"No I didn't—" She hesitated. "But Alice, the tweeny, was up, and she told me this morning she saw a ghost outside. But she's a bit daft, like. I don't know if she dreamt it."

"I'll speak to Alice," Pitt replied with a smile. "It may be important. Thank you."

Very slowly she smiled back. "If you'll wait in the morning room, I'll tell Mr. Lutterworth as you're 'ere . . . sir."

The room they were shown to was unusually gracious, not merely that the owner had money, but he also had far better taste than perhaps he knew. Pitt had time only to glance at the watercolors on the walls. They were certainly valuable, the sale of any one of them would have fed a family for a decade, but they were also genuinely beautiful, and entirely right in their setting, wooing the eye, not assaulting it.

Alfred Lutterworth was in his late fifties with a fresh complexion, at the moment considerably flushed, and a rim of smooth white hair around a shining head. He was of good height and solidly built, with the assured stance of a self-made man. His face was strong featured. In a gentleman it might have been considered handsome, but there was something both belligerent and uncertain in it that betrayed his sense of not belonging, for all his wealth.

"My maid tells me you're 'ere about Mrs. Shaw bein' murdered in that fire," Lutterworth said with a strong Lancashire accent. "That right? Them girls reads penny dreadfuls in the cupboard under the stairs an' 'as imaginations like the worst kind o' novelists."

"Yes sir, I'm afraid it is true," Pitt replied. He introduced himself and Murdo, and explained the reason for their questions.

"Bad business," Lutterworth said grimly. "She was a good woman. Too good for most o' the likes o' them 'round 'ere. 'Ceptin' Maude Dalgetty. She's another—no side to 'er, none at all. Civil to everyone." He shook his head. "But I didn't see a thing. Waited up till I 'eard Flora come 'ome, that were twenty afore midnight. Then I turned the light down and went to sleep sound, until the fire bells woke me. Could 'a marched an army past in the street before that an' I'd not 'ave 'eard 'em."

"Flora is Miss Lutterworth?" Pitt asked, although he already knew from the Highgate police's information.

"That's right, me daughter. She was out with some friends at a lecture and slide show down at St. Alban's Road. That's just south of 'ere, beyond the church."

Murdo stiffened to attention.

"Did she walk home, sir?" Pitt asked.

"It's only a few steps." Lutterworth's deep-set, rather good eyes regarded Pitt sharply, expecting criticism. "She's a healthy lass."

"I would like to ask her if she saw anything." Pitt kept his voice level. "Women can be very observant."

"You mean nosey," Lutterworth agreed ruefully. "Aye. My late wife, God rest 'er, noticed an 'undred things about folk I never did. An' she was right, nine times out o' ten." For a moment his memory was so clear it obliterated the police in his house or the smell of water on burnt brick and wood still acrid in the air, in spite of the closed windows. From the momentary softness in his eyes and the half smile on his lips they bore nothing but sweetness. Then he recalled the present. "Aye—if you want to." He reached over to the mantel and pulled the knob of the bell set on the wall. It was porcelain, and painted with miniature flowers. An instant later the parlormaid appeared at the door.

"Tell Miss Flora as I want 'er, Polly," he ordered. "To speak to the police."

"Yes sir." And she departed hastily, whisking her skirts around the door as she closed it again.

"Uppity, that lass," Lutterworth said under his breath. "Got opinions; but she's 'andsome enough, and that's what parlormaids 'as to be. And I suppose one can't blame 'er."

Flora Lutterworth must have been impelled as much by curiosity as her servants, because she came obediently even though her high chin and refusal to meet her father's eyes, coupled with a fire in her cheeks equal to his, suggested they had very recently had a heated difference of opinion about something, which was still unresolved.

She was a fine-looking girl, tall and slender with wide eyes and a cloud of dark hair. She avoided traditional beauty by the angularity of her cheekbones and surprisingly crooked front teeth. It was a face of strong character, and Pitt was not in the least surprised she had quarreled with her father. He could imagine a hundred subjects on which she would have fierce opinions at odds with his—everything from which pages of the newspaper she should be permitted to read to the price of a hat, or the time she came home, and with whom.

"Good afternoon, Miss Lutterworth," he said courteously. "No doubt you are fully aware of the tragedy last night. May I ask you, did you see anyone on your way home from the lecture, either a stranger or someone you know?"

"Someone I know?" The thought obviously startled her.

"If you did, we should like to speak to them in case they saw or heard anything." It was at least partly the truth. There was no point in making her feel as if she would automatically be accusing someone.

"Ah." Her face cleared. "I saw Dr. Shaw's trap go past just as we were leaving the Howards'."

"How do you know it was his?"

"No one else around here has one like that." She had no trace of Lancashire in her voice. Apparently her father had paid for elocution lessons so she should sound the lady he wished her, and even in his temper, now that her attention was engaged elsewhere, his eyes rested on her with warmth. "Anyway," she continued, "I could see his face quite clearly in the carriage lamps."

"Anyone else?" Pitt asked.

"You mean coming this way? Well, Mr. Lindsay came a few moments after us—I was walking with Mr. Arroway and the Misses Barking. They went on up to the Grove in Highgate itself. Mr. and Mrs. Dalgetty were just ahead of us. I don't recall anyone else. I'm sorry."

He pressed her for further descriptions of the evening and the names of everyone attending, but learned nothing that he felt would be of use. The occasion had ended a little too early for the fire setter, and in all probability he, or she, would have waited until such a function was well over before venturing out. They must have supposed themselves to have several hours at least.

He thanked her, asked permission to speak to the tweeny and the rest of the staff, and accordingly he and Murdo were shown to the housekeeper's sitting room, where he heard the twelve-year-old between maid's story of seeing a ghost with burning yellow eyes flitting between the bushes in next-door's garden. She did not know what time it was. The middle of the night. She had heard the clock in the hall strike ever so many times, and there was no one else about at all, all the gas lamps on the landing below were dimmed right down and she daren't call anyone, terrified as she was. She had crept back to bed and put the covers over her head, and that was all she knew, she swore it.

Pitt thanked her gently—she was only a few years older than his own daughter, Jemima—and told her she had been a great help. She blushed and bobbed a curtsey, losing her balance a little, then retreated in some confusion. It was the first time in her life that an adult had listened to her seriously.

"Do you reckon that was our murderer, Inspector?" Murdo

asked as they came out onto the footpath again. "That girl's ghost?"

"A moving light in Shaw's garden? Probably. We'll have to follow up all the people Flora Lutterworth saw as she left the lecture. One of them may have seen somebody."

"Very observant young lady, very sensible, I thought," Murdo said, then colored pink. "I mean she recounted it all very clearly. No, er, no melodrama."

"None at all," Pitt agreed with the shadow of a smile. "A young woman of spirit, I think. She may well have had more to say if her father were not present. I imagine they do not see eye to eye on everything."

Murdo opened his mouth to reply, then found himself in confusion as to what he wanted to say, and swallowed hard without saying anything.

Pitt's smile widened and he increased his rather gangling pace up the pavement towards the house of Amos Lindsay, where the widower Dr. Shaw was taking refuge, being not only bereaved but now also homeless.

The house was far smaller than the Lutterworths', and as soon as they were inside they could not help being aware it was also of highly eccentric character. The owner was apparently at one time an explorer and anthropologist. Carvings of varied nature and origin decked the walls, crowded together on shelves and tables, and even stood in huddles on the floor. From Pitt's very restricted knowledge he took them to be either African or central Asian. He saw nothing Egyptian, Oriental or from the Americas, nothing that had the subtle but familiar smoothness of the classicism that was the heritage of western European culture. There was something alien in it, a barbaric rawness at odds with the very conventional Victorian middle-class interior architecture.

They were conducted in by a manservant with an accent Pitt could not place and a skin no darker than many Englishmen's, but of an unusual smoothness, and hair that might have been drawn on his head with India ink. His manners were impeccable.

Amos Lindsay himself was eminently English in appearance, short, stocky and white-haired, and yet totally unlike

Pascoe. Where Pascoe was essentially an idealist harking back to an age of medieval chivalry in Europe, Lindsay was a man of insatiable and indiscriminate curiosity—and irreverence for establishment, as his furnishings showed. But his mind was voyaging outward to the mysteries of savagery and the unknown. His skin was deep furrowed both by the dominant nature of his features and by the severity of tropical sun. His eyes were small and shrewd, those of a realist, not a dreamer. His whole aspect acknowledged humor and the absurdities of life.

Now he was very grave and met Pitt and Murdo in his study, having no use for a morning room.

"Good evening," he said civilly. "Dr. Shaw is in the withdrawing room. I hope you will not ask him a lot of idiotic questions that anyone else could answer."

"No sir," Pitt assured him. "Perhaps towards that end you might answer a few for us before we meet Dr. Shaw?"

"Of course. Although I cannot imagine what you think there is to learn from us. But since you are here, you must suppose, in spite of the unlikelihood of it, that it was in some way criminal." He looked acutely at Pitt. "I went to bed at nine; I rise early. I neither saw nor heard anything, nor did my domestic staff. I have already asked them because quite naturally they were alarmed and distressed by the noise of the fire. I have no idea what manner of person might do such a thing with intent, nor any sane reason why. But then the mind of man is capable of almost any contortion or delusion whatever."

"Do you know Dr. and Mrs. Shaw well?"

Lindsay was unsurprised. "I know him well. He is one of the few local men I find it easy to converse with. Open-minded, not pickled in tradition like most around here. A man of considerable intelligence and wit. Not common qualities—and not always appreciated."

"And Mrs. Shaw?" Pitt continued.

"Not so well. One doesn't, of course. Can't discuss with a woman in the same way as with a man. But she was a fine woman; sensible, compassionate, modest without unctuousness, no humbug about her. All the best female qualities."

"What did she look like?"

"What?" Lindsay was obviously surprised. Then his face creased into a comic mixture of humor and indecision. "Matter of opinion, I suppose. Dark, good features, bit heavy in the—" He colored and his hands waved vaguely in the air. Pitt judged they would have described the curve of hips, had not his sense of propriety stopped him. "Good eyes, intelligent and mild. Sounds like a horse—I apologize. Handsome woman, that's my judgment. And she walked well. No doubt you'll talk to the Worlingham sisters, her aunts; Clemency resembles Celeste a trifle, not Angeline."

"Thank you. Perhaps we should meet Dr. Shaw now?"

"Of course." And without further speech he led them back into the hall, and then with a brief warning knock he opened the withdrawing room door.

Pitt ignored the remarkable curios on the walls, and his eyes went immediately to the man standing by the hearth, whose face was drained of emotion, but whose body was still tense, waiting for some action or demand upon it. He turned as he heard the door latch, but there was no interest in his eyes, only acknowledgment of duty. His skin had the pallor of shock, pinched at the sides of the lips and bruised around the eye sockets. His features were strong, and even bereavement in such fearful circumstances could not remove the wit and intelligence from him, nor the caustic individualism Pitt had heard others speak of.

"Good evening, Dr. Shaw," Pitt said formally. "I am Inspector Pitt, from Bow Street, and this is Constable Murdo from the local station. I regret it is necessary that we ask you some distressing questions—"

"Of course." Shaw cut off his explanations. As Murdo had said, he was a police surgeon and he understood. "Ask what you must. But first, tell me what you know. Are you sure it was arson?"

"Yes sir. There is no possibility that the fire started simultaneously in four different places, all accessible from the outside, and with no normal household reason, such as a spark from the hearth or a candle spilled in a bedroom or on the stairs."

"Where did they start?" Shaw was curious now and unable to remain standing on the spot. He began to move about, first to one table, then another, automatically straightening things, compulsively making them tidier.

Pitt stood where he was, near the sofa.

"The fire chief says it was in the curtains," he replied. "In every case."

Shaw's face showed skepticism, quick and even now with a vestige of humor and critical perception which must normally be characteristic in him. "How does he know that? There wasn't much"—he swallowed—"left of my home."

"Pattern of the burning," Pitt answered gravely. "What was completely consumed, what was damaged but still partially standing; and where rubble and glass falls shows to some extent where the heat was greatest first."

Shaw shook himself impatiently. "Yes, of course. Stupid question. I'm sorry." He passed a strong, well-shaped hand over his brow, pushing straight fair hair out of his way. "What do you want from me?"

"What time were you called out, sir, and by whom?" He was half aware of Murdo by the door, pencil and notebook in hand.

"I didn't look at the clock," Shaw answered. "About quarter past eleven. Mrs. Wolcott was in childbirth—her husband went to a neighbor's with a telephone."

"Where do they live?"

"Over in Kentish Town." He had an excellent voice with clear diction and a timbre that was unique and remarkably pleasing. "I took the trap and drove. I was there all night until the child was delivered. I was on the way home about five o'clock when the police met me—and told me what had happened—and that Clemency was dead."

Pitt had seen many people in the first hours of loss; it had often been his duty to bear the news. It never failed to distress him.

"It's ironic," Shaw continued, not looking at anyone. "She had intended to go out with Maude Dalgetty and spend the night with friends in Kensington. It was canceled at the last moment. And Mrs. Wolcott was not due for another week. I should have been at home, and Clemency away." He did not add the obvious conclusion. It hung in the silent room. Lindsay stood somber and motionless. Murdo glanced at Pitt and his thoughts were naked for a moment in his face. Pitt knew them already.

"Who was aware that Mrs. Shaw had changed her mind, sir?" he asked.

Shaw met his eyes. "No one but Maude Dalgetty and myself," he replied. "And I assume John Dalgetty. I don't know who else they told. But they didn't know about Mrs. Wolcott. No one did."

Lindsay was standing beside him. He put his hand on Shaw's shoulder in a steadying gesture of friendship. "You have a distinctive trap, Stephen. Whoever it was may have seen you leave and supposed the house empty."

"Then why burn it?" Shaw said grimly.

Lindsay tightened his grip. "God knows! Why do pyromaniacs do anything? Hatred of those who have more than they? A sense of power—to watch the flames? I don't know."

Pitt would not bother to ask whether the home was insured, or for how much; it would be easier and more accurate to inquire through the insurance companies—and less offensive.

There was a knock on the door and the manservant reappeared.

"Yes?" Lindsay said irritably.

"The vicar and his wife have called to convey their condolences to Dr. Shaw, sir, and to offer comfort. Shall I ask them to wait?"

Lindsay turned to Pitt, not for his permission, of course, but to see if he had finished any painful questioning and might now retreat.

Pitt hesitated for a moment, uncertain whether there was anything further he could learn from Shaw now, or if in common humanity he should allow whatever religious comfort there might be and defer his own questions. Perhaps he would actually learn more of Shaw by watching him with those who knew him and had known his wife.

"Inspector?" Lindsay pressed him.

"Of course," Pitt conceded, although from the expression

of defiance and something close to alarm in Shaw's face, he doubted the vicar's religious comfort was what he presently desired.

Lindsay nodded and the manservant withdrew, a moment later ushering in a mild, very earnest man in clerical garb. He looked as if he had been athletic in his youth, but now in his forties had become a little lax. There was too much diffidence in him for good looks, but there was nothing of malice or arrogance in his regular features and rather indecisive mouth. His surface attempt at calm masked a deep nervousness, and the occasion was obviously far from being his element.

He was accompanied by a woman with a plain, intelligent face, a little too heavy of eyebrow and strong of nose to be appealing to most people, but a good-natured mouth. In contrast to her husband she projected an intense energy, and it was all directed towards Shaw. She barely saw Lindsay or Pitt, and made no accommodation to them in her manner. Murdo was invisible.

"Ah . . . hem—" The vicar was plainly confused to see the police still there. He had prepared what he was going to say, and now it did not fit the circumstances and he had nothing else in reserve. "Ah . . . Reverend Hector Clitheridge." He introduced himself awkwardly. "My wife, Eulalia." He indicated the woman beside him, waving his hand, thick wristed and with white cuffs a size too large.

Then he turned to Shaw and his expression altered. He was apparently laboring under some difficulty. He wavered between natural distaste and alarm, and hard-won resolution.

"My dear Shaw, how can I say how sorry I am for this tragedy." He took half a step forward. "Quite appalling. In the midst of life we are in death. How fragile is human existence in this vale of tears. Suddenly we are struck down. How may we comfort you?"

"Not with platitudes, dammit!" Shaw said tartly.

"Yes, well—I'm sure . . ." Clitheridge floundered, his face pink.

"People only say some things so often because they are true, Dr. Shaw," Mrs. Clitheridge said with an eager smile, her eyes on Shaw's face. "How else can we express our feelings for you, and our desire to offer consolation."

"Yes quite—quite," Clitheridge added unnecessarily. "I will take care of any—any, er . . . arrangements you care to—er . . . Of course it is soon—er . . ." He tailed off, looking at the floor.

"Thank you," Shaw cut across. "I'll let you know."

"Of course. Of course." Clitheridge was patently relieved.

"In the meantime, dear doctor . . ." Mrs. Clitheridge took a step forward, her eyes bright, her back very straight under her dark bombazine, as if she were approaching something exciting and a little dangerous. "In the meantime, we offer you our condolences, and please feel you may call upon us for anything at all, any task that you would prefer not to perform yourself. My time is yours."

Shaw looked across at her and the ghost of a smile touched his face. "Thank you, Eulalia. I am sure you mean it kindly."

The blush deepened in her face, but she said no more. The use of her Christian name was a familiarity, particularly in front of such social inferiors as the police. Pitt thought from the lift of Shaw's brows that even now he had done it deliberately, an automatic instinct to sweep away pretense.

For a moment Pitt saw them all in a different light, six people in a room, all concerned with the violent death of a woman very close to them, trying to find comfort for themselves and each other, and they observed all the social niceties, masked all the simplicity of real emotion with talk of letters and rituals. And the old habits and reactions were there too: Clitheridge's reliance on quoting predictable Scriptures, Eulalia's stepping in for him. Something in her was wakened to a sharper life by Shaw's personality, and it both pleased and disturbed her. Duty won. Perhaps duty always won.

From Shaw's tight body and restless movements none of it reached more than a surface, intellectual humor in him. The ache underneath he would bear utterly alone—unless Lindsay had some frank expression that could bridge the gulf.

Pitt stepped back out of the center of the floor and stood next to the patterned curtains, watching. He glanced at Murdo to make sure he did the same.

"Are you going to remain here with Mr. Lindsay?" Eulalia inquired solicitously of Shaw. "I assure you, you would be most welcome at the parsonage, if you wish. And you could remain as long as suited you—until . . . er, of course you will purchase another house—"

"Not yet, my dear, not yet," Clitheridge said in a loud whisper. "First we must, er, organize—deal with the—er, spiritual—"

"Nonsense!" she hissed back at him. "The poor man has to sleep somewhere. One cannot deal with emotions until one has accommodated the creature."

"It is the other way 'round, Lally!" He was getting cross. "Please allow me—"

"Thank you." Shaw interrupted, swinging around from the small table where he had been fingering an ornament. "I shall remain with Amos. But I am sensible of your kindness—and you are perfectly correct, Eulalia, as always. One can grieve far more adequately in some physical comfort. There is no advantage whatsoever in having to worry about where to sleep or what to eat."

Clitheridge bridled, but offered no demur; the opposition was far too much for him.

He was saved from further argument by the manservant's reappearance to announce yet more callers.

"Mr. and Mrs. Hatch, sir." There was no question as to whether they should be received. Pitt was curious.

"Of course." Lindsay nodded.

The couple who were admitted a moment later were soberly, even starkly dressed, she in total black, he in a winged collar, black tie and high-buttoned suit of indeterminate dark shade. His face was composed in extreme gravity, tight-lipped, pale, and his eyes brilliant with contained emotion. It was a countenance that caught Pitt's attention with its intensity as passionate as Shaw's, and yet by every innate inclination different—guarded and inward of thought where Shaw was rash and quickly expressive; abstemious and melancholy where Shaw was full of vitality and a wild humor; and yet the possibilities of depth were the same, the power of emotion.

But it was Mrs. Hatch who came forward first, ignoring

everyone else and going straight to Shaw, which seemed to be what he expected. He put both arms around her and held her.

"My dear Prudence."

"Oh, Stephen, this is quite dreadful." She accepted his embrace without hesitation. "How can it have happened? I was sure Clemency was in London with the Bosinneys. At least thank God you were not there!"

Shaw said nothing. For once he had no answer.

There was an uncomfortable silence as if others who felt the emotions less deeply were embarrassed by their exclusion and would rather not have witnessed them.

"Mrs. Shaw's sister," Murdo whispered, leaning closer to Pitt. "Both ladies are daughters of the late Theophilus Worlingham."

Pitt had never heard of Theophilus Worlingham, but apparently he was a person of some repute from the awe in Murdo's voice.

Josiah Hatch cleared his throat to draw the episode to a conclusion. Proprieties must be observed, and he had become aware of the shadowy figures of Pitt and Murdo in the unlit corner of the room, not part of the event, and yet intrusively present.

"We must comfort ourselves with faith," he continued. He looked sideways at Clitheridge. "I am sure the vicar has already spoken words of strength to you." It sounded almost like a charge, as if he were not sure at all. "This is a time when we call upon our inner resources and remember that God is with us, even in the valley of the shadow, and His will shall be done."

It was a statement at once banal and unarguable, and yet he was painfully sincere.

As if catching some honesty in the man, Shaw pushed Prudence away gently and answered him.

"Thank you, Josiah. It is a relief to me to know you will be there to sustain Prudence."

"Of course," Hatch agreed. "It is a man's godly duty to support women through their times of grief and affliction. They are naturally weaker, and more sensitive to such things. It is their gentleness and the purity of their minds which make them so perfectly suited to motherhood and the nurturing of tender youth, so we must thank God for it. I remember dear Bishop Worlingham saying so much to that effect when I was a young man."

He did not look at any of them, but to some distance of his own memory. "I shall never cease to be grateful for the time in my youth I spent with him." A spasm of pain crossed his face. "My own father's refusal to allow me to enter the church was almost offset by that great man's tutelage of me in the ways of the spirit and the path of true Christianity."

He looked at his wife. "Your grandfather, my dear, was as close to a saint as we are like to see in this poor world. He is very sadly missed—sadly indeed. He would have known precisely how to deal with a loss like this, what to say to each of us to explain divine wisdom so we should all be at peace with it."

"Indeed—indeed," Clitheridge said inadequately.

Hatch looked at Lindsay. "Before your time, sir, which is your misfortune. Bishop Augustus Worlingham was quite remarkable, a great Christian gentleman and benefactor to uncounted men and women, both materially and spiritually. His influence was incalculable." He leaned forward a fraction, his face creased with earnestness. "No one can say how many are now following a righteous path because of his life here on this earth. I know of dozens myself." He stared at Lindsay. "The Misses Wycombe, all three of them, went to nurse the sick entirely on his inspiration, and Mr. Bartford took the cloth and set up a mission in Africa. No one can measure the domestic happiness resulting from his counsel on the proper place and duties of women in the home. A far wider area than merely Highgate has been blessed by his life . . ."

Lindsay looked nonplussed, but did not interrupt. Perhaps he could think of nothing adequate to say.

Shaw clenched his teeth and looked at the ceiling.

Mrs. Hatch bit her lip and glanced nervously at Shaw.

Hatch plunged on, a new eagerness in his voice, his eyes bright. "No doubt you have heard of the window we are dedicating to him in St. Anne's Church? It is planned already and we need only a little more money. It is a representation of the bishop himself, as the prophet Jeremiah, teaching the people from the Old Testament; with angels at his shoulders."

Shaw's jaw clenched, and he refrained from saying anything with apparent difficulty.

"Yes—yes, I heard," Lindsay said hastily. He was patently embarrassed. He glanced at Shaw, now moving as if he could barely contain the pent-up energy inside him. "I am sure it will be a beautiful window, and much admired."

"That is hardly the point," Hatch said sharply, his mouth puckering with anger. "Beauty is not at issue, my dear sir. It is the upliftment of souls. It is the saving of lives from sin and ignorance, it is to remind the faithful what journey it is we make, and to what end." He shook his head a little as if to rid himself of the immediacy of the very solid materiality around him. "Bishop Worlingham was a righteous man, with a great understanding of the order of things, our place in God's purpose. We permit his influence to be lost at our peril. This window will be a monument to him, towards which people will raise their eyes every Sunday, and through which God's holy light will pour in upon them."

"For heaven's sake, man, the light would come through whatever window you put in the wall," Shaw snapped at last. "In fact you'd get most of it if you stood outside in the grave-yard in the fresh air."

"I was speaking figuratively," Hatch replied with suppressed fury in his eyes. "Must you see everything in such earthbound terms? At least in this terrible time of bereavement, lift your soul to eternal things." He blinked fiercely, his lips white and his voice trembling. "God knows, this is dreadful enough."

The momentary quarrel vanished and grief replaced anger. Shaw stood motionless, the first time he had been totally still since Pitt had arrived.

"Yes—I—" He could not bring himself to apologize. "Yes, of course. The police are here. It was arson."

"What?" Hatch was aghast. The blood fled from his face and he swayed a little on his feet. Lindsay moved towards him in case he should fall. Prudence swung back and held out her arms, then the meaning of what Shaw had said struck her and she also stood appalled.

"Arson! You mean someone set fire to the house intentionally?"

"That is right."

"So it was"—she swallowed, composing herself with difficulty—"murder."

"Yes." Shaw put his hand on her shoulder. "I'm sorry, my dear. But that is what the police are here for."

For the first time both she and Hatch turned their attention to Pitt with a mixture of alarm and distaste. Hatch squared his shoulders and addressed Pitt with difficulty, ignoring Murdo.

"Sir, there is nothing whatsoever that we can tell you. If indeed it was deliberate, then look to some vagabond. In the meantime, leave us to bear our grief in private, in the name of humanity."

It was late and Pitt was tired, hungry and weary of pain, the stench of stale smoke, and the itch of ash inside his clothes. He had no more questions to ask. He had seen the forensic evidence and learned what little there was to be concluded from it. It was no vagabond responsible; it was carefully laid with intent to destroy, probably to kill—but by whom? Either way the answer would lie in the hearts of the people who knew Stephen and Clemency Shaw, perhaps someone he had already seen, or heard mentioned.

"Yes sir," he agreed with a sense of relief. "Thank you for your attention." He said this last to Shaw and Lindsay. "When I learn anything I shall inform you."

"What?" Shaw screwed up his face. "Oh—yes, of course. Goodnight—er—Inspector."

Pitt and Murdo withdrew and a few minutes later were walking up the quiet street by the light of Murdo's lantern, back towards Highgate Police Station, and for Pitt a long hansom ride home.

"Do you reckon it was Mrs. Shaw or the doctor they were after?" Murdo asked after they had gone a couple of hundred yards and the night wind was blowing with a touch of frost in their faces.

"Either," Pitt replied. "But if it was Mrs. Shaw, then it seems so far only Mr. and Mrs. Dalgetty, and the good doctor himself, knew she was at home."

"Lot of people might want to kill a doctor, I suppose," Murdo said thoughtfully. "I imagine doctors get to know a lot of folks' secrets, one way or another."

"Indeed," Pitt agreed, shivering and quickening his pace a little. "And if that is so, the doctor may know who it is—and they may try again."

CHAPTER
TWO

Charlotte had done half the linen and her arm was tired with the weight of the flatiron. She had stitched three pillowcases and mended Jemima's best dress. Now she had stuffed it in her needlework basket and pushed it all away where it could not be seen, at least not at a casual glance, which was the most Pitt would give the corner of the room when he came in.

It was already nearly nine o'clock and she had long been straining at every creak and bump waiting for him. Now she tried to take her mind from it, and sat on the floor in a most undignified position, reading *Jane Eyre*. When Pitt did come at last she was quite unaware of it until he had taken off his overcoat and hung it up and was standing in the doorway.

"Oh, Thomas!" She put the book aside and scrambled to her feet, disentangling her skirt with considerable difficulty. "Thomas, where on earth have you been? You smell terrible."

"A fire," he replied, kissing her, touching only her face with his lips, not holding her where the smut and grime would soil her dress.

She heard the weariness in his voice, and something more, an experience of tragedy.

"A fire?" she asked, holding his gaze. "Did someone die in it?"

"A woman."

She looked up at his face. "Murder?"

"Yes."

She hesitated, seeing the crumpled, grimy clothes, still wet in places from the afternoon's rain, and then the expression in his eyes.

"Do you want to eat, wash, or tell me about it?"

He smiled. There was something faintly ludicrous in her candor, especially after the careful manners of the Clitheridges and the Hatches.

"A cup of tea, my boots off, and then later hot water," he replied honestly.

She accepted that as declining to talk, and hurried through to the kitchen, her stockinged feet making no sound on the linoleum of the passage, or the scrubbed boards of the kitchen floor. The range was hot, as always, and she put the kettle back on the hob and cut a slice of bread, buttered it and spread it with jam. She knew he would want it when he saw it.

He followed her through and unintentionally stood in her way.

"Where was it?" she asked.

"Highgate," he said as she walked around him to get the mugs.

"Highgate? That's not your area."

"No, but they are sure this was arson, and the local station sent for us straightaway."

Charlotte had deduced that much from the smell of smoke and the smudges on his clothes, but she forbore from mentioning it.

"It was the home of a doctor," he went on. "He was out on a call, a woman in childbirth unexpectedly early, but his wife was at home. She had canceled a trip to the city at the last moment. It was she who was burned."

The kettle was boiling and Charlotte heated the pot, then made the tea and set it to brew. He sat down gratefully and she sat opposite him.

"Was she young?" she said quietly.

"About forty."

"What was her name?"

"Clemency Shaw."

"Could it not have been an accident? There are lots of accidental fires, a candle dropped, a spark from an unguarded hearth, someone smoking a cigar and not putting it out properly." She poured the tea and pushed one of the mugs towards him.

"On the curtains of four separate rooms, downstairs, at midnight?" He took his tea and sipped it and burned his tongue. He bit into the bread and jam quickly.

"Oh." She thought of waking in the night to the roar and the heat, and knowing what it was, and that you were trapped. How much more dreadful to think someone else had lit it deliberately, knowing you were there, meaning to burn you to death. The thought was so fearful that for a moment she felt a little sick.

Pitt was too tired to notice.

"We don't know yet if they meant to kill Mrs. Shaw—or her husband." He tried the tea again.

She realized he must have felt all that she was now imagining. His mind would have conjured the same pictures, only more vividly; he had seen the charred rubble, the heat still radiating from it, the smoke still filling the air and stinging the eyes and throat.

"You can't do any more tonight, Thomas. She isn't in any pain now, and you cannot touch the grief," she said gently. "There is always somebody hurting somewhere, and we cannot take their pain." She rose to her feet again. "It doesn't help." She brushed his hand with hers as she passed. "I'll get a bowl of hot water and you can wash. Then come to bed. It will be morning soon enough."

Pitt left as soon as he had eaten breakfast, and Charlotte began the routine of domestic chores. The children, Jemima and Daniel, were seen off to their respective lessons at the same school along the road, and Gracie the maid began the dusting and sweeping. The heavy work, scrubbing floors, beating the carpets and carrying the coal and coke for the cooker, was done by Mrs. Hoare, who came in three days a week.

Charlotte resumed the ironing, and when she had finished

that, began on pastry baking, the daily making of bread, and was about to begin washing and preparing jars for jam when there was a clatter at the door. Gracie dropped her broom and ran to answer it, and returned a moment later breathless, her thin little face alight with excitement.

"Oh, ma'am, it's Lady Ashworth back—I mean, Mrs. Radley—back from 'er 'oneymoon—an' lookin' so grand—an' 'appy."

Indeed, Emily was only a few steps behind, laden with beautiful parcels wrapped in paper and ribbons, and swirling huge skirts of noisy taffeta in a glorious shade of pale water green. Her fair hair showed in the fine curls Charlotte had envied since childhood, and her skin was rosy fair from sun and pleasure.

She dropped everything on the kitchen table, ignoring the jars, and threw her arms around Charlotte, hugging her so fiercely she almost lost her balance.

"Oh, I have missed you," she said exuberantly. "It's wonderful to be home again. I've got so much to tell you, I couldn't have borne it if you had been out. I haven't had any letters from you for ages—of course I haven't had any letters at all since we left Rome. It is so boring at sea—unless there is a scandal or something among the passengers. And there wasn't. Charlotte, how can anyone spend all their lives playing bezique and baccarat and swapping silly stories with each other, and seeing who has the newest bustle or the most elegant hair? I was nearly driven mad by it." She disengaged herself and sat down on one of the kitchen chairs.

Gracie was standing rooted to the spot, her eyes huge, her imagination whirling as she pictured ships full of card-playing aristocrats with marvelous clothes. Her broom was still propped against the wall in the passageway and her duster stuffed in the waist of her apron.

"Here!" Emily picked up the smallest of the packages and offered it to her. "Gracie, I brought you a shawl from Naples."

Gracie was overcome. She stared at Emily as if she had materialized by magic in front of her. She was too overwhelmed even to speak. Her small hands locked onto the package so tightly it was fortunate it was fabric, or it might have broken.

"Open it!" Emily commanded.

At last Gracie found words. "Fer me, my lady? It's fer me?"

"Of course it's for you," Emily told her. "When you go to church, or out walking, you must put it 'round your shoulders, and when someone admires you, tell them it came from the Bay of Naples and was a gift from a friend."

"Oh—" Gracie undid the paper with fumbling fingers, then as the ripple of blue, gold and magenta silk fell out, let her breath go in a sigh of ecstasy. Suddenly she recalled her duty and shot off back to the hallway and her broom, clutching her treasure.

Charlotte smiled with a lift of happiness that would probably not be exceeded by any other gift Emily might bring, even for Jemima or Daniel.

"That was very thoughtful," she said quietly.

"Nonsense." Emily dismissed it, a trifle embarrassed herself. She had inherited a respectable fortune from her first husband, the shawl had cost a trifle—it was so small a thing to give so much pleasure. She spread out the other parcels and found the one with Charlotte's name on it. "Here—please open it. The rest are for Thomas and the children. Then tell me everything. What have you done since your last letter? Have you had any adventures? Have you met anyone interesting, or scandalous? Are you working on a case?"

Charlotte smiled sweetly and benignly, and ignoring the questions, opened the parcel, laying aside the wrapping paper neatly, both to tantalize Emily and because it was far too pretty to tear. She would keep it and use it at Christmas. Inside were three trailing bouquets of handmade silk flowers that were so lush and magnificent she gasped with amazement when she saw them. They would make the most ordinary hat look fit for a duchess, or in the folds of a skirt make a simple taffeta dress into a ball gown. One was in pastel pinks, one blazing reds, and the third all the shades between flamingo and flame.

"Oh, Emily. You're a genius." Her mind raced through all the things she could do with them, apart from the sheer pleasure of turning them over and over in her hand and dreaming, which was a joy in itself if she never got any further. "Oh, thank you! They are exquisite."

Emily was glowing with satisfaction. "I shall bring the paintings of Florence next time. But now I brought Thomas a dozen silk handkerchiefs—with his initials on."

"He'll adore them," Charlotte said with absolute certainty. "Now tell me about your trip—everything you can that isn't terribly private." She did not mean to ask Emily if she were happy, nor would she have. Marrying Jack Radley had been a wild and very personal decision. He had no money and no prospects; after George Ashworth, who had had both, and a title as well, it was a radical social change. And she had certainly loved George and felt his death profoundly. Yet Jack, whose reputation was dubious, had proved that his charm was not nearly as shallow as it appeared at first. He was a loyal friend, with courage as well as humor and imagination, and was prepared to take risks in a cause he believed right.

"Put on the kettle," Emily ordered. "And have you got pastry baking?" She sniffed. "It smells delicious."

Charlotte obeyed, and then settled to listen.

Emily had written regularly, except for the last few weeks, which had been spent at sea on the long, late-summer voyage home from Naples to London. They had sailed slowly by intent, calling at many ports, but she had not mailed letters, believing they would not reach Charlotte before she did herself. Now the words poured out in descriptions of Sardinia, the Balearic Isles, North Africa, Gibraltar, Portugal, northern Spain and the Atlantic coast of France.

To Charlotte they were magical places, immeasurably distant from Bloomsbury and the busy streets of London, housework and domestic duties, children, and Pitt's recounting of his day. She would never see them, and half of her regretted it and would love to have watched the brilliant light on colored walls, smelled the spice and fruit and dust in the air, felt the heat and heard the different rhythm of foreign tongues. They would have filled her imagination and enriched her memory for years. But she could have the best of them through Emily's recounting, and do it without the seasickness, the weariness of long cramped coach rides, highly irregular sanitation and a wide variety of insects which Emily described in repulsive detail.

Through it all there emerged a sharper, kinder and less romantic picture of Jack, and Charlotte found many of her anxieties slipping away.

"Now that you're home, are you going to stay in the city?" she asked, looking at Emily's face, flushed with color from sun and wind but tired around the eyes. "Or are you going to the country?" She had inherited a large house in its own parklands, in trust for her son from her marriage to Lord Ashworth.

"Oh, no," Emily said quickly. "At least—" She made a small, rueful face. "I don't know. It's very different now we're not on a planned journey with something new to see or to do each day, and somewhere we have to be by nightfall. This is the beginning of real life." She looked down at her hands, small and strong and unlined on the table. "I'm a little frightened in case suddenly we're not sure what to say to each other—or even what to do to fill the day. It's going to be so different. There isn't any crisis anymore." She sniffed rather elegantly and smiled directly at Charlotte. "Before we were married there was always some terrible event pressing us to act—first George's death, and then the murders in Hanover Close." She raised her fair eyebrows hopefully and her blue eyes were wide, but they knew each other far too well for even Emily to feign innocence. "I don't suppose Thomas has a case we could help with?"

Charlotte burst into laughter, even though she knew Emily was serious and that all the past cases in which they had played a part were fraught with tragedy, and some danger as well as any sense of adventure there may have been.

"No. There was a very terrible case while you were away."

"You didn't tell me!" Emily's expression was full of accusation and incredulity. "What? What sort of case? Why didn't you write to me about it?"

"Because you would have been too worried to enjoy your honeymoon, and I wanted you to have a perfect time seeing all the glories of Paris and Italy, not thinking about people having their throats cut in a London fog," Charlotte answered honestly. "But I will certainly tell you now, if you wish."

"Of course I wish! But first get me some more tea."

"We could have luncheon," Charlotte suggested. "I have cold meat and fresh pickle—will that do?"

"Very well—but talk while you're getting it," Emily instructed. She did not offer to help; they had both been raised to expect marriage to gentlemen of their own social status who would provide them with homes and suitable domestic servants for all house and kitchen labor. Charlotte had married dreadfully beneath herself—to a policeman—and learned to do her own work. Emily had married equally far above herself, to an aristocrat with a fortune, and she had not even been *in* a kitchen in years, except Charlotte's; and although she knew how to approve or disapprove a menu for anyone from a country squire to the Queen herself, she had no idea, and no wish for one, as to how it should be made.

"Have you been to see Great-Aunt Vespasia yet?" Charlotte asked as she carved the meat.

Great-Aunt Vespasia was actually George's aunt, and no immediate relative to either of them, but they had both learned to love and admire her more deeply than any of their own family. She had been one of the great beauties of her generation. Now she was close to eighty, and with wealth and social position assured she had both the power and the indifference to opinion to conduct herself as she pleased, to espouse every cause her conscience dictated or her sympathies called for. She dressed in the height of fashion, and could charm the prime minister, or the dustman—or freeze them both at twenty paces with a look of ice.

"No," Emily replied. "I thought of going this afternoon. Does Aunt Vespasia know about this case?"

Charlotte smiled smugly. "Oh yes. She was involved. In fact she lent me her carriage and footman for the final confrontation—" She let it hang in the air deliberately.

Emily glared at her.

Blithely Charlotte refilled the kettle and turned to the cupboard to find the pickle. She even thought of humming a little tune, but decided against it on the ground that she could not sing very well—and Emily could.

Emily began to drum her fingers on the scrubbed-clean wooden tabletop.

"A member of Parliament was found lashed to a lamppost on Westminster Bridge. . . ." Charlotte began to recount the whole story, at first with relish, then with awe, and finally with horror and pity. When she had finished the meal was done and it was early afternoon.

Emily said very little, reaching her hands across the table to clasp Charlotte's arm with her fingers. "You could have been killed!" she said angrily, but there were tears in her eyes. "You must never do such a mad thing again! I suppose whatever I think of to say to you, Thomas will already have said it? I trust he scolded you to within an inch of your life?"

"It was not necessary," Charlotte said honestly. "I was quite aware of it all myself. Are you ready to go and see Aunt Vespasia?"

"Certainly. But you are not. You must change out of that very plain stuff dress and put on something more appealing."

"To do the ironing?"

"Nonsense. You are coming with me. It will do you good. It is a lovely day and the drive will be excellent."

Charlotte gave duty a brief thought, then submitted to temptation.

"Yes—if you wish. It will only take me a few moments to change. Gracie!" And she hurried out to find the maid and request her to prepare the children's tea for their return and peel the vegetables for the main evening meal.

Lady Vespasia Cumming-Gould lived in a spacious, fashionable house, and her door was opened by a maid in a crisp uniform with lace-trimmed cap and apron. She recognized Charlotte and Emily immediately and showed them in without the usual formalities of prevarication. There was no question as to whether they would be received. Her ladyship was not only very fond of them both, she was also acutely bored with the chatter of society and the endless minutiae of etiquette.

Vespasia was sitting in her private withdrawing room, very sparsely furnished by current standards of taste—no heavy oak tables, no overstuffed sofas and no fringes on the curtains. Instead it was reminiscent of a far earlier age, when Vespasia herself was born, the high empire of Napoleon Bonaparte, before the Battle of Waterloo, the clean lines of the Georgian era and the austerity of a long, desperate war for survival. One of her uncles had died in Nelson's navy at Trafalgar. Now even the Iron Duke was dead and Wellington a name in history books, and those who fought in the Crimea forty years later were old men now.

Vespasia was sitting upright on a hard-backed Chippendale chair, her dove-gray gown high at the neck, touched with French lace, and four ropes of pearls hanging almost to her waist. She did not bother with the pretense of indifference. Her smile was full of delight.

"Emily, my dear. How very well you look. I'm so pleased you have come. You shall tell me everything you enjoyed. The tedious parts you may omit, no doubt they were just the same as when I was there and it is quite unnecessary that any of us should endure them again. Charlotte, you will live through it all a second time and ask all the pertinent questions. Come, sit down."

They both went to her, kissed her in turn, then took the places she indicated.

"Agatha," she commanded the maid. "You will bring tea. Cucumber sandwiches, if you please—and then have Cook make some fresh scones with—I think—raspberry jam, and of course cream."

"Yes, my lady." Agatha nodded obediently.

"In an hour and a half," Vespasia added. "We have much to hear."

Whether they would stay so long was not open to argument, nor if any other chance caller should be admitted. Lady Vespasia was not at home to anyone else.

"You may begin," Vespasia said, her eyes bright with a mixture of anticipation and laughter.

Nearly two hours later the tea table was empty and Emily finally could think of nothing else whatever to add.

"And now what are you going to do?" Vespasia inquired with interest.

Emily looked down at the carpet. "I don't know. I suppose I could become involved in good works of some sort. I could be patron of the local committee for the care of fallen women!"

"I doubt it," Charlotte said dryly. "You are not Lady Ashworth anymore. You'd have to be an ordinary member."

Emily made a face at her. "I have no intention of becoming either. I don't mind the fallen women—it's the committee members I cannot abide. I want a proper cause, something to do better than pontificate on the state of others. You never did answer me properly when I asked you what Thomas was doing at the moment?"

"Indeed." Vespasia looked at Charlotte hopefully also. "What is he doing? I trust he is not in Whitechapel? The newspapers are being very critical of the police at the moment. Last year they were loud in their praises, and all blame went to the mobs in Trafalgar Square in the riots. Now the boot is on the other foot, and they are calling for Sir Charles Warren's resignation."

Emily shivered. "I imagine they are frightened—I think I should be if I lived in that sort of area. They criticize everyone—even the Queen. People are saying she does not appear enough, and the Prince of Wales is far too light-minded and spends too much money. And of course the Duke of Clarence behaves like an ass—but if his father lives as long as the Queen, poor Clarence will be in a bath chair before he sees the throne."

"That is not a satisfactory excuse." Vespasia's lips moved in the tiniest smile, then she turned to Charlotte again. "You have not told us if Thomas is working on this Whitechapel affair."

"No. He is in Highgate, but I know very little about the case," Charlotte confessed. "In fact it has only just begun—"

"The very best place for us to become acquainted with it," Emily said, her enthusiasm returning. "What is it?"

Charlotte looked at their expectant faces and wished she had more to tell.

"It was a fire," she said bleakly. "A house was burned and a woman died in it. Her husband was out on a medical call—he is a doctor—and the servants' wing was the last to be damaged and they were all rescued."

"Is that all?" Emily was obviously disappointed.

"I told you it was only the very beginning," Charlotte apologized. "Thomas came home reeking of smoke and with fine ash in his clothes. He looked drained of all energy and terribly sad. She was supposed to have gone out, but it was canceled at the last moment."

"So it should have been the husband who was at home," Vespasia concluded. "I assume it was arson, or Thomas would not have been called. Was the intended victim the husband—or was it he who set the fire?"

"It would seem that he was the intended victim," Charlotte agreed. "With the best will in the world, I cannot see any way in which we could"—she smiled with a touch of self-mockery —"meddle."

"Who was she?" Emily asked quietly. "Do you know anything about her?"

"No, nothing at all, except that people spoke well of her. But then they usually do of the dead. It is expected, even required."

"That sounds totally vacuous," Vespasia said wearily. "And tells neither Thomas nor us anything about her at all—only that her friends are conventional. What was her name?"

"Clemency Shaw."

"Clemency Shaw?" Vespasia's voice quickened with recognition. "That name is familiar, I believe. If it is the same person, then she is—was—indeed a good woman. Her death is a tragedy, and unless someone else takes over her work, a great many people will suffer."

"Thomas said nothing of any work." Charlotte was acutely interested herself now. "Perhaps he doesn't know. What work was it?"

Emily sat forward in her chair, waiting eagerly.

"It may not be the same person," Vespasia warned.

"But if it is?"

"Then she has begun a fight to get certain laws changed regarding the ownership of slum housing," Vespasia answered gravely, her face expressing what she knew from her own experience of the near impossibility of overcoming such vested interests. "Many of the worst, where there is appalling over-crowding and no sanitation at all, are owned by people of wealth and social standing. If it were more readily known, some minimal standards might be enforced."

"And who is in its way?" Emily was practical as always.

"I cannot give you a detailed answer," Vespasia replied. "But if you are determined to pursue it, then we should go and visit Somerset Carlisle, who will be able to tell us." Even as she spoke she was already rising to her feet and preparing to leave.

Charlotte caught Emily's eye with a flash of amusement, and they also rose.

"What an excellent idea," Charlotte agreed.

Emily hesitated only a moment. "Is it not an unsuitable time to call upon anyone, Aunt Vespasia?"

"Most unsuitable," Vespasia agreed. "That is why it will do very well. We shall be highly unlikely to find anyone else there." And without continuing the discussion she rang the bell for her maid to call Emily's carriage so they might travel together.

Charlotte had a moment's hesitation; she was not dressed well enough to call upon a member of Parliament. Usually for anything approaching such formality in the past she had borrowed a gown from Emily, or Aunt Vespasia herself, suitably made over to fit her, even if by strategic pins here and there. But she had known Somerset Carlisle for several years, and always in connection with some passionate cause when there was little thought of social niceties, only the matter in hand. Anyway, neither Emily nor Vespasia were taking the slightest notice of protests and if she did not catch them up she would be left behind, and she would have gone in her kitchen pinafore rather than that.

Somerset Carlisle was at home in his study working on papers of some political importance, and for anyone less than Vespasia his footman would politely have refused them entrance. However, he had an appreciation for the dramatic and a knowledge of his master's past crusades in one cause or another, and he was quite aware that Lady Vespasia Cumming-Gould had frequently been involved in them one way or another; indeed she was an effective ally for whom he had great regard.

Accordingly he conducted all three ladies to the study door and knocked before opening it and announcing their presence.

Somerset Carlisle was not young, nor yet middle-aged; quite possibly he never would be, but would pass directly from where he was now into a wiry and unmellowed old age. He was full of nervous energy, his winged eyebrows and thin, mercurial face never seemed completely in repose.

His study reflected his nature. It was full of books on all manner of subjects, both for his work and for his wide personal interests. The few spaces on the walls were crammed with paintings and curios, beautiful, and probably of financial value. The deep Georgian windows shed excellent light, and for winter or evening work there were several gas brackets both on the walls and pendant from the ceiling. A long-legged marmalade cat was stretched out in ecstatic sleep in the best chair in front of the fire. The desk itself was piled with papers in no imaginable sort of order.

Somerset Carlisle put his pen into the stand and rose to greet them with obvious delight, coming around the desk, knocking off a pile of letters and ignoring them completely as they cascaded to the floor. The cat did not stir.

He took the immaculately gloved hand that Vespasia offered him.

"Lady Cumming-Gould. How very nice to see you." He met her eyes with a spark of humor. "No doubt you have some urgent injustice to fight, or you would not have come without warning. Lady Ashworth—and Mrs. Pitt—now I know something is afoot! Please sit down. I—" He looked around for some place of comfort to offer them, and failed. Gently he removed the cat and placed it on the seat of his own chair behind the desk. It stretched luxuriously and resettled itself.

Vespasia took the chair and Charlotte and Emily sat on the upright chairs opposite. Carlisle remained standing. No one bothered to correct him that Emily was now plain Mrs. Jack Radley. There was time enough for that later.

Vespasia came to the point quickly.

"A woman has died in a fire which was not accidental. We know little other than that, except that her name was Clemency

Shaw—" She stopped, seeing the look of distress that had touched his face the moment she said the name. "You knew her?"

"Yes—mostly by repute," he answered, his voice low, his eyes searching their faces, seeing the surprise and the heightened tension as he spoke. "I only met her twice. She was a quiet woman, still uncertain of how best to achieve her aims and unused to battling the intricacies of civil law, but there was an intense dedication in her and an honesty I admired very much. I believe she cared for the reforms she desired more than her own dignity or the opinions of her friends or acquaintances. I am truly grieved that she is dead. Have you no idea how it happened?" The last question he addressed to Charlotte. He had known Pitt for many years, in fact since he himself had been involved in a bizarre murder.

"It was arson," she replied. "She was at home because a trip into town had been unexpectedly canceled, and her husband was out on a medical emergency. Otherwise he would have died, and not she."

"So her death was accidental." He made it almost a question, but not quite.

"Someone might have been watching and known." Charlotte would not leave it so quickly. "What was she fighting for—what reforms? Who would want her to fail?"

Carlisle smiled bitterly. "Almost anyone who has invested in slum property and raked in exorbitant rents for letting it to whole families a room at a time, sometimes even two or three families." He winced. "Or for sweatshops, gin mills, brothels, even opium dens. Very profitable indeed. You'd be surprised by some of the people who make money that way."

"How did Mrs. Shaw threaten them?" Vespasia asked. "Precisely what did she wish to do about it? Or should I say, what did she have the slightest realistic prospect of doing?"

"She wanted to change the law so that owners could be easily traced, instead of hiding behind companies and lawyers so they are virtually anonymous."

"Wouldn't it be better to make some law as to occupancy and sanitation?" Emily asked reasonably.

Carlisle laughed. "If you limit occupancy all you would do is put even more people out into the street. And how would you police it?"

"Oh—"

"And you'd never get a law passed on sanitation." His voice hardened. "People in power tend to believe that the poor have the sanitation they deserve, and if you gave them better, within a month they would have it back to its present state. It is easier for them to take their own luxury with a quiet conscience. Even so, to do anything about it would cost millions of pounds—"

"But each individual owner—" Emily argued. "They would have millions. At least over time—"

"Such a law would never be passed through Parliament." He smiled as he said it, but there was anger in his eyes and his hands by his sides were tight. "You forget who votes for them."

Again Emily said nothing. There were only two political parties with any chance of forming a government, and neither of them would espouse such a law easily, and no women had the franchise, the poor were ill organized and largely illiterate. The implication was too obvious.

Carlisle gave a little grunt that was almost a laugh. "That is why Mrs. Shaw was attempting to make it possible to discover without difficulty who owned such places. If it were public, social pressure would do a great deal that the law cannot."

"But don't social pressures come from the same people who vote?" Charlotte asked; then knew the moment she had said it that it was not so. Women did not vote, and subtle though it was, a very great deal of society was governed one way or another by women. Men might do all manner of things if they were sufficiently discreet, indulge tastes they would not acknowledge even to their fellows. But publicly and in the domestic tranquillity of their homes they would deplore such affronts to the fabric of a civilized people.

Carlisle saw the realization in her face and did not bother to explain.

"How perceptive of Mrs. Shaw," Vespasia said quietly. "I imagine she made certain enemies?"

"There was some . . . apprehension," he agreed. "But I don't believe she had as yet succeeded well enough to cause actual anxiety."

"Might she have, had she lived?" Charlotte asked with intense seriousness. She found herself regretting Clemency Shaw's death not only with the impartial pity for any loss but because she could never meet her, and the more she heard, the more strongly she felt she would have liked her very much.

Carlisle considered for a moment before replying. It was not a time for empty compliments. He had known enough of political life and the power of financial interests, and had been close enough to several murders, not to dismiss the possibility that Clemency Shaw had been burned to death to keep her from continuing in a crusade, however unlikely it seemed that she would affect the course of law, or of public opinion.

Charlotte, Emily and Vespasia all waited in silence.

"Yes," he said eventually. "She was a remarkable woman. She believed passionately in what she was doing, and that kind of honesty sometimes moves people where logic fails. There was no hypocrisy in her, no—" He frowned very slightly as he searched for precisely the words to convey the impression upon him of a woman he had met only twice, and yet who had marked him indelibly. "No sense that she was a woman seeking a cause to fight, or some worthy works to fill her time. There was nothing she wanted for herself; her whole heart was on easing the distress of those in filthy and overcrowded housing."

He saw Vespasia wince and knew it was pity rather than distaste.

"She hated slum landlords with a contempt that could make you feel guilty for having a roof over your own head." He smiled awkwardly, a crooked gesture very charming in his oddly crooked face. "I am very grieved that she is dead." He looked at Charlotte. "I presume Thomas is on the case, which is why you know about it?"

"Yes."

"And you intend to meddle?" The last observation was addressed to all three of them.

Vespasia sniffed a little at his choice of word, but she did not disagree in essence. "You could have expressed yourself more fortunately," she said with a very slight lift of her shoulders.

"Yes we do." Emily was forthright. Unlike Clemency Shaw, she was quite definitely looking for something to do, but that was no reason why she should not do it well. "I don't yet know how."

"Good." He had no doubts. "If I can be of assistance, please call on me. I had a great admiration for Clemency Shaw. I should like to see whoever murdered her rot in Coldbath Fields, or some similar place."

"They'll hang him," Vespasia said harshly. She knew Carlisle did not approve of the rope; it was too final, and there were too many mistakes. She did not herself, but she was a realist.

He looked at her levelly, but made no remark. The issue had been discussed before and they knew each other's feelings. A wealth of experience lay in common, other tragedies, errors and knowledge of pain. Crime was seldom a single act, or the fault of a single person.

"That is not a reason to leave it undone." Charlotte rose to her feet. "When I learn more I shall tell you."

"Be careful," Carlisle warned, going to the door ahead of her and holding it open while they went through, first Vespasia, her head high, her back very stiff, then Emily close behind, lastly Charlotte. He put his hand on her arm as she passed him. "You will be disturbing very powerful people who have a great deal at stake. If they have already murdered Clemency, they will not spare you."

"I shall be,",she said with conviction, although she had no idea what she was going to do that would be the slightest use. "I shall merely gather information."

He looked at her skeptically, having been involved in several of her past meddlings, but he relaxed his grip and escorted them to the door and out into the sunlit street where Emily's carriage was waiting.

As soon as the horses began to move Emily spoke.

"I shall discover whatever I can about Mrs. Shaw and her struggles to have new laws passed to disclose who owns derelict property. I am sure if I think hard I must have some acquaintances who would know."

"You are a new bride," Vespasia cautioned her gently. "Your husband may have rather different expectations of his first weeks at home from honeymoon."

"Ah—" Emily let out her breath, but it was only a hesitation in her flight of thought. "Yes—well that will have to be got around. I shall deal with it. Charlotte, you had better be discreet about it, but discover everything you can from Thomas. We must be aware of all the facts."

They did not wait at Vespasia's house but wished Vespasia good-bye and watched her alight and climb the steps to the front door, which was opened before her by the waiting maid. She went in with an absentminded word of thanks, still deep in thought. There were many social evils she had fought against in the long years since her widowhood. She enjoyed battle and she was prepared to take risks and she no longer cared greatly what others thought of her, if she believed herself to be in a just cause. Which was not that the loss of friends, or their disapproval, did not hurt her.

But now it was Emily who occupied her mind. She was far more vulnerable, not only to the emotions of her new husband, who might well wish her to be more decorous in her behavior, but also to the whims of society, which loved innovations in fashion, something to marvel at and whisper about, but hated anything that threatened to disturb the underlying stability of its members' familiar and extremely comfortable lives.

Charlotte parted from Emily at her own door after a brief hug, and heard the carriage clatter away as she went up the scrubbed steps into the hall. It smelled warm and clean; the sounds of the street were muffled almost to silence. She stood still for a moment. She could just hear Gracie chopping something on a board in the kitchen, and singing to herself. She felt an overwhelming sense of safety, and then gratitude. It was hers, all of it. She did not have to share it with anyone except her own family. No one would put up the rent or threaten her with eviction. There was running water in the kitchen, the range burned hot, and in the parlor and bedrooms there were fires. Sewage ran away unseen, and the garden was sweet with grass and flowers.

It was very easy to live here every day and forget the uncounted people who had no place warm enough, free of filth and smells, where they could be safe and have privacy enough for dignity.

Clemency Shaw must have been a most unusual woman to have cared so much for those in tenements and slums. In fact she was remarkable even to have known of their existence. Most well-bred women knew only what they were told, or read in such parts of the newspapers or periodicals as were considered suitable. Charlotte herself had not had any idea until Pitt had shown her the very edges of an utterly different world, and to begin with she had hated him for it.

Then she'd felt angry. There was a horrible irony that Clemency Shaw should be murdered by the destruction of her home, and whoever had caused it, Charlotte intended to find and expose, and their sordid and greedy motives with them. If Clemency Shaw's life could not bring attention to the evil of slum profiteers, then Charlotte would do all in her power to see that her death did.

Emily was bent on a similar purpose, but for slightly different reasons, and in an utterly different fashion. She entered the hallway of her spacious and extremely elegant house in a swirl of skirts and petticoats and flung off her hat, rearranging her hair to look even more casually flattering, fair tendrils curling on her neck and cheeks, and composed her face into an expression of tenderness touched with grief.

Her new husband was already at home, which she knew from the identity of the footman who had opened the door for her. Had Jack been out, Arthur would have been with him.

She pushed open the withdrawing room doors and made a dramatic entrance.

He was sitting by the fire with a tea tray on the low table and his feet up on the stool. The crumpets were already gone; there was only a ring of butter on the plate.

He smiled with warmth when he heard her and stood up courteously. Then he saw the expression on her face and suddenly his pleasure turned to concern.

"Emily—what is it? Is something wrong with Charlotte? Is she ill—is it Thomas?"

"No—no." She flew to his arms and put her head on his shoulder, partly so he would not meet her eyes. She was not entirely sure how far she could deceive Jack successfully. He was too much like her; he also had survived on his charm and very considerable good looks and he was aware of all the tricks and how to perform them. And it was also because she found herself still very much in love with him, and it was a most comfortable feeling. But she had better explain herself before he became alarmed. "No, Charlotte is perfectly well. But Thomas is engaged on a case which distresses her deeply—and I find I feel the same. A woman was burned to death—a brave and very good woman who was fighting to expose a vicious social evil. Great-Aunt Vespasia is most upset as well." Now she could abandon subterfuge and face him squarely.

"Jack, I feel we should do what we can to help—"

He smoothed her hair gently, kissed her, then with wide eyes and barely the beginning of a smile, met her gaze.

"Oh yes? And how shall we do that?"

She made a rapid change of tactics. Drama was not going to win. She smiled back. "I'm not sure—" She bit her lip. "What do you think?"

"What social evil?" he said guardedly. He knew Emily better than she realized.

"Slum owners who charge exorbitant rents for filthy and crowded tenements—Clemency Shaw wanted to make them answerable to public opinion by not being able to be anonymous behind rent collectors and companies and things."

He was silent for so long she began to wonder if he had heard her.

"Jack?"

"Yes," he said at last. "Yes we will—but together. You cannot do anything alone, Emily. We shall be threatening some very powerful people—there are millions of pounds—you'd be surprised how many fortunes are seated in St. Giles and the Devil's Acre—and the misery there."

She smiled very slightly; the thought was ugly and there flashed through her mind the faces of people she had known in her days with George. She had accepted them easily then; it never occurred to her to wonder where their incomes were generated. Certain people simply had money; it was a state of affairs that had always existed. Now she was less innocent, and it was not a comfortable feeling.

Jack was still holding her. He brushed one finger gently over her forehead, pushing back a wisp of hair.

"Still want to go on?" he asked.

She was startled how clearly he had understood her thoughts, and the twinges of both guilt and apprehension they had aroused.

"Of course." She did not move; it was extremely pleasant remaining in his arms. "There is no possible way to retreat now. What should I say to Great-Aunt Vespasia, or Charlotte—and more important, what should I say to myself?"

His smile widened and he kissed her gently, and then gradually with passion.

When she thought about money again, it was a faraway thing to be dealt with another day, real and important then, but for now there were other, better things.

CHAPTER
THREE

Because Pitt had been sent for from the Bow Street station, and did not belong to Highgate, he reported the incident to his own superior officer, a man whom he both respected for his professional ability and liked for his candor and lack of pretension. Perhaps because Drummond was a gentleman by birth and had sufficient financial means not to have to concern himself with it, he did not feel the compulsion to prove his position.

He greeted Pitt with pleasure, interest quickening his lean face.

"Well?" he asked, standing up from his desk, not as a courtesy, which would have been absurd to a junior, even though he had offered Pitt considerable promotion. Pitt had declined it, because although he could dearly have used the money, he would have hated being behind a desk directing other men in the investigations. He wanted to see the people, watch faces, hear the inflections of a voice, the gestures and movements of the body. It was people who gave him both his pleasure and his pain, and the reality of his work. To give instructions to others and shuffle reports would rob him of the chance to exercise the real skills he possessed. To decline it had been Charlotte's decision as well as his, made because she knew him well enough to understand his happiness, and prefer it to the extra salary. It was one of those rarely-spoken-of generosities which deepened his sense of sharing with her and the knowledge that her commitment was still one of love.

Micah Drummond was regarding him with curiosity.

"Arson," Pitt replied. "I have looked through the physical evidence, such as it is, and there seems no doubt. There is too little left of the body to learn anything useful, but from the remains of the building the firemen say at least four separate fires were started, so whoever it was was determined to succeed."

Drummond winced and his eyes reflected his distress.

"And you say it was a woman who was found?"

"There seems little doubt it was a Mrs. Clemency Shaw." And he explained what they had learned from the brief investigations in the community of the immediate area, and from the Highgate police, including their natural inquiry into all the members of the small crowd which had turned out in the alarm and commotion to stand huddled in the background and stare. Perhaps among the sympathizers and offerers of help there had been one there to thrill at the glory of the flames and feel a vicarious power in their consuming destruction? Arsonists did not stay, but those touched with a certain madness did.

Drummond resumed his own seat behind his desk and waved Pitt to the most comfortable leather-upholstered chair opposite. It was an agreeable room, full of light and air from the large window. The walls were lined with bookshelves, except for the area around the fireplace, and the desk was polished oak, as beautiful as it was functional.

"Was it intended to have been the husband?" Drummond came straight to the point. "What do you know about him?"

Pitt tilted back in the chair and crossed his legs. "A doctor. An intelligent, articulate man, apparently open-minded and outspoken, but I haven't found time to look into his medical reputation yet."

"Your own feelings?" Drummond looked at him a little sideways.

Pitt smiled. "I liked the man, but then I've liked a few people who have committed murder, when desperate, frightened or injured enough. It would be so much easier if we could either like or dislike people and be decided about it; but I keep having to change my mind, and complicate my feelings by doing both at the same time in wildly differing proportions, as each new act and explanations for it emerge. It's such hard work." His smile broadened.

Drummond sighed and rolled his eyes upward in mock exasperation.

"A simple opinion, Pitt!"

"I should think he's an excellent candidate for murder," Pitt replied. "I can think of dozens of reasons why someone might want to silence a doctor, especially this one."

"A medical secret?" Drummond raised his eyebrows high. "Surely doctors keep such confidences anyway? Are you thinking of something discovered inadvertently and not bound by such an ethical code? For example . . . ?"

"There are many possibilities." Pitt shrugged, choosing at random. "A contagious disease which he would be obliged to report—plague, yellow fever—"

"Rubbish," Drummond interrupted. "Yellow fever in Highgate? And if that were so he would have reported it by now. Possibly a congenital disease such as syphilis, although that is unlikely. How about insanity? A man might well kill to keep that out of public knowledge, or even the knowledge of his immediate family, or prospective family, if he planned an advantageous marriage. Look into that, Pitt."

"I will."

Drummond warmed to the subject, leaning back a little in his chair and putting his elbows on the arms and his fingertips together in a steeple. "Maybe he knew of an illegitimate birth, or an abortion. For that matter maybe he performed one!"

"Why wait until now?" Pitt said reasonably. "If he's just done it, it will be among the patients he's visited in the last day or two; and anyway, why? If it was illegal he would be even less likely to speak of it, or make any record, than the woman. He has more to lose."

"What about the husband or father?"

Pitt shook his head. "Unlikely. If he didn't know about it beforehand, then he would probably be the one she was most anxious to keep it from. If he then discovered it, or learned it from her, the last way to keep it discreet would be to murder the doctor and cause all his affairs to be investigated by the police."

"Come on, Pitt," Drummond said dryly. "You know as well as I do that people in the grip of powerful emotions don't think like that—or half our crimes of impulse would never be committed, probably three quarters. They don't think; they feel—overwhelming rage, or fear, or simply confusion and a desire to lash out at someone and blame them for the pain they are suffering."

"All right," Pitt conceded, knowing he was right. "But I still think there are lots of other motives more probable. Shaw is a man of passionate convictions. I believe he would act on them, and devil take the consequences—"

"You do like him," Drummond said again with a wry smile, and knowledge of some unspoken hurt in his own past.

No reply was called for.

"He may have knowledge of a crime," Pitt said instead, following his own thoughts. "A death, perhaps of someone in terminal illness and great pain—"

"A merciful killing?" Drummond's expression quickened. "Possible. And occurring to me as someone who likes him less and perhaps has a clearer view, he may have assisted in a killing for less unselfish reasons, and the principle mover has grown nervous lest his accomplice becomes careless, or more likely from your description of Shaw as a man with nerve and passion, blackmail him. That would be an excellent cause for murder."

Pitt would like to have denied such a thought, but it was eminently logical, and to dismiss it would be ridiculous.

Drummond was watching him, his eyes curious.

"Perhaps," Pitt agreed aloud, and saw a small smile curl Drummond's lips. "But knowledge gained simply because of his professional skill is in my opinion more likely."

"What about a purely personal motive?" Drummond asked. "Jealousy, greed, revenge? Could there be another woman, or another man in love with his wife? Didn't you say he was expecting to be at home, and she not?"

"Yes." Pitt's mind was filled with all sorts of ugly possibilities, dark among them the Worlingham money, and the pretty face of Flora Lutterworth, whose father resented her frequent, private visits to Dr. Shaw.

"You need to have a great deal more." Drummond stood up and walked over towards the window, his hands in his pockets. He turned to face Pitt. "The possibilities are numerous—either for the murder of the wife, which happened, or for the murder of Shaw, which may have been attempted. It could be a very long, sad job. Heaven knows what other sins and tragedies you'll find—or what they will do to hide them. That's what I hate about investigation—all the other lives we overturn on the way." He poked his hands deeper into his pockets. "Where are you going to begin?"

"At the Highgate police station," Pitt replied, standing up also. "He was the local police surgeon—"

"You omitted to mention that."

Pitt smiled broadly. "Makes the knowledge without complicity look a trifle more likely, doesn't it?"

"Granted," Drummond said graciously. "Don't get carried away with it. What then?"

"Go to the local hospital and see what they think of him there, and his colleagues."

"You won't get much." Drummond shrugged. "They usually speak well of each other regardless. Imply that any one of them could have made an error, and they all close ranks like soldiers facing the enemy."

"There'll be something to read between the lines." Pitt knew what Drummond meant, but there was always the turn of a phrase, the overcompensation, the excessive fairness that betrayed layers of meaning and emotion beneath, conflicts of judgment or old desires. "Then I'll see his servants. They may have direct evidence, although that would be a lot to hope for. But they may also have seen or heard something that will lead to a lie, an inconsistency, an act concealed, someone where they should not have been." As he said it he thought of all the past frailties he had unearthed, foolishness and petty spites that had little or nothing to do with the crime, yet had broken old relationships, forged new ones, hurt and confused and changed. There were occasions when he hated the sheer intrusion of investigation. But the alternative was worse.

"Keep me advised, Pitt." Drummond was watching him, perhaps guessing his thoughts. "I want to know."

"Yes sir, I will."

Drummond smiled at the unusual formality, then nodded a dismissal, and Pitt left, going downstairs and out of the front doors to the pavement of Bow Street, where he caught a hansom north to Highgate. It was an extravagance, but the force would pay. He sat back inside the cab and stretched out his legs as far as possible. It was an agreeable feeling bowling along, not thinking of the cost.

The cab took him through the tangle of streets up from the river, across High Holborn to the Grey's Inn Road, north through Bloomsbury and Kentish Town into Highgate.

At the police station he found Murdo waiting for him impatiently, having already sifted through all the police reports of the last two years and separating all those in which Shaw had played a significant part. Now he stood in the middle of the room, uncarpeted, furnished with a wooden table and three hard-backed chairs. His fair hair was ruffled and his tunic undone at the neck. He was keen to acquit himself well, and in truth the case touched him deeply, but at the back of his mind was the knowledge that when it was all over Pitt would return to Bow Street. He would be left here in Highgate to resume working with his local colleagues, who were at present still acutely conscious of an outsider, and stung by resentment that it had been considered necessary.

"There they are, sir," he said as soon as Pitt was in the door. "All the cases he had the slightest to do with that could amount to anything, even those of disturbing the Queen's peace." He pointed his finger to one of the piles. "That's those. A few bloody noses, a broken rib and one broken foot where a carriage wheel went over it, and there was a fight afterwards between the man with the foot and the coachman. Can't see anybody but a madman murdering him over that."

"Neither can I," Pitt agreed. "And I don't think we're dealing with a madman. Fire was too well set, four lots of curtains, and all away from the servants' quarters, none of the windows overlooked by a footman or a maid up late, all rooms that would normally be closed after the master and mistress had gone to bed, no hallways or landings which might be seen by a servant checking doors were locked or a maid fetching a late cup of tea for someone. No, Murdo, I think our man with the oil and the matches is sane enough."

Murdo shivered and his face lost a little of its color. "It's a very ugly thing, Mr. Pitt. Someone must have felt a great passion to do it."

"And I doubt we'll find him in this lot." Pitt picked up the larger pile which Murdo had sorted for him. "Unless it's a death Shaw knew something very odd about. By the way, did you look into the demise of the late Theophilus Worlingham yet?"

"Oh, yes sir." Murdo was eager now. Obviously it was a task he had performed well and was waiting to recount it.

Pitt raised his eyebrows expectantly.

Murdo launched into his account, and Pitt sat down behind the desk, crossing his legs.

"Very sudden," Murdo began, still standing and hunching his shoulders a trifle in dramatic concentration. "He had always been a man of great physical energy and excellent health, what you might call a 'muscular Christian' I believe—" He colored slightly at his own audacity in using such a term about his superiors, and because it was an expression he had only heard twice before. "His vigor was a matter of some pride to him," he added as explanation, as the thought suddenly occurred to him that Pitt might be unfamiliar with the term.

Pitt nodded and hid his smile.

Murdo relaxed. "He fell ill with what they took to be a slight chill. No one worried unduly, although apparently Mr. Worlingham himself was irritated that he should be no stronger than most. Dr. Shaw called upon him and prescribed aromatic oils to inhale to reduce the congestion, and a light diet, which did not please him at all, and that he should remain in bed—and give up smoking cigars, which also annoyed him very much. He made no comment as to a mustard plaster—" Murdo screwed up his face in surprise and shook his head. "That's what my mam always used on us. Anyway, he got no better, but Shaw didn't call again. And three days later his daughter Clemency, the one who was murdered, visited and found him dead in his study, which is on the ground floor of his house, and the French doors open. He was lying stretched out on the carpet and according to the bobby as was called out, with a terrible look on his face."

"Why were the police sent for?" Pitt asked. After all, it was ostensibly a family tragedy. Death was hardly a rarity.

Murdo did not need to glance at his notes. "Oh—because o' the terrible look on his face, the French doors being open, and there was a great amount of money in the house, even twenty pounds in Treasury notes clutched in his hand, and they couldn't unlock his fingers of it!" Murdo's face was pink with triumph. He waited for Pitt's reaction.

"How very curious." Pitt gave it generously. "And it was Clemency Shaw who found him?"

"Yes sir!"

"Did anyone know whether any money was missing?"

"No sir, that's what's so peculiar. He had drawn out seven thousand, four hundred and eighty-three pounds from the bank." Murdo's face was pale again and a little pinched at the thought of such a fortune. It would have bought him a house and kept him in comfort till middle age if he never earned another penny. "It was all there! In Treasury notes, tied up in bundles in the desk drawer, which wasn't even locked. It takes a lot of explaining, sir."

"It does indeed," Pitt said with feeling. "One can only presume he intended to make a very large purchase, in cash, or to pay a debt of extraordinary size, which he did not wish to do in a more usual manner with a draft. But why—I have no idea."

"Do you suppose his daughter knew, sir—I mean, Mrs. Shaw?"

"Possibly," Pitt conceded. "But didn't Theophilus die at least two years ago?"

Murdo's triumph faded. "Yes sir, two years and three months."

"And what was the cause on the death certificate?"

"An apoplectic seizure, sir."

"Who signed it?"

"Not Shaw." Murdo shook his head fractionally. "He was the first on the scene, naturally, since Theophilus was his father-in-law, and it was his wife who found him. But just because of that, he called in someone else to confirm his opinion and sign the certificate."

"Very circumspect," Pitt agreed wryly. "There was a great deal of money in the estate, I believe. The amount withdrawn was only a small part of his total possessions. That's another thing you might look into, the precise degree and disposition of the Worlingham fortune."

"Yes sir, I will immediately."

Pitt held up his hand. "What about these other cases Shaw was involved with? Do you know about any of them?"

"Only three firsthand, sir; and none of them is anything out of the way. One was old Mr. Freemantle, who got a bit tiddley at the mayor's Christmas dinner party and got into a quarrel with Mr. Tiplady and pushed him down the steps of the Red Lion." He tried to keep his expression respectful, and failed.

"Ah—" Pitt let out his breath in a sigh of satisfaction. "And Shaw was called to attend to the resulting injuries?"

"Yes sir. Mr. Freemantle fell over by hisself and had to be helped home. I reckon if he'd been a less important gentleman he'd 'ave cooled off the night in a cell! Mr. Tiplady had a few bruises and a nasty cut on his head, bled all over the place and gave them all a fright. Looked as white as a ghost, he did. Sobered him up better than a bucket of cold water!" His lips curled up in a smile of immeasurable satisfaction and his eyes danced. Then full memory returned and the light died. "Filthy temper the next day. Came in here shouting and carrying on, blamed Dr. Shaw for the headache he had, said he hadn't been properly treated, but I reckon he was just furious 'cause we'd all seen him make a right fool of hisself on the town hall steps. Dr. Shaw told him to take more water with it next time, and go home till he'd slept it off."

Pitt did not bother to pursue it. A man does not murder a

doctor because the doctor speaks rather plainly about his de-bauchery and the consequent embarrassments.

"And the others?"

"Mr. Parkinson, Obadiah Parkinson, that is, got robbed up Swan's Lane one evening. That's up by the cemetery," he added in case Pitt did not know. "He was hit rather hard and the bobby that found him called Dr. Shaw, but there's nothing in that. He just took a good look at him, then said it was concussion and took him home in his own trap. Mr. Parkinson was very obliged."

Pitt put the two files aside and picked up the third.

"Death of the Armitage boy," Murdo said. "Very sad in-deed, that. Dray horse took fright at something and bolted. Young Albert was killed instantly. Very sad. He was a good lad, and not more than fourteen."

Pitt thanked him and dispatched him to go and pursue the Worlingham money, then he began to read the rest of the files on the desk in front of him. They were all similar cases, some tragic, some carrying an element of farce, pomposity exposed by the frailties of the flesh. Perhaps domestic tragedy lay behind some of the reports of bruising and broken bones, it was even possible that some of the autopsies which read as pneumonia or heart failure concealed a darker cause, an act of violence; but there was nothing in the notes here in front of him to indicate it. If Shaw had seen something he had not reported it in any official channel. There were seven deaths in all, and even on a second and third reading, Pitt could find nothing suspicious in any of them.

Finally he abandoned it, and after informing the desk ser-geant of his intention, he stepped out into the rapidly chilling afternoon air and walked briskly to the St. Pancras Infirmary, glancing briefly across the road at the Smallpox Hospital, then climbed the steps to the wide front entrance. He was already inside when he remembered to straighten his jacket, polish his boots on the backs of his trouser legs, transfer half the collected string, wax, coins, folded pieces of paper and Emily's silk hand-kerchief from one pocket to the other to balance the bulges a trifle, his fingers hesitating on the handkerchief's exquisite tex-

ture just a second longer than necessary. Then he put his tie a
little nearer center and ran his fingers through his hair, leaving
it conspicuously worse. Then he marched to the superintendent's
office and rapped sharply on the door.

It was opened by a young man with fair hair and a narrow,
anxious face.

"Yes?" he said, peering at Pitt.

Pitt produced his card, an extravagance which always gave
him a tingle of pleasure.

"Inspector Thomas Pitt, Bow Street Police," the young man
read aloud with alarm. "Good gracious. What can you possibly
want here? There is nothing amiss, I assure you, nothing at all.
Everything is in most excellent order." He had no intention of
allowing Pitt in. They remained standing in the doorway.

"I do not doubt it," Pitt soothed him. "I have come to make
some confidential inquiries about a doctor who I believe has
worked here—"

"All our doctors are fine men." The protest was instant. "If
there has been any impropriety—"

"None that I know of," Pitt interrupted. Drummond was
right, it was going to be exceedingly difficult to elicit anything
but panicky mutual defense. "There has been a most serious
threat against his life." That was true, in essence if not precisely
the way he implied it. "You may be able to help us discover
who is responsible."

"Against his life? Oh, dear me, how monstrous. No one here
would dream of such a thing. We save lives." The young man
picked nervously at his tie, which was apparently in danger of
throttling him.

"You must occasionally have failures," Pitt pointed out.

"Well—well, of course. We cannot work miracles. That
would be quite unreasonable. But I assure you—"

"Yes—yes!" Pitt cut across him. "May I speak with the gov-
ernor?"

The man bridled. "If you must! But I assure you we have
no knowledge of such a threat, or we should have informed the
police. The superintendent is a very busy man, very busy indeed."

"I am impressed," Pitt lied. "However if this person succeeds in carrying out his threat, and murders the doctor in
question, as well as his current victim, then your superintendent
will be even busier, because there will be fewer physicians to do
the work . . ." He allowed the train of thought to tail off as the
man in front of him was alternately pink with annoyance and
then white with horror.

However, the harassed superintendent, a lugubrious man
with long mustaches and receding hair, could tell Pitt nothing
about Shaw that advanced his knowledge. He was far more
agreeable than Pitt expected, having no sense of his own importance, only of the magnitude of the task before him in
battling disease for which he knew no cure; ignorance that
swamped the small inroads of literacy; and a perception of
cleanliness where there was too little pure water, too many
people, no sanitation and frequently no outlet to a sewer,
drains overflowed and rats were everywhere. If the Queen's
consort could die of typhoid carried by poor drains, living in
his own palace, what struggle was there to be waged in the
houses of the ordinary, and the poor, let alone the slums of
the destitute?

He escorted Pitt into his small, untidy office, which smelled
faintly of soap and paper. The window was very small, and both
gas lamps were lit and made a slight hissing sound. He invited
Pitt to sit down.

"Nothing," he said regretfully. "Shaw is a damn good doctor, sometimes gifted. Seen him sit up all day and all night and
all the next day with a sick man, and weep when he loses a
mother and child." A smile spread across his lantern face. "And
seen him bawl out a pompous old fool for wasting his time."
He sighed. "And worse than that to a man who could have fed
his children on milk and fruit, and didn't. Poor little beggars
were twisted up with rickets. Never seen a man so furious as
Shaw that day. He was shaking with passion and white to the
lips." He took a deep breath and tilted back in his chair and
looked at Pitt with surprisingly sharp eyes. "I like the man. I'm
damned sorry about his wife. Is that why you're here—because
you think the fire was meant for him?"

"It seems possible," Pitt replied. "Did he have any deep differences of opinion with his colleagues, that you know of?"

"Ha!" The superintendent barked out his laughter. "Ha! If you can ask that you don't know Shaw. Of course he did—with everyone: colleagues, nurses, administrative staff—me." His eyes were alive with a dark amusement. "And I knew of them all—I should imagine everyone within earshot did. He doesn't know the meaning of discretion—at least where his temper is concerned." He slid down off the tilt of his chair and sat up straight, looking at Pitt more intently. "I don't mean on medical matters, of course. He's closer than an oyster with a confidence. Never betrayed a secret even in consultation for another opinion. I doubt he's ever spoken a word of gossip in his life. But got a temper like an Indian curry when he sees injustice or humbug." He shrugged his bony shoulders. "He's not always right—but when he's proved wrong he'll usually come 'round, albeit not immediately."

"Is he well liked?"

The superintendent smiled at Pitt. "I'll not insult you with a generous fiction. Those who like him, like him very much. I am one of them. But there are a good few he's offended with what they consider uncalled-for brusqueness or frankness when it amounts to rudeness, interference or undermining their position." His gaunt, good-humored face showed the tolerance of years of battles and defeats. "There are many men who don't care to be proved wrong and shown a better way, especially in front of others. And the harder and longer they stick to their first position, the bigger fools they look when they finally have to back away from it and turn around." His smile grew broader. "And Shaw is frequently less than tactful in the way he goes about it. His wit is often quicker than his perception of people's feelings. More than once I've seen him set the room laughing at someone's expense, and known from the look on a man's face that he'd pay for it dearly one day. Few men care to be the butt of a joke; they'd rather be struck in the face than laughed at."

Pitt tried to make his voice casual, and knew immediately that it was a wasted effort. "Anyone in particular?"

"Not enough to set fire to the man's house," the superintendent replied, looking at Pitt wide-eyed and candid.

There was no point in fencing with the man and Pitt did not insult him by trying "The names of those most offended?" he asked. "It will be something at least to eliminate them now. The house is gutted and Mrs. Shaw is dead. Someone set the fires."

The superintendent's face lost its humor as if it had been wiped away with a sponge, and somberness replaced it. He made no struggle.

"Fennady couldn't abide him," he replied, leaning back and beginning what was obviously a catalogue, but there was still more comprehension than judgment in his voice. "They quarreled over everything from the state of the monarchy to the state of the drains, and all issues between. And Nimmons. Nimmons is an old man with old ideas which he had no inclination to change. Shaw taught him some better ways, but unfortunately he did it in front of the patient, who promptly transferred his custom, bringing his very large family with him."

"Tactless," Pitt agreed.

"His middle name." The superintendent sighed. "But he saved the man's life. And there's Henshaw—he's young and full of new ideas, and Shaw can't be bothered with them either, says they are untried and too risky. The man's as contrary as an army mule at times. Henshaw lost his temper, but I don't think he really bears any resentment. That's all I can give you."

"No tact, no discretion with his colleagues, but how about impropriety with his patients?" Pitt was not yet ready to give up.

"Shaw?" The superintendent's eyebrows rose. "Damn your realism, but I suppose you have to. Not that I know of, but he's a charming and vigorous man. Not impossible some woman imagined more than there was."

He was interrupted by a sharp tap on the door.

"Come in," he said with a glance of apology at Pitt.

The same fair young man who had so disapproved of Pitt poked his head around the door with a look of equal distaste on his face.

"Mr. Marchant is here, sir." He ignored Pitt very pointedly. "From the town hall," he added for good measure.

"Tell him I'll be there in a few minutes," the superintendent replied without any haste.

"From the town hall," the young man repeated. "It is important—sir."

"So is this," the superintendent said very distinctly, without shifting his position at all. "Man's life might hang on it." Then he smiled lugubriously at the double meaning. "And the longer you stand there, Spooner, the longer it will be before I am finished here and can come and see Marchant! Get out man, and deliver the message!"

Spooner withdrew with umbrage, closing the door as sharply as he dared.

The superintendent turned to Pitt again with a slight shake of his head.

"Shaw . . ." Pitt prompted.

"Not impossible some woman fell in love with him," the superintendent resumed, shaking his head. "It happens. Odd relationship, doctor and patient, so personal, and yet so practical and in some ways remote. Wouldn't be the first time it has got out of hand, or been misunderstood by a husband, or a father." He pushed out his lip. "It's no secret Alfred Lutterworth thinks his daughter sees a damned sight too much of Shaw, and insists on doing it alone, and won't discuss what passes between them, or what her ailment might be. Handsome girl, and great expectations. Old Lutterworth made a fortune in cotton. Don't know if anyone else has his eyes on her. Don't live in Highgate myself."

"Thank you, sir," Pitt said sincerely. "You've given me a great deal of your time, and been some help at least in eliminating certain possibilities."

"I don't envy you your job," the superintendent replied. "I thought mine was hard, but I fear yours will be harder. Good day to you."

When Pitt left the hospital the autumn evening was dark and the gas lamps were already lit. It was now October, and a few early leaves crunched under his feet as he strode towards the intersection where he could get a cab. The air had a clarity and sharpness that promised frost in a week or two. The stars shone in pinpricks of light infinitely far away, flickering and sparking in the cold. Out here in Highgate there was no fog from the river, no smoke in the air from factories or densely packed houses huddled back-to-back. He could smell the wind blowing off the fields and hear a dog barking in the distance. One day he must take Charlotte and the children for a week in the country. She had not been away from Bloomsbury for a long time. She would love it. He began to think of small economies he could make, ways he could save enough for it to be possible, and the expression on her face when he could tell her. He would keep it to himself until he was sure.

He strode out along the footpath and was so lost in thought that the first cab passed him by and was over the rise in the hill and disappearing before he realized it.

In the morning he returned to Highgate to see if Murdo had discovered anything of interest, but he was already out hot on the scent, and had left only the briefest notes to that effect. Pitt thanked the desk sergeant, who still grudged him his interference in a local matter which he believed they could well have handled themselves. Pitt left and went back to the hospital to speak to the Shaws' butler.

The man was propped up in bed looking haggard, his eyes deep socketed with shock and pain, his face unshaved and his left arm bound in bandages. There were raw grazes on his face and one scab beginning to form. It was unnecessary for the doctor to tell Pitt that the man had been badly burned.

Pitt stood by the bedside and in spite of the fact that it was blood, carbolic, sweat and the faint odor of chloroform that he could smell in the air, the sharp stench of smoke and wet cinders came back to him as if he had stood by the ruined house only a few minutes since, and then seen the charred wreck of Clemency Shaw's body lying on a stretcher in the morgue, barely recognizable as human. The anger inside him knotted his stomach and his chest till he found it hard to form the words in his mouth or force the breath to make speech.

"Mr. Burdin?"

The butler opened his eyes and looked at Pitt with no interest.

"Mr. Burdin, I am Inspector Pitt of the Metropolitan Police. I have come to Highgate to find out who set the fire that burned Dr. Shaw's house—" He did not mention Clemency. Perhaps the man had not been told. This would be a cruel and unnecessary shock. He should be informed with gentleness, by someone prepared to stay with him, perhaps even to treat his grief if it worsened his condition.

"I don't know," Burdin said hoarsely, his lungs still seared by the smoke. "I saw nothing, heard nothing till Jenny started screaming out. Jenny's the housemaid. Her bedroom's nearest the main house."

"We did not imagine you had seen the fires started." Pitt tried to sound reassuring. "Or that you knew anything obvious. But there may have been something which, on reflection, could be of importance—perhaps when put together with other things. May I ask you some questions?" It was a polite fiction to seek permission, but the man was badly shocked, and in pain.

"Of course." Burdin's voice dropped to a croak. "But I've already been thinking, turning it over and over in my mind." His face furrowed now with renewed effort. "But I don't remember anything different at all—not a thing. Everything was just as—" The breath caught in his throat and he began to cough as the raw lining hurt anew.

Pitt was confused for a moment, panic growing inside him as the man's face suffused with blood as he struggled for air, tears streaming down his cheeks. He stared around for help, and there was none. Then he saw water on the table in the corner and reached for it, tipping it into a cup clumsily in his haste. He clasped Burdin around the shoulders and eased him up and put the cup to his lips. At first he choked on it, spluttering it over himself, then at last enough trickled down his burning throat and cooled it. The pain was eased and he lay back, exhausted. It would be cruel and pointless to require him to speak again. But the questions must be asked.

"Don't speak," Pitt said firmly. "Turn your hand palm up if the answer is yes, and down if it is no."

Burdin smiled weakly and turned his palm up.

"Good. Did anyone call on the doctor at his house that day, other than his surgery appointments?"

Palm up.

"Tradesmen or business?"

Palm down.

"Personal acquaintance?"

Palm on its side.

"Family?"

Palm up.

"The Worlingham sisters?"

Palm down, very definitely.

"Mr. or Mrs. Hatch?"

Palm up.

"Mrs. Hatch?"

Palm down.

"Mr. Hatch? Was there a quarrel, raised voices, unpleasantness?" Although Pitt could think of nothing that could aggravate a temperamental difference into murder.

Burdin shrugged fractionally and turned his hand on its side.

"Not more than usual?" Pitt guessed.

Burdin smiled and there was a flicker of something like humor in his eyes, but again he shrugged. He did not know.

"Anyone else call?"

Palm up.

"Local person?"

Palm up and raised a little.

"Very local? Mr. Lindsay?"

Burdin's face relaxed in a smile, the palm remained up.

"Anyone else that you know of?"

Palm down.

He thought of asking if there was any mail that might be unusual or of interest, but what would such a thing be? How could anyone recognize it?

"Did Dr. Shaw seem anxious or disturbed about anything that day?"

The palm was down, but indecisive, hovering above the bed cover.

Pitt took a guess, drawn from what he had observed of Shaw's temperament. "Angry? Was he angry about something?"

The palm came up quickly.

"Thank you, Mr. Burdin. If you think of anything else, comments, a letter, unusual arrangements, please tell the hospital and write it down for me. I shall come immediately. I hope you recover quickly."

Burdin smiled and closed his eyes. Even that small effort had tired him.

Pitt left, angry himself at so much physical pain, and helpless because he could do nothing for it, and he had learned little he felt of use. He imagined Shaw and Hatch probably quarreled fairly regularly, simply because their natures were utterly different. They would almost certainly perceive any issue with opposite views.

The Shaws' cook was in a far less serious state of health, and he left the hospital and took a hansom for the short ride down Highgate Hill and through Holloway to the Seven Sisters Road and the house of her relatives, which Murdo had given him. It was small, neat and shabby, exactly what he expected, and he was permitted in only with reluctance and after considerable argument.

He found the cook sitting up in bed in the best bedroom, wrapped around more against the indecency of being visited by a strange man than to prevent any chill. She had been burned on one arm and had lost some of her hair, giving her a lopsided, plucked look which had it been less tragic would have been funny. As it was Pitt had difficulty in maintaining a perfectly sober expression.

The niece, bustling with offense, remained obtrusively present every moment of the time.

"Mrs. Babbage?" Pitt began. All cooks were given the courtesy title of "Mrs." whether they were married or not.

She looked at him with alarm and her hand flew to her mouth to stifle a shriek.

"I mean you no harm, Mrs. Babbage—"

"Who are you? What do you want? I don't know you." She craned upwards as if his mere presence threatened her with some physical danger.

He sat down quickly on a small bedroom chair just behind him and tried to be disarming. She was obviously still in an extreme state of shock, emotional if not from her injuries which appeared to be relatively slight.

"I am Inspector Pitt," he said, introducing himself, avoiding the word *police*. He knew how respectable servants hated even an association with crime as tenuous as the presence of the police. "It is my duty to do what I can to discover how the fire started."

"Not in my kitchen!" she said so loudly it startled her niece, who drew her breath in in a loud gasp. "Don't you go accusing me, or Doris! I know how to tend a stove. Never had so much as a coal fall out, I 'aven't; never mind burnin' down an 'ole 'ouse."

"We know that, Mrs. Babbage," he said soothingly. "It did not begin in the kitchen."

She looked a trifle mollified, but still her eyes were wide and wary and she twisted a rag of a handkerchief around and around in her fingers till the flesh of them was red with the friction. She was afraid to believe him, suspecting a trap.

"It was begun deliberately, in the curtains of four different ground-floor rooms," he elaborated.

"Nobody would do such a thing," she whispered, winding the handkerchief even more tightly. "What do you come to me for?"

"Because you might have seen something odd that day, noticed someone unusual hanging around—" Even as he said it he knew it was hopeless. She was too shocked to recall anything, and he himself did not believe it had been a tramp or a casual vagrant. It was too careful; it spoke of a deep hatred, or insatiable greed, or fear of some intolerable loss. It came back to his

mind again with renewed force: what did Stephen Shaw know—
and about whom?

"I didn't see nothin'." She began to weep, dabbing at her
eyes, her voice rising again. "I mind me own business. I don't
ask no questions an' I don't listen be'ind no doors. An' I don't
give meself airs to think things about the master nor the mistress—"

"Oh?" Pitt said instantly. "That's very commendable. I suppose some cooks do?"

" 'Course they do."

"Really? Like what, for example?" He endeavored to look
puzzled. "If you were that sort, what may you have wondered?"

She drew herself up in virtue and glared at him over the top
of her large hand, wrapped around with the sodden handkerchief.

"Well, if I were that sort—which I in't—I might 'ave wondered why we let one of the maids go, when there weren't
nothin' wrong wiv 'er, and why we 'aven't 'ad salmon like we
used to, nor a good leg o' pork neither—an' I might 'ave asked
Burdin why we 'aven't 'ad a decent case o' claret come inter the
'ouse in six months."

"But of course you didn't," Pitt said judiciously, hiding the
shadow of a smile. "Dr. Shaw is very fortunate to have such a
discreet cook in his household."

"Oh, I don't know as I can cook for 'im anymore!" She
started sniffing again violently. "Jenny's given 'er notice an' as
soon as she's fit she'll go back 'ome ter Somerset where she
comes from. An' Doris in't no more'n a chit of a thing—thirteen
mebbe. An' poor Mr. Burdin's so bad who can say if 'e'll ever
be the same again? No, I got ter be in a respectable 'ouse, for
me nerves."

There was no purpose in arguing with her, and for the time
being Shaw had no need of servants—there was no house for
them to live in or to wait upon. And apart from that, Pitt's mind
was racing with the very interesting fact that the Shaws had
apparently reduced their standard of living recently, to the degree that the cook had noticed it and it had set her mind wondering.

He stood up, wished her well, thanked the niece, and took his departure. Next he went in search of Jenny and Doris, neither of whom were burned more than superficially and more suffering from shock and fright and some considerable pain, but not in danger of relapse, as might be the case with Burdin.

He found them in the parsonage, in the care of Lally Clitheridge, who needed no explanation of his call.

But even after careful questioning they could tell him nothing of use. They had seen no one unusual in the neighborhood; the house had been exactly as it was at any other time. It had been a very ordinary day until they were roused, Jenny by the smell of smoke as she lay awake, thinking of some matter she blushed to recall and would not name, and Doris by Jenny's screams.

He thanked them and went out as dusk was falling and walked briskly southwards to Woodsome Road and the home of the woman who came in daily to do the heavy work, a Mrs. Colter. It was a small house but the windows were clean and the step scrubbed so immaculately he avoided putting his boots on it out of respect.

The door was opened by a big, comfortable woman with a broad-cheeked face, an ample bosom, and an apron tied tightly around her waist, the pocket stuffed full of odds and ends and her hair trailing out of a hasty knot on the back of her neck.

"Who are you?" she said in surprise, but there was no ill nature in it. "I dunno you, do I?"

"Mrs. Colter?" Pitt removed his rather worn hat, now a little crooked in the crown.

"That's me. It don't tell me who you are!"

"Thomas Pitt, from the Metropolitan Police—"

"Oh—" Her eyes widened. "You'll be about poor Dr. Shaw's fire, then. What a terrible thing. She was a good woman, was Mrs. Shaw. I'm real grieved about that. Come in. I daresay you're cold—an' 'ungry, mebbe?"

Pitt stepped in, wiping his feet carefully on the mat before going onto the polished linoleum floor. He almost bent and took his boots off, as he would have done at home. A smell of rich stew assailed him, delicate with onions and the sweetness of fresh carrots and turnips.

"Yes," he said with feeling. "Yes I am."

"Well I don't know as I can 'elp you." She led the way back and he followed after. To sit in a room with that aroma, and not eat, would be very hard. Her generous figure strode ahead of him and into the small, scrubbed kitchen, a huge pot simmering on the back of the stove filling the air with steam and warmth. "But I'll try," she added.

"Thank you." Pitt sat down on one of the chairs and wished she meant the stew, not information.

"They say it were deliberate," she said, taking the lid off the pot and giving its contents a brisk stir with a wooden ladle. "Although 'ow anybody could bring theirselves to do such a thing I'm sure I don't know."

"You said 'how,' Mrs. Colter, not 'why,' " Pitt observed, inhaling deeply and letting it out in a sigh. "You can think of reasons why?"

"In't much meat in it," she said dubiously. "Just a bit o' skirt o' mutton."

"You have no ideas why, Mrs. Colter?"

" 'Cos I in't got the money for more, o' course," she said, looking at him as if he were simple, but still not unkindly.

Pitt blushed. He was well used enough to poverty not to have made such an idiotic remark, or one so condescending.

"I mean why anyone should set fire to Dr. and Mrs. Shaw's house!"

"You want some?" She held up the ladle.

"Yes please, I would."

"Lots o' reasons." She began to dish up a generous portion in a large basin. "Revenge, for one. There's them as says 'e should'a looked after Mr. Theophilus Worlingham better'n 'e did. Although I always thought Mr. Theophilus would wind 'isself up into a fit and die one day. An' 'e did. But then that don't mean everyone sees it that way." She put the bowl down in front of him and handed him a spoon to eat with. It was mostly potatoes, onions, carrots and a little sweet turnip with a few stray ends of meat, but it was hot and full of flavor.

"Thank you very much," he said, accepting the bowl.

"Don't think it'd 'ave much to do wiv it." She dismissed the notion. "Mr. Lutterworth was fair furious with Dr. Shaw, on account of 'is daughter, Miss Flora, nippin' ter see 'im all hours, discreet like, not through the reg'lar surgery. But Mrs. Shaw weren't worried, so I don't suppose there were nothin' in it as there shouldn't 'a bin. Leastways, not much. I think Dr. Shaw and Mrs. Shaw kept their own ways a lot. Good friends, like, but maybe not a lot more."

"That's very observant of you, Mrs. Colter," Pitt said doubtfully.

"Need more salt?" she asked.

"No thank you; it's perfect."

"Not really." She shook her head.

"Yes it is. It doesn't need a thing added," he assured her.

"Don't take much ter see when people is used ter each other, and respects, but don't mind if the other gets fond o' someone else."

"And Dr. and Mrs. Shaw were fond of someone else?" Pitt's spoon stopped in midair, even the stew forgotten.

"Not as I know of. But Mrs. Shaw went off up to the city day after day, and 'e wished 'er well and never cared nor worried as who she went wiv; or that the vicar's wife came all over unnecessary every time Dr. Shaw smiled at 'er."

This time Pitt could not dismiss his amusement, and bent his head over the dish at least to conceal the worst of it.

"Indeed?" he said after another mouthful. "Do you think Dr. Shaw was aware of this?"

"Bless you, no. Blind as a bat, 'e is, to other people's feelin's o' that nature. But Mrs. Shaw, she saw it, an' I think she were kind o' sorry for 'er. 'E's a bit of a poor fish, the Reverend. Means well. But 'e's no man, compared wi' the doctor. Still," she sighed, "that's 'ow it is, in't it?" She regarded his empty bowl. "You want some more?"

He considered the family she had to feed and pushed the plate away from him.

"No thank you, Mrs. Colter. That answered the need perfectly. Very fine flavor."

She colored a little pink. She was unused to compliments, and pleased and awkward at the same time.

"It's nuthin' but ordinary." She turned away to give it a fierce stir.

"Ordinary to you, maybe." He rose from the table and pushed the chair back in, something he would not have bothered to do at home. "But I'm much obliged to you. Is there anything else you can think of that might have bearing on the fire?"

She shrugged. "There's always the Worlingham money, I suppose. Though I don't see 'ow. Don't think the doctor cared that much about it, and they ain't got no children, poor souls."

"Thank you, Mrs. Colter. You've been most helpful."

"Don't see that I 'ave. Any fool could'a told you as much, but if it pleases you, then I'm glad. I 'ope you catch whoever done it." She sniffed hard and turned her back to stir the pot again. "She were a fine woman, an' I grieve sorely that she's gorn—an' in such an 'orrible way."

"I will, Mrs. Colter," he said rather recklessly, and then when he was out on the footpath in the sharp evening air, wished he had been more reserved. He had not the faintest idea who had crept around cutting the glass, pouring oil on curtains and lighting those fires.

In the morning he returned to Highgate immediately, turning the case over and over in his mind on the long journey. He had told Charlotte of the progress he had made, largely negative, because she had asked him. She had taken an interest in the case beyond his expectations, because as yet there was little human drama of the sort which usually engaged her emotions. She gave him no explanation, except that she was sorry for the dead woman. It was a fearful way to die.

He had assured her that in all probability Clemency Shaw had been overcome by smoke long before any flames reached her. It was even possible she had not woken.

Charlotte had been much comforted by it, and since he had already told her his progress was minimal, she had asked him no more. Instead she turned to her own business of the day, giving volleys of instructions to Gracie, who stood wide-eyed and fascinated in the kitchen doorway.

Pitt stopped the hansom at Amos Lindsay's house, paid him off, and walked up to the front door. It was opened by the black-haired manservant again and Pitt asked if he might speak with Dr. Shaw.

"Dr. Shaw is out on call"—the briefest of hesitations—"sir."

"Is Mr. Lindsay at home?"

"If you care to come in I shall inquire if he will receive you." The manservant stood aside. "Who shall I say is calling?"

Did he really not remember, or was he being deliberately condescending?

"Inspector Thomas Pitt, of the Metropolitan Police," he replied a little tartly.

"Indeed." The manservant bowed so slightly only the light moving across his glistening head determined it at all. "Will you be so good as to wait here? I shall return forthwith." And without bothering to see if Pitt would do as he was bidden, he walked rapidly and almost silently towards the back of the house.

Pitt had time to stare again around the hall with its fierce and exotic mixture of art and mementos. There were no paintings, nothing of the nature of European culture. The statuary was wooden or ivory, the lines alien, looking uneasy in the traditional dimensions of the room with its paneling and squared windows letting in the dull light of an October morning. The spears should have been held in dark hands, the headdresses moving, instead of pinned immobile against the very English oak. Pitt found himself wondering what an unimaginably different life Amos Lindsay had lived in countries so unlike anything Highgate or its residents could envision. What had he seen, and done; whom had he known? Was it something learned there which had prompted his political views which Pascoe so abhorred?

His speculation was cut short by the manservant reappearing, regarding him with mild disapproval.

"Mr. Lindsay will see you in his study, if you will come this way." This time he omitted the "sir" altogether.

In the study Amos Lindsay stood with his back to a brisk

fire, his face pink under his marvelous white hair. He did not look in the least displeased to see Pitt.

"Come in," he said, ignoring the manservant, who withdrew soundlessly. "What can I do for you? Shaw's out. No idea how long, can't measure the sick. What can I add to your knowledge? I wish I knew something. It's all very miserable."

Pitt glanced back towards the hallway and its relics. "You must have seen a good deal of violence at one time and another." It was more an observation than a question. He thought of Great-Aunt Vespasia's friend, Zenobia Gunne, who also had trekked into Africa, and sailed uncharted rivers and lived in strange villages, with people no European had seen before.

Lindsay was watching him curiously. "I have," he conceded. "But it never became ordinary to me, nor did I cease to find violent death shocking. When you live in another land, Mr. Pitt, no matter how strange it may seem at first, it is a very short time until its people become your own, and their grief and their laughter touches you as deeply. All the differences on earth are a shadow, compared with the sameness. And to tell you the truth, I have felt more akin to a black man dancing naked but for his paint, under the moon, or a yellow woman holding her frightened child, than I ever have to Josiah Hatch and his kind pontificating about the place of women and how it is God's will that they should suffer in childbirth." He pulled a face and his remarkably mobile features made it the more grotesque. "And a Christian doctor doesn't interfere with it! Punishment of Eve, and all that. All right, I know he is in the majority here." He looked straight at Pitt with eyes blue as the sky, and almost hidden by the folds of his lids, as if he were still screwing them up against some tropical sun.

Pitt smiled. He thought quite possibly he would feel the same, had he ever been out of England.

"Did you ever meet a lady named Zenobia Gunne on your travels—" He got no further because Lindsay's face was full of light and incredulity.

"Nobby Gunne! Of course I know her! Met her in a village in Ashanti once—way back in '69. Wonderful woman! How on earth do you know her?" The happiness fled from his face and was replaced by alarm. "Dear God! She's not been—"

"No! No," Pitt said hastily. "I met her through a relative of my sister-in-law. At least a few months ago she was in excellent health, and spirits."

"Thank heaven!" Lindsay waved at Pitt to sit down. "Now what can we do about Stephen Shaw, poor devil? This is a very ugly situation." He poked at the fire vigorously, then replaced the fire iron set and sat down in the other chair. "He was extremely fond of Clemency, you know. Not a great passion—if it ever was, it had long passed—but he liked her, liked her deeply. And it is not given to many men to like their wives. She was a woman of rare intelligence, you know?" He raised his eyebrows and his small vivid eyes searched Pitt's countenance.

Pitt thought of Charlotte. Immediately her face filled his mind, and he was overwhelmed with how much he also liked his wife. The friendship was in its own way as precious as the love, and perhaps a greater gift, something born of time and sharing, of small jokes well understood, of helping each other through anxiety or sorrow, seeing the weaknesses and the strengths and caring for both.

But if for Stephen Shaw the passion had gone, and he was a passionate man, then could it have been kindled elsewhere? Would friendship, however deep, survive that whirlwind of hunger? He wanted to believe so; instinctively he had liked Shaw.

But the woman, whoever she was—she would not feel such constraints. Indeed she might seethe with jealousy, and the fact that Shaw still liked and admired his wife might make that frail outer control snap—and result in murder.

Lindsay was staring at him, waiting for a reponse more tangible than the thoughtful expression on his face.

"Indeed," Pitt said aloud, looking up again. "It would be natural if he found it hard at present to think of who might hold him in such enmity, or feel they had enough to gain from either his death or his wife's. But since you know him well, you may be able to give more suggestions, unpleasant as it would be. At least we might exclude some people. . ." He left the sentence hanging in the air, hoping it would be unnecessary to press any further.

Lindsay was too intelligent to need or wish for any more prompting. His eyes wandered over the relics here in the room. Perhaps he was thinking of other lands, other peoples with the same passions, less colored and confused by the masks of civilization.

"Stephen has certainly made enemies," he said quietly. "People of strong convictions usually do, especially if they are as articulate about them as he is. I am afraid he has little patience with fools, and even less with hypocrites—of which this society provides a great many, in one form or another." He shook his head. A coal settled in the fire with a shower of sparks. "The more we think we are sophisticated sometimes the sillier we get—and certainly the more idle people there are with nothing to fill their minds except making moral rules for everyone else, the more hypocrisy there is as to who keeps them and who doesn't."

Pitt envisioned a savage society in the sun on vast plains with the flat-topped trees he had seen in paintings, and grass huts, drum music and imprisoning heat—a culture that had not changed since memory's record began. What had Lindsay done there, how had he lived? Had he taken an African wife, and loved her? What had brought him back to Highgate on the outskirts of London and the heart of the Empire with its white gloves, carriages, engraved calling cards, gas lamps, maids in starched aprons, little old ladies, portraits of bishops, stained-glass windows—and murder?

"Whom in particular may he have offended?" He looked at Lindsay curiously.

Lindsay's face was suddenly wreathed in smiles. "Good heavens, man—everyone. Celeste and Angeline think he failed to treat Theophilus with proper attention, and that if he had not, the old fool would still be alive—"

"And would he?"

Lindsay's eyebrows shot up. "God knows. I doubt it. What can you do for an apoplectic seizure? He couldn't sit 'round the clock with him."

"Who else?"

"Alfred Lutterworth thinks Flora is enamored of him—which she may well be. She's in and out of the house often enough, and sees Stephen on her own, out of normal surgery hours. She may imagine other people don't know—but they most certainly do. Lutterworth thinks Stephen is seducing her with an eye to the money, of which there is a very great deal." The bland look of slight amusement on his face made Pitt think that the idea of Shaw murdering his wife because she stood in the way of such a marriage had not crossed his mind. His weathered face, so lined it reflected every expression, was touched with pity and a shadow of something like contempt, without its cruelty—but there was no fear in it.

"And of course Lally Clitheridge is appalled by his opinions," Lindsay went on, his smile broadening. "And fascinated by his vitality. He is ten times the man poor old Hector is, or ever will be. Prudence Hatch is fond of him—and frightened of him—for some reason I haven't discovered. Josiah can't abide him for a dozen reasons that are inherent in his nature—and Stephen's. Quinton Pascoe, who sells beautiful and romantic books, reviews them, and quite genuinely loves them, thinks Stephen is an irresponsible iconoclast—because he supports John Dalgetty and his avant-garde views of literature, or at least he supports his freedom to express them, regardless of whom they offend."

"Do they offend people?" Pitt asked, curious for himself as well as for any importance it might have. Surely no literary disapproval could be powerful enough to motivate murder? Ill temper, dislike, contempt, but surely only a madman kills over a matter of taste?

"Grossly." Lindsay noted Pitt's skepticism and there was a light of irony in his own eyes. "You have to understand Pascoe and Dalgetty. Ideals, the expression of thought and the arts of creation and communication are their lives." He shrugged. "But you asked me who hated Stephen from time to time—not who I thought would actually set fire to his house with the intent of burning him to death. If I knew anyone I thought would do that

I should have told you long before you came to the door asking."

Pitt acknowledged it with a grimace, and was about to pursue the matter when the manservant reappeared to announce that Mr. Dalgetty had called to ask if Lindsay would receive him. Lindsay glanced at Pitt with a flash of amusement, then indicated his agreement.

A moment later John Dalgetty came in, obviously having assumed Lindsay was alone. He launched into speech immediately, his voice ringing with enthusiasm. He was a dark man of medium stature and high, almost vertical forehead, fine eyes, and a shock of hair which was now receding a little. He was very casually dressed with a loose black cravat tied in what had probably been a bow when he set out that morning. Now it was merely a bundle. His jacket was overlong and loose, and the whole effect was extremely untidy, but had a certain panache.

"Quite brilliant!" He waved his hands. "Just what Highgate needs—indeed the whole of London! Shake up some of these tired old ideas, make people think. That's what matters, you know—freedom from the rigid, the orthodox that ossifies the faculties of invention and discovery." He frowned, leaning a little forward in his urgency. "Man is a creature full of the power of the mind, if only we free it from the shackles of fear. Terrified of the new, quaking at the prospect of making a mistake. What do a few mistakes matter?" He hunched his shoulders high. "If in the end we discover and name some new truth? Cowards— that's what we're fast becoming. A nation of intellectual cowards—too timorous to undertake an adventure into unknown regions of thought or knowledge." He swung one arm wide towards an Ashanti spear on the wall. "How would our Empire be if all our voyagers of the seas or explorers of the lands had been too afraid of anything new to circumnavigate the earth, or venture into the dark continents of Africa and India?" He poked his fingers at the floor. "Right here in England, that's where! And the world"—he flung out his hand dramatically—"would belong to the French, or the Spanish, or God knows whom. And here we are leaving all the voyages of the mind to the Germans, or whomever, because we are afraid of treading on a few toes. Have you seen Pascoe? He's practically foaming at the mouth because of your monograph on the wrongs of the ownership of the means of production! Of course it's brilliant. Full of new ideas, new concepts of community and the proper division of wealth. I shall review it as widely as—oh—" Suddenly he noticed Pitt and his face fell with amazement, then as quickly filled with curiosity. "I beg your pardon, sir, I was unaware Mr. Lindsay had company. John Dalgetty." He bowed very slightly. "Seller of rare books and reviewer of literature, and I hope, disseminator of ideas."

"Thomas Pitt," Pitt replied. "Inspector of police, and I hope discoverer of truth, or at least a measurable portion of it—we will never know it all, but sometimes enough to assist what serves as justice."

"Good gracious me." Dalgetty laughed aloud, but there was considerable nervousness in it as well as humor. "A policeman with an extraordinary turn of phrase. Are you making fun of me, sir?"

"Not at all," Pitt replied sincerely. "The truth of a crime, its causes and its effects, are far beyond us to reach. But we may, if we are diligent and lucky, discover who committed it, and at least some portion of why."

"Oh—ah—yes, indeed. Very terrible." Dalgetty drew his black brows down and shook his head a little. "A fine woman. Didn't know her closely myself, always seemed to be busy with matters of her own, good works and so forth. But excellent reputation." He looked at Pitt with something almost like a challenge. "Never heard a word against her from anyone. Great friend of my wife's, always conversing with one another. Tragic loss. I wish I could help, but I know nothing at all, absolutely nothing."

Pitt was inclined to believe him, but he asked a few questions in case there was some small fact in among the enthusiasm and opinions. He learned nothing, and some fifteen minutes after Dalgetty departed, still muttering praises of the monograph, Stephen Shaw himself returned, full of energy, coming in like a gale, flinging doors open and leaving them swinging. But Pitt saw the shadows under his eyes and the strain in the lines around his mouth.

"Good afternoon, Dr. Shaw," he said quietly. "I am sorry to intrude again, but there are many questions I need to ask."

"Of course." Shaw absentmindedly straightened the Ashanti spear, and then moved to the bookcase and leveled a couple of volumes. "But I've already told you everything I can think of."

"Someone lit those fires deliberately, Dr. Shaw," Pitt reminded him.

Shaw winced and looked at Pitt. "I know that. If I had the faintest idea, don't you think I'd tell you?"

"What about your patients? Have you treated anyone for any disease that they might wish to conceal—"

"For God's sake, what?" Shaw stared at him, eyes wide. "If it were contagious I should report it, regardless of what they wished! If it were insanity I should have them committed!"

"What about syphilis?"

Shaw stopped in mid movement, his arms in the air. "Touché," he said very quietly. "Both contagious and causing insanity in the end. And I should very probably keep silence. I certainly should not make it public." A flicker of irony crossed his face. "It is not passed by shaking hands or sharing a glass of wine, nor is the insanity secret or homicidal."

"And have you treated any such cases?" Pitt smiled blandly, and had no intention of allowing Shaw to sidestep an answer.

"If I had, I should not break a patient's confidence now." Shaw looked back at him with candor and complete defiance. "Nor will I discuss with you any other medical confidence I may have received—on any subject."

"Then we may be some considerable time discovering who murdered your wife, Dr. Shaw." Pitt looked at him coolly. "But I will not stop trying, whatever I have to overturn to find the truth. Apart from the fact that it is my job—the more I hear of her, the more I believe she deserves it."

Shaw's face paled and the muscles tightened in his neck and his mouth pulled thin as if he had been caught by some necessary inner pain, but he did not speak.

Pitt knew he was wounding, and hated it, but to withhold now might make it worse in the close future.

"And if, as seems probable, it was not your wife the murderer was after," he went on, "but yourself, then he—or she—will very possibly try again. I assume you have considered that?"

Shaw's face was white.

"I have, Mr. Pitt," he said very quietly. "But I cannot break my code of medical ethics on that chance—even were it a certainty. To betray my patients would not necessarily save me—and it is not a bargain I am prepared to make. Whatever you learn, you will have to do it in some other way."

Pitt was not surprised. It was what he had expected of the man, and in spite of the frustration, he would have been at least in part disappointed had he received more.

He glanced at Lindsay's face, pink in the reflected firelight, and saw a deep affection in it and a certain wry satisfaction. He too would have suffered a loss had Shaw been willing to speak.

"Then I had better continue with it in my own way," Pitt accepted, standing a little straighter. "Good day, Mr. Lindsay, and thank you for your frankness. Good day, Dr. Shaw."

"Good day, sir," Lindsay replied with unusual courtesy, and Shaw stood silent by the bookshelves.

The manservant returned and showed him out into the autumn sunlight, thin and gold, and the wind scurrying dry leaves along the footpath. It took him half an hour's brisk walk before he found a hansom to take him back into the city.

CHAPTER

FOUR

Charlotte did not enjoy the public omnibus, but to hire a hansom cab all the way from Bloomsbury to her mother's home on Cater Street was an unwarranted extravagance; and should there be any little surplus for her to spend, there were better things that might be done with it. Particularly she had in mind a new gown on which to wear Emily's silk flowers. Not, of course, that a cab fare would purchase even one sleeve of such a thing, but it was a beginning. And with Emily home again, there might arise an occasion to wear such a gown.

In the meantime she climbed aboard the omnibus, gave the conductor her fare, and squeezed between a remarkably stout woman with a wheeze like a bellows and a short man whose gloomy stare into the middle distance of his thoughts threatened to take him beyond his stop, unless he were traveling to the end of the line.

"Excuse me." Charlotte sat down firmly, and they were both obliged to make way for her, the large woman with a creak of whalebone and rattle of taffeta, the man in silence.

She alighted presently and walked in mild, blustery wind the two hundred yards along the street to the house where she had been born and grown up, and where seven years ago she had met Pitt, and scandalized the neighbors by marrying him. Her mother, who had been trying unsuccessfully to find a husband for her ever since she had been seventeen, had accepted the match with more grace than Charlotte had imagined possible. Perhaps it was not unmixed with a certain relief? And although Caroline Ellison was every bit as traditional, as ambitious for her daughters, and as sensitive to the opinions of her peers as anyone else, she did love her children and ultimately realized that their happiness might lie in places she herself would never have considered even tolerable.

Now even she admitted to a considerable fondness for Thomas Pitt, even if she still preferred not to tell all her acquaintances what he did as an occupation. Her mother-in-law, on the other hand, had never ceased to find it a social disaster, nor lost an opportunity to say so.

Charlotte mounted the steps and rang the bell. She had barely time to step back before it opened and Maddock the butler ushered her in.

"Good afternoon, Miss Charlotte. How very pleasant to see you. Mrs. Ellison will be delighted. She is in the withdrawing room, and at the moment has no other callers. Shall I take your coat?"

"Good afternoon, Maddock. Yes, if you please. Is everyone well?"

"Quite well, thank you," he replied automatically. It was not expected that one would reply that the cook had rheumatism in her knees, or that the housemaid had sniffles and the kitchen maid had twisted her ankle staggering in with the coke scuttle. Ladies were not concerned in such downstairs matters. He had never really grasped that Charlotte was no longer a "lady" in the sense in which she had been when she grew up in this house.

In the long-familiar withdrawing room Caroline was sitting idly poking at a piece of embroidery, her mind quite absent from it; and Grandmama was staring at her irritably, trying to think of a sufficiently stinging remark to make. When she was a girl embroidery was done with meticulous care, and if one were unfortunate enough to be a widow with no husband to please, that was an affliction to be borne with dignity and some grace, but one still did things with proper attention.

"If you continue in that manner you will stitch your fingers, and get blood on the linen," she said just as the door opened and Charlotte was announced. "And then it will be good for nothing."

"It is good for very little anyway," Caroline replied. Then she became aware of the extra presence.

"Charlotte!" She dropped the whole lot, needle, linen, frame and threads, on the floor and rose to her feet with delight—and relief. "My dear, how nice to see you. You look very well. How are the children?"

"In excellent health, Mama." Charlotte hugged her mother. "And you?" She turned to her grandmother. "Grandmama? How are you?" She knew the catalogue of complaint that would follow, but it would be less offensive if it were asked for than if it were not.

"I suffer," the old lady replied, looking Charlotte up and down with sharp, black eyes. She snorted. She was a small, stout woman with a beaked nose, which in her youth had been considered aristocratic, at least by those most kindly disposed towards her. "I am lame—and deaf—which if you came to visit us more often you would know without having to ask."

"I do know, Grandmama," Charlotte replied, determined to be agreeable. "I asked only to show you that I care."

"Indeed," the old woman grunted. "Well sit down and tell us something of interest. I am also bored. Although I have been bored ever since your grandfather died—and for some time before, come to that. It is the lot of women of good breeding to be bored. Your mother is bored also, although she has not learned to resign herself to it as I have. She has developed no skill at it. She does bad embroidery. I cannot see well enough to embroider anymore, but when I could, it was perfect."

"You will have tea." Caroline smiled across her mother-in-law's head. These conversations had been part of her life for twenty years, and she accepted them with good grace. Actually, she was seldom bored; when the first grief of her widowhood had passed she had discovered new and most interesting pursuits. She had found herself free to read the newspapers for the first time in her life, any pages she wished. She had learned a little of politics and current affairs, social issues of debate, and she had joined societies which discussed all manner of things.

She was finding time heavy this afternoon simply because she had decided to spend the time at home with the old lady, and they had until now received no callers.

"Please." Charlotte accepted, seating herself in her favorite chair.

Caroline rang for the maid and ordered tea, sandwiches, cakes and fresh scones and jam, then settled to hear whatever news Charlotte might have, and to tell her of a philosophical group she had recently joined.

The tea came, was poured and passed, and the maid retired.

"You will have seen Emily, no doubt." Grandmama made it a statement, and her face was screwed up with disapproval. "In my day widows did not marry again the moment their poor husbands were cold in the ground. Unseemly haste. Most unseemly. And it's not even as if she were bettering herself. Stupid girl. That I could understand, at least. But Jack Radley! Who on earth are the Radleys? I ask you!"

Charlotte ignored the whole matter. She was confident Jack Radley would flatter the old lady and she would melt like butter on a hot crumpet. It was simply not worth trying to argue the point now. And of course whatever Emily had brought her from Europe she would criticize, but she would be pleased all the same, and show it off relentlessly.

As if aware of Charlotte's well-controlled temper the old lady swiveled around and glared at her over the top of her eyeglasses.

"And what are you doing with yourself these days, miss? Still meddling in your husband's affairs? If there is anything in the world that is totally and inexcusably vulgar, it is curiosity about other people's domestic tragedies. I told you at the time no good would come of it." Again she snorted spitefully and settled back a little in her seat. "Detective, indeed!"

"I am not involved in Thomas's present case, Grandmama." Charlotte took a fifth cucumber sandwich and ate it with relish. They really were delicious, thin as wafers, and sweet and crisp.

"Good," the old woman said with satisfaction. "You eat too much. It is unladylike. You have lost all the refinement of manner you used to have. I blame you, Caroline! You should never have allowed this to happen. If she had been my daughter she would not have been permitted to marry beneath her!"

Caroline had long ago ceased to defend herself from such remarks, and she did not wish to quarrel, even though she was provoked. In fact it gave her a certain satisfaction to catch her mother-in-law's beady eyes and smile sweetly back at her, and see the irritation in them.

"Unfortunately I had not your skill," she said gently. "I managed very well with Emily—but Charlotte defeated me."

The old lady was temporarily beaten. "Hah!" she said, at a loss for words.

Charlotte hid her smile, and took another sip of tea.

"Given up meddling, have you?" The old lady renewed the attack. "Emily will be disappointed!"

Charlotte sipped her tea again.

"All cutpurses and thieves, I suppose," Grandmama continued. "Been demoted, has he?"

Finally Charlotte was drawn, in spite of her resolution.

"No. It is arson and murder. A very respectable woman has been burned to death in Highgate. In fact her grandfather was a bishop," she added with something unpleasantly like triumph.

The old lady looked at her guardedly. "What bishop would that be? Sounds unlikely to me."

"Bishop Worlingham," Charlotte replied immediately.

"Bishop Worlingham! Augustus Worlingham?" The old lady's eyes snapped sharp with interest; she leaned forward in her chair and thumped her black walking stick on the ground. "Answer me, girl! Augustus Worlingham?"

"I imagine so." Charlotte could not remember Pitt having mentioned the bishop's Christian name. "There surely cannot be two."

"Don't be impertinent!" But the old lady was too excited to be more than cursorily critical. "I used to know his daughters, Celeste and Angeline. So they still live in Highgate. Well why not? Very fortunate area. I should go and call upon them, convey my condolences upon their loss."

"You can't!" Caroline was appalled. "You've never mentioned them before—you cannot have called upon them in years!"

"And is that any cause not to comfort them now in their distress?" the old lady demanded, eyebrows high, searching for reason in an unreasonable house. "I shall go this very afternoon. It is quite early. You may accompany me if you wish." She hauled herself to her feet. "As long as you do not in any circumstances display a vulgar curiosity." And she stumped past the tea trolley and out of the withdrawing room without so much as glancing behind her to see what reaction her remarks had provoked.

Charlotte looked at her mother, undecided whether to declare herself or not. The idea of meeting people so close to Clemency Shaw was strongly appealing, even though she believed the person who had connived her death, whoever had lit the taper, was someone threatened by her work to expose slum profiteers to the public knowledge.

Caroline drew in her breath, then her expression of incredulity turned rapidly through contemplation to shamefaced interest.

"Ah—" She breathed in and out again slowly. "I really don't think we should permit her to go alone, do you? I have no idea what she might say." She bit her lip to suppress a smile. "And curiosity is so vulgar."

"Perfectly terrible," Charlotte agreed, rising to her feet and clasping her reticule, ready for departure.

They made the considerable ride to Highgate in close to silence. Once Charlotte asked the old lady if she could inform them of her acquaintance with the Worlingham sisters, and anything about their present situation, but the reply was scant, and in a tone that discouraged further inquiry.

"They were neither prettier nor plainer than most," the old lady said, as if the question had been fatuous. "I never heard any scandal about them—which may mean they were virtuous, or merely that no opportunity for misbehavior offered itself. They were the daughters of a bishop, after all."

"I was not seeking scandal." Charlotte was irritated by the

implication. "I simply wondered what nature of people they were."

"Bereaved," came the reply. "That is why I am calling upon them. I suspect you of mere curiosity, which is a character failing of a most distasteful sort. I hope you will not embarrass me when we are there?"

Charlotte gasped at the sheer effrontery of it. She knew perfectly well the old lady had not called on the Worlinghams in thirty years, and assuredly would not now had Clemency died in a more ordinary fashion. For once a suitably stinging reply eluded her, and she rode the remainder of the journey in silence.

The Worlingham house in Fitzroy Park, Highgate, was imposing from the outside, solid with ornate door and windows, and large enough to accommodate a very considerable family and full staff of indoor servants.

Inside, when they were admitted by a statuesque parlormaid, it was even more opulent, if now a little shabby in various places. Charlotte, well behind her mother and grandmother, had opportunity to glance around with a more lingering eye. The hall was unusually large, paneled in oak, and hung with portraits of varying age, but no plates underneath to tell their names. An instant suspicion crossed Charlotte's mind that they were not ancestral Worlinghams at all, merely dressing to awe a visitor. In the place of honor where the main light shone on it was by far the largest portrait, that of an elderly gentleman in very current dress. His broad face was pink fleshed, his silver hair grew far back on his sloping forehead and curled up over his ears, forming an almost luminous aureole around his head. His eyes were blue under heavy lids, and his chin was wide; but his most remarkable feature was the benign, complacent and supremely confident smile on his lips. Under this the plate was legible even as Charlotte walked past it to the morning room door. BISHOP AUGUSTUS T. WORLINGHAM.

The maid departed to inquire whether they would be received, and Grandmama bent herself stiffly to sit in one of the chairs, staring around at the room critically. The pictures here were gloomy landscapes, framed samplers with such mottoes as "Vanity, vanity, all is vanity," in cross-stitch; "The price of a good woman is above rubies," framed in wood; and "God sees all," with an eye in satin and stem stitches.

Caroline pulled a face.

Charlotte imagined the two sisters as girls sitting on a sabbath afternoon in silence, carefully sewing such things, all fingers and thumbs, hating every moment of it, wondering how long until tea when Papa would read the Scriptures to them; they would answer dutifully, and then after prayers be released to go to bed.

Grandmama cleared her throat and looked with disfavor at an enormous glass case filled with stuffed and mounted birds.

The antimacassars were stitched in brown upon linen, and all a trifle crooked.

The parlormaid returned to say that the Misses Worlingham would be charmed to receive them, and accordingly they followed her back across the hall and into the cavernous withdrawing room hung with five chandeliers. Only two of these were lit, and the parquet wooden floors were strewn with an assortment of Oriental rugs of several different shades and designs, all a fraction paler where the pile had been worn with constant tread, from the door to the sofa and chairs, and to a distinct patch in front of the fire, as if someone had habitually stood there. Charlotte remembered with an odd mixture of anger and loss how her father had stood in front of the fire in winter, warming himself, oblivious of the fact that he was keeping it from everyone else. The late Bishop Worlingham, no doubt, had done the same. And his daughters would not have raised their voices to object, nor would his wife when she was alive. It brought a sharp flavor of youth, being at home with her parents and sisters, the callowness and the safety of those times, taken for granted then. She glanced at Caroline, but Caroline was watching Grandmama as she sailed up to the elder of the Misses Worlingham.

"My dear Miss Worlingham, I was so sorry to hear of your bereavement. I had to come and offer my condolences in person, rather than simply write a letter. You must feel quite dreadful."

Celeste Worlingham, a woman in her late fifties with strong features, dark brown eyes and a face which in her youth must

have been handsome rather than pretty, now looked both confused and curious. The marks of shock were visible in the
strained lines around her mouth and the stiff carriage of her neck,
but she had admirable composure, and would not give in to
unseemly grief, at least not in public, and she considered this
public. Obviously she did not recall even the barest acquaintance
with any of her visitors, but a lifetime of good manners overrode
all.

"Most kind of you, Mrs. Ellison. Of course Angeline and I
are very grieved, but as Christians we learn to bear such loss
with fortitude—and faith."

"Naturally," Grandmama agreed, a trifle perfunctorily.
"May I introduce to you my daughter-in-law, Mrs. Caroline
Ellison, and my granddaughter, Mrs. Pitt."

Everyone exchanged courtesies and Grandmama fixed her
eyes on Celeste, then changed her mind and looked at Angeline,
a younger, fairer woman with mild features and a comfortable,
domestic look. Grandmama swayed back and forth on her feet
and planted her stick heavily on the carpet and leaned on it.

"Please sit down, Mrs. Ellison," Angeline said immediately.
"May we offer you some refreshment? A tizanne, perhaps."

"How kind," Grandmama accepted with near alacrity, pulling Caroline sharply by the skirt so she also was obliged to sit
on the fat red sofa a step behind her. "You are as thoughtful as
ever," Grandmama added for good measure.

Angeline reached for the hand bell and rang it with a sharp,
tinkling sound, and almost as soon as she had replaced it on the
table the maid appeared. She requested a tizanne, then changed
her mind and asked for tea for all of them.

Grandmama sank back in her seat, set her stick between her
own voluminous skirts and Caroline's, and rather belatedly
masked a look of satisfaction with concern again.

"I imagine your dear brother will be a great strength to you,
and of course you to him," she said unctuously. "He must be
most distressed. It is at such a time that families must support
each other."

"Exactly what our father the bishop used to say," Angeline
agreed, leaning forward a little, her black dress creasing across

her ample bosom. "He was such a remarkable man. The family is the strength of the nation, he used to say. And a virtuous and obedient woman is the heart of the family. And dear Clemency was certainly that."

"Poor Theophilus passed on," Celeste said with a touch of asperity. "I am surprised you did not know. It was in *The Times*."

For an instant Grandmama was confounded. It was no use saying she did not read obituaries; no one would have believed her. Births, deaths, marriages and the Court calendar were all that gentlewomen did read. Too much of the rest was sensational, contentious or otherwise unsuitable.

"I am so sorry," Caroline murmured reluctantly. "When was it?"

"Two years ago," Celeste answered with a slight shiver. "It was very sudden, such a shock to us."

Caroline looked at Grandmama. "That will have been when you were ill yourself, and we did not wish to distress you. I imagine by the time you were recovered we had forgotten we had not told you."

Grandmama refused to be obliged for the rescue. Charlotte was moved to admiration for her mother. She would have allowed the old lady to flounder.

"That is the obvious explanation," Grandmama agreed, staring at Celeste and defying her to disbelieve.

A flicker of respect, and of a certain dry humor, crossed Celeste's intelligent face.

"Doubtless."

"It was very sudden indeed." Angeline had not noticed the exchange at all. "I am afraid we were inclined to blame poor Stephen—that is, Dr. Shaw. He is our nephew-in-law, you know? Indeed I almost said as much, that he had given Theophilus insufficient care. Now I feel ashamed of myself, when the poor man is bereaved himself, and in such terrible circumstances."

"Fire." Grandmama shook her head. "How can such a thing have happened? A careless servant? I've always said servants are nothing like they used to be—they're slovenly, impertinent and careless of detail. It is quite terrible. I don't know what the world is coming to. I don't suppose she had this new electrical lighting, did she? I don't trust that at all. Dangerous stuff. Meddling with the forces of nature."

"Oh, certainly not," Angeline said quickly. "It was gas, like ours." She barely glanced at the chandelier. Then she looked wistful and a little abashed. "Although I did see an advertisement for an electric corset the other day, and wondered what it might do." She looked at Charlotte hopefully.

Charlotte had no idea; her mind had been on Theophilus and his unexpected death.

"I am sorry, Miss Worlingham, I did not see it. It sounds most uncomfortable—"

"Not to say dangerous," Grandmama snapped. She not only disapproved of electricity, she disapproved even more of being interrupted in what she considered to be her conversation. "And absurd," she added. "A bedpost and a maid with a good strong arm was sufficient for us—and we had waists a man could put his hands 'round—or at least could think of such a thing." She swiveled back to Celeste. "What a mercy her husband was not also killed," she said with a perfectly straight face, not even a flicker or a blush. "How did it happen?"

Caroline closed her eyes and Grandmama surreptitiously poked her with her stick to keep her from intervening.

Charlotte let out a sigh.

Celeste looked taken aback.

"He was out on a call," Angeline answered with total candor. "A confinement a little earlier than expected. He is a doctor, you know, in many ways a fine man, in spite of—" She stopped as abruptly as she had begun, a tinge of pride creeping up her cheeks. "Oh dear, I do beg your pardon. One should not speak ill, our dear father was always saying that. Such a wonderful man!" She sighed and smiled, staring mistily into some distance within her mind. "It was such a privilege to have lived in the same house with him and been of service, caring for him, seeing that he was looked after as such a man should be."

Charlotte looked at the plump, fair figure with its benign face, a blurred echo of her sister's, softer, and more obviously vulnerable. She must have had suitors as a young woman. Surely she would rather have accepted one of them than spend her life ministering to her father's needs, had she been permitted the chance. There were parents who kept their daughters at home as permanent servants, unpaid but for their keep, unable to give notice because they had no other means of support, ever dutiful, obedient, ever loving—and at the same time hating, as all prisoners do—until it was too late to leave even when the doors were at last opened by death.

Was Angeline Worlingham one of these? Indeed, were they both?

"And your brother also." Grandmama was unstoppable; her beadlike eyes were bright and she sat upright with attention. "Another fine man. Tragic he should die so young. What was the cause?"

"Mama-in-law!" Caroline was aghast. "I really think we—Oh!" She gave a little squeal as the old lady's stick poked her leg with a sharp pain.

"Have you the hiccups?" Grandmama inquired blandly. "Take a little more of your tea." She returned to Celeste. "You were telling us of poor Theophilus's passing. What a loss!"

"We do not know the cause," Celeste said with chill. "It appears it may have been an apoplectic seizure of some sort, but we are not perfectly sure."

"It was poor Clemency who found him," Angeline added. "That is another thing for which I hold Stephen responsible. Sometimes he is a touch too free in his ideas. He expects too much."

"All men expect too much," Grandmama opined sententiously.

Angeline blushed furiously and looked at the floor; even Celeste looked uncomfortable.

This time Caroline ignored all strictures and spoke.

"That was a most unfortunate turn of phase," she apologized. "I am sure that you meant it was unfair to expect Clemency to cope with the discovery of her father's death, especially when it was quite unexpected."

"Oh—of course." Angeline collected herself with a gasp of relief. "He had been ill for a few days, but we had not presumed it serious. Stephen paid scant regard to it. Of course"—she drew down her brows and lowered her voice confidentially—"they were not as close as they might have been, in spite of being father- and son-in-law. Theophilus disapproved of some of Stephen's ideas."

"We all disapprove of them," Celeste said with asperity. "But they were social and theological matters, not upon the subject of medicine. He is a very competent doctor. Everyone says so."

"Indeed, he has many patients," Angeline added eagerly, her plump hands fingering the beads at her bosom. "Young Miss Lutterworth would not go to anyone else."

"Flora Lutterworth is no better than she should be," Celeste said darkly. "She consults him at every fit and turn, and I have my own opinions that she would be a good deal less afflicted with whatever malady it is had Stephen a wart on the end of his nose, or a squint in one eye."

"Nobody knows what it is," Angeline whispered. "She looks as healthy as a horse to me. Of course they are very *nouveau riche*," she added, explaining to Caroline and Charlotte. "Working-class really, for all that money. Alfred Lutterworth made it in cotton mills in Lancashire and only came down here when he sold them. He tries to act the gentleman, but of course everyone knows."

Charlotte was unreasonably irritated; after all, this was the world in which she had grown up, and at one time might have thought similarly herself.

"Knows what?" she inquired with an edge to her voice.

"Why, that he made his money in trade," Angeline said with surprise. "It is really quite obvious, my dear. He has brought up his daughter to sound like a lady, but speech is not all, is it?"

"Certainly not," Charlotte agreed dryly. "Many who sound like ladies are anything but."

Angeline took no double meaning and settled back in her seat with satisfaction, rearranging her skirts a trifle. "More tea?" she inquired, holding up the silver pot with its ornate, swan neck spout.

They were interrupted by the parlormaid's return to announce that the vicar and Mrs. Clitheridge had called.

Celeste glanced at Grandmama, and realized she had not the slightest intention of leaving.

"Please show them in," Celeste instructed with a lift of one of her heavy eyebrows. She did not glance at Angeline; humor was not something they were able to share, their perceptions were too different. "And bring more tea."

Hector Clitheridge was solid and bland, with the sort of face that in his youth had been handsome, but was now marred by constant anxiety and a nervousness which had scored lines in his cheeks and taken the ease and directness out of his eyes. He came forward now in a rush to express his condolences yet again, and then was startled to find an additional three women there whom he did not know.

His wife, on the other hand, was quite homely and probably even in her very best years could only have offered no more charms than a freshness of complexion and a good head of hair. But her back was straight, she could well have walked with a pile of books on her head without losing any, and her eye was calm, her manner composed. Her voice was unusually low and agreeable.

"My dear Celeste—Angeline. I know we have already expressed our sympathies and offered our services, but the vicar thought we should call again, merely to assure you that we are most sincere. So often people say these things as a matter of custom, and one does not care to take them up on it for precisely that reason. Some people avoid the bereaved, which is scarcely Christian."

"Quite," her husband agreed, relief flooding his face. "If there is anything we can do for you?" He looked from one to the other of them as if he awaited a suggestion.

Celeste introduced them to the company already present, and everyone exchanged greetings.

"How very kind," Clitheridge said, smiling at Grandmama. His hands fiddled with his badly tied tie, making it worse. "Surely a sign of true friendship when one comes in times of grief. Have you known the Misses Worlingham long? I do not recall having seen you here before."

"Forty years," Grandmama said promptly.

"Oh my goodness, how very fine. You must be exceedingly fond of each other."

"And it is thirty of them since we last saw you." Celeste finally lost her temper. It was apparent from her face that Grandmama mildly amused her, but the vicar's waving hands and bland words irritated her beyond bearing. "So kind of you to have come just now when we are suffering a dramatic loss."

Charlotte heard the sarcasm in her tone, and could see in the strong, intelligent face that none of the motives or excuses had passed her by.

Grandmama sniffed indignantly. "I told you, I did not read of poor Theophilus's death. If I had I would surely have come then. It is the least one can do."

"And at Papa's death too, no doubt," Celeste said with a very slight smile. "Except perhaps you did not read of that either?"

"Oh, Celeste. Don't be ridiculous." Angeline's eyes were very wide. "Everyone heard of Papa's passing. He was a bishop, after all, and a most distinguished one. He was respected by absolutely everybody!"

Caroline attempted to rescue Grandmama.

"I think perhaps when someone passes in the fullness of their years, it is not quite the same grief as when a younger person is cut off," she offered.

Grandmama swung around and glared at her, and Caroline colored faintly, more with annoyance at herself than apology.

The vicar fidgeted from one foot to the other, opened his mouth to say something, then realized it was a family dispute, and retreated hastily.

Charlotte spoke at last.

"I came because I had heard of Mrs. Shaw's magnificent work attempting to improve the housing standards of the poor," she said into the silence. "I have several friends who held her in the very highest esteem, and feel her loss is one to the whole community. She was a very fine woman."

There was utter silence. The vicar cleared his throat nervously. Angeline gave a little gasp, then put her handkerchief to her mouth and stifled it. Grandmama swiveled around in her seat with a crackle of taffeta and glared at Charlotte.

"I beg your pardon?" Celeste said huskily.

Charlotte realized with a hollowness, and a rush of blood up her cheeks, that obviously Clemency's work was unknown to her family, and to her vicar. But it was impossible to retreat; she had left herself no room at all. There was nothing to do but advance and hope for the best.

"I said she was a very fine woman," she repeated with a rather forced smile. "Her efforts to improve the living standards of the poor were greatly admired."

"I fear you are laboring under a misapprehension, Mrs. . . . er—Pitt," Celeste replied, now that she had recovered her poise. "Clemency was not concerned in any such matter. She did her ordinary duties such as any Christian woman will do. She took soup and the like, preserves and so on, to the deserving poor about the neighborhood, but so do we all. No one does as much as Angeline. She is always busy with some such thing. Indeed, I serve on several committees to assist young women who have—er—fallen into difficult circumstances and lost their character. You appear to have poor Clemency confused with someone else—I have not the slightest idea who."

"Nor I," Angeline added.

"It sounds a very virtuous work," Mrs. Clitheridge put in tentatively. "And most courageous."

"Quite unsuitable, my dear." The vicar shook his head. "I am sure dear Clemency would not have done such a thing."

"So am I." Celeste finished the subject with a chilly stare at Charlotte, her rather heavy brows raised very slightly. "Nevertheless, it was gracious of you to call. I am sure your mistake was perfectly genuine."

"Perfectly," Charlotte assured her. "My informants were the daughter of a duke and a member of Parliament."

Celeste was taken aback. "Indeed? You have some notable acquaintances—"

"Thank you." Charlotte inclined her head as if accepting a compliment.

"There must be another lady by the same name," the vicar suggested soothingly. "It seems unlikely, and yet what other explanation is there?"

"You must be right, my dear." His wife touched his arm with approval. "It seems obvious now. Of course that is what has happened."

"It all seems to be quite unimportant." Grandmama reasserted her influence on the conversation. "My acquaintance is with you, and has been since our youth. I should like to pay my respects at the funeral, and should be greatly indebted if you would inform me as to when it is."

"Oh certainly," the vicar answered before either of the Misses Worlingham had time. "How kind of you. Yes—it is to be held in St. Anne's, next Thursday at two o'clock in the afternoon."

"I am obliged." Grandmama was suddenly very gracious.

The door opened again and the parlormaid announced Mr. and Mrs. Hatch, and was followed immediately by a woman of about the same height as Angeline, and with a considerable resemblance to her in feature. The nose was a trifle more pronounced, the eyes had not faded, nor the hair, and she was obviously a generation younger, yet there was much in the bearing that was like, and she too wore the total black of mourning.

Her husband, only a step behind her, was of medium height and extreme gravity. He reminded Charlotte quite strongly of pictures of Mr. Gladstone, the great Liberal prime minister, in his earlier years. There was the same dedicated purpose in his stare, the same look of total rectitude and certainty in his own convictions. His side whiskers were less bristling and his nose of less grand proportions; still, the impression was sharp.

"My dear Prudence." Celeste greeted Mrs. Hatch with outstretched hands.

"Aunt Celeste." Prudence went to her and they kissed each other lightly, then she moved to her Aunt Angeline, and was kissed more closely and held a moment longer.

Josiah was more formal, but his condolences seemed every

bit as sincere. In fact he looked quite obviously distressed; his face was pale and there was a drawn appearance to the skin about his mouth. His emotions were apparently very deep and he kept them in control with some effort.

"The whole situation is quite dreadful," he said fixedly, looking at no one in particular. "Everywhere there is moral decline and decay. Young people in confusion, not knowing whom or what to admire anymore, women unprotected—" His voice was thick with distress. "Look at this unspeakable business in Whitechapel. Bestial—quite bestial. A sign of the chaos of our times—rising anarchy, the Queen closed up in Osborne ignoring us all, the Prince of Wales squandering his time and money in gambling and loose living, the Duke of Clarence worse." Still he looked at no one, his mind consumed with his inner vision. His body was motionless, but there was great strength in it, a feeling of waiting power. "The coarsest and most absurd ideas are being propagated and there is one tragedy after another. Everything has begun to slip ever since the dear bishop died. What a terrible loss that was." For a moment a look of sheer anguish crossed his features as if he gazed upon the end of a golden age, and all that followed must be darker and lonelier. His hands clenched in front of him, large knuckled and powerful. "And no one remotely near his stature has arisen to carry God's light for the rest of us."

"Theophilus . . ." Angeline said tentatively, then stopped. His look of contempt froze the words before they were formed.

"He was a good man," Prudence said loyally.

"Of course he was," her husband agreed. "But not his father's equal, not by a very long way. He was a pygmy in comparison." A strange mixture of grief and contempt crossed his face, then a zeal that had a wild beauty, almost visionary. "The bishop was a saint! He had wisdom incomparable with any of us. He understood the order of things as they should be, he had the insight into God's ways and how we should live His word." He smiled briefly. "How often I have heard him give counsel to men—and to women. Always his advice was wise and of spiritual and moral upliftment."

Angeline sighed gently and reached for her handkerchief, a wisp of cambric and lace.

"Men be upright," he continued. "Be utterly honest in your dealings, preside over your families, instruct your wives and children in the teachings of God. Women be obedient and virtuous, be diligent in your labors and they shall be your crown in heaven."

Charlotte shifted uncomfortably in her chair. The strength of his emotion was so obvious she could not dismiss it, but the sentiment was one she longed to quarrel with.

"Love your children and teach them by your example," Hatch went on, unaware of her, or anyone else. "Be chaste—and above all, be dutiful and be loyal to your family; therein lies your happiness and the happiness of the world."

"Amen," Angeline said with a sweet smile, her eyes raised as if in thought she could feel her father somewhere above her. "Thank you, Josiah, you have again reminded one of the purpose and reason for life. I don't know what we should do without you. I do not mean to speak slightly of Theophilus, but more than once I have thought you were Papa's true spiritual heir."

The color spread up his cheeks and for a moment there seemed to be tears in his eyes.

"Thank you, my dear Angeline. No man alive could wish for a finer compliment, and I swear to you, I shall endeavor to live worthily of it."

She beamed at him.

"The window?" Celeste said quietly, her face also softer and an expression of pleasure filling her eyes. "How is it progressing?"

"Very well," he answered after a sharp sniff and a shake of his head. "Very well indeed. It is most gratifying to see how everyone in Highgate, and far beyond, wishes to remember him and give all they can. I think they truly realize that these are dark times full of the doubts and misguided philosophies that these days pass as some kind of greater freedom. If we do not show very plainly what is the right way, God's way, then many souls will perish, and drag the innocent down with them."

"You are so very right, Josiah," Celeste put in.

"Indeed," Angeline nodded. "Indeed you are."

"And this window will be a powerful influence." He would not be cut off before he had spoken his mind, even by agreement. "People will look at it, and remember what a great man Bishop Worlingham was, and revere his teachings. It is one of the achievements of my life, if I may say so, to perpetuate his name and the good works that he performed in his mortal existence here."

"I'm sure we are all indebted to you," Angeline said heartily. "And Papa's work will not die as long as you are alive."

"Indeed we are most grateful," Celeste agreed. "I'm sure Theophilus would say so too, were he alive to do so."

"Such a loss," Clitheridge said awkwardly, two spots of pink coloring his cheeks.

His wife put her hand on his arm and her grip was surprisingly firm; Charlotte could see the white of her knuckles.

A pinched expression crossed Josiah Hatch's face, drawing tight the corners of his mouth, and he blinked several times. It seemed a mixture of sudden envy and disapproval.

"Ah—I—I would have expected Theophilus to initiate such a project himself," he said with wide eyes. "I am sometimes tempted to think, indeed I cannot avoid it, that Theophilus did not truly appreciate what an outstanding man his father was. Perhaps he was too close to him to realize how far above that of others were his thoughts and his ideals, how profound his perception."

It seemed no one had anything to add to this, and there were several moments of uncomfortable silence.

"Ahem!" The vicar cleared his throat. "I think, if you will excuse me, we will leave you, and go and visit Mrs. Hardy. Such a sad case, so difficult to know what to say to be of comfort. Good day, ladies." He bowed rather generally in the visitors' direction. "Good day to you, Josiah. Come, Eulalia." And taking his wife by the arm he went rather hastily out into the hallway and they heard the front door open and close again.

"Such a kind man—so kind," Angeline said almost as if she were pronouncing an incantation. "And so is dear Lally, of course. Such a strength to him—and to us all."

Charlotte thought that perhaps without her the vicar would collapse into incomprehensibility, but she forbore from saying so.

"He preaches a very good sermon," Celeste said with faint surprise. "He is really very learned, you know. It doesn't come through in his conversation, but perhaps that is as well. It doesn't do to overwhelm people with more learning than they can understand. It offers neither comfort nor instruction."

"How very true," Prudence agreed. "In fact I admit at times I do not know what he is talking about. But Josiah assures me it is all extremely good sense, don't you, my dear?"

"So it is," he said decisively, nodding his head a little, but there was no warmth in his tone. "He is always up to date on what the learned doctors of theology have said, and frequently quotes their works; and he is always correct, because I have taken the liberty of checking." He glanced briefly at the three visitors. "I have a considerable library, you know. And I have made it my business to take such periodicals as are enlightening and enlarging to the mind."

"Very commendable." Grandmama was frustrated with her enforced silence for so long. "I presume Theophilus inherited the bishop's library?"

"He did not." Celeste corrected her instantly. "I did."

"Celeste wrote up all Papa's sermons and notes for him," Angeline explained. "And of course Theophilus was not interested in books," she went on, looking with a nervous glance at Prudence. "He preferred paintings. He had a great many very fine paintings, mostly landscapes, you know? Lots of cows and water and trees and things. Very restful."

"Charming," Caroline said, simply for something to add to the conversation. "Are they oils or watercolors?"

"Watercolors, I believe. His taste was excellent, so I am told. His collection is worth a great deal."

Charlotte was curious to know if Clemency had inherited it, or Prudence; but her family had already disgraced itself more than enough for one day. And she did not believe that the motive for Clemency's murder, which they had all skirted delicately around mentioning, was money. Far more likely was the dangerous and radical reform she so passionately worked for—and apparently so secretly. Why had she not told even her aunts and her sister? Surely it was something to be proud of, most particularly with such a history of service as her grandfather's?

Her speculation was cut short by the parlormaid arriving yet again to announce Dr. Stephen Shaw. And again, he was so hard on her heels that she almost bumped into him as she turned to leave. He was not above average height and of strong but not stocky build, but it was the vitality in his face that dominated everything else and made the others in the room seem composed of browns and grays. Even tragedy, which had left its mark on him in shadows around his eyes and more deeply scored lines around his mouth, did not drain from him the inner energy.

" 'Afternoon, Aunt Celeste, Aunt Angeline." His voice was excellent with a resonance and a diction full of character and yet in no way eccentric. "Josiah—Prudence." He gave her a light kiss on the cheek, more a gesture than anything else, but a shadow of irritation crossed Hatch's face. There was the bleakest ficker of amusement in Shaw's eyes as he turned to look at Grandmama, Caroline and Charlotte.

"Mrs. Ellison," Celeste explained, introducing Grandmama. "She was a friend of ours some forty years ago. She called to give us her condolences."

"Indeed." The shadow of a smile became more distinct around his mouth. "For the bishop, for Theophilus, or for Clemency?"

"Stephen—you should not speak flippantly of such matters," Celeste said sharply. "It is most unseemly. You will allow people to take the wrong notion."

Without waiting for invitation he sat down in the largest chair.

"My dear aunt, there is nothing in creation I can do to prevent people from taking the wrong notion, if that is what they wish to do." He swung around to face Grandmama. "Most civil of you. You must have a great deal of news to catch up on— after such a space."

Neither the implication nor his amusement were lost on Grandmama, but she refused to acknowledge them even by an excuse. "My daughter-in-law, Mrs. Caroline Ellison," she said coldly. "And my granddaughter, Mrs. Pitt."

"How do you do." Shaw inclined his head courteously to Caroline. Then as he looked at Charlotte, a flash of interest crossed his features, as though he saw in her face something unusual.

"How do you do, Mrs. Pitt. Surely you are not acquainted with the Misses Worlingham also?"

Hatch opened his mouth to say something, but Charlotte cut across him.

"Not until today; but of course the bishop was much admired by repute."

"How excellently you choose your words, Mrs. Pitt. I presume you did not know him personally either?"

"Of course she didn't!" Hatch snapped. "He has been gone about ten years—to our misfortune."

"Let us hope it was not to his." Shaw smiled at Charlotte with his back to his brother-in-law.

"How dare you!" Hatch was furious, spots of color mottling his cheeks. He was still standing and he glared down at Shaw. "We are all more than tired of hearing your irreverent and critical remarks. You may imagine some twisted modicum of what you are pleased to call humor excuses anything at all—but it does not. You make a mock of too much. You encourage people to be light-minded and jeer at the things they should most value. That you could not appreciate the virtue of Bishop Worlingham says more about your own shallowness and triviality than it does about the magnitide of his character!"

"I think you are being a trifle harsh, Josiah," his wife said soothingly. "I daresay Stephen did not mean anything by it."

"Of course he did." Hatch would not be placated. "He is always making derisory remarks which he imagines to be amusing." His voice rose and he looked at Celeste. "He did not even wish to donate to the window. Can you imagine? And he supports that wretched man Lindsay in his revolutionary paper which questions the very foundations of decent society."

"No it doesn't," Shaw said. "It merely puts out certain ideas on reform which would distribute wealth more equitably."

"More equitably than what?" Hatch demanded. "Our present system? That amounts to overthrow of the government—in fact, revolution, as I said."

"No it does not." Shaw was overtly annoyed now and he swung around in his chair to face Hatch. "They believe in a gradual change, through legislation, to a system of collectivist state ownership of the means of producing wealth, with workers' control—full employment and appropriation of unearned increment—"

"I don't know what you are talking about, Stephen," Angeline said with her face screwed up in concentration.

"Neither do I," Celeste agreed. "Are you speaking about George Bernard Shaw and those fearful Webbs?"

"He is talking about anarchy and the total change or loss of everything you know!" Hatch replied with very real anger.

This was far deeper than the reopening of an old family quarrel. They were profound issues of morality. And turning from him to Shaw, Charlotte believed that in his eyes also she saw a fire of seriousness beneath the perception of a very surface absurdity. Humor was always with him, it was deep in all the lines of his face, but it was only the outer garment of a passionate mind.

"People can get away with anything these days," Grandmama said unhelpfully. "In my youth, Bernard Shaw, Mr. Webb, and their like would have been put in prison before they were permitted to speak of such ideas—but today they are quite openly quoted. And of course Mrs. Webb is quite beyond the pale."

"Be quiet," Caroline said sharply. "You are making bad into worse."

"It is already worse," the old lady retorted in a stage whisper audible to everyone in the room.

"Oh dear." Angeline wrung her hands nervously, looking from one to the other of her nephews-in-law.

Charlotte attempted to repair some of the damage.

"Mr. Hatch, do you not think that when people read the ideas proposed in these pamphlets they will consider them, and if they are truly evil or preposterous then they will see them for what they are, and reject them out of hand? After all, is it not better they should know what they stand for and so find them the more repellent and frightening, than merely by our recounting of them? Truth cannot but benefit from the comparison."

Hatch stopped with his breath drawn in and his mouth open. Her premise was one he could not possibly deny, and yet to do so would rob him of his argument against Shaw.

For seconds the silence hung. A carriage rattled past the street going up Highgate Hill. A snatch of song came from somewhere upstairs and was hushed instantly, presumably some young housemaid disciplined for levity.

"You are very young, Mrs. Pitt," Hatch said at last. "I fear you do not fully grasp the weakness of some people, how easily greed, ignorance and envy can draw them to espouse values that are quite obviously false to those of us who have had the advantage of a moral upbringing. Unfortunately there are an increasing number"— here he shot a bright, hard glance at Shaw—"who confuse freedom with license and thus behave completely irresponsibly. We have just such a person here, named John Dalgetty, who keeps a shop of sorts, selling books and pamphlets, some of which pander to the lowest possible tastes, some which excite flighty minds to dwell on subjects with which they are quite unable to deal, questions of philosophy disruptive both to the individual and to society."

"Josiah would have a censor to tell everyone what they may read and what they may not." Shaw turned to Charlotte, his arms wide, his eyebrows raised. "No one would have had a new idea, or questioned an old one, since Noah landed on Ararat. There would be no inventors, no explorations of the mind, nothing to challenge or excite, nothing to stretch the boundaries of thought. No one would do anything that hadn't been done before. There would certainly be no Empire."

"Balderdash," Charlotte said frankly, then blanched at her temerity. Aunt Vespasia might be able to get away with such candor, but she had neither the social status nor the beauty for it. But it was too late to withdraw it. "I mean, you will never stop people from having radical thoughts, or from speaking them—"

Shaw started to laugh. It was a rich, wonderful sound; even around all the black crepes and the somber faces, it was full of joy.

"How can I argue with you?" He controlled his mirth with difficulty. The room seemed alight with his presence. "You are the perfect argument for your case. Obviously not even Josiah's presence in person can stop you from saying precisely what comes into your mind."

"I apologize," she said, uncertain whether to be offended, embarrassed, or to laugh with him. Grandmama was outraged, probably because Charlotte was the center of attention; Caroline was mortified; and Angeline, Celeste and Prudence were struck dumb. Josiah Hatch struggled between conflicting emotions so powerful he dared not put them into speech. "I was extremely discourteous," she added. "Whatever my opinions, they were not asked for, and I should not have expressed them so forcefully."

"You should not have expressed them at all," Grandmama snapped, sitting bolt upright and glaring at her. "I always said your marriage would do you no good—and heaven knows you were wayward enough to begin with. Now you are a disaster. I should not have brought you."

Charlotte would have liked to retort that she should not have come herself—but it was not the time, and perhaps there was no such time.

Shaw came to Caroline's rescue.

"I am delighted that you did, Mrs. Ellison. I am exceedingly tired of the polite but meaningless conversation of people who wish to express their sympathy but endlessly repeat each other simply because there is nothing anyone can say that is deep enough." His face lightened. "Words do not encompass it, nor do they bridge the gap between those who grieve and those who do not. It is a relief to talk of something else."

Suddenly the memory of Somerset Carlisle and the sorrow in his face was as clear in Charlotte's mind as if he had been here in the room with them.

"May I speak privately with you, Dr. Shaw?"

"Really!" Prudence murmured in amazement.

"Well . . ." Angeline fluttered her hands as if to brush something away.

"Charlotte," Caroline said warningly.

The same smile touched Shaw's mouth with amusement.

"Certainly. We shall repair to the library." He glanced at Celeste. "And leave the door open," he added deliberately, and watched her scowl with irritation. A protest rose to her lips, and she abandoned it; the explanation of what she had not thought, or implied, was worse than its absence. She shot him a look of intense annoyance.

He held the door open for Charlotte and then as she swept out, chin high, he followed her and strode ahead. Since she had no idea where she was going, he led the way to the library, which turned out to be as impressive and pompous as the hall, with cases and cases of leather-bound books in brown and burgundy and dark green, all lettered with gold. Pious scripts were framed in mahogany on the free wall space, and there was a large picture of some high church dignitary above the mantelpiece, carved in marble and inset with quartz pillars supporting the shelf. Massive leather-covered chairs occupied much of the dark green carpet, giving the whole room a claustrophobic feeling. A large bronze statue of a lion ornamented the one table. The curtains, like those in the withdrawing room, were heavily fringed, tied back with fringed sashes, and splayed carefully over the floor at their base.

"Not a room to put you at your ease, is it?" Shaw met her eyes very directly. "But then that was never the intention." A smile curled the corners of his mouth. "Are you impressed?"

"That was the intention?" She smiled back.

"Oh assuredly. And are you?"

"I'm impressed with how much money he must have had." She was perfectly frank without even considering it. He was a man whose honesty demanded from her exactly the same. "All these leather-bound books. There must be a hundred pounds' worth in every case. The contents of the whole room would keep an average family for at least two years—food, gaslight, a new outfit for every season, coal enough to keep them thoroughly warm, roast beef every Sunday and goose for Christmas, and pay a housemaid to boot."

"Indeed it is, but the good bishop did not see it that way. Books are not only the source of knowledge, but the display of them is the symbol of it." He made a slight gesture of distaste with his shoulders, and paced over to the mantel, and back again, straightening the bronze as he passed it.

"You were not fond of him," she said with a half smile.

Again his face was unwaveringly direct. In any other man she might have felt it bold, but it was so obviously part of his nature only the most conceited woman would have interpreted it so.

"I disagreed with him about almost everything." He waved his hands. "Not, of course, that that is the same thing. I do not mean to equivocate. I apologize. No, I was not fond of him. Some beliefs are fundamental, and color everything that a man is."

"Or a woman," she added.

His smile was sudden and illuminated his entire face. "Of course. Again, I apologize. It is very avant-garde to suppose that women think at all; I am surprised you mention it. You must keep most unusual company. Are you related to the policeman Pitt who is investigating the fire?"

She noticed that he did not say "Clemency's death," and the flicker of pain in his moment of hesitation was not lost on her. He might mask the hurt, but the second's glimpse of it showed a side of him that she liked even better.

"Yes—he is my husband." It was the only time she had admitted it when she was involving herself in a case. Every other time she had used her anonymity to gain an advantage. And also, the wives of policemen were not received in society, any more than would be the tradesmen's wives. Commerce was considered vulgar; trade was beneath mention. In fact the very necessity of earning money at all was not spoken of in the best circles. One simply presumed it came from lands or investments. Labor was honest and good for the soul, and the morals; but the more leisure one had, the greater status one possessed.

He stood perfectly still for a moment, and the very unnaturalness of it in him spoke a kind of pain.

"Is that why you came—to learn more information about us? And brought your mother and grandmother too!"

The only possible answer was the truth. Any alternatives, however laced with honesty, would jar on his ear and degrade them both.

"I think curiosity may well be why Grandmama came. Mama, I think, came with her to try to make it a little less—awful." She stood facing him across the table with its rampant bronze lion. "I came because I heard from Lady Vespasia Cumming-Gould, and Mr. Somerset Carlisle, that Mrs. Shaw was a most remarkable person who had given much time to fighting against the power of slum landlords, that she wished to change the law to make them more accessible to public awareness."

They were standing barely a yard from each other and she was acutely aware of his total attention.

"Mr. Carlisle said she had an unusual passion and unselfishness about it," she went on. "She was not looking for personal praise nor for a cause to occupy herself, but that she simply cared. I felt such a woman's death should not go unsolved, nor people who would murder her in order to protect their miserable money remain unexposed—and perhaps scandal of that might even further her work. But your aunts tell me she was not involved in anything of that kind. So it seems I have the wrong Clemency Shaw."

"No you have not." Now his voice was very quiet and he moved at last, turning a little away from her towards the mantelpiece and the fire. "She did not choose to tell anyone else what she was doing. She had her reasons."

"But you knew?"

"Oh yes. She trusted me. We had been"—he hesitated, choosing his word carefully—"friends . . . for a long time."

She wondered why he chose the term. Did it mean they had been more than merely lovers—or something less—or both?

He turned back and looked directly at her, without bother-

ing to disguise the grief in his face, nor its nature. She thought
he did mean "friends," and not more.

"She was a remarkable woman." He used her own words.
"I admired her very much. She had an extraordinary inner courage. She could know things, and face them squarely, that would
have crushed most people." He drew in his breath and let it out
slowly. "There is a terrible empty space where she used to be, a
goodness no longer here."

She wanted to move forward and touch him, put her hand
over his and convey her empathy in the simplest and most immediate way. But such a gesture would be bold, intrusively intimate between a man and a woman who had met only moments
ago. All she could do was stand on the spot and repeat the words
anyone would use.

"I'm sorry, truly I am sorry."

He swung his hands out wide, then starting pacing the floor
again. He did not bother to thank her; such trivialities could be
taken for granted between them.

"I should be very glad if you learned anything." Quite automatically he adjusted the heavy curtains to remove a crooked
fold, then swung back to face her. "If I can help, tell me how,
and I shall do it."

"I will."

His smile returned for an instant, full of warmth.

"Thank you. Now let us return and see if Josiah and the
aunts have been totally scandalized—unless, of course, there is
something else you wish to say?"

"No—not at all. I simply desired to know if I was mistaken
in my beliefs, or if there were two people with such an unusual
name."

"Then we may leave the wild seductiveness of the bishop's
library"—he glanced around it with a rueful smile—"and return
to the propriety of the withdrawing room. Really, you know,
Mrs. Pitt, we should have conducted this interview in the conservatory. They have a magnificent one here, full of wrought
iron stands with palms and ferns and potted flowers. It would
have given them so much more to be shocked about."

She regarded him with interest. "You enjoy shocking them, don't you?"

His expression was a curious mixture of impatience and pity.

"I am a doctor, Mrs. Pitt; I see a great deal of real suffering. I get impatient with the unnecessary pain imposed by hypocrisy and idle imaginations which have nothing better to do than speculate unkindly and create pain where there need be none. Yes, I hate idiotic pretense and I blow it away where I can."

"But what do your aunts know of your reality?"

"Nothing," he admitted, pulling his face into a rueful smile. "They grew up here. They have neither of them ever left this house except to make social calls or to attend suitable functions and charitable meetings which never see the objects of their efforts. The old bishop kept them here after his wife died; Celeste to write his letters, read to him, look up reference works for his sermons and discourses and to keep him company when he wished to talk. She also plays the piano, loudly when she is in a temper, and rather badly, but he couldn't tell. He liked the idea of music, but he was indifferent to its practice."

Even standing in the doorway his intense inner energy was such that he could not keep entirely still. "Angeline took care of all his domestic needs and ran the household, and read romantic novels in brown paper wrappers when no one was looking. They never kept a housekeeper. He considered it a woman's place and her fulfillment to keep a home for a man and make it a haven of peace and security." He waved his hands, strong and neat. "Free from all the evils and soil of the outer world with its vulgarity and greed. And Angeline has done precisely that—all her life. I suppose one should hardly blame her if she knows nothing else. I stand reproved. Neither her ignorance nor her sometime fatuity are her fault."

"They must have had suitors?" Charlotte said before she thought.

He was tidying the curtains automatically and straightened up to look at her.

"Of course. But he saw them off in short shrift, and made sure the call of duty drowned out everything else."

Charlotte saw a world of disappointment and domestic details, suppressed and confused passions forever overlaid by pious words and the irresistible pressures of ignorance, fear and guilt; duty always winning in the end. Whatever the Worlingham sisters did to occupy their minds and justify the arid years of their lives was to be pitied, not added to further by blame.

"I don't think I would have cared for the bishop either," she said with a tight smile. "Although I suppose he is like a great many. They are certainly not the only daughters whose lives have been spent so, with father—or mother. I have known several."

"And I," he agreed.

Perhaps the conversation might have gone further had not Caroline and Grandmama appeared in the doorway of the withdrawing room across the hall and seen them.

"Ah, good," Caroline said immediately. "You are ready to leave. We were just saying good-bye to the Misses Worlingham. Mr. and Mrs. Hatch have already gone." She looked at Shaw. "May we extend our condolences to you, Dr. Shaw, and apologize for intruding upon a family occasion. You have been most courteous. Come, Charlotte."

"Good afternoon, Dr. Shaw." Charlotte held out her hand and he took it immediately, holding it till she felt the warmth of him through her gloves.

"Thank you for coming, Mrs. Pitt. I look forward to our meeting again. Good day to you."

"Perhaps I should—" Charlotte glanced towards the withdrawing room door.

"Nonsense!" Grandmama snapped. "We have said all that is necessary. It is time we left." And she marched out of the front door, held open for them by a footman; the parlormaid was presumably occupied in the kitchen.

"Well?" Grandmama demanded when they were seated in the carriage.

"I beg your pardon?" Charlotte pretended mystification.

"What did you ask Shaw, and what did he say, child?" Grandmama said impatiently. "Don't affect to be stupid with me. Awkward you may be, and certainly lacking in any degree of subtlety whatever, but you are not without native wit. What did that man say to you?"

"That Clemency was precisely what I had supposed her," Charlotte replied. "But that she preferred to keep her work for the poor a private matter, even from her family, and he would be most obliged if I learned anything about who murdered her."

"Indeed," Grandmama said dubiously. "He took an uncommonly long time to say so little. I shouldn't be the slightest bit surprised if he did it himself. There is a great deal of money in the Worlingham family, you know, and Theophilus's share, as the only son, passed to his daughters equally. Shaw stands to inherit everything poor Clemency had." She rearranged her skirts more carefully. "And according to Celeste, even that is not sufficient for him. He has set his cap on that young Flora Lutterworth, and she is little better than she should be, chasing after him, seeing him in private goodness knows how many times a month. Her father is furious. He has ambitions for her a great deal higher than a widowed doctor twice her age and of no particular background. Caroline, please move yourself farther to the left; you have not left me sufficient room. Thank you." She settled herself again. "They have quarreled over it quite obviously, to any discerning eye. And I daresay Mrs. Clitheridge has had a word with her, in a motherly sort of way. It is part of the vicar's duty to care for the moral welfare of his flock."

"What makes you think that?" Caroline said with a frown.

"For goodness sake, use your wits!" Grandmama glared at her. "You heard Angeline say Lally Clitheridge and Flora Lutterworth had had a heated and most unpleasant exchange, and were hardly on speaking terms with one another. No doubt that was what it was about—anyone could deduce that, without being a detective." She turned a malevolent eye on Charlotte. "No—your doctor friend had every reason to have done away with his wife—and no doubt he did. Mark my words."

CHAPTER
FIVE

Charlotte dreaded Grandmama's attending the funeral of Clemency Shaw, but long as she considered the matter, she devised no way of preventing her. When she called upon them next she did suggest tentatively that perhaps in the tragic circumstances it would be better if the affair were as private as possible. The old lady gave that the contemptuous dismissal it deserved.

"Don't be absurd, child." She looked at Charlotte down her nose. This was an achievement in itself since she was considerably shorter than Charlotte, even when they were both seated, as they now were in the withdrawing room by the fire. "Sometimes I despair of your intelligence," she added for good measure. "You display absolutely not a jot at times. Everyone will be there. Do you really imagine people will pass up such an opportunity to gossip at domestic disaster and make distasteful speculations? It is just the time when your friends should show a bold face and make it apparent to everyone that they are with you and support you in your distress—and believe you perfectly innocent of—of anything at all."

It was such a ridiculous argument Charlotte did not bother to make a reply. It would change nothing except Grandmama's temper, and that for the worse.

Emily did not go, to her chagrin. But dearly as she would like to have, she acknowledged that her motive was purely curiosity, and she herself felt it would be indecent. The more she thought of Clemency Shaw, the more she became determined to do all she could that her work might continue, as the best tribute she could pay her, and she would not spoil it by an act of self-indulgence.

However she did offer to lend Charlotte a black dress. It was certainly a season old, but nonetheless extraordinarily handsome, cut in black velvet and stitched with an embroidery of leaves and ferns on the lapels of the jacket and around the hem of the skirt. Tacked in at the back was the name of the maker, Maison Worth, the most fashionable house in Europe.

Bless Emily!

And also offered was the use of her carriage so Charlotte would not be obliged either to hire one or to ride on the omnibus to Cater Street and go with Caroline and the old lady.

She had shared with Pitt both the few scraps of definite information and the large and very general impressions she had gained.

He was sitting in the armchair beside the parlor fire, his feet stretched out on the fender, watching through half-closed eyes the flames jumping in the grate.

"I shall go to the funeral," she added in a tone that was only half a statement and left room for him to contradict if he wished—not because she thought he would, but as a matter of policy.

He looked up, and as far as she could judge in the firelight his eyes were bright, his expression one of tolerance, even a curious kind of conspiracy.

"I shall be in some respects in a better position than you to observe," she went on. "After all, to most of them I shall be another mourner and they will assume I am there to grieve—which the more I know of Clemency Shaw, the more truly I am. Whereas those who know you will think of the police, and remember that it was murder, and that there is so much more yet ahead of them that will be exceedingly unpleasant, if not actually tragic."

"You don't need to convince me," he said with a smile, and she realized he was very gently laughing at her.

She relaxed and leaned back in her chair, reaching out her foot to touch his, toe to toe.

"Thank you."

"Be careful," he warned. "Remember, it is not just grief—it is murder."

"I will," she promised. "I'm going in Emily's carriage."

He grinned. "Of course."

Charlotte was not by any means the first to arrive. As she alighted with Emily's footman handing her down, she saw Josiah and Prudence Hatch ahead of her passing through the gate and up the path towards the vestry entrance. They were both dressed in black as one would expect, Josiah with his hat in his hand and the cold wind ruffling his hair. They walked side by side, staring straight in front of them, stiff backed. Even from behind, Charlotte could tell that they had quarreled over something and were each isolated in a cocoon of anger.

Ahead of them and passing through the doors as Charlotte crossed the pavement was Alfred Lutterworth, alone. Either Flora was not coming or she had accompanied someone else. It struck Charlotte as unusual. She would have to inquire, as discreetly as possible, after the cause.

She was welcomed at the door by a curate, probably in his late twenties, thin, rather homely of feature, but with such animation and concern in his expression that she warmed to him immediately.

"Good morning, ma'am." He spoke quietly but without the reverential singsong which she always felt to be more a matter of show that of sincerity. "Where would you care to sit? Are you alone, or expecting someone?"

A thought ran through Charlotte's mind to say she was alone, but she resisted the temptation. "I am expecting my mother and grandmother—"

He moved to go with her. "Then perhaps you would like the pew here to the right? Did you know Mrs. Shaw well?" The innocence of his manner and the traces of grief in his face robbed his question of any offense.

"No," she replied with complete honesty. "I knew her only

by repute, but all I hear of her only quickens my admiration."
She saw the puzzlement in his eyes and hastened to clarify to a
degree which surprised her. "My husband is in charge of the
investigation into the fire. I took an interest in it, and learned
from a friend who is a member of Parliament about the work
Mrs. Shaw did to fight against the exploitation of the poor. She
was very modest about it, but she had both courage and compassion of a remarkable degree. I wish to be here to pay my
respects—" She stopped abruptly, seeing the distress in his face.
Indeed he seemed to be far more moved by grief than were
either of Clemency's aunts, or her sister, when Charlotte had
visited them two days before.

He mastered his feelings with difficulty, and did not apologize. She liked him the better for it. Why should one apologize
for grief at a funeral? In silence he showed her to the pew, met
her eyes once in a look for which words would have been unnecessary, then returned to the doorway, holding his head high.

He was just in time to greet Somerset Carlisle, looking thin
and a trifle tired, and Great-Aunt Vespasia, wearing magnificent
black with osprey feathers in her hat, sideswept at a marvelous
angle, and a black gown of silk and barathea cut to exaggerate
both her height and the elegance of her bearing. It was asym-
metrical, as was the very ultimate in fashion. She carried an eb-
ony stick with a silver handle, but refused to lean on it. She
spoke very briefly to the curate, explained who she was, but not
why she had chosen to come, and then walked past him with
great dignity, took out her lorgnette and surveyed the body of
the church. She saw Charlotte after only a moment, and lost
further interest in anyone else. She took Somerset Carlisle's arm
and instructed him to lead her to Charlotte's pew, thus making
it impossible for Caroline or Grandmama to join her when they
arrived a few moments later.

Charlotte did not attempt to explain. She simply smiled with
great sweetness, then bent her head in an attitude of prayer—to
conceal her smile.

After several minutes she raised her eyes again, and saw well
in front of her the white head of Amos Lindsay, and beside him
Stephen Shaw. She could only imagine the turmoil of emotions

that must be in him as he saw the agitated figure of Hector Clitheridge flapping about like a wounded crow. His wife was in handsome and serviceable black in the front row, trying to reassure him, alternately smiling and looking appropriately somber. The organ was playing slowly, either because the organist considered it the correct tempo for a funeral or because she could not find the notes. The result was a sense of uncertainty and a loss of rhythm.

The pews were filling up. Quinton Pascoe passed up the aisle, finding himself a seat as far as possible from John Dalgetty and his wife. Nowhere among the forest of black hats of every shape and decoration could Charlotte see any that looked as if they might belong to Celeste or Angeline Worlingham.

The organ changed pitch abruptly and the service began. Clitheridge was intensely nervous; his voice cracked into falsetto and back again. Twice he lost his place in what must surely be long-familiar passages and fumbled to regain himself, only making his mistake the more obvious. Charlotte ached for him, and heard Aunt Vespasia beside her sigh with exasperation. Somerset Carlisle buried his face in his hands, but whether he was thinking of Clemency, or the vicar, she did not know.

Charlotte found her own attention wandering. It was probably the safest thing to do; Clitheridge was unbearable, and the young curate was so full of genuine distress she found it too harrowing to look at him. Instead her eyes roamed upward over and across traceries of stone, plaques of long-dead worthies, and eventually, with a jolt of returning memory, to the Worlingham window with its almost completed picture of the late bishop in the thin disguise of Jeremiah, surrounded by other patriarchs and topped by an angel. She recognized the bishop quite easily. The face was indistinct—the medium enforced it—but the thick curls of white hair, so like an aureole in the glass with the light shining through, was exactly like the portrait in the family hallway and it was unmistakable. It was a remarkably handsome memorial and must have cost a sizable sum. No wonder Josiah Hatch was proud of it.

At last the formal part of the service was over and with immense relief the final amen was said, and the congregation rose to follow the coffin out into the graveyard, where they all stood huddled in a bitter west wind while the body was interred.

Charlotte shivered and moved a little closer to Aunt Vespasia, and behind her half a step, to shield her from the gusts, which if the sky had been less clear, would surely have carried snow. She stared across the open grave with Clitheridge standing at the edge, his cassock whipping around his ankles and his face strained with embarrassment and apprehension. A couple of yards away Alfred Lutterworth was planted squarely, ignoring the cold, his face somber in reflection, his thoughts unreadable. Next to him, but several feet away, Stephen Shaw was folded in a mixture of private anger and grief, the emotion so deep in his face only the crudest of strangers would have intruded. Amos Lindsay stood silently at his elbow.

Josiah Hatch was taking control of the pallbearers. He was a sidesman and used to some responsibility. His expression was grim, but he did his duty meticulously and not a word or a movement was omitted or performed without ceremony. It was done to an exactness that honored the dead and preserved the importance above all of the litany and tradition of the church.

Clitheridge was obviously relieved to allow someone else to take over, however pedantic. Only the curate seemed less than pleased. His bony features and wide mouth reflected some impatience that appeared to increase his grief.

Charlotte had been quite correct, there were about fifty people present, most of them men, and quite definitely neither Angeline nor Celeste Worlingham were among them; nor was Flora Lutterworth.

"Why are the Worlinghams not here?" she whispered to Aunt Vespasia as they turned at last, cold to the bone, and made their way back to the carriages for the short ride to the funeral supper. She had not been specifically invited, but she fully intended to go. They passed Pitt standing near the gate, so discreet as to be almost invisible. He might have been one of the pallbearers or an undertaker's assistant, except that his gloves were odd, there was a bulge in one pocket of his coat, and his boots were brown. She smiled at him quickly as they passed, and saw an answering warmth in his face, then continued on her way to the carriage.

"I daresay the bishop did not consider it suitable," Aunt Vespasia replied. "Many people don't. Quite idiotic, of course. Women are every bit as strong as men in coping with tragedy and the more distressing weaknesses of the flesh. In fact in many cases stronger—they have to be, or none of us would have more than one child, and certainly never care for the sick!"

"But the bishop is dead," Charlotte pointed out. "And has been for ten years."

"My dear, the bishop will never be dead as far as his daughters are concerned. They lived under his roof for over forty years of their lives, and obeyed every rule of conduct he set out for them. And I gather he had very precise opinions about everything. They are not likely to break the habit now, least of all in a time of bereavement when one most wishes to cling to the familiar."

"Oh—" Charlotte had not thought of that, but now some recollection returned to her of other families where it had been considered too much strain on delicate sensibilities. Fits of the vapors detracted rather seriously from the proper solemnity due to the dead. "Is that why Flora Lutterworth isn't here either?" That seemed dubious to her, but not impossible. Alfred Lutterworth apparently had great ambitions towards gentility, and all that might seem well-bred.

"I imagine so," Vespasia replied with the ghost of a smile. They were at the carriages. Caroline and Grandmama were somewhere behind them. Charlotte glanced over her shoulder and saw Caroline talking to Josiah Hatch with intense concentration, and Grandmama was staring at Charlotte with a look like thunder.

"Are you waiting?" Vespasia asked, her silver eyebrows raised.

"Certainly not!" Charlotte waved her arm imperiously and Emily's coachman moved his horses forward. "They have their own equipage." It gave her a childish satisfaction to say it aloud. "I shall follow you. I assume the Misses Worlingham will be up to the occasion of the funeral supper?"

"Of course." Now Vespasia's smile was undisguised. "That is the social event—this was merely the necessary preamble." And she accepted her footman's hand and mounted the step into her carriage, after handing to the crossing sweeper, a child of no more than ten or eleven years, a halfpenny, for which he thanked her loudly, and pushed his broom through another pile of manure. The door was closed behind her and a moment later it drew away.

Charlotte did the same, and was still behind her when they alighted outside the imposing and now familiar Worlingham house, all its blinds drawn and black crepe fluttering from the door. The roadway was liberally spread with straw to silence the horses' hooves, out of respect for the dead, and the wheels made barely a sound as the coachman drove away to wait.

Inside everything had been prepared to the last detail. The huge dining room was festooned with black crepe till it looked as if some enormous spider had been followed by a chimney fire and an extremely clumsy sweep. White lilies, which must have cost enough to feed an ordinary family for a week, were arranged with some artistry on the table, and in a porcelain vase on the jardiniere. The table itself was set with a magnificent array of baked meats, sandwiches, fruits and confectionary, bottles of wine in baskets, suitably dusty from the cellar and carrying labels to satisfy even the most discriminating connoisseur. Some of the Port was very old indeed. The bishop must have laid it down in his prime, and forgotten it.

Celeste and Angeline stood side by side, both dressed in black bombazine. Celeste's was stitched with jet beads and had a fall of velvet over the front and caught up in the bustle. It was a fraction tight at the bosom. Angeline's was draped over the shoulders with heavy black lace fastened with a jet pin set with tiny pearls, a very traditional mourning brooch. The lace was also echoed across the stomach and under the bombazine bustle; only the most discriminating would know it was last year's arrangement of folds. And it was even tighter around the bosom. Charlotte guessed they had performed the same service at Theophilus's funeral, and perhaps at the bishop's as well. A clever dressmaker could do a great deal, and from observation it seemed, like many wealthy people, the Worlingham sisters liked their economies.

Celeste greeted them with deep solemnity, as if she had been a duchess receiving callers, standing stiff-backed, inclining her head a fraction and repeating everyone's names as though they were of significant importance. Angeline kept a lace-edged handkerchief in her hand and dabbed at her cheek occasionally, echoing the last two words of everything Celeste said.

"Good afternoon, Mrs. Pitt." Celeste moved her hand an inch in recognition of a relative stranger of no discernible rank.

"Mrs. Pitt," Angeline repeated, smiling uncertainly.

"Gracious of you to come to express your condolences."

"Gracious." Angeline chose the first word this time.

"Lady Vespasia Cumming-Gould." Celeste was startled, and for once the fact that she was a bishop's daughter seemed unimpressive. "How—how generous of you to come. I am sure our late father would have been quite touched."

"Quite touched," Angeline added eagerly.

"There would be no reason for him to be," Vespasia said with a cool smile and very direct stare. "I came entirely on Clemency Shaw's behalf. She was a very fine woman of both courage and conscience—a rare-enough combination. I am truly grieved that she is gone."

Celeste was lost for words. She knew nothing of Clemency to warrant such an extraordinary tribute.

"Oh!" Angeline gave a little gasp and clutched the handkerchief more tightly, then dabbed at a tear that started down her pink cheek. "Poor Clemency," she whispered almost inaudibly.

Vespasia did not linger for any further trivialities that could only be painful, and led the way into the dining room. Somerset Carlisle, immediately behind her, was so used to speaking gently with the inarticulate he had no trouble murmuring something kind but meaningless and following them in.

There were some thirty people there already. Charlotte recognized several from her own previous brief meetings at the Worlinghams', others she deduced from Pitt's description as she had done in the church.

She looked at the table, pretending to be engrossed in admiring it, as Caroline and Grandmama came in. Grandmama was scowling and waving her stick in front of her to the considerable peril of anyone within range. She did not particularly want Charlotte with her, but she was furious at being left behind. It lacked the respect due to her.

It was a gracious room, very large, with fine windows all ornately curtained, a dark marble fireplace, an oak sideboard and serving table and a dresser with a Crown Derby tea service set out for display, all reds, blues and golds.

The main table was exquisitely appointed, crystal with a coat of arms engraved on the side of each goblet, silver polished till it reflected every facet of the chandelier, also monogrammed with an ornate Gothic W, and linen embroidered in white with both crest and monogram. The porcelain serving platters were blue-and-gold-rimmed Minton; Charlotte remembered the pattern from the details of such knowledge her mother had taught her, in the days when she attended such functions where information of the sort was required in the would-be bride.

"They never put all this out for her when she was alive," Shaw said at her elbow. "But then I suppose, God help us, we never had the entire neighborhood in to dine, especially all at once."

"It often helps grief to do something with a special effort," Charlotte answered him quietly. "Perhaps even a trifle to excess. We do not all cope with our losses in the same way."

"What a very charitable view," he said gloomily. "If I had not already met you before, and heard you be most excruciatingly candid, I would suspect you of hypocrisy."

"Then you would do me an injustice," she said quickly. "I meant what I said. If I wished to be critical I could think of several things to comment on, but that is not one of them."

"Oh!" His fair eyebrows rose. "What would you choose?" The faintest smile lit his eyes. "If, of course, you wished to be critical."

"Should I wish to be, and you are still interested, I shall let you know," she replied without the slightest rancor. Then remembering that it was his bereavement more than anyone else's, and not wishing to seem to cut him, even in so small a way, she leaned a little closer and whispered, "Celeste's gown is a trifle tight, and should have been let out under the arms. The gentleman I take to be Mr. Dalgetty needs a haircut, and Mrs. Hatch has odd gloves, which is probably why she has taken one off and is carrying it."

His smile was immediate and filled with warmth.

"What acute observation! Did you learn it being married to the police, or is it a natural gift?"

"I think it comes from being a woman," she replied. "When I was single I had so little to do that observation of other people formed a very large part of the day. It is more entertaining than embroidery and painting bad watercolors."

"I thought women spent their time gossiping and doing good works," he whispered back, the humor still in his eyes, not masking the pain but contrasting with it so he seemed alive and intensely vulnerable.

"We do," she assured him. "But you have to have something to gossip about, if it is to be any fun at all. And doing good work is deadly, because one does it with such an air of condescension it is more to justify oneself than to benefit anyone else. I should have to be very desperate indeed before a visit from a society lady bringing me a jar of honey would do more than make we want to spit at her—which of course I could not afford to do at all." She was exaggerating, but his smile was ample reward, and she was perfectly sure he knew the truth was both homelier and kinder, at least much of the time.

Before he could reply their attention was drawn to Celeste a few feet away from them, still playing the duchess. Alfred Lutterworth was standing in front of her with Flora by his side, and Celeste had just cut them dead, meeting their eyes and then moving on as if they were servants and not to be spoken to. The color flared up Lutterworth's cheeks and Flora looked for a moment as if she would weep.

"Damn her!" Shaw said savagely under his breath, then added a simile from the farmyard that was extremely unkind, and unfair to the animal in question. Without excusing himself to Charlotte he walked forward, treading on a thin woman's dress and ignoring her.

"Good afternoon, Lutterworth," he said loudly. "Good of you to come. I appreciate it. Good afternoon, Miss Lutterworth. Thank you for being here—not the sort of thing one would choose, except in friendship."

Flora smiled uncertainly, then saw the candor in his eyes and regained her composure.

"We would hardly do less, Dr. Shaw. We feel for you very much."

Shaw indicated Charlotte. "Do you know Mrs. Pitt?" He introduced them and they all made formal acknowledgment of each other. The tension evaporated, but Celeste, who could not have failed to hear the exchange, as must everyone else in their half of the room, was stiff-faced and tight-lipped. Shaw ignored her and continued a loud, inconsequential conversation, drawing in Charlotte as an ally, willingly or not.

Ten minutes later both the group and the conversation had changed. Caroline and Grandmama had joined them, and Charlotte was listening to an extremely handsome woman in her middle forties with shining hair piled most fashionably high, magnificent dark eyes, and a black hat which would have been daring two years ago. Her face was beginning to lose the bloom of youth, but there was still enough beauty to cause several people to look at her more than once, albeit a type of beauty more characteristic of hotter climates than the restrained English rose—especially those bred in the genteel gardens of Highgate. She had been introduced as Maude Dalgetty, and Charlotte liked her more the longer she spoke. She seemed a woman too contented within herself to bear any malice towards others, and there were none of the small barbs of callousness or idleness in her comments.

Charlotte was surprised when Josiah Hatch joined them, and it was immediately apparent from the softening of his grim expression that he held her in considerable esteem. He looked at Charlotte with little interest and even that was prepared to be critical. He already suspected she had come either out of curiosity, which he considered intolerable, or because she was a friend of Shaw's of whom he would be bound to disapprove. However, when he turned to Maude Dalgetty the angle of his body eased, even the rigidity of his collar seemed less constricting.

"Mrs. Dalgetty, I'm so pleased you were able to come." He sought for something else to add, perhaps more personal, and failed to find it.

"Of course, Mr. Hatch." She smiled at him and he unbent even more, finding a very small smile himself. "I was very fond of Clemency; I think she was one of the best women I knew."

Hatch paled again, the blood leaving his cheeks. "Indeed," he said huskily, then cleared his throat with a rasping breath. "There was very much in her to praise—a virtuous woman, neither immodest nor unmindful of all her duties, and yet with good humor at all times. It is a great tragedy her life—was—" His face hardened again and he shot a glance across the table to where Shaw's fair head could be seen bending a little to listen to a stout woman wearing a tiny hat. "Was in so many ways wasted. She could have had so much more." He left it hanging in the air, ambiguous as to whether he was referring to Shaw or Clemency's longevity.

Maude Dalgetty chose to interpret it as the latter.

"Indeed it is," she agreed with a sad shake of her head. "Poor Dr. Shaw. This must be appalling for him, and yet I can think of nothing at all that one could do to help. It is a miserable feeling to see grief and be unable even to reach it, let alone offer anything of comfort."

"Your compassion does you credit," he said quickly. "But do not distress yourself too deeply on his behalf; he is unworthy of it." All the tightness returned to his body, his shoulders cramped in the black fabric of his coat seemed to strain at the seams. "He has characteristics it would be inappropriate I should mention in front of you, dear lady, but I assure you I speak from knowledge." His voice shook a little, whether from weariness or emotion it was impossible to say. "He treats with mockery and insult all that is worthiest of reverence in our society. Indeed he would spread slander about the finest of us, did not some of us, your husband among them, prevent him."

He looked at Maude intently. "I disagree with all your husband's principles as far as publishing is concerned, as you well

know; but I stand by him in the defense of a lady's good
name—"

Maude Dalgetty's fine arched brows rose in surprise and interest.

"A lady's good name! Good gracious, was Dr. Shaw speaking ill of someone? You surprise me."

"That is because you do not know him." Hatch was
warming to the subject. "And your mind is too fine to imagine
ill of people unless it is proved right before you." His cheeks
were quite pink. "But I soon put him in his place, and your
husband added to my words, most eloquently, although I flatter
myself that what I said to him was sufficient."

"John did?" Her husky voice lifted in surprise. "How very
unusual. You almost make me think it was me Dr. Shaw spoke
ill of."

Hatch colored furiously and his breath quickened; his large
hands were clenched by his sides.

Standing well within earshot, Charlotte was certain that it
had indeed been Maude Dalgetty Shaw had spoken ill of, truly
or not, and she wished intensely there were some way to learn
what he had said, and why.

Hatch moved a little, turning his back half towards Charlotte. Since she did not wish to be conspicuous in her interest,
she allowed herself to be excluded, and drifted towards Lally
Clitheridge and Celeste. But before she reached them they separated and Lally accosted Flora Lutterworth, circumspectly but
very definitely.

"How good of you to come, my dear Flora." Her tone was
at once warm and acutely condescending, like a duchess interviewing a prospective daughter-in-law. "You are charmingly
softhearted—a nice virtue in a girl, if not carried to indiscretion."

Flora stared at her, opened her mouth to reply, and was lost
for any words that would express her feelings.

"And modesty as well," Lally continued. "I am so glad you
do not argue, my dear. Indiscretion can be the ruin of a girl,
indeed has been of many. But I am sure your father will have
told you that."

Flora blushed. Obviously the quarrel had not yet been healed.

"You must heed him, you know." Lally was equally perceptive, and placed her arm in Flora's as if in confidence. "He has your very best interest at heart. You are very young, and inexperienced in society and the ways in which people assess each other. An unwise act now, and you may well be considered a girl of less than complete virtue—which would ruin all the excellent chances you have for a fine future." She nodded very slightly. "I hope you understand me, my dear."

Flora stared at her. "No—I don't think I do," she said coolly, but her face was very tight and her knuckles were white where she clasped her handkerchief.

"Then I must explain." Lally leaned a little closer. "Dr. Shaw is a very charming man, but at times rather too outspoken in his opinions and rash in his respect for other people's judgment. Such things are acceptable in a man, especially a professional man—"

"I find Dr. Shaw perfectly agreeable." Flora defended him hotly. "I have received nothing but kindness at his hands. If you disagree with his opinions, that is your affair, Mrs. Clitheridge. You must tell him so. Pray do not concern me with the matter."

"You misunderstand me." Lally was plainly annoyed. "I am concerned for your reputation, my dear—which is frankly in some need of repair."

"Then your quarrel is with those who speak ill of me," Flora retorted. "I have done nothing to warrant it."

"Of course not!" Lally said sharply. "I know that. It is not what you have done, it is your indiscretion in appearance. I warn you as your vicar's wife. He finds the matter difficult to discuss with a young lady, but he is concerned for your welfare."

"Then please thank him for me." Flora looked at her very directly, her cheeks pink, her eyes blazing. "And assure him that neither my body nor my soul are in any jeopardy. You may consider your duty well acquitted." And with a tight little smile she inclined her head politely and walked away, leaving Lally standing in the center of the room, her mouth in a thin line of anger.

Charlotte moved backward hastily in case Lally should realize she had been listening. As she swung around, she came face-to-face with Great-Aunt Vespasia, who had been waiting until she had her attention, her eyebrows raised in curiosity, her mouth touched with humor.

"Eavesdropping?" she said under her breath.

"Yes," Charlotte admitted. "Most interesting. Flora Lutterworth and the vicar's wife, having a spat over Dr. Shaw."

"Indeed? Who is for him and who against?"

"Oh, both for him—very much. I rather think that is the trouble."

Vespasia's smile widened, but it was not without pity. "How very interesting—and wildly unsuitable. Poor Mrs. Clitheridge, she seems worthy of better stuff than the vicar. I am hardly surprised she is drawn elsewhere, even if her virtue forbids she follow." She took Charlotte by the arm and moved away from the two women now close behind them. She was able to resume a normal speaking voice. "Do you think you have learned anything else? I do not find it easy to believe the vicar's wife set fire to the house out of unrequited love for the doctor—although it is not impossible."

"Or Flora Lutterworth, for that matter," Charlotte added. "And perhaps it is not unrequited. Flora will have a great deal of money when her father dies."

"And you think the Worlingham money is not sufficient for Dr. Shaw, and he has eyes on Lutterworth's as well?" Vespasia asked.

Charlotte thought of her conversation with Stephen Shaw, of the energy in him, the humor, the intense feeling of inner honesty that still lingered with her. It was a painful idea. And she did not wish to think Clemency Shaw had spent her life married to such a man. And surely she would have known.

"No," she said aloud. "I believe it may all have to do with Clemency's work against slum owners. But Thomas thinks it is here in Highgate, and that really it was Dr. Shaw himself who was the intended victim. So naturally I shall observe all I can, and tell him of it, whether I can see any sense in it or not."

"Very proper of you." Now Vespasia did not even attempt

to hide her amusement. "Perhaps it was Shaw himself who killed his wife—I imagine Thomas has thought of that, even if you have not."

"Why should I not think of it also?" Charlotte said briskly, but under her breath.

"Because you like him, my dear; and I believe your feeling is more than returned. Good afternoon, Dr. Shaw." As she spoke Shaw had come back and was standing in front of them, courteous to Vespasia, but his attention principally upon Charlotte.

Aware of Vespasia's remarks, Charlotte found herself coloring, her cheeks hot.

"Lady Cumming-Gould." He inclined his head politely. "I appreciate your coming. I'm sure Clemency would have been pleased." He winced as if saying her name aloud had touched a nerve. "You are one of the few here who have not come out of curiosity, the social desire to be seen, or sheer greed for the best repast the Worlinghams have laid out since Theophilus died."

Amos Lindsay materialized at Shaw's elbow. "Really, Stephen, sometimes you do yourself less than justice in expressing your thoughts. A great many people are here for more commendable reasons." His words were directed not to curbing Shaw but to excusing him to Vespasia and Charlotte.

"Nevertheless we must eat," Shaw said rather ungraciously. "Mrs. Pitt—may I offer you a slice of pheasant in aspic? It looks repulsive, but I am assured it is delicious."

"No thank you," Charlotte declined rather crisply. "I do not feel any compulsion to eat, or indeed any desire."

"I apologize," he said immediately, and his smile was so unforced she found her anger evaporated. She felt for his distress, whatever the nature of his love for Clemency. This was a time of grief for him when he would probably far rather have been alone than standing being polite to a crowd of people of widely varying emotions from family bereavement, in Prudence, right to social obligation like Alfred Lutterworth, or even vulgar curiosity, as was ill-hidden on the faces of several people whose names Charlotte did not know. And it was even possible one of them might be Clemency's murderer.

"There is no need," she said, answering his smile. "You have every cause to find us intrusive and extremely trying. It is we who should apologize."

He reached out his hand as if he would have touched her, so much more immediate a communication than words. Then he remembered at the last moment that it was inappropriate, and withdrew, but she felt almost as if he had, the desire was so plain in his eyes. It was a gesture of both gratitude and understanding. For an instant he had not been alone.

"You are very gracious, Mrs. Pitt," he said aloud. "Lady Cumming-Gould, may I offer you anything, or are you also less than hungry?"

Vespasia gave him her goblet. "You may bring me another glass of claret," she answered graciously. "I imagine it has been in the cellar since the bishop's time. It is excellent."

"With pleasure." He took the goblet and withdrew.

He was replaced within moments by Celeste and Angeline, still presiding over the gathering like a duchess and her lady-in-waiting. Prudence Hatch brought up the rear, her face very pale and her eyes pink rimmed. Charlotte remembered with a sharp pang of pity that Clemency had been her sister. Were it Emily who had been burned to death, she did not think she could be here with any composure at all; in fact she would probably be at home unable to stop weeping, and the idea of being civil to a lot of comparative strangers would be unbearable. She smiled at Prudence with all the gentleness she could convey, and met only a numb and confused stare. Perhaps shock was still anesthetizing at least some of the pain? The reality of it would come later in the days of loneliness, the mornings when she woke and remembered.

But Celeste was busy being the bishop's daughter and conducting the funeral supper as it should be done. The conversation should be elevated and suitable to the occasion. Maude Dalgetty had mentioned a romantic novel of no literary pretension at all, and must be put in her place.

"I don't mind the servants reading that sort of thing, as long as their work is satisfactory of course; but such books really have no merit at all."

Beside her a curious mixture of expressions crossed Prudence's face: first alarm, then embarrassment, then a kind of obscure satisfaction.

"And a lady of any breeding is far better without them," Celeste went on. "They really are totally trivial and encourage the most superficial of emotions."

Angeline became very pink. "I think you are too critical, Celeste. Not all romances are as shallow as you suggest. I recently—I mean, I learned of one entitled *Lady Pamela's Secret*, which was very moving and most sensitively written."

"You what?" Celeste's eyebrows rose in utter contempt.

"Some of them reflect what many people feel . . ." Angeline began, then tailed off under Celeste's icy stare.

"I'm sure I don't know any women who feel anything of the sort." Celeste was not prepared to let it go. "Such fancies are entirely spurious." She turned to Maude, apparently oblivious of Prudence's scarlet face and wide eyes. "Mrs. Dalgetty, I am sure with your literary background, your husband's tastes, that you found it so? Girls like Flora Lutterworth, for example . . . But then her status in Highgate is very recent; her background is in trade, poor girl—which of course she cannot help, but neither can she change it."

Maude Dalgetty met Celeste's gaze with complete candor. "Actually it makes me think of my own youth, Miss Worlingham, and I thoroughly enjoyed *Lady Pamela's Secret*. Also I considered it quite well written—without pretensions and with a considerable sensitivity."

Prudence blushed painfully and stared at the carpet.

"Good gracious," Celeste replied flatly, making it very obvious she was thinking something far less civil. "Dear me."

Shaw had returned with Vespasia's glass of claret and she took it from him with a nod of thanks. He looked from one to another of them and noticed Prudence's high color.

"Are you all right, Prudence?" he asked with more solicitude than tact.

"Ah!" She jumped nervously and met his concerned expression with alarm, and colored even more deeply.

"Are you all right?" he repeated. "Would you like to retire for a while, perhaps lie down?"

"No. No, I am perfectly—oh—" She sniffed fiercely. "Oh dear—"

Amos Lindsay came up behind her, glanced at Shaw, then took her by the elbow. "Come, my dear," he said gently. "Perhaps a little air. Please allow me to help you." And without waiting for her to make up her mind, he assisted her away from the crush and out of the door towards some private part of the house.

"Poor soul," Angeline said softly. "She and Clemency were very fond of each other."

"We were all fond of her," Celeste added, and for a moment she too looked into some distance far away, or within her memory, and her face reflected sadness and hurt. Charlotte wondered how much her managerial attitude and abrasively condescending manner were her way of coping with loss, not only of a niece but perhaps of all the opportunities for affection she had missed, or forfeited, over the years. She had probably loved her father at the time, admired him, been grateful for the ample provision of home, gowns, servants, social position; and also hated him for all the things her duty had cost her.

"I mean the family," Celeste added, looking at Shaw with sudden distaste. "There are ties of blood which no one else can understand—particularly in a family with a heritage like ours." Shaw winced but she ignored him. "I never cease to be grateful for our blessings, nor to realize the responsibility they carry. Our dear father, Clemency's grandfather, was one of the world's great men. I think outside those of us of his blood, only Josiah truly appreciates what a marvelous man he was."

"You are quite right," Shaw said abruptly. "I certainly didn't and don't now. . . . I think he was an opinionated, domineering, sententious and thoroughly selfish old hypocrite—"

"How dare you!" Celeste was furious. Her face purpled and her whole body shook, the jet beads on her bosom scintillating in the light of the chandeliers. "If you do not apologize this instant I shall demand you leave this house."

"Oh, Stephen, really." Angeline moved from one foot to the

other nervously. "You go too far, you know. That is unforgivable. Papa was a veritable saint."

Charlotte struggled for something to say, anything that would retrieve an awful situation. Privately she thought Shaw might well be right, but he had no business to say so here, or now. She was still searching her brain wildly when Aunt Vespasia came to the rescue.

"Saints are seldom easy to live with," she said in the appalled silence. "Least of all by those who are obliged to put up with them every day. Not that I am granting that the late Bishop Worlingham was necessarily a saint," she added as Shaw's face darkened. She held up her hand elegantly and her expression was enough to freeze the rebuttal on his lips. "But no doubt he was a man of decided opinions—and such people always arouse controversy, thank heaven. Who wills a nation of sheep who bleat agreement to everything that is said to them?"

Shaw's temper subsided, and both Celeste and Angeline seemed to feel that honor had been served. Charlotte grabbed for some harmless subject, and heard herself complimenting Celeste on the lilies displayed on the table, rather as if laid out above a coffin.

"Beautiful," she repeated fatuously. "Where did you find such perfect blooms?"

"Oh, we grow them," Angeline put in, gushing with relief. "In our conservatory, you know. They require a lot of attention—" She told them all at some length exactly how they were planted, fertilized and cared for. They all listened in sheer gratitude for the respite from unpleasantness.

When Angeline finally ran out of anything to add, they murmured politely and drifted away, pretending to have caught the eye of another acquaintance. Charlotte found herself with Maude Dalgetty again, and then when she went to see if Prudence was recovered, with John Dalgetty, listening to him expound on the latest article he had reviewed, on the subject of liberty of expression.

"One of the sacred principles of civilized men, Mrs. Pitt," he said, leaning towards her, his face intent. "The tragedy is that there are so many well-meaning but ignorant and frightened

people who would bind us in the chains of old ideas. Take Quinton Pascoe." He nodded towards Pascoe very slightly, to be sure
Charlotte knew to whom he was referring. "A good man, in his
own way, but terrified of a new thought." He waved his arm.
"Which wouldn't matter if he were only limiting himself, but
he wants to imprison all our minds in what he believes to be
best for us." His voice rose in outrage at the very conception.

Charlotte felt a strong sympathy with him. She could clearly
recall her indignation when her father had forbidden her the
newspaper, as he had all his daughters, and she felt as if all the
interest and excitement in the world were passing her by and
she was shut out from it. She had bribed the butler to pass her
the political pages, without her parents' knowledge, and pored
over them, reading every word and visualizing the people and
events in minute detail. To have robbed her of it would have
been like shutting all the windows in the house and drawing the
curtains.

"I quite agree with you," she said with feeling. "Thought
should never be imprisoned nor anyone told they may not believe as they choose."

"How right you are, Mrs. Pitt! Unfortunately, not everyone
is able to see it as you do. Pascoe, and those like him, would set
themselves up to decide what people may learn, and what they
may not. He is not personally an unpleasant man—far from it,
you would find him charming—yet the arrogance of the man is
beyond belief."

Apparently Pascoe had heard his name mentioned. He pushed
his way between two men discussing finance and faced Dalgetty,
his eyes hot with anger.

"It is not arrogance, Dalgetty." His voice was low but only
just in control. "It is a sense of responsibility. To publish every
single thing that comes into your hand, regardless of what it is
or whom it may hurt, is not freedom; it is an abuse of the art of
printing. It is no better than a fool who stands on the corner of
the street and shouts out whatever enters his thoughts—be it
true or false—"

"And who is to judge whether it is true or false?" Dalgetty
demanded. "You? Are you to be the final arbiter of what the

world shall believe? Who are you to judge what we may hope for or aspire to? How dare you?" His eyes blazed with the sheer monstrosity of any mere human limiting the dreams of mankind.

Pascoe was equally enraged. His whole body quivered with frustrated fury at Dalgetty's obtuseness and willful failure to grasp the real meaning.

"You are utterly wrong!" he shouted, his skin suffusing with color. "It has nothing whatsoever to do with limiting aspiration or dreams—as well you know. But it does have to do with not creating nightmares." He swung his arms wildly, catching the top of a nearby woman's feathered hat and knocking it over her eye, and quite oblivious of it. "What you do not have the right to do is topple the dreams of others by making mock of them— yes—it is you who are arrogant, not I."

"You pygmy!" Dalgetty shouted back. "You nincompoop. You are talking complete balderdash—which perfectly reflects your muddled thinking. It is an impossibility to build a new idea except at the expense of part of the old—by the very fact that it *is* new."

"And what if your new idea is ugly and dangerous?" Pascoe demanded furiously, his hand chopping the air. "And adds nothing to human knowledge or happiness? Ah? Nincompoop. You are an intellectual child—and a spiritual and moral vandal. You are—"

At this point the heated voices had drawn everyone's attention, all other conversation had ceased and Hector Clitheridge was wading towards them in extreme agitation, his clothes flapping, his arms waving in the air and his face expressing extreme embarrassment and a kind of desperate confusion.

"Mr. Pascoe! Please!" he implored. "Gentlemen!" he turned to Dalgetty. "Please remember poor Dr. Shaw—"

That was the last thing he should have said. The very name was as a red rag to a bull for Pascoe.

"A perfect case in point," he said triumphantly. "A very precise example! He rushes in—"

"Exactly!" Dalgetty chopped the air with his hands in excitement. "He is an honest man who abhors idolatry. Especially the worship of the unworthy, the dishonorable, the valueless—"

"Who says it is valueless?" Pascoe jumped up and down on the spot, his voice rising to falsetto in triumph. "Do you set yourself up to decide what may be kept, and what destroyed? Eh?"

Now Dalgetty lost his temper completely. "You incompetent!" he shouted, scarlet-cheeked. "You double-dyed ass! You—"

"Mr. Dalgetty!" Clitheridge pleaded futilely. "Mr.—"

Eulalia came to the rescue, her face set in firm lines of disapproval. For an instant she reminded Charlotte of a particularly strict nanny. She ignored Dalgetty except for one glare. "Mr. Pascoe." Her voice was determined and under perfect control. "You are behaving disgracefully. This is a funeral supper—have you completely forgotten yourself? You are not usually without any sense of what is fitting, or of how much distress you may be causing to innocent people, already injured by circumstance."

Pascoe's bearing changed. He looked crestfallen and thoroughly abashed. But she had no intention of leaving any blow unstruck.

"Imagine how poor Prudence feels. Is one tragedy not enough?"

"Oh, I am sorry." Pascoe was shocked at himself and his penitence was transparently sincere. Dalgetty no longer entered even the edge of his thoughts. "I am mortified that I should have been so utterly thoughtless. How can I apologize?"

"You can't." Eulalia was relentless. "But you should try." She turned to Dalgetty, who was looking decidedly apprehensive. "You, of course, I do not expect to have any sensitivity towards the feelings of others. Liberty is your god, and I sometimes think you are prepared to sacrifice anyone at all on its shrine."

"That is unfair." He was sincerely aggrieved. "Quite unfair. I desire to liberate, not to injure—I wish only to do good."

"Indeed?" Her eyebrows shot up. "Then you are singularly unsuccessful. You should most seriously reconsider your assumptions—and your resulting behavior. You are a foolish man." And having delivered herself of her most formidable tirade to date, she was flushed, and handsomer than at any time since she was a bride. She was also rather alarmed at what she had dared to say, and the fact that she had rescued the whole assembly from a miserable and acutely embarrassing situation was only just becoming apparent to her. She blushed as she saw every eye on her, and retreated hastily. For once it would be ridiculous to pretend she had merely been helping her husband. He was standing with his hands in the air and his mouth open, but intensely relieved, and also alarmed and a little resentful.

"Bravo, Lally," Shaw said quietly. "You are quite magnificent. We are all duly chastened." He bowed very slightly in a small, quaintly courteous gesture, then moved to stand beside Charlotte.

Again Eulalia colored hotly. This time it was obviously with pleasure, but so acute and unaccustomed it was painful to see.

"Really—" Clitheridge protested. No one heard what he was going to say next, if indeed he knew himself. He was interrupted by Shaw.

"You make me feel as if we are all in the nursery again. Perhaps that is where we should be." He looked at Dalgetty and Pascoe and there was humor in his face rather than anger. If he resented Clemency's funeral being interrupted by such a scene there was no trace of it in his expression. In fact Charlotte thought it might even have been a relief to him from the pain of the reality. He looked set now to prolong the tension and make matters worse.

"I think it is long past time we all grew out of it," she said briskly, taking Shaw by the arm. "Don't you, Dr. Shaw? Squabbling is quite fun at times, but this is a selfish and totally inappropriate place for it. We should be adult enough to think of others, as well as ourselves. I am sure you agree?" She was not sure at all, but she did not intend to allow him the opportunity to say so. "You have already told me about the magnificent conservatory the Misses Worlingham have, and I have seen the lilies on the table. Perhaps you would be generous enough to show it me now?"

"I should be delighted," he said with enthusiasm. "I cannot think of anything I should rather do." And he took her hand in his and placed it on his arm, leading her through the room to the far side. She glanced backwards only once, and saw a look of fury and dislike on Lally Clitheridge's face so intense the memory of it remained with her the rest of the day. It was still powerful in her mind when she finally returned home to Bloomsbury, and gave Pitt her account of the day, and her impressions of it.

CHAPTER
SIX

Pitt woke in the middle of the night to hear a loud, repeated banging which through the unraveling layers of sleep he realized was at the front door. He climbed out of bed, feeling Charlotte stirring beside him.

"Door," he mumbled, reaching for his clothes. There was no point in hoping it was simply a matter of information he could accept, then go back to the warm oblivion of sleep. Anyone banging so fiercely and repeatedly wanted his presence. He pulled on trousers and socks; his boots were in front of the kitchen stove. He attempted to tuck in his shirttails, and lost them. He padded downstairs, turned up the gas on the lamp in the hall, and unbolted the front door.

The chill of the damp night air made him shiver, but it was a small discomfort compared with the sight of Murdo's ashen face and the bull's-eye lantern high in his hand, which threw its yellow light on the paving stones and into the mist around him. It picked out the dark shape of a hansom cab waiting at the curb beyond, the horse's flanks steaming, the cabby shrouded in his cloak.

Before he could ask, Murdo blurted it out, his voice cracking a little.

"There's another fire!" He forgot the "sir." He looked very young, the freckles standing out on his fair skin in its unnatural pallor. "Amos Lindsay's house."

"Bad?" Pitt asked, although he knew.

"Terrible." Murdo kept his voice under control with difficulty. "I never saw anything like it—you can feel the heat a hundred yards up the road; fair hurts your eye to look at it. God—how can anyone do that?"

"Come in," Pitt said quickly. The night air was cold.

Murdo hesitated.

"My boots are in the kitchen." Pitt turned and left him to do as he pleased. He heard the latch close and Murdo tiptoeing heavily after him.

In the kitchen he put up the gas and sat on the hard-backed chair, reaching for his boots and then lacing them tightly. Murdo came in as far as the stove, relishing the warmth. His eyes went over the clean wood, the china gleaming on the dresser, and he caught the smell of laundry drying on the airing rail winched up towards the ceiling above them. Unconsciously the lines in his young face were already less desperate.

Charlotte appeared in the doorway in her nightgown, her bare feet having made no sound on the linoleum.

Pitt smiled at her bleakly.

"What is it?" she asked, glancing at Murdo and back at Pitt.

"Fire," he said simply.

"Where?"

"Amos Lindsay's. Go back to bed," he said gently. "You'll get cold."

She stood white-faced. Her hair was dark over her shoulders, copper where the gaslight caught it.

"Who was in the house?" she asked Murdo.

"I dunno, ma'am. We aren't sure. They was trying to get the servants out, but the heat was terrible, scorch the hair off—" He stopped, realizing he was speaking to a woman and probably should not be saying such things.

"What?" she demanded.

He looked miserable and guilty for his clumsiness. He stared at Pitt, who was now ready to go.

"Eyebrows, ma'am," he answered miserably, and she knew he was too shocked to equivocate.

Pitt kissed Charlotte quickly on the cheek and pushed her

back. "Go to bed," he said again. "Standing here catching a chill won't help anyone."

"Can you tell me if—" Then she realized what she was asking. To dispatch someone with a message, simply to allay her fears, or confirm them, would be a ridiculous waste of manpower, when there were urgent things to be done, injured and perhaps bereaved people to help. "I'm sorry."

He smiled, an instant of understanding, then turned and went out with Murdo and pulled the front door closed behind him.

"What about Shaw?" he asked as they climbed up into the cab and it started forward immediately. It was obviously quite unnecessary to tell the cabby where they were going. Within moments the horse had broken from a trot into a canter and its hooves rang on the stones as the cab swayed and turned, throwing them from one wall to the other, and against each other, with some violence.

"I don't know, sir, impossible to tell. The place is an inferno. We 'aven't seen 'im—it looks bad."

"Lindsay?"

"Nor 'im neither."

"Dear God, what a mess!" Pitt said under his breath as the cab lurched around a corner, the wheels lifting for an instant and landing hard on the cobbles again with a jar that shook his bones.

It was a long, wretched ride to Highgate and they neither of them spoke again. There was nothing to say; each was consumed in his own imagination of the furnace they were racing towards, and the memory of Clemency Shaw's charred body removed from another ruin so shortly before.

The red glow was visible through the cab window as soon as they turned the last corner of Kentish Town Road onto Highgate Road. In Highgate Rise the horse jerked to a halt and the cabby leaped down and threw the door open.

"I can't take yer no further!"

Pitt climbed out and the heat hit him, enveloping him in stinging, acrid, smut-filled, roaring chaos. The whole sky seemed red with the towering brilliance of it. Showers of sparks exploded in the air, white and yellow, flying hundreds of feet up, then falling in dying cinders. The street was congested with fire engines, horses plunging and crying out in terror as debris fell around them. Men clung onto them, trying to steady them amid the confusion. There were hoses connected up to the Highgate Ponds, and men struggled with leather buckets, passing them from hand to hand, but all they were doing was protecting the nearest other houses. Nothing could save Lindsay's house now. Even as Pitt and Murdo stood in the road a great section of the top story collapsed, the beams exploded and fell in rapid succession and a huge gout of flame fifty feet high went soaring upwards, the heat of it driving them back to the far pavement and behind the hedge, even as far as they were from the house.

One of the fire engine horses screamed as a length of wood fell across its back and the smell of burning hair and flesh filled the immediate air. It plunged forward, tearing its reins out of the fireman's hands. Another man, almost too quick for thought, caught up a bucket of water and threw it over the beast, quenching in one act both the heat and the pain.

Pitt ran forward and caught the animal, throwing all his weight against its charge, and it shuddered to a halt. Murdo, who had grown up on a farm, took off his jacket, squashed it into another bucket of water, then slapped it onto the beast's back and held it.

The chief fireman was coming towards Pitt, his face a mask of smoke stains. Only the eyes showed through, red-rimmed and desperate. His eyebrows were singed and there were angry red weals under the blackened grime. His clothes were torn and soiled almost beyond recognition by water and the charring of heat and debris.

"We've got the servants out!" he shouted, then spluttered into coughing and controlled himself with difficulty. He waved them farther back and they followed him to where there was a faint touch of coolness of night air softening the heat and the stench, and the roaring and crashing of masonry and the explosion of wood were less deafening. His face was haggard, not only with sorrow but with his own failure. "But we didn't get either of the two gentlemen." It was unnecessary to add that it was now beyond hope, it was apparent to anyone at all. Nothing could be alive in that conflagration.

Pitt had known it, yet to hear it from someone else who spoke from years of such hope and struggle gave him a sudden gaping emptiness inside that took him by surprise. He realized only now how much he had been drawn to Shaw, even though he accepted that he might have murdered Clemency. Or perhaps it was only his brain that accepted it, his inner judgment always denied it. And with Amos Lindsay there had been no suspicion, only interest, and a little blossom of warmth because he had known Nobby Gunne. Now there was only a sense of sharp pain for the destruction. Anger would come later when the wound was less consuming.

He turned to Murdo and saw the shock and misery in his face. He was young and very new to murder and its sudden, violent loss. Pitt took him by the arm.

"Come on," he said quietly. "We failed to prevent this, but we've got to get him before he does any more. Or her," he added. "It could be a woman."

Murdo was still stunned. "What woman would ever do that?" He jerked his hand back, but he did not turn.

"Women are just as capable of passion and hatred as men," Pitt replied. "And of violence, given the means."

"Oh no, sir—" Murdo began instinctively, the argument born of his own memories. Sharp tongues, yes; and a box on the ears; certainly greed at times, and coldness; nagging, bossiness and a great deal of criticism; and mind-staggering, speech-robbing unfairness. But not violence like this—

Memory returned, crowding in on Pitt, and he spoke with surprise.

"Some of the most gruesome murders I've ever worked on were committed by women, Murdo. And some of them I understood very well—when I knew why—and pitied. We know so little about this case—none of the real passions underneath it—"

"We know the Worlinghams have a great deal of money, and so does old Lutterworth." Murdo struggled to gather everything in his mind. "We know—we know Pascoe and Dalgetty hate each other, although what that has to do with Mrs. Shaw . . ." He trailed off, searching for something more relevant.

"We know Lindsay wrote pro-Fabian essays—although that has nothing to do with Mrs. Shaw either—but the doctor approved it."

"That's hardly a passion to kindle a funeral pyre like that," Pitt said bitterly. "No, Murdo. We don't know very much. But dear God—we're going to find out." He swung around and walked back towards the fire chief, who was now directing his men to saving the houses in the immediate vicinity.

"Have you any idea if it was set the same way?" Pitt shouted.

The fire chief turned a filthy, miserable face to him.

"Probably. It went up very quick. Two people called us—one saw it from the street at the front, towards the town, the other down towards Holly Village and half at the back. That's at least two places. From the speed of it I daresay there was more."

"But you got the servants out? How? Why not Lindsay and Shaw? Were the fires all in the main house?"

"Looks like it. Although by the time we got here it was spread pretty well all over. Got one man badly burned and another with a broken leg getting the servants out."

"Where are they now?"

"Dunno. Some feller in a nightshirt and cassock was running 'round trying to help, and getting in the way. Good-hearted, I suppose—but a damn nuisance. Woman with 'im 'ad more sense. 'Nother couple over off to the side, looked white as ghosts—woman weeping—but they brought blankets. 'Bin too busy to watch 'em when they're safe out. Now, I'll answer your questions tomorrer—"

"Did you get the horse out?" Pitt did not know why he asked it, except some dim memory of terrified animals in another fire long ago in his youth.

"Horse?" The fire chief frowned. "What horse?"

"The doctor's horse—for his trap."

"Charlie!" the fire chief yelled at a soaked and filthy man who was walking a few yards away, limping badly. "Charlie!"

"Sir?" Charlie stopped and came over towards them, his eyebrows scorched, his eyes red-rimmed and exhausted.

"You were 'round the back—did you get the horse?"

"Weren't no 'orse, sir. I looked special. Can't bear a good animal burnt."

"Yes there was," Pitt argued. "Dr. Shaw has a trap, for his calls—"

"No trap neither, sir." Charlie was adamant. "Stable was still standing when I got there. No 'orse and no trap. Either they was kept somewhere else—or they're out."

Out! Was it possible Shaw was not here at all, that once again the fire had not caught him? In all this fearful pyre could only Amos Lindsay be dead?

Who would know? Who could he ask? He turned around in the red night, still loud with the crackling of sparks and the roar and boom of flame. He could see at the far edge of the tangle of engines, horses, water buckets, ladders, and weary and injured men, the two black figures of Josiah and Prudence Hatch, a little apart from each other, huddled in a private and separate misery. The cassocked figure of Clitheridge was striding along, skirts flying, a flask in his outstretched hand, and Lally was rewrapping a blanket around the shoulders of a tiny kitchen girl who was shuddering so violently Pitt could see it even through the smoke and the melee. Lindsay's manservant with the polished hair stood alone, stupefied, like a person upright in his sleep.

Pitt skirted around the horses and buckets and the men still working, and started towards the far side. He was off the opposite pavement and in the middle of the road when he heard the clatter of hooves and looked automatically up the street towards Highgate center to see who it was. There was no purpose in more fire engines now—and anyway there was no sound of bells.

It was a trap, horse almost at a gallop, wheels racing and jumping in their speed and recklessness. Pitt knew long before he saw him that it was Shaw, and he felt an intense relief, followed the instant after by a new darkness. If Shaw was alive, then it was still possible he had set both fires, first to kill Clemency, now to kill Lindsay. Why Lindsay? Perhaps in the few days he had stayed with Lindsay, Shaw had betrayed himself by a word, an expression, even something unsaid when it should have been? It was a sickening thought, and yet honesty could not dismiss it.

"Pitt!" Shaw almost fell off the step of the trap and took no trouble even to tie the rein, leaving the horse to go where it would. He grabbed Pitt by the arm, almost swinging him off his feet. "Pitt! For God's sake, what's happened? Where's Amos? Where are the staff?" His face was so gaunt with horror it was impossible not to be moved by it.

Pitt put out his hand to steady him. "The servants are all right, but I'm afraid Lindsay was not brought out. I'm sorry."

"No! No!" The cry was torn from Shaw and he plunged forward, bumping into people, knocking them aside in his headlong race towards the flames.

After a moment's stupefaction Pitt ran after him, leaping a water hose and accidentally sending a fireman flying. He caught Shaw so close to the building the heat was immense and the roaring of the flames seemed almost around them. He brought him to the ground, driving the wind out of him.

"You can't do anything!" he shouted above the din. "You'll only get killed yourself!"

Shaw coughed and struggled to get up. "Amos is in there!" His voice was close to hysteria. "I've got to—" Then he stopped, on his hands and knees facing the blaze, and realization came to him at last that it was utterly futile. Something inside him collapsed and he made no resistance when Pitt pulled him to his feet.

"Come back, or you'll get burned," Pitt said gently.

"What?" Shaw was still staring at the violence of the flames. They were so close the heat was hurting their skin, and the brightness made him screw up his eyes, but he seemed only peripherally aware of it.

"Come back!" Pitt shouted as a beam fell in with a crash and an explosion of sparks. Without thinking he took Shaw by the arms and pulled him as if he had been a frightened animal. For a moment he was afraid Shaw was going to fall over, then at last he obeyed, stumbling a little, careless if he hurt himself.

Pitt wanted to say something of comfort, but what was there? Amos Lindsay was dead, the one man who had seemed to understand Shaw and not be offended by his abrasiveness, who saw beyond the words to the mind and its intent. It was Shaw's second terrible bereavement in less than two weeks. There was nothing to say that would not be fatuous and offensive, only betraying a complete failure to understand anything of his true pain. Silence at least did not intrude, but it left Pitt feeling helpless and inadequate.

Clitheridge was floundering over towards them, a look of dedication and terror on his face. He obviously had not the faintest idea what to say or do, except that he was determined not to flinch from his duty. At the last moment he was saved by events. The horse in the trap took flight as a piece of burning debris shot past it and it reared up and twisted around.

That at least was something Clitheridge understood. He abandoned Shaw, for whom he could do nothing and whose grief appalled and embarrassed him, and reached instead for the horse, holding the rein close to its head and throwing all his considerable weight against the momentum of its lunge.

"Whoa! Steady—steady now. It's all right—steady, girl. Hold hard!" And miraculously for once he was completely successful. The animal stopped and stood still, shuddering and rolling its eyes. "Steady," he said again, full of relief, and began to lead it across the road, away from the roar and heat, and away from Shaw.

"The servants." At last Shaw spoke. He twisted around on one foot and swayed a little. "What about the servants? Where are they? Are they hurt?"

"Not seriously," Pitt replied. "They'll be all right."

Clitheridge was still across the street with the horse and trap, leading it away, but Oliphant the curate was coming towards them, his thin face lit by the glare from the flames, his figure gawky in a coat whose shoulders were too big. He stopped in front of them and his voice was quiet and certain.

"Dr. Shaw; I lodge with Mrs. Turner up on West Hill. She has other rooms and you'd be welcome to stay there as long as you choose. There is nothing you can do here, and I think a strong cup of tea, some hot water to wash in, and then sleep would help you to face tomorrow."

Shaw opened his mouth to argue, then realized that Oliphant had not offered facile words of comfort. He had offered practical help and reminded him that there was another day ahead, and regardless of pain or shock, there would be duties, things to do that would be useful and have meaning.

"I—" He struggled for the practical. "I have no—nothing— it is all gone—again—"

"Of course," Oliphant agreed. "I have an extra nightshirt you are welcome to, and a razor, soap, a clean shirt. Anything I have is yours."

Shaw tried to cling to the moment, as if something could still be retrieved, some horror undone that would become fixed if he were to leave. It was as though accepting it made it true. Pitt knew the feeling, irrational and yet so strong it held one to the scene of tragedy because to move was to acknowledge it and allow it to be real.

"The servants," Shaw said again. "What about them? Where are they to sleep? I must—" He turned one way and another, frantic for some action to help, and saw none.

Oliphant nodded, his face red in the flames' reflection, his voice level. "Mary and Mrs. Wiggins will stay with Mr. and Mrs. Hatch, and Jones will stay with Mr. Clitheridge."

Shaw stared at him. Two firemen went past supporting a third between them.

"We shall begin to search for new positions for them in the morning." Oliphant held out his hand. "There are plenty of people who want good, reliable help that has been well trained. Don't worry about it. They are frightened, but not hurt. They need sleep and the assurance that they will not be put on the street."

Shaw looked at him incredulously.

"Come," Oliphant repeated. "You cannot help here—"

"I can't just—just walk away!" Shaw protested. "My friend is in that—" He stared helplessly at the blaze, now redder and sinking as the last of the wood crumbled away inside and the masonry collapsed inward. He searched for words to explain the tumult of emotions inside him, and failed. There were tears in the grime on his face. His hands clenched at his sides and jerked as if he still longed to move violently, and had no idea where or how.

"Yes you can leave it," Oliphant insisted. "There is no one left here; but tomorrow there will be people who need you—sick, frightened people who trust you to be there and use the knowledge you have to help them."

Shaw stared at him, horror in his face turning to a slow amazement. Then finally, without speaking, he followed him obediently, his shoulders sagging, his feet slow, as if he were bruised, and intensely, painfully tired.

Pitt watched him go and felt a racking mixture of emotions inside himself; pity for Shaw's grief and the stunning pain he obviously felt, fury at the fearful waste of it, and a kind of anger because he did not know who to blame for it all, who to cherish and who to want to hunt and see punished. It was like having a dam pent up inside him and the pressure of confusion ached to burst in some easy and total action, and yet there was none.

The building crashed in sparks again as another wall subsided. Two firemen were shouting at each other.

Finally he left them and retraced his own steps to look for Murdo and begin the miserable task of questioning the closest neighbors to see if any of them had seen or heard anything before the fire, anyone close to Lindsay's house, any light, any movement.

Murdo was amazed by how tumultuous were his feelings about accompanying Pitt to the Lutterworths'. Away from the immediate heat of the fire his face hurt where the skin was a little scorched, his eyes stung and watered from the smoke, even his throat ached from it, and there was a large and painful blister forming on his hand where he had been struck by a flying cinder. But his body was chilled, and inside the coat Oliphant had found for him, he was shivering and clenched with cold.

He thought of the huge, dark house of the Lutterworths, of the splendor inside it, carpets, pictures, velvet curtains bound with sashes and splayed on the floor like overlong skirts. He had only ever seen such luxury at the Worlinghams' themselves, and theirs was a lot older, and worn in one or two places. The Lutterworths' was all new.

But far sharper in his mind, and making him clench his sore hands before he remembered the blister, was the memory of Flora Lutterworth with her wide, dark eyes, so very direct, the proud way she carried her head, chin high. He had noticed her hands especially; he always remarked hands, and hers were the most beautiful he had ever seen, slender, with tapering fingers and perfect nails, not plump and useless like those of so many ladies of quality—like the Misses Worlingham, for example.

The more he thought of Flora the lighter his feet were on the frosty pavement, and the more wildly his stomach lurched at the prospect of Pitt knocking on the front door with its brass lion's head, until he disturbed the entire household and brought the footman to let them in, furious and full of contempt, so they could stand dripping and filthy on the clean carpet till Lutterworth himself was roused and came down. Then Pitt would ask him a lot of intrusive questions that would all be pointless in the end, and could have waited until morning anyway.

They were actually on the step when he finally spoke.

"Wouldn't it be better to wait until morning?" he said breathlessly. He was still very wary of Pitt. At times he admired him, at others he was torn by old loyalties, parochial and deep rooted, understanding his colleagues' resentment and sense of having been undervalued and passed by. But most often he was lost in his own eagerness to solve the case and he thought of nothing but how could he help, what could he contribute to their knowledge. He was gaining a measure of respect for Pitt's patience and his observation of people. Some of his conclusions had escaped Murdo. He had had no notion how Pitt knew of some of the exchanges between Pascoe and Dalgetty—until Pitt had quite openly recounted how Mrs. Pitt had attended the funeral supper and repeated back to him all her impressions. In that moment Murdo had ceased to dislike Pitt; it was impossible to dislike a man who was so candid about his deductions. He could easily have pretended a superior ability, and Murdo knew a good many who would have.

Pitt's reply was unnecessary, both because Murdo knew perfectly well what it would be, and because the front door swung open the moment after Pitt knocked and Alfred Lutterworth himself stood in the lighted hall, hastily but fully dressed. Only his neck without a tie and his ill-matched coat and trousers betrayed that he had already been up. Perhaps he had been one of the many who had crowded around the edge of the fire, anxious, curious, concerned, some offering help—or to see the job done to its bitter conclusion.

"Lindsay's 'ouse." He made it a statement rather than a question. "Poor devil. 'E was a good man. What about Shaw—did they get 'im this time?"

"You believe it was Shaw they were after, sir?" Pitt stepped in and Murdo followed him nervously.

Lutterworth closed the door behind them. "Do you take me for a fool, man? Who else would they be after, first 'is own 'ouse, and now Lindsay's? Don't stand there. You'd best come in, although there's nowt I can tell yer." His northern accent was more pronounced in his emotion. "If I'd seen anyone you'd not 'ave 'ad to come seekin' me, I'd'a gone seekin' you."

Pitt followed him and Murdo came a step behind. The withdrawing room was cold, the ashes of the fire already dark, but Flora was standing beside it. She was also fully dressed, in a gray, winter gown, her face pale and her hair tied back with a silk kerchief. Murdo felt himself suddenly excruciatingly awkward, not knowing what to do with his feet, where to put his painful, dirty hands.

"Good evening, Inspector." She looked at Pitt courteously, then at Murdo with something he thought was a smile. "Good evening, Constable Murdo."

She had remembered his name. His heart lurched. It had been a smile—hadn't it?

"Good evening, Miss Lutterworth." His voice sounded husky and ended in a squeak.

"Can we help, Inspector?" She turned to Pitt again. "Does anyone . . . need shelter?" Her eyes pleaded with him to tell her the answer to the question she had not asked.

Murdo drew breath to tell her, but Pitt cut across him and he was left openmouthed.

"Your father thinks the fire was deliberately set, in order to kill Dr. Shaw." Pitt was watching her, waiting for reaction.

Murdo was furious. He saw the last trace of color leave her face and he would have rushed forward to save her from collapsing, had he dared. In that instant he loathed Pitt for his brutality, and Lutterworth himself for not having protected her, he whose duty and privilege it was.

She bit her lip to stop it trembling and her eyes filled with tears. She turned away to hide them.

"No need to cry for 'im, girl," Lutterworth said gently. " 'E was no use to you, nor to 'is poor wife neither. 'E was a greedy man, with no sense o' right nor wrong. Save your tears for poor Amos Lindsay. 'E was a good-enough chap, in 'is own way. A bit blunt, but none the worse for that. Don't take on." Then he swung around to Pitt. "Mind you could'a chosen your time and your words better! Clumsy great fool!"

Murdo was in an agony of indecision. Should he offer her his handkerchief? It had been clean this morning, as it was every morning, but it must smell terrible with smoke now; and anyway, wouldn't she think him impertinent, overfamiliar?

Her shoulders were trembling and she sobbed without sound. She looked so hurt, like a woman and a child at once.

He could bear it no longer. He pulled the handkerchief out of his pocket, dropping keys and a pencil along with it, and went forward to give it to her, arm outstretched. He no longer cared what Pitt thought, or what detective strategy he might be using. He also hated Shaw, with an utterly new emotion that had never touched him before, because Flora wept for him with such heartbreak.

"He in't dead, miss," he said bluntly. "He was out on a call somewhere an' 'e's terrible upset—but he in't even hurt. Mr. Oliphant, the curate, took him back to his lodgings for the night. Please don't cry like that—"

Lutterworth's face was dark. "You said he was dead." He swung around, accusing Pitt.

"No, Mr. Lutterworth," Pitt contradicted. "You assumed it.

I am deeply sorry to say that Mr. Lindsay is dead. But Dr. Shaw is perfectly well."

"Out again?" Lutterworth was staring at Flora now, his brows drawn down, his mouth tight. "I'll lay odds that bounder struck the match 'imself."

Flora jerked up, her face tearstained, Murdo's handkerchief clasped in her fingers, but now her eyes were wide with fury.

"That's a terrible thing to say, and you have no right even to think it, let alone to put it into words! It is completely irresponsible!"

"Oh, and you know all about responsibility, of course, girl," Lutterworth retorted, by now regardless of Pitt or Murdo. His face was suffused with color and his voice thick in his emotion. "Creepin' in and out at all hours to see 'im—imagining I don't know. For heaven's sake, 'alf Highgate knows! And talk about it over the teacups, like you were some common whore—"

Murdo gasped as if the word had struck him physically. He would rather have sustained a dozen blows from a thief or a drunkard than have such a term used of Flora. Were it any other man he would have knocked him to the ground—but he was helpless.

"—and I've nothing with which to call them liars!" Lutterworth was anguished with impotent fury himself, and anyone but Murdo would have pitied him. "Dear God—if your mother were alive she'd weep 'erself sick to see you. First time since she died I 'aven't grieved she weren't 'ere with me—the very first time . . ."

Flora stared at him and stood even straighter. She drew a breath to defend herself, her cheeks scarlet, her eyes burning. Then her face filled with misery and she remained silent.

"Nothing to say?" he demanded. "No excuses? No—what a fine man he is, if only I knew 'im like you do, eh?"

"You do me an injustice, Papa," she said stiffly. "And yourself also. I am sorry you think so ill of me, but you must believe what you will."

"Don't you come high and mighty with me, girl." Lutterworth's face was torn between anger and pain. Had she been looking at him more closely she might have seen the pride as he gazed at her, and the shattered hope. But his words were unfortunate. "I'm your father, not some tomfool lad following after you. You're not too big to send to your room, if I have to. An' I'll approve any man that sets 'is cap at you, or you'll not so much as give 'im the time o' day. Do you hear me, girl?"

She was trembling. "I'm sure everyone in the house hears you, Papa, including the tweeny in the attic—"

His face flushed purple with anger.

"—but if anyone does me the honor of courting me," she went on before he had mustered the words, "I shall most certainly seek your approval. But if I love him, I'll marry him whether you like him or not." She turned to Murdo, and with a barely shaking voice thanked him for informing her that Dr. Shaw was alive and well. Then, still clutching his handkerchief, she swept out and they heard her footsteps go across the hall and up the stairs.

Lutterworth was too wretched and too embarrassed to apologize or seek polite excuses for such a scene.

"I can't tell you anything you don't know for yourselves," he said brusquely when the silence returned. "I 'eard the alarm and went out to see, same as 'alf the street, but I didn't see nor 'ear anything before that. Now I'll be going back to my bed and you'd best get about your business. Good night to you."

"Good night sir," they replied quietly, and found their own way to the door.

It was not the only quarrel they witnessed that night.

Pascoe was too distressed to see them, and his servant refused on his behalf. They trudged in silence and little expectation of learning anything useful, first to the Hatches' house to question Lindsay's maid, who was bundled up in blankets and shaking so violently she could not hold a cup steady in her hand. She could tell them nothing except that she had woken to the sound of fire bells and had been so terrified she did not know what to do. A fireman had come to the window and carried her out, across the roof of the house and down a long ladder to the garden, where she had been soaked with water from a hose, no doubt by accident.

At this point her teeth were chattering on the edge of the cup and Pitt recognized that she was unlikely to know anything useful, and was beyond being able to tell him anyway. Not even the prospect of a clue towards who had burned two houses to the ground, with their occupants inside, prompted him to press her any further.

When she had been escorted upstairs to bed, he turned to Josiah Hatch, who was gaunt faced, eyes fixed in horror at the vision within his mind.

Pitt watched him anxiously, he seemed so close to retreating into himself with shock. Perhaps to be forced to speak and think of and answer questions of fact would be less of a torture than one might suppose. It would draw him from the contemplation of the enormity of destruction, and from the flicker in the muscles in his eyelids and the corners of his mouth, the fear of the evil which now was so obviously still in their midst.

"What time did you retire this evening, Mr. Hatch?" he began.

"Ugh?" Hatch recalled himself to the present with difficulty. "Oh—late—I did not look at the clock. I was in deep contemplation of what I had been reading."

"I heard you come up the stairs at about quarter to two," Prudence put in very quietly, looking first at her husband and then at Pitt.

He turned a blank face towards her. "I disturbed you? I'm sorry, that was the last thing I intended."

"Oh no, my dear! I had been roused by one of the children. Elizabeth had a nightmare. I had merely not yet gone back to sleep."

"Is she well this morning?"

Prudence's face relaxed into the ghost of a smile. "Of course. It was simply an ill dream. Children do have them, you know— quite often. All she required was a little reassurance."

"Could not one of the older children have given her that without disturbing you?" He frowned, seizing on the matter as if it were important. "Nan is fifteen! In another few years she may have children of her own."

"There is a world of difference between fifteen and twenty, Josiah. I can remember when I was fifteen." The tiny smile returned again, soft and sad. "I knew nothing—and I imagined I knew everything. There were entire regions—continents of experience of which I had not the faintest conception."

Pitt wondered what particular ignorances were in her mind. He thought perhaps those of marriage, the responsibility after the romance had cooled, the obedience, and perhaps the bearing of children—but he could have been wrong. It might have been worldly things, quite outside the home, other struggles or tragedies she had seen and coped with.

Hatch apparently did not know what she referred to either. He frowned at her in incomprehension for a few moments longer, then turned to Pitt again.

"I saw nothing of any import." He answered the question before it was asked. "I was in my study, reading from the work of St. Augustine." The muscles in his jaw and neck tightened and some inner dream took hold of him. "The words of men who have sought after God in other ages are a great enlightenment to us—and comfort. There has always been powerful evil in the world, and will be as long as the soul of man is as weak and beset by temptations as it is." He looked at Pitt again. "But I am afraid I can be of no assistance to you. My mind and my senses were totally absorbed in contemplation and study."

"How terrible," Prudence said to no one in particular, "that you were awake in your study, reading of the very essence of the conflict between good and evil." She shivered and held her arms close around herself. "And only a few hundred yards away, someone was setting a fire that murdered poor Mr. Lindsay— and but for a stroke of good fortune, would have murdered poor Stephen as well."

"There are mighty forces of evil here in Highgate." He stared straight ahead of him again, as if he could see the pattern in the space between the jardiniere with its gold chrysanthemums and the stitched sampler on the wall with the words of the Twenty-third Psalm. "Wickedness has been entertained, and invited to take up its abode with us," he went on.

"Do you know by whom, Mr. Hatch?" It was surely a futile question, and yet Pitt felt impelled to ask it. Murdo behind him, silent until now, shifted uncomfortably from one foot to the other.

Hatch looked around in surprise. "God forgive him and give him peace, by Lindsay himself. He spread dark ideas of revolution and anarchy, overthrow of the order of things as they are. He wanted some new society where individual ownership of property was done away and men were no longer rewarded according to their ability and effort but given a common wage regardless. It would do away with self-reliance, diligence, industry and responsibility—all the virtues which have made the Empire great and the nation the envy of all the Christian world." His face was pinched with anger at the distortion, and grief for all that would be lost. "And John Dalgetty published them—to his dishonor—but he is a foolish man forever pursuing what he imagines is justice and a kind of freedom of the mind that has become all important to him, consuming all his better judgment. In his frenzy he deludes others."

He looked at Pitt. "Poor Pascoe has done all he can to dissuade him, and then to prevent him by public opinion, and even the law; but he is puny against the tide of inquisitiveness and disobedience in mankind and the passion for novelty—always novelty." His body was clenched under his clothes, aching with tension. "Novelty at any price! New sciences, a new social order, new art—we are insatiable. The minute we have seen a thing, we want to cast it aside and find something else. We worship freedom as if it were some infinite good. But you cannot escape morality—freedom from the consequence of your acts is the great delusion at the core of all this"—he flung his hand out—"this frenzy for newness—and for irresponsibility. We have been from the first a race that hungers for forbidden knowledge and would eat the fruit of sin and death. God commanded our first parents to abstain, and they would not. What chance has poor Quinton Pascoe?"

His face tightened and a look of defeat washed his whole countenance with pain. "And Stephen in his arrogance upheld Dalgetty and made mock of Pascoe and his attempts to protect the weak and the sensitive from the cruder expressions of ideas that could only injure and frighten at best—and at worst deprave. Mockery of the truth, of all man's past aspirations to higher good, is one of the Evil One's most fearsome weapons, and God help him, Stephen has been more than willing to use it."

"Josiah—I think you speak too harshly," Prudence protested. "I know Stephen speaks foolishly at times, but there is no cruelty in him—"

He turned around to her, his face grim, his eyes burning. "You know him very little, my dear. You see only the best. That is to your credit—and it is what I intend shall continue, but be counseled by me: I have heard him say much that I shall never repeat to you, which has been both cruel and degraded. He has a contempt for the virtues which you most admire."

"Oh, Josiah, are you sure? Could you not perhaps have misunderstood him? He has an unfortunate sense of humor at times—and—"

"I could not!" He was absolute. "I am perfectly capable of telling when he is attempting to be amusing and when he means what he says, however superficially he covers it with lightness. The essence of mockery, Prudence, is that it should make good people laugh at what they would otherwise have taken seriously and loved—to make moral purity, labor, hope, and belief in people, seem ridiculous to them—things of jest to be derided."

Prudence opened her mouth to refute what he was saying; then recalling some other knowledge, some fact until then secondary, she colored with embarrassment and looked down at the floor. Pitt was aware of her misery as if she had touched him, but he had no idea what caused it. She wanted to defend Shaw, but why? Affection, simple compassion because she believed his suffering to be genuine, or some other reason unguessed by him yet? And what held her back?

"I regret we cannot help you," Hatch said civilly, but he could not mask the exhaustion in his voice, nor the shock in his eyes. He was on the point of collapse, and it was nearly four in the morning.

Pitt gave up. "Thank you for your time now, and your courtesy. We will not keep you up longer. Good night, sir—Mrs. Hatch."

Outside the night was black and the wind whined in the darkness, glaring red over towards the ruins of Amos Lindsay's house. The street was still full of fire engines, and firemen were walking the horses up and down to keep them from chilling.

"Go home," Pitt said to Murdo, stamping his feet on the ice around the pavement. "Get a few hours' sleep and I'll see you at the station at ten."

"Yes sir. Do you think Shaw did it himself, sir? To cover the murder of his wife?"

Pitt looked at Murdo's scorched and miserable face. He knew what he was thinking.

"Over Flora Lutterworth? Possibly. She's a handsome girl, and can expect a lot of money. But I doubt Flora had any part in it. Now go home and sleep—and get that hand attended to. If that blister breaks and you get it dirty, God knows what infection you could get. Good night, Murdo."

"Good night, sir." And Murdo turned and made his way hastily across the road and past the firemen up towards Highgate.

It took Pitt nearly half an hour to find a cab, and then he only succeeded because some late-night junketer had failed to pay his fare and the cabby was standing on the pavement calling after him instead of making a hasty return to his own bed. He grumbled, and asked for extra, but since Bloomsbury was more or less on his way, he weighed exhaustion against profit and came out on the side of profit.

Charlotte came flying down the stairs almost before Pitt had the door shut, a shawl caught half around her shoulders and no slippers on. She stared at him, waiting for the answer.

"Amos Lindsay's dead," he said, taking off his boots and moving frozen toes inside his socks. Really he ought to put his socks in the kitchen to dry out. "Shaw was out on a call again. He got back soon after we arrived." His coat fell off the hook

behind him and landed in a heap on the floor. He was too tired
to care. "The servants are all right."

She hesitated only a moment, absorbing the knowledge.
Then she came down the rest of the stairs and put her arms
around him, her head against his shoulder. There was no need
to talk now; all she could think of was relief, and how cold he
was, and dirty, and tired. She wanted to hold him and ease out
the horror, make him warm again and let him sleep, as if he had
been a child.

"The bed's warm," she said at last.

"I'm covered in smut and the smell of smoke," he answered,
stroking her hair.

"I'll wash the sheets," she said without moving.

"You'll have to soak them," he warned.

"I know. What time do you have to go back?"

"I told Murdo ten o'clock."

"Then don't stand here shivering." She stood back and held
out her hand.

Silently he followed her upstairs and as soon as his outer
clothes were off, fell gratefully into the warm sheets and held
her close to him. Within minutes he was asleep.

Pitt slept late and when he woke Charlotte was already up.
He dressed quickly and was downstairs for hot water to shave
within five minutes and at the breakfast table in ten to share the
meal with his children. This was a rare pleasure, since he was
too often gone when they ate.

"Good morning, Jemima," he said formally. "Good morning, Daniel."

"Good morning, Papa," they replied as he sat down. Daniel
stopped eating his porridge, spoon in the air, a drop of milk on
his chin. His face was soft and the features still barely formed.
His baby teeth were even and perfectly formed. He had Pitt's
dark curls—unlike Jemima, two years older, who had her mother's auburn coloring, but her hair had to be tied in rags all night
if it were to curl.

"Eat your porridge," Jemima ordered him, taking another
spoonful of her own. She was inquisitive, bossy, fiercely pro-

tective of him, and seldom stopped talking. "You'll get cold in school if you don't!"

Pitt hid a smile, wondering where she had picked up that piece of information.

Daniel obeyed. He had learned in his four years of life that it was a lot easier in the long run than arguing, and his nature was not quarrelsome or assertive, except over issues that mattered, like who had how much pudding, or that the wooden fire engine was his, not hers, and that since he was the boy he had the right to walk on the outside. And the hoop was also his— and the stick that went with it.

She was agreeable to most of these, except walking on the outside—she was older, and taller, and therefore it only made sense that she should.

"Are you working on a very important case, Papa?" Jemima asked, her eyes wide. She was very proud of her father, and everything he did was important.

He smiled at her. Sometimes she looked so like Charlotte must have at the same age, the same soft little mouth, stubborn chin and demanding eyes.

"Yes—away up in Highgate."

"Somebody dead?" she asked. She had very little idea what "dead" meant, but she had heard the word many times, and she and Charlotte and Daniel had buried several dead birds in the garden. But she could not remember all that Charlotte had told her, except it was all right and something to do with heaven.

Pitt met Charlotte's eyes over Jemima's head. She nodded.

"Yes," he replied.

"Are you going to solve it?" Jemima continued.

"I hope so."

"I'm going to be a detective when I grow up," she said, taking another spoonful of her porridge. "I shall solve cases as well."

"So shall I," Daniel added.

Charlotte passed Pitt his porridge and they continued in gentle conversation until it was time for him to leave. He kissed the children—Daniel was still just young enough not to object—kissed Charlotte, who definitely did not object, and put on his boots, which she had remembered to bring in this morning to warm, and took his leave.

Outside it was one of those crisp autumn mornings when the air is cold, tingling in the nostrils, but the sky is blue and the crackle of frost under the feet is a sharp, pleasing sound.

He went first to Bow Street to report to Micah Drummond.

"Another fire?" Drummond frowned, standing by his window looking over the wet rooftops towards the river. The morning sunlight made everything gleam in gray and silver and there was mist only over the water itself. "Still they didn't get Shaw?" He turned back and met Pitt's eyes. "Makes one think."

"He was very distressed." Pitt remembered the night before with an ache of pity.

Drummond did not answer that. He knew Pitt felt it unarguably and they both knew all the possibilities that rose from it.

"I suppose the Highgate police are looking into all the known arsonists in the area, methods and patterns and so on? Made a note of all the people who turned out to watch, in case it's a pyromaniac who just lights them for the love of it?"

"Very keen," Pitt said ruefully.

"But you think it's a deliberate murder?" Drummond eyed him curiously.

"I think so."

"Bit of pressure to get this cleared up." Drummond was at his desk now, and his long fingers played idly with the copper-handled paper knife. "Need you back here. They've taken half a dozen men for this Whitechapel business. I suppose you've seen the newspapers?"

"I saw the letter to Mr. Lusk," Pitt said grimly. "With the human kidney in it, and purported to come 'from hell.' I should think he may be right. Anyone who can kill and mutilate repeatedly like this must live in hell, and carry it with him."

"Pity aside," Drummond said very seriously, "people are beginning to panic. Whitechapel is deserted as soon as it's dusk, people are calling for the commissioner to resign, the newspapers are getting more and more sensational. One woman died from a heart attack with the latest edition in her hand." Drummond sighed in a twisted unhappiness, his eyes on Pitt's. "They don't joke about it in the music halls, you know. People usually make jokes about what frightens them most—it's a way of defusing it. But this is too bad even for that."

"Don't they?" Curiously, that meant more to Pitt than all the sensational press and posters. It was an indication of the depth of fear in the ordinary people. He smiled lopsidedly. "Haven't had much time to go to the halls lately."

Drummond acknowledged the jibe with the good nature with which it was intended.

"Do what you can with this Highgate business, Pitt, and keep me informed."

"Yes sir."

This time instead of taking a hansom, Pitt walked briskly down to the Embankment and caught a train. He got off at the Highgate Road station, putting the few pence difference aside towards Charlotte's holiday. It was a beginning. He walked up Highgate Rise to the police station.

He was greeted with very guarded civility.

"Mornin' sir." Their faces were grave and resentful, and yet there was a certain satisfaction in them.

"Good morning," he replied, waiting for the explanation. "Discovered something?"

"Yes sir. We got an arsonist who done this kind o' thing before. Never killed anyone, but reckon that was more luck than anything. Method's the same—fuel oil. Done it over Kentish Town way up 'til now, but that's only a step away. Got too 'ot for 'im there an' 'e moved north, I reckon."

Pitt was startled and he tried without success to keep the disbelief out of his face. "Have you arrested him?"

"Not yet, but we will. We know 'is name an' where 'e lodges. Only a matter of time." The man smiled and met Pitt's eyes. "Seems like they didn't need to send a top officer from Bow Street to 'elp us. We done it ourselves: just solid police work—checkin' an' knowin' our area. Mebbe you'd best go an' give them an 'and in Whitechapel—seems this Jack the Ripper's got the 'ole city in a state o' terror."

"Takin' photographs o' the dead women's eyes," another constable added unhelpfully. " 'Cause they reckon that the last thing a person sees is there at the back o' their eyes, if you can just get it. But we got no corpses worth mentioning—poor devils."

"And we've got no murderer worth mentioning yet either," Pitt added. He remembered to exercise some tact just in time. He still had to work with these men. "I expect you are already looking into who owned the other property this arsonist burned? In case there is insurance fraud."

The officer blushed and lied. "Yes sir, seein' into that today."

"I thought so." Pitt looked back at him without a flicker. "Arsonists sometimes have a reason beyond just watching the flames and feeling their own power. Meanwhile I'll get on with the other possibilities. Where's Murdo?"

"In the duty room, sir."

"Thank you."

Pitt found Murdo waiting for him just inside the door of the duty room. He looked tired and had his hand bandaged and held stiffly at his side. He still looked uncertain whether to like Pitt or resent him, and he had not forgotten Pitt's treatment of Flora Lutterworth, nor his own inability to prevent it. All his emotions were bare in his face, and Pitt was reminded again how young he was.

"Anything new, apart from the arsonist?" he asked automatically.

"No sir, except the fire chief says this was just like the last one—but I reckon you know that."

"Fuel oil?"

"Yes sir, most likely—and started in at least three places."

"Then we'll go and see if Pascoe is fit to talk to this morning."

"Yes sir."

Quinton Pascoe was up and dressed, sitting beside a roaring fire in his withdrawing room, but he still looked cold, possibly from tiredness. There were dark circles under his eyes and his hands were knotted in his lap. He seemed older than Pitt had thought when they last met, and for all his stocky body, less robust.

"Come in, Inspector, Constable," he said without rising. "I am sorry I was not able to see you last night, but I really cannot tell you anything anyway. I took a little laudanum—I have been most distressed over the turn of events lately, and I wished to get a good night of rest." He looked at Pitt hopefully, searching to see if he understood. "So much ugliness," he said with a shake of his head. "I seem to be losing all the time. It puts me in mind of the end of King Arthur's table, when the knights go out one by one to seek the Holy Grail, and all the honor and companionship begins to crumble apart. Loyalties were ended. It seems to me that a certain kind of nobility died with the end of chivalry, and courage for its own sake, the idealism that believes in true virtue and is prepared to fight and to die to preserve it, and counts the privilege of battle the only reward."

Murdo looked nonplussed.

Pitt struggled with memory of *Morte d'Arthur* and *Idylls of the King*, and thought perhaps he saw a shred of what Pascoe meant.

"Was your distress due to Mrs. Shaw's death?" Pitt asked. "Or other concerns as well? You spoke of evil—a general sense—"

"That was quite appalling." Pascoe's face looked drained, as if he were totally confused and overcome by events. "But there are other things as well." He shook his head a little and frowned. "I know I keep returning to John Dalgetty, but his attitude towards deriding the old values and breaking them down in order to build new . . ." He looked at Pitt. "I don't condemn all new ideas, not at all. But so many of the things he advocates are destructive."

Pitt did not reply, knowing there was no good response and choosing to listen.

Pascoe's eyes wrinkled up. "He questions all the foundations we have built up over centuries, he casts doubt on the very origin of man and God, he makes the young believe they are invulnerable to the evil of false ideals, the corrosion of cynicism and irresponsibility—and at the same time strips them of the armor of faith. They want to break up and change things without thought. They think they can have things without laboring for them." He bit his lip and scowled. "What can we do, Mr. Pitt? I have lain awake in the night and wrestled with it, and I know less now than when I started."

He stood up and walked towards the window, then swung around and came back again.

"I have been to him, of course, pleaded with him to withhold some of the publications he sells, asked him not to praise some of the works he does, especially this Fabian political philosophy. But to no avail." He waved his hands. "All he says is that information is sacred and all men must have the right to hear and judge for themselves what they believe—and similarly, everyone must be free to put forward any ideas they please, be they true or false, good or evil, creative or destructive. And nothing I say dissuades him. And of course Shaw encourages him with his ideas of what is humorous, when it is really at other people's expense."

Murdo was unused to such passion over ideas. He shifted uncomfortably from one foot to the other.

"The thing is," Pascoe continued intently, "people do not always know when he is joking. Take that wretched business of Lindsay. I am profoundly grieved he is dead—and I did not dislike him personally, you understand—but I felt he was deeply wrong to have written that monograph. There are foolish people, you know"—he searched Pitt's face—"who believe this new nonsense about a political order which promises justice by taking away private property and paying everyone the same, regardless of how clever or how diligent they are. I don't suppose you've read this miserable Irishman, George Bernard Shaw? He writes so divisively, as if he were trying to stir up contention and make people dissatisfied. He talks of people with large appetites and no dinner at one end, and at the other, people with large dinners and no appetites. And of course he is all for freedom of speech." He laughed sharply. "He would be, wouldn't he? He wants to be able to say anything he pleases himself. And Lindsay reported him."

He stopped suddenly. "I'm sorry. I know nothing that can be of help to you, and I do not wish to speak ill of others when such an issue is at stake, especially the dead. I slept deeply until I was awoken by the fire bells, and poor Lindsay's house was a bonfire in the sky."

Pitt and Murdo left, each in his own thoughts as they stepped out of the shelter of the porch into the icy wind. All through an unfruitful visit to the Clitheridges they said nothing to each other. Lindsay's manservant could give them no help as to the origin of the fire, only that he had woken when the smell of smoke had penetrated his quarters, at the back of the house, by which time the main building was burning fiercely and his attempts to rescue his master were hopeless. He had opened the connecting door to be met by a wall of flame, and even as he sat hunched in Clitheridge's armchair, his face bore mute witness to the dedication of his efforts. His skin was red and wealed with blisters, his hands were bound in thin gauze and linen, and were useless to him.

"Dr. Shaw was 'round here early this morning to put balm on them and bind them for him," Lally said with shining admiration in her eyes. "I don't know how he can find the strength, after this new tragedy. He was so fond of Amos Lindsay, you know, apart from the sheer horror of it. I think he must be the strongest man I know."

There had been a bleak look of defeat in Clitheridge's face for an instant as she spoke, and Pitt had imagined a world of frustration, petty inadequacies and fear of other people's raw emotion that must have been the vicar's lot. He was not a man to whom passion came easily; rather the slow-burning, inner turmoil of repressed feelings, too much thought and too much uncertainty. In that instant he felt an overwhelming pity for him; and then turning and seeing Lally's eager, self-critical face, for her also. She was drawn to Shaw in spite of herself, trying to explain it in acceptable terms of admiration for his virtues, and knowing it was immeasurably deeper than that and quite different.

They left having learned nothing that seemed of use, except

Oliphant's address, where they discovered that Shaw was out on a call.

At the Red Lion public house they ate hot steak and kidney pudding with a rich suet crust which was light as foam, and green vegetables, then a thick fruit pie and a glass of cider.

Murdo leaned back in his chair, his face flushed with physical well-being.

Pitt rose to his feet, to Murdo's chagrin.

"The Misses Worlingham," he announced. "By the way, do we know who reported the fire? It seems no one we know saw it till the engines were here, except Lindsay's manservant, and he was too busy trying to get Lindsay out."

"Yes sir, a man over in Holly Village was away from home in Holloway." He flushed faintly as he searched for the right word. "An assignation. He saw the glow, and being in mind of the first fire he knew what it was and called the engine." Reluctantly he followed Pitt out into the wind again. "Sir, what do you expect to learn from the Misses Worlingham?"

"I don't know. Something about Shaw and Clemency, perhaps; or Theophilus's death."

"Do you think Theophilus was murdered?" Murdo's voice changed and he faltered in his stride as the thought occurred to him. "Do you think Shaw killed him so his wife would inherit sooner? Then he killed his wife? That's dreadful. But why Lindsay, sir? What had he to gain from that? Surely he wouldn't have done it as a blind, just because it was—pointless." The enormity of it made him shudder and nearly miss his footstep on the path.

"I doubt it," Pitt replied, stretching his pace to keep warm and pulling his muffler tighter around his neck. It was cold enough to snow. "But he's stayed with Lindsay for several days. Lindsay's no fool. If Shaw made a mistake, betrayed himself in some way by a word, or an omission, Lindsay would have seen it and understood what it meant. He may have said nothing at the time, but Shaw, knowing his own guilt and fearing discovery, may have been frightened by the smallest thing, and acted immediately to protect himself."

Murdo hunched his shoulders and his face tightened as the

ugliness of the thought caught hold of his mind. He looked cold and miserable in spite of his burned face.

"Do you think so, sir?"

"I don't know, but it's possible. We can't ignore it."

"It's brutal."

"Burning people to death is brutal." Pitt clenched his teeth against the wind stinging the flesh and creeping into every ill-covered corner of neck and wrist and ankle. "We're not looking for a moderate or squeamish man—or woman."

Murdo looked away, refusing to meet Pitt's eyes or even guess his thoughts when he spoke of women and these crimes. "There must be other motives," he said doggedly. "Shaw's a doctor. He could have treated all kinds of diseases, deaths that someone wants hidden—or at least the way of it. What if someone else murdered Theophilus Worlingham?"

"Who?" Pitt asked.

"Mrs. Shaw? She would inherit."

"And then burned herself to death—and Lindsay?" Pitt said sarcastically.

Murdo restrained an angry answer with difficulty. Pitt was his superior and he dared not be openly rude, but the unhappiness inside him wanted to lash out. Every time Pitt mentioned motive Flora's face came back to his mind, flushed with anger, lovely, full of fire to defend Shaw.

Pitt's voice broke through his thoughts.

"But you are right; there is a whole area of motive we haven't even begun to uncover. God knows what ugly or tragic secrets. We've got to get Shaw to tell us."

They were almost at the Worlinghams' house and nothing more was said until they were in the morning room by the fire. Angeline was sitting upright in the large armchair and Celeste was standing behind her.

"I'm sure I don't know what we can tell you, Mr. Pitt," Celeste said quietly. She looked older than the last time he had seen her; there were lines of strain around her eyes and mouth and her hair was pulled back more severely in an unflattering fashion. But it made the strength of her face more apparent.

Angeline, on the other hand, looked pale and puffy, and the softer shape of her jaw, sagging a little, showed her irresolution. There were signs of weeping in the redness of her eyelids, and she looked tremulous enough to weep again now.

"We were asleep," Angeline added. "This is terrible! What is happening to us? Who would do these things?"

"Perhaps if we learn why, we will also know who." Pitt guided them towards the subject he wanted.

"Why?" Angeline blinked. "We don't know!"

"You may, Miss Worlingham—without realizing it. There is money involved, inheritances . . ."

"Our money?" Celeste said the word unconsciously.

"Your brother Theophilus's money, to be exact," Pitt corrected her. "But yes, Worlingham money. I know it is intrusive, but it is necessary that we know; can you tell us all you remember of your brother's death, Miss Worlingham?" He looked from one to the other of them, making sure they knew he included them both.

"It was very sudden," Celeste's features hardened, her mouth forming a thin, judgmental line. "I am afraid I agree with Angeline: Stephen did not care for him as we would have wished. Theophilus was in the most excellent health."

"If you had known him," Angeline added, "you would have been as shocked as we were. He was such a—" She searched her memory for the vision of him as he had been. "He was so vigorous." She smiled tearfully. "He was so alive. He always knew what to do. He was so decisive, you know, a natural leader, like Papa. He believed in health in the mind and a lot of exercise and fresh air for the body—for men, of course. Not ladies. Theophilus always knew the right answer, and what one should believe. He was not Papa's equal, of course, but still I never knew him when he was mistaken about anything that mattered." She sniffed hard and reached for a wholly inadequate wisp of a handkerchief. "We always doubted the manner of his death, one may as well say so now. It was not natural, not for Theophilus."

"What was the cause, Miss Worlingham?"

"Stephen said it was apoplexy," Celeste answered coldly. "But of course we have only his word for that."

"Who found him?" Pitt pressed, although he already knew.

"Clemency." Celeste's eyes opened wide. "Do you believe Stephen killed him, and then when he realized that Clemency knew what he had done, he killed her also? And then poor Mr. Lindsay. Dear heaven." She shivered convulsively. "How evil— how monstrously evil. He shall not come into this house again— not set foot over the step!"

"Of course not, dear." Angeline sniffed noisily. "Mr. Pitt will arrest him, and he will be put in prison."

"Hanged," Celeste corrected grimly.

"Oh dear." Angeline was horrified. "How dreadful—thank heaven Papa did not live to see it. Someone in our family hanged." She began to weep, her shoulders bent, her body huddled in frightened misery.

"Stephen Shaw is not in our family!" Celeste snapped. "He is not and never was a Worlingham. It is Clemency's misfortune that she married him, but she became a Shaw—he is not one of us."

"It is still dreadful. We have never had such shame anywhere near us, even by marriage," Angeline protested. "The name of Worlingham has been synonymous with honor and dignity of the highest order. Just imagine what poor Papa would have felt if the slightest spot of dishonor had touched his name. He never did anything in his entire life to merit an ugly word. And now his son has been murdered—and his granddaughter—and her husband will be hanged. He would have died of shame."

Pitt let her continue because he was curious to see how easily and completely they both accepted that Shaw was guilty. Now he must impress on them that it was only one of several possibilities.

"There is no need to distress yourself yet, Miss Worlingham. Your brother's death may well have been apoplexy, just as Dr. Shaw said, and we do not know that he is guilty of anything yet. It may have nothing to do with money. It may well be that he has treated some medical case which he realized involved a crime, or some disease that the sufferer would kill to keep secret."

Angeline looked up sharply. "You mean insanity? Someone

is mad, and Stephen knows about it? Then why doesn't he say? They ought to be locked up in Bedlam, with other lunatics. He shouldn't allow them to go around free—where they can burn people to death."

Pitt opened his mouth to explain to her that perhaps the person only thought Shaw knew. Then he looked at the mounting hysteria in her, and at Celeste's tense eyes, and decided it would be a waste of time.

"It is only a possibility," he said levelly. "It may be someone's death was not natural, and Dr. Shaw knew of it, or suspected it. There are many other motives, perhaps even some we have not yet thought of."

"You are frightening me," Angeline said in a small, shaky voice. "I am very confused. Did Stephen kill anyone, or not?"

"No one knows," Celeste answered her. "It is the police's job to find out."

Pitt asked them several more questions, indirectly about Shaw or Theophilus, but learned nothing more. When they left, the sky had cleared and the wind was even colder. Pitt and Murdo walked side by side in silence till they reached Oliphant's lodging house and at last found Shaw sitting in the front parlor by the fire writing up notes at a rolltop desk. He looked tired, his eyes ringed around with dark hollows and his skin pale, almost papery in quality. There was grief in the sag of his shoulders and the nervous energy in him was transmuted into tension, and jumpiness of his hands.

"There is no point in asking me who I treated or for what ailment," he said tersely as soon as he saw Pitt. "Even if I knew of some disease that would prompt someone to kill me, there is certainly nothing that would cause anyone to harm poor Amos. But then I suppose he died because I was in his house." His voice broke; he found the words so hard to say. "First Clemency—and now Amos. Yes, I suppose you are right; if I really knew who it was, I would do something about it—I don't know what. Perhaps not tell you—but something."

Pitt sat down in the chair nearest him without being asked, and Murdo stood discreetly by the door.

"Think, Dr. Shaw," he said quietly, looking at the exhausted figure opposite him and hating the need to remind him of his role in the tragedy. "Please think of anything you and Amos Lindsay discussed while you were in his house. It is possible that you were aware of some fact that, had you understood it, would have told you who set the first fire."

Shaw looked up, a spark of interest in his eyes for the first time since they had entered the room. "And you think perhaps Amos understood it—and the murderer knew?"

"It's possible," Pitt replied carefully. "You knew him well, didn't you? Was he the sort of man who might have gone to them himself—perhaps seeking proof?"

Suddenly Shaw's eyes brimmed with tears and he turned away, his voice thick with emotion. "Yes," he said so quietly Pitt barely heard him. "Yes—he was. And God help me, I've no idea who he saw or where he went when I was there. I was so wrapped up in my own grief and anger I didn't see and I didn't ask."

"Then please think now, Dr. Shaw." Pitt rose to his feet, moved more by pity not to intrude on a very obvious distress than the sort of impersonal curiosity his profession dictated. "And if you remember anything at all, come and tell me—no one else."

"I will." Shaw seemed sunk within himself again, almost as if Pitt and Murdo had already left.

Outside in the late-afternoon sun, pale and already touched with the dying fire of autumn, Murdo looked at Pitt, his eyes narrowed against the cold.

"Do you think that's what happened, sir: Mr. Lindsay realized who did it—and went looking for proof?"

"God knows," Pitt replied. "What did he see that we haven't?"

Murdo shook his head and together, hands deep in pockets, they trudged back along the footpath towards the Highgate police station.

CHAPTER
SEVEN

Charlotte was deeply distressed that Lindsay had died in the second fire. Her relief that Shaw had escaped was like a healing on the surface of the first fear, but underneath that skin of sudden ease there ached the loss of a man she had seen and liked so very shortly since. She had noticed his kindness, especially to Shaw at his most abrasive. Perhaps he was the only one who understood his grief for Clemency, and the biting knowledge that she might have died in his place; that some enmity he had earned, incited, somehow induced, had sparked that inferno.

And now Amos Lindsay was gone too, burned beyond recognition.

How must Shaw be feeling this morning? Grieved—bewildered—guilty that yet another had suffered a death meant for him—frightened in case this was not the end? Would there go on being fires, more and more deaths until his own? Did he look at everyone and wonder? Was he even now searching his memory, his records, to guess whose secret was so devastating they would murder to keep it? Or did he already know—but feel bound by some professional ethic to guard it even at this price?

She felt the need for more furious action while the questions raced through her thoughts. She stripped the beds and threw the sheets and pillowcases down the stairs, adding nightshirts for all the family, and towels; then followed them down, carrying armfuls into the scullery, off the kitchen, where she filled both tubs with water and added soap to one, screwed the mangle between them, and began the laundry. She was in one of her oldest dresses, sleeves rolled up and a pinafore around her waist, scrubbing fiercely, and she let her mind return to the problem again.

For all the possible motives to murder Shaw, including money, love, hate and revenge (if indeed someone believed him guilty of medical neglect, Theophilus Worlingham or anyone else), her thoughts still returned to Clemency and her battle against slum profiteers.

She was up to her elbows in suds, her pinafore soaked, and her hair falling out of its pins, when the front doorbell rang. Fishmonger's boy, she thought. Gracie will get it.

A moment later Gracie came flying back up the corridor, her feet clattering on the linoleum. She swung around the kitchen doorway, breathless, her eyes wide with amazement, awe and horror as she saw her mistress.

"Lady Vespasia Cumming-Gould!" she said squeakily. "She's right 'ere be'ind me, ma'am! I couldn't put 'er in the parlor, ma'am; she wouldn't stay!"

And indeed Great-Aunt Vespasia was on Gracie's heels, elegant and very upright in a dark teal gown embroidered in silver on the lapels, and carrying a silver-topped cane. These days she was seldom without it. Her eyes took in the kitchen, scrubbed table, newly blacked range, rows of blue-and-white china on the dresser, earthenware polished brown and cream, steaming tubs in the scullery beyond, and Charlotte like a particularly harassed and untidy laundrymaid.

Charlotte froze. Gracie was already transfixed to the spot as Vespasia swept past her.

Vespasia regarded the mangle with curiosity.

"What in heaven's name is that contraption?" she inquired with her eyebrows raised. "It looks like something that should have belonged to the Spanish Inquisition."

"A mangle," Charlotte replied, brushing her hair back with her arm. "You push the clothes through it and it squeezes out the soap and water."

"I am greatly relieved to hear it." Vespasia sat down at the table, unconsciously arranging her skirts with one hand. She looked at the mangle again. "Very commendable. But what are you going to do about this second fire in Highgate? I presume you are going to do something? Whatever the reasons for it, it does not alter the fact that Clemency Shaw is dead, and deserves a better epitaph than that she was murdered in error for her husband."

Charlotte wiped her hands and came to the table, ignoring the sheets still soaking in the tub. "I am not sure that she was. Would you like a cup of tea?"

"I would. What makes you believe that? Why should anyone murder poor Amos Lindsay, if not in an attempt to get rid of Shaw more successfully than last time?"

Charlotte glanced at Gracie, who at last moved from the doorway and reached for the kettle.

"Maybe they were afraid Shaw had realized who they were, or that he might realize?" she suggested, sitting down opposite Vespasia. "He may well have all the information, if he knew how to add it up and see the pattern. After all, he knew what Clemency was doing; she may have left papers which he had seen. In fact, that may be why they chose fire. To destroy not only Clemency but all the evidence she had collected."

Vespasia straightened a little. "Indeed, that is something I had not considered. It is foolish, because it makes no difference to her, poor creature, but I should prefer not to believe she did not even die in her own right. If Shaw knows already who it is, why does he not say so? Surely he has not yet worked it out, and certainly has no proof. You do not suggest he is in any kind of collusion with them?"

"No—"

Behind Charlotte, Gracie was rather nervously heating the teapot and spooning in tea from the caddie. She had never prepared anything for someone of Great-Aunt Vespasia's importance before. She wished to make it exactly right, and she did not know what exactly right might be. Also she was listening to everything that was said. She was horrified by and very proud of Pitt's occupation, and of Charlotte's occasional involvement.

"I assume Thomas has already thought of everything that

we have," Vespasia continued. "Therefore for us to pursue that line would be fruitless—"

Gracie brought the tea, set it on the table, the cup rattling and slopping in her shaking hands. She made a half curtsey to Vespasia.

"Thank you." Vespasia acknowledged it graciously. She was not in the habit of thanking servants, but this was obviously different. The child was in a state of nervous awe.

Gracie blushed and withdrew to take up the laundry where Charlotte had left off. Vespasia wiped out her saucer with the napkin Charlotte handed her.

Charlotte made her decision.

"I shall learn what I can about Clemency's work, who she met, what course she followed from the time she began to care so much, and somewhere I shall cross the path of whoever caused these fires."

Vespasia sipped her tea. "And how do you intend to do it so you survive to share your discoveries with the rest of us?"

"By saying nothing whatever about reform," Charlotte replied, her plan very imperfectly formed. "I shall begin with the local parish—" Her mind went back to her youth, when she and her sisters had trailed dutifully behind Caroline doing "good works," visiting the sick or elderly, offering soup and preserves and kind words. It was part of a gentlewoman's life. In all probability Clemency had done the same, and then seen a deeper pain and not turned away from it with complacency or resignation, but questioned and began the fight.

Vespasia was looking at her critically. "Do you imagine that will be sufficient to safeguard you?"

"If he murders every woman who is involved in visiting or inquiring after the parish poor, he will need a bigger conflagration than the great fire of London," Charlotte replied with decision. "Anyway," she added rather more practically, "I shall be a long way from the kind of person who owns the properties. I shall simply start where Clemency started. Long before I discover whatever someone murdered to keep, I shall draw other people in, you and Emily—and of course Thomas." Then suddenly she thought she might be being presumptuous. Vespasia had not said she wished to be involved in such a way. Charlotte looked at her anxiously.

Vespasia sipped her tea again and her eyes were bright over the rim of her cup.

"Emily and I already have plans," she said, setting the cup down in its saucer and looking over Charlotte's shoulder at Gracie, who was self-consciously scrubbing at the washboard, her shoulders hunched. "If you think it advisable not to go alone, leave the children with your mother for a few days and take your maid with you."

Gracie stopped in mid-motion, laundry dripping in the sink, her back bent, her hands in the air. She let out a long sigh of exquisite anticipation. She was going to detect—with the mistress! It would be the biggest adventure of her entire life!

Charlotte was incredulous. "Gracie!"

"And why not?" Vespasia inquired. "It would appear quite natural. I shall lend you my second carriage and Percival to drive it for you. There is no point in doing it if you do not do it as well as possible. I am concerned in the matter. My admiration for Clemency Shaw is considerable. I shall require you to inform me of your findings, if any. Naturally you will also tell Thomas. I have no intention of allowing the whole thing to be swallowed up in public assumption that the intended victim was Stephen Shaw, and Clemency's death can be dismissed as an error, however tragic. Oh!" Her face fell with sudden awful comprehension. "Do you think it is conceivable that that is why poor Lindsay was murdered? So we might well assume Clemency's death was unintended? How cold-bloodedly deliberate."

"I am going to find out," Charlotte said quietly with a little shiver. "As soon as Percival arrives with the carriage, I shall take the children to Mama's, and we shall begin."

"Fetch what they require," Vespasia commanded. "And I shall take them with me on my return. I have no errands until this evening when the House rises."

Charlotte got to her feet. "Somerset Carlisle?"

"Just so. If we are to fight against the slum profiteers, we require to know the exact state of the law, and what it is most reasonable to expect we may achieve. One may assume that Clemency did much the same, and discovered some weakness in their position. We need to know what it was."

Gracie was scrubbing so hard the board was rattling in the tub.

"Stop that now, child!" Vespasia ordered. "I can hardly hear myself think! Put it through that contraption and hang it up. I am sure it is clean enough. For goodness sake, they are only bed sheets! Then when you have done that, go and tidy yourself up and put on a coat, and a hat if you have one. Your mistress will require you to accompany her to Highgate."

"Yes ma'am!" Gracie heaved the entire lot of linen up, standing on tiptoe to get it clear of the water, dropped it in the clean water in the opposite tub, pulled the plug, then began to pay it through the mangle, winding like fury in her excitement.

Vespasia seemed completely unaware that she had just given a complete hour's instructions to someone else's servant. It seemed common sense, and that was sufficient to justify it.

"Go upstairs to the nursery and pack whatever is necessary," she continued, speaking to Charlotte in almost the same tone of voice. "For several days. You do not want to be anxious for them while you are endeavoring to unravel this matter."

Charlotte obeyed with a very slight smile. She did not resent being ordered around; it was what she would have done anyway, and the familiarity with which Vespasia did it was a kind of affection, also an unspoken trust that they were involved in the affair together and desired the same end.

Upstairs she found Jemima solemnly practicing her writing. She had progressed from the stage of rather carefully drawing letters and now she did them with some abandon, confident she was making words, and of their meaning. Sums she was considerably less fond of.

Daniel was still struggling, and with immeasurable superiority now and again Jemima gave him assistance, explaining carefully precisely what he must do, and why. He bore it with placid good nature, imitating her round script and concealing both his ignorance and his admiration behind a frown of attention. It can be very difficult being four and having a sister two years older.

"You are going to stay with Grandmama for a few days," Charlotte informed them with a bright smile. "You will enjoy it very much. You can take your lessons with you if you wish, but you don't have to do them more than an hour or two in the mornings. I shall explain why you are not at school. If you are good, Grandmama might take you for a carriage ride, to the zoo perhaps?"

She had their immediate cooperation, as she had intended. "You will be going with Great-Aunt Vespasia, who is ready to take you as soon as you are packed. She is a very important lady indeed, and you must do everything exactly as she tells you."

"Who is Great Vepsia?" Daniel asked curiously, his face puckered up trying to remember. "I only 'member Aunt Emily."

"She is Aunt Emily's aunt," Charlotte simplified for the sake of clarity, and to avoid mentioning George, whom Jemima at least could recall quite clearly. She did not understand death, except in relation to small animals, but she knew loss.

Daniel seemed satisfied, and rapidly Charlotte set about putting into a Gladstone bag everything they would require. When it was fastened she made sure they were clean and wrapped up in coats and that their gloves were attached to their cuffs, their shoes buttoned, their hair brushed and their scarves tied. Then she took them downstairs to where Vespasia was waiting, still seated in the kitchen chair.

They greeted her very formally, Daniel half a step behind Jemima, but as she took out her lorgnette to regard them, they were so fascinated by it they forgot to be shy. Charlotte had no qualms as she watched them mount into the carriage, with considerable assistance from the footman, and depart along the street.

Gracie was so excited she could hardly hold her comb in her hand to tidy her hair, and her fingers slipped and made a knot in the strings of her bonnet which she would probably have to cut with scissors ever to get it off again. But what did it matter? She was going with the mistress to help her detect! She had very little clear idea of what it would involve, but it would absolutely without question be marvelously interesting and very important. She might learn secrets and make discoveries concerning issues of such magnitude that people were prepared to commit murder in their cause. And possibly it would even be dangerous.

Of course she would walk a couple of steps behind, and only speak when she was invited to; but she would watch and listen all the time, and notice everything that anyone said or did, even the way their faces looked. Maybe she would notice something vital that no one else did.

It was some two hours later when Charlotte and Gracie descended from the second carriage. They were handed down by Percival, to Gracie's intense delight; she had never ridden in a proper carriage before, still less been assisted by another servant. They walked up the path to St. Anne's Church side by side at Charlotte's insistence, in hope of finding someone there who might guide them in matters of parish relief, and thus to a more precise knowledge of Clemency Shaw's interest in housing.

Charlotte had given the matter a good deal of thought. She did not wish to be open about her intentions and it had been necessary to construct a believable story. She had tussled with the problem without success until Gracie, biting her lip and not wishing to be impertinent, had suggested they inquire about a relative who had been thrown on the parish as a result of widowhood, which they had just heard about and were anxious to help.

Charlotte had thought this so unlikely to be true that even Hector Clitheridge would doubt it, but then Gracie had pointed out that her Aunt Bertha had been in just such a predicament, and Gracie had indeed heard about it only two weeks ago. Then Charlotte realized what she meant, and seized upon the idea instantly.

"O' course me Aunt Bertha din't live in 'Ighgate," Gracie said honestly. "She lived in Clerkenwell—but then they dunno that."

And so after learning that there was no one in at the parsonage, they repaired to the church of St. Anne's itself, and found Lally Clitheridge arranging flowers in the vestry. She turned at the sound of the door opening, a look of welcome on her face. Then she recognized Charlotte and the smile froze. She kept the Michaelmas daisy in her hand and did not move from the bench.

"Good afternoon, Mrs. Pitt. Are you looking for someone?"

"I expect you could help me, if you would be so kind," Charlotte answered, forcing a warmth into her voice which did not come naturally in the face of Lally's chill gaze.

"Indeed?" Lally looked beyond her at Gracie with slightly raised brows. "Is this lady with you?"

"She is my maid." Charlotte was conscious as she said it of sounding a trifle pompous, but there was no other reasonable answer.

"Good gracious!" Lally's eyebrows shot up. "Are you unwell?"

"I am perfectly well, thank you." It was becoming harder and harder to keep an amiability in her tone. She wanted to tell Lally she owed her no account of her arrangements and would give none, but that would defeat her purpose. She needed at the least an ally, better still a friend. "It is on Gracie's behalf we are here," she continued her civil tone with an effort. "She has just heard that her uncle has died and left her aunt in very poor circumstances, most probably a charge on the parish. Perhaps you would be kind enough to tell me which of the ladies in the neighborhood have been most involved in charitable works and might know of her whereabouts."

Lally was quite obviously torn between her dislike for Charlotte and her compassion for Gracie, who was staring at her belligerently, but Lally apparently took it for well-controlled grief.

"You do not know her address?" She looked past Charlotte as if she had not been there. It was an excellent compromise.

Gracie's mind was quick. "I know 'er old 'ouse, ma'am; but I'm afraid wot wif poor Uncle Albert bein' took so sudden, and not much put by, that they might'a bin put out on the street. They'd 'ave no one to turn to, 'ceptin the parish."

Lally's face softened. "There's been no Albert buried in this parish, child; not in more than a year. And believe me, I mark every burial. It is part of my Christian duty, as well as my wish. Are you sure it is here in Highgate?"

Gracie did not look at Charlotte, but she was acutely conscious of her a foot or two away.

"Oh, yes ma'am," she replied earnestly. "I'm sure that's wot they said. Per'aps if you would just tell us the names o' the other ladies as 'elps them as is in trouble, we could ask an' mebbe they'd know, like?" She smiled appealingly, putting to the front of her mind their purpose in having come; it was, after all, the greater loyalty. This must be what detecting involved, learning facts people were reluctant to tell you.

Lally was won over, in spite of herself. Still ignoring Charlotte she directed her answer to Gracie.

"Of course. Mrs. Hatch may be able to assist you, or Mrs. Dalgetty, or Mrs. Simpson, Mrs. Braithwaite or Miss Crombie. Would you like their addresses?"

"Oh, yes ma'am, if you'd be so good?"

"Of course." Lally fished in her reticule for a piece of paper, and failed to find a pencil.

Charlotte produced one and handed it to her. She took it in silence, wrote for several moments, then gave the slip to Gracie, who took it, still without looking at Charlotte, and held on to it tightly. She thanked Lally with a slight curtsey. "That's ever so kind of you, ma'am."

"Not at all," Lally said generously. Then her expression clouded over again and she looked at Charlotte. "Good day, Mrs. Pitt. I hope you are successful." She passed back the pencil. "Now if you will excuse me I have several vases of flowers to finish and then some calls to make." And she turned her back on them and began furiously poking daisies into the rolled-up wire mesh in the vase, sticking them in at all angles.

Side by side Charlotte and Gracie left, eyes downcast until they were outside. Then immediately Gracie pushed the paper at Charlotte with a glow of triumph.

Charlotte took it and read it. "You did expertly, Gracie," she said sincerely. "I couldn't have managed without you!"

Gracie flushed with pleasure. "What does it say, ma'am? I carsn't read that kind o' writin'."

Charlotte looked at the sprawling cursive script. "It is exactly what we want," she answered approvingly. "The names and addresses of several of the women who might know where Clemency Shaw began her work. We shall start immediately with Maude Dalgetty. I rather liked her manner at the funeral. I think she may be a sensible woman and generous spirited. She was a friend of Clemency's and so, I expect, inclined to help us."

And so it proved. Maude Dalgetty was both sensible and desirous to help. She welcomed them into a withdrawing room full of sunlight and bowls of late roses. The room had a graciousness of proportion and was elegantly furnished, although many of the pieces were beginning to show wear. There were little knots and gaps in some of the fringes around lamps and the sashes on the curtains, and some of the crystals were missing from the chandelier. But the warmth was unmistakable. The books were used—here was one open on the side table. There was a large sewing basket with mending and embroidery clearly visible. The painting above the mantelpiece was a portrait of Maude herself, probably done a dozen years earlier, sitting in a garden on a summer day, the light on her skin and hair. She certainly had been a remarkable beauty, and much of it was left, even if a little more amply proportioned.

Two cats lay curled up together in a single ball of fur by the fire, sound asleep.

"How may I help you?" Maude said as soon as they were in. She paid no less attention to Gracie than to Charlotte. "Would you like a cup of tea?"

It was, strictly speaking, too early for such a thing, but Charlotte judged it was sincerely offered and since she was thirsty and had eaten no lunch, and she imagined Gracie was the same, she accepted.

Maude ordered it from the maid, then inquired again how she might help.

Charlotte hesitated. Sitting in this warm room looking at Maude's intelligent face she was uncertain whether to risk telling her the truth rather than a concocted lie, however plausible. Then she recalled Clemency's death, and Lindsay's so soon after, and changed her mind. Wherever the heart of the murders lay, there were tentacles of it here. An unwitting word by even an innocent person might provoke more violence. It was one of the ugliest changes in the aftermath of murder that instinctive trusts disappeared. One looked for betrayal and suspected every answer of being a lie, every careless or angry word of hiding greed or hatred, every guarded comment of concealing envy.

"Gracie has recently heard that an aunt of hers in this locality has been widowed," she explained. "She fears she may be in straitened circumstances, perhaps even to the degree of being put out on the street."

Maude's face showed immediate concern but she did not interrupt.

"If she has fallen on the care of the parish then perhaps you know what has become of her?" Charlotte tried to put the urgency into her voice that she would have felt had it been true, and saw the compassion in Maude's eyes, and hated herself for the duplicity. She hurried on to cover it in speech. "And if you do not, then someone else may? I believe that the late Mrs. Shaw concerned herself greatly with such cases?" She felt her cheeks burn. This was the kind of deception she most despised.

Maude tightened her lips and blinked several times to control the very obvious grief that flooded her face.

"Indeed she did," she said gently. "But if she had any record of whom she helped it will have been destroyed when the house was burned." She turned to Gracie, since it was Gracie whose aunt they were speaking of. "The only other person likely to know would be the curate, Matthew Oliphant. I think she confided in him and he gave her counsel, and possibly even help. She spoke very little of her work, but I know she felt more deeply about it as time passed. Most of it was not within the parish, you know? I am not at all sure she would have been directly involved with a local loss. You might be better advised to ask Mrs. Hatch, or perhaps Mrs. Wetherell."

The maid returned with tea and the most delicious sandwiches, made with the thinnest of bread and tomato cut into minute cubes so there was nothing squashy in them and no stringy skins to embarrass the eater. For several minutes Charlotte abandoned the purpose of her visit and simply enjoyed them. Gracie, who had never even seen anything so fine, let alone tasted it, was absolutely spellbound.

It was early afternoon and becoming overcast when Percival drew up the carriage outside the lodging house where Matthew Oliphant lived. He handed down Charlotte, and then Gracie, and watched them walk up the path and knock on the door before he returned to the carriage seat and prepared to wait.

The door was opened by a maid who advised them that Mr. Oliphant was in the sitting room and would no doubt receive them, since he seemed to receive everyone.

They reached the sitting room, an impersonal place furnished with extreme conservatism, armchairs with antimacassars, a portrait of the Queen over the mantel and one of Mr. Gladstone on the far wall, several samplers of religious texts, three stuffed birds under glass, an arrangement of dried flowers, a stuffed weasel in a case, and two aspidistras. They reminded Charlotte immediately of the sort of things that had been left over after everyone else had taken what they liked. She could not imagine the person who would willingly have selected these. Certainly not Matthew Oliphant, with his humorous, imaginative face, rising in his chair to greet them, leaving his Bible open on the table; nor Stephen Shaw, busy writing at the rolltop desk by the window. He stood up also when he saw Charlotte, surprise and pleasure in his face.

"Mrs. Pitt, how charming to see you." He came towards her, his hand extended. He glanced at Gracie, who was standing well back, smitten with shyness now they were dealing with gentlemen.

"Good afternoon, Dr. Shaw," Charlotte replied, hastily concealing her chagrin. How could she question the curate with Shaw himself present? Her whole plan of action would have to be changed. "This is Gracie, my maid—" She could think of no explanation for her presence, so she did not try. "Good afternoon, Mr. Oliphant."

"Good afternoon, Mrs. Pitt. If—if you wish to be alone with the doctor, I can quite easily excuse myself. My room is not cold; I can pursue my studies there."

Charlotte knew from the temperature of the hallway that that was almost certainly a fiction.

"Not at all, Mr. Oliphant. Please remain. This is your home and I should be most uncomfortable to have driven you away from the fire."

"What may I do for you, Mrs. Pitt?" Shaw asked, frowning at her in grave concern. "I hope you are as well as you seem? And your maid?"

"We are very well, thank you. Our visit has nothing to do with your profession, Dr. Shaw." There was now no purpose whatsoever in continuing with the tale of Gracie's uncle. He would see through it and despise them both, not only for the lie, but for the inadequacy of it. "I did not come about myself." She faced him boldly, meeting his eyes and being considerably disconcerted by the acute intelligence in them, and the directness of his gaze back at her. She took a deep breath and plunged on. "I have determined to pursue the work that your late wife was involved in regarding the housing of the poor, and their conditions. I would like to learn where she began, so I may begin in the same place."

There was a full minute's total silence. Matthew Oliphant stood by the fire with the Bible in his hand, his knuckles white where he grasped it, his face pale, then flushed. Gracie was rooted to the spot. Shaw's expression flashed from amazement to disbelief, and then suspicion.

"Why?" he said guardedly. "If you have some passion to work with the poor or the dispossessed what is wrong with those in your own neighborhood?" His voice hovered on the edge of sarcasm. "Surely there are some? London is teeming with poor. Do you live in some area so select you have to come to Highgate to find anyone in need?"

Charlotte could think of no answer. "You are being unnecessarily rude, Dr. Shaw." She heard herself mimicking Aunt Vespasia's tone, and thought for an awful moment that she sounded ridiculous. Then she saw Shaw's face and the sudden color of shame in his cheeks.

"I apologize, Mrs. Pitt. Of course I am." He was contrite. "Please forgive me." He did not mention either his bereavement or the loss of his friend; as an excuse it would have been cheap and beneath him.

She smiled at him with all the warmth and deep empathy that she felt for him, and the very considerable liking. "The matter is forgotten." She dismissed it charmingly. "Can you help me? I should be so obliged. Her crusade is one in which I should like to become involved myself, and draw others. It would be foolish not to profit from what she has already done. She has earned much admiration."

Very slowly, wordlessly, Matthew Oliphant sat down again and opened his Bible, upside down.

"Do you?" Shaw frowned in some inner concentration. "I cannot see that it will be much advantage to you. She worked alone, so far as I know. She certainly did not work with the parish ladies, or the vicar." He sighed. "Not that poor old Clitheridge could fight his way out of a wet paper bag!" He looked at her gravely, a kind of laughing admiration in his eyes she found a trifle discomfitting. One or two rather absurd thoughts flashed through her mind, and she dismissed them hastily, a flush in her cheeks.

"Nevertheless I should like to try," she insisted.

"Mrs. Pitt," he said gently. "I can tell you almost nothing, only that Clemency cared very much about reforming the laws. In fact I think she cared more about them than almost anything else." His face pinched a little. "But if, as I suspect, what you are really seeking is to discover who set fire to my house, you will not accomplish it this way. It is I who was meant to die in that fire, as it was when poor Amos died."

She was at once fiercely sorry for him and extraordinarily angry.

"Indeed?" Her eyebrows shot up. "How arrogant of you! Do you assume that no one else could possibly be important enough in the scheme of things, and only you arouse enough passion or fear to be murdered?"

It was one sting too much. His temper exploded.

"Clemency was one of the finest women alive. If you had known her, instead of arriving the moment she was dead, you wouldn't have to be told." He was leaning forward a little, his shoulders tight and hunched. "She did nothing to incur the kind of insane hatred that burns down houses and risks the lives of everyone in them. For heaven's sake if you must meddle—at least do it efficiently!"

"I am trying to!" she shouted back. "But you are determined to obstruct me. One would almost think you did not want it solved." She pointed at him sharply. "You won't help. You won't tell the police anything. You stick to your wretched confidences as if they were secrets of state. What do you imagine that we are going to do with them, except catch a murderer?"

He jerked very upright, back straight. "I don't know any secrets that will catch anyone but a few unfortunate devils who would rather keep their diseases private than have them spread 'round the neighborhood for every able and nosy busybody to turn over and speculate on," he shouted back. "Dear God— don't you think I want him caught—whoever he is? He murdered my wife and my best friend—and I may be next."

"Don't give yourself airs," she said coldly, because suddenly her anger had evaporated and she was feeling guilty for being so ruthless, but she did not know how to get out of the situation she had created. "Unless you know who it is, as it appears poor Mr. Lindsay did, you are probably not in danger at all."

He threw an ashtray into the corner of the room, where it splintered and lay in pieces, then he walked out, slamming the door.

Gracie was still standing on the spot, her eyes like saucers.

Oliphant looked up from his Bible and at last realized it was upside down. He closed it quickly and stood up.

"Mrs. Pitt," he said very softly. "I know where Mrs. Shaw began, and some of where it led her. If you wish, I will take you."

Charlotte looked at his bony, agreeable face, and the quiet

pain in it, and felt ashamed of her outburst for its noise and self-indulgence.

"Thank you, Mr. Oliphant, I should be very grateful."

Percival drove them; it was well beyond the area of Highgate and into Upper Holloway. They stopped at a narrow street and alighted from the carriage, once again leaving it to wait. Charlotte looked around. The houses were cheek by jowl, one room upstairs and one down, to judge by the width, but there may have been more at the back beyond view. The doors were all closed and the steps scrubbed and whitestoned. It was not appreciably poorer than the street on which she and Pitt had lived when they were first married.

"Come." Oliphant set out along the pavement and almost immediately turned in along an alley that Charlotte had not observed before. Here it was dank and a chill draft blew on their faces, carrying the smell of raw sewage and drains.

Charlotte coughed and reached for her handkerchief—even Gracie put her hand up to her face—but they hurried after him till he emerged in a small, dim courtyard and crossed it, warning them to step over the open gutters. At the far side he knocked on a paint-peeled door and waited.

After several minutes it was opened by a girl of fourteen or fifteen with a gray-white face and fair hair greasy with dirt. Her eyes were pink-rimmed and there was a flicker of fear in the defiance with which she spoke.

"Yeah? 'Oo are yer?"

"Is Mrs. Bradley at home?" he asked quietly, opening his coat a fraction to show his clerical collar.

Her face softened in relief. "Yeah, Ma's in bed. She took poorly again. The doc were 'ere yest'dy an' 'e give 'er some med'cine, but it don't do no good."

"May I come in and see her?" Oliphant requested.

"Yeah, I s'pose. But don' wake 'er if she's sleepin'."

"I won't," he promised, and held the door wide for Charlotte and Gracie to enter.

Inside the narrow room was cold. Damp seeped through wallpaper, staining it with mold, and the air had an odor that was sour and clung in the back of the throat. There was no tap or standpipe, and a bucket in the corner covered with a make-shift lid served the purposes of nature. Rickety stairs led up-wards through a gap in the ceiling and Oliphant went up first, cautioning Charlotte and Gracie to wait their turn in case the weight of more than one person should collapse them.

Charlotte emerged into a bedroom with two wooden cots, both heaped with blankets. In one lay a woman who at a glance might have been Charlotte's mother's age. Her face was gaunt, her skin withered and papery, and her eyes so hollow the bones of her brow seemed almost skull-like.

Then as Charlotte moved closer she saw the fair hair and the skin of her neck above the patched nightshirt, and realized she was probably no more than thirty. There was a handkerchief with blood on it grasped loosely in the thin hand.

The three of them stood in silence for several minutes, staring at the sleeping woman, each racked with silent, impotent pity.

Downstairs again, Charlotte turned to Oliphant and the girl.

"We must do something! Who owns this—this heap of timber? It's not fit for horses, let alone women to live in. He should be prosecuted. We will begin straightaway. Who collects the rent?"

The girl was as white as flour; her whole body shook.

"Don't do that, please miss! I beg yer, don't turn us aht. Me ma'll die if yer put 'er in the street—and me an' Alice and Becky'll 'ave ter go inter the poor 'ouse. Please don't. We aven't done nuthin' wrong, honest we 'aven't. We paid the rent—I swear."

"I don't want to put you out." Charlotte was aghast. "I want to force whoever owns this place to make it fit to live in."

The girl looked at her with disbelief.

"Wotcher mean? If we makes a fuss 'e'll 'ave us aht. There's plenty more as'd be glad ter 'ave it—an' we'll 'ave ter go souf into—w'ere it'll be worse. Please miss, don't do it!"

"Worse?" Charlotte said slowly. "But he should make this—this fit to live in. You should have water at least, and drainage. No wonder your mother is ill—"

"She'll get better—jus' let 'er sleep a bit. We're all right, miss. Just leave us be."

"But if—"

"That's wot 'appened ter Bessie Jones. She complained, an' now she's gorn ter live in St. Giles, an' she ain't got no more'n a corner o' the room to 'erself. You let be—please miss."

Her fear was so palpable that Charlotte could do no more than promise to say nothing, to swear it in front of Matthew Oliphant, and leave shivering and by now aware of a rising nausea in her stomach, and an anger so tight it made all the muscles in her body ache.

"Tomorrow I'll take you to St. Giles," Oliphant said quietly when they were out in the main street again. "If you want to go."

"I want to go." Charlotte said the words without hesitation—if she had thought for even a moment she might have lost her resolve.

"Did you go there with Clemency also?" she asked more gently, trying to imagine the journey she was copying, thinking of Clemency's distress as she must have seen sights just like these. "I expect she was very moved?"

He turned to her. His face was curiously luminous with memory that for all its bleakness held some beauty for him that still shone in his mind and warmed him till he was temporarily oblivious of the street or the cold.

"Yes—we came here," he answered with sweetness in his voice. "And then to St. Giles, and from there eastwards into Mile End and Whitechapel—" He might have been speaking of the pillared ruins of Isfahan, or the Golden Road to Samarkand, so did his tongue caress the words.

Charlotte hesitated only a moment before plunging on, ignoring what was suddenly so obvious to her.

"Then could you tell me where she went last?"

"If I could, Mrs. Pitt, I would have offered," he said gravely, his cheeks pink. "I only knew the general direction, because I was not with her when she found Bessie Jones. I only know that she did, because she told me afterwards. Would to God I had been." He strove to master his anguish, and almost succeeded. "Maybe I could have saved her." His voice cracked and finished husky and almost inaudible.

Charlotte could not argue, although perhaps by then Clemency had already frightened those landlords and owners whose greed had eaten into them until they had destroyed her.

Oliphant turned away, struggling for control. "But if you wish to go there, I shall try to take you—as long as you understand the risk. If we find the same place, then—" He stopped; the conclusion was not needed.

"You are not afraid?" she asked, not as a challenge but because she was certain that he was not. He was harrowed by feelings, almost laid naked by them, and yet fear was not among them—anger, pity, indignation, loss, but not fear.

He turned back to her, his face for a moment almost beautiful with the power of his caring.

"You wish to continue Clemency's work, Mrs. Pitt—and I think perhaps even more than that, you wish to learn who killed her, and expose them. So do I."

She did not answer; it was hardly necessary. She caught a sudden glimpse of how much he had cared for Clemency. He would never have spoken; she was a married woman, older than he and of higher social station. Anything more than friendship was impossible. But that had not altered his feeling, nor taken anything from his loss.

She smiled at him, politely, as if she had seen no more than anyone else, and thanked him for his help. She and Gracie would be most obliged.

Naturally she explained to Pitt what she was doing, and to what end. She might have evaded it had not Vespasia taken the children to Caroline, but their absence had to be explained and she was in no mood to equivocate.

She did not tell him what manner of place she would be going to because nothing in her experience could have foreseen where the following two days would take her. She, Oliphant and Gracie were driven by Percival from street to street, forever narrower, darker and more foul, following the decline of the unfortunate Bessie Jones. Gracie was of inestimable help because she had seen such places before and she understood the desperation that makes men and women accept such treatment rather than lose their frail hold on space and shelter, however poor, and be driven out into the streets to be huddled in doorways shuddering with cold, exposed to the rain and casual violence.

Finally in the later afternoon of the third day they found Bessie Jones, as Clemency Shaw had done before them. It was in the heart of Mile End, off the Whitechapel Road. There seemed to be an unusual number of police around.

Bessie was crouching in the corner of a room no more than twelve feet by sixteen, and occupied by three families, one in each corner. There were about sixteen people in all, including two babies in arms, which cried constantly. There was a blackened potbellied stove against one wall, but it was barely alight. There were buckets for the necessities of nature, but no drain to empty either that or any other waste, except the one in the courtyard, which overflowed and the stench filled the air, catching in the throat, soiling the clothes, the hair and the skin. There was no running water. For washing, cooking, drinking, it all had to be fetched in a pail from a standpipe three hundred yards away along the street.

There was no furniture except one broken wooden chair. People slept in what scraps of rag and blanket they could gather together for warmth; men, women and children, with nothing between them and the boards of the floor but more rags and loose ends of oakum, and the dross of the cloth industry too wretched even to remake into drab for the workhouse.

Above the crying of children, the snoring of an old man asleep under the broken window, boarded with a loose piece of linoleum, was the constant squeaking and scuttling of rats. On the floor below were the raucous sounds of a gin mill and the shouts of drunkards as they fought, swore and sang snatches of bawdy songs. Two women lay senseless in the gutter and a sailor relieved himself against the wall.

Below street level, in ill-lit cellars, ninety-eight women and girls sat shoulder to shoulder in a sweatshop stitching shirts for a few pence a day. It was better than the match factory with its phosphorous poisoning.

Upstairs a brothel prepared for the evening trade. Twenty yards away rows of men lay in bunks, their bodies rotting, their minds adrift in the sweet dreams of opium.

Bessie Jones was worn out, exhausted by the fruitless fight, and glad now at least to be under shelter from the rain and to have a stove to creep close to in the night, and two slices of bread to eat.

Charlotte emptied her purse and felt it a gross and futile thing to have done, but the money burned her hand.

In all of it she had followed the path that Clemency Shaw had taken, and she had felt as she must have felt, but she had learned nothing as to who might have killed her, although why was only too apparent. If the ownership of such places was accredited publicly there would be some who would not care, they had no reputation or status to lose. But there were surely those who drew their money from such abysmal suffering, and who would pay dearly to keep it secret, and call it by some other name. To say one owned property implied estates somewhere in the shires; farmlands might be envisioned, rich earth yielding food, cattle, timber—not the misery, crime and disease Charlotte and Gracie had seen these few days.

When she reached home she stripped off all her clothes, even her shift and pantaloons, and put them all in the wash, and told Gracie to do the same. She could not imagine any soap that would cleanse them of the odor of filth—her imagination would always furnish it as long as the memory lasted—but the sheer act of boiling and scrubbing would help.

"What are you going ter do, ma'am?" Gracie asked, wide-eyed and husky. Even she had never seen such wretchedness.

"We are going to discover who owns these abominable places," Charlotte replied grimly.

"An' one of 'em murdered Miss Clemency," Gracie added,

passing over her clothes and wrapping herself in Charlotte's old gown. The waist of it was around her hips and the skirt trailed on the floor. She looked such a child Charlotte had a moment of guilt for involving her in this fearful pursuit.

"I believe so. Are you afraid?"

"Yes ma'am." Gracie's thin little face hardened. "But I in't stoppin' 'ere. I'm going' ter 'elp yer, never doubt that, an' nob'dy in't going' ter stop me. Nor I in't going' ter let yer go there on yer own, neither."

Charlotte gave her a great hug, taking her utterly by surprise so she blushed fiercely with pleasure.

"I wouldn't dream of going without you," Charlotte said candidly.

While Charlotte and Gracie were following the path of Clemency Shaw, Jack Radley looked up one of his less reputable friends from his gambling days, before he had met Emily, and persuaded him that it would be both interesting and profitable to take a turn around some of the worst rented accommodation in London. Anton was very dubious about the interest it would afford, but since Jack promised him his silver cigar cutter—he had given up the habit anyway—he understood the profit readily enough, and agreed to do it.

Jack absolutely forbade Emily to go with them, and for the first time in their relationship he brooked no argument whatsoever.

"You may not come," he said with a charming smile and completely steady eyes.

"But—" she began, smiling back at him, searching for a lightness in him, a softness in his expression which would allow her to win him over. To her surprise she found none. "But—" she began again, looking for an argument in her favor.

"You may not come, Emily." There was not a flicker in his eyes and no yielding in his mouth. "It will be dangerous, if we have any success, and you would be in the way. Remember the reason we are doing this, and don't argue the toss. It is a waste of time, because whatever you say, you are not coming."

She drew in a deep breath. "Very well," she conceded with as much grace as she could muster. "If that is what you wish."

"It is better than that, my love," he said with the first edge of a smile. "It is an order."

When he and Anton had departed, leaving her on the door-step, she felt completely betrayed. Then as she gave the matter more reasoned consideration, she realized that he had done it to protect her from both the unpleasantness of the journey and the distress of what she would inevitably see; and she was pleased that he showed such concern. She had no desire to be taken for granted. And while she did not like being denied or counter-manded, she also did not like being able to prevail over his wishes. Getting your own way too often can be singularly un-satisfying.

With an idle afternoon on her hands, and a mind teeming with questions, she ordered the other carriage. After dressing extremely carefully in a new gown from Salon Worth in Paris, a deep thunder blue which flattered her fair coloring, and em-broidered lavishly in blouse front and around the hem, she set out to visit a certain lady whose wealth and family interests were greater than her scruples. This she knew from high society friends she had met in the past, at places where breeding and money were of far more account than personal affection or any form of regard.

Emily alighted and climbed the steps at the Park Lane ad-dress. When the door was opened, she presented her card and stood her ground while a slightly disconcerted parlormaid read it. It was one of Emily's old ones from before her remarriage, and still read "The Viscountess Ashworth," which was very much more impressive than "Mrs. Jack Radley."

Normally a lady would have left her card so the lady of the house might in turn leave hers and they would agree on a future time to meet, but Emily was clearly not going to depart. The parlormaid was obliged either to ask her to go or to invite her in. The title left her only one choice.

"Please come in, my lady, and I will see if Lady Priscilla will receive you."

Emily accepted graciously, and head high, walked through

the large hallway decked with family portraits, even a suit of armor on a stand. She took her place in the morning room in front of the fire, until the maid returned and ushered her upstairs into the first-story boudoir, the sitting room specially reserved for ladies.

It was an exquisite room, decorated in the Oriental style, which had become popular lately, and full of chinoiserie of every sort: lacquer boxes, an embroidered silk screen, landscape paintings where mountains floated above mists and waterfalls and tiny figures like black dots traveled on interminable roads. There was a glass-shelved cupboard containing at least twenty jade and ivory figures, and two carved ivory fans like frozen white lace.

Lady Priscilla herself was perhaps fifty, thin and with black hair of an unnatural depth that only her fondest friends imagined to be her own. She was wearing magenta and rose, also embroidered, but perfectly symmetrical. She knew it was a mistake as soon as she saw Emily.

"Lady Ashworth!" she exclaimed with courteous surprise. "How charming of you to have called upon me—and how unexpected."

Emily knew perfectly well she meant "how uncouth and without the appropriate warning," but she had come with a highly practical purpose in mind, and had no intention of jeopardizing it with impulsive words.

"I wished to find you alone," Emily replied with a slight inclining of her head. "I would like some confidential advice, and it suddenly occurred to me that no one in London would be better able to give it than you."

"Good gracious. How you flatter me!" Lady Priscilla exclaimed, but her overriding expression was not vain so much as curious. "Whatever do I know that you do not know quite as well yourself?" She smiled. "A little scandal, perhaps—but surely you have not come alone at this time of day for that."

"I am not averse to it." Emily sat down on the chair indicated. "But that is not why I am here. It is counsel I want, in certain matters in which I now have the freedom to be my own mistress—" She let it hang in the air, and saw Priscilla's sharp face quicken with interest.

"Your own mistress? Of course I heard of Lord Ashworth's death—" She composed her features to the appropriate solicitude. "My dear, how awful. I am so sorry."

"It was some time ago now." Emily brushed it aside. "I have remarried, you know—"

"But your card."

"Oh—did I give you one of the old ones? How careless of me. I do apologize. I am getting so shortsighted these days."

It was on Priscilla's tongue to say "A small pair of spectacles, perhaps?" but she did not wish to be too offensive in case she did not learn the cause for Emily's consulting her, and then how could she relate it to others?

"It is of no consequence," she murmured.

Emily smiled dazzlingly. "How gracious of you."

"If I can help?" Priscilla offered intently.

"Oh I'm sure." Emily settled a little farther into her seat. This could have been quite entertaining, but she must not lose sight of her reason for coming. Clemency Shaw's death was enough to sober any amusement. "I have a certain amount of money at my disposal, and I should like to invest it profitably, and if possible where it is both safe and reasonably discreet."

"Oh—" Priscilla let out her breath slowly, a dawn of comprehension in her face. "You would like it to return you some profit, but be inaccessible to your family. And you are married again?"

"I am." Silently Emily thought of Jack, and apologized to him. "Hence the need for the utmost . . . discretion."

"Absolute secrecy," Priscilla assured her, her eyes alight. "I can advise you very well; you certainly came to the right person."

"I knew it," Emily said with triumph in her voice, not for investment, but because she was on the brink of discovering exactly what she sought. "I knew you were the very best person. What should I do with it? I have quite a substantial amount, you understand?"

"Property," Priscilla replied without hesitation.

Emily schooled her face very carefully into disappointment.

"Property? But then anyone who wished could ascertain exactly what I owned, and what income it brought me—which is precisely what I wish to avoid!"

"Oh my dear—don't be naive!" Priscilla waved her hands, dismissing the very idea. "I don't mean domestic residences in Primrose Hill. I mean two or three blocks of old tenements in Mile End or Wapping, or St. Giles."

"Wapping?" Emily said with careful incredulity. "What on earth would that be worth to me?"

"A fortune," Priscilla replied. "Place it in the hands of a good business manager, who will see that it is let advantageously, and that the rent is collected every week or month, and it will double your outlay in no time."

Emily frowned. "Really? How on earth would rent for places like that amount to much? Only the poorest people live in such areas, don't they? They could hardly pay the kind of rents I should wish."

"Oh yes they can," Priscilla assured her. "If there are enough of them, it will be most profitable, I promise you."

"Enough?"

"Certainly. Ask no questions as to what people do, and what profit they in turn can make, then you can let every room in the building to a dozen people, and they will sublet it, and so on. There is always someone who will pay more, believe me."

"I am not sure I should care to be associated with such a place," Emily demurred. "It is not—something—"

"Ha!" Priscilla laughed aloud. "Who would? That is why you do it through a business manager, and a solicitor, and his employees, and a rent collector, and so on. No one will ever know it is you who owns it, except your own man of affairs, and he will certainly never tell anyone. That is his purpose."

"Are you sure?" Emily widened her eyes. "Does anyone else do such a thing?"

"Of course. Dozens of people."

"Who—for instance?"

"My dear, don't be so indiscreet. You will make yourself highly unpopular if you ask such questions. They are protected, just as you will be. I promise you, no one will know."

"It is only a matter of—" Emily shrugged her shoulders high

and opened her eyes innocently. "Really—people might not understand. There is nothing illegal, I presume?"

"Of course not. Apart from having no desire to break the law"—Priscilla smiled and pursed her lips—"these are all highly respectable people with positions to maintain—it also would be very foolish." She spread elegant hands wide, palms upwards, her rings momentarily hidden. "Anyway, it is quite unnecessary. There is no law to prevent your doing everything I suggest. And believe me, my dear, the profits are exceedingly good."

"Is there any risk?" Emily said lightly. "I mean—there are people agitating for reforms of one sort or another. Might one end up losing it all—or on the other hand being exposed to public dislike, if—"

"None at all," Priscilla said with a laugh. "I don't know what reformers you have heard of, but they have not even a ghost of a chance of bringing about any real changes—not in the areas I propose. New houses will be built here and there, in manufacturing towns, but it will not affect the properties we are concerned with. There will always be slums, my dear, and there will always be people with nowhere else to live."

Emily felt such a passion of revulsion she found it almost impossible to hide it. She looked down to conceal her face, and searched in her reticule for a handkerchief, then blew her nose a good deal less delicately than was ladylike. Then she felt sufficiently composed to meet Priscilla's eyes again and try to make the loathing in her own look like anxiety.

"I thought it was such slums that reformers were involved in?"

Now the contempt in Priscilla's face was easily readable.

"You are being timid for no reason, Emily." The use of her name added an infinite condescension to Priscilla's words. "There are very powerful people involved. It would not only be quite pointless trying to ruin them, it would be extremely dangerous. No one will cause more than a little inconvenience, I promise, and that will be dealt with without your needing even to know about it, much less involve yourself."

Emily leaned back and forced a smile to her face, although it felt more like the baring of teeth. She met Priscilla's gaze without a flicker though inside she was burning with a hatred that made her want to react with physical violence.

"You have told me precisely what I wished to know. And I am sure you are totally reliable and unquestionably are fully aware what you are dealing with. No doubt we will meet again on the matter, or at least you will hear from me. Thank you so much for sparing me your time."

Priscilla smiled more widely as Emily rose to her feet. "I am always happy to be of assistance to a friend. When you have realized your assets and decided what you would like to invest, come back and I shall put you in touch with the best person to help you, and to be utterly discreet."

Money was not mentioned, but Emily knew perfectly well it was understood, and she was equally sure Priscilla herself took a proportion for her services.

"Of course." Emily inclined her head very slightly. "You have been most gracious; I shall not forget it." And she took her leave and went out of the house into the cold air of the street where even the manure on the cobbles could not spoil its comparative sweetness to her.

"Take me home," she told the coachman as he handed her up. "Immediately."

When Jack returned tired and dirty, his face ashen, she was waiting for him. He was just as somber, with an underlying anger equal to hers.

He stopped in the hallway where she had come from the withdrawing room to meet him. She still found his step on the black-and-white flagstones quickened her heart and the sound of his voice as the footman took his coat made her smile. She looked at him and searched his dark gray eyes, with the curling lashes she had marveled at—and envied—when they first met. She had considered him far too conscious of his own charm. Now that she knew him better, she still found him just as engaging, but knew the man behind the manners and liked him immensely. He was an excellent friend, and she knew the supreme value of that.

"Was it very bad?" She did not waste words in foolish questions like "How are you?" She could see in his face how he was, that he had been exhausted and hurt and was as violently angry as she, and as impotent to change or destroy the offenders or to help the victims.

"Beyond anything I can convey in words," he replied. "I'll be lucky if I can get the smell out of my clothes or the taste out of my throat. And I don't think I'll ever completely lose the picture of their misery. I can see their faces every time I close my eyes as if they were painted on the inside of my eyelids." He looked around the huge hallway with its flagged floor, oak-paneled walls, the sweeping staircase up to a gallery, the paintings, the vases laden with flowers two and three feet tall, the huge carved furniture with gleaming wood and the umbrella stand with five silver- and horn-handled sticks.

Emily knew what he was thinking; the same thoughts had passed through her head more than once. But it was George's house, Ashworth heritage, and belonged to her son Edward, not to her except as a trust until he was of age. Jack knew that too, but they both still felt a taste of guilt that they enjoyed its luxury as easily as if it had been theirs, which in all practical ways it was.

"Come into the withdrawing room and sit down," she said gently. "Albert can draw you a bath. Tell me what you learned."

Taking her arm he went with her and in a quiet, very grave voice he described where Anton had taken him. He chose few words, not wanting to harass her nor to relive the horror and the helpless pity he had felt himself, not the nauseating disgust. He told her of rat-and-lice-infected tenements where the walls dripped and hung with mold, of open sewers and drains and piles of refuse. Many rooms were occupied by fifteen or twenty people, all ages and both sexes, without privacy or sanitation of any kind, without water or drainage. In some the roofs or windows were in such disrepair the rain came in; and yet the rent was collected every week without fail. Some desperate people sublet even the few square yards they had, in order to maintain their own payments.

He forbore from describing the conditions in the sweatshops

where women and girls worked beneath street level, by gaslight or candlelight and without ventilation, eighteen hours a day stitching shirts or gloves or dresses for people who inhabited another world.

He did not go into any detail about the brothels, the gin mills and the narrow, fetid rooms where men found oblivion in opium; he simply stated their existence. By the time he had said all he needed to, to share the burden and feel her understanding, her anguish at the same things, her equal sense of outrage and helplessness, Albert had been twice to say his bath was getting cold, and had finally come a third time to say that a fresh bath had been drawn.

There were in bed, close together and almost ready for sleep, when she finally told him what she had done, where she had been, and what she had learned.

Vespasia took the questions to Somerset Carlisle, when the parliamentary business of the day was done. It was after eleven in the evening chill with a rising fog when she finally reached her home. She was tired, but too filled with concern to sleep. Part of her thoughts were turned towards the matters she had raised with him, but a good deal of her anxiety was for Charlotte. It was not untouched with guilt, lest by suggestion, the offer of Percival and the carriage, and the ready ease with which she had taken the children to Caroline Ellison, that she had enabled Charlotte to embark on a course which might become personally dangerous. At the time she had simply thought of Clemency Shaw and the appalling injustice of her death. For once she had allowed anger to outweigh judgment, and had sent the woman she was most fond of into considerable risk. It was true; she cared for Charlotte as much as anyone, now her own daughter was dead. And more than that; she liked her—enjoyed her company, her humor, her courage. It was not only rash, it was completely irresponsible. She had not even consulted Thomas, and he of all people had a right to know.

But it was not her nature to spend time over what could not be undone. She must bear it—and take the blame should there be any. There was no purpose to be served in speaking or writing to Thomas now; Charlotte would tell him, or not, as she wished; and he would prevent her from continuing, or not, as he was able. Vespasia's meddling now would only compound the error.

But she found it hard to sleep.

The following evening they met at Vespasia's house for dinner, and to compare notes upon what they had learned, but primarily to hear from Somerset Carlisle the state of the law they must fight, deal with, and change if possible.

Emily and Jack arrived early. Emily was less glamorously dressed than Vespasia could remember her being since she had ceased mourning for George. Jack looked tired; there were lines of strain on his normally handsome face and the humor was absent from his eyes. He was courteous, from habit, but even the usual compliments were not on his lips.

Charlotte was late, and Vespasia was beginning to feel anxious, her mind wandering from the trivial conversation they maintained until the business of the evening could be shared.

Somerset Carlisle came in, grim-faced. He glanced at Vespasia, then Emily and Jack, and forbore from asking where Charlotte was.

But Charlotte finally arrived, brought by Percival and the returned carriage. She was breathless, tired, and her hair markedly less well done than customarily. Vespasia was so overwhelmingly relieved to see her all she could do was criticize her for being late. She dared not to show her emotions; it would have been most unseemly.

They repaired to the dining room and dinner was served.

Each reported what he or she had seen and done, cursorily and with no unnecessary description; the facts were fearful enough. They did not speak as if they had been tired, sickened or endangered themselves. What they had seen dwarfed self-pity or praise.

When the last was finished they turned as one to Somerset Carlisle.

Pale-faced, weary of heart, he explained the law to them as
he had ascertained it. He confirmed what they already knew:
that is was almost impossible to discover who owned property
if the owner wished to remain anonymous, and that the law
required nothing to assist the tenant or shield him. There were
no basic requirements of fitness for habitation concerning water,
sewage, shelter or any other facility. There were no means of
redress regarding payment of rents or freedom from eviction.

"Then we must change the law," Vespasia said when he had
finished. "We will continue where Clemency Shaw was cut off
by her murderers."

"It may be dangerous," Somerset Carlisle warned. "We will
be disturbing powerful people. The little I have learned so far
indicates there are members of great families who come by at
least part of their income that way, some industrialists with vast
fortunes reinvested. It has not failed to touch others of ambition
and greed, men who can be tempted and who have favors to
sell—members of the House, judges of court. It will be a very
hard struggle—and with no easy victories."

"That is a pity," Vespasia said without even consulting the
others by so much as a glance. "But it is irrelevant."

"We need more people in power." Carlisle glanced at Jack.
"More men in Parliament prepared to risk a comfortable seat by
fighting against the vested interests."

Jack did not reply, but he spoke little the rest of the evening,
and all the way home he was deep in thought.

CHAPTER
EIGHT

Pitt and Murdo were working from early in the morning until long after dark pursuing every scrap of material evidence until there was nothing else to learn. The Highgate police themselves were still searching for the arsonist they were convinced was guilty, but as yet they had not found him, although they felt that every day's inquiry brought them closer. There had been other fires started in similar manner: an empty house in Kentish Town, a stable in Hampstead, a small villa to the north in Crouch End. They questioned every source of fuel oil within a three-mile radius of Highgate, but discovered no purchases other than those which were accounted for by normal household needs. They asked every medical practitioner if they had treated burns not explained to their certain knowledge. They counseled with neighboring police and fire forces on the name, present where-abouts, past history and methods of every other person known to have committed arson in the last ten years, and learned nothing of use.

Pitt and Murdo also delved into the value, insurance and ownership of all the houses that had been burned, and found nothing in common. Then they asked into the dispositions in wills and testaments of Clemency Shaw and Amos Lindsay. Clemency bequeathed everything of which she died possessed to her husband, Stephen Robert Shaw, with the solitary exception of a few personal items to friends; and Amos Lindsay left his works of art, his books and the mementos of his travels also to Stephen Shaw, and the house itself most surprisingly to Matthew Oliphant, a startling and unexplained gift of which Pitt entirely approved. It was just one more evidence of a kind and most unconventional man.

He knew that Charlotte was busy, but since she was traveling in Great-Aunt Vespasia's carriage, and with her footman in attendance, he was satisfied there was no danger involved. He thought there was also little profit, since she had told him she was pursuing Clemency Shaw's last known journeys, and he was quite sure, since Lindsay's death, that Clemency had been killed by chance and the true intended victim was Stephen Shaw.

So the morning after the dinner at Vespasia's house in which they had learned the extent and nature of the law, Charlotte dressed herself in tidy but unremarkable clothes. This was not in the least difficult, since that description encompassed the greater part of her wardrobe. She then waited for Emily and Jack to arrive.

They came surprisingly early. She had not honestly thought Emily rose at an hour to make this possible, but Emily was at the door before nine, looking her usual fashionable self, with Jack only a pace behind her, dressed in plain, undistinguished browns.

"It won't do," Charlotte said immediately.

"I am quite aware that it won't." Emily came in, gave her a quick peck on the cheek and made her way to the kitchen. "I am only half awake. For pity's sake have Gracie put on the kettle. I shall have to borrow something of yours. Everything of mine looks as if it cost at least as much as it did—which of course was the intention. Have you got a brown dress? I look terrible in brown."

"No I haven't," Charlotte said a little stiffly. "But I have two dark plum-colored ones, and you would look just as terrible in either of them."

Emily broke into laughter, her face lighting up and some of the tiredness vanishing.

"Thank you, my dear. How charming of you. Do they both fit you, or might one of them be small enough for me?"

"No." Charlotte joined in the mood, her eyes wide, preventing herself from smiling back with difficulty. "They will be excellent 'round the waist, but too big in the bosom!"

"Liar!" Emily shot back. "They will bag around the waist, and I shall trip over the skirts. Either will do excellently. I shall go and change while you make the tea. Are we taking Gracie as well? It will hardly be a pleasant adventure for her."

"Please ma'am?" Gracie said urgently. She had tasted the excitement of the chase, of being included, and was bold enough to plead her own cause. "I can 'elp. I unnerstand them people."

"Of course," Charlotte said quickly. "If you wish. But you must stay close to us at all times. If you don't there is no accounting for what may happen to you."

"Oh I will, ma'am," she promised, her sober little face as grave as if she were swearing an oath. "An' I'll watch an' listen. Sometimes I knows w'en people is tellin' lies."

Half an hour later the four of them set out in Emily's second carriage on the journey to Mile End to trace the ownership of the tenement house to which Charlotte had followed the trail of Clemency Shaw. Their first intent was to discover the rent collector and learn from him for whom he did this miserable duty.

She had made note of the exact location. Even so it took them some time to find it again; the streets were narrow and took careful negotiation through the moil of costers' barrows, old clothes carts, peddlers, vegetable wagons and clusters of people buying, selling and begging. So many of the byways looked alike; pavements wide enough to allow the passage of only one person; the cobbled centers, often with open gutters meandering through them filled with the night's waste; the jettied houses leaning far out over the street, some so close at the top as to block out most of the daylight. One could imagine people in the upper stories being able to all but shake hands across the divide, if they leaned out far enough, and were minded to do so.

The wood was pitted where sections were rotten and had fallen away, the plaster was dark with stains of old leakage and rising dampness from the stones, and here and there ancient pargetting made half-broken patterns or insignia.

People stood in doorways, dark forms huddled together, faces catching the light now and then as one or another moved.

Emily reached out and took Jack's hand. The teeming, fathomless despair of it frightened her. She had never felt quite this kind of inadequacy. There were so many. There was a child running along beside them, begging. He was no older than her own son sitting at home in his schoolroom struggling with learning his multiplication tables and looking forward to luncheon, apart from the obligatory rice pudding which he loathed, and the afternoon, when he could play.

Jack fished in his pockets for a coin and threw it for the boy. The child dived on it as it rolled almost under the carriage wheels and for a sickening moment Emily thought he would be crushed. But he emerged an instant later, jubilant, clutching the coin in a filthy hand and biting his teeth on it to check its metal.

Within moments a dozen more urchins were close around them, calling out, stretching their hands, fighting each other to reach them first. Older men appeared. There were catcalls, jeers, threats; and all the time the crowd closing in till the horses could barely make their way forward and the coachman was afraid to urge them in case he crushed the weight of yelling, writhing, shoving humanity.

"Oh my God!" Jack looked ashen, realizing suddenly what he had done. Frantically he turned out his pockets for more.

Emily was thoroughly frightened. She hunched down on the seat, closer to his side. There seemed to be clamoring, reaching people all around them, hands grasping, faces contorted with hunger and hatred.

Gracie was wrapped with her shawl around her, wide-eyed, frozen.

Charlotte did not know what Jack intended that would help, but she emptied out her own few coins to add to his.

He took them without hesitation and forcing the window open flung them as far behind the coach as he could.

Instantly the crowd parted and dived where the coins had fallen. The coachman urged the horses forward and they were free, clattering down the road, wheels hissing on the damp surface.

Jack fell back on the seat, still pale, but the beginning of a smile on his lips.

Emily straightened up and turned to look at him, her eyes very bright and her color returned. Now as well as pity and fear, there was a new, sharp admiration.

Charlotte too felt a very pleasant respect which had not been there before.

When they reached the tenement it was decided Charlotte and Gracie should go in, since they were familiar to the occupants. To send more might appear like a show of force and produce quite the opposite effect from the one they wished.

"Mr. Thickett?" A small group of drab women looked from one to another. "Dunno w'ere 'e comes from. 'E jus' comes every week and takes the money."

"Is it his house?" Charlotte asked.

" 'Ow the 'ell der we know?" a toothless woman said angrily. "An' why der you care, eh? Wot's it ter you? 'Oo are yer any'ow, comin' 'ere arskin' questions?"

"We pays our rent an' we don' make no trouble," another added, folding fat arms over an even fatter bosom. It was a vaguely threatening stance, although she held no weapon nor had any within reach. It was the way she rocked very slightly on her feet and stared fiercely at Charlotte's face. She was a woman with little left to lose, and she knew it.

"We wanna rent," Gracie said quickly. "We've bin put aht o' our own place, an' we gotta find summink else quick. We can't wait till rent day; we gotta find it now."

"Oh—why dincher say so?" The woman looked at Charlotte with a mixture of pity and exasperation. "Proud, are yer? Stupid, more like. Fallen on 'ard times, 'ave yer, livin' too 'igh on the 'og—an' now yer gotta come down in the world? 'Appens to lots of folk. Well, Thickett don't come today, but fer a consideration I'll tell yer w'ere ter find 'im—"

"We're on 'ard times," Gracie said plaintively.

"Yeah? Well your 'ard times in't the same as my 'ard times." The woman's pale mouth twisted into a sneer. "I in't arskin' money. O' course you in't got no money, or yer wouldn't be 'ere— but I'll 'ave yer 'at." She looked at Charlotte, then at her hands and saw their size, and looked instead at Gracie's brown woollen shawl. "An' 'er shawl. Then I'll tell yer w'ere ter go."

"You can have the hat now." Charlotte took it off as she spoke. "And the shawl if we find Thickett where you say. If we don't—" She hesitated, a threat on her lips, then looked at the hard disillusioned face and knew its futility. "Then you'll do without," she ended.

"Yeah?" The woman's voice was steeped in years of experience. "An' w'en yer've got Thickett yer goin' ter come back 'ere ter give me yer shawl. Wotcher take me for, eh? Shawl now, or no Thickett."

"Garn," Gracie said with withering scorn. "Take the 'at and be 'appy. No Thickett, no 'at. She may look like gentry, but she's mean w'en she's crossed—an' she's crossed right now! Wotsa matter wiv yer—yer stupid or suffink? Take the 'at and give us Thickett." Her little face was tight with disgust and concentration. She was on an adventure and prepared to risk everything to win.

The woman saw her different mettle, heard the familiar vowels in her voice and knew she was dealing with one more her own kind. She dropped the bluff, shrugging her heavy shoulders. It had been a reasonable attempt, and you could not blame one for trying.

"Yer'll find Thickett in Sceptre Street, big 'ouse on the corner o' Usk. Go ter ve back an' ask fer Tom Thickett, an' say it's ter give 'im rent. They'll let yer in, an' if yer says aught abaht money e'll listen ter yer." She snatched the hat out of Charlotte's hands and ran her fingers over it appreciatively, her lips pursed in concentration. "If yer on 'ard times, 'ock a few o' these and yer'll 'ave enough ter eat for days. 'Ard times. Yer don' know 'ard times from nuffin'."

No one argued with her. They knew their poverty was affected for the occasion and a lie excusable only by its brevity, and their own flicker of knowledge as to what its reality would be.

Back in the carriage, huddled against the chill, they rode still slowly to Sceptre Street as the woman had told them. The thor-

oughfare was wider, the houses on each side broader fronted
and not jettied across the roadway, but the gutters still rolled
with waste and smelled raw and sour, and Charlotte wondered
if she would ever be able to get the stains out of the bottom of
her skirts. Emily would probably throw hers away. She would
have to make some recompense to Gracie for this. She looked
across at her thin body, as upright as Aunt Vespasia, in her own
way, but a full head shorter. Her face, with its still childish softness of skin, was more alive with excitement than she had ever
seen it before.

They stepped down at the designated corner and crossed the
footpath, wider here, and knocked on the door. When a tousle-
headed maid answered they asked for Mr. Thickett, stating very
clearly that it was a matter of money, and some urgency to it,
Gracie putting in a dramatic sniff. They were permitted to enter
and led to a chilly room apparently used for storing furniture
and for such occasional meetings as this. Several chests and old
chairs were piled recklessly on top of each other, and there was
a table missing a leg and a bundle of curtains which seemed to
have rotted in places with damp. The whole smelled musty and
Emily pulled a face as soon as they were inside.

There was no place to sit down, and she remembered with
a jolt that they were supplicants now, seeking a favor of this
man and in no position to be anything but crawlingly civil. Only
the remembrance of Clemency Shaw's death, the charred corpse
in her imagination, enabled her to do it.

"He won't tell us the owner," she whispered quickly. "He
thinks he has the whip hand of us if we are here to beg half a
room from him."

"You're right, m'lady," Gracie whispered back, unable to
forget the title even here. "If 'e's a rent collector 'e'll be a bully—
they always is—an' like as not big wif it. 'E won't do nuffin' fer
nobody less'n 'e 'as ter."

For a moment they were all caught in confusion. The first
story would no longer serve. Then Jack smiled just as they heard
heavy footsteps along the passageway and the door opened to
show a big man, barrel-chested, with a hatchet face, jutting nose

and small, round, clever eyes. He hooked his thumbs in his waistcoat, which was once beige but was now mottled and faded with years of misuse.

"Well?" He surveyed them with mild curiosity. He had only one yardstick by which he measured people. Could they pay the rent, either by means already in their possession or by some they could earn, steal or sublet to obtain. He looked at the women also, not as possessors of money or labor force worth considering, but to see if they were handsome or young enough to earn their livings on the street. He judged them all handsome enough, but only Gracie to have the necessary realism. The other two, and it showed plainly in his face, would have to come down a good deal further in the world before they were accommodating enough to please a paying customer. However, a friendliness made up for a lot of flaws, in fact almost anything except age.

On the other hand, Jack looked like a dandy, in spite of his rather well-worn clothes. They might be old, but that did not disguise the flair with which he tied his cravat, or the good cut of the shoulders and the lie of the lapels. No, here was a man who knew and liked the good things. If he was on hard times he would make no worker: his hands, smooth, well-manicured and gloveless, attested to that. But then he did look shrewd, and there was an air about him of easiness, a charm. He might make an excellent trickster, well able to live on his arts. And he would not be the first gentleman to do that—by a long way.

"So yer want a room?" he said mildly. "I daresay as I can find yer one. Mebbe if yer can pay fer it, one all ter yerselves, like. 'Ow abaht five shillin's a week?"

Jack's lip curled with distaste and he reached out and put his hand on Emily's arm. "Actually you mistake our purpose," he said very frankly, looking at Thickett with hard eyes. "I represent Smurfitt, Taylor and Mordue, Solicitors. My name is John Consterdine." He saw Thickett's face tighten in a mixture of anger and caution. "There is a suit due to be heard regarding property upon which there have been acts of negligence which bear responsibility for considerable loss. Since you collect the rents for this property, we assume you own it, and therefore are liable—"

"No I don't!" Thickett's eyes narrowed and he tightened his body defensively. "I collect rents, that's all. Just collect. That's an honest job and yer got no business wi' me. I can't 'elp yer."

"I am not in need of help, Mr. Thickett," Jack said with considerable aplomb. "It is you, if you own the property, who will shortly be in prison for undischarged debt—"

"Oh no I won't. I don't own nuffin but this 'ouse, which in't 'ad nuffin wrong wif it fer years. Anyway"—he screwed up his face in new appraisal, his native common sensed returning, now the first alarm had worn off—"if yer a lawyer, 'oo are they? Lawyers' clerks, eh?" He jabbed a powerful finger towards Emily, Charlotte and Gracie.

Jack answered with transparent honesty.

"This is my wife, this is my sister-in-law, and this is her maid. I brought them because I knew you would be little likely to see me alone, having a good idea who I was and why I came. And circumstances proved me right. You took us for a family on hard fortune and needing to rent your rooms. The law requires that I serve papers on you—" He made as if to reach into his inside pocket.

"No it don't," Thickett said rapidly. "I don't own no buildings; like I said, I just collect the rents—"

"And put them in your pocket," Jack finished for him. "Good. You'll likely have a nice fund somewhere to pay the costs—"

"All I 'ave is me wage wot I'm paid for it. I give all the rest, ceptin' my bit, over."

"Oh yes?" Jack's eyebrows went up disbelievingly. "To whom?"

"Ter ve manager, o' course. Ter 'im wot manages the business fer 'o'ever owns all them buildings along Lisbon Street."

"Indeed? And who is he?" The disbelief was still there.

"I dunno. W'ere the 'ell are you from? D'yer think people 'oo 'as places like vat puts their names on the door? Yer daft, or suffink?"

"The manager," Jack backtracked adeptly. "Of course the owner wouldn't tell the likes of you, if you don't report to him—who is the manager?' I'm going to serve these papers on someone."

"Mr. Buffery, Fred Buffery. Yer'll find 'im at Nicholas Street, over be'ind the brewery, vat's w'ere 'e does business. Yer go an' serve yer papers on 'im. It in't nuffink ter do wi' me. I just take the rents. It's a job—like yours."

Jack did not bother to dispute it with him. They had what they wanted and he had no desire to remain. Without expressing any civilities he opened the door and they all left, finding the carriage a few houses away, and proceeding to the next address.

Here they were informed that Mr. Buffery was taking luncheon at the neighboring public house, the Goat and Compasses, and they decided it would be an excellent time to do the same. Emily particularly was fascinated. She had never been inside such an establishment before, and Charlotte had only in more salubrious neighborhoods, and that on infrequent occasions.

Inside was noisy with laughter, voices in excited and often bawdy conversation, and the clink of glasses and crockery. It smelled of ale, sweat, sawdust, vinegar and boiled vegetables.

Jack hesitated. This was not a suitable place for ladies, the thought was as plain on his face as if he had spoken it.

"Nonsense," Emily said fiercely just behind him. "We are all extremely hungry. Are you going to refuse to get us luncheon?"

"Yes I am—in this place," he said firmly. "We'll find something better, even if it's a pie stall. We can get Mr. Buffery when he returns to his office."

"I'm staying here," Emily retorted. "I want to see—it's all part of what we are doing."

"No it isn't." He took her arm. "We need Buffery to tell us who he manages the building for; we don't need this place. I'm not going to argue about it, Emily. You are coming out."

"But Jack—"

Before the altercation could proceed any further Gracie slid forward and grasped the bartender waiting on the next table, pulling his sleeve till he turned to see what was upsetting his balance.

"Please mister," she appealed to him with wide eyes. "Is Mr. Buffery in 'ere? I can't 'ear 'is voice, an' I don't see too well. E's me uncle an' I got a message fer 'im."

"Give it ter me, girl, an' I'll give it 'im," the bartender said not unkindly.

"Oh I carsn't do that, mister, it'd be more 'n me life's worf. Me pa'd tan me summink wicked."

" 'Ere, I'll take yer. E's over 'ere in the corner. Don't you bovver 'im now, mind. I'll not 'ave me customers bovvered. You give yer message, then scarper, right?"

"Yes mister. Thank yer, mister." And she allowed him to lead her over to the far corner, where a man with a red face and golden red hair was seated behind a small table and a plate generously spread with succulent pie and crisp pickles and a large slice of ripe cheese. Two tankards of ale stood a hand's reach away.

"Uncle Fred?" she began, for the bartender's benefit, hoping fervently at least Charlotte, if not all of them, were immediately behind her.

Buffery looked at her with irritation.

"I in't yer uncle. Go and bother someone else. I in't interested in your sort. If I want a woman I'll find me own, a lot sassier than you—and I don't give ter beggars."

" 'Ere!" the bartender said angrily. "You said as 'e were yer uncle."

"So 'e is," Gracie said desperately. "Me pa said as ter tell 'im me gramma's took bad, an' we need money fer 'elp for 'er. She's that cold."

"That right?" the bartender demanded, turning to Buffery. "You runnin' out on yer own ma?"

By this time Charlotte, Emily and Jack were all behind Gracie. She felt the warmth of relief flood through her. She sniffed fiercely, half afraid, half determined to play this for all it was worth.

"Yer got all them 'ouses, Uncle Fred, all Lisbon Street

mostly. You can find Gramma a nice place w'ere she can be warm. She's real bad. Ma'll look after 'er, if'n yer just find a better place. We got water on all the walls an' it's cold summink awful."

"I in't yer Uncle Fred," Buffery said furiously. "I in't never seen yer before. Git out of 'ere. 'Ere—take this!" He thrust a sixpence at her. "Now get out of 'ere."

Gracie ignored the sixpence, with difficulty, and burst into tears—with ease.

"That won't buy more'n one night. Then wot'll we do? Yer got all the 'ouses on Lisbon Street. Why can't yer get Ma and Pa a room in one of 'em, so we can keep dry? I'll work, honest I will. We'll pay yer."

"They in't my 'ouses, yer little fool!" Buffery was embarrassed now as other diners turned to look at the spectacle. "D'yer think I'd be 'ere eatin' cold pie and drinkin' ale if I got the rents fer that lot? I jus' manages the bus'ness of 'em. Now get aht an' leave me alone, yer little bleeder. I in't never seen yer an' I got no ma wot's sick."

Gracie was saved further dramatic effort by Jack stepping forward and pretending to be a lawyer's clerk again, entirely unconnected with Gracie, and offering his services to dispatch her on her way. Buffery accepted eagerly, very aware now of his associates and neighbors staring at him. His discomfort offered a better sideshow than many of the running patterers who sang ballads of the latest news or scandal. This was immediate and the afflicted one was known to them.

When Buffery had identified himself, Jack told Gracie to leave, which she did rapidly and with deep gratitude, after picking up the sixpence. Jack then proceeded to threaten him with lawsuits as accessory to fraud, and Buffery was ready to swear blind that he did not own the buildings in Lisbon Street, and prove it if necessary before the lawyer who took the rent money from him every month, less his own miserable pittance for the service he performed.

After a brief luncheon, early afternoon found them in the offices on Bethnal Green Road of Fulsom and Son, Penrose and Fulsom, a small room up narrow stairs where Jack insisted on going alone. He returned after a chilly half hour. Emily and Charlotte and Gracie were wrapped in carriage rugs, Gracie still glowing from her triumph in the public house, and the subsequent praise she had received.

They spent until dark trying to track down the property management company whose name Jack had elicited, by a mixture of lies and trickery from the seedy little Mr. Penrose, but eventually were obliged to return home unsuccessful.

Charlotte intended to recount the day's events to Pitt, but when he arrived home late, lines of weariness deep in his face, and in his eyes a mixture of eagerness and total bafflement, she set aside her own news and asked after his.

He sat down at the kitchen table and picked up the mug of tea she had automatically put before him, but instead of drinking it he simply warmed his hands holding it, and began to talk.

"We want to Shaw's solicitors today and read Clemency's will. The estate was left to Shaw, as we had been told, all except a few personal items to friends. The most remarkable was her Bible, which she left to Matthew Oliphant, the curate."

Charlotte could see nothing very odd in this. One might well leave a Bible to one's minister, especially if he were as sincere and thoughtful as Oliphant. She could almost certainly have had no idea of his feelings for her; they had been so desperately private. She recalled his bony, vulnerable face as clearly as if she had seen it a few moments ago.

Why was Pitt so concerned? It seemed ordinary enough. She looked at him, waiting.

"Of course the Bible was destroyed in the fire." He leaned forward a little, elbows on the table, his face puckered in concentration. "But the solicitor had seen it—it was an extraordinary thing, leather bound, tooled in gold and with a hasp and lock on it which he thought must be brass, but he wasn't sure." His eyes were bright with the recollection. "And inside every initial letter of a chapter was illuminated in color and gold leaf with the most exquisite tiny paintings." He smiled slowly. "As if one glimpsed a vision of heaven or hell through lighted keyholes. She showed it to him just once, so he would know what item he was dealing with and there could be no mistake. It had been her grandfather's." His face shadowed for a moment with distaste. "Not Worlingham, on the other side." Then the awareness of the present returned and with it the waste and the destruction. His face was suddenly blank and the light died out of it. "It must have been marvelous, and worth a great deal. But of course it's gone with everything else."

He looked at her, puzzled and anxious. "But why on earth should she leave it to Oliphant? He's not even the vicar, he's only a curate. He almost certainly won't stay there in Highgate. If he gets a living it will be elsewhere—possibly even in a different county."

Charlotte knew the answer immediately and without any effort of reasoning. It was as obvious to her as to any woman who had loved and not dared to show it, as she had once, ages ago, before Pitt. She had been infatuated with Dominic Corde, her eldest sister's husband, when Sarah was alive and they all lived in Cater Street. Of course that had died as delusion became reality and impossible, agonizing love resolved into a fairly simple friendship. But she thought that for Clemency Shaw it had remained achingly real. Matthew Oliphant's character was not a sham she had painted on by dream, as Charlotte had with Dominic. He was not handsome, dashing, there at every turn in her life; he was at least fifteen years her junior, a struggling curate with barely the means of subsistence, and to the kindest eye he was a little plain and far from graceful.

And yet a spirit burned inside him. In the face of other people's agony Clitheridge was totally inadequate, graceless, inarticulate and left on the outside untouched. Oliphant's compassion robbed him of awkwardness because he felt the pain as if it were his own and pity taught his tongue.

The answer was clear. Clemency had loved him just as much as he had loved her, and been equally unable to show it even in the slightest way, except when she was dead to leave him something of infinite value to her, and yet which would not seem so very remarkable that it would hurt his reputation. A Bible, not a painting or an ornament or some other article which would betray an unseemly emotion, just a Bible—to the curate. Only those who had seen it would know—and perhaps that would be the solicitor—and Stephen Shaw.

Pitt was staring at her across the table.

"Charlotte?"

She looked up at him, smiling a very little, suddenly a tightness in her throat.

"He loved her too, you know," she said, swallowing hard. "I realized that when he was helping me to follow Bessie Jones and those awful houses. He knew the way she went."

Pitt put the cup down and reached to take her hands, gently, holding them and touching her fingers one by one. There was no need to say anything else, and he did not wish to.

In fact it was the following morning, just before he left, that he told her the other thing that had so troubled him. He was tying up his boots at the front door and she was holding his coat.

"The lawyers have sorted the estate already. It's quite simple. There is no money—only a couple of hundred pounds left."

"What?" She felt she must have misunderstood him.

He straightened up and she helped him on with the coat.

"There is no money left," he repeated. "All the Worlingham money she inherited is gone, except about two hundred and fourteen pounds and fifteen shillings."

"But I thought there was a lot—I mean, wasn't Theophilus rich?"

"Extremely. And all of it went to his two daughters, Prudence Hatch and Clemency Shaw. But Clemency has none left."

There was one ugly thought which she had to speak because it would haunt her mind anyway. "Did Shaw spend it?"

"No—the solicitor says definitely not. Clemency herself paid huge drafts to all kinds of people—individuals and societies."

"Whatever for?" said Charlotte, although the beginning of an idea was plain in her mind, as she could see that it was in his also. "Housing reform?"

"Yes—most of it that the solicitor knew about, but there is a great deal he cannot trace—to individuals he has never heard of."

"Are you going to find them?"

"Of course. Although I don't think it has anything to do with the fire. I still believe that was intended for Shaw, although I haven't even the beginning of proof as to why."

"And Amos Lindsay?"

He shrugged. "Because he knew, or guessed, who was responsible; perhaps from something Shaw said, without realizing its significance himself. Or even uglier and perhaps more likely, whoever it is is still after Shaw, and that fire was a failed attempt to kill him also." He pulled his muffler off the hook and put it around his neck, the ends hanging loosely. "And of course it is still not impossible Shaw set them himself: the first to kill Clemency, the second to kill Lindsay because in some way he had betrayed himself to him—or feared he had."

"That's vile!" she said fiercely. "After Lindsay had been his closest friend. And why? Why should Shaw murder Clemency? You just said there was no money to inherit."

He hated saying it, and the revulsion showed in his face as he formed the words. "Precisely because there is no money. If it was all gone, and he needed more, then Flora Lutterworth was young, very pretty and the sole heiress to the biggest fortune in Highgate. And she is certainly very fond of him—to the point where it is the cause of local gossip."

"Oh," she said very quietly, unable to find anything to refute what he said, although she refused to believe it unless there was inescapable proof.

He kissed her very gently, and she knew he understood what she felt, and shared it. Then he left, and she turned immediately and went upstairs to dress for the day's journey with Emily, Jack and Gracie.

It took all morning to trace the management company, and a mixture of evasions and trickery to elicit from them the name of the solicitors, this time a highly reputable firm in the City which took care of the affairs of the company which actually owned the properties in Lisbon Street, and also several others.

At two o'clock they were all seated in the warm and extremely comfortable offices of Messrs Warburg, Warburg, Boddy and Boddy, awaiting Mr. Boddy Senior's return from an extended luncheon with a client. Grave young clerks perched on stools writing in perfect copperplate script on documents of vellum, which had scarlet seals dangling from them. Errand boys scurried on silent feet, discreet and obedient, and a wrinkled man in a stiff, winged collar kept a careful eye on them, never moving from his wooden chair behind the desk. Gracie, who had never been in an office of any sort before, was fascinated and her eyes followed every movement.

Eventually Mr. Boddy returned, he was silver-haired, smooth-faced, impeccably bland in voice and manner. He disregarded the women and addressed himself solely to Jack. It seemed he had not moved with the times and recognized that women now had a legal entity. To him they were still appendages to a man's property: his pleasure possibly, his responsibility certainly, but not to be informed or consulted.

Charlotte bristled and Emily took a step forward, but Jack's hand stayed her and as a matter of tactics she obeyed. In the last two days she had learned a quite new respect for his ability to read character and to obtain information.

But Mr. Boddy was of an entirely different mettle than those they had dealt with to date. He was smooth, quite certain of his own safety from suit of any kind, and his calm, unctuous face did not flicker when he explained with barely civil condescension that yes, he handled affairs of property and rent for certain clients but he was not at liberty to name them nor give any particulars whatsoever. Yes, most certainly Mrs. Shaw had called upon him with similar questions, and he had been equally unable to answer her. He was profoundly grieved that she should have met so tragic a fate—his eyes remained chill and expressionless—please accept his sincerest condolences, but the facts remained.

This was a murder inquiry, Jack explained. He was acting

on behalf of persons, whom he also was unable to name, and would Mr. Boddy prefer it if the police came and asked these questions?

Mr. Boddy did not take kindly to threats. Was Jack aware that the persons who owned these properties were among the most powerful in the City, and had friends they could call upon, if need be, to protect their interests? Some of these said people had high positions and were able to give, or to withhold, favors, which might make a considerable difference to the agreeability of one's life and the prospect of one's future advancement in profession, finance or society.

Jack raised his eyebrows and asked with very slight surprise if Mr. Boddy was telling him that these people to whom he was referring were so embarrassed by their ownership of the property in question that they were prepared to damage the reputation or interests of anyone who might inquire.

"You must assume whatever you will, Mr. Radley," Boddy replied with a tight smile. "I am not answerable for your situation, I have discharged my duty towards you. Now I have further clients to see. Good day to you."

And with that they were obliged to depart with no more than the company name, which they had already gleaned from the management. No names were given and no principals—the matter was not described in any way, except by the rather amorphous threat.

"Odious little person," Aunt Vespasia replied when they told her. "But what we might have expected. If he were to repeat names to any Tom, Dick and Harry who came to the door, he would not have lasted long as lawyer to the kind of people who own such properties." She had already ordered tea and they were sitting around the fire in her withdrawing room, thawing out from the chill both of the weather outside and of their disappointment at having met, at least for the time being, what seemed to be a dead end. Even Gracie was permitted, on this occasion, to sit with them and to take tea, but she said nothing at all. Instead she stared with huge eyes at the paintings on the walls, the delicate furniture with its satin-smooth surfaces, and when she dared, at Vespasia herself, who was sitting upright, her silver hair coiled immaculately on the crown of her head, great pearl drops in her ears, ecru-colored French lace at her throat and in long ruffles over her thin, tapered hands, bright with diamonds. Gracie had never seen anyone so splendid in all her life, and to be sitting in her house taking tea with her was probably the most memorable thing she would ever do.

"But he did say he'd seen Clemency," Charlotte pointed out. "He didn't make the slightest attempt to conceal it. He was as bold as brass, and twice as smooth. He probably told whoever owns it that she had been there, and what she meant to do. I would dearly like to have hit him as hard as I could."

"Impractical," Emily said, biting her lip. "But so would I, preferably with an exceedingly sharp umbrella point. But how can we find who owns this company? Surely there must be a way?"

"Perhaps Thomas could," Vespasia suggested, frowning slightly. "Commerce is not something with which I have any familiarity. It is at times like these I regret my lack of knowledge of certain aspects of society. Charlotte?"

"I don't know whether he could." She was sharply reminded of the previous evening. "But he doesn't think there is any purpose. He is quite convinced that Dr. Shaw is the intended victim, not Clemency."

"He may well be right," Vespasia conceded. "It does not alter the fact that Clemency was fighting a battle in which we believe intensely, and that since she is dead there is no one else, so far as we know. The abuse is intolerable, for the wretchedness of its victims, and for the abysmal humbug. Nothing irks my temper like hypocrisy. I should like to rip the masks off these sanctimonious faces, for the sheer pleasure of doing it."

"We are with you," Jack said instantly. "I didn't know I had it in me to be so angry, but at the moment I find it hard to think of much else."

A very slight smile touched Vespasia's lips and she regarded him with considerable approval. He seemed unaware of it, but it gave Emily a feeling of warmth that startled her, and she realized how much it mattered to her that Vespasia should think well of him. She found herself smiling back.

Charlotte thought of Pitt still struggling with Shaw's patients, seeking for the one piece of knowledge that was so hideous it had led to two murders, and might lead to more, until Shaw himself was dead. But she still felt it was Clemency that had been meant to die in that first fire, and the second was merely to cover it. The murderer in act might be any one of dozens of arsonists for hire, but the murderer in spirit was whoever owned those fearful, rotting, teeming tenements in Lisbon Street, and was afraid of the public embarrassment Clemency would expose him to when she succeeded in her quest.

"We don't know how to find who owns a company." She set her cup down and stared at Vespasia. "But surely Mr. Carlisle will—or he will know someone else who does. If necessary we must hire someone."

"I will speak to him," Vespasia agreed. "I think he will see that the matter is of some urgency. He may be persuaded to set aside other tasks and pursue this."

And so he did, and the following evening reported to them, again in Vespasia's withdrawing room. He looked startled and a little confused when he was shown in by the footman. His usual wry humor was sharp in his eyes, but there was a smoothness in his face as if surprise had ironed out the customary lines deep around his mouth.

He gave the greetings of courtesy briefly and accepted Vespasia's offer of a seat. They all stared at him, aware that he bore extraordinary news, but they could only guess at its nature.

Vespasia's silver-gray eyes dared him to indulge in histrionics. Words of caution were superfluous.

"You may begin," she informed him.

"The company which owns the buildings is in turn owned by another company." He told the story without embroidery, just the bare details that were required in order for it to make sense, looking from one to another of them, including Gracie, so that she might feel equally involved. "I called upon certain people who owe me favors, or will wish for my goodwill in the future, and managed to learn the names of the holders of stock in this second company. There is only one of them still alive—in fact only one has been alive for several years. Even when the company was formed in 1873, from the remnants of another similar company, and that apparently in the same way from an even earlier one, even in 1873 the other holders of stock were either absent from the country indefinitely or of such age and state of health as to be incapable of active interest."

Vespasia fixed him firmly with her level, penetrating gaze, but he had no guilt of unnecessary drama, and he continued in his own pace.

"This one person who was active and who signed all necessary documents I succeeded in visiting. She is an elderly lady, unmarried, and therefore always mistress of her own property, such as it is, and only acts as go-between, holding shares in name but hardly in any act. Her income is sufficient to keep her in some form of comfort, but certainly not luxury. It was obvious as soon as I was through the door that the bulk of the money, which will amount to several thousands each year, was going somewhere else."

Jack shifted in his chair and Emily drew in her breath expectantly.

"I told her who I was." Carlisle blushed faintly. "She was extremely impressed. The government, especially when expressed as Her Majesty's instrument for ruling her people, and the church, are the two fixed and immutable forces for good in this lady's world."

Charlotte made a leap of imagination. "You are not saying that the person for whom she acts is a member of Parliament, are you?"

Vespasia stiffened.

Emily leaned forward, waiting.

Jack drew in his breath, and Charlotte had her hands clenched in her lap.

Carlisle smiled broadly, showing excellent teeth. "No, but you are almost right. He is—or was—a most distinguished member of the church—in fact, Bishop Augustus Worlingham!"

Emily gasped. Even Vespasia gave a little squeak of amazement.

"What?" Charlotte was incredulous, then she began to laugh a little hysterically, wild, absurd humor welling up inside her, black as the charred ruins of Shaw's house. She could scarcely grasp the horror Clemency must have felt when she came this far. And surely she had? She had found this innocent, befuddled old lady who had funneled the slum rents, the waves of misery and sin, into her own family coffers to make the bishop's house warm and rich, and to buy the roasts and wine she and her sister ate, to clothe them in silk and be waited upon by servants.

No wonder Clemency spent all her inheritance, hundreds of pounds at a time, uncounted, to right his wrongs.

Had Theophilus known? What about Angeline and Celeste? Did they know where the family money came from, even while they sought donations from the people of Highgate to build a stained-glass window to their bishop's memory?

She imagined what Shaw would make of this when he knew. And surely one day he would? It would become public knowledge when Clemency's murderer was tried—then she stopped. But if the owner were Bishop Worlingham—he was long dead, ten years ago—and Theophilus too. The income was Clemency's—and for Prudence, Angeline and Celeste. Would they really murder their sister and niece to protect their family money? Surely Clemency would not have revealed the truth? Would she?

Or would she? Had they had a fearful quarrel and she had told them precisely the cost of their comfort, and that she meant to fight for a law to expose all such men as the bishop to the public obloquy and disgust they deserved?

Yes—it was not inconceivable Celeste at least might kill to prevent that. Her whole life had been used up caring for the bishop. She had denied herself husband and children in order to stay at his side and obey his every command, write out his letters and sermons, look up his references, play the piano for his relaxation, read aloud to him when his eyes were tired, always his gracious and unpaid servant. It was a total sacrifice of her own will, all her choices eaten up in his. She must justify it—he must remain worthy of such a gift, or her life became ridiculous, a thing thrown away for no cause.

Perhaps Pitt was right, and it was close to home, the heart as well as the act in Highgate all the time.

They were all watching her, seeing in her eyes her racing thoughts and in the shadows across her face the plunges from anger to pity to dawning realization.

"Bishop Augustus Worlingham," Somerset Carlisle repeated, letting each syllable fall with full value. "The whole of Lisbon Street was owned, very tortuously and with extreme secrecy, by the 'good' bishop, and when he died, inherited by Theophilus, Celeste and Angeline. I presume he provided for his daughters so generously because they had spent their lives as his servants, and certainly they would have no other means of support and it would be beyond any expectation, reasonable or unreasonable, that they might marry at that point—or would wish to by then. I looked up his will, by the way. Two thirds went to Theophilus, the other third, plus the house, which is worth a great deal of course, to the sisters. That would be more than enough to keep them in better than comfort for the rest of their lives."

"Then Theophilus must have had a fortune," Emily said with surprise.

"He inherited one," Carlisle agreed. "But he lived extremely well, according to what I heard; ate well, had one of the finest cellars in London, and collected paintings, some of which he donated to local museums and other institutions. All the same, he left a very handsome sum indeed to each of his daughters when he died unexpectedly."

"So Clemency had a great deal of money," Vespasia said, almost to herself. "Until she began to give it away. Do we know when that was?" She looked at Jack, then at Carlisle.

"The lawyer would not say when she was there," Jack replied, his lips tightening at remembrance of his frustration and the lawyer's bland, supercilious face.

"Her fight to get some alteration in the disclosure of ownership began about six months ago," Carlisle said somberly.

"And she made her first large donation to a charitable shelter for the poor at about the same time. I would hazard a guess that that is when she discovered her grandfather was the owner she had sought."

"Poor Clemency." Charlotte remembered the sad trail of sick women and children, gaunt and hopeless men which she herself had followed from Shaw's patient list in Highgate, down through worse and worse houses and tenements till she at last found Bessie Jones huddled in one corner of an overcrowded and filthy room. Clemency had followed the same course, seen the same wretched faces, the illness and the resignation. And then she had started upwards towards the owners, as they had done.

"We must not let the fight die with her," Jack said, sitting a little more upright in his chair. "Worlingham may be dead, but there are scores, perhaps hundreds of others. She knew that, and she would have given her life to exposing them—" He stopped. "And I still think she may have died because of it. We were warned specifically that there are powerful people who could make us, if we are discreet and withdraw, or break us if we persist. Obviously Worlingham himself did not kill her, but one of the other owners may well have. They have a great deal to lose—and I don't imagine Clemency paid any heed to threats. There was too much passion in her, and revulsion for her own inheritance. Nothing but death would have stopped her."

"What can we do?" Emily looked at Vespasia, then at Carlisle.

Carlisle's face was very grave and he drew his brows down in thought.

"I'm not sure. The forces against it are very large; they are vested interests, a great deal of money. Lots of powerful families may not be sure where all their income originates. Nor will they be in any haste to embarrass their friends."

"We need a voice in Parliament," Vespasia said with decision. "I know we have one." She glanced at Carlisle. "We need more. We need someone new, who will address this matter in particular. Jack—you are doing nothing whatever but enjoying yourself. Your honeymoon is over. It is time you were useful."

Jack stared at her as if she had risen out of the ground in front of him. Their eyes met, hers steady silver-gray and absolutely unflinching, his dark gray-blue, long-lashed and wide in total incredulity. Then gradually the amazement passed into the beginning of an idea. His hands tightened on the arm of his chair. Still his gaze never left hers, nor did hers waver for a second.

No one else moved or made the tiniest sound. Emily all but held her breath.

"Yes," Jack said at last. "What an excellent idea. Where do I begin?"

CHAPTER
NINE

Charlotte had recounted to Pitt at least the salient points of her experiences searching for the ownership of the buildings in Lisbon Street, and when she made the shattering discovery not only that it was the Worlingham family themselves, but that Clemency had learned it several months before she died, she poured it all out to him the moment she arrived home. She saw his coat in the hall and without even taking off her hat she raced down the corridor to the kitchen.

"Thomas. Thomas—Lisbon Street was owned by Bishop Worlingham himself! Now the family takes all the rents. Clemency discovered it. She knew!"

"What?" He stared at her, half turned in his seat, his eyes wide.

"Bishop Worlingham owned Lisbon Street," she said again. "All those slums and gin houses were his! Now they belong to the rest of the family—and Clemency discovered it. That's why she felt so awful." She sat down in a heap in the chair opposite him, skirts awry, and leaned across the table towards him. "That's probably why she worked so hard at undoing it all. Just think how she must have felt." She closed her eyes and put her head in her hands, elbows on the table. "Oh!"

"Poor Clemency," Pitt said very quietly. "What a very remarkable woman. I wish I could have known her."

"So do I," Charlotte agreed through her fingers. "Why do we so often get to know about people only when it's too late?"

It was a question to which she expected no answer. They both knew that they would have had no occasion to know of Clemency Shaw had she not been murdered, and it required no words to convey their understanding.

It was another half hour before she even remembered to tell him that Jack was seriously considering standing for Parliament.

"Really?" His voice rose in surprise and he looked at her carefully to make sure she was not making some obscure joke.

"Oh yes—I think it's excellent. He ought to do something or they'll both be bored to pieces." She grinned. "We cannot meddle in all your cases."

He let out a snort and refrained from comment. But there was a sense of deep comfort in him, experiences and emotions shared, horror, exultation, pity, anger, at times fear, all the multitude of feelings that are roused by terrible events, common purpose, and the unique bond that comes of sharing.

Consequently, when he joined Murdo at the Highgate Police Station the next day there were several things he had to tell him, most of which only added to Murdo's growing anxiety about Flora Lutterworth. He thought of their few brief and rather stilted conversations, the hot silences, the clumsiness he felt standing there in her magnificent house, his boots shining like huge wedges of coal, his uniform buttons so obviously marking him out as a policeman, an intruder of the most unwelcome sort. And always her face came back burning across his mind, wide-eyed, fair-skinned with that wonderful color in her cheeks, so proud and full of courage. Surely she must be one of the most beautiful women he could ever see? But there was far more than beauty to her; there was spirit and gentleness. She was so very alive, it was as if she could smell winds and flowers he only imagined, see beyond his everyday horizons into a brighter, more important world, hear melodies of which he only knew the beat.

And yet he also knew she was afraid. He longed to protect her, and was agonizingly aware than he could not. He did not understand the nature of what threatened her, only that it was connected with Clemency Shaw's death, and now with Lindsay's as well.

And with a part of him he refused even to listen to, in spite of its still, cold voice in his brain, he was also aware that her role in it might not be entirely innocent. He would not even think that she was personally involved, perhaps actually to blame. But he had heard the rumors, seen the looks and blushes and the secrecy; he knew there was a special relationship between Flora and Stephen Shaw, one so definite that her father was furious about it, yet she felt it so precious to her she was prepared to brave his anger and defy him.

Murdo was confused. He had never felt jealousy of this muddled nature before, at once so sure she had done nothing shameful, and yet unable to deny to himself that there was a real and deep emotion inside her towards Shaw.

And of course the alternative fear was large; perhaps it was its very size which blocked out the other even more hideous thought—that Alfred Lutterworth was responsible for the attempts on Shaw's life. There were two possible reasons for this, both quite believable, and both ruinous.

The one he refused to think was that Shaw had dishonored Flora, or even knew of some fearful shame in her life, perhaps an illegitimate child, or worse, an abortion; and Lutterworth had tried to kill him when somehow he had learned of it—to keep him silent. He could hardly hope for a fine marriage for her if such a thing were known—in fact no marriage at all would be possible. She would grow old alone, rich, excluded, whispered about and forever an object of pity or contempt.

At the thought of it Murdo was ready to kill Shaw himself. His fists were clenched so tight his nails, short as they were, bit into the flesh of his palms. That thought must be cast out, obliterated from his mind. What betrayal that he would let it enter—even for an instant.

He hated himself even for having thought it. Shaw was pestering her; she was young and very lovely. He lusted after her, and she was too innocent to see how vile he was. That was far more like it. And of course there was her father's money. Shaw had already spent all his wife's money—and there was extraordinary evidence for that. Inspector Pitt had found out just yesterday that Clemency Shaw's money was all gone. Yes—that made perfect sense—Shaw was after Flora's money!

And Alfred Lutterworth had a great deal of money. That thought was also wretched. Murdo was a constable, and likely to remain so for a long time; he was only twenty-four. He earned enough to keep himself in something like decency, he ate three times a day and had a pleasant room and clean clothes, but it was as far from the splendor of Alfred Lutterworth's house as Lutterworth's was in turn from what Murdo imagined of the Queen's castle at Windsor. And Lutterworth might as well cast eyes upon one of the princesses as Murdo upon Flora.

It was with a finality of despair that he forced the last thought, the one prompted by Inspector Pitt's wife's discovery of the ownership of some of the worst slum tenements by old Bishop Worlingham. Murdo was not so very amazed. He had long known that some outwardly respectable people could have very ugly secrets, especially where money was concerned. But what Pitt had not mentioned was that if Mrs. Shaw, poor lady, had discovered who owned those particular houses, she might also have discovered who owned several others. Pitt had mentioned members of Parliament, titled families, even justices of the courts. Had he not also thought of retired industrialists who wanted to enter society and needed a good continuing income, and might not be too particular as to where their money was invested?

Alfred Lutterworth might well have been in every bit as much danger from Clemency Shaw as the Worlinghams were— in fact more. Clemency might protect her own—it appeared she had. But why should she protect Lutterworth? He had every reason to kill her—and if Lindsay had guessed this, to kill him too.

That is, if he owned slum property too. And how could they ever find that out? They could hardly trace the ownership of every piece of rotten plaster and sagging timber in London, every blind alley, open drain and crumbling pile of masonry, every wretched home of cold and frightened people. He knew because he had tried. He blushed hot at the memory of it; it was a kind of betrayal that he had let the thought take root in his mind and had asked questions about Lutterworth's finances, the source of his income and if it could involve rents. But it was not as easy as he had imagined. Money came from companies, but what did those companies do? Time had been short, and he had no official instructions to give his questions the force of law.

Nothing had been resolved; he was simply uncertain and appallingly conscious of his guilt. Nothing he could even imagine doing would remove the ache of fear and imagination at the back of his mind.

He saw Flora's face in his heart's eye and all the pain and the shame she would feel burned through him till he could hardly bear it. He was even glad to hear Pitt's footsteps return and to be told their duty for the morning. Part of him was still outraged that they sent an outsider—did they think Highgate's own men were incompetent? And part of him was immensely grateful that the responsibility was not theirs. This was a very ugly case, and the resolution seemed as far off now as it had when they were standing in the wet street staring at the smoldering remains of Shaw's house, long before the taper was struck to set Lindsay's alight.

"Yes sir?" he said automatically as Pitt came around the corner and into the foyer where he was standing. "Where to, sir?"

"Mr. Alfred Lutterworth's, I think," Pitt barely hesitated on his way out. He had been to the local superintendent, as a matter of courtesy, and on the small chance that something had occurred that Murdo did not know about, some thread worth following.

But the superintendent had looked at him with his habitual disfavor and reported with some satisfaction another fire, in Kentish town, a possible lead on the arsonist he personally was sure was the guilty party in all cases, and rather a negative report on house insurance and the unlikelihood of either Shaw or Lindsay being involved in fire for the purposes of fraud.

"Well I hardly imagined Lindsay burned himself to death to claim the insurance!" Pitt had snapped back.

"No sir," the superintendent had said coldly, his eyes wide.

"Neither did we. But then we are confident the fires were all set by the arsonist in Kentish Town—sir."

"Indeed." Pitt had been noncommittal. "Odd there were only two houses that were occupied."

"Well he didn't know Shaw's was—did he?" the superintendent had said irritably. "Shaw was out, and everyone thought Mrs. Shaw was too. She only canceled at the last minute."

"The only people who thought Mrs. Shaw was out were the people who knew her," Pitt had said with satisfaction.

The superintendent had glared at him and returned to his desk, leaving Pitt to go out of the door in silence.

Now he was ready to go and probe and watch and listen to people, where his true art lay. He had days ago given up expecting things to tell him anything. Murdo's heart sank, but there was no escaping duty. He followed Pitt and caught up with him, and together they walked along the damp, leaf-scattered footpath towards the Lutterworths' house.

They were admitted by the maid and shown into the morning room, where there was a brisk fire burning and a bowl of tawny chrysanthemums on the heavy Tudor dresser. Neither of them sat, although it was nearly quarter of an hour before Lutterworth appeared, closely followed by Flora, dressed in a dark blue stuff gown and looking pale but composed. She glanced at Murdo only once, and her eyes flickered away immediately, a faint, self-conscious flush on her cheeks.

Murdo remained in a bitterly painful silence. He longed to help her; he wanted to hit out at someone—Shaw, Lutterworth for allowing all this to happen and not protecting her, and Pitt for forging blindly ahead with his duty, regardless of the chaos it caused.

For an instant he hated Pitt for not hurting as much as he did, as if he were oblivious of pain; then he looked sideways for just a moment at him, and realized his error. Pitt's face was tense; there were shadows under his eyes and the fine lines in his skin were all weary and conscious of realms of suffering past and to come, and of his inability to heal it.

Murdo let out his breath in a sigh, and kept silent.

Lutterworth faced them across the expensive Turkish carpet. None of them sat.

"Well, what is it now?" he demanded. "I know nowt I 'aven't told you. I've no idea why anyone killed poor old Lindsay, unless it was Shaw, because the old man saw through 'im and 'ad to be silenced. Or it were that daft Pascoe, because 'e thought as Lindsay were an anarchist.

"Take that 'orse." He pointed to a fine figurine on the mantel shelf. "Bought that wi' me first big year's profit, when the mill started to do well. Got a fine consignment o' cloth and sold it ourselves—in the Cape. Turned a pretty penny, did that. Got the 'orse to remind me o' me early days when me and Ellen, that's Flora's mother"—he took a deep breath and let it out slowly to give himself time to regain his composure—"when me and Ellen went courtin'. Didn't 'ave no carriage. We used to ride an 'orse like that—'er up in front o' me, an me be'ind wi' me arms 'round 'er. Them was good days. Every time I look at that 'orse I think o' them—like I could still see the sunlight through the trees on the dry earth and smell the 'orse's warm body and the 'ay in the wind, an' see the blossom in the 'edges like fallen snow, sweet as 'oney, and my Ellen's 'air brighter'n a peeled chestnut—an' 'ear 'er laugh."

He stood motionless, enveloped in the past. No one wanted to be the first to invade with the ugliness and immediacy of the present.

It was Pitt who broke the spell, and with words Murdo had not foreseen.

"What past do you think Mr. Lindsay recalled in his African artifacts, Mr. Lutterworth?"

"I don't know." Lutterworth smiled ruefully. " 'Is wife, mebbe. That's what most men remember."

"His wife!" Pitt was startled. "I didn't know Lindsay was married."

"No—well, no reason why you should." Lutterworth looked faintly sorry. " 'E didn't tell everyone. She died a long time ago—twenty years or more. Reckon as that's why 'e came 'ome. Not that 'e said so, mind."

"Were there any children?"

"Several, I think."

"Where are they? They've not come forward. His will didn't mention any."

"It wouldn't. They're in Africa."

"That wouldn't stop them inheriting."

"What—an 'ouse in 'Ighgate and a few books and mementos of Africa!" Lutterworth was smiling at some deep inner satisfaction.

"Why not?" Pitt demanded. "There were a great many books, some on anthropology must be worth a great deal."

"Not to them." Lutterworth's lips smiled grimly.

"Why not? And there's the house!"

"Not much use to a black man who lives in a jungle." Lutterworth looked at Pitt with dour satisfaction, savoring the surprise on his face. "That's it—Lindsay's wife was African, beautiful woman, black as your 'at. I saw a picture of 'er once. He showed me. I was talking about my Ellen, an' 'e showed me. Never saw a gentler face in me life. Couldn't pronounce 'er name, even when 'e said it slow, but 'e told me it meant some kind o' river bird."

"Did anyone else know about her?"

"No idea. He may have told Shaw. I suppose you 'aven't arrested him yet?"

"Papa!" Flora spoke for the first time, a cry of protest torn out in spite of herself.

"An' I'll not 'ave a word about it from you, my girl," Lutterworth said fiercely. " 'E's done enough damage to you already. Your name's a byword 'round 'ere, runnin' after 'im like a lovesick parlormaid."

Flora blushed scarlet and fumbled for words to defend herself, and found none.

Murdo was in an agony of impotence. Had Lutterworth glanced at him he would have been startled by the fury in his eyes, but he was occupied with the irresponsibility he saw in his daughter.

"Well what do you want wi' me?" he snapped at Pitt. "Not to hear about Amos Lindsay's dead wife—poor devil."

"No," Pitt agreed. "Actually I came to ask you about what properties you own in the city."

"What?" Lutterworth was so utterly taken aback it was hard not to believe he was as startled as he seemed. "What in heaven's name are you talking about, man? What property?"

"Housing, to be exact." Pitt was watching him closely, but even Murdo who cared more intensely about this case than about anything else he could remember, did not see a flicker of fear or comprehension in Lutterworth's face.

"I own this 'ouse, lock, stock and barrel, and the ground it stands on." Lutterworth unconsciously stiffened a fraction and pulled his shoulders straighter. "And I own a couple o' rows o' terraced 'ouses outside o' Manchester. Built 'em for my workers, I did. And good 'ouses they are, solid as the earth beneath 'em. Don't let water, chimneys don't smoke, privies in every back garden, an' a standpipe to every one of 'em. Can't say fairer than that."

"And that's all the property you own, Mr. Lutterworth?" Pitt's voice was lighter, a thread of relief in it already. "Could you prove that?"

"I could if I were minded to." Lutterworth was eyeing him curiously, his hands pushed deep into his pockets. "But why should I?"

"Because the cause of Mrs. Shaw's murder, and Mr. Lindsay's, may lie in the ownership of property in London," Pitt replied, glancing for less than a second at Flora, and away again.

"Balderdash!" Lutterworth said briskly. "If you ask me, Shaw killed 'is wife so 'e could be free to come after my Flora, and then 'e killed Lindsay because Lindsay knew what 'e was up to. Give 'imself away somehow—bragging, I shouldn't wonder, and went too far. Well 'e'll damn well not marry Flora—for my money, or anything else. I won't let 'er—and 'e'll not wait till I'm gone for 'er, I'll be bound."

"Papa!" Flora would not be hushed anymore, by discretion or filial duty or even the embarrassment which flamed scarlet up her cheeks now. "You are saying wicked things which are quite untrue."

"I'll not have argument." He rounded on her, his own color

high. "Can you tell me you haven't been seeing 'im, sneaking in and out of his house when you thought no one was looking?"

She was on the verge of tears and Murdo tensed as if to step forward, but Pitt shot him a stony glare, his face tight.

Murdo longed to save her so desperately his body ached with the fierceness of his effort to control himself, but he had no idea what to say or do. It all had a dreadful inevitability, like a stone that has already started falling and must complete its journey.

"It was not illicit." She chose her words carefully, doing her best to ignore Pitt and Murdo standing like intrusive furniture in the room, and all her attention was focused on her father. "It was . . . was just—private."

Lutterworth's face was distorted with pain as well as fury. She was the one person left in the world he loved, and she had betrayed herself, and so wounded him where he could not bear it.

"Secret!" he shouted, pounding his fist on the back of the armchair beside him. "Decent women don't creep in the back door o' men's houses to see them in secret. Was Mrs. Shaw there? Was she? And don't lie to me, girl. Was she in the room with you—all the time?"

Flora's voice was a whisper, so strained it was barely heard. "No."

"O' course she wasn't!" He threw out the words in a mixture of anguish because they were true and a desperate kind of triumph that at least she had not lied. "I know that. I know she'd gone out because half Highgate knows it. But I'll tell you this, my girl—I don't care what Highgate says, or all London society either—they can call you anything they can lay their tongues to. I'll not let you marry Shaw—and that's final."

"I don't want to marry him!" The tears were running down her face now. Her hand flew to her mouth and she bit her teeth on her finger as if the physical pain relieved her distress. "He's my doctor!"

"He's my doctor too." Lutterworth had not yet understood the change in her. "I don't go creeping in at the back door after him. I go to him openly, like an honest man."

"You don't have the same complaint as I do." Her voice was choked with tears and she refused to look at any of them, least of all Murdo. "He allowed me to go whenever I was in pain—and he—"

"Pain?" Lutterworth was horrified, all his anger drained away, leaving him pale and frightened. "What sort of pain? What's wrong with you?" Already he moved towards her as if she were about to collapse. "Flora? Flora, what is it? We'll get the best doctors in England. Why didn't you tell me, girl?"

She turned away from him, hunching her shoulders. "It's not an illness. It's just—please let me be! Leave me a little decency. Do I have to detail my most private discomforts in front of policemen?"

Lutterworth had forgotten Pitt and Murdo. Now he swung around, ready to attack them for their crassness, then only just in time remembered that it was he who had demanded the explanation of her, not they.

"I have no property in London, Mr. Pitt, and if you want me to prove it to you I daresay I can." His face set hard and he balanced squarely on his feet. "My finances are open to you whenever you care to look at them. My daughter has nothing to tell you about her relationship with her doctor. It is a perfectly correct matter, but it is private, and is privileged to remain so. It is only decent." He met Pitt's eyes defiantly. "I am sure you would not wish your wife's medical condition to be the subject of other men's conversation. I know nothing further with which I can help you. I wish you good day." And he stepped over and rang the bell to have the maid show them out.

Pitt dispatched Murdo to question Shaw's previous servants again. The butler was recovering slowly and so was able to speak more lucidly. He might recall some details which he had been too shocked and in too much pain to think of before. Also Lindsay's manservant might be more forthcoming on a second or third attempt. Pitt most especially wanted to know what the man knew of Lindsay's last two days before the fire. Something, a word or an act, must have precipitated it. All the pieces gathered from one place and another might point to an answer.

Pitt himself returned to the boardinghouse, where he intended to wait for Shaw as long as might be necessary, and question the man until he learned some answers, however long that took, and however brutal it required him to be.

The landlady was getting used to people coming to the door and asking for Dr. Shaw, and to several of them requesting to sit in the parlor and wait for him to return. She treated Pitt with sympathy, having forgotten who he was, and regarding him as one of the doctor's patients, in need of a gentle word and a hot cup of tea.

He accepted both with a slight twinge of conscience, and warmed himself in front of the fire for twenty minutes until Shaw came in in a whirl of activity, setting his bag down on the chair by the desk, his stick up against the wall, having forgotten to put it in the hall stand, his hat on top of the desk and his coat where the landlady was waiting to take it from him. She picked up the rest of his apparel, scarf, gloves, hat and stick, and took them all out as if it were her custom and her pleasure. It seemed she had already developed a certain fondness for him even in these few days.

Shaw faced Pitt with some surprise, a guardedness in his eyes, but no dislike.

" 'Morning Pitt, what is it now? Have you discovered something?" He stood near the center of the room, hands in his pockets, and yet giving the appearance of being so balanced on his feet that he was ready for some intense action, only waiting to know what it might be. "Well, what is it, man? What have you learned?"

Pitt wished he had something to tell him, for Shaw's own sake, and because he felt so inadequate that he still had almost no idea who had started the fires or why, or even beyond question whether it was Shaw who was the intended victim or Clemency. He had begun by being sure it was Shaw; now with Charlotte's conviction that it was Clemency's activities to expose slum profiteers which had provoked it, his own certainty was shaken. But there was no point in lying; it was shabby and they both deserved better.

"I'm afraid I don't know anything further." He saw Shaw's face tighten and a keenness die from his eyes. "I'm sorry," he added unhappily. "The forensic evidence tells me nothing except that the fire was started in four separate places in your house and three in Mr. Lindsay's, with some kind of fuel oil, probably ordinary lamp oil, poured onto the curtains in the downstairs rooms where it would catch quickly, climb upwards taking the whole window embrasure, and then any wooden furniture."

Shaw frowned. "How did they get in? We'd have heard breaking glass. And I certainly didn't leave any downstairs windows open."

"It isn't very difficult to cut glass," Pitt pointed out. "You can do it silently if you stick a piece of paper over it with a little glue. In the criminal fraternity they call it 'star glazing.' Of course they use it to reach in and undo the catch rather than to pour in oil and drop a taper."

"You think it was an ordinary thief turned assassin?" Shaw's brows rose in incredulity. "Why, for heaven's sake? It doesn't make any sense!" There was disappointment in his face, primarily in Pitt for having thought of nothing better than this.

Pitt was stung. Even though Shaw might be the murderer himself, and he hated to acknowledge that thought, he still respected the man and wanted his good opinion in return.

"I don't think it was an ordinary thief at all," he said quickly. "I am simply saying that there is a very ordinary method of cutting glass without making a noise. Unfortunately, in the mass of shattered glass, bricks, rubble and timbers around it was impossible to say whether that was done or not. Everything was trodden on by the firemen or broken by falling masonry. If there was any cut glass rather than broken it was long since destroyed. Not that it would have told us anything, except that he came prepared in skills as well as materials—which is fairly obvious anyway."

"So?" Shaw stared at him across the expanse of the worn, homely carpet and the comfortable chairs. "If you know nothing more, what are you here for? You haven't come simply to tell me that."

Pitt kept his temper with an effort and tried to order his thoughts.

"Something precipitated the fire in Amos Lindsay's house," he began levelly, fixing his eyes on Shaw's, at the same time sitting down in one of the big easy chairs, letting Shaw know that he intended the discussion to be a long and detailed one. "You were staying with him for the few days preceding; whatever happened you may have noticed, something which you could now recall, if you tried."

The skepticism vanished out of Shaw's face and was replaced by thought, which quickly deepened into concentration. He sat down in the opposite chair and crossed his legs, regarding Pitt through narrowed eyes.

"You think it was Lindsay they meant to kill?" A flicker of emotion crossed his face with peculiar pain, half hope and a release from guilt, half a new darkness of unknown violence and forces not guessed at yet. "Not me?"

"I don't know." Pitt pulled his mouth into a grimace that had been intended as a wry smile but died before humor touched it. "There are several possibilities." He took the wild risk of being honest. It crossed his mind to wonder what good an attempt at deception would do anyway. Shaw was neither gullible nor innocent enough to be taken in. "Possibly the first fire was meant for Mrs. Shaw, and the second was because either you or Lindsay had discovered who it was—or they feared you had—"

"I certainly haven't!" Shaw interrupted. "If I had I'd have told you. For heaven's sake, man, what do you— Oh!" His whole body sagged in the chair. "Of course—you have to suspect me. You'd be incompetent not to." He said it as if he could not believe it himself, as if he were repeating a rather bad joke. "But why should I kill poor Amos? He was about the best friend I had." Suddenly his voice faltered and he looked away to hide the emotion that filled his face. If he was acting, he was superb. But Pitt had known men before who killed someone they loved to save their own lives. He could not afford to spare Shaw the only answer that made sense.

"Because during the time you stayed with him you said or did something that betrayed yourself to him," he replied. "And when you knew that he understood, you had to kill him because you could not trust him to keep silent—not forever, when it meant the noose for you."

Shaw opened his mouth to protest, then the color drained from his skin as he realized how terribly rational it was. He could not sweep it away as preposterous, and the words fled before he began.

"Or the other possibilities," Pitt continued, "are that you said something which led him to learn, or deduce, who it was—without his mentioning it to you. That person became aware that Lindsay knew—perhaps he made further inquiries, or even faced them with it—and to preserve themselves, they killed him."

"What? For heaven's sake." Shaw sat upright, staring at Pitt. "If I had said anything at all that threw any light on it, he would have said so to me at the time, and then we should have reported it to you."

"Would you." Pitt said it with such heavy doubt that it was not a question. "Even if it concerned one of your patients? Or someone you had thought to be a close friend—or even family?" He did not need to add that Shaw was related in one degree or another to all the Worlinghams.

Shaw shifted his position in the chair, his strong, neat hands lying on the arms. Neither of them spoke, but remained staring at each other. Past conversations were recalled like living entities between them: Pitt's struggle to get Shaw to reveal any medical knowledge that might point to motive; Shaw's steady and unswerving refusal.

Finally Shaw spoke slowly, his voice soft and very carefully controlled.

"Do you think I could have told Amos anything I would not tell you?"

"I doubt you would tell him anything you considered a confidence," Pitt answered frankly. "But you could have spoken to him far more than to me, you were a guest in his house, and you were friends." He saw the pain flash across Shaw's face again and found it hard to imagine it was not real. But emotions are very complex, and sometimes survival can cut across others that are very deep, the wrenching of which never ceases to hurt. "In ordinary speech, a word dropped in passing in the course of your day, an expression of success over a patient recovered, or relapsed, and then at another time mention of where you had been—any number of things, which added together gave him some insight. Perhaps it was not total, merely something he wanted to pursue—and in doing so forewarned the murderer that he knew."

Shaw shivered and a spasm of distaste crossed his features.

"I think I liked Amos Lindsay as much as any man alive," he said very quietly. "If I knew who had burned him to death, I should expose them to every punishment the law allows." He looked away, as if to conceal the tenderness in his face. "He was a good man; wise, patient, honest not only with others but with himself, which is far rarer, generous in his means and his judgments. I never heard him make a hasty or ill-natured assessment of another man. And there wasn't a shred of hypocrisy in him."

He looked back at Pitt, his eyes direct and urgent. "He hated cant, and wasn't afraid to show it for what it was. Dear God, how I'm going to miss him. He was the only man around here I could talk to for hours on end about any subject under the sun—new ideas in medicine, old ideas in art, political theory, social order and change." He smiled suddenly, a luminous expression full of joy as fragile as sunlight. "A good wine or cheese, a beautiful woman, the opera, even a good horse—other religions, other people's customs—and not be afraid to say exactly what I thought."

He slid down a little in his chair and put his hands together, fingertips to fingertips. "Couldn't do that with anyone else here. Clitheridge is such a complete fool he can't express an opinion on anything." He let his breath out in a snort. "He's terrified of offending. Josiah has opinions on everything, mostly old Bishop Worlingham's. He wanted to take the cloth, you know." He looked at Pitt quizzically, to see what he made of the idea, whether he understood. "Studied under the old bastard, took everything he said as holy writ, adopted his entire philosophy, like a suit of clothes ready-made. I must say it fitted him to the quarter inch." He pulled a face. "But he was the only son, and his father had a flourishing business and he demanded poor Josiah take it over when he fell ill. The mother and sisters were dependent; there was nothing else he could do."

He sighed, still watching Pitt. "But he never lost the passion for the church. When he dies his ghost will come back to haunt us dressed in miter and robes, or perhaps a Dominican habit. He considers all argument heresy.

"Pascoe's a nice enough old fossil, but his ideas are wrapped in the romance of the Middle Ages, or more accurately the age of King Arthur, Lancelot, the Song of Roland, and other beautiful but unlikely epics. Dalgetty's full of ideas, but such a crusader for liberality of thought I find myself taking the opposing view simply to bring him back to some sort of moderation. Maude has more sense. Have you met her? Excellent woman." His mouth twitched at the corners as if at last he had found something that truly pleased him, something without shadow. "She used to be an artist's model, you know—in her youth. Magnificent body, and not coy about it. That was all before she met Dalgetty and became respectable—which I think her soul always was. But she's never lost her sense of proportion or humor, or turned her nose up at her old friends. She still goes back to Mile End now and again, taking them gifts."

Pitt was stunned, not only at the fact, but that Shaw should know, and now be telling him.

Shaw was watching him, laughing inwardly at the surprise in his face.

"Does Dalgetty know?" Pitt asked after a moment or two.

"Oh certainly. And he doesn't care in the slightest, to his eternal credit. Of course he couldn't spread it around, for her sake. She very much wants to be the respectable woman she appears. And if Highgate society knew they'd crucify her. Which would be their loss. She's worth any ten of them. Funnily enough, Josiah, for all his narrow limits, knows that. He admires her as if she were a plaster saint. Some part of his judgment must be good after all."

"And how did you find out about her modeling?" Pitt asked, his mind scrambling after explanations, trying to fit this new piece in to make sense of all the rest, and failing. Was it conceivable Dalgetty had tried to kill Shaw to keep this secret? He hardly seemed like a man who cared so desperately for social status—he did enough to jeopardize it quite deliberately with his liberal reviews. And yet that was fashionable in certain literary quarters—not the same thing as posing naked for young men to paint, and all the world to see. Could he love his wife so much he would murder to keep the respectability she enjoyed?

"By accident." Shaw was watching him with bright, amused eyes. "I was making a medical call on an artist on hard times, and he tried to pay me with a painting of Maude. I didn't take it, but I would like to have. Apart from the irony of it, it was damned good—but someone would have seen it. My heaven, she was a handsome woman. Still is, for that matter."

"Does Dalgetty know that you know this?" Pitt was curious whether he would believe the answer, either way.

"I've no idea," Shaw replied with apparent candor. "Maude does—I told her."

"And was she distressed?"

"A trifle embarrassed at first; then she saw the humor of it, and knew that I'd not tell anyone."

"You told me," Pitt pointed out.

"You are hardly Highgate society." Shaw was equally blunt, but there was no cruelty in his face. Highgate society was not something he admired, nor did he consider exclusion from it to be any disadvantage. "And I judge you not to be a man who would ruin her reputation for no reason but malice—or a loose tongue."

Pitt smiled in spite of himself. "Thank you, Doctor," he said with undisguised irony. "Now if you would turn your attention to the few days you were staying at Mr. Lindsay's house, especially the last forty-eight hours before the fire. Can you remember any conversations you had with him about the first fire, about Mrs. Shaw, or about anyone who could possibly be connected with a reason to kill her, or you?"

Shaw pulled a bleak face and the humor died from his eyes.

"That covers just about everyone, since I haven't any idea why anyone should hate me enough to burn me to death. Of course I've quarreled with people now and again—who hasn't? But no sane person bears grudges over a difference of opinion."

"I don't mean a general philosophy, Doctor." Pitt held him to the point. The answer might lie in his memory. Something had triggered in a murderer's mind the need to protect himself— or herself—so violently that the person had risked exposure by killing again. "Recall which patients you saw those last few days; you must have notes if you can't remember. What times did you come and go, when did you eat? What did you say to each other at table? Think!"

Shaw slumped in his chair and his face became lost in an effort of concentration. Pitt did not interrupt or prompt him.

"I remember Clitheridge came on the Thursday," Shaw said at last. "Early in the evening, just as we were about to dine. I had been out to see a man with stones. He was in great pain. I knew they would pass in time, but I wished there was more I could do to ease him. I came home very tired—the last thing I wanted was a lot of platitudes from the vicar. I'm afraid I was rude to him. He intends well, but he never gets to the point; he goes 'round and 'round things without saying what he means. I've begun to wonder if he really does mean anything, or if he thinks in the same idiotic homilies he speaks. Perhaps he's empty, and there's no one inside?" He sniffed. "Poor Lally."

Pitt allowed him to resume in his own time.

"Amos was civil to him." Shaw continued after a moment. "I suppose he picked up my errors and omissions rather often, especially in the last few weeks." Again the deep pain suffused his face, and Pitt felt like an intruder sitting so close to him. Shaw drew a deep breath. "Clitheridge went off as soon as he had satisfied his duty. I don't remember that we talked about anything in particular. I wasn't really listening. But I do remember the next day, the day before the fire, that both Pascoe and Dalgetty called, because Amos told me about it over dinner. It was about that damn monograph, of course. Dalgetty wanted him to do another, longer one on the new social order, all wrapped 'round in the essential message that freedom to explore the mind is the most sacred thing of all, and knowledge itself is the holiest thing, and every man's God-given right." He leaned forward a little again, his eyes searching Pitt's face, trying to deduce his reaction. Apparently he saw nothing but interest, and continued more quietly.

"Of course Pascoe told him he was irresponsible, that he was undermining the fabric of Christianity and feeding dangerous and frightening ideas to people who did not want them and would not know what to do with them. He seemed to have got the idea that Amos was propagating seeds of revolution and anarchy. Which had an element of truth. I think Dalgetty was interested in the Fabian Society and its ideas on public owner-ship of the means of production, and more or less equal remu-neration for all work"—he laughed sharply—"with the exception of unique minds, of course—by which I gather they mean phi-losophers and artists."

Pitt was compelled to smile as well. "Was Lindsay interested in such ideas?" he asked.

"Interested, yes—in agreement, I doubt. But he did approve of their beliefs in appropriation of capital wealth that perpetuates the extreme differences between the propertied classes and the workers."

"Did he quarrel with Pascoe?" It seemed a remote motive, but he could not leave it unmentioned.

"Yes—but I think it was more flash than heat. Pascoe is a born crusader; he's always tilting at something—mostly wind-mills. If it hadn't been poor Amos, it would have been someone else."

The faint flicker of motive receded. "Were there any other callers, so far as you know?"

"Only Oliphant, the curate. He came to see me. He made it seem like a general call out of concern for my welfare, and I expect it was. He's a decent chap; I find myself liking him more each time I see him. Never really noticed him before this, but most of the parishioners speak well of him."

" 'He made it seem,' " Pitt prompted.

"Oh—well, he asked several questions about Clemency and her charity work on slum ownership. He wanted to know if she'd said anything to me about what she'd accomplished. Well of course she did. Not every day, just now and again. Actually she managed very little. There are some extremely powerful people who own most of the worst—and most profitable—streets. Financiers, industrialists, members of society, old families—"

"Did she mention any to you that you might have repeated to Oliphant, and thus Lindsay?" Pitt jumped at the thought, slender as it was, and Charlotte's face came to his mind, eyes bright, chin determined as she set out to trace Clemency's steps.

Shaw smiled bleakly. "I honestly don't remember, I'm sorry. I wasn't paying much attention. I tried to be civil because he was so earnest and he obviously cared, but I thought he was wasting his time—and mine." He drew his brows together. "Do you really think Clemency was actually a threat to someone? She hadn't a dog in hell's chance of getting a law passed to disclose who profited out of slum tenements, you know. The worst she could have done would be to get herself sued for slander by some outraged industrialist—"

"Which you would not have liked," Pitt pointed out quietly. "It would have cost you all you possess, including your reputation, and presumably your livelihood."

Shaw laughed harshly. "Touché, Inspector. That may look like a perfect motive for me—but if you think she'd have done that, and left me exposed, you didn't know Clem. She wasn't a foolish woman and she understood money and reputation." His eyes were bright with a sad humor close to tears. "Far better than anyone will know now. You won't understand how much I miss her—and why should I try to explain? I stopped being in love with her long ago—but I think I liked Clem better than anyone else I've ever known—even Amos. She and Maude were good friends. She knew all about the modeling—and didn't give a damn." He stood up slowly, as if his body ached.

"I'm sorry, Pitt. I have no idea who killed Clem—or Amos, but if I did I should tell you immediately—in the middle of the night, if that's when it occurred to me. Now get out of here and go and dig somewhere else. I've got to eat something, and then go out on more calls. The sick can't wait."

———

The following morning Pitt was disturbed by a loud banging on his front door so urgent he dropped his toast and marmalade and swung up from the kitchen chair and along the hallway in half a dozen strides. In his mind the horror of fire was already gaping at him, nightmarish, and he had a sick premonition that this time it would be the lodging house, and the gentle curate, who found the right words to touch grief, would be in the ashes. It hurt him almost intolerably.

He yanked the door open and saw Murdo standing on the step, damp and miserable in the predawn light. The gas lamp a little beyond him to the left gave him the remnants of a halo in the mist.

"I'm sorry sir, but I thought I should tell you—just in case it has to do with it—sir," he said wretchedly. His words were unexplained, but apparently made sense to him.

"What are you talking about?" Pitt demanded, beginning to hope it was not fire after all.

"The fight, sir." Murdo shifted from one foot to the other, patently wishing he had not come. What had begun as a good idea now seemed a very bad one. "Mr. Pascoe and Mr. Dalgetty. Mrs. Dalgetty told the station sergeant last night, but I only just learned of it half an hour ago. Seems they didn't take it serious—"

"What fight?" Pitt pulled his coat off the hook by the door. "If they fought last night couldn't it have waited till after breakfast?" He scowled. "What do you mean, fight? Did they hurt each other?" He found the idea absurd and faintly amusing. "Does it really matter? They are always quarreling—it seems to be part of their way of life. It seems to give them a kind of validity."

"No sir." Murdo looked even more miserable. "They're planning to fight this morning—at dawn, sir."

"Don't be ridiculous!" Pitt snapped. "Who on earth is going to get out of a warm bed at dawn and plan to have a quarrel? Somebody's having a very ill considered joke at your expense." He turned to hang up his coat again.

"No sir," Murdo said stolidly. "They already had the quarrel, yesterday. The fight is this morning at sunrise—in the field between Highgate Road and the cemetery—with swords."

Pitt grasped for one more wild instant at the concept of a joke, saw in Murdo's face that it was not, and lost his temper.

"Hell's teeth!" he said furiously. "We've got two houses in ruins, charred bodies of two brave, kind people—others injured and terrified—and two bloody idiots want to fight a duel over some damnable piece of paper." He snatched the coat back again and pushed Murdo off the step onto the pavement, slamming the door. The cab Murdo had come in was only a few yards away. "Come on!" Pitt yanked the door open and climbed in. "Highgate Road!" he shouted. "I'll show these two prancing fools what a real fight is! I'll arrest them for disturbing the Queen's peace!"

Murdo scrambled in beside him, falling sideways as the cab jerked into motion and only just catching the door as it swung away. "I don't suppose they'll hurt each other," he said lamely.

"Pity." Pitt was totally without sympathy. "Serve them both right if they were skewered like puddings!" And he rode the rest of the way in furious silence, Murdo not daring to make any further suggestions.

Eventually the cab came to an abrupt halt and Pitt threw open the door and jumped out, leaving the fare to Murdo to pay, and set off across the path through the field, Highgate Road to his left and the wall of the magnificent cemetery to his right. Three hundred yards ahead of him, paced out on the grass, their figures squat in the distance, were five people.

The solid figure of Quinton Pascoe was standing, feet a little apart, a cape slung over one shoulder, the cold, early sun, clear as springwater, on his shock of white hair. In front of him the dew was heavy on the bent heads of the grass, giving the leaves a strange hint of turquoise as the light refracted.

No more than half a dozen yards away, John Dalgetty, dark-headed, his back to the sun, the shadow masking his face, stood with one arm thrown back and a long object raised as if he were about to charge. Pitt thought at first it was a walking stick. The whole thing was palpably ridiculous. He started to run towards them as fast as his long legs would carry him.

Standing well back were two gentlemen in black frock coats, a little apart from each other. Presumably they were acting as seconds. Another man, who had taken his coat off—for no apparent reason, it was a distinctly chilly morning—was standing in shirtsleeves and shouting first at Pascoe, then at Dalgetty. His voice came to Pitt across the distance, but not his words.

With a flourish Pascoe swung his cloak around his arm and threw it onto the ground in a heap, regardless of the damp. His second rushed to pick it up and held it in front of him, rather like a shield.

Dalgetty, who had no cloak, chose to keep his coat on. He flourished the stick, or whatever it was, again, and let out a cry of "Liberty!" and lunged forward at a run.

"Honor!" Pascoe shouted back, and brandishing something long and pale in his hand, ran forward as well. They met with a clash in the middle and Dalgetty slipped as his polished boots failed to take purchase on the wet grass.

Pascoe turned swiftly and only just missed spearing him through the chest. Instead he succeeded in tearing a long piece from Dalgetty's jacket and thoroughly enraging him. Dalgetty wielded what Pitt could now see was a sword stick, and dealt Pascoe a nasty blow across the shoulders.

"Stop it!" Pitt bellowed as loudly as his lungs would bear. He was running towards them, but he was still a hundred and fifty yards away, and no one paid him the slightest attention. "Stop it at once!"

Pascoe was startled, not by Pitt but by the blow, which must have hurt considerably. He stepped back a pace, shouted, "In the name of chivalry!" and swiped sideways with his ancient and very blunt sword, possibly an ill-cared-for relic of Waterloo, or some such battle.

Dalgetty, with a modern sword stick, sharp as a needle, parried the blow so fiercely the neglected metal broke off halfway up and flew in an arc, catching him across the cheek and opening up a scarlet weal which spurted blood down his coat front.

"You antiquated old fool!" he spluttered, startled and extremely angry. "You fossilized bigot! No man stands in the path of progress! A medieval mind like you won't stop one single good idea whose time has come! Think you can imprison the imagination of man in your old-fashioned ideas! Rubbish!" He swung his broken sword high in the air so wildly the singing sound of it was audible to Pitt even above the rasping of his own breath and the thud of his feet. It missed Pascoe by an inch, and clipped a tuft off the top of his silver head and sent it flying like thistledown.

Pitt tore off his coat and threw it over Dalgetty.

"Stop it!" he roared, and caught him across the chest with his shoulder, sending them both to the ground. The broken sword stick went flying bright in the sun to fall, end down, quivering in the ground a dozen yards away.

Pitt picked himself up and disregarded Dalgetty totally. He did not bother to straighten his clothes and dust off the earth and grass. He faced a shaken, weaponless and very startled Pascoe.

By this time Murdo had dealt with the cab driver and run across the field to join them. He stood aghast at the spectacle, helpless to know what do to.

Pitt glared at Pascoe.

"What on earth do you think you're doing?" he demanded at the top of his voice. "Two people are dead already, God knows who did it, or why—and you are out here trying to murder each other over some idiotic monograph that nobody will read anyway! I should charge you both with assault with a deadly weapon!"

Pascoe was deeply affronted. Blood was seeping through the tear across the shoulder of his shirt and he was clearly in some pain.

"You cannot possibly do that!" his voice was high and loud. "It was a gentleman's difference of opinion!" He jerked his hand up wildly. "Dalgetty is a desecrator of values, a man without judgment or discretion. He propagates the vulgar and destructive and what he imagines to be the cause of freedom, but which is actually license, indiscipline and the victory of the ugly and the dangerous." He waved both arms, nearly decapitating Murdo, who had moved closer. "But I do not lay any charge against him. He attacked me with my full permission—so you cannot arrest him." He stopped with some triumph and stared at Pitt out of bright round eyes.

Dalgetty climbed awkwardly to his feet, fighting his way out of Pitt's coat, his cheek streaming blood.

"Neither do I lay charge against Mr. Pascoe," he said, reaching for a handkerchief. "He is a misguided and ignorant old fool who wants to ban any idea that didn't begin in the Middle Ages. He will stop any freedom of ideas, any flight of the imagination, any discovery of anything new whatsoever. He would keep us believing the earth is flat and the sun revolves around it. But I do not charge him with attacking me—we attacked each other. You are merely a bystander who chose to interfere in something which is none of your affair. You owe us an apology, sir!"

Pitt was livid. But he knew that without a complaint he could not make an arrest that would be prosecuted.

"On the contrary," he said with sudden freezing contempt. "You owe me a considerable gratitude that I prevented you from injuring each other seriously, even fatally. If you can scramble your wits together long enough, think what that would have done to your cause—not to mention your lives from now on."

The possibility, which clearly had not occurred to either of them, stopped the next outburst before it began, and when one of the seconds stepped forward nervously, Pitt opened his mouth to round on him for his utter irresponsibility.

But before he could continue on his tirade the other second shouted out and swung around, pointing where across the field from the Highgate direction were rapidly advancing five figures, strung out a dozen yards from each other. The first was obviously, even at that distance, the vigorous, arm-swinging Stephen Shaw, black bag in his hand, coattails flying. Behind him loped the ungainly but surprisingly rapid figure of Hector Clitheridge, and running after him, waving and calling out, his wife, Eulalia. Separated by a slightly longer space was a grim figure with scarf and hat which Pitt guessed to be Josiah Hatch, but he was too distant to distinguish features. And presumably the woman behind him, just breaking into a run, was Prudence.

"Thank God," one of the seconds gasped. "The doctor—"

"And why in God's name didn't you call him before you began, you incompetent ass?" Pitt shouted at him. "If you are going to second in a duel, at least do it properly! It could have meant the difference between a man living or dying!"

The man was stung at last by the injustice of it, and the thoroughgoing fear that Pitt was right.

"Because my principal forbade me," he retaliated, pulling himself up very straight.

"I'll wager he did," Pitt agreed, looking at Dalgetty, now dripping blood freely and very pasty-faced; then at Pascoe holding his arm limply and beginning to shake from cold and shock. "Knew damned well he'd prevent this piece of idiocy!"

As he spoke Shaw came to a halt beside them, staring from one to the other of the two injured men, then at Pitt.

"Is there a crime?" he said briskly. "Is any of this palaver"—he waved his hands, dropping the bag to the ground—"needed for evidence?"

"Not unless they want to sue each other," Pitt said disgustedly. He could not even charge them with disturbing the peace, since they were out in the middle of a field and no one else was even aware of their having left their beds. The rest of Highgate was presumably taking its breakfast quietly in its dining rooms, pouring its tea, reading the morning papers and totally unaffected.

Shaw looked at the two participants and made the instant decision that Dalgetty was in the more urgent need of help, since he seemed to be suffering from shock whereas Pascoe was merely in pain, and accordingly began his work. He had done no more than open his bag when Clitheridge arrived, acutely distressed and embarrassed.

"What on earth has happened?" he demanded. "Is somebody hurt?"

"Of course somebody's hurt, you fool!" Shaw said furiously. "Here, hold him up." He gestured at Dalgetty, who was covered in blood and was beginning to look as if he might buckle at the knees.

Clitheridge obeyed gladly, his face flooding with relief at some definite task he could turn himself to. He grasped Dalgetty, who rather awkwardly leaned against him.

"What happened?" Clitheridge made one more effort to understand, because it was his spiritual duty. "Has there been an accident?"

Lally had reached them now and her mind seized the situation immediately.

"Oh, how stupid," she said in exasperation. "I never thought you'd be so very childish—and now you've really hurt each other. And does that prove which of you is right? It only proves you are both extremely stubborn. Which all Highgate knew anyway." She swung around to Shaw, her face very slightly flushed. "What can I do to be of assistance, Doctor?" By that time Josiah Hatch had also reached them, but she disregarded him. "Do you need linen?" She peered in his bag, then at the extent of the bloodstains, which were increasing with every minute. "How about water? Brandy?"

"Nobody's going to pass out," he said sharply, glaring at Dalgetty. "For heaven's sake put him down!" he ordered Clitheridge, who was bearing most of Dalgetty's weight now. "Yes, please, Lally—get some more linen. I'd better tie some of this up before we move them. I've got enough alcohol to disinfect."

Prudence Hatch arrived breathlessly, gasping as she came to a halt. "This is awful! What on earth possessed you?" she demanded. "As if we haven't enough grief."

"A man who believes in his principles is sometimes obliged to fight in order to preserve them," Josiah said grimly. "The price of virtue is eternal vigilance."

"That is freedom," his wife corrected him.

"What?" he demanded, his brows drawing down sharply.

"The price of *freedom* is eternal vigilance," she replied. "You said virtue." Without being told she was taking a piece of clean cloth out of Shaw's bag, unfolding it and soaking it in clean spirit from one of his bottles. "Sit down!" she commanded Pascoe smartly, and as soon as he did, she began to clean away the torn outer clothing and then the blood till she could see the ragged tear in the flesh. Then she held the pad of cloth to it and pushed firmly.

He winced and let out a squeak as the spirit hit the open wound, but no one took any notice of him.

"Freedom and virtue are not the same thing at all," Hatch

argued with profound feeling, his face intent, his eyes alight. To
him the issue obviously far outweighed the ephemeral abrasions
of the encounter. "That is precisely what Mr. Pascoe risked his
life to defend!"

"Balderdash!" Shaw snapped. "Virtue isn't in any danger—
and prancing about on the heath with swords certainly isn't going to defend anything at all."

"There is no legal way to prevent the pernicious views and
the dangerous and degrading ideas he propagates," Pascoe
shouted across Prudence's instructions, his lips white with pain.

Lally was already setting off again towards the road on her
errand. Her upright figure, shoulders back, was well on its way.

"There should be." Hatch shook his head. "It is part of our
modern sickness that we admire everything new, regardless of
its merit." His voice rose a little and he chopped his hands in
the air. "We get hold of any new thought, rush to print any idea
that overturns and makes mock of the past, the values that have
served our forefathers and upon which we have built our nation
and carried the faith of Christ to other lands and peoples." His
shoulders were hunched with the intensity of his emotion. "Mr.
Pascoe is one of the few men in our time who has the courage
and the vision to fight, however futilely, against the tide of man's
own intellectual arrogance, his indiscriminate greed for everything new without thought as to its value, or the result of our
espousing it."

"This is not the place for a sermon, Josiah." Shaw was busy
working on Dalgetty's cheek and did not even look up at him.
Murdo was assisting him with considerable competence. "Especially the arrant rubbish you're talking," he went on. "Half
these old ideas you're rehearsing are fossilized walls of cant and
hypocrisy protecting a lot of rogues from the light of day. It's
long past time a few questions were asked and a few shoddy
pretenses shown for what they are."

Hatch was so pale he might have been the one wounded. He
looked at Shaw's back with a loathing so intense it was unnerv-
ing that Shaw was oblivious of it.

"You would have every beautiful and virtuous thing stripped
naked and paraded for the lewd and the ignorant to soil—and

yet at the same time you would not protect the innocent from the mockery and the godless innovations of those who have no values, but constant titillation and endless lust of the mind. You are a destroyer, Stephen, a man whose eyes see only the futile and whose hand holds only the worthless."

Shaw's fingers stopped, the swab motionless, a white blob half soaked with scarlet. Dalgetty was still shaking. Maude Dalgetty had appeared from somewhere while no one was watching the path across the field.

Shaw faced Hatch. There was dangerous temper in every line of his face and the energy built up in the muscles of his body till he seemed ready to break into some violent motion.

"It would give me great pleasure," he said almost between his teeth, "to meet you here myself, tomorrow at dawn, and knock you senseless. But I don't settle my arguments that way. It decides nothing. I shall show you what a fool you are by stripping away the layers of pretense, the lies and the illusions—"

Pitt was aware of Prudence, frozen, her face ashen pale, her eyes fixed on Shaw's lips as if he were about to pronounce the name of some mortal illness whose diagnosis she had long dreaded.

Maude Dalgetty, on the other hand, looked only a little impatient. There was no fear in her at all. And John Dalgetty, half lying on the ground, looked aware only of his own pain and the predicament he had got himself into. He looked at his wife with a definite anxiety, but it was obvious he was nervous of her anger, not for her safety or for Shaw in temper ruining her long-woven reputation.

Pitt had seen all he needed. Dalgetty had no fear of Shaw—Prudence was terrified.

"The whited sepulchers—" Shaw said viciously, two spots of color high on his cheeks. "The—"

"This is not the time," Pitt interrupted, putting himself physically between them. "There's more than enough blood spilled already—and enough pain. Doctor, get on with treating your patients. Mr. Hatch, perhaps you would be good enough to go back to the street and fetch some conveyance so we can carry Mr. Pascoe and Mr. Dalgetty back to their respective homes. If you want to pursue the quarrel on the merits or necessities for censorship, then do it at a more fortunate time—and in a more civilized manner."

For a moment he thought neither of them was going to take any notice of him. They stood glaring at each other with the violence of feeling as ugly as that between Pascoe and Dalgetty. Then slowly Shaw relaxed, and as if Hatch had suddenly ceased to be of any importance, turned his back on him and bent down to Dalgetty's wound again.

Hatch, his face like gray granite, his eyes blazing, swiveled on his heel, tearing up the grass, and marched along the footpath back towards the road.

Maude Dalgetty went, not to her husband, with whom she was obviously out of patience, but to Prudence Hatch, and gently put her arm around her.

CHAPTER

TEN

"I suppose we should have expected it—had we bothered to take the matter seriously at all," Aunt Vespasia said when Charlotte told her about the duel in the field. "One might have hoped they would have more sense, but had they any proportion in things in the first place, they would not have become involved in such extremes of opinion. Some men lose track of reality so easily."

"Thomas said they were both injured," Charlotte went on. "Quite unpleasantly. I knew they said a great deal about the subject of freedom of expression, and the need to censor certain ideas in the public interest, but I did not expect it to come to actual physical harm. Thomas was very angry indeed—it all seems so farcical, in the face of real tragedy."

Vespasia sat very upright and her concentration seemed to be entirely inward, as if she did not see the graciousness of the room around her, or the gentle movement of the bronzing beech leaves outside the window, dappling the light.

"Failure, disillusion and love rejected can all make us behave in ways that seem absurd, my dear—perhaps loneliness most of all. It does not lessen the pain in the slightest, even if you are one who is able to laugh while you weep. I have thought at times that laughter is man's greatest salvation—and at other times that it is what damns him beneath the animals. Beasts may kill one another, they may ignore the sick or distressed—but they never mock. Blasphemy is a peculiarly human ability."

Charlotte was confused for a moment. Vespasia had taken the thought much further than anything she had intended. Perhaps she had overdramatized the scene.

"The whole quarrel was about the rights of censorship," she said, starting to explain herself. "That wretched monograph of Amos Lindsay's, which is academic now, since the poor man is dead anyway."

Vespasia stood up and walked over towards the window.

"I thought it was the question as to whether some men have the right to make mock of other men's gods, because they believe them to be either vicious or absurd—or simply irrelevant."

"One has the right to question them," Charlotte said with irritation. "One must, or there will be no progress of ideas, no reforming. The most senseless ideologies could be taught, and if we cannot challenge them, how are we to know whether they are good or evil? How can we test our ideas except by thinking—and talking?"

"We cannot," Vespasia replied. "But there are many ways of doing it. And we must take responsibility for what we destroy, as well as for what we create. Now tell me, what was it Thomas said about Prudence Hatch being so mesmerized with fright? Did she imagine Shaw was going to let slip some appalling secret?"

"That is what Thomas thought—but he has never persuaded Shaw to tell him anything at all that would indicate any secret he knows worth killing to hide."

Vespasia turned to face Charlotte.

"You have met the man—is he a fool?"

Charlotte thought for several seconds, visualizing Shaw's dynamic face with its quick, clear eyes, the power in him, the vitality that almost overflowed.

"He's extremely intelligent," she replied frankly.

"I daresay," Vespasia agreed dryly. "That is not the same thing. Many people have high intelligence and no wisdom at all. You have not answered me."

Charlotte smiled very slightly. "No, Aunt Vespasia, I am not sure that I can. I don't think I know."

"Then perhaps you had better find out." Vespasia arched her brows very gently but her eyes were unwavering.

Very reluctantly Charlotte rose to her feet, a quiver of excitement inside her, and a very real sense of fear which was getting larger with every moment. This time she could not hide behind a play of innocence as she had done so often in the past when meddling in Pitt's cases. Nor would she go with some slight disguise as she had often done, the pretense of being some gentlewoman of no account, up from the country, and insinuate herself into a situation, then observe. Shaw clearly knew exactly who she was and the precise nature of her interest. To try to deceive him would be ridiculous and demean them both.

She must go, if she went at all, quite openly as herself, frank about her reasons, asking questions without opportunity of camouflage or retreat. How could she possibly behave in such a way that it would be anything but intrusive and impertinent— and hideously insensitive?

It was on the edge of her tongue to make an excuse, simply say all that was in her mind; then she saw Vespasia's slender shoulders stiff as a general commanding a charge to battle, and her eyes as steady as a governess controlling a nursery. Insubordination was not even to be considered. Vespasia had already understood all her arguments, and would accept none of them.

" 'England expects that every man will do his duty,' " Charlotte said with a ghost of a smile.

A spark of laughter lit Vespasia's eyes.

"Quite," she agreed relentlessly. "You may take my carriage."

"Thank you, Aunt Vespasia."

Charlotte arrived at the lodging house where Shaw was temporarily resident exactly as the landlady was serving luncheon. This was ill-mannered in the extreme, but most practical. It was probably the only time when she could have found him present and not either in the act of repacking his bag to leave again or trying to catch up with his notes and messages.

He was obviously surprised to see her, when the landlady showed her in, but the expression on his face showed far more pleasure than irritation. If he minded being interrupted in his meal he hid it with great skill.

"Mrs. Pitt. How very agreeable to see you." He rose, setting his napkin aside, and came around to greet her, holding out his hand and taking hers in a strong, warm grip.

"I apologize for calling at such an inconvenient time." She was embarrassed already, and she had not yet even begun. "Please do not allow me to spoil your luncheon." It was a fatuous remark. She had already done so by her mere presence. Whatever she said, he would not allow her to wait in the parlor while he ate in the dining room, and even if he were to, it could hardly be a comfortable repast in such circumstances. She felt her face coloring with awareness of the clumsy way she had begun. How could she possibly ask him all the intimate and personal questions she wished? Whether she ever learned if he was a fool—in Aunt Vespasia's terms of reference—she herself most certainly was.

"Have you eaten?" he asked, still holding her hand.

She seized the opportunity he offered.

"No—no, I have somehow mislaid time this morning, and it is much later than I had realized." It was a lie, but a very convenient one.

"Then Mrs. Turner will fetch you something, if you care to join me." He indicated the table set for one. Whatever other lodgers there were resident, they appeared to take their midday meal elsewhere.

"I would not dream of inconveniencing Mrs. Turner." She had only one answer open to her. She cooked herself; she knew perfectly well any woman with the slightest economy in mind did not prepare more than she knew would be required. "She cannot have been expecting me. But I should be most happy to take a cup of tea, and perhaps a few slices of bread and butter— if she would be so good. I had a late breakfast, and do not wish for a full meal." That was not true either, but it would serve. She had eaten a considerable number of tomato sandwiches at Aunt Vespasia's.

He swung his arms wide in an expansive gesture and walked over to the bell, pulling it sharply.

"Excellent," he agreed, smiling because he knew as well as she did that they were reaching a compromise of courtesy and truth. "Mrs. Turner!" His voice rang through the room and must have been clearly audible to her long before she had even entered the hall, let alone the dining room.

"Yes, Dr. Shaw?" she said patiently as she opened the door.

"Ah! Mrs. Turner, can you bring a pot of tea for Mrs. Pitt—and perhaps a few slices of bread and butter. She is not in need of luncheon, but some slight refreshment would be most welcome."

Mrs. Turner shook her head in a mixture of doubt and acceptance, glanced once at Charlotte, then hurried away to do as she was requested.

"Sit down, sit down," Shaw offered, drawing out a chair for her and holding it while she made herself comfortable.

"Please continue with your meal." She meant it as more than good manners. She knew he worked hard, and hated to think of him obliged to eat his boiled mutton, potatoes, vegetables and caper sauce cold.

He returned to his own seat and began to eat again with considerable appetite.

"What can I do for you, Mrs. Pitt?" It was a simple question and no more than courtesy dictated. Yet meeting his eyes across the polished wood set with dried flowers, a silver cruet stand and assorted handmade doilies, she knew any evasion would meet his immediate knowledge, and contempt.

She did not want to make a fool of herself in his estimation. She was surprised how painful the idea was. And yet she must say something quickly. He was watching her and waiting. His expression had a remarkable warmth; he was not seeking to find the slightest fault with her, and her sudden realization of that only made it worse. Old memories of other men who had admired her, more than admired, came back with a peculiar sharpness, and a sense of guilt which she had thought forgotten.

She found herself telling the truth because it was the only thing that was tolerable.

"I followed Mrs. Shaw's work," she said slowly. "I began with the parish council, where I learned very little."

"You would," he agreed, his eyes puzzled. "She started from my patients. There was one in particular who did not get better, regardless of my treatment of her. Clemency was concerned, and when she visited her she began to realized it was the condition of the house, the damp, the cold, the lack of clean water and any sanitation. She never would recover as long as she lived there. I could have told her that, but I didn't because I knew there was nothing that could be done to better it, and it would only cause her distress. Clem felt people's misery very much. She was a remarkable woman."

"Yes I know," Charlotte said quickly. "I went to those same houses—and I asked the same questions she had. I have learned why they didn't complain to the landlord—and what happened to those who did."

Mrs. Turner knocked briskly on the door, opened it and brought in a tray with teapot, cup and saucer and a plate of thin bread and butter. She put it down on the table, was thanked, and departed.

Charlotte poured herself a cup of tea, and Shaw resumed his meal.

"They got evicted and had to seek accommodation even less clean or warm," Charlotte continued. "I followed them down the scale from one slum to another, until I saw what I think may be the worst there is, short of sleeping in doorways and gutters. I was going to say I don't know how people survive—but of course they don't. The weak die."

He said nothing, but she knew from his face that he understood it even better than she did, and felt the same helplessness, the anger that it should be, the desire to lash out at someone—preferably the clean and comfortable who chose to laugh and look the other way—and the same pity that haunted both of them whenever the eyes closed and the mind relaxed vigilance, when the hollow faces came back, dull with hunger and dirt and weariness.

"I followed her all the way to one particular street she went where the houses were so crammed with people old and young, men and women, children and even babies, all together without privacy or sanitation, twenty or thirty in a room." She ate a piece of bread and butter because it had been provided— memory robbed her of appetite. "Along the corridor and up the stairs was a brothel. Down two doors was a gin mill with drunken women rolling about on the steps and in the gutter. In the basement was a sweatshop where women worked eighteen hours a day without daylight or air—" She stopped, but again she saw in his eyes that he knew these places; if not this particular one, then a dozen others like it.

"I discovered how hard it is to find out who owns such buildings," she continued. "They are hidden by rent collectors, companies, managers, lawyers' offices, and more companies. At the very end there are powerful people. I was warned that I would make enemies, people who could make life most unpleasant for me, if I persisted in trying to embarrass them."

He smiled bleakly, but still did not interrupt. She knew without question that he believed her. Perhaps Clemency had shared the same discoveries and the same feelings with him.

"Did they threaten her also?" she asked. "Do you know how close she came to learning names of people who might have been afraid she would make their ownership public?"

He had stopped eating altogether, and now he looked down at his plate, his face shadowed, a painful mixture of emotions conflicting within him.

"You think it was Clem they meant to kill in the fire, don't you?"

"I did," she admitted, and saw him stiffen. His eyes lifted instantly and met hers, searching, startled. "Now I'm not sure," she finished. "Why should anyone wish to kill you? And please don't give me an evasive answer. This is too serious to play games with words. Clemency and Amos Lindsay are dead already. Are you sure there will be no more? What about Mrs. Turner and Mr. Oliphant?"

He winced as if she had struck him, and the pain in his eyes was dark, the tightening of his lips undisguised. The knife and fork slid from his hands.

"Do you imagine I haven't thought? I've been through every

case I have treated in the last five years. There isn't a single one that it would be even sane to suspect of murder, let alone anything one would pursue."

There was no point in turning back now, even though no doubt Thomas had already asked exactly the same questions.

"Every death?" she said quietly. "Are you sure absolutely every death was natural? Couldn't one of them, somewhere, be murder?"

A half-unbelieving smile curled the corners of his lips.

"And you think whoever did it may fear I knew—or may come to realize that—and is trying to kill me to keep me silent?" He was not accepting the idea, simply turning over the possibility of it and finding it hard to fit into the medicine he knew, the ordinary domestic release or tragedy of death.

"Couldn't it be so?" she asked, trying to keep the urgency out of her voice. "Aren't there any deaths which could have been profitable to someone?"

He said nothing, and she knew he was remembering, and each one had its own pain. Each patient who had died had been some kind of failure for him, small or great, inevitable or shocking.

A new thought occurred to her. "Perhaps it was an accident and they covered it up, and they are afraid you realized the truth, and then they became afraid you would suspect them of having done it intentionally."

"You have a melodramatic idea of death, Mrs. Pitt," he said softly. "Usually it is simple: a fever that does not break but exhausts the body and burns it out; or a hacking cough that ends in hemorrhage and greater and greater weakness until there is no strength left. Sometimes it is a child, or a young person, perhaps a woman worn down by work and too many childbirths, or a man who has labored in the cold and the wet till his lungs are wasted. Sometimes it's a fat man with apoplexy, or a baby that was never strong enough to live. Surprisingly often in the very end it is peaceful."

She looked at his face, the memories so plain in his eyes, the grief not for the dead but for the confusion, anger and pain of those left behind; his inability to help them, even to touch the loneliness of that sudden, awful void when the soul of someone you love leaves the shell and gradually even the echo of life goes and it becomes only clay in the form of a person but without the substance—like a cold hearth when the fire is gone.

"But not always," she said with regret, hating to have to pursue it. "Some people fight all the way, and some relatives don't accept. Might there not be someone who felt you did not do all you could? Perhaps not from malice, simply neglect, or ignorance?" She said it with a small, sad smile, and so gently he could not think that she believed it herself.

A pucker formed between his brows and he met her eyes with a mild amusement.

"No one has ever showed anything beyond a natural distress. People are often angry, if death is unexpected; angry because fate has robbed them and they have to have something to blame, but it passes; and to be honest no one has suggested I could have done more."

"No one?" She looked at him very carefully, but there was no evasion in his eyes, no faint color of deceit in his cheeks. "Not even the Misses Worlingham—over Theophilus's death?"

"Oh—" He let out his breath in a sigh. "But that is just their way. They are among those who find it hard to accept that someone as . . . as full of opinion and as sound as Theophilus could die. He was always so much in evidence. If there was any subject under discussion, Theophilus would express his views, with lots of words and with great certainty that he was right."

"And of course Angeline and Celeste agreed with him—" she prompted.

He laughed sharply. "Of course. Unless he was out of sympathy with his father. The late bishop's opinions took precedence over everyone else's."

"And did they disagree overmuch?"

"Very little. Only things of no importance, like tastes and pastimes—whether to collect books or paintings; whether to wear brown or gray; whether to serve claret or burgundy, mutton or pork, fish or game; whether chinoiserie was good taste—

or bad. Nothing that mattered. They were in perfect accord on moral duties, the place and virtue of women, and the manner in which society should be governed, and by whom."

"I don't think I should have cared for Theophilus much," she said without thinking first and recalling that he had been Shaw's father-in-law. The description of him sounded so much like Uncle Eustace March, and her memories of him were touched with conflicting emotions, all of them shades of dislike.

He smiled at her broadly, for a moment all thought of death banished, and nothing there but his intense pleasure in her company.

"You would have loathed him," he assured her. "I did."

An element in her wanted to laugh, to see only the easy and absurd in it; but she could not forget the virulence in Celeste's face as she had spoken of her brother's death, and the way Angeline had echoed it with equal sincerity.

"What did he die of, and why was it so sudden?"

"A seizure of the brain," he replied, this time looking up and meeting her eyes with complete candor. "He suffered occasional severe headaches, great heat of the blood, dizziness and once or twice apoplectic fits. And of course now and again gout. A week before he died he had a spasm of temporary blindness. It only lasted a day, but it frightened him profoundly. I think he looked on it as a presage of death—"

"He was right." She bit her lip, trying to find the words to ask without implying blame. It was difficult. "Did you know that at the time?"

"I thought it was possible. I didn't expect it so soon. Why?"

"Could you have prevented it—if you had been sure?"

"No. No doctor knows how to prevent a seizure of the brain. Of course not all seizures are fatal. Very often a patient loses the use of one side of his body—or perhaps his speech, or his sight— but will live on for years. Some people have several seizures before the one that kills them. Some lie paralyzed and unable to speak for years—but as far as one can tell, perfectly conscious and aware of what is going on around them."

"How terrible—like death, but without its peace." She shivered. "Could that have happened to Theophilus?"

"It could. But he went with the first seizure. Perhaps that was not so unlucky."

"Did you tell Angeline and Celeste that?"

His brows rose in slight surprise, perhaps at his own omission.

"No—no, I didn't." He pulled a face. "I suppose it is a trifle late now. They would think I was making excuses."

"Yes," she agreed. "They blame you—but how bitterly I don't know."

"For heaven's sake!" He exploded, amazement filling his eyes. "You don't imagine Angeline and Celeste crept around in the dark and set fire to my house hoping to burn me to death because they think I could have saved Theophilus? That's preposterous!"

"Someone did."

The hilarity vanished and left only the hurt.

"I know—but not over Theophilus."

"Are you absolutely positive? Is it not possible that his death was murder—and someone is afraid you may realize it, and then know who killed him? After all, the circumstances were extraordinary."

He looked at her with disbelief which was almost comic, his eyes wide, his mouth open. Then gradually the thought became less absurd and he realized the darkness of it. He picked up his knife and fork again and began to eat automatically, thinking.

"No," he said at last. "If it was murder, which I don't believe, then it was perfect. I never suspected a thing—and I still don't. And who would want to kill him anyway? He was insufferable, but then so are a lot of people. And neither Prudence nor Clemency wanted his money."

"Are you sure?" she said gently.

His hand came up; he stopped eating and smiled at her with sudden charm, a light of sheer pleasure in his eyes.

"Certainly. Clemency was giving her money away as fast as she could—and Prudence has quite sufficient from her books."

"Books?" Charlotte was totally confused. "What books?"

"Well, *Lady Pamela's Secret* for one," he said, now grinning broadly. "She writes romances—oh, under another name, of course. But she is really very successful. Josiah would have apoplexy if he knew. So would Celeste—for utterly different reasons."

"Are you sure?" Charlotte was delighted, and incredulous.

"Of course I'm sure. Clemency managed the business for her—to keep it out of Josiah's knowledge. I suppose I shall have to now."

"Good gracious." She wanted to giggle, it was all so richly absurd, but there was too much else pressing in on both of them.

"All right." She sobered herself with an effort. "If it was not over Theophilus, either personally or his money, over what then?"

"I don't know. I've racked my brain, gone over and over everything I can think of, real or imaginary, that could cause anyone to hate or fear me enough to take the awful step of murder. Even the risk—" He stopped and a shred of the old irony came back. "Not that it has proved to be much of a risk. The police don't seem to have any more idea who it was now than they did the first night."

She defended Pitt in a moment of instinct, and then regretted it.

"You mean they have not told you of anything? That does not mean they don't know—"

His head jerked up, his eyes wide.

"Nor have they told me," she said quickly.

But he had understood the difference.

"Of course. I was too hasty. They seem so candid, but then they would hardly tell me. I must be one of their chief suspects—which is absurd to me, but I suppose quite reasonable to them."

There was nothing else for her to say to him, no other questions she could think of to ask. And yet she could not answer Aunt Vespasia's question yet. Was he a fool, in her sense—blind to some emotional value that any woman would have seen?

"Thank you for sparing me so much time, Dr. Shaw." She rose from the table. "I realize my questions are impertinent." She smiled in apology and saw the quick response in his face. "I asked them only because having followed Clemency's path I have such a respect for her that I care very much that whoever killed her should be found—and I intend to see that her work is continued. My brother-in-law is actually considering standing for Parliament—he and my sister were so moved by what they learned, I think they will not rest until they are engaged in doing what they can to have such a law passed as she suggested."

He stood also, as a matter of courtesy, and came around to pull her chair back so she might move the more easily.

"You are wasting your time, Mrs. Pitt," he said very quietly. It was not in the tone of a criticism, but rather of regret, as if he had said exactly the same words before, for the same reasons—and not been believed then either. It was as if Clemency were in the room with them, a benign ghost whom they both liked. There was no sense of intrusion, simply a treasured presence who did not resent their moments of friendship, not even the warmth in the touch of his hand on Charlotte's arm, his closeness to her as he bade her good-bye, nor the quick, soft brightness of his eyes as he watched her departing figure down the front steps and up into the carriage, helped by Vespasia's footman. He remained in the hallway, straight-backed, long after the carriage had turned the corner before eventually he closed the door and returned to the dining room.

Charlotte had instructed the coachman to drive to the Worlingham house. It did sound unlikely that either Celeste or Angeline would have attempted to kill Shaw, however derelict they believed him to have been in the matter of Theophilus's death. And yet Clemency, and thus Shaw, had inherited a great deal of money because of it. It was a motive which could not be disregarded. And the more she thought of it, the more did it seem the only sensible alternative if it were not some powerful owner of tenements who feared the exposure she might bring. Was that realistic? Who else's name had she uncovered, apart from her own grandfather's?

In the search surely she must have found others, if not before Worlingham's, then afterwards? That had been the beginning of her total commitment to change the law, which would mean highly unwelcome attention to quite a number of people. Somerset Carlisle had mentioned aristocratic families, bankers, judges, diplomats, men in public life who could ill afford such a source of income to be common knowledge. And the lawyer with the smug face had been so sure his clients would exercise violence of their own sort to keep themselves anonymous he had been prepared to use threats.

But who had gone so far out of the ordinary social or financial avenues of power as to commit murder? Was there any way whatsoever they could learn? Visions floated into her mind of searching the figures of the criminal world for the arsonist, and trying to force him to confess his employer. It would be hopeless, but for a wild element of luck.

How would they ever know? Had Clemency been rash enough to confront him? Surely not. What would be the purpose?

And she had not exposed the Worlinghams, that much was certain. They could hardly be building the magnificent memorial window to him, and having the Archbishop of York dedicate it, were there the slightest breath of scandal around his name.

Had Theophilus known? Certainly Clemency had not told him because he had died long before she came anywhere near her conclusion, in fact before she became closely involved in the matter at all. Had he ever questioned where the family money came from, or had he simply been happy to accept its lavish bounty, smile, and leave everything well covered?

And Angeline and Celeste?

The carriage was already drawing up at the magnificent entrance. In a moment the footman would be opening the door and she would climb out and ascend the steps. She would have to have some excuse for calling. It was early; it would be unlikely for anyone else to be there. She was hardly a friend, merely the granddaughter of a past acquaintance, and an unfortunate reminder of murder and the police, and other such terrible secret evils.

The front door swung wide and the parlormaid looked at her with polite and chilly inquiry.

Charlotte did not even have a card to present!

She smiled charmingly.

"Good afternoon. I am continuing some of the work of the late Mrs. Shaw, and I should so much like to tell the Misses Worlingham how much I admired her. Are they receiving this afternoon?"

The parlormaid was too well trained to turn away someone who might present an oasis of interest in two extremely monotonous lives. The Misses Worlingham hardly ever went out, except to church. What they saw of the world was what came to their door.

Since there was no card, the parlormaid put down the silver card tray on the hall table and stepped back to allow Charlotte inside.

"If you would care to wait, ma'am, I shall inquire. Who shall I say is calling?"

"Mrs. Pitt. The Misses Worlingham are acquainted with my grandmother, Mrs. Ellison. We are all admirers of the family." That was stretching the truth a great deal—the only one Charlotte admired in the slightest was Clemency—but that was indeed enough if spread fine to cover them all.

She was shown into the hall, with its marvelous tessellated floor and its dominating picture of the bishop, his pink face supremely confident, beaming with almost luminous satisfaction down at all who crossed his threshold. The other portraits receded into obscurity, acolytes, a congregation, not principals. Pity there was no portrait of Theophilus; she would like to have seen his face, made some judgment of him, the mouth, the eyes, seen some link between the bishop and his daughters. She imagined him as utterly unlike Shaw as possible, two men unintelligible to each other by the very cast of their natures.

The parlormaid returned and told Charlotte that she would be received—a shade coolly, from her demeanor.

Angeline and Celeste were in the withdrawing room in very much the same postures as they had been when she had called with Caroline and Grandmama. They were wearing afternoon gowns in black similar to the ones they had worn then, good quality, a little strained at the seams, decorated with beads and, in Angeline's case, black feathers also, very discreetly. Celeste wore jet earrings and a necklace, very long, dangling over her rather handsome bosom and winking in the light, its facets turning as she breathed.

"Good afternoon, Mrs. Pitt," she said with a formal nod of her head. "It is kind of you to come to tell us how much you admired poor Clemency. But I thought you expressed yourself very fully on the subject when you were here before. And I may remind you, you were under some misapprehension as to her work for the less fortunate."

"I am sure it was a mistake, dear," Angeline put in hastily. "Mrs Pitt will not have meant to distress us or cause anxiety." She smiled at Charlotte. "Will you?"

"There is nothing I have learned of Mrs. Shaw which could make you anything but profoundly proud of her," Charlotte replied, looking very levelly at Angeline and watching her face for the slightest flicker of knowledge.

"Learned?" Angeline was confused, but that was the only emotion Charlotte could identify in her bland features.

"Oh yes," she answered, accepting the seat which was only half offered, and sitting herself down comfortably well in the back of the lush, tasseled and brocaded cushions. She had no intention of leaving until she had said all she could think of and watched their reactions minutely. This house had been bought and furnished with agony. The old bishop had known it; had Theophilus? And far more recently and more to the point, had these two innocent-looking sisters? Was it conceivable Clemency had come home in her desperate distress when she first learned beyond doubt where her inheritance had been made, and faced them with it? And if she had, what would they have done?

Perhaps fire, secretly and in the night, burning to its terrible conclusion, when they were safely back in their own beds, was just the weapon they might choose. It was horrible to think of, close, like suffocation, and terrifying as the change from mildness to hatred in a face you have known all your life.

Had these women, who had given the whole of their lives, wasted their youth and their mature womanhood pandering to their father, killed to protect that same reputation—and their own comfort in a community they had led for over half a century? It was not inconceivable.

"I heard so well of her from other people," Charlotte went on, her voice sounding gushing in her ears, artificial and a little too highly pitched. Was she foolish to have come here alone? No—that was stupid. It was the middle of the day, and Aunt Vespasia's coachman and footman were outside.

But did they know that?

Yes of course they did. They would hardly imagine she had walked here.

But she might have come on the public omnibus. She frequently traveled on it.

"Which other people?" Celeste said with raised eyebrows. "I hardly thought poor Clemency was known outside the parish."

"Oh indeed she was." Charlotte swallowed the lump in her throat and tried to sound normal. Her hands were shaking, so she clasped them together, digging her nails into her palms. "Mr. Somerset Carlisle spoke of her in the highest terms possible—he is a noted member of Parliament, you know. And Lady Vespasia Cumming-Gould also. In fact I was speaking to her only this morning, telling her I should call upon you this afternoon, and she lent me her carriage, for my convenience. She is determined that Mrs. Shaw shall not be forgotten, nor her work perish." She saw Celeste's heavy face darken. "And of course there are others," she plowed on. "But she was so discreet, perhaps she was too modest to tell you much herself?"

"She told us nothing," Celeste replied. "Because I believe, Mrs. Pitt, that there was nothing to tell. Clemency did the sort of kindnesses among the poor that all the women of our family have always done." She lifted her chin a fraction and her tone became more condescending. "We were raised in a very Christian household, as I daresay you are aware. We were taught as children to care for those less fortunate, whether through their own indigence or not. Our father told us not to judge, merely to serve."

Charlotte found it hard to hold her tongue. She ached to tell them precisely what she thought of the bishop's charity.

"Modesty is one of the most attractive of all the virtues," she said aloud, gritting her teeth. "It seems that she said nothing to you of her work to have the laws changed with regard to the ownership of the very worst of slum properties."

There was nothing at all in either of their faces that looked like even comprehension, let alone fear.

"Slum properties?" Angeline was utterly confused.

"The ownership of them," Charlotte continued, her voice sounding dry and very forced. "At present it is almost impossible to discern who is the true owner."

"Why should anyone wish to know?" Angeline asked. "It seems an extraordinary and purposeless piece of knowledge."

"Because the conditions are appalling." Charlotte murmured her answer and tried to make it as gentle as was appropriate to two elderly women who knew nothing of the world beyond their house, the church and a few of the people in the parish. It would be grossly unfair now to blame them for an ignorance which it was far too late for them to remedy. The whole pattern of their lives, which had been set for them by others, had never been questioned or disturbed.

"Of course we know that the poor suffer," Angeline said with a frown. "But that has always been so, and is surely inevitable. That is the purpose of charity—to relieve suffering as much as we can."

"A good deal of it could be prevented, if other people did not exercise their greed at the expense of the poor." Charlotte sought for words they would understand to explain the devastating poverty she had seen. She looked at the total lack of comprehension on their faces. "When people are poor already, they are much more prone to illness, which makes them unable to work, and they become poorer still. They are evicted from decent housing and have to seek whatever they can get." She was simplifying drastically, but a long explanation of circumstances they had never imagined would only lose their emotion. "Landlords know their plight and offer them room without light or air, without running water or any sanitary facilities—"

"Then why do they take them?" Angeline opened her eyes

wide in inquiry. "Perhaps they do not want such things, as we would?"

"They want the best they can get," Charlotte said simply. "And very often that is merely a place where they can shelter and lie down—and perhaps, if they are lucky, share a stove with others so they can cook."

"That doesn't sound too bad," Celeste replied. "If that is all they can afford."

Charlotte put forward the one fact she knew would reach the bishop's daughters.

"Men, women and children all in the same room?" She stared straight into Celeste's strong, clever face. "With no lavatory but a bucket in the corner—for all of them—and nowhere to change clothes in privacy, or to wash—and no way of sleeping alone?"

Charlotte saw all the horror she could have wished.

"Oh, my dear! You don't mean that?" Angeline was shocked. "That is—quite uncivilized . . . and certainly unchristian!"

"Of course it is," Charlotte agreed. "But they have no alternative, except the street, which would be even worse."

Celeste looked distressed. It was not beyond her imagination to think of such conditions and feel at least a shadow of their wretchedness, but she was still at a loss to see what purpose could be served by making the owners known.

"The owners cannot make more space," she said slowly. "Nor solve the problems of poverty. Why should you wish to discover who they are?"

"Because the owners are making a very large profit indeed," Charlotte replied. "And if their names were public, they might be shamed into maintaining the buildings so they are at least clean and dry, instead of having mold on the walls and timbers rotting."

It was beyond the experience of either Celeste or Angeline. They had spent all their lives in this gracious house with every comfort that money and status could supply. They had never seen rot, never smelled it, had no conception of a running gutter or open sewerage.

Charlotte drew breath to try to depict it in words, and was

prevented from beginning by the parlormaid returning to announce the arrival of Prudence Hatch and Mrs. Clitheridge.

They came in together, Prudence looking a little strained and unable to stand or to sit with any repose. Lally Clitheridge was charming to Celeste, full of smiles to Angeline; and then when she turned to where Charlotte had risen to her feet, recognizing her before introductions were made, her face froze and she became icily polite, her eyes hard and a brittle timbre to her voice.

"Good afternoon, Mrs. Pitt. How surprising to see you here again so soon. I had not thought you such a personal friend."

Celeste invited them to be seated, and they all obeyed, rearranging skirts.

"She came to express her admiration for Clemency," Angeline said with a slight nervous cough. "It seems Clemency really did look into the question of people making extreme profits out of the wretchedness of some of the poor. We really had no idea. She was so very modest about it."

"Indeed?" Lally raised her eyebrows and looked at Charlotte with frank disbelief. "I had not realized you were acquainted with Clemency at all—let alone to the degree where you know more of her than her family."

Charlotte was stung by the manner more than the words. Lally Clitheridge was regarding her with the air one might show a rival who had tricked one out of a deserved advantage.

"I did not know her, Mrs. Clitheridge. But I know those who did. And why she chose to share her concern with them and not with her family and neighbors I am unaware—but possibly it was because they were almost as concerned as she and they understood and respected her feelings."

"Good gracious." Lally's voice rose in amazement and offense. "Your intrusion knows no bounds. Now you suggest she did not trust her own family—but chose instead these friends of yours, whom you have been careful not to name."

"Really, Lally," Prudence said gently, knotting her hands together in her lap. "You are distressing yourself unnecessarily. You have allowed Flora Lutterworth to upset you too much." She glanced at Charlotte. "We have had a rather distasteful encounter, and I am afraid hasty words were said. That young woman's behavior is quite shameless where poor Stephen is concerned. She is obsessed with him, and does not seem able to comport herself with any restraint at all—even now."

"Oh dear—that again." Angeline sighed and shook her head. "Well of course she has no breeding, poor soul, what can you expect? And raised virtually without a mother. I dare say there is no one to instruct her how to behave. Her father is in trade, after all and he's from the north; you could hardly expect him to have the least idea."

"No amount of money in the world makes up for lack of breeding," Celeste agreed. "But people will insist upon trying."

"Exactly," Charlotte said with a voice that cut like acid. "People with breeding can lie, cheat, steal or sell their daughters to obtain money, but people who only have money can never acquire breeding, no matter what they do."

There was a silence that was like thunder, prickling the air and touching the skin in a cold sweat.

Charlotte looked at their faces one by one. She was quite sure, although there was no proof whatever, that neither Celeste nor Angeline had even the shadow of an idea where their family money came from. Nor did she believe that money was at the root of Prudence's fear. She looked aghast now, but not for herself; her hands were quite still, even loose in her lap. She was staring at Charlotte in total incomprehension, for her devastating rudeness, not because she was afraid of her.

Lally Clitheridge was dumbfounded.

"I thought Stephen Shaw was the rudest person I had ever met," she said with a tremor in her voice. "But you leave him standing. You are totally extraordinary."

There was only one possible thing to say.

"Thank you." Charlotte did not flinch in the slightest. "Next time I see him I shall tell him of your words. I am sure he will be most comforted."

Lally's face tightened, almost as if she had been struck—and quite suddenly and ridiculously Charlotte realized the root of her enmity. She was intensely jealous. She might regard Shaw as verbally reckless, full of dangerous and unwelcome ideas, but she was also fascinated by him, drawn from her pedestrian and dutiful life with the vicar towards something that promised excitement, danger, and a vitality and confidence that must be like elixir in the desert of her days.

Now the whole charade not only made Charlotte angry but stirred her to pity for its futility and the pointless courage of Lally's crusade to make Clitheridge into something he was not, to do his duty when he was swamped by it, constantly to push him, support him, tell him what to say. And for her daydreams of a man so much more alive, the vigor that horrified and enchanted her, and the hatred she felt for Charlotte because Shaw was drawn to her, as easily and hopelessly as Lally was to Shaw.

It was all so futile.

And yet she could hardly take the words back, that would only make it worse by allowing everyone to see that she understood. The only possible thing now was to leave. Accordingly she rose to her feet.

"Thank you, Miss Worlingham, for permitting me to express my admiration for Clemency's work, and to assure you that despite any dangers, or any threats that may be made, I will continue with every effort at my command. It did not die with her, nor will it ever. Miss Angeline." She withdrew her hand, clutched her reticule a trifle more closely, and turned to leave.

"What do you mean, Mrs. Pitt?" Prudence stood up and came forward. "Are you saying that you believe Clemency was murdered by someone who—who objected to this work you say she was doing?"

"It seems very likely, Mrs. Hatch."

"Stuff and nonsense," Celeste said sharply. "Or are you suggesting that Amos Lindsay was involved in it as well?"

"Not so far as I know—" Charlotte began, and was cut off instantly.

"Of course not," Celeste agreed, rising to her feet also. Her skirt was puckered but she was unaware of it in her annoyance. "Mr. Lindsay was no doubt murdered for his radical political views, this Fabian Society and all these dreadful pamphlets he writes and supports." She glared at Charlotte. "He associated with people who have all sorts of wild ideas: socialism, anarchy, even revolution. There are some very sinister plots being laid in our times. There is murder far more abominable than the fires here in Highgate, fearful as they were. One does not read the newspapers, of course. But one cannot help but be aware of what is going on—people talk about it, even here. Some madman is loose in Whitechapel ripping women apart and disfiguring them in the most fearful way—and the police seem powerless either to catch him or prevent him." Her face was white as she spoke and no one could fail to feel her horror rippling out in the room like coldness from a door opened on ice.

"I am sure you are right, Celeste." Angeline seemed to withdraw into herself as if she would retreat from these new and terrible forces that threatened them all. "The world is changing. People are thinking quite new and very dangerous ideas. It sometimes seems to me as if everything we have is threatened." She shook her head and pulled at her black shawl to put it more closely around her shoulders, as if it could protect her. "And I really believe from the way Stephen speaks that he quite admires this talk of overthrowing the old order and setting up those Fabian ideas."

"Oh, I'm sure he doesn't," Lally contradicted strongly, her face pink and her eyes very bright. "I know he liked Mr. Lindsay, but he certainly never agreed with his ideas. They are quite revolutionary. Mr. Lindsay was reading some of the essays and pamphlets and things by that fearful Mrs. Bezant who helped to put the match girls up to refusing to work. You remember that in April—or was it May? I mean, if people refuse to work, where will we all be?"

Charlotte was powerfully tempted to put forward her own political views, in favor of Mrs. Bezant and explaining the plight of the match girls, their physical suffering, the necrosis of the facial bones from breathing the phosphorus; but this was neither the time nor were these the people. Instead she turned to Lally with interest.

"Do you believe they were political murders, Mrs. Clitheridge? That poor Mrs. Shaw was killed because of her agitation for slum reform? You know I think you may well be correct. In fact it is what I believe myself, and have been saying so for some time."

Lally was very much put out of composure by having to agree with Charlotte, but she could not backtrack now.

"I would not have put it quite in those terms," she said, bridling. "But I suppose that is what I think. After all, it makes by far the most sense out of things. What other reason could there be?"

"Well there are others who have suggested more personal forms of passion," Prudence pointed out, frowning at Charlotte. "Perhaps Mr. Lutterworth, because of Dr. Shaw's involvement with Flora—if, of course, it was Stephen he meant to kill, not poor Clemency."

"Then why would he kill Mr. Lindsay?" Angeline shook her head. "Mr. Lindsay certainly never did her any harm."

"Because he knew something, of course." Prudence's face tightened in impatience. "That does not take a great deal of guessing."

They were all standing close together near the door, the sunlight slanting between the curtains and the blinds making a bright patch behind them and causing the black crepes to look faintly dusty.

"I am surprised the police have not worked it out yet," Lally added, glancing at Charlotte. "But then I suppose they are not a very superior class of person—or they would not be employed in such work. I mean, if they were clever enough to do something better—they would, wouldn't they?"

Charlotte could accommodate a certain amount of insult to herself and keep her temper, but insult to Pitt was different. Again her anger slipped out of control.

"There are only a certain number of people who are willing to spend their time, and sometimes to risk their lives, digging into the sin and tragedy of other people's affairs and uncovering the violence in them," she said acidly, staring at Lally, her eyes wide. "So many people who look the picture of rectitude on the outside and pretend to civic virtue have inner lives that are thoroughly sordid, greedy and full of lies." She looked from one to another of them, and was satisfied to see alarm, even fear in some of their faces, most especially Prudence's. And seeing it she instantly relented and was ashamed. It was not Prudence she had intended to hurt.

But again there was no verbal retreat, only physical, and this time she excused herself, bade them farewell and swept out, head high, twitching her skirts smartly over the step. A few moments later she was back in Aunt Vespasia's carriage and once again going towards Stephen Shaw's lodgings. There were now far more questions she wished to ask him. Perhaps it really was all to do with radical political ideas, not merely Clemency's slum profiteers, but Lindsay's socialist beliefs as well. She had never asked him if Lindsay knew about Clemency's work, or if it had taken her to the new Fabian Society; it simply had not occurred to her.

Mrs. Turner admitted her again with no surprise, and told her that the doctor was out on a call but she expected him back shortly, and if Charlotte cared to wait in the parlor she was welcome. She was brought yet another pot of tea, set out on a brand-new Japanese lacquer tray.

She poured herself a cup of tea and sat sipping it. Could Shaw really know anything that someone would kill to keep secret? Pitt had said little to her about the other patients he had investigated. Shaw seemed so certain all the deaths he had attended were natural—but then if he were in conspiracy with someone, he would say that. Was it possible he had helped someone to murder, either by actually providing the means, or simply by concealing it afterwards? Would he?

She recalled his face to mind easily, the strength in him, and the conviction. Yes—if he believed it to be right, she had no doubt he would. He was quite capable of exercising his powers. If ever a man had the courage of his convictions it was Stephen Shaw.

But did he believe it was right—or could ever be? No, surely not. Not even a violent or insane person? Or someone with a painful and incurable disease?

She had no idea if he was treating such a person. Pitt must have thought of all this too—surely?

She had resolved nothing when some thirty minutes later

Shaw burst in, half throwing his case into the corner and flinging his jacket over the back of the chair. He swung around,
startled to see her, but his expression lit with delight and he
made no pretense of indifference.

"Mrs. Pitt! What fortune brings you back here again so soon?
Have you discovered something?" There was humor in his eyes,
and a little anxiety, but nothing disguised his liking for her.

"I have just been visiting the Misses Worlingham," she answered, and saw the instant appreciation of all that that meant
in his face. "I was not especially welcome," she said in answer
to his unspoken question. "In fact Mrs. Clitheridge, who called
at the same time, has taken a strong dislike to me. But as a result
of certain conversation that took place, several other thoughts
come to my mind."

"Indeed? And what are they? I see Mrs. Turner gave you
some tea. Is there any left? I am as dry as one of poor Amos's
wooden gods." He reached for the pot and lifted it experimen-
tally. It was obvious from the weight that there was considerable
liquid left in it. "Ah—good." He poured out her used cup in the
slop bowl, rinsed it from the hot water jug, and proceeded to
pour himself some tea. "What did Celeste and Angeline say that
sparked these new ideas? I must admit, the thought intrigues
me."

"Well, there is always money," she began slowly. "The
Worlinghams have a great deal of money, which Clemency must
have inherited, along with Prudence, when Theophilus died.

He met her eyes with total candor, even a black laughter
without a shred of rancor at her for the suggestion.

"And you think I might have murdered poor Clem to get
my hands on it?" he asked. "I assure you, there isn't a penny
left—she gave it all away." He moved restlessly around the
room, poking at a cushion, setting a book straight on a shelf so
it did not stand out from the rest. "When her will is probated
you will see that for the last few months she had been obliged
to me even for a dress allowance. I promise you, Mrs. Pitt, I
shall inherit nothing from the Worlingham estate except a couple
of dressmakers' bills and a milliner's account. Which I shall be
happy to settle."

"Given it all away?" Charlotte affected surprise. Pitt had already told her that Clemency had given her money away.

"All of it," he repeated. "Mostly to societies for slum clearance, help to the extremely poor, housing improvement, sanitation, and of course the battle to get the law changed to make ownership easily traceable. She went through thirty thousand pounds in less than a year. She just gave it away until there was no more." His face was illuminated with a kind of pride and a fierce gentleness.

Charlotte asked the next question without even stopping to weigh it. She had to know, and it seemed so easy and natural to ask.

"Did she tell you why? I mean, did she tell you where the Worlingham money came from?"

His mouth curled downward and his eyes were full of bitter laughter.

"Where the old bastard got it from? Oh, yes—when she discovered it she was devastated." He walked over and stood with his back to the mantel. "I remember the night she came home after she found out. She was so pale I thought she would pass out, but she was white with fury, and shame." He looked at Charlotte, his eyes very steady on hers. "All evening she paced the floor back and forth, talking about it, and nothing I could say could take away the guilt from her. She was distraught. She must have been up half the night—" He bit his lip and looked downwards. "And I'm ashamed to say I was so tired from being up the night before that I slept. But I knew in the morning she had been weeping. All I could do was tell her that whatever her decision, I would support her. She took two more days to decide that she would not face Celeste and Angeline with it."

He jerked up again, his foot kicking against the brass fender around the hearth. "What good would it do? They had no responsibility for it. They gave their whole lives to looking after and pandering to that old swine. They couldn't bear it now to think it had all been a farce, all the goodness they thought was there a whited sepulcher if ever there was one!"

"But she told Prudence," Charlotte said quietly, remembering the haunting fear and the guilt in Prudence's eyes.

He frowned at her, his expression clouded where she had expected to see something a little like relief.

"No." He was quite definite. "No, she certainly didn't tell Prudence. What could she do, except be plagued with shame too?"

"But she is," Charlotte said, still gently. She was filled with sorrow, catching some glimpse of how it would torment Prudence, when her husband admired the bishop almost to hero worship. What a terrible burden to live with, and never to let slip, even by hint or implication. Prudence must be a very strong woman with deep loyalty to keep such a secret. "She must find it almost unendurable," she added.

"She doesn't know!" he insisted. "Clem never told her—just because it would be, as you say, unendurable. Old Josiah thinks the bishop was the next thing to a saint—God help him. The bloody window was all his idea—"

"Yes, she does," Charlotte argued, leaning a little forward. "I saw it in her eyes looking at Angeline and Celeste. She's terrified of it coming out, and she's desperately ashamed of it."

They sat across the table staring at each other, equally determined they were in the right, until slowly Shaw's face cleared and understanding was so plain in him she spoke automatically.

"What? What have you realized?"

"Prudence doesn't know anything about the Worlingham money. That's not what she is afraid of—the stupid woman—"

"Then what?" She resented his calling her stupid, but this was not the time to take it up. "What is she afraid of?"

"Josiah—and her family's contempt and indignation—"

"For what?" she interrupted him again. "What is it?"

"Prudence has six children." He smiled ruefully, full of pity. "Her confinements were very hard. The first time she was in pain for twenty-three hours before the child was delivered. The second time looked like being similar, so I offered her anesthetic—and she took it."

"Anesthetic—" Suddenly she too began to see what terrified Prudence. She remembered Josiah Hatch's remarks about women and the travail of childbirth, and it being God's will. He would, like many men, consider it an evasion of Christian responsibility to dull the pain with medical anesthesia. Most doctors would not even offer it. And Shaw had allowed Prudence her choice, without asking or telling her husband—and she was living in mortal fear now that he might break his silence and betray her to her husband.

"I see," she said with a sigh. "How tragic—and absurd." She could recall her own pain of childbirth only dimly. Nature is merciful in expunging the recollection in all save a small corner of the mind, and hers had not been harsh, compared with many. "Poor Prudence. You would never tell him—would you?" She knew as she said it that the question was unnecessary. In fact, she was grateful he was not angry even that she asked.

He smiled and did not answer.

She changed the subject.

"Do you think it would be acceptable for me to come to Amos Lindsay's funeral? I liked him, even though I knew him for so short a while."

His face softened again, and for a moment the full magnitude of his hurt was naked.

"I should like it very much if you did. I shall speak the eulogy. The whole affair will be awful—Clitheridge will behave like a fool, he always does when anything real is involved. Lally will probably have to pick up the pieces. Oliphant will be as good as he is allowed to be, and Josiah will be the same pompous, blind ass he always is. I shall loathe every moment of it. I will almost certainly quarrel with Josiah because I can't help it. The more sycophantic he is about the damn bishop the angrier I shall be, and the more I shall want to shout from the pulpit what an obscene old sinner he was—and not even decent sins of passion or appetite—just cold, complacent greed and the love of dominion over other people."

Without thinking she put out her hand and touched his arm. "But you won't."

He smiled reluctantly and stood immobile lest she move.

"I shall try to behave like the model mourner and friend—even if it chokes me. Josiah and I have had enough quarreling—but he does tempt me sorely. He lives in a totally spurious world and I can't bear his cant! I know better, Charlotte. I hate lies;

they rob us of the real good by covering it over with so many coats of sickening excuses and evasions until what was really beautiful, brave, or clean, is distorted and devalued." His voice shook with the intensity of his feeling. "I hate hypocrites! And the church seems to spawn them like abscesses, eating away at real virtue—like Matthew Oliphant's."

She was a little embarrassed; his emotion was so transparent and she could feel the vitality of him under her hand as if he filled the room.

She moved away carefully, not to break the moment.

"Then I shall see you at the funeral tomorrow. We shall both behave properly—however hard it is for us. I shall not quarrel with Mrs. Clitheridge, although I should dearly like to, and you will not tell Josiah what you think of the bishop. We shall simply mourn a good friend who died before his time." And without looking at him again she walked very straight-backed and very gracefully to the parlor door, and out into the hallway.

CHAPTER

ELEVEN

It had taken Murdo two days of anxiety and doubt, lurching hope and black despair before he found an excuse to call on Flora Lutterworth. And it took him at least half an hour to wash, shave and dress himself in immaculately clean clothes, pressed to perfection, his buttons polished—he hated his buttons because they made his rank so obvious, but since they were inescapable, they had better be clean and bright.

He had thought of going quite frankly to express his admiration for her, then blushed scarlet as he imagined how she would laugh at him for his presumption. And then she would be thoroughly annoyed that a policeman, of all the miserable trades—and not even a senior one—should dare to think of such a thing, let alone express it. He had lain awake burning with shame over that.

No, the only way was to find some professional excuse, and then in the course of speaking to her, slip in that she had his deepest admiration, and then retreat with as much grace as possible.

So at twenty-five minutes past nine he knocked on the door of the Lutterworth house. When the maid answered, he asked if he might see Miss Flora Lutterworth, to seek her aid in an official matter.

He tripped over the step on the way in, and was sure the maid was giggling at his clumsiness. He was angry and blushing at the same time and already wished he had not come. It was doomed to failure. He was making a fool of himself and she would only despise him.

"If you'll wait in the morning room, I'll see if Miss Lutterworth'll see you," the maid said, smoothing her white starched apron over her hips. She thought he was very agreeable, nice eyes and very clean-looking, not like some she could name, but she wasn't for having him get above himself. But when he had finished with Miss Flora, she would make sure it was she who showed him out. She wouldn't mind if he asked her to take a walk in the park on her half day off.

"Thank you." He stood in the middle of the carpet, twisting his helmet in his hands, and waited while she went. For a wild moment he thought of simply leaving, but his feet stayed leadenly on the floor and while his mind took flight and was halfway back to the station, his body remained, one moment hot, the next cold, in the Lutterworths' elegant morning room.

Flora came in looking flushed and devastatingly pretty, her eyes shining. She was dressed in a deep rose-pink which was quite the most distinguished and becoming gown he had ever seen. His heart beat so hard he felt sure the shaking of his body must be visible to her, and his mouth was completely dry.

"Good morning, Constable Murdo," she said sweetly.

"G—good morning, ma'am." His voice croaked and squeaked alternatively. She must think him a complete fool. He drew in a deep breath, and then let it out without speaking.

"What can I do for you, Constable?" She sat down in the largest chair and her skirts billowed around her. She gazed at him most disconcertingly.

"Ah—" He found it easier to look away. "Er, ma'am—" He fixed his eyes on the carpet and the prepared words came out in a rush. "Is it possible, ma'am, that some young gentleman, who admired you very much, might have misunderstood your visits to Dr. Shaw, and become very jealous—ma'am?" He dared not look up at her. She must see through this ruse, which had sounded so plausible alone in his room. Now it was horribly transparent.

"I don't think so, Constable Murdo," she said after considering it for a moment. "I really don't know of any young gentlemen who have such powerful feelings about me that they would entertain such . . . jealousy. It doesn't seem likely."

Without thinking he looked up at her and spoke. "Oh yes, ma'am—if a gentleman had kept your company, socially of course, and met you a number of times, he might well be moved to—to such passions—that—" He felt himself blushing furiously, but unable to move his eyes from hers.

"Do you think so?" she said innocently. She lowered her eyes demurely. "That would suppose him to be in love with me, Constable—to quite an intense degree. Surely you don't believe that is so?"

He plunged in—he would never in his wildest dreams have a better opportunity. "I don't know whether it is, ma'am—but it would be very easy to believe. If it is not so now, it will be— There are bound to be many gentlemen who would give everything they possessed to have the chance to earn your affections. I mean—er—" She was looking at him with a most curious smile, half interested and half amused. He knew he had betrayed himself and felt as if there were nothing in the world he wanted so much as to run away, and yet his feet were rooted to the floor.

Her smiled widened. "How very charming of you, Constable," she said softly. "You say it as if you really believed I were quite beautiful and exciting. It is certainly the nicest thing anyone has told me for as long as I can remember."

He had no idea what to say, no idea at all. He simply smiled back at her and felt happy and ridiculous.

"I cannot think of anyone who might entertain such emotions that they could have harmed Dr. Shaw on my account," she went on, sitting up very straight. "I am sure I have not encouraged anyone. But of course the matter is very serious, I know. I promise you I shall think about it hard, and then I shall tell you."

"May I call in a few days' time to learn what you have to say?" he asked.

The corners of her mouth curled up in a tiny smile.

"I think, if you don't mind, Constable, I would rather discuss it somewhere where Papa will not overhear us. He does tend to misunderstand me at times—only in my best interest, of course. Perhaps you would be good enough to take a short walk with me along Bromwich Walk? The weather is still most pleasant and it would not be disagreeable. If you would meet me at the parsonage end, the day after tomorrow, we might walk up to Highgate, and perhaps find a lemonade stall to refresh ourselves?"

"I—" His voice would hardly obey him, his heart was so high in his throat and there was a curious, singing happiness all through his veins. "I'm sure that would be most—" He wanted to say "marvelous" but it was much too forward. "Most satisfactory, ma'am." He should get that silly smile off his face, but it would not go.

"I'm so glad," she said, rising to her feet and passing so close to him he could smell the scent of flowers and hear the soft rustle of the fabric of her skirts. "Good day, Constable Murdo."

He gulped and swallowed hard. "G-good day, Miss Lutterworth."

"An artists' model?" Micah Drummond's eyes widened and there was laughter in them, and a wry appreciation. "Maude Dalgetty was that Maude!"

Now it was Pitt's turn to be startled. "You know of her?"

"Certainly." Drummond was standing by the window in his office, the autumn sunlight streaming in, making bright patterns on the carpet. "She was one of the great beauties—of a certain sort, of course." His smile widened. "Perhaps not quite your generation, Pitt. But believe me, any young gentleman who attended the music halls and bought the odd artistic postcard knew the face—and other attributes—of Maude Racine. She was more than just handsome; there was a kind of generosity in her, a warmth. I'm delighted to hear she married someone who loves her and found a respectable domestic life. I imagine it was what she always wanted, after the fun was over and it came time to leave the boards."

Pitt found himself smiling too. He had liked Maude Dalgetty, and she had been a friend of Clemency Shaw.

"And you have ruled her out?" Drummond pursued. "Not that I can imagine Maude caring passionately enough about her reputation to kill anyone to preserve it. There was never anything of the hypocrite in her in the old days. Are you equally sure about the husband—John Dalgetty? No evasions, Pitt!"

Pitt leaned against the mantel shelf and faced Drummond squarely.

"Absolutely," he said without a flicker. "Dalgetty believes passionately in total freedom of speech. That is what the idiotic affair in the field was about. No censorship, everything open and public, say and write what you please, all the new and daring ideas you can think of. The people who matter most to him wouldn't cut him because his wife was on the stage and posed for pictures without certain of her clothes."

"But she would care," Drummond argued. "Didn't you say she works in the parish, attends church and is part of an extremely respectable community?"

"Yes I did." Pitt put his hands in his pockets. One of Emily's silk handkerchiefs was in his breast pocket and he had folded it to show slightly. Drummond's eyes had caught it, and it gave him a slow satisfaction which more than made up for the cold, early ride on the public omnibus, so he could add a few more pence to the economy for Charlotte's holiday.

"But the only person who knew," he went on, "so far as I am aware, was Shaw—and, I presume, Clemency. And Clemency was her friend—and Shaw wouldn't tell anyone." Then a flash of memory returned. "Except in a fit of anger because Josiah Hatch thinks Maude is the finest woman he's ever met." His eyes widened. "And he's such a rigid creature—with all the old bishop's ideas about the purity and virtue of women, and of course their duties as the guardians of the sanctity of the home as an island from the vile realities of the outer world. I can well imagine Shaw giving the lie to that, as a piece of cant he couldn't abide. But I still think he wouldn't actually betray her—simply tell."

"I'm inclined to agree with you." Drummond pursed his lips. "No reason to suspect Pascoe—no motive we know of. You've ruled out Prudence Hatch, because Shaw would never betray her medical secrets." Drummond's eyes were bright. "Please convey my compliments to Charlotte." He slid down a little in his chair and rested his feet on the desk. "The vicar is an ass, you say, but you know of no quarrel with Shaw, except that his wife is titillated by the man's virility—hardly enough to drive a clergyman to multiple arson and murder. You don't think Mrs. Clitheridge could be so besotted with Shaw, and have been rejected, to the point where she tried to murder him in fury?" He was watching Pitt's expression as he spoke. "All right—no. Nor, I assume, would she have killed Mrs. Shaw in jealousy. No—I thought not. What about Lutterworth, over his daughter?"

"Possible," Pitt conceded doubtfully. Lutterworth's broad, powerful face came back to his mind, and the expression of rage in it when he mentioned Shaw's name, and Flora's. There was no question he loved his daughter profoundly, and had the depth of emotion and the determination of character to carry through such an act, if he thought there were justification. "Yes, he is possible. Or he was—I think he knows now that Flora's connection with the doctor was purely a medical one."

"Then why the sneaking in and out instead of going to the usual surgery?" Drummond persisted.

"Because of the nature of her complaint. It is personal, and she is highly sensitive about it, didn't want anyone else to know. Not difficult to understand."

Drummond, who had a wife and daughters himself, did not need to make further comment.

"Who does that leave?"

"Hatch—but he and Shaw have quarreled over one thing or another for years, and you don't kill someone suddenly over a basic difference in temperament and philosophy. Or the elderly Worlingham sisters—if they really believed that he was responsible for Theophilus's death—"

"And do they?" Drummond only half believed it, and it was obvious in his face. "Would they really feel so strongly about it? Seems more likely to me they might have killed him to keep him quiet over the real source of the Worlingham money. That I could believe."

"Shaw says Clemency didn't tell them," Pitt replied, although it seemed far more likely to him also. "But perhaps he didn't know she had. She might have done it the night before she died. I need to find what precipitated the first murder. Something happened that day—or the day immediately before—that frightened or angered someone beyond enduring. Something changed the situation so drastically that what had been at the worst difficult, but maybe not even that, suddenly became so threatening or so intolerably unjust to them, they exploded into murder—"

"What did happen that day?" Drummond was watching him closely.

"I don't know," Pitt confessed. "I've been concentrating on Shaw, and he won't tell me anything. Of course, it is still possible he killed Clemency himself, set the fire before he left, and killed Amos Lindsay because somehow he had betrayed himself by a word, or an omission, and Lindsay knew what he'd done. They were friends—but I don't believe Lindsay would have kept silent once he was sure Shaw was guilty." It was a peculiarly repugnant thought, but honesty compelled that he allow it.

Drummond saw the reluctance in him.

"Not the first time you've liked a murderer, Pitt—nor I, for that matter. Life would be a great deal easier at times, if we could like all the heroes and dislike all the villains. Or personally I'd settle for simply not pitying the villains as much as I do the victims half the time."

"I can't always tell the difference." Pitt smiled sadly. "I've known murderers I've felt were victims as much as anyone in the whole affair. And if it turns out to be Angeline and Celeste, I may well this time too. The old bishop filled their lives, dominated them from childhood, laid out for them exactly the kind of women he expected them to be, and made it virtually impossible for them to be anything else. I gather he drove away all suitors and kept Celeste to be his intellectual companion, and Angeline to be his housekeeper and hostess when necessary. By the time he died they were far too old to marry, and totally dependent on his views, his social status and his money. If Clemency, in her outrage, threatened to destroy everything on which their lives were built, and faced them not only with old age in total public disgrace but a negation of everything they believed in and which justified the past, it is not hard to understand why they might have conspired to kill her. To them she was not only a mortal threat but a traitor to her family. They might consider her ultimate disloyalty to be a sin that warranted death."

"They might well," Drummond agreed. "Other than that you are left with some as yet unnamed slum profiteer who was threatened by Clemency's uncovering work. I suppose you have looked into who else's tenements she was interested in? What about Lutterworth? You said he's socially ambitious—especially for Flora—and wants to leave his trade roots behind and marry her into society? Slum profiteering wouldn't help that." He pulled a sour face. "Although I'm not sure it would entirely hurt it either. A good few of the aristocracy made their money in highly questionable ways."

"Undoubtedly," Pitt agreed. "But they do it discreetly. Vice they will overlook, vulgarity they may accept—with reluctance, if there is enough money attached—but indiscretion never."

"You're getting very cynical, Pitt." Drummond was smiling as he said it.

Pitt shrugged. "All I can find out about Lutterworth is that his money was in the north, and he sold nearly all his interests. There never was any in London that I can trace."

"What about the political aspect?" Drummond would not give up yet. "Could Clemency have been murdered because of some other connection with Dalgetty and his Fabian tracts—and Lindsay the same?"

"I haven't traced any connection." Pitt screwed up his face. "But certainly Clemency knew Lindsay, and they liked each other. But since they are both dead, it is impossible to know what they spoke about, unless Shaw knows and can be persuaded to tell us. And since both houses are burnt to the ground, there are no papers to find."

"You might have to go and speak to some of the other members of the society—"

"I will, if it comes to that; but today I'm going to Lindsay's funeral. And perhaps I can discover what Clemency did on her last day or two alive, who she spoke to and what happened that made someone so angry or so frightened that they killed her."

"Report to me afterwards, will you? I want to know."

"Yes sir. Now I must leave, or I shall be late. I hate funerals. I hate them most of all when I look around the faces of the mourners and think that one of them murdered him—or her."

Charlotte also was preparing to attend the funeral, but she was startled to have received a hand-addressed note from Emily to say that not only would she and Jack attend, and for convenience would pick Charlotte up in their carriage at ten o'clock, but that Great-Aunt Vespasia also would come. No explanation was given, nor when they arrived, since it was now five minutes past nine, would there be any opportunity to decline the arrangements or ask for any alternative.

"Thank heaven at least Mama and Grandmama are remaining at home." Charlotte folded the note and put it in her sewing basket, where Pitt would not find it, simply as a matter of habit. Of course he would ultimately know they had all attended, but there was no way she would be able to pretend to Pitt it was a matter of personal grief, although she had liked Lindsay. They were going because they were curious, and still felt they could discover something of meaning about Lindsay's death, and Clemency's. And that Pitt might not approve of.

Perhaps Emily knew something already? She and Jack had said they would probe the political questions, and Jack had made some contact with the Liberal party with a view to standing for Parliament when a vacant seat arose that would accept him as a candidate. And if he were truly serious about continuing Clemency's work, he might also have met with the Fabians and others with strong socialist beliefs—not, of course, that they had the slightest chance of returning a member to the House. But ideas were necessary, whether to argue for or against.

She was busy dressing her hair and unconsciously trying to make the very best of her appearance. She did not realize till she had been there half an hour and was still not entirely satisfied, just what an effort she was making. She blushed at her own vanity, and foolishness, and dismissed the wrenching thoughts of Stephen Shaw from her mind.

"Gracie!"

Gracie materialized from the landing, a duster in her hand, her face bright.

"Yes, ma'am?"

"Would you like to come to Mr. Lindsay's funeral with me?"

"Oh yes, ma'am! When is it, ma'am?"

"In about quarter of an hour—at least that is when we shall be leaving. Mrs. Radley is taking us in her carriage."

Gracie's face fell and she had to swallow hard on the sudden lump in her throat.

"I 'aven't finished me work, ma'am. There's still the stairs to do, and Miss Jemima's room. The dust settles jus' the same though she in't there right now. An' I in't changed proper. Me black dress in't pressed right—"

"That dress is dark enough." Charlotte looked at Gracie's ordinary gray stuff working dress. It was quite drab enough for mourning. Really, one day when she could afford it she should get her a nice bright blue one. "And you can forget the housework. It'll not go away—you can do it tomorrow; it'll all be the same in the end."

"Are you sure, ma'am?" Gracie had never been told to forget dusting before, and her eyes were like stars at the thought of just letting it wait—and instead going off on another expedition of detecting.

"Yes I'm sure," Charlotte replied. "Now go and do your hair and find your coat. We mustn't be late."

"Oh yes, ma'am. I will this minute, ma'am." And before Charlotte could add anything she was gone, her feet clattering up the attic stairs to her room.

Emily arrived precisely when she said she would, bursting in in a wildly elegant black gown cut in the latest lines, decorated with jet beading and not entirely suitable for a funeral, in that although the lace neckline was so high as to be almost to the ears, the main fabric of the dress was definitely a trifle fine, showing the pearliness of skin in an unmistakable gleam more fit for a soiree than a church. Her hat was very rakish, in spite of the veil, and her color was beautifully high in her cheeks. It was not difficult to believe that Emily was a new bride.

Charlotte was so happy for her she found it hard to disapprove, sensible though that would have been, and appropriate.

Jack was a couple of steps behind, immaculately dressed as always, and perhaps a little easier now about his tailor's bills. But there was also a new confidence about him too, not built solely on charm and the need to please, but upon some inner happiness that required no second person's approbation. Charlotte thought at first it was a reflection of his relationship with Emily. Then as soon as he spoke, she realized it was deeper than that; it was a purpose within himself, a thing radiating outward.

He kissed Charlotte lightly on the cheek.

"I have met with the Parliamentary party and I think they will accept me as a candidate!" he said with a broad smile. "As soon as a suitable by-election occurs I shall stand."

"Congratulations," Charlotte said with a great bubble of happiness welling up inside her. "We shall do everything we can to help you to succeed." She looked at Emily and saw the intense satisfaction in her face also, and the gleam of pride. "Absolutely everything. Even holding my tongue, should it be the last resort. Now we must go to Amos Lindsay's funeral. I think it is part of our cause. I don't know why, but I am convinced he died in connection with Clemency's death."

"Of course," Emily agreed. "It doesn't make any sense otherwise. The same person must have killed both of them. I still think it is politics. Clemency ruffled a great many feathers. The more I investigate what she was doing, and planning to do, the more I discover how fierce was her determination and how many people could be smeared with the taint of very dirty money indeed. Are you sure the Worlingham sisters did not know what she was doing?"

"No—not absolutely," Charlotte confessed. "I don't think so. But Celeste is a better actress than Angeline, whom I find very hard to think guilty, she seems so transparent, and so unworldly—even ineffectual. I can't think of her being efficient enough, or coolheaded enough, to have planned and laid those fires."

"But Celeste would," Emily pressed. "After all, they have more to lose than anyone."

"Except Shaw," Jack pointed out. "Clemency was giving away the Worlingham money hand over fist. As it happens she had given all her share away before she died—but you have only Shaw's word for it that he knew that. He may have thought little of what she was doing and killed her to stop her while there was still some left, and only learned afterwards that he was too late."

Charlotte turned to look at him. It was an extremely ugly thought which she had not until this moment seen, but it was undeniable. No one else knew what Clemency had been doing; there had been only Shaw's own word for it that he had known all along. Perhaps he hadn't? Perhaps he had found out only a day or two before Clemency's death, and it was that discovery which suddenly presented him with the prospect of losing his extremely comfortable position both financially, for certain, and socially, if she should make it public. It was a very good motive for murder indeed.

She said nothing, a chilling, rather sick feeling inside her.

"I'm sorry," Jack said gently. "But it had to be considered."

Charlotte swallowed hard and found it difficult. Shaw's fair, intense and blazingly honest face was before her inner eye. She was surprised how much it hurt.

"Gracie is coming with us." She looked away from them towards the door, as if the business of going were urgent and must be attended to. "I think she deserves to."

"Of course," Emily agreed. "I wish I thought we should really learn something—but all I can reasonably hope for is a strong instinct. Although we might manage to ask some pertinent questions at the funerary dinner afterwards. Are you invited?"

"I think so." Charlotte remembered very clearly Shaw's invitation, and his wish that she should be there, one person with whom he could feel an identity of candor. She thrust it from her mind. "Come on, or we shall be late!"

The funeral was a bright, windy affair with more than two hundred people packing the small church for the formal, very stilted service conducted by Clitheridge. Only the organ music was faultless, flowing in rich, throbbing waves over the solemn heads and engulfing them in the comfort of a momentary unity while they sang. The sun streamed through the stained-glass windows in a glory of color falling like jewels on the floor and across the rigid backs and heads and all the variegated textures of black.

Upon leaving Charlotte noticed a man of unusual appearance sitting close to the back, with his chin in the air and seemingly more interested in the ceiling than the other mourners. It was not that his features were particularly startling so much as the intelligence and humor in his expression, irreverent as it was. His hair was fiercely bright auburn and although he was sitting, he appeared to be quite a slight man. She certainly had not seen him before, and she hesitated out of curiosity.

"Is there something about me which troubles you, ma'am?" he asked, swiveling suddenly around to face her, and speaking with a distinctly Irish voice.

She collected her wits with an effort and replied with aplomb.

"Not in the least, sir. Any man as intent upon heaven as you deserves to be left to his contemplation—"

"It was not heaven, ma'am," he said indignantly. "It was the ceiling that had my attention." Then he realized she knew that as well as he, and had been irking him on purpose, and his face relaxed into a charming smile.

"George Bernard Shaw, ma'am. I was a friend of Amos Lindsay's. And were you also?"

"Yes I was." She stretched the truth a fraction. "And I am very sorry he is gone."

"Indeed." He was instantly sober again. "It's a sad and stupid waste."

Further conversation was made impossible by the press of

people desiring to leave the church, and Charlotte nodded politely and excused herself, leaving him to resume his contemplation.

At least half the mourners followed the coffin out into the sharp, sunny graveyard where the wet earth was dug and the ground was already sprinkled over with fallen leaves, gold and bronze on the green of the grass.

Aunt Vespasia, dressed in deep lavender (she refused to wear black), stood next to Charlotte, her chin high, her shoulders square, her hand gripping fiercely her silver-handled cane. She loathed it, but she was obliged to lean on it for support as Clitheridge droned on about the inevitability of death and the frailty of man.

"Fool," she said under her breath. "Why on earth do vicars imagine God cannot be spoken to in simple language and needs everything explained to Him in at least three different ways? I always imagine God as the last person to be impressed by long words or to be deceived by specious excuses. For heaven's sake, He made us. He knows perfectly well that we are fragile, stupid, glorious, grubby and brave." She poked her stick into the ground viciously. "And He certainly does not want these fanfaronades. Get on with it, man! Inter the poor creature and let us go and speak well of him in some comfort!"

Charlotte closed her eyes, wincing in case someone had heard. Vespasia's voice was not loud, but it was piercingly clear with immaculate enunciation. She heard a very soft "Here, here" behind her and involuntarily turned. She met Stephen Shaw's level blue eyes, bright with pain, and belying the smile on his lips.

She turned back to the grave again immediately, and saw Lally Clitheridge's look of steel-hard jealousy, but it aroused more pity in her than anger. Had she been married to Hector Clitheridge there would certainly have been moments when she too might have dreamed wild, impermissible dreams, and hated anyone who broke their fantastic surface, however ridiculous or slight.

Clitheridge was still wittering on, as if he could not bear to let the moment go, as though delaying the final replacing of the earth somehow extended a part of Amos Lindsay.

Oliphant was restive, moving his weight from one foot to the other, conscious of the grief and the indignity of it.

At the far end of the grave Alfred Lutterworth stood bare-headed, the wind ruffling his ring of white hair, and close beside him, her hand on his arm, Flora looked young and very pretty. The wind had put a touch of color into her cheeks, and the anxiety seemed to have gone from her expression. Even while Charlotte watched she saw Lutterworth place his hand over hers and tighten it a fraction.

Over her shoulder to the left, at the edge of the graveyard, Constable Murdo stood as upright as a sentry on duty, his buttons shining in the sun. Presumably he was here to observe everyone, but Charlotte never saw his gaze waver from Flora. For all that he seemed to observe, she might have been the only person present.

She saw Pitt only for a moment, a lean shadow somewhere near the vestry, trailing the ends of a muffler in the breeze. He turned towards her and smiled. Perhaps he had known she would come. For the space of an instant the crowd disappeared and there was no one else there. It was as if he had touched her. Then he turned and went on towards the yew hedge and the shadows. She knew he would be watching everything, expressions, gestures, whose eyes met whose, who spoke, who avoided speaking. She wondered if anything she had learned and told him was any use at all.

Maude Dalgetty was standing near the head of the grave. She was a little plumper than in her heyday, and the lines were quite clear in her face, but were all upward, generous and marked by humor. She was still a beauty, and perhaps always would be. In repose, as she was now, there was nothing sour in her features, nothing that spoke of regret.

Beside her, John Dalgetty stood very straight, avoiding even the slightest glance to where Quinton Pascoe stood equally rigid, doing his duty by a man he had liked but quarreled with fiercely. It was the attitude of a soldier at the grave of a fallen enemy.

Dalgetty's was the pose of a soldier also, but he was mourning a warrior in a mutual cause. Never once in the service did they acknowledge each other.

Josiah Hatch was bareheaded, as were all the men, and looked pinched as if the wind bit into his bones. Prudence was not with him; neither were the Worlingham sisters. They still held to the belief that ladies did not attend the church funeral or the graveside.

At last Clitheridge wound to a close, and the gravediggers began to replace the earth.

"Thank God," Shaw said behind Charlotte. "You are coming to the funeral luncheon, aren't you?"

"Of course," Charlotte accepted.

Vespasia turned around very slowly and regarded Shaw with cool interest.

He bowed. "Good morning, Lady Cumming-Gould. It is most gracious of you to come, especially on a day so late in the season when the wind is sharp. I am sure Amos would have appreciated it."

Vespasia's eyes flickered very slightly with an amusement almost invisible.

"Are you?"

He understood, and as always the candor was on his tongue instantly.

"You came because of Clemency." He had known he was right, but he saw it in her face. "It is not pity which brings you here, and you are right, the dead are beyond our emotions. It is anger. You are still determined to learn who killed her, and why."

"How perceptive of you," Vespasia agreed. "I am."

All the light vanished from his face, the frail humor like sunlight through snow. "So am I."

"Then we had better proceed to the funerary meal." She lifted her hand very slightly and immediately he offered her his arm. "Thank you," she accepted, and, her hat almost sweeping his shoulder in its magnificent arc, she sailed down the path towards her waiting carriage.

As had been done for Clemency, this gathering was held in the Worlingham house also, from very mixed motives. It was impossible to do it, as would have been customary, in Lindsay's own home, since it was a mere jumble of scarred beams resting at violent angles amid the heaps of burned and broken brick. His dearest friend, Shaw, was in no better a position. He could hardly offer to hold it in Mrs. Turner's lodging house. It was not large enough and was occupied by several other people who could not be expected to have their house disrupted for such an event.

The choice rested between the Worlinghams' and the vicarage. As soon as they realized that, Celeste and Angeline offered the use of their home, and of their servants to make all the necessary provisions. It was a matter of duty. They had not cared for Amos Lindsay, and cared still less for his opinions, but they were the bishop's daughters, and the leaders of Christian society in Highgate. Position must come before personal feelings, especially towards the dead.

All this they made plain, in case anyone should mistakenly imagine they supported anything that Amos Lindsay had said or done.

They received everyone at the double doorway into the dining room, where the huge mahogany table was spread with every kind of baked meat and cold delicacy. The centerpiece was formed of lilies with a heavy, languorous perfume which instantly reminded Charlotte of somnolence, and eventually decay. The blinds were partially drawn, because today at least the house was in mourning, and black crepe was trailed suitably over pictures and texts on the walls, and around the newel posts of the stairs and over the door lintels.

The formal proceedings were very carefully laid out. It would have been impossible to seat everyone, and anyway since Shaw had invited extra people as the whim took him (including Pitt, to the deep indignation of the Worlingham sisters and the vicar), the servants did not know in advance how many there would be.

Therefore the food was set out so that people might be served by the butler and maids who were standing waiting discreetly just beyond the door, and then stand and speak with each other, commiserate, gossip and generally praise the dead until it should be time for a few prepared words, first by the vicar, then by Shaw as the departed's closest friend. And of course they could partake of a few of the very best bottles of Port wine, or something a little lighter for the women. Claret was served with the meal.

"I don't know how we are going to learn anything now," Emily said with a frown of disappointment. "Everyone is doing precisely what one would expect. Clitheridge looks incompetent and harassed, his wife is trying to compensate for him all the time, while being aware of you and Dr. Shaw, and if looks had any effect your hair would have frizzled on your head and dropped out, and your dress would hang on your back in scorched rags."

"Can you blame her?" Charlotte whispered back. "The vicar doesn't exactly make one's pulse race, does he."

"Don't be vulgar. No he doesn't. I would rather have the good doctor any day—unless, of course, he murdered his wife."

Charlotte had no effective answer for that, knowing it could be true, however much it hurt, so she turned around sharply and poked Emily in the ribs, as if by accident.

"Humph," Emily said in total comprehension.

Flora Lutterworth was on her father's arm, her veil drawn back so she might eat, and there was color in her cheeks and a faintly smug smile on her pretty mouth. Charlotte was curious to know what had caused it.

Across the room at the far side, Pitt saw it too, and had a very good idea it had something to do with Murdo. He considered it highly likely that Murdo would not find it so difficult to pursue Miss Lutterworth. In fact he might very well discover that it happened in spite of any ideas of his own, and it would all be much easier than he had feared.

Pitt was dressed unusually smartly for him. His collar was neat, his tie perfectly straight—at least so far—and he had nothing in his jacket pockets except a clean handkerchief (Emily's silk one was only for show), a short pencil and a piece of folded paper so he might make notes if he wished. That was quite redundant, because he never did; it was something he thought an efficient policeman ought to have.

He realized Shaw had invited him precisely to annoy Angeline and Celeste. It was a way of establishing that although the function was held in the Worlingham house, this was Amos Lindsay's funerary dinner, and he, Shaw, was the host and would invite whom he chose. To that end he stood at the head of the table, very square on his feet, and behaved as if the servants offering the baked meats and claret were his own. He welcomed the guests, especially Pitt. He did not glance once at the grim faces of Angeline and Celeste, who were in black bombazine and jet beads, standing behind him and a trifle to one side. They smiled guardedly at those they approved of, such as Josiah and Prudence Hatch, Quinton Pascoe, and Aunt Vespasia; nodded civilly to those they tolerated, like the Lutterworths, or Emily and Jack; and totally ignored those whose presence they knew to be a calculated affront, such as Pitt and Charlotte—although since they came separately and did not speak to each other, the sisters did not immediately connect them.

Pitt took his delicious cold game pie, jugged hare, and brown bread and butter and homemade pickle, liberally apportioned, and his glass of claret, finding them extraordinarily difficult to manage, and wandered around half overhearing conversations, and closely observing faces—those who were speaking, and more particularly those who were alone and unaware they were being observed.

What had been the precise course of events on the day or two before Clemency Shaw's death? Some time earlier she had discovered the source of the Worlingham money, and spread and given away her own inheritance, almost entirely to relieve the distress of those who were the victims of appalling misery, either directly to assist them, or indirectly to fight the laws which presently enabled owners to take their excess profits so discreetly that their names were never known nor their public reputations smeared with their true behavior.

When had she shared this with Shaw? Or had he discovered

it some way of his own, perhaps only when her money was gone, and they had had a furious quarrel? Or had he been wiser than that, and pretended to agree— No. If he had hidden his response, it must have been because he thought there was still a substantial majority of the money left—enough to be worth killing her to save.

He looked across the heads of two women talking, to where Shaw still stood at the head of the table, smiling and nodding, talking to Maude Dalgetty. He looked very tense; his shoulders were tight under the fabric of his black jacket, as if he longed to break into action, punch the air, stride backward and forward, do anything to use that wild anger inside him. Pitt found it hard to believe he would have contained his temper so well that Clemency, who must have known his every expression, inflection of voice, gesture, would not have understood the power of his rage, and thus at least some shadow of her own danger.

What must she have thought when Josiah Hatch announced that there was going to be a stained-glass window put in the church dedicated to the old bishop, and depicting him as one of the early Christian saints? What an intolerable irony. What self-control had enabled her to keep silent? And she had done so. It had been a public announcement, and if she had given even the slightest hint that she knew some hideous secret, as a member of the family she would have been listened to, even if not entirely believed.

Was it conceivable that everyone had kept silent about it—a conspiracy?

He looked around the room at the somber faces. All were suitably grim for the occasion: Clitheridge harassed and nervous; Lally smoothing things over, fussing around Shaw; Pascoe and Dalgetty studiously avoiding each other, but still padded out by bandages under their mourning clothes—Dalgetty's cheek stitched and plastered. Matthew Oliphant was speaking quietly, a word of comfort, a gesture of warmth or reassurance; Josiah Hatch's face was white except where the wind had whipped his cheeks; Prudence was more relaxed than earlier, her fear gone. Angeline and Celeste were quietly angry; the Lutterworths were still being socially patronized. No, he could not believe in a conspiracy among such disparate people. Too many of them had no interest in protecting the reputation of the Worlinghams. Dalgetty would have delighted in spreading such a richly ironic tale, the ultimate freedom to speak against the established order of things—even if only to infuriate Pascoe.

And Amos Lindsay, with his Fabian socialist sympathies, would surely have laughed loud and long, and made no secret of it at all.

No—assuredly nothing had been said when the window was announced. And all plans had gone ahead for it, money had been raised, the glass purchased and the artists and glaziers engaged. The Archbishop of York had been invited to dedicate it and all Highgate and half ecclesiastical north London would be there at the ceremony.

Pitt sipped his claret. It was extremely good. The old bishop must have laid down a remarkable cellar, as well as everything else. Ten years after his death, Theophilus's share gone, and there was still this quality to draw on for an affair which was not really more than a duty for Celeste and Angeline.

The Worlingham window must be costing a very considerable amount of money, and according to the family, part of the purpose of it was to show the great regard in which the whole of Highgate had held the bishop. Therefore it was to be funded with public money, collected from the parish, and any other people whose remembrance of him was so clear that they wished to contribute.

Who had organized that? Celeste? Angeline? No—it had been Josiah Hatch. Of course, it would be a man. They would hardly leave such a public and financial matter to elderly ladies. And it would be more seemly if it did not come from one of the immediate family. That left the two grandsons-in-law—Hatch and Shaw. Hatch was a church sidesman, and had a reverence for the bishop that exceeded even that of his daughters. He was the old bishop's true spiritual heir.

Anyway, the idea of Stephen Shaw working on such a scheme was ludicrous. He had disliked the bishop strongly in his lifetime, and now on learning of the true source of his wealth, he whose daily work took him to the victims of such greed, despised him with a passion.

Pitt wondered what Shaw had said to Hatch, when Hatch asked him for a contribution. That must have been a rich moment: Hatch holding out his hand for money for a memorial window depicting the bishop as a saint; and Shaw newly aware that the bishop's fortune came from the wretchedness of thousands, even the exploitation and death of many—and his wife had just given away every penny she inherited to right at least a fraction of the wrongs.

Had Shaw kept his temper—and a still tongue?

Pitt looked again across the crowd at that passionate, dynamic face with its ruthless honesty.

Surely not?

Shaw was banging the table, his glass high in his other hand.

Gradually the buzz of conversation died and everyone turned towards him.

"Ladies and gentlemen," he said in a clear, ringing voice. "We are met here today, at the kind invitation of Miss Celeste and Miss Angeline Worlingham, to honor our departed friend, Amos Lindsay. It is appropriate that we say a few words about him, to remember him as he was."

There was a faintly uncomfortable shifting of weight in the room, a creaking of whalebone stays, the faint rattle of taffeta, someone's shoes squeaking, an exhalation of breath.

"The vicar spoke of him in church," Shaw went on, his voice a little louder. "He praised his virtues, or perhaps it would be more accurate to say he praised a list of virtues which it is customary to attribute to the dead, and no one ever argues and says, 'Well, no, actually, he wasn't like that at all.' " He raised his glass a little higher. "But I am! I want us to drink in remembrance of the man as he really was, not some hygienic, dehumanized plaster replica of him, robbed of all his weaknesses, and so of all his triumphs."

"Really—" Clitheridge looked pale and dithered between stepping forward and interrupting physically—and the more restrained action of simply remonstrating, and hoping Shaw's better taste would prevail. "I mean—don't you think—?"

"No I don't," Shaw said briskly. "I hate the pious whimperings about his being a pillar of the community, a God-fearing man and beloved of us all. Have you no honesty left in your souls? Can you stand here and say you all loved Amos Lindsay? Balderdash!"

There was an audible gasp of indrawn breath this time, and Clitheridge turned around desperately as if he were hoping some miraculous rescue might be at hand.

"Quinton Pascoe was afraid of him, and was horrified by his writings. He would have had him censored, had he been able."

There was a slight rustle and murmur as everyone swiveled to look at Pascoe, who turned bright pink. But before he could protest, Shaw went on.

"And Aunt Celeste and Aunt Angeline abhorred everything he stood for. They were—and still are—convinced that his Fabian views are unchristian and, if allowed to proliferate though society, will bring about the end of everything that is civilized and beneficial to mankind—or at any rate to that class of it to which we belong, which is all that matters to them, because it is all they know. It is all their sainted father ever allowed them to know."

"You are drunk!" Celeste said in a furious whisper which carried right around the room.

"On the contrary, I am extremely sober," he replied, looking up at the glass in his hand. "Even Theophilus's best burgundy has not affected me—because I have not drunk enough of it. And as for his superb Port—I have not even touched it yet. The very least I owe poor Amos is to have my thoughts collected when I speak of him—although God knows I have enough provocation to get drunk. My wife, my best friend and my house have all been taken from me in the last few weeks. And even the police, with all their diligence, don't seem to have the faintest idea by whom."

"This is most undignified," Prudence said very quietly, but still her voice carried so at least a dozen people heard her.

"You wanted to speak of Mr. Lindsay," Oliphant prompted Shaw.

Shaw's face changed. He lowered the glass and put it on the table.

"Yes, thank you for reminding me. This is not the time or the occasion for my losses. We are here to remember Amos—truly and vividly as the living man really was. We do him a hideous disservice to paint him in pastel colors and gloss over the failures, and the victories."

"We should not speak ill of the dead, Stephen," Angeline said after clearing her throat. "It is most unchristian, and quite unnecessary. I am sure we were all very fond of Mr. Lindsay and thought only the best of him."

"No you didn't," he contradicted her. "Did you know he married an African woman? Black as the ace of spades—and beautiful as the summer night. And he had children—but they are all still in Africa."

"Really, Stephen—this is quite irresponsible!" Celeste stepped forward and took him firmly by the elbow. "The man is not here to defend himself—"

Shaw shook her loose, bumping her abruptly.

"God dammit, he doesn't need a defense!" he shouted. "Marrying an African is not a sin! He did have sins—plenty of them—" He flung his arms expressively. "When he was young he was violent, he drank too much, he took advantage of fools, especially rich ones, and he took women that most certainly weren't his." His face screwed up with intensity and his voice dropped. "But he also had compassion, after he'd learned pain himself: he was never a liar, nor a bigot." He looked around at them all. "He never spread gossip and he could keep a secret to the grave. He had no pretensions and he knew a hypocrite when he saw one—and loathed all forms of cant."

"I really think—" Clitheridge began, flapping his hands as if he would attract everyone's attention away from Shaw. "Really—I—"

"You can pontificate all you like over everyone else." Shaw's voice was very loud now. "But Amos was my friend, and I shall speak of him as he really was. I'm sick of hearing platitudes and lies, sick and weary to my heart of it! You couldn't even speak of poor Clem honestly. You mouthed a lot of pious phrases that meant nothing at all, said nothing of what she was really like.

You made her sound as if she were a quiet, submissive, ignorant little woman who wore her life away being obedient, looking after me and doing useless good works among the parish poor. You made her seem colorless, cowardly of spirit and dull of mind. She wasn't!" He was so furious now, and so torn by grief, that his face was suffused with color, his eyes were bright and his whole body trembled. Even Celeste dared not interfere.

"That was nothing like Clem. She had more courage than all the rest of you put together—and more honesty!"

With difficulty Pitt tore his attention from Shaw and looked around at the other faces. Was there any one of them reflecting fear of what Shaw was going to say next? There was anxiety in Angeline's face, and distaste in Celeste's, but he could not see the dread that would have been there had they known of Clemency's discovery.

There was nothing in Prudence's profile either, and nothing in the half outline of Josiah except rigid contempt.

"God knows how she was born a Worlingham," Shaw went on, his fist clenched tight, his body hunched as if waiting to explode into motion. "Old Theophilus was a pretentious, greedy old hypocrite—and a coward to the last—"

"How dare you!" Celeste was too angry to consider any vestige of propriety left. "Theophilus was a fine, upright man who lived honestly and charitably all his life. It is you who are greedy and a coward! If you had treated him properly, as you should have, both as his son-in-law and as his doctor, then he would probably be alive today!"

"Indeed he would," Angeline added, her face quivering. "He was a noble man, and always did his duty."

"He died groveling on the floor with fistfuls of money spread all around him, tens of thousands of pounds!" Shaw exploded at last. "If anybody killed him, it was probably whoever was blackmailing him!"

There was a stunned and appalled silence. For deafening seconds no one even drew breath. Then there was a shriek from Angeline, a stifled sob from Prudence.

"Dear heaven!" Lally spoke at last.

"What on earth are you saying?" Lutterworth demanded.

"This is outrageous! Theophilus Worlingham was an outstanding man in the community, and you can have no possible grounds for saying such a thing! You didn't find him, did you? Who says there was all this money? Perhaps he had a major purchase in mind."

Shaw's face was blazing with derision. "With seven thousand, four hundred and eighty-three pounds—in cash?"

"Perhaps he kept his money in the house?" Oliphant suggested quietly. "Some people do. He may have been counting it when he was taken by a seizure. It was a seizure he died of, wasn't it?"

"Yes it was," Shaw agreed. "But it was flung all over the room, and there were five notes clutched in his hand, thrust out before him as if he were trying to give it to someone. Everything indicated he hadn't been alone."

"That is a monstrous lie!" Celeste found her voice at last. "Quite wicked, and you know it! He was utterly alone, poor man. It was Clemency who found him, and called you."

"Clem found him, and called me, certainly," Shaw agreed. "But he was lying in his study, with the French doors open onto the garden—and who is to say she was the first person there? He was already almost cold when she arrived."

"For God's sake, man!" Josiah Hatch burst out. "You are speaking about your father-in-law—and the Misses Worlingham's brother! Have you no decency left at all?"

"Decency!" Shaw turned on him. "There's nothing indecent in speaking about death. He was lying on the floor, purple-faced, his eyes bulging out of his head, his body chill, and five hundred pounds in Treasury notes held so fast in his hand we couldn't remove them to lay him out. What is indecent is where the bloody money came from!"

Everyone began to shift uncomfortably, half afraid to look at each other, and yet unable to help it. Eyes met eyes and then slid away again. Someone coughed.

"Blackmail?" someone said aloud. "Not Theophilus!"

A woman giggled nervously and her gloved hand flew to her mouth to suppress the sound.

There was a sharp sibilance of whispering, cut off instantly.

"Hector?" Lally's voice was clear.

Clitheridge looked red-faced and utterly wretched. Some force beyond himself seemed to propel him forward to where Shaw stood at the head of the table, Celeste a little behind him and to his right, white to the lips and shaking with rage.

"Ahem!" Clitheridge cleared his throat. "Ahem—I—er . . ." He looked around wildly for rescue, and found none. He looked at Lally once more, his face now scarlet, and gave up. "I—er—I am afraid I was the one with—with, er—Theophilus when he died—er, at least shortly before. He—er—" He cleared his throat violently again as if he had some obstruction in it. "He—er—he sent a message for me to come to him—with one of the—er—choirboys who had—er—" He looked imploringly at Lally, and met implacable resolve. He gasped for air, and continued in abysmal misery. "I read the message and went over to his house straightaway—it sounded most urgent. I—er—I found him in a state of great excitement, quite unlike anything I had ever seen." He shut his eyes and his voice rose to a squeak as he relived the utter horror of it. "He was beside himself. He kept spluttering and choking and waving his hands in the air. There were piles of Treasury notes on his desk. I could not even hazard a guess how much money. He was frantic. He looked very unwell and I implored him to allow me to send for the doctor, but he would not hear of it. I am not sure he even grasped what I was saying. He kept on insisting he had a sin to confess." Clitheridge's eyes were rolling like a frightened horse and he looked everywhere but at the Worlinghams. The sweat broke out on his brow and lip and his hands were wringing each other so hard his knuckles were white.

"He kept on thrusting the money at me and begging me to take it—for the church—for the poor—for anything. And he wanted me to hear his confession . . ." His voice trailed away, too agonized at the memory to find words anymore, as if his throat had closed.

"Lies!" Celeste said loudly. "Absolute lies! Theophilus never had anything to be ashamed of. He must have been having a seizure, and you misunderstood everything. Why in heaven's name didn't you call the doctor yourself, you fool!"

Clitheridge found his tongue again. "He was not having a seizure," he said indignantly. "He was lunging after me, trying to grasp hold of me and force me to take the money, all of it! There were thousands of pounds! And he wanted me to hear his confession. I was—I was mortified with embarrassment. I have never seen anything so—so—so horrifying in my life."

"What in God's name did you do?" Lutterworth demanded.

"I—er—" Clitheridge swallowed convulsively. "I—I ran! I simply fled out of that ghastly room, through the French windows—and across the garden—all the way back to the vicarage."

"And told Lally, who promptly covered up for you—as usual," Shaw finished. "Leaving Theophilus to fall into a seizure and die all by himself—clutching the money. Very Christian!" Still, honesty moderated contempt. "Not that you could have saved him—"

Clitheridge had collapsed within himself, guilty, hideously embarrassed and overcome with failure. Only Lally took any notice of him, and she patted him absently as she would a child.

"But all the money—?" Prudence demanded. She was confused and appalled. "What was all the money for? It doesn't make sense. He didn't keep money at home. And what happened to it?"

"I put it back in the bank, where it came from," Shaw answered her.

Angeline was on the edge of tears.

"But what was it for? Why would poor Theophilus take all his money out of the bank? Did he really mean to give it all to the church? How noble of him! How like him!" She swallowed hard. "How like Papa too! Stephen—you should have done as he wished. It was very wrong of you to put it back in the bank. Of course I understand why—so Prudence and Clemency could inherit it all, not just the house and the investments—but it was still very wrong of you."

"God Almighty!" Shaw shouted. "You idiot woman! Theophilus wanted to give it to the church to buy his salvation! It was blood money! It came from slum tenements—every penny of it wrung out of the poor, the keepers of brothels, the distilling in gin mills, the masters of sweatshops and the sellers of opium in narrow little dormitories where addicts lie in rows and smoke themselves into oblivion. That's where the Worlingham money comes from. The old bishop bled every drop of it out of Lisbon

Street, and God knows how many others like it—and built this damn great palace of complacency for himself and his family."

Angeline held both her hands to her mouth, knuckles white, tears running down her face. Celeste did not even look at her. They were quite separate in their overwhelming shock and the ruin of their world. She stood strong-faced, staring into some distance beyond everyone present, hatred and an immense, intolerable anger hardening inside her.

"Theophilus knew it," Shaw went on relentlessly. "And in the end when he thought he was dying it terrified the hell out of him. He tried to give it back—and it was too late. I didn't know it then—I didn't even know that ass Clitheridge had been there, or what the money was for. I simply put it in the bank because it was Theophilus's, and shouldn't be left lying around. I only discovered where it came from when Clemency did—and told me. She gave it all away in shame—and to make whatever reparation she could—"

"That's a lie! Satan speaks in your mouth!" Josiah Hatch lunged forward, his face scarlet, his hands outstretched like talons to grip Shaw by the throat and choke the life out of him, and stop his terrible words forever. "You blasphemer! You deserve to die—I don't know why God has not struck you down. Except that He uses us poor men to do His work." Already he had carried Shaw to the ground with the fierceness of his attack and his own despair.

Pitt charged through the crowd, which was standing motionless and aghast. He thrust them aside, men and women alike, and grasped at Hatch's shoulders, trying to pull him back, but Hatch had the strength of devotion, even martyrdom if need be.

Pitt was shouting at him, but he knew even as he did so that Hatch could not hear him.

"You devil!" Hatch spoke from between his teeth. "You blasphemer! If I let you live you'll soil every clean and pure thing. You'll spew up your filthy ideas over all the good work that has been done—plant seeds of doubt where there used to be faith. You'll tell your obscene lies about the bishop and make people laugh at him, deride him where they used to revere him."

He was weeping as he spoke, his hands still scrabbling at Shaw's throat, his hair fallen forward over his brow, his face purple. "It is better that one man should die than a whole people wither in unbelief. You must be cast out—you pollute and destroy. You should be thrown into the sea—with a millstone 'round your neck. Better you'd never been born than drag other people down to hell with you."

Pitt hit him as hard as he could across the side of the head, and after a brief moment of convulsing, wild arms flailing and his mouth working without sound, Josiah Hatch fell to the ground and lay still, his eyes closed, his hands clasped like claws.

Jack Radley pushed his way from the side of the room and came to Pitt's aid, bending over Hatch and holding him.

Celeste fainted and Oliphant eased her to the ground.

Angeline was weeping like a child, lost, alone and utterly bereft.

Prudence was frozen as if all life had left her.

"Get Constable Murdo!" Pitt ordered.

No one moved.

Pitt jerked up to repeat his command, and saw out of the corner of his eye Emily going towards the hallway and the front door, where Murdo was patrolling.

At last life returned to the assembly. Taffeta rustled, whalebone creaked, there was a sighing of breath and the women moved a little closer to the men.

Shaw climbed to his feet, white-faced, his eyes like holes in his head. Everyone turned away, except Charlotte. She moved towards him. He was shaking. He did not even attempt to straighten his clothes. His hair was standing out in tufts, his necktie was under one ear and his collar was torn. His jacket was dusty and one sleeve was ripped from the armhole, and there were deep scratches on his face.

"It was Josiah!" His voice was husky in his bruised throat. "Josiah killed Clem—and Amos. He wanted to kill me." He looked strained and there was confusion in his eyes.

"Yes," she agreed, her voice soft and very level. "He wanted to kill you all the time. Lindsay and Clem were only mistakes—because you were out of the house. Although perhaps he didn't mind if he got Amos as well—he had no reason to suppose he was out, as he did with Clemency."

"But why?" He looked hurt, like a child who has been struck for no reason. "We quarreled, but it wasn't serious—"

"Not for you." She found it suddenly very painful to speak. She knew how deeply it would hurt him, and yet she could not evade it. "But you mocked him—"

"Good God, Charlotte—he asked for it! He was a hypocrite— all his values were absurd. He half worshiped old Worlingham, who was a greedy, vicious and thoroughly corrupt man, posing as a saint—and not only robbing people blind but robbing the destitute. Josiah spent his life praising and preaching lies."

"But they were precious to him," she repeated.

"Lies! Charlotte—they were lies!"

"I know that." She held his gaze in an uncompromising stare, and saw the distress in his, the incomprehension, and the terrible depth of caring.

It was a bitter blow she was going to deal him, and yet it was the only way to healing, if he accepted it.

"But we all need our heroes, and our dreams—real or false. And before you destroy someone else's dreams, if they have built their lives on them, you have to put something in their place. Before, Dr. Shaw." She saw him wince at her formality. "Not afterwards. Then it is too late. Being an iconoclast, destroying false idols—or those you think are false—is great fun, and gives you a wonderful feeling of moral superiority. But there is a high price to speaking the truth. You are free to say what you choose—and probably this has to be so, if there is to be any growth of ideas at all—but you are responsible for what happens because you speak it."

"Charlotte—"

"But you spoke it without thinking, or caring—and walked away." She did not moderate her words at all. "You thought truth was enough. It isn't. Josiah at least could not live with it— and perhaps you should have thought of that. You knew him well enough—you've been his brother-in-law for twenty years."

"But—" Now there was no disguising any of his sudden, newfound pain. He cared intensely what she thought of him, and he could see the criticism in her face. He searched for approval, even a shred; understanding, a white, pure love of truth for its own sake. And he saw at last only what was there—the knowledge that with power comes responsibility.

"You had the power to see," she said, moving a step away from him. "You had the words, the vision—and you knew you were stronger than he was. You destroyed his idols, without thinking what would happen to him without them."

He opened his mouth to protest again, but it was a cry of loneliness and the beginning of a new and bitter understanding. Slowly he turned away and looked at Josiah, who was now regaining his senses and being hauled to his feet by Pitt and Jack Radley. Somewhere in the hallway Emily was bringing Constable Murdo in, carrying handcuffs.

Shaw still could not face Angeline and Celeste, but he held out his hands to Prudence

"I'm sorry," he said very quietly. "I am truly sorry."

She stood motionless for a moment, unable to decide. Then slowly she extended her hands to him, and he clasped them and held them.

Charlotte turned away and pushed between the crowd to find Great-Aunt Vespasia.

Vespasia sighed and took Charlotte's arm.

"A very dangerous game—the ruin of dreams, however foolish," she murmured. "Too often we think because we cannot see them that they do not have the power to destroy—and yet our lives are built upon them. Poor Hatch—such a deluded man, such false idols. And yet we cannot tear them down with impunity. Shaw has much to account for."

"He knows," Charlotte said quietly, raw with regret herself. "I told him so."

Vespasia tightened her hand on Charlotte's. There was no need for words.

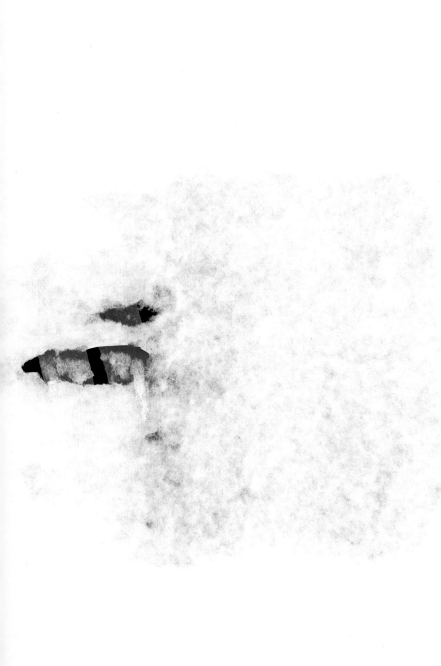

THE PSYCHOLOGY
OF SUICIDE

THE PSYCHOLOGY
OF SUICIDE

Edwin S. Shneidman, PH.D.

Fellow, Center for Advanced Study in the Behavioral Sciences, Stanford, California

Norman L. Farberow, PH.D.

Co-Director, Suicide Prevention Center, Los Angeles; Principal Investigator, Central Research Unit, Veterans Administration Center, Los Angeles; Clinical Professor of Psychiatry (Psychology), University of Southern California School of Medicine

Robert E. Litman, M.D.

Co-Director and Chief Psychiatrist, Suicide Prevention Center, Los Angeles; Professor of Psychiatry, University of Southern California School of Medicine

New York
Science House
1970

Library of Congress Catalog Card Number: 75-84841
Standard Book Number: 87668-027-9

FORMAT BY HARVEY DUKE

Manufactured by Haddon Craftsmen, Inc.
Scranton, Pennsylvania

To The Memory of
Louis I. Dublin
Pioneer in Suicidology

FOREWORD

The deliberate invention of new institutionalized social behavior based on scientifically disciplined forethought does not yet come easily even to modern technological man. The transition from the long-held faith in an inherently regulated homeostatic society to an active society of responsibility-accepting, self-studying, and self-directing people is only beginning. Yet these assertive trends toward the use of validated knowledge not only to inform but also to create social practice are demonstratively visible. Certainly they are apparent in the contemporary medical response to human distress and particularly in that specific behavior of distress expressed as contemplated, attempted, or completed suicide.

Over a decade ago, two psychologists, Dr. Edwin Shneidman and Dr. Norman Farberow, became an unique social happening. They began to define themselves as one manifestation of how society ought to respond to the suicidal behavior of individuals. The immediate motivation was to save lives, but as with so much of human despair that threatens or makes others uneasy and therefore is intentionally hidden, structurally isolated, or culturally transformed from being troubled into troublemaking, it was necessary also to make suicidal distress socially visible as well as conceptually acceptable as a signal for help. The social visibility of distress and the associated response of reparation and help could then lead to the use of the disciplined imagination, of rationality, to understand, to study, and then to inform distress-reducing and distress-preventing action.

A social invention, the Suicide Prevention Center of Los Angeles, consequently came into being. It is at least Janus-faced, one aspect being intimately related to the urban space in which so much of man's unhappiness is now occurring. The inward-directed face looks into the University of Southern California and the School of Medicine and provides the awareness and the integration of the knowledge and resources that, as the book illustrates, have been brought to the study of suicide.

The evaluation and assessment of an innovated social organization itself is as important as the judgment of its actions and effects

in its investing society. From its beginning, the Suicide Prevention Center was designed to make possible the noncompetitive collaboration of many disciplines. Dr. Robert Litman, a psychiatrist, became Co-Director, and the plan to involve a wide range of professional practitioners, caretakers, and social gatekeepers in the research, training, and helping functions of the Center was formulated.

The National Institute of Mental Health underwrote a generous grant to establish the Center as an innovative demonstration project in suicide prevention and study. The late Dr. Harold Hildreth, a well-known psychologist associated with the National Institute of Mental Health, energetically supported the Center and gave much of his time and intellectual resources to the developing years of the organization.

Under the aegis of these innovating men, the Center constantly studied itself, seeking to maintain its own creative balance between stability and invention and change. It is particularly necessary for those social organizations formed primarily to respond to psychological needs, either reparative or developmental, to apply to themselves as effectively as possible the contemporary knowledge about human behavior. Otherwise they may transform the human energy brought to them by the members of the organization into inefficient, ineffective, or, even worse, into destructive action either in the interactions of people inside the organization or also between the transactions of the organization and the people who come to it for help. In responding to this necessity for behaviorally sophisticated self-study, the Suicide Center has effectively refuted that it is always darkest under the lamp.

This collection of readings is the outcome of the history and of the social process of many committed and thinking people who have responded to and who have tried to understand those among us who try to die or who try not to live. But this volume on suicide may also be a primer for those of us who are trying to be alive.

Edward Stainbrook, PH.D., M.D.
Professor of Human Behavior
School of Medicine
University of Southern California

PREFACE

For over ten happy and productive years (1955-1966) the three of us were "suicidal" together. In that decade, we initiated, organized, and administered the Los Angeles Suicide Prevention Center; we authored or edited, separately and jointly, some 80 publications, including four books; and, perhaps most importantly, we experienced—each stimulated by the other—a continual daily pursuit of fresh ideas and new clinical and intellectual adventures—all relating to the prevention of unnecessary deaths.

This present volume is a sampler—a collection of "readings" from among our publications of that period. The contents are organized under eight headings: theory and taxonomy, administration and organization, statistics and demography, diagnosis and evaluation—general, diagnosis and evaluation—specific clinical groups, therapy and treatment, forensic and professional issues, biography and literature, and book reviews. We have advertently tried, in this volume, to reprint materials which originally appeared in somewhat out-of-the-way sources.

The large majority of the 44 chapters was written by one or more of the three of us; eleven of the chapters were co-authored with one or more of the three of us by a dozen of our colleagues. We express our special gratitude to them: Samuel M. Heilig, Charles Neuringer and Norman D. Tabachnick of the Los Angeles Suicide Prevention Center; Sidney Cohen, Allen Darbonne, Calista Leonard, Theodore L. McEvoy, and John W. McKelligott of the Veterans Administration Center in Los Angeles; Theodore J. Curphey of the Los Angeles County Coroners Office; Daniel M. Ogilvie and Philip J. Stone of Harvard University; and Philip Mandelkorn of *Time* magazine.

On the Acknowledgment Page we have listed the publishers and journals to whom we are indebted for their permission to allow us to reproduce the pieces in this volume. The complete bibliographic reference for each item is given on the first page of each chapter.

The nature of our joint efforts has been such that they could not have been pursued without the active support of at least four major organizations, to whom we wish to express our special indebtedness

and appreciation: the Veterans Administration, both the Central Office in Washington, D.C., and the Los Angeles Center; the Office of the Los Angeles County Chief Medical Examiner-Coroner, specifically Dr. Theodore J. Curphey; the National Institute of Mental Health, especially the late Dr. Harold M. Hildreth, for initiating, sustaining and supporting NIMH Grant MH-128 from 1958 to 1969; and the University of Southern California School of Medicine, especially Deans Clayton Loosli and Roger Egeberg and Dr. Edward Stainbrook, Chairman of the Department of Psychiatry.

A number of lovely and willing helpers, in a number of different places, assisted in a number of ways in the preparation of this book. It is a pleasure to thank them. They are: Kay Smith (at the Los Angeles Suicide Prevention Center), China Jessup (at the National Institute of Mental Health), Lynne Beale and Frances Rodgers (at Harvard), Isabelle Brown and Patricia Tankard (at the Massachusetts General Hospital), Florence Boitano and Sara Frank (at the NIMH San Francisco Regional Office), and Helen Lowrance and Priscilla Jones (at the Center for Advanced Study in the Behavioral Sciences).

Appropriately, this volume will convey some aspects of our separate interests, our different emphases and our individual styles. But, more importantly from our point of view, we hope that it will not fail to communicate the extent of our shared endeavors and our common concerns.

E.S.S.
N.L.F.
R.E.L.

Stanford and
Los Angeles,
California
1970

ACKNOWLEDGMENTS

Appreciation is acknowledged to the following for permission to reproduce materials which appear in this volume.

CHAPTER 1:
Reprinted from Robert W. White (ed.), *The Study of Lives* (New York: Atherton Press, 1963); also printed in the *International Journal of Psychiatry, 2*:167–200, 1966, and in H. L. P. Resnik (ed.), *Suicidal Behaviors* (Boston: Little, Brown and Co., 1968). The discussions are reprinted from the *International Journal of Psychiatry*.

CHAPTER 2:
Reprinted from *Journal of Consulting Psychology, 28*:95–106, 1964.

CHAPTER 3:
Reprinted from E. S. Shneidman and N. L. Farberow (eds.), *Clues to Suicide* (New York: McGraw-Hill Book Co., 1957).

CHAPTER 4:
Reprinted from George Gerbner *et al.* (eds.), *The Analysis of Communication Content* (New York: John Wiley and Sons, 1969).

CHAPTER 5:
Reprinted from *The American Journal of Public Health, 55*:21–26, 1965.

CHAPTER 6:
Reprinted from *Community Mental Health Journal, 4*:287–295, 1968.

CHAPTER 7:
Reprinted from *Public Affairs Pamphlet No. 406* (New York: Public Affairs Committee, 1967).

CHAPTER 8:
Reprinted from *Bulletin of Suicidology*, pp. 2-7, July 1967, and from Norman L. Farberow (ed.), *Proceedings: Fourth International Conference for Suicide Prevention* (Los Angeles, California: DelMar Publishing Company, 1968).

CHAPTER 9:
Reprinted from *Journal of General Psychology, 56*:251–256, 1957.

CHAPTER 10:
Reprinted from E. S. Shneidman and N. L. Farberow (eds.), *Clues to Suicide* (New York: McGraw-Hill Book Co., 1957).

CHAPTER 11:
Reprinted from the *Journal of Projective Techniques, 22*:211–228, 1958.

CHAPTER 12:
Reprinted from Norman L. Farberow and Edwin S. Shneidman (eds.), *The Cry for Help* (New York: McGraw-Hill Book Co., 1961).

CHAPTER 13:
Reprinted from Henry P. David and J. C. Brengelmann (eds.), *Perspectives in Personality Research* (New York: Springer Publishing Co., 1960; German edition, Geneva: Hans Huber Verlag, 1960).

CHAPTER 14:
Reprinted from Philip J. Stone, Dexter C. Dunphy, Marshall S. Smith, and Daniel M. Ogilvie (eds.), *The General Inquirer: A Computer Approach to Content Analysis* (Cambridge, Massachusetts: The M.I.T. Press, 1966).

CHAPTER 15:
Reprinted from Norman L. Farberow and Edwin S. Shneidman (eds.),
The Cry for Help (New York: McGraw-Hill Book Co., 1961).

CHAPTER 16:
Reprinted from *Techniques in Crisis Intervention: A Training Manual*
(Los Angeles, California: Suicide Prevention Center, Inc., 1968).

CHAPTER 17:
Reprinted from L. E. Abt and S. L. Weisman (eds.), *Acting Out* (New
York: Grune and Stratton, 1965).

CHAPTER 18:
Reprinted from *Medical Bulletin No. 8 (MB-8)* (Washington, D.C.: Veterans Administration, February, 1962).

CHAPTER 19:
Reprinted from *Medical Bulletin No. 9 (MB-9)* (Washington, D.C.: Veterans Administration, February, 1963).

CHAPTER 20:
Reprinted from the *Journal of Abnormal Psychology, 71*: 287–299, 1966.

CHAPTER 21:
Reprinted from *The Journal of The American Medical Association, 195*:
422–428, 1966.

CHAPTER 22:
Reprinted from *The Journal of Nervous and Mental Disease, 142*:32–44,
1966.

CHAPTER 23:
Reprinted from E. S. Shneidman and N. L. Farberow (eds.), *Clues to
Suicide* (New York: McGraw-Hill Book Company, 1957).

CHAPTER 24:
Reprinted from E. S. Shneidman and N. L. Farberow (eds.), *Clues to
Suicide* (New York: McGraw-Hill Book Company, 1957).

CHAPTER 25:
Reprinted from *American Journal of Nursing, 65*:10–15, 1965 and from
Bulletin of Suicidology, December, 1968, 19–25.

CHAPTER 26:
Reprinted from *Archives of General Psychiatry, 11*:282–285, 1964.

CHAPTER 27:
Reprinted from *California Medicine, 104*:168–174, 1966.

CHAPTER 28:
Reprinted from *Zeitschrift für Präventiv Medizin, 10*:488–498, 1965.

CHAPTER 29:
Reprinted from *American Journal of Psychotherapy, 19*:570–576, 1965.

CHAPTER 30:
Reprinted from *The Journal of the American Medical Association, 184*:
924–929, 1963.

CHAPTER 31:
Reprinted from Norman L. Farberow and Edwin S. Shneidman (eds.),
The Cry for Help (New York: McGraw-Hill Book Company, 1961).

CHAPTER 32:
From the Los Angeles Suicide Prevention Center. Mimeographed, 1966.

CHAPTER 33:
Reprinted from *Police*, 10: 14–18, 1966.

CHAPTER 34:
Reprinted from 246 Federal Supplement 368 (D. La., 1965). Some names
have been changed.

CHAPTER 35:

Reprinted from Norman L. Farberow (ed.), *Taboo Topics* (New York: Atherton Press, 1963).

CHAPTER 36:

Reprinted from the *Journal of Forensic Sciences, 13*: 33–45, 1968.

CHAPTER 37:

Reprinted from Edwin S. Shneidman (ed.), *Essays in Self-Destruction* (New York: Science House, 1967).

CHAPTER 38:

Presented at the Melville-Hawthorne Conference, Williams College, September 5, 1966. Reprinted from Howard P. Vincent (ed.), *Melville and Hawthorne in the Berkshires* (Kent, Ohio: Kent State University Press, 1966).

CHAPTER 39:

Reprinted from *Contemporary Psychology, 8*:177–180, 1963.

CHAPTER 40:

Reprinted from *Contemporary Psychology 9*:414–416, 1964; also reprinted in *Social Case Work, 45*:481–482, 1964.

CHAPTER 41:

Reprinted from *Contemporary Psychology, 9*:370–371, 1964.

CHAPTER 42:

Reprinted from *Contemporary Psychology, 10*:553–554, 1965.

CHAPTER 43:

Reprinted from *American Journal of Psychiatry, 123*:501–502, 1966.

CHAPTER 44:

Reprinted from *Contemporary Psychology, 12*:449–450, 1967.

CONTENTS

THE PSYCHOLOGY
OF SUICIDE

PART I
THEORY
AND TAXONOMY

Chapter 1
ORIENTATIONS TOWARD DEATH
Edwin S. Shneidman

This chapter presents a psychologically oriented classification of death. Inasmuch as the present conceptualization of death embodies semantic confusions, a set of new concepts is proposed: cessation, *the final and irreversible stopping of consciousness;* interruption, *the stopping of consciousness with the expectation and actuality of further conscious experiences; and* continuation, *experiencing the stream of temporally contiguous conscious events. Primary importance is given to the role of the individual in his own death. All deaths are classified as* intentional, subintentional, *or* unintentional, *depending on the decedent's conscious and unconscious roles in effecting or hastening his own demise. A "psychological autopsy" of Melville's Captain Ahab is included to illustrate these concepts.*

It is both stimulating and depressing to contemplate the fact that at this period in man's history, when, at long last, one can find a few genuine indications of straightforward discussions and investigations of death, these pursuits come at the time of man's terrible new-found capacity to destroy his works and to decimate his kind. For these reasons, it may be said that a special kind of intellectual and affective permissiveness, born out of a sense of urgency, now exists for man's greater understanding of his own death and destruction.

For the past few years, a number of us engaged in activities related to the prevention of suicide have habitually looked upon instances of suicidal phenomena as manifestations of a major scourge, involving, as they inevitably do, untimely death for the victim and generally stigmatized lives for the survivors. My own special interest in the classification of death phenomena is one outcome of this group concern with suicidal behaviors. The purpose of this chapter is to stimulate a rethinking of conventional notions of death and suicide. A further purpose is to attempt to create a psychologically oriented classification of death phenomena—an ordering based in large part on the role of the individual in his own demise.

Reflections on death, including suicide, are found in some of man's earliest written works. Death and suicide have been depicted and refined in various ways; numerous misconceptions have grown up around these topics. These proliferated intellectual overgrowths are not the specimens that we wish to describe here. Rather, we have to see them as encumbering underbrush that must be cleared away before we can come to the heart of the problem. This is the task to which I now turn.

"Idols," or False Notions About Death and Suicide

This section might have been entitled "A Few Aphorisms Concerning the Interpretation of Suicide and the Nature of Death." Such a heading would, of course, be a minor variation of a theme in Bacon's *Novum Organum*. As in Bacon's day, there are "idols and false notions which are now in possession of the human understanding." Bacon enumerated four classes of "idols" (or fallacies) : Idols of the Tribe, Idols of the Cave, Idols of the Market Place, and Idols of the Theater. Of particular interest to us in the present context are the Idols of the Cave—"the idols of the individual man, for everyone . . . has a cave or den of his own, which refracts and discolors the light of nature."[1] In respect to suicide and death each person figuratively builds for himself, in relation to the cryptic topics of life and death, his own (mis)-conceptual vault of beliefs, understandings, and orientations—"Idols of the Grave," as I will call them. Further, I would propose five subcategories of these Idols of the Grave, specifically as they concern: (1) the role of classification or taxonomy in treating dying or suicidal people; (2) the classification of suicidal phenomena; (3) the relationships between suicidal and death phenomena; (4) the classification of death phenomena; and (5) the concept of death itself.

THE IDOL THAT MAXIMALLY EFFECTIVE PROGRAMS OF PREVENTION AND TREATMENT CAN BE DEVELOPED IN THE ABSENCE OF TAXONOMIC UNDERSTANDING. Although one's associations to the word taxonomy—the discipline whose purpose it is to develop concise methods for classifying knowledge—are primarily to the fields of botany and zoology, I wish to focus on the role of taxonomy in the healing arts and sciences. It has been axiomatic in these disciplines that definitive therapies or cures stem from accurate

diagnosis and that accurate diagnoses can hardly exist in the absence of meaningful (including taxonomic) understanding of the phenomena. Before one can meaningfully and efficiently treat, protect, and help, one must understand; paradoxically, however, the heart of understanding lies in meaningful classification. In the area of mental health (especially in the areas concerning death and suicide), meaningful taxonomies would seem to be the professionals' *sine qua non* for effective diagnosis, prevention, and treatment. All this is not to imply that there have not been classifications of death and suicidal phenomena but rather to suggest that we must continue to attend to the classificatory aspect of our enterprise if we mean to increase, over the years, our effectiveness—an effectiveness that must rest on expanded understanding.

THE IDOL THAT THE PRESENT CLASSIFICATIONS OF SUICIDAL PHENOMENA ARE MEANINGFUL. The use of an illustration may be the best introduction to this topic. A women of around thirty years of age was seen on the ward of a large general hospital after she had been returned from surgery. She had, a few hours before, shot herself in the head with a .22 caliber revolver, the result being that she had enucleated an eye and torn away part of her frontal lobe. Emergency surgical and medical procedures had been employed. When she was seen in bed subsequent to surgery, her head was enveloped in bandages, and the appropriate tubes and needles were in her. Her chart indicated that she had attempted to kill herself, the diagnosis being "attempted suicide." It happened that in the next bed there was another young woman of about the same age. She had been permitted to occupy the bed for a few hours to "rest" prior to going home, having come to the hospital that day because she had cut her left wrist with a razor blade. The physical trauma was relatively superficial and required but two stitches. She had had, she said, absolutely no lethal intention, but had definitely wished to jolt her husband into attending to what she wanted to say to him about his drinking habits. Her words to him had been, "Look at me, I'm bleeding." She had taken this course after she had, in conversation with her husband, previously threatened suicide. Her chart, too, indicated a diagnosis of "attempted suicide."

Common sense should tell us that if we obtained scientific data from these two cases—psychiatric anamnestic data, psychological

test data, etc.—and then grouped these materials under the single rubric of "attempted suicide," we would obviously run the risk of masking precisely the differences that we might wish to explore. Common sense might further tell us that the first woman could most appropriately be labeled as a case of "committed suicide" (even though she was alive), and the second woman as "nonsuicidal" (even though she had cut her wrist with a razor blade). But, aside from the issue of what would be the most appropriate diagnosis in each case, it still seems evident that combining these two cases—and hundreds of similar instances—under the common heading of "attempted suicide" might definitely limit rather than extend the range of our potential understanding.

Individuals with clear lethal intention, as well as those with ambivalent or no lethal intention, are currently grouped under the heading of attempted suicide: We know that individuals can attempt to attempt, attempt to commit, attempt to be nonsuicidal. All this comes about largely because of oversimplification as to types of causes and a confusion between modes and purpose. (The law punishes the holdup man with the unloaded or toy gun precisely because the victim must assume that the bandit has, by virtue of his holding a "gun," covered himself with the semantic mantle "gunman.") One who cries "help" while holding a razor blade is deemed by society to be suicidal. Although it is true that the act of putting a shotgun in one's mouth and pulling the trigger with one's toe is almost always related to lethal self-intention, this particular relationship between method and intent does not hold for most other methods, such as ingesting barbiturates or cutting oneself with a razor. In most cases the intentions may range all the way from deadly ones, through the wide variety of ambivalences, rescue fantasies, cries for help, and psychic indecisions, all the way to clearly formulated nonlethal intention in which a semantic usurpation of a "suicidal" mode has been consciously employed.

It may not be inaccurate to state that in this century there have been two major theoretical approaches to suicide: the sociological and the psychological, identified with the names of Durkheim and Freud, respectively. Durkheim's delineation of etiological types of suicide—anomic, altruistic, and egoistic—is probably the best-known classification.[2] For my part, I have often felt that this famous typology of suicidal behaviors has behaved like a brilliantly con-

ceived sociologic motorcycle (anomie) with two psychological side-cars, performing effectively in textbooks for over half a century, but running low on power in clinics, hospitals, and consultation rooms. This classification epitomizes some of the strengths and shortcomings of any study based almost entirely on a social, normative, tabular, nomothetic approach. It is probably fair to say, however, that Durkheim was not so much interested in suicide per se as he was in the explication of his general sociological method.

Freud's psychological formulation of suicide, as hostility directed toward the introjected love object—what I have called "murder in the 180th degree"—was more a brilliant inductive encompassment than an empirical, scientific particularization.[3] This concept was given its most far-reaching exposition by Karl Menninger, who, in *Man Against Himself,* not only outlined four types of suicide—chronic, focal, organic, and actual—but also proposed three basic psychological components: the wish to kill, the wish to be killed, and the wish to die.[4]

Neither of these two theoretical approaches to the nature and causes of suicide constitutes the classification most common in everyday clinical use. That distinction belongs to a rather homely, supposedly common-sense division, which in its barest form implies that all humanity can be divided into two groupings, suicidal and nonsuicidal, and then divides the suicidal category into committed, attempted, and threatened.[5] Although the second classification is superior to the suicidal-versus-nonsuicidal view of life, that it is not theoretically or practically adequate for understanding and treatment is one of the main tenets of this chapter. It may well be that the word "suicide" currently has too many loose, contradictory meanings to be scientifically or clinically useful.

THE IDOL THAT LIVING AND DYING ARE SEPARATE. Living and dying have too often been seen erroneously as distinct, separate, almost dichotomous activities. To correct this view one can enunciate another, which might be called the psychodynamics of dying. One of its tenets is that in cases where an individual is dying over a period of time, which may vary from hours to years in persons who "linger" in terminal illnesses, this interval is a psychologically consistent extension of styles of coping, defending, adjusting, interacting, and other modes of behavior that have characterized that

individual during most of his life up to that time. Feifel says, "A man's birth is an uncontrolled event in his life, but the manner of his departure from life bears a definite relation to his philosophy of life and death. We are mistaken to consider death as a purely biological event. The attitudes concerning it and its meaning for the individual can serve as an important organizing principle in determining how he conducts himself in life." How an individual dies should no less reflect his personal philosophy, the goodness of his personal adjustment, his sense of fruition, fulfillment, self-realization. Feifel further states that ". . . types of reactions to impending death are a function of interweaving factors. Some of the significant ones appear to be . . . the psychological maturity of the individual; the kind of coping techniques available to him; variables of religious orientation, age, socioeconomic status, etc.; severity of the organic process; and the attitudes of the significant persons in the patient's world."[6]

Dr. Arthur P. Noyes is reported to have said, "As we grow older, we grow more like ourselves." I believe that this illuminating but somewhat cryptic remark can also be taken to mean that during the dying period, the individual displays behaviors and attitudes that contain great fealty to his lifelong orientations and beliefs. Draper says: "Each man dies in a notably personal way."[7] Suicidal and/or dying behaviors do not exist *in vacuo*, but are an integral part of the life style of the individual.[8]

THE IDOL THAT THE TRADITIONAL CLASSIFICATION OF DEATH PHENOM-ENA IS CLEAR. *The International Classification of the Causes of Death* lists 137 causes, such as pneumonia, meningitis, malignant neoplasms, myocardial infarctions; but, in contrast, there are only four commonly recognized *modes* of death: *natural death, accident, suicide,* and *homicide.* In some cases, cause of death is used synonymously to indicate the natural cause of death. Thus, the standard U. S. Public Health Service Certificate of Death has a space to enter cause of death (implying the mode as natural) and, in addition, provides opportunity to indicate accident, suicide, or homicide. Apparently, it is implied that these four modes of death constitute the final ordering into which each of us must be classified. The fact that some of us do not fit easily into one of these four crypts is the substance for this section.

The shortcoming of the common classification is that in its over-simplification and failure to take into account certain necessary dimensions it often poses serious problems in classifying deaths meaningfully. The basic ambiguities can be seen most clearly by focusing on the distinctions between natural (intrasomatic) and accidental (extrasomatic) deaths. On the face of it, the argument can be advanced that most deaths, especially in the younger years, are unnatural. Perhaps only in the cases of death of old age might the termination of life legitimately be called natural. Let us examine the substance of some of these confusions. If an individual (who wishes to continue living) has his skull invaded by a lethal object, his death is called accidental; if another individual (who also wishes to continue living) is invaded by a lethal virus, his death is called natural. An individual who torments an animal into killing him is said to have died an accidental death, whereas an individual who torments a drunken companion into killing him is called a homicidal victim. An individual who has an artery burst in his brain is said to have died with a cerebral-vascular accident, whereas it might make more sense to call it a cerebral-vascular natural death. What has been confusing in this traditional approach is that the individual has been viewed as a kind of biological *object* (rather than psychological, social, biological organism), and as a consequence, the role of the individual in his own demise has been omitted.

THE IDOL THAT THE CONCEPT "DEATH" IS ITSELF OPERATIONALLY SOUND. We come now to what for some may be the most radical and iconoclastic aspect of our presentation so far, specifically the suggestion that a major portion of the concept of "death" is operationally meaningless and ought therefore to be eschewed. Let the reader ask the question of the author: "Do you mean to say that you wish to discuss suicidal phenomena and orientations toward death without the concept of death?" The author's answer is in the affirmative, based, he believes, on compelling reasons. Essentially, these reasons are epistemological; that is, they have to do with the process of knowing and the question of what it is that we can know. Our main source of quotable strength—and we shall have occasion later to refer to him in a very different context—is the physicist Percy W. Bridgman. Essentially, his concept is that death is not

experienceable, that if one could experience it, one would not be dead. One can experience another's dying and another's death and his own dying—although he can never be sure—but no man can experience his own death.

In his book *The Intelligent Individual and Society*, Bridgman states this view as follows:

> There are certain kinks in our thinking which are of such universal occurrence as to constitute essential limitations. Thus the urge to think of my own death as some form of my experience is almost irresistible. However, it requires only to be said for me to admit that my own death cannot be a form of experience, for if I could still experience, then by definition it would not be death. Operationally my own death is a fundamentally different thing from the death of another in the same way that my own feelings mean something fundamentally different from the feelings of another. The death of another I can experience; there are certain methods of recognizing death and certain properties of death that affect my actions in the case of others. Again it need not bother us to discover that the concept of death in another is not sharp, and situations may arise in practice where it is difficult to say whether the organism is dead or not, particularly if one sticks to the demand that "death" must be such a thing that when the organism is once dead it cannot live again. This demand rests on mystical feelings, and there is no reason why the demand should be honored in framing the definition of death. . . . My own death is such a different thing that it might well have a different word, and perhaps eventually will. There is no operation by which I can decide whether I am dead; "I am always alive."[9]

This pragmatic view of death—in the strict philosophical sense of pragmatism—is stated most succinctly (in a side remark about death) by the father of pragmatism. Peirce, in discussing metaphysics, says:

> We start then, with nothing, pure zero. But this is not the nothing of negation. For *not* means *other than*, and *other* is merely a synonym of the ordinal numeral *second*. As such it implies a first; while the present pure zero is prior

to every first. The nothing of negation is the nothing of death, which also comes *second to,* or after, everything.[10]

Two further thoughts on death as experience. Not only, as we have seen, is death misconceived as an experience, but (1) it is further misconceived as a bitter or calamitous experience, and (2) it is still further misconceived as an *act,* as though dying were something that one had to do. On the contrary, dying can be a supreme passivity rather than the supreme act or activity. It will be done for you; dying is one thing that no one has to "do."[11]

In addition to this philosophical aspect of the situation, there is also the reflection that one's own death is really psychologically inconceivable. Possibly the most appropriate quotation in this connection is from the twentieth-century giant of depth psychology. In his paper "Thoughts for the Times on War and Death," Freud wrote:

> Our own death is indeed unimaginable, and whenever we make the attempt to imagine it we can conceive that we really survive as spectators. Hence the psychoanalytic school could venture on the assertion that at bottom no one believes in his own death, or to put the thing in another way, in the unconscious every one of us is convinced of his own immortality.[12]

Indeed, the word "death" has become a repository for pervasive logical and epistemological confusions—"Idols of the Dead." The first order of business might well be to clarify the concepts currently embedded in our notions of death. For my part, I would wish to eschew, where possible, the concept of death and, instead, use concepts and terms that are operationally viable. This is the text of the present section, the content of the next section, and the burden of this chapter.

Cessation, Termination, Interruption, and Continuation

In the preceding section, I have been critical of some current concepts relating to suicide and death. In this section I wish to propose a tentative psychological classification of all behaviors involving demise. Two sets of key concepts are involved: The first

is made up of the terms cessation, termination, interruption, and continuation; the second, of the terms intentioned, subintentioned, unintentioned, and contraintentioned. At this point, our first tasks are those of definition.

CESSATION. The key concept in this chapter is the idea of "cessation."[13] In this context, cessation has a psychological, specifically introspective referent. Our definition of "cessation" is that it is the stopping of the potentiality of any (further) conscious experience. "Death"—some form of termination—is the universal and ubiquitous ending of all living things; but only man, by virtue of his verbally reportable introspective mental life, can conceptualize, fear, and suffer cessation. Cessation refers to the last line of the last scene of the last act of the last drama of that actor. It should be immediately obvious that different individuals—and any particular individual at different times—can have a variety of attitudes and orientations toward their cessations. The next section contains an explication of possible orientations toward cessation. Cessation is used here not as a synonym for the word death, but rather as its operationally defined substitute. Also, in order to have a shorthand term for cessation, I shall use the term "Psyde," referring, so to speak, to the demise of the psychic processes—the final stopping of the individual consciousness, as far as we know.[14]

TERMINATION. The concept of "termination"—which is defined as the stopping of the physiological functions of the body—is needed because there can occur the stopping of the potentiality of conscious experience (cessation) which is not temporally coincident with the stopping of the functions of the body. Our shorthand word for termination is "Somize," referring to the demise of the soma. Consider the report of the following incident: A young man was, while riding as a passenger on a motorcycle, hit by an automobile and thrown several yards through the air. He landed on his head at a curbside. At the hospital, this case was regarded as remarkable, because, although his skull was crushed and although he showed no evidence of any conscious experience and even had a rather complete absence of reflexes, he was kept alive for many days by means of intravenous feeding, catheter relief, and many other life-extending pieces of mechanical apparatus. Eventually he "expired." The

conceptual point to be made in this context is that he suffered cessation the moment that his head hit the pavement. So, although he had ceased, he had not terminated, in that he continued to breathe. No one would have thought to suggest that he be buried or cremated as long as he was still breathing. A further point can be made: The operational definition (or criterion) for termination can be put at the stopping of the exchange of gases between the human organism and his environment; that is, an individual may be said to be terminated when, if a mirror is put to his mouth, there is no frosting on the glass—the subsequent growth of his beard or other activities do not matter.[15] If cessation relates to the psychological personality, then termination has to do with the biological organism. It is useful to distinguish between cessation and termination. We all know that it is possible for an individual to put a gun to his head, planning to "blow his brains out" (termination) and yet *believe* that he will be at his own funeral, that he will be able to check whether or not his widow follows the instructions in his suicide note (without cessation). In order not to be entrapped by the confusion that exists in many minds concerning these two concepts, we must clarify them in our own.

INTERRUPTION. The third concept of this group is that of interruption, which relates not to termination but to cessation. If cessation has to do with the stopping of the potentiality of any conscious experience, then interruption is in a sense its opposite, in that "interruption" is defined as the stopping of consciousness with the actuality, and usually the expectation, of further conscious experiences. It is a kind of temporary cessation. The best example of an interruption state is being asleep; others are being under an anaesthetic, in an alcoholic stupor, in a diabetic coma, in an epileptic seizure, and, on another level, being in a fugue, amnesic, or dissociative state. The primary purpose of introducing the notion of interruption states is to provide a concept whereby data—especially those that could be obtained from experimental situations—might serve as paradigms, analogues, models, or patterns for certain cessation conditions. For example—and more will be said about this later—it might be possible to devise paradigms having to do with sleep behavior that will give us fresh leads and new insights into suicidal behaviors, which a direct approach would not yield.

CONTINUATION. When one works with suicidal people clinically and investigates, through "psychological autopsies," cases of suicide, one often gets the impression that individuals who, in point of fact, have killed themselves, have not necessarily "committed suicide." That is to say, in some cases, it seems that the person's intention was not to embrace death but rather to find surcease from external or internalized aspects of life. In the context of this chapter, we shall call the process of living "continuation." "Continuation" can be defined as experiencing, in the absence of interruption, the stream of temporally contiguous conscious events. From this point of view, our lives are made up of one series of alternating continuation and interruption states.

One might find a group of nonlethally oriented "suicide attempters"—each of whom wished to postpone cessation—who, individually, might manifest quite different patterns of orientation toward continuation. The nuances of these patterns might well include the following: (1) patterns of ambivalence (coexistent wishes to live and to die, including rescue fantasies, gambles with death, and cries for help); (2) the state of hopefulness or hopelessness, and accompanying feelings of psychological impotence; (3) patterns of self-righteousness, indignation, inner resourcefulness, defeat, and ennui; (4) orientations toward the next temporal interval, whether one of blandness, inertia, habit, interest, anticipation, expectation, or demand; (5) intensity of thought and action in relation to continuation, ranging from absent (no thought about it), through fleeting fantasy, concern, obsession, and rash behavior outburst, to deliberate performance. Continuation is the converse of cessation. It would be important to know, in any particular case, how an individual's attitudes toward continuation interacted with his orientations toward cessation. In addition to this, we could say that a comprehensive study of suicidal phenomena should include concern for nonsuicidal phenomena and such perverse questions as what a specific individual has to live for or why a specific individual does not commit suicide.

Basic Orientations Toward Cessation

The operation that gives meaning to the phrase "basic orientation toward cessation" has to do with the role of the individual in his own demise. By "role of the individual" is meant his overt and

covert behaviors and nonbehaviors that reflect conscious and unconscious attributes relevant to his cessation. These include at least the following: his attitudes and beliefs about death, cessation, hereafter, and rebirth; his ways of thinking; his need systems, including his needs for achievement, affiliation, autonomy, and dominance; his dyadic relationships, especially the subtleties of dependencies and hostilities in relation to the significant people in his life; the hopefulness and hopelessness in the responses of these people to his cries for help; the constellation and balance of ego activity and ego passivity; his orientations toward continuation states. To know these facts about a person would well require a comprehensive psychological understanding of his personality.

Four subcategories relating to the role of the individual in his own demise are suggested: intentioned, subintentioned, unintentioned, and contraintentioned.

INTENTIONED. By intentioned, I refer to those cases in which the individual plays a direct and conscious role in his own demise. These cases do not refer to persons who wish for "death" or termination, but rather to those who actively precipitate their cessation. (Of course, cessation cannot be avoided by anyone. The entire issue is one of timing and involves postponing and hastening.) In terms of the traditional categories of death, no currently labeled accidental or natural deaths would be called intentioned, some homicidal deaths might be called intentioned, and most (but, importantly, not all) suicidal deaths would be called intentioned. In relation to the term "suicide," intentioned cases may be said to have *committed* suicide. Using the word "Psyde" to represent cessation, we can list a number of subcategories: (1) Psyde-seekers; (2) Psyde-initiators; (3) Psyde-ignorers; and (4) Psyde-darers.

1. *Psyde-seeker.* A Psyde-seeker is one who, during the time that he can be so labeled, has consciously verbalized to himself his wish for an ending to all conscious experience and behaves in order to achieve this end. The operational criteria for a Psyde-seeker lie not primarily in the method he uses—razor, barbiturate, carbon monoxide—but in the fact that the method *in his mind* is calculated to bring him cessation; and, whatever his rescue fantasies or cries for help may be, he does the act in such a manner and site that rescue (or intervention) is realistically unlikely or impossible. In

all, he has a predominantly unambivalent intention or orientation toward cessation during that period. The phrase "during that period" is meant to convey the notion that individuals' orientations toward cessation shift and change over time.[16] A person who was a Psyde-seeker yesterday and made a most serious suicidal act then, could not today be forced to participate in activities that might cost him his life. It is known clinically—as supported by our experience at the Suicide Prevention Center—that many individuals are "suicidal" for only a relatively brief period of time; so that if they can be given appropriate sanctuary, they will no longer seek Psyde and will wish to continue to live as long as possible.

2. *Psyde-initiator*.[17] A Psyde-initiator is a Psyde-seeker, but sufficiently different to warrant a separate label. A Psyde-initiator believes that he will suffer cessation in the fairly near future—a matter of days or weeks—or he believes that he is failing and, not wishing to accommodate himself to a new (and less effective and less virile) image of himself, does not wish to let "it" happen to him. Rather, *he* wants to play a role in its occurrence. Thus he will do it for himself, at his own time, and on his own terms. In our investigations at the Veterans Administration Central Research Unit for the Study of Unpredicted Death we find, on occasion, a case in which an older person, hospitalized in a general medical hospital, in the terminal stages of a fatal disease will, with remarkable and totally unexpected energy and strength, take the tubes and needles out of himself, climb over the bed rails, lift a heavy window, and throw himself to the ground several stories below. What is most prototypical about such an individual is that when one looks at his previous occupational history one sees that he has never been fired —he has always quit. In either case, the person ends up unemployed, but the role he has played in the process is different.[18]

3. *Psyde-ignorer*. Consider the following suicide note: "Good-by, kid. You couldn't help it. Tell that brother of yours, when he gets to where I'm going, I hope I'm a foreman down there; I might be able to do something for him." Although it is true that suicide notes that contain any reference to a hereafter, a continued existence, or a reunion with dead loved ones are relatively very rare (see Appendix to *Clues to Suicide*[19]), it is also true that some people who kill themselves believe, as part of their total system of beliefs, that one can effect termination without involving cessation.

They seem to ignore the fact that, so far as we know, termination always involves cessation. One can note that even those in our contemporary society who espouse belief in a hereafter as part of their religious tenets still label a person who has shot himself to death as suicidal. This is probably so primarily because, whatever *really* happens after termination, the survivors are still left to live (and usually to mourn) in the undeniable physical absence of the person who killed himself. Thus, this subcategory of Psyde-ignorer, or, perhaps better, Psyde-transcender, contains those persons who, from our point of view, effect their own termination and cessation but who, from their point of view, effect only their termination and continue to exist in some manner or another.

This paragraph is not meant necessarily to deny a (logical) possibility of continuation after cessation (life after death), but the concept of Psyde-ignoring (or something similar to it) is a firm necessity in any systematic classification of this type; otherwise we will put ourselves in the untenable position of making exactly comparable a man's shooting his head off in the belief and hope that he will soon meet his dead wife in heaven and a man's taking a trip from one city to another with the purpose and expectation of being reunited with his spouse. Obviously, these two acts are so vastly different in their effects (on the person concerned and on others who know him) that they cannot be equated. Therefore, independent of the individual's convictions that killing oneself does not result in cessation but is simply a transition to another life, we must superimpose our belief that cessation is necessarily final as far as the human personality that we can know is concerned.

4. *Psyde-darer.* A Psyde-darer is an individual who, to use gamblers' terms, bets his continuation (i.e., his life) on the objective probability of as few as five out of six chances that he will survive. Regardless of the outcome, an individual who plays Russian Roulette is a Psyde-darer at that time. In addition to the objective probabilities that exist, the concept of a Psyde-darer also involves subjective probabilities of the same order of magnitude. Thus, a person with little skill as a pilot who attempts to fly an airplane or one with unpracticed coordination who attempts to walk along the ledge of a roof of a tall building may be classified as a Psyde-darer. The rule of thumb is that it is not what he does, but the background (of skill, prowess, and evaluation of his own abilities)

against which he does it, that matters. In a sense the Psyde-darer is only a partial, or fractional, cessation-seeker; but since each lethal fraction contained within the gambling situation is completely lethal, it seems most meaningful to classify such an act within the intention category.

SUBINTENTIONED. Subintentioned cessation behaviors relate to those instances in which the individual plays an indirect, covert, partial, or unconscious role in his own demise. That individuals may play an unconscious role in their own failures and act inimically to their own best welfare seem to be facts too well documented from psychoanalytic and general clinical practice to ignore. Often cessation is hastened by the individual's seeming carelessness, imprudence, foolhardiness, forgetfulness, amnesia, lack of judgment, or other psychological mechanisms. This concept of subintentioned demise is similar, in some ways, to Karl Menninger's concepts of chronic, focal, and organic suicides, except that Menninger's ideas have to do with self-defeating ways of continuing to live, whereas the notion of subintentioned cessation is a description of a way of stopping the process of living. Included in this subintention category would be many patterns of mismanagement and brink-of-death living that result in cessation. In terms of the traditional classification of modes of death (natural, accident, homicide, and suicide), some instances of all four types can be subsumed under this category, depending on the particular details of each case. In relation to the term suicide, subintentioned cases may be said to have *permitted* suicide.

Subintentioned cessation involves what might be called the psychosomatics of death: that is, cases in which essentially psychological processes (like fear, anxiety, derring-do, hate, etc.) seem to play some role in exacerbating the catabolic or physiological processes that bring on termination[20] (and necessarily cessation), as well as those cases in which the individual seems to play an indirect, largely unconscious role in inviting or hastening cessation itself.[21] The Psyde groups for the subintentioned category are, tentatively, as follows: (1) Psyde-chancer; (2) Psyde-hastener; (3) Psyde-capitulator; and (4) Psyde-experimenter.

(1) *Psyde-chancer.* The Psyde-darer, Psyde-chancer, and Psyde-experimenter are all on a continuum of chance expectation and

chance possibility of cessation. The difference lies in the combination of objective and subjective probabilities. If a Psyde-darer has only five chances out of six of continuing, then a Psyde-chancer would have chances significantly greater than that, but still involving a realistic risk of cessation. It should be pointed out that these categories are largely independent of the method used, in that most methods (like the use of razor blades or barbiturates) can, depending on the exact place of the cut, the depth of the cut, and the realistic and calculated expectations for intervention and rescue by others, legitimately be thought of as intentioned, subintentioned, unintentioned, or contraintentioned—depending on these circumstances. Individuals who "leave it up to chance," who "gamble with death,"[22] who "half-intend to do it" are the subintentioned Psyde-chancers.

(2) *Psyde-hastener.* The basic assumption is that in all cessation activities the critical question (on the assumption that cessation will occur to everyone) is when, so that, in a sense, all intentioned and subintentioned activities are hastening. The Psyde-hastener refers to the individual who unconsciously exacerbates a physiological disequilibrium so that his cessation (which would, in ordinary terms, be called a natural death) is expedited. This can be done either in terms of the "style" in which he lives (the abuse of his body, usually through alcohol, drugs, exposure, or malnutrition) or, in cases where there is a specific physiological imbalance, through the mismanagement of prescribed remedial procedures. Examples of the latter would be the diabetic who "mismanages" his diet or his insulin, the individual with cirrhosis who "mismanages" his alcoholic intake, the Berger's disease patient who "mismanages" his nicotine intake. Very closely allied to the Psyde-hastener in the Psyde-facilitator, who, while he is ill and his psychic energies are low, is somehow more than passively unresisting to cessation, and "makes it easy" for termination (and accompanying cessation) to occur. Some unexpected deaths in hospitals may be of this nature. The excellent paper of Weisman and Hackett explores this area.[23]

(3) *Psyde-capitulator.* A Psyde-capitulator is a person who, by virtue of some strong emotion, usually his fear of death, plays a psychological role in effecting his termination. In a sense, he gives in to death or he scares himself to death. This type of death in-

cludes voodoo deaths; the type of death reported among Indians and Mexicans from southwestern U.S. railroad hospitals, where the patients thought that people who went to hospitals went there to die, and being hospitalized was thus cause in itself for great alarm; and some of the cases reported from Boston by Weisman and Hackett. All of these individuals play a psychological role in the psychosomatics of their termination and cessation.

(4) *Psyde-experimenter*. A Psyde-experimenter is a person who often lives "on the brink of death," who consciously wishes neither interruption nor cessation, but—usually by use of (or addiction to) alcohol and/or barbiturates—seems to wish a chronically altered, usually befogged continuation state. Psyde-experimenters seem to wish to remain conscious but to be benumbed or drugged. They will often "experiment" with their self-prescribed dosages (always in the direction of increasing the effect of the dosage), taking some chances of extending the benumbed conscious states into interruption (coma) states and even taking some chances (usually without much concern, in a kind of lackadaisical way) of running some minimal but real risk of extending the interruption states into cessation. When this type of death occurs, it is traditionally thought of as accidental.

UNINTENTIONED. Unintentioned cessation describes those occurrences in which, for all intents and purposes, the person psychologically plays no significant role in his own demise. He is, at the time of his cessation, "going about his business" (even though he may be lying in a hospital), with no conscious intention of effecting or hastening cessation and no strong conscious drive in this direction. What happens is that "something from the outside"—the outside of his mind—occurs. This "something" might be a cerebral-vascular accident, a myocardial infarction, a neoplastic growth, some malfunction, some catabolism, some invasion—whether by bullet or by virus—which, for him, has lethal consequences. "It" happens to "him." Inasmuch as all that anyone can do in regard to cessation is to attempt some manipulation along a temporal dimension (i.e., to hasten or to postpone it), one might suppose that unintentioned is synonymous only with "postponer," but it appears that there are other possible attitudes—welcoming, accepting, resisting, disdaining, and the like—all within the unintentioned category.

In terms of the traditional categories of death, most natural, accidental, and homicidal deaths would be called unintentioned, and no presently labeled suicidal deaths would be so called. In relation to the term "suicidal," unintentioned cases may be said to have *omitted* suicide.

The Psyde categories for unintentioned cessation are: (1) Psyde-welcomer; (2) Psyde-acceptor; (3) Psyde-postponer; (4) Psyde-disdainer; and (5) Psyde-fearer.

(1) *Psyde-welcomer.* A Psyde-welcomer is one who, although playing no discernible (conscious or unconscious) role in either hastening or facilitating his own cessation, could honestly report an introspective position of welcoming the end to his life. Very old people, especially after a long, painful, debilitating illness, report that they would welcome "the end."

(2) *Psyde-acceptor.* The slight difference between a Psyde-welcomer and a Psyde-acceptor lies in the nuance of activity and passivity that distinguishes them. The Psyde-acceptor is one who has accepted the imminence of his cessation and "is resigned to his own fate." In this, he may be relatively passive, philosophical, resigned, heroic, realistic, or mature, depending on "the spirit" in which this enormous acceptance is made.

(3) *Psyde-postponer.* Most of the time most of us are acute Psyde-postponers. Psyde-postponing is the habitual, indeed the unthinking, orientation of most humans toward cessation. The Psyde-postponer is one who, to the extent that he is oriented toward or concerned with cessation at all, wishes that it would not occur in anything like the foreseeable future and further wishes that it would not occur for as long as possible (this Psyde-postponing orientation should not be confused with the ubiquitous human fantasies of immortality).

(4) *Psyde-disdainer.* Some individuals, during those moments when they consciously contemplate cessation, are disdainful of the concept and feel that they are above being involved in the cessation of the vital processes that it implies. They are, in a sense, supercilious toward death. It may well be that most young people in our culture, independent of their fears about death, are habitually Psyde-disdainers, as well as they might be—for a while.[24]

(5) *Psyde-fearer.* A Psyde-fearer is one who is fearful of death and of the topics relating to death. He may literally be phobic

about this topic.[25] He fights the notion of cessation, seeing reified death as a feared and hated enemy. This position may be related to conscious wishes for omnipotence and to great cathexis to one's social and physical potency. Hypochondriacs, fearing illnesses and assault, are perhaps also Psyde-fearers. (A person who, when physically well, is a Psyde-fearer might, when physically ill, become a Psyde-facilitator.)

Imagine five people, all older men on the same ward of a hospital, all dying of cancer, none playing an active or unconscious role in his own cessation. Yet it is still possible to distinguish among them different orientations toward cessation: One wishes not to die and is exerting his "will to live" (Psyde-postponer) ; another is resigned to his cessation (Psyde-acceptor) ; the third is disdainful of what is occurring to him and will not believe that death can "take him" (Psyde-disdainer) ; still another, although not taking any steps in the direction of hastening his end, does at this point in his illness welcome it (Psyde-welcomer) ; and the fifth is most fearful about the topic of death and the implication of cessation and forbids anyone to speak of it in his presence (Psyde-fearer).

CONTRAINTENTIONED. It is, of course, possible to shout "Fire!" in the absence of a conflagration, or "Stop thief!" in the absence of a crime. It is also possible, figuratively or literally, to shout or to murmur—the intensity of the cry does not seem to matter in some cases—"Suicide!" in the clear absence of any lethal intention. (I shall, of course, eschew the words "suicide attempt" and "suicide threat," having already indicated that either of these can range from great lethal intent, through ambivalent lethal intent, to no lethal intent.) One common result of shouting "Fire!" or "Stop thief!" is that these calls mobilize others; indeed, they put society (or certain members of society) in a position where it has no choice but to act in certain directions. An individual who uses the semantic blanket of "Suicide!" with a conscious absence of any lethal intention I shall term as one who has employed contraintentioned—advertently noncessation—behavior. From a strictly logical point of view, it might be argued that contraintentioned behaviors belong within the unintentioned category. I believe, however, that there are sufficient reasons to warrant a separate category, if only to

point up the fact that individuals can usurp the labels and the semantic trappings of death, especially of suicide and, at the same time, have a clear, conscious intention not to commit suicide and not to run any risk of cessation.

Among the contraintentioned individuals there are, by definition, no cessation or related postmortem states and hence no comparable traditional modes of death. In relation to the term suicide, contra-intention cases may be said to have *remitted* (in the sense of having "refrained from") suicide.

The Psyde subcategories that we distinguish among the contra-intentioned cases are (1) Psyde-feigner and (2) Psyde-threatener.

(1) *Psyde-feigner.* A Psyde-feigner is one who feigns or simu-lates what appears to be a self-directed advertent movement toward cessation. Examples are the ingesting of water from a previously emptied iodine bottle or using a razor blade with no lethal or near-lethal possibility or intent. Psyde-feigning involves some overt behavior on the part of the individual.

(2) *Psyde-threatener.* A Psyde-threatener is a person who, with the conscious intention of avoiding cessation, uses the threat of his cessation (and the other's respect for that threat) with the aim of achieving some of the secondary gains which go with cessation-oriented behavior. These gains usually have to do with activating other persons—usually the "significant other" person in the neurotic dyadic relationship in which the individual is involved.

Two additional comments, both obvious, should be made about contraintentioned behavior. The first is that what are ordinarily called "suicide attempts" may range in their potential lethality from absent to severe.[26] I do not wish to imply for a moment that all so-called suicide attempts should be thought of as contraintentioned; quite the contrary. Thus, each case of barbiturate ingestion or wrist-cutting, or even of the use of carbon monoxide in an auto, must be evaluated in terms of the details of that case, so that it can be assessed accurately—as of that time—in terms of its in-tentioned, subintentioned, unintentioned, and contraintentioned components. The second comment is that those who work with peo-ple who have "attempted suicide," especially those people seen as having manifested contraintentioned behavior, must guard against their own tendencies to assume a pejorative attitude toward these behaviors. It is all too easy to say that an individual *only* attempted

suicide or to dismiss the case as beneath the need for human compassion, if one assesses the act as contraintentioned. It should be
obvious that no act that involves, even merely semantically, cessation behavior is other than a genuine psychiatric crisis. Too often
we confuse treatment of suicidal individuals with attending to the
physical trauma forgetting that meaningful treatment has to be
essentially in terms of the person's personality and the frustrations, duress, fears, and threats that he experiences in his living
relationships. An unquestioned contraintentioned act merits fully
as much professional attention as any other maladaptive behavior;
a cry for help should never be disregarded, not only for humani-
tarian reasons, but also because we know that the unattended cries
tend to become more shrill, and the movement on the lethality
scale from cry to cry is, unfortunately, in the lethal direction.

An Example of an Equivocal Death

It might be most appropriate to conclude this chapter by presenting, by way of example, some excerpts from a singularly interesting case. I have chosen this from a uniquely comprehensive
study of death and lives by Herman Melville. It is the case of the
equivocal death—was it accident, suicide, or what—of Melville's
tortured, obsessively possessed, fury-driven, cetusized man: Captain Ahab of the "Pequod."[27]

The procedure called the "psychological autopsy" (used at the
Suicide Prevention Center) involves obtaining psychological data
about the behaviors and statements of the deceased in the days
before his death, from which information an extrapolation of intention is made over the moments of, and the moments directly
preceding, his cessation. In the case of Captain Ahab, I shall proceed as though I were preparing a report for an imaginary Nantucket coroner, including some sort of recommendation as to what
labelings would be the most appropriate on his imaginary death
certificate. The focus will be an attempt to come to some kind of
resolution concerning Ahab's intention types and Psyde categories.
But first, some facts: specifically how did the end of his life occur?

FACTS. For Ahab's death, we have the following account (from Chapter 135) of his last actions: "The harpoon was darted; the stricken
whale flew forward; with igniting velocity the line ran through the

groove;—ran foul. Ahab stooped to clear it; he did clear it; but
the flying turn caught him round the neck, and voicelessly as
Turkish mutes bowstring their victim, he was shot out of the boat,
ere the crew knew he was gone. . . ." On first thought, it might
sound as though Ahab's death were pure accident, an unintentioned death, the cessation of a Psyde-postponer; but let us see
where our second thoughts lead us. Perhaps there is more.

BACKGROUND. It is possible to view *Moby Dick* as a great, sonorous
Mahlerlike symphony—*Das Lied von der See*—not primarily about
the joy of life nor the pessimism engendered by a crushing fate,
but rather as a dramatic and poetic explication of the psychodynamics of death. And, within the context of this thought, is it not
possible that Moby Dick, the great *white* whale, represents the
punishment of death itself? In Chapter 28, when Ahab makes his
first appearance on the "Pequod" at sea, the word "white" is used
three times in one paragraph to describe Ahab: a head-to-toe scar
on Ahab's body, "lividly whitish"; an allusion to a "white sailor,"
in the context of Captain Ahab's being laid out for burial; and
"the barbaric white leg upon which he partly stood." Everywhere,
reference to the pallor of death; and if there is still any question,
the case for "white death" is made explicit in the discussion of
the whiteness of the whale (Chapter 42), in which we are told:
"It cannot well be doubted, that the one visible quality in the aspect
of the dead which most appals the gazer, is the marble pallor lingering there; as if indeed that pallor were as much like the badge of
consternation in the other world, as of mortal trepidation here. And
from that pallor of the dead, we borrow the expressive hue of the
shroud in which we wrap them. Nor even in our superstitions do we
fail to throw the same snowy mantle round our phantoms; all
ghosts rising in a milk-white fog—Yea, while these terrors seize us,
let us add that even the king of terrors, when personified by the
evangelist, rides on his pallid horse."

And if the great white whale is death, then is not the sea itself
the vessel of death? Melville sets this tone for his entire heroic
narrative in his stunning opening passage:

> Call me Ishmael. Some years ago—never mind how long
> precisely—having little or no money in my purse, and
> nothing particular to interest me on shore, I thought I

would sail about a little and see the watery part of the world. It is a way I have of driving off the spleen, and regulating the circulation. Whenever I find myself growing grim about the mouth; whenever it is a damp, drizzly November in my soul; whenever I find myself involuntarily pausing before coffin warehouses, and bringing up the rear of every funeral I meet; and especially whenever my hypos get such an upper hand of me, that it requires a strong moral principle to prevent me from deliberately stepping into the street, and methodically knocking people's hats off—then, I account it high time to get to sea as soon as I can. This is my substitute for pistol and ball. With a philosophical flourish Cato throws himself upon his sword; I quietly take to the ship. . . .

And again, much later, in the description of the blacksmith (Chapter 112), we read:

Death seems the only desirable sequel for a career like this; but Death is only a launching into the region of the strange Untried; it is but the first salutation to the possibilities of the immense Remote, the Wild, the Watery, the Unshored; therefore, to the death-longing eyes of such men, who still have left in them some interior compunctions against suicide, does the all-contributed and all-receptive ocean alluringly spread forth his whole plain of unimaginable, taking terrors, and wonderful, new-life adventures; and from the hearts of infinite Pacifics, the thousand mermaids sing to them—"Come hither, broken-hearted; here is another life without the guilt of intermediate death; here are wonders supernatural, without dying for them. Come hither! bury thyself in a life which, to your now equally abhorred and abhorring, landed world, is more oblivious than death. Come hither! put up *thy* grave-stone, too, within the churchyard, and come hither, till we marry thee!"

If any case is to be made for subintention—Psyde-chancing, Psyde-hastening, Psyde-capitulating, Psyde-experimenting behavior patterns—then, at the least, two further background issues need to be involved: the concept of unconscious motivation and the concept of ambivalence. Ahab's chronicler would not have, in principle,

resisted the concept of subintention, on the grounds of its involving unconscious motivation, for (in Chapter 41) he says:

> ... Such a crew, so officered, seemed specially picked and packed by some infernal fatality to help him to his monomaniac revenge. How it was that they so aboundingly responded to the old man's ire—by what evil magic their souls were possessed, that at times his hate seemed almost theirs; the White Whale as much their insufferable foe as his; how all this came to be—what the White Whale was to them, or how to their unconscious understandings, also, in some dim, unsuspected way, he might have seemed the gliding great demon of the seas of life—all this to explain, would be to dive deeper than Ishmael can go. The subterranean miner that works in us all, how can one tell whither leads his shaft by the ever shifting, muffled sound of his pick? ...

That which is most sharply and most accurately characteristic of the subintentioned person—namely, the ubiquitous ambivalence, the pervasive psychological coexistence of logical incompatibles—is seen vividly in the following internal dialogue of life and death, of flesh and fixture, (as reported in Chapter 51) within Ahab:

> Walking the deck with quick, side-lunging strides, Ahab commanded the t'gallant sails and royals to be set, and every stunsail spread. The best man in the ship must take the helm. Then, with every mast-head manned, the piled-up craft rolled down before the wind. The strange, up-heaving, lifting tendency of the taff-rail breeze filling the hollows of so many sails, made the buoyant, hovering deck to feel like air beneath the feet; while still she rushed along, as if two antagonistic influences were struggling in her—one to mount direct to heaven, the other to drive yawingly to some horizontal goal. And had you watched Ahab's face that night, you would have thought that in him also two different things were warring. While his one live leg made lively echoes along the deck, every stroke of his dead limb sounded like a coffin-tap. On life and death this old man walked. ...

And within Ahab, toward Moby Dick, there were deep ambiguities.

METHOD. In any psychological autopsy it is important to examine the method or the instrument of death and, especially, the victim's understandings and subjective estimations of its lethal works. Ahab was garroted by a free-swinging whale-line. We are warned (in Chapter 60) that ". . . the least tangle or kink in the coiling would, in running out, infallibly take somebody's arm, leg, or entire body off . . ."; we are forewarned ". . . of this man or that man being taken out of the boat by the line, and lost"; and we are warned again, "All men live enveloped in whale-lines. All are born with halters round their necks; but it is only when caught in the swift, sudden turn of death, that mortals realize the silent, subtle, ever-present perils of life." Ahab knew all this; nor was he a careless, accident-prone man. The apothecary knows his deadly drugs; the sportsman knows the danger of his weapons; the whaler captain—that very whaler captain who, instead of remaining on his quarter-deck, jumped to "the active perils of the chase" in a whale-boat manned by his "smuggled on board" crew—ought to know his whale-lines.

QUESTIONS. Having described the precise circumstances of Ahab's death, and having mentioned some background issues deemed to be relevant, I would now pose some questions concerning his demise: Was Ahab's death more than simple accident? Was there more intention than unintention? Was Ahab's orientation in relation to death entirely that of Psyde-postponing? Are there discernible subsurface psychologic currents that can be fathomed and charted, and is there related information that can be dredged and brought to the surface? Specifically, can Ahab's death be described as victim-precipitated homicide; that is, is this an instance in which the victim stands up to subjectively calculated overwhelming odds, inviting destruction by the other? Let us see.

EXTRACTS. Ahab lead a fairly well-documented existence, especially insofar as the dark side of his life was concerned. *Moby Dick* abounds with references to various funereal topics: sleep, coffins, burials, soul, life-after-death, suicide, cemeteries, death, and re-birth.

But—as in a psychological autopsy—we are primarily interested in interview data from everyone who had known the deceased, es-

pecially in what our informants can tell us about Ahab's personality, insofar as his orientations toward death are known. It should be recognized that in some important ways Captain Ahab's psychological autopsy will be a truncated and atypical one, especially with respect to the range of informants; there is no information from spouse, parents, progeny, siblings, collaterals, neighbors; there are only mates, some of the more articulate shipboard subordinates, captains of ships met at sea, and, with terrifying biblical certitude, Elijah.

As we know, all the possible informants, listed below, save Ishmael, perished with Captain Ahab and are technically not available for interview. Only Ishmael's observations are direct; all else is second-hand through Ishmael, colored by Ishmael, and perhaps with no more veridicality than Plato's reports of Socrates. We shall have to trust Ishmael to be an accurate and perceptive reporter.

Our primary informant, Ishmael, reflected about Captain Ahab in twenty-five separate chapters (specifically Chapters 16, 22, 27, 28, 30, 33, 34, 36, 41, 44, 46, 50, 51, 52, 73, 100, 106, 115, 116, 123, 126, 128, 130, 132, and 133). Starbuck, the chief mate of the "Pequod," is next: there are nine separate encounters with, or reports about, his captain (in Chapters 36, 38, 51, 118, 119, 123, 132, 134, and 135). Next is Stubb, the second mate, with seven separate anecdotes (to be found in Chapters 28, 31, 36, 73, 121, 134, and 135). All the others are represented by one or two bits of information apiece: Elijah (in Chapters 19 and 21); Gabriel of the "Jeroboam" (Chapter 71); Bunger, the ship's surgeon of the "Samuel Enderby" (100); the blacksmith (113); the Captain of the "Bachelor" (115); Flask, the third mate (121); the Manxman (125); and the carpenter (127).

Knowing that the limitations of space simply do not permit me to document the essence of each informant's remarks, either with appropriate quotations or abbreviated résumés, how can I summarize all the data? Perhaps my best course would be to concentrate on the general features that one would look for in any psychological autopsy. Thus, the information distilled from interviews with Ishmael, Starbuck, Stubb, and all the others, might, in a dialogue of questions and answers, take the following form.

1. Hidden psychosis? Not at the beginning of the voyage, but

certainly at the end (and indeed from Chapter 36 on—"the chick that's in him picks the shell. 'Twill soon be out.") the madness in Ahab was blatant, open, known. His monomania was the official creed of his ship. Along with his other symptoms, his psychiatric syndrome was crowned with a paranoid fixation. But what matters in Ahab is not so much the bizarrely shaped psychological iceberg that many saw above the surface, but rather the hugeness of the gyroscopically immovable subsurface mass of other-destruction and self-destruction. We know the poems about fire and ice. Ahab is a torrid, burning, fiery iceberg.

2. Disguised depression? Ahab was openly morbid and downcast. His was not exactly psychotic depression, nor can we call it reactive depression for it transcended the bounds of that definition. Perhaps best it might be called a "character depression," in that it infused his brain like the let-go blood from a series of small strokes in the hemisphere.

3. Talk of death? The morbid talk of death and killing runs through reports about Ahab like an *idée fixe*.

4. Previous suicide attempts? None is reported.

5. Disposition of belongings? Ahab, after forty solitary years at sea, had little in the way of self-possessions or interpersonal belongings. His wife, he said, was already a widow; his interest in the possible profits from the voyage was nil; his withdrawal from meaningful material possessions (and his loss of joy with them) is perhaps best indicated by his flinging his "still lighted pipe into the sea" and dashing his quadrant to the deck—both rash acts for a sailor-captain.

In Ahab's conscious mind, he wanted to kill—but have we not said that self-destruction can be other-destruction in the 180th degree? Figuratively speaking, the barb of the harpoon was pointed toward him; his brain thought a thrust, but his arm executed a retroflex. Was his death "accident"? If he had survived his psychodynamically freighted voyage and had returned unharmed to Nantucket's pier, *that* would have been true accident. Men can die for nothing—most men do; but some few big-jointed men can give their lives for an internalized something: Ahab would not have missed this opportunity for the world.

What further evidence can be cited bearing on the issue of sub-intentioned cessation? With his three harpooners before him, with

their harpoons turned up like goblets, Ahab (in Chapter 36) commands them, in this maritime immolation scene, as follows: "Drink, ye harpooneers! drink and swear, ye men that man the deathful whaleboat's bow—Death to Moby Dick! God hunt us all, if we do not hunt Moby Dick to his death!" Kill or be killed; punish or be retributed; murder or suicide—how the two are intertwined.

In Ahab's case, we have no suicide note or other holograph of death, but, *mirabile dictu,* we do have (in Chapter 135) Ahab's last thoughts:

> I turn my body from the sun. . . . Oh, lonely death on lonely life! Oh, now I feel my topmost greatness lies in my topmost grief. Ho, ho! from all your furthest bounds, pour ye now in, ye bold billows of my whole foregone life, and top this one piled comber of my death! Towards thee I roll, thou all-destroying but unconquering whale; to the last I grapple with thee; from hell's heart I stab at thee; for hate's sake I spit my last breath at thee. Sink all coffins and all hearses to one common pool! and since neither can be mine, let me then tow to pieces, while still chasing thee, though tied to thee, thou damned whale! *Thus,* I give up the spear!

What is to be particularly noted in this is the prescience of Ahab. "I spit my last breath at thee," he says. How does he know that it is to be his *last* breath? Where are the sources of his premonitions? What are the contents of his subintentions? Does this not remind us of Radney, the chief mate of the "Town-Ho" (Chapter 54) who behaved as if he "sought to run more than half way to meet his doom"? Is this not exactly what the tantalizer says to his "all-destroying but unconquering" executioner in cases of victim-precipitated homicide?

RECOMMENDATION. It is suggested that Captain Ahab's demise was goal-seeking behavior that made obsessed life *or* subintentioned death relatively unimportant to him, compared with the great press for the discharge of his monomania of hate. He dared, and made, that murderous death-white whale kill him. He could not rest until he was so taken. (Did Satan *provoke* God into banishing him?) Ahab invited cessation by the risks that he ran; he was a Psyde-chancer. He permitted suicide. Consider Ahab's psychological position: What could he have done, to what purpose would any further

voyages have been, if he *had* killed the symbol of his search? It was, from Ahab's point of view, the time; and in his unconscious wish, it was the "appropriate death." *In nomine ceti albini!*

Discussions

AVERY D. WEISMAN: As one of America's leading authorities on suicide, Dr. Edwin Shneidman is understandably impatient with the prevalence of false notions about death and suicide. In fact, he thinks that the word *suicide* is too ambiguous to be either scientifically or clinically significant. He also wants to avoid the term *death* and to replace it with operational terms. Like other investigators of suicide and death, he is deeply aware that the line that divides living from dying is often difficult to determine. Semantic confusion, oversimplification, prejudice, and unexamined assumption impose still further obstacles to understanding.

Dr. Shneidman's central concept is that of *cessation.* It refers to conscious experience. An analogous concept, *termination,* applies to physiological functions. The relation of cessation to termination is approximately that between psychic death and physical death. While termination presumably puts an end to conscious experience, it is possible for cessation to occur without concomitant termination. This distinction underscores the contrast between extinction of individual consciousness and objective death as an inescapable fact of nature.

Dr. Shneidman focuses on the concept of cessation, and shows how people may, knowingly or not, bring about or delay their own cessation. Thus, there are cessation-fearers, cessation-ignorers, cessation-postponers, and so forth. According to the degree to which a person's conscious motivation participates in his own cessation, he distinguishes between intentioned, subintentioned, unintentioned, and contraintentioned acts.

CONCEPTS OF DEATH. It is extremely difficult to learn what people think about death and dying. Not only are most people burdened by assumptions and prejudices that have been uncritically absorbed in the course of life, but their personal attitudes toward death are likely to change as they grow older, fall sick, and are themselves threatened with death.

The concept of cessation allows us to recognize how people affirm

the reality of death at various stages of life and under different circumstances. Patients are not expected to say *what* death means to them, or *how* they expect to die. Although Dr. Shneidman's classification of cessation behavior is largely contingent upon reports and observations made by sophisticated, observant investigators, the choice of category is broad enough to reduce unwarranted inferences. He demonstrates that *cessation attitudes are not necessarily suicidal, nor is there a specific cessation attitude for suicide.* With equal relevance, cessation attitudes are both vital and lethal, covering a wide range of comprehensive versions of life as well as death.

Perhaps the most prevalent concept of death is that it is an unmitigated evil, never to be sought, always to be avoided as long as possible. Although cessation and termination cannot be postponed indefinitely, most people also believe that suicide is wrong—far more than those who believe that suicide is a sickness. Even sophisticated thinkers find that death is deplorable, and that hastening the inevitable is a sign of disability or defeat, not merely of disease. In Dr. Shneidman's sense, most of us are *doomed* to be cessation-postponers and cessation-fearers. Mankind concedes the universality of objective death, but still regards personal extinction either as an illusion or a tragic fault. Because Dr. Shneidman shows that the inner attitude of suicidal patients cannot be reduced to a single formula, he urges us to think again about our conventional notions of life and death.

APPROPRIATE DEATH. In 1961, Dr. Thomas Hackett and I reported a group of patients who approached death with a minimum of anxiety and conflict.[28] Several of our patients anticipated death as a fitting solution to their problems. It was apparent that for some people death is not deplorable, but desirable as a means of attaining resolution of conflict, fulfillment of desire, and rewarding quiescence. We termed this concept *appropriate death.*

Although we were quite explicit about our meaning, so strong are the forces of habit and prejudice that the concept of appropriate death has been misunderstood in different ways. First, it is not intended to be merely a poetic metaphor, or a sentimental afterthought when someone has died. Second, appropriate death has no etiological significance. It is not a conspiracy of emotional, social,

and biological forces that come together and dispose patients to an unwelcome death. Third, we understood that because the world is filled with so many needless and meaningless deaths it is difficult to imagine that death can ever be either acceptable or appropriate. The judgment about whether or not death was appropriate could not be made with finality, nor could we dogmatically declare that death was wholly acceptable to our patients. We defined an appropriate death as one in which there is reduction of conflict, compatibility with the ego ideal, continuity of significant relationships, and consummation of prevailing wishes. In short, an appropriate death is one which a person might choose for himself, had he an option. Death is therefore a harmonious end point of motivated acts within the context of the ego ideal. It is not merely conclusive; it is consummatory.

It is quite simple to define appropriate death in whatever way we choose. It is another matter when we try to discover if there are appropriate and acceptable deaths among patients who are not "predilected" to death and who manage to survive.

We can ask a hypothetical question: If no one died until he chose to, who would ever be ready for death? For the vigorous, healthy adult, the question is clearly unthinkable, because his affiliation with life is so strong. However, there are other people, for example, the chronically ill and the extremely aged, in whom the margin between life and death is obscure. They may be quite willing to slip into oblivion, without being either depressed or suicidal. But to be willing to die is not equivalent to being able to die. Death may be acceptable, and not appropriate, or it may be appropriate, and not acceptable. We have known a patient who survived a series of hazardous operations for brain abscess. Despite numerous post-operative complications, he recovered. Three weeks after hospital discharge, he committed suicide. Evidently, his "drive to survive" persisted during his hospital weeks, but collapsed shortly after discharge! What kind of cessation was this? Had he died in the hospital, his death would have been subintentioned or unintentioned. He was a cessation-acceptor at this time. After discharge, he became a successful cessation-seeker. We may speculate that he was not suicidal in the hospital because he was cared for with unusual dedication and was not expected to fulfill social obligations. After discharge, however, he was once again a homeless drifter, living on

the margins of life. No one can tell if this patient, deep in his mind, expected to destroy himself, nor can we be sure whether he was a cessation-welcomer or a cessation-fearer. In other words, although Dr. Shneidman has provided us with a valuable system of taxonomy, it is still not quite operational. We require quite a bit of understanding of a patient's attitude toward survival before we can appraise his attitude toward extinction.

Any concept of death is a version of life. The range of possible deaths is a catalogue that depicts many kinds of acceptability and appropriateness. Because there is a difference between cessation and termination, some kinds of death may be highly appropriate in the interpersonal and intrapersonal dimension, without involving a suitable impersonal or biological termination. We have studied several patients in whom social and emotional factors were consistent with both an acceptable and appropriate death, and yet they did not die. Naturally, we do not understand the specific biological, social, and emotional conjunction that eventuates in death. The concept of appropriate death does not require this kind of information. It does require that cessation and termination have a meaning in the life style of a patient, that a patient does not die merely as a passive victim of a disease, and that dying is a positive act that protects his responsibility.

SUICIDE AND APPROPRIATE DEATH. What is the relation of suicide to appropriate death? Is it not an appropriate death that a suicidal patient wants to bring about? Does each variety of cessation correspond to a different context in which death is appropriate? Suicidal patients seek harmony, relief, and resolution of conflict. They apparently choose to extinguish themselves in order to find an idealized version of life.

Despite their similarities, suicide and appropriate death differ. There are, to be sure, many illustrious men who have chosen to terminate their life rather than to survive with diminished creative powers. There are many other instances in which murder may be defensible. Whether a man's life is always his to dispense with is a moral question, and cannot be decided by psychiatrists or psychologists. Knowledge of the psychopathology of suicide is still rudimentary, but we have reason to believe, with Dr. Shneidman, that self-destruction may be "murder in the 180th degree." In other

words, a suicidal act may replace and relieve a homicidal fantasy. Moreover, suicidal impulses are inconstant. A man who is suicidal today may find the idea unthinkable tomorrow. In suicide there are critical phases; one part of a person takes over the autonomy of the rest, and decrees its extinction—usually in opposition to his life style, his ego ideal, and the longitudinal meaning of his life.

A suicidal patient has *appropriated* death, without achieving an appropriate death. The availability of suicide carries many people through sleepless nights, but I doubt if many people choose suicide, quietly and dispassionately, as the culmination of a life plan. Any of us may choose suicide rather than suffer the tyranny of disease or despotic forces, but those people who do destroy themselves are usually suffering from an inner agony, not an external crisis.

The statement, "I have nothing more to live for," may be a sentiment expressed by someone whose feasible work is done, or, in contrast, an utterance wrung out in a moment of despair. Despite verbal similarity, one statement is an expression of quiescence, the other, of pain. This is the interface where Dr. Shneidman's work and our own will meet. We are deeply appreciative of the contributions that he and his colleagues have made to these basic problems.

KARL MENNINGER: There is much in the lives of individuals and communities that is puzzling: bickerings, hatreds, and fightings over trivia, useless waste and self-destructiveness. People extend themselves to injure others, and expend time, trouble, and energy in shortening that pitifully small recess from oblivion that we call life. As if lacking aught else to destroy or failing to accomplish it, many turn their weapons directly upon themselves.

DEATH INSTINCT. It was such observations as this that led Sigmund Freud to the formulation of the theory of a drive toward self-destruction, which he called the death instinct. There exist from the beginning in all of us strong propensities toward self-destruction and these come to fruition as actual suicide only in exceptional cases in which many circumstances and factors combine to make it possible.

Freud makes the further assumption that the life and death instincts—let us call them the constructive and destructive tendencies of the personality—are in constant conflict and interaction

just as are similar opposing forces in the concepts of physics, chemistry, and biology. To create and to destroy, to build up and to tear down, these are the anabolism and the catabolism of the personality, no less than of the cells and the corpuscles—the two directions in which the same energies exert themselves.

These forces, originally directed inward and related to the intimate problems of the self, continuously tend to be directed outwardly, focused on other environmental objects. Managed with sufficient skill and with the maintenance of a certain balance and control, this may resolve in growth, development, social integration. An incomplete turning outward of the self-directed destructiveness *and* also of the constructiveness with which we are—by hypothesis —born, results, of course, in permanent lack of development. Instead of dealing with people such individuals avoid them. Instead of fighting their enemies, such individuals fight themselves; instead of loving friends or music or the building of a house, such persons love only themselves. Hate and love are the emotional representatives of the destructive and constructive tendencies.

But no one evolves so completely as to be entirely free from the upsurge of the self-destructive tendencies; indeed, the phenomena of life, the behavior peculiar to different individuals, may be said to express the result of the measures taken to control these conflicting factors. An equilibrium of sorts, oftentimes very unstable, is achieved, maintained until disturbed by new developments in the environment that cause a rearrangement with perhaps quite different outcome.

Freud repeatedly emphasized that the manifestations of the self-destructive instinct were never nakedly visible. In the first place, the self-destructive instincts get turned in an outward direction by the very process of life, and in the second place, they get neutralized in the very process of living. Self-destruction in the operational sense is a result of a return, as it were, of the self-destructive tendencies to the original object. It is not *quite* the original object as a rule, because the object of redirected aggression, aggression reflected back upon the self, is usually the body. And since a part of the body may be offered up as a substitute for the whole, this partial suicide, as we have called it, is a way of averting total suicide. But if that part of the body is a vital part, the partial suicide becomes actual suicide.

On this basis we can understand how it can be that some people kill themselves quickly and some slowly and some not at all, why some contribute to their own deaths and others withstand valiantly and brilliantly external assaults upon their lives to which their fellows would have quickly succumbed. So much of this, however, takes place automatically and unconsciously that it will seem at first blush like an impossible task to dissect the details of a particular bargain or compromise between the life and death instincts.

Early in my professional career I was impressed with the central position in all psychiatry held by the phenomenon of suicide. It is considered irrational in most cultures; in some societies it is unknown; it is strangely overprevalent in certain very civilized countries. It increases with prosperity. Rationalized as it may be by intellectuals, its occurrence is always somewhat uncanny, incredible, inexplicable. It is a little difficult for survivors to conceive of anyone having been *quite* so hopeless, *quite* so heartless, *quite* so unrealistic. It is, indeed, a last act, an irreparable, irreversible, final blow. Its dreadfulness, its aggressive impact, is felt by relatives and friends and physicians, which, of course, was partly its victim's intent.

THREE COMPONENTS IN THE SUICIDAL ACT. First of all suicide is obviously a *murder*. In the German language it is, literally, a murder of the self (*Selbstmord*), and in all the earlier philological equivalents the idea of murder is implicit.

But suicide is also a murder committed *by* the self as murderer. It is a death in which are combined in one person the murderer and the murdered. We know that the motives for murder vary enormously; so do the motives for wishing to be murdered, which is quite another matter and not nearly as absurd as it may sound. For since in suicide there is a self that submits to the murder and would appear to be desirous of doing so, we must seek the motives of this strange submission.

If the reader will picture to himself a battlefield scene in which a wounded man is suffering greatly and begs someone to kill him, he will readily appreciate that the feelings of the *murderer* would be very different, depending upon whether he were a friend or a foe of the wounded man; those of the man who desires to be murdered, that is, to be put out of his agony, however, would be the same in either case.

In many suicides it is quite apparent that one of these contributing factors is stronger than the other. One sees people who want to die but cannot take the step against themselves; they fling themselves in front of trains, or like King Saul and Brutus, they beseech their armor bearers to slay them.

Probably no suicide is consummated unless—in addition to these wishes to kill and be killed—the suicidal person also wishes to die—using the word "wish" here to relate to the resultant of motivational factors, conscious and unconscious wishes. Many suicides, in spite of the violence of the attack upon themselves and in spite of the corresponding surrender, paradoxically seem to be unwilling to die. Every hospital intern has labored in the emergency ward with would-be-suicides, who beg him to save their lives. The fact that dying and being murdered achieve the same end so far as personal extinction is concerned, leads the practical-minded individual to think, "If a person wants to murder himself, or if he feels so badly about something that he is willing to be murdered, then he surely must want to die." But the illustration just given is only one of many indications that this is not so. Murdering or being murdered entails factors of violence, while dying relates to a surrender of one's life and happiness. In attempted suicide the wish to die may or may not be present, or may be to quite a variable degree, as Shneidman has described in his concepts of cessation, termination, interruption, and continuation. Freud emphasized the fact that instincts were never conscious and that we should not equate the death instinct with the wish to die or the life instinct with the wish to live. What I am proposing is that many other factors enter the formula. Stengel and others have pointed out how a certain amount of play-acting is always involved whereby the drama of suicide is played with a childish and unrealistic King's X cross: "It really isn't going to happen even though I am doing it." "I am doing it not to end all but to portray all." "I am showing what I have suffered." "I am dramatizing the need I have for help." Such feelings as this represent a wish to live, despite the actions that seem to indicate a wish to die.

Suicide must thus be regarded as a peculiar kind of death that entails three basic internal elements and many modifying ones. There is the element of dying, the element of killing, and the element of being killed. Each is a condensation for which there exist com-

plexes of motive, unconscious and conscious. What we call a suicide is for the individual himself an attempt to burst into life or to save his life. It may be to avoid something far more dreadful, to avoid committing murder or going mad. After all, the reasoning processes of the suicidally impelled person cannot be expected to be logical or rational or even consistent. From my own point of view the suicidal determination—determination, I say, in fantasy, not enactment, not motivation—the suicidal determination as such, the surrender of all hope, is a final catastrophe of dissolution, which the organism so greatly dreads. In a sense suicide is a flight from death, using death in a very broad sense.

SOME ADDITIONAL COMMENTS ON METHODS AND PREVENTION. In the end each man kills himself in his own selected way, fast or slow, soon or late. We all feel this, vaguely; there are so many occasions to witness it before our eyes. The methods are legion and it is these that attract our attention. Some of them interest surgeons, some of them interest lawyers and priests, some of them interest heart specialists, some of them interest sociologists. All of them must interest the man who sees the personality as a totality and medicine as the healing of the nations.

I believe that our best defense against self-destructiveness lies in the courageous application of intelligence to human phenomenology. If such is our nature, it were better that we knew it and knew it in all its protean manifestations. To see all forms of self-destruction from the standpoint of their dominant principles would seem to be logical progress toward self-preservation and toward a unified view of medical science.

KOJI SATO: It is a great pleasure for me to add some comments to Dr. Shneidman's stimulating paper. I have been thinking of the death of Zen masters. Even Zen masters have their individuality, and their ways of leaving this world are different from one another. I wrote for our journal *Psychologia*—an International Journal of Psychology in the Orient—a paper entitled "Deaths of Zen masters" (Vol. 7, Nos. 3, 4, 1964). Master Gempo Yamamoto's way of passing away is specially interesting in Shneidman's classification. After the Master reached his ninetieth birthday, he was thinking of closing the curtain of his puppet show in this world. He began fasting a

number of times. But his disciples begged him to live more. At last, at the end of 1960, he seemed to leave this world and began fasting. Seigen Tanaka, one of his layman disciples, begged him to stop fasting, but was struck by the old Master with all his might. Tanaka, however, succeeded in persuading him to stop it for the reason that it was the end of the year and the Master's death would make much trouble to many people. Next year Tanaka visited the Master on May 28, and the Master said, "I was thinking of leaving today; it is the day of my master's death; I have nothing to say, just hold my hand," and grasped his hand firmly. When Tanaka told him that he would come again on June 5, the Master laughed, saying, "I will see you at the main hall of Ryutakuji Temple." At one o'clock on the night of June 3, the Master requested a cup of wine from his attendant monk, took it and showed his enjoyment. After ten minutes he said briefly: "I am going out on a journey, prepare my clothing," and lay down and passed away at 1:15 A.M. in his ninety-sixth year. Someone said it was suicide, but it is quite sure it was not a usual suicide. The fruit was ripe enough. Usually ripe fruits fall down unintentionally, but this fruit fell down intentionally, being ripe enough.

ROBERT E. LITMAN: Shneidman applies psychodynamic concepts to the classification of deaths. The result is a new scientific view of self-destruction avoiding the sociolegal connotations of suicide.

The academic reader will enjoy this essay for its polished literary style and marks of philosophic erudition. But style should not obscure the essential content, which is a bold proposal that the prevailing classification of death, honored by centuries of use, should be discarded as unclear in favor of a new classification that assigns the deceased into categories according to his orientation toward death.

The traditional classification of death has served the sociolegal need to assign blame for every death, either to God (natural, accident) or man (homicide, suicide). By analogy with homicide, suicide might be "justifiable" (as in heroic self-sacrifice), "excusable" (as in simple carelessness), or "culpable" (a deliberate social wrong). The concept of the role of the individual in his own demise cuts across these categories and serves a different need, that of furthering the scientific understanding of self-destruction.

IS SUICIDE A USEFUL TERM? Shneidman suggests, "It may well be that the word *suicide* currently has too many loose and contradictory meanings to be scientifically or clinically useful."

This is a statement with which I must agree. As a term, *suicide* leads more to scientific confusion than to clarity. In clincial practice the word *suicide* has an affectual shock value that is useful in a few limited communication situations but often leads to ambiguous discourse and misunderstanding between practitioners. In talking about suicidal behavior, it promotes clarity if the clinician specifies whether the given act, thought, impulse, or affect was mildly suicidal, moderately suicidal, or seriously suicidal. Suicide is not a unitary syndrome, but rather a collection of different acts by dissimilar people for various motives.

However, I do not feel that the community is ready for a new taxonomy of death. Rather we should encourage the legal profession, coroners, and police officials to use the customary and accepted classifications more consistently and conscientiously. By contrast, behavioral scientists working in the vanguard of research on self-destruction do need new designs for ordering their observations. To classify certain people as "death-seekers," "death-darers," "death-experimenters," and the like, is dramatically descriptive and stimulates new views of human lives and deaths.

Because the distinction between death and cessation seems to me to be too finely philosophical to be pertinent for taxonomy, I would recommend dropping the term *Psyde,* especially since other workers may share my own prejudice against neologisms in favor of plain English. (For example, many of us deplore the translation of Sigmund Freud's *Das Ich* as *the ego*; it should be *the I*.)

IS IT DYNAMIC? "The operation that gives meaning to the phrase 'basic orientation toward cessation' has to do with the role of the individual in his own demise. By 'role of the individual' is meant his overt and covert behaviors and nonbehaviors that reflect conscious and unconscious attributes relevant to his cessation."

By his concept "role of the individual" Shneidman ties "orientation" to behavior (and nonbehavior). These behaviors are understood to reflect all the multidetermined complexity of shifting drives and defenses ambivalently balanced against each other. Obviously the whole purpose of this classification is to introduce

psychodynamic concepts into the descriptive terminology of death. For this effort the essay deserves general recognition and evaluation.

Probably the greatest difficulty from the standpoint of personality dynamics involves Shneidman's snapshot focus on a limited unit of time. By tying "orientation" to action behavior, the concept freezes psychodynamics at one particular moment of time, that moment appropriate to the behavior "relevant to his cessation." Although this focus on a segment of time and a segment of behavior-action is in some respects artificial and does not do justice to the complexity of total personality, it provides a tremendous gain in clarity and, we hope, in useful diagnostic divisions. A difficulty in the path of clinical application is that over periods of time patients tend to change, sometimes rapidly, in their orientations and behaviors.

DID AHAB COMMIT SUICIDE? When a seagoing vessel or an airship is lost, there is an inquiry to determine what happened and to assign blame. In this context the traditional suicide concepts retain some validity. Some of us may serve as consultants for such investigations. What should we say if it is learned that a disaster with great loss of life occurred as a direct result of certain unusual actions of the captain, actions that contradict the lifelong habits, training, ethical attitudes, and responsibilities of the captain? What if, before the event, the captain behaved strangely, with symptoms of depression and even madness? We would ask ourselves, was the captain suicidal? If we do our duty conscientiously, some such deaths will be labeled suicide.

Then what of the crew and passengers? Are not all of us who travel in automobiles, ships, and airplanes death-chancers? In order to live with any freedom of action, we must constantly consciously place our lives somewhat in jeopardy, chancing death one way or another.

In my opinion, Captain Ahab was more than a death-chancer (which we all are); he was at least a death-darer. There is good evidence that he was, during the last moments of his life, a death-seeker. Was his death accidental? A board of inquiry to whom the facts were disclosed, as Shneidman has reported them, might well consider carefully, deliberate at length, and then conclude that this

death was "probable suicide." Then, having completed the legal requirement, the board could seek further scientific enlightenment by reconstructing the Captain's orientation toward his own cessation and that of his ship and its crew.

Reply to Discussants

EDWIN S. SHNEIDMAN: When I first read these comments to my paper, my primary reaction was an affective one. I was emotionally moved, especially by the tinges of a pervasive feeling that I was reading about someone who was already dead. I experienced a transcendent narcissism that was quickly and mysteriously transformed into feelings of concomitant depression and humility. It may be that part of this feeling stemmed from the fact that this essay was written by me during a period the passing of which I have constantly mourned. Specifically, it was written in 1961–1962, the year of the greatest intellectual excitement of my life, when I was privileged to be a U. S. Public Health Service Special Research Fellow at Harvard University, studing with that incomparable man, Professor Henry A. Murray; and this feeling was also based in part on the fact that these ideas are already old ones for me—and in that sense represent some of my "dead" thoughts.

As I think about my own essay, and the insightful and generous comments that have been made about it, I believe that my own interests—which began with the discovery of several hundred suicide notes in the vaults of the Los Angeles Coroner's Office in 1949—have moved from (1) a specific concern with suicide, to (2) a broader interest in death, and currently to (3) a deep interest in and concern with what I consider to be a still wider topic, namely, inimical patterns of living. By this I have in mind the multitudinous ways in which an individual can reduce, truncate, demean, narrow, shorten, or destroy his own life. I personally prefer not to talk about "substitute suicide," but, rather, straightforwardly, to talk about inimical patterns of behavior—of which killing oneself is the most extreme. My own current interests concern the various orientations to life, of which one's orientations to death are one significant aspect. Growing out of my own thoughts on cessation, interruption,

and altered continuation, one facet of my own current research work has to do with aspects of interruption, specifically with the intensive study of the sleep patterns of a small number of suicidal and nonsuicidal subjects night-by-night over the period of the past three years. In *Essays in Self-Destruction*, I have a chapter entitled "Sleep and Self-Destruction," in which I give a first report of some of the relationships between interruption patterns and orientations toward cessation. I can also report that my interest in Melville has been intensified one-hundredfold by my thoughts about orientations toward life and death subsequent to my writing the Ahab section of this paper. I have, in the last several months, read through the eleven novels and collections of stories by Melville, cataloguing every reference to any aspect of cessation, interruption, or altered continuation—I now have a few thousand such punch cards—and attempting to relate what Melville did in each of his books to what was going on in his own life at the time, specifically, his own partial deaths, withdrawal from society, decrease in public productivity, and the like. I feel that the labors involved in this hobby have already come to a meaningful fruition in my own increased understandings of human nature, and I would hope someday to publish on this topic.

Chapter 2
SUICIDE, SLEEP, AND DEATH
Edwin S. Shneidman

Growing out of the work at the Los Angeles Suicide Prevention Center, a theoretical reexamination of the concepts of death and suicide is proposed. In lieu of these two terms, other concepts are are developed: cessation (final); interruption (periodical); and continuation (modal, partial, critical, and focal). Examples of behaviors and psychological states for each of these are given. A set of cross-behavioral congruencies, focusing especially on the similarities between sleep phenomena (seen as interruption) and self-destructive phenomena (seen as cessation), is developed under the headings of beliefs, motives, affective states, cognitive patterns, sociocultural influences, and the like. In addition, relevant sources of data—primarily from a variety of types of personal documents and anamnestic data—for each type of behavior are suggested. The focus of the paper is on the investigation of cessation (death and suicidal) phenomena through the study of paradigmatically useful interruption and continuation states.

> . . . the men, women, the children; the old with the young, the decrepit with the lusty—all equal before sleep, death's brother.
>
> JOSEPH CONRAD, *Lord Jim*

In the last few years there has been an awakening of interest in sleep; a lively concern with the topic of death;[1] and serious attempts at suicide research, our own included.[2] This paper, advertently speculative and discursive, grows out of our work at the Los Angeles Suicide Prevention Center and is an attempt to apply some insights from each of these areas (sleep, death, and suicide) to the others. My primary purpose is to present an overview of some possibly productive parallels between sleep phenomena and death (particularly suicidal) phenomena.

Theoretical Background

DEATH AND SUICIDE. In the previous chapter of this book, I attempted, in greater detail than is possible here, to indicate some of

the conceptual shortcomings inherent in our current notions of death and suicide.[3] Briefly stated, the current classification of suicidal behaviors (into committed, attempted, threatened, and non-suicidal) groups together different forms of behavior in a way that is often more confusing than clarifying. The most obvious shortcoming is that various individuals, all labeled or diagnosed as "threatened suicide," "attempted suicide," or even "committed suicide," can have behaved with marked differences in their lethality intentions and their dyadic purposes. The obfuscatory effects of combining anamnestic and psychological data from a variety of intentional types and pretending that they can be placed under one rubric (for example, "attempted suicide") are incalculable.

And if "suicide" is poorly dimensionalized, "death" is even more so. The current classification of modes of death (into the four crypts of natural, accidental, suicide, and homicide) is found to be obscuring primarily because this remarkably apsychological seventeenth-century classification rather completely omits the role of the individual in his own demise. What is the difference to the individual whether he is invaded by a lethal bullet (homicide), a lethal steering wheel (accident) or a lethal virus (natural), if in all of these cases he did not want this event to happen? And what of the unconscious or covert ways in which an individual may participate in his being invaded by virus, wheel, or bullet? In addition, if this were not enough, the concept of "death" itself, as Bridgman has pointed out, is operationally unpalatable, in that no individual can experience his own death—if he could, then he would not be dead—and he can never even be certain that he is dying—in that he might recover or be saved.[4]

CESSATION, TERMINATION, INTERRUPTION, AND CONTINUATION. In light of all these depressing considerations concerning the obfuscatory nature of our current conceptualizations of death and suicide, I have proposed a classification of "orientations toward cessation" which attempts to encompass the range of possible psychological postures that one might have toward one's own demise.[5] In this scheme, cessation is defined as the stopping of the potentiality of any (further) conscious experience. It is the last introspective bit in the last scene of the last act of that individual. In order to understand the role of cessation, three additional concepts—termination,

interruption, and continuation—seem to be required. These terms can be defined as follows:

Termination is the stopping of the physiological functions of the body, specifically the stopping of the exchange of gasses between the organism and his environment. Although termination carries with it cessation, it is, of course, possible (in an individual with a crushed skull, for example) for cessation to occur for that individual hours or days prior to the occurrence of his termination.

Interruption is defined as the stopping of consciousness with the actuality, and usually the expectation, of further conscious experiences. It is, to use two contradictory terms, a kind of "temporary cessation."

Continuation is the experiencing, in the absence of interruption, the stream of temporally contiguous conscious events.[6] Our psychological lives are thus made up of a series of alternating continuation and interruption states; the end, the nothingness, the naughtment, the conclusion of the conscious life is cessation.

SLEEP. In terms of our definitions above, sleep is an excellent example of an interruption state. Other interruption states include being under an anaesthetic, in an alcholoic stupor, in a diabetic coma, epileptic seizure, fainting spell, and the like. It is interesting to note that the opening sentence in the first edition of Kleitman's book *Sleep and Wakefulness* is:

> Sleep is commonly looked upon as a periodic temporary cessation, or interruption, of the waking state which is the prevalent mode of existence for the healthy human adult.[7]

Our task now is to generate psychological and sociological similarities between sleep phenomena (viewed as *interruption* phenomena) and death phenomena (viewed as *cessation* phenomena), attempting to show how various interruption states (for which data are *relatively* easy to obtain) might be related as conceptual analogies or paradigms (or even metaphors) to various cessation behaviors.

Overview of Conceptual Scheme

Most of the remainder of this short paper will be occupied with an explication of Chart I. I shall begin by pointing out some of its salient features.

What contents are subsumed under the headings? The major heading of the chart has to do with alterations of behavioral and psychological states. Two kinds of alteration states are delineated: *discontinuation* (Part I) and *continuation* (Part II).

Under discontinuation states (I) we see the following listed:

A. *Final* discontinuations, which are permanent and are synonymous with "cessation" as defined above. The relevant sources of data are suicide notes, wills, letters written in the context of death, and the like.

B. *Periodical* discontinuations—in the sense that they have a characteristic periodicity (that is, occur from time to time)—are temporary and are synonymous with "interruption" states as defined above. For this category, the relevant sources of data of what we call "interruption notes," that is, materials that we elicit—just as we have previously elicited simulated suicide notes[8]—by asking individuals to write notes within the context of an interruption state, that is just before or just after sleep, anaesthesia, and so forth.

C. *Intermedial* discontinuation states are posited in order to take account of those behaviors and states of mind having to do with the internal debates between life and death, with gambles with death,[9] and with the ubiquitous ambivalences between living and dying that we constantly see in our patients at the Suicide Prevention Center. These intermedial states (such as near-cessation or trend toward cessation) also call our attention to the continuum of vitality-of-consciousness, ranging between cessation and ardent living, which we see in a range of people.

In this connection Henry A. Murray has stated:

> A personality is a full Congress of orators and pressure-groups, of children, demagogues, communists, isolationists, war-mongers, mugwumps, grafters, log-rollers, lobbyists, Caesars and Christs, Machiavellis and Judases, Tories and Promethean revolutionists.[10]

This is a most useful figure of speech. It reminds us that some individuals are in a chronic internal debate with themselves regarding life and death, a kind of lethal filibuster; also that there are as in Congress, committees of the mind; that we often refer vital issues to "the other house" (the significant other) for final outcome; and, finally, that actions of the personality are rarely a matter of one

internal voice but rather a Congress of voices, and that many a seemingly dichotomous action, the result of complicated internal debates, is launched by a bare majority vote.

Under continuation behaviors (II), we have mentioned (D) *modal* continuation states, (E) *focal* continuation states, (F) *partial* discontinuation states and (G) *critical* continuation states.

D. By *modal* continuation states, we mean the way in which a person continues being more or less himself, with only those changes that are gradual, that is, changes over time and between psychological "stages of man."[11] The sources for these modal behaviors for an individual would be his ordinary letters to relatives and friends, diaries, and special communications that might be called "credo statements."

E. The *focal* continuation behaviors are especially important. They relate to acutely altered continuation states, that is, relatively short-term (mesotemporal) changes in the quality of consciousness; the best examples are being intoxicated or drugged *and* remaining conscious. Conscious malingering, role-playing, spying, and feigning also belong in this category. Another way individuals alter their conscious states is by what might be called *unplugging,* that is, by drifting, idling, seceding, or uncorking, such as "having a good read," "ducking into a movie," going on vacation or a *Wanderjahr,* staying in bed, watching Westerns on television, or, more actively, going on an escapade, a binge, or an orgy, having a brief affair—in short, plugging oneself out by means of escape or removal activities, as opposed to staying in it and "sweating it out."

F. *Partial* continuation states have to do with withdrawals by the individual from society and withdrawal by society from the individual. In another context, Murray has implied that one may suffer a cessation of a part of psychic life, such as cessation of affect (for example, feeling almost dead), or the cessation of an orientation of conscious life (for example, the cessation of social life, dead to the outer world, or of spiritual life, dead to the inner world). For example, writing of Melville, Murray states:

> He abdicated to the conscience he condemned, and his ship *Pequod,* in sinking, carried down with it the conscience he aspired to, represented by the skyhawk, the bird of heaven. With his ideal drowned, life from then on was load, and time stood still. All he had denied to love he

CHART I

SCHEMATIC CHART OF INTERRELATIONS AMONG

ALTERATION

I. DISCONTINUATION BEHAVIORS

	A. FINAL Permanent (Cessation)	B. PERIODICAL Temporary (Interruption)	

ALTERATION
STATES

C. INTERMEDIAL

RELATED PSYCHOLOGICAL STATES	Naughtment Cessation Death Demise	Near Cessation Trend toward cessation	Sleep Unconsciousness Anesthesia Stupor Fainting Seizures

CROSS- BEHAVIORAL CONGRUENCIES	1. MOTIVATIONAL ROLES (of individual in his own alteration): Intentioned, subintentioned, unintentioned, and contraintentioned. 2. COSMOLOGICAL BELIEFS: Beliefs about natural and supernatural world; God, prayer, hereafter, reunion, survival after death, etc. 3. AFFECTIVE STATES, especially the sequence and order of both positive and negative affect states. 4. COGNITIVE STYLES: Individual's idiosyncratic log-		

RELEVANT SOURCES OF DATA	Suicide notes Wills Letters written in context of death	Materials reflecting ambivalence, role of chance, and internal debate	"Interruption notes" written in context of sleep, anesthetic, EST.

ANAMNESTIC,

CESSATION-INTERRUPTION-CONTINUATION BEHAVIORS

BEHAVIORS

II. CONTINUATION BEHAVIORS

	D. MODAL	E. FOCAL *Acutely Altered* *Continuation States*

F. PARTIAL CONTINUATIONS AND DISCONTINUA- TIONS		G. CRITICAL (*Endings*)	

Sensory
  anesthesia
Motor paralysis
Affectlessness
Withdrawals
Psychoses
Dissociations
Fugue states
Amnesias
	Modal behaviors
	  together with
	  shifts and
	  changes with
	  age and
	  "stages of
	  man"
		Grief
		Bereavement
		Mourning
		Nostalgia
		Longing
			Intoxication
			Drugged states
			  (LSD, etc.)
			Hypnosis
			Anoxia
			Malingering
			Role playing
			Spying
			Feigning
			Unplugging

ical styles and his private epistemology (contralogic); ways of concluding.

5. PHENOMENOLOGICAL ASPECTS: Defining the self; coded messages; death and sleep as a resource; as a threat to competence, etc.
6. STRUCTURAL FEATURES: Inexperienceability of death and sleep enforced and middle states; metaphenomena; the postego.
7. SOCIO-CULTURAL CHARACTERISTICS: Modal times and places; taboos and sanctions; artifacts and rituals; deviant patterns; class differences.

Conspicuous
  lacunae in
  modal com-
  munication
  patterns
	Ordinary
	  letters to
	  relatives and
	  friends
	Diaries
	Credo
	  statements
		Communica-
		  tions re divorce,
		  death of loved
		  one, gradua-
		  tion, leaving
		  job, changing
		  locale
			Communica-
			  tions during
			  or about
			  special state

INTERVIEW AND DYADIC MATERIALS

(POSTSELF)

gave, throughout a martyrdom of forty years, to death. "But hark ye yet again—the little lower layer" Melville's capitulation in the face of overwhelming odds was limited to the sphere of action. His embattled soul refused surrender and lived on, breathing back defiance, disputing "to the last gasp" of his "earthquake life" the sovereignty of that inscrutable authority in him.[12]

The relevant sources of psychological data are both positive (diaries, reports, etc.) and negative, in that they might consist of conspicuous lacunae in the individual's modal communication patterns.

G. *Critical* continuation episodes. These are alterations of the human condition that we can refer to as "endings," that is, conclusions of phases of life; closing off of episodes in one's life in which there are irreversible breaking of physical stimuli, psychological events, interpersonal relationships, and living patterns. They involve irreparable losses, over and above the manner in which we become habituated to the passage (and loss) of temporal units. Examples of such endings involve at least the following: graduation from school, leaving a job, moving from one city to another, being discharged from the service, leaving or changing jobs, divorcing a spouse, experiencing the death of a loved one, having property destroyed or stolen, and the like. "Endings" are like "little deaths."

We turn now to a necessarily brief discussion of those features that, in our present view, cut across (or are common to, or may be used as bridges between) the varieties of discontinuation and continuation behaviors. We have somewhat arbitrarily grouped these similarities under seven headings (indicated as the Cross-Behavioral Congruencies in Chart I) and shall, in the following paragraphs, touch upon each one.

Some Motivational Similarities Between Death and Sleep

We have already indicated our uneasiness with the current classification of death, primarily that the roles of the individual in his own demise are omitted. It is possible to envisage a variety of roles that an individual can play in relation to his own discontinuation (cessation and interruption)[13] or altered continuation. Thus, at any given moment in his life, an individual will have certain motivational orientations both in reference to his interruption and to his cessation.[14] For purposes of developing this scheme, four categories,

relating to the role of the individual in his own alteration, are suggested. They are: *intentioned, subintentioned, unintentioned,* and *contraintentioned.* An overview of some basic orientations toward cessation and the related interruption and altered continuation states is presented in Table I. A more detailed discussion of these orientations is presented in Chapter 5.

The Role of Cosmological Beliefs in Death, Sleep, and Drugs

A frequent question, from both lay and professional people, about suicide, concerns the role of religion. A not too inaccurate reply would hold that religious beliefs inhibit suicide—and facilitate it. But, more importantly, it is probably neither unfair nor inaccurate to state that no previous study that uses as its "religious" variables the categories of Protestant, Catholic, Jewish, and the tabulations of church-going behavior is worth serious attention. Apparently not so obviously, what would seem to be needed would be studies relating self-destructive behaviors to the operational features of religious beliefs, including a detailed explication of the subject's present belief systems in relation to an omnipotent God, the efficacy of prayer, the existence of an hereafter, the possibility of reunion with departed loved ones, and the like. These cosmological beliefs would seem to play a role in suicidal behavior, in the "death-work" that a dying person has to do, and in his attitudes toward sleep.

The Roles of Affective States in Death and Sleep

Out of our thoughts of the possible relationships between cessation behavior (e.g., suicide) and interruption behaviors (e.g., sleep), we have begun, at the Suicide Prevention Center, a program of research that we call a Sleep Study. In this study, we are especially interested in affective states—most particularly what Murray calls the temporal sequence of positive and negative affective states.[15] For us, this means that we believe that individuals may have idiosyncratic temporal *orders* of certain affective states leading to specific actions, and that for each individual the reappearance of the initial stages of such a sequence may be prodromal to certain acute behaviors by that individual. Thus we are interested, following Murray's suggestions, in the macrotemporal ordering of affective states (over a period of weeks), the mesotemporal ordering (during a day), and the microtemporal ordering (for example, in the

TABLE I

SOME MOTIVATIONAL CONGRUENCIES AMONG CESSATION, INTERRUPTION, AND
CONTINUATION STATES

Role of the individual in his own alteration	Discontinuation behaviors		Continuation behaviors
	Basic orientations toward cessation	Related interruption states	Related altered continuation states
Intentioned (Individual plays direct or conscious role in his alteration	Seeker Initiator Ignorer Darer	Most sleep phenomena Voluntary unconsciousness Elective anesthesia Drugs and alcohol (used for interruption) Insomnia (as inability)	Intoxication Drugged states LSD, psilocybin, etc.) Hypnosis
Subintentioned (Indirect, covert, partial, or unconscious role)	Chancer Hastener Facilitater Capitulater Experimenter	Some fatigue-sleep states Some alcoholic stupors Some diabetic comas Some barbiturate comas	Alcoholic delirium Schizophrenia (?) Amnesic states Fugue states Dissociative states Escapades, binges, etc.
Unintentioned (Plays no significant role)	Welcomer Accepter Postponer Disdainer Fearer	Involuntary unconsciousness Some comas Some fainting Seizures	Febrile delirium Organic states Anoxic states
Contraintentioned (Employs "semantic blanket" of altered state with conscious intention of avoiding it)	Feigner Contemplater	Feigned sleep Feigned unconsciousness Feigned death	Malingering Role playing Spying

minutes before the sleep interruption or alcoholic altered continuation).

As part of this larger sleep study, a Sleep Form, based in part on items from Kleitman and from Hildreth, has been developed.[16]

This form includes 30-some items relating to the number of hours of sleep, quality of sleep, number of awakenings, record of alcohol or drugs, and, especially, the affective states upon retiring and upon awakening. The purpose of this Sleep Form is to tap nightly fluctuations of an individual's sleep (interruption) behaviors so that they can be related to his daily fluctuations in his drug and alcohol (altered continuation) behaviors and to his behaviors vis-à-vis suicide (cessation). This procedure, which permits comparisons between variations, is, of course, a use of Mill's Method of Concomitant Variation. Records of six subjects, mailed in daily for a period of over a year, have been obtained.

In one case, at the Suicide Prevention Center, in a particularly tragic chain of unfortunate circumstances, a 67-year-old widow who was a participant in the Sleep Study committed suicide. She sent in Sleep Forms for over 40 nights until the day of her self-inflicted death. Inspection of the data indicated that there was no decline (including the night before her death) in the *number* of hours of reported sleep, but there was a conspicuous change in her waking affective state. It was noteworthy that just before her death, her feelings upon going to bed changed from an almost constant feeling of depression to being "matter of fact" and that she recorded that she thought of sleep as an "escape from the world," "a reunion with loved ones," and as "a temporary death." All through the 40-day period she reported "sleeping well"; what was most remarkable were her feelings upon awakening. She reported feeling "discouraged," "wishing she were dead," "having no hope," and "miserable."

The point can be made that had she survived this suicide attempt —she died in the hospital after being in coma for 3 days—and had we, at any future time, seen any beginning repetition of her previous prior-to-suicide attempt temporal sequence of affective states relative to sleeping and waking we could have then taken appropriate measures to save her life.

Some Cognitive Similarities Between Sleep and Death

We have talked about cessation, endings, little deaths, interruptions—all of these terms that involve some sort of resolution. We shall now introduce another term: "conclusions." And, apropos of the cognitive aspects of death and sleep, we shall reflect that the

phrase "coming to conclusions" has at least two meanings: (1) *modus operandi* of an individual's cognitive styles, that is, the ways in which he "concludifies" his syllogisms-of-everyday-life; and (2) the ways in which he concludes aspects of his life (like the end of a day, or the end of a marriage). The two may be related. In relation to the cognitive aspects of suicide, we have reported elsewhere a method that involves a delineation of an individual's idiologics— by means of a tabulation of his "idiosyncracies of reasoning" (such as irrelevant premises, equivocation, stranded predicates, etc.) and his "cognitive maneuvers" (such as his summarizing, alleging, digressing, etc.)—and then constructing that individual's contra-logic, that is, his private epistemology or his unverbalized logical conceptions in terms of which his idiologics makes sense to him.[17] We assert that an individual's private epistemology (his contra-logic) is not irrelevant to his attitudes toward death, suicide, sleep, drugs, and the like. And if this is so, it becomes useful to do an analysis of an individual's everyday logicisizing—his syllogizing or concludifying—so as to arrive at an understanding of the manner in which he will habitually cognize his way through a psychologically stressful situation. Our logical analysis of suicide notes has led us to believe that more than one individual has killed himself—given his (mis-)perception of the facts (and his distorted premises)— by making unnecessary ideological leaps into oblivion.

Some Phenomenological Similarities Between Death and Sleep

We know that death can have various personal meanings to different people—as punishment, as separation, as reunion, as a lover and so forth,[18]—and that suicide can have six different meanings to a half-dozen individuals each of whom shoots out his brains. It is also so that sleep has different meanings to different people at different times: as a replenishment, as a nice long nap, as a bothersome interruption of one's activities, as a chance to dream, an escape from pain, a temporary death, an escape from the world, a pleasant way to pass the time, reunion with loved ones, and the like.[19]

Some phenomenological similarities between sleep and death include the following: (1) aspects of "defining the self" in both death and sleep; (2) the presence of coded messages in both sleep and dying behaviors; (3) the possibility of viewing both sleep and

death as a resource; (4) aspects that threaten the sense of competence in death and sleep, especially in relation to insomnia.[20]

Some Structural Similarities Between Death and Sleep

THE BASIC OPERATIONAL SIMILARITY OF BOTH: AN INDIVIDUAL CANNOT EXPERIENCE HIS OWN DEATH OR SLEEP. Bridgman has indicated that, in any discussion of death, it is necessary to distinguish between private experiences and public experiences; between my being asleep and your being asleep, between my death and your death; that is, between the individual as he experiences himself (I_s) and the individual as he is experienced by other (I_o).[21] Thus, an individual can never hear himself snore nor can he experience his own death, for, if he were in a position to have this experience, he would in fact not be asleep or dead. One can, of course, at the present moment, experience the future anticipation of what will happen after one is dead, but this present moment experiencing is limited to an I_s experience.[22]

The reader may have noted in Chart I the word "Postself" stretching like a band below the various continuation behavior states. In any comprehensive description of the various orientations that an individual might have toward his own cessation, it seems important to include the attitudes of the living person toward those aspects of him that "survive" after his cessation—his after-death reputation, impact, influence; his legacy; his image in the memory of his survivors. This concept of the living individual's psychological investment in his after-death "existence" I have labeled the "postego" or postself; it refers to an individual's postcontinuation. It is possible to distinguish a variety of postego orientations, ways in which an individual can view the continuation of his this-world personality; for example, he can conceptualize himself as (1) endless, (2) immortal, (3) finite, (4) residual, (5) meaningless, and the like.[23]

THE ROLE OF "ENFORCED STATES" IN BOTH SLEEP AND DEATH. One can immediately see some possibilities of focusing on some similarities among data from studies of sleep deprivation, insomnia, electrocoma treatment, seizures, some anaesthesia studies, studies of dying patients, and the like, by viewing individuals who have been de-

prived of sleep as experiencing not sleep deprivation but *enforced* (as opposed to elective or casual) continuation; individuals deprived of consciousness (through EST, seizures, etc.) as undergoing *enforced* interruption; and individuals who were dying or threatened with death (by homicide, terminal disease, etc.) as reacting to the imminence of *enforced* cessation.[24]

BOTH SLEEP AND SUICIDE CAN BE SEEN AS METAPHENOMENA. Both sleep and suicide can be seen as metaphenomena, that is, as secondary reactions to more substantive occurrences. Sleep, for example, can be seen as a resonating (or secondary) reaction to what might be called "unvigilance." (Oswald, discusses the role of vigilance, as distinguished from consciousness, in sleep.[25]) And surely some suicidal occurrences can be seen as metaphenomena. My own current view of many suicidal acts is that they can be seen to represent metacrises.[26] That is to say, on the one hand we hear reported almost every "reason" for suicide (ill health, being jilted, loss of fortune, pregnancy, loss of job, school grades, etc.—some certainly more persuasive than others) and on the other hand, we hear of the circumstances in which "we simply can't imagine why he did it." It may well be that the substantive reasons (whatever they are) are almost never sufficient cause. What seems to happen in some cases is that the individual becomes disturbed (over ill health, loss of work, etc.) and then develops a panic reaction (a metacrisis) to his perception that he is disturbed. He becomes agitated over the fact that he is anxious. At the time of the greatest resonating perturbation the content that sparked the original disturbances may not be at all uppermost in his mind. Suicide may represent a reaction to an overwhelming crisis that is itself a reaction to another substantively bound crisis; a panic reaction to the individual's feeling that things are getting out of control.[27] It may well be that often suicide is a metacritical act, representing a reverberating crisis, with its own (essentially content-free) autonomy.

Some Sociocultural Similarities Between Death and Sleep

Recently, Aubert and White and Naegle have written on the sociology of sleep.[28] A number of the attributes that they cite as sociological characteristics of sleep can be applied almost directly as characteristics of death, dying, and suicidal behaviors. Among

the sociocultural similarities between death and sleep, the following can be cited: (1) modal times and locations for both death and sleep; (2) taboos and sanctions in relation to both death and sleep; (3) artifacts and rituals in both death and sleep; (4) elements of social disengagement in both; (5) aspects of communion rites in both. Limitations of space do not permit a more detailed elaboration of these congruencies but the reader of the Naegle and Aubert and White articles can readily see their applications to death phenomena if he approaches these articles with that set in mind.

An Illustrative Cessation Note

Some of the concepts presented in this paper can be illustrated by a suicide note (obtained from the office of the Los Angeles County Chief Medical Examiner-Coroner). This note was written by a 72-year-old white, Protestant, divorced female, who killed herself with an overdose of Seconal. The note, addressed to her attorneys, is presented here because, more than most suicide notes, it contains references to cessation (death), interruption (sleep), altered continuation (drugs), modal continuation (self-image), and postcontinuation (concern with the postself). This poignant document is slightly edited and all persons and place names have been changed.

Suicide Note	Comments
Dear Bill and Bob: Since Thursday, I have been in such extreme pain that no amount of medication will bring it under control.	Relates to focally altered continuation state.
If I could only sleep. I honestly think that only complete sedation would stop it. But what doctor would agree to such a treatment. This they are willing to do only in terminal cases.	Yearning for interruption . . . and for cessation.
I have thought about this a great deal. There are so many reasons why I regret this action, especially since my daughter passed away.	Related to her "internal debate." Relates to an "ending" in her life.
I had such great hopes of doing all the creative things that nature seemed to bless me with. I used to say what a wonderful life I would have when I retired. That, when I got tired of writing, I could play the piano; and then I had my paint brushes ready and waiting for me. I have enjoyed a small degree of success in my painting.	Relates to modal continuation behavior.

Suicide Note

Now with this added problem of glaucoma, and a bad right arm, I can no longer paint. I was never meant to be idle. I have always had a drive to do more and better things in no matter what form it took.

I think this action hurts me most because of my friends, Betty Brown and family. Of course no one in the family would ever let my Aunt Susan know the real reason. She knows that I have had two heart attacks; let her believe that was the reason.

Perhaps if I were willing to live on strong pain killers, I might be able to get by on drugs, but who wants to live in a fog?

I would like to ask a favor. My legal name is Jones. I did not have it changed at the time of my divorce. Would you thus have the death certificate and grave marker made out in the name of Mrs. Mary M. Jones. I want to be remembered this way. There are papers in my safety deposit box proving that I am one and the same, so there should be no complications with Social Security, etc. And please do not let my dear neighbors next door know the truth.

Surely there must be a justifiable Mercy death. In sorrow and deep regret,
         Mary

Comments

Partial continuation-discontinuation state; credo statement.

Instructional; concern with others.

Addicts and alcoholics do live in a fog (an altered continuation state.)

Concern with her post-self

Relates to the way she wishes to live and die . . . and to how she wishes to be remembered (her postself).

Chapter 3
THE LOGIC OF SUICIDE
Edwin S. Shneidman and Norman L. Farberow

Four types of suicidal phenomena, distinguished by different styles of logical thinking, together with their respective psychological characteristics, are described. The four logical styles include: normal logic, contaminated logic, catalogic, and paleologic. In addition, a fundamental distinction is made between I_s (the individual as he experiences himself) and I_o (the individual as he is experienced by others). Some of the semantic confusions that result from overlooking this distinction, and their implications for understanding suicidal phenomena, are discussed.

On superficial thought, one of the outstanding characteristics of the suicidal act is that it is illogical. Yet one can take the position that there is an implicit syllogism or argument in the suicidal act. Although we cannot be sure that our logical reconstructions of suicidal logic are correct, it remains that the suicidal person behaves *as if* he had reasoned and had come to certain—albeit, generally unacceptable—conclusions.[1]

Parenthetically, it is recognized that suicidal reasoning has unconscious motivations and psychodynamic determinants, but those areas are not the subject of this paper. This logical analysis of suicide is not an alternative to a psychodynamic accounting but rather is meant to provide a formal framework within which the specific nature of the psychodynamics must be specified. Thus, the purpose of this paper is to elucidate some details of suicidal logic. The implication is that if one knew the lethal modes of reasoning and the suppressed premises (or beliefs) that lead to a deadly conclusion, then one might have effective clues to use in the prediction and prevention of suicide.

The materials for the development of this paper come from the more than 700 suicide notes we have collected as part of our larger study on the psychology of suicide.

In formal, or traditional, logic there are a number of errors, called logical fallacies, that can be made. One of many types of fallacy is illustrated in the deductive logic implicit in schizophrenic thinking

—first described by Storch and then by von Domarus and recently called "paleologic" by Arieti.[2] In normal logic, before identity can be made, certain conditions have to be satisfied. "Paleologic" sweeps aside these conditions and arrives at fallacious identities. Two examples of this type of reasoning, from von Domarus, can be given. "Switzerland loves freedom; I love freedom; therefore I am Switzerland" and "The Virgin Mary was a virgin; I am a virgin; therefore I am the Virgin Mary."[3]

Another type of logical fallacy, other than the deductive fallacy, wherein the error is dependent on the form of the argument, is the semantic fallacy, wherein the error is dependent on the meaning of the terms occurring in the premises or conclusion. Our examination of the suicide notes indicated that the fallacies of reasoning committed were primarily of this latter type. An example of a semantic fallacy is as follows: "Nothing is better than hard work; a small effort is better than nothing; therefore a small effort is better than hard work." Here the fallacy is not dependent upon the form of the argument but rather on the ambiguous meaning of a specific term, namely, "nothing." Another example of a semantic fallacy, this time with suicidal content, is as follows: "If anybody kills himself then he will get attention; I will kill myself; therefore I will get attention." Deductively, this argument is sound, but the fallacy is concealed in the concepts contained in the word "I." Here the logical role of this pronoun is related to the psychology of the conception of the self.

We see then that in addition to the logic of the normal person and the "paleologic" of the schizophrenic person, we have the reasoning of the suicidal person. We call this type of thinking "destructive logic" or "catalogic." It is destructive not only in the sense that it disregards the classical rules for semantic clarity and formal reasoning but also in that it destroys the logician.

As a result of our analysis of the semantic qualities exhibited in the suicidal notes, it appeared that the logic could be understood best in terms of two implied components of the "I," or the self. The first we call I_s. This is the self as experienced by the individual himself. I_s refers to the person's own experiences, his pains and aches, and sensations and feelings. He says in the note "I can see you crying" and adds (by implication from the tenor of the rest of the note) "I'll be glad this is going to trouble you." The second

aspect of the semantic self is called I_o. This is the individual as he feels himself thought of or experienced by others. This would be what he considers his reputation, based on other people's attitudes, other people's actions, ideas, remarks; that is, what others think of him. This comes out in the notes in the extreme concern with practical and trivial details, such as the repair of the automobile, the distribution of goods, the canceling of appointments, and so forth. The suicide says in effect, "I_o will get attention, that is, certain other people will cry, go to a funeral, sing hymns, relive memories, and the like." But he also implies or states that even after death, I_s will go through these experiences, that is, "I will be cried over; I will be attended to"—as though the individual would be able to experience these occurrences. This is the heart of the semantic fallacy or ambiguity.[4]

More accurately, it is not a fallacy in the words of the reasoning, but rather it is a fallacious identification. Hence, we call it a *psychosemantic fallacy*. Parenthetically, we believe that this confusion or ambiguity might indeed occur whenever an individual thinks about his death, whether by suicide or otherwise. It may arise because an individual cannot imagine his own death, his own cessation of experience, a state in which there is no more I_s after death. A rare example wherein an individual experienced both the I_o satisfactions of the response from others, as well as the I_s satisfactions of experiencing the reactions of others to his death, is in *Tom Sawyer*, when the boys hide out in the balcony of the church and listen to their own funeral service; but it must be pointed out that they could do this only because they were in point of fact not dead.

This semantic confusion in suicidal logic is similar to the "atmosphere effect" described by Woodworth and Sells.[5] They describe the tendency of individuals to accept negative conclusions because of the negative impression created by the premises. An example would be: "None of my relatives is wealthy; no wealthy person loves me; therefore none of my relatives loves me." In the present context, we label this the "noose effect," that is, it is Thorndike's well-known "halo effect" which has slipped.

The question of the role of anticipation and anticipatory goal responses arises. There is a form of satisfaction to I_s in the following sense: although it is true that I_s ceases to exist after death and thus could not be the subject of the remorse felt toward I_o at that

time, I_s can experience a satisfaction through the anticip
the remorse felt toward I_o. This anticipation, of course, tak
before death, when I_s still exists. It is a fallacy because i
to achieve the anticipation (of the pleasurable experience), he cannot achieve the result (experience it), except that the anticipation
of pleasure can itself be a pleasure. It is this psychologic reward
which may be one of the prime motivating aspects of suicide. Also,
it has been said that all motivations of suicide (both psychodynamic
and sociologic) involve anticipation of rejection. An individual's
taking of his own life can thus be a way of protecting himself from
anticipated punishment and trauma. There may be implications in
the above for an exploration of suicide from the point of view of
learning-theory concepts.

Some important exceptions to our general hypothesis about suicidal logic can be given. They are three in number:

1. Some individuals desire nothingness—surcease from pain—
and do not confuse I_s with I_o. They apparently understand that, with
the commission of suicide, I_s will cease. They realistically face the
termination of I_s. Such an individual says, "I cannot stand this
excruciating pain." We call these individuals "surcease suicides."
Our work with suicide notes of the more aged persons illustrates
this phenomenon.

2. Another exception is those individuals who believe in the
continuation of I_s, that is, a belief in a life after death or a hereafter.
In this case, owing to the belief in the continued I_s, the psychosemantic ambiguity with I_o need not arise. They say in their notes
that they will come back and haunt the individual, or that they will
be looking down from above, or they will see loved ones in heaven.
This means that beliefs in the hereafter are often very relevant
to the suicidal logic, inasmuch as an individual who believes in a
life after death, may not commit the semantic fallacy discussed in
this chapter. Also related to this category are persons who put an
emphasis on the I_o. Examples would be the kamikaze pilots of the
last war, Seneca's suicide at his emperor's suggestion, and so forth.
We call these "cultural suicides."

3. A third exception to the above generalizations would be in
relation to individuals who are schizophrenic. One obvious implication of this statement is that not all suicide is psychotic. Certainly
some psychotics do commit suicide (and, although in the minority,

they are the most unpredictable of all suicides). Here, the hypothesis concerning suicidal logic would be subservient to the notions of schizophrenic "paleologic"; one would expect the reasoning of a schizophrenic suicide to reflect more the semantics and logic of the schizophrenic than of the suicide.

How may these instances of suicidal semantic confusion be identified? The following criteria can be stated, although they are not definite and provide only the initial clues that may indicate that the suicidal semantic fallacy is being committed.

1. Concern with minor details, trivia, and neutral statements in the suicide note would be one indication that the semantic fallacy is being committed.

2. Another indication would be concern with the direct or indirect reaction of others, specifically what explicit thoughts are being entertained toward the individual. For example, "Don't think badly of me."

The following two criteria are negative criteria:

3. Concern with one's own suffering and physical discomfiture or pain, where the focus is on ending it all, would seem to indicate that this error or confusion is not taking place.

4. An indication of the belief in a hereafter also would tend to preclude the presence of this semantic error.

Thus it is possible to diagram four types of suicide, each with its own implications for treatment, as indicated in Table 1.

What evidence do we have for this general hypothesis about suicidal logic? We believe that we have some empirical, experimental data that are relevant to it. In another publication we have compared thirty-three genuine suicide notes left by Caucasian, Protestant, native-born males between the ages of twenty-five and fifty-nine, with an equal number of suicide notes elicited from comparable nonsuicidal subjects matched man-for-man in terms of similar occupations and in terms of almost identical chronological age.[6]

These sixty-six notes were analyzed in terms of "discomfort," "relief," and "neutral" statements as defined by O. Hobart Mowrer.[7] We assumed that the Discomfort-Relief Quotient (DRQ) would reflect the ways in which an individual expressed feelings about himself. Specifically, we believed that discomfort and relief statements could be held to be comparable to our I_s concept and that neutral statements could be thought similar to our I_o concept.

TABLE I

OUTLINE OF TYPES OF SUICIDE AND SUGGESTED TREATMENTS

Logical Type	Personal Characteristics	Psychologic Label	Suggested Mode of Treatment
Catalogic: the logic is destructive; it confuses the self as experienced by the self with the self as experienced by others	Individuals who are lonely, feel helpless and fearful, and feel pessimistic about making meaningful personal relationships	*Referred suicides:* the confusion in logic and in the identification is "referred" (like referred pain) from other root problems	Dynamic psychotherapy wherein the goal would be to supply the patient with a meaningful, rewarding relationship, so that his search for identification would be stabilized
Normal logic: the reasoning is acceptable according to Aristotelian standards	Individuals who are older, or widowed, or who are in physical pain	*Surcease suicides:* persons desire surcease from pain and reason that death will give them this	Treatment is in terms of giving freedom from pain through analgesics and sedatives, and providing companionship by means of active milieu therapy
Contaminated logic: the logical or semantic error is in the emphasis on the self as experienced by others	Individuals whose beliefs permit them to view suicide as a transition to another life or as a means of saving reputation	*Cultural suicides:* their concept of death plays a primary role in the suicide	Treatment has to do with deeply entrenched religious and cultural beliefs and would have to deal with and clarify the semantic implications of the concept of death
Paleologic: makes logical identifications in terms of attributes of the predicates rather than of the subjects	Individuals who are delusional and/or hallucinatory	*Psychotic suicides:* not all suicides are psychotic, but psychotics can be unpredictably suicidal	Treatment has to do primarily with the psychosis and only subsequently with suicidal tendencies; treatment would include protecting the individual from his own impulses

A sample scoring by Dr. Mowrer of the discomfort (D), relief (R), and neutral thought units (N) in one suicide note is reproduced below:

> Dearest Mary:/Well, dear—it's the end of the trail for
> D
> me./It has been a fairly long and reasonably pleasant life,
> all in all—especially fine that part in which you played a
> R   R
> part./ You have been wonderful./No man could have
> R
> asked for a better wife than you have been./
>
> Please understand that if I didn't feel that this course
> would be the best for you and the girls I certainly would
> D
> have waited for nature to take her course./It would not
> D
> have been long anyhow,/for the clot I coughed up was
> from the lungs and I know there's activity there—of an
> D
> ominous nature./
>
> D
> Be good to your mother, girls./You have the finest
> R
> mother in the world;/even as I have had the most wonder-
> R
> ful wife and two wonderful daughters./ Bye-by Mary,
> N   R
> Betty, and Helen./How I do love you all./And may God
> R
> help and guide you from here on in./Daddy.[9]

The results of our analyses were as follows: the total number of mutually agreed-upon thought units as a result of this joint procedure was 553. Of this total there were 369 in the thirty-three genuine notes and 184 in the thirty-three elicited notes; the χ^2 was 8.7, significant beyond the .01 level, indicating that the genuine-note writers were significantly more verbose.

For the *discomfort* (tension, pain, hostility) statements, the genuine notes had 226 and the simulated notes had 137; the χ^2 was 9.5, significant beyond the .01 level and indicating that the genuine-note writers expressed significantly more discomfiture.

For the *relief* (pleasant, warm, loving) statements, the genuine

notes had 65 and the pseudo notes had 34; the χ^2 was .06, which was not significant, indicating that neither the genuine- nor the pseudonote writers expressed more relief.

For *neutral* statements, the genuine notes had 78 and the pseudonotes had 13; the χ^2 was 17.7, significant beyond the .01 level and indicating that the genuine-note writers expressed a significantly greater number of neutral statements. The content of these neutral statements typically had to do with giving instructions and admonitions and sometimes included lists of things to do.

The focus of our attention was on the difference in the neutral statements between the genuine suicide notes and the simulated suicide notes. This was so for two reasons: there was no significant statistical difference in the relief statements between the two sets of notes, and although there was a difference with regard to the greater amount of discomfort shown by the two kinds of suicide notes, it was also true that, when we analyzed the differences in quality of affect relating to the discomfort statements between the two groups, we noted that the discomfort statements in the genuine notes were characterized more by deeper feelings of hatred, vengeance, and self-blame, as compared with the more mildly negative statements of the simulated notes. We were forced to conclude that the quality of the discomfort statements is not accurately represented in the Mowrer scoring system.

We interpret the larger number of neutral statements on the part of the genuine-note writers as indicative of unrealistic feelings of omnipotence and omnipresence on the part of the suicidal individual. He cannot successfully imagine his own death and his own complete cessation. It also epitomizes the illogicality of the entire suicidal deed—thinking simultaneously and contradictorily of being absent and of giving orders as though one were going to be present to enforce them. Although the suicide is able to imagine his absence from the scene more successfully than the nonsuicide, he shows, paradoxically, the greater inability to comprehend his complete cessation of influence and effect. The larger number of neutral statements in the genuine notes—wherein reputation, or the self as experienced by others, is the primary characteristic—would seem definitely to imply this paradox.

To the extent that these neutral statements do indeed contain implied semantic confusions, we have support from our data for

the hypothesis that the logical processes of the genuinely suicidal person are characterized (at least to a statistically significant extent greater than in the case of nonsuicidal individuals given a suicidal *Aufgabe*) by proneness to commit the particular kind of psychosemantic fallacy discussed in this chapter. Specifically, we mean the suicide's confusion relating to the concept of the self revolving around the multiple logical components and meanings contained in the pronoun I, *das Ich,* the ego.

One may speculate about the psychological significance of the confused suicidal logic. It may well be the confusion reflects his problems having to do primarily with identification. It is this fallacious identification between the self as experienced by the self (I_s) and the self as it feels itself experienced by others (I_o) that enables the suicide to accept erroneous premises and invalid conclusions and that accounts for his making his tragic deductive leap into oblivion.

Chapter 4
CONTENT ANALYSIS OF SUICIDAL LOGIC
Edwin S. Shneidman

*This chapter proposes a method for analyzing aspects of an
individual's cognitive or mentational styles, especially the ways in
which he comes to his conclusions (called* concludifying*). The
individual's logical styles are then related to other aspects of his
general personality functioning. The method is developed in terms
of four main sections: (1) idio-logic (made up of idiosyncrasies
of reasoning and cognitive maneuvers); (2) contra-logic (in which
the individual's epistemology is inferred); (3) psycho-logic
(which relates the individual's thinking styles to his more general
personality traits); and (4) pedago-logic (which attempts to
construct an optimal communication or teaching approach, tailor-
made to the individual's logical style). Various illustrations are
employed: the Kennedy-Nixon debates, items from the*
Congressional Record, *and genuine suicide notes.*

> ". . . everybody conceives himself
> to be proficient in the art of
> reasoning. . . ."
> > Charles Sanders Peirce

> ". . . we cannot call a man
> illogical for acting on the
> basis of what he feels to be
> true."
> > Kenneth D. Burke

> "Everything we do seems to be
> reasonable . . . at the time we
> are doing it."
> > Donald Snygg and Arthur Combs

The purpose of this paper is to suggest a method of analyzing
certain aspects of an individual's cognitive styles and to relate
these analyses to relevant aspects of his general personality functioning.

As a beginning, we assume that thought is a common characteristic of all humans (excluding neonates and unconscious persons).

Each person does something that we call thinking, reasoning, cerebrating, deducing, inducing, syllogizing, coming to conclusions, inferring, and the like.

The most general term for these processes is "concludifying" (i.e., coming to conclusions). It includes all the mentational processes—cognitive maneuvers, logical gambits, sequences of associations, modes of induction, making deductive inferences—by which an individual can arrive at a firm or tentative conclusion.

Our second assumption is that individuals think in various *ways,* that is, that each individual has, along with his culturally common ways of thinking, some patterns of thinking that he may share with some other individuals and some that are unique to him. There is no one way of thinking, but there are many ways or patterns of thinking.

It has been asserted that there are modes of thinking that are peculiar to cultures;[1] we believe that, in addition, within each culture there are individual idiosyncratic patterns of thinking that, in their totality, are then characteristic of (currently unrecognized) groups of individuals within that culture. We recognize that two or more persons might reach different conclusions for reasons other than their different logical patterns—for example, by beginning with different premises or by different selections and distortions of the evidence—but, nonetheless, in the present context, the focus of our interest is on the forms of thought (and the consequences created by nuances of difference in these forms) rather than on the premises of the contents of thought.

Each individual has, along with culturally common ways of concludifying, some ways of thinking that he shares in common with others in that culture and some that are absolutely idiosyncratic for him. Thus, ways of thinking (like other aspects of personality functioning) can be viewed in terms of those characteristics that are universal, ubiquitous, and unique. There is not one way of thinking, but there are many ways. In this chapter, we are not talking about "correct" thinking or argument. People don't just make mistakes in their apparent logic; there are good reasons for their seeming to be unreasonable. Thus, we are interested primarily in the processes of concludifying in which an individual thinker engages. By illuminating the characteristics of an individual's cognitive processes we might then infer the psychological "reasons" (as

well as his personality characteristics) that, for him, are consistent with his reasoning as he does. Note that we are little concerned with the notion of "error" in reasoning. "Error" has usually implied a departure from a particular (theoretical) standard of thinking, usually that attributed to Aristotle when he was thinking about thinking. "Reasoning," to quote William James, "is always for a subjective interest." The "marriage" between an individual's patterns of thinking and other aspects of that individual's personality is binding whether "in sickness or in health." We are interested in how people *do* think, not in how they *ought* to think.

Our third assumption is that if one knew the idiosyncratic characteristics of an individual's cognitive processes, he would then be in a position to infer other facts about that individual, especially what that individual's view of causality and order are, as well as certain personality characteristics that are consistent with that individual's modes of reasoning. And, by virtue of this knowledge, he would be in a position to enhance (or to frustrate) communication with that individual.

In this approach to the logics of communication there are four major categories of analysis, as follows: idio-logic, contra-logic, psycho-logic, and pedago-logic.

Idio-Logic

In this system, idio-logic has to do with the individual's styles of thinking, referring to all those things that might be said—given the text of some original verbatim material (such as a political speech, a suicide note, a psychological test protocol, etc.) by that person—about the syllogistic structure, the idiosyncrasies of either induction or deduction, the forms of the explicit or implied premises, the gaps in reasoning or unwarranted conclusions, and so forth,—indeed, anything that a logically oriented investigator who understood this approach could wring from a manuscript if he put his mind to it. These idio-logical attributes are made up of two kinds of items: (1) *aspects of reasoning*, which include all those categories that would traditionally be subsumed under "logical fallacies" (but which we see not as fallacies but simply as idiosyncrasies), that relate essentially to the individual's inductive and deductive gambits and tactics; and (2) *cognitive maneuvers*, which describe the style of the development of thought, dealing

especially with the flow of argumentation and with the cognitive interstices between the specific aspects of reasoning.

As will be noted from Table I, the aspects of reasoning are divided among categories, as follows: (1) idiosyncracies of relevance (e.g., irrelevant premises, *argumentum ad populum*, false cause); (2) idiosyncracies of meaning (e.g., equivocation, indirect contact, etc.); (3) enthymematic idiosyncracies (e.g., contestable suppressed premises, suppressed conclusion); (4) idiosyncracies of logical structure (isolated predicate and isolated term); and (5) idiosyncracies of logical interrelations (e.g., contradiction, truth-type confusion, etc.)

The cognitive maneuvers (Table II) are divided among absolute statements (e.g., to allege, to deny); qualified statements (to modify, to accept conditionally, etc.); initiating a new notion (e.g., to branch out, to interrupt, to digress, etc.); continuing a previous notion (e.g., to elaborate by phrase, to agree, to repeat, etc.).

Together, these aspects of reasoning and cognitive maneuvers represent an attempt to explicate all the idiosyncracies of concludifying that an individual might manifest in his flow of thought. It seemed obvious that this general approach could be exemplified in an analysis of aberrant or "error-filled" materials. Previous studies of disturbed suicidal individuals and psychiatric patients supported this contention.[2] That this approach was also applicable to the analysis of well-functioning individuals was in part demonstrated by an analysis of the Kennedy-Nixon "Great Debates" of 1960[3] if not by an analysis of a small group of Harvard undergraduates (in press).

The numerals listed on Tables I and II are the percentages taken from a detailed analysis of first two (of the four) 1960 Kennedy-Nixon debate sessions. In this context, all that they are meant to demonstrate is that the distributions of the aspects of reasoning and the cognitive maneuvers of these two specific individuals were sufficiently different as to distinguish them from each other, and further, to identify the separate logical styles of each. It was evident that Kennedy and Nixon were concludifying in very different ways; that is to say, independent of the *content* of their thoughts or the issues they were discussing, each would *process* the issue through his mind in ways quite different from the other. Given

any issue, each would tend to cerebrate it in his own way and, perforce, come to *somewhat* different conclusions.

By way of illustration, consider the following genuine suicide note, written just before her self-inflicted gun-shot death by a 23-year-old Caucasion Protestant female—in which the notations above the content of the note refer to the headings in Table I and II:

Dear Folks:

II-D   II-D   I-F   II-C1
I know this won't seem the right thing to you but from

I-F,II-D   II-D   I-F,I-J   39
where I stand it seems like the best solution, considering

II-A,II-B,I-J
what is inevitably in store for the future.

      46   10
You know I am in debt. Probably not deeply compared

          II-C1   I-E 10
to a lot of people but at least they have certain abilities, a
skill or trade, or talents with which to make a financial

                  I-E   I-F
recovery. Yes, I am still working but only "by the grace of
the gods." You know how I feel about working where there
are a lot of girls I never could stand their cattiness and I

      II-D
couldn't hope to be lucky enough again to find work where
I had my own office & still have someone to rely on like

       47
Betty. And above all, most jobs don't pay as well as this

                                   7
one for comparable work. I get so tired, at typing for instance, that I couldn't hold a straight typist position. I

                             I-F
wish I had the social position & "know how" to keep this

   I-H
job. That way I wouldn't worry myself into such a dither

                    46
that I make stupid errors. Sometimes they're just from
trying too hard to turn out a perfect copy to please someone. With 3 separate offices served by one board its pretty
hard to locate people for their calls. And when I do find
them they don't want to take them—for which I really

          I-H,II-B   II-C2
can't blame them as some of them are ascenine. But when
the calls come in on the bd I have to dispatch them one

II-D
way or another & the fellows don't seem to realize that.

I-A
Some girls can talk about their work to their girlfriends
II-C1   II-D
and make it sound humorous but I guess it sounds like com-
42
plaining the way I talk. And when I mention anything to
Betty, either in fun or in an effort to correct a situation, it
42.1
gets all over the office like wildfire. Now, when I sit there
paying attention to the board or my work the fellows
9,II-C2
think I'm purposely being unfriendly. But just what is
I-H
there to talk about when you get tired of the same old questions & comments on the weather, "how are you," "working hard or hardly working?" & you know better than to
say very much about things they're interested in or concerned about. I've usually tried to either kid the person
I-K
concerned about whatever it is or just shut up about it because if one goes about telling the other persons business
II-C2
that can cause trouble. However, the kidding, or even a
friendly interest, sometimes, can hurt. So where are you?
Might just as say very little and appear uncooperative or
whatever they think.

12.1   II-A,I-J,I-H
Due to these & many, many more frustrations from the
board & other causes I have become much more nervous
I-D
than I was. You know what the medicine I was taking did
to me so far as my being extremely keyed up, irritable,
etc. was concerned. Now I feel just about as depressed as
I was keyed up then. I couldn't even talk coherently at
I-H
times, and now I'm too concerned about my financial af-
42
fairs to know what it is safe to say. How I wish I could
I-F   I-F
make "small talk" or "party chatter" like some girls do.

II-C2
But I can't compete with most of them for many reasons
& after trying to enter into social activities with kids in
my age range, especially the past year, I find that I can't

28
compete with most of them. Even if I had all the clothes
42.1
to look the part I still wouldn't be able to act the part.
Sorry I'm such a disappointment to you folks.

I-A   I-H   I-A
I'm saying these things so you'll understand why it's
47
so futile for me to even hope for a better job. And as long
as I go on living there will be "working conditions" when
there are so many other better places for the money. I
I-A,I-D
don't mean to sound unappreciative of all you folks have
10
done all thru the years to keep us kids well & healthy. It's
I-F,7,I-J
just that I can't see the sense in putting money into a los-
19   12.1
ing game. I know I'm a psycho somatic—that's just it.

II-A
One reason for doing this now that that Bill will be back
& wants his .22.

9
But the primary reason is one I think you already
know—Mike. I love him more than anyone knows & it may
I-D   II-C2   5
sound silly to you but I can't go on without him. What is
there thats worth living for without him?

An analysis of the idio-logic of that suicide note indicates there were forty-seven instances of thirteen different aspects of reasoning and twenty-seven instances of fifteen different cognitive maneuvers. The aspects of reasoning that appeared most frequently were I-F, argumentum ad populum, eight instances; II-A, equivocation, five; and 2-D, indirect context, nine. For purposes of illustration within this paper, I shall use but two of the aspects of reasoning: I-F, argumentum ad populum, and II-D, indirect context.

A brief explication of *argumentum ad populum* (I-F) is as follows:

Definition: An appeal to affective dispositions and attributes of one's audience, where such dispositions and attitudes are extraneous to the concepts incorporated in the conclusion. The speaker attempts to influence his audience to accept his conclusion or position by citing certain real or alleged states that, while not part of

TABLE I

ASPECTS OF REASONING

	Kennedy	Nixon
I. Idiosyncrasies of Relevance Those features of the argumentative style invoking the intrusion of conceptual elements extraneous to the argument.		
A. *Irrelevant Premise*: Premise is irrelevant to the conclusion it is purportedly instrumental in establishing.	8.7%	4.9%
B. *Irrelevant Conclusion*: Conclusion is irrelevant to the major body of premises that purportedly establish it.	7.4	2.6
C. *Argumentum Ad Baculum*: Appeal to force or fear in one or more premises where the conclusion in question does not involve these concepts.	1.7	.0
D. *Argumentum Ad Hominen*: Appeal to real or alleged attributes of the person or agency from which a given assertion issued in attempting to establish the truth or falsity of that assertion.	.9	3.8
E. *Argumentum Ad Misericordiam*: Appeal to pity for oneself or for an individual involved in the conclusion where such a sentiment is extraneous to the concepts incorporated in the conclusion.	.9	.4
F. *Argumentum Ad Populum*: Appeal to already present attitudes of one's audience where such attitudes are extraneous to the concepts incorporated in the conclusion.	3.4	12.0
G. *Argumentum Ad Verecundium*: Appeal to authority whose assertions corroborate or establish the conclusion where no premises are asserted to the effect that the authority is dependable or sound.	1.7	.0
H. *False or Undeveloped Cause*: Falsely judging or implying a causal relationship to hold between two events.	1.3	3.7
J. *Complex Question*: A premise or conclusion of an argument contains a qualifying clause or phrase, the appropriateness or adequacy of which has not been established.	.0	1.9
K. *Derogation*: A premise or conclusion containing an implicit derogation of an individual or group, where the concepts expressing derogation are neither relevant nor substantiated.	.9	4.9
II. Idiosyncrasies of Meaning		
A. *Equivocation*: The use of a word or phrase that can be taken in either of two different senses.	6.6	2.2
B. *Amphiboly*: An unusual or clumsy grammatical structure obscuring the content of the assertion incorporating it.	4.8	3.0
C.1 *Complete Opposition*: Phrasing indicating an opposition or disjointedness of elements that are in fact opposed and disjointed.	2.6	.7
C.2 *Incomplete Opposition*: Phrasing indicating an opposition or disjointedness of elements that are in fact not opposed or disjointed.	—	—

TABLE I *continued*

	Kennedy	Nixon
D. *Indirect Context*: Indirect phrasing rather than direct phrasing in contexts where the latter is appropriate.	—	—
E. *Mixed Modes*: Context contains two or more of the following modes within the same context: descriptive, normative, or emotive-personal.	—	—
III. Enthymematic Idiosyncrasies Argument contains suppressed premise or conclusion.		
A. *Contestable Suppressed Premise*: A suppressed premise, necessary for rectifying initial validity of argument, is contestable.	5.2	3.7
B. *False Suppressed Premise*: A suppressed premise necessary for rectifying initial invalidity of argument is false, either logically or empirically.	2.6	3.0
C. *Plausible Suppressed Premise*: A suppressed premise necessary for rectifying initial invalidity of argument is plausible but not obvious.	3.8	2.2
D. *Suppressed Conclusion*: The conclusion, while determined by the context of discussion, is never explicitly asserted, so that the point allegedly established by the argument is not brought clearly into focus.	.4	.7
IV. Idiosyncrasies of Logical Structure *Isolated Predicate:* A predicate occurs in a premise that occurs neither in the remaining premises nor in the conclusion, the function of such recurrence being to bind or relate the isolated predicate to other predicates, and *Isolated Term:* A predicate occurs in the conclusion that does not occur in the premise.	42.0	41.6
V. Idiosyncrasies of Logical Interrelations		
A.1 *Truth-Type Confusion*: A confusion between unquestionable assertions on the one hand—logically true assertions and definitions—with empirical assertions on the other hand.	2.2	6.4
A.2 *Logical-Type Confusion*: Confusion between general and specific or between abstract and concrete.	—	—
B. *Contradiction*: Making conflicting or contradictory assertions.	.9	.7
C. *Identification of A Conditional Assertion with Its Antecedent*: Treating an assertion of the form "If A, then B" as equivalent to A.	.0	1.5
D. *Illicit Distribution of Negation*: Treating an assertion of the form "It is false that if A, then B" as equivalent to "If A, then it is false that B."	.9	.0
E. *Illicit Derivation of Normative from Descriptive*: To derive a normative statement from a descriptive, that is a statement of the form, "It is necessary that X," "One should do X," "X ought to be", from ordinary descriptive statements, that is, statements containing no words expressing imperativeness.	2.2	.7
Total	100%	100%

TABLE II

COGNITIVE MANEUVERS

		Kennedy	Nixon
1a.	To switch from a normative to a descriptive mode	.3%	.6%
1b.	To switch from a normative to an emotive or personal mode	.3	.1
2a.	To switch from a descriptive to a normative mode	.1	1.0
2b.	To switch from a descriptive to an emotive or personal mode	6.6	5.2
3a.	To switch from an emotive or personal mode to a descriptive one	4.6	3.0
3b.	To switch from an emotive or personal mode to a normative one	.4	.6
5.	To enlarge or elaborate the preceding, relevantly or irrelevantly	7.9	6.0
7.	To use an example, relevantly or irrelevantly	2.3	2.7
8.	To deduce or purport to deduce from the preceding	2.8	3.4
9.	To change emphasis, with continuity or warrant, or without continuity or warrant	2.2	1.5
10.	To make a distinction between two preceding notions, a preceding notion and a new notion, or between two new notions, with or without warrant, justification, relevance	4.1	5.9
11.	To branch out	4.3	2.9
12.1	To synthesize or summarize	4.1	3.0
14.	To obscure or equivocate by phrasing or context	6.9	4.6
16.	To smuggle a debatable point into a context which is semantically alien to it	5.8	8.4
17.	To paraphrase or otherwise render as equivalent statements that, in general, are not to be taken as syntactically identical, with or without warrant	1.7	2.4
21.	To give a premise or assumption for a statement explicit or implicit in the preceding	5.0	5.8
25.	To be irrelevant	7.3	9.6
26.	To repeat or rephrase	1.7	1.2
28.	To allege but not substantiate	4.4	6.3
31.	To deny or reject with or without warrant	2.8	2.7
35.	To agree with the whole but take issue with a part, implicitly or explicitly	1.0	1.3
37.	To shift focus from subject to audience	.0	.0
39.	To accept conditionally	2.9	1.6
41.	To render another's assertion stronger or weaker by paraphrase	.3	2.0
42.	To digress	.4	1.3
42.1	To initiate discontinuities	4.3	2.0
43.	To resolve discontinuities	.0	.0
44.	To perpetuate or aggravate discontinuities	1.5	.4
46.	To go toward greater specificity	4.8	5.8
47.	To go toward greater generality	1.4	.7
48.	To transfer or attempt to transfer authority or responsibility	1.5	.9
50.	To attack	3.4	3.8
53.	To introduce a new notion	.0	.0
54.	Others (of less than 1% each)	2.9	2.9
	Total percentage	100%	100%
	Total number of units	725	678

the objective content of his conclusion, are consonant with and elicit certain "folk beliefs," attitudes, or appraisals held by his audience and, by their very familiarity, function to blunt any more critical or objective assessment of the speaker's conclusion or position.

Example: "I think that in common decency and common honesty, so long as the Senator from Utah knows what the obvious error is which has been deleted, he should tell the Senate." (*Congressional Record,* McCarthy, 1954/15849/2.9)

Discussion: The phrase, "in common decency and honesty," is used here as an emotional appeal to the body of Senators present— an appeal that is extraneous to the issue of whether the Senator from Utah has provided adequate grounds for his behavior. Whether or not the Senator's behavior is in violation of most men's or most Senators' behavior is in violation of most men's or most Senators' conception of "common decency and honesty" is an open but irrelevant question.

Indirect context—Aspect of Reasoning (II-D)—:

Definition: The speaker uses contexts of the form "I think that . . . ," "It seems that . . . , " "It looks like . . . ," etc.,—indirect contexts—as premises in an argument in which the conclusion is in "direct" form, that is, is not relativized to appearances or beliefs, but is absolute. The speaker tends to relativize premises to himself (or to some other agency), while drawing conclusions that are not relativized. He weakens his premises to induce their acceptance and purports to derive a stronger conclusion than logically follows. He conceives of statements of the form, say, "I think that P" as logically equivalent to statements of the form "P" and uses the relativized statements in places where the nonrelativized or "direct" form is logically required or contextually more appropriate.

Example: "I think that in common decency and common honesty, so long as the Senator from Utah knows what the obvious error is which has been deleted, he should tell the Senate." (*Congressional Record,* McCarthy, 1954/1584/2.9)

Discussion: The preface, "I think that . . ." relativizes the above assertion to the speaker. That is, if we take the "direct" part of the above, that is, the part starting with "in common decency . . . ," then the appropriateness, plausibility, or truth of this latter assertion could be discussed by sociologists, legal philosophers, legal

scholars, ministers, and others, while the entire quoted assertion McCarthy makes, framed in indirect discourse, could be discussed only by a lie-detection expert or McCarthy's closest confidants.

The final construction of the individual's idio-logic is essentially an exercise in English exposition. One gives the greatest emphasis to the aspects of reasoning that appear most often, or seem to be "most important" in that subject style of thinking.

One additional example: a very brief suicide note, "I love everybody but my darling wife has killed me." Its implied conclusion—in light of the deed which followed it—is: Therefore, I kill myself. In this short note one can detect two idiosyncracies of reasoning: equivocation (II-A) and false suppressed premise (III-B). The definition of equivocation is: A word or phrase is used that can be taken in either of two different senses in a given context; or else in repeated use of a word or phrase, the sense of that word or phrase changes; the speaker does not fix the meaning of his terms; he leaves the interpretation open; he does not give necessary elaboration to fix unambiguously the meaning, or else he shifts from one meaning to another.

In terms of that suicide note, the implied conclusion (Therefore, I kill myself) is suppressed in the actual suicide note, but the note is taken as giving grounds, rationale, premises, warrant, and the like, for the writer's taking his own life. The equivocation occurs with the word, "kill," which in the premises has the sense of "violated," "betrayed,"—that is, "killed" in the figurative sense—while "kill" in the conclusion is lethally literal in its meaning.

The definition of false suppressed premise is: A suppressed premise, necessary for rectifying initial invalidity of an argument, is false. The speaker tends to omit explicit mention of positions or assumptions that are central to his exposition and that, moreover, are almost totally idiosyncratic to him, being neither shared by others nor independently defendable. In the case of the brief suicide note, the false suppressed premises is: For any person X and for any person Y, if X loves Y and Y kills X, then X kills X.

The following are examples—using actual suicide notes—of some of the cognitive maneuvers: (1) To allege but not substantiate (to make an assertion, which is nonobvious yet contextually important, whose context contains no premise that would tend to establish it): "I cannot live any longer, I do not wish to live any longer. Death is

better than living. Sometimes it is the best." (2) To deny or reject with or without warrant: ". . . and mother, I wish that you hadn't called me a liar, and said I was just like George, *as I am not.*" (3) To move toward greater generality: ". . . and about William, I want to dismiss every idea about him. I don't like him any more than a companion; for a while I thought I did, but no more—in fact, I am quite tired of him, as you know. *I get tired of everyone after a while.*" (4) To transfer authority or responsibility. (The speaker shifts to another person the responsibility for defending a position or handling a difficulty when it would appear incumbent upon the speaker to defend the position or eliminate the difficulty) : "You alone know the answer. Your inhuman acts are the answer. Just search your mind and soul." (5) To cite a premise belatedly: "Do not hesitate to tell any of our friends that I took this step of my own free will; I am not ashamed of it. *There is no reason why I should continue to suffer with no hope of recovery.*" (6) To repeat or rephrase: "I cannot live any longer. I do not wish to live any longer."

Contra-Logic

From the tabulations of an individual's idio-logic, his contra-logic—which represents his private epistemological and metaphysical view of the universe—may then be inferred. Under the assumption that there is a rationale behind each individual's reasoning, this procedure permits us to assert (or to estimate) what that rationale is, and thereby, to understand his reasons for his reasoning as he does. Contra-logic is our reconstruction of an individual's private, usually unarticulated notions of causality and purpose, which would make his idio-logic seem errorless to him. The contra-logic serves to nullify or contravene or "explain" that individual's idio-logic and makes it sensible—for him. It answers the questions: What must that person's beliefs about the nature of the universe be in order for him to manifest the styles of thinking that he does, that is, what are his underlying (and unverbalized) epistemological and metaphysical systems that are consistent with his ways of moving cognitively in the world? In the same sense that every person has an idio-logical structure that can be explicated, there is for each individual a complimentary contra-logical position that can be inferred.

An example will serve to clarify the concept of contra-logic: A patient in a disturbed mental hospital ward—an example cited by Von Domarus[4] and repeated by Arieti[5]—unexpectedly yells, "I am Switzerland." The reconstructed syllogism reads: I want to leave this locked ward—I love freedom; Switzerland loves freedom; (therefore) I am Switzerland. His idio-logic is one of reasoning in terms of attributes of the predicate, but his style of reasoning would make "sense" to us (and does make sense to him) if it were the case (or if one supplied the implicit premise) that there were only *one* member to a class, that is, that Switzerland is the only entity that loves freedom. That is the contra-logic that explains this idio-logic, for in that case, it would follow without logical error that anyone who then loved freedom would, of necessity, have to be Switzerland. (The psychological concomitants of such a state are mentioned under psycho-logic, below).

Some other examples of contra-logics, using a variety of kinds of individuals—a suicide, a Jekyll-and-Hyde homosexual, a chess champion, some noted political figures—are published in previous discussions of this method.[6]

Let us continue our analysis of that one suicide note from the 23-year-old girl: The contra-logic of *argumentum ad populum* is, as follows:

Definition: It follows that one believes that: The acceptability or truth of a conclusion or position is not, and should not be, strictly a function of so-called "objective considerations," for any conclusion or position can be adequately assessed only in light of what the "going beliefs" and attitudes of the society are. Thus, the eliciting of these beliefs and attitudes by means of folk homilies, idioms, shiboleths, and the like is appropriate to assessment of the conclusion, that is, a conclusion is not independent of the whole nexus of societal beliefs, rather it is to be judged only in light of them, hence their elicitation is always appropriate. Truth is conventional and relative to society; it is not absolute or "extrasocietal." Concurrence of other men's views with the speaker's views is more important than concurrence of the speaker's views with the objective world.

The contra-logic of indirect context is, as follows:

Definition: It follows that one believes that statements of the form "I think that P" are logically equivalent to statements of the

form "P"; that is, indirect statements are logically on a par with direct statements. All knowledge is relative—relative to man, society, and so forth—that is, to the perceiver or the asserter. There is no world or reality distant from our perceptions. There is no objective truth independent of, or in any way transcending, what any given man conjectures, surmises, believes. A statement of the form "P" is to be understood as elliptical for "I think that P," that is, everything is indexed to the speaker.

We turn again to the note from the suicidal girl, this time to see what can be said about her contra-logic. Keeping in mind her use of argumentum ad populum and indirect context, the following might be said about her underlying idiosyncratic epistemological and metaphysical view of the universe:

There is no objective truth; what seems to be true for the observer is to be taken as true in fact (indirect context, II-D). Validation of one's beliefs is obtained by concurrence of those beliefs with prevalent societal beliefs and attitudes, that is, one is correct in one's beliefs if others agree with them (*argumentum ad populum*, I-F). Everything that one asserts is already implicit in one's beliefs; if someone disagrees with you, it is because his beliefs are different from your own (not because he may be reasoning differently) and there is nothing to negotiate (complex question, I-J). Everything is relative to underlying assumptions (cognitive maneuver 39, to accept conditionally).

Psycho-Logic

The concept of psycho-logic refers to those overt and covert aspects of personality that are related to—reflective of, are of a piece with, grow out of, create, or participate with—the individual's styles of thinking. The psycho-logic answers the question: What kind of a person would he have to be (in relation to his mentational psychological traits) in order for him to have the view-of-the-world that he does (contra-logic) as manifested in his ways of thinking (idio-logic). That an individual's ways of thinking and aspects of his personality (psycho-logic) are synchronous should come as no surprise to any student of human nature.

What aspects of personality are included under the psycho-logic? In the present context we can be interested only in those psychological aspects that are reflective of the individual's ways of think-

ing, that is, reflections of his mentational functionings. No claims as to the manifestations of characteristics in other-than-mentational areas of activity, such as physical, sexual, or social areas, can be made. Further, it should be stated that only with the most severe reservations can one generalize from an individual's mentational behaviors in any one specific situation to his entire logical armanentarium.

To return to our "Switzerland" example of the man who (idio-logically) reasoned in terms of attributes of the predicate, and who (contra-logically) assumed that there was only one member to a class: That type of reasoning (psycho-logically) reflects a mental state in which the focus of attention is narrowed (in this case to one attribute of a class), his inner freedom to widen or broaden the boundaries of the focus of attention is rather rigidly fixed. In such a state one might expect to see some of the following characteristics or symptoms: intense concentration or conflict; withdrawal from others; oblivion to ordinary stumuli; hypesthesia—even catatonic behavior.

Keeping in mind the restrictions indicated above, a set of men-tational psychological traits—that is, those psychological traits that can easily be related to patterns of thinking—is proposed. These traits are indicated in Table III.

To return again to our 23-year-old suicide girl: A summary of the psycho-logic for this girl might read: The subject is relativistic and fearful of commitment (indirect context, II-D) ; she is needful of approval from others and attempts to elicit that approval when-ever possible (*argumentum ad populum*, I-F) ; she tends to be dis-trustful and, if opposed, is untractable and rigid (complex question, I-J).

Pedago-Logic

The pedago-logic (relating to the process of education or instruc-tion or pedagogy) can be seen as a possible practical application of this method. If the idio-logic explicates an individual's styles of thinking, and the contra-logic describes his underlying philosophy of the universe, and the psycho-logic details his personality traits related to thinking, then the pedago-logic is a prescription that per-mits us to modify the process of communication or instruction for that person so as to maximize his opportunities for learning. To use

Table III

MENTATIONAL PSYCHOLOGICAL TRAITS

A. *Scope* (or *Range*): Wide-ranged diverse, broad-scoped *vs.* narrow-ranged, focused, specialized. Generally, the compass of foci of concern: large, medium, small.

A.1 Global, holistic, totality; molar, large units *vs.* molecular, detailed, atomistic.

A.2 Combinatory, extrapolating, seeing implications *vs.* concrete, unimaginative.

B. *Discreetness:* Dichotomous, binary, either-or *vs.* continuous, neutralistic, both-and, n'chotomous.

C. *Flexibility:* Flexible, adaptable, mobile *vs.* fixed, inflexible, firm, rigid.

D. *Certainty:* Dogmatic certainty, affirmation *vs.* uncertainty, indecision, doubt, equivocation.

E. *Autism:* Good reality orienation, nonautistic *vs.* poor reality orientation, projection of standards, autistic. Generally: realistic (certain), realistic (possible, probable), unrealistic (impossible).

F. *Creativity:* Creative, original; novel, new *vs.* conforming, commonplace, banal.

G. *Bias:* Objective, unprejudiced *vs.* prejudiced, infusion of affect, subjective. Also: reductive (derogatory), neutral, elevative (laudatory).

H. *Consistency:* Consistent, reliable, predictable *vs.* variable, unreliable, inconsistent, unpredictable, fluctuating.

I. *Accord:* Builds on past achievement, extends accepted position, accepts present authorities, constructive *vs.* contrary, iconoclastic, perverse, negative, naysayer, destructive.

J. *Organization:* Systematic, organized, methodical *vs.* unsystematic, disorganized, unmethodical, loose, scattered, disjointed.

K. *Directiveness:* Goal-directed, planful, purposeful *vs.* lacking in direction, planless, purposelessness. Generally: compulsive persistence, appropriate persistence, impersistence (abandoning goal).

L. *Activity:* Aggressive, involved, adventurous, assertive, taking initiative *vs.* passive, acquiescent, receptive, detached, timid, letting happen (lethargic), not taking initiative generally: proactive (taking initiative), reactive, inactive (apathy).

M. *Spontaneity:* Spontaneous, uninhibited *vs.* constructed inhibited, controlled.

N. *Precision:* Definite, precise, clear-cut *vs.* indefinite, vague, amorphous.

O. *Pursuit:* Tenacious, perseverating, single-minded *vs.* changeable, labile, easily diverted.

P. *Orientation:* Action or fact-oriented, practical, unreflective, extrinsic reward-oriented *vs.* mentation-oriented, contemplative, theoretical, philosophic, intrinsic reward-oriented.

Q. *Awareness:* Awareness of own cognitive activity *vs.* unawareness of own cognitive activity.

an analogy: everyone who moves at all can be said to locomote, but individuals locomote in many various ways. In this sense, the pedago-logic provides a way of "limping along" with the individual; it is a custom-fitted prosthetic device intended to facilitate his potential for locomotion. In the usual learning situation, there are at least two major aspects present: the substantive (what is being taught), and the process (the way in which the "what" is presented—the

teacher's way or the textbook's way). Most of us adjust to the way
of the text or the teacher, but our grasp of content would be even
greater if the content were presented *our* way, in a textbook custom-
made to reflect our styles of cognizing. A good military aide soon
learns to tailor the briefings for his General to fit the General's ways
of thinking; a master coach adapts his teachings to the styles of his
star players, so that he can maximize their potentials for performance. The pedago-logic is a prescription for maximizing (or mini-
mizing) communication.

The "thrust" of the concept of the pedago-logic is perhaps illustrated best by using an example involving individuals of limited
intellectual capacity. We—Peter Tripodes and I—made a few visits
to a state hospital for the mentally retarded where we recorded our
conversations with a small number of below-normal young adults.
We routinely asked questions intended to elicit some sort of concludifying responses, such as "Why do you think so?" in relation to
such topics of interest as privileges, visiting hours, dances, work,
release from hospital, and the like. We then analyzed the kinds of
idio-logics displayed by our subjects. Our thought—based on the
notion that there are different ways to conceptualize (and thus to
teach) *subtraction*—was to construct a few (three or four) simple
textbooks teaching subtraction in the logical styles "consistent" with
the three or four main types of logical styles we found among these
subjects. Our hypothesis was that learning (measured by rate, level
of difficulty, retention, etc.) using these "tailor-made" texts would be
superior to learning from any one set (including their present set)
of textbooks, simply because in the latter case some of the students
would have to try to adapt to a style of presentation not peculiarly
their own.[7]

Although we did not have the opportunity to complete this study,
the thoughts that stimulated its initiation may help to clarify the
concept of resonating to another's logical styles. This same principle ought to apply, with even greater usefulness perhaps, in the
school situation, or with military, industrial, or governmental personnel, especially in briefing leaders at the top-most levels. (Conversely, if one were meeting an opponent in a debate or at a
bargaining table or in an international arena, it would behoove one
to know that individual's logical styles [as well as one's own] in

order more effectively to counter and to outmaneuver him—to beat him with his own game).

A summary of the pedago-logic of the 23-year-old girl's suicide note might include the following: The subject will either agree with you immediately or disagree with you forever, requiring a feeling of commonality in underlying beliefs in order to communicate with you (indirect context, II-D). This feeling of commonality can often be elicited by your suggesting that your own beliefs are commonly held by others (*argumentum ad populum*, I-F). In the absence of such a feeling of commonality, she will tend to be oblivious to anything you might say thereafter (complex question, I-J). A summary of the analysis of her logics is presented in Table IV.

Returning, for the last time, to our I-am-Switzerland friend, one might concentrate on widening his intellective blinders, for example to show him (if it were possible) that were countries other than Switzerland that loved freedom (e.g., Denmark, Israel, etc.) and that there were other-than-countries, that is, people who loved freedom (e.g., Jefferson, Lincoln, Paine, LaFayette, etc.)—to break through, at the least, the narrow notion of Switzerland = freedom, and freedom = Switzerland. On the other hand, his very rigidity and inflexibility might militate against his effectively listening to any argument not isomorphic with his own fixed beliefs. It is interesting to contemplate his reaction to your responding to his "I am Switzerland" with "I am Switzerland too," to which, if you possessed (and held) the keys to his locked ward he might then say, "No, you are really Germany." Using this kind of language, you might then reply: "All right then, let's negotiate. At least, let's draw up a nonaggression pact." But obviously, the most meaningful as well as the most direct response to his saying "I am Switzerland" would be to say— with seeming irrelevance, but with piercing perspicacity: "I know that you want your freedom from this locked ward, and we'll see what we can do, you and I." Then you would be talking his logic and he would know that someone had truly understood him.

Summary

As with any aspect of human personality, it is useful to consider man's mentational styles, following Murray and Kluckhohn,[8] in the terms of (1) which are common of all men—universal; (2) which

Table IV

Aspect of Reasoning	Idio-logic	Contra-logic	Psycho-logic	Pedago-logic
Indirect Context (II-D)	Relativizes assertions to own or other's perceptions; concerned with the appearance of events rather than the events themselves.	There is no world or reality distinct from perceptions. There is no objective truth; there is only conjecture, surmisal, belief, etc.	Relativistic; fearful of commitment, feels divorced from reality, alienated from others.	This individual will see no objective grounds for your assertions, but will regard them as idiosyncratic to your point of view or attitude.
Argumentum ad Populum (I-F)	Appeals to affective dispositions and attitudes by the use of idiomatic expressions.	Truth is conventional and relative to society; societal attitudes are important determinants of truth and appropriateness.	Insecure; needy of approval; opportunistic.	This individual will tend to be responsive to the emotional content in metaphors, slogans, idioms, etc., and other devices which connote widespread acceptance of your position.
Complex Question (I-J)	Uses phrasings that "beg" some critical points at issue, by assuming that these points have already been established.	A position or conclusion cannot be negotiated or established by argument or proof, but is already incorporated in all one's assertions.	Distrustful, rigid, intractable, refractory. Tends to be fatalistic and tenacious.	In communicating with this individual, be fully explicit in making your point or she will tend to ignore it, having made up her mind beforehand.

are present in some men—ubiquitous; and (3) which are present in none other than one man—unique. In this paper we have attempted to indicate our belief that what is *universal* about mentational styles is that every human (perhaps other than neonates and decorticated persons) engages in some forms of concludifying; what is *ubiquitous* about mentation is that there is a finite number of general patterns (combinations or styles) of logical behaviors (which can be conceptualized in terms of the relative frequencies and clusterings of idiosyncrasies of reasoning and cognitive maneuvers); and what is *unique* are the special nuances of patterning or styles of thought that specially characterize any particular individual's logical style.

All this is conceptualized in terms of a four-part scheme: (1) idio-logic—which explicates the details of a man's logical styles; (2) contra-logic—which attempts to explain why his reasoning seems reasonable to him (by citing what appears to be his underlying philosophies of causal relations which would "explain" his logical styles; (3) psycho-logic—which surmizes which traits of human personality might well be found with (or are consistent with) the idiosyncratic logical styles and the underlying epistemology of that individual; and (4) pedago-logic—which extrapolates from the other three and suggests what logical styles might be employed (by a teacher or mentor or aide) with an individual so as to communicate and teach (or conversely, to frustrate and thwart) that individual most effectively.

The general approach is one of attempting, without prejudgment, to understand the net results of an individual's ways of thinking by examining, in terms of logical, epistemological, and selected psychological dimensions, what manner of mind it was from which those results had come.

PART II
ADMINISTRATION
AND ORGANIZATION

Chapter 5
FEASIBILITIES OF THE LOS ANGELES SUICIDE PREVENTION CENTER
Edwin S. Shneidman and Norman L. Farberow

Reconceptualization of some timeworn (and inadequate) concepts concerning suicide has resulted in a clinical experiment in lifesaving. The Los Angeles Suicide Prevention Center, now with more than a decade of experience, has demonstrated the feasibility of offering around-the-clock crisis intervention using a multiprofessional approach. Some twelve specific suicide prevention feasibilities are listed. Aspects of the training and research programs are enumerated.

The Suicide Prevention Center opened its telephones and its doors in Los Angeles to patients on September 1, 1958, in an abandoned and structurally condemned building on the grounds of the Los Angeles County General Hospital. The inauguration of the Los Angeles Suicide Prevention Center was preceded by about a decade of interest, study, focus, and concern with the topics of suicide and suicide prevention.[1] From 1955 on, our work was supported by a research grant from the National Institute of Mental Health.[2] It might be said that in large measure the present Center grew out of our experience under that research grant, of being unable, in clear conscience, to conduct purely research activities on the wards of a large hospital without feeling, at the same time, deeply involved with direct and consultative lifesaving service functions. The research grant was preceded by six years of working (mostly weekends and nights) primarily with suicide note materials that we had discovered in the vaults of the Los Angeles County Coroner's office and later with nonsuicidal (control) materials we had begun to generate ourselves.

How far we have come since the day in 1949 when we discovered those hundreds of genuine suicide notes in the Coroner's files is not for us to say, but we do believe that it would be most appropriate, now, several years after the formal establishment of the Suicide Prevention Center, to give some public accounting of our organization and some of our past activities and activities in process.

If we are a demonstration project, then let us ask (rhetorically) what it is that we have demonstrated. Primarily, we believe that we have demonstrated certain important *feasibilities*. Webster's Dictionary defines "feasible" as "capable of being done or carried out; practicable, possible; also as reasonable or capable of being used or dealt with successfully." The remainder of this paper is a brief discussion of each of several feasibilities. As an overview, we shall list a dozen of them. We propose that our experiences at the Suicide Prevention Center in Los Angeles over the last several years have demonstrated *the feasibility of:*

1. Preventing suicide
2. Generating communicable clues to suicide
3. Doing social research on this topic
4. Using active therapeutic techniques, often involving the "significant other"
5. Acting as a consultation service for established health agencies
6. Working with great mutual usefulness with the Chief Medical Examiner-Coroner, especially by use of the "Psychological Autopsy" procedure
7. Having an around-the-clock service
8. Employing a truly multiprofessional approach
9. Reconceptualizing some timeworn (and inadequate) concepts of suicide and death
10. "Un-booing" some unnecessary taboos
11. Conducting training programs on suicide prevention
12. Operating a specifically focused suicide prevention center.

The Feasibility of Preventing Suicide

We might say that if we have learned anything from our decade of work on this topic, we have learned that, happily, most individuals who are acutely suicidal are so for only a relatively short period, and that, even during the time they are suicidal, they are extremely ambivalent about living and dying. If the techniques for identifying these individuals before rash acts are taken can be disseminated and if there are agencies, like the Suicide Prevention Center, in the community that can throw resources in on the side of life and

give the individual some temporary surcease or sanctuary, then after a short time most individuals can go on, voluntarily and willingly, to live useful and creative lives. We know that it is feasible to prevent suicide.[3]

Everybody dies; the only question is when, not if. Suicidal deaths are premature and *untimely*. At the Suicide Prevention Center we have demonstrated that in practically every case they need not occur; that they are *un*necessary. Nor does the individual who commits suicide limit his rash act to himself. Suicides often, by the very nature of their death in our society, put their skeletons in their survivors' closets. From this we see why suicide is a community mental health problem, responsible for the perturbation in many people, a perturbation made visible perhaps years later, in the clinics and the hospitals.

The Feasibility of Generating Communicable Prodromal Clues to Suicide

The essential nature of suicide is not clearly understood. It is not a single disease entity. In our work at the Suicide Prevention Center and the Veterans Administration Central Research Unit for the Study of Unpredicted Death, we have used various techniques: retrospective studies of committed suicides, psychological autopsies, cross-sectional studies of now-alive patients, and prospective studies of individuals who have attempted or threatened suicide. These studies reveal that most persons go through a discernable prodromal phase during which they reveal, consciously or unconsciously, their potentially suicidal tendencies. This communication is sometimes explicit, sometimes it is cryptic and in code, and even sometimes the communicator is unaware of the significance of his own behaviors. Our task is to make the content and nature of these prodromal clues explicit, as people in cancer prevention have publicized such clues of malignancy as "bleeding from an aperture" or "an unhealing skin blemish." Our studies have indicated that one primary target group for this information is the physician, in that at least one-third of the individuals who commit suicide have seen a physician within six months prior to the act. We estimate that "cries for help" in relation to suicide occur perhaps 500,000 times a year in the United States. We believe that the experiences of the

staff at the SPC and the many other individuals who have trained with us, have demonstrated the feasibility of communicating knowledge about known prodromal clues of suicide to other professional and interested lay people.[4]

The Feasibility of Conducing Research on This Topic

If we accept the notion that service and training improve largely to the extent that they receive nourishment from research findings, then a comprehensive program of suicide prevention must include not only the saving of lives today but the investigation of why individuals take their lives—so that more lives can be saved more expeditiously tomorrow. The question is, is it possible (that is, permissible) to do meaningful research in this area. Our experience at the LA SPC, in the Veterans Administration, with local, state, and national health agencies, and in relation to press, radio, and television people all indicate a growing feasibility of both large- and small-scale research (and clinical) activities on the topics of suicide and suicide prevention.

Although one might be taxed to think of a more worthy goal than that of saving lives, nevertheless the *raison d' être* of the SPC is its research and investigatory functions. The research goal addresses itself to the more profound questions: Why are people self-destructive? What are the dimensions of self-destruction? And what are the parameters within a human personality (actively engaged in a social milieu) that relate to self-destruction? There is a constant search for better procedures, techniques, and notions as to how to save more lives more expeditiously through a better understanding of the self-destructive processes in man. The research activities at the SPC have been pursued by most of the members of the staff, who, out of their own intiative and their own interests, have asked questions and have attempted to resolve them. We shall list the areas of our research interests in the terms of publications by members of the SPC staff.

TYPES OF SUICIDAL SUBJECTS. We have been concerned with suicide and age, specifically, as follows: in adolescents and children;[5] and in the aged;[6] with suicide among various diagnostic groups, including schizophrenic patients;[7] among patients with malignant neoplasms;[8] among cardiovascular patients;[9] and in patients suffer-

ing from anxiety and depression.[10] We have examined suicide in various settings, including suicide in mental hospitals;[11] suicide prevention in general hospitals;[12] and suicide in the community;[13] attempted, threatened, and committed suicides;[14] and suicide in some special groups, such as suicide in a Nisei woman;[15] and specified characteristics of callers to the SPC who refuse to identify themselves, whom we have labeled no-name callers;[16] also, we have done some follow-up studies.[17]

PUBLICATIONS ADDRESSED TO VARIOUS PROFESSIONAL GROUPS. The dissemination of information about suicide among various groups, especially to the gatekeepers who stand in the position early to recognize suicide or effectively to treat it, has always been considered important. Thus, we have written articles about suicide and the police,[18] suicide and the physician,[19] suicide in general practice,[20] suicide prevention for nurses,[21] the social worker in suicide prevention,[22] the medical-legal aspects of suicide prevention,[23] and the clergy's responsibility in suicide prevention.[24]

PSYCHODYNAMICS OF SUICIDAL PERSONS. Studies focused on investigations into the intrapsychic and interpersonal aspects of the suicidal person resulted in the following publications: the immobilization response to suicidal behavior,[25] observations on attempted suicide,[26] interpersonal relations in suicide attempts,[27] countertransference aspects in suicide attempts,[28] failure and masochism in suicide,[29] and acting-out suicide.[30] The book *The Cry for Help* is primarily concerned with the psychodynamics of suicidal persons.[31]

ASPECTS OF THE SUICIDAL CRISIS. Studies of suicidal crisis include writings on emergency response to suicidal crises,[32] insights obtained through analysis of genuine and simulated suicide notes[33] and through the analysis of psychological tests,[34] sociopsychological aspects of the suicidal crisis,[35] and aspects of the suicidal crisis from the staff members' point of view.[36] The book *Clues to Suicide* explores various aspects of the suicidal crisis.[37]

ADMINISTRATIVE ASPECTS OF SUICIDE PREVENTION. Some of our writings have related to the Center itself,[38] on how to establish a center,[39] or on the feasibilities of suicide prevention.[40] Other papers

in this general area include one on suicide prevention around the clock[41] and the operation of a telephone answering service.[42]

THEORETICAL ASPECTS OF SUICIDE. Writings on the theoretical aspects of suicide include discursive pieces, encyclopedia articles, and attempts at definition and taxonomy. Specifically, they include an overview of the suicide problem,[43] the psychology of suicide,[44] the definition of suicide,[45] a discussion of the relationships between suicide and death,[46] suicide as crisis or catastrophe,[47] the assessment of suicidal potential,[48] the logical or cognitive aspects of suicide,[49] a taxonomy of orientations toward death,[50] a study of accidents as subintentioned deaths or suicidal equivalents,[51] sleep and its relationship to suicidal phenomena,[52] and a comprehensive study of Freud's thoughts on the topic of suicide.[53]

The Feasibility of Using Active Therapeutic Techniques

A fundamental assumption in the clinical operation of the Suicide Prevention Center has been that it would involve essentially short-term treatment, viewing the suicidal situation as a crisis period. For this reason, the Center serves primarily as a resource where immediate attention for the emergency is provided by means of diagnostic and referral services. It was recognized that this would be necessary in order to attend to the needs of many people rather than to focus on the long-term treatment of just a few. This dictates our need for active intervention. It follows that an important feature in the clinical work with suicidal patients is the involvement of the "significant other" in the treatment situation. Most of our cases are persons in conflict with others and the suicidal situation is the resultant of interpersonal (or dyadic) tensions. To work with only the one party neglects this aspect and makes the treatment procedure incomplete. We have been active also in involving friends, family, and community agencies, and in recommending hospitalization when we assess the lethality risk as high and the potential rescuers' capacities as not adequate.[54]

The Feasibility of Acting as a Consultation Service for Established Health Agencies

To operate as a short-term emergency clinic requires close integration and liaison with other resources within the community to

whom patients can be sent for various appropriate longer-term therapeutic, rehabilitative, or environmental care. The Suicide Prevention Center has established liaison with and integrated closely with other agencies in the community, including the city and county health departments, police and sheriff departments, Welfare Planning Council, and State Department of Mental Hygiene. In addition, there has been contact with more than fifty health and welfare agencies in our county who, having heard of the Center, telephone for consultation or are a resource for direct referrals for extended treatment. At first there was reluctance on the part of many social agencies to accept even the lowest-risk suicidal individuals. However, with referrals that included an evaluation of suicidal potential and the knowledge that consultation by telephone would be readily available, a greater willingness has occurred among the agencies in accepting referrals. Also the demonstration of the capability of our own staff in working with suicidal persons encouraged workers in other agencies to do the same.

The Feasibility of Working with Great Mutual Usefulness with the Chief Medical Examiner-Coroner, Especially by Use of the "Psychological Autopsy" Procedure

Special mention should be made of the liaison with Dr. T. Curphey, the Los Angeles County Chief Medical Examiner-Coroner, with whom, as Deputy Coroners, many of the staff of the Suicide Prevention Center work closely. Vital services and research functions are carried out in the coroner's office through the investigation of cases of equivocal deaths, that is, cases in which the mode of death was uncertain but possibly suicidal. We call this process the "Psychological Autopsy."[55] The staff members investigate the cases by obtaining a psychological picture of the deceased by interviewing surivivors (especially concerning the victim's motivations in relation to lethal outcome) and adding this information to the other data available to the coroner, allowing him to make a more meaningful certification as to the mode of death. Through the coroner's office also much important research data have been gathered for use in various investigations into suicide in the community. Dr. Curphey has reported the *therapeutic* effects of our contacts with these bereaved survivors.[56]

The Feasibility of Having an Around-the-Clock Service, Using Other-than-Fully Professional Personnel

The Suicide Prevention Center operates with a relatively small staff, fewer than a dozen full- and part-time professionals, not counting trainees in various fields. The Center began as an 8-to-5, Monday-through-Friday operation. It soon became clear that a 24-hour service would have to be provided to the community. We have met this problem by carefully selecting and thoroughly training young people—mostly graduate students in the field of psychology, sociology, nursing, social work, and other related fields—who have already assumed a professional attitude and who are trainable in attitudes, procedures, and techniques required in working with suicidal persons. Volunteers have assumed a major role in the clinical operation of the Center.[57]

The Feasibility of Employing a Truly Multiprofessional Approach

At the Suicide Prevention Center, individuals from various disciplines and points of view work congenially together. These include psychologists, sociologists, nurses, social workers, psychiatrists, clergymen, and others. Each, of course, has his special skills, but what needs to be noted is that our experience has demonstrated that members of each speciality can, independently—feeling free to ask consultation from each other—deal appropriately with suicidal persons, calling from our common funds of knowledge.[58]

Out of our feelings that no one profession or point of view has a stranglehold on truth, we have, from 1963 to 1967, invited Fellows to the Suicide Prevention Center each year "to contemplate suicide and to think about death." Typically, these are individuals from various fields in the social and behavioral sciences whose broad interests and knowledge in depth of their own fields permit them and us to have mutually catalyzing dialogues. Since 1963, the following individuals (alphabetized) have been Fellows at the SPC: Kresten Bjerg: Psychology;[59] Warren Breed: Sociology;[60] Jacques Choron: Philosophy;[61] James Diggory: Psychology;[62] Harold Garfinkel: Sociology;[63] Erving Goffman: Sociology; Gerald Heard: Philosophy;[64] Jonathan Jenness: Anthropology; Kenshiro Ohara: Social Psychiatry; Stephen Pepper: Philosophy;[65] Harvey Sacks: Sociology;[66] and Elsa Whalley: Psychology.[67] The return to the SPC in terms of ideas and a sense of intellectual stimulation has been enor-

mous. The Fellows have been one of the most rewarding features of the entire SPC effort. The book *Essays in Self-Destruction* presents essays by these Fellows as well as by a number of distinguished visitors to the Center.[68]

The Feasibility of Reconceptualizing Some Timeworn (and Inadequate) Concepts of Suicide and Death

We believe in the importance of both relatively short-span empirical research with almost immediate applicability and payoff, and also in the advisability of long-range research thinking where the potentiality of payoff may be more problematic but, in implications of the payoff, more exciting. In the fields of suicide and death, we are concerned about the serious questions of *definition* and *classification*.[69] The usual coroner's classification of modes of death (natural, accidental, suicide, and homicide) is a remarkably *a*psychological classification that omits the role of the individual in his own demise. Nonetheless it is a classification that is required by custom based on the habit of centuries; it is often inconsistent and contradictory when applied to special cases. We need new thoughts on this topic. And our time-honored classification of suicidal behaviors into committed suicide, attempted suicide, and threatened suicide groups together as "suicidal" a number of very different forms of behavior (in relation to both intention and motivation), which can, with profit, be separated and designated more clearly.[70] Appropriate taxonomies of suicide and death need to be made the explicit topic of reflection and investigation. Our field calls for some thoughtful long-range iconoquestioning.

The Feasibility of "Un-Booing" Some Unnecessary Taboos

The theme of the book *Taboo Topics*[71] and of the chapter on suicide within it[72] is that given concerted effort and "derring-do," given what Prof. Charles Osgood of Illinois called "the ability to run uphill," given the internally accepted assignment that a neglected topic merits investigation or that a problem area begs to be solved—given all these, then the feasibility of what we call "un-booing" some unnecessary taboos becomes manifest. At the Suicide Prevention Center, we have reflected as to whether we just happened to "come along at the right time" or whether we had played some active role in creating a more permissive *Zeitgeist* in relation to suicide study.

We believe an accurate appraisal would probably indicate both.
But we have learned in our work over the past several years that one
need not run scared and that, with proper obeisance to the social
amenities, one can, in the service of suicide prevention, ask people
to write simulated suicide notes, participate in psychological autopsies, answer questions about their suicidal behaviors—all of which
on first blush would seem to be taboo.

The Feasibility of Conducting Training Programs on Suicide Prevention

Of equal importance with the existence of a suicide prevention
agency in a community is the training and education of both lay and
professional personnel in relation to suicide prevention. Like fire
prevention, it is everybody's problem. Recognizing this, the Suicide
Prevention Center in Los Angeles has placed appropriate emphasis
upon training and educational activities, directed toward pre- and
postprofessional persons, and toward the public at large. In line
with our recognition of the importance of the training function we
have encouraged professional persons who are interested in establishing suicide prevention centers in their own communities throughout the United States to come to our center and to spend time with
us, receiving intensive training especially in clinical procedures
relating to the assessment of lethality and to appropriate referral
and therapeutic techniques. We know that the problem of training
in this country is well beyond the capacity of any one center and
we now see the feasibility of training trainers; that is, of sharing
what we know with dozens of groups spread through the various
regions of the country, who can, with us, serve as regional training
centers and regional resource agencies, as more and more local
communities recognize their needs and responsibilities to establish
their own suicide prevention agencies.

The Feasibility of Operating a Specifically Focused Suicide Prevention Center

It is legitimate to ask why there should be a separate suicide
prevention center. We know that in most communities there are
already available facilities such as hospitals, clinics, social work
agencies, professional persons, and, more recently, emergency
psychiatric centers. Cannot these resources be used optimally to

take care of suicidal persons? Our advocacy of a separate suicide prevention center is consistent with our belief that the suicidal crisis has unique features, relating especially to the dramatically heightened intra- and interpersonal crisis in which life and death frequently hang in the balance. Focused resources are needed for these focused emergencies. The suicide prevention center is conceived as an emergency psychosocial first-aid center—we have compared it with a lifeguard station on a dangerous beach—with its special resources and specially trained personnel geared to meet the specific needs of both the individual and his significant others at the moments of special crisis. Suicide is, of course, not only the individual's problem. It is the family's problem, and it is the community's problem. We have referred to the ugly backwash of disrupted mental health created in the family and in the community by a suicidal death. Society faces its legitimate challenge of meeting the suicidal person's needs quickly and efficiently. Justice Benjamin Cardozo, in 1923, stated: "A cry of distress is a summons to rescue." This ringing statement can stand as the credo of an enlightened democratic society, whose keystone lies in its heightened evaluation of each human life.

We believe that there is a new and vocal group in America: it is those of us who are passionate about the need and the feasibility of effectively reducing the unnecessary present suicide rates. The place for each of us to do this is in our community. The time is now.

Chapter 6
NONPROFESSIONAL VOLUNTEERS IN A SUICIDE PREVENTION CENTER

Samuel M. Heilig, Norman L. Farberow, Robert E. Litman, and Edwin S. Shneidman

Roles are now being developed in which the concerned citizen can play an active and positive force for the mental health of the community. The volunteers' participation has lead to a pilot training program designed to staff the telephone answering service of the LA SPC. The success of the volunteer program made it apparent that, with careful selection and rigorous training and supervision, nonprofessional volunteers can make a significant contribution in a crisis center.

An important current focus of interest in the mental health field has been the development of theory and principles of community mental health and community psychiatry. Bellak has called this development the third major revolution in the history of psychiatry.[1] He defines community psychiatry as "the resolve to view the individuals' psychiatric problems within the frame of reference of the community and *vice versa*."[2] A significant aspect of this development has been the involvement of the community and its members in the concern for its own mental health. The citizen as well as the mental health professional must play an active role in the mental health of the community.

More specifically, roles are now being developed in which the citizen is an active, positive force for the mental health of the community and its members, including direct therapeutic interaction with its emotionally disturbed individuals. This conception of the citizen's role is markedly different from the approach in years gone by. In the past, the volunteer's participation in such activities had been considered ancillary and indirect. Work with patients in direct one-to-one relationship was unusual.

Review of Literature

Review of the literature indicates that volunteers have been used in the mental health field in a limited way for a long period. Frank,[3]

Fechner and Parke,[4] Evans,[5] and Haddock and Dundon[6] discuss the volunteer in mental hospitals, stressing their importance as bridges to the community. However, the use of the volunteer is described in traditional roles of entertainment and clerical activities.

The history of this approach is best outlined in the American Psychiatric Association Report, "The Volunteer and the Psychiatric Patient," published in 1959. This report includes a survey that indicated that 46 percent, or 525 out of 1140 state hospitals, private hospitals, private schools, clinics, state schools, general hospitals, VA hospitals, county hospitals, and workshops had some sort of volunteer program, utilizing about 100,000 volunteers. The report indicates, however, that the volunteer was used mainly in providing incidental services such as entertainment, dances, and parties, bringing gifts, taking patients on walks, and assisting in ward activities. Volunteers disliked clerical assignments and preferred direct contact with patients. The report also indicated that the major contribution of volunteer programs is the bridge that is established between mental hospitals and the community, both in giving patients a link with the outside world and helping enlighten communities about mental illness. A bibliography of 59 articles published mostly in the late forties and early fifties is listed in the report.

Lee reports the use of volunteers in court as an aid to relatives of patients appearing for commitment.[7] He indicates the program was very successful in helping both relatives and hospital during this difficult initial hospitalization period. Vail and Karlins report on a decade of volunteer services in Minnesota between 1952 and 1962, pointing out that over 5000 volunteers are now being used in mental institutions.[8] They describe the movement toward increased use of volunteers as a result of (1) recognition of the basic brutal fact of man-power needs, and (2) recognition that the skills involved in the alleviation of human misery are, in their essence, not technical but simply human.[9] They also point out that members of the clinical professions take on the function of teaching and supervising volunteers who provide actual services, thereby increasing the use of professional skills. Mills reports a program for training volunteers that describes the cardinal points to be con-

sidered in preparation of nonprofessionals for the traditional activities in mental health.[10]

Bellak, in his comprehensive *Handbook for Community Psychiatry*, covers many of the newer developments in the field.[11] However, the viewpoint toward volunteers seems to remain unchanged or, at best, only slightly modified. Beckenstein, in his chapter on the New State Hospital, discusses voluntary organizations in terms of volunteers conducting half-way houses, or sheltered workshops or forming committees to contact employers.[12] Bierer comes closer to our concepts in his paper on the Marlborough Experiment, referring to the Therapeutic Social Club, the Self-Governed Community Hostel and to "Neurotics Nomine" (patients who visit other patients).[13] These arrangements, however, all refer to efforts to utilize the therapeutic forces within the patients to help themselves and others. Bellak does talk about imparting psychiatric understanding, not only to general practitioners and nonpsychiatric residents, but to other key groups in the community such as clergy, teachers, lawyers, and police.[14] In general, volunteers have been considered useful, but adjunctive, with their use in therapeutic roles as yet unexplored.

Maya Pines discusses the need for more imaginative use of personnel in mental health centers.[15] She describes the work in mental health centers in slum areas of New York, where people indigenous to the area and familiar with the culture, are used to work directly with people who need help.

The programs referred to above described the use of volunteers in hospital situations primarily. The emphasis in the programs has been on the use of volunteers in ways and in activities that were considerably different from the contacts provided by the trained professional person. The use of nonprofessional volunteers to perform the same functions as trained persons had not been attempted in any organized way.

An extensive project to train lay people to perform a psychotherapeutic function was developed by Margaret J. Rioch, Charmian Elkes, and Arden A. Flint in 1960. The project was seen as one of a growing number of experiments attempting to deal with the manpower problem. The first year of the program was reported by the investigation in the *American Journal of Orthopsychiatry,*

1963,[16] and the results of the two-year training program plus two years follow-up were reported in U.S. Department of Health, Education and Welfare, Public Health Service Publication No. 1254.[17] The project concerned the training of a group of "housewives" as psychotherapists. Their results are reported in more detail below because of the pertinence of their program to ours.

The program focused intensively on teaching the techniques of psychotherapy, with little stress on theory. The procedures of recruitment and selection are outlined in detail. The group of eight finally selected were all females with an average age of 43; one widowed, with all others married; and all with children. Their husbands were professionals or executives, all were college graduates, three with advanced degrees. Six had held paying jobs. Training consisted of four separate semesters of group presentations, seminars, and individual supervision. The trainees started interviewing in their third week, and tapes of interviews were used in teaching. The group started at first with "normal" controls and later went to "real" patients. Among the biggest difficulties for the trainees was to learn how to be "professional" rather than social, to pursue areas of anxiety rather than to avoid them. The trainees had in-service training in a number of different agencies such as the probation office, juvenile court, clinics, university counseling center, social service agencies, public high schools, junior college, universities or colleges, and one hospital.

The success of the program was evidenced by the fact that at the end of the training period all trainees found paid positions in either a mental health clinic, high school, college, state hospital, adolescent service, or experimental hospital ward. All intended to continue working indefinitely.

The project was considered to have demonstrated (1) that it was possible to add to the source of manpower in a mental health field by using this hitherto unexplored group; (2) that it pointed out another avenue of approach for transition from one phase of life to another for the middle-aged woman; and (3) that it was possible to offer adequate training in psychotherapy with a minimum of destructive competition and a maximum of successful on-the-job training. Various rating procedures were developed and both objective and outside ratings of the performance of the volunteers indicated a high level of performance. It should be pointed out that

this group was selected and trained for eventual paid mental work rather than for unpaid volunteer service. In the Suicide Prevention Center volunteers have been trained but not with the goal of future paid professional employment.

In the United States there are also self-help groups of volunteers in organizations that serve mental health functions. AA is probably the best known of these, and there are others for ex-mental hospital patients, such as Recovery Incorporated. These are useful and effective groups for many people, and they operate without a professional orientation. Centers for suicide prevention, such as Rescue, Inc., in Boston, Friends in Miami, and the National Save-a-Life League in New York, have developed staffs using nonprofessional volunteers. Resnik's report on the experiences of Friends in Miami serves to emphasize some of the problems connected with selection. Essentially, he found that when selection and training procedures were not worked out carefully beforehand it resulted in a disturbingly high number of emotionally upset people who were attracted to the field by their own special needs.

On the other hand, in Europe nonprofessional volunteers have been used in suicide prevention centers for more than a decade. Organizations like the Samaritans in England and the Outstretched Hand in various countries on the continent have often started around a nucleus of a minister and some of his parishioners, and have operated successfully. Many of these groups call on professional consultation available within the community as needed.

The report that follows, of the selection, training, and use of lay volunteers to provide direct clinical service in evaluation and handling of suicidal crises, most closely parallels the project described by Rioch. The volunteers have been used to support a professional team of psychiatrists, psychologists, and psychiatric social workers in the Suicide Prevention Center of Los Angeles.

Procedures for Selection

The volunteers were referred to the Center from several sources. The Executive Director of the Los Angeles County Mental Health Association assisted in the selection, and members of the staff and professional colleagues referred others. The primary procedure for evaluation of the volunteer was the interview. The volunteer was seen by a least three professional persons on the staff of the Center

and evaluated by each. The volunteer was accepted only if all three agreed on the suitability. In addition, the candidates were asked to take the MMPI and to write out an autobiography. The MMPI was used primarily to fill in information which was not covered within the interview and to serve as a rough check on the impression of the personality status of the candidate.

Criteria for Selection

No prior set of criteria existed at the time the program was initiated for appropriate selection of volunteers in such activities. As a result, some criteria were set up *a priori* and used as general guidelines. These were: maturity, responsibility, motivation, sensitivity, willingness to accept training and supervision, and ability to get along well in a group.

The main criteria were maturity and responsibility. Persons working with individuals in a suicidal crisis need to be able to view such situations in their proper perspective and to provide the caller with a feeling of depth of experience and understanding. Stability in occupation and interpersonal relationships and evidence of good judgment in their own lives was sought.

Motivation was evaluated, in terms of the reasons the candidate was applying for such work. Frequently it was a result of children in school, time for further self-development, and an unwillingness to become involved in the usual run of teas, bridge games, or charity affairs. Most often the person did not see suicide, per se, as focally fascinating, but rather was attracted by the prospect of working directly with people and by what seemed to be a real opportunity to learn and to develop. Motivation was also examined in terms of willingness to give time and effort consistently over a long period. This was required not only for the training period but also for the subsequent work schedule.

Sensitivity to the multiple levels on which humans function was an important criterion. It was not necessary for the person to know dynamics but there had to be an indication that dynamics in self and other was an accepted framework of thought.

Inasmuch as the candidate would be required to interact constantly with staff and other volunteers, the ability to work as a member of a team, and to get along well with a group was another selection criterion. Persons judged to be disruptive, hypercritical,

complaining, or rigid and not able to adapt readily to new situations were excluded early.

An important characteristic was the ability to accept training and supervision. Such persons indicated they did not know all the problems involved but were willing to learn. Certain volunteers were avoided. The SPC had received many calls prior to starting the program from persons who wished to volunteer. Often they were people looking for a way to gratify their egos and to push their own individual conceptions of human problems and their solution. Their investment was frequently in such areas as astrology, hypnotism, spiritualism, numerology, and graphology. Often such persons were emotionally disturbed themselves—rigid, inflexible, and tenuously organized. It was felt that such persons would not serve the agency, they would use it.

Volunteers Selected

Ten nonprofessional volunteers out of 16 applicants were selected. All were women, although not by design. Men simply were not available during the daytime when the Center planned on using the volunteers.

The women were primarily in their 30's and early 40's. All were married and had children who were grown or in school. All were in the middle or upper class socioeconomically. One woman had recently worked as a nursery school teacher, the rest were housewives. Two had had recent office experience.

In spouses' occupations, two were skilled craftsmen, three ran or owned successful businesses, two were physicians, one was a psychiatrist, and the remaining three were a lawyer, a banker, and an engineer. Although the women were not selected on this basis, all had some college training, six having received a Bachelor's degree. In general, their college education was in the liberal arts. None had any prior training or experience in mental health work. An interesting feature of the group was that six of the ten women had had a satisfactory experience in psychotherapy. One of the women was still in active treatment and it was with her therapist's approval that she participated in the program.

Of the six not used, three were evaluated as unsuitable. Two wanted to be coordinators of the program or to direct it. They were semiprofessionals, having had some professional training and

experience although not enough fully to qualify at a professional level. One woman was considered unsuitable because of immaturity and low threshold for anxiety. Three otherwise suitable candidates were unable, because of family and other commitments, to contribute the investment of time and energy required. These three asked to be reconsidered for similar future training programs in the hope that their time demands would then permit them.

The Training Program

The training program was considered an additional opportunity for evaluation especially of motivation. It also gave the volunteers an opportunity to check their own feelings about investment of time and commitment of self in the program. The training program consisted of two major divisions, a formal lecture and discussion program, and an in-service training apprenticeship. The formal lecture and discussion program was held two days a week for five weeks. All of the regular staff of the Center participated allowing the group the opportunity to hear various points of view of many disciplines. The last hour of each day was used for group discussion of the material presented. It became an hour in which the group often aired their own feelings about suicide and death.

The content of the formal presentations covered three main areas: (1) theoretical material about the meaning of suicidal behavior; (2) methods and techniques for handling the suicidal crisis; and (3) case histories and clinical material. In the theoretical area, concepts such as communication, ambivalence, significant other, reaction to death and dying, and other areas pertinent to suicide were discussed. In addition, basic aspects of personality, adjustment, and defense mechanisms were presented. In the area of methods and technique, emphasis was placed on the problems of establishing and maintaining rapport in a telephone interview, evaluation of the suicide potentiality, identifying and focusing on the significant problems, assessing personality strengths and weaknesses, utilization of personal and community resources, and initiation of a helpful action.

One useful procedure in the training was to listen to a call being taken by one of the regular staff. During the fifth week several of the volunteers began to take their own calls under supervision, which they would then bring back to the group for discussion.

Following the five-week training program, a roster was formed with two volunteers assigned to each day of the week. One member of the staff served as supervisor and teacher of each pair, and the volunteer was instructed to discuss each case with her supervisor before making a disposition. The case supervision served mainly as a teaching and supportive arrangement for the volunteer, but also offered the staff an opportunity for close evaluation of the work of the volunteers.

During the apprentice-training experience with the staff supervisors, all the volunteers met once weekly in group discussion of their cases, the program, and their own feelings and reactions to the work. A cohesive, enthusiastic group feeling developed that was in marked contrast to the atmosphere of the earlier meetings during the formal training program. The women became quite enthusiastic about the work and were eager to learn more. After several weeks they asked not only for suggestions for continued reading, but also for more lectures on such topics as personality development, interviewing technique, neurosis and mental illness, and the process of therapy.

With the continuing interest in learning and growth experience the volunteers were invited to sit in when a staff member interviewed in person the patient they had talked with on the telephone. After some months, some women began to see an occasional patient in the office and to provide brief counseling service in selected cases. In addition, if a volunteer showed a special interest in any of the activities of the Center, an effort was made to include them. For example, some women helped in several of the on-going research projects, and one volunteer sat in as a regular observer in a group therapy. It seemed to be especially important to allow the volunteer to expand her interests and activities and not to restrict her to a routine function.

Several women volunteered to work more than one day per week. Four women came in two days a week, and one women came in three days a week. All were invited to participate in the regular Friday morning staff meetings of the Center, and many did.

Interaction with Staff

The volunteers interacted well with the regular professional staff both in working relationships and in informal contacts. They

all used staff members readily for supervision and consultation on cases. If the assigned supervisor was busy, the volunteer had little hesitancy in seeking out another professional staff member. Supervisors were rotated for the volunteers every three months in order to provide exposure to the different styles and points of view of the staff therapists. The volunteers participated in the coffee breaks, informal staff discussions, and group lunches. Nevertheless, they always tended to identify themselves as a group and their closest relationships at the Center have been with each other.

In the beginning of the program there was some resistance within some members of the staff to the heavy demands of the training program, an extra burden in an already heavy work schedule. Doubts were voiced about whether or not the volunteers would be able to do enough work to warrant all the extra effort. Several of the volunteers also asked if it was worth the agency's time to spend so much effort and energy in their training. When the volunteers did begin to take calls, relieving the pressure of clinical work on the regular staff, there was general agreement that the early demands on staff time were well compensated. Indeed, some of the staff who were supervising the more eager volunteers became interested in developing their abilities and spent extra time in their supervisory sessions with them.

One Year Later

During the first year, the volunteers worked eagerly and enthusiastically, handling approximately one third of the calls from the community. Out of 1,808 new daytime calls for 1965, the volunteers took 680 calls, or 38 percent. Monthly, the highest percentage of calls, 54 percent, was taken in July while the lowest percentage, 22 percent, came in October, 1965. In July, many of the regular staff took vacations, throwing more of the case load to the volunteers. In October, new students began to take calls, ordinarily taken by the volunteers.

Volunteers' View

An effort was made to determine the reaction of the volunteers to their 13 months' experience in the program by asking them to fill out a short questionnaire. A summary of the responses follows:

1. "You came to the program with personal desires, expectations,

etc. Which have been met and how?" The most frequent response to this question, given by five of the seven volunteers was, phrased in different ways, the hope of making a significant contribution. This was generally stated in terms of feeling helpful, being useful, and feeling of both giving and receiving. The second most frequent response (4/7) was the hope that some form of self-development would occur through the experience. This might come about by learning new things, developing new skills, being exposed to intellectual stimulation, and the like. Two people indicated the strong attraction in the possibility of self-development through the enactment of a new role and the gathering of new experiences. This included the feeling that this might be an opportunity to utilize inner resources and allow feelings of real self to come through. It was apparent that some search for feelings of identity was in process. Two volunteers mentioned specifically their search for a place to express maternal and philanthropic needs. One person talked about a need to be with people who were "warm and admirable" and another talked of curiosity about herself and whether or not she as well as other housewives could be trained to be useful in such a function.

2. "What expectations had not been met and why not?" None of the volunteers indicated any disappointment in their expectations about the program. One person did express discouragement in feelings about herself as a therapist and the fact that her own aspirations in that direction had not been realized. One volunteer pointed to the difficulty set in the intrinsic program; we set paradoxical roles, altruistic volunteer vs. pseudo-professional. One represents denial of aspirations, the other affirms them.

3. "How has the work or program affected you? What impact if any has it had on you and your activities, values, thinking, aspirations, and so forth?" Most of the answers to this question stressed the feeling that the experience has made them more sensitive and understanding of others' problems. Four people talked about feeling more tolerant of others, that people are the same regardless of what kind of background they have, and that they have developed a sense of empathy toward the behavior and feelings of others. A number of people noted changes that had occurred among themselves. Five people talked, for example, about changes in values about what's good or right; coming to terms with death and living, and a growth

in learning about the self; a feeling of being a better mother, friend, with more strength in values, thinking and aspirations; more self-confidence in dealing with people; and a reaffirmation of identity based upon acceptance of self and aspirations. Two people specifically indicated a rise in confidence in dealing with and meeting other people. Two people talked about a desire to continue their own growth through further schooling. Two persons also talked about becoming aware of the difference between being an expert and a nonexpert and therefore realizing how little is known. One person talked about a feeling of being useful, another talked about living and enjoying the present more as a result of learning how to work with others in distress. Two people mentioned that their relationships with their husbands have been affected and perhaps improved. One understands her husband's work better, and another passes on some of the techniques to her husband, who is able to use them in his own work with other people. One person contrasted the experience with analysis but felt that there was more change in the latter. It is apparent that many of the women, however, felt the same kind of self-development and growth that occurs in going through an intensive therapy or analysis. Tolerance, self-directed questioning, and seeking for further understanding of one's own aspirations, desires, and motivations resulted.

The most frequent suggestion for improvement was for continued training either through presentation of cases or formal lectures. Refresher courses were suggested by six people. Two people suggested the use of taped interviews over a longer period of time as helpful in training. One person asked for more frequent evaluation of her work to learn how well she was doing and to avoid mistakes. Another asked for early explanation of the purely mechanical procedures, such as use of telephone, filling out of forms, and so on. Another volunteer felt that the exposures to new speakers in related fields presenting new ideas would be useful. She also suggested that the availability of staff was the most important aspect for her and would be for new volunteers.

Another volunteer talked at length about the need of the staff to think through carefully and clearly the definitions of role and limitations of goals for the volunteers. This applies not only to what the volunteers themselves have as their own aspiration, but also what the Center can provide. Thus the staff needs to be explicit

about what the volunteer can expect from the program. Warning should be given to new volunteers that aspirations will be heightened. Occasionally the need for dismissal of a volunteer arises. The volunteer should be prepared for this. A school was suggested using courses and various clinics, *à la* Rioch, to train paid mental health nonprofessionals.

Six volunteers expressed either explicitly or implicitly the wish to continue working in the Center. Three of these indicated that they wished at the same time to return to school and receive more professional training. Two volunteers saw within their continuing work at the Center the possibilities of new learning experiences, such as with group therapy and help in future training of volunteers. One volunteer was uncertain about her future role.

Some Pros and Cons

The volunteers showed strengths in particular aspects of the suicide prevention work. They did well in obtaining necessary information about the patient's current situation and stress, the details about suicide plans and ideas, and evaluating suicide potential. Another task that the volunteers did well was in mobilizing the patient's resources during the crisis. They did not hesitate to make the time-consuming effort to enlist family and friends, and to contact personal physicians, ministers, and therapists, when they were available.

The volunteers frequently offered a relationship to the patient that was on a more direct, friendly level than that of professionals; this seemed especially important in those cases in which contact rather than authority seemed more important. This is similar to experiences of the Samaritans in England, where "befriending" by the worker is seen as most significant in helping suicidal persons.

One special difficulty in connection with the volunteers occurred on days when, for one reason or another, few calls came and there was little work. It was found to be demoralizing for a volunteer to come to the Center and not have anything to do. It is interesting in this context to note than on those days when the staff feared the volunteers were being overworked, there was never any complaint from the volunteers. They would, however, not hesitate to complain when they did not have work.

One general disadvantage refers to size of staff and communica-

tion difficulties. Adding a significant number of new people to any program of activity complicates many of the organizational and communication procedures. For example, in using volunteers the responsibility for a case might be shared by one or more volunteers and a supervisor, and there was often the simple problem of knowing where the record was when it was needed. Most important was the problem of keeping current in communications about cases that were shared. This is really not a criticism or consequence of volunteers *per se*, but rather a comment on size. Its relevance is that using volunteers in an organization frequently increases precipitously the number of people involved.

One significant unanticipated problem has emerged—the problem of identity and self-concept. As the volunteers have grown in experience and skills, they have developed as mental health counselors. While they feel hampered by their lack of formal training, this does not lessen their sense of identity with the mental health area. In our Center this feeling was constantly encouraged by attitude and precept so that the volunteers readily adopted the professional stance. Volunteer status has, therefore, begun to lose some of its appeal. Some of the women have mentioned the recognition and prestige that comes through the simple process of payment. They also see themselves doing very much the same functions that many of the paid regular staff are performing.

A partial answer lies in a further sense of accomplishment and reward. Recognition might be offered with the establishment of an intermediate level in the professional area that would identify these trained volunteers as capable of giving expert service for payment rendered. Certainly the need for such skills remains high. As shown by Rioch, there is more than enough room for such workers in the hierarchy of mental health activities. The regular staff of any agency must also undertake the task of providing further growth experiences. Some possibilities are: training of subsequent volunteers in the same agency; participation in the clinical activities of the Center, such as brief or emergency psychotherapy, longer-term rehabilitative psychotherapy, group therapy, intake, and history gathering; involvement in research activities in the agency.

Fundamental to the planning for use of volunteers must be a clear conception of the need they will meet. The program then can be task oriented. For example, at the Suicide Prevention Center the

need was to have more help in handling an increasing number of calls from suicidal people. With this need explicit at the outset, enlistment, selection, and training could be focused. The volunteer too, could be clear whether or not she wanted to do this particular work.

Probably most important was staff interest, enthusiasm, direction, and coordination. The staff accepted wholeheartedly the volunteers as to-be-trained peers, with no sign of fence-guarding. The director may be a key factor in that his enthusiasm or lack of it influences the morale and attitudes of the group.

Summary

In summary, it is important to note that nonprofessional mental health volunteers, carefully selected, trained, and supervised, contribute a valuable service in direct patient activities. They seem to function, in our experience, especially well in supplementing and assuming many of the responsibilities in patient-therapist interaction. Of course, these comments must be limited to situations in which the nonprofessional volunteer works in regular collaboration with the professional staff. This is one model only for use of such volunteers. The above comments cannot be applied to volunteers who work independently in self-help groups with professionals supporting their work, rather than the volunteers supporting the work of the professionals. Much needs yet to be learned about the optimal structure of the predominantly volunteer staffed agency. Limited experience to date with such widely scattered centers in Pasadena; Seattle; Orlando, Florida; and England indicate that a crucial factor lies in strong, enthusiastic, and devoted leadership.

In the mental health field, in general, it is apparent that nonprofessional volunteers, trained in crisis intervention techniques and personal counseling, can occupy an important place in the profession and make a significant contribution to the mental health of the community.

Chapter 7
HOW TO PREVENT SUICIDE
Edwin S. Shneidman and Philip Mandelkorn

The toll of suicide cannot be communicated in the statistics. It affects the lives of one out of ten people in this country. The calculated waste of lives lost unnecessarily and the irrevocable damage to survivors have demanded that a man's despair in his suicidal crisis be heard and that a positive choice to live be offered. Americans have begun to hear the cries for help. By 1966, more than 100 suicide prevention centers were functioning in communities across the land. In 1966, the Federal government established an NIMH Center for Studies of Suicide Prevention, which supports research into suicide, its clues, causes, and prevention.

Before you finish reading this page, someone in the United States will try to kill himself. At least 60 Americans will have taken their own lives by this time tomorrow. More than 25,000 persons in the United States killed themselves last year, and nine times that many attempted suicide. Many of those who attempted will try again, a number with lethal success. And here's the irony: Except for a very few, all of the people who commit suicide want desperately to live.

At one time or another almost everyone contemplates suicide. It is one of several choices open to man. Yet any debate of suicide's sin or merit is best left to the academicians, the theologians, and the philosophers. Few suicidal persons would listen closely. Most of these deeply troubled men, women, and children are submerged in their own despair.

No single group, nor color, nor class of people is free from self-inflicted death. Rich or poor, male or female, Christian or Jew, black or white, young or old—to some extent every category of man suffers death by suicide. However, there appear to be some statistical differences. In the United States, the number of men who kill themselves is three times higher than that of women (though women attempt suicide more often than men) ; whites twice that of Negroes; college students half again as much as their noncollege counterparts (for collegians, suicide is the third leading cause of death—only

accidents and cancer take more lives) ; single people twice that of those married; and among adults, it is more frequently the elderly who kill themselves.

Suicides are much less accurately reported in some places than others; nevertheless, suicide is among the ten leading causes of death in the United States. Of every 100,000 persons in this country, each year 11 choose suicide. In contrast, Hungary has 26.8 suicides per 100,000; Austria, 21.7; Czechoslovakia, 21.3; Finland, 19.2; West Germany and Sweden, 18.5; Switzerland, 16.8; Japan, 16.1; and France, 15.5. Most other countries report suicide rates lower than the United States, including Italy, 5.3, and Ireland, 2.5.

The most typical American suicide is a white Protestant male in his forties, married with two children. He is a breadwinner and a taxpayer. The sorrow his untimely preventable death brings to his family cannot be totaled, but the financial burden on his family and community is considerable. Costs begin with the city or county ambulance fee. The cost of the coroner's time and facilities soon follows. Widows' and survivors' benefits and insurance must be added. Then there is the heightened probability of subsequent indigent relief. Recent studies indicate that the surviving children of suicide victims more often require mental health care. Mental and physical care for a suicide's survivors usually must be provided by the city or county to whom the suicide has irrevocably bequeathed this responsibility.

Over the years, a suicide can cost his community at least $50,000. Counting all the taxes that he would have paid over the next quarter century, in the end, a suicide may cost his community a great deal more.

Why Do Men Kill Themselves?

For troubled men, each day is different. Why do men kill themselves? This is the first question asked by anyone who knew the person who committed suicide. Certainly he was tragically upset. But this alone does not explain why he took his own life. So many other people carry heavier burdens in their daily lives, yet persevere. What made this person different from those others? Why did he give up? Men have been puzzled by suicide for centuries. Only in the last 50 or 60 years, however, have any scientifically tenable explanations taken shape.

One theory still highly regarded today was proposed initially by the French sociologist Emile Durkheim, late in the nineteenth century. Suicide, he asserted, is the result of society's strength or weakness of control over the individual. According to Durkheim, there are three basic types of suicide, each a result of man's relationship to his society. In one instance, the "altruistic" suicide is literally required by society. Here, the customs or rules of the group demand suicide under certain circumstances. Historically, Japanese committing hara-kiri are examples of altruistic suicides. Hindu widows who willingly cremated themselves on the funeral pyres of their husbands were also examples of altruistic suicide. In such instances, however, the persons had little choice. Self-inflicted death was honorable; continuing to live was ignominious. Society dictated their action and, as individuals, they were not strong enough to defy custom.

Most suicides in the United States are "egoistic"—Durkheim's second category. Contrary to the circumstances of an altruistic suicide, egoistic suicide occurs when the individual has too few ties with his community. Demands, in this case to live, don't reach him. Thus, proportionately, more men who are on their own kill themselves than do church or family members.

Finally, Durkheim called "anomic" those suicides that occur when the accustomed relationship between an individual and his society is suddenly shattered. The shocking, immediate loss of a job, a close friend, or a fortune is thought capable of precipitating anomic suicides; or, conversely, poor men surprised by sudden wealth, have also, it has been asserted, been shocked into anomic suicide.[1]

As Durkheim detailed the sociology of suicide, so Freud fathered psychological explanations. To him, suicide was essentially within the mind. Since men ambivalently identify with the objects of their own love, when they are frustrated the aggressive side of the ambivalence will be directed against the internalized person. Psychoanalytically, suicide can thus be seen as murder in the 180th degree.

While these perceptive men, half a century ago, evolved their own distinctive theories to explain suicide, authorities today are melding these theories. As an outgrowth of Durkheim's original thinking, sociologists now feel they can explain suicide in the United States as partly resulting from the peculiarities of this culture. Dr. Herbert

Hendin has written that suicide is a "barometer of social tension."[2] The psychologists meanwhile understand suicide in terms of various levels of pressure on men, which sometimes parlay into suicide. Thus, a primary cause for suicide might be a traumatic experience during early childhood or youth, a physical handicap, or any of various fundamental psychological disturbances. An individual may be so affected by any of these primary problems, that his outlook, manner of thought, or perspective will sustain further impetus to commit suicide.

With these underlying tensions pulsing inside a person who is already somewhat suicidal, the end of a love affair, a failed examination, a serious illness, almost any unfortunate experience can precipitate an attempt at self-destruction.

Suicide Notes

Fortunately, no one is 100 percent suicidal. Psychologists today realize that even the most ardent death wish is ambivalent. People cut their throats and plead to be saved at the same moment. Suicide notes often illustrate the fatal illogic of the suicidal person, the mixing of cross-purposed desires: "Dear Mary, I hate you. Love, John." "I'm tired. There must be something fine for you. Love, Bill." These simple, but pathetic messages are actual suicide notes. Like the iceberg's tip above the surface, they hint at the awesome mass below. When a man is suicidal, his perspective freezes. He wants to live, but can see no way. His logic is confused, but he cannot clear his head. He stumbles into death, still gasping for life, even in those last moments when he tries to write down how he feels.

Though overflowing with genuine emotion, a suicide note is usually written with a specious logic that demonstrates the confusion of its author. These notes often instruct someone to do something in the future. There is the implication that the suicidal person will be there to insure that his orders are carried out. Other notes reflect a sad desire to punish persons close to the suicide, as if he would be able to observe the pity and tears he has created. Employing bizarre logic, still others identify their own death with suffering, and kill themselves because they are suffering.

No one knows what it is like to be dead. At best, one can only imagine what it would be like if one were alive to watch—an in-

visible personality—at one's own funeral. Often, such an attractive fantasy intoxicates the suicidal mind, and tips the scale to death. But until the very moment that the bullet or barbiturate finally snuffs out life's last breath—while the ground is rushing up—the suicidal person terribly wants to live. No doubt, he also wants to die. But it is an ambivalent wish—to die and to live. Until he dies, a suicide is begging to be saved. Before his death, the suicidal person leaves a trail of subtle and obvious hints of his intentions. Every suicide attempt is a serious cry for help.

This cry can be heard, and suicide can be prevented—reason enough for communities to establish suicide prevention services. Since people who kill themselves also want to live, and since their acute suicidal states are temporary—that is, given the opportunity to clear their heads, almost all would choose to live—help should be offered to the suicidal. The increasing financial cost of a suicide to a community simply underscores compassion's plea for suicide prevention. And there is yet another reason.

Prevailing Attitudes

The victims of suicide are not only those who die by their own hands. The families—the wives or husbands, brothers and sisters, parents, and especially the children—of a suicide are undoubtedly stigmatized. There is an onus associated with suicide that has nothing to do with the loss of life. A suicide in the family irrevocably affects the relatives. The mode of death forever after is mentioned by the family in whispers, if it is mentioned at all. They would rather their loved ones die of almost any other cause, no matter how painful or expensive. There is a taint, a stigma, an aura of shame that envelops the family of the suicide and marks even the closest friends and associates. The guileless remark, "her father committed suicide," is never forgotten by anyone who hears it. Suicide is never totally forgiven.

People have been killing themselves since the beginnings of recorded history, probably ever since there has been the species. Yet, the action has always been condemned, with only occasional and specific exceptions, by most other men. And suicide is still very much taboo today.

Probably the present attitude stems from the long history of suicide's condemnation. Suicide is and always has been an action

FACTS AND FABLES ON SUICIDE

FABLE: People who talk about suicide don't commit suicide.

FACT: Of any ten persons who kill themselves, eight have given definite warnings of their suicidal intentions.

FABLE: Suicide happens without warning.

FACT: Studies reveal that the suicidal person gives many clues and warnings regarding his suicidal intentions.

FABLE: Suicidal people are fully intent on dying.

FACT: Most suicidal people are undecided about living or dying, and they "gamble with death," leaving it to others to save them. Almost no one commits suicide without letting others know how he is feeling.

FABLE: Once a person is suicidal, he is suicidal forever.

FACT: Individuals who wish to kill themselves are suicidal only for a limited period of time.

FABLE: Improvement following a suicidal crisis means that the suicidal risk is over.

FACT: Most suicides occur within about three months following the beginning of "improvement," when the individual has the energy to put his morbid thoughts and feelings into effect.

FABLE: Suicide strikes much more often among the rich—or, conversely, it occurs almost exclusively among the poor.

FACT: Suicide is neither the rich man's disease nor the poor man's curse. Suicide is very "democratic" and is represented proportionately among all levels of society.

FABLE: Suicide is inherited or "runs in the family."

FACT: Suicide does not run in families. It is an individual pattern.

FABLE: All suicidal individuals are mentally ill, and suicide always is the act of a psychotic person.

FACT: Studies of hundreds of genuine suicide notes indicate that although the suicidal person is extremely unhappy, he is not necessarily mentally ill.

From *Some Facts about Suicide* by E. S. Shneidman and N. L. Farberow, Washington, D. C., PHS Publication No. 852, U. S. Government Printing Office, 1961.

that contradicts the valuation of human life, a basic democratic and social ethic. Throughout the years, various societies have responded to this insult by many crude and cruel means. The bodies of suicides have been dragged through the streets, hung naked upside-down for public view, and impaled on a stake at a public crossroads. The dead man could not be punished, of course. But his widow and children could be. Early English practice was to censure the suicide's family formally, deny the body burial in the church or city cemetery, and confiscate the survivor's property.

As a violation of one of the Ten Commandments, suicide has been called a crime against God, a heinous offense punishable in hell, of course, but also in man's courts.

Some Enlightenment

With the rise of humanism in the eighteenth century, attitudes toward the suicidal person shifted. He came to be seen, not as a malicious criminal, but as a lunatic. As such, he fared little better, though. The mentally disturbed have been treated as society's pariahs until only recently. Even today, they are not fully accepted.

But times and attitudes have changed. Scientists have come to take a more enlightened stand on suicide, notably in the last few decades. Although the act of suicide is still socially taboo in the Western world, fortunately education and mental health advances have encouraged its study, and the effective treatment of the suicidal has begun. Most of the early state laws outlawing suicide and punishing attempts have subsequently been revoked. Those still on the books are rarely enforced. The courts have begun to interpret suicidal deaths as results of mental disturbance. In the wake of current professional studies and news articles on their findings, the public is beginning to realize that suicides can be prevented.

Suicide Prevention Services

Americans have begun to hear the cries for help from their troubled relatives, neighbors, and friends. Suicide prevention services are being developed throughout the country. In 1966 the federal government established a national Center for Studies of Suicide Prevention within the National Institute of Mental Health (NIMH). Its purposes are many. The Center concentrates on catalyzing more active suicide prevention activities across the land. Both impetus

and information are offered to those communities considering suicide prevention. The Center supports further research into suicide—its clues, its causes, and, hopefully, its prevention. By emphasizing suicide research and training and by encouraging the growth of suicide prevention activities, it aims, hopefully, in the not too distant future, to reduce the number of suicides in the United States.

Finally, suicide prevention has become a science. Suicidology now attracts professionals of varied disciplines—psychology, psychiatry, sociology, social work, nursing, health education, and public health among others. Currently, Fellowships in Suicidology are being offered at Johns Hopkins University supported by a five-year grant from NIMH.

Early History

The path to this achievement was first roughly cut by devoted laymen and then it took years of paving. Motivated by the compassion of their usually nonprofessional founders, the first suicide prevention services in the United States began operating early in this century. Probably the original, and still well-known, suicide prevention operation is the National Save-A-Life League established in 1906 in New York City by the late Baptist minister, Harry Warren. His son, Harry Warren, Jr., now heads the League, essentially a lay organization. Boston's Rescue, Incorporated, is a church-sponsored suicide prevention service, organized in 1959 by Catholic Father Kenneth Murphy. Rescue, Incorporated, employs the volunteer services of 70 clergymen and professionals. Suicidal persons who have learned about these organizations through the local press frequently call them. The counselors then try to arrange personal interviews, use the basic techniques of psychological therapy, and, if necessary, refer the troubled callers on for psychiatric care.

These agencies have been effective, but hardly sufficient. With thousands of people intentionally killing themselves in this country every month, the need for more systematic suicide prevention on a national scale is obvious.

The Los Angeles Center

The first step in this needed direction was made in Los Angeles in 1958. With grants from the NIMH, the Los Angeles Center

slowly grew into the first full-scale, scientifically oriented suicide prevention operation. It has a staff of psychiatrists, psychologists, and social workers, plus a number of carefully selected and trained lay volunteers who help man the telephones. The Los Angeles Center's operation has become so widely known that during a typical month more than 500 persons contact the 24-hour suicide prevention service for help.

In recent years, suicide prevention activities have quickly spread across the country. In 1958 there were three comprehensive suicide prevention centers in operation. Today, less than a decade later, there are 100 functioning in 26 states. The trend continues. Hundreds of new services will be operating before another decade passes. The reason that so many are going to such lengths is easy to explain: *The lives of people who are suicidal can be saved.*

Clues to Suicide

Almost everyone who seriously intends suicide leaves clues to his imminent action. Sometimes there are broad hints; sometimes only subtle changes in behavior. But the suicide decision is usually not impulsive. Most often, it is premeditated. Although it might be done on impulse, and to others appear capricious, in fact, usually suicide is a decision that is given long consideration. It is not impossible, then, to spot a potential suicide if one only knows what to look for.

Fully three-fourths of all those who commit suicide have seen a physician within at least four months of the day on which they take their lives. When people are suicidal, a state of mind that comes and goes, there is no single trait by which all of them can be characterized. Always, however, they are disturbed, and often they are depressed. They feel hopeless about the direction of their lives and helpless to do anything about it. Under the mammoth weight of their own pessimism, they sink to their death.

Usually their attitude reflects itself in various verbal or behavioral "clues." Most obvious are the self-pitying cries of those who threaten, "I'm going to kill myself." They usually mean it, at least unconsciously. They just haven't decided how or when. If conditions in the suicidal person's life do not change, he will soon set the time and choose the method of his death. *All verbal indications should be taken seriously.* Dejected or angry asides such as "I want

to die. This is the last straw . . . my family would be better off without me . . . I won't be around much longer for you to put up with"—all are real clues to suicide, and too seldom taken as such.

There are also behavioral hints, some quite obvious. A suicide attempt, no matter how feeble or unlikely to succeed, is the starkest testimony of the suicidal state. "She just wanted attention," is the exasperated comment that often follows a suicide attempt. Indeed, that is exactly what she wanted. Without it, she may well succeed in her next attempt. Four out of five persons who kill themselves have attempted to do so at least one time previously. Of course, there are less pointed behavioral clues to suicide. Though not so readily discerned, they predict a suicide quite accurately. Once a person has finally decided to kill himself, he begins to act "differently." He may withdraw to become almost monklike and contemplative. He may drastically reduce eating or refrain from conversation and ignore normal sexual drives. He may either sleep more soundly or suffer from insomnia. He may have a will drawn up, or, often, act as if he were going on a long and distant trip. In the final days of his life, frequently he gives away what for him have been highly valued material possessions. College students give away their skis, watches, and cameras. Wealthier men and women make outright money grants of cash to relatives and friends.

Occasionally, the situation itself may be the final straw, and is the crucial indicator of imminent suicide. People already suffering from suffocating depressions often kill themselves on learning—or believing erroneously—they have a malignant tumor. Singly, any of these rather unexpected acts or remarks is not particularly significant, but clustered, they predict suicide.

These are the clues to suicide. They are not too difficult to recognize. But it is not so easy to determine just how close the troubled person actually is to a suicide attempt. Trained professional or volunteer staff members of any suicide prevention service can prevent a suicide.

The Phone Rings

Active suicide prevention begins when the telephone rings. Surprisingly few calls are made by cranks. Of all the calls received at the well-publicized Los Angeles Suicide Prevention Center, fully 99 percent are sincere. A third of them are made by people who,

though distressed, are far from actually attempting to take their lives. At least 10 percent of all calls are made by people moderately to seriously suicidal, and of these one out of six callers is on the verge of death.

When a worried man or woman calls the publicized telephone number of the suicide prevention service just to talk to someone, to share his problems, the staff person on duty begins immediately to assess the caller's degree of "lethality." Cold statistics help at the outset. The staff man knows that elderly, single men are more apt to commit suicide than young married women callers. He tries to evaluate the *stress* the person making the call is under. He asks questions gauged to uncover whether the caller is stable or not, if he has a history of suicide attempts, what his *life style* is, and if there are any symptoms that would indicate that suicide is imminent. Finally, and most important, the staff member must discover just how specific is the caller's *plan* to kill himself. Has he planned the day and hour of his suicide? And just how will he accomplish it? Here, it is important to know which method the caller has chosen; shooting one's self with a gun that lies loaded in the next room at the moment of the call is a much more lethal scheme than a vague plan to purchase some sleep medicine at a drug store.

A person who is vaguely considering ending it all may be quite serious. But the suicidal situation is not yet urgent. By contrast, an old man, depressed and lonely, withdrawn and confused, who plans suicide at a specific time with a gun or barbiturates now in hand presents a suicidal situation of extreme urgency to the suicide prevention worker.

These cases are the most serious at the moment of call. Here, the telephone therapist cannot hope to solve all the problems that a deeply troubled person faces. But even this highly imminent suicide can be averted, because suicidal crises can be managed. Professionally trained people who work in suicide prevention services realize that their goals must be limited. For the suicide prevention staff worker the primary goal is to stop the caller from killing himself, not to remake his personality. In most cases, the caller is suffering from any of a wide range of psychological problems, sometimes coupled to body ills. But curing all the caller's troubles, no matter how serious, is not the major intention of a suicide prevention service. When a man is foundering a lifeline must be thrown to him.

It is neither the time nor the task of the rescuer to teach the drowning man to swim or to improve his stroke. Thus, suicide prevention need have only limited mental health goals. Similarly, an active suicide prevention service has a limited goal. It provides a ready contact between the community's highly disturbed citizens and the established helping agencies which are available for them.

When a person calls to say that he or she is contemplating suicide, the voice of the suicide prevention worker on the other end can become the caller's lifeline. Callers have shot themselves to death while talking to a suicide prevention worker. Others have held loaded pistols to their temples.

The first telephone interview often spells the difference between life and death. The staff person who answers the phone must immediately establish some continuing communication with the caller, maintaining even the most tenuous of relationships. ("How did you get into this trouble?" he'll ask the caller. "What are some of the solutions that you've thought about?") At the same time, he begins to determine the lethality of the suicidal situation. ("Have you thought how you would do it?" "When?") As communication continues, the staff member must work toward establishing rapport with the caller while keeping the interview from becoming simply conversational. In fact, the caller must be made to feel he is being interviewed by a sympathetic, knowledgeable authority who can help.

If the situation is highly critical, the staffer must come up with an answer right there on the telephone. Frequently, with suicidal persons, life has lost its shadings. Every issue is either black or white, yes or no, life or death. Sometimes the caller can be persuaded to see his problem in a broader perspective. In other cases, the staff therapist might be able to "arrange" things for the suicidal caller. Simply setting up an interview with a staff psychiatrist, psychologist, social worker, or volunteer may provide the tension relief needed to ease a critical suicidal situation.

The Suicidal Crisis

Suicidal crises almost always concern two people: the suicidal person and the "significant other." The telephone therapist must determine who this is: father, wife, mother, lover, or whoever. Then an interview is arranged, if possible, to see both. It does little

good to counsel a suicidal person who will return a few hours later to the relationship that has just driven him to the brink of self-inflicted death. The "significant other" person in his life must be made aware of the situation, and, if possible, become involved in the life-saving efforts. In most cases, these "others" show surprise, concern, and a willingness to help—at least to some extent; in some cases, they must be disregarded or even circumvented.

Sometimes, really only a little help is needed during the period of the suicidal crisis. A person who verges on suicide also clings to life. All of his problems cannot be erased in a telephone call during the middle of the night to a staffman at a suicide prevention service. Should the posture of the "significant other" momentarily shift in this crucial relationship, there is no guarantee that the story will have a happy ending. But the suicide for the moment, has been averted. Fortunately, people are not permanently suicidal. Even for those whose daily lives are as gloomy as the black despair inside their minds, the suicidal mood ebbs and flows like the tides.

Suicide Research

Study of suicide begun during the early part of this century has evolved into study of its prevention. Authorities from a number of widely varying disciplines are contributing to man's knowledge on suicide. Research continues along avenues seemingly far apart. But their goals essentially are the same: to save lives and to improve mental health. While a range of specialists continues to refine the overall methods of suicide prevention, still another group of scientists is searching for the chemical links between man's mental and physiological circumstances.

One aim is to develop effective antidepressant drugs. NIMH Director Dr. Stanley F. Yolles believes that these drugs will help save the lives of potential suicides who are suffering from blinding depressions.[3] Three-quarters of them visit physicians within months of taking their lives. By training physicians to spot the clues to suicide and arming them with such drugs, suicidal crises can be postponed and suicides can be averted.

Of course drugs will not stop all suicides. However, if they help postpone the irrevocable act, suicide prevention activities will do the rest. Anthropologists, sociologists, health educators, philosophers, and social workers today work alongside psychiatrists and

psychologists in suicide prevention centers. Together, these professionals continue to shed new light on the subject even as they save the lives of the troubled people calling for help. Research continues on many fronts. For example, investigators are studying the relationship of sleep to suicide. Some people escape into long and peaceful sleep just before they kill themselves. Others suffer from insomnia. The key seems to lie in the quality of sleep and the individual's attitudes toward his own sleep.

Another body of research probes the tendency to suicide that may be related to an individual's peculiarities of reasoning. Suicide notes clearly indicate that many suicides are at least in part the result of faulty reasoning. Those whose thoughts are without shades of meaning will not consider depression a passing mood. When *life* is black, *death* is the only answer. Still others regularly employ a spurious logic that can trip them over life's edge.

Today's newly operating suicide prevention services are helping to explain why men kill themselves. Combined with biochemical advances toward eliminating depression, suicide prevention has begun to take effect. All of these activities aim at reducing the suicide rate in the United States. Before that happens, the nation's suicide rate may very well appear to rise. As suicide prevention takes hold across the country, more accurate and standard methods of reporting suicides will become the practice. *Reported* suicide totals may rise for a while.

Accurate Reports Needed

At present, suicide is not uniformly reported. What constitutes suicide in one county, city, or state is often not the same for the coroner in the neighboring area. Some coroners report as suicides only those deaths which are accompanied by suicide notes. In all cases, coroners and physicians are under pressure in their communities to certify suicides as accidental or natural deaths.

The families of suicide victims are loath to have self-inflicted death accurately reported. Many of them petition coroners to change their rulings to accidental or natural death. In three-quarters of these cases insurance money hangs in the balance. Some life-insurance policies will not pay their face value for death by suicide.

One method of improving suicide reporting is by "Psychological

Autopsy." This procedure was begun by Dr. Theodore Curphey, Los Angeles Chief Medical Examiner-Coroner.[4] The coroner may invite members of the local suicide prevention service to investigate a death if he is uncertain about certifying it as an accident or a suicide. Since it is now known that suicidal persons almost invariably leave clues to their intentions days or weeks before they act, these "death investigation teams" often accurately uncover the true mode of death. The clues are gleaned by carefully assessing the information gathered from interviewing members of the deceased's family, friends, coworkers, physicians, and others.

Death investigation teams attempt to discover whether the deceased actually *intended* to die during those last days of his life. If the investigators learn that prior to death the deceased was very depressed, had seen a physician recently, and had spoken or acted in such a way that had indicated he was suicidal, this can be established.

Sometimes, what appear to be suicides are actually accidental deaths. Death investigation teams in these cases help the family survivors avoid the stigma of suicide. But it is equally important that death by suicide be accurately certified. The scientific community demands accurate death certification, a crucial ingredient in further research. Suicide prevention requires honest reporting. Recording suicides accurately is fair to all citizens, and ultimately will help to improve the community's mental health.

Subintentioned Death

There is still another aspect of death which does not appear on death certificates today. This is the "subintentioned" death. Among the modes of death listed today—natural, accident, suicide, and homicide (called the NASH classification)—there is no space for the subintentioned death. But authorities now realize that those same pressures that work fatally on the victims of suicide sometimes move more subtly.

No one knows how many accidental and natural deaths are caused by the subintentioned wish to die. Some people want to die, but have not reached that state where they will act consciously on a suicidal desire. Instead, they begin to live more carelessly and unconsciously imperil their lives. A chronically ill person who stops taking his life-

saving medicine is an example. Depressed college students who drive recklessly are others. Fate, they seem to be saying, will make the crucial decision. But they are giving death the edge.

Generally today, these deaths are ruled as accidental. But it has been proposed that the prior attitude of the victim toward his death be assessed as *intentioned, subintentioned,* or *unintentioned*—and thus reported on the death certificate in addition to the usual cause and mode of death.

Some people are eating away at their own lives. If they do not have the resolve to commit suicide overtly, they can still offer up their lives to chance. Sooner or later, many of them will succeed in killing themselves . . . or *permit* some disease to kill them. Whether these subintentioned deaths are called accidental or natural, they are nonetheless results of death-oriented behavior. Suicide prevention efforts can also save many of these death-prone persons.

Community Service Planning

There is no doubt that carefully established suicide prevention services pay off in lives and money saved. Community mental health improves as a result. Each community should tailor a suicide prevention service to its own needs. It should be emphasized that there is no single pattern or organization yet proved to be overall better or more successful than another. A suicide prevention service can be organized to operate autonomously or as a unit of the community's mental health facilities. It can be part of an emergency hospital or tied to the local university or mental health clinic. However, it seems evident that the apparent pattern for the future is that many suicide prevention services will be an integral part of the community's comprehensive mental health center—a logical site for them. In any case, suicide prevention requires planning, interest, and time.

Ideally, any new service will be staffed with at least one, and, hopefully, two professional persons such as psychiatrists, psychologists, or psychiatric social workers. A professional psychiatric consultant should be available to the service at least for a few hours each week.

The rest of the staff may be nonprofessional volunteers. Experience has proved that lay volunteers can be very effective staff members *if* they are *carefully selected,* and *rigorously trained.* Gen-

erally, housewives who are mature, usually over 40, and have weathered psychological storms within their own lives are potentially good members. For example, women who have lost children through accident or disease and have since adjusted to these personal tragedies often are compassionate, resilient, and unafraid staff members. As a rule, it may be a good idea not to select people who have suffered psychotic breakdowns or who themselves at one time attempted suicide, or who appear overzealously interested in suicide.

A suicide prevention service cannot open shop all at once like a supermarket. Rather, the entire process, if it would be successful, must be gradually and tactfully woven into the community. From the beginning, the organizers must solicit help—at the very least, cooperation—from the city or county medical authorities. The hospitals, the coroner's office, and the police chief should know about the beginning of any suicide prevention service. In fact, suicide prevention needs their help. This is reasonable, since the new service ultimately will ease police and hospital emergency room work loads. But on occasion, the suicide prevention service will have to call on them for help. The local press, radio, and television should be informed about what's afoot and asked to cooperate. If a story breaks before the budding suicide prevention service is ready, this premature news could be disastrous.

Of course, the city government must know what plans are being made. If city officials are not the initial sponsors of such a community service, certainly their endorsement should be heartily pursued. Without local cooperation, successful suicide prevention is practically impossible.

Obtaining Funds

It is certainly impossible without adequate funds. There is no avoiding the hard fact that effective suicide prevention costs money. A carefully planned service will turn to every possible avenue for funds. Since the local citizenry will gain the most, they might be approached to help finance a new suicide prevention service. Local philanthropies, local government, and private citizens usually will contribute. There are many foundations in the country that aim their grants toward local mental health undertakings.[5] Suicide prevention services might also qualify for federal aid. As a com-

ponent of a comprehensive community mental health center, a new suicide prevention activity might qualify for NIMH construction and staffing funds under the Community Mental Health Services Act of 1963 (P. L. 88-164). Requests for federal support for suicide prevention, research, training, and demonstration (but not for direct service) may be sent to the Center for Studies of Suicide Prevention at the NIMH, Chevy Chase, Md.

Staff Training

Once the plans are off the ground, the local service staff must be trained. The team core of two professionals will find visits to currently operating suicide prevention operations both educational and stimulating. After a relatively brief period of such indoctrination, these core members will be able to select and train their volunteers. Their training, which must be allotted at least three months' time, might consist of required study of the literature on suicide coupled to more active indoctrination. In one form of training, called psychodrama, volunteers assume the roles of various types of suicidal persons and hold conversations with the staff therapist. Another method employs tapes of actual calls to operating suicide prevention services. A tape is stopped in the midst of the conversation, and a volunteer is asked how he would continue the handling of the call. By starting the tape again he can immediately check his response with that of an expert.

A name for the service must be selected—one that is easy to remember and comes straight to the point. Here, perhaps, it is better to be direct. Suicide should not be euphemized. The words *suicide prevention* could well be part of the organization's name, whether it is called a clinic, service, unit, office, corporation, foundation, institute, bureau, or center. A deeply troubled person on the verge of self-destruction usually has neither the patience nor the inclination to search through the telephone book trying to find the name of the organization designed to save his life. It would be a good idea to have the emergency suicide prevention telephone number listed at the front of the telephone book together with other emergency numbers.

Well before the service is ready to take calls, local community sources should be informed. Local physicians, clergymen, police, government officials, and businessmen's clubs should be told. At the

same time, the science writer for large newspapers or the city editors for smaller papers should be informed. The public will learn quickly about the new service.

A Beginning

Then calls will begin, and lives will be saved—which is, after all, the purpose of suicide prevention.

Today, hundreds of thousands of people are frightened and alone. They live in what Melville called ". . . a damp, drizzly November of my soul." For them it seems that death is closing in. They see no other way. Active, increasingly effective suicide prevention services offer the suicidal person a fresh grasp on life. They promise no panacea. Life's burdens will continue. But troubled men can persevere. The services now spreading across the country can show him that life is not so narrow—and, more importantly, that death is not the answer.

Suicide is a tragic and unnecessary waste. Fortunately now, it can, with appropriate measures, be prevented.

Chapter 8
RECENT DEVELOPMENTS IN SUICIDE PREVENTION
Edwin S. Shneidman

The national Center for the Studies of Suicide Prevention, recently established by the National Institute of Mental Health, is described. The primary goal of the NIMH CSSP is to effect a reduction in the suicide rate of this country. Four main routes to the reduction of suicidal deaths are proposed. A comprehensive ten-point national program—subsumed under the three broad categories of prevention, intervention, and postvention—is outlined.

This brief description of the NIMH Center for Studies of Suicide Prevention focuses on its current goals and the actual and potential resources it hopes to offer to individuals and institutions concerned with suicide prevention throughout the country.

The Center for the Studies of Suicide Prevention was established within the NIMH in 1966 to support the development of the nation's capability to prevent suicide. Within the NIMH, the Center represents a new concept for NIMH functioning. It is a center focusing on a substantive problem, embracing, as it were, the conceptual catchment area of self-destruction.

The goal of the NIMH Center for Studies of Suicide Prevention is to effect a reduction in the suicide rate of this country. Suicide is now the leading cause of unnecessary and stigmatizing deaths and a comprehensive national suicide prevention program is a first order of mental health business.

In general, there are four main avenues or routes to the reduction of suicidal deaths. They are:

1. *Increase the acumen for recognition of potential suicide among all potential rescuers.* The key to the reduction of suicide lies in recognition and diagnosis—the perception of the premonitory signs and clues. It is typical for most individuals who are suicidal to cast some verbal or behavioral shadows before them. Prevention lies in recognition. The task of early case-finding must be shared by both professionals and lay people. The "early signs" of suicide must be

known to each physician, clergyman, policeman, and educator in the land—and to each spouse, parent, neighbor, and friend.

2. *Facilitate the ease with which each citizen can utter a cry for help.* The tabooed nature of suicide must be recognized. Part of a successful program of suicide prevention lies in reducing the taboos and in giving a greater permissiveness to citizens in distress to seek help and to make their plight a legitimate reason for treatment and assistance.

3. *Provide resources for responding to the suicidal crisis.* Both facilities and personnel will be needed. The personnel will need to acquire relevant skills and appropriate attitudes. Management and treatment of the suicidal individual and his "significant others," within their own cultural setting, will be required to effect a reduction of the suicide rate.

4. *Disseminate the facts about suicide.* Much mythology and erroneous folklore exist concerning suicidal phenomena. One of the first tasks is to disseminate the solidly known facts (as opposed to the fables) to all citizens—in much the same way as health facts, about cancer, for example, have been publicized in this country.

In overview, the NIMH Center for Studies of Suicide Prevention will have five basic functions:

1. The Center will serve as the focal point within the Institute to coordinate and direct activities throughout the nation in support of research, pilot studies, training, information, and consultation aimed at furthering basic knowledge about suicide and improving techniques for helping the suicidal individual.

2. The Center will compile and disseminate information and training material designed to assist mental health personnel, clergy, police, educators, and others in obtaining a better understanding of suicidal actions and learning to utilize research findings.

3. The Center will assist in developing and experimenting with a variety of regional and local programs and organizational models to coordinate emergency services and techniques of prevention, case finding, treatment, training, and research.

4. The Center will maintain liaison with studies and programs on suicide prevention undertaken by other agencies, both national and international.

5. The Center will promote and maintain the application of research findings by state and local mental health agencies.

In the planning that preceded the establishment of the Center for Studies of Suicide Prevention in its present form, a ten-point comprehensive national suicide prevention program was outlined. The ten separate aspects of the national suicide prevention program were subsumed under three more general conceptual headings:

a. Prevention (to come *before*), that is, to do those things that will avert or ward off the inimical event or make it unnecessary or impossible to occur. This includes what is, in conventional public health parlance, called "primary prevention."

b. Intervention (to come *during* or *between*), that is, to do those things during the crisis that will mollify or reduce the intensity of the crisis or event that has already begun to occur; or to do those things that come between the present crisis and any possible future one, with the goal of making the occurrence of a future crisis less likely. This is conventionally referred to as "secondary prevention."

c. Postvention (to come *after*), that is, to do those things after the dire event has occurred that either (i) serve to mollify the aftereffects of the event in the victim, or (ii) deal with the inimical sequelae in other persons effected by the event (for example, in the case of committed suicide, to deal with the mental health needs of the survivor-victims). This is often called "tertiary prevention."

The ten aspects of the national program follow:

Prevention

1. *An active NIMH program of research and training grants.* This aspect of the comprehensive suicide prevention program would include stimulating, catalyzing, promoting, and supporting especially promising and needed research projects. Also, training grants should be made available for special training in suicide prevention, for regional training activities, symposia, and the like.

Pedestrian and repetitious studies especially should be avoided in the awarding of research grants. On the other hand, there are several special current interest and research areas in suicide in which research might very well be supported and interest in these areas might be stimulated. These include: adolescent and child suicides; biochemistry of suicide, including the study of stress and depression; stressful interpersonal relationships and suicide; cognitive aspects of suicide; the study of accidents, homicide, and self-destructive life styles; intensive longitudinal personality studies, especially

relating to inimical behaviors; suicide and terminal illness; the effects of environmental deprivation and stress; studies of the use of volunteer personnel; studies of various organizational and funding patterns for suicide prevention activities; studies of "psychological autopsies"; and the investigation of equivocal and unequivocal deaths.

The conceptual catchment area of a national prevention program is no less than the scientific study of self-destruction in man. It includes subtle (covert and subintentioned) forms of self-destruction as well as overt ones; it encompasses partial deaths and self-destructive behaviors as well as obvious suicide; and it should be concerned with global death and mass self-destruction as well as individual suicide. In short, it related to all the ways in which man, as an individual and in collectivities, truncates and demeans, as well as shortens, his finite life.

2. *Special programs for the "gatekeepers" of suicide prevention.* An important key to suicide prevention lies in detection and diagnosis. One of the most important findings from past experience is that practically every person who kills himself gives some verbal or behavioral clues of his intention to do so. These prodromal clues are often in "code," are cryptic or disguised, but nonetheless they are clues, and one can learn to recognize them. These are the "handles" to prevention. In practice, a variety of people hear the presuicidal clues—spouse, friend, neighbor, clergyman, policeman, bartender, physician, employer, and others; however, it is a most important fact that more than 65 percent of all individuals who commit suicide have seen a physician (usually a general practitioner) within four months of the event. It is therefore crucial to have a program for physicians in detecting and diagnosing potential suicides.

Special programs, tailor-made for clergymen, policemen, educators, and others, should also be prepared. It is planned to produce training materials addressed to these target groups in the form of appropriate brochures, long-playing records, films, programmed learning schedules, and special publications.

3. *Carefully prepared programs in massive public education.* This is probably the most important single item for effective suicide prevention and at the same time one of the most difficult to put into practice in ways that would be both acceptable and effective. One major avenue to the reduction of suicidal deaths is to use the lay

citizen for first-line detection and diagnosis. A rough model of such lay cooperation may be found in cancer detection, in which more and more citizens know the prodromal clues for cancer. The same model, with appropriate changes, might well be adopted in suicide prevention.

A study of mass public education might be done initially in a few carefully preselected communities. This study should involve experts in epidemiology, biostatistics, and especially in the communication media. This type of study should be preceded by a long-term comprehensive study of the actual state of suicidal (and suicidal equivalent) incidents in those areas. Public education should include planned and careful use of all the public media: schools, TV, newspapers, radio, advertisements, placards. Such education should be carried on in appropriate usual and unusual places, such as doctors' offices, pool halls, public lavatories, and the like.

One or two cities might be selected for large-scale pilot projects (or one or two sections of cities might be selected with equal catchment areas). The effects and effectiveness of such a program of public education should be observed through scientifically controlled studies. This can be achieved, in part, by selecting other cities (or sections of cities) that are comparable, in terms of the major variables, to the experimental cities.

Although such a program of mass public education would seem to be very important in any full-scale assault on the problem of suicide, the unanticipated effects of publicizing and popularizing the topic of suicide prevention would have to be constantly appraised during any mass-education efforts. We do not know what either the short-term or the long-term effects of such a program might be. These effects, in turn, become a legitimate subject for serious study in which consultants in sociology would play an important role.

Intervention

4. *Support of studies of special groups and the development of new techniques.* In addition to general support for a variety of research projects, there needs to be special focus and attention on certain issues or groups that, either because of their unusual interest or their paradigmatic character, merit special support. This category would include support for such topics as suicide among chil-

dren, the Negro, American Indians, the aged, college students, the addicted, and so on. In addition, there ought to be some special attention to the development of new and improved techniques for effectively offering help to the needful citizen: the scientific exploration and refinement of psychotherapy techniques for the suicidal person; the development of improved procedures for the delivery of services; the wider applications of currently known skills and procedures; the more effective use of existing and potential community resources; developing the special relationships that exist between suicide prevention efforts and the community mental health centers —to mention but a few.

5. *The development of a cadre of trained, dedicated professionals.* There do not exist, at present, trained professionals in sufficient number to man the proposed and projected projects in suicide prevention. There is an acute need for the creation of a core of individuals who might then direct and staff the suicide prevention programs in the NIMH central office, in the regional offices, and in the communities throughout the country. It should be pointed out that what is being proposed here is that individuals be given sufficient training in the basic ideas, facts, and skills relating to suicide and suicide prevention so that they can then act more meaningfully in their administrative and technical capacities. This aspect of the NIMH suicide prevention program will be implemented by establishing multidisciplinary Fellowships in Suicidology. These individuals must be carefully selected from those who have either done research in suicide or evinced a special interest in this field, and then given special opportunities for further training in suicidology. There is every reason to believe that such a program should be multidisciplinary. It would strengthen the program to have people with M.D.'s, Ph.D.'s, M.S.W.'s, and M.P.H.'s in such a program. The Ph.D.'s should come from a number of fields, especially psychology and sociology. The multidisciplinary aspect is especially important in that a variety of points of view are desired, a catholicity of interests is necessary, and the goal of this training is to provide administrative leadership, not primarily to create therapists in suicide prevention.

6. *Special programs for the selection and training of volunteers.* The manpower situation in suicide prevention is such that it not only makes good sense, but it is an operational necessity to employ other than paid or professional personnel as front-line responders of

initial contacts to a suicide prevention center. Further, it now seems apparent that nonprofessional persons, provided they are carefully screened, adequately trained and effectively supervised, can provide an excellent source of needed personnel. Whether or not one agrees with Dr. Louis Dublin that the introduction of the volunteer into the suicide prevention scene was the single most important development in the past several years, it nonetheless remains a fact that close attention to the possible use of volunteer personnel and careful study of improved methods for recruitment, selection, training, supervision, and evaluation of volunteers is an integral part of a comprehensive national program.[1]

Postvention

7. *A redefinition and refinement of statistics on suicide.* It is generally agreed that current statistics on suicide are grossly inadequate and that comparisons of suicidal incidents between cities, between states, and between countries, based on available figures, are at best sometimes inaccurate and often obfuscatory and misleading. The current inaccuracies are due to many reasons, including the following: (*a*) confusion as to how to certify equivocal deaths, as, for example, those that lie between suicide and accident; (*b*) dissembling on the part of police and physicians who wish to protect the family, and public officials who wish to protect the reputation of their community; (*c*) inaccurate record-keeping, in which the data that could be known and ascertained simply is not accurately tabulated; (*d*) the inadequacies of the present concepts. More will be said of this last point in the paragraphs below.

Two additional points should be made in relation to statistics: An opportunity exists in this program to introduce improved classifications and to conduct pilot studies to determine (for the first time) the veridical suicide rates in some selected communities; and further, the specter exists that unless there is a refinement of the concepts related to self-destruction, there will never be accuracy of reporting, because the present concepts are simply not strong enough accurately to reflect the events that they are purported to represent.

The NIMH Suicide Prevention Advisory Committee might suggest new concepts, a comprehensive program for uniform national record-keeping, and refinement and redefinition of statistics on self-destruction.

8. *A special program for followup of suicide attempts.* We know that about eight out of ten people who commit suicide have previously attempted or threatened it, but the data relating to the percentage of people who have attempted or threatened suicide and who subsequently commit suicide are contradictory and equivocal. The primary purpose of this program would be to prevent the committing of suicide. Some people who commit suicide do so the first time they attempt it, but the more common pattern is that of a series of attempts, with increasing lethality. Too many reports of suicide are of individuals who have been previously sewn up or pumped out and released, only to complete the task within hours. Like the program for the gatekeepers, and the support of suicide prevention centers, and the program in public education, this program also is meant to "nibble" at the suicide problem and to help effect a reduction in the suicide rate.

These studies might be conducted in two or three preselected sites at which the conditions are propitious for success, especially in cooperating hospitals, police departments, and public health facilities. The actual followup could be done by a variety of types of personnel, including public health nurses, social workers, psychologists, and the like. The data already available from the work of Robins, Tuckman, and Stengel would serve as a beginning for further and better understanding.[2]

There is great confusion about the relationship between attempted suicide and committed suicide. (This confusion exists largely because clinicians and investigators fail to think in terms of lethality. A suicidal event—whether a threat, an attempt, or a commission—is best understood in terms of its lethal intention, rather than its method.) We need to know the characteristics of those attempters who are highly lethal, as opposed to the characteristics of those with low lethality. Obviously, prevention of suicidal deaths lies in dealing with the former.

It might be well to pattern the followup proceduces for suicide attempts roughly after that of VD or TB followup, and look forward to the time when suicide attempt followup can be built into the Public Health Service. The followup could be seen as "postcrisis followup" and would be a legitimate aspect of a comprehensive approach to suicide prevention. It is known that the most dangerous period after a suicide attempt occurs within three months. A

followup procedure might be one effective way of saving some lives.

9. *A special followup program for the survivor-victims of individuals who have committed suicide.* It is not inaccurate to state that, from the point of view of the survivor, there are two kinds of deaths: all the deaths from cancer, heart ailment, accident, and the like, on the one hand, and suicidal deaths on the other. If one stops to consider the kind of grief-work and mourning an individual experiences on the death of a loved one who dies from a natural or accidental cause on the one hand and then thinks of the kind of grief one has to live with for the rest of his life if his parent or spouse has committed suicide, the contrast is clear. The individual who commits suicide often sentences the survivor to be obsessed for the rest of his life about the suicidal death. The suicide puts his skeleton in the survivors' psychological closets. No other kind of death in our society creates such lasting emotional scars as does a suicidal death. A comprehensive suicide prevention program should attend to the psychological needs of the stigmatized survivors, especially children who survive a parent who has committed suicide.

Although this aspect of the program is not especially directed toward reducing suicide, it nevertheless relates to the survivors of the suicidal death and is directly in the center of mental health concern. Today each citizen enjoys many rights in this country; we would hope that among these rights he might be granted the right to lead an unstigmatized life, especially a life unstigmatized by the suicidal death of a parent or a spouse.

Studies of the effects of suicides on survivors need to be done. Two kinds of studies immediately suggest themselves: retrospective studies of individuals one of whose family has committed suicide one, five, ten, or twenty years ago; and prospective studies of those who have experienced the suicide of a member of the immediate family in the very recent past. These studies would record the effects on the survivor through the years.

We do not at present know the "cost" of each suicide in terms of the deleterious mental effects on the survivors—how many survivors of a father's or a mother's suicide subsequently need mental hospitalization or other mental health care. To ascertain what these facts are, we need to develop special ways for effectively helping individuals who have suffered this kind of traumatic loss. Just as there are better and worse ways of responding, for example, to the

loss of a limb or to blindness, so we must develop better ways to help survivors respond to the grim facts of suicide in their family and thus to reduce the overall mental health toll.

Special research projects should be elicited, encouraged, and supported in the field of suicidal sequelae—that is, the effects of suicide on the survivors, and efforts should be made to mollify these effects.

10. *A rigorous program for the evaluation of the effectiveness of suicide prevention activities.* Quite obviously, it is an extremely thorny methodological problem in epidemiology to test or to prove the effectiveness of a program in suicide prevention. Nevertheless, efforts to evaluate effective suicide prevention activities must, from both a scientific and moral point of view, be a part of a comprehensive suicide prevention program from its very beginning. Without this feature of rigorous evaluation there can be no accounting by NIMH, either to itself or to Congress, or to the scientific communities.

This aspect of the program can be implemented best by consultation with people in biometry, in epidemiology, in sociological methodology, in research design, and in statistics.

The basic issues in a suicide prevention program are encompassed in this question: What can a local suicide prevention program do that will lower the suicide rate of the people of that community, and how can we find out whether this is being accomplished?

A priori, there are two kinds of criteria for judging the effectiveness of suicide prevention programs. The primary, and by far the more important criterion, is the reduction of suicidal deaths (and the unequivocal demonstration thereof). The secondary criterion (a large and potentially fruitful field for development) would include outcomes short of or different from the clear-cut demonstration of the saving of a life, but nonetheless relevant to the entire area of suicide prevention—especially as suicide prevention lies imbedded in the larger field of mental health. As a beginning, one might suggest the following as possibly relevant secondary criteria: a decrease in the lethality of an individual; an increase in his mental health or psychological well-being; a decrease in the taboo or stigma of suicide; an increase in the amount of coordination among the mental health agencies in the community; improved conceptualizations and methods for gathering data; increased dissemination of information relating to suicide prevention.

A program for evaluation cannot be tacked on to research efforts, but it must be built into the program from the beginning. The evaluation aspect of a comprehensive suicide prevention program is critical, both scientifically and morally, and should be one of the initial—and sustained—features of the program.

In suicide prevention, as in many other fields, needs usually run ahead of knowledge; urgency for service often precedes understanding. A comprehensive program for suicide prevention can therefore include immediate application of present knowledge, with the goal of saving lives. Just as there are fire stations throughout our country, there ought to be suicide prevention centers in every part of the land. Communities throughout the country should be encouraged to establish some kind of suicide prevention activity. We need immediately to initiate new life-saving activities. Even in our present state of knowledge, before we know all that we are going to learn, we know enough to feel confident that we can apply currently known facts and principles with a reasonable anticipation of reducing the suicide rate. The Community Mental Health Centers will, in many cases, furnish an excellent vehicle for relating suicide prevention activities to organized community programs.

It should be recognized that there will undoubtedly be a variety of organizational and funding models for suicide prevention activities, each growing out of the needs and peculiarities of the local community. Some suicide prevention units will be operated in conjunction with a general hospital, some with an emergency room, a psychiatric clinic, or a welfare bureau, and some will operate autonomously. NIMH's responsibility may best be discharged by its serving in a consultative capacity to requesting communities as they plan the services especially suited to their needs.

The ten-point program for suicide prevention outlined above is a mutual enterprise whose successful development depends on the active interest, support, and activities of suicidologists throughout the country.

PART III
STATISTICS
AND DEMOGRAPHY

Chapter 9
A PSYCHOLOGICAL APPROACH TO THE STUDY OF SUICIDE NOTES
Edwin S. Shneidman and Norman L. Farberow

This study focuses on the stability and meaningfulness of the Mowrer Discomfort-Relief Quotient (DRQ) by comparing two sets of written documents: a group of thirty-three genuine suicide notes and an equal number of matched simulated suicide notes, the latter elicited from nonsuicidal subjects. The main findings of this comparison indicate that the genuine suicide note is characterized by a relatively greater amount of hate-of-other and self-blame and by attempts to leave specific instructions and restrictions on those left behind. The use of the DRQ itself, as a technique for studying suicidal phenomena, seemed to be of limited usefulness.

Purpose

The selection of the optimal mode of analysis of such psychological materials as personal documents, thematic protocols, case work records, psychotherapy sessions, and the like, often poses a serious methodological problem for many psychological investigators. The Discomfort-Relief Quotient, with which Mowrer's name is closely associated, offers a succinct method for noting comparisons either between sessions of the same individual or among different subjects.[1] Mowrer's technique divides any content under study into thought units that are scored for their discomfort, relief, or neutral quality; the DRQ is obtained by finding the ratio of the discomfort units to the discomfort plus relief units. Mowrer's own published researches with the DRQ seemed to be encouraging and seemed to point up the usefulness of this device. However, one of the few publications dealing with an application of the DRQ to a grossly disturbed group of subjects yielded rather equivocal results in that the DRQ was found to be uncorrelated with tension in these psychotic subjects. The effect of these paradoxical results was somewhat mollified in light of the interpretation that schizophrenics may not feel or show discomfort or anxiety as it would be felt or shown by disturbed nonpsychotic subjects.

The present study seeks to shed additional light on the stability

and meaningfulness of the DRQ by comparing two sets of written documents: a group of genuine suicidal notes, and a group of "suicide" notes elicited by us from nonsuicidal subjects. There are, thus, two purposes of the present study: one, to measure the usefulness of the DRQ concept for these materials; and two—if the DRQ is useful—to obtain additional information about the phenomena of suicide.

Materials and Subjects

It should be stated here that the present study is only one aspect of a larger project.[2] In the course of a long-term study on suicide being conducted in the Los Angeles area, suicide notes, psychological tests, and psychiatric case history data on persons who had committed suicide were collected. This paper is concerned with the suicide notes, the method of analysis of which presented a serious problem of choice. Mowrer's method seemed potentially fruitful and was attempted. The notes are being analyzed from several other theoretical points of view as well.

For this study two groups of thirty-three notes were used. Group 1 consisted of genuine suicide notes, written by individuals just before they took their own lives (and found by the police). Group 2 consisted of notes, written by nonsuicidal and nondepressed subjects, who, at the authors' request, wrote the "suicide" note that they would write assuming they were at the point of taking their own lives. These latter elicited notes are called "simulated" notes.

The genuine notes were secured from the Los Angeles County Coroner. That office keeps a file on every suicide committed in Los Angeles County. With the kind permission of the Coroner, 721 suicide notes have been collected to date from the folders of about 7,000 suicides in Los Angeles County in the last ten years.[3] In the present sample, one in every seven individuals who commit suicide, or about 12 to 15 percent, leave suicide notes. Prior analysis of the data, however, has shown that individuals who leave notes are almost identical in economic, social, cultural, and personal factors with those who do not leave notes.

Procedure

Employing the logic of Mill's Methods of Difference and of Residues, that is, attempting to ascertain what it was that characterized

suicidal notes not per se, but over and above other written communications,[4] the design of the experiment called for comparison with nonsuicidal suicidelike notes. These seemed to offer the most potentialities for a pointed and relevant comparison.

For the present investigation, the aim was to compare two groups as homogeneous as possible. For this reason thirty-three subjects who were male, Caucasian, Protestant, married, native-born, and between the ages of 25 to 59 were selected from among the more than 700 genuine note writers. The comparison subjects, also thirty-three in number, were matched from all these variables, employing a man-for-man matching system in which each genuine note writer had a simulated note writer counterpart who was within five years of his age and whose occupation was identical or at least in the same general occupational class. The simulated notes were obtained from such diverse sources as labor unions, fraternal organizations, and universities. Recognizing the moral and ethical overtones associated with the topic of suicide, certain precautions were exercised. Each subject was first given a short personality questionnaire and any indication that he had ever been depressed, emotionally disturbed, or would be perturbed by having to think of suicide, led to his being asked, instead, to write about the happiest experience of his life. If he indicated that he would not be upset by such a request he was asked to write the note he would write "if he were about to take his own life."

In terms of procedure, the sixty-six notes were typed and coded and then scored, without knowledge of the true category of the note, by the present authors for discomfort thought units, relief thought units, and neutral thought units according to Mowrer's method.

Results

The results will be discussed under two headings: first, the interrater reliability in scoring all the notes in terms of discomfort, relief, and neutral thought units; and second, the comparisons between the genuine and simulated suicide notes on the basis of joint scoring.

For purposes of determining reliabilities, all sixty-six notes were employed. Two raters were involved. The first step in determining the interrater reliability was to find the number of separate thought

units in each note that was agreed upon as a thought unit. In the sixty-six notes, one rater found a total of 600 thought units and the other rater found 619. Of these, 528 thought units, or 86 percent, were rated in common. Of these 528 thought units, 375 or 71 percent were scored identically by the two raters as discomfort, relief, or neutral. Chi square (from the three-by-three table) was 154.73—far in excess of the .01 level of significance, and indicated that the interrater scoring was similar beyond chance. By use of Tschuprow's formula,[5] the significance of the agreements between the two raters in scoring the individual thought units was next determined and found to be .38—indicating a fair amount of agreement between the two raters that was real or true.

The differences between the genuine and simulated notes were next examined. At this point the two raters pooled their judgments and arrived at a single DRQ label for each thought unit in each of the sixty-six notes. Considerable help in this was obtained from a sample scoring of a few of the notes as scored by Dr. Mowrer in a personal communication.[6] These samples served as models for the scoring of notes whenever any differences of opinion arose.

The total number of mutually agreed-upon thought units was 553. Of this total there were 369 in the thirty-three genuine notes and 184 in the thirty-three elicited notes; the χ^2 was 8.7, significant beyond the .01 level and indicating that the genuine note writers expressed significantly more discomfiture.

For the relief statements, the genuine notes had sixty-five and the pseudo had thirty-four; the χ^2 was .06, which was not significant, indicating that neither the genuine nor the simulated notes contained more relief.

For the neutral statements, the genuine notes had seventy-eight and the pseudo had thirteen; the χ^2 was 17.7, significant beyond the .01 level and indicating that the genuine note writers expressed a significantly greater number of neutral statements. The content of these neutral statements typically had to do with giving instructions and admonitions and sometimes included lists of things to do.

In comparing the DRQ's the genuine note quotient was .78 and the pseudo note quotient was .80. The critical ratio was not significant.

Discussion

In this paper, the discussion of the suicide notes will be solely in terms of Mowrer's concepts of discomfort, relief, and neutral thought units. The tentative and limited nature of these findings—based as they are on only thirty-three suicidal notes—should be kept in mind. Another caution is that only about 12 to 15 percent of all individual's who commit suicide in Los Angeles County leave notes. Thus, there may be undetermined sampling errors, although a comparison of available statistical data such as sex, race, age, nativity, religion, and the like, indicated that the groups were similar in these respects.

In terms of the similar quotients, Mowrer says that the DRQ indicates drive. He states: "It is the record of all the tensions that creep into the record." According to the above results, it would appear either that individuals can empathize with the suicidal state quite accurately even to the point of simulated affect, or that the quotient, itself, is not as sensitive a measure as one might need for a suicidal-pseudosuicidal note comparison.[7]

The larger number of neutral statements on the part of the genuine note writers may indicate an unrealistic feeling of omnipotence and omnipresence on the part of the suicidal individual. One individual who committed suicide stated: "You are to cremate my body. This is an order." This statement almost epitomizes the illogicality of the entire suicidal deed: to think simultaneously (and contradictorally) of killing oneself and of giving orders as though one were going to be present to enforce them.

Not only was there a greater amount of discomfort shown by the genuine suicide notes (according to the number of thought units), but when the difference in the quality of affect of the discomfort statements between the two groups was analyzed, it was noted that the discomfort statements in the genuine notes were characterized more by deeper feelings of hatred, vengeance, and self-blame as compared with the more mildly negative statements of the simulated note group. Thus, the quality of the discomfort statements is not accurately represented in the Mowrer scoring system.

Summary

The Mowrer concepts of discomfort and relief and the DRQ seem

to be interesting but of limited value for the study of suicide by means of suicide notes.

Within the limits of the usefulness of Mowrer's concepts to the present data, it is possible to state that the suicidal person is an individual who, when he is really faced with the prospect of seriously considering leaving this world, departs with a blast of hate and self-blame and an attempt to leave definite instructions and restrictions on those he has purposely left behind.

Chapter 10
SUICIDE AND AGE
Norman L. Farberow and Edwin S. Shneidman

Are there stable relationships between chronological age and under-lying suicidal psychodynamics? A number of suicide notes—489 from men and 130 from women, divided into three age groups (20 to 39, 40 to 59, and 60 and over)—were analyzed in terms of Menninger's three concepts of the wish to kill, the wish to be killed, and the wish to die. In general, for both sexes, the intensity of the wish to kill and the wish to be killed decreases with advancing age, while the intensity of the wish to die increases with age. The constellations of psychodynamics motivating individuals to commit suicide seem to be different in each of the three major age groupings.

Suicide is a phenomenon that does not limit itself to any particular age. Statistics show it as an ever-increasing proportionate problem with the advance in age, the phenomenon occurring in all ages from the young child to the very old adult. There are many speculations about the psychodynamics of suicide. It has been noted, in our examination of these formulations, that there have been no differentiations in these theories for the age of the suicidal person, the assumption generally being made such psychodynamic formulations as are proposed apply to all suicides regardless of age. The authors' investigations to date have caused them to question this assumption, and this study is an attempt to determine whether the question raised, that is, whether the dynamics, or the pattern of dynamics, varies with the age of the suicidal subject, is a legitimate and necessary one.

The material used in this particular study to investigate this question consisted of suicide notes obtained from the Los Angeles County Coroner's Office. Of the more than 700 notes collected covering the years from 1944 to 1953, 619 notes, consisting of all the notes written by the male and female, Caucasian, native-born suicide-note writers, were examined in this study.[1] The males (489 notes) ranged in age from twenty through ninety-six, while the females (130 notes) ranged in age from twenty through seventy-eight.

For this study, a number of the various theories most frequently found in the psychiatric and psychologic literature were examined. On the basis of this survey, Karl Menninger's theory of suicide, as described in his book *Man Against Himself*, was selected.[2] This theory lent itself to the purpose of the present study; that is, it broadly categorized the assumed psychodynamic motivations underlying the act of killing oneself, and the motivations were readily inferred from the raw data of the study—the suicide notes. Menninger's theory states that there are three components to the suicidal act and that all are present in varying degrees in any given case. These three components are (1) the wish to kill, (2) the wish to be killed, and (3) the wish to die. In translating these three components operationally, considerable help was obtained from a written communication from Dr. Menninger in which he stated, ". . . I think you might use as a very rough criterion, conscious hate, conscious guilt feelings, and conscious hopelessness, or discouragement as roughly determining the three components that I suggested." In further describing his three factors in his book, Menninger uses additional descriptive terms, such as, for "wish to kill"—aggression, accusation, blame, eliminating, driving away, disposing of, annihilating, and revenge; for "wish to be killed"—submission, masochism, self-blame, and self-accusation; and for "wish to die"—hopelessness, fear, fatigue, and despair. References to illness and pain as motives for doing away with the self were included in the last component.

All 619 notes were grouped according to the age of the writer into three age groups, twenty to thirty-nine, forty to fifty-nine, and sixty and over, or what might be broadly conceived as young, middle-aged, and older groups (Table 1). The notes were then classified under one of the above three categories, or in an unclassifiable

TABLE 1

DISTRIBUTION OF MALE AND FEMALE SUICIDE-NOTE WRITERS
ACCORDING TO AGE

Ages	Male	Female	Total
20-39	99	38	137
40-59	215	52	267
60+	175	40	215
Total	489	130	619

category if the note did not give enough information to allow any classification. Though Menninger hypothesizes that all three of these factors, in varying strengths, are present in each suicidal act, the procedure was followed of classifying each note in terms of one component, that is, the major, predominant motive that was judged to be expressed. This was done to focus more clearly on any changes in motivations that might appear in the notes for the various ages.

The following notes are examples of the four rubrics into which all of the notes were categorized. They are not chosen as characteristic of any particular age group, but are selected to illustrate each of the categories.

Wish to Kill
> *Male, married, age 53.*

1.

I hereby Will all the property to my son, anything that you can get as Jane did not have anything in the place. She just took me for a ride. If she gives you any trouble find Joe as she has checked up on Jim and a lot of other. See Jack 1000 Main Street. She will tell you or her little girl that Oscar and her have been living together out at her place as man and wife. Also go to the Beach and see how long her and Jim lived here as man and wife. You know where I said to look. I have 2 small policys (that Insurance I mean) they made out to you.

> *John Smith*

2.

Jane:

You 25¢ chippy I hope this makes you happy. All the time that you could spend here you had to be shacked up with someone else. Now you tell me to get the hell out from the bar. You have brought this on your self. When ever you think that you can be married to me 9 mo. and only live with me 1½ mo. the rest of the time you have been sleeping with some one else. I could go from here to and through the state of Washington and find out with who and what day & nite you spent with some other man, and now you are telling me to get the hell out.

> *John*

Wish to Be Killed

  Female, married, age 24.

I've proved to be a miserable wife, mother and homemaker—not even a decent companion. Johnny and Jane deserve much more than I can ever offer. I can't take it any longer. This is a terrible thing for me to do, but perhaps in the end it will be all for the best. I hope so.

Mary

Wish to Die

  Male, divorced, age 50.

To The Police—

This is a very simple case of suicide. I owe nothing to anyone, including the World; and I ask nothing from anyone. I'm fifty years old, have lived violently but never committed a crime.

I've just had enough. Since no one depends upon me, I don't see why I shouldn't do as I please. I've done my duty to my Country in both World Wars, and also I've served well in industry. My papers are in the brown leather wallet in my gray bag.

If you would be so good as to send these papers to my brother, his address is: John Smith, 100 Main Street.

I enclose five dollars to cover cost of mailing. Perhaps some of you who belong to the American Legion will honor my request.

I haven't a thing against anybody. But, I've been in three major wars and another little insurrection, and I'm pretty tired.

This note is in the same large envelope with several other letters— all stamped. Will you please mail them for me? There are no secrets in them. However, if you open them, please seal them up again and send them on. They are to the people I love and who love me. Thanks.

George Smith

Unclassifiable

  Female, widowed, age 70.

In case of my death notify Charles Smith, Smith Funeral Home, 100 Main Street.

This letter to be opened by him.

Mary Jones

It is my wish that my funeral be strictly private. Just a minister to say a prayer for me.

TABLE 2

NUMBER AND PERCENTAGES OF 489 MALE SUICIDE NOTES CLASSIFIED
ACCORDING TO MENNINGER'S HYPOTHESIS

Ages	To Kill		To Be Killed		To Die		Unclassifiable	
	Number	%	Number	%	Number	%	Number	%
20-39	31	31	27	27	23	23	18	18
40-59	50	23	35	16	75	35	55	26
60+	20	11	18	10	99	57	38	22
Total	101	21	80	16	197	40	111	23

The notes were classified independently by the two authors and the reliability of their ratings was checked by means of a χ^2 analysis. A four-by-four contingency table was formed, in terms of the four categories used. That the two judges agreed quite well in their classification of the notes is shown by the fact that the obtained χ^2 was 751.47, which, for 9 degrees of freedom, is significant beyond the .001 level. When the obtained χ^2 is expressed in terms of Tschuprow's coefficient,[3] a value of .64 is obtained, which constitutes a substantial correlation. After reliability in scoring was ascertained, those notes in which discrepancies in scoring had appeared were reread, and the differences resolved so that a single classification was obtained. The percentage of notes scored as wish to kill, be killed, to die, or unclassifiable were then computed for each age group of note writer. These results may be seen for males and females in Tables 2 and 3 respectively.

The general trend for each of the components indicated that the two factors, the wish to kill and the wish to be killed, decreased with age, and the factor, wish to die, increased with age. The category of

TABLE 3

NUMBER AND PERCENTAGES OF 130 FEMALE SUICIDE NOTES CLASSIFIED
ACCORDING TO MENNINGER'S HYPOTHESIS

Ages	To Kill		To Be Killed		To Die		Unclassifiable	
	Number	%	Number	%	Number	%	Number	%
20-39	12	32	8	21	8	21	10	26
40-59	15	29	9	17	15	29	13	25
60+	6	15	2	5	30	75	2	5
Total	33	25	19	15	53	41	25	19

"unclassifiable" was scored for about one-quarter of the notes for each age group.

The specific trend for each of the individual motives for the male suicide-note writers showed that the wish to kill appeared in 31 percent of the notes of the young group, declined to 23 percent for the middle age group, and then fell to 11 percent in the notes of the older group. The differences between the proportions in the various age groups indicated no significant difference between the young and the middle age group, but the differences between the middle age and the older groups, and between the young and older age group, were statistically significant (Table 4).

TABLE 4

CRITICAL RATIOS BETWEEN PROPORTIONS OF AGE GROUPS OF MALE
AND FEMALE SUICIDE-NOTE WRITERS

Age Groups	To Kill		To Be Killed		To Die	
	M	F	M	F	M	F
Young—middle age	1.47	0.30	2.15*	0.48	2.25*	0.88
Middle age—older	3.23†	1.66	1.78	1.92	4.43†	4.95†
Young—older	3.83†	1.80	3.40†	2.15*	6.02†	5.68†

* A t value of 1.968 is necessary for significance at the 5% level.
† A t value of 2.592 is necessary for significance at the 1% level.

The wish to be killed appeared in 27 percent of the notes of the young group, fell to 16 percent for the middle age group, and then to 10 percent for the older group. The differences between the proportions for the young and the middle age and between the young and the older groups were found to be statistically significant, but the difference between the middle age and the older groups was not.

The wish to die appeared in 23 percent of the notes of the young group, increased to 35 percent for the middle age group, and rose to 57 percent in the older age group. Here, all the differences between the various age groups were found to be statistically significant.

At first glance, the general trend for the women's notes seems to follow somewhat the same pattern, with the wish to kill and to be killed decreasing with advancing age and the wish to die increasing with advancing age. The difference between these proportions, however, is statistically significant only between the young and the older group for the factor "wish to be killed," and between the middle

age and the older, and the young and the older, age groups for the factor, "wish to die" (Table 4).

It is apparent that the results of this study emphasize the meaningfulness of the question raised at the beginning of this chapter; that is, that the pattern or the constellation of the various dynamics motivating the suicidal person tends to show marked shifts depending on his age. The pattern for the male suicide-note writers, particularly, changes with age. As may be seen from Table 2, the younger males are expressing all the factors fairly equally—31, 27, and 23 percent for wish to kill, to be killed, or die, respectively. The older males, however, are expressing the wish to kill and to be killed only 11 and 10 percent of the time, respectively, while the wish to die appears in 57 percent of their notes. Another way of stating this is by combining the data for the wish to kill and to be killed (the intense affects) and contrasting these with the percentage for the wish to die (the more chronic and less intense affect). The younger males then show the wish to kill and be killed in 58 percent of their notes and the wish to die in 23 percent. The pattern reverses itself in the older age group with 21 percent and 57 percent, respectively. One must conclude that the younger males, between twenty and thirty-nine, apparently are much more concerned than the older males, sixty and above, with the highly charged, more affect-laden, and, at the same time, more transient motives, "kill" or "be killed." They are inclined to be much more intensely angry and hostile, full of hate and bitterness toward another person; or more depressed, self-disparaging, self-abasing, and guilt-ridden than the older males. In the suicide of older men these more interpersonal motives seem to decrease in intensity and the affect shifts to the less acute but more chronic feelings of discouragement—pain, illness, mild despair, and so on. The older suicide is tired, either of life or of pain and suffering, and he writes that he is physically and/or mentally exhausted. The scores of the middle age group point up the trends in the shifts of these motives, showing that the anger and hostility tend to persist longer and to appear in the notes fairly often through the age of fifty-nine, before the frequency begins to lessen noticeably. On the other hand, the guilt and self-blame lessens markedly by age thirty-nine and then does not decrease much more after that.

While for the female suicide-note writers the pattern does not

show the same distinct shifts in all factors as for the male note writers, there are the same relative shifts in the patterns for the various age groups (Table 3). Thus, the younger females also show somewhat the same percentages of motives—32, 21, and 21 for wish to kill, to be killed, and to die, respectively, and then a very marked shift in the older age group to percentages of 15, 5, and 75, respectively. Or again, it might be stated that the wishes to kill and to be killed appear in 53 percent of the notes as contrasted to 21 percent for wish to die for the younger females, with the pattern reversing itself even more markedly, with 20 and 75 percent, respectively, for the older females.

However, viewed from age group to age group, the feelings of anger and hostility do not change remarkably (statistically) with advancing age, but tend to persist in somewhat the same proportions regardless of whether the woman is young, middle-aged, or old. The older women do tend, however, to show much less guilt and self-blame, and considerably more discouragement, despair, feelings of being a burden, and depressed feelings about pain and illness than the younger women. Again the middle age group gives some clues as to the time when these shifts occur. Their scores indicate that it is at age sixty and above that guilt decreases to a point significantly less than the younger group expresses, and that the decline up to that age is a gradual and apparently steady one. The despair and discouragement increase tremendously once age sixty is passed, whereas from ages twenty to fifty-nine there is not too much difference in its presence as a motive for the destruction of the self.

Some words of caution should be expressed at this point. One cannot help but wonder whether the results would have been changed much if it were possible to know the motives in the "unclassifiable" notes. Twenty-three percent and 19 percent male and female notes, respectively, could not be classified, and if these notes had fallen primarily into any one of the other categories, they would have caused a marked change in the pattern. Certainly, this must be kept in mind in drawing any conclusions. However, the trends themselves seem remarkably consistent and the probability must also be considered that the already noted trends might have been further emphasized. One other caution to be kept in mind is that these results are based upon a "selected" sample, namely, suicide-

note writers. In Los Angeles County, note writers make up around 15 percent of the total number of people who commit suicide and may not actually be representative of the total group. However, comparisons of sociologic, economic, and other available statistics indicated that the suicide-note writers seemed to be similar to the entire group of suicidal individuals in Los Angeles County for the period studied.

It should be stated here that the results of this study do not in any way indicate that Menninger's hypotheses are invalid for different ages. This study is not designed to test the validity of this theory, but simply takes advantage of its operational usefulness in serving as a vehicle for examining the motives expressed in the notes. As stated earlier, Menninger emphasizes that these are elements that are all present in all suicides, but in varying degrees, a fact that actually is verified by the date. These results do stress the important fact, however, that apparently the pattern of the motives shifts and that there is a relationship between these changes with differences in age. They also point to a need to reexamine and to modify the current theories about suicide in order to take into account the variations in the constellations of dynamics of the suicidal patient, depending upon his age. It seems possible to draw some immediate practical implications for treatment and management of the suicidal person.

In general, when persons between twenty and thirty-nine years of age come to the attention of the therapist because of suicidal urges or attempts, the therapist might expect to find the more intense interpersonal motives operating in over half of his patients, while the chronic depressive feelings will be dominant in only about one-quarter of the cases. The method of choice for treatment, once the necessary medical measures have been taken, seems to be a type of dynamic psychotherapy. The aim would be to provide patients with the opportunity for working out and gaining insight into the tensions and the intense feelings that had been operating in their interpersonal relationships. In the case of older patients, both male and female, the therapist must be prepared to institute more of the environmental and milieu therapy and to treat with the purpose of offering a great deal of physical relief for pain and suffering. In addition to providing analgesics and sedatives, he

must be prepared to offer much support aimed at relieving feelings of discouragement, of uselessness, and of being a burden. This means he may have to take a much more active part than generally he might by actually entering into the patient's environment in dealing with relatives and friends in helping to reestablish fading environmental bonds and lost feelings of usefulness and belonging.

Chapter 11
SUICIDAL AND NONSUICIDAL HEROES
Edwin S. Shneidman and Norman L. Farberow

The Thematic Apperception Test (TAT), analyzed in terms of attributes of the story heroes, is used to explore suicidal thoughts and feelings. Suggestions are made for modifications of the picture thematic technique in the exploration of human self-destructiveness.

This article presents a report of the results of some Thematic Apperception Text (TAT) data obtained from subjects who either attempted or committed suicide and compares them with a similar data obtained from nonsuicidal subjects. It is interesting to note, after surveying the literature on the TAT, that this preliminary report is among the very few papers on the topic of suicide and the TAT. This is all the more surprising when one considers that an individual's attempting or committing suicide offers an unusual, although tragic, opportunity for comparing psychological test results with an incontrovertible behavioral variable. This is not to deny the fact that the "incontrovertible behavioral variable"—that certain individuals have committed suicide—in itself reflects a complex set of phenomena, and that there are thorny methodological problems involved in relating a series of fantasy projections to a multidetermined behavioral variable. Nevertheless, the reasons for the relative neglect of this important area are likely to be found in the difficulty in obtaining the data, rather than in the lack of importance of the topic.

Literature

That portion of the TAT literature directly concerned with suicide can be cited in terms of a relatively small number of references. There are, first off, some published clinical reports of individuals, for whom TAT protocols are available, who attempted or committed suicide. Holzberg, Cahen, and Wilk presented the case history and psychological test data (TAT, as well as a Rorschach, Wechsler-Bellevue, Draw-A-Person, P-F Study, and MMPI) on one 24-year-old male who was tested three days before he committed suicide.[1] Tomkins, in his text on the TAT, discusses

suicide as one of the possible sequelae of the disrupted relationship
(pages 164 through 170) and, in addition, presents a most instructive intense analysis of one TAT protocol that contains suicidal
content in one story but not in the others (pages 184 through 194).[2]
Rizzo, in an Italian journal, presents one case of an attempted
suicide in which the TAT (and the Rorschach test) are compared
with data from narcoanalysis and existential analysis. The abstract
of this article—the article itself was not seen—states cryptically
that "agreement could not be reached."[3] Finally, Kahn has presented a paper, for which there is a published abstract, in which he
compared the clinical data of two attempted suicide patients. These
data included the TAT, the Rorschach test, and his own Symbol
Arrangement test. He reports that "there was general agreement
among the test findings. . . ."[4]

There are very few research studies involving the TAT and
suicide. Broida obtained the responses to TAT Card 3BM (as well
as to Card IV of the Rorschach and the D scale of the MMPI) from
twenty "known suicidal" mental hygiene clinic subjects and an
equal number of nonsuicidal controls, matched for age, diagnostic
classification, educational level, and the like. In terms of the TAT
results, he found no difference in thema between the responses of
the two groups of subjects to the one TAT card.[5] Crasilneck, in an
unpublished dissertation, indicated that he studied sixty-six subjects hospitalized subsequent to a suicidal attempt. The TAT was
administered, in addition to the Wechsler-Bellevue and the Rorschach test. His two groups were "suicidal" and "pseudosuicidal" patients. The criteria in his study were nine indices that he had
evolved. On the TAT he found no differences between the two
groups in terms of aggression toward others or aggression by
others. The suicidal group had more aggression toward the self,
more degrees of depression, and more impulsive anxiety than the
pseudosuicidal groups.[6]

Background

How best to analyze TAT protocols? It is always possible to
parry this question by indicating that the optimal method for
analyzing a TAT protocol depends in large part on the particular
purposes and characteristics of the project in which the TAT proto-

col is being analyzed. But this does not entirely do it. In *Thematic Test Analysis*, for example, sixteen different interpretative approaches have been brought together focused around a single case —and there are as many more not included in that text.[7] It is interesting to note that—in contrast to the history in America of the rather sacrosanct Rorschach test in which one finds only more or less minor variations of Rorschach's original themes—American psychologists have felt extremely free to devise many ways of interpreting (or even modifying) the test materials of the TAT since the time of its first appearance in the technical literature. The TAT has been everybody's baby. Elsewhere, we have indicated the various published methods for analyzing the TAT may be subsumed under five general types, as follows: the normative, tabular, statistical; the hero-oriented; the intuitive, clinical, psychoanalytic; the interpersonal, psychodramatic; and the perceptual or formal.[8] It was felt that, by and large, the best "general" system was a combination of all of these. However, it can be pointed out that one characteristic of all these approaches was that the attributes of the story teller (the subject) were inferred (by one process or another) from the attributes of the test protocol data. This procedure, which characterizes most of the published methods of interpreting the TAT, is, of course, not the only possible one. Another possibility is that of delineating the characteristics of the TAT protocol *itself* and then, if one wishes, relating these delineations to variables that pertain to the subjects (such as their psychiatric diagnoses, the length of stay in psychotherapy, whether or not they had committed suicide, and so forth). This latter course seems, at first consideration, to be much more conservative, but by virtue of staying closer to the test data, it would seem to offer the possibility of higher reliability and greater freedom from the usual asumptions that are made whenever one leaps from psychological test data to the prediction, postdiction or "paridiction" of behavior.[9] Friedman has made the same point in his articles in which he Q-sorts the outstanding qualities of the TAT story *hero's* behavior, rather than those of the story teller.[10] It is also interesting to note that in many ways this focus on the attributes of the hero is, historically, very much attuned to Murray's own initial approach, which was essentially a delineation of the needs of and press on the TAT story hero. One is tempted

here to make the comment that the methods have come a full circle
—back to Murray's first insights.[11]

At any rate, this present study is not an attempt to infer the
attributes of the suicidal and nonsuicidal subjects (what kind of
a person is he?) directly from their TAT protocols but rather it
is an attempt to relate the characteristics of the chief protagonists
in the subjects' TAT stories (what kind of TAT heroes does he
describe?) with their suicidal and nonsuicidal behavior.

Subjects

In all, the TAT heroes of ninety-three subjects were studied in
this project.[12] Simply for clarity of exposition, the subjects will be
described as belonging to two sets.

Set No. 1, consisting of forty-eight protocols, is from a previous
study by Friedman and had been described by him as follows:

> The sample consisted of 48 white, male Ss—16 nor-
> mals, 16 psychoneurotics, and 16 paranoid schizophrenics.
> The three groups were roughly equated as to age and
> education. The paranoid schizophrenic group consisted
> exclusively of hospitalized patients with a psychiatric
> diagnosis of paranoid schizophrenia at the time of testing.
> The neurotic group was composed of nonhospitalized sub-
> jects who were undergoing some form of psychotherapy.
> All but one member of this group were veterans of World
> War II who had received a service-connected diagnosis of
> psychoneurosis and all had an existing neurotic diagnosis
> at the time of testing. No one was included in this group
> if a previous diagnosis of psychosis had been made. The
> utilization of a group undergoing psychotherapy was con-
> sidered feasible since, in all cases, the number and type of
> contacts were not sufficient to produce any marked
> change. At the time of examination, the Ss were deemed
> representative of a neurotic population. The normals were
> people who seemed to be functioning effectively socially
> and occupationally, who felt no serious maladjustment
> within themselves, and who had no history of psychiatric
> treatment.[13]

Set No. 2 consisted of forty-five TAT protocols of subjects in
the following categories: sixteen neurotic males who had attempted

suicide; sixteen neurotic females who had attempted suicide; eight schizophrenic males who had attempted suicide; and five neurotic males who had committed suicide. The distribution of these forty-five subjects, together with Friedman's forty-eight nonsuicidal subjects, are presented schematically in Table I. The chronological

TABLE I—Subjects Used in This Study

	FEMALE		MALE		
	Attempted Suicide	Nonsuicidal		Attempted Suicide	Committed Suicide
N O R M A L		A Male Normal Nonsui. N-16*			
N E U R O T I C	F Female Neurotic Att. Sui. N-16	B Male Neurotic Nonsui. N-16*	B' Male Neurotic Nonsui. N-3	D Male Neurotic Att. Sui. N-16	G Male Neurotic Com. Sui. N-5
P S Y C H O T I C		C Male Schizo- phrenic Nonsui. N-16*	C' Male Schizo- phrenic Nonsui. N-3	E Male Schizo- phrenic Att. Sui. N-8	

* These subjects came from Friedman's study.

age, religious affiliation, occupation, and diagnosis of each of the subjects are presented in Table II. All subjects are Caucasian.

The TAT records in Set. No. 2 were obtained as part of a more inclusive study of suicide.[14]

The *completed* suicide TAT protocols were obtained by checking all the names of individuals who committed suicide in Los Angeles County in the period 1945–1957, obtained from the Los Angeles County Coroner's Office—about 9,000 names—against all the names of individuals who had ever been in any of the state mental hospitals, Veterans Administration mental hospitals, or mental

TABLE II—Ages, Religious Affiliations, Occupations, and Diagnoses of Subjects

Group	No.	Ages	Religion	Occupation	Diagnoses
A—Normal Nonsuicidal males	16	22-45; mean, 31.4	Not indicated	Artisans, sales-people, factory workers, etc.	All subjects diagnosed as "normal."
B—Neurotic, Nonsuicidal males	16	23-42; mean, 30.8	Not indicated	Artisans, sales-people, tech-nicians, etc.	11 anxiety neuroses, 2 anxiety hys-terias, 2 mixed neuroses, 1 obsessive-com-pulsive
B'—Neurotic Nonsuicidal males	3	26.31, 33	All Prot-estant	Salesman, waiter, and machinist	1 mixed neurosis with compulsive trends, 1 anxiety reaction with ir-ritable colon syn-drome, and 1 passive-depen-dency reaction with psycho-physiologic skin reaction
C—Schizophrenic, Nonsuicidal males	16	20-42; mean, 30.8	Not indicated	Artisans, semi-skilled workers, laborers, etc.	All subjects diag-nosed as "para-noid schizo-phrenic."
C'—Schizophrenic, Nonsuicidal males	3	22, 26, 29	All Prot-estant	Student, un-skilled laborer, and unempl.	1 paranoid schizo-phrenic, 1 undif-ferentiated schizophrenic, and 1 catatonic schizophrenic
D—Neurotic Attempted suicide, males	16	29-48; mean, 36.3	7 Prot. 5 Cath. 4 Jew.	Artisans, sales-people, tech-nicians, laborers, etc.	5 depressive reac-tions, 4 anxiety reactions, 3 pas-sive-dependent personalities, 2 passive-aggres-sive personalities 1 inadequate per-sonality, 1 dis-sociative reaction
E—Schizophrenic, Attempted suicide, males	8	22-44; mean, 30.7	4 Prot. 3 Cath. 1 Jew.	Engineer, salesman, mechanic, student, 3 laborers	3 paranoid schizo-phrenia, 4 undif-ferentiated schizophrenia, 1 psychotic depres-sive reaction

Group	No.	Ages	Religion	Occupation	Diagnoses
F—Neurotic Attempted suicide, Females	16	23-56; mean, 35.5	11 Prot. 4 Cath. 1 Jew.	11 housewives, 3 secretaries, 2 technicians	6 passive-aggressive personalities, 3 anxiety reactions, 2 depressive reactions, 2 hysterical personalities, 2 masochistic characters, 1 oral character
G—Neurotic, Committed suicide, males	5	29-44; mean, 38.4	3 Prot. 2 Jew.	2 salesmen, actor, writer, clerk	3 anxiety reaction, 2 depressive reaction

sanataria in the Southern California area—about 150,000 names. In this manner, TAT protocols of nineteen individuals (positively identified as being the same individuals who had committed suicide) were obtained. From these, we selected those five TAT protocols for male Caucasian nonpsychotic individuals who could be matched with Friedman's neurotic nonsuicidal subjects and for whom, in addition, the temporal interval between the date of the TAT protocol and the date of the actual suicide was not more than one year.

The male and female *neurotic attempted* suicide TAT protocols were obtained by one of the clinical psychologists working with us on the overall suicide project, who tested individuals who had made recent suicide attempts.[15] The actual testing was done at the Los Angeles County General Hospital, the Mount Sinai Hospital, the UCLA Medical Center, or in an office of one of several psychiatrists in private practice. A group of sixteen TAT protocols from Caucasian male subjects who had attempted suicide and had been diagnosed as neurotic was selected. A similar group of sixteen neurotic female records was compiled. The selection of these two groups of neurotic attempted suicide records was done so as to come as close as possible (in terms of age, occupational status, and diagnoses) to Friedman's neurotic nonsuicidal group. These data have been presented in Table II.

It should also be pointed out (for whatever implications are involved) that strict comparability between the committed suicide and the attempted suicide TAT protocols does not exist, inasmuch

as the individuals in the suicide group were tested within a year *before* the fatal suicidal episode, whereas the attempted suicide group were all tested within a week *after* the suicidal episode (in a hospital or clinic situation at a time when the suicide attempt was prominent in the consciousness of the subject)—so that the resultants of the attempt itself, of the survival from the attempt, of the possible secondary gains from the attempt, and so forth, all may be reflected, in ways unknown to us, in these TAT protocols.

The *psychotic attempted* suicide TAT protocols were obtained from individuals who were, by virtue of a recent suicide attempt, on "Suicide Status" at a large Veterans Administration Neuropsychiatric Hospital, and who were, further, diagnosed as psychotic.

The TAT was only one of several tests administered to the male and female neurotic and psychotic attempted suicidal subjects.[16] In addition, other psychological test protocols, a comprehensive psychiatric anamnesis,[17] and—as described in Footnote 16—an elicited suicide note were obtained from each attempted suicide subject tested or interviewed for this project.

Procedure

The Q-sort technique of Stephenson was employed.[18] This procedure gives a single composite description of the personality characteristics of an individual, in this case, the TAT hero. As set up in this study, it was the sorter's task to distribute eighty statements describing the personality characteristics of the TAT hero of each protocol into nine piles approximating a normal distribution. The number of items in each of the nine steps was as follows: 4, 6, 10, 12, 16, 12, 10, 6, and 4. The polarities of the distribution were "most characteristic" and "least characteristic" of the TAT hero.[19]

The Q-sorting for all ninety-nine subjects in this study was done by one individual.[20] Each sorting, of course, used the same set of eighty statements. These statements, devised and previously published by Friedman,[21] are designed to reflect the traits, attributes, feelings and emotions, experiences, behavior tendencies, and goals and orientations generally attributed to TAT heroes.[22]

It should be stated that the sortings were done "blindly"—that is, without knowledge by the sorter as to the identity or classification of the subjects whose TAT heroes he was sorting. In the case of the first set (male normal, neurotic, and psychotic nonsuicidal

subjects), Friedman himself took pains to avoid the possibility of contamination of his ratings. In the case of the second set (male and female neurotic and psychotic attempted and committed suicide subjects), the topic of suicide was never mentioned and even the sex of the subjects was not indicated. The authors avoided contaminating the rater by communicating with him (until after the study was completed) only through a third party (a Department Chairman at a local university) using only university stationery, and giving no information except that all the subjects were Caucasian and between the ages of 21 and 55.

Results

The statistical results[23] will be reported in terms of the following five headings: (I) Reliabilities, (II) Within-Group Correlations, (III) Between-Group Correlations, (IV) High Relationships among Individual Items, and (V) Judgments as to Sex and Diagnosis.

1. RELIABILITIES. The statistical findings pertaining to reliabilities are presented under three headings: (A) Interrater Reliabilities, (B) Intragroup Reliabilities, and (C) Intrarater Reliabilities.

A. *Interrater Reliabilities.* In one of the reports of his previous study, Friedman presented some reliability figures for his three groups (normal, neurotic, and psychotic)—Groups A, B, and C in our Table I. He stated as follows:

> Five judges were selected, all of whom had experience with the TAT. Each judge was given a sheet of instructions for rating, the rating procedures were discussed, and the judges sorted one sample protocol with the author to get a general impression of the task. Ten records, both normal and deviant, were selected at random. The author rated each of the ten records and secured two other judges' ratings for each record so that there were three ratings or sorts for each record.
> Since three judges rated each record, judge A's sort could be correlated with judge B's and C's, and judge B's and C's with each other. The three reliability coefficients (AB, AC, BC), each reflecting the degree of agreement between the two judges in characterizing the TAT hero, were computed by means of the product-moment correlation formula suggested by Cronbach for use when the

score of all persons have the same mean and variance as in the case of Q-sort data. The 30 reliability coefficients obtained from the three correlations for each of the ten records range from .37 to .88 with a mean correlation of .72 and a median of .75. When computing the average correlation by the method of z-transformation of a correlation coefficient, the reliability figure was .74. The frequency distribution of interrater reliability coefficients was as indicated (in Table III) below.

The obtained correlations compare favorably with other studies reported in the literature dealing with similar types of ratings, and indicate that judgments on this type of material can be reliably made.

TABLE III—Frequency Distribution of Friedman's Inter-Rater
Reliability Coefficients

Reliability Coefficient	Frequency
.80 to .89	4
.70 to .79	19
.60 to .69	4
.50 to .59	1
.40 to .49	1
.30 to .39	1

As an extension of the above interrater reliability figures reported by Friedman, we asked Friedman to Q-sort blindly (as described in the "Procedure," above) three nonsuicidal male neurotic subjects and three nonsuicidal male psychotic subjects. We believe that these six subjects[24] are similar and comparable to the (nonsuicidal) neurotic and psychotic subjects described by Friedman in his article.[25] These six neurotic and psychotic subjects are labelled B′ and C′, respectibely, in Table I. We then asked two skilled clinicians, both experienced with the TAT, to do blind Q-sorts of the same six protocols, sorting Friedman's eighty items according to his instructions for sorting in terms of the TAT hero. The distribution of these eighteen correlations among the three judges (Friedman and two clinicians selected by us) on these six protocols is as indicated in Table IV. This procedure thus replicates the procedure employed by Friedman, as described above. As indicated in Tables IV and V, the range of correlations was from −.30 to .68, with a mean correlation of .34, and a median correlation of .42.

B. *Intragroup Reliabilities*. We also correlated Friedman's sort-

TABLE IV—Inter-Rater Reliability Coefficients from the Present Study

	Friedman & Clin. I	Friedman & Clin. II	Clin. I & Clin. II
	.13	.34	.49
Group B′	.49	−.30	−.26
	.55	.63	.47
	.61	.16	.14
Group C′	.55	.08	.39
	.62	.68	.49

TABLE V—Frequency Distribution of Inter-Rater Reliability Coefficients from Present Study

Reliability Coefficient	Frequency
.60 to .69	4
.50 to .59	2
.40 to .49	4
.30 to .39	2
.20 to .29	
.10 to .19	3
.00 to .09	1
−.01 to −.09	
−.10 to −.19	
−.20 to −.29	1
−.30 to −.39	1

ings of the three nonsuicidal neurotic records that we had sent him (B′) with his previous sortings of his sixteen nonsuicidal neurotic records (B) and we correlated his sortings of the three nonsuicidal psychotic records we sent him (C′) with his previous sortings of his sixteen nonsuicidal psychotic records (C). These correlations are indicated in Tables VI and VII, respectively. As shown, the

TABLE VI—Reliability Coefficients Between B′ and B

Group B	B′-1	B′-2	B′-3
1	.22	.37	−.20
2	.16	.50	−.08
3	.31	−.11	.22
4	.02	−.05	−.05
5	.09	.55	−.21
6	.30	.10	.05
7	.22	−.30	.23
8	.16	−.16	−.07
9	.23	−.17	−.05
10	.18	−.12	.02
11	.10	−.32	.31
12	.58	.30	.01
13	.15	.00	.07
14	.20	.18	−.27
15	.20	−.01	.05
16	−.01	−.10	−.12

TABLE VII—Reliability Coefficients Between C′ and C

Group C	C′-1	C′-2	C′-3
1	.14	.25	.14
2	.31	.38	−.18
3	−.32	−.19	.34
4	.32	−.14	.15
5	.34	.02	.00
6	.23	.08	.01
7	.54	.26	.14
8	.10	.00	.47
9	−.37	−.05	.21
10	.16	.04	.08
11	−.11	−.12	.07
12	.26	.07	−.10
13	−.22	−.01	.61
14	−.19	−.26	.21
15	.04	.28	.50
16	.16	.21	−.03

correlations range from −.37 to .61, with a median correlation of zero. In light of these correlations, we intercorrelated Friedman's sortings within the three B′ records and also his sortings within the three C′ records, with the results as shown in Table VII.

C. *Intrarater Reliabilities.* We were also interested in intrarater reliabilities. To obtain these, we asked Friedman, four weeks after he had completed the fifty-one Q-sorts to rerate five records. We randomly selected one group (Group D, the neurotic male attempted suicide group) from among the seven groups of subjects (Groups A through G, Table I), and from this selected group, chose randomly

TABLE VIII—Reliability Coefficients Between B′ and C′

B′ vs B′	
B′-1 vs B′-2	.10
B′-1 vs B′-3	.14
B′-2 vs B′-3	−.12

C′ vs C′	
C′-1 vs C′-2	.57
C′-1 vs C′-3	.00
C′-2 vs C′-3	.08

TABLE IX—Intrarater Reliability Coefficients

Subject	Rating 1 vs Rating 2
D-105	.74
D-106	.78
D-108	.78
D-109	.75
D-111	.78

five records. The results of this rerating procedure are given in Table IX. As can be seen, the correlations ranged from .74 to .78, with a median of .78.

2. WITHIN-GROUP CORRELATIONS. A. *Within-Group Correlations Reported by Friedman.* Friedman's reports of his within-groups findings were as follows: within Normal (Group A), .261; within Neurotic (Group B), .245; and within Psychotic (Group C), .119.

B. *Within-Group Correlations Obtained in the Present Study.* The statistics for the 638 within-group correlations of the seven groups (Groups A through G) are presented in Table X.[26] As indicated in

TABLE X—Frequency Distribution of Within-Group Correlation Coefficients

Correlation Coefficient	A	B	C	D	E	F	G
.75 to .79						2	
.70 to .74	2					6	
.65 to .69		1				3	
.60 to .64	3	1	2	2		2	
.55 to .59	4	1	2	3	1	6	
.50 to .54	7	6	5	4	1	8	
.45 to .49	8	13	2	5	2	5	1
.40 to .44	9	8	7	1		10	
.35 to .39	7	9	4	8		12	
.30 to .34	11	16	7	11	5	8	
.25 to .29	10	9	7	14	2	5	
.20 to .24	13	12	8	2	2	8	2
.15 to .19	8	9	8	12	2	4	2
.10 to .14	14	5	14	9	1	4	2
.05 to .09	8	10	6	8	3	4	
.01 to .04	2	3	9	4	1	4	
.00	1	3	2	3		1	
−.01 to −.04	6	3	7	4	1	2	
−.05 to −.09	2	4	12	10	2	9	1
−.10 to −.14	2	4	2	5		5	
−.15 to −.19	2	1	5	1	1	4	
−.20 to −.24	1		5	4	1	1	
−.25 to −.29		1	1	3	3		1
−.30 to −.34		1	1	2		2	1
−.35 to −.39				1		3	
−.40 to −.44			3	2			
−.45 to −.49				1		2	
−.50 to −.54							
−.55 to −.59			1	1			
−.60 to −.64							
−.65 to −.69							
Total	120	120	120	120	28	120	10
Median Corr. Coeff.	.25	.26	.11	.15	.17	.30	.14

the table, the median correlations range from .11 to .30; the ranges of correlations for each of the seven columns are also indicated. In order to ascertain whether or not there were any significant differences between any of the within-groups statistics, the correlation coefficients were recorded as raw scores and Mood's Median Test was applied.[27] Statistical analysis indicated that the combined median for the seven groups (which was .21) was significant at the .01 level, with six degrees of freedom. A further extension of the Median Test therefore seemed justified to see where the differences between the individual groups lay. The results of this analysis, as shown in Table XI, indicate that among the twenty-one possible comparisons of the seven groups there were six pairs that are statistically different at the .01 level of confidence, and three pairs significant at the .05 level. The six pairs at the .01 level are as follows: (A vs. C) nonsuicidal normals vs. nonsuicidal psychotics; (A vs. D) nonsuicidal normals vs. neurotic attempted suicides; (B vs. C) nonsuicidal neurotics vs. nonsuicidal psychotics; (B vs. D) nonsuicidal neurotics vs. neurotic attempted suicides; (C vs. F) nonsuicidal psychotics vs. female neurotic attempted suicides; and (D vs. F) neurotic male attempted suicides vs.

TABLE XI—Significant Differences Among the Seven Groups
in Relation to Within-Group Data

Groups	Obtained χ^2	P	.01	.05
A vs B	0.0172	.90		
A vs C	13.1405	.01	x	
A vs D	6.6671	.01	x	
A vs E	1.6335	.30		
A vs F	0.0692	.80		
A vs G	4.0475	.05		x
B vs C	15.0512	.01	x	
B vs D	8.0672	.01	x	
B vs E	2.064	.20		
B vs F	0.000	—		
B vs G	4.5023	.05		x
C vs D	0.8711	.50		
C vs E	0.4157	.70		
C vs F	16.0568	.01	x	
C vs G	0.3192	.70		
D vs E	0.000	—		
D vs F	9.469	.01	x	
D vs G	0.2463	.90		
E vs F	2.2241	.20		
E vs G	0.8179	.50		
F vs G	4.6769	.05		x

neurotic female attempted suicides. One set of within-group correlations of each of these six pairs is statistically different from the other set in relation to the within-group correlation distributions, indicating that one set is either significantly more or significantly less homogeneous than the other set.

3. BETWEEN-GROUP CORRELATIONS. A. *Between-Group Correlations Reported by Friedman.* Friedman has reported the following between-group correlations for his nonsuicidal normal, neurotic, and psychotic groups (Group A, B, and C): normal vs. neurotic, .114; normal vs. psychotic, .110; and neurotic vs. psychotic, .154. Concerning these correlations, Friedman has stated, "The higher mean correlation between the neurotic and paranoid schizophrenic groups suggests a greater similarity between these two groups and a greater relative dissimilarity to the normal TAT."[28]

B. *Between-Group Correlations in the Present Study.* As indicated in Table XII, the median correlations for the twenty-one columns of between-group correlations range from −.03 to .23.[29] To ascertain whether or not these obtained correlations were significantly different from zero, the Wallace-Snedecor Tables for Significant Coefficients of Correlations were used.[30] To avoid excessive chance occurrences, only those intergroup correlations that exceeded the .01 level of confidence were accepted as being significant. As indicated by the asterisks in Table XII, there were four sets of comparisons in which significant differences were found between the Q-sortings for the members of the two groups represented in the between-group comparisons. These four groups are: (B vs. D), neurotic nonsuicidal males vs. neurotic attempted suicide males; (B vs. F), neurotic nonsuicidal males vs. neurotic attempted suicide females; (D vs. F), neurotic attempted suicide males vs. neurotic attempted suicide females; and (E vs. F), psychotic attempted suicide males vs. neurotic attempted suicide females. These results are of most interest to the clinically oriented reader.

4. HIGH RELATIONSHIPS AMONG INDIVIDUAL ITEMS. Each of the eighty items was Q-sorted according to a nine category continuum ranging from zero (least characteristic) to eight (most charateristic). Inasmuch as we knew how many items were in each category, we could assign a probability with which a particular item would fall

TABLE XII—Frequency Distribution of Between-Group Correlation Coefficients

Correlation Coefficient	AB	AC	AD	AE	AF	AG	BC	BD	BE	BF	BG	CD	CE	CF	CG	DE	DF	DG	EF	EG	FG
.75 to .79												1							1		
.70 to .74												2					7	1	1		
.65 to .69			3		1		1	2				4				1	8	1	5	1	3
.60 to .64		4	3				6	4	1	1		7					7	3	4		1
.55 to .59		3					6	8	1	1		6	1	1			12	3	9	1	3
.50 to .54	2	2	2	2	3		4	10	1	10	3	10	2	5	1	2	14	3	4	3	3
.45 to .49	8	10	5	2	4	4	8	12	6	7	1	7	2	8	3	2	22	6	9	1	4
.40 to .44	11	7	6	2	6	7	11	14	9	18	3	17	6	7	3	3	8	8	8	3	3
.35 to .39	10	17	10	7	8	6	18	25	12	16	6	22	6	11	6	9	19	3	13	3	3
.30 to .34	16	7	7	5	14	7	17	29	13	17	7	22	6	18	3	9	17	7	8	4	7
.25 to .29	20	16	6	8	10	7	21	21	10	27	6	19	11	18	4	10	20	2	7	1	2
.20 to .24	29	22	21	7	22	4	21	18	12	21	4	19	10	20	8	12	17	7	5	2	7
.15 to .19	23	21	18	5	11	7	18	17	13	27	7	12	7	19	8	9	22	3	11	1	5
.10 to .14	24	22	20	8	12	4	22	16	13	19	10	18	8	10	4	12	9	7	8		4
.05 to .09	20	21	19	10	11	8	21	8	3	13	5	5	10	20	5	8	9	6	7	2	6
.01 to .04	21	21	12	4	8	1				18	3			12	9	10	7	1	1	3	3
.00	9	10	13	1	5	0	5	12	3	9	1	18	2	14	2	9	4	6	1	3	2
−.01 to −.04	14	16	14	7	16	3	11	15	7	4	5	12	5	5	2	4	10	5	6	3	3
−.05 to −.09	10	14	23	8	12	2	9	9	10	9	6	14	9	16	6	2	8	2	4	2	6
−.10 to −.14	14	12	21	9	19	6	15	15	4	10	4	16	8	14	3	6	7	4	4	1	5
−.15 to −.19	7	10	15	9	17	4	8	5	3	15	4	7	7	9	2	3	3	3	4		5
−.20 to −.24	5	5	13	9	29	2	2	7	3	3	4	5	3	12	3	5	8	3	6		2
−.25 to −.29	4	7	8	11	12	5	7	3	3	3	1	4	8	9	3	3	2	1	1		3
−.30 to −.34	1	6	6	2	18	2	3	1		1		3	2	10		1	2			2	1
−.35 to −.39	3	1	4	4	10	1	3	1		2		2	2	5	2	8	2				
−.40 to −.44	5		4	6	2			1	1	1			1	2		3	4	2	2		1
−.45 to −.49			2	2	2		1	2		2		1		2				1			
−.50 to −.54		1	1		2			1		2				2		3					
−.55 to −.59		1			2									1							
−.60 to −.64																					
−.65 to −.69																	1				
Total	256	256	256	128	256	80	256	256	128	256	80	256	128	256	80	128	256	80	128	40	80
Median	.12	.10	.01	−.03	.01	.16	.15	.18	.15	.22	.12	.11	.07	.11	.10	.16	.22	.08	.23	.10	.13
Difference*								Yes		Yes							Yes		Yes		

* Significant difference between members of the two groups comprising the between-group comparison.

in any of the nine categories. It was decided that only categories 0, 1, 2, and 6, 7, 8 would be taken as indicative of least characteristic and most characteristic respectively of the subject within a group. The scores for all the individuals within a group were totaled for each item. If the item had either an extremely high or an extremely low total score, indicating that the rater had given most individuals of that group either a 0, 1, 2, or a 6, 7, 8 rating for that item, then that item was selected for further analysis. By means of "An Extended Table of Chi-Square for Two Degrees of Freedom for Use in Combined Probabilities from Independent Samples"[31], the probability for each rating of an item thus chosen was changed into a Chi-square with two degrees of freedom. To see if a particular item was significant, the Chi-squares representing the ratings of a particular item for all people in a single group were added and the level of significance was established. The results are shown in Table XIII. It was decided, in order to avoid

TABLE XIII—Items of Possible Significance

Level of Significance	Groups						
	A	B	C	D	E	F	G
.01	2*	13	42	33	10	31*	
	7*	14			47	42	
	33	31*			51	47	
	44	42				60	
	48*	66				77*	
	55*	74					
		75					
		79					
.02	12*				37*		1*

* The asterisk indicates that the item is one sorted as "Least Characteristic" of the TAT hero.

excessive chance occurrences, to accept only items that were significant at a .02 level of confidence or better. Further, in order to ascertain whether or not the *number* of items significant at the .02 level or better within each group was above chance, it was necessary to ascertain the probability with which that particular number of items could occur by chance within a group of eighty occurrences. These figures are shown in Table XIV and indicate that four or more items within a group are necessary to have a significant number of items at the .02 level or better.

TABLE XIV—Probability Table for Chance Significance
at the .01 Level with 80 Items

No. of Items	Probability
0	.406570
1	.365913
2	.164661
3	.049398
4	.011115
5	.002001
6	.000300
7	.000039
8	.000009

As indicated in Table XIII, there were four groups in which four
or more items were found: (A) nonsuicidal normals, 7 items; (B)
nonsuicidal neurotics, 8 items; (E) psychotic attempted suicides,
4 items; and (F) female neurotic attempted suicides, 5 items. These
items are listed in Table XV.[32]

5. JUDGMENTS AS TO SEX AND DIAGNOSIS. After Friedman had done

TABLE XV—Significant "Most Characteristic" and
"Least Characteristic" Items

Group	Least	Most	Item No.	Item
A		x	2	Works hard to achieve a desired goal
		x	7	Gets very interested in things
		x	12*	A serious person
	x		33	Sometimes thinks about suicide
	x		44	Tries to get even with people
		x	48	Thinks how nice it would be to be a success
		x	55	Concerned about future
B	x		13	Gets drunk
	x		14	Gambles
		x	31	Feels blue and downhearted
	x		42	Has good control over emotions
	x		66	Spoiled by parents
	x		74	Rarely asks mother's permission to do things
	x		75	Follows father's advice
	x		79	Helped by father's guidance
E	x		10*	Has a good imagination
		x	37*	Sometimes feels like crying
	x		47*	Thinks about enjoyable things
	x		51*	Looks at the bright side of things
F		x	31	Feels blue and downhearted
	x		42	Has good control over emotions
	x		47	Thinks about enjoyable things
	x		60	Does what other people advise
		x	77	Dislikes being told what to do

* Significant at the .02 level; all other items significant at the .01 level

TABLE XVI—Chi-Square Distribution for
Male-Female Judgments*

		Actual		
		Male	Female	
Obtained	Male	29	7	36
	Female	6	9	15
		35	16	51

* Chi-Square equal 6.335, significant at the .05 level. Yates' correction was used for the obtained frequencies.

the blind Q-sorts of the fifty-one TAT protocols, we then asked him to indicate his opinion whether the *storyteller* in each case was male or female. No clues were given him as to the number of men and women in the total sample. The facts were that there were thirty-five men and sixteen women. Friedman's blind analysis resulted in judgments of thirty-six men and fifteen women of which twenty-nine out of the thirty-five men were correctly labeled and nine out of the sixteen women were correctly labeled. The Chi-square for this distribution is 6.335, significant at the .05 level. These data are shown in Table XVI.

In addition, we asked Friedman to sort blindly for diagnostic categories. We did this by limiting his blind judgments to the following groups: Group D, male neurotic attempted suicide; Group G, male neurotic committed suicide; and Group B', male neurotic nonsuicide. The number of individuals in these three groups were sixteen, five, and three respectively. All subjects were, as indicated, male and neurotic. Friedman was asked to indicate whether in his judgment each storyteller was one of three categories: an attempted suicide, a committed suicide, or nonsuicidal. The Chi-square distribution of Friedman's judgments in this connection are presented in Table XVII.

TABLE XVII—Chi-Square Distribution
for Diagnostic Judgments*

		Actual		
		Non-Suic'l	Comm. Suic	Attem. Suic	
	Nonsuicidal	2	1	9	12
Obtained	Committed Suicide	1	1	4	6
	Attempted Suicide	0	3	3	6
		3	5	16	24

* Chi-Square not computed because of small number of cases in six of the cells, but, by inspection, it does not appear to be significant.

Discussion

Inasmuch as this study, concerned as it is with the TAT, is essentially about fantasy, we felt that we would like to take advantage of this fact and indicate some of our own fantasies in relation to this paper. When we conceived of doing this particular study, we had, as one does at the beginning of any project, a number of hypotheses, notions, and even aspirations for our data. (We tried, of course, to eliminate any systematic biases or prejudgments that might influence the results.) In reflecting back on what we were thinking at the beginning of the study, it seems that we covertly had the naïve hope that our results would be something as follows: that our reliabilities would be perfect; that the within-group correlations would be plus 1.00, indicating complete homogeneity within each group; and that the between-group correlations would be around zero, indicating these homogeneous groups were indeed different from one another. We could then, of course, describe in some detail those clinically useful attributes that nature (and statistics) had shown us had accrued to each of the seven groups. Clinicians would then have new and practical clues to sharpen their diagnostic acumen and to enable them to distinguish among nonsuicide, attempted suicide, committed suicide, neurotic, psychotic, male, female, and the like.

Actually, some results pertaining to suicide *per se* were obtained and are indicated in the previous section[33]. But the primary point for discussion of this study must be directed not toward the clinical aspects of suicide but rather toward the implications for methodology and the implications for picture thematic projective testing in general. What we began as a study of the TATs of suicidal subjects resulted primarily in a study of the TAT itself.

The TAT has, of course, been manipulated along different dimensions. In the first place, Murray himself devised the TAT materials so that there was contained within them a continuum from more ambiguous stimuli to more structured stimuli. We have indicated in the section on "Background" that the TAT became everybody's baby and this constitutes the second way in which the TAT was varied; namely, in terms of the modifications of the TAT materials for specific kinds of subjects. Thus we find TAT modifications for Negroes, Navahos, Utes, paraplegics, Michigan adoles-

cents, Korean prisoners of war, and others. There is still a third dimension along which the TAT can vary, that is, in terms of specific personality categories. In other studies it has been found that *composite* judgments of entire protocols usually lead to generally poor results.[34] Rather, what seems to be called for are *specific* projective materials, which are devised and used for *particular* personality functions, for example, a separate "test" to elicit amounts and patterns of hostility; and similarly with passivity, sexuality, and the like.

At the begining of the present study it seemed to us that the technique of evaluating the attributes of the *hero* offered an unusual opportunity to stick close to the given data and thus to obtain interjudge reliabilities based on phenotypes. What we had not anticipated was that one cannot collate or average or add heroes. Consider: the clinician's usual diagnostic task is comparable to seeing a play, for example *Hamlet*, and then divining Shakespeare's personality attributes. In the hero-oriented approach, the task is to see *Hamlet* and then to describe, in some systematic way, Hamlet's personality characteristics. But, if on a single day the clinician were to see *Hamlet, Love's Labor Lost, Othello, Measure For Measure, King Lear*, and *All's Well That Ends Well*—how could he then give a *single* description of the chief protaganist of *all* these plays? Unfortunately, this was the judge's task in the present study.

The recommendation at this point is that protocols be separated into their respective stories and judgments be made across the protocols in terms of single stories, that is, all the heroes described in the stories given to Card 6BM would be judged, the heroes of 7BM, 13MF, and so forth, and then the correlations could be made. Further, following along the lines of Little's suggestions, we would intend to design specific sets of picture thematic stimulus materials, to investigate hostility feelings, suicidal feelings, and the like.

Although, for us, the results of this study have been disappointing in that they have told us less about suicide than we would have wanted to learn, they opened new vistas for exploring suicide (and other aspects of human functioning) by pointing to modifications of the picture thematic technique that may be useful in the exploration of human personality.

Summary

There are many ways in which TAT protocols are interpreted, although most of these ways have in common the fact that they are concerned with the attributes of the subject who tells the story. Another way that the TAT protocols can be handled is in terms of the attributes of the hero within the TAT story. This study employs the latter technique.

The attributes of the TAT heroes of ninety-three TAT protocols were rated—by means of an eighty-item, nine-step Q-sort proce-dure—by a single judge. There were seven groups of subjects, as follows: sixteen each nonsuicidal normal, neurotic, and psychotic males; sixteen neurotic males who had attempted suicide; five neurotic males who committed suicide; eight psychotic males who attempted suicide; and sixteen neurotic females who attempted suicide.

Interrater reliabilities (among three raters) yielded a median correlation of .75 in a previous study and a median correlation of .42 in the present study. Interrater reliabilities (of one rater on five protocols, four weeks apart) showed a median correlation of .78.

The median correlations of the seven sets of within-group cor-relations ranged from .11 to .30, indicating that none of the seven groups was outstandingly homogeneous.

Of the 21 possible between-group comparisons—whose median correlations ranged from −.03 to .23—in the following four pairs of groups, one of each pair was found to be significantly different from the other group in that pair: normal males vs. neurotic male attempted suicide; normal males vs. neurotic female attempted suicide; neurotic male attempted suicide vs. neurotic fe-male attempted suicide; and, psychotic male attempted suicide vs. neurotic female attempted suicide. It would appear that the most obvious differences occurred between the sortings for the heroes of male vs. female subjects, and, next in order, between the sortings for the heroes of normal vs. disturbed (but not necessarily sui-cidal) subjects.

The judge was able to make overall judgments as to the sex of the subjects better than chance, but he could not evaluate the suicidal or nonsuicidal status of the subjects better than chance expectation.

After an evaluation of the statistical results, it was felt that sorting for the attributes of the TAT hero had yielded, in the over-all, disappointing results insofar as suicide was concerned. It was believed that these results occurred primarily because it is difficult to sort for *one* hero from several TAT stories within a single TAT protocol.

Two suggestions were made: to sort for the attributes of the TAT hero card-by-card, that is, by taking the same card through all the protocols; and, to develop specific sets of picture thematic stimulus materials designed to tap the range of responses along the dimensions of a *single* aspect of personality functioning (such as aggression, passivity, homosexuality, suicidal feelings, and the like).

Chapter 12
ATTEMPTED AND COMMITTED SUICIDES
Edwin S. Shneidman and Norman L. Farberow

*There is a generally held assumption that there are important
differences between attempted and committed suicides. This study
presents empirical data from a survey of both committed and
attempted suicide conducted in Los Angeles County in 1957. The
breakdown of characteristics such as sex, marital status, method
of suicidal behavior, socioeconomic status, and given reason
for the suicidal act sharply point up differences that are
important in planning for prevention and rescue operations.*

The purpose of this chapter is to present the comparative results
of a survey of persons who attempted suicide and persons who committed suicide, specifically during the year 1957 in Los Angeles
County. Because the data on attempted suicides for a large-scale
metropolitan community have been heretofore relatively unavailable (most of the data on this group has been obtained from
selected and unavoidably biased sample populations), the characteristics of suicide attempters have generally had to be inferred
or extrapolated. This survey, however, presents some empirically
derived data about attempted suicide and, in addition, by virtue
of obtaining similar data on the persons who committed suicide in
Los Angeles County during the same period, permits a number
of comparisons between the two groups.

In the scientific literature, the terms *suicide* and *suicidal* are
often found to have varied and ambiguous meanings. The greatest
confusion seems to exist between two specific implications of the
term, namely, suicide meaning (1) killing oneself (i.e., commiting
suicide) and (2) injuring oneself in a suicidelike way with more
or less lethal intention (i.e., attempting suicide). Many examples
of scientific studies can be given in which nonsuicidal subjects are
contrasted with suicidal subjects, the latter consisting of both
attempted and committed cases. In these instances, the implicit
assumption is that there are no important differences between the
attempted and committed groups, the two somehow being rendered

similar by the semantic blanket of the word *suicide*. On the other hand, some writers have pointed out that it is dangerous to make assumptions about the relationships between attempted and committed suicide, in that one cannot a priori assume either that they are the same or that they are different.[1] Although there are several noteworthy surveys of committed suicide, the data on attempted suicides are much more sparse. This is probably so because fairly accurate data for attempted suicides are relatively difficult to come by, whereas statistics for committed suicides are relatively easy, often misleadingly easy, to obtain.

The sociological aproach to the explication of data on *committed* suicide is, by now, a time-honored tradition. It includes what is probably the best known single work on the topic of suicide, Durkheim's *Le Suicide*, which, when it was published in France in 1897, established a model for sociological research generally.[2] There have been many subsequent studies of this genre. Some of the best known of these are the monographs or books on committed suicide by Cavan,[3] Schmid,[4] Sainsbury,[5] Yap,[6] Henry and Short,[7] and the compilations of Dublin and Bunzel.[8] All these fall within the ecological tradition of taking a plot of ground—a city or a country—and figuratively or literally reproducing its map several times to show its socially shady (and topographically shaded) areas and their many relationships to suicide rates. We believe that it might be a fundamental methodological error simply to assume that the characteristics of the population that commits suicide are the same as those of the population that attempts suicide. Stengel and Cook, in their studies of attempted suicide in London (based on subjects admitted to five hospitals), have raised this same question.[9] The matter is definitely one for empirical investigation. The difficulties in obtaining reliable data concerning attempted suicides probably result in large part from the fact that persons who do not lose their lives either cover up their own attempts or have their attempts covered up for them by others. Perhaps the best sources of such information would be physicians and hospitals in a large metropolitan community. This is the task to which we, in the study being reported in this chapter, addressed ourselves. Our own motivation in making this study of attempted suicides was to obtain a base line for our operations at the SPC so that our sample

of subjects at the SPC would represent *pro rata* the population of *attempted* suicides in the Los Angeles community.

Data were collected for both completed suicides and attempted suicides for Los Angeles County for the calendar year 1957.[10] For the *completed* suicides, the data were obtained from the Los Angeles coroner's office. By county law, all persons who die by suicide, homicide, or accident or unattended by a physician for 90 days must be certified by the coroner's office. Equivocal cases of suicide (as in deaths by marginal doses of barbiturates in an apparently nonsuicidal person) are currently investigated by the Suicide Team of the SPC. In 1957, the certification of suicide was made solely by the coroner and his deputies and may contain unknown errors. Nonetheless, our procedure was to search the coroner's records, make a note of each person indicated as having committed suicide in 1957, and then examine each folder, abstract each case, and translate the data onto our forms. For each case, information was obtained in the following categories: sex, age, race, nativity, marital status, occupation, time in the Los Angeles community, method of suicide, presence or absence of suicide note, serology (especially ethanol), with whom the victim had been living, the type of dwelling (house, apartment, hotel, etc.), and the address.

For the *attempted* suicides, the sources of our data were three: (1) the physicians in the Los Angeles area, (2) the total records for 1957 of the Los Angeles County General Hospital, and (3) the sixteen Los Angeles municipal emergency hospitals. We shall describe the data obtained from the physicians first. This type of study, we believe, had never been done before. The greatest untapped sources of information about attempted suicides, we thought, were the physicians in the community. It was thought that probably the majority of persons who attempted suicide were seen by their personal or family physicians, were treated medically, and were returned to their routine functioning in the community without any information being recorded in any official document in the community. Our experience in the investigation of committed suicides at the SPC supported this notion. Other investigators too have pointed out that large numbers of suicidal persons had been treated by their family physicians.[11]

Working closely with the two medical associations in Los Angeles

County, we contacted each of the 6,602 Doctor of Medicine (M.D.) members of the Los Angeles County Medical Association and each of the 1,534 Doctor of Osteopathy (D.O.) members of the Los Angeles County Osteopathic Society. Our letter, describing the project and asking their cooperation, was accompanied by a cover letter from the president of the respective organization, which, in the case of the LACMA, stated: "The purpose of this letter is to endorse the enclosed project, which is concerned with the problem of suicide prevention in Los Angeles County. The plan for this project was presented to the Council of the Los Angeles County Medical Association and has received its unqualified approval. You are urged to cooperate with this project, the results of which will be extremely important to the community and to all physicians." We enclosed a card, asking each physician to report "the total number of individuals seen professionally because of an actual suicide attempt," from Jan. 1, 1957, to Apr. 30, 1958.[12] In the cover letter, suicide attempt was defined as an actual act (such as cutting wrists or ingesting barbiturates) and was not to include either suicide threats or any cases in which the subject did not survive the attempt, so as to avoid any duplication with the coroner's data. Further, if the number of such cases seen in 1957 was zero, it was requested that the card be returned (with the number zero on it) so that a complete tabulation might be made. All this mail material was sent out by Addressograph, and addressed, stamped envelopes were provided for the return mail.

The percentage of returns can be commented upon. Of the 6,602 letters to M.D.s, we received over 5,000 responses (77 percent), and of the 1,534 letters to D.O.s, we received over 1,000 responses (66 percent). This kind of response to a mail survey from physicians is in itself noteworthy and reflects the interest in this topic. The exact breakdown of number of responses and number of patients reported is given in Table I.

As these cards were returned to us, we followed the response by sending each physician who had reported one or more suicide attempts one questionnaire for each attempted suicide that he had reported. The questions to be answered for each patient were sex, age, race, religion, date of suicide attempt, marital status, previous contacts with physician, previous suicide attempts, method of suicide attempts, whether other physicians were involved, whether

TABLE I—Survey Returns from Physicians and Attempted Suicide Cases Reported, Los Angeles County, 1957

Group	Letters Sent Out	Cards Returned	Zero Attempted Suicides Reported	One or More Attempted Suicides Reported	Average Number of Attempted Suicides Seen by Physicians	Estimate of Attempted Suicides Treated*
D.O.	1,534	1,004(66%)	679	325	2.22	826
H.D.	6,602	5,048 77%)	3,665	1,383	2.26	3,061
Total	8,136	6,052(71%)	4,344	1,708	2.24	3,887

* The figures in this column have been corrected for two factors by subtracting proportionately for the 4 extra months (January through April, 1958) for which the physicians reported and by adding proportionately for the percentages of M.D.s and D.O.s (23 and 34%, respectively) who did not report at all.

the patient was hospitalized for the attempt, what reasons the patient gave for the attempt, the disposition by the physician, medication, how the patient was saved, the physician's rating of the seriousness of the attempt, the patient's occupation and estimated income, the patient's aproximate address, and the nature of the physician's own practice; the patient's name was not asked. The number of returns from these questionnaires is indicated in Table II.

As indicated above, other than physicians, our sources of information about suicide attempts in Los Angeles were the county and city hospitals. Los Angeles County General Hospital is an approximately 3,000-bed general, medical, surgical, and neuropsychiatric hospital. A large number of patients who attempt suicide are

TABLE II—Number of Questionnaires Returned by Physicians on Attempted Suicides, Los Angeles County, 1957

Group	Number of Questionnaires Sent Out	Number of Physicians Replying	Number of Patients Reported	Number of Questionnaires Used*
D.O.	302	178	263	163
M.D.	1,287	461	714	470
Total	1,589	639	977	633

* This column represents the total number of usable questionnaires on the basis of the completeness of information contained within them.

taken, usually by emergency ambulance, to LACGH. The files of all patients discharged from this hospital in 1957 with the diagnosis of attempted suicide were examined, and the necessary data were abstracted. The names of patients who were identified as having come from the emergency hospitals were eliminated from the tabulation in order to eliminate duplication. In all, 494 cases of attempted suicide (210 men and 284 women) were obtained.

The Los Angeles city emergency hospital system has a large central receiving unit and fifteen branch hospitals scattered throughout strategic areas of the city to treat the many and varied emergency cases that occur in a large metropolitan community. More than 200,000 records for 1957 were individually examined for all cases marked either suicide attempt or possible suicide attempt and all cases where the injury seemed to indicate a suicidal attempt (such as wrist cutting or ingestion of lye in an adult), and the pertinent available data were abstracted. Since these hospitals are emergency in nature, the amount of data available from their records was necessarily brief, but information for 1,525 suicide attempts for 1957 (498 males and 1,027 females) was obtained. Thus the total number of attempted suicides found for 1957 was 5,906; 3,887 reported by physicians and 2,019 obtained from the records of the county and city hospitals.

How thoroughly do these figures represent Los Angeles County for 1957? There are two main sources of error to be kept in mind. First, there are those persons who attempt suicide and who never reach a physician or a hospital, either because their wounds or their illness are not severe enough to bring them to the attention of a physician or because they somehow obtain family care or self-care; second, there are a number of small private emergency hospitals scattered throughout the city that are not represented in this report. To have gone to their files would have entailed inordinate expenditure of time and effort. Over and above this, it was felt that the persons treated in them were, for the most part, obtained in response to the letter to the physicians who staff these hospitals. So far as number is concerned, it is felt that relatively few additional cases would have been obtained. The number obtained, 5,906, represents, we believe, a fair but undoubtedly conservative figure for the number of attempted suicides in Los Angeles County in 1957.

In 1957, there were, according to the official records of the coroner's office, 768 persons who *committed* suicide. (This represented a slight increase in number from previous years within the last decade but a slight decrease in rate in relation to the growing total population.) During this same calendar year, the number of *attempted* suicides reported to us by physicians and obtained from hospital records was 5,906. The ratio of attempted suicides to committed suicides was 7.69:1 (5,906:768), or approximately 8:1.

Sociological Data

The sociological data will be discussed in separate categories, as presented in Table III, and will include sex, race, age, marital status, occupation, religion, and nativity.

SEX. The difference in the percentage distribution between the two sexes is a most striking one: for committed suicides the percentage of males and females are 70 and 30, respectively, whereas for attempted suicides the percentages for males and females are 31 and 69—an almost exact reversal. These proportions of male to female (approximately 2⅓:1 for committed suicide and 1:2⅓ for attempted suicide) are somewhat lower than many of the estimated proportions suggested by other investigatiors (4:1 and 1:5 for "commits" and "attempts," respectively). These figures also contain interesting implications, especially in regard to the percentage of attempts who go on to commit suicide (and, conversely, the percentage of commits who have previously attempted suicide). From our previous work with male veterans (hospitalized in Veterans Administration neuropsychiatric hospitals) we have found that almost 80 percent of persons who committed suicide had previously attempted or threatened it. It would appear that the percentage of males who attempt and subsequently commit suicide is different from the percentage of females and that individual instances of attempted suicide must be evaluated, by and large, quite differently in males and in females.

RACE. Among the committed suicides, more than nine out of every ten persons were white (95 percent), whereas Negroes committed about 3 percent of the suicides. These percentages compare with the

TABLE III—Percentage Distribution by Sex of Sociological Factors
for Committed and Attempted Suicides
in Los Angeles County, 1957

Sociological Factors	Committed Suicide, %*			Attempted Suicide, %*		
	Male (n=540)	Female (n=228)	Total (n=768)	Male (n=828)	Female (n=1,824)	Total (n=2,652)
Sex	70	30	100	31	69	100
Race						
Caucasian	94	98	95	89	88	89
Negro	3	1	3	8	7	8
Oriental	2	. . .	1	1	1	1
Other and don't know	1	1	1	3	3	2
Age						
10-19	2	1	1	6	8	8
20-29	10	9	9	27	29	28
30-39	19	21	20	27	28	28
40-49	21	25	23	17	18	17
50-59	20	19	20	12	8	9
60-69	14	18	15	5	4	4
70-79	9	7	9	2	2	2
80-89	4	1	3	1	0	0
90 and over	0	0	0	0	0	0
Don't know	0	0	0	2	3	3
Marital Status						
Single	15	9	13	32	21	25
Married	53	48	52	46	58	54
Divorced	13	14	13	7	7	7
Widowed	6	20	11	3	4	4
Separated	8	7	8	6	5	5
Other and don't know	4	2	4	7	5	5
Occupation						
Professional	7	8	7	4	3	4
Semiprofessional	3	0	2	3	1	2
Artisan	10	4	7	6	2	3
White-collar	14	3	11	7	1	3
Clerical	4	13	6	3	9	7
Skilled	17	3	13	19	4	9
Semiskilled	12	2	9	12	7	8
Unskilled	25	10	20	15	6	9
Student	2	0	2	2	3	3
Housewife	0	50	16	1	45	31
Don't know	6	7	6	28	19	22

TABLE III—(*continued*)

Sociological Factors	Committed Suicide, %*			Attempted Suicide, %*		
	Male (n=540)	*Female (n=228)*	*Total (n=768)*	*Male (n=828)*	*Female (n=1,824)*	*Total (n=2,652)*
Religion						
Protestant	1	1	1			
Catholic	2	1	1			
Jewish	1	1	1			
Other	1	1	0			
Don't know	95	97	96			
Nativity						
North America	82	84	83			
Mexico	1	1	1			
Scandinavia	1	1	1			
Italy and Spain	1	0	1			
Europe (outside Scandinavia, Italy, and Spain)	11	10	10			
Orient	1	0	1			
Other	1	2	1			
Don't know	2	2	2			
Subject living with						
Spouse	44	42	44			
Parents	5	3	4			
Siblings	1	2	2			
Progeny	1	7	3			
Friends	2	2	2			
Self	22	20	21			
Other	4	7	5			
Don't Know	21	17	19			
Was subject referred for subsequent treatment?						
Yes				44	63	53
No				1	3	2
Don't know				55	35	44
To whom was subject referred?						
Psychiatrist				45	20	25
Psychologist					2	1
Social services				1	3	3
Medical services				3	2	2
Other				4	4	4
Don't know				32	28	29
Hospital				15	41	36

* All figures add up to 100% (approximately) within each subcategory.

national statistics for 1957, which show the same proportion of races. The attempted suicides also show a high proportion of whites, though the percentage (89 percent) is not quite so high as for the commits (95 percent). There are proportionately more Negroes who attempt suicide than commit it (8 versus 3 percent).

Unfortunately, the percentages of racial distribution in Los Angeles County for 1957 were not available, and no comments can be made about the relative racial proportions of committed and attempted suicides within the county.

AGE. Except for a small percentage of attempted suicides (3 percent), chronological age was known for practically every case. The committed suicides and attempted suicides showed marked variation in age distribution. Both male and female commits show a modal age of forty-two, whereas among the attempted suicides the peak occurs at age thirty-two for males and twenty-seven for females. For both sexes, attempts in the sixties and above are relatively rare compared with commits (6 versus 27 percent). There are more attempts among both sexes in their twenties and thirties than there are commits (56 versus 29 percent). Indeed, more than three times as many females in their twenties attempt suicide rather than commit it (29 versus 9 percent). In general, the older the person, the more likely the suicidal behavior will have lethal consequences. (It is well known that suicide *rate*, especially in males, goes up with each decade after age fifty.)

Some additional specific details about age can be given. The *number* of males (as contrasted with females) who kill themselves remains relatively high as one goes into the upper age bracket, even in the eighties. This, of course, would indicate that the rate for males goes up in Los Angeles County as it does in the national statistics. At the other extreme it is of some sad interest to note that 11 of the 768 committed suicides (1 percent) were age nineteen or younger, the youngest being eleven. However, among the attempted suicides, as much as 8 percent of the attempts occurred below age twenty, and of these, about 1 percent occurred below age fifteen. At around age forty there are about three times as many attempts by females as by males, but this ratio decreases until the numbers are about the same at age seventy and over.

Among the committed suicides only 10 percent occur below age thirty, whereas 36 percent of the attempted suicides occur below this age; further, less than one-third of the committed suicides (30 percent) have occurred before age forty, whereas two-thirds of the attempted suicides (64 percent) have occurred before this age. Conversely, one-fourth (27 percent) of the committed suicides occur after age sixty, whereas only 6 percent of the attempts occur after this age.

MARITAL STATUS. Even discounting the percentages of both attempts and commits who are in their teens and twenties, it is still surprising to see the relatively large percentage of both attempts (54 percent) and commits (52 percent) of both sexes who are married. However, in Los Angeles County, 64 percent of persons of all ages are married, so this category contributes proportionately less than its share. Proportionately fewer single persons (13 percent) commit suicide (there are 19 percent single persons in Los Angeles County), but proportionately more single persons attempt suicide (25 percent). The divorced and separated groups contribute disproportionately to the committed suicides (13 and 8 percent, respectively) as compared with these categories in the population of Los Angeles County (5 and 4 percent, respectively). The divorced and separated groups among the attempted suicides are approximately the same as the Los Angeles County population (7 and 5 percent, respectively). Widowed persons accounted for 11 percent of the committed suicides and 4 percent of the attempted suicides, as compared with 9 percent in the county population, indicating that the widowed generally are more lethal in their suicidal activity. It is of further interest to note that about five times as many widows commit suicide as attempt suicide (20 versus 4 percent), whereas about twice as many widowers commit suicide as attempt suicide (6 versus 3 percent).

When the attempts are compared further with the commits, we see that, although about the same percentage of each are married, about twice as many single persons attempt as commit suicide (25 versus 13 percent). The divorced, separated, and widowed groups commit suicide twice as often as they attempt it (32 versus 16 percent). It seems probable that the losses and disturbances in dyadic relationships occurring among the older groups, in

which more divorced, separated, and widowed appear, are also more likely to result in more lethal suicidal behavior.

OCCUPATION. The commits and attempts seem essentially similar in occupation; that is, if the percentages of males and females in each occupational group of attempts and commits are compared, it is seen that the percentages tend to be the same. This statement is based on the assumption that the obtained percentage of "don't knows" (6 percent of the commits and 22 per cent of the attempts) would distribute itself proportionately among the various categories. The main differences seem to be that more white-collar males commit suicide than attempt it (14 versus 7 percent); more unskilled males commit suicide than attempt it (25 versus 15 percent); more professional women commit suicide than attempt it (8 versus 3 percent); and more semiskilled women attempt suicide than commit it (7 versus 2 percent). The largest single category for both female "commits" and female "attempts" is housewife (50 and 45 percent, respectively). In general, among the committed suicides, the unskilled, semiskilled, and skilled laboring groups make up 42 percent, and white-collar and clerical workers contribute 17 percent of the total committed suicides. Among the attempted suicides, these groups contribute 26 and 10 percent, respectively.

Efforts were made to compare these figures with the occupational distribution in Los Angeles County generally (see Table IV). In Los Angeles County 25 percent of the population are in occupations labeled professional, technical, managerial, proprietor, and kindred occupations. If the professional and semiprofessional are combined in our listings, we find only 9 percent of the commits in these groups, so in Los Angeles it appears that the higher status groups do not provide a higher proportion of committed suicides, as has been stated elsewhere.[13] As the data from the various socioeconomic areas in Los Angeles County (as shown in Table VII also indicate, the commission of suicide is neither the rich man's curse nor the poor man's disease.

RELIGION. The death certificate (and other data in the coroner's office) in California does not indicate religion. Sometimes one can make a rather astute guess from the name of the cemetery

TABLE IV

Percentage Distribution by Sex in Occupations in
Los Angeles County (1950 Census)

Occupation	Male, %	Female, %	Total, %
Professional, technical, etc.	12	14	12
Farmers, farm managers	1	—	1
Managers, proprietors	15	6	12
Clerical	7	32	15
Sales workers	10	9	9
Craftsmen, foremen, etc.	22	2	16
Operators, etc.	18	16	17
Private household workers	1	7	2
Service workers, except household	7	12	9
Farm laborers, unpaid family workers	0	0	0
Farm laborers, except unpaid laborers and foremen	1	—	1
Laborers, except farm and mining	6	—	5
Not reported*	1	1	1

* Nonlabor force is not included above. Percentages do include housewives, students, and retired persons.

or mortuary, but this is not always so. Our data on religion for the committed suicides are predominately in the "don't know" category, and thus no comparisons between commits and attempts are possible. This (we rationalize) may be just as well, inasmuch as the question of religious affiliation is by no means so simple as some writers seem to have assumed it to be. Take, for example, the deceivingly simple question: Is the person a Catholic? Does one mean: Were his parents Catholic? Was he baptized a Catholic? Is he currently attending mass and confession? Does he himself have questions and doubts about his belief? Especially in this area, simple tabulations along a single dimension can mask a great deal of meaningful data.

NATIVITY. The place of birth of those who attempted suicide was not indicated in sufficient number, so comparisons with committed suicides cannot be made. Among the commit group more than 80 percent were born in the United States, and the next highest single percentage, around 10 percent, were born in European countries other than Italy, Spain, or Scandinavia.

WITH WHOM WAS THE SUBJECT LIVING? In this table there is information for committed suicides only. The information indicates

that 44 percent of the men and 42 percent of the women were living with their spouse and that 22 percent of the men and 20 percent of the women were living by themselves. Thirteen percent of the males and 21 percent of the females were living with others (parents, siblings, progeny, etc.). These data do not lend support to the common assertion that suicide is primarily an isolated event. Rather they tend to show suicidal behavior as a dyadic, interpersonal event and indicate that many persons who committed suicide (whether male or female) were living with their spouses, generally in an apartment setting. These figures are all the more striking when one remembers that approximately 15 percent of this group are single.

WAS THE SUBJECT REFERRED FOR TREATMENT AND TO WHOM? These data refer, of course, to the attempted suicides. The information indicates that at least 44 percent of the men and 84 percent of the women were referred for subsequent treatment. Of these percentages, 45 percent of the men and 20 percent of the women were referred specifically to a psychiatrist for treatment. It is surprising to see the small percentages referred to social service agencies. Most women were referred to a hospital for treatment, which may reflect the need for treatment (such as gastric lavage) of their most frequent suicide attempt method, barbiturate ingestion.

Suicide Data

The suicide data will be discussed in the categories presented in Table V and will include month of suicide, day of suicide, time (hour) of suicide, serology, method of suicide, presence of suicide note, seriousness of suicidal action, and "reason" for suicidal behavior. For the last two rubrics, the information for the attempted suicides is for only those cases reported by the physicians, inasmuch as these data were not available from municipal and county hospital records.

MONTH OF SUICIDE. The data do not show any significant temporal variations in suicidal phenomena by month. February is the lowest month (5 percent), and most other months vary between 8 and 9 percent. Although December and January have the highest percentages (11 and 10 percent, respectively), the variation is not sig-

nificant. Among the attempted suicides, the lowest month is April (5 percent) ; most other months again vary between 8 and 9 percent.

DAY AND HOUR OF SUICIDE. There does not seem to be any significant variation for either committed or attempted suicides in terms of the day selected for the suicidal behavior. Our data do not bear out the notion of "blue Monday" or any other single day as being a peak period for suicidal behavior. (Although it is one of the greater frequency days for attempts, it is one of the lower frequency days for committed.) As for the hour when suicides are committed or attempted, there are not sufficient data to warrant any conclusions.

METHOD OF SUICIDE. On an a priori basis, one would expect differences in the methods used by persons who die and persons who do not, and these differences are found empirically. By and large, suicidal methods can be divided into two groups: those in which the point of no return is reached precipitously, and those in which the point of no return is reached gradually. The former, which include gunshot wounds, hanging, and jumping, are identified almost exclusively with committed suicide, whereas wrist-cutting and throat-cutting are identified almost entirely with attempted suicide. There are some exceptions: carbon monoxide poisoning, although not precipitously effective, is, for males, the third cause of suicidal death after gunshot wounds and hanging. A second major exception is barbiturates, which occupies an important role as a method in both attempted and committed suicides. For women it is clearly the first method for both attempted and committed suicides; for men it is the first-ranking method for attempted suicides and the fourth-ranking method for committed suicides. As indicated above, there are marked sex differences in method for committing suicide. Males use guns 41 percent of the time, whereas women use them only 18 percent of the time. Women use barbiturates 46 percent of the time to kill themselves, whereas men use them 13 percent of the time. Men also use hanging and carbon monoxide poisoning more often than women. Among the attempts, males use cutting (26 versus 15 percent) and guns more often (5 versus 1 percent) than females. Women use barbiturates more often than men (59 versus 34 percent).

Two points seem to stand out from these data: the sex differences,

TABLE V—Percentage Distribution by Sex of Suicide Data for Committed and Attempted Suicides in Los Angeles County, 1957

Suicidal Factors	Committed Suicide, %*			Attempted Suicide, %*		
	Male (n=540)	Female (n=228)	Total (n=768)	Male (n=828)	Female (n=1,824)	Total (n=2,652)
Month of suicide						
January	10	8	10	7	10	9
February	5	5	5	10	9	9
March	8	6	8	9	8	8
April	8	10	8	6	5	5
May	9	9	9	8	8	8
June	8	10	8	7	10	9
July	7	6	7	7	9	8
August	9	10	9	10	9	10
September	8	7	8	10	9	9
October	8	10	8	9	7	8
November	9	8	8	7	9	8
December	10	11	11	9	8	8
Day of suicide						
Monday	12	13	12	15	14	15
Tuesday	13	12	13	15	13	14
Wednesday	13	10	12	15	13	13
Thursday	16	16	16	10	11	11
Friday	13	16	14	12	12	12
Saturday	12	13	12	14	12	12
Sunday	14	14	14	13	12	13
Don't know	6	7	7	7	13	11
Time of suicide						
6 A.M.-12 noon	12	11	12			
12 noon-6 P.M.	18	11	16			
6 P.M.-Midnight	11	11	11			
Midnight-6 P.M.	8	7	8			
Don't know	51	60	53			
Method of suicide						
Cut wrist	1	0	1	20	12	15
Cut throat	1	3	2	6	2	3
Gunshot, head	35	14	29	2	—	1
Gunshot, other	6	4	6	3	1	2
Barbiturates	13	46	23	34	54	48
Poisoning	4	6	4	9	9	9
Hanging	16	7	13	2	1	1
Jumping	3	4	3	1	1	1
Drowning	1	4	2	0	0	0
Carbon monoxide, auto	14	6	11	2	—	1
Illuminating gas	2	2	2	4	3	3
Stabbing	1	1	1	1	1	1
Other and don't know	3	2	3	15	17	16

Suicidal Factors	Committed Suicide, %*			Attempted Suicide, %*		
	Male (n=540)	Female (n=228)	Total (n=768)	Male (n=828)	Female (n=1,824)	Total (n=2,652)
Suicide note						
Yes	35	39	36	2	1	1
No	65	61	64	98	99	99
Serology at death						
Ethanol absent	28	23	25			
Less than 1.5 ethanol	11	4	9			
More than 1.5 ethanol	13	7	9			
Don't know, ethanol	2	1	2			
Barbiturate present	9	33	20			
Poison present	2	2	2			
Carbon monoxide present	9	3	7			
Combinations (of above)	5	9	6			
Don't know	21	18	20			
Seriousness of suicidal action						
Really wanted to die				36	27	29
Undecided; left survival up to chance				23	19	20
Expected to be saved, did not intend to die				25	40	37
Don't know or not indicated				16	14	14
"Reasons" indicated for suicidal action						
Ill physical health	26	20	24	8	4	5
Ill mental health	9	18	12	4	3	3
Love affair	2	1	2	2	3	4
Jealousy, anger, rage	1	3	1	1	1	1
Death of other	2	5	3	2	1	1
Loneliness	1	1	1	1	2	2
Marital difficulties	15	9	13	11	29	24
Business, employment, finances	8	1	6	10	1	3
Psychological depression	13	16	14	9	20	18
Guilt over sexuality	0	0	0	1	1	1
Other and don't know	23	26	24	51	35	38
How subject was saved						
Subject asked someone for help or came for help				18	26	24
Someone stopped subject				9	10	10
Someone found subject				72	64	65

* All figures add up to 100% (approximately) in each subcategory.

with greater lethality for males from use of methods in which the point of no return is reached quickly; and the ubiquitous and significant role of barbiturates in suicidal behavior, emphasizing the need for careful precautions in prescribing these drugs.

Compared with national figures for rates by method of committing suicide, as supplied by the National Office of Vital Statistics, U.S. Department of Health, Education, and Welfare, the Los Angeles County rates by method of committed suicide do not differ significantly. There are, of course, no national rates for attempted suicide. There does tend to be a somewhat greater rate for deaths by carbon monoxide poisoning in Los Angeles (1.6 Los Angeles versus 0.8 U.S.), which may reflect the greater concentration of automobiles in the Los Angeles area. Generally, the rates by method for committed and attempted suicide found in Los Angeles County would probably apply in most large metropolitan areas. It is of interest to note that methods for committing and attempting suicide change over the years, so problems of control that were predominant two or three decades ago (especially caustics and poisons) have now changed to the problem of controlling barbiturates.

SUICIDE NOTE. It is of interest that 35 percent of the males and 39 percent of the females left suicide notes. This figure is somewhat more than what has been reported by other investigators.[14] The percentages may differ for several reasons: official attitude toward the notes as public documents, varying standards for certification of suicide by coroners, and the like. The small percentage of attempt notes is a result of the fact that notes from this group are not public property in Los Angeles County but remain in the possession of the attempter or the rescuer.[15] It may be sufficient to mention in passing that suicide notes offer an unusual opportunity for the investigator to obtain some important insights into the thoughts and feelings of suicidal persons, written as they are within the context of suicidal behavior. In other publications we have analyzed the content of suicide notes from various points of view.[16]

SEROLOGY. Serology is, of course, available only in the cases of committed suicide. It is of interest to note that 24 percent of the committed males had some ethanol content, and 11 percent of the

females had some ethanol content. The presence of other chemicals, such as barbiturates, poisons, and carbon monoxide, simply reflected the method of committed suicide.

SERIOUSNESS OF SUICIDAL ACTION. In the questionnaire to the physicians, we asked the doctors to check the seriousness of the specific suicide attempt. Although we are well aware that the reliability of these ratings is open to much question, there are some very interesting tendencies to be commented upon. Of the males who made suicide attempts 36 percent were adjudged as really wanting to die, with 23 percent leaving survival up to chance. Only 25 percent of the male attempters were adjudged as expecting to be saved. Among the females the physicians thought that only 27 percent really wanted to die, 19 percent left survival up to chance, and 40 percent definitely expected to be saved. This points up the seriousness of the phenomenon of attempted suicide and also the important role of the rescuer in the actual saving of lives.

"REASONS" FOR SUICIDAL BEHAVIOR. Although it is believed that the reasons for suicide cited in this section are not reliable scientific data, they are nevertheless presented for their general interest value. The sources of the reasons for the commits were the police reports and deputy coroner reports (as obtained from witnesses) on file at the coroner's office; the source for the reasons for the attempts was the questionnaire filled out by physicians. An additional, and much better source, for reasons are the suicide notes themselves, as indicated in another publication.[17] We believe that the reasons for suicide derived in this manner at best reflect only the more superficial, precipitating causes for suicidal behavior and leave untold the more important sustaining causes, primary causes, and the like. With these preliminary comments out of the way, we can see that, among men who commit suicide, ill health, marital difficulties, and psychological depression, the latter of which might well cut across the first two, are given as the three main reasons. Among women who commit suicide, physical ill health, mental ill health, and depression are given. What the police and the coroner have told is almost a tautology; namely, that persons who hurt (are in pain) and who are depressed are suicidal.

Among attempted suicides ill health does not rank high (except for males), but rather such causes as marital difficulties and depression are given most often for both sexes and financial and employment difficulties are added for men.

HOW THE SUBJECT WAS SAVED. The information given by the physicans indicates that the largest percentage (72 percent of the men and 64 percent of the women) were found by someone, usually the spouse. Twenty-four percent of those who attempted suicide actually asked for help.

Ecological Data

We wished to plot the distributions of attempted and committed suicides within the socioeconomic geographic areas of Los Angeles County. First, of course, we needed to obtain each subject's address. For committed suicides we obtained the address from the death certificate, and for attempted suicides we obtained the address either from hospital records or from the physicians' questionnaires. In the questionnaires, in which we did not ask for the patient's name, we obtained the address by asking the following: "Do not indicate the patient's exact address. Instead, indicate the street number within the same 100 block, the correct postal zone, and the subsection. Address is important so that a careful ecological distribution of suicide attempts can be made and used for planning purposes, etc." The procedure was then (1) to translate each address into the correct census tract, (2) to translate the census tract into 1 of 100 study areas, and (3) to translate each study area into 1 of 9 area types.[18] These terms merit some explanation. Los Angeles County consists of several hundred census tracts, which shift with different census activities. In order to give some stability to the changing patterns (for research and planning purposes), the Los Angeles Welfare Planning Council made an extensive study of the census data of Los Angeles County and then, on the basis of the analyses, divided the county into 100 relatively stable, relatively homogeneous study areas (based on such factors as average economic income, average educational level, percentage of home ownership, and occupational levels). It then distributed these 100 study areas (on the basis of an intensive investigation of urbanization and social rank) among nine general Area Types. The

names and descriptions of these nine Area Types are given by the council as follows.[19]

AREA TYPE I, MOST ADVANTAGED SUBURBS (FOUR AREAS). Familiarity with the neighborhoods in this area confirms the fact that it has many social advantages: fine schools, effective churches, plenty of play space for the many children in large backyards with many swimming pools, safe street play areas, riding stables, and a high percentage of college-trained persons who provide a reservoir of potential volunteer leadership for activities such as scouting. The area is definitely suburban and will remain so indefinitely, for most of the persons living there earn their living by commuting fifteen miles or more to the cities of Los Angeles, Pasadena, Burbank, and Glendale. Single-family detached dwellings predominate.

AREA TYPE II, MOST ADVANTAGED RESIDENTIAL COMMUNITIES (FOURTEEN AREAS). Fine houses, spacious yards, many recreational facilities, churches, and good schools are found. The community is somewhat older. There is a tremendous reservoir of city-wide leadership owing to the presence of the University of California at Los Angeles. Some commercial establishments may be found here, such as exclusive restaurants, shops, and nightclubs.

AREA TYPE III, MOST ADVANTAGED APARTMENT HOUSE AREAS (FIVE AREAS). This area is well built up, with a fairly high population density owing to the apartment house pattern. Few children but many professional persons are found here. There is a city-wide shopping center.

AREA TYPE IV, MODERATELY ADVANTAGED SUBURBS (THIRTEEN AREAS). Some older estates are found in the area, but recent subdivision into tract housing is most common. Spacious yards and play space prevail. An abundance of volunteer leadership, many churches of the neighborhood variety, and good though crowded schools are found. Commuting imposes special problems on families who live there. Young veteran families and white-collar and skilled workers predominate.

AREA TYPE V, MODERATELY ADVANTAGED NATURAL COMMUNITIES (THIRTY-FOUR AREAS). This type includes more than one-third of all

the areas in Los Angeles County. Housing is moderately new and
of the single-family type, with small yards and restricted play
space. The area is fully built up. There are a variety of churches
and schools in the area. Leadership is fairly abundant, community
organization is well developed. There is little industry. The distance to Los Angeles city center is ten miles. There is a wide range
of occupations represented.

AREA TYPE VI, MODERATELY ADVANTAGED MULTIPLE-DWELLING AREAS
(EIGHT AREAS). Population density is greater in this area because
of the multiple-family dwellings. Space is limited to recreational
facilities. There are many older persons, many on smaller incomes,
and fewer children. This area shows port-of-entry characteristics,
and converted dwellings are seen.

AREA TYPE VII, LEAST ADVANTAGED RURAL AREA (ONE AREA). Only
one area, an unincorporated part of Los Angeles County, was included in this group. It is still the center of the dairy industry.
There are pockets of older, substandard Mexican-American housing
surrounded by much open space still devoted to agriculture or lying
waste. Low-cost tract housing is filling up some of the open spaces.
Community organization is weak. Leadership is somewhat limited
because of the lower educational attainments of the residents.
Churches tend to be of the evangelical variety.

AREA TYPE VIII, LEAST ADVANTAGED INDUSTRIAL COMMUNITIES (FOUR-
TEEN AREAS). Area 17 (San Pedro), part of the harbor of Los
Angeles, is typical of this area type. Population density is moderate,
with few yards and many multiple dwellings. Shipping and industry are associated with blighted neighborhoods, skid row districts,
and the like. There is need for outside help to solve problems.
Housing projects, nationality and minority groups in distinctive
numbers, settlement houses, boys' clubs, and missions are found.

AREA TYPE IX, LEAST ADVANTAGED ROOMING HOUSE AND APARTMENT
AREAS (SEVEN AREAS). Older houses have been converted to rooming houses or apartments. There are buildings in the rear, and
apartment houses are run-down. There is no play space, and much

blight is found where industry and business have encroached on housing areas. Minority groups (Negroes, Mexican-Americans, Chinese, Japanese) predominate here. The population is declining, and community consciousness is weak. There are churches of many sects. Leadership is limited and needs to be supplemented from the outside by professional agencies, settlements, and so forth.

The distribution of attempted and committed suicides among these nine socioeconomic area types is indicated in Table VI. Also in Table VI are the percentage of total population within each area type and the ratios of committed and attempted suicides (per 100,000 population) for each area type. For attempted suicides, the total again is for that part (2,652) of the total population of attempters in Los Angeles County (5,906) on which information was available. The columns of numbers of attempted suicides and percentage of total attempted suicides in Table VI therefore do not give exact attempted suicide population figures but do provide pro-portionate results, which allow the areas to be compared with one another. The percentage distribution of both attempted and com-mitted suicides among the nine Area Types is for the most part consistent with the percentage distribution of population within Los Angeles County. There are some notable exceptions, specifically in Area IV (moderately advantaged suburbs), which contains 21 percent of the population but only 12 percent of the committed and attempted suicides. Area V (moderately advantaged natural communities) contributes less than its share of attempted suicides, 20 percent out of 31 percent of the population. Area VI (mod-erately advantaged apartment areas), which contains 7 percent of the population, contributes somewhat more than its share of committed suicides, 11 percent, and a still higher share of the attempted suicides, 14 percent.

Another way to view these data is to note the *rates* of committed and attempted suicide for each area type (number per 100,000 total Los Angeles County population). Among the committed suicides, we find the rate in Area III (most advantaged apartment house areas) and Area VI (moderately advantaged apartment house areas) is fairly high (22 and 21 percent, respectively). Both Area III and Area VI have relatively high proportions of females and of widowed and divorced persons. The lowest rates, 3 and 8 percent, appear

TABLE VI—Distribution of Total Population and Attempted and
Committed Suicides Among Area Types, Los Angeles County, 1957

Area Type	Population*	% of Total Population	No. of Committed Suicides	% of Total Committed Suicides	Ratio of Committed Suicide to Area Population (per 100,000)	No. of Attempted Suicides	% of Total Attempted Suicides	Ratio of Attempted Suicide to Area Population (per 100,000)†
I	265,180	5	31	4	.00012	129	5	.00049
II	828,884	16	132	17	.00016	452	17	.00055
III	200,279	4	44	6	.00022	118	4	.00059
IV	1,097,822	21	93	12	.00008	327	12	.00030
V	1,673,977	31	236	31	.00014	538	20	.00032
VI	392,863	7	84	11	.00021	379	14	.00100
VII	119,000	2	4	1	.00003	20	1	.00017
VIII	529,354	10	68	9	.00013	255	10	.00048
IX	192,989	4	37	5	.00019	193	7	.00100
Area Unknown			39	5		241	9	
Total	5,300,348	100	768	100	(av.=.00014)	2,652	100	(av.=.00054)

* Population based on 1957 figures from a special census of Los Angeles County.
† Rates presented in this column are approximately 45% of their true value, inasmuch as 2,652 of the total population of 5,906 attempted suicides are represented (assuming proportionate distribution among the nine area types of the uncharted attempted suicides).

TABLE VII—Some Salient Characteristics of Committed and
Attempted Suicides, Los Angeles County, 1957

Characteristic	Committed Suicide	Attempted Suicide
Sex	More males	More females
Race	For both sexes, almost entirely Caucasian	For both sexes, predominantly Caucasian
Age	For both sexes, greatest number in forties; for males, continues proportionately high in sixties and over	For both sexes, greatest number in twenties and thirties
Marital status	For both sexes, large percentage married (though low proportionately), more divorced, separated, and widowed; for females, high proportion of widowed	For both sexes, large percentage married (though low proportionately), high proportion single
Occupation	For females, high proportion of housewives; for males, high proportion skilled and unskilled	For females, high proportion of housewives; for males, high proportion skilled, semiskilled, and unskilled
Nativity	For both sexes, predominantly native-born	For both sexes, predominantly native-born
Method of suicide	For males, mostly gunshot wounds, hanging, carbon monoxide; for females, mostly barbiturates and gunshot wounds	For both sexes, mostly barbiturates, some wrist cutting
"Reason" for suicide	For both sexes, ill health, depression; for males, marital difficulties	For both sexes, marital difficulties, depression; for males, financial and employment difficulties.
Socioeconomic areas	For both sexes, highest in apartment areas of all types (most, moderately, and least advantaged)	For both sexes, highest in apartment areas, particularly least and moderately advantaged

in Areas VII and IV (least advantaged rural areas and moderately advantaged suburbs, respectively). Both of these areas have high well-knit family concentrations.

In relation to attempted suicides, Areas VII (least advantaged rural area), IV (moderately advantaged suburbs), and V (moderately advantaged natural communities) are relatively low in their rates. Again, all these areas contain a relatively high percentage of married persons with family-type dwellings and well-developed community organization. On the other hand, Area IX (least advan-

taged apartment areas) and Area VI (moderately advantaged apartment areas), which have relatively higher percentages of single persons, have proportionately higher rates of suicidal attempts. It thus appears that there is some tendency for a high rate of both committed and attempted suicides to be associated with apartment living, especially among widowed and separated females. Even Area III, a luxury apartment house area, has a higher rate of attempts. Apparently this factor cuts across social class factors and applies to lower, middle, and, to some extent, upper socioeconomic strata. These figures raise some interesting questions for city planners, especially in Los Angeles, where there is a noticeable trend toward building large apartment communities. One would have to investigate what is cause and what is effect: Does apartment living exacerbate suicidal impulses, or do suicidal persons gravitate to apartments? Nonetheless a thought might be given to enhancing the community features in any large apartment ediflce.

What general sociological comparisons can be made between attempted suicides and committed suicides (for Los Angeles County for 1957)? Table VII summarizes most of the preceding material by presenting some of the salient features of the data presented in this chapter. From this table, it is possible to delineate *modal* (or *typical*) portraits of the suicide committer and the suicide attempter, if the reader will keep in mind the important cautions that these are oversimplified; they refer only to statistically outstanding features, and in a clinical or emergency setting each case must be decided from its own idiosyncracies. With these cautionary comments in mind, we may say the following:

The *modal suicide attempter* is likely to be (1) female, (2) Caucasian, (3) in her twenties or thirties, probably the former, (4) most likely married or single, (5) a housewife, and (6) native-born, and to (7) attempt suicide by barbiturates, (8) give as a "reason" marital difficulties or depression, and (9) live in an apartment in an apartment house area.

By way of contrast, the *modal suicide committer* is likely to be (1) male, (2) Caucasian, (3) in his forties or older, (4) married, (5) a skilled or unskilled worker, and (6) native-born, and to (7) commit suicide by gunshot wounds, hanging, or carbon monoxide poisoning, (8) give as a reason ill health, depression, or marital

difficulties, and (9) live in an apartment in an apartment house area.

One point now seems evident: on the basis of the statistical study of sociological factors presented in this chapter, it appears that one cannot combine attempted suicides and committed suicides (and call them both suicidal) without masking a good number of differences, which can, in themselves, be extremely important. A corollary is that studies investigating selected samples of attempted suicides should not, in seeking other sources of information, match their data from committed suicides on the assumption that the two are essentially the same.

Chapter 13
A SOCIOPSYCHOLOGICAL INVESTIGATION OF SUICIDE

Edwin S. Shneidman and Norman L. Farberow

This study compares two major kinds of data—sociological and psychological—for individuals who committed suicide in Los Angeles in 1956–1958. The sociological information for 948 indivduals was derived from census tract and Welfare Planning Council data and, among other items, indicated the socioeconomic status of each individual. The psychological information consisted of analyses of the suicide notes of 768 individuals who killed themselves. Among the findings of the study, two were of special interest: (1) the percentages of individuals who committed suicide at each of the major socioeconomic levels were almost identical with the total percentages of citizens who lived at each of those levels. Suicide is thus "democratic," being proportionately represented at each socioeconomic stratum in the society. And (2) the reasons (given in the suicide notes) were different among the various socioeconomic levels. The major implication of the study is that the phenomena of suicide must be viewed as an admixture of both social and psychological elements; one needs both Durkheim and Freud in order to explain self-destructive phenomena.

There are several rather distinct approaches to the investigation of the phenomena of suicide—the ecologic, anthropologic, psychiatric, and psychoanalytic points of view immediately come to mind. Of these, perhaps the best-known approach to the analysis of suicidal data is that which is generally called "sociological." This approach to understanding suicide has, by now, a time-honored tradition and includes what is probably the best-known single work on the topic, Durkheim's *Le Suicide*.[1] Durkheim's work on suicide in France established a model for sociological investigations of suicide—and also delineated an essentially psychological classification of types of suicides (anomic, altruistic, and egoistic). There have been many subsequent studies of this genre. The monographs and books by Cavan on suicide in Chicago,[2] of Schmid

on suicide in Seattle and Minneapolis,[3] of Sainsbury on suicide in London,[4] of Dublin and Bunzel,[5] and of Henry and Short on suicide in the United States[6] all fall within the sociological tradition of taking a plot of ground—a city or a country—and figuratively or literally reproducing its map several times to show its socially shady (and topographically shaded) areas and their multifarious relationships to suicide rates. This kind of study certainly has the merit of employing the available sociological and suicidal data, but it also has the characteristic of being focused in its conclusions on generalizations about suicide that are necessarily couched in socio-economic terminology. One result of this outcome is that the individual who has aspirations for effecting any kind of reduction in suicide rates is limited in his range of possible actions by virtue of the fact that he is given little information about the highly individual and personal *psychological* aspects of the suicidal behaviors.

It was in an effort to fill this lack that the present project was undertaken. In essence, the purpose of the study reported in this paper is to *juxtapose psychological and sociological suicidal data* (for the same community and for the same temporal interval) *so that congruencies between the two sets of data*—the "data of the individual" and the "data of the social structure"—*might be indicated and their relationships to suicidal data might be explored.*

Overview of the Data

This study, which explores both sociological and psychological data relating to suicide, utilizes data from a specific, large metropolitan area—Los Angeles County—and, except where specifically noted, one time—calendar year 1957.

In the interests of clarity of exposition, a brief description of the different kinds of data employed in this study will be given at this point.

Sociological information, which will consist of data from each of the nine types of sociocultural-economic areas (called Area Types) into which Los Angeles County has been divided. The Los Angeles Welfare Planning Council did an extensive study of the census data of Los Angeles County; then, on the basis of their analyses, divided the County into 100 relatively stable, relatively homogeneous "study areas" (based on such factors as average eco-

nomic income, average educational level, percentage of home ownership, occupational levels, and the like), and, finally, distributed
these 100 study areas (on the basis of an analysis of "urbanization"
and "social rank") among nine Area Types, as follows: Most advantaged suburbs, most advantaged residential communities, most
advantaged apartment house areas, moderately advantaged suburbs, moderately advantaged natural communities, moderately advantaged multiple-dwelling areas, least advantaged rural areas, least
advantaged industrial communities, and least advantaged rooming-
house and apartment areas. The data for these nine Area Types
constitute the basic sociological data for this study.

Some population data for each of the nine sociological Area Types
is indicated in Table I, below. These data come from a Welfare
Planning Council Report entitled "Fact Sheets on 100 Study Areas,
Los Angeles County, June, 1957" and were collated into the nine
Area Types by the present writers. The column captions in Table
I can be described as follows: "% of Population" refers to the number of people in each Area Type compared to the total population
of Los Angeles County; "% Youth" refers to the number of individuals over 65 years of age of the total number of individuals of
that Area; "% Minority" is defined by the Planning Council as
"Negroes, other races, and whites with Spanish surnames"; and
"% Change" refers to the increase or decrease in population in that
specific area since the 1950 Census.

Suicidal Information

The Coroner's files were searched, and each of the 768 cases
certified during 1957 as "Suicide" (for a total of 9,770 cases processed by the Coroner in 1957) was examined. The following items
were abstracted for each case: sex, race, age, marital status, occupation, length of time in Los Angeles County, presence or absence
of suicide note, and street address. The victim's street address was
coded for Study Area and then for Area Type.

The distribution of the 768 suicides in Los Angeles County in 1957
among the nine Area Types is indicated in Table II. The reader will
note that the percentages of suicide compared to the total number of
suicides within each Area Type (keeping in mind that 5 percent
of the suicides could not be located by Area Type) *are remarkably
similar* to the percentages of the total population contained within

TABLE I—Population Data For Nine Area Types
Los Angeles County, 1957

Area Type	Name	No. of Areas	Population	% of Popul.	% of Youth	% 20-65	% Aged	% Minority	% Change
I	Most Advantaged Suburbs	4	265,180	5%	35%	61%	4%	1%	49%
II	Most Advantaged Residential Communities	14	828,884	16%	24%	68%	8%	3%	23%
III	Most Advantaged Apartment House Areas	5	200,279	4%	21%	65%	4%	3%	3%
IV	Moderately Advantaged Suburbs	13	1,097,822	21%	40%	56%	4%	9%	124%
V	Moderately Advantaged Natural Communities	34	1,673,977	31%	31%	62%	7%	6%	24%
VI	Moderately Advantaged Apartment Areas	8	392,863	7%	18%	68%	14%	13%	−4%
VII	Least Advantaged Rural Areas	1	119,000	2%	42%	56%	2%	9%	177%
VIII	Least Advantaged Industrial Communities	14	529,354	10%	36%	58%	6%	34%	3%
IX	Least Advantaged Apartment Areas	7	192,989	4%	28%	61%	11%	59%	−20%
TOTAL OR AVERAGE		100	5,300,348	100%	31%	61%	8%	15%	42%

each Area Type, with the possible exceptions of Area Types IV and VI. More significant are the nine ratios of numbers of suicide to the numbers of people within each Area Type. In this column one sees that the range of ratios is from 3 per 100,000 population to 22 per 100,000 population, with an average rate of 14 per 100,000— somewhat higher than the national average of 9.8. Statistically, the

TABLE II—Suicide Information
Los Angeles County, 1957

Area Type	Name	Population	% of Popul.	No. of Suicides	% of Total Suicides	Ratio of No. Suicides to Pop. in that Area Type
I	Most Advantaged Suburbs	265,180	5%	31	4%	.00012
II	Most Advantaged Residential Communities	828,884	16%	132	17%	.00016
III	Most Advantaged Apartment House Areas	200,279	4%	44	6%	.00022
IV	Moderately Advantaged Suburbs	1,097,822	21%	93	12%	.00008
V	Moderately Advantaged Natural Communities	1,673,977	31%	236	31%	.00014
VI	Moderately Advantaged Apartment Areas	392,863	7%	84	11%	.00021
VII	Least Advantaged Rural Areas	119,000	2%	4	1%	.00003
VIII	Least Advantaged Industrial Communities	529,354	10%	68	9%	.00013
IX	Least Advantaged Apartment Areas	192,989	4%	37	5%	.00019
Area Unknown				39	5%	
TOTAL		5,300,348	100%	768	100%	Av.=.00014

differences among the ratios of the nine Area Types were significant.[7] The major differences were that Area Type IV was low in suicide rate, and Area Types III and VI were relatively high. It is of interest to note that both high suicide Area Types are apartment house areas.

The suicidal data were examined for statistically significant differences within the total suicidal population among the nine Area Types for four items: race, sex, age, and marital status. The findings are shown in Table III. In the Table, each "Hi" or "Low" indicates a greater or lesser proportion, respectively, within an overall statistically significant difference for the specific Area Type indicated.

There were no statistically significant differences for *race* of suicidal individuals among the nine Area Types. More than 90 percent of all individuals who committed suicide in Los Angeles County in 1957 were Caucasian. No single Area Type contained more than 2 percent other-than-Caucasians among the suicide population. Comparison with the "% Minority" column of Table I— especially for Area Types VIII and IX—indicates that minority groups are not proportionately represented in the suicide statistics. One partial explanation is that the Planning Council data for the Area Types includes individuals with Spanish surnames (ostensibly to include the Los Angeles Mexican population) within the minority figures, whereas the Coroner's Office automatically classifies a Mexican-American as a Caucasian. Even so, the percentage of Negroes in Area Types VIII and IX is many times higher than the 1 percent of Negro suicides in those areas of Los Angeles County.

For *sex*, there were statistically significant differences in male-female ratio within some of the Area Types.[8] Inspection of the data revealed that these differences occurred in two Area Types: Area Type III (Most advantaged apartment house areas) had a greater number of female suicides than would be expected and a smaller number of male suicides than would be expected; and Area Type VIII (Least advantaged industrial communities) had a smaller number of female suicides than would be expected on the basis of the overall male-female suicide distribution throughout the County.

There were no statistically significant differences for *age* groups of suicidal individuals among the nine Area Types.

For *marital status* of suicided individuals, there were statistically

TABLE III—High and Low Proportions for Sex, and Marital
Status of Suicides, Los Angeles County, 1957

Area Type	Name	SUICIDE RATE	SEX		MARITAL STATUS		
			Male	Female	Sgl.	Mar.	Div./Wid.
I	Most Advantaged Suburbs						Low
II	Most Advantaged Residential Communities						
III	Most Advantaged Apartment House Areas	Hi	Low	Hi		Low	Hi
IV	Moderately Advantaged Suburbs	Low					
V	Moderately Advantaged Natural Communities					Hi	Low
VI	Moderately Advantaged Apartment Areas	Hi				Low	Hi
VII	Least Advantaged Rural Areas						
VIII	Least Advantaged Industrial Communities			Low	Low		
IX	Least Advantaged Apartment Areas				Hi	Low	

significant differences among the nine Area Types.[9] These differences occurred in six of the Area Types. In Area Type I there
were fewer Widowed and Divorced; in Area Type III there were
fewer Married and more Widowed and Divorced; in Area Type V
there were more Married and fewer Widowed and Divorced; in
Area Type VI the pattern was the same as in Area Type III; in

Area Type VIII there were fewer Single; and in Area Type IX there were more Single and fewer Married.

Psychological Information

One might ask, rhetorically, what are the sources from which one ordinarily obtains "psychological" information about an individual? The conventional answers would include such sources as anamneses, psychological test protocols, psychotherapy notes, interview records, and the like. An unconventional response—but one most relevant when one is dealing with a population of individuals each of whom has committed suicide—would be *suicide notes*. On the face of it, genuine suicide notes (written, typically, within a few minutes before the individual kills himself, and sometimes actually written as the individual is dying) constitute an unusual opportunity to obtain data concerning the ideation and the affect of the suicidal person. One can make a strong case for the position that if the psychology of the suicidal individual appears in any sort of record, it might, on a common-sense basis, be expected to be found in the document the individual composed directly within the context of the suicidal act.

It is of interest that an exhaustive survey of the bibliography on suicide since 1897 (prepared by the present writers) reveals that the literature on suicide notes is, by and large, a very recent one. With the exception of a monograph on suicide notes by Morgenthaler and Steinberg (which reproduces 47 suicide notes obtained in Berne, Switzerland, during the period 1928 to 1935) published in 1945,[10] the remaining few references to studies involving notes are all within the past two years: an article and some book chapters by Shneidman and Farberow;[11] an article by Tuckman, Kleiner, and Lavell;[12] and an article by Osgood and Walker.[13] The outline employed to analyze suicide notes in the present study (as indicated in Table IV) includes the "content categories" used by Osgood and Walker.

All 948 genuine suicide notes were analyzed by one rater. This individual, a psychologist, had no knowledge of the race, address, and the like of the note-writer—as a matter of record, the rater had no information about the purpose of the study at all. In addition, 100 (of the 948) suicide notes were rated independently of

TABLE IV—Outline for Analysis of "Psychology" of Suicide Notes

A. *ADDRESSEE OF SUICIDE NOTE*

1. No address
2. To Whom it may concern
3. Police
4. Spouse
5. Parent
6. Child
7. Sibling
8. Friend
9. Specific, but not able to ascertain
10. Other: (Specify)

B. *REASONS STATED IN SUICIDE NOTE*

11. No reason stated
12. Ill health, illness, physical disability, symptoms, pain
13. Rejection by another; jilted; unloved; not understood; can't live without you
14. Finances, money, bills, debts
15. Job, occupation, unemployment
16. Ennui, tired of life
17. No point in living; not worth trying
18. Interest in death, other world, hereafter
19. To "join" a (deceased) loved one
20. As a "way out," reached end, couldn't go on
21. Isolation, loneliness
22. Love triangle (other man, woman)
23. Confusion, depression, fear anxiety
24. Being persecuted; hearing voices; losing mind
25. Sex
26. Other: (Specify)

C. *AFFECT INDICATED IN SUICIDE NOTE*

31. No affect
32. Hostility, criticism, blame, revenge
33. Absolution of other, giving forgiveness (of specific persons)
34. Sorrow, seeking forgiveness (from specific persons)
35. Seeking forgiveness from deity
36. Self-depreciation, self-derogation, self-criticism, guilt, self-blame (fault) better off without me
37. Love, idealization, praise, defense
38. Other: (Specify)

D. *SPECIFIC CONTENT OTHER THAN AFFECT*

51. No specific content other than affect
52. Mention of religion, fate, life, world, death (abstraction)
53. Goodbye, farewell
54. Reference to suicidal act, no one responsible
55. Reference to suicide note
56. Instructions re money, business, power of attorney, funeral expenses
57. Instructions re insurance
58. Instructions re material possessions
59. Instructions re children
60. Instructions re own remains
61. Instructions re notification of others
62. Instructions re message to others
63. Other: (Specify)

E. *GENERAL FOCUS OF THE SUICIDE NOTE*

71. Primarily *reason* for suicide
72. Primarily *affect*
73. Primarily *instructions*
74. Primarily *abstractions*
75. Primarily *content other than affect*
76. Primarily *reflecting own confusion*
77. Extremely short; cryptic; enigmatic
78. Other: (Specify) No content

the initial rating by another rater, so that some indications of interrater reliability—discussed below—might be obtained.

In this study, psychological variables were educed by analyzing each suicide note in terms of the following scheme:

1. To whom the suicide note was addressed (e.g., spouse, parent, child, etc.) This rubric was intended to yield the interpersonal involvements, the directions of dyadic relationships, and the like.

2. Reasons for suicide explicitly stated in the note (e.g., ill health, rejection, finances, etc.) This category described the victim's stated conscious "reasons" for killing himself.

3. Affect indicated (or implied) in the suicide note (e.g., anger, sorrow, affection, etc.)

4. Content other than affect (e.g., did the note include reference to money and insurance, material possessions, disposition of remains, etc.) The purpose here was to get at the victim's main concerns at the time—whether these concerns were with himself, with others, with material possessions, with death, and so forth.

5. The general focus of the suicide note (i.e., did the note focus on the reason, on affect, or on instructions). The purpose here was to obtain an indication of the overall tenor of the individual's last communication.

A listing of all the scoring categories is given in Table IV.

There are two methodological questions concerning the suicide notes that need to be mentioned. They are: (1) Are the results obtained by the present scoring system replicable with another rater? (2) Are the suicide-note writers representative of the total population of individuals who committed suicide?

1. *Interjudge reliability.* As a check upon the reliability of the categorizing, 100 of the suicide notes were reanalyzed by another judge. All but nine were categorized as they had been previously, yielding a reliability figure that indicated that the two analyzers scored the notes in essentially the same manner.[14]

2. *Representativeness of suicide-note writers.* A statistical comparison by distribution by sex, age categories, and marital status between (a) the 1957 suicide-note writers and (b) the 1957 suicides minus the note writers indicated that the two groups were similar, that is, there were no statistically significant differences between the two groups in any of these three categories. These results concerning the representativeness of suicide notes are consistent with

data in relation to the 721 suicide notes collected over a ten-year period, that ". . . the socioeconomic statistics of the note-writing group have been compared with the similar data from the non-note-writing group and the two groups have been found to be essentially the same."[15] In the study reported by Tuckman, Kleiner, and Lavell, in which they indicate, in relation to 165 suicide notes collected over a five-year period, that "A comparison of those who left notes with those who did not showed no significant difference between the two groups with respect to age, race, sex, employment, marital status, physical condition, mental condition, history of mental illness, place of suicide, reported causes of unusual circumstances preceding the suicide, medical care and supervision, and history of previous attempts or threats."[16]

The heart of the psychological data is in the analysis of the suicide notes. What did the statistical analyses of the scorings of the notes yield? Were there any indications of statistically significant differences in "psychology," as revealed in note content, among the nine different sociological Area Types? The results indicated that in two of the five aspects of suicide note analysis—Reasons for suicide and Affect—there were significant results.[17] The specific differences for the details of note content in the Reasons and Affect categories among the nine Area Types are indicated in Table V and are discussed below.

Area Type I—Most Advantaged Suburbs: 5 percent of the population; 4 percent of the suicides; 12/100,000 suicide rate; less than 1 percent minority groups; small proportionate percentage of Widowed and Divorced.

In their suicide notes they more often than other Area Types give reasons for their suicide, and these reasons are not concerned with ill health or rejection or finances, but rather with such reasons—in this wealthy group—as "tired of life," "as a way out," "no point in living," "can't go on"—almost as though, to stretch a point, they were surfeited with life itself. (Without commenting on the reported differences in the national suicide rates between two countries with obviously different standards of living—for example, Spain and Sweden—it would be a most interesting study—apropos the findings reported in this paragraph—to analyze the differences in the content of the suicide notes in the two countries.) One implication of this finding is that thoroughgoing suicide prevention not

TABLE V—Results From Psychological Analysis of Suicide Notes

Area Type	Name	REASONS FOR SUICIDE				AFFECT OR EMOTION			
		None	Health	Rejection	Tired of Life	None	Absolution	Self Deprec.	Affection
I	Most Advantaged Suburbs	Low			Hi				
II	Most Advantaged Residential Communities		Low	Low					
III	Most Advantaged Apartment House Areas		Hi				Hi		
IV	Moderately Advantaged Suburbs		Low			Low		Low	Hi
V	Moderately Advantaged Natural Communities	Low		Hi					Low
VI	Moderately Advantaged Apartment Areas			Low					
VII	Least Advantaged Rural Areas								
VIII	Least Advantaged Industrial Communities					Hi			Low
IX	Least Advantaged Apartment Areas	Hi				Hi			Low

only will have to concern itself with intrapsychic and sociological factors, but, eventually, will have to deal with the basic cultural values as well.

Two sample Area Type I suicide notes are reproduced below:

A. No funeral. Please leave the body to science. William Smith

B. I'm sorry. Don't both with a post. It's sodium cyanide. At 11:12

TABLE VI—Sociological, Suicidal, and Psychological Data,
Los Angeles County, 1957

| | SOCIOLOGICAL INFORMATION | | | SUICIDAL INFORMATION | | | | PSYCHOLOGICAL INFORMATION | |
Area Type	Area Name	Population	% of Popu.	No. Sui	% of Sui	Sui Rate	Sex Marital	Stated Reason for Suicide	Affect or Emotion in Suicide Note
I	Most adv. suburbs	265,180	5%	31	4%	12		Hi Tired of life Hi Reasons given	
II	Most adv. resid. com.	828,884	16%	132	17%	16		Low Ill health Low Rejection	
III	Most adv. apartment house areas	200,279	4%	44	6%	22	Hi Females Hi Wid, Div. Low Married	Hi Ill health	Hi Absolution
IV	Moderately advantaged suburbs	1,097,822	21%	93	12%	8		Low Ill health	Hi Affection Low Self-depreciation Hi general Affect
V	Mod. adv. natural communities	1,673,977	31%	236	31%	14	Hi Married Low Wid, Div.	Hi Rejection Hi Reasons given	Low Affection & love
VI	Mod. adv. apt. areas	392,863	7%	84	11%	21	Hi Wid, Div. Low Married	Low Rejection	
VII	Least adv. rural areas	119,000	2%	4	1%	3			
VIII	Least adv. ind. com.	529,354	10%	68	9%	13	Hi Males Low Singles		Low general Affect Low Affection & love
IX	Least adv. apt. areas	192,989	4%	37	5%	19	Low Males Hi Singles	Low Reasons given	Low general Affect Low Affection & love

Area Type II—Most Advantaged Residential Communities: 16 percent of the population; 17 percent of the suicides; 16/100,000 suicide rate; also no minorities.

The suicide notes of this group give little indication of the psychology of the note writers. The notes show no particular affect or lack of it and the focus of the notes is rather general in nature. Reasons for suicide are not often given and when given they are conspicuously lacking in any reference to ill health or feelings of rejection or loneliness. This Area Type contains a large percentage of 40-to-49-year-olds who are relatively financially independent and successful, and their notes may reflect this quality in the apparent lack of any special need for communicating the reasons, instructions or emotions relative to the suicidal act.

Two sample Area Type II notes are reproduced below:

    A. Don't take life too seriously. You'll never get out of
       it alive anyway. Mary Smith
    B. [On Beverly Hilton Hotel stationery]
       Nobody to blame. Call YO 12345

Area Type III—Most Advantaged Apartment House Areas: 4 percent of the population, 6 percent of the suicides, 22/100,000 suicide rate, low minority percentage, a greater proportionate percentage of female suicides in that Area Type; larger proportionate percentage of Widowed and Divorced and smaller proportionate percentage of Married.

The outstanding characteristic of the suicide notes from this Area Type is that the content of the suicide notes are conspicuously filled with reasons of ill health (physical disability, symptoms, pain) —as though much of the reason for their existence is dependent on their body and its functioning—and the affect expressed is focused, more than in any other Area Type, on Absolution (giving forgiveness, etc.). One gets the picture of self-centered, pontifical people assuaging their deep intrapsychic conflicts with ready assumption of guilt and blame and with rationalizations of physical pain. As can be seen, they have, in many ways, more in common with some Moderately and Least Advantaged Area Types than with the other two Most Advantaged (I and II) Area Types.

A typical Area Type III suicide note is reproduced below:

To All My Friends:
> Please forgive me and thanks for all your kindness.
> My courage has run out. In the face of poor health, deserted by my sisters, and persistent cruelty of my husband I have no further reason to keep fighting.
> All my life I have tried to be decent. I have worked hard to make a marriage out of puny material. To be deserted at such a time of my life is too disillusioning and too harsh. It is more than I can bear. I just feel that those who should be close to me are like "rats deserting a sinking ship." Therefore I do not want any of them (my sisters or my husband) near me in death or to have any part of my possessions.
> But I do appreciate the goodness and the kindness of my friends, my doctors and my lawyer—it kept me going up to this point.
> Goodbye and try to remember me at my best.

Area Type IV—Moderately Advantaged Suburbs: 21 percent of the population; 12 percent of the suicides; 8/100,000 suicide rate; almost no minority population.

Suicide notes of individuals from this Area Type differ in many ways from Area Type I, the Most Advantaged Suburbans. The suicide notes indicate many reasons for suicide but they are conspicuously low in listing ill health as a reason for suicide. Their notes contain a great deal of feeling—there is rarely a note with no affect—but the affect infrequently includes Self-Depreciation (self-derogation, self-criticism, guilt, self-blame). Most often they include such emotions as Affection (love, idealization of others, praise, defense of the other, etc.). The overall impression is that these note-writers are individuals in their 30's, living in Moderately Advantaged Suburban areas, who are very much involved in the feelings of interpersonal relationships. Their suicides are not for health or money but rather have to do with love—and the converse of love, hostility, although this would be more from inference than from actual content of the notes. These are individuals who manifest the conflicts of love and hate and who, along with the individuals in Area Type V, could probably be most helped by psychotherapeutic intervention.

An Area Type IV suicide note is given below:

Mary:

Here is the note you wanted giving you power of attorney for the house and everything else (including all of *your* bills.)

I hope that my insurance will get you out of the whole mess that you got us both in.

This isn't hard for me to do because it's probably the only way I'll ever get rid of you, we both know how the California courts only see the women's side.

My only hope is that you can raise Junior to be as honest and as good as he is right now.

I think that Junior and Betty and George are really the only things in the world that I'll miss. Please take good care of them.

Good luck, Bill

P.S. I love you Junior, and thank you Betty for all you've done for me and Junior. Love   Daddy.

Area Type V—Moderately Advantaged Natural Communities: 31 percent of the population; 31 percent of the suicides; 14/100,000 suicide rate; low minority percentage; high proportionate percentage of Marriage, and low proportionate percentage of Widowed and Divorced. The communities in this Area Type are the "little cities" within the greater Los Angeles community.

Their suicide notes show that they very often give reasons for suicide and, interestingly enough, the reasons mentioned in their notes more often have to do with feelings of Rejection by another, (not being understood, feelings of isolation, loneliness, loss of love, etc.). Curiously enough, their notes also contain a conspicuously low percentage of affection toward the note recipient, even though many of them are married. They have been rejected and they are very angry—it would appear, possibly angry at themselves. Here again, as with the individuals in Area IV, the possibilities for psychotherapeutic help through insight, resolution of feelings, and the like appear to be important.

Below are two notes written by the same individual from this Area Type:

Dear Mary:

Be sure you hold fast to what you think you have now. I go with no bitterness toward you only pity and love.

I pray this example will be the means of you going forward in life in the right way. Take good care of Junior and love him, do not vent your spite out on him when things do not go your way. Here are my car keys. If Dad will grant my one wish this car is yours.   Mother

This Ten dollars is from what I earned last week, part of it I mean. Nothing to do with Dad's money. I've left him $70 more than he would have done for me if the shoe had been on the other foot.

Dear Bill:

Please do not have a lot of hypocrisy such as burial etc. Give my carcass to a hospital or cremate it.

If you have a spark of honesty in you and you love our son try and arrange for him to live with George and Mary, where he will be happy and raised in a decent home. He will never be happy with you.

Here's what money I've left. I've sent Henrys to him and I've left Mary ten dollars out of it what I earned last week.

Goodbye and God bless you.   Betty

Area Type VI—Moderately Advantaged Apartment Areas: 7 percent of the population; 11 percent of the suicides; 21/100,000 suicide rate; small minority population; low proportionate percentage of Married suicides and high proportionate percentage of Widowed and Divorced. This is a suicidal group weighted primarily in the nonmarried direction.

In terms of the reasons given in the suicide notes, Rejection is indicated less often than any other Area Type except Area Type II. It is interesting to note that Area VI has the next to the highest percentage of suicide of any Area Type in Los Angeles County. (Area III is highest with a rate of 22/100,000.) It is also interesting to see that the three highest suicidal ratios (22, 21, and 19 out of 100,000 population) occur in the three Apartment House Areas— Area Type III, VI, and IX, respectively—even though the psychology of the suicide notes obtained from these three Area Types seem not to be similar in emphasis.

Two simple suicide notes are reproduced below:

A. Dear Mary. I am so sick and disgusted cant get well
so do the best you can. So sorry cant take it no longer.

Cremate my body no flowers no minister. Just cremate
me the least expense. My all my love to all of you. Bill

B. Bill. Im sorry but I had this all made out and decided
when you called. A hell of a day today. Thanks for the
call. But call George. Henry

Area Type VII—Least Advantaged Rural Areas: 2 percent of
the population; 1 percent of the suicides; small minority population;
3/100,000 suicide rate.

The psychological characteristics of the suicide notes for Area
Type VII were not subjected to statistical analysis (and not included in the overall statistical analyses) inasmuch as this Area
Type includes only one Study Area, and had only 2 percent of the
population.

Area Type VIII—Least Advantaged Industrial Communities: 10
percent of the population; 9 percent of the suicides; 13/100,000
suicide rate; fairly large minority population; low proportionate
percentage of Single individuals. More often than any other area,
except Area Type IX, no affect is indicated in the notes and,
further, again along with Area Type IV there is a conspicuous
absence of affection. The focus of their suicide notes is quite clear:
it is primarily on Instructions, in this case, to the relatives. These
instructions have to do primarily with material possessions, the
notification of others, and the disposition of the victim's remains.
The notes give the impression of matter-of-fact directives having
to do with the mundane and material aspects of a hard existence.

Two notes from Area Type VIII are given below:

A. To Whom It May Concern: I live at 100 Main Street,
Los Angeles, California. In case of extreme emergency,
please notify my daughter, Mary B. Jones, Box 100,
San Diego, California. In my apartment there is a
letter to her giving all necessary instructions about
what to do with my affairs. I have a checking account
with the National Bank, 1st Street Branch, Los
Angeles. It is my wish that all of my friends listed
in my address book be notified. I am a Protestant.
Belong to no lodges now. My apartment rent is paid
to the 15th of next month. William B. Smith

B. Robert:

BE ALERT. . . CLOSE THE DOOR. . . NOW HEAR THIS. . . . BE ALERT. By the time you read this, I shall have *disposed* of *myself*. (I can only guess your reaction. If its bad, massage your crotch and breathe deeply). FINISH READING: I felt better when I decided, several weeks ago. Too many adjustments to make. Ten years ago may have been able to do it. Too rigid now. Too many crystalizations. Too late to utilize the recently acquired revelation that many years ago, fear of world obstructed and stunted natural drives and imagination. Just the one fear was enough. World as total. Not individuals as such. When complete jerks make up this world.

First, check in my room. I may have goofed. If I did, I'll kill myself. That's a joke. Come on relax. You have things to do.

If you want to avoid Mom knowing (boy, am I burdening you) . . get hold of the police—and tell them to co-operate, to *quietly* come and take me to city facility. I should have passed out from strangulation about five hours ago, so only necessary to cart me away.

Pull this off!! To ease your mind, tell Pop. Then both of you tell Mom I took off and you don't know where—say Merchant Marine

The V.A. can bury me. Pop has my papers. They ship me out of town don't bother to go. In fact don't bother anyway. It's incredibly stupid the way people mourn the dead. My only regret is that I didn't have the world by the balls. If you don't, *you* suffer. Remember that.

You may doubt this letter, Robert. Satisfy your curiosity . . but don't immediately hate me for imposing on you. Get things done. You can even stay home from work. I could have gone away and done it. But for once, let this ass hole family be practical. I would have taken my car.—but now you have it.

If (I hate that word) I am dead, pull yourself together and do the things I said.

So help me if you go into the bathroom during the

night and read this before you are supposed to, I'll
kill you. Two cars and all.

Area Type IX—Least Advantaged Apartment Areas: 4 percent
of the population; 5 percent of the suicides; 19/100,000 suicide rate;
very high minority population; high proportionate percentage of
Single persons; and low proportionate percentage of Married.

The suicide notes written in this Area Type are conspicuously low
in the Reasons for suicide given and in Affect shown. The only exception to this is that where affect is shown at all the emotion of
Affection is noticeably absent. As in Area Type VIII, the notes
from this Area Type are concerned largely with Instructions having
to do with the workaday details; things for people to do, things to
get, things to fix, things to put aright. These notes—unaddressed as
they are in many cases—seem to be directed to the world at large,
a world which from the victim's point of view has probably been
harsh and unrewarding.

A sample suicide note from Area Type IX is reproduced below:

My name is William B. Smith. In case of my death I am
leaving everything I have in this room to Mr. Henry
B. Jones. His address is 100 Main Street, Los Angeles,
Calforina. YO-12345.   W.B.S.

Implications

If a light touch is not inappropriate, it is relevant to state that
when Ralph Rackstraw says, in *H.M.S. Pinafore,* that "Love burns
as brightly in the fo'c'sle as it does on the quarterdeck," he may
have been misleading his mess-mates by limiting their attentions
to the quantitative variations in brightness, whereas, it may be,
rather, that love (and other emotions as well) burn *differently* in
Area Type IV and Area Type VIII. There can be no doubt that the
concerns with everyday living, the details of existence that press
for obsessive rumination, the pervasive milieu that the individual
sees as "life" are indeed different in many important qualitative respects in Area Type I and Area Type IX. Recent comprehensive
studies cutting across social strata, such as the Kinsey investigations of patterns of sexual behavior,[18] have made it clear that the
socioeconomic factors play important roles in determining the patterns of demonstrations of emotion—causing either their taboo or

their open acceptance. Other studies, such as the Yale studies of alcoholism, have revealed similar analyses with fairly specific patterns of the expressions of alcoholic symptom among different socioeconomic levels. Further, the study by Hollingshead and Redlich on social class and mental illness demonstrated that mentally-ill individuals of different social classes not only fall heir to different modes to treatment but more importantly, for the present context, also actually present different types of emotional maladaptation, in part related to the social class membership of the mentally ill person.[19] The data from this research are in line with the studies cited above in indicating that the emotions expressed by suicidal persons will vary more or less consistently within different socioeconomic areas, and that the patterns for expression of these emotions will be reflective of the nature of the social class position of which the victims are members. Not only are different *methods* (i.e., shooting, hanging, jumping, etc.) obviously used in suicide, but people apparently commit suicide in different *ways*, that is, with expression or denial of affection, with mention or avoidance of specific reasons, and the like, some of which are definitely related to the socioeconomic level (or, in this study, Area Type) to which they belong.

What clues for prevention or treatment of suicide can be gathered from this study? It may well be that in an individual consultation with a potentially suicidal person, there must be some cognizance taken of his social class membership and some recognition given to the implications that follow such awareness. Why should Area Type I people—with all the material advantages—be "tired of life"? Is there really more physical sickness in Area Type III, or is there a large element of hypochondriasis? What is the meaning of the affection indicated by the Area Type IV suicides? And why are the Area Type V suicides conspicuously rejected? (Or, why do they feel that they are?) And Area Types VIII and IX: How could one hope to treat their suicidal impulses without taking into account their lack of dyadic relationships and their obvious difficulties in expressing affection or finding someone to express affection to? All these are some of the sociopsychological implications from these data. Another implication from the findings relates to traditional psychotherapy. It is that psychotherapeutic techniques might be most effective (in the total population of potentially suicidal individuals) for those persons who come from the *moderately* advan-

taged area types (IV, V, and VI) and who are concerned with affection and rejection (and apparently with the resolution of conflicts of feelings) rather than for individuals in either the most advantaged or least advantaged area types.

But if there is any single implication from this study it is that the occurrences of suicide—those enigmatic acts of complete self-destruction—are events neither exclusively of the psyche nor of the society, but rather are events that can be understood best in terms of the admixture of both—as sociopsychological phenomena.

Chapter 14
A COMPUTER ANALYSIS OF SUICIDE NOTES
Daniel M. Ogilvie, Philip J. Stone, and Edwin S. Shneidman

Thirty-three pairs of genuine and simulated suicide notes were analyzed by use of the General Inquirer, using a specially prepared dictionary of tag words. Genuine notes more often contained specific information, used names of people and places and things, and gave instruction concrete enough to be carried out. By contrast, the simulated notes contained a greater number of "thinking" words, suggesting a different order of indecision.

The Notes and the Problem

Thirty-three genuine and 33 simulated suicide notes were made available to members of the research team by Shneidman.[1] The genuine notes were selected from 721 suicide notes collected from folders of suicide cases in Los Angeles county for the ten-year period of 1945 to 1954. This sample included only those notes written by suicide victims who were male, Caucasian, Protestant, native-born, and between the ages of 25 and 59. For comparative purposes, simulated suicide notes were obtained from nonsuicidal individuals who were all also male, Caucasian, Protestant, and native-born, and who were matched with genuine note-writers with respect to age and occupational level. The simulated note-writers were instructed to make their notes sound as real as possible, to write as if they were actually planning to take their own life. Through the use of the General Inquirer, we were able to distinguish between genuine and simulated suicide notes.

THE DICTIONARY. The dictionary used in this study was the Harvard II Psychosociological Dictionary (forerunner of our current dictionary.)[2] That category system, like the Harvard III Dictionary, was divided into first-order tags (discrete, independent categories) and second-order tags (nonindependent categories). The first-order tags were subdivided into *ROLES, OBJECTS, EMOTIONAL STATES,* and *ACTIONS.* All Things were either *ROLES* or *OB-*

JECTS, and all Processes were either *EMOTIONAL STATES* or
ACTIONS. The second-order tags were classified as referring to
either *INSTITUTIONS, STATUSES, QUALITIES*, or *SYMBOLIC
REFERENTS*.

FIRST INSPECTION OF TAG SCORE DIFFERENCES. The genuine and simulated notes were processed separately. The tags that appeared to
differentiate between the sets (total difference of .03 percent or
greater) are presented in Table I.

Roughly summarizing the differences revealed in Table I, we
found that the genuine suicide notes are slightly more diversified

TABLE I—Tags That Discriminate Between Genuine and
Simulated Notes

FIRST-ORDER TAGS
Things

ROLES		OBJECTS	
(Genuine)	(Simulated)	(Genuine)	(Simulated)
SELF*	SELVES	ARTIFACT	
OTHER		PLACE	
MALE-ROLE			
FEMALE-ROLE			

Processes

EMOTIONAL STATES		ACTIONS	
(Genuine)	(Simulated)	(Genuine)	(Simulated)
	ANXIETY-FAIL	COMMUNICATE	THINK
	ANXIETY-UNABLE	POSSESS	SENSE
	DISTRESS	GET	IF
		ATTACK	NOT
			MOVE
			AVOID
			DIRECT
			GOALS

SECOND-ORDER TAGS

INSTITUTIONS		STATUSES	
(Genuine)	(Simulated)	(Genuine)	(Simulated)
	ACADEMIC	HIGHER-STATUS	

QUALITIES		SYMBOLIC REFERENTS	
(Genuine)	(Simulated)	(Genuine)	(Simulated)
QUANTITY-REFERENCE		SEX-THEME	DEATH-THEME
BAD		MALE-THEME	UNDERSTATE

*Tags that appear in this table are those that had comparatively "high" counts
for the set (genuine or simulated) under which they are listed.

in their use of the eight general categories in our theoretical scheme. With the exception of *EMOTIONAL STATES* and *INSTI-TUTIONS*, the genuine notes have relatively higher counts on some tags under all categories. On the other hand, the simulated notes do not have any higher scores in the following categories: *OB-JECTS, STATUSES*, and *QUALITIES*. Moreover, the simulated notes make relatively little use of the *ROLES* category.

More specifically, the greatest difference seems to be that the genuine note-writers concentrate more heavily on tags referring to Things (*ROLES* and *OBJECTS*) and *qualities*, whereas the simulated note-writers have their heaviest concentration on tags referring to Processes. The use of tags under Things and *qualities* by genuine note-writers appears to represent a greater emphasis on specifics. On the other hand, the high counts on tags under Processes might well reflect a more general use of words indicating the operation of cognitive processes for the simulated note-writers (words such as think, sense, if, goals). Another difference between the two types of notes is the tendency for the genuine notes to use sentences with words referring to themselves in the first person and to others (male and females), whereas the simulated note-writers tend to refer more to themselves and others simultaneously by using the word "we." Equally interesting is the complete absence of tags under *EMOTIONAL STATES* for the genuine notes. This reflects a relative lack of direct references to emotion. Also we find that the genuine notes are high on the symbolic tags SEX-THEME and MALE-THEME, possibly indicating an underlying concern with sex that is not recognized on the conscious level.

LEFTOVER REVELATIONS. The words that were not found in the dictionary and thereby were printed out as leftovers were reviewed. First it was found that the dictionary defined a higher percentage of words in the simulated notes (92 percent) than were defined for the genuine notes (86 percent). In other words, 8 percent of the words in the simulated notes were not defined, whereas 14 percent of the words from the genuine notes went without definition. In addition to this finding, the words in the two lists differed in content. Specifically, 64 percent of the leftover words from the genuine notes could be classified in one of the following five categories:

proper names, places, objects, numbers, and time. By contrast, only 32 percent of the leftover words from the simulated notes could be classified under these categories. This finding supports one of our initial interpretations of the differences on tag counts between the two sets of notes. That is, the genuine note-writers used very specific, concrete references in their messages.

RETRIEVING AND JUDGING SENTENCES. Previous to processing the genuine and simulated notes, they had been coded and syntax marked. For our purposes, this was important in two respects. First, pronouns could be identified. If the writer referred to his sister by using the pronoun "you," the information that "you" meant sister and sister meant female was not lost. Second, since sentence "parts" (subject, verb, object, and so on) had been specified, initial tag-score differences between the sets of notes were further divided into differences with respect to parts of speech. For example, the summary score for the tag FEMALE-ROLE revealed that genuine note-writers referred to females more frequently than did simulated note-writers. Further inspection of the printout revealed that the greatest difference lay in the genuine notes' references to females in the *subject* position of the sentence (154 occurrences of female as subject for the genuine notes compared to 64 occurrences for the simulated notes). Making use of this rather substantial difference, we retrieved all sentences from both sets of notes that matched our Female-as-Subject specification.

Working from the printout of the retrieval of these sentences, we found that all sentences from both genuine and simulated notes could be classified under one of the following three categories:

1. Writer is making a request or is giving an instruction or command to a woman.
   Examples: You (female) get in touch with Mary Jones (female) at once.
   You (female) please get a lawyer.
   You (female) be happy.
   You (female) teach him (son) to grow into a fine man.

2. Writer is giving information or expressing opinions (given as information) about a woman.

Examples: She lives close by.

Soon she (daughter) will dominate you.

She packed her bag.

Mother meant good.

3. A woman has acted upon the writer, over and above straight information.

Examples: She kept after me.

Helen (female) gave it (pen) to me.

And (wife) left me.

But she (mother) drove me to my grave.

Table II gives the percentage distribution of sentences retrieved and classified from both genuine and simulated notes with respect to these categories.

TABLE II—Classifications of "Female-as-Subject" Retrievals

	Genuine	Simulated
Instruction	29%	45%
Information	55%	50%
Female acting upon writer	15%	06%
	n=152	n=64

Independently rated by three judges not familiar with the materials with 95 percent agreement.

We see that genuine note-writers gave a smaller percentage of instructions to females, but they had a higher percentage of sentences giving information about women and sentences implying that a woman had directed action toward the writer. The latter two findings seemed reasonable, but the first finding created difficulties insofar as it was incongruent with our evolving notion of a suicide victim's terse concreteness. An investigation of those sentences in which the writer was giving commands or instructions indicated that they could be further classified into two relatively clear categories. These categories were

1. Instructions are of a specific nature.

Examples: You (female) tell my folks.

You (female) please take care of my bills.

2. Instructions are of an unreasonable or vague nature.

Examples: You (female) do not be mean with me, please.

You (female) find a new life for yourself.

Three judges who were not familiar with the materials independently judged these "instruction" sentences as belonging either in the *specific* or *vague* categories. There was complete agreement among raters. The results showed that when genuine writers gave instructions, 55 percent of these instructions were specific and direct. Only 25 percent of the instructions given by the simulated note-writers had this quality; the other 75 percent were of a vague, noninstrumental nature.

Moving away from the women in the lives of genuine and simulated suicide note-writers, we recall that another difference between the two sets of notes appeared when we considered tags under the Processes division of first-order tags. The simulated notes were overrepresented by tags falling under this division. Quite generally, we remarked that this might reflect a greater use of decision-making words on the part of the pretenders. To investigate this possibility further, we chose to concentrate on sentences that were retrieved on the basis of containing words that had been defined by the tag THINK. Fifty-nine sentences were recovered from the genuine set compared to 54 sentences from the simulated set.[3] It was noted from these retrievals that two types of words were responsible for raising the tag count for THINK. The first type included words such as think, recall, reason, remember, explain, consider, decide, and so forth. The second type included the words know, knew, known. Normally when words in the first list are used in a sentence they serve to indicate that the writer is attempting to solve a problem or is using his reasoning processes in some way, for instance, "I am thinking of all the problems we have shared." On the other hand, when "know" is used in a sentence, it indicates that a problem has been solved, knowledge has been gained, a decision has been made; for example, "I knew that if I went to the doctor, I would. . . ."

This distinction within the category THINK differentiated between the genuine and simulated notes in the following manner. Fifty-eight percent of the genuine notes originally retrieved as matching the specification THINK contained a form of the word "know." When the distribution is viewed in a slightly different manner, nineteen of the thirty-three genuine notes contained sentences using a form of the word "know." By contrast, only eight of the thirty-three simulated suicide notes contained "know" sentences.

We may conclude that the simulated note-writers tended to use

words indicating the operation of problem-solving modes, whereas the genuine note-writers' use of the word "know" reflects the fact that a final decision has been made. Partial substantiation of this view is gained when we recall that, along with the tag THINK, other tags referring to intellectual processes (SENSE, IF, ACADEMIC) were more frequently used by the simulated note-writers than by the genuine note-writers.

Discussion and Summary

Before summarizing the results of our analysis, it is instructive to review briefly the results of these same paired notes in an analysis conducted by Gottschalk and Gleser.[4] By using a hand method of classifying words into objects, processes, spatial relations, and so forth (a method similar to our computer method), they summarized that the categories of words that typify genuine suicide notes include a relatively high percentage of references to people and things, places or spatial relations, and a relatively low percentage of references to cognitive processes. We too found that genuine notes had a relatively high percentage of references to people, places, and things when we (1) compared the frequencies of tags under *ROLES* and *OBJECTS* and (2) compared the two lists of leftover words. The results of our analysis of *specific* versus *vague* requests made by the note-writers using "Female-as-Subject" warrant us to note the possibility that the genuine note-writers not only made more specific mention of names, places, and objects but they were much more specific in their entire final communicative attempt than were the simulated note-writers. Again, in line with Gottschalk and Gleser's findings, we pointed out that the simulated note-writers used a large number of words that were defined by the tags indicating the use of cognitive processes. The results of the analysis of the tag THINK and the high counts on tags SENSE, IF, and ACADEMIC for the simulated note-writers added support to this finding. Contrasting these results for simulated note-writers we found that the genuine suicide note-writers tended to use the word "know" more often. This finding can also be viewed as another example of the genuine note-writers' specificity as opposed to the generality of the simulated notes.

As a demonstration of the usefulness of these findings in discriminating between the genuine and simulated notes, Stone carried out

the following procedure. First he developed a discriminant function for distinguishing between the first fifteen pairs of notes. The three factors that, when combined, best discriminated between these pairs were (1) references to concrete things, persons, and places (higher for genuine notes); (2) use of the word "love" in the text (higher for genuine notes); (3) total number of references to processes of thought and decision (higher for simulated notes). The first and third criteria were taken from the findings just discussed. The addition of the second factor (use of the word "love") was the result of further exploration of the text-word differences between these fifteen documents.

The discriminant function developed from these factors was simple and straightforward: the score on the third measure was subtracted from the sum of the scores of the first two measures. This index correctly discriminated thirteen of the fifteen pairs of notes.

Stone, who was not familiar with the remaining eighteen pairs of notes, then applied the discriminant function to them. After making his predictions on the basis of the index scores, we found that he had correctly separated seventeen of the eighteen paired notes.

More elaborate functions for discriminating between real and simulated suicide notes could be obtained by combining stepwise multiple regression techniques with tree-building procedures. Our further explorations have shown that the task becomes much more difficult, however, if the notes are not available in matched pairs, as they were for Stone. Assuming that age and socioeconomic information is available, a more realistic procedure would be to collect more notes and develop separate discrimination formulas and norms as needed for each major age and socioeconomic group.

In summary, the question asked at the outset of this study was "Can we find differences between genuine suicide notes and simulated suicide notes by using the General Inquirer procedures?" We found that we could find differences and that those differences were substantial. More often than was true of the simulated notes, genuine notes contained specific information, used names of people, places, and things, made frequent mention of women, and gave instructions to others that were concrete enough to be actually carried out. By contrast, the simulated suicide notes contained a greater percentage of "thinking" words, suggesting that the issue of suicide was being pondered, reasoned with, and probably rationalized.

PART IV
DIAGNOSIS
AND EVALUATION:
GENERAL

Chapter 15
EMERGENCY EVALUATION OF
SUICIDAL POTENTIAL
Robert E. Litman and Norman L. Farberow

On occasion, a rapid assessment of an individual's self-destructive potentiality is required. Certain factual data are important: age and sex, onset of self-destructive behavior, availability and lethality of possible self-destructive method, recent losses, history of recent medical and therapeutic encounters, and available resources. In addition, a number of evaluative judgments should be made regarding the quality of communication, the nature of the feelings expressed, the reactions of significant others, and the personality status of the potential victim. Following the evaluation, appropriate courses of action can be recommended.

At times, professional persons in the mental health field (psychiatrists, psychologists, social workers, etc.) are asked to make a rapid assessment of someone's self-destructive potential. This is illustrated most dramatically by telephone requests for immediate consultation and advice. These calls may come from a variety of sources, such as persons engaged in medical, legal, educational, or social welfare activities, who request an evaluation of suicidal clues in a patient or client; they may come from a concerned spouse, relative, or friend; or they may come directly from the self-destructive persons themselves.

The professional person's role in answering such emergency consultation requests can be divided into three phases. First he obtains necessary information, then he forms an evaluative judgment of the situation, and finally he recommends appropriate action. He may, for example, recommend immediate hospitalization for a case; or he may interpret the suicidal communication as having low lethal potentiality and recommend outpatient treatment. Frequently he makes arrangements for additional evaluative interviews with the aim of developing a more definitive treatment plan.

As a method of assembling information, the telephone interview under emergency pressures has definite shortcomings. There is a

tendency for the most dramatic and emotionally disturbing aspects of the picture to obscure other equally relevant elements. Several important questions may remain unanswered. The consultant may recommend a course of action based on incomplete data when actually more complete information was potentially available.

A systematic approach to the problem of obtaining the most pertinent indicators of self-destructive danger (or safety) within a limited amount of time is provided by a schedule of areas that should be explored during the interview. The following short schedule, derived from the experience of the staff of the Suicide Prevention Center, focuses on matters the evaluator wants to know about immediately. The first group of questions is factual and can be answered in one or two words with occasional brief amplification (e.g., age, sex, recent illnesses, loss of spouse). The second group of questions is evaluative and requires special training and skill in interviewing and diagnosis (e.g., is there depression, psychosis, ability to communicate).

The main items in the schedule are outlined below. This is followed by a discussion of their relevance to the problem of evaluating self-destructive potentiality. Some case illustrations are then provided as examples of the application of the schedule.

Short Schedule for Assessment of Self-Destructive Potentiality

I Case history: factual
   A. Age and sex
   B. Onset of self-destructive behavior: chronic, repetitive pattern, or recent behavior change? Any prior suicide attempts or threats?
   C. Method of possible self-injury: availability, lethality?
   D. Recent loss of loved person: death, separation, divorce?
   E. Medical symptoms: history of recent illness or surgery?
   F. Resources: available relatives or friends, financial status?

II Judgmental-evaluative
   A. Status of communication with patient
   B. Kinds of feeling expressed
   C. Reactions of referring person
   D. Personality status and diagnostic impression

Case History: Factual

AGE AND SEX. The age and sex of the patient are generally the first items of information to be considered. These two facts provide a framework within which the emergency classification and appraisal of self-destructive persons can proceed. At all ages, suicidal communications from males arouse more concern than similar communications from females, and, in general, the older the person, the more serious is the self-destructive potentiality. Moreover, the danger increases with age much more for males than for females. We have rarely encountered a nonlethally intended suicidal action in a man over fifty. Thus, a self-destructive communication from or about a person in this age and sex group immediately raises suspicion of a high-risk situation, and the burden of proof that this is not an emergency rests upon the other data that can be obtained.

By contrast, the group of young females, aged fifteen to thirty-five, provides the largest number of self-destructive nonlethal communications and suicidal attempts, that is, the least number of completed suicides. In this group, the goal of influencing another person's behavior, with little or no intention to die, is more often prominent. Other factors involved in the lower emergency danger rating for women are their choice of less violent methods of self-injury (pills rather than guns) and their greater willingness to communicate (ask for help and accept it). In the middle-aged and older female group, suicidal threats and attempts tend to become more serious.

ONSET OF SELF-DESTRUCTIVE BEHAVIOR. As a general rule, the more acute and precipitous the onset of the self-destructive behavior, the better the ultimate prognosis and, paradoxically, the greater the need for active intervention. Thus, a history of recent personality change combined with a history of recent actual suicidal attempts is a major danger signal for the immediate future. If there has been a pattern of repetitive self-destructive behavior over a long period of time, the eventual outlook may be extremely pessimistic, especially as the potential victim grows older and the condition gradually grows worse. However, in such chronic cases, al-

though emergency intervention may be necessary for the immediate situation, it usually has no lasting effect, and a more gradual long-term rehabilitation plan must be formulated in addition. A crucial point in the evaluation is whether the person with a chronic, repetitive self-destructive pattern has completely exhausted his emotional resources.

METHOD OF POSSIBLE SELF-INJURY. The method of self-injury proposed by the patient sometimes reflects the degree of emergency. In general, a specific choice of time, place, and method for the proposed suicide is a serious indication, but if the method is aspirin ingestion or cold pills, the emergency is dissipated. By contrast, the person who owns a gun and proposes to use it against himself should be the object of immediate emergency efforts, if not toward him, at least toward removing the gun. Similarly, ideas of jumping from a high place should be taken more seriously and may call for questions as to where the person is, and the like. Nearly all pills used to produce sleep can be lethal in large amounts, but the rapid-acting barbiturates, such as pentobarbital and secobarbital, are by far the most effective for suicide.

RECENT LOSS OF LOVED PERSON. Many suicide attempts, especially in young persons, occur after the separation from a spouse or a loved one. In these circumstances, self-destructive behavior is often undertaken with ambivalent feelings. The wish to die is balanced by a wish to live and to be rescued and reunited with the loved person. Frequently, these suicide attempts are successful as a form of adaptational behavior in that they do serve to bring the loved person back. On the other hand, in many of these gambles with death, death wins. When there has been a definite loss of a loved person, such as a spouse, parent, child, lover, or mistress, within the previous year (by death, divorce, or separation), the potentiality for self-destruction is increased. Certain persons, such as some widows of ages forty to sixty who have been extremely dependent on their husbands, display exaggerated mourning and grief reactions associated with strong self-destructive urges.

MEDICAL SYMPTOMS. A history of recent hospitalization or medical consultation may indicate increased self-destructiveness, especially

in older persons. Medical conditions most often associated with suicidal reactions are psychosomatic diseases, polysurgery, malignant tumors, and various symptoms associated with depression. Some indicators of depression are anorexia, weight loss, sleeplessness, fatigue, impotence, loss of sexual desire, and hypochondriacal preoccupation, especially cancerophobia. When a chronic debilitating disease such as cancer actually exists, suicidal reactions tend to be precipitated by incidents that the patient interprets as rejection from family and physician.

RESOURCES. Often the attitudes of spouse, relative, or friend may mean the difference between life or death for persons involved in symbiotic relationships. A consultant wants to know who brings the patient to the attention of helping authorities and why? Are there relatives in the picture? Is there a history of solidarity with spouse, relatives, or friends? Or, contrariwise, is there a history of instability, constant ambivalent relationships, desertion, and distrust? Financial resources need to be included in the evaluation, as these determine to some extent what types of treatment are available. A recent loss of job or sudden drop in financial status may constitute a traumatic loss to certain persons, especially middle-aged men and career women. Persons who have a lifelong history of direct self-destructiveness, as illustrated by unstable interpersonal relationships, alcoholism, impulsivity, and hostile dependency, often reach a crisis in the fourth or fifth decade when they find that they have exhausted themselves financially and interpersonally; they are, so to speak, emotionally bankrupt. After a long pattern of suicidal gestures, this may be the point when such persons actually do commit suicide.

Judgmental-Evaluative

STATUS OF COMMUNICATION WITH PATIENT. For a person struggling with strong currents of self-destructiveness, the life line is one of unbroken communication with other persons. When a patient is able to express his troubled feelings and cry for help, the self-destructive danger may be high, but it is never so extreme as when the patient has given up and withdrawn and is no longer communicating. A warm, receptive, hopeful, encouraging, responsive

attitude by the consultant will help to keep the communication line intact. Repeated telephone connections with the patient can help to weather a short period of crisis. Usually, an emergency self-destructive situation is ominously foreshadowed by a break in the communication, canceled appointments, unanswered telephone calls, and silence.

The most perplexing problem is presented by those self-destructive persons who reject offers of consultation, assistance, or therapy. With a life at stake, how can we help someone against his own will? This represents a most complicated medical and legal problem. However, in a limited number of experiences with this situation the SPC staff has found that often the hostile attitudes, objections, and resistances of the potentially self-destructive person were relatively superficial and would melt away when exposed to sympathetic, firm, consistent, and coordinated helping efforts.

KINDS OF FEELINGS EXPRESSED. Typical presuicidal communications include verbal statements such as "I am tired of life," "I mean to end it all," "my family would be better off without me," or "soon I won't be around." On a behavioral level, efforts to put business and social affairs in order, the making out of a will, and unusual preparations as if for an absence may have a similar significance. Suicidal threats designed primarily to taunt or punish the recipient or to gain a distinct goal or advantageous objective (for example, to force a marriage or obtain a therapeutic abortion) carry a relatively low emergency lethal valence. The affective state associated with these communications should be evaluated. The most serious suicidal potential is associated with feelings of helplessness and hopelessness, exhaustion and failure, and the feeling "I just want out." A combination of agitation and confusion, however, particularly in a person who has had a previous psychotic episode, may constitute an emergency. When the predominant feeling is one of frustration, anger, or rage, without overwhelming confusion, the lethal danger is generally somewhat less.

REACTIONS OF REFERRING PERSON. If the referring person is a spouse, relative, friend or other lay person, a number of possible reactions require evaluation. First, are there indications of a close and ambi-

valent symbiotic relationship and, if so, is it possible that the referring person is actually also disturbed? Does the referring person's attitude reflect a need to have a sick, dependent partner leaning upon him? Is there an attitude of rejection and a desire to get rid of the potentially suicidal person? A defensive, paranoid, rigid, punishing, moralistic, or hopelessly dependent attitude on the part of the referring person indicates that little help can be expected from that source, although attempts should be made nevertheless to secure as much cooperation as possible. It is generally encouraging when the referring person expresses sympathy and concern for the patient, together with an admission of his own sense of helplessness in the situation and need for assistance. Often the referring person, with guidance and advice, can be a source of strength and support in the emergency situation.

Professional persons sometimes express an exaggerated or disproportionate degree of anxiety over a relatively mild self-destructive communication from a patient or client. Reassurance from a consultant will often encourage such persons or agencies to proceed with their own appropriate techniques. On the other hand, some emotional reaction is expected from the referring person, no matter what their professional training and experience, because emotions activated by suicide go very deep in human psychology, well beyond the usual concept of countertransference. This also applies to calls from professional psychotherapists, whose requests for consultation bring up special problems. When a referring psychotherapist indicates no feelings of personal concern about his potentially self-destructive patient, one wonders whether the therapist's judgment and insight can be relied upon for purposes of evaluation. If the therapist recognizes feelings of annoyance or irritation with the patient in himself and can discuss them with the consultant, this in itself reduces one's feelings about the immediate suicidal potentiality of the patient. If the psychotherapist reports honest feelings of helplessness in himself and a breaking off of communication between himself and the patient, then it would appear that an emergency situation has developed and it is time for some sort of active intervention. In these situations, the source of the difficulty may be some specific countertransference problem in the therapist, which can be resolved by a supervisory consultation. Often the SPC has

provided, in addition to such consultations, needed practical information about community resources, available clinics, methods of hospitalization, commitment procedures, etc.

PERSONALITY STATUS AND DIAGNOSTIC IMPRESSION. Much of the information that might be subsumed under this heading has already been discussed above. What should be reemphasized is the importance of evaluating the possible presence of psychotic thinking and severe depressive affect. If either of these indicators is present, and especially if combined with alcoholism, the question of emergency hospitalization must be seriously considered. One asks about previous hospitalization for mental illness and looks for the various symptoms of disordered thinking (confusion, disorientation, delusions, disturbed body image, etc.). One wants to know, in addition, about past periods of elation or depression and the extent of the depression. The course and outcome of previous psychotherapy efforts should be ascertained. A previous pattern of failure in therapy is a danger signal.

Illustrative Cases

The above schedule includes the most important immediate emergency indicators for evaluation of suicidal danger. However, patterns of suicidal behavior vary. The following examples illustrate how different items of the schedule carry different weights, depending on the total context.

CASE 1

A supervisor of nurses called the SPC. A 23-year-old female staff nurse, Mrs. F., had been on sick leave for a week and had returned to work obviously depressed. The supervisor asked a few questions, and Mrs. F. revealed that she had made a serious suicide attempt with barbiturate capsules because her husband had left her to go to Las Vegas with another woman. Because of the suicide attempt her husband had returned to her to help her. However, Mrs. F. was afraid he might still leave her. The nursing supervisor was told that this was not an emergency, and an appointment was made to see this nurse the next day. She was interviewed and accepted at the SPC for psychotherapy.

Comment. Completed suicide occurs infrequently in young married women, even though this group contributes most heavily to the number of suicide threats and suicide attempts. In 90 percent of the cases, rejection by a man is the source of the self-destructive behavior, although occasionally the rejection is from a parent. This patient's pattern of self-destructive behavior indicates that she needs serious evaluation and eventual treatment, although the method of threatened self-injury (sleeping pills) is of low lethality in this age group. We judged that this was not an acute emergency case because (1) the lost love object, the husband, had returned, (2) the patient was able to communicate her feelings to her supervisor, and (3) her usual personality was described as compliant, conscientious, and obsessive rather than alcoholic and impulsive; she was described as nonpsychotic. The prognosis for immediate and long-range treatment was deemed to be excellent. In general, most suicide threats made by young women are because of rejection in love and are of low lethality. The exceptions to this rule are persons with schizoid and schizophrenic personalities.

CASE 2

A social worker called from the Bureau of Public Assistance about a 19-year-old girl, who was recently discharged from a state hospital with the diagnosis of schizophrenia, improved. Although she was working part time and making a better adjustment than before, this girl expressed to the worker her feelings that life was not worth living. She had previously made a suicide attempt by cutting her wrist with a razor blade. The girl led a very lonely life. Her foster mother was often hostile toward her and threatened to have her sent back to the hospital. The social worker was told that, although this was not an emergency situation, nevertheless the suicidal danger was high and considerable care, effort, and activity were called for in this case.

Comment. Concern was expressed about this patient because this type of case carries with it a chronic risk of suicide. However, the main problem is schizophrenia and not suicide. The diagnosis of chronic schizophrenic reaction is extremely important because the proportion of suicides is high from this category and the prediction

of suicide in this group is difficult. The previous self-destructiveness together with the recent communication of a wish to die indicates a serious chronic suicidal danger. Nevertheless, the girl should not be considered a permanent candidate for hospitalization. The patient's best chance for improvement in the underlying schizophrenic process is through working at a job, living in the community, and having a supportive relationship with the social worker. We recommended that the social worker continue casework with the girl, looking forward to a long-term relationship in which she would give the girl someone to talk to and some psychological and practical support in organizing her life. Continuing consultation with the SPC was offered. The rejecting attitudes of the foster mother might be changed by some guidance and counseling.

CASE 3

Mrs. V. called the SPC as a self-referral from a family service agency. She had called the agency about her husband, who is an engineer in an aircraft plant. According to his wife, he is a compulsive gambler who lives in a dream world of his own and refuses to recognize the damage he was doing by his gambling and to accept psychiatric help. She had threatened to divorce him many times, and now she was desperate. The previous day her husband hold her he had worked out a plan whereby he would commit suicide so that Mrs. V. could collect the insurance and pay off their debts, which, however, were more than the insurance would cover. Mrs. V. suspected that her husband's real plan was to gamble his pay check in the hope of getting enough money to keep the house. They had one child, and she was pregnant with another. Her plan was to have him committed so she could collect his pay check and use the money to straighten out their financial situation.

Comment. Suicidal communication in men should be taken a great deal more seriously than similar communications in women. In this case more information was needed about the husband and quickly. The actual facts gathered indicated that he was working in a responsible position, which contradicted the wife's implication that he was in a dream world or nearly psychotic. Possibly the main disturbance in the family centered in the wife rather than in the

husband. The pattern of gambling, unaccompanied by severe alcoholism or acute depression, does not usually lead to suicide in young men. The husband was called and was told that his wife was worried about him and had asked us to call. The impression gained while talking to him was that he was not depressed, not psychotic, and not suicidal. He did feel that he and his wife needed some sort of help and accepted an appointment to come to the office for an evaluation interview and possible referral for marriage counseling.

CASE 4

Sometimes one particular element of the schedule stands out and overshadows all the others. An example is the immediate danger when a lethal weapon is not only at hand but is presented as the threatened suicidal method. A certified clinical psychologist, who practices in an outlying community, called to report this problem. The previous night he had been asked to see a 19-year-old man whose mother and father had recently separated as a prelude to divorce. The young man had become moody and depressed. The preceding afternoon he had locked himself in his room with a .22 rifle and threatened to kill himself. The psychologist was called; he was able to talk to the young man through the locked door and thought he had established a relationship. He made an appointment for the young man to come to his office the next day. When the patient did not show up, the psychologist called the home and learned that the young man was again locked in his room with the gun. According to the psychologist, this man had made no previous destructive actions, had made regular progress in school, and displayed no schizophrenic disturbance in thinking.

Comment. This was evaluated as an emergency situation that carried an excellent prognosis for the long run, provided the short-term danger was negotiated successfully. The psychologist was advised to secure the cooperation of the father, the mother, all members of the family, friends, clergyman, indeed everyone who might be able to communicate with the young man, and return with them to the house. The primary immediate aim was to persuade him to give up the gun and to remove it from the house. This done, efforts toward establishing a therapeutic relationship could be renewed.

This was accomplished, with the SPC continuing to act as consultant to the therapist as needed.

CASE 5

> Key indicators of suicidal danger in persons who have made suicidal communications are the presence of alcoholism or clinical depression in someone over age forty. A physician in general practice called because a 50-year-old woman in his office seemed quite depressed. She had been an alcoholic for fifteen or twenty years, had been three times divorced, had been taking large amounts of barbiturates for more than a year, and was now asking for a large prescription. In answer to our questions, the physician reported a history of several surgical operations in the last few years and said that she was out of money and out of friends. She said that she didn't care whether she lived or died. In fact, she wished she was dead. He added that he was worried about her and he didn't know what he could do to help her.

Comment. Dependent persons who have led unstable lives and who tend to collect frustrations and disappointments and soothe them with alcohol and barbiturates generally make unsuccessful suicidal attempts when they are younger, but these attempts become more serious in the later stages of life and should be taken seriously. This case was deemed an emergeny, and we suggested to the physician that he send the woman to our office immediately, which he did. She was seen by us on a supportive basis and responded well for several weeks to a good deal of encouragement along with energizing drugs and mild sedation. However, she lapsed into depression again when it became clear to her that her current boyfriend had no intention of marrying her. At this point she was willing to accept hospitalization at a state hospital.

CASE 6

> On the referral of the mental hygiene counselor of the superior court, two sisters called for help about their father, a 52-year-old construction foreman, who was periodically an alcoholic and was threatening to commit suicide by shooting himself on his birthday (the next day).

Comment. This situation was regarded as an emergency. Age and sex were in the high suicide range, and the recent onset of self-destructive behavior, highly lethal method, and repetitive pattern of alcoholism further indicated an emergency. In addition, one got the impression of a man who was agitatedly depressed. On the positive side, the resources were not exhausted, there was still communication by the patient, and it seemed that with quick action a tragedy might be forestalled and the outcome might be good. A physician in the neighborhood was called and informed about the circumstances. On our recommendation, the physician together with the daughters and the man's two brothers went to the house, and there was a series of consultations back and forth between the family and the physician and the SPC. With this intervention, the patient's mood improved considerably. He expressed the feeling that he had thought everybody had deserted him and hated him. He was touched by the display of family affection and concern. Hospitalization was not necessary, but continued observation was recommended.

CASE 7

> The wife of a 51-year-old photographer, who had made a recent mild suicide attempt and was treated at the county hospital, sent a letter to the hospital at his suggestion, stating that her husband had become depressed again. She begged for advice and help, and the letter was referred to the SPC. We called the husband, who reacted with great gratitude and appreciation to the idea that we were concerned about him. He talked for almost an hour on the phone to the social worker.

Comment. Although the patient was depressed, it was not felt that this was an emergency because of his willingness to communicate and his desire for help. Most persons who call the SPC for help for themselves seldom represent emergencies. We have found that such persons can be given an appointment for the next day, or often several days in advance, and they will keep it. Usually we make a series of telephone calls to keep in communication with the patient until they are able to come to see us. It is only when communication is broken off that we become alarmed and feel that an emergency situation may have developed. The patient appeared the next day

for psychiatric interview and psychological testing and was found to be extremely depressed. Hospitalization was recommended and accepted.

Summary

In response to a request for emergency consultation regarding a problem of potential self-destruction, the consultant must obtain the most pertinent information, evaluate the situation, and recommend a course of action, all within a limited time. The use of a short schedule, specifying the questions to ask and the areas of information to explore, facilitates the consultation process. Use of the schedule tends to correct distortions induced by the limitation of time, the pressures of anxiety and other emotions, and certain technical restrictions inherent in such consultations. Several typical problem situations involving self-destructive potentiality are discussed in terms of the emergency evaluation procedure and the recommended plans of action.

Chapter 16
EVALUATION AND MANAGEMENT OF SUICIDAL PERSONS

Norman L. Farberow, Samuel M. Heilig, and Robert E. Litman

This is the Los Angeles Suicide Prevention Center's training manual designed primarily to teach volunteers the techniques of telephone evaluation and emergency management. Three main characteristics of the suicidal situation are discussed: crisis, ambivalence, and the communication of the feelings of hopelessness and helplessness. Based upon a set of basic principles for suicide prevention, a step-by-step procedure for evaluating suicidal potentiality is outlined and illustrated with a number of typical telephone calls for help.

Suicide is one of the most difficult problems confronting persons in the helping professions. This applies not only to the professional therapist but to all the occupations concerned with health and well-being of the public. It is rare that any psychiatrist, psychologist, social worker, nurse, physician, clergyman, policeman, or educator can conduct his affairs without at some time being faced with the need to evaluate and handle a suicidal situation.

Confusion often accompanies the use of the term *suicide*. The result of this confusion is the indiscriminate application of the term *suicidal* to patients with the implication that all persons are of equal lethal danger. Experience has shown that suicidal persons vary in lethal potentiality from minimal to highly serious, and that each person requires careful evaluation on his own merits.

Prominent Aspects of the Suicidal Situation

Crisis. The suicidal person is usually in the midst of a crisis. Crisis has been defined (by Webster) as a "turning point in the course of a situation," and "a situation whose outcome decides whether possible bad consequences will follow." Gerald Caplan has defined crisis as a "disorganization of homeostasis (when faced with a problem) . . . which cannot be solved quickly by the indi-

vidual's normal range of problem-solving mechanisms." For the person in a suicidal crisis, the principal factors are the overwhelming importance of an intolerable problem and the feelings of hopelessness and helplessness. The pressure of these feelings force him toward some actions for immediate resolution. These actions may be maladaptive, as in suicide attempts.

Crisis provides an unusual opportunity for therapeutic intervention. It is in the nature of crisis that it cannot be tolerated indefinitely. Therefore, the initiation and timing of therapeutic efforts during the crisis can influence the situation toward a good outcome.

Ambivalence. One of the most prominent features characterizing the suicidal person is ambivalence, expressed through feelings of wanting to die and wanting to live, both occurring at the same time. An example of ambivalence is the person who ingests a lethal dose of barbiturates and then calls someone for rescue before he loses consciousness. The relationship and strength of the two opposing impulses to live and to die will vary for different persons, and also within the same person under different conditions. Most people have a stronger wish to live than to die. It is this fact of ambivalence that makes suicide prevention possible. In working with a suicidal person it is necessary to evaluate both motives and their relationship to each other and to ally oneself on the side of the fluctuating wish to live.

Communication. Suicidal activity is frequently a last-ditch method of expressing feelings of desperation and helplessness. Suicidal people are reduced to this method when they feel unable to cope with a problem and that others are not attending to or denying their need for help. The suicidal behavior thus becomes a desperate means to claim the attention that they feel they have lost. The communication aspect may be in terms of verbal statements such as "I no longer want to live" or "I am going to kill myself"; or it may be in terms of actions such as the procuring of pills or guns, a sudden decision to prepare a will, or the giving away of treasured possessions. The communication may also be either direct or indirect and to a specific person or to the world in general. When it is indirect it is necessary to recognize the intent of the disguised message and to understand the real content of the communication. Recognition of the communication aspects of suicidal behavior

facilitates a more accurate evaluation of the various factors in the situation and allows for a more appropriate and helpful response.

The Worker in Suicide Prevention

The Effect of the Suicidal Communication. The suicidal situation can further be understood in terms of the effect upon the recipients of the communication. For example, the communications may arouse feelings of sympathy, anxiety, anger, hostility, and the like, among family or friends. These feelings, arising out of reactions of helplessness under the continued barrage of desperate communications, are often projected into the situation and attributed to the patient. Similar feelings may be aroused within the worker unless he can anticipate and counteract such reactions in himself. Another feeling of which the worker must be aware is the feeling of omnipotence, the feeling of being able to solve all the problems and meet all the demands of the patient. This is, of course, impossible, but the delusion is fostered because of the intense dependency transferred to him by the patient.

On the other hand, some suicidal situations will arouse within the worker feelings of anxiety and questions of adequacy to handle the critical situations. While a moderate level of anxiety is appropriate, too much anxiety may seriously hamper the worker, especially if it is transmitted to the patient who, at this point, is depending upon the worker to help him solve his problems. If the suicidal person, who feels helpless and lost, perceives excess anxiety within the worker he may lose his confidence in the possibility of being helped. The worker may begin in the area of suicide prevention with much anxiety, but experience has shown that he soon learns to handle his own feelings of concern and develops markedly in self-confidence.

Feelings About Death. Death is a part of life and living, but in our culture it has always been surrounded by powerful taboos. These taboos and the feelings they arouse may affect the worker and even interfere in the interaction with the patient, unless the worker is sensitive to his own feelings about death. Whatever his own feelings, the worker must avoid any tendencies toward moralistic attitudes toward death and suicide. The worker's point of view, within the professional situation, must be that death is to be postponed, if possible.

Basic Principles of Suicide Prevention

The following comments are offered as guidelines for effective and comfortable functioning in working with the suicidal patient. It is, of course, impossible to anticipate every situation, but the principles pertain to most situations.

In most cases, suicidal crises will go through several stages of resource activity. In the early stages, the person first comes to the attention of family, relatives, and friends. In the second stage, he will come into contact with first-line resources, such as family physician, clergyman, police, lawyers, school personnel, and public health nurses. If the suicidal tendencies persist, the third line of resources is called into play, the professional person and agency. The professions involved will include psychiatry, psychology, psychiatric social work, and psychiatric nursing. Agencies in the community most often involved will be mental hospitals, general hospitals, psychiatric clinics, social work agencies, and various service agencies such as family service, vocational rehabilitation, and employment offices. Probably, with the current development of community mental health centers and the movement toward more immediate response to both physical and emotional illnesses, the professional persons and agencies will be contacted earlier and more directly.

The handling of a telephone call from suicidal persons generally involves six steps. They may or may not occur simultaneously.
1. Establishing a relationship, maintaining contact, and obtaining information
2. Identification and clarification of the focal problems
3. Evaluation of the suicidal potential
4. Assessment of strength and resources
5. Mobilization of patients' and others' resources
6. Formulation of a therapy plan and the initiation of the appropriate actions.

Each of the steps is discussed in detail below.

1. Establishing a Relationship, Maintaining Contact, and Obtaining Information. In general, the worker should be patient, interested, self-assured, hopeful, and knowledgeable. He will want to communicate by his attitude that the person has done the right thing in calling and that the worker is able and willing to help. By the fact of his call, the patient has indicated a desire for help with

his problems. He should be accepted without challenge or criticism and allowed to tell his story in his own way, the worker confining himself to listening carefully to the information that is volunteered. The response, both in terms of attitude and tone on the telephone, will make a significant impact.

Often, because the patient will not have a clear idea of the agencies' functions, it will be necessary to make clear the services offered. For example, the patient may request financial aid or a home visit, and, if these are not part of the service, this must be unhesitatingly stated.

A call should be initiated with a clear identification of the worker, and a request for the name and telephone number of the caller. Names and phone numbers of interested other persons such as family, physicians, close friends, or others who might be possible resources in the situation should also be obtained. The worker's immediate goal is to obtain information to be used in an evaluation of the suicidal potentiality. This is usually best accomplished by asking, including direct specific questions, about his suicidal feelings. It is the patient's reason for calling and to talk about it without undue anxiety is helpful in reducing the patient's own fear of his suicidal impulses.

2. Identification and Clarification of Focal Problems. The suicidal patient often displays a profound sense of confusion, chaos, and disorganization. He is unclear about his main problem and has become lost in details. One of the most important services of the worker is to help the patient recognize and order the central and the secondary problems. For example, a woman caller presented a profusion of symptoms with feelings of worthlessness, despair, and inadequacy, accompanied by incessant weeping. Questioning revealed that her main problem lay in her relationships with her husband. A statement to this effect provided her with an authoritative definition of her central conflict and she was now able to address herself to this identified problem more effectively.

In some instances the caller may be clear about his central problem, but indicate that he has exhausted all his own alternatives for solution. The worker, as an objective outsider, might be able to provide a number of additional alternatives for the patient to consider.

3. Evaluation of Suicide Potential. The suicide potential refers

to the degree of probability that the patient may act out with self-destructive behavior in the immediate or relatively near future. A number of criteria to evaluate suicide potentiality have been developed. Suicidal potentiality will vary from minimal, in which there is no danger of loss of life, to maximal, in which the possibility of death occurring is great.

As soon as the worker begins to talk with the person, he has assumed the responsibility of preventing his suicide. To do so the worker must have an accurate evaluation of the lethal risk within the suicidal behavior. The plan of action formulated by the worker will depend upon the evaluation of the suicidal risk and on the appraisal of the patient's personality and resources. The criteria for evaluation of suicide potential follow:

a. *Age and sex.* Both statistics and experience have indicated that the suicide rate for committed suicide rises with increasing age, and that men are more likely to kill themselves than women. Age and sex are useful, therefore, in evaluating the caller. A communication from an older male tends to be most dangerous; from a young female, least dangerous. A communication from an older woman, however, is more dangerous than from a younger boy. Young people do kill themselves, even if the original aim may be to manipulate and control other people and not to die. Age and sex thus offer a general framework for evaluating the suicidal situation, but each case requires further individual appraisal, in which the criteria which follow are most useful.

b. *Suicide plan.* This is probably the most significant of the criteria of suicide potentiality. Three main elements should be considered in appraising the suicide plan. These are (i) the lethality of the proposed method, (ii) availability of the means, and (iii) specificity of the details. A method involving a gun or jumping or hanging will be of higher lethality than one that depends on the use of pills or wrist-cutting. If the gun is at hand, the threat of its use must be taken more seriously than when the person talks about shooting himself but has no gun immediately available. In addition, if the person indicates by many specific details that he has spent time and ingenuity in planning his method, the seriousness of the suicidal risk rises markedly.

Another factor in the rating of the suicide plan arises when the details are obviously bizarre. Further evaluation of the plan will

depend in large degree upon the patient's diagnosis. Psychotic people with the idea of suicide are high risks and often make bizarre attempts as a result of psychotic ideation.

c. *Stress*. Information about the precipitating stress usually is obtained in answer to the question, "Why are you calling at this time?" The precipitating stresses may be either or both inter- or intrapersonal, such as loss of a loved person by death, divorce, or separation; loss of job, money, prestige, or status; physical illness, sickness, surgery, accident, loss of limb; threat of prosecution, criminal involvement or exposure, and the like. Sometimes, increased anxiety and tension appear as a result of success, such as promotion on the job and increased responsibilities. Stress must always be evaluated from the patient's point of view and not from the worker's or society's point of view. What might be considered minimal stress by a worker might be felt as severe for the patient. The relationship noted between stress and symptoms (next criterion) is useful in evaluating prognosis. In general, if stress and symptoms are great, the action response of the worker must be high. In contrast, if symptoms are severe, but stress is low, either the story may be incomplete or the person is chronically unstable.

d. *Symptoms*. Suicidal symptoms occur in many different psychological states. Among the most common are depression, psychosis, and agitation. Evidence of a severe depressive state may be elicited with questions about sleep disorder, anorexia, weight loss, withdrawal, loss of interest, apathy and despondency, severe feelings of hopelessness and helplessness, and feelings of physical and psychological exhaustion. Psychotic states will be characterized by delusions, hallucinations, loss of contact or disorientation, or highly unusual ideas and experiences. Agitated states will show tension, anxiety, guilt, shame, poor impulse control, and feelings of rage, anger, hostility, and revenge. Of most significance is the state of agitated depression in which the person may feel that he is unable to tolerate the pressure of his feelings and anxieties and exhibits marked tension, fearfulness, restlessness, and pressure of speech. The patient feels he must act out in some direction in order to obtain some relief from his feelings. Alcoholics, homosexuals, and drug addicts tend to be high suicidal risks.

e. *Resources*. The patient's environmental resources are often critical in determining whether or not the patient will live. Inquiry

should be for resources that can be used to support him through the severe suicidal crisis. These may consist of family, relatives, close friends, physicians, or clergymen. If the patient is already in contact with a therapeutic agency or a professional therapist, the first consideration should be the possibility of referral back to the therapist or agency. Another resource may be the patient's work, especially when it provides him with self-esteem and gratifying relationships. Related to this is the patient's financial status, which may determine the feasibility of immediate physical and psychological care.

Sometimes the patient and family try to keep the suicidal situation a secret, or even to deny its existence. This attempt at secrecy and denial, in general, must be vigorously counteracted and the suicidal situation deals with openly and frankly. A general principle is that it is usually better both for the worker and for the patient when the responsibility for a suicidal patient is shared by as many people as possible. This gives the patient the feeling he lacks, that others are interested and ready to help him. Where there are no apparent sources of support, the situation may be considered ominous. The same evaluation may be applied when resources are available but have been exhausted, as when family and friends have turned away and now refuse to be concerned with the suicidal patient.

f. Life style. This criterion, in the sense of a global overview of the person's functioning, refers to a stable versus an unstable existence, and includes an evaluation of the suicidal behavior of the patient as acute or chronic. The stable person will indicate a consistent work history, stable marital and family relationships, and no history of prior suicidal behavior. If serious attempts were made in the past, the current suicidal situation may usually be rated more dangerous. The unstable personality may include severe character disorders, borderline psychotics, and persons with repeated difficulties in main areas of life functioning, such as interpersonal relationships, employment, frequent hospitalization, and the like. Acute suicidal behavior may be found in either a stable or an unstable personality; chronic suicidal behavior is found only in an unstable person. In stable personalities undergoing a suicidal crisis the reaction of the worker is appropriately highly responsive, active, and invested. In unstable persons, the worker generally must

be more cautious in his approach. His main object will be to clarify and simplify, to restore order to the confused person's life, and to help him stay in an interpersonal relationship with a meaningful person or resource.

g. Communication aspects. The communication aspects of the suicidal situation are revealing. The most important question is whether or not communication still exists between the suicidal person and other people. The most alarming signal is one that the communication with the suicidal person has been completely severed. This would be an indication to the worker that the suicidal person has reached the limits of his external resources and has lessened considerably the possibility of rescuing activity.

The form of the communication may be significant. In type, the communication may be either verbal or nonverbal, and, in content, it may be either direct or indirect. The most serious indication in the suicidal situation is when the person engages in nonverbal and indirect suicidal communication. These "action communications" imply that the interchange between the suicidal person and others around him is unclear and that there is a high probability of acting out of the suicidal impulses. In addition, if the recipient of the communication has strong tendencies toward denial, it may be very difficult for him to appreciate or even recognize the suicidal nature of the communications. In general, one of the primary goals of the worker is to clarify the communications among all who are involved.

The content of the communications may be directed to one or more significant persons in his environment with accusations, expressions of hostility, blame, and implied and overt demands for changes in behavior and feelings on the part of the others. Other communications may express feelings of guilt, inadequacy, worthlessness, or indications of strong anxiety and tension. When the communication is directed to specific persons, the reactions of these persons is important in the evaluation of the suicidal danger. These reactions are detailed in the following section.

h. Reactions of significant other. The significant other may be judged by the worker either as nonhelpful, or even injurious, in the situation and therefore no possible assistance for the patient; or he may be seen as helpful and a significant resource for rescue. The nonhelpful significant others either reject the patient or deny the suicidal behavior itself and withdraw both psychologically and

physically from continued communication. The significant other may resent the increased demands, the insistence on gratification of dependency needs, the dictum to change his behavior. In other cases, one may see helpless, indecisive, and ambivalent behavior on the part of the significant other and the strong feeling that he does not know what the next step is and has given up. This latter reaction of hopelessness gives the suicidal person the feeling that aid is not available from a previously dependable source and may increase the patient's own feelings of hopelessness.

By contrast, a helpful reaction from the significant other is one in which the significant other recognizes the communication, is aware of the problem that needs to be dealt with, and seeks help for the patient. This is an indication to the patient that his communications are being attended to and that someone is doing something to provide help for him.

i. Medical status. The medical situation of the patient may reveal additional important information for evaluating the suicidal potentiality. The patient, for example, may be suffering from a chronic, debilitating illness that has involved considerable change in self-image and self-concept. For persons with chronic illness, the relationship with their physician, their family, or a hospital will be of most importance. It is a positive sign if the patient continues to see these as resources for help.

The patient may be suffering from ungrounded fears of a fatal illness, such as cancer or brain tumor, and indicate a preoccupation with death and dying. There may be a history of many repeated unsuccessful experiences with doctors or a pattern of failure in previous therapy. These symptoms are of importance because of their possible effect on the significant others and doctors, exhausting them as resources for the patient.

In general, no single criterion need be alarming, with the possible exception of one: having a very lethal and specific plan for suicide. Rather, the evaluation of suicidal potential should be based on the general pattern of all the above criteria within the individual case. For example, feelings of exhaustion and loss of resources might well have different implications in two patients of different ages. Thus, a 25-year-old married man stated that he was tired, depressed, and was having vague ideas about committing suicide by

driving into a freeway abutment. There was no history of prior suicidal behavior. He reported difficulty in his marriage and talked of separation, but he was still in contact with his wife and was still able to work on a job that he has had for many years. This case was considered a low suicide risk. A contrasting case of high risk was a 64-year-old man with a history of alcoholism who reported he had made a serious suicide attempt one year ago and was saved when someone unexpectedly walked in and found him comatose. He recounted a history of three failures in marriage, and many job changes in the past year. He further stated that his physical health had been failing, that he had no family left, and that he was thinking of killing himself with a gun he had in his house.

4. *Assessment of Patient's Strengths and Resources.* It is as important to assess the patient's strengths and resources as it is to evaluate the pathological aspects of the picture. Frequently the patient will present alarming serious negative feelings and behaviors. These may be mitigated, however, by a number of positive features still present within the situation. For example, one indication of important internal resources may be the patient's reaction to the worker's first attempts to focus the interview. If the patient is able to respond to the worker, accepting suggestions and directions, this is an important hopeful sign. Improvement in mood and thinking within the course of one interview is a positive sign and indicates the patient's ability to respond to profferred help.

5. & 6. *Mobilization of Resources, and Treatment and Handling of the Suicidal Situation.* The plan formulated for the patient will be determined by the evaluation of the patient's suicidal status and the information obtained about him and his resources. In general, those cases with the higher suicidal potential will require the most activity on the part of the worker. An evaluation of acute suicidal potential in a situation that appears out of control will usually require immediate hospitalization. In our experience, however, only 13 percent of the cases require this action. Most calls received by the worker are of low suicidal risk. Many of them can be handled satisfactorily by simply providing sympathetic and understanding listening with perhaps counseling and advice.

Most cases, however, will require more action on the part of the worker, usually in the process of referring the patient to another

resource in the community. The type of referral will depend upon the evaluation of the problem. The referral may be to either a non-professional or a professional resource or to both.

If the call comes at night, the worker should keep in mind that most problems are magnified when seen in the nighttime hours. An immediate goal would be to help the patient get through the night. The goal should be to get sufficient information to determine if it is a high risk emergency requiring an immediate action.

In the highly unusual event that a person is calling in the midst of his suicide attempt (less than 7 percent of the calls), as much information as is necessary to identify the patient or the caller should be obtained and the informant should be instructed either to take the patient to an emergency hospital, to call his personal physican, to call an ambulance, or to call the police. The overriding aim at that time is to provide the patient with immediate medical attention.

At this point it is important to note an important aspect of the worker's responsibility. The worker might make a referral for the patient to one of the other resources within the community, but the responsibility for the patient remains his until this responsibility is assumed by the other resource. The patient is thus *transferred* rather than *referred*. The worker must not assume his responsibility has been discharged until he is assured that the patient has been accepted elsewhere.

In general, if there is any question or doubt about the evaluation of the suicidal situation of the patient, he should be referred to a professional person for a complete evaluation. A patient with a suicidal problem that is not immediately serious but who presents emotional disturbances may be referred to a psychiatric clinic, private therapist, or a family agency. Usually such resources will require a waiting period and the referral to such agencies will depend upon whether or not the patient can sustain the interim period. A resource book showing available psychiatric and social agencies in the community is especially useful.

For the worker in suicide prevention, there will always appear, despite experience and knowledge, some cases that will arouse anxiety and tension within him. The most constructive way to handle the feelings is through consultation with colleagues, which generally provides at least two measures of help. Not only is there a sharing

of anxiety and responsibility, but there is benefit from discussion of the problem, which may offer further insights and alternative solutions to the problem. Consultation must not be used, however, as a device for "passing the buck."

Resources

The following are detailed suggestions about general and community resources for use in suicidal situations. Any one or combinations of these resources should be considered as imaginatively and constructively as possible. The worker should not allow himself to be constrained by conventional practices.

1. *Family.* The family is often neglected as a resource but is one of the most valuable at the time of crisis. The patient should be encouraged to discuss his situation and problems with his family. If it is considered important that someone be with the patient during the crisis, the family members should be called and apprised of the situation even though the patient may be reluctant. The patient is usually informed first that his family will be called. Also, the family must be involved in accepting responsibilities for the emergency and in helping the patient get the treatment that has been recommended.

2. *Friends.* Close friends often can be used in the same way families have been used. For example, the patient can be encouraged to have a friend stay with him during a difficult period. The friend may also be helpful in talking things out and in giving a feeling of support.

3. *Family physician.* People often turn to their family doctors for help and physicians often serve as supportive authority figures. The patient usually has a good relationship with his doctor and should be encouraged to discuss his problems with him. Physicians can also be helpful in cases where medication or hospitalization is required.

4. *Clergy.* If the caller is close to his church he should be encouraged to discuss his situation with his clergyman.

5. *Employer.* When the patient's occupation is involved and there is considerable question about his feelings or self-esteem because of vocational difficulties, the patient can be encouraged to talk about these difficulties with his employer.

6. *Police.* Police should be utilized only in cases of clear and immediate emergency; for example, if the suicide attempt is about to occur or has occurred. The patient may need prompt medical attention and the police are often the ones who can procure it for him most quickly. The police are able to take the responsibility for involvement with a patient and may hospitalize when necessary. It should be remembered, however, that the police are not to be used simply as an ambulance or transportation system. As a general rule, the police should be involved as little as possible, but when the decision to use them is made it should be carried through with firmness and dispatch. The two main criteria will be the helplessness and injury of the patient.

7. *Emergency hospital.* Usually the patient or his family or the caller will know of private emergency hospitals in his area. The worker should know about city and county hospitals available for emergency medical treatment hospitalization. The police will generally use city and county hospitals.

8. *Own agency.* The worker may wish to refer the patient to his own agency in those cases in which it is felt there is a high suicide potential and in which there is a need for more intensive, careful, further evaluation. Giving the patient an appointment gives the patient a task and a purpose to his immediate future. This resource, of course, can be used only when the agency includes facilities for personal interview and evaluation.

9. *Social work agencies and community psychiatric clinics.* In those cases in which the suicide danger has been evaluated as low or perhaps not even the primary problem, a referral to a family service agency or community psychiatric clinic can be considered. These are often the treatment medium of choice for patients in whom the underlying problem may be seen as marital discord, family conflict, or chronic personal and social maladjustment. The worker should be familiar with the social work agencies or community psychiatric clinics within the community and referrals can be made to those near the patient. Often, a referral to an agency that works primarily with persons of the patient's own religion is more desirable. Other considerations are fees and hours that will be compatible with the patient's situation.

10. *Private therapists.* Some calls are from people looking for psychiatric treatment. The worker should be familiar with private

therapists for appropriate recommendation in such cases. If the patient indicates that he is already in treatment, he should be encouraged to return to his own therapist.

11. *Psychiatric hospital.* If the community contains a psychiatric hospital or a general hospital with a psychiatric ward where patients can be hospitalized, a liaison with such facilities is most important. Generally, referral to such a resource is made when it is thought the patient is so disturbed that he might seriously harm himself or others, and/or he is so disorganized he can no longer exercise judgment or direction of his affairs. It might be necessary to have family or friends take the patient to the hospital if the patient himself is incapable of getting there.

Some Typical Calls

Following are some illustrations of what may be considered typical calls:

> 1. A woman, between 30 and 40 years old, calls at night saying that she doesn't understand why she feels so depressed. She states she is alone, complains of not being able to sleep, having troubled thoughts, and feeling that she needs to talk to someone. Sometimes she will say that she really doesn't want to kill herself but she has had suicidal thoughts over many months or years. She may be agitated, depressed, weeping, as if she is having a hysterical breakdown. She may be demanding and asks what can be done to help her right now, because she feels she is not able to get through the night. Questioning will reveal she has had many similar episodes before. Probably she is reacting to some interpersonal conflict such as argument with a family member or close friend.

It is best to listen patiently and wait for the opportunity to point out realistically that things look worse at night, but that it is not the best time when she can get help for herself. She should be advised to call her doctor or social work agency or clinic in the morning, so as to arrange a program of help for herself. It may be helpful to suggest that she call a close friend or relative to come and be with her during this difficult night.

> 2. A woman sounds as if she were between 20 and 35 years old, but who will not identify herself. She asks

what can the Suicide Prevention Center do for a person who doesn't want to live anymore, and generally takes a challenging position. The caller sounds controlled, makes vague allusions to a long-standing problem, and wants to know what you can do about it. Frequently, these no-name callers are either in psychotherapy or have recently interrupted psychotherapy.

The worker should point out that the caller has responsibility to clarify his request and cooperate if he is to receive help. You must know who he is and about his situation before you can assist him. If he tells you he has a therapist, and who he is, you should refer him back to the therapist. Tell him that you will call the therapist to notify him that the patient has called you.

3. A woman between 40 and 55 calls about herself, complaining that she is very depressed, feels lonely and tired, and feels that no one is interested in her. She talks about many physical and medical problems. She says that she feels her doctor is not helping her enough and that her husband is not paying enough attention to her. She will say that she feels like her life is over, and there is no point in continuing to live.

An effort should be made to talk with the husband and to discuss with him how his wife is feeling. Both the patient and the husband should be encouraged to talk with the family physician at the first opportunity about the patient's depression. You may offer to call the physician too, if they wish, in order to enlist his aid. If none of these resources seems available the patient may be asked to call the SPC for an appointment.

4. A man between 18 and 30 sounds evasive and anxious on the phone and is reluctant to give his name. He talks about having a problem that he is hesitant to identify, and states he is calling for help because the only solution he can think of is to kill himself. His suicide plan will be an impulsive one, like smashing his car up on the freeway, or cutting himself with a razor blade. This man often has a personal problem about which he feels guilty, such as homosexuality.

This patient should be encouraged to seek help for himself. You should commend him for having done the right thing in calling you

as a beginning effort to get help for himself. You might suggest a resource to which he might go, such as a psychiatric clinic, private therapist, physician, or school counselor.

5. A man between 25 and 40 complains that his life is just a mess because of his bungling. He talks about having gotten himself into such a jam, either financially or with his family or on the job, that he feels the only way out is to kill himself. Often, he will be reacting to a specific, recent setback in his life.

He should be told that he is reacting to a specific stress, and that he needs help with that particular problem about which he feels helpless and hopeless. He should be reminded that he was able to function well before he had this setback, that he is suffering from a depression that is most often time-limited and temporary and that he needs help to get back on his feet again. He should be encouraged to call the SPC during regular office hours for an appointment.

6. A man about 50 or over sounds very depressed and discouraged and seems apologetic about calling and troubling you. He may complain about a physical problem that has prevented his working, and feels now that he is beyond help. His general feelings about himself are that he is old and infirm and a burden on others. When asked what his suicidal thoughts are he talks about specific plans for killing himself.

Friends, family, and resources should be mobilized and involved. The patient should be told that help is available to him. He should be told to call the SPC for an appointment and his family should be impressed with the need to follow through. If he fails to call, then a staff member of the SPC should be alerted to call him back to arrange an appointment.

7. A family member or friend calls about a person who is described as depressed, withdrawn, or has shown some behavioral or personality change. The patient may have told them that he is planning to kill himself and even discussed a specific plan with them; or, he may have generally talked about wanting to end his life. The caller is asking how serious the situation is and what he should do.

The caller should be advised to contact the patient and let him know he is concerned about him and trying to get help. He should be told to have the patient call you, so that the patient will have the feeling that help is being obtained for him, and, also, you will have an opportunity to evaluate the situation with the patient. You should maintain your contact with the initial caller and keep him apprised of what is happening, maintaining him as a resource to help, if need be. The recommendation to the patient will depend on the evaluation of the lethal potentiality.

8. The caller is a neighbor or friend and is concerned about someone he knows. He may be reluctant to identify himself or to involve himself in any responsibility but requests that you do something about the person he is concerned about. He is not able to give too much detail or information about the situation that concerns him.

You should get as much information as you can and encourage him to let the person know that he is concerned for him and to advise the patient to call you. You should point out that it would be unrealistic for you simply to call someone without being able to say who notified you. The caller should be told that it is his responsibility to be involved, if he is really concerned about a person who is suicidal. Often, such a caller will ask you to make a home visit, to which you may reply that it is impossible for you to leave the phone inasmuch as you are on duty.

9. A physician, minister, police officer, or similar person in a position of responsibility calls about a case. Frequently, the call is about someone who has just been rescued after a suicide attempt.

Get as much information as possible to evaluate the situation. If the patient is still threatening suicide, hospitalization should be considered. If the patient seems calmed down and under control, then he should be encouraged to seek professional help. Your informant should be encouraged to demonstrate his continued interest in the patient, if he is able to do so. The patient or family should be advised to call the SPC for an appointment, if more information is needed to make an appropriate referral.

10. A person calls and demands to speak to a specific staff member.

Unless there is an extreme emergency, you should talk with the patient yourself, seek to help if you can with the current problem, and ask the patient to call the staff member in the morning. If, however, the emergency is great, you can call the staff member and ask him to call the patient.

> 11. The caller tells you about a neighbor or family member who is being physically restrained from attempting suicide, and the patient cannot be left unattended. The patient is described as psychotic and determined to kill himself.

The caller should be advised to take the patient to the psychiatric unit of the General Hospital. It should be emphasized that harmful drugs or objects should be removed from the patient's environment and someone should always be with him.

> 12. A call comes in from someone who is attempting suicide while telling you about it.

You should keep the person on the phone. Get his name, phone number, address, and information about his attempt. Try to learn specifically what he has ingested or what he is doing. Call the police and identify yourself as a member of the SPC staff and give them all the pertinent information and ask them to investigate.

Chapter 17
SUICIDE AS ACTING OUT
Robert E. Litman

This paper considers suicide as a clinical manifestation of acting out. Through a series of case examples from the Los Angeles Suicide Prevention Center, the paper explicates various kinds of problems in the unconscious and their behavioral manifestations, as they relate to suicide attempts. The clinical categories include transference acting out, malignant masochism, ego weakness, neurotic symbiotic unions, and so on. Suicide is viewed as a planned act, reflecting a "nonverbal translation of unconscious conflict."

Acting out is an essential element of suicide. In some clinical situations, for example, the emergency evaluation of suicidal persons by Suicide Prevention Center therapists, the potential of the patient for acting out is a critical factor in determining the therapeutic procedure.

The observations and conclusions described here are derived from two main methodological approaches to suicide. One is the "psychological autopsy" method of retrospective reconstruction of the life situation and suicidal behaviors of persons who have committed suicide in Los Angeles County during recent years. As part of the investigations, which were conducted in cooperation with the Chief Medical Examiner-Coroner's Office, we interviewed relatives, friends, employers, and physicians of the deceased.[1] The interviews included several hundred with psychotherapists of patients who committed suicide.

The second source of data has been the clinical experiences of the staff of the Suicide Prevention Center at Los Angeles with almost 10,000 living suicidal persons.[2] Slightly more than half of these persons called the around-the-clock emergency telephone service for help for themselves.[3] The other calls were initiated by relatives, friends, or professional persons who were worried about a patient or client.

These two approaches to suicide investigation are complemen-

tary. Each has advantages and disadvantages. Retrospective interviews about individuals who committed suicide are subject to the distortions and omissions of informants. On the other hand, inferences based on interviews with living suicidal patients can be applied to committed suicides only with caution. Patients are slightly suicidal, moderately suicidal, or seriously suicidal. There are essential differences between slightly suicidal people and seriously suicidal people.[4] For example, therapists who deal with slightly suicidal patients tend to be impressed by their manipulations, exploitations, and hostility. By contrast, therapists who review cases of suicide or treat seriously suicidal patients tend to be impressed by their hopelessness, confusion, and terrible suffering.

Acting out may be defined as "any act which attempts to resolve an internal conflict by translating the unverbalized statement of conflict into action—the latter being ego-syntonic, although the consequence is alien," or, more briefly, "Acting out is a generally nonverbal translation of an unconscious conflict."[5] In the next section I will briefly present three histories typical of suicide, with emphasis on the internal conflict and the process of translation into suicide action.

Typical Suicides

   Case 1: Mr. A, age 51, shot himself with a rifle through his heart, while sitting in his automobile, at approximately 8 A.M. He had been a real estate salesman who led a conventional life, ambitiously oriented toward financial success, which, to him, was especially important, since he felt inadequate at times because he lacked a college education. During a short period, about four months before his death, he lost three important business transactions that he had counted on, and following this loss he became morose, depressed, irritable and despondent, and he began to drink, mostly beer, rather heavily. He became indecisive and began to talk about changing to some different type of work.

   This disturbed his wife. Although there was no obvious marital disharmony, in recent years they had grown apart. The children were grown, and her main interest was religious. There had been almost no sexual intercourse for several years. The wife had Mr. A examined by a physi-

cian, who diagnosed high blood pressure and prescribed an antihypertensive drug. She tried to interest Mr. A in church affairs, but he did not attend regularly.

One week prior to Mr. A's death his wife, concerned about his lethargy, sleeplessness, lack of appetite, and hopeless attitude, telephoned the physician, who said that the patient should have more activity. Two days before his death Mr. A went to a department store and bought a rifle, which he left in his car. The night before his death he talked to a clergyman for several hours, mostly about his failure and anxiety. He woke around 5 A.M. and went for a walk, during which he unwrapped the gun and loaded it. Then he returned for breakfast. At his wife's request, they prayed. Then he went for another walk, again to his automobile, and this time he shot himself.

Later, his wife found several notes, torn up in small pieces in the wastebasket. Apparently he wrote the notes before going for a walk at 5 A.M. and tore them up when he returned for breakfast at 7. When reassembled, the notes read, "Honey, I am unable to take this any longer. God have mercy on my soul. I'm sorry, but I am unable to go on living in the condition I am in. Please be brave. Sorry that life turned out this way. I hope you can find a better life without me. I know I must be nuts. Life isn't worth living, and I have to go through hell every day that I have been through."

After the death Mrs. A wondered if she had been in some way responsible. She herself had been feeling let down and depressed. She said they had no financial problems. Mr. A's father had died in an accident on the thirteenth of the month, which was the date Mr. A committed suicide.

We infer that the main internal conflict concerned Mr. A's feeling that he could not live up to the demands of his conscience, of God, and of his wife. There might have been an identification with his dead father involved in choosing the exact day of his death. He had evidently considered suicide for some time, gradually moving toward the final act.

Case 2: Mrs. B, age 47, died in her home from an overdose of barbiturates. She had been a well-educated and ex-

tremely intelligent woman, who, for most of her life, was anxious and worried, especially about her health. She inherited a good deal of money from her father and never worked. She felt lonely and insecure, ostensibly because she was unable to establish stable relationships with men. She had been divorced twice. Over the years she had seen several psychiatrists, each time for a few consultations, and each time she terminated the therapy, usually, she said, because the doctor was too cold and impersonal. She had been taking sleeping pills for many years.

Each time a love relationship was severed, she went through a period of depression and twice had made suicide attempts with barbiturates. About a month before her death she consulted a psychiatrist because of weight loss, sleeplessness, and acutely depressive feelings, brought on, she thought, by news that her divorced husband had remarried. The psychiatrist recommended more consultations with him, but she failed to keep her appointment, and he did not call her. On the day of her death she consulted her family physician, who was alarmed by the serious weight loss and said that he would have to do a careful diagnostic study, since she might be suffering from some organic illness, possibly even a tumor. That night she took a fatal overdose of sleeping pills, leaving a note, which said she couldn't face a lingering death from cancer. An autopsy showed no tumor, and no particular organic illness.

This patient's main unconscious problem seemed to revolve around her need for love, which was in conflict with her fear of intimacy. Her life pattern seemed to act out a memory of briefly being close to someone and then separating. There was some evidence that she unconsciously hoped to be rescued from the last suicide action, as she had previously been rescued, for she communicated clues to suicide to several people. It was known that she had saved up a large number of pills over a long period of time, with the idea that some day she might use these pills for suicide.

Case 3: Individuals who have survived a very serious suicide action, which in all probability, should have resulted in death, may be an exceptionally good source

of information on the psychology of suicide. Mr. C, aged 62, shot himself in the head with a pistol. Apparently the shell was defective, for it produced very little power and the bullet, after breaking through the skull, lodged in the meninges, barely penetrating the brain, causing minimal damage. Mr. C had been a successful commercial artist. One year previously he suffered a small cerebro-vascular accident. This did not impair his ability to walk, speak, or think, but it did leave him with a tremor, which disabled him as an artist. He had previously been divorced from his wife, and he lived with his aged mother.

During his year of unemployment Mr. C. became increasingly depressed. He felt he was no good, that he was a burden on his mother, and he could not accept his status as an ex-artist. He rehearsed shooting himself with the pistol, unloaded.[6] Finally, he took a room in a motel, so that his mother would not be disturbed by the shot, and fired the bullet into his brain. He was shocked to find himself still alive. He staggered out of the room into the lobby, where help was summoned. When interviewed the next day, he was not suicidal. After his discharge from the hospital he obtained work as a gardener and made a good adjustment. He seemed to have completely lost his former identity as an artist. Two years later he was well and happy.

His internal conflict seemed to center around feelings of self-depreciation and guilt and an inability to accept loss of status. Unconsciously he was dissatisfied with living with his mother, but was unable to leave her. When he shot himself, he had a thought that it was like destroying a badly injured horse. After the suicide attempt he seemed to feel that he had been reborn, with a new identity.

The Psychology of Suicide Acts

These case examples illustrate that suicide acts, as a general rule, are not sudden, unpredictable, impulsive, momentary, or random acts. In most cases, the suicide plan has been developed gradually and rehearsed in fantasy and preliminary action. In nearly every case of suicide there is evidence of crisis, conflict, ambivalence, mixed motivations, and multiple determinants.

Emotional crises occur from time to time in all lives when people face problems, which temporarily are beyond their ability to solve. Situations that threaten the continuity of our mental, physical, and social equilibrium are powerful sources of stress. Confrontations with death, ill health, loss of love, or change in social status are typical examples. The person under stress feels restless, uneasy, painfully tense, and unable to adapt. At first, suicide is only one of many possible reactions. The individual tries Solution A, Solution B, Solution C, Solution D, and feels no improvement. He thinks of Solutions E, F, G, H, and I and imagines no improvement. Finally he comes to Solution S—suicide. He struggles against it, abandons it, tries other thoughts, other actions. Sometimes nothing helps. The person loses hope and returns repeatedly to thoughts of suicide. His thinking grows more distorted, constricted, confused, and desperate, and as the suicide act is rehearsed in fantasy and in preliminary actions, the act acquires momentum and an autonomous pressure for completion.

Contributions to an act of suicide come from all psychological levels and structures and from the external environment. There is no simple or single psychological formula that applies to all suicides.

Some of the more important unconscious fantasy systems that contribute to suicide take the form of wishes, as follows: (1) a tired wish for surcease, escape, sleep, death; (2) a guilty wish for punishment, sacrifice, to make restitution; (3) a hostile wish for revenge, power, control, murder; (4) an erotic wish for passionate surrender, the greatest ecstasy, reunion with the loved dead; (5) a hopeful wish for life, for rescue, rebirth, a new start.

Suicide is usually associated with failure of important ego functions, such as orientation in the external world, understanding causes and effects, and the control of dangerous wishes. There tends to be a narrowing and constriction of ego span and ego capacity. Frequently the feeling of hopelessness is so severe as to amount to a cognitive defect.

Certain superego attitudes dispose toward suicide. Among these are inability to accept help because of pride, and an all-or-nothing view of life, which suggests suicide to a person who is losing. The histories of many suicides indicate that there were pathological identifications with hostile parents or nuclear identifications with loved persons who died.[7]

Finally, there is a social factor in every suicide. Some meaning is supplied by the cultural, religious, and sociological milieu that provides a context for suicide. More specifically, suicide occurs within a nexus of interpersonal relations and communicates a message, most often a "cry for help." The people around the potential suicide play an important role in the outcome, either by acts of commission, ommission, or both.

> Example: A husband came home at 3 A.M. to find his wife unconscious, an empty sleeping pill container in the waste paper basket, and on the table a note, "Wake me if you love me." He threw the note down and left. She died. Such acts of desertion, as well as acts of rescue, suggest a mutual acting out.

Varieties of Acting Out

The acting out in suicide manifests itself somewhat differently in various clinical categories. Without attempting a complete survey, I will discuss briefly some aspects as follows: (1) suicide with minimal acting out; (2) acting out in the transference; (3) malignant masochism and schizophrenia; (4) special ego weakness; (5) alcoholism; (6) symbiotic union; (7) depression.

Suicide with minimal acting out. Indications of minimal acting out would be an absence of crisis, personality change, and ego-splitting; and the presence of adequate reality testing, verbalization of the essential conflicts, and a general sense of continuity between the total personality and the suicide act. By such criteria "appropriate" suicides do occur among the old and very sick, but are relatively rare. Some people leave careful notes, which indicate guilt over exhausting the resources of the family in a useless and painful survival. Often the aged have great ambivalence over killing themselves, on one hand wishing for surcease but, on the other hand, feeling paralyzed to act. For instance, an old man wrote, "I'm going to try to die of carbon monoxide. I hope it works this time." In terminal diseases suicide is often precipitated by an abrupt or unfeeling family decision to move the patient from his home to a nursing facility. The patient acts out his panic, loss of identity, and anger at being dispossessed.

Transference acting out. Approximately 10 percent of suicides in Los Angeles have talked with a psychiatrist or other mental

health specialist within two months before the death. For a few
of the patients, the contact was only brief and meaningless, but for
a majority there had been a therapeutic relationship with transference and countertransference aspects. The suicide of persons
who were in therapy tended with great regularity to occur at a
time of separation between patient and doctor. Frequently the
separation was caused by an absence of the doctor due to travel or
vacation, or it was brought about by an interruption or termination
of treatment. Many of the patients had very recently been discharged from psychiatric hospitals. Therapists agreed that the
transference feelings of the patients were "I have been abandoned."
A subsidiary fantasy was "It is hopeless. Doctors cannot or will
not help me."

That patients feel abandoned by their therapists is well known to
the staff of the Suicide Prevention Center. Of approximately 1,700
night calls in 1963, almost a third were from persons who had a
therapist. These people called the Suicide Prevention Center instead of their own therapists because of transference feelings,
usually of being abandoned. They said, "My doctor is tired of me."
"I don't want to impose on the doctor any longer." "He doesn't
want to see me anymore." Sometimes the patient had abandoned
the doctor. "He gets too personal and upsets me too much." The
most seriously suicidal persons are not those who feel angry and
want "to show the doctor" or make him "feel sorry." The most
serious cases seem to be living out a memory-fantasy of being
abandoned and left to die.

Malignant masochism. Some patients in therapy commit suicide
as a form of negative therapeutic reaction. These cases are rare but
extremely tragic, not only for the patient, but for the therapist.
Superego pathology is especially prominent in these patients. They
give a history of either a loved dead parent for whom they long,
or an incorporated hostile parent who demands death as the only
way of obtaining love.

> *Case 4:* A young woman, diagnosed as a schizophrenic,
> had been a demon in a psychiatric hospital for many
> months because of her uncontrolled self-destructive be-
> havior, which included repeated episodes of cutting up
> her arms and neck with broken glass, bottles, windows, or
> whatever she could use. Finally, one of the resident doc-

tors took a special interest in her and began to see her every day. After a few months there was a dramatic change. She stopped cutting herself and began to wash regularly, dress neatly, and use make-up. One day he complimented her on the changes. That night she hanged herself.[8] One element of her history was the story that her mother had savagely abused the girl when she was about three years old, and the mother had a psychotic break.

Schizophrenia. Schizophrenic patients who commit suicide usually have a history of previous suicide attempts or threats, and have had periods of confused behavior, with occasional outbursts of poorly organized action. Because schizophrenics misinterpret the actions of others and are dominated by their own fantasies, they may suicide unpredictably. They make up the only group of suicides that occur without any prior indication to the therapist of withdrawal, separation, or breaking off of communication. For example, a schizophrenic ran away from a psychiatric hospital and jumped from a high building because he felt that his death would save his family from persecution by the FBI and the communists. Most of the bizarre suicides, such as jumping into a cement mixer, self-incineration, nailing self to a cross, and diving head first from a bridge onto a freeway are acts of schizophrenics. Since many suicidal schizophrenics are also potentially homicidal, there is some danger for rescuers who try to interrupt the destructive acts.

Ego Weakness. Reports on individuals who committed suicide indicate that there was a change in the ego of the deceased. Informants say, "He was different." "Her whole personality changed." Patients who survive very serious suicide attempts often report, "It was like I was in a dream." "I couldn't think straight." "I felt I had to do it." A woman who cut her wrists said, "Usually I feel weak but at the moment I was cutting my wrists, I felt strong, purposeful and punishing. My arm seemed to belong to someone else. Then the blood came, and I was myself again."[9]

A few suicides, less than 5 percent, result from impulsive panic behavior. For example, a man arrested after a homosexual act suddenly darted away in handcuffs from police officers and threw himself under the wheels of a passing truck. Such guilt-panic suicides occur once or twice a month in jails in Los Angeles. After

a disaster there may be impulsive suicides. For instance, a husband whose wife was killed in an automobile accident slipped away from the crowd and hanged himself. The unconscious conflicts seem to center around guilt.

A substantial minority of suicides are catalyzed by the ego weakening action of alcohol and other drugs. Alcohol greatly reduces the self-preservative functions of the ego and allows latent suicidal fantasies to emerge into consciousness and latent actions to be acted out.

Alcoholism. Suicide actions occur frequently in alcoholic characters, not only because of the ego weakening effects of alcohol, but also because the alcoholic character contains strong self-destructive elements. Many chronic alcoholics become depressed, realizing that the years of alcoholism have cost them friends, love, and financial success. Some authorities say that the alcoholic must "hit bottom." This period of crisis is frequently associated with suicidal action, so that for any group of alcoholics, about 5 percent may be expected sooner or later to commit suicide. In periodic alcoholics, suicide is most apt to occur toward the end of a binge and is associated with tremendous guilt and self-reproach. In chronic alcoholics who have come to the end of their psychological rope, failure and escape fantasies predominate.

Symbiotic union. Many people, including those who appear to have made a normal life adjustment, have, in reality, never successfully completed the separation-individuation stage of development and retain a considerable parasitic need to lean upon the ego of others. If the symbiotic association is dissolved, the individual feels abandoned, helpless, and terribly threatened, and he feels an urge to take action, which may include suicide. Often the actions are addressed directly to the partner as a message, "You can't leave me, I need you, you must stay." Much depends upon how the partner responds. Often both partners in a symbiotic union become depressed and suicidal together, each signaling by action but not by words the feeling, "I am terribly frightened of the impending breakup, but I can do nothing about it."

Depressive suicide. When depressives struggle to express their feelings, they report, "I feel empty, sick, dead, terrified." "I can't stand the suffering." "I feel hopeless that any improvement can

occur." Four ominous signs of suicide potentiality in depressives are: (1) an impatient, agitated attitude that something must be done immediately; (2) a detailed, feasible, lethal suicide plan; (3) pride, suspicion, and hyperindependence as character traits; (4) isolation, withdrawal, living alone, or living with someone so emotionally removed from the suicidal person that the patient, in effect, is living alone. The act of suicide often expresses in action a conflict between wishes to fail, give up and rest on one side, and a demanding ambition on the other. The act says, "Leave me alone, I am sorry but I can't do what you want me to do. I have to do what I want to do."

Importance of Suicide Plan

Depressions are characterized by exhaustion of energy, psychomotor retardation, and paralysis of will. How can the depressed, immobilized patient initiate and carry out a decisive self-destructive act? In my opinion, the essential mechanism is ego-splitting. A fragment of ego, dissociated from the preoccupied major part, becomes the nucleus for acting out. The unconscious conflicts are translated into acting out through the intermediary stage of the suicide plan.

During painful crises, thoughts of suicide provide temporary relief from tension. From such thoughts and numerous other psychic elements, including wishes, memories, fantasies, identifications, defenses, and partial adaptations, the suicide plan is formed. It is crystallized, strengthened, and reinforced by repetitions in imagination and by verbal extensions such as promises, threats, and declarations. At first the plan seems alien and dangerous to the individual himself and provokes anxiety. Gradually, the suicide plan acquires an autonomous structure within the ego, more or less dissociated from the rest of the self and tolerated as ego-syntonic.

Various preliminary actions are initiated. For example, a weapon is chosen or the suicidal act is rehearsed. Although further elaboration may be suspended for days or months, the suicide plan has acquired some of the qualities of an incomplete or interrupted on-going act. Such interrupted acts have an autonomous momentum toward completion.

Case 5: A stable, middle-aged professional man became extremely disturbed when his wife asked for a divorce. He quit working, made vague threats toward her, and then developed over a period of months a complicated suicide plan with midnight, December 31st, as the deadline. Since the marriage had been unhappy and his wife lacked beauty and charm, I asked him why he felt she was indispensable. He answered that by now his wife had nothing to do with it. "I said I would kill myself, and I am going to do what I said I would do." He agreed that the plan sounded crazy; yet, "to myself, doctor, I just don't feel crazy." The patient acted out his plan, plunging a stiletto into his heart. His life was saved by open heart surgery, and he was no longer suicidal. The act had been completed.

The concept of a relatively autonomous suicide plan is of special importance to professional persons working in emergency centers, hospital admitting services, or wherever a therapeutic disposition must be determined for suicidal patients. In evaluating the danger of acting out, the details of the suicide plan: place, time, method, purpose, deadlines, and commitments, should be reviewed with the patient.

Summary
1. Acting out is an essential element of suicide.
2. The internal conflicts that are translated into suicide actions are varied, complex, and multidimensional. Id, ego, superego, and environment all contribute to each suicidal act.
3. Features of typical suicides are reported. Some specific suicide syndromes are reviewed. These include: Suicide with minimal acting out, transference suicide, schizophrenia, alcoholism, special ego states, neurotic symbiotic unions, and depression.
4. Suicide acts begin as fantasy attempts to resolve crises. The fantasies evolve gradually into a suicide plan, which is rehearsed in imagination and in anticipatory actions.
5. The suicide act itself acquires momentum and an autonomous pressure toward completion. This factor is of special importance for therapists who evaluate patients in emergency centers or hospital admitting units.

PART V
DIAGNOSIS
AND EVALUATION:
SPECIFIC CLINICAL GROUPS

Chapter 18
SUICIDAL RISK AMONG SCHIZOPHRENIC PATIENTS

Norman L. Farberow, Edwin S. Shneidman, and Calista V. Leonard

Thirty cases, selected from among 190 schizophrenic individuals who committed suicide in Veteran Administration psychiatric hospitals throughout the United States in the years 1955–1958, were matched man-for-man with thirty schizophrenic patients who did not commit suicide. All available data were analyzed and a "Psychological Autopsy" was conducted for each of the sixty cases. Three subtypes of schizophrenic suicidal patients were distinguished: dependent-satisfied, dependent-dissatisfied and unaccepting. For each of these three types, the typical hospital course, prodromal clues, patient's attitudes toward hospitalization and illness, reactions under stress, and attitudes toward discharge were delineated. In addition, specific recommendations were given for the management of each of the three types of hospitalized schizophrenic patient.

Introduction

This report is concerned exclusively with the problem of preventing suicide among those patients in a psychiatric hospital who have been diagnosed as schizophrenic.[1] The information contained herein is based upon the results obtained to date from a continuing nationwide research project on the problem of unpredicted deaths being conducted currently at the VA Central Research Unit for the Study of Unpredicted Deaths, VA Center, Los Angeles.

In the entire country, most individuals who commit suicide do so outside of a hospital setting; however, if they survive they are often brought to a hospital subsequent to a suicide attempt. Although a relatively small percentage of suicides occurs within the hospital itself, the identification and treatment of those hospital patients who are the potential suicides (so that special prevention and treatment can be instituted) is one of the problems of major

concern to any hospital staff. This is a particularly difficult problem among the group of patients diagnosed as schizophrenic, which has the highest suicide rate among psychiatric hospital patients. This chapter presents the results of a detailed study of suicidal behavior in schizophrenic psychiatric hospital patients, and offers clues for identification and suggestions for prevention of such suicidal behavior.

Procedures and Results

Suicidal and nonsuicidal records since 1950 from almost each of the 192 VA hospitals and domiciliaries in the VA system have been forwarded to the Central Research Unit. Statistical comparisons were made of the identifying characteristics of all the individuals whose records were received.

In the records from psychiatric hospitals, the largest single diagnostic group (comprising 70 percent of the total suicidal records) was made up of individuals diagnosed as "schizophrenic." In order to conduct intensive individual analyses, a group of thirty schizophrenic individuals (male, Caucasian, only in order to concentrate on the predominant group) was randomly selected from the 190 schizophrenic suicide cases occurring during the 4 years from 1955 to 1958. This sample group was found to represent proportionately the age, race, religious, diagnostic characteristics, and geographical distribution of the larger group, and is thus considered representative of schizophrenic patients in VA psychiatric hospitals who kill themselves. Each of the thirty schizophrenic suicide cases was then matched man-for-man (in terms of age, religion, year of hospitalization, location of hospital, etc.), with a comparable schizophrenic control case in which suicide did not occur. Control cases were obtained from the control (nonsuicidal) cases also on file at the Central Research Unit. Comparison of the length of hospitalization of the two groups indicated no significant differences between them. The range for length of hospitalization for both groups was from one month to approximately twenty years, with about half of each group hospitalized for one year or less.

A four-step procedure was followed in analyzing the sixty cases: (1) A detailed and comprehensive abstract was prepared of each patient's case history, his course in the hospital, and all available recorded information about him. (2) An intensive "psychological

autopsy" (lasting three to four hours) was held for each case by a team of psychologists and psychiatrists in order to determine which characteristics differentiated the suicide case from the nonsuicide case.[2] During the "psychological autopsy" all available information concerning the case was presented to the consulting group except the last few entries in the case history, which were withheld so that the group was not informed whether the case was a suicide or a control. This procedure (sometimes called the technique of "blind analysis") is such that the team did not know whether the case was a suicide or a nonsuicide case, but was nevertheless required on the basis of information presented to predict which type of case it was and to give the reasons for so deciding. This eliminates the bias which would have existed had the group known whether or not the specific case being studied was a suicide. (3) A summary sheet was prepared by the team during the "psychological autopsy" noting the course of the illness and treatment given, the psychodynamics inferred from the patient's behavior, characteristics of the patient's behavior within the hospital, and any clues that might have been indicators of possible suicide or lack of potential suicidal behavior. Following preparation of the summary sheet, participants predicted the outcome of the case, that is, whether it was a suicide or control. The identity of the case was then revealed to them and the clues that had been elicited were further discussed in light of the known outcome, and the "clues" obtained from the case were recorded. (4) Basic similarities and differences between suicide schizophrenics and nonsuicide schizophrenics and suggestions for management were extracted and synthesized on the basis of the total information compiled during the case abstractions and the "psychological autopsies." These similarities and differences were formulated in behavioral empirical terms, avoiding purely psychodynamic concepts. This procedure of synthesis occurred several times during the months that the sixty cases were examined.

Among the thirty schizophrenic[3] patients who committed suicide —and were subjects of intensive analysis—three subtypes could be distinguished, which we labeled as (1) the *unaccepting* suicidal patient $(N=10)$, (2) the *dependent-satisfied* suicidal patient $(N=12)$, and (3) the *dependent-dissatisfied* suicidal patient $(N=8)$. In addition, (4) the behavior of the *nonsuicidal* schizophrenic control patient is presented for contrast. For all four types

of schizophrenic psychiatric hospital patients, their total behaviors seemed to be amenable to categorization in terms of three headings: (1) patient's attitudes toward hospitalization and illness; (2) patient's behavior pattern under stress; and (3) patient's attitudes toward his out-of-the-hospital environment and toward release from the hospital. The following descriptions of the four types of patients are presented in terms of these three categories. In addition, a special section is included with suggestions for management of suicidal behavior for each type of patient based on the results of this investigation.

The Unaccepting Schizophrenic Suicidal Patient

The first type of schizophrenic suicidal patient can be labeled the *Unaccepting* Patient.

PATIENT'S ATTITUDES TOWARD HOSPITALIZATION AND ILLNESS. In terms of the first categorization this kind of individual resisted or rejected the hospitalization and did not believe (or could not admit) that he was mentally ill—in spite of the fact that he was often grossly disturbed and delusional on admission to the hospital. The Unaccepting Patients were frequently omnipotent in their delusions, insisting that there was nothing wrong with them, and demanding to be released from the hospital. They were exceedingly restless, hyperactive, impulsive, and were occasionally demanding and assaultive in their behavior. These patients showed a remarkable absence of the feelings of guilt or inadequacy and of the somatic complaints (and requests for treatment) that were so conspicuously present in the other types of suicide patients. The Unaccepting Patients appeared to have little insight into their illnesses, yet the severity of illness on admission tended to be high, with an obvious and urgent need for hospitalization. They showed much resistance to the hospital and to accepting the idea that there was anything wrong with them.

PATIENT'S BEHAVIOR PATTERN UNDER STRESS. For these patients the distinguishing features of the second categorization was an agitated, acting-out behavior pattern under stress (frequently requiring the use of sedation, wetpacks, or restraints). A previous history of suicidal activity or ideation was present in about half of these cases.

The possibility of overt and aggressive physical acting-out behavior was quite apparent to staff members and, indeed, the comment was made, with some cases, that homicide might have been a possibility, as well as suicide.

It should be emphasized that even under stress there was an absence of expressions of inadequacy or inferiority and an absence of somatic complaints (in contrast to other types of suicidal patients); rather the patient seemed to feel that there was nothing at all wrong with him. His reaction under stress was primarily one of great agitation and restlessness with occasional impulsivity, assaultiveness, and antagonistic behavior toward others.

During the course of hospitalization, tranquilizing drugs were used for these patients with a calming effect that allowed passes and leaves to be considered fairly rapidly. It appeared that while these patients "improved" in the hospital, in that they became somewhat more cooperative, they never really lost their basic resistance to hospitalization. Their insight into their illness was limited and their later cooperation with the hospital seemed to be aimed at getting out of the hospital.

Although tranquilizing drugs were most helpful in calming these disturbed Unaccepting Patients, this "calming" apparently did not reduce their suicidal potential. Many were still receiving tranquilizers either at the time of the suicide or shortly before. These patients had improved with tranquilizing drugs and at the time of death were in fairly good contact with reality. The tranquilizing action of the drugs may have made the patient appear better than he actually was, and may have permitted passes and leaves to be given prematurely. This statement is not to be interpreted as a criticism of the use of tranquilizing medications—which seemed in many cases to be most helpful to disturbed patients—but is instead a caution that the tranquilized patient has not necessarily learned new methods for coping with his stresses or his illness.

ATTITUDES TOWARD OUT-OF-THE-HOSPITAL ENVIRONMENT AND TOWARD RELEASE FROM THE HOSPITAL. Whenever passes and leaves were considered, these (Unaccepting) patients seemed to be in a particularly difficult position. They frequently felt that they could do all right away from the hospital and were anxious to leave. Many had unrealistically optimistic plans about the future. In addition,

they showed very little anxiety or tension about going out on passes or leaves. This provided considerable incentive on the part of the hospital to release the patient even though social service investigation might not have been as complete as might ordinarily be desirable. However, it was apparent that premature release of this type of patient was particularly hazardous. On the one hand, they could not accept hospitalization, and if, in addition, their home environment was unbearably stressful, they would face an intolerable situation either way they moved. With the restless, impulsive, acting-out type of behavior these patients had shown under stress, they were not able passively to accept a difficult home situation, nor would they accept return to the hospital. Yet they had to *do* something about their situation, and self-destruction became the action chosen. In almost all cases, suicide occurred at a time when there was some remission of their illness, and under circumstances that indicated that there had been considerable planning and organization in bringing about their own deaths. With the majority of the Unaccepting Patients, suicide occurred while on pass or leave.

MANAGEMENT OF SUICIDAL BEHAVIOR IN THE UNACCEPTING PATIENT. Inasmuch as the Unaccepting Patient is resistive of hospitalization and often has little insight into his illness, control of suicidal behavior appears particularly difficult. Since he is often quieted rapidly with tranquilizing medications and is anxious to leave, the problem of when to give passes or leaves may be crucial, and his *home environment* may be of vital importance. Some suggestions follow:

1. Considerable social service investigation and careful evaluation of the patient's home environment is particularly indicated *before* release of patient on pass or leave.

2. Orientation of family members to the patient's illness is necessary. Many family members seem to lack understanding and may place undue pressure on the patient upon his release from the hospital because he seems improved.

3. Although ideally this type of patient should be provided with the opportunity to learn new ways of coping with outside stresses, this may prove difficult since he has little recognition of his illness. The necessity for providing a supportive home environment for him is therefore apparent. If his home environment does not seem to

be supportive, a substitute outside environment is needed for the Unaccepting Patient.

4. If the home environment appears potentially stressful, yet the calculated risk of releasing the patient on pass or leave must be taken, the patient's family should be made aware of the suicidal risk and instructed to avail themselves quickly of social work contacts or rehospitalization. The family should be informed especially that any increase in physical agitation such as restlessness, pacing, or insomnia, are warnings of possible suicidal action.

For the Unaccepting Patient who must remain in the hospital, it appears of primary importance to give him some hope of an eventual release into an outside environment that he will look forward to. The Unaccepting Patient is not content to accept hospitalization.

In summary, the following can be said about the management of the Unaccepting schizophrenic (potentially suicidal) Patient: There is increased suicidal risk as he improves. If he must remain in the hospital, he should be given the hope of eventual release into an environment which will be supportive. If he seems well enough for passes or leaves away from the hospital, he must not be released into a stressful environment. He will want to leave because he is now "improved" but this does not mean he can handle outside stresses. A careful evaluation should include examination of his home situation, his work situation, and his outside interpersonal contacts, and a substitute environment must be found or very close supervision must be provided to avoid exacerbation of suicidal tendencies.

It should be reemphasized that the Unaccepting Patient is not only resistive of hospitalization, but his past behavior pattern under stress has been impulsive, restless, and demanding. If he is returned to what is for him stressful environment, this dangerous reaction pattern may reappear.

The Dependent-Satisfied Schizophrenic Suicidal Patient

The second type of schizophrenic patient who committed suicide was labeled the *Dependent-Satisfied* Patient.

ATTITUDES TOWARD HOSPITALIZATION AND ILLNESS. These patients were characterized by a high degree of dependency on the hospital

and seemed fairly "satisfied" with their hospitalization. They usually realized they were ill (many were voluntary admissions), and were depending on the hospital for help in their illness. They seemed to feel safer in the hospital and liked the attention and reassurance provided although they were not particularly demanding about it. They might show an attachment for some staff member such as a nurse, therapist, or doctor, and were interested in the type of treatment given, about which they were seldom critical. They would ask for some special type of treatment on occasion—such as sedation or seclusion or some form of medication for a somatic complaint. In general, however, their behavior in the hospital was quiet, cooperative, and best characterized as that of a "good hospital patient." The suicide of this type of patient frequently came as a surprise and shock to staff members.

BEHAVIOR PATTERN UNDER STRESS. In the hospital these patients were usually quiet and cooperative, apparently because hospitalization was for them a fairly successful means of coping with stress. However, a study of their previous behavior before entering the hospital, on admission to the hospital, or while on pass or leave, revealed an agitated behavior pattern. This was manifested by considerable tension, anxiety, and restlessness. They were overtly depressed and often expressed feelings of guilt and inadequacy. A previous history of suicidal ideation or activity was present in three-fourths of the subjects in this group. Frequently on admission they were greatly upset, depressed, tearful, and begging for something to help them control their feelings. Some were physically assaultive under stress and apologetic after they were calm again. While still under stress they needed attention and reassurance and manifested somatic complaints. They requested treatment of various kinds, such as sedation, restraint, or seclusion, to help them control their impulses. They might also ask for certain kinds of therapy or work assignments. It should be strongly emphasized that this disturbed behavior disappeared as the patient improved in the hospital, and the patient's quiet hospital behavior belied the extent of his agitated behavior out of the hospital.

Tranquilizing drugs were given to all twelve patients during the course of their hospitalization and seemed to be very helpful in calming most of them. Nine of these patients were receiving tran-

quilizing drugs at the time of suicide. Shock therapy had been given to half of these patients and one had just finished a course of shock treatment at the time of suicide. Group or individual psychotherapy had been part of the treatment for half of these patients.

ATTITUDES TOWARD OUT-OF-THE-HOSPITAL ENVIRONMENT AND TO-WARD RELEASE FROM THE HOSPITAL. Most of the Dependent-Satisfied Patients seemed to improve in the hospital and as they did so their behavior became deceptively "nonsuicidal." It was only when passes or leaves away from the hospital were considered or given that there was a return of the tension and anxiety previously shown under stress. Many of these patients were released on pass or trial visit to what appeared to be a fairly optimal environment (a supportive wife or parents, a job held open for the patient during his hospitalization, and so forth). However, on close investigation it was evident that the patient felt conflict and ambivalence about his home environment and that it was *to him* a very stressful situation. All of these patients showed some tension or anxiety as passes and leaves were considered or given and all but two committed suicide while on pass or furlough. These patients were not considered delusional or hallucinatory and were felt to be in fairly good contact at the time of their suicide.

Assessment of suicidal potentiality in these patients was particularly difficult during the "psychological autopsies"; however, it became increasingly apparent that suicidal risk was based on the extreme importance of hospitalization to these patients. They seemed relatively satisfied in the hospital and they simply could not be separated safely from the hospital until they had found another sanctuary that was acceptable to them, or until they had learned new means of coping with outside stresses.

MANAGEMENT OF SUICIDAL BEHAVIOR IN THE DEPENDENT-SATISFIED PATIENT.

1. The extreme importance of hospitalization for this type of patient was apparent. This patient is often deceptively quiet, co-operative, and nonsuicidal as he improves in the hospital, but his basic dependence on the hospital and lack of ability to control his impulses away from the hospital has not changed.

2. Hospitalization for the Dependent-Satisfied Patient is needed

for protection against his own impulses until he has another sanctuary that is acceptable to him, or until he has learned new methods of coping with stress in the outside environment. In many of the suicide cases, early passes or leaves were given in spite of direct statements by the patient that he feared he would be unable to control his impulses away from the hospital, and in spite of anxiety, tension, and remission of illness that would occur with the giving of passes. (Note that this pattern is not usually shown by the Unaccepting (Suicide) Patient, who is looking forward to leaving the hospital.)

3. It is dangerous to assume that because a suicidal patient has improved in the hospital he is therefore well enough to be released into the same stressful environment from which he was originally hospitalized. The use of symptomatic treatment only—usually tranquilizing drugs—which reduces disturbance, anxiety, and depression in the hospital does not necessarily provide the patient with better means to cope with the stresses of life away from the hospital.

4. Psychological testing is useful before giving passes or leaves, in order to determine whether the improvement shown in the patient represents genuine improvement—or whether the underlying conflicts are still present with the possibility that his suicidal tendencies will flare up again when he leaves the hospital.

5. There is a need for a close (and sometimes long) protective association with the hospital and a gradual release of this patient into a new environment that he can genuinely accept. Unlike the Unaccepting Patient who is resistive to being held in the hospital, the Dependent-Satisfied Patient is quite willing to stay and the problem seems to be how to get him safely out of the hospital once he has shown improvement.

6. Before even a gradual release of this patient from the hospital, a careful evaluation of the home environment must be made from two standpoints: (a) a realistic evaluation must be made through social service investigation to determine the supportiveness of the home environment; and (b) most importantly, an evaluation of the stressfulness of the home environment must be made from the standpoint of the patient's own feelings and attitudes. This cannot be overemphasized. In the Dependent-Satisfied Patient, suicide almost always seemed to result because the stressfulness (for the

patient) of leaving the protection of the hospital had not been fully appreciated by staff members. Regardless of the reality of the situation from the standpoint of others, if the patients feels the home situation to be unbearably stressful, then it is nonsupportive. Anxiety and tension about leaving the hospital was shown by all Dependent-Satisfied suicide cases. If there is any question, it is safest to allow the Dependent-Satisfied Patient to remain in the hospital.

To recapitulate, the management of the Dependent-Satisfied schizophrenic (potentially suicidal) patient can be described as follows: This patient does not seem suicidal as long as he stays *in the hospital,* but if there is any tension or anxiety about passes or leaves away from the hospital, there is suicidal risk. This patient is often deceptively nonsuicidal as he "improves" in the hospital under tranquilizing drugs, but he cannot be released safely on pass or leave; he needs hospital protection against his own impulses (and usually asks for this protection) until he can be gradually released into another sanctuary that he can accept, or until he has learned new defenses against stress *outside the hospital.* It should be emphasized that no matter how realistically supportive the home environment seems, if the patient—who may look deceptively non-suicidal—shows tension or anxiety at the thought of leaving, the separation from the hospital must be made very cautiously, with particular attention to "open channels of communication" (so that the patient is free to express his anxieties and the hospital and family are free to receive them). In addition, the family should be especially advised to be ready and willing to return the patient to the hospital as soon as "things do not appear to be going well." They should be especially alert for any suicidal threat (no matter how mild) and for increases in physical agitation, such as pacing, restlessness, nervousness, or inability to sleep.

The Dependent-Dissatisfied Schizophrenic Suicidal Patient

The patient of this third type, called the *Dependent-Dissatisfied* Suicidal Patient ($N=8$), was in some ways very similar to the Dependent-Satisfied Patient.

ATTITUDES TOWARD HOSPITALIZATION AND ILLNESS. The Dependent-Dissatisfied Patient (like the Dependent-Satisfied Suicide Patient)

was very dependent on the hospital. This type of patient usually realized he was ill and was depending on the hospital for help. However (in contrast to the Dependent-Satisfied Patient) the Dependent-Dissatisfied Patient apparently began to feel, after a while, that the hospital was not giving him the help he needed. Thus, instead of becoming quiet and appearing "nonsuicidal" in the hospital, these patients became increasingly tense and depressed, with frequent expressions of feelings of guilt, inadequacy, or worthlessness. This type of patient was still very reluctant to leave the hospital and showed this clearly by constant demands and great need for attention and reassurance from the hospital. This demanding, needful behavior is described more fully below.

BEHAVIOR PATTERN UNDER STRESS. Under stress, the Dependent-Dissatisfied Patient (like the Dependent-Satisfied Patient) showed much restlessness, anxiety, and depression. Some were voluntary hospital admissions in an agitated state with tearfulness, delusions, fear of loss of control, and expressions of guilt or unworthiness. A history of suicidal activity or ideation was present in all but one of the members of this group.

In the hospital this type of patient frequently had periods of quiet behavior (lasting from a few days, in some cases, to several months in others). However, these were followed by a return of the agitated behavior with an increase in restlessness, suicidal ideation, somatic complaints (and demands for treatment of somatic complaints), criticism, hostility, and threats to elope or leave the hospital against medical advice. The threats to leave the hospital were seldom carried out, however, since the patient was most reluctant to leave. There were increased demands for attention and reassurance: wanting to see the doctor, the nurse, the chaplain; asking for unnecessary physical examinations or dental work; requesting sedation, seclusion, therapy of various kinds, and so forth. In many cases these patients made excessively self-centered demands for attention that were simply impossible to satisfy. Statements such as "Nothing is being done for me," "Other people don't like me—I should end it all," "There is no place for me anywhere," were frequent and were further indications of intense dissatisfaction. As noted above, this disturbed activity might be followed by an opposite reaction of overly cooperative, quiet, hopeful, oversubmissive be-

havior, as the patient tried (with apparent desperation) to find a way to meet his needs. The agitated, disturbed behavior would return again, however.

This demanding, time-consuming, attention-getting behavior, was often irritating and disturbing to the hospital staff and to other patients as well, and this patient was on occasion referred to as the hospital "pest." Any manifestation of such reactions of annoyance or hostility on the part of the hospital staff or other patients, however, would just intensify the plight of the dissatisfied patient. He had clearly indicated his inability to handle his tensions outside the hospital, yet he had been unable to find the help he needed in the hospital. He literally had no place to go since he could not leave the hospital, nor could he tolerate his anxieties and unsatisfied needs in the hospital. Nearly all of the Dependent-Dissatisfied Patients committed suicide in the hospital. (This is in marked contrast to the Dependent-Satisfied group, wherein all but two killed themselves outside of the hospital.) All the Dependent-Dissatisfied Suicide Patients were on tranquilizer drugs at the time of the suicide, and all were considered in good contact with reality at the time—some left suicide notes.

ATTITUDES TOWARD OUT-OF-THE-HOSPITAL ENVIRONMENT AND TOWARD RELEASE FROM THE HOSPITAL. By and large, the Dependent-Dissatisfied Patient appeared to be an individual who "couldn't leave the hospital," yet seemed to have given up hope of being helped in the hospital. Often these patients felt (with some justification) that they were not liked by others ("Nobody likes me," "The doctors think I'm making this up," "This is the only way out"). There was much resistance to passes or leaves away from the hospital and much tension and anxiety should separation from the hospital be considered or implemented in any way. Considerable ambivalence was shown by the patient toward his home and frequently the people in his home environment appeared to feel ambivalent toward him. The patient appeared to be unhappy both in the hospital and out of the hospital and seemed to feel that no one was interested in him or trying to help him. The ambivalence felt by the patient toward hospital and home seemed to be the precipitating factor in suicidal behavior rather than merely separation from the hospital as was

the case with the Dependent-Satisfied Patient. If his situation remained unrelieved he would do something about it himself and
suicide was the action chosen.

MANAGEMENT OF SUICIDAL BEHAVIOR IN THE DEPENDENT-DISSATISFIED
PATIENT. The problem of management of suicidal behavior in this
patient rests in the recognition of the extreme importance of the
hospital to him and of his inability to leave it. The first steps in the
control of suicidal behavior depend upon giving him the excessive
emotional support he needs in the hospital. If this can be accomplished then the problem of releasing him safely from the hospital
would seem to be the same as that outlined in the preceding paragraphs for the Dependent-Satisfied Patient.

Suggestions for the immediate control of suicidal behavior in the
Dependent-Dissatisfied Patient are:

1. Alerting the hospital staff to the fact that repeated suicidal
threats or "mild" suicide attempts that are attention-getting devices
must be taken seriously. The fact that this behavior is a demand
for attention does not mean that the patient will not kill himself.
Just such attention-getting behavior preceded many actual suicides
—and suicide almost always occurred in the hospital in the Dependent-Dissatisfied Patient.

2. Often the instituting of any new treatment or medication gives
this patient temporary relief and improvement.

3. Sympathetic recognition by the hospital staff that the excessively complaining, demanding, depressed behavior of the dissatisfied patient is an expression of desperate, although excessive,
need for care and support.

4. The establishment of a "Buddy System" in which carefully
selected volunteers might act as "Big Brothers" for the patient.
This might be a valuable adjunct to other hospital and therapeutic
procedures. The main purpose of this relationship would be to convey to the patient a sense of interest, a feeling of belief in his own
worthwhileness and his own integrity—and meanwhile to protect
him from his own self-destructive impulses. This might also help
to satisfy, at least temporarily, some of the excessive needs for
attention and reassurance in this type of patient.

In summary, the management of the Dependent-Dissatisfied
(potentially suicidal) Patient should take the following into ac-

count: The complaining, depressed, restless, attention-seeking behavior of this overly dependent patient is a desperate plea for emotional reassurance and attention. Even though this may have been
going on for some time, it does not mean he won't commit suicide.
If he does not get this help he is demanding, he may, indeed,
eventually kill himself—and if this occurs it will probably be in the
hospital. His situation is precarious. If he is not satisfied in the
hospital or out of the hospital, he really has "no place to go" and
he must do something about his plight. Although suicidal ideation
or threats may seem to be attention-getting devices, they must be
taken seriously; suicidal precautions should be observed. Temporary
measures that may reduce suicidal potential are: Beginning any
new treatment or medication; assigning a "buddy" to him; giving
him as much as possible the extra attention he demands, and above
all, providing sympathy and understanding even though his behavior may make this most difficult for those around him. The long-
range control of suicidal behavior would seem to rest on securing a
satisfactory adjustment in the hospital, and then applying the suggestions for control of suicidal behavior which are listed in the
preceding section for the Dependent-Satisfied Patient.

The Nonsuicidal (Control) Schizophrenic Patient

By way of contrast to the above-detailed three types of schizophrenic patients who did commit suicide, those schizophrenic patients (the Control cases) who did not commit suicide ($N=30$) fell
into two distinct groups. The first group ($N=16$) was quite homogeneous and was labeled the Marginal (Nonsuicidal) Control Patient. The second consisted of a mixed group that showed some
characteristics of the Marginal Control group and some characteristics of the suicide groups.

MARGINAL (NONSUICIDAL) CONTROL PATIENT

Attitudes Toward Hospitalization and Illness. The attitude of
these patients toward hospitalization was almost indifferent, as
if it were a transient episode in their lives. They seemed to be somewhat indifferent to hospitalization and to the awareness of their
own illness. These patients seemed able to function outside the hospital in a marginal way and often hospitalization had been precipitated by some unusual incident or stress in the employment

situation or by a chance arrest for vagrancy, or after an alcoholic episode. These patients seldom asked for anything and did not particularly seem to need attention or reassurance. They seemed somewhat indifferent to their treatment and to the hospital staff. This is in contrast to the suicidal patients who were either overly resisting or overly dependent on hospitalization.

Behavior Pattern Under Stress. Although these patients were often delusional, hallucinatory, preoccupied or withdrawn, they seemed able to make a somewhat passive (or marginal) adjustment to their own disordered mental processes and thus showed fewer subjective indications of stress or acute discomfort. They seldom manifested somatic complaints or asked for any sort of treatment. They were seldom assaultive, impulsive, or restless, and rarely expressed feelings of inferiority or inadequacy. By and large, the Marginal Controls did not do a number of things that characterized the suicide cases: They did not demand to leave the hospital, they did not pace the corridors or strike their fists against walls. They did not need constant reassurance or continually ask to see the doctor or the nurse or the chaplain, and the like. They seemed accepting and somewhat indifferent to their hospital care.

The course in the hospital was characterized by very little disturbance and seemed to be in large part a matter of custodial care. The patient frequently improved in the hospital surroundings with or without tranquilizing drugs. These patients did not seem particularly disturbed about being in the hospital, nor did they seem particularly dependent on the hospital. Rather, they seemed to be somewhat indifferent to the episode.

Attitudes Toward Out-of-the-Hospital Environment and Toward Release From the Hospital. When passes or leaves were suggested or instituted, there was little tension or distress shown by the patient. They seemed somewhat indifferent to the out-of-the-hospital environment and to the problems of getting along away from the supportive hospital environment. There had never been a particularly severe pattern of disturbance and the patient seemed able ordinarily to accept the stresses of life somewhat passively. Upon release from the hospital they were able to resume the same marginal adjustment that had been characteristic of them before hospitalization. It seemed probable that they might be admitted to a hospital again at some time in the future should outside circum-

stances exacerbate their illness or bring them to the attention of others, but that the hospitalization would again be primarily a matter of temporary custodial care.

MIXED GROUP

The rest of the Control patients ($N=14$) consisted of a mixed group in which some patients showed characteristics that were quite similar to those of the Marginal (Nonsuicidal) Control Patients. There were enough differences, however, that it was not felt justified to group them in the larger homogeneous group described above. On the other hand, some patients in this mixed group greatly resembled one of the suicidal types. The fact that the person was not a suicide seemed to be due primarily to an unusually supportive environment at home and to unusually careful precautions about release from the hospital. The findings in these cases were carefully studied and form the basis of some of the recommendations for management procedure that are given in the preceding sections on the three suicidal types of patients.

Concluding Comments

Many interesting findings emerged from this intensive analysis of suicide in the hospitalized schizophrenic patient. It was evident that rather than a single type of schizophrenic suicidal patient there are three primary types with quite different behavioral characteristics. Recognition of suicidal potential and institution of appropriate preventive procedures depend very much on the type of patient. These different types are described in detail in the preceding sections and, in addition, have been translated into briefer checklist form. One of the more interesting and encouraging findings of this study was that regardless of type of suicidal patient, suicide occurred in almost all cases after there had been a remission of illness. Had it been found (as was anticipated before the study began) that suicide occurred in the depth of the psychotic process, prevention and treatment would seem much more difficult. However, this was not the case. The suicide instead seemed to occur when patients were *improved* and when they seemed to be thrown by their inability to tolerate what was for them an inordinately stressful life situation from which they could see "no other way out." This may be related to the oft-repeated speculations that a psychosis may

well serve as a "safety valve" resource for some individuals. However, that these patients were in fair contact with reality and able to plan and organize their actions is most encouraging from the standpoint of treatment methods and prevention of suicidal behavior in other schizophrenic patients.

Nothing in the text of this report is intended to suggest or imply to hospital personnel that they should in their performance feel it necessary to "run scared," or in any way to give up the considerable advantages to patients (and to staff) of progressive psychiatric treatment methods (such as open wards, liberal use of passes, legitimate and careful use of medications, use of community resources employment of "half-way" centers, day hospitals, etc.). Rather, this report is intended to add support to these procedures by offering assistance with the identification of high-risk predischarge patients and suggestions for a program specifically designed to diminish that risk.

Chapter 19
SUICIDE AMONG PATIENTS WITH MALIGNANT NEOPLASMS

Norman L. Farberow, Edwin S. Shneidman, and Calista V. Leonard

Thirty-two cases, from twenty-three Veterans Administration GM&S hospitals throughout the country, of veterans with cancer who committed suicide during the years 1955–1960, were compared with an equal number of matching nonsuicidal individuals. Detailed case history data were prepared for each case. In addition, a "Psychological Autopsy" was conducted on all sixty-four cases. Data were analyzed in terms of the patient's attitudes toward the hospital, the hospital's attitudes toward the patient, the patient's attitudes toward his illness, indicators of emotional disturbance in the patient, the nature of the patient's home and family relationships, and the role of pain and discomfort in the patient's illness. A distinguishable group, labeled the dependent-dissatisfied suicide, was described. Also, the characteristics of a group of "implementers" (those who take their own fate into their own hands) were outlined. In general, high suicidal potential was found in the following: older men with cancer of the throat; younger men with Hodgkin's disease or leukemia; or a person of any age with cancer concomitant with heightened stress, severe anxiety, low tolerance for pain. Suicide can occur in all stages of the disease, especially in individuals who are alert and oriented, who feel that they have no emotional support, and who believe that their psychological and physical resources are exhausted.

Cancer continues to kill thousands of persons in the United States each year. In 1958, the Bureau of Vital Statistics indicated that malignant neoplasms was the cause of death for more than 254,000 persons and that it ranked as second among the list of killers. In 1958 the Veterans Administration treated more than 35,000 cases with diagnoses of cancer, a number that ranks it third in diseases treated in the VA. Cancer in all its aspects—physiological, histo-

logical, and psychological—ranks high in importance as an area for systematic research.

In a recent report investigating the problems of suicide, it was determined that cases with diagnoses of malignant neoplasms contributed disproportionately to the total number of suicides. Thus, over a nine-year period, 1950–1958 inclusive, of the total number of cases that committed suicide in GM&S hospitals, the percentage of cases with a diagnosis of cancer was 17 percent. However, in the total case load in all VA hospitals, cancer cases generally comprised only 6 to 7 percent. An intensive investigation of cancer patients who committed suicide was deemed important for the possibility of increasing understanding and furthering the prevention of suicide within hospitals.

Procedures

The total number of cases $(N=32)$ with cancer who had committed suicide during the years 1955–1960, which had been reposited with the Central Research Unit, was selected for study. A set $(N=32)$ of control cases was selected, which were matched with the suicide cases, man for man insofar as possible, on the basis of the following characteristics: (1) diagnosis: the same organ for the primary site of the cancer; (2) severity: the same degree of severity of the disease (rated on a 3-point scale—critical, fair, and good—by a medical consultant); (3) age: plus or minus five years in most cases; (4) sex: all male; (5) religion: Protestant, Catholic, Jewish, or not stated; (6) race: all Caucasian.

The cancer cases came from twenty-three GM&S hospitals scattered throughout the country. When possible, a control case from the same hospital or the same geographic area was used. However, because of the number of criteria upon which matching was attempted, the control cases reposited with the Central Research Unit could not supply the exact number of matched cases required, so that most (25) were obtained from the files of Wadsworth GM&S hospital in Los Angeles, California.

A four-step procedure was followed in analyzing each case:

1. A detailed and comprehensive abstract was prepared of each patient's case history, his course in the hospital, and all the available recorded information about him. This required exhaustive

review of the patient's medical folder, doctors' notes, nurses' notes, consultants' notes, psychological and social work histories, when available, and all other material incorporated into the files. It might be noted here that obtaining an adequate picture of the patient as a person was very difficult. These were primarily medical folders and thus usually presented a very complete history of the disease, but very little about the personality of the person who had the disease. While efforts to obtain a complete picture of the patient were frustrated, it was recognized that this was the same handicap under which any ward physician operated and thus he would have to make his judgments about the suicide potentiality on the same dearth of information as the investigators.

2. An intensive "psychological autopsy" was held for each case in which the abstract was presented to a medical consultant and a group of psychologists, including the coprincipal investigators, nurses, and social workers, for the purpose of differentiating the characteristics of the suicide case from the control case.[1] The procedure followed was to present to the assembled group all of the information except for the last few entries in the case history so that the group did not know whether the case was a suicide or control. Each member of the group would then judge whether the case was a suicide or control and indicate his levels of confidence in his decision. If, in his judgment, it was a suicide, he also "guessed" at what the probable method was. Thus, in this step, it was necessary for each person to make his judgment solely on the basis of the information presented without depending upon prior information, knowledge, biases, or prejudices because of knowing the kind of case.

3. A summary sheet was prepared during the "psychological autopsy," which categorized the most pertinent features of each case and noted the characteristics of the patients, behavior within the hospital, and particularly any clues that might have been indicators of possible suicide or lack of suicidal behavior. The summary included such general headings as: (*a*) details of admission; (*b*) summary of course of illness; (*c*) patient's attitudes toward illness and toward hospitalization; (*d*) indications of mental or psychological disturbance in the patient; (*e*) hospital attitudes toward patients; (*f*) efficacy of treatment procedures; (*g*) role of pain

and discomfort; (*h*) nature of patient's relationships with his family; (*i*) deficit factors; (*j*) clues for or against suicide; (*k*) if suicide, how prevention could have been effected.

Following the preparation of the summary and the prediction of the outcome, that is, whether it was a suicide or control, the identity of the case was revealed and the clues that had been elicited were reviewed in light of the known outcome. The lesson learned was then recorded.

4. In the final step, basic similarities and differences between suicidal cancer cases and nonsuicidal cancer cases were extracted and synthesized on the basis of the total information compiled during the "psychological autopsies."

Description of Populations

The characteristics of the two groups, suicides and nonsuicide controls, are described as follows:

The distribution of ages in the suicide group has a mean of 53 years with a range from 25 to 74. The mean of the control group is also 53 with a range from 21 to 76. If the age distribution in the suicide group is broken down into three age groups, under 45, 45–64, 65 and over, the percentages falling in each category are 34, 34, and 32 percent respectively. This contrasts with the age distribution of cancer cases in VA hospitals, which shows that 16 percent of the total discharge group fall in the below age 45 group, 41 percent fall between ages 45–64, and 42 percent are in the 65 and over group.[2] Thus, there is a larger younger group among the suicides while the middle and older age groups among the suicides are somewhat smaller. It is of interest to note, however, that six of the eleven cases in the 45–64 group fall between ages 60 and 64. If these were added to the older group, the age group of 60 and over would contain sixteen suicides or 50 percent of the suicide group. It is apparent that there is a bimodal distribution among the suicides, with one group made up of younger patients below 45, and a second group made up of older patients, 60 and over.

The religious distribution among the suicide group showed 18 Protestants, 7 Catholics, 6 Jewish, and one unknown. Among the controls, despite efforts to match exactly for each case, the distribution of religions showed 19 Protestants, 9 Catholics, and 4 Jewish. The variation between the two groups is insignificant.

The distribution of diagnoses among the suicide cases is shown in Table I below. These may be contrasted with the distribution of deaths among VA patients with the same diagnoses.

Table I indicates that among the younger group, under 45, the lymphatic and hemapoietic cancers contribute most of the suicides (54 percent). In the older group, if the larynx and pharynx regions are considered together as general neck region, 50 percent fall in this category. This contrasts with the distribution of cancer among the cases in the VA in which lymphatic and hemapoietic cancers comprised 34 percent of the younger age group, and cancers of the larynx, pharynx, (and buccal) areas comprised only 10 percent of the older age groups. This suggests that such diseases as Hodgkins and leukemia, contribute disproportionately to suicide cases in the younger suicide group, while cancer of the larynx and pharynx (or neck region) contribute disproportionately to suicide cases of the older group.

In the 45-to-64 age group ($N=11$), cancers of the intestines, and bronchus, trachea, and lungs, contributed 63 percent or almost two thirds of the suicide cases in this age group. In the total VA population of cancer cases, this group makes up only 29 percent.

The suicide and control cases were rated for severity of disease or prognosis on a rough three-point scale—critical, fair, and good. Among the suicide cases twenty-nine were rated as critical, three as poor, and none as fair. Among the control cases thirty were rated as critical, one as poor, and one as fair. All but two of the control cases died. These two were discharged MHB. Five control cases who died listed as the cause of death something other than cancer, four cases from bronchial pneumonia, and one case from cerebral vascular accident.

Among the suicide group the two methods most frequently used were jumping and cutting. Thus twelve persons (37 percent) jumped, and nine persons (28 percent) cut or stabbed themselves. One person cut himself severely before he jumped. Four persons (12 percent) shot themselves, three out of the hospital, and one in the hospital when the patient brought a gun with him when he returned from pass. Two persons (6 percent) hanged themselves; two persons (6 percent) took poison (out of the hospital) and one set fire to himself (in the hospital). The method is not known for two persons who killed themselves outside the hospital.

TABLE I

Number and Percentage of Patients with Malignant Neoplasms, by Primary Site, Who Committed Suicide

DIAGNOSES	TOTAL			AGES Under 45			AGES 45-64			AGES 65 and Over		
	N	S %	VA* %	N	S %	VA* %	N	S %	VA* %	N	S %	VA* %
Buccal cavity and pharynx	3	9	6	0	0	4	2	18	6	1	10	5
Stomach	1	3	7	1	9	4	0	0	6	0	0	9
Intestine, except rectum	4	13	6	0	0	6	4	36	6	0	0	6
Rectum	0	0	6	0	0	3	0	0	4	0	0	6
Other digestive organs	2	6	10	0	0	7	1	9	11	1	10	9
Larynx	4	13	2	0	0	1	0	0	2	4	40	4
Bronchus and trachea, lung	5	16	28	1	9	16	3	27	34	1	10	26
Other respiratory organs, including secondary and unspecified as to primary	0	0	-	0	0	-	0	0	-	0	0	-
Breast	0	0	-	0	0	1	0	0	-	0	0	-
Female genital organs	0	0	-	0	0	1	0	0	-	0	0	-
Prostate	1	3	5	0	0	-	0	0	4	1	10	10
Other male genital organs	1	3	1	1	9	5	0	0	-	0	0	-
Bladder and other urinary organs	3	9	5	1	9	2	1	9	5	1	10	7
Skin, includes melanoma	1	3	2	1	9	4	0	0	1	0	0	2
Brain, eye, nervous system, and endocrine glands	1	3	4	0	0	12	0	0	4	1	10	2
Bone and connective tissue	0	0	1	0	0	3	0	0	1	0	0	-
Lymphatic and hematopoietic	6	19	11	6	54	26	0	0	1	0	0	8
All other malignancy of unspecified site and other secondary	0	0	6	0	0	5	0	0	6	0	0	6
TOTAL	32	100%	100%	11	99%	100%	11	99%	100%	10	100%	100%

* Percent of patients in VA hospitals who died from malignant neoplasms during calendar year 1959.

A terminal condition in the disease had been reached by six of the nine persons who used cutting; five of the twelve persons who jumped; one of the four gunshot wounds; one of the two hanging cases; one of the two poison cases; and by the man who set fire to himself. It is of interest to note that even though persons may be considered terminally ill and in the final stages of the disease, weakened and practically unable to move, they are still able to use a variety of methods to kill themselves, some of these methods requiring effort, energy, and considerable planning.

Results

Comparison of the two groups, suicide cancer cases and nonsuicide (control) cancer cases, was made from the summaries. The results are presented below in two sections: First, areas or specific factors are compared for significant differences or lack of them between the total group of suicides versus the controls; second, a detailed description is presented of the relatively homogeneous subgroups of suicides and controls that could be distinguished and characterized. A final section describes the concept of the "Implementer," which has evolved from the study and may have specific meaning for evaluation of suicidal potentiality.

TOTAL GROUP COMPARISONS OF SUICIDES VERSUS CONTROLS

Patient's Attitudes Toward Illness. One factor investigated in this area was whether or not the patient knew his diagnosis. Although there were specific indications in eighteen suicide cases versus only nine control cases that patients were aware of their diagnoses, caution must be exercised against the inference that knowing one has the dread disease of cancer is more likely to lead to suicide. It seems probable that most of the control cases knew their diagnosis too, but because of the fact that they were not so emotionally distressed by their illness, it was not noted in their records. Twenty-five of the suicide cases seemed quite distressed by their illness, contrasted with fifteen control cases.

Patient's Attitudes Toward the Hospital. This area proved to be one of the more reliable indicators of possible suicidal behavior. The pattern that emerged as significant was the attitude on the part of the suicidal patient (as compared with the nonsuicidal) of involvement in his treatment with an apparent need to control and

direct it, in many cases with complaining, demanding behavior. Such patients apparently were active enough in this direction that notations appeared in their hospital records indicating requests, refusals, or other involvement in the treatment procedures. Such notes were absent in the large majority of control cases and the asumption drawn is that the controls were more accepting of whatever treatment was given and so did not induce similar notations in their records. These results became the nucleus of the concept of the "Implementer," which is discussed in a separate section that follows later.

Hospital Attitudes Toward Patients. For most patients, both suicides and controls, the hospital's attitude seemed to be primarily one of efficient medical treatment. However, among the suicide cases there was a group of difficult patients, described elsewhere in this report as "Dependent Dissatisfied," whose behavior apparently made it realistically difficult for the hospital to maintain an objective attitude. Notes suggestive of irritation crept into these records on occasion.

Indications of Emotional Disturbance in the Patient. This section noted the evidence for emotional disturbance in the patient along with the number of psychiatric consultations held. The results served to emphasize the need for increased awareness on the part of the staff of the psychological as well as physical distress in cancer patients. Indications of unusual emotional disturbance appeared in twenty of the suicide cases as contrasted with ten of the controls. Psychiatric consultations were held in six suicides and four control cases. However, the need for psychiatric consultation in an additional fourteen of the suicide patients was apparent (as compared with an additional six control cases). These would have been most helpful to the staff as well as the patient, with a resulting lessening of management problems. Among the ten control cases in which there was psychological distress, the hospital provided not only psychiatric consultations but other supportive treatments that appeared to be, in part, responsible for the nonsuicide outcome of the case.

Nature of Patient's Home and Family Relationships. Among the suicides and controls there were practically no differences in marital status, with about one-half of both groups married, about one-fourth single, and one-fourth widowed, divorced, or separated.

There were, however, important differences between the two groups in the interpersonal relationships in the home and family. Among the 17 married suicides, twelve were noted as having some difficulty, tension, or anxiety in the family life, while only three of the nineteen married controls appeared to have similar difficulty. Among some of the suicides who were married and in whose records there was an indication of difficulty, there were such additional burdens for the patient to bear as financial problems, preschool-age children at home, and other stresses over and above the trauma of the terminal illnes. In sixteen of the married controls there were specific indications in the folders of supportive wives and comfort in the home environment. It was not possible to distinguish differences in this area between suicides and controls for the single, widowed, divorced, or separated cases because of lack of information.

Role of Pain and Discomfort in Patient's Illness. When the study was initiated it was felt this question might be crucial in differentiating between suicide versus nonsuicide cancer cases. Evaluating the degree of pain or discomfort from hospital records was difficult because of individual differences in the patient's reactions as well as differences in the disease process. Three bases for judgment were used: (1) the patient's own reaction to pain as indicated by behavioral notes in the record; (2) the presence in the nurses' or doctors' notes of indications that the patient seemed more disturbed by pain or discomfort than they felt he should be; this was based on the feeling that the staff was experienced with persons in pain and would recognize unusual cases of high or low pain tolerance; (3) evaluation of each matched suicide and control pair in terms of the pain and discomfort which might be attributable to the disease site itself. Thus twelve of the thirty-two pairs were judged to be alike in degree of tolerance to pain and discomfort associated with that disease site. However, in sixteen pairs the suicide cases showed much less ability to tolerate pain while in four pairs the controls showed somewhat less tolerance for pain.

In reviewing the thirty-two pairs of matched suicides and controls there seemed to be no specific patterns of pain distress for particular diagnostic groups. Some cases of cancer of the larynx showed little pain, others showed much; some cases of cancer of the lung showed little pain, others showed much; and similarly for other

disease sites. It seemed as though the physical disease was less important in the extent of pain and discomfort experienced than was the patient's psychological reaction to the disease process.

Patient's Confusion and Awareness During Illness. One of the first questions that arose in this study was whether suicide was more likely to occur when the patient is in a state of confusion. Confusion was found in eight of the suicide and fifteen of the controls, so this does not appear to be a distinguishing factor. Indeed, the presence of quiet confusion came to be used as a tentative clue against suicide. In the eight cases of suicide in which confusion was reported, the suicide did not occur during the confused period but rather when the patient was alert and oriented.

Suicide in Terminal State. An impression held prior to the research proved to be erroneous. It had been thought that if a patient were terminal, he would be unable to commit suicide even if he wished to because of his reduced physical capacity. From this study it is apparent that suicide can occur even in the most terminal state. For example, two of the suicides occurred in patients who were in oxygen tents and in very weakened condition. Another patient was immobilized in a Stryker frame and partially paralyzed, but was able to set fire to himself with lighter fluid which he distributed across his chest. Suicide occurred in sixteen patients who were terminal. It can be seen that the intention to commit rather than physical strength is the important variable.

Deficit Factors. Attempts were made to assess the following deficit factors for each patient: sensory loss, operations, artificial devices present (tracheotomy, feeding tube, catheter, etc.), loss of ability to eat solids, loss of voice, and difficulty in breathing, swallowing, and the like. In general, there was a slight tendency for more suicides to have one or more deficit factors than the controls. Only six of the suicides had none of the above deficit factors listed, while ten of the controls had none. In addition, the suicidal potentiality was raised when the patient showed psychological discomfort or some indication of disturbance of interpersonal relationships along with the deficit factors. It appeared entirely possible that such patients assessed or weighed the deficit factors in their lives against the positive factors and came up with a suicidal decision. A man who is not comfortable at home and who is not comfortable in the hospital because of his deteriorated physical condition may

feel he has no other resources for relief and comfort. This appears to be especially true if he is the type of person who is not accepting of his environment and the deficit factors in life, and who will not quietly accept what fate has dealt to him. This serves to emphasize the possibility that additional psychological support in the medical hospital may be one of the decisive factors influencing patients with terminal illness to live out their lives. It may be, indeed, that psychological or emotional support would contribute sufficiently to the patient's comfort that his illness would not appear unbearable for him.

Suicide Attempts, Threats, and Depression. Nine suicide cases had threatened suicide (most of them while in the hospital) and one of these had made a previous suicide attempt. In contrast, only one control case threatened suicide. Although the difference is statistically significant, it can readily be seen that the presence of suicide threats is not in itself sufficient to distinguish the large number of potential suicides. (Reports of suicide threats that were found in the Investigation Report and not in the body of the clinical folders were not counted since these threats were not reported to the staff until later, and it was felt that this information would not be available to the hospital staffs in similar cases). Many of the nine suicides who threatened did so directly to staff members. Almost all of these threats were made by patients who were described as complaining and irritable, and the suicide threat was apparently seen more as a plea for attention than an indication of danger. While this feeling appears to have some validity, it is most important to note that this does not mean that the person who threatens suicide for the purpose of getting attention and special treatment may not go on to commit suicide if things become too intolerable for him.

In addition, two suicide patients were noted to be talking about the possibility of suicide but were not making clear-cut suicide threats. Two other suicide patients were closely watched by the hospital, apparently because the possibility of suicidal action had been aroused in the staff's mind. These four patients are not included with the group of nine suicide patients who had a clear history of suicide threat. It is of interest to note that homicide threats were also made by two patients who threatened suicide.

Depression alone does not distinguish the potential suicide from

the control patient although there is a tendency for the suicidal patient to be more severely depressed. Fifteen suicide patients and eighteen control patients had no notations of depression in their records. However, when the factors of complaining behavior and agitation are considered along with depression, differences begin to emerge. This pattern is discussed more fully in the next section on the Dependent Dissatisfied Suicide and the Passive (Nonsuicide) Control.

THE DEPENDENT DISSATISFIED SUICIDE AND THE PASSIVE (NONSUICIDE) CONTROL. Two groups, one among the suicides and the other among the controls, seemed to group themselves into separate and relatively distinct subgroups.

The Dependent Dissatisfied Suicide. One large group of suicide patients ($N = 13$) emerged with a relatively homogeneous pattern, both in terms of personality characteristics and to some extent in terms of age and diagnosis (most above age 60 with cancer of the neck region). This group was called "Dependent Dissatisfied" because its characteristics were so similar to the general pattern previously described for one of the groups of schizophrenic suicides (see *Medical Bulletin MB-8,* dated Feb., 1962). The thirteen suicide cancer cases who were "dependent dissatisfied" were characterized primarily by emotional disturbance in relation to their illness and to their hospital care. Following are some of the notations concerning the behavior of these patients: "Patient has mentioned suicide but this appears to be hysteria," "Patient is just upset about having to come back into the hospital," "Patient appears to be exaggerating his pain," "Patient appears to be 'using' the hospital." This reaction on the part of the staff was more than understandable upon study of the record. These patients were immature, demanding, complaining, irritable, hostile, difficult ward problems. All of these patients were greatly disturbed about their illness.

Many had different ideas about the treatment or medication they should be receiving and such notations in the record, as the following, were frequently found: "Patient insists he is cold; refused blankets, wants heat pad instead," "Patient refused Demerol for pain, insists aspirin gives him more relief," "Patient insisting on special medication for sleep. Doctor contacted but when nurse re-

turned a few minutes later, patient was asleep." It should be noted that among this group of patients one-half were receiving placebos, and among those who were not specifically noted as receiving placebos, it was judged that they might have reacted positively to them.

In reviewing the past history of these patients, a history of somatic complaints before admission to the hospital was present in ten of the thirteen patients of this group. In addition, all of these patients appeared to have somatic complaints while in the hospital that the staff felt were excessive considering the stressfulness of the illness. Reactions of irritability on the part of the busy staff to the demands for more attention occurred. (This picture is in direct contrast with the group of nonsuicide patients labeled "passive control" in whom similar emotionally disturbed ward management problems and psychological upset were absent.) Nine of the thirteen suicide patients either made suicide threats or spoke about suicide, and two also threatened homicide. Neuropsychiatric consultations were judged as needed in all cases, although only three were held. In these three the suicide threats were minimized by the staff.

Some sensory loss was present in five of these patients. Voice loss occurred in four of the cancers of the throat area, and in most of these the patient did not respond well to the special training that the hospital attempted to provide. Deafness was present in five cases, and failing vision was present in one. Although these figures are small, there is a tendency for this group to have more sensory impairment than occurs for the rest of the suicides and the control group generally.

Eight of these patients were terminal while five patients carried a prognosis of "critical" and were judged to have two to six months or more to live.

In summary, the "dependent dissatisfied" patient was easily recognized by the staff of the hospital as the demanding, agitated, difficult patient who wanted attention and special treatment and who insisted upon getting it.

The Passive (Nonsuicide) Control. Nineteen of the controls formed a fairly homogeneous group. The characteristics they shared appeared to have little bearing upon their disease. Rather, the factors that distinguished the group were passivity, quiet acceptance of the hospital, adherence to ward routine, and a nondemanding

and uncomplaining attitude. These were "good" patients as evidenced by the fact that there were practically no entries in the records that were of a behavioral nature. Ages in this group varied from 21 to 76. All diagnostic categories were represented including one case of cancer of the epiglottis and one case of cancer of the thyroid. All nineteen cases expired from the disease. Almost without exception there was no indication in the folder of any past history of maladjustment. Neuropsychiatric consultations were not held and they did not seem to be needed. The only indication of possible suicidal potential was in three patients in whom there was depression. In nine of these patients there was some confusion, which set in during the terminal stages, but the confusion seemed to be the result of physical deterioration and there was no indication of psychological upset or confusion. Ten of the cases were alert until death occurred. Although in many cases the illness itself was highly stressful with indications that there should have been more pain and discomfort, these patients were able to bear physical discomfort with relatively little disturbance.

EQUIVOCAL GROUPS

Mixed Suicide Group. Nineteen suicides could not be clearly classified as "Dependent Dissatisfied" nor could they be separated into meaningful subgroups on the basis of the limited behavioral information in the folders. Seven were quiet and uncomplaining although the physical distress seemed unusually severe in some cases. The remaining twelve showed varying degrees of agitation but none approached the "Dependent Dissatisfied" in this characteristic, or the quality of the agitation was not the same. Four of the suicides in the mixed group were quite agitated, but did not appear to be overly willful or complaining. These were relatively young married men with small children and their agitation seemed due, in part, to concern about the welfare of their families. In only one of the hospital records of these young men was it clear that Social Service facilities had been made available, yet there seems little question that this assistance would have been most welcome in helping these patients adapt to their terminal illness. These four young men gave many indications of their distress concerning the home situation and their need for emotional support from the hospital.

The mixed group of nineteen suicides consisted of men from all

walks of life in whom there seemed to be an apparent exhaustion of resources—physical, emotional, or both. In some cases there were definite clues to possible suicidal behavior such as agitation, depression, and emotional disturbance. In some cases, however, it is difficult to see how the staff could have foreseen this suicidal action or what measures could possibly have been taken to prevent the suicide.

Agitated Controls. Thirteen of the controls showed much agitation and their resemblance to the suicidal group was alarmingly close. These patients frequently had a history of emotional maladjustment and their hospital course was marked by emotional agitation and disturbance above and beyond what might be expected from the disease itself. Indeed, three of these patients could appropriately be labeled "Dependent Dissatisfied" although the outcome was control and not suicide. It was evident from the hospital record that these patients enjoyed extremely supportive attention from the hospital staffs and from their families, and without this support a suicidal action might well have occurred. In many cases the patient's personal distress was recognized and psychological consultations were held for some. The wisdom of these hospitals in providing additional emotional support for such agitated patients is seen not only in the nonsuicidal outcome but also in the indications of lessened distress in the patient.

THE IMPLEMENTER. As this study progressed it became increasingly apparent that an important behavioral characteristic was present in most of the suicide cases and was absent in most of the control cases. This characteristic we have labeled "Implementing Behavior." When it became apparent that this might be an important differentiating characteristic, special rating forms were given to those attending the case conferences and were filled out before the outcome of the case was known. The difference in the two groups proved to be statistically significant on the basis of these rating forms. Those cases that had already been completed before the form was developed were then reviewed and especially rated for "Implementing Behavior." The "Implementer" is a person in whom there is apparently an active need to control his environment. In the hospital record this would be manifested by behavior such as refusals of some treatments, demands for other treatments, re-

quests for change of ward, insistence on receiving passes, or other notations of an active interest in directing his situation. This was assumed to reflect a need to control or direct the life situation to meet the patient's own wishes. This is not to say that only suicides are interested in what happens to them, but rather to say that in hospital records the presence of many such entries in the nurses' or doctors' notes may reveal the presence of a strong need to control the environment that is not found in the usual patient. Although the information concerning the patient's personal life was minimal and made it difficult to ascertain whether this same characteristic was present in his prehospital record, there were some indications that this was so. It thus seemed to reflect an enduring personality characteristic rather than one that had developed with the onset of a terminal illness. In contrast, the majority of control cases did not show this "Implementing Behavior." They seemed to be accepting of whatever treatment was given and content to adapt to the additional stresses and strains imposed by their illness and changes in their lives.

Discussion

Suicide is a particularly taboo subject in our society, and cancer also tends to arouse feelings of disquiet and displeasure. For these reasons and others this study was not a simple one.

In the records, the medical history, including the course of the illness, was usually very completely presented. However, the personality of the patient, his interpersonal relationships, and his attitudes toward his disease were either frustratingly absent or sketchily noted. With persistence and careful sifting of every available note it was possible to obtain a picture of the patient and the kind of person he was, but it must be admitted that the data are often sparse.

The primary intent of the study was to determine whether clues could be found that would help identify the potential suicide and thus facilitate the prevention of suicide among patients with malignancies. This was not with a view to prolonging their last painful hours but with the hope that it might be possible to learn new means of making such persons sufficiently comfortable psychologically that suicide would not be contemplated.

While it was known that suicide occurs disproportionately more

often among cancer patients before the study was initiated (it was one reason for selecting this group for intensive study) the recurrent question was why some patients committed suicide while others chose to live out their lives. This study indicates that it does not depend only on the site or nature of the disease, or the amount of pain or suffering to be tolerated, but rather on the fundamental psychological organization of the patient. Closely related to the above is the perplexing question, "Why does a person at the threshold of death commit suicide?" It may be that the value of life is lessened for the man who knows its duration is short and that its content will be filled with pain and discomfort. What may be more pertinent, psychologically such persons are subjected to severe if not total disruption of their life pattern, a slow dissolution of their body image, a frontal attack on their self-concept, and a tremendous strain on their interpersonal relationships. The illness demands that old familiar patterns of relating to important others be discarded and new ones formed. The most extensive and intensive of sick roles is imposed with many implications interpersonally, especially in the area of dependency. For some persons the adaptation and the adjustment to the changed life is made without too much strain. For others there is great difficulty, sometimes amounting almost to total denial and rejection of the role. The acceptance and adaptation to the new requirements for living seemed especially difficult for the person we have called the "Implementer." These men insisted on maintaining their old concepts of self. This seemed to be at least partially expressed in an active need to control and direct their destinies. If they were unable to affect the ultimate end of the disease they could at least set the time and the terms of their death to some extent.

What could the physician and the hospital have done to prevent the suicide? Some suggestions are presented and discussed below. Some of these stem from the data directly while others emerged from the intensive discussions of the cases by the research staff with the medical consultant.

Identification of the potential suicide is the first preventive step. An attempt has been made to identify these patients and these factors are summarized in the summary.

Suicide in the hospital is the responsibility of all staff. Physicians, nurses, aides, and other members of the hospital organization, such

as administration, housekeeping, and security, bear the responsibility in greater or lesser degree. The communication channels between all members must be kept open so that observation and information can be readily transmitted. In several cases in the study it was felt that a breakdown had occurred in the communication between aide, nurse, and physician, and that this had played a significant role in the suicide.

The psychological status of the terminally ill patient was found to be most important. Such a patient should never be alienated from human contacts. Transfer to a private room to "await death" invariably was detrimental. Even though the doctor may be able to do little to alter the course of the disease, he can do much to promote a warm, understanding relationship. He should proffer support and assistance in every way to allay physical and psychological discomfort. The physicians' personal feelings of inadequacy or even self-blame may be aroused when faced with the treatment of the patient with widespread metastases. Such a patient must never be "written off" by a doctor who is pressed for time and who feels that his skills can best be used by his concentrating on those whose physical state can be improved. The loss of interest and involvement can be felt by the dying and may be interpreted as a final rejection and help precipitate a suicidal decision.

Every hospital and interpersonal resource should be mobilized to carry the patient through his last days. Psychiatric consultation for diagnostic and therapeutic aid could have been helpful in the mangement of many of the patients in the suicide group. Supportive psychotherapy and pastoral assistance can be impressively helpful. In general, his psychological defense mechanisms should be reinforced. Whether it is denial of the imminently inevitable, or a frank discussion of his impending death, it is important that the relationship and the implied support be provided. Some patients in the suicide group had lost every reason to remain alive. Family, friends, physical comfort, spiritual meaning, and hope had gone. What must be done is to give such a person a reason to live until the moment of death.

The judicious use of tranquilizing drugs not only reduces anxiety, but also potentiates the effect of narcotics and analgesics. An occasional patient will require antidepressant medication. In some instances a reluctance to give an obviously dying person sufficient

analgesics and narcotics to keep him comfortable was observed. The dangers of producing addiction to opiates was mentioned as the reason. Although this is a complex problem in the patient with chronic pain, the problem of addicting a critically ill cancer patient seems academic.

Summary

From an intensive study of sixty-four records of patients with diagnoses of malignant neoplasms, half of whom had committed suicide and half of whom were carefully matched nonsuicide controls, clues for identification and recognition of suicide potential were obtained. These clues may be used by a hospital staff in determining those cancer patients who may be likely to commit suicide:

1. *High Suicide Potential.* Older men with cancer of the throat and neck region; younger men with Hodgkins or leukemia. Regardless of age or disease site, there is suicidal potential if all or most of the following factors are present:

  a. Emotional stress—over and above the physical and psychological aspects of the disease process itself. This might be in the form of:
  b. Severe depression, anxiety, dejection, mood swings, agitation, over-dependence.
  c. Low tolerance for pain and discomfort.
  d. Excessive demanding and complaining behavior with strong need for attention and reassurance.
  e. Controlling and directing activity (e.g., insistent requests or refusals of treatment and medications).
  f. Relative alertness and orientation.
  g. Exhaustion of resources, physical and emotional, including feeling of lack of support and attention from family or hospital.
  h. Prior and present suicidal threats or attempts (including obviously manipulative suicide threats).

2. *Low Suicide Potential.* This control (nonsuicidal) patient quietly accepts whatever treatment the hospital provides without indication of disturbance or agitation. Regardless of the stressfulness of the disease process, this patient seems psychologically quiet, comfortable, and at ease. He seems at peace with the environment

even though he may be in physical distress and in a terminal stage of the illness.

3. *Equivocal Suicide Potential.* Characteristics of both high and low suicide potential groups appeared, for example, agitation, depression or stoicism, calm, and the like. The nonsuicide outcome for some patients seemed directly related to the recognition and treatment of the psychological distress by hospital and home figures.

Suicide Can Occur In:

All stages of the disease, including the most terminal of physical conditions.

Cases in which there is relatively little pain or discomfort from the illness as well as those in which there is much.

Persons who are alert and oriented rather than confused.

Persons who have the feeling (whether appropriate or not) of no further emotional support either in or out of the hospital.

Persons who feel their psychological and physical resources have been exhausted.

Chapter 20
SUICIDE AMONG PATIENTS WITH ANXIETY OR DEPRESSIVE REACTIONS
Norman L. Farberow and Theodore L. McEvoy

Analysis of records of Veterans Administration General Medical and Surgical patients with anxiety or depressive reactions, half of whom had committed suicide, and the rest of whom were matched nonsuicidal controls, showed that suicides and nonsuicides were sufficiently differentiated on each of twenty-three feeling and behavior items. Also most of the cases could be categorized into patterns relating to their interpersonal, intrapsychic, and societal ties and conflicts. An important measure against suicide is evidence that members of the hospital staff are interested in and concerned about the patient.

Depression has been noted as a characteristic symptom in most suicide cases.[1] Anxiety has also been indicated as a prominent feature.[2] When these symptoms are so marked that they can be characterized as psychoneurotic syndromes, suicide can be expected to occur proportionally more often among persons so classified.

A survey of cases of suicide[3] occurring among patients in the Veterans Administration General Medical and Surgical Hospitals indicated that a large number of the suicides were patients with diagnoses of anxiety reaction or depressive reaction, both on neuropsychiatric, and on medical and/or surgical wards.[4] This number, however, was smaller than would be expected proportionally from the total number of such cases. A study of patients with a diagnosis of anxiety or depressive reaction who killed themselves was undertaken to determine the identifying personality characteristics and behavioral features of such a group.

Procedures

For both clinical and practical reasons, the two groups of cases, anxiety reaction and depressive reaction, were combined into one

group for this study. This was done in order to have a large enough number of cases for statistically meaningful comparisons, and because it was recognized that the two diagnoses are similar enough dynamically often to be combined into one diagnosis of anxiety-depressive reaction.

Preliminary investigation identified nineteen anxiety-reaction cases and twenty-four depressive-reaction cases that had ended with death by suicide. For each of these cases, a control case was selected, matched for age (plus or minus 3 years), sex (all male), race (all Caucasian), religion (Protestant, Catholic, or Jewish), and diagnosis (anxiety reaction or depressive reaction as either primary or secondary diagnosis). The source of data for this study included all the available clinical information contained in the patient's clinical and correspondence folders.

The following steps were used in analyzing the eighty-six cases (43 suicides and 43 controls): (1) A detailed chronological abstract was prepared for each patient from the case history, doctor's and nurse's notes, psychological test results, ancillary therapists' reports, and all other available data.[5] (2) A "psychological autopsy"[6] was held for each case by a group of research psychologists and a psychiatrist.[7] During the "psychological autopsy" the final outcome of the case was withheld from the research staff until after the "clues" had been identified and the predictions about the outcome had been made. (3) Summary sheets recorded the findings of the research staff. (4) A checklist was evolved grouping the identifying clues into general categories. (5) Each of the eighty-six cases was again reviewed and assessed for the presence or absence of each of these clues. The frequency of the clues among the suicide cases was compared with the frequencies among the control cases (Chi-square). (6) The cases were further analyzed by patterns that had been tentatively identified among the suicidal and nonsuicidal groups. The clues were also applied to the subgroups to determine their applicability.

The analyses thus provided two kinds of information: (1) the identification of clues that (statistically) significantly differentiated anxiety and depressive suicide cases from nonsuicide cases, and (2) the identification of patterns that seemed to characterize subgroups of suicidal and nonsuicidal anxiety and depressive cases.

DESCRIPTION OF THE POPULATION

Groups. The suicidal and the control groups each consisted of forty-three patients, nineteen with a primary diagnosis of anxiety reaction and twenty-four with a diagnosis of depressive reaction.[8]

Population characteristics. The population characteristics of the groups may be seen in Table I.

TABLE I—Characteristics of Anxiety and Depressive
Reaction Patients

Characteristics	Anxiety		Depressive	
	Suicide $N=19$	Control $N=19$	Suicide $N=24$	Control $N=24$
Age				
Range	30-69	30-70	33-66	28-64
Median	49	48	50	46
Religion				
Protestant	10	10	20	20
Catholic	7	7	4	4
Jewish	2	2	0	0
Length of stay in hospital				
Less than 1 month	7	11	12	11
3 months	8	6	7	7
6 months	2	0	1	3
1 year	2	1	3	2
More than 1 year	0	1	1	1
Diagnosis				
Primary	14	8	15	14
Primary (but listed secondary)	3	3	3	2
Secondary to medical diagnosis	2	8	6	8

Age was a controlled variable, so the age distributions for the suicides and controls are similar.[9] Median ages for the anxiety and depressive suicides are 49 and 50, respectively. Thirty-five percent of the suicide cases fall in the decade from 55 to 64, indicating, as in the general population, that suicide is a greater problem within the older age brackets. The religious distribution of the population shows the usual higher number of Protestants, and fewer Catholics and Jews. Table I indicates that the suicides and controls were in the hospital for relatively similar periods of time.

The diagnosis of anxiety reaction or depressive reaction was either the primary or the sole diagnosis in thirty-five of the suicide cases and in twenty-seven of the control cases (a difference not statistically significant). This includes six cases among the suicides and five among the controls in which the diagnosis was listed as secondary, but which, in the judgment of the psychiatrist, was the primary condition. In these cases the listed primary diagnosis was an historical one and did not play a role in the current situation of the patients.

In the remaining cases the diagnosis of anxiety or depressive reaction was secondary to a medical situation. The anxiety suicides had primary medical diagnoses of bronchitis and visceroptosis. The anxiety controls had primary medical diagnoses of ulcer, hemorrhoids, fever, hypochondriasis, stenosis of the larynx, pulmonary fibrosis, and hernia surgery.

The depressive suicides had primary medical diagnoses of asthma, bronchiectasis, hypertension, palsy, cancer, and schizoid condition. The depressive controls had primary medical diagnoses of cardiac hypertension (2), arthritis, diabetes, tuberculosis and cancer (2).

One hundred twenty-nine anxiety and depressive cases had to be reviewed in order to obtain the required forty-three control cases. In only fifty-six of these 129 cases (43%) was the diagnosis of anxiety reaction or depressive reaction the primary or sole diagnosis. (This contrasts with the ratio of thirty-five cases among the 43 suicides, 81%.) Apparently many patients in a general medical and surgical hospital will receive a diagnosis of anxiety or depressive reaction secondary to a medical problem. Thus, a random sample of "control" patients rather than the matched sample used in this study might have demonstrated many more differences between the suicide and nonsuicide cases. By using a matched sample the task of differentiating between the two groups focused on the more subtle and complex differences rather than the more obvious differences.

Although the groups were not matched on marital status, the differences among them were not significant. Twenty-six of the suicides were married, nine were single, and eight were divorced, separated, or widowed. Among the controls, twenty-four were married, six were single, and thirteen were divorced, separated or widowed.

TABLE II

Methods Used to Commit Suicide Among Anxiety
and Depressive Patients

Method	In hospital	Out of hospital	Total
Jumping	17	1	18
Cutting	5	0	5
Gunshot wound	0	5	5
Hanging	4	3	7
Drowning	1	2	3
Carbon-monoxide	0	2	2
Jump/train	1	1	2
Strangulation	1	0	1
Total	29	14	43

Table II shows that fourteen of the patients committed suicide while on leave, pass, or trial visit; twenty-nine killed themselves in the hospital. The choice of suicide method reflected the hospital status of the patient. Most of the patients in the hospital jumped, while most of the patients out of the hospital shot themselves.

Results

PREDICTIONS OF SUICIDAL OUTCOME. The blind predictions of suicidal or nonsuicidal outcome of the eighty-six cases in staff conferences were analyzed using five raters who had attended and predicted in 35 percent or more of the case conferences.

The results indicated that the suicides were more readily identified than the controls (79% versus 64%). The researchers were unanimously correct in their predictions in twenty-one of the anxiety and eighteen of the depressive cases. These were about equally divided among suicides and controls in the anxiety group, but the depressive group showed twice as many "correct" predictions for the suicides as for the controls. Six cases were false positives; that is, two of the anxiety cases and four of the depressives, all controls, were incorrectly predicted to be suicides by all members of the research staff. One case did become a suicidal victim sixty-five days after discharge; another was subsequently hospitalized in a state of deep coma following a suicidal attempt by drug ingestion. Five of these false positive cases had histories of prior suicidal

TABLE III—Clues Used for and Against Suicide of Anxiety and Depressive Patients with Significance of Difference in Occurrence for Suicidal and Control Patients

Clue	Chi-square
Clues for:	
1. Conflict over impending industrial or occupational change	0.19
2. Poor work history	1.28
3. Disturbed by potential marital or "significant other" change	0.56
4. Disturbed sexual adjustment	5.20^3
5. Change in family unity	8.12^4
6. Discomfort at home or on pass	9.64^4
7. Social isolation	4.67^3
8. "Character" disorders (alcoholism, drug addiction, etc.)	0.75
9. Disabling organic illness	1.89
10. Deterioration of body image	0.05
11. Poor prognosis	18.90^5
12. Felt rejected by hospital	$—^1$
13. Negative reaction to hospital staff	3.14^2
14. Not gratified in hospital	$—^1$
15. Patient "rejected" hospital	6.41^3
16. Positive hospital attitude toward patient	2.35
17. Negative hospital attitude toward patient	2.35
18. Severe psychiatric symptoms	7.77^4
19. Excessive dependency	0.19
20. Ineffective somatic symptoms	3.44^2
21. Ineffective usual defenses	3.26
22. Recent loss of emotional support from significant person or agency	0.23
23. Suicidal history	10.61^4
Clues against:	
1. No occupational difficulties	—
2. Family support	—

Clue	Chi-square
Clues against:	
3. Agency support	—
4. Positive response to agency support	—
5. Social (other) support	0.24
6. No acute psychological crisis apparent	1.69
7. No psychological symptoms	3.26^2
8. Recognizes problems as psychogenic	5.65^3
9. Has plans for the future	5.20^3
10. Adapting well to crisis or illness	1.29
11. Blames others without insight	0.14
12. History of dissociative reaction	0.62
13. Alcoholism is a refuge	—
14. History of "resolved" anxiety or depressive episodes	—
15. Effective obsessive-compulsive defenses	1.02
16. Possible psychotic break	0.43
17. Prominent somatic complaints	0.69
18. Confusion, e.g., toxic, organic, DT's	$—^1$
19. Feels well physically	5.20^3
20. Lack of suffering from organic causes	0.75
Feeling and behavior symptoms for suicide:	
1. Sleeplessness	20.79^4
2. Hostility	3.22^2
3. Agitation	12.01^4
4. Tension	9.63^4
5. Nervousness	13.31^5
6. Worries	11.01^5
7. Crying, tearful	1.87
8. Marked anxiety	13.31^5
9. Marked depression	8.94^4
10. Emotional lability	1.08
11. Hopelessness	2.82

[1] … number of important data.   [2] $p \leq .10$.   [3] $p \leq .05$.   [4] $p \leq .01$.   [5] $p \leq .001$.

behavior. There were no false negatives, that is, cases actually suicidal which were unanimously predicted to be controls.

CLUE ANALYSIS. At each psychological autopsy the staff was required to specify the clues that contributed to their decision that the case was a suicide or nonsuicide control. These clues were organized into clinically meaningful groups and compiled into a 43-item checklist (see Table III). Each of the eighty-six cases was again reviewed and assessed for the presence or absence of each of the general clues. The suicides and nonsuicide controls were then compared to determine the differences, if any.

Fifteen of the forty-three clues significantly differentiated between the suicide and control cases. One additional general clue, "feeling and behavior symptoms prominent during hospitalization," was broken down into eleven clues of specific behavioral symptoms and these were also analyzed. Of these, eight were significantly differentiating.

GENERAL DIFFERENTIATING CLUES. The fifteen general clues are as follows:

Poor prognosis. Among the suicide patients, response to therapy was very poor with usually no appreciable alleviation of psychological symptoms. In the cases with prominent medical problems, the long-term prognosis for the disease was always guarded.

Suicidal history. A history of suicidal behavior (i.e., threats, ruminations, attempts) was more common among the patients who killed themselves than among those who did not. Many of those persons had thus "identified" themselves as potentially suicidal patients. Of the controls with suicidal histories, several might have been considered suicidal clinically even though they had not, at the time of the investigation, killed themselves.

Discomfort at home on pass. Suicidal patients more often found their conflicts exacerbated when released home on leave or pass.

Changes in family unity. Significantly greater among suicides, this clue reflects the lack of support, understanding, or acceptance the patients felt from his family, with no visitors (recorded) while in the hospital, negative changes in marital relationship, etc.

Severe psychiatric symptoms. Although all of the cases, control and suicide, exhibited some psychiatric symptoms (each had a

diagnosis of anxiety reaction or depressive reaction), the suicide cases showed significantly more severe symptoms more frequently. These symptoms included marked thinking disorders, such as irrational preoccupations and severe phobias, sometimes even raising the question of incipient psychotic processes.

Negative reaction to hospital. The suicidal patient more often did not experience effective alleviation of his problems or conflicts. Because the hospital did not meet his needs the patient was often demanding, cantankerous, or made attempts to elope and generally was a "problem" patient.

Severe sexual disturbances. These disturbances, more common among suicides, accompanied the indications of increasing marital discord, as expressed in problems of frigidity, impotence, infidelity, and the like. The symptoms also reflected a general deterioration in a significant interpersonal relationship.

Social isolation. As a discriminating clue, this was more characteristic of one group of suicides discussed later under the pattern of "egoistic" suicides. Social isolation characterized persons who had no important relationships in their functioning.

Relative ineffectiveness of somatic complaints in binding anxiety or depression. The potentiality for suicide seemed increased when anxious or depressed persons did not possess alternative means of expressing their problem, such as through somatic symptoms.

Ineffectiveness of usual psychological defenses. For the suicides, previously operative defenses, such as compulsive characteristics, denial, projection, and the like, no longer seemed effective, and control of anxiety and depression seemed lessened.

Negative reaction to the staff. Not only did the suicides react negatively to their hospitalization (Clue 6) but they were often negative to staff members, and openly hostile, disparaging, and uncooperative significantly more often than control patients.

Adaptation to illness. This clue, contraindicatory of suicide, reflected a successful resolution or adjustment to an illness or psychological conflict. It implies that suicide, as a mode of adjustment, increased in probability as other methods of adjustment or adaptation were not effective.

Physical well-being. This clue, also a contraindicator of suicide, included the notions of general freedom from continuous discomfort

and lack of suffering from organic causes. In general, the controls responded well to therapy and hence were not plagued with continuous physical distress.

Plans for future. This clue also contraindicates suicide. The ability to make plans for the future relates in general to evidence of adaptability. It is also related to more favorable prognosis and was significantly more characteristic of the control group.

No psychological symptoms. This "negative" clue characterized the control cases. Freedom from marked or prolonged symptomatology was compatible with rapid and favorable response to treatment.

A general clue, "feeling and behavior symptoms prominent during hospitalization," was examined for its subsymptoms. Eight of these were found to discriminate significantly as clues for suicide between the suicide and the nonsuicide cases. In general, the clues give a picture of highly intensified anxiety and depressive symptoms, such as sleeplessness, agitation, worry, tension, and so forth.

DRUGS. Medications were noted as the cases were reviewed. An attempt to relate the role of the medications to the illnesses and suicide was discarded because of the sparsity of the information. The patients, unlike a group of schizophrenics studied previously were in the hospital a much shorter length of time and data were much less complete.[10] In general, the depressive cases showed little difference in treatment by drugs, with approximately equal numbers of both suicides and controls receiving tranquilizers or hypnotics and sedatives. The anxiety-suicide cases, however, were treated more often with tranquilizers, while the controls tended to receive more hypnotics and sedatives.

PATTERN ANALYSIS. Utilizing the prepared abstracts, the data collected during the psychological autopsies, and the original files, all eighty-six cases were reviewed. Four relatively clear patterns could be established among sixty-five of the eighty-six cases, two characterizing primarily suicidal persons, one primarily control, and one found equally often among both suicides and controls. In addition, another group of seven cases seemed to approach a fifth pattern among the suicides, but is only tentatively identified because of its

small size. Fourteen residual cases could not be classified in any category. The distribution of the patients in the patterns are shown in Table IV.

TABLE IV—Number of Anxiety and Depressive Suicides and Controls in Obtained Patterns

Patterns	Anxiety		Depressive		Total		Total
	Sui-cide	Con-trol	Sui-cide	Con-trol	Sui-cide	Con-trol	
Object-loss	7	2	8	1	15	3	18
Involutional	4	1	7	4	11	5	16
Medical	0	9	3	4	3	13	16
Egoistic	6	5	2	2	8	7	15
Preegoistic	1	1	0	5	1	6	7
	18	18	20	16	38	34	72

The patterns are labeled according to the apparent predominant characteristic of each group. Each of the patterns is discussed in detail below:

THE OBJECT-LOSS PATTERN. "I can't give up hope that she will change her mind." The distinguishing characteristic of this primarily suicidal group was that it was interpersonally based with each patient feeling that he was in danger of losing a "love object." It was also true that in some of these cases there was the additional factor that the patient was anxious about his job and felt threatened because of possible occupational failure. However, in no case was there just an industrial conflict, while in all cases there were signs of marital and interpersonal discord. The prominence of vocational conflicts increased roughly with age.

Eighteen cases (15 suicides, 3 controls, $p < .01$) of the total eighty-six cases in the study fell into this pattern. Most of the patients were younger, with a median age of 36 and range of 30 to 49. Suicidal activity was very prominent in this group, especially during the prehospitalization crisis. Thirteen of the eighteen cases (72%) had known suicidal histories.

Fifteen men were married at the time of their hospitalization; the three others were about to be married. The conflicts centered

mostly around impending divorce, separation, childbirth rivalry, infidelity of spouse, guilt over extramarital affairs, and "questionable paternity." Along with these marital difficulties was evidence of sexual disturbance such as masturbatory guilt, sexual incompatibility, homosexual panic, feelings of inadequacy and conflict over masculine role, feeling "repelled" by sex, and feeling of "sin." These sexual conflicts were usually acute and were present in the object-loss pattern significantly more often than in the other three patterns ($p < .01$).

The social and marital adjustment was characterized by marked dependency on the spouse or significant other (16 of the 18 cases, $p < .05$). Peer relationships showed feelings of social inadequacy and fears about competing. Work adjustments were typically marred by feelings of guilt, failure, and inadequacy. In every case, the patient was hospitalized because of psychological difficulties (marital and vocational conflicts). In only three of the eighteen cases were there also organic or medical problems, and these responded to medical treatment readily.

In the hospital the cases were marked by unrelieved emotional distress, seen in sleeplessness, tension, and agitation. There was unfavorable response to hospital treatment and in many cases their conditions worsened. Although considerably disturbed emotionally, they were, for the most part, free of physical discomfort or pain. Two of the three controls in this group were identified by the staff as false positives. Both had made prior suicidal attempts, and one made a subsequent attempt.

Characteristically, this group of patients experienced trouble on passes (13 out of 18 cases, $p < .05$), frequently returning early or with exacerbated symptoms. This reflected their feeling of loss of interpersonal support and relationships with other significant persons. In addition, these patients were self-centered, obsessively preoccupied with their own problems, unable to entertain any significant change in the status quo, nor to work out a constructive resolution for their future.

Example. A 37-year-old married man was first admitted to a Veterans Administration hospital with the chief complaint of "personality changes in the last four months." According to the patient, he had been constantly employed, carefree, good-natured, and happy-go-lucky. However, in the four months prior to admission,

his personality and behavior had changed and he had become withdrawn, unable to sleep, and had had suicidal thoughts. The patient's wife had been involved in an extramarital affair, which the patient had successfully denied to himself, until she finally made it clear to him that she intended to obtain a divorce. The patient had an extremely dependent relationship with his wife which she was apparently unable to tolerate further.

During the hospital stay, the patient was unable to make any plans that would include the loss of his wife. However, she refused all attempts at reconcilation and proceeded with divorce actions. He made a number of veiled suicide threats, such as asking about insurance payments in cases of suicidal death. The patient went home on a week-end pass about sixty-five days after admission. While on pass, he went to an amusement park and shot himself with a rifle in a nearby deserted shooting gallery.

THE INVOLUTIONAL PATTERN. This group of patients, principally suicidal cases, was made up of older men who were reacting with strong emotional disturbances to a threat to their psychological integrity. The threat centered primarily around industrial or occupational failures and the fear of losing economic independence. Other "threats" included sudden illnesses or failing health (resulting in severe limitations to occupational or social activities), and recent changes in the marital or family relationship, such as the loss of sex drive, impotence, frigidity in the spouse, or the loss of children through marriage or death. Characteristically, these men had previously achieved a satisfactory social adjustment, had been productive persons, and had only rarely been physically ill. This group was similar to the object-loss cases but without the excessive dependency that characterized the latter group. They had been "sucessful" husbands and workers for many years in adult life.

Sixteen cases (11 suicides and 5 controls, $p < .10$) fell into the "involutional" pattern. Most of the patients were older (median age 58, range 46 to 66). Nine of the sixteen cases (seven suicides and two controls) in this group had histories of prior suicidal behavior.

All sixteen patients in this group experienced a severe reaction to changes in their perception of themselves as effective men with ability to be economically independent. Ten suicides and two control

patients had been working until just prior to hospitalization. Nine of the suicides were facing imminent retirement, business failure, or loss of work due to "nervousness." In three cases there had been a gradual approach to retirement and, as their effectiveness diminished, there was a corresponding increase in depression and feelings of bitterness and hopelessness.

All the men in this group were married. The conflicts centering in the home situation, along with recent physical illness or psychosomatic problems, contributed considerably to their pervasive feelings of failure and inadequacy. Among the suicides, there were two cases of impotence, three cases of rejection by their wives, two cases in which the child married and left, and three cases with recent illness of the wife.

In the hospital the most prominent syndrome of this group might be best described as an agitated depression. Insomnia, tension, hyperactivity, chronic anxiety, and worry were prominent features. While often pleasant and cooperative on approach, the patients in this group were generally too wrapped up in their own concerns to socialize easily. Behavioral symptoms characteristic of this group were sleeplessness, agitation, tension, nervousness, marked anxiety, and marked depression. Two of the control cases were identified by the staff as false positives. One of these men was a clear suicidal risk who later voluntarily returned to the hospital because he was fearful of killing himself.

These cases were not chronic patients, many of them never having been hospitalized before. This is compatible with the finding that, as a group, these men had achieved reasonably satisfactory work records and were, in many ways, "solid citizens."

Example. A 50-year-old used-car salesman, married and with two grown children, was hospitalized for a severe depressive reaction. The patient had always been "nervous" but had never been hospitalized or treated for any psychiatric disorder. The patient had been in business for himself but had recently developed the unfounded idea that he was "losing out." He was chronically hypersensitive about his lack of formal education and tended to feel inferior because of this. There had been a recent change in the family structure when his daughter had married and his son had left home for college. Never a person with broad interests or social outlets, he had increasingly drawn in upon himself and his

home life, and, at the same time, became less able to make major decisions without his wife's support.

The patient entered the hospital with a variety of vague somatic complaints. There was considerable apathy and melancholy with expressions of feelings of worthlessness, unworthiness, and doubts about his sanity. In the hospital, the patient was cooperative but clearly depressed. He was treated with tranquilizers, hydrotherapy, and corrective and occupational therapy but showed little progress. About thirty-seven days after admission, the wife requested that the patient be given a weekend pass since his daughter and son-in-law were visiting. The patient appeared pleased, but while home, without warning, he took the family car, drove to an isolated spot, and hanged himself.

THE MEDICAL PATTERN. The most outstanding feature of this pattern of primarily control patients was that the focal problem seemed to be a medical one with the psychological reactions as secondary manifestations of the illness. When adjustment problems were noted they were moderate, characterological, heterogeneous, and showed no commonality of pattern. A little more than one fourth of the control group fell into this pattern. One may wonder how many of the suicide cases in this group received their psychiatric diagnosis after the fact. However, from a general survey of admissions to general medical and surgical hospitals of cases with primary or secondary diagnoses of anxiety or depressive reaction, it may be estimated that such persons actually account for 50 percent or more of such admissions.

Sixteen of the eighty-six cases in the study (13 controls and 3 suicides) fell into this category. The age range for this group was wide, from 30 years to 67 years, with a median age of 56. Within the pattern, the depression cases tended to be older, with a mean age of 59 as compared with 47 for the anxiety cases. Suicidal activity had occurred in all three of the suicide cases in this group but in none of the nonsuicide cases.

Without exception, these men had successfully adjusted to work and to important interpersonal relationships. Thirteen of the sixteen patients in this group were married at the time of their hospitalization, including all three of the suicide cases. Of the three not married, one was an elderly widower who made his

home with a daughter, and the other was a happily divorced man with ten children and many close family ties. In only two cases were there indications of marital conflicts, but in neither of these was the hospitalization precipitated by or related to these conflicts.

The one characteristic that unified this heterogeneous group was that each patient was admitted to the hospital for a legitimate medical or surgical problem requiring hospital care. The anxiety or depressive reactions were clearly secondary manifestations of the physical illnesses and these conditions improved along with their general improvement in health.

Almost without exception the nonsuicide patients responded rapidly to therapy, improved quickly in both physical and psychological areas, and were "good" patients—quiet, cooperative, and responsive. Only the three suicide cases differed to some degree, being older men with more serious and lasting illnesses. The suicides seemed to be direct consequences of attempts to cope with the organic illness. The extent of the accompanying depression and suicidal behavior was not recognized.

Example. A 58-year-old man, living with his second wife, had two grown stepchildren who were married and lived outside his home. The patient was a postal employee with many years of service. His health was generally good until age 51, when he entered the hospital for possible pneumonia. There was no significant organic disease found. His complaints of pain were associated with a mild osteoarthritis of the spine. The patient was anxious on admission but rapidly became asymptomatic.

At age 59, the patient reentered the hospital following a coronary infarction. He was somewhat concerned and mildly depressed about the effect of his illness on his position at the post office. However, the heart condition responded well to treatment and social service resolved his occupational concerns. The patient's symptoms rapidly abated and he was discharged with maximum hospital benefit.

THE EGOISTIC PATTERN. "The individual ego asserts itself to excess in the face of the social ego and at its expense. . . . Egoistic suicide is the special type of suicide springing from excessive individualism."[11]

The most remarkable aspect of this group of patients, distributed

equally among suicides and controls, was the small degree of integration of the patients into society. The men were chronic "loners," or social isolates, with apparently few or no important relationships. Their diagnoses might be questioned, for there were relatively few of the reactive features found among the object-loss, involutional, and medical cases. In some cases, they were marginally psychotic with a strong hypochondriacal overlay. However, they did appear to be chronically anxious or depressed and most displayed character-disorder symptoms. They showed obsessive health concern, bodily preoccupations, and self-pity. Prevention of suicide among these patients would have been difficult. Those who killed themselves did so without an observable psychological crisis or specific precipitating circumstances.

Fifteen of the eighty-six cases in the study (eight suicides and seven controls) fell into this category. The ages ranged from 42 years to 70 years, with a median age of 56 years.

The social isolation of these men was further reflected in their pre- and inhospital histories. Occupational adjustment was poor. Only one (a control case) of the fifteen men was employed at the time of hospital admission. The other fourteen men had work records that, for the most part, were both erratic and unskilled. Some had been unemployed as many as ten to twenty years. One man had not worked for forty years of his adult life.

Important familial or other usual close relationships were lacking. None of the men was living with a spouse at the time of the last hospitalization. Several patients had transient superficial contacts with a sibling or a grown child, but did not live with such a person. Three persons had been public wards for over ten years. Sexual relationships were infrequent, with some sexual contacts with prostitutes noted among some of the younger men. Several men were divorced, all of them for many years. Two men who were separated had not obtained divorces apparently for religious reasons, but had lived alone for many years.

The patients came to the hospital for a wide variety of reasons, some somatic and medical, and others having vague organic bases or none at all. The hospital picture was generally one of chronic and obsessive bodily preoccupation among these patients. It may be theoretically meaningful that persons whose adjustment was so marginal socially and who invested so little interest or energy in

other persons or work should show excessive self-interest and bodily preoccupation. On the ward, these men showed tendencies to remain alone, aloof, disinterested, uncooperative, and negativistic to the staff. The long-range prognosis for improvement or changes was poor in eleven of the fifteen cases. Interestingly, not one of the patients perceived his problem as psychogenic.

It was difficult to detect clues that would alert the professional person to the probability of suicide among these men. There was a slight tendency toward greater degrees of emotional disturbance among the suicidal patients. Typical of their behavior were notes indicating that they were uncooperative, fearful of surgery, refused preoperative care, refused treatment at times, made a number of AMA requests, refused social service, and demanded therapy or other help intermittently.

Example. A 67-year-old man, born in Norway, came to the United States as a young man, leaving his family in Norway. In World War I, he served in the army overseas for six months. In the 1920's, after three children, the patient was divorced by his wife because of excessive use of alcohol. The patient's social adjustment apparently deteriorated and he entered a Veterans Administration hospital for the first time in 1942, suffering from delirium tremens. From 1942 until 1957, he lived either in a Veterans Administration domiciliary or Veterans Administration hospital with only occasional contacts with his daughter.

The patient had a series of medical hospitalizations for a variety of somatic complaints without any active disease or clear-cut precipitating circumstances for hospitalization. During his final hospital stay, the patient was restless, agitated, demanding, and asocial. He was antagonistic toward the staff and tended to try their patience. One day he was missing from his ward and was later found to have drowned himself in a nearby river.

THE PREEOGISTIC PATTERN. A small but unique group of seven younger patients had many characteristics very similar to the "egoistic" suicide cases, but only one committed suicide. All but one of them were considered suicidal by the research team. These cases ranged in age from 28 years to 46 years, with a median age of 36 years. In this respect they were much younger than the "egoistic" cases. Five of the seven cases had suicidal histories.

None of the seven patients was living with a spouse at the time of the last hospitalization, although four had been married and were now either divorced or separated. All seven were decidedly passive and dependent in their social adjustment. Only two of the seven men had an adequate work record; the rest were economically dependent on family or pension. Although younger men, they were "old" and appeared to have little interest in anything. They indulged excessively in alcohol or drugs and were preoccupied with bodily symptoms and complaints.

RESIDUAL CASES. Fourteen cases (five suicide and nine control) could not be placed into any of the patterns identified. Among the suicides, either the data were too scarce for classification or the patients tended to display features common to several of the patterns described. The control cases, mostly younger men in their forties, had entered the hospital with a variety of somatic complaints but with no organic illness. Each seemed to look to the hospital for relief of some minor concern or as a refuge from a current crisis. They displayed little symptomatic disturbance in the hospital and recovery was, in most cases, both quick and uneventful. Six of the nine control cases were readily identified as nonsuicidal.

Discussion

Suicide occurs most often in persons who are in a disturbed emotional state. The task of predicting suicide potentially among anxious or depressed neurotic patients, by definition emotionally perturbed, becomes an especially difficult one. Even among such persons, accurate prediction is relatively infrequent. Its infrequency, however, emphasizes its seriousness and widespread impact when it does occur.

The task is one of identifying, within an already more susceptible group, those patients who might have higher suicidal potentiality. One goal of this study was to facilitate this identification by the specification of clues and patterns more frequently associated with suicidal behavior. Such patients might then be marked for special suicide prevention measures. It is probably true that the use of the clues and patterns might tend, in some instances, to

encompass too many patients. However, this may be neither inappropriate nor inefficient. The delineation of a group with probably higher suicidal potentiality does not assume that all such patients would kill themselves. Even among patients identified by a prior suicide attempt[12] or other prior suicide behavior[13] less than 10 percent go on to commit suicide. However, it is also true that suicidal events are more probable among persons in this group than among other nonsuicidal patients or nonpatients.[14] Once the more susceptible group has been identified, it follows that, as in many similar examples of physical disease, further intensive exploration can be made and appropriate preventive measures can more effectively be applied.

Some remarks about the results may be made:

1. In general, for identification purposes the suicidal patient is the more severely disturbed patient, both psychologically and behaviorally. Although all the patients had psychoneurotic diagnoses, the suicide patient had psychiatric symptoms that were more severe, with more depression, anxiety, tension, hostility, and agitation than the controls. Where there were physical complications, such as an illness, infection, or somatic disorder, there seemed to be no relief from treatment, thus adding to the discomfort and distress of the patient. Withdrawal, agitation, sleeplessness, sexual disturbances, and the like, exacerbated already deteriorated relationships. Withdrawal from, or insistent, intrusive demands on both staff and other patients reflected and produced strong negative feelings.

How useful is the general clue that the suicidal patients are the more seriously disturbed patients? Many neuropsychiatric patients are severely disturbed at one time or another. However, it is unlikely there are many patients, especially among the neurotics, who show such marked aberrations for a prolonged time. When the other clues are added, such as age, prior suicidal behavior, current self-destructive ideation, feelings of hopelessness even in the hospital, the possibility of identifying a potential suicidal acting-out increases greatly.

2. Another important suicidal indicator was a history of prior suicidal behavior, including thoughts of death, fantasies of rescue, expressions of "having had it," as well as an actual attempt, as

noted in previous studies.[14] Apparently, a person who has used this mode of behavior in the past is likely to use it again, and to carry the act through to completion.

3. Most of the suicide cases in this study were patients who were on neuropsychiatric wards within general medical and surgical hospitals. Others, however, entered the hospital for a physical illness and, while in the hospital, developed a neurotic reaction. Thus, eight out of the forty-three suicide cases (18%) had a diagnosis of anxiety or depressive reaction as the secondary diagnosis to a physical illness. The physician and other hospital staff on the ward, not just the psychiatrist and neuropsychiatric personnel, must be alert to the danger of suicide among their patients who develop severe anxiety and depression reactions. When this occurs, especially among older patients, a psychiatric consultation would be helpful in evaluating the suicidal danger. Besides giving the patient evidence of interest and concern on the part of the hospital staff, it helps the physician with recommendations and gives him the feeling of sharing the responsibility in the making of what might be a critical decision.

4. More than one third of the suicides were 55 years or older. This is of interest in that, generally, it has been thought that neurotic cases tended to be younger. It thus paralleled the often-reported finding among the general population that the suicidal danger increases with white males as they grow older.[15]

Within the tentatively identified patterns, there are theoretical as well as practical observations. In terms of age, the object-loss group was the only consistently young group (median age of 36). The involutional and egoistic groups were almost all older (median ages of 58 and 56, respectively). While the medical group included some younger people, it was also predominantly older (median age of 56).

One might speculate about a psychodynamic relationship between the object-loss and involutional groups. Despite the age difference there were marked similarities. In both groups there were severe blows to self-esteem and psychological integrity stemming either from the direct interpersonal relationship with a love-object or from functioning in the occupational area. In both groups there were feelings of inadequacy, worthlessness, inability, and uselessness. In the younger group marital and sexual problems

predominated, and some, but fewer, occupational problems. In the involutional group occupational difficulties predominated, with some, but fewer, marital and sexual problems.

Patients in the involutional group were not as passive dependent as those in the object-loss group. They seemed to have lived their lives with less disturbance and with obviously greater adjustment up to the time their current difficulty arose. While still essentially passive-dependent persons, they had been able to find appropriate life partners and work, and thus to effect a "good" adjustment for most of their lives. When a severe blow to their self-esteem occurred, either through the loss of a job, demotion, through a physical illness that pushed them into a dependency state, or through some sexual difficulty, for example, loss of virility, their defenses were shaken. They reacted with one of the more marked clues for suicide, an agitated depression that could not be relieved, filled with preoccupation, sleeplessness, tension, and worry.

The egoistic group was a much more puzzling group in that their disturbed psychological states seemed to occur without any significant precipitating event. These were borderline or schizoid persons who seemed more to exist on the fringe of society rather than to live in and be a part of it. In the hospital, too, they remained aloof from the staff and other patients, continuing their noninteractive ways. Within this group, although there were as many suicides as there were controls, there seemed to be a few recognizable differences between them. The suicides made many more demands from the hospital. They were excessively dependent, incapable of being gratified, complaining, manipulating, protesting, and rejecting. The hospital was no haven, but probably no place could have been. The suicidal patients within this group also seemed to become suicidal without precipitating cause. However, within the hospital, the two clues that seemed most useful for identification were the presence of prior or current suicidal behavior, either in threats or ruminations, and the excessive complaining, dissatisfied behavior they exhibited.

The medical group probably makes up around half of all those who receive either a primary or secondary diagnosis of anxiety or depressive reaction in general medical and surgical hospitals. Characteristically their emotional reaction was focused around a physical problem that apparently made them anxious and depressed

enough to warrant a neuropsychiatric diagnosis. But they differed from the other groups, especially the involutional, in one important aspect. In relation to their physical illness, they were relieved by the treatment they obtained and their symptoms subsided. The medical group also stood out from the other patients in that their interpersonal relationships were satisfactory, their marital relationships secure, and their sexual relationships gratifying. When emotional strain occurs between partners, a physical illness tends to take on many more subtle dynamic implications and may well become much more recalcitrant to treatment. Within a secure relationship, the physical illness tends to respond to treatment, anxiety diminishes, and relief can occur.

The preegoistic group of patients closely resembles the egoistic patients in life style. These groups differed from each other, however, in two aspects of their psychosocial adjustment: the preegoistic men were much younger and they were still on the fringe of social interaction. Their (lack of) social adjustment had not yet jelled or become brittle or chronic. The preegoistic men were also still close enough to remnants of relationships to resort to communication and "cries for help." Perhaps the more isolated and older "egoistic" men gave such little warning of their intentions because they lacked any important persons with whom to communicate.

Although the results of this study were obtained on a specific group, veterans with diagnoses of anxiety reaction or depressive reaction in general medical and surgical hospitals, the conclusions seem consistent with and generalizable to other public and private hospital populations.[16] In general, suicide may be seen as an aberrant, unusual, and complex phenomenon, arising out of intense inter- and intrapersonal needs. A feeling of identity and a meaningful self-concept are most important: When these are threatened, the very foundations of man's reasons for existence seem shaken, his hopes recede, and a sense of emptiness and loss pervades the individual. Tension mounts, straining the usual coping mechanisms and defenses. The struggle within each person becomes a measure of his tension tolerance. Because this level of tolerance fluctuates, the picture will vary and we will see "suicidal" persons swing up and down in their depressive feelings and emotionally disturbed behavior.

While the above formulations would seem to apply primarily to persons in the object-loss and involutional patterns, they also fit in part to those in the egoistic pattern. Although these men have largely withdrawn from society and their source of self-esteem does not depend so much upon relationships with others, they seem highly self-centered with a focus on bodily functioning and personal needs. When disruptions occur in these areas, they too react with self-destructive behavior.

Our results do not tell us why suicide is selected as a way out rather than some other resolution. To understand this would require knowing much more in depth about each individual in the study. Our results do tell us that, for the most part, suicide is preventable. Of most significance is that as the person struggles with his feelings, overt behavioral signs appear. These help identify and delineate the suicidal patient. Second, there is a fluctuation in the self-destructive impulses so that there is usually time and opportunity for intervention to occur. Third, ambivalence is always present and the man communicates his wish to live and to be saved at the same time he declares that he wants to die. Fourth, those measures aimed at restoring and supporting feelings of self-esteem, such as interest, concern, recognition, and acceptance on the part of the staff seem crucial. As Kline states:

> Warm rapport and time spent with the patient, even though it does not seem productive of important "insights," is the most valuable type of psychotherapy. It is not necessary constantly to attempt to stimulate the patient to conversation or participation. Simple human presence is important of itself. It is to be expected that the patient will over and over again ask for reassurance and although this will eventually become boring or even irritating to the personnel it is important that such reassurance be provided.[17]

Encouragement of the patient into as many other activities and adjunct therapies as possible is important. Direct discussion of suicidal tendencies with the patient helps give him the feeling he is understood.

It is also important that the family be integrated with the treatment process. The physician, psychiatrist, or psychiatric social worker can play a crucial role in informing the family about the

patient's condition and the suicidal danger, and in enlisting their aid. If the family cannot help, this must be recognized and the patient made aware of the probability that he cannot find, and should not seek, support there. Discharge to the family, or to the same environment that fostered his disturbance, without any change having occurred in that environment, merely invites a recurrence of the disturbance and potential suicidal acting out.

Chapter 21
SUICIDE AMONG CARDIOVASCULAR PATIENTS

Norman L. Farberow, John W. McKelligott,
Sidney Cohen, and Allen Darbonne

Intensive examination of cases of patients with respiratory and cardiac disease who committed suicide while in Veterans Administration General Medical and Surgical Hospitals, and of control cases matched in diagnosis, severity of illness, age, religion, and other factors, revealed a number of personality and behavior items that significantly differentiated between them. In general, the suicides seemed more emotionally disturbed, had poorer relationships with hospital staff and family, and were seen as "problem" patients because of their provoking, complaining, and demanding behavior. One major pattern of behavior emerged that was named the "dependent-dissatisfied" pattern. A number of suggestions are offered for prevention.

A survey of suicide among patients in general medical and surgical hospitals, and tuberculosis hospitals in the Veterans Administration, indicated that, except for cases with primary neuro-psychiatric diagnoses, the greatest numbers occurred among patients with long-term, serious illnesses, such as malignant neoplasms, and respiratory and circulatory disorders. In light of these facts, a series of investigations of these groups has been undertaken, and studies of suicide among patients with malignant neoplasms and neuro-psychiatric diagnosis have been reported.[1] This investigation focuses on patients in VA General Medical and Surgical Hospitals with cardiorespiratory illnesses who commit suicide. For this study patients with primary diagnoses of respiratory and cardiac illnesses are combined into the one general syndrome because symptoms such as dyspnea, tachycardia, and chest pain are common to both. It has the aim of identifying personality patterns and behavioral clues that might be useful in the understanding and prevention of suicide. The studies are part of a continuing investigation of suicide being carried out by the Veterans Administration Central Research Unit for the Study of Unpredicted Deaths.

Although the specific problem of suicide has not previously

been investigated among patients with respiratory and circulatory illnesses, the number of studies reporting on personality or emotional aspects of these illnesses is voluminous. A few of the relevant ones only are mentioned. Berle, Merrill, and Sparer may be referred to for reviews of the extensive literature on tuberculosis and personality.[2] Vernier *et al*[3] report a large-scale investigation of the psychosocial aspects of the tuberculosis patient. They describe the patient who adjusts well to the hospital as being older, more passive, and less intelligent than the patient who makes a poor adjustment. The "good" patient is apparently a person whose needs are being adequately met in the rather regimented, closely supervised atmosphere of the tuberculosis ward. The patient who makes a good community adjustment after discharge is the one who had a comparatively poor adjustment to hospitalization and relatively poor response to treatment for tuberculosis.

Albee felt that patients with tuberculosis, whom he compared with those other chronic illnesses, for example, arthritis, ulcer, and the like, were not as depressed or hypochondriacal.[4] He found no relation between the degree of emotional deviation and severity of the illness. Hawkins and co-workers compared tuberculosis patients with employees working at the same sanitarium.[5] They felt the patients had experienced a concentration of domestic strife, residential and occupational changes, and personal crises in the two years prior to contracting tuberculosis. Their tuberculosis group also evidenced significantly more psychoneurotic symptoms.

Knapp and Nemetz studied 406 episodes of acute asthmatic attacks in nine patients and concluded that, aside from a preoccupation with the physical aspects of the illness, the psychological concomitants that appeared most often were depressive features, a sense of sadness, helplessness, and hopelessness.[6] In a study of five patients with bronchial asthma who died, Kraft and associates felt that the excessive hostility that was conspicuous in the precipitation of their asthmatic attacks was so strong that it literally "choked them to death."[7] The patients felt driven further and further from their prior level of adjustment until it seemed as if death was the only way out. Figuratively, the patients killed themselves through their asthma, but more literally, one of the patients put her affairs in order and then stopped all medication. Another, knowing it would be fatal, took aspirin.

Webb and Lawton, investigating by means of anamnesis and the Szondi test, found that patients with primary obstructive pulmonary emphysema displayed many traits previously noted in the bronchial asthma group, namely, hypersensitivity, passivity, immaturity, and insecurity.[8] They also found tendencies toward self-effacement, concealment, and unobtrusiveness. The emphysema patients exhibited a more fickle, unstable emotional bond to worldly objects, both personal and material, than did the control groups.

There are also many studies of patients with cardiac disease investigating the relationship between the disease and personality. To cite a few, Duncan and Stevenson found that their patients with tachycardia or auricular fibrillation showed common personality traits of chronic anxiety, poorly expressed hostility, and compulsive behavior.[9] Arlow felt the fear of death was not the sole content in anxiety attacks of patients with angina pectoris.[10] Rather, the angina attack becomes the focus and point of discharge for earlier significant anxieties. Kaplan concluded that the emotional implications of cardiac disease will vary and will depend mainly upon the personality structure and life situations of the individual.[11] Cleveland and Johnson describe reactions to the trauma of a heart attack, such as profuse anxiety and fear.[12] The latter was related to the threat of imminent death or loss of physical capacity, or both. If, however, the initial attack is weathered, anxiety may be dissipated and adequate defenses instituted to cope with the imposed stress.

Procedures

For this study, ninety patients with cardiorespiratory illnesses, forty-five suicides and forty-five nonsuicide controls, were studied. Among the suicides, thirty were patients with primary diagnoses of respiratory disease. Patients with carcinoma of the lungs were not used, having been included in a previous study of suicide among patients with malignant neoplasms. Six respiratory cases (four Negroes and two Orientals) were excluded to avoid the complications of subcultural factors. The thirty suicide cases used in the study were the remaining total number of suicides among the patients with respiratory illnesses on file in the Central Research Unit. Fifteen suicides were patients with a primary diagnosis of cardiac disease. Each case of suicide was matched with a nonsuicide

control case that was selected on a man-for-man basis using the following variables: (1) disease—the same principal diagnosis; (2) age—plus or minus five years; (3) sex—all male; (4) race—all white; and (5) religion.

The study was terminated after fifteen suicides and fifteen controls among cardiac cases had been reviewed because of their similarity to the respiratory cases. This impression was verified statistically when comparisons between the respiratory and cardiac protocols yielded a nonsignificant number of differentiating items. In addition the fifteen suicide cardiac cases were compared with the remaining suicide cardiac disease cases, thirty-seven arteriosclerotic heart disease (ASHD) and three rheumatic heart disease (RHD), for age, diagnosis, and religion. No significant differences between the study group and the remaining cases were found, so that the groups of cases used can be considered a representative sample, within these characteristics. An additional twenty cases with a primary diagnosis of hypertensive cardiovascular disease (HCVD) are not represented. Even though a check showed that many of the ASHD cases also had a secondary diagnosis of HCVD (38%) and vice versa (50%), the study group still can not be considered representative of, nor should conclusions be applied to the HCVD cases.

The intensive analysis of each patient's chart used the procedure of the "psychological autopsy," described elsewhere.[13] Briefly, the six-step procedure consisted of the following: (1) the preparation of an abstract of each case; (2) blind presentation (without indication whether the case was a suicide or a control) to a research team; (3) a judgment by each person as to whether the case was a suicide or control, and the reasons why; (4) completion of a summary protocol evaluating the physical disease and personality factors obtained and the clues used for determining suicide or control status of the case; (5) disclosure of the outcome, suicide or control, and a discussion of the facilitating or misleading elements; and (6) synthesis of the similarities and differences between the suicidal and nonsuicidal cases.

Description of the Population

The essential characteristics of the suicide and control population are shown in Table I.

Diagnosis.—The principal diagnoses in the matched suicidal and

TABLE I—Characteristics of Suicide (S) and NonSuicide Control (C) General Medical and Surgical Hospital Patients With Cardiorespiratory Illnesses

Variables	Pulmonary Tuberculosis S 15	Pulmonary Tuberculosis C 15	Pulmonary Emphysema S 13	Pulmonary Emphysema C 13	Asthmatic Bronchitis S 2	Asthmatic Bronchitis C 2	Total S 30	Total C 30	Cardiac ASHD S 13	Cardiac ASHD C 13	Cardiac RHD S 2	Cardiac RHD C 2	Cardiac Total S 15	Cardiac Total C 15	Grand Total S 45	Grand Total C 45
No.																
Age																
70-79	0	0	0	2	0	0	0	2	1	0	0	0	1	0	1	2
60-69	5	5	9	8	2	2	16	15	7	9	0	0	7	9	23	24
50-59	3	3	4	3	0	0	7	6	5	4	1	1	6	5	13	11
40-49	1	2	0	0	0	0	1	2	0	0	0	0	0	0	1	2
30-39	5	5	0	0	0	0	5	5	0	0	0	1	0	1	5	6
20-29	1	0	0	0	0	0	1	0	0	0	1	0	1	0	2	0
Religion																
Protestant	6	6	9	9	2	2	17	17	6	6	1	1	7	7	24	24
Catholic	8	8	3	4[1]	0	0	11	12	7	7	1	1	8	8	19	20
Jew	0	0	0	0	0	0	0	0	0	0	0	0	0	0	0	0
Other or none	1	1	1	0	0	0	2	1	0	0	0	0	0	0	2	1
Marital Status																
Single	3	4	1	1	1	0	5	5	2	1	0	0	2	1	7	6
Married	5	8	7	10	1	1	13	19	7	8	1	0	8	8	21	27
Divorced	5	2	3	0	0	1	8	3	2	2	0	2	2	4	10	7
Separated	1	0	1	0	0	0	2	0	1	1	0	0	1	1	3	1
Widowed	1	1	1	2	0	0	2	3	1	1	1	0	2	1	4	4
No. of Hospitalizations																
1	1	4	2	2	0	1	3	7	5	5	1	0	6	5	9	12
2	1	3	2	6	0	0	3	9	2	1	0	1	2	2	5	11
3	5	2	3	1	1	0	9	3	1	2	0	1	1	3	10	6
4	0	3	1	0	0	1	1	4	1	2	0	0	1	2	2	6
5	4	2	2	0	0	0	6	2	1	0	1	0	2	0	8	2
>5	4	1	3	4	1	0	8	5	3	3	0	0	3	3	11	8
Severity of Illness																
Far advanced or severe	13	13	11	11	2	2	26	26	6	7	1	1	7	8	33	34
Moderately advanced or less	2	2	2	2	0	0	4	4	7	6	1	1	8	7	12	11
Method of Suicide																
Jump	6		8		1		15		9		1		10		25	
Cut	4		3		0		7		0		1		1		8	
Hang	2		2		0		4		3		0		3		7	
Gunshot wound	2		0		1		3		1		0		1		4	
Poison	1		0		0		1		0		0		0		1	

[1] One Russian Orthodox suicide was matched with a Catholic control.

control respiratory groups were as follows: pulmonary tuberculosis (15 cases), pulmonary emphysema (13 cases), and asthmatic bronchitis (2 cases). Among the matched suicidal circulatory groups, the principal diagnoses were arteriosclerotic heart disease (13 cases), rheumatic heart disease (2 cases).

Age.—The median ages for the subcategories were 52 for the tuberculosis patients, 63 for the emphysema group, and 62 for the ASHD patients. Among the controls, thirty-five (twenty-four respiratory and 11 circulatory cases) died; ten (6 respiratory and 4 circulatory cases) were discharged after receiving maximum hospital benefit.

The age distribution of the study group was compared with that of all the patients within the VA General Medical and Surgical Hospitals with the above principal diagnoses. In the total population, median ages were 47 for tuberculosis patients, 65 for emphysema patients and 66 for ASHD patients. Thus, no significant differences between the total population and our study population appeared.

Religion.—All suicides were matched for stated religion, except for one Russian Orthodox suicide case, which was matched with one Catholic control.

Marital Status.—Among the suicides, most of the patients in the emphysema and ASHD groups were married. There was a slight tendency for more tuberculosis patients to be divorced or single. The marital distribution for the suicidal respiratory patients was similar to the total VA population.

Number of Hospitalizations.—Three of the thirty patients with respiratory disease and six of the fifteen patients with circulatory disease committed suicide during their first VA hospitalization. The impact of a heart attack on the personality of the patient has been noted before.[14] In our study, fourteen of the thirty patients with respiratory illness survived five or more hospitalizations before they killed themselves, while five of the fifteen suicidal patients with heart disease had five or more hospitalizations.

Length of Illness.—The median length of time the suicides were ill of a respiratory disease, that is, from date of first diagnosis to date of death, was four years four months. The range was from two months to twenty-three years two months. The median length of time the controls were ill of respiratory disease was four years

eleven months. The median length of time the suicide circulatory cases were ill was eleven months, with a range from one week to nine years three months. The range was from one week to thirty-four years two months. For cardiac control cases the median was one year one month, with a range from seven days to twenty-seven years nine months.

Severity of the Illness.—The severity of the illness was determined either by the ward doctor's evaluation as listed in the file or by the judgment of the research staff medical consultant. In our study, it is apparent that among the patients with respiratory disease, those who kill themselves are more often severely ill (see Table I). Although data on the percentage of severely ill patients among the population of VA respiratory cases do not exist, it is highly unlikely that 85 percent would fall into this category. Among the cardiac cases about half were considered moderately or less seriously ill. From this and from the fact that the control cases had diagnoses equally severe, it is apparent that while the severity of the illness may play a role, it is not crucial to the decision to kill oneself.

Method of Suicide.—Most of the patients (25 of 45) committed suicide by jumping, the method most commonly used in general hospitals. Cutting (eight patients) and hanging (seven patients) occurred next most often. Four patients shot themselves while on pass. One patient used poison by bringing a can of hydrogen cyanide gas with him when he returned from a pass and allowing the gas to escape into his room at night. He hung a sign on his door asking not to be disturbed and warning the personnel to be careful on entering.

Results

Judges.—Five members were consistently present at the respiratory research conferences and three were also present at the heart conferences. Their "proficiency" in predicting the suicide and control cases was recorded. The guesses varied from 68 percent to 82 percent correct for each of the individual researchers.

In forty-eight of the cases (53%) there was unanimous agreement about the correct outcome; nineteen were suicides and twenty-nine were controls. The outcome in fourteen cases (16%) was unanimously predicted wrong; seven of these patients were suicides and seven were controls.

TABLE II—Accuracy of Prediction of Suicidal or Nonsuicidal Outcome of Cases by Research Conference Members

	Accuracy					
	Suicides		Controls		Total	
Judges[1]	No.	%	No.	%	No.	%
1	18/33	55	28/33	85	46/66	70
2	34/40	85	31/39	79	65/79	82
3	28/41	68	29/36	81	57/77	74
4	9/15	60	10/13	77	19/28	68
5	7/10	70	8/10	80	15/20	75
Unanimous right	19/45	42	29/45	64	48/90	53
Unanimous wrong	7/45	16	7/45	16	14/90	16

[1] All judges were present for the respiratory conferences; judges 1-3 were present for the cardiac conferences.

General Results.—A protocol containing 107 items was used to summarize the research group's impressions for each case at the end of each conference on respiratory cases. This protocol was modified for the circulatory cases and nonapplicable items eliminated so that it contained sixty-seven items. Judgments on the items were made before outcome of the case was revealed. By means of a chi-square analysis, the significance of the differences for the items between all the suicide and nonsuicide cases was determined. Thirty-three items were found to be statistically significant ($P < 0.05$), a number greater than would be expected to occur by chance. In addition, five items that could be scored for the respiratory cases but not for the circulatory cases (because of lack of information) were significant (Table III).

The thirty-eight significant items were then subgrouped into the following general categories of behavior or feelings:

Emotional Status in Hospital.—The suicides were more emotionally disturbed both prior to and while in the hospital. They seemed to be more hostile, anxious, agitated, apprehensive, depressed, and distressed over their illness than the controls. They had disturbances in body image and seemed more defeated by their illnesses. They were also seen as more often dependent and complaining than the controls, creating disturbances on the ward that labeled them as "bad" patients. It is, therefore, not surprising that more psychiatric consultations were requested for them. The suicides were most often judged by the research staff to be in need of psy-

TABLE III—Items Significantly Differentiating Between Suicidal
and Nonsuicidal Patients With Respiratory or Cardiac Illness

Items	X^2 Value
Significant at 0.0005 Level	
Patient felt hospital was not supportive	37.04
Patient was indifferent or hostile to hospital	22.49
Psychiatric consultation would have been helpful	17.40
Hospital low in support	16.01
Agitated	14.98
Depressed	14.70
Felt defeated by illness[1]	11.59
Apprehensive	11.40
Dependent-dissatisfied	10.87
Significant at 0.005 Level	
Hospital uninterested or unaccepting	10.44
Complaining	10.00
Distressed	9.65
Psychiatric consultation requested	7.98
Intolerant of pain and discomfort	7.97
Dependent personality	7.77
Insomnia	7.70
Known changes of psychological significance between hospitalizations[1]	7.18
Significant at 0.025 Level	
Felt he was getting worse	6.04
Less often struggling to overcome illness	5.05
Dependent upon hospital	4.88
Less alert and aware	4.87
Less family support[1]	4.65
Inadequate interpersonal relations with other patients and staff	4.45
Quiet or withdrawn[1]	4.43
Given placebos	4.38
Average implementer rating	4.09
Hostility	3.87
Significant at 0.05 Level	
Significant change in body image	3.80
Previous suicidal threats and attempts	3.73
Anxious	3.69
Requested repeat medications	3.62
Confusion from disease[1]	3.51
Impulsive	3.39
"Bad" patient	3.34
Service connected	3.26
Three or more hospitalizations	2.99
Less ill at end of report than controls	2.89
Not cooperative with hospital	2.89

[1] Significant for patients with respiratory illness only.

chiatric consultations, even when these had not been requested. At the same time the suicides were seen as more alert and aware than the controls. When confusion did occur, it was more likely to be of emotional origin. Within the respiratory group only, the suicides were noted to be more withdrawn.

Physical Status.—The suicides required more frequent hospitalizations than the controls. During their hospitalization, they more often had symptoms of insomnia. They were given more placebos from which they often obtained relief.

Reactions to the Illness.—The suicides were seen as more distressed over their illness. They felt they were getting worse, and struggled less to overcome it. Among the respiratory group, they seemed to feel defeated by the illness more often.

Patient's Attitude Toward the Hospital.—The suicides had poorer interpersonal relationships with the staff and the patients than the controls and saw the hospital as hostile and indifferent toward them. They did not feel they could count on the hospital for support, even though they were judged more dependent on it. The suicides more often request medications, made more frequent demands, and were considered less cooperative than the controls.

Hospital's Attitude Toward the Patient.—The hospital apparently saw these patients as "bad" ward problems and reacted to them with hostility or indifference, offering less support to them than to the controls. Notes of irritation, and of watching the patient to see if he was feigning pain or discomfort or seeking attention were found more frequently in the records of the suicides.

Family Relationships.—Little information was available in the medical records about family relationships. One impression was that suicidal patients with pulmonary disease more often lacked family support while in the hospital than the controls.

Nonsignificant Items.—A number of items that had originally been included on the basis of prior experience, interest, or hypothesis did not yield significant differences when the suicidal and control groups were compared. It is possible, however, that this was due to lack of information rather than a true lack of significance. Among these items were those related to military history, educational status, or occupational history. Although other investigators have speculated that retirement contributes to a loss of feeling of pur-

posefulness, the category of "retired from work" did not yield a significant difference. Items related to financial status were also not significant, with the suicides in neither better nor poorer financial condition than the controls.

Recreational or outside interest while in the hospital did not differentiate between suicidal or control patients. Isolation as a result of the illness, the length of stay during the final hospitalization, and the efficacy of the medical treatment procedures all were statistically nonsignificant.

Among the personality items, there were no differences among the two groups in terms of alcoholism or drug addiction. Insofar as could be judged, there seemed to be no differences in religious interest. Whether the patient was able to see his family more often because of geographical proximity, or was isolated as a result of the illness, also was not differentiating.

Some physical aspects of the illnesses were also checked to see if they played an important role in the suicide. The assumption that the suicidal patient would experience more difficulty in breathing was not confirmed. There were no differences between the two groups in the amount of pain and discomfort experienced but tolerance to pain or discomfort was less in the suicidal patients.

The Dependent-Dissatisfied Person.—A consistent personality pattern emerged among the suicides that might be labeled, tentatively, the dependent-dissatisfied personality. Those cases that combined a high level of both dependency and complaining behavior presented a significant suicidal pattern ($P < 0.001$). Twenty-six of the suicides fit this pattern whereas only ten controls did. (One of the ten controls had previously made a serious suicide attempt.) The opposite combination of low ratings on both dependency and dissatisfaction was equally predictive of nonsuicidal outcome. Twenty-five controls and eight suicides were low in both variables. Individuals rated high in either area and low in the other were approximately equally distributed between suicides and controls.

The dependent-dissatisfied person, in general, seemed to be disturbed in his relationships both outside and in the hospital. Family history showed more divorces and separations, less family support, and premature returns from passes. In the hospital this patient was often described as hostile, agitated, apprehensive, depressed, com-

plaining, and distressed over his illness. He was constantly demanding some kind of activity or behavior on the part of the hospital
personnel that represented special attention.

False Negatives.—Seven patients who were actually suicides were
judged controls by the reviewing research team. It was considered
important to reexamine these "missed" cases and note what might
have been misleading. These cases were rated moderate to high in
dependency but low in dissatisfaction characteristics in the research
conferences. In their behavior in the hospital, the patients complained little and were not aggressive. They seemed to be relatively
inactive and did not display much agitation. Their behavior did not
undergo any change toward the end of the illness. In their past experiences, they revealed a more or less stable work record with no
suicidal history. They did not appear to be very depressed, nor did
they need psychiatric consultations because of emotional disturbance. Their relationships with the patients and staff of the
hospital seemed to be adequate. They did display a high level of apprehension, which, however, was related to pain and discomfort
and seemed appropriate to the severity of the illness. In general,
these patients were remarkably similar in behavior and in their
response to the stress of their illness to most of the controls. In many
cases the suicidal death came as a complete surprise, both to the
hospital staff and to the research team.

False Positives.—There were also seven cases of controls that
were judged to be suicides by all the research team. These cases
showed a suicidal history, some degree of hostility and agitation, depression, apprehension, impulsivity, feelings of defeat, and the like.
In general, they seemed very similar to the dependent-dissatisfied
cases. One of the main reasons why these cases were taken as
suicides was the fact that they were much more complaining, demanding, and were greater ward problems than most of the controls. However, they also seemed to receive support from hospital
and family.

Comment

Suicide is the end result of a number of antecedent conditions.
Often, a prominent contributor to these conditions is the stress of
physical illness. This study focused on patients with cardiorespiratory disease who were thus exposed to one kind of physical syn-

drome: long-term, generally debilitating, pulmonary or cardiac illness. Most patients with cardiorespiratory diseases do not kill themselves; only a small number do. The question is whether it is possible to delineate within this particular group those characteristics that might point to patients with a higher potentiality for suicide.

In our study thirty-eight suicidal "identifying" items were obtained from illness, population, personality, and behavioral data on patients who had already killed themselves. Further studies, it is hoped, will help to sharpen as well as to eliminate some of the items. At this point, however, it seems desirable to be overinclusive of items (and therefore of patients) in pursuing the goal of identification of suicidal potentiality. It would seem better to err on the side of overinclusion than to be exclusive and to miss patients. Only a small percentage of the persons identified as "potentially suicidal" would probably go on to kill themselves. It is precisely this group, however, that contributes the greatest number of later lethal acting-out cases. Identification of such a person does not mean that strict suicide precautions should automatically and arbitrarily be imposed. It does mean that the index of alertness in hospital personnel should be raised about suspicious subsequent behavior of the people in this group.

With these preliminary comments, what characteristics have been specified and what suggestion can be made to prevent suicidal behavior?

1. In general, a heightened emotional disturbance emerged as one of the more significant clues. This does not mean that the patient was psychotic, grossly disturbed, or even a markedly confused person. Most patients show some emotional disturbance in an understandable and appropriate reaction to a physical disease, such as in patients with severe pulmonary illness or in cardiac patients who are suffering their first heart attack. Dovenmeuhle and Verwoerdt have pointed out that the first onset of cardiac disease, whether mild or severe, is apt to be accompanied by marked depressive symptoms.[15] In our study the emotional disturbance was a matter of degree. The people who committed suicide were more agitated, depressed, anxious, and distressed than the controls. They were noted to be vociferous, complaining, and upsetting to the staff. They were continually dissatisfied and demanding. If a judgment

had been made, they would have been called "bad" patients. They were ambivalent in their relationships with people; they wanted support but made themselves obnoxious and defeated attempts to be helped. At times they would withdraw, angry and disappointed by the rebuffs that they themselves elicited.

2. External support, whether from family or from the hospital personnel, was a distinct deterrent to suicide. We believe that many suicides are averted when depressed, chronically suffering patients know that other people care. Suicide can be a hostile act and an accusatory communication directed against the cold, rejecting survivors. Seriously ill patients in pain often consider their own self-destruction; the restraining influence is frequently "I can't do this to my family." When outside supports are unavailable and the patient literally "has nothing left to live for," the hospital must serve as the friendly, interested "family." It is our impression that when the hospital ward was manned by personnel who looked upon their patients as people and were concerned with their welfare, that the incidence of suicide was low. Where the attitude of the staff was impersonal, distant, or uninterested, the potentiality of suicide increased.

3. The communication processes within a hospital can serve as an antisuicide device. It is now well known that the suicidal patient gives prior indications of his intent by word or behavior. If an aide or nurse receives such a communication, it should be transmitted to the responsible physician. He may wish to obtain a psychiatric opinion, thus sharing the responsibility and obtaining information about the suicide potential of the patient.

4. The greater use of ancillary professional personnel would be helpful. The psychiatrist, psychologist, or psychiatric social worker may be called on to deal with the death wishes and thoughts expressed by the patient. They can also be of assistance in the management of psychological problems connected with habituation or addiction to analgesics, overdependency upon oxygen or the positive pressure apparatus, panic states when the patient comes to realize his prognosis, difficult behavior, or sudden, unaccountable mood swings.

5. The suicidal group was more concerned with their body functions and were less able to tolerate pain than the controls. The

significance of their physical distress seemed more troubling to them. The control group seemed to have as much pain but its meaning was less ominous to them. Dyspnea, which had originally been assumed to be an important factor in predicting suicide, did not emerge as such. It had been thought that an inability to draw an effortless breath would be an important psycholgoical as well as physiological stress. This may still be so, but those who eventually committed suicide were no more dyspneic than their controls. (The study design, it will be recalled, matched patients on severity of illness.) Weiss's symptom of "sighing respiration," anticipated in the suicides because of their greater emotional disturbance, was not evident, probably because the symptom could not be differentiated from dyspnea stemming directly from the disease.[16]

6. The false negatives, those cases judged incorrectly to be controls who turned out to be suicide, deserve special mention. Their suicidal termination came as a complete surprise to the members of the research conference, for their story and what could be learned of their character structure were very similar to the nonsuicidal patients. Two possible explanations occur. One is that relatively intact personalities, when faced with a difficult period of impending death, may make a "rational" decision to destroy themselves. A second explanation might be that their apparent "normal" personality is merely the reflection of inadequate hospital records. It may be worthwhile to restudy these cases, interview the survivors, and determine whether or not their "normal" personality was simply due to sparse information.

In this regard we can confirm the paucity of personality information in many general hospital records. Consideration might be given to the obtaining of pertinent sociopsychiatric data during the admissions procedure; this could be done by giving the patient or his relatives a questionnaire to complete, which could be filed in his chart.

7. Certain simple procedures might prevent an occasional suicide. For example, the bathroom is a relatively private place where suicidal activities are often instigated. A few precautions, such as stops on the windows allowing them to be opened only a few inches, or safety screens, might be sufficient deterrent to prevent an impulsive suicide or the completion of a planned suicide. Rooms can

be inspected for the elimination of overhead bars from which a hanging can be consummated. Experience has shown that such practical safeguards are effective, especially in deterring impulsive suicides.

8. The most important antisuicidal measures remain the sensitivity and alertness of the staff to the suicidal danger and the indication of interest and concern for the patient as a person.

Chapter 22
CASE HISTORY AND NEUROPSYCHIATRIC HOSPITALIZATION FACTORS IN SUICIDE
Norman L. Farberow, Edwin S. Shneidman, and Charles Neuringer

A retrospective study of 218 suicides and 220 controls was conducted at the Veterans Administration Central Research Unit and the Suicide Prevention Center, both in Los Angeles. The study focused on sociological matrix data, especially information relating to early experiences that might highlight important developmental sequences specific to suicide. Among the statistically significant items found were population statistics, clinical diagnoses, early childhood factors, marital histories, educational achievements, military history, prehospital difficulties, and behavior patterns in the hospital.

The phenomena of suicide have been studied from many aspects, but in general two primary approaches have been identified with the sociological and psychological points of view. The sociological approach has focused on large-scale accumulations of data about people who have committed suicide. The extensive surveys by Morselli, Durkheim, and Halbwachs,[1] and the more specialized studies of Cavan, Schmid and Von Arsdol, and Yap[2] have concentrated on differences in frequencies and proportions of suicide among large population groups distinguished by such factors as age, sex, religion, socioecomonic status, race, marital status, and occupation. There are very few sociological studies of attempted or threatened suicides, probably because most governments do not systematically collect data about them; indeed, in most jurisdictions official reports of suicide attempts or threats are not required.

Most psychological studies are attempts to examine the motivation, dynamics, and personality characteristics of the suicidal person. Most of these data come from living people who have threatened suicide or who attempted suicide and survived. Freud, Menninger, N.D.C. Lewis, Ringel, Stengel and Cook, Shneidman, and

others have speculated on the intrapsychic characteristics of people who attempt suicide.[3] A few psychological studies have attempted to assemble data on people who completed suicide—from documents and from the accounts of people who knew the deceased.[4] The scarcity of such reports reflects the difficulties of collecting important psychological data on persons who are already dead.

The line between the two areas has grown steadily less defined. Psychologists refer to social factors in their theoretical formulations of the causation of suicide (e.g., economic, political, and religious conflicts, depressions in reaction to loss of status, blows to self-concept, dependency frustration in reactions to divorce, separation, or death) ; while sociologists rely heavily on psychological mechanisms to explain the link between "social forces" and individual self-destruction (cf. Durkheim's "egoistic" suicide in which the person no longer finds anything of value in his social environment, hence no *raison d'être* for himself; or "anomic" suicide in which social restraints on aspiration are removed, so that individuals are no longer content with what they have genuinely achieved or can reasonably get).

The present study is part of a larger program of investigation of the social and psychological aspects of suicide being carried out in the Central Research Unit of the Veterans Administration and the Suicide Prevention Center of Los Angeles. One significant part of this program has been the intensive examination of small nosological groups in which suicide has occurred, such as patients with diagnoses of schizophrenia, anxiety, depression, cancer, cardiac and respiratory diseases. Large-scale investigations have examined the sociological and psychological characteristics of committed and attempted suicides in Los Angeles and various aspects of committed suicides in the Veterans Administration. This study attempts to combine both large- and small-scale approaches in a detailed examination of sociopsychological case history data and recorded hospital behavior as found in the files of neuropsychiatric hospital veterans who committed suicide.

The extensive case records of veterans who had committed suicide since 1950 while on VA hospital rolls were deposited within the Central Research Unit for examination and study. Cases were obtained from the almost two hundred neuropsychiatric, general medical and surgical, and tuberculosis hospitals and domiciliaries

which make up the Veterans Administration hospital system. Control cases were collected at the same time by requiring that when a suicide case was sent to the Central Research Unit it be accompanied by the case record—the next one in file—of a discharged veteran who had not committed suicide. The case record included all of the summaries, reports, and notes on the patient, such as case histories, doctors' notes, nurses' notes, laboratory studies, psychology reports, social work investigations, and correspondence files. Also included were all the ancillary therapies found in today's hospitals, that is, educational, industrial, vocational, and correctional therapies.

The task set for the present study was to find any empirical relationships between a person's taking his own life and historical and/or hospital events in his life. If it can be assumed that particular experiences during a lifetime have profound and lasting effects on a person, it would be hoped that these experiences would be revealed in the data accumulated about patients in neuropsychiatric hospitals and that they might be delineated in such a way so as to differentiate suicidal patients from nonsuicidal patients. If so, the identification of such "suicide-significant" characteristics within a person's life should shed considerable light on the complex and confused problem of suicide. In addition, if hospital experiences serve to differentiate suicidal from nonsuicidal veterans, the exposition of such events might serve to facilitate early recognition and precaution.

Procedures

COLLECTION OF DATA. In order to collect, categorize, and record the data available within the case records, it was first necessary to prepare a protocol that would abstract all of the essential data contained in the hospital case record in a form suitable for electronic machine processing. Items to be included in the protocol were obtained from three sources. The first was the social histories themselves. Fifteen social histories were chosen at random and items were extracted from the case records using a critical incident technique. The frequency with which each item appeared in the case history was tabulated. Items that occurred five or more times were included.

A second source of items was the typical social history schedules that have been developed over many years and are in common use. These were scanned and items judged to be significant in the sociopsychological development of an individual were selected.

The third source was the personnel of the Central Research Unit and the Suicide Prevention Center who were asked to contribute items they felt to be important. These items were thus based on the experiences of persons who had been working in the area of suicide for several years.

More than one thousand items covering a varied range of topics such as parental background, educational experiences, marital history, and behavior in the hospital were gathered in a preliminary form. All the items were phrased positively and, except for those that required numerical answers, were worded so that they could be answered with "yes," "no," "don't know," "doesn't apply," or "no information." The form then underwent a series of revisions. Ambiguities in phrasing, unclear words, and repetitive items were eliminated by the judges' evaluations of the clarity and explicitness of the items. For each revision the form was tried out by having several raters abstract a case, after which there was a discussion of each item. This procedure was repeated a total of seven times until a schedule, called "Form G" and containing 540 items, was finally evolved and deemed acceptable.

The reliability of Form G was tested by asking four judges to abstract the same five cases chosen at random from the files. The percentage of agreement on the ratings was computed and found to range from .89 to .91 with a mean of .91, a level of reliability that was considered adequate.

POPULATION. Four hundred and thirty-eight case records of male neuropsychiatric hospital patients were examined. (Only male patients were used inasmuch as only two percent of VA neuropsychiatric hospital population are females and it was decided not to confound the data with the proportionally few available female suicide cases.) Of these, 218 were records of mental hospital patients who had committed suicide while on hospital rolls. These cases, selected randomly, were a large sample (55 percent) of the total number of neuropsychiatric hospital suicide records ($N = 393$) that had been received at the Central Research Unit at the time of

the study. The control group was composed of 220 cases of neuro-psychiatric hospital patients who had not committed suicide, randomly selected from the control cases available.

In order adequately to generalize any results obtained from the comparisons between the suicides and controls, it was necessary that the control group used in this study be a representative sample of the total Veterans Administration neuropsychiatric patient population. The control cases were therefore compared with the general Veterans Administration neuropsychiatric population on the characteristics of age, race, and diagnosis. Data for these characteristics were supplied by the VA Biometrics Service. When the distributions of the age, race, and diagnosis of the study control population were compared with those of the total VA neuropsychiatric population, no significant differences were found. Our control cases thus seemed to be an adequate representative sample of the VA neuropsychiatric hospital population at large.

ABSTRACTING OF CASES. The names of all the suicide cases were typed on cards and then shuffled. The resulting randomized sequence of names was typed onto a list. The same procedure was followed for the controls. The abstractors were then instructed randomly to select cases to abstract from the two lists. The abstracting of the suicide and control cases was alternated in order to control for learning effects. All the abstractors were graduate students in clinical psychology, who were trained by the authors in the use of the protocol and the procedures to be followed in the abstracting.[5]

Results

CHARACTERISTICS OF THE SUICIDAL GROUP. Of the 218 suicides studied, 132 persons (60 percent) committed suicide while out of the hospital, i.e., on leave, on trial visit, on pass, or AWOL. The remaining eighty-six patients (40 percent) committed suicide in the hospital or on the hospital grounds. Eighty-six patients (40 percent) committed suicide by hanging, forty-nine (22 percent) by gunshot, and twenty-one (10 percent) by jumping from a high place. The methods used by the remaining sixty-two patients (28 percent) were evenly distributed among the many other modalities of self-destruction.[6]

TABLE I—Items Significantly Differentiating Suicide and Non-Suicide (Control) Patients[1]

No.[2]	Item	Suicide N=218			Control N=220			χ^2 [4]
		Yes	No	Total[3]	Yes	No	Total[3]	
01-46	S's mother was a housewife.	95	123	218	59	161	220	12.80
01-59	S's father had a nervous breakdown.	11	207	218	1	219	220	7.02
01-67	S's mother had a nervous breakdown.	22	89	111	5	82	87	7.05
02-53	It was reported that S felt guilty about childhood masturbation.	25	193	218	9	211	220	7.33
02-55	As a child S had friends of the same sex.	64	154	218	36	184	220	9.76
02-68	S is preoccupied or obsessed with sex.	45	173	218	21	199	220	9.68
03-29	S and spouse share leisure-time activities.	21	17	38	8	30	38	8.00
03-30	While S was married, he stayed away from home evenings.	7	25	32	20	16	36	9.00
03-64	It was reported that S has had strange religious visions and experiences.	40	61	101	17	57	74	4.60
03-68	S finished college.	22	183	205	8	175	183	4.59
03-69	S was a poor student.	38	99	137	49	46	95	12.44
03-80	S was only a farmer.	15	186	201	6	200	206	4.30
04-28	While S was in the service, he was in front line combat.	39	127	166	45	79	124	4.99
04-53	It was reported that S had frequent physical ill-nesses.	26	84	110	41	54	95	7.80
04-54	S has had a prior nervous breakdown or psychotic illness.	106	81	187	73	91	164	4.66
04-55	S has had surgery (excluding tonsil and appendix removal)	66	101	167	84	72	156	6.03
04-56	It was reported that S suffers from ulcers at the present time.	7	89	96	24	75	99	11.14
04-57	S suffers from heart disease.	19	191	210	52	155	207	17.83
04-62	It was reported that S has been in one or more accidents (excluding motor vehicle accidents).	33	36	69	57	21	78	8.67

Code	Description						
04-64	It was reported that S has had a serious physical illness.	42	84	126	103	54	157	27.52
04-67	S has an alcoholic problem.	56	144	200	80	117	197	6.44
04-68	S has had a psychotic break in which he either had hallucinations or delusions.	164	45	209	106	84	190	22.20
04-80	It was reported that S has had severe depressions while in the hospital.	121	55	176	34	88	122	46.09
05-38	S received individual psychotherapy during his last psychiatric hospitalization.	59	129	188	27	166	193	15.38
05-41	S received group psychotherapy during his last psychiatric hospitalization.	67	120	187	20	172	192	32.86
05-44	S received therapeutic brain surgery (lobotomy, lobectomy, etc.) during his last psychiatric hospitalization.	7	210	217	0	213	213	4.92
05-45	S was on a tranquilizer drug therapy regime during his last psychiatric hospitalization.	159	52	211	116	91	207	36.37
05-47	S received electroshock therapy during last psychiatric hospitalization.	68	146	214	24	187	211	24.71
05-50	S received insulin coma therapy during last psychiatric hospitalization.	32	178	210	15	195	210	6.92
05-53	S received educational therapy during last psychiatric hospitalization.	51	147	198	32	153	185	4.03
05-54	S received physical therapy during last psychiatric hospitalization.	94	104	198	59	136	195	11.45
05-55	S received corrective therapy during last psychiatric hospitalization.	99	96	195	67	121	188	8.25
05-56	S received occupational therapy during last psychiatric hospitalization.	167	37	204	100	90	190	37.70
05-57	S complained if tranquilizers were not prescribed for him.	26	86	112	3	103	106	17.72
05-61	While S was in the hospital he was visited more than once by relatives (other than spouse).	123	62	185	91	81	172	6.23
05-62	S was allowed to go on passes during his last psychiatric hospitalization.	162	51	213	105	98	203	26.08
05-65	Did S return to the hospital early from trial visits voluntarily?	32	34	66	12	37	49	6.00
05-66	Did S become anxious while on trial visits?	47	9	56	8	36	44	35.57

TABLE I—*Continued*

No.[2]	Item	Suicide N=218			Control N=220			χ^2 [4]
		Yes	No	Total[3]	Yes	No	Total[3]	
05-67	Did S elope (AWOL) from the hospital or his ward?	94	114	208	37	171	208	67.92
05-69	It was reported that S paced on the ward and/or was considered hyperactive.	103	59	162	46	91	137	25.27
05-80	S was violent at times and had to be restrained during his last psychiatric hospitalization.	67	125	192	43	161	204	8.67
06-10	S got into fist fights with the other patients.	63	139	202	32	169	201	12.11
06-11	It was reported that S had crying spells.	61	60	121	41	72	113	4.14
06-12	S was described as being withdrawn and/or mute during his last psychiatric hospitalization.	133	64	197	79	100	179	19.73
06-13	Was it ever mentioned that S was considered to be suicidal during his last psychiatric hospitalization?	121	93	214	42	171	213	62.18
06-14	Suicidal threats made by S were recorded during his last psychiatric hospitalization.	87	112	199	20	181	201	57.35
06-15	Suicidal attempts made by S were recorded during his last psychiatric hospitalization.	51	149	200	3	199	202	47.43
06-16	If S was ever on suicidal status (maximum security), was he taken off this status at a later date?	94	23	117	31	30	61	15.18
06-42	Chronic brain syndrome due to cerebral arteriosclerosis.	10	208	218	30	190	220	6.32
06-51	Manic depressive psychosis.	18	200	218	7	213	220	4.31
06-54	Schizophrenic reaction, hebephrenic type.	30	188	218	16	204	220	4.21
06-56	Schizophrenic reaction, paranoid type.	103	115	218	67	153	220	12.22
06-57	Schizophrenic reaction, undifferentiated type.	67	151	218	43	177	220	6.66
06-70	Psychoneurotic disorder, anxiety reaction.	26	192	218	43	177	220	4.21
06-76	Personality disorder, inadequate personality.	2	216	218	10	210	220	4.11
07-08	Personality disorder, aggressive personality.	3	215	218	14	206	220	5.99
07-59	Number of Ss making suicide attempts.	83	135	218	17	203	220	60.88

Item	Description						
08-36	S has obsessive thoughts or compulsions.	96	61	157	51	69	120	8.52
08-39	S is depressed.	142	45	187	86	72	158	16.58
11-08	S has never demanded to leave the hospital.	98	106	204	126	74	200	8.55
11-09	Doesn't seem to realize he is really ill.	116	81	197	93	99	192	3.85
11-14	S on occasion demanded to be released from the hospital.	104	99	203	75	125	200	7.15
11-17	Has been loud and demanding on occasion.	84	116	200	62	133	195	3.99
11-18	Has on occasion been assaultive toward a staff member.	58	149	207	31	173	204	9.21
11-19	Has seldom asked for any kind of treatment or medication.	122	84	206	142	61	203	4.68
11-20	S seems to feel safer in the hospital.	97	34	131	54	57	111	15.27
11-26	S does not really want to leave the hospital.	67	67	134	30	94	124	16.97
11-29	Needs constant attention and reassurance.	48	133	181	32	153	185	3.97
11-32	Not restless.	76	135	211	123	76	199	26.00
11-33	Not impulsive.	92	111	203	129	55	184	23.02
11-35	Seldom expresses any feelings of inadequacy or inferiority.	125	74	199	163	29	192	23.33
11-36	Is usually isolated and withdrawn.	111	92	203	86	110	196	4.20
11-38	Has been extremely restless on occasion.	126	79	205	78	117	195	17.44
11-39	On occasion has impulsively assaulted others, struck fists against wall, etc.	78	134	212	38	166	204	16.04
11-45	Has in past on some occasion impulsively struck things, overturned tables, etc.	65	134	199	25	167	192	20.05
11-47	Has on occasion expressed feelings of lack of personal worth and inadequacy.	87	103	190	49	129	178	12.28
11-49	Has previous history of suicidal activity and has been suicidal in hospital on occasion.	66	134	200	7	181	188	53.31
11-50	Is frequently restless, pacing.	90	115	205	27	173	200	44.73
11-51	Can be very impulsive on occasion.	116	83	199	60	124	184	24.17
11-53	Has frequently expressed feelings of lack of personal worth and inadequacy.	58	140	198	19	178	197	22.90
11-55	Has previous history of suicidal activity and has threatened suicide in the hospital or has made mild attempts.	66	134	200	5	184	189	58.89
11-59	S has never tried to elope.	113	99	212	170	43	213	32.82

TABLE I—Continued

No.[2]	Item	Suicide N=218			Control N=220			χ^2[4]
		Yes	No	Total[3]	Yes	No	Total[3]	
11-62	Shows no particular tension or anxiety with passes and leaves away from hospital.	60	85	145	89	22	111	36.60
11-63	Feels he can do all right away from the hospital.	88	46	134	114	15	129	17.57
11-64	Has mixed feelings toward home environment.	101	30	131	72	54	126	10.63
11-65	S has eloped or demanded to leave the hospital.	115	94	209	72	139	211	17.60
11-66	Although quieter with tranquilizing drugs, patient does not seem to have learned new methods of coping with home environment.	106	15	121	55	18	73	3.95
11-67	S is being released into same environment from which he was originally hospitalized.	77	62	139	126	39	165	13.89
11-68	Shows some tension and anxiety with passes and leaves away from the hospital.	89	52	141	29	81	110	31.71
11-69	Has on occasion said that he was afraid he couldn't control his impulses away from the hospital.	23	133	156	7	157	164	9.06
11-73	S is much happier in the hospital than out.	51	63	114	20	76	96	12.10
11-74	Resists passes and leaves away from the hospital, shows tension and anxiety with them.	24	141	165	7	130	137	6.20
11-77	S has threatened to elope or go AMA but doesn't really want to leave the hospital.	18	137	155	7	148	155	4.32
11-78	Tranquilizing drugs don't seem to do much for S; still unhappy most of the time.	84	44	128	31	40	71	7.98
11-79	S is unhappy in hospital and out of hospital too.	110	33	143	52	58	110	22.20

[1] By chi-square.

[2] Numbers refer to card and item number in original protocol.

[3] "Total" is the sum of frequencies of "yes" and "no." Differences between "Total" and "N" shows the number of cases lost to "doesn't apply," "don't know," and "no information" categories.

[4] Chi-squares (χ^2) at various significance levels for one degree of freedom are: $<.05 = 3.84$; $<.01 = 6.64$.

Ninety patients (41 percent) had made a previous suicide attempt. It is likely that this is a minimal figure in that some attempts did not find their way into the records. Ninety-four patients (43 percent) had made previous suicide threats. Of the previous attempts, 23 percent had been by wrist slashing and 15 percent by hanging.

One hundred and eighteen (54 percent) of the suicide cases were reported as being psychiatrically "improved" at the time of the suicide. Discharge plans were being made for thirty-one patients (14 percent) of the individuals who committed suicide. Eighty-one patients (37 percent) had never been considered suicidal and had given no signs or indications of impending suicidal action, according to the records. Some verbal communication of the suicidal intention could be found retrospectively in 30 percent of the cases. Twenty-two (10 percent) of the suicides were in individual psychotherapy; eighteen (8 percent) were in group psychotherapy; and 114 (52 percent) were on tranquilizers at the time of the suicide. Between 37 and 74 percent of the suicidal patients were involved in one or another of the adjunctive therapies at the time of their suicide.

When the behavioral manifestations prior to the suicide were tabulated, agitation, depression, withdrawal, sleep trouble, complaints about health, and difficulty in thinking and concentrating were found, in that order, to be the most frequent prodromal clues. Unfortunately, for most patients the records did not allow a clear specification of the precipitating cause for the suicide.

COMPARISON OF SUICIDAL GROUP WITH CONTROLS. The suicide group was compared with the nonsuicide control group by: (1) Chi-squares and (2) *t*-tests between items.

One hundred and eight statistically significant items were found (a number greater than that expected to occur by chance, using the .05 level of significance). These 108 items are presented in Tables I-III. The statistically significant items indicate that the suicides differ from the controls in the following areas:

Population characteristics: The suicidal patients were younger than the controls when they first entered the mental hospital, mean age 36 vs. mean age 45. There were more single men among the suicidal group, and more divorced or separated men among the

controls. No differences were found in the distributions of race, religion, and other population characteristics.

Diagnoses: The suicidal patients had more diagnoses of psychosis (schizophrenia and manic-depressive) while the controls had

TABLE II—Items Significantly Differentiating Suicide and Non-Suicide (Control) Patients[1]

No.[2]		Suicide N=218	Control N=220	df	χ^2
01-15-16	*Marital Status*				
	single	109	67	5	22.64[4]
	married	74	89		
	divorced	19	30		
	divorced and remarried	7	18		
	separated	6	13		
	widowed	3	3		
	Total	218	220		
01-28	*Parental Mortality*				
	father alive now	24	27	4	8.98[3]
	mother alive now	48	40		
	both parents alive now	83	57		
	both parents dead now	49	71		
	no information	14	25		
	Total	218	220		
03-77	*S's Intellectual Level*				
	above normal	48	21	3	12.46[4]
	normal	120	108		
	below normal	26	39		
	no information	24	52		
	Total	218	220		
04-24-25	*Branch of Service*				
	army	142	172	6	11.03[3]
	navy	39	29		
	marine corps	13	6		
	air force	21	9		
	coast guard	2	2		
	other	1	1		
	unknown	0	1		
	Total	218	220		
04-30	*Highest rank in the armed forces*				
	private or apprentice seaman	35	48	3	13.72[4]
	middle ranks	104	101		
	officers–2nd Lt. or Ensign or above	17	8		
	unknown	62	63		
	Total	218	220		

[1] By chi-square.
[2] The numbers refer to card and item numbers in original protocol.
[3] $p < .05$.
[4] $p < .01$.

more acute and chronic brain syndrome diagnoses and neurotic and personality disorder diagnoses.

Early childhood: More suicides had both their parents alive at the time of the death (they died younger than the controls). More suicides had parents who had been in psychiatric difficulties themselves. The suicides had fewer difficulties in school and more friends of the opposite sex than did the controls.

Marital histories: There were fewer divorces and remarriages among the suicides. They tended to spend more of their leisure time with their wives and to be home more often. The suicides seemed to feel that family obligations were important.

Educational achievements: More suicides went further in school; more finished college; and more were considered to be above normal in intellectual functioning.

Military history: Consistent with their higher educational achievement, more of the suicides achieved higher ranks in the armed forces. There were more suicides who had served in the Marine Corps and Air Force, while more controls had served in the Army.

Prehospital difficulties: Prior to hospitalization, the suicides had more strange religious visions, hallucinations, prior nervous breakdowns, delusions, and obsessive thoughts and compulsions than did the controls. The controls had more frequent physical illness, surgery, ulcers, heart disease, alcoholism, enuresis, and more chronic stomach difficulties than did the suicides.

Experience and behavior in the hospital: The suicides seemed subject to depressions that were more severe, and thus spent more time in the hospital than the controls (in spite of their premature deaths). During their more lengthy stay they received more psychotherapy, both individual and group, more lobotomies (during the early part of the 1950 decade), and more of the adjunct therapies than the controls. They received tranquilizers more often and were more likely to complain if the tranquilizers were not prescribed for them. More suicides requested to be put in restraints. They were visited by relatives more often and were allowed to go out on pass more often. When they did they were likely to return from pass early, reporting extreme anxiety while away from the hospital. On the other hand, more suicides eloped from the hospital.

The suicides showed violent behavior in the hospital more often, required restraints more often, had more fist-fights with other

patients, and had more crying spells than the control patients. They also showed the other extreme of such behavior in becoming withdrawn and mute more often. They made more suicide attempts and threats while in the hospital than did the controls.

The suicidal patients seemed to have the more marked ambivalent feelings about the hospital, more often demanding to leave it, failing to acknowledge or accept their illness, and at the same time demanding constant attention and reassurance. They expressed feelings of inadequacy and inferiority more often and seemed to feel safe in

TABLE III—Items Significantly Differentiating Suicide and
Non-Suicide (Control) Patients[1]

No.[2]		Suicide N = 218	Control N = 220	t-value[3]
01-9-10	Age at the time case history was taken			
	Mean	35.52	44.54	6.94
	S.D.	11.25	15.14	
01-11-12	Age at the time of death			
	Mean	39.72	67.25	16.19
	S.D.	12.20	11.21	
03-13	Number of times S has been married			
	Mean	.75	1.06	4.47
	S.D.	.69	.86	
03-14-15	Number of children from previous marriages			
	Mean	.32	.83	2.83
	S.D.	.75	1.30	
03-66-67	Highest school grade completed by S			
	Mean	10.85	9.67	3.28
	S.D.	3.54	3.55	
05-30-32	Total number of months that S has been in a psychiatric hospital			
	Mean	44.96	31.75	2.13
	S.D.	61.94	63.40	
05-33-35	Number of months of S's last psychiatric hospitalization			
	Mean	33.55	20.25	2.89
	S.D.	55.80	41.07	
07-59-60	Number of suicide attempts			
	Mean	.37	.07	7.50
	S.D.	.48	.27	

[1] By t-test.
[2] The numbers refer to card and item numbers in original protocol.
[3] t-ratios significant at .05=1.96 and .01=2.58.

the hospital. Although they demanded tranquilizers more often, they did not tend to improve with their use.

Discussion

The method used in this study of large-scale comparison of data obtained from case records of neuropsychiatric hospital patients explored the possibility of discovering significant suicidal information within the sociopsychological matrix. Of particular interest was the possibility of obtaining information relating to early experiences that might highlight important developmental events or influences specific to suicide.

Although a great amount of data was gathered, a relatively small number of the items that discriminated between the suicides and the controls referred to developmental or early life-history events. Several reasons may account for this. First, there may simply be a lack of sufficient information in the records. A number of items in the protocol with high frequencies of "don't know" and "no information" responses related to early history. Many of the items might have been marked "don't know" because the information was not specifically stated in negative form, and the rater used that category rather than the "no" category. A second reason might be that the kind of information found in the case records of neuropsychiatric hospital patients does not include the data that would be most meaningful in relationship to suicide.

However, a few differences in early history and many differences in adult behaviors were found between the two groups. These latter differentiating characteristics were most often observed in the hospital behavior, thus providing some overt clues for identification and the opportunity for prevention of suicide.

In general, the suicidal patient in a neuropsychiatric hospital seemed to be more seriously psychiatrically ill, with the illness showing more acute phases and more extremes in behavior. The psychiatric picture fluctuated more often between both ends of the continuum, with behavior such as restlessness, hyperactivity, agitation, pacing at one end, and severe depression, isolation, muteness, and withdrawal at the other. As a result, the suicidal patients tended to receive the more serious psychiatric diagnoses, such as schizophrenia and manic-depressive psychosis, while the controls received more diagnoses of organicity or neurotic disorders.

In the hospital the suicidal patients seemed to make more demands upon hospital personnel, to complain and criticize treatment for which they had themselves asked, to show marked ambivalence about leaving the security of the hospital, and to have a constant need for reassurance and support. The suicides required the more extreme treatment methods such as insulin coma, lobotomy, and electric shock therapy. They also received more attention from the staff and participated in more therapy activities such as individual and group psychotherapy, educational therapy, and occupational therapy. On the other hand, the controls seemed to require less care and less extensive treatment, both direct and ancillary. They were seen as neither so extensively nor intensively (psychiatrically) ill, with symptoms that were not so extreme. If anything, the control patient seemed to be less involved and less concerned with his immediate surroundings. He seemed able to exist and function within his surroundings with less conflict, even though still displaying psychiatric symptoms. The data thus show that suicide occurs among the sicker patients, those with more serious psychiatric symptoms and with a history of acting out more often, including suicide attempts, threats, and other suicidal behavior. If other identifying information about personality and behavior is added, it becomes possible to focus appropriate preventive activities by the hospital staff on individual cases.

From the few early history and prehospital items that differentiated between the suicides and the controls, some comments may be made about the personality development of the suicidal patient. The items suggest that the suicidal patients had marked conflict within the dependence-independence area, with most of the disturbance stemming from strong, ungratified dependency needs and strained interpersonal relationships. In his personality development, the suicidal person seemed to have been in closer and more intense relationships with other persons than the control. The patients in the suicide group seemed to have an extremely strong need to please, to conform, and to be liked, and much of their involvement and investment with others seemed based upon attempts to win approval and recognition. They apparently needed the support of others more strongly, and their feelings of self seemed to be dependent on the persons in whom they had invested themselves. By their reactions when interpersonal crises occurred, one might

speculate that any threat to this relationship was felt as equivalent to destruction. As adults, the suicidal patients were very involved with their wives, spent more time with them, and were home more often. The suicidal patients at the same time seemed to be over-strivers. They had a strong need to succeed that seemed overdetermined, with an emphasis on achievement that carried into many areas such as education, military service, and vocation.

The picture obtained here of an unresolved dependence-independence conflict is somewhat consistent with the results of other studies. Based on extensive examination of schizophrenic,[7] malignant neoplasm,[8] respiratory,[9] and anxiety and depressive[10] patients who later committed suicide, and who were matched with control groups of similar but nonsuicidal patients, a characteristic pattern among suicides that has been tentatively labeled the "dependent-dissatisfied" person has emerged. As the name indicates, the patients within these studies who committed suicide showed both the dependency and the dissatisfaction with their lives that was found within the subjects in the present study. The "dependent-dissatisfied" person was that person who was continually complaining, demanding, insisting, and controlling. He showed inflexibility and lack of adaptability, continually repeating his demands on others regardless of their effect on them. He turned to hospital and staff for support but continually succeeded in alienating them with his insatiable demands for special attention. He seemed to need constantly repeated evidence of self-worth from outside sources in order to maintain his own feelings of self-esteem. However, his own activity continually pushed him into a more difficult "bind," for as he increased his demands, his sources of gratification were exhausted and became more rejecting, forcing the patient to increase his demands still more.

Stanton and Schwartz studied the sociopsychological environment of the mental hospital and emphasized the need to understand not only the patient but the patient in his milieu, especially his "sick" milieu.[11] The present study, as well as the previous ones, adds substantiation to this viewpoint, with the caution that the milieu must be understood in terms of its significance to each patient individually. What is felt as support and a high level of care by one patient may be seen as a rejecting attitude and inefficient procedure by another. The latter may, as a result, become suicidal. Apparently,

however, he will in this process give many clues, thus making prevention feasible.

A retrospective study such as this fulfills a useful purpose if it provides some data for intensive examination, some clues for theoretical formulations, and some directives for further research. Our results have shown that in dealing with suicidal patients in mental hospitals, we are contending with the most seriously ill patients, the ones who are the biggest hospital problems and the most difficult to treat. Short-range preventive programs are possible, however, for these patients do tend to identify themselves sufficiently while in the hospital. The program for prevention does not seem easy for it has been found that these patients develop skills for provoking rejection and thus bring about the state they dread most: loneliness and the feeling that no one, not even the hospital nor its staff, cares. It is difficult to give extra and special attention to patients who are insatiably demanding and ungrateful.

Long-range predictive and preventive programs are yet to be accomplished. Some clues have been obtained about early development, but much further research needs to be carried out. One possibility for further study is to identify "dependent-dissatisfied" persons among current patients of neuropsychiatric hospitals and to carry out interviews in depth, obtaining anamnestic and personality data. These cases can then be followed for several years, giving a past, present, and future to the data collected. Such results hopefully will provide, literally, a future for them as well as for other suicidal patients.[12]

PART VI
THERAPY
AND TREATMENT

Chapter 23
TREATMENT OF THE POTENTIALLY SUICIDAL PATIENT

Robert E. Litman

*Two aspects of office treatment of suicidal patients are discussed:
(1) the initial interview in cases in which suicidal thoughts
are the presenting complaint, and (2) suicidal crises in on-going
psychotherapy. Clinical vignettes containing various clues to
suicidal potential and ways in which to handle suicidal crises
are presented. The advantages, as well as the risks, of office
treatment of suicidal persons are discussed. The importance
of open communication between therapist and patient and of
consultation with colleagues on the part of the therapist is
emphasized.*

Psychiatrists recognize potentially suicidal patients by various
objective clues such as self-destructive threats or fantasies, recent
suicidal attempts, complaints of pain, suffering, and hopelessness,
and physical signs of depression such as sleeplessness, anorexia,
and weight loss. In addition, psychotherapists are sometimes alerted
subjectively by their own intuition that the patient is suicidal.

Under favorable circumstances, some such patients can be treated
successfully in office practice, although the task is difficult and
complicated. This chapter presents some clinical experiences with
suicidal patients. Two aspects are selected for discussion: (1) the
initial psychiatric interview when suicidal intentions constitute the
presenting complaint; and (2) suicidal crises that complicate psychotherapy that has already been under way for some time.

When a patient's wish to continue living balances precariously for
a time against a strong wish to commit suicide, then relatively
minor, often accidental, adverse environmental influences may be
decisively fatal. For example, a salesman, age thirty-five, became
despondent when his wife asked for a divorce to marry his best
friend. The patient obtained sleeping tablets from his family
physician, who recognized the depression and referred him to a
psychiatrist. However, the patient canceled his appointment. One
afternoon after conference with his wife's lawyer, the patient felt

extremely depressed and acutely suicidal. He tried to see his brother, who was out of his office, and then his father, who was also out. He called the psychiatrist, who was busy in consultation. Finally, he called his wife at home, but her line was busy. Feeling completely isolated and estranged, he took the pills. After several hours the psychiatrist returned the patient's call, but there was no answer. Since it was now late afternoon, the psychiatrist called the home. The wife became concerned, went to her husband's office and found him there unconscious. The patient later reported that, had any of his calls been completed, he would not have taken the pills then. This example emphasizes how a series of fortuitous factors can be important in allowing a patient's suicidal wish to become a suicidal action, and equally accidental factors can prevent the suicidal action from becoming a suicidal death.

A general prerequisite condition for successful office psychotherapy with such a patient is that a psychotherapeutic relationship be established early and maintained consistently during the suicidal crisis, so that the patient is able to appeal for help and so that the therapist is able to perceive and respond to the appeal until the suicidal urges have abated. At moments of crisis, the psychiatrist must be able to throw his weight into the balance on the side of survival.

Ordinarily, in the first therapeutic interview with a new patient the psychiatrist feels no pressure with regard to time. He lets the patient unfold his story pretty much in his own way, while the psychiatrist waits for insight into the patient's personality and character before making some specific explanation or interpretation. When, however, strong suicidal urges are revealed at the first examination rather different tactics are called for. After taking a careful history of the onset and progress of the suicidal feeling, I usually express sympathy toward the patient's feeling of loneliness and painful depression and give a strong, positive, optimistic outlook with regard to treatment, without specifying in detail just what kind of treatment I have in mind. I feel justified in my optimism for I am reasonably confident that through one therapeutic agency or another, or a combination of several, the patient will be feeling much improved within a few weeks or months. In addition to psychotherapy and appropriate drugs, I think of such measures as environmental manipulation through interviews with

friends and relatives, hospitalization when indicated, and, if necessary, electrical cerebral stimulation.

If the suicidal trend is severe, the patient should be seen daily. The patient's response to such an optimistic approach may be taken as a rough prognostic guide to the feasibility of office psychotherapy. The outlook is favorable when patients feel relieved after the first interview, with decreased tension and a slight lift in mood, and quickly form a dependent transference relationship to the therapist.

The following case illustrates this approach. A forty-eight-year-old associate professor at an Eastern school became depressed when an expected promotion was withheld. At the same time, his wife received a special award for research. The patient became suicidal when he learned that his promotion had probably been blocked by the very dean whom he most idealized. At faculty meetings the patient felt an almost uncontrollable urge to confess his (minor) academic sins and to resign. One suicidal attempt by gas in his apartment was prevented by his wife's unexpected return. The next day, he abruptly left town and came to Los Angeles, preoccupied with thoughts of suicide. Friends persuaded him to see a psychiatrist. I listened to his story and expressed sympathy for his frustration and confusion. I assured him that depressions of this type are always self-limited, the only danger being suicide. I predicted that with psychiatric treatment the depression could be lifted in one to three months. After that, of course, we would have the problem of trying to understand the personality factors that made him vulnerable to a depressive reaction. That second phase of the treatment might take many months or years. I arranged to see him the next day. The patient was tearfully grateful for the reassurance. That night he slept well for the first time in weeks. Because he was better each day I did not hospitalize him or further consider shock treatment. This was an excellent case for office psychotherapy. The patient appealed for help, it was offered him, and he accepted it gratefully. At the same time, friends were giving assistance. After three months the patient improved sufficiently to take a job in Los Angeles and later send for his wife. Still later, as the patient's treatment progressed, he had several periods of depression that were successfully interpreted as transference frustration reactions.

If the suicidal patient makes no emotional response to the therapist during the first few hours, the hazards of office psychotherapy are greatly increased. I prefer to hospitalize such patients for further evaluation, especially if there are indications pointing to schizophrenia, alcoholism, or impulsive psychopathic tendencies. For example, a thirty-five-year-old man came to the office with his wife. During his treatment with a psychiatrist in another city he had made two unsuccessful suicide attempts. The wife said she worried about him when he got a shifty, withdrawn look in his eyes. The patient himself blandly denied any suicidal wishes or suicidal thoughts. His face was immobile. He minimized the previous therapy and the previous suicide attempts with little affect. I said I knew he must be quite depressed and asked him to come back the next day but he refused to do so. He wanted treatment once a month, which I felt was not feasible. Three weeks later I learned that he was in treatment with a very competent psychiatrist once a week. Two weeks after that, several hours before his psychiatric appointment, in his wife's absence he neatly stuffed his nose and ears with cotton to avoid a mess and killed himself with a pistol. The psychiatrist had no indication of the suicidal intent.

Another example: a forty-five-year-old divorcee had a history of alcoholism and promiscuous sexual behavior. The one stable and rewarding influence in her life was her work. She owned and managed a telephone exchange. When she first learned that her recent hoarseness was due to a malignant laryngeal tumor requiring a vocal cord resection, she became extremely depressed and talked of suicide. A psychiatrist recommended hospitalization, but she rebelled at the locked doors of the psychiatric ward and her relatives agreed with her. The psychiatrist somewhat reluctantly saw her as an office patient. Two nights before the scheduled operation, she got drunk on alcohol and committed suicide by drinking cleaning fluid. Experience teaches that schizophrenics, alcoholics, and impulsive psychopaths can be completely unpredictable with regard to suicide.

Occasionally the psychiatrist, hoping to establish a therapeutic relationship in time, may decide to take the risk of office psychotherapy even in those unpromising cases where the patient denies his need for help with indifference or even hostility to the therapist. One is tempted to take a chance when the patient is the only bread-

winner for many dependents or when the patient is prominent in some social or political or business activity and feels that his career might be hurt by a record of psychiatric hospitalization. Sometimes the patient and family flatly refuse a recommendation of hospitalization. Then the therapist is advised to make it clear, preferably in writing, that the risk is acknowledged by all concerned. In such a situation I think it is essential that the patient have someone in the family or some friend to whom he is able to appeal for help during an acute short-lived suicidal crisis. The therapist can use this friend or relative as an ancillary therapist during dangerous periods in the treatment. If ambivalent feelings between the patient and the ancillary therapist threaten to complicate the situation further, it may become necessary to refer the relative or friend to another psychiatrist for support in his role as assistant therapist.

Sometimes the psychiatrist first meets his patient when the latter is in the hospital recovering from an unsuccessful attempt at suicide. One may then encounter what in another context has been called "the moment of truth," which should be seized with all possible decision and dispatch. Because of heightened apprehension and guilt, the patient, spouse, and key relatives and friends may reveal information and feelings that have eluded therapeutic efforts for years.

For example, a forty-year-old woman had been in psychotherapy for five years because of a street phobia and a fear of being alone. Finally, her husband began to hint that he was tired of her clinging. At the same time her therapist admitted that he was getting nowhere with her and suggested termination. She attempted suicide by taking a large number of sleeping capsules that she had been saving for some weeks. As she lay in a coma, her husband confessed to me the secret that several people had suspected but the patient had never mentioned to her therapist. The husband had been having an affair with the patient's sister, a steady visitor to the home, for six years. The patient's repression of this problem was responsible in large measure for her anxiety symptoms. This patient could not be treated in office practice because she could not return to face the truth at home. She required a long period of hospitalization.

In such cases, suicidal preoccupations and suicidal attempts announce a situation of emotional bankruptcy. Death appeals as a

last resort to dependent persons who have alienated their relatives and exhausted their friends. Checking through their social relationships one finds no remaining assets. Such people usually have no special talents and no special interests. They have existed as emotional parasites and now the host has deserted them. My experience using office psychotherapy with such people has been unfavorable. Rehabilitation usually involves a relatively long period of inpatient, institutional care, even though such persons are not psychotic. If the patient is wealthy, this would mean a hospital, preferably in some distant location. For patients of lesser financial resources, the local social agencies should be investigated. Patients often establish a strong dependent transference relationship to an institution, such as the Veterans Administration or the university clinic, and gain a source of confidence from this transference. Group therapy experience can help such patients develop more independent social techniques. On the other hand, such patients in individual office treatment are apt to go into a chronic suicidal crisis and make unending demands which strain the psychiatrist's patience and lead him finally to reject the patient. At best, this is another failure for the patient and, at worst, it means another suicidal attempt.

It sometimes happens that a good working therapeutic relationship established in the first interviews becomes dangerously attenuated in subsequent hours. This calls for renewed efforts from the therapist, as illustrated by the following case: A twenty-eight-year-old housewife reluctantly sought therapy at the urging of an old friend, a social worker. Without emotion the patient said that she had been depressed for a year and had saved about thirty sleeping capsules for her eventual suicide. She told of a deprived childhood at the hands of a rejecting mother and described how she had survived by growing tough, and had endured marriage by virtue of her husband's exceptional personality qualities, which were directly opposite to hers. He was a retiring, sensitive, commercially successful painter who fled from any family strife to his art. The patient carried the brunt of family leadership. She had always taken great pride in her physical beauty, but her pregnancy one year before had ruined her figure. Without special emphasis, she mentioned that her child was probably mentally retarded. The therapist interrupted with exclamations of sympathy and thrust a box of tissue into the woman's surprised hands. She burst into tears and cried

throughout the rest of the hour. Later she angrily protested that she had been tricked. But an emotional relationship had been established and the danger of suicide subsided. However, the patient did not give up her pills. Several months later, the feelings of utter hopelessness returned. Specialists had pronounced the baby hopelessly retarded. Plastic surgery on her breasts was unsuccessful and made her figure worse. Her only friend was out of town. The patient was indifferent to the therapist and preoccupied with thoughts of taking the pills. She dreamed of death. When she was late for an appointment, the therapist noted in himself anxiety and an urge to call her home for reassurance that she was not lying in a coma. The therapist did the following things: He told the patient he was worried about her and asked her to come for an extra hour. He called her husband and asked him to come out of his studio for a while to aid his wife. The husband was astonished to learn that the woman on whom he always leaned was having an emotional breakdown. He responded manfully to the therapist's appeal that for a change he should act as a protective parent toward his wife. She in turn was gratified by his response. The therapist got in touch with appropriate social agencies and encouraged the patient in plans for special placement for the child. With these activities, the patient's interest in therapy (and life) was renewed, and the suicidal urges decreased.

In any office psychotherapy, from the most superficial to the most intensive, an acute suicidal crisis precludes further progress until a more stable intrapsychic balance is achieved. Ideally the therapist will search for the various conscious and unconscious sources of the disturbance and explain the trouble to the patient. The interpretation of suicidal threats and fantasies as transference hostility toward the therapist can be overdone. Often these crises are desperate appeals for love and protection. When strong self-destructive urges appear as a phase of therapy, important and pertinent information is elicited by a careful self-examination on the part of the therapist for feelings of rejection toward the patient and covert wishes that the therapy be interrupted or terminated, which the patient takes as a death wish. In such an emergency, the use of consultation and supervision to check the therapist's countertransference is strongly recommended. This tends to relieve the therapist's anxiety and promote a more realistic appraisal of the

situation with appropriate activity. At times explanations or interpretations in words are not suitable for the suicidal patient who has regressed to a paratactic form of logic and cannot understand ordinary communication. Interpretations are clearer when phrased as actions, for instance, increasing the frequency and length of the hours, or alerting relatives to the need for some special treatment of the patient, or taking the patient to a hospital. A consultant may be helpful in sharing the responsibility for such a drastic change in treatment as removing the patient to a hospital. It cannot be denied that such activity tends to increase the regressive dependent transference and may prolong the therapy. On the other hand, the therapist who is dealing with such deeply unconscious destructive feelings as those involved in suicide needs to have the feeling himself that the therapy is timeless, as the unconscious is timeless. Many of the suicidal crises occurring in therapy are precipitated by unconscious impatience in the therapist toward his patient or the patient's unconscious. Suicidal patients demand a great deal from the therapist in terms of time, effort, and responsibility. In return, the therapist should make sure that he has the time available and that he is paid a satisfactory fee. Two or three suicidal patients at one time are more than enough for any man's practice. The availability of excellent psychiatric hospital facilities for suicidal patients can ease the strain of therapy with such patients considerably.

The disadvantage of drugs, electric treatments, and hospitalization in general is that they provide essentially passive remedies for problems that often require active resolution. If patients are discharged abruptly from the hospital to return to their original conflicts the cycle of hopelessness and suicide may be repeated. The advantage of office psychotherapy is that it encourages the patient toward solving his problems himself, which promotes self-confidence and self-respect. Psychotherapy aims at changes in character, which are then reflected by changes in the patient's environment, leading to more satisfactions in life. Ideally, the hospital and the office provide complementary phases of the patient's treatment.

In summary, office psychotherapy of suicidal patients offers a greater reward for the patient but it carries an increased risk for, and imposes a special responsibility on, the psychiatrist. The risk is minimized when there is open emotional communication between the patient and the therapist. Office treatment is especially suitable

for patients who form a dependent relationship toward the therapist early in treatment. However, extremely dependent or emotionally bankrupt patients may require the nurturing influence of a hospital or clinic for successful rehabilitation. The psychiatrist should be optimistic, patient, flexible, and resourceful. When confronted with a suicidal crisis, the therapist should carefully check his counter-transference, preferably with the aid of a consultant. In suicidal emergencies, aid for the patient should be solicited without hesitation from appropriate relatives, friends, and social agencies. The hospital and the office can provide complementary phases in the successful treatment of suicidal patients.

Chapter 24
THE SUICIDAL CRISIS IN PSYCHOTHERAPY
Norman L. Farberow

*Two psychotherapy sessions for each of two patients are
described, with emphasis on the suicidal crises that occurred in
them. Four general conclusions are drawn: emergencies were
met by increasing the activity of the therapist; the meanings of
hospitalization for both the patient and the therapist are
several and subtle; the therapist needs to recognize his own
emotional duress during the suicidal crisis of his patient; and
medical consultation during a suicidal crisis is especially important.*

Probably no single event in the course of psychotherapy carries
so much emotional impact and requires so much skill, knowledge,
sensitivity, ability, and fortitude on the part of the therapist as a
suicidal crisis in his patient. While the whole course of therapy
constantly demands the right word or the best response from the
therapist, this demand seems especially heightened by the drama
of the suicidal crisis, where there is the suspense of a threat to
kill or the immediacy of a gesture toward self-destruction. Often
there is not even time to consider what has gone wrong in the
therapy and why the crisis has developed. This is the time, instead,
when the questions of what to do and how to do it crowd in: How
serious is this impulse, should the patient be sent to the hospital
without delay, and, if so, how should one get him there? What will
stay his hand before he acts so that the crisis can be worked
through; what words does he need? What happens if his psychotherapy is interrupted at this point? What will this crisis do to the
future course of his therapy? The answers will vary, too, with
whether the patient is being seen in private practice or in a clinic
setting; with the therapist's willingness to undergo the emotional
strain and the increased demands of this period; with the evaluation of the patient's ego strengths, his resiliency, the intensity and
force of the suicidal urge; with the length of time in treatment,
the rapport established, and the diagnosis of the patient.

It is true that no single course of action can be prescribed that
would fit all cases. Probably, if any were to be suggested at all, the

safest and surest one would be to place the patient within the protective walls of a hospital. But sometimes the most conservative approach is not the most productive one, and in some cases one is tempted to take the calculated risk of continuing to treat the patient in his present situation when the tensions and the conflicts immediately at hand can be worked through and understood. It is difficult to specify the factors that determine which cases will be helped by being sent to the hospital and which should continue in an outpatient therapy setting. As is so often the case, however, the determination of the best method of treatment cannot wait upon the exhaustive scientific examinations of the phenomenon under consideration. Service must be rendered while research goes on. Perhaps, however, by continued examination, appraisal, and review and by discussion, comparison, and sharing of experiences, the goal of prevention of the needless loss of life by self-destruction may be approached.

This chapter shares with the reader a detailed account of two therapy sessions for each of two veterans who were patients in a mental hygiene clinic. During their therapy suicidal crises occurred. (All identifying information has been removed in order to preserve anonymity.) It is important here to emphasize that these crises occurred after therapy had been in progress for some time—about three to four months. This chapter is limited to a discussion of suicidal crisis under these special conditions, that is, when it occurs in psychotherapy and when the therapy is already in process. Neither of these cases had come to therapy originally as a result of suicidal tendencies, but rather because of severe anxiety attacks, with symptoms that had not included suicidal tendencies.

The cases were in two distinctly different diagnostic categories and the methods used in handling the crises were markedly different. In the first case, the approach was mainly interpretive, uncovering; in the second, it was mainly supportive and reassuring. These examples, of course, do not imply that the techniques employed in each of the cases are the best methods of handling suicidal crises in therapy. Rather, they are presented in order to provide the reader with a description of at least two of the many kinds of suicidal crises and to provoke interest in and discussion about this problem.

Mr. S.

The patient was a 33-year-old white male who might be classified as an emotionally unstable, immature person with primarily obsessive-compulsive defenses. When he first came to the clinic, he was in the midst of an extreme anxiety attack amounting almost to panic. He was referred to the neuropsychiatric hospital, where he spent approximately six months and then returned to the clinic. At the time of the reopening of his case, he was in the process of separating from his wife and one child, and he remained in a highly emotional, disturbed state for some time. He was making a marginal economic and social adjustment, living for some time in slums and skid row areas and rooming with friends from the hospital. He showed very little motivation toward seeking any kind of employment, and spent most of the time bemoaning the fact of his separation and impending divorce. He found little satisfaction in any of his personal relationships and showed considerable disturbance in his sexual functioning at the time.

Therapy was soon established on a twice-a-week basis, with the patient irregular in attendance, either missing his appointments or wandering in at some time other than his appointed hour. He was ambivalent about therapy, demanding, pleading for more time, and then not showing up for the extra sessions granted him. He showed marked mood swings, in one hour presenting a happy, cheerful front, and in the next, a swing to apathy and depression. Therapy proceeded on a limited insight level, with the focus of the discussion on the relationship between him and his wife, and with some references to the genetic sources of his difficulties in his past relationships with his mother.

At the time of the suicidal crisis the patient was receiving frequent notices from his wife's lawyers about arrangements for a divorce. The therapist had to be away from the office for three days, during which time it was arranged to have the patient tested. When the therapist returned, the patient was very depressed and announced he was returning to the hopsital. However, he returned the next day and stated he had moved in with his parents. The next two sessions were filled with anger and bitterness toward his wife. Sessions 16 and 17 follow in detail. The patient announced that he had almost committed suicide the night before session 16.

THERAPY INTERVIEW 16. The patient came in slowly. I could barely hear him because he spoke in an extremely low tone and in very brief sentences. He looked very depressed and apathetic. He said, "I have just one thing on my mind. I almost did it Friday night. I don't know why I stopped. I've really been sick these past few days, afraid to fall asleep. When I do, I have the most miserable dreams."

I asked what had happened to make it worse right now. He said, "The other night I went out with Jimmy and two other fellows." At this point, he began to talk a little louder. "I went to several bars and finally ended at one in our old neighborhood. I saw my father-in-law there with a strange woman. I didn't go over to him and he didn't come over to me. I always did suspect that he was playing around. We went to some other clubs, picked up one couple and went to a party. We took off from there and went to another party and finally left there around four or five o'clock. I had a lousy time. I slept most of the next day and watched TV a little. Then the idea got into my head and I felt that I really wanted to do it. I thought I might write some things just to get them off my mind. The pencil wouldn't keep up with my mind, there were too many things to say. I was going to take some stuff that I knew we had in the medicine chest. I thought, and thought, and thought all day, and just thought about my wife, about this guy, Joe, and how much I hated their guts. I think that night I dreamed I was beating up on him and I was thinking of so many different ways that I would like to. I guess I feel pretty bitter toward him and toward my wife. They stole the last possession I had." I asked what this was and he said it was pride. I asked him to explain. He said, "Pride—that I was right and that others were wrong. Other people kept telling me that you can't trust a woman. I wanted to show them that they were wrong."

I said, "Why do you have to kill or hurt yourself because of that?" and he said, "She took the last thing that I had. There is nothing left to live for." I said, "You want to hurt her and the only way you can do this is through hurting yourself. You feel this is the only way that you can get at her." The patient protested. This wasn't true—he really didn't want to hurt her. He started all over again, "I've lost all my possessions," and so forth. "I can't even call on God."

I said, "You have been wanting to get back at her and hurt her

and you have been telling me how you have been unable to. Maybe this is the way you feel you can hurt her." The patient disregarded me and said, "To think that it is me, me. I don't even ask, why me, any more. This is the kind of thing that you read about, or that you hear on the radio. I notice that I don't give a goddam any more. I don't feel like fighting. I don't feel like anything else. There is nothing left to live for, just to come here, and I hate that because I know I have to leave."

The patient was talking louder, and with a little more vigor. I asked how he had felt on seeing his father-in-law. He said, "I was uncomfortable. I remember I started telling myself, 'That's where she got it,' but no, that's not the answer. I think I'm beyond sour grapes now."

I went back to my main point and said again, "The most important thing in the world for you was the feeling you wanted to get back at your wife, and this is the way you felt you could do it best." Again the patient paid no attention and, instead, looked rather wistfully at me and asked if I had been in touch with his wife. I said I had not, and asked why he wanted me to be. He didn't answer for a while. Finally he said, "I know it's childish, wishful thinking, but I had the feeling that maybe you would make everything all right, maybe you would get us both back together again. But I know I don't have the feeling that things can be patched up. Because of this one thing, things can never be the same." He then continued, "I can't go on like this. I'm living in a void." Our time was up. I ended the session and made arrangements to see him the next day.

THERAPY INTERVIEW 17. Patient came in late in the afternoon, looking better. He said he felt better today, he had had a long sleep. I asked why he felt better and he said, "I could share my troubles with someone." I said that wasn't all of the reason. The patient said, "I slept all day yesterday and worked around the yard. I spent some time with Jimmy, just talking. I got a little depressed at his house." I asked again what it was that made him feel better, since nothing had changed for him since yesterday. He said, "Sometime last night I changed. I must have had fifty different dreams. I started thinking that I wanted to snap out of it. I really don't know how it's changed. I don't think I feel any different about my wife or about Joe." I said, "How do you feel about yourself?" He

said, "I don't want to die. I just want to get out of this void." I asked, "Was it anything that happened here yesterday?" He answered, "I feel, mainly, it was the unburdening. I wanted to tell someone. You were the only one I could talk to without feeling like a stupid ass. Not sympathetic, but understanding. Also, yesterday was the first time I ever realized exactly how I felt about my wife and about Joe. It must be good to cuss somebody out instead of mulling and mulling. There was no one else to talk to. I couldn't get any real satisfaction out of talking to Jimmy."

I asked, "What are your feelings toward your wife and toward Joe?" He said, "I really hate them. I hold her responsible for my present condition. I just can't seem to get proper satisfaction— she's dragging me down. I'm angry and I'm frustrated, and I have to fight the world as well as her. She wasn't helping me, she was only adding to my burden."

I said, "You felt if you could only hurt yourself, you would be hurting her, and in this way, you'd get back at her." He said, "I guess I felt guilty about feeling that way, but the strongest feeling that I had was the feeling that I couldn't hurt her. I wanted to be in the position to say 'No.' I made overtures toward her, hoping she'd come back and then I could reject her. I do know of one way now that I could hurt her, through her father. I just thought of it, but I don't like to hurt and I don't want to be hurt."

With this patient, interpretations were direct and pointed, with the focus on the dynamic of the patient's anger at his wife, his need to hurt her, and his method of accomplishing this, that is, by hurting himself. It is, of course, impossible to say how effective these interpretations were. At the time, the feeling was that they were not making much of an impression upon him, and yet, in session 17, he did return with his anger more appropriately directed at the external objects, his wife and her boy friend, Joe. It would still be difficult to evaluate how much of the subsequent behavior was due primarily to these interpretations, for in the effort to stem the tide of his self-aggressive feelings many other factors were introduced into the therapy: an immediate increase in sessions to five a week, lengthening of time as needed, increased therapist activity and participation in the discussion, and permission to call the therapist at any time the patient felt the need. The interest and concern of

the therapist were undoubtedly powerful, if unmeasurable, influences in relieving the situation. The daily sessions were continued for about a week, when the intensity of the emotions around this crisis seemed to have subsided. Then the sessions were gradually spaced out until the former frequency of twice a week was reached.

Briefly, the further course of therapy was relatively uneventful, with the patient remaining in therapy for an additional thirty-three interviews, by which time he had found work and was seriously involved with a new girl friend.

Mr. R.

This patient was a 28-year-old, white, married male who might be classified as conversion reaction in a basically schizoid personality. He had been in therapy at the clinic several times previously, one of these periods lasting over a year. One of his main complaints, which he felt had begun three years earlier after an operation on his ears, was a condition that he described as a "shaking of the neck." His previous therapists had described their treatment methods as conducted on a superficial basis with some minor attempts at insight and with the aim of strengthening his intellectual defenses. The patient was able to reduce his chronically high level of anxiety and partly to work through his fears concerning his feeling that he was not much of a man. His therapist also stated that though marked concern over homosexual interests was present, this area was avoided when some evidence of psychotic defenses started to appear. The patient was out of therapy for about a year and a half and then returned because of a severe anxiety attack centering around the responsibilities of a new baby, a new house, and the rush of added work in his seasonal job. The present course of therapy was instituted on a once-a-week basis and was conducted on a supportive level, with few interpretations except to repeat and to strengthen his intellectual defenses. The patient improved, and interruption was once again being considered when another seasonal trend in the patient's work caused an exacerbation of the patient's symptoms and an increase in anxiety that mounted almost to panic. The patient became obsessed with feelings of inadequacy in his work, entered into a deep, depressed period, and entertained serious suicidal thoughts. The following therapy sessions are practically verbatim reports of the two therapy hours that occurred at

the onset of his agitated depression. This emotional disturbance actually persisted for about two months, during the early part of which he was seen practically every day and during which time there were frequent telephone calls at night to the therapist at his home.

THERAPY INTERVIEW 12. I had not expected the patient at this hour. He came in as an emergency. He was very depressed, and to some slight extent, agitated. He started out saying, "I have been feeling terrible with headaches and pains that just continue in the back of my neck. I haven't been able to sleep for nights. I haven't been able to do the work. They [the patient's fellow workers] ask me a question and I can't answer. I was the same way at the trial when I got confused and didn't understand what they were asking me. [Patient had recently instituted civil suit for damages incurred in an automobile accident.] The doctor gave me some pills [APC's] but they didn't do any good.

"I had to go to the doctor for an operation on the tip of my penis. It's still spraying. The people at work are trying to snap me out of this. They know that I'm not feeling well. I don't even feel I have the right to feel sick. There's so much stuff at the office that I get confused." The patient began to cry, but regained his control quickly. He went on, "I went to a party, though I didn't want to go. I didn't enjoy myself. I quit smoking because I thought this would help me through the holiday. Maybe I was getting so tense because of smoking too much, but when I was at the trial and had to wait for the lawyer, I got so nervous I had to go down and get some smokes. The trial is over already. We had a trial just in front of the judge last Wednesday. He hasn't given his decision. Tuesday night we were at the lawyer's and Wednesday I was on the witness stand, under cross-examination, for two or three hours." I asked how this had gone and how he had felt. He said, "I felt fairly good. I became afraid that my neck was going to be held responsible for the numbness that I had been having in my hand. My lawyer told me little things to say that weren't exactly the truth, and I either forgot them, or else I felt I couldn't tell any untruth while there on the stand."

I asked how the operation had gone. He said, "I really didn't want

to take all that time, but my 'stream-line' was so bad that it sprayed all over. I had to sit on the toilet in order to take a leak."

He said, "I get self-conscious," and I asked what it was that made him feel this way. He said, "It's my short penis, my big nose, and when I walk, I bounce along. It's my blond eyebrows and my light beard." I asked what these, put together, meant he was afraid of, and he said he was afraid of life. I asked what it was, specifically, he was afraid of, and he replied, "Probably I'm afraid I'm not man enough, but I don't want to believe that.

"Lately, I've lost all my sexual drive with my wife. I've heard that this means a guy's going to have a nervous breakdown." I told him this was not true. I stated it was possible to have a lot of anxiety and still be able to function. I also told him that people frequently lose their sex drive when they are very anxious. He said he had thought of committing suicide, and I told him I was glad he had come in to see me first, and was talking about it with me. He went on, "I'm so anxious. I can't hear the questions that other people ask me. I feel guilty because another fellow is doing my work."

Arrangements were made to see him the next day.

THERAPY INTERVIEW 13. The patient came in very slowly. "I didn't go to work today because I've been feeling very bad. I think I'm going crazy. Is there something I can do about it? Maybe I ought to go to the hospital." I asked what was making him feel bad and he said, "These pains in my head and this tension. It's as if bands are pulled real tight around my head. I can't sleep and I can't eat. I can't do my job. I can't go to the store, I can't do anything. I know I'm worse than before. When I went to see the doctor, I was afraid to sit in the reception room. I've been making my wife nervous, moping around the house. I was really going to commit suicide today. First, I took all my pills and then I went for a long ride up the boulevard. I was going to get a hose but couldn't find any. I went to the drugstore and got a quart of beer and a scratch pad to write my wife a note. I parked on a deserted street and started writing the note and then my pen ran out of ink. I had to laugh. I drank some more of the beer and felt a little bit better, and then felt that I just didn't have the guts to go through with it. When I

went home, my wife gave me a list of things to get in the store, and I took some films into the drugstore. Afterwards, the lady across the street came over and played with the kids."

I asked what the reason was for this wanting to kill himself. He said "It was my shattered childhood. I didn't have a father to instill any confidence. I want my wife to remarry to someone who likes children. Then the thought came that no one likes a child as much as his own folks. When I kissed my wife and child good-bye this morning, I really hated to go. Then I thought, 'I've got to hang around to take care of my boy and of my wife.'" He began to cry again. "When I was young I had asthma and I was oversensitive. The war worried me a lot. Being cooped up in that house for five days [in combat, the patient was trapped for five days in no man's land], I couldn't eat or sleep. I can't relax, I can't concentrate. I'm thinking only of myself."

I asked what it was right now that made everything seem so terrible. He said, "I can't do my job, I'm a failure." To him, this meant that he was a complete failure, and I pointed out how he was seeing everything in black and white, and that he was feeling that if he couldn't do his job, he was worthless. He said he felt like an outcast. I pointed out all of the things that he had been able to do— how well he actually had been able to function despite the tension he had been feeling. I mentioned his house, his wife, his child, his job, but the patient was unconvinced. "At work, even if you're half dead, you're supposed to go in at this time. Other times I can call in if I'm sick and it's okay, but I'm afraid of what others will think now.

"I can't feel friendly or be friendly to others. I have to wait and see if they like me first." I said he felt people had to like him and if they didn't, they'd hate him. It was an all-or-none process, just like the other thing.

He talked about his operation for circumcision when he was young. Dr. C. had said, "I've never seen one like that before." The patient thought he was referring to how small his penis was. When he came home after the operation, his folks went out. He got sick, and the lady next door had to come in to change the dressing for him. "I got out of bed too soon and started swimming too soon. My stepfather punished me once by making me stand on a stool naked and raising the widow shade far enough so that my sexual organ

was exposed to the outside. He took me out of bed one night when I was only half asleep because I didn't do the dishes right. He was always tearing me down, always belittling me. At camp one summer the boys were swimming and took off their trunks. One fellow pointed to my genital and said, 'Look at the way it's shrunk up.'"

I asked what this meant to him, and he said, "It means I'm less stable." I wondered what this referred to. He said he and a girl were swimming one day and she swam between his legs. As she came up she said to him, "Get that stabilizer out of the way." I asked what "stable" meant for him and he said it meant being a more solid individual.

I said he was wondering if perhaps he were a woman, or like a woman. The patient denied this vehemently, and I told him his inability to work at this point did not mean that he was a woman.

As I ended the session, the patient said he still felt anxious and said he thought perhaps I should send him to the hospital. I replied that we could always send him to the hospital later if he needed it and that, though I recognized how strong his feelings were and how bad he felt, we would talk about it here and try to understand what was making him feel so bad. I told him I felt confident in his strength to pull through this period of strain. He could call me at any time, day or night, if he wished. I also reassured him directly, telling him these things would pass and that he would get better. I pointed out how he had felt bad in the past and it had always gotten better. I made an appointment to see him the next day.

The therapy that followed with Mr. R. in the next week and a half consisted of almost daily sessions and numerous telephone calls from him. The interviews were much the same, with the activity of the therapist directed at offering support and reassurance. During this time the seasonal rush in the patient's employment passed and the pressure the patient had felt was considerably lessened. However, the guilt feelings remained strong; he felt he had let his fellow employees down, and he assumed they were looking down on him. These feelings were relieved partly by some intellectual discussion of his fears. He was encouraged to talk over his feelings and his fears with his wife and was surprised to find she accepted him even though he had admitted his fears to her. The patient's depression lasted approximately two months, with the last month

indicating steady relief of his feelings. Therapy was gradually reduced to the former once-a-week basis. The telephone calls ceased without further comment. The patient was seen for about two more months, during which time he seemed to have become stabilized, both emotionally and vocationally. At the time of termination, the patient stated that the therapist had made one very significant comment to him during his depression. This was the statement that the therapist had confidence in the patient's ability to stand the strain of that period.

The calculated risk is much more apparent in this case than with Mr. S. This patient, in contrast to Mr. S., had a much more tenuous ego organization and poorer defenses, which indicated a psychotic substructure. These signs are significant as danger signals in suicidal tendencies because of the added difficulty in the prediction and control of psychotics. Moreover, the patient himself had asked for the sanctuary of the hospital, and the way was open for the most obvious and recommended procedure without the usual accompanying difficulties of convincing the patient, conferring with relatives, arranging with the hospital, and the like. Nevertheless, there were factors that seemed to warrant taking the chance of outpatient therapy. A review of the patient's past history revealed assets that could be counted on. Despite the evidence of some psychotic substructure, the patient showed a considerable—even surprising, in the light of his family history—amount of ego strength. He had finished high school, had been a good athlete—a star in some sports (even though it was compensatory behavior)—and had worked consistently since the war. He had gone through a difficult stretch of war service, experiencing a great amount of combat without an emotional breakdown requiring hospitalization. He had married and was raising a family. On the negative side were the indications of psychotic functioning, the history of a short period in a mental hospital since the service, and the seriousness, as well as the tenacity, of the depressive feelings. A strong factor in the decision not to hospitalize him was the feeling of the therapist that to accede to the patient's request for hospitalization was to agree that he was weak, ineffectual, and inadequate. It was exactly this feeling that was being combated in his therapy. Another important consideration was that if sent to the hospital the patient could no longer be

seen by his therapist, and therapy would be interrupted for an indefinite period of time.

At least four important conclusions emerge from the consideration of the experiences of both the patients and the therapist in these two cases.

1. In both cases, treatment to meet the emergencies was changed by greatly increasing the activity of the therapist. This included increasing the frequency of the meetings, lengthening the time of each meeting if possible, inviting and being available for telephone calls at any time, day or night, and participating more in the discussions in each session. All this activity was designed to give the patient a feeling of sincere concern and interest by the therapist in his welfare.

2. Commitment to the hospital must be evaluated by the therapist from the points of view of the two people most immediately involved, first, the patient, whose safety and health must at all times be the primary consideration, and second, the therapist. Thus, hospitalization may have several meanings to the patient, even diametrically opposed ones. The patient may obtain a feeling of security and comfort, knowing that he is being protected from the terrible conflicts that may be raging inside him; or he may be disappointed and crushed, feeling that his therapist, too, does not consider him strong enough to cope with his feelings. The therapist must weigh these and any other feelings he may sense in the patient, such as those of rejection and abandonment, as probable reactions to such a move. For the therapist, commitment to the hospital involves the interruption of therapy and the alteration, and frequently the relinquishing, of the therapeutic plans for the patient. The therapist must search his own motivations thoroughly for any narcissistic and omnipotent feelings that may be influencing his judgment of the status of the patient before he makes a decision to continue his therapy with the patient or to hospitalize him.

3. One of the most important factors influencing the decision of the therapist is his own willingness and ability to undergo the emotional strain during the period of the suicidal crisis. This includes accepting the increased demands on his time and attention, the intrusion into his private life, and the requirement that he be available at all times. The therapist must be willing to accept the ten-

sion of not knowing what might be happening while his patient is out of sight and sound. He must be able to bear the weighty responsibility if his calculation of the risk was in error and his patient does succeed in taking his own life.

4. Inasmuch as in the suicidal crisis there is always the possibility, no matter how remote, that the patient may succeed in taking his own life, it is especially important for the nonmedical therapist that the medical profession be a part of the total treatment picture.

Chapter 25
PREVENTING SUICIDE
Edwin S. Shneidman

This paper, addressed primarily to physicans and nurses, is based on two assumptions: that individuals who are moving toward suicide are deeply ambivalent (and wish to be rescued) and that, typically, suicide never occurs without prodromata and premonitory clues. Prevention of suicide lies in seeing (or hearing) these clues. The premonitory clues to suicide are (1) verbal, (2) behavioral, (3) situational, and (4) syndromatic. Four types of syndromatic clues are listed: depressed, disoriented, defiant, and dependent-dissatisfied. " 'All' that is required [for suicide prevention] are sharp eyes and ears, good intuition, a pinch of wisdom, and ability to act appropriately, and a deep resolve."

In almost every case of suicide, there are hints of the act to come, and physicians and nurses are in a special position to pick up the hints and to prevent the act. They come into contact, in many different settings, with many human beings at especially stressful times in their lives.

A suicide is an especially unhappy event for helping personnel. Although one can, in part, train and inure oneself to deal with the sick and even the dying patient, the abruptness and needlessness of a suicidal act leaves the nurse, the physician, and other survivors with many unanswered questions, many deeply troubling thoughts and feelings.

Currently, the major bottleneck in suicide prevention is not remediation, for there are fairly well-known and effective treatment procedures for many types of suicidal states; rather it is in diagnosis and identification.[1]

Assumptions

A few straightforward assumptions are necessary in suicide prevention. Some of them are:

Individuals who are intent on killing themselves still wish very much to be rescued or to have their deaths prevented. Suicide prevention consists essentially in recognizing that the potential victim

is "in balance" between his wishes to live and his wishes to die, then throwing one's efforts on the side of life.

Suicide prevention depends on the active and forthright behavior of the potential rescuer.

Most individuals who are about to commit suicide are acutely conscious of their intention to do so. They may, of course, be very secretive and not communicate their intentions directly. On the other hand, the suicidally inclined person may actually be unaware of his own lethal potentialities, but nonetheless may give many indirect hints of his unconscious intentions.

Practically all suicidal behaviors stem from a sense of isolation and from feelings of some intolerable emotion on the part of the victim. By and large, suicide is an act to stop an intolerable existence. But each individual defines "intolerable" in his own way. Difficulties, stresses, or disappointments that might be easy for one individual to handle might very well be intolerable for someone else—in *his* frame of mind. In order to anticipate and prevent suicide one must understand what "intolerable" means to the other person. Thus, any "precipitating cause"—being neglected, fearing or having cancer (the fear and actuality can be equally lethal), feeling helpless or hopeless, feeling "boxed-in"—may be intolerable for *that* person.

Although committing suicide is certainly an all-or-none action, thinking about the act ahead of time is a complicated, undecided, internal debate. Many a black-or-white action is taken on a barely pass vote. Professor Henry Murray of Harvard University has written that "a personality is a full Congress" of the mind. In preventing suicide, one looks for any indications in the individual representing the dark side of his internal life-and-death debate. We are so often surprised at "unexpected" suicides because we fail to take into account just this principle that the suicidal action is a decision resulting from an internal debate of many voices, some for life and some for death. Thus we hear all sorts of post-mortem statements like "He seemed in good spirits" or "He was looking forward to some event next week," not recognizing that these, in themselves, represent only one aspect of the total picture.

In almost every case, there are precursors to suicide, which are called "prodromal clues." In the "psychological autopsies" that have been done at the Suicide Prevention Center in Los Angeles—

in which, by interview with survivors of questionable accident or suicide deaths, they attempt to reconstruct the intention of the deceased in relation to death—it was found that very few suicides occur without casting some shadows before them. The concept of prodromal clues for suicide is certainly an old idea; it is really not very different from what Robert Burton, over three hundred years ago in 1652, in his famous *Anatomy of Melancholy,* called "the prognostics of melancholy, or signs of things to come." These prodromal clues typically exist for a few days to some weeks before the actual suicide. Recognition of these clues is a necessary first step to lifesaving.

Suicide prevention is like fire prevention. It is not the main mission of any hospital, nursing home, or other institution, but it is the minimum ever-present peripheral responsibility of each professional; and when the minimal signs of possible fire or suicide are seen, then there are no excuses for holding back on lifesaving measures. The difference between fire prevention and suicide prevention is that the prodromal clues for fire prevention have become an acceptable part of our common-sense folk knowledge; we must also make the clues for suicide a part of our general knowledge.

Clues to Potential Suicide

In general, the prodromal clues to suicide may be classified in terms of four broad types: verbal, behavioral, situational, and syndromatic.

VERBAL. Among the verbal clues we can distinguish between the direct and the indirect. Examples of direct verbal communications would be such statements as "I'm going to commit suicide," "If such and such happens, I'll kill myself," "I'm going to end it all," "I want to die," and so on. Examples of indirect verbal communications would be such statements as "Goodbye," "Farewell," "I've had it," "I can't stand it any longer," "It's too much to put up with," "You'd be better off without me," and, in general, any statements that mirror the individual's intention to stop his intolerable existence.

Some indirect verbal communications can be somewhat more subtle. We all know that in human communication, our words tell only part of the story, and often the main "message" has to be

decoded. Every parent or spouse learns to decode the language of loved ones and to understand what they really mean. In a similar vein, many presuicidal communications have to be decoded. An example might be a patient who says to a nurse who is leaving on her vacation, "Goodbye, Miss Jones, I won't be here when you come back." If some time afterward she, knowing that the patient is not scheduled to be transferred or discharged prior to her return, thinks about that conversation, she might do well to telephone her hospital.

Other examples are such statements as, "I won't be around much longer for you to put up with," "This is the last shot you'll ever give me," or "This is the last time I'll ever be here," a statement which reflects the patient's private knowledge of his decision to kill himself. Another example is, "How does one leave her body to the medical school?" The latter should never be answered with factual information until after one has found out why the question is being asked, and whose body is being talked about. Individuals often ask for suicide prevention information for a "friend" or "relative" when they are actually inquiring about themselves.

BEHAVIORAL. Among the behavioral clues, we can distinguish the direct and the indirect. The clearest examples of direct behavioral communications of the intention to kill oneself is a "practice run," an actual suicide attempt of whatever seriousness. Any action that uses instruments conventionally associated with suicide (such as razors, ropes, pills, and the like), regardless of whether or not it could have any lethal outcome, must be interpreted as a direct behavioral "cry for help" and an indication that the person is putting us on our alert. Often, the nonlethal suicide attempt is meant to communicate deeper suicidal intentions. By and large, suicide attempts must be taken seriously as indications of personal crisis and of more severe suicide potentiality.

In general, indirect behavioral communications are such actions as equivalents of a trip or putting affairs into order. Thus the making of a will under certain peculiar and special circumstances can be an indirect clue to suicidal intention. Buying a casket at the time of another's funeral should always be inquired after most carefully and, if necessary, prompt action (like hospitalization) taken. Giving away prized possessions like a watch, earrings, golf clubs, or

heirlooms should be looked on as a possible prodromal clue to suicide.

SITUATIONAL. On occasion the situation itself cries out for attention, especially when there is a variety of stresses. For example, when a patient is extremely anxious about surgery, or when he has been notified that he has a malignancy, when he is scheduled for mutilative surgery, when he is frightened by hospitalization itself, or when outside factors (like family discord, for example, or finances) are a problem—all these are situational. If the doctor or nurse is sensitive to the fact that the situation constitutes a "psychological emergency" for that patient, then he is in a key position to perform lifesaving work. His actions might take the form of sympathetic conversation, or special surveillance of that patient by keeping him with some specially assigned person, or by requesting consultation, or by moving him so that he does not have access to windows at lethal heights. At the least, the nurse should make notations of her behavioral observations in the chart.

To be a suicide diagnostician, one must combine separate symptoms and recognize *and label* a suicidal syndrome in a situation in which no one symptom by itself would necessarily lead one to think of a possible suicide.

In this paper we shall highlight syndromatic clues for suicide in a medical and surgical hospital setting, although these clues may also be used in other settings. First, it can be said that patient status is stressful for many persons. Everyone who has ever been a patient knows the fantasies of anxiety, fear, and regression that are attendant on illness or surgery. For some in the patient role (especially in a hospital), as the outer world recedes, the fantasy life becomes more active; conflicts and inadequacies and fears may then begin to play a larger and disproportionate role. The point for suicide prevention is that one must try to be aware especially of those patients who are prone to be psychologically overreactive and, being so, are more apt to explode irrationally into suicidal behavior.

SYNDROMATIC. What are the syndromes—the constellations of symptoms—for suicide? Labels for four of them could be: depressed, disoriented, defiant, and dependent-dissatisfied.

Depressed. The syndrome of depression is, by and large, made up of symptoms that reflect the shifting of the individual's psychological interests from aspects of his interpersonal life to aspects of his private psychological life, to some intrapsychic crisis within himself. For example, the individual is less interested in food, he loses his appetite, and thus loses weight. Or, his regular patterns of sleeping and waking becomes disrupted, so that he suffers from lack of energy in the daytime and then sleeplessness and early awakening. The habitual or regular patterns of social and sexual response also tend to change, and the individual loses interest in others. His rate or pace or speed of talking, walking, and doing the activities of his everyday life slows down. At the same time there is increased preoccupation with internal (intrapsychic) conflicts and problems. The individual is withdrawn, apathetic, apprehensive and anxious, often "blue" and even tearful, somewhat unreachable and seemingly uncaring.

Depression can be seen too in an individual's decreased willingness to communicate. Talking comes harder, there are fewer spontaneous remarks, answers are shorter or even monosyllabic, the facial expressions are less lively, the posture is more drooped, gestures are less animated, the gait is less springy, and the individual's mind seems occupied and elsewhere.

An additional symptom of the syndrome of depression is detachment, or withdrawing from life. This might be evidenced by behavior that would reflect attitudes, such as "I don't care," "What does it matter," "It's no use anyway." If an individual feels helpless he is certainly frightened, although he may fight for some control or safety; but if he feels hopeless, then the heart is out of him, and life is a burden, and he is only a spectator to a dreary life that does not involve him.

First aid in suicide prevention is directed to counteracting the individual's feelings of hopelessness. Dr. Robert Litman, chief psychiatrist of the Los Angeles Suicide Prevention Center, has said that "Psychological support is transmitted by a firm and hopeful attitude. We convey the impression that the problem which seems to the patient to be overwhelming, dominating his entire personality, and completely insidious, is commonplace and quite familiar to us and we have seen many people make a complete recovery.

Hope is a commodity of which we have plenty and we dispense it freely."[2]

It is of course pointless to say "Cheer up" to a depressed person, inasmuch as the problem is that he simply cannot. On the other hand, the effectiveness of the "self-fulfilling prophecy" should never be underestimated. Often an integral part of anyone's climb out of a depression is his faith and the faith of individuals around him that he is going to make it. Just as hopelessness breeds hopelessness, hope—to some extent—breeds hope.

Oftentimes, the syndrome of depression does not seem especially difficult to diagnose. What may be more difficult—and very much related to suicide—is the apparent improvement after a severe depression, when the individual's pace of speech and action picks up a little. The tendency then is for everyone to think that he is cured and to relax vigilance. In reality the situation may be much more dangerous; the individual now has the psychic energy with which to kill himself that he may not have had when he was in the depths of his depression. By far, most suicides relating to depression occur within a short period (a few days to 3 months) after the individual has made an apparent turn for the better. A good rule is that any significant change in behavior, even if it looks like improvement, should be assessed as a possible prodromal index for suicide.

Although depression is the most important single prodromal syndrome for suicide—occurring to some degree in approximately one-third of all suicides—it is not the only one.

Disoriented. Disoriented people are apt to be delusional or hallucinatory, and the suicidal danger is that they may respond to commands or voices or experiences that other people cannot share. When a disoriented person expresses any suicidal notions, it is important to take him as a most serious suicidal risk, for he may be in constant danger of taking his own life, not only to cut out those parts of himself that he finds intolerable, but also to respond to the commands of hallucinated voices to kill himself. What makes such a person potentially explosive and particularly hard to predict is that the trigger mechanism may depend on a crazed thought, a hallucinated command, or a fleeting intense fear within a delusional system.

Disoriented states may be clearly organic, such as delirium

tremens, certain toxic states, certain drug withdrawal states. Individuals with chronic brain syndromes and cerebral arteriosclerosis may become disoriented. On the other hand, there is the whole spectrum of schizophrenic and schizoaffective disorders, in which the role of organic factors is neither clearly established nor completely accepted. Nonetheless, professional personnel should especially note individuals who manifest some degree of nocturnal disorientation, but who have relative diurnal lucidity. Those physicians who see the patients only during the daytime are apt to miss these cases, particularly if they do not read nurses' notes.

Suicides in general hospitals have occurred among nonpsychiatric patients with subtle organic syndromes, especially those in which symptoms of disorientation are manifested. One should look, too, for the presence of bizarre behavior, fear of death, and clouding of the patient's understanding and awareness. The nurse might well be especially alert to any general hospital patient who has any previous neuropsychiatric history, especially when there are the signs of an acute brain syndrome. Although dyspnea is not a symptom in the syndrome related to disorientation, the presence of severe dyspnea, especially if it is unimproved by treatment in the hospital, has been found to correlate with suicide in hospitals.

When an individual is labeled psychotic, he is almost always disoriented in one sphere or another. Even if he knows where he is and what the date is, he may be off base about who he is, especially if one asks him more or less "philosophic" questions, like "What is the meaning of life?" His thinking processes will seem peculiar, and the words of his speech will have some special or idiosyncratic characteristics. In general, whether or not such patients are transferred to psychiatric wards or psychiatric hospitals, they should—in terms of suicide prevention—be given special care and surveillance, including consultation. Special physical arrangements should be made for them, such as removal of access to operable screens and windows, removal of objects of self-destruction and the like.

Defiant. The Welsh poet, Dylan Thomas, wrote, "Do not go gentle into that good night. . . . rage, rage against the dying of the light." Many of us remember, usually from high school literature, Henley's *Invictus,* "I am the master of my fate: I am the captain of my soul." The point is that many individuals, no matter how miserable their circumstances or how painful their lives, attempt to retain some

shred of control over their own fate. Thus a man dying of cancer may, rather than passively capitulate to the disease, choose to play one last active role in his own life by picking the time of his death; so that even in a terminal state (when the staff may believe that he doesn't have the energy to get out of bed), he lifts a heavy window and throws himself out to his death. In this sense, he is willful or defiant.

This kind of individual is an "implementer."[3] Such a person is described as one who has an active need to control his environment. Typically, he would never be fired from any job; he would quit. In a hospital he would attempt to control his environment by refusing some treatments, demanding others, requesting changes, insisting on privileges, and indulging in many other activities indicating some inner need to direct and control his life situation. These individuals are often seen as having low frustration tolerance, being fairly set and rigid in their ways, being somewhat arbitrary and, in general, showing a great oversensitivity to outside control. The last is probably a reflection of their own inability to handle their inner stresses.

Certainly, not every individual who poses ward management problems needs to be seen as suicidal, but what personnel should look for is the somewhat agitated concern of a patient with controlling his own fate. Suicide is one way of "calling the shot." The nurse can play a lifesaving role with such a person by recognizing his psychological problems and by enduring his controlling (and irritating) behavior—indeed, by being the willing target of his berating and demanding behavior and thus permitting him to expend his energies in this way, rather than in suicidal activities. Her willingness to be a permissible target for these feelings and, more, her sympathetic behavior in giving attention and reassurance even in the face of difficult behavior are in the tradition of the nurturing nurse, even though this can be a difficult role continually to fulfill.

Dependent-dissatisfied. Imagine being married to someone on whom you are deeply emotionally dependent, in a situation in which you are terribly dissatisfied with your being dependent. It would be in many ways like being "painted into a corner"—there is no place to go.

This is the pattern we have labeled "dependent-dissatisfied."[4]

Such an individual is very dependent on the hospital, realizing he is ill and depending on the hospital to help him; however, he is dissatisfied with being dependent and comes to feel that the hospital is not giving him the help he thinks he needs. Such patients become increasingly tense and depressed, with frequent expressions of guilt and inadequacy. They have emotional disturbances in relation to their illnesses and to their hospital care. Like the "implementer," they make demands and have great need for attention and reassurance. They have a number of somatic complaints, as well as complaints about the hospital. They threaten to leave the hospital against medical advice. They ask to see the doctor, the chaplain, the chief nurse. They request additional therapies of various kinds. They make statements like, "Nothing is being done for me" or "The doctors think I am making this up."

The reactions of irritability on the part of busy staff are not too surprising in view of the difficult behavior of such patients. Tensions in these patients may go up especially at the time of pending discharge from the hospital. Suicide prevention by hospital staff consists of responding to the emotional needs and giving emotional support to these individuals. With such patients the patience of Job is required. Any suicide threats or attempts on the part of such patients, no matter how "mild" or attention-getting, should be taken seriously. Their demand for attention may lead them to suicide. Hospital staff can often, by instituting some sort of new treatment procedure or medication, give this type of patient temporary relief or a feeling of improvement. But most of all, the sympathetic recognition on the part of hospital staff that the complaining, demanding, exasperating behavior of the dependent-dissatisfied patient is an expression of his own inner feelings of desperation may be the best route to preventing his suicide.

Co-Workers, Family, Friends

Suicide is "democratic." It touches both patients and staff, unlettered and educated, rich and poor—almost proportionately. As for sex ratio, the statistics are interesting: Most studies have shown that in Western countries more men than women commit suicide, but a recent study indicates that in certain kinds of hospital settings like neuropsychiatric hospitals, a proportionately larger

percentage of women kill themselves.⁵ The information in this paper is meant to apply not only to patients, but to colleagues, and even to members of our families as well. The point is that only by being free to see the possibility of suicidal potential in everybody can suicide prevention of anybody really become effective.

In our society, we are especially loathe to suspect suicide in individuals of some stature or status. For example, of the physicians who commit suicide, some could easily be saved if they would be treated (hospitalized, for example) like ordinary citizens in distress. Needless to say, the point of view that appropriate treatment might cause him professional embarrassment should never be invoked in such a way so as to risk a life being lost.

In general, we should not "run scared" about suicide. In the last analysis, suicides are, fortunately, infrequent events. On the other hand, if we have even unclear suspicions of suicidal potential in another person, we do well to have "the courage of our own confusions" and take the appropriate steps.

These appropriate steps may include notifying others, obtaining consultation, alerting those concerned with the potentially suicidal person (including relatives and friends), getting the person to a sanctuary in a psychiatric ward or hospital. Certainly, we don't want to holler "Fire" unnecessarily, but we should be able to interpret the clues, erring, if necessary, on the "liberal" side. We may feel chagrined if we turn in a false alarm, but we would feel very much worse if we were too timid to pull the switch that might have prevented a real tragedy.

Earlier in this paper the role of the potential rescuer was mentioned. One implication of this is that professionals must be aware of their own reactions and their own personalities, especially in relation to certain patients. For example, does he have the insight to recognize his tendency to be irritated at a querulous and demanding patient and thus to ignore his presuicidal communications? Every rescue operation is a dialogue: Someone cries for help and someone else must be willing to hear him and be capable of responding to him. Otherwise the victim may die because of the potential rescuer's unresponsiveness.

We must develop in ourselves a special attitude for suicide prevention. Each individual can be a lifesaver, a one-person com-

mittee to prevent suicide. Happily, elaborate pieces of mechanical equipment are not needed; "all" that is required are sharp eyes and ears, good intuition, a pinch of wisdom, an ability to act appropriately, and a deep resolve.

Chapter 26
IMMOBILIZATION RESPONSE TO SUICIDAL BEHAVIOR
Robert E. Litman

When a suicidal communication is perceived by a potential rescuer but is avoided, denied, or repressed, the consequences may be tragic. The potential rescuer may be immobilized, with possible solutions to the problem remaining unconscious to him. Interpersonal relationships in which the "significant other" is seen as essential to survival and separation is seen as death or disaster to both may respond well to emergency intervention by a rescuing third party.

Certain aspects of self-destructive behavior can be understood as an appeal for help in an intolerable situation made to one or more potential rescuers.[1] Often the response of the person who receives such a communication is crucial for life or death. When the responses are inadequate, what are the reasons?

The concept "suicide" comprises such a wide variety of complex social-psychological phenomena that most investigators have limited themselves to special aspects.

For example, Stengel emphasized the social effects of suicidal behavior.[2] Ordinarily suicide threats or attempts have a powerful social effect, tending automatically to induce or "release" rescuing activity from the environment. Indeed, much of the rationale of a Suicide Prevention Center is provided by observations indicating that potentially self-destructive persons are ambivalent about death.[3] They communicate their suicidal preoccupation. Then others can give aid.

In a recent study of suicide in St. Louis, Robins and co-workers found suicidal communications were made by more than two-thirds of the deceased.[4] The persons receiving the communications became anxious, tense, and concerned. Generally they felt helpless to act, especially since professionals offered little or no guidance. According to Robins, failure to act resulted primarily from ignorance of what to do.

Meerloo, on the other hand, reported a series of cases in which the suicide victims were willed to death by the conscious hostility of their partners who committed "psychic mentacide."[5] Jensen and Petty recognized in every suicidal act a desire to be rescued but indicated that potential rescuers must have available surplus libido to be effective.[6] Tabachnick discussed the complex interpersonal dynamics and countertransference reactions that sometimes block freedom of personal action to aid another.[7]

The focus of this investigation are those unfortunate cases in which a suicidal communication is made to an "other" within a close interpersonal relationship. The tragedy is that the suicidal communication is perceived but conscious recognition of its significance is avoided, denied, and repressed. Possible solutions to the problem remain unconscious. The potential rescuer is immobilized. Such situations are common in suicide prevention center experience. These four cases were chosen for this report because a dream of the immobilized potential rescuer provided psychoanalytic understanding of his dilemma.

Case 1 After an unhappy childhood, followed by ten years of a disappointing childless marriage, Mary A met John B, a shy, introverted graduate student who was seven years younger than she. Mary divorced her unloved first husband to marry Mr. B, who left his mother's apron strings to become attached to his wife. In order to make the change he had about a year of psychotherapy. Mary worked in a lab while he studied for his doctor's degree.

After several years, the balance of their quiet lives was decisively disturbed by two events. First, Mary became pregnant. Mr. B reacted with withdrawal, confusion, anxiety, and impotence. The pregnancy terminated with a spontaneous miscarriage, but Mr. B's potency did not return. They never discussed this problem. Apparently each felt the other should talk about it first.

Secondly, Mr. B received his degree and got a well-paying job, and Mary quit work. She then became aware of extreme nervous tension and the development of phobias. She was afraid to drive her car alone. She demanded more and more special attention from Mr. B. Both partners in the marriage were depressed but did not discuss it with each other. Mary consulted an internist for a series of diagnostic medical examinations, and insisted that Mr. B accompany her to the office each time. This precipitated several

quarrels. During one of these Mr. B committed suicide by hanging. Two weeks before Mr. B's death, Mary dreamed as follows:

"I walked out onto a high balcony and was horrified to see that John had fallen over the balcony railing and was dangling. He was holding onto the leash of our dog, Prince. The leash was tight around the dog's neck and was choking the dog. I stood paralyzed, not knowing what to do. If I did not act, the dog would be choked to death; if I cut the leash, John would fall and be killed on the pavement below. I woke up terrified and choking."

In the morning, Mary told this dream to her husband with the interpretation that she made herself. "I felt that I was the dog being choked by our marriage, but I couldn't end the marriage because it would kill you, John."

Mr. B made no comment and the dream was forgotten. When she discovered Mr. B's suicide, Mary was at first astonished and disbelieving. A full day passed by until she suddenly recalled this dream, and with the recollection came the knowledge that she had recognized her husband's suicidal state and by her subsequent actions was guilty of his death. She then made a suicide attempt with barbiturates and, following that, was brought for psychiatric treatment.

At the time of the dream, Mary knew that the marriage was collapsing and had considered the possibility of going back to work. John, she could see, vacillated between moods of humble ingratiation, with servile efforts to please her, and moods of withdrawal and depression. He talked about death several times. She took it to be in connection with the death of a friend. In the dream, she opens the door and walks out on the balcony of a high building. She associates to the doctor's office where she took a thyroid test. The doctor is a man she can depend on and lean on. She recalls her pregnancy and miscarriage. John liked to take the dog for a walk. Sometimes he said he lived a dog's life. He brought her slippers to her and lit her cigarettes, but she could not depend on him to be a man. "I just didn't feel I could be a mother to him any more, the way I used to be. I was worn out, having a nervous breakdown myself." (The dog?) She had always wanted a dog and as soon as she could she got a big dog, a Labrador Retriever. "This dog is very sensitive to my moods and very close to me." There were many associations as to how the dog can sense what she is feeling.

The dream resembles those of a traumatic neurosis. The problem is represented clearly, and the dream ends with paralysis, immobilization, and unmastered anxiety. The approaching dissolution of her marriage is felt as an overwhelming trauma and is associated with the miscarriage and previous traumatic separations from her pets and her mother. The symbolism of the leash as it appears in this dream recalls the umbilical cord. The dreamer identifies herself with the baby-mother symbiosis and she cannot cut the cord.

Mary might have saved her husband (and herself) after the dream by seeking out professional help. The dream hints at that solution in the associations to the doctor's office and the doctor and her attempts to bring her husband with her to the doctor's office. Two main problems interfered with her unconscious efforts to alert the doctor and get his help for her husband. First was the absence of verbal communication between husband and wife. They were incapable of discussing feelings; their mutual sensitivity was limited to nonverbal exchange—like that between master and dog, mother and baby, and thus was extremely susceptible to repression. As we unearthed, in diaries and from friends, additional evidence of Mr. B's death preoccupation, Mary was continually surprised. Secondly, an action to resolve the symbiotic relationship (symbolized by cutting the leash) was specifically traumatic to Mary, overwhelming her efforts at ego mastery. Instead of calling in a third party to cut the cord, she was compelled helplessly to maintain the symbiosis. What is illustrated here is not so much hostile psychic homicide (Meerloo) as a mutual race toward suicide by two regressed dependent people.

Case 2 Mrs. C and Mrs. D had grown to be close friends while both were patients on a small psychiatric ward that specialized in milieu therapy. Mrs. D committed suicide with her husband's pistol while on a trial leave of absence from the hospital. Mrs. C had been discharged several weeks before, but continued coming to the hospital for day care activities. During this interim period, about a week before the suicide, she reported the following dream to her therapist.

"Mrs. D tied me to a tree trunk with a rope and danced around. She piled branches around me and set them on fire. Then she was tangled in the rope, too, and we were caught. I was helpless and frightened." Associations: Mrs. D is much younger than Mrs. C and reminds

her of her daughter, who is a dancer. Once when they were young, this daughter tied her sister to a tree with a rope. Mrs. D at times thinks she killed her baby. Some of the patients say she really did. Mrs. C adds that she and Mrs. D have been very close in the hospital. Right now Mrs. C feels that the two of them will never get well. The fire reminds her that when she used to take barbiturates to a state of coma, she set the bed on fire. After a long silence she confesses that she and Mrs. D have discussed ways to commit suicide, for instance, to run out in front of a car or take barbiturates or by hanging. Mrs. D says that these are all female ways of killing oneself and like everything female it is ineffective. The men do it better. The rope reminds Mrs. C of sex. She thinks of homosexuality. Mrs. C feels that she is more feminine than Mrs. D. More silence, then she asks anxiously if she should warn the doctor that Mrs. D will kill herself.

Here again we see the close connection symbolized by the rope. There is also the anxious immobility and the difficulty in communication (secrecy from the therapist). Mrs. C knows unconsciously that Mrs. D is in danger, but she is unable to mobilize her own ego sufficiently to recognize the danger consciously and warn the therapist directly. Instead, she places herself in the situation of danger in the dream and is helpless.

Case 3 On the advice of her doctor, Mrs. E called the Suicide Prevention Center regarding her husband. She said they were a successful televison writing team. In the last year they had been having bad luck and some financial reverses, but the main trouble was a steadily increasing depressive attitude on the part of the husband. For several months he had been unable to work, constantly on sleeping pills, almost bedridden. He had talked repeatedly of death and suicide. She said, "Last night I had a horrible dream. I guess that is why I decided to call you today. I dreamed that I or my husband was dead, or both of us were dead, by hanging. I was so confused—I couldn't tell which of us was which, or which of us was dead, and who had killed us, or had we killed each other."

The telephone interview revealed that she, too, had become depressed and she felt helpless to contend with her problems. I suggested emergency hospitalization for the husband. She rejected it, giving many reasons, principally emphasizing denial of the seriousness of the situation and anxiety about making any decisive moves.

The earliest appointment she would accept was for the next day at 1 P.M. The next morning she took the car to be washed and serviced and while she was gone, her husband ingested an overdose of pills and was dying when she returned.

On learning of this, I went immediately to the home of Mrs. E and found her profoundly depressed and suicidal. Her feelings were a mixture of guilt, anger, perplexity, and confusion. She was obsessed with the thought "If I hadn't told him we were going to see a psychiatrist, maybe he would not have done this."

I was impressed by the strong identification with her husband, the intense mutual dependency, and the unwillingness to accept any type of interruption in the relationship.

Case 4 The situation and dream are in some ways similar to the first three with, however, a happier outcome. The dreamer is a psychiatrist in psychoanalysis. He dreams:

"I am in my office; the lighting is dim and it seems smoggy. I am waiting for my patient, Mrs. F, who is late. I try to make a phone call but I cannot. There is much anxiety. I wake up coughing."

The smoggy office reminds him that he feels tired and sick today; maybe he is catching cold. He would like to leave Los Angeles. Mrs. F seldom comes late. Lately she has been quite uncommunicative. Her resistance takes the form of sitting silently for minutes on end and looking at him expectantly. He has interpreted the hostility with no effect. Once, years ago, she made a suicide attempt. Suicide! He had not realized he was concerned that she might attempt suicide. But only last week she talked longingly of death. He decides Mrs. F is quite depressed. The phone call would be to Mrs. F or maybe the doctor's analyst.

Note the traumatic quality of the dream, ending in anxious immobilization. The telephone, which links the doctor with his patient and his analyst, symbolizes the leash, the umbilical cord. The dream eloquently represents the block in verbal communication. Something in the relationship with Mrs. F is activating in the doctor a regressed traumatic situation that he can verbalize only with difficulty. He realizes that he has been hoping that Mrs. F would spontaneously recover and make the first move toward reconciliation. He decides to discuss the case with a third person (a consultant).

Comment

The concept of symbiotic relationships between human beings was formulated by Balint and popularized by Benedek, Mahler, and others.[8] The extension of this concept, which originally applied to the mother and child, to relationships between adults, has recently been reviewed by Pollock.[9]

The above case reports illuminate briefly some aspects of crises, precipitated by the breakdown of neurotic symbiotic unions between adults. These are interpersonal relationships in which regressive elements predominate. There is a great deal of mutual identification; psychic representations of self and object are frequently fused. The other person is experienced as essential to survival, and a separation or divergence from the other is equated with death or disaster to both. It is as if there were an umbilical cord uniting the partners. In dreams, this may be symbolized by a leash, cord, rope, or telephone. To cut this umbilical connection is felt as dangerous and extremely traumatic. Both of the partners are immobilized under conditions of great tension and discomfort. Communication of feelings between the partners is primarily by action and gesture rather than words. "He knows what I'm thinking without my saying it."

Both partners wait for some action from the other to resolve the painful stalemate. Danger signals are exchanged but not acknowledged as such. The eventual breakthrough into action tends to be explosive and quite destructive especially when the content of the unacknowledged communications included references to suicide.

An analysis of the routes by which couples drift or are propelled into this crisis pattern is beyond the scope of this paper. Nor is it appropriate here to discuss the treatment. In general, persons involved in a symbiotic race toward suicide respond well to emergency psychotherapy. The exhaustion of the stronger partner is the final signal for emergency intervention by a rescuing third person—friend, therapist, or consultant.[10]

Chapter 27
MANAGEMENT OF SUICIDAL PATIENTS IN MEDICAL PRACTICE
Robert E. Litman

Suicidal crises are best understood as late stages in the progressive breakdown of adaptational behavior in emotionally exhausted patients. The premonitory symptoms of suicide include verbal communications, suicide attempts, symptomatic actions, depression, treatment failure, excessive emotional reactions to specific disease states, and panic reaction.

Of persons who committed suicide, 75 percent had seen a physician within six months. To recognize and evaluate suicide danger the physician must not be afraid to question the patient directly about his suicidal plans. The average physician encounters half a dozen suicidal patients a year and may have ten to twelve suicides in his practice during a long career.

In treating suicidal patients, the physician should maintain his medical attitude. The patients need emergency medical care including appropriate drugs. Free communication between patient and physician is very important. This may take some extra time. Patients benefit from emergency psychological support and stimulation toward constructive action. Family, friends, and community agencies should be mobilized to aid the patient. For seriously suicidal patients, consultation is recommended and treatment in hospital is advisable.

"Prevention is a watchword of modern medicine."[1] This attitude has led in recent years to increasing emphasis on the role of physicians in preventing suicide. Undoubtedly suicide describes a group of actions and events of great variety and complexity, but the focus of this communcation is on recognizing, evaluating, and treating suicidal patients in medical practice.

It is based upon shared experiences and discussions with the staff of the Suicide Prevention Center at Los Angeles, especially with Drs. Farberow, Shneidman, and Tabachnick, my associates for many years.[2] Additional observations and other points of view can be found in articles by Bennett, Mintz, Motto and Greene, Offenkrantz, Robins and co-workers, and Vail.[3]

Who are the suicidal patients? How are they defined? Commonly, the term *suicidal* is applied ambiguously not only to actions of self-murder, self-injury, and self-neglect, but also to threats, communications, and thoughts about self-destruction. What are the relationships among these different suicidal behaviors?

In California, medical examiners and coroners certified approximately 2,800 deaths as suicide in 1963. Suicide was the ninth leading category of death. About 10 percent of the suicides were old and sick persons, weary after sixty-five years or more of life. But the great majority of these deaths occurred in young and middle-aged persons with great potentialities and responsibilities. For example, in colleges, on ships at sea and in factories, suicide was the third leading cause of death. Families, physicians, and the community felt these suicides unnecessary, unreasonable, and uniquely tragic. How can they be explained?

In medical practice, suicide is best understood as the final stage of a progressive breakdown of adaptational behavior occurring in an emotionally exhausted patient. Rough analogies may be drawn to states of physiological collapse; for example, in heat stroke or in untreated adrenal insufficiency. In these examples there is a progressive failure of physiological adjustment with the appearance of premonitory symptoms and signs leading to a potentially fatal crisis. Thoughts of suicide, suicide attempts, and numerous kinds of suicidal communications are part of the prodromal symptomatology of suicidal crises.[4]

Emotional crises occur from time to time in all lives when people face problems that are temporarily beyond their ability to solve. Situations that threaten the continuity of mental, physical, and social equilibrium are powerful stressors. Confrontations with death, ill health, loss of love, or change in social status are typical examples. The person under stress feels restless, uneasy, painfully tense, and unable to adapt.[5]

Prodromal Suicidal Clues

There are a number of prodromal clues:

1. Verbal communications. In more than half of the suicide deaths, there is a history of previous, spontaneous, suicidal communications. These statements were direct: "I am going to shoot

myself." "I wish I were dead." Or they were indirect: "You would be better off without me." "How do you leave your body to the medical school?" Sometimes such comments are made directly to a physician, but more often the physician receives the information from frightened friends and relatives who want advice on how to respond to these messages. The most significant interpretation of suicidal communications is that they represent "cries for help." As such, they tend to activate intense emotional responses in persons receiving the communications. More often than not the suicidal situation involves several people.

It should be added that many suicidal patients do not express their self-destructive thoughts spontaneously but will do so if they are asked.

2. Suicide attempts. In one-third of the suicide deaths, there is a history of previous suicide attempts. These are intentional self-injuries made in an emotional context resembling suicide. Surveys indicate that physicians in California see about eight suicide attempts for every suicide. Approximately 20 percent of persons who attempt suicide repeat action of this type at least once. About 5 percent of the attempters eventually kill themselves. Half of these deaths occur within a year of the previous attempt, sometimes within hours.

Considering the sizable mortality rate, physicians who treat surgical and medical self-injuries should ask about obvious sources of emotional stress as soon as possible after the self-injury. For a limited time the shock of the suicide attempt causes families and individuals to report truthfully about vital conflicts and embarrassing problems that ordinarily are hidden or distorted by half truths. The disinterested, preoccupied, or timid physician loses a golden opportunity to bring concealed problems out into the open where they can be dealt with more effectively.

3. Symptomatic actions. Some suicidal persons communicate their plans by actions. One man bought two caskets, one for his wife who had just died. A student gave away his sports equipment, saying, "I won't need this any more." In struggling against suicidal feelings, some persons take dare-devil chances, and they may have a series of accidents or near misses. Increased alcohol intake and irregular attendance at work are common. Requests for increasing

amounts of strong sedatives and rapid-acting sleep producers are ominous premonitory clues to suicide.

4. Depression. This syndrome is of major importance to physicians because of its frequency, serious disability, danger to life— and good response to treatment.[6] Suicide should be considered as a possibility whenever depressive symptoms are reported. The symptoms are physiological, psychological, and social. In all areas the ability to enjoy is lost or seriously disrupted.

Physiological symptoms include sleep disorder, especially sleeplessness; appetite disorder, especially loss of appetite; constipation, dry mouth, headaches, other aches and pains; and fatigue. The psychological symptoms include loss of energy, loss of initiative and absence of interest in usual pleasures, such as sex, sports, books, and television. The mood is sad and often guilty, with low self-esteem. Patients tend to feel hopeless and helpless. These emotions are experienced as painful and uncomfortable.

Social withdrawal completes the picture. The patient loses interest in social gatherings and other people, although he may try at times to pretend interest. Often physicians or families suggest a vacation. The realization by the patient that he is unable to enjoy a vacation may be the last straw that precipitates a suicidal crisis.

The depressive syndrome tends to have a discreet onset and a limited duration. Older patients usually have had previous depressive episodes. A family history of depression is common.

5. Treatment failures. In medical practice, suicidal crises tend to be associated with treatment failures. For example, Workman's Compensation has paid a number of death claims recently on workers who remained disabled after treatment for back strain, then killed themselves. Suicide reports often allude to vague abdominal pains or causalgias, persisting after numerous surgical operations. Diseases that impair respiration—for example, emphysema or lymphoma of the neck and mediastinum—are more often associated with suicide than are other chronic illnesses.

6. Excessive reactions. Some attention should be directed toward patients who have an excessive emotional preoccupation with some specific condition, such as pregnancy, obesity, or cancer. Even if the patient does not have the particular condition, the negative results of medical examinations should be carefully and repeatedly explained to such patients. It is particularly ironic when a suicide note

gives "cancer" as the reason for the act but the autopsy shows no signs of the disease. In suicide histories dread of heart attacks occurs more commonly than actual coronary occlusions.

7. *Panic reactions.* About 5 percent of suicides result from sudden blind panic. Examples: A male school teacher charged with homosexuality dived, in handcuffs, under the wheels of a passing truck. An older man, confused and frightened in an unfamiliar hospital room, jumped out of the window. After an automobile accident, while rescuers attended his badly hurt wife, the uninjured husband wandered off and hanged himself.

Evaluation of Suicidal Potentiality

Persons who are considering suicide as a potential solution to life crises seek out physicians, hoping for answers less extreme than suicide. Seventy-five percent of suicides had seen a physician within six months of the death. Unfortunately, patients do not ordinarily reveal spontaneously that they are in suicidal crises. This information emerges readily, however, if the physician asks for it, especially if there is a preexisting patient-physician relationship of confidence and trust. When he notes prodromal clues to suicide, the physician must decide how to proceed.[7]

Usually, the most tactful and informative technique is to approach the suicidal motivation gradually through a series of questions, working from the more general to the more specific. Such a series of questions might be something like this: "How is your life going? How are you feeling in general? How are your spirits—your mental outlook—your hopes?" If the answers indicate low spirits or pessimistic attitudes or much tension or confusion, another series of questions might be something like this: "Do you wish you could be out of it? Would you like sometimes to give up? Ever wish you were dead?"

If the answers to the above are suggestively affirmative, then a third series of questions might be: "Have you thought of ending your life? How close are you now to suicide? How would you do it? What is your plan?"

1. *Suicide plan.* The most important, single element in evaluating the immediate suicide emergency is the patient's suicide plan, including the proposed method, place, and time. If the patient has decided upon a specific, highly lethal method of suicide with an

instrument that is readily available to him, there is a serious emergency. Usually, patients will talk to an interested physician about the details of their suicide plans, although sometimes this information is obtained from friends or relatives. We take it seriously when a patient sets a deadline for his action; for instance, his fiftieth birthday, retirement day, or an anniversary. Vague suicide plans are somewhat reassuring, as are plans to use methods of relatively low lethality, such as aspirin ingestion.

Direct denials are usually truthful and can be relied on, at least temporarily. "Yes, I thought of suicide, but I would never do it because of my children." "For me, suicide is impossible because of my religion." "I would leave town first." The exceptions to this rule—that is, patients who dissemble to friendly physicians—are nearly always obvious psychiatric cases, usually with a history of psychiatric hospitalization.

Physicians who hesitate to ask such direct questions about suicide because of possible harmful effects on patients should be reassured by the experience of the staff of the Suicide Prevention Center in Los Angeles. In interviews with 10,000 suicidal patients and reviews of 3,000 suicide deaths, we found no evidence that such questions had ever harmed patients.

2. *Severity of symptoms.* Danger signals are: Severe agitation with depression; helplessness, combined with a frantic need to do something; hopelessness that gets worse in response to helping efforts from others; confusion; paranoid trends with persecution delusions or homicidal threats. Five percent of suicidal patients are also potentially homicidal.

3. *Basic personality.* Suicidal crises vary in emergency force, according to the patient's character. Persons who have led stable, responsible lives generally respond well to treatment and return to their previous levels. Because of the favorable prognosis, such persons should be the objects of extremely zealous suicide prevention efforts. At present about half of the persons who kill themselves are of that order. Sometimes high social position, public prominence, or professional success is a barrier between patients and the help they need. Examples are physicians, military leaders, and political figures. Many lives would be saved if persons in crises could accept help without stigma.

By contrast, many unstable, immature, addictive, alcoholic, and

deviant persons are chronically on the edge of self-destruction. These patients benefit less from emergency first aid. They need consistent firm direction and long-range rehabilitation.

4. *Precipitating stress.* If the suicidal crisis is a reaction to an overwhelming, sudden stress, the patient needs emergency protection and support but may recover rapidly and spontaneously. This is analogous to heat stroke collapse. If the suicidal crisis represents an internal decompensation with no special external stress, the patient may need special study and special treatment, presumably by a psychiatrist. This is analogous to a physiological crisis due to adrenal cortical insufficiency.

5. *Resources.* These include physical, financial, and interpersonal assets. The willingness and ability of other persons to aid the patient often is the difference between life and death. Some patients are emotionally bankrupt, and this must be taken into account. For example, many alcoholics, after years of self-destructive behavior that has alienated family and friends, "hit bottom" and are highly suicidal.

6. *Special indicators.* These include such factors as family history of suicide, recent suicide of a close friend or relative, anniversary of a divorce or of a death in the family, complete social isolation, history of psychiatric treatment, especially recent discharge from a mental hospital, and recent suicide attempt, unrecognized or untreated.

Management of Suicidal Patients

The physician is not expected to function as a psychiatrist or skilled psychotherapist. In his practice, however, he should always maintain a *medical attitude.* This means that the physician helps whenever possible and does nothing to make matters worse. Sometimes self-destructive patients are uncooperative, provocative, and hostile. Such behavior makes the physician's task more difficult, but should be regarded as symptomatic rather than taken personally. The average physician will encounter half a dozen potentially suicidal patients a year and have ten to twelve suicides in his practice during a long career. Suicide prevention is not his daily preoccupation but rather an occasional opportunity. The management of suicidal crises includes emergency medical and psychological support, plus consultation and referral in appropriate cases, and

a special effort to keep in touch with patients while they are still suicidal.

EMERGENCY MEDICAL CARE. Suicidal patients require extra time, not only for examination but for management and follow-up care. Some suicidal depressions are precipitated by drugs, such as reserpine and occasionally antibiotics, or by withdrawal from sedatives or alcohol. Sometimes virus infections, nutritional deficiencies, or hormonal disturbances are important factors. Often changes in previous medical treatment plans are indicated.

It takes extra time to reassure the anxious patient or explain to the suspicious. Some physicians wisely schedule emotionally disturbed patients at the end of consultation hours, so that extra time is available if needed. If a patient requires excessive time in the office or makes repeated emergency nighttime telephone calls, it may well be a signal to transfer the patient to a psychiatrist or to put him in a hospital.

USE OF DRUGS. Drugs are an essential part of the medical management of suicidal patients. For sleepless patients the rapid-acting barbiturates and other strong hypnotics are wonder drugs. They give an exhausted patient a chance to rest and recover. But these drugs are being misused. There were over a thousand deaths from barbiturates in California last year, most of them due to drugs prescribed by physicians. Prescriptions should not be dispensed or refilled casually. Repeated requests for hypnotics by a patient should warn the physician to review the case and possibly get consultation.

Tranquilizers, psychic stimulants, and psychic energizers are used freely in our clinic. Recent articles review present information on choice of drugs and dosage.[8] This field is new and changing rapidly. During the last year we have been giving moderately anxious patients the tranquilizer chlordiazepoxide, 30 to 100 mg a day. Agitated patients have received phenothiazines: Chlorprothixene, 75 to 200 mg a day, or thioridazine, 30 to 100 mg a day. Depressed patients were usually given amitriptyline, 30 to 150 mg, or imipramine, 30 to 200 mg daily.

I dispense tablets and psychotherapy simultaneously. I tell patients, "The drug industry spent a fortune developing these pills

for you and millions of other patients like you." Side effects, such as dry mouth, are predicted, and the patient is instructed to call me daily or every other day to report. This facilitates our communication and provides for follow-up. Usually the patient gets better. If he feels worse on medication, I think seriously of getting him into a hospital.[9]

EMERGENCY PSYCHOLOGICAL SUPPORT. Because of his position of trust and authority, the physician is ideally suited to give emergency psychological first aid. This includes: (1) establishing communication with the patient; (2) reminding him of his identity; (3) involving family and friends; and (4) stimulating toward constructive action.

Suicidal patients are, by the nature of their response to their difficulties, isolated and alienated from other people who could help them. They feel "different," changed for the worse, worthless. By taking the time to talk with him, the physician helps the patient to reestablish communication with the rest of the world. Psychological support is transmitted by a firm and hopeful attitude. Although the physician recognizes sympathetically that to the patient his problem is overwhelming and insoluble, at the same time he indicates that he has seen many other patients in similar crises who eventually recovered completely. Hope is a powerful medicine that should never be withheld.

The process of taking a medical history is in itself therapeutic. In reviewing his history, the patient is reminded of what he was in the past and who he is now—husband, worker, father, and the like. Thus he recreates his sense of personal continuity and identity. In answering questions about his present problems, the patient widens his view of the world, alternative possibilities can be explored, and additional solutions are suggested. If the physician can help the patient break his overwhelming, giant-size problem down into several smaller, clearly stated, and logically organized, man-size problems, it helps him overcome his panic and confusion.

THE USE OF FAMILY AND FRIENDS. One of the key problems in suicide prevention is the appropriate use of families and friends. It is suggested that whenever possible the family physician talk to the relatives or friends of the patient who is in a suicidal crisis, especially

if it is evaluated as an emergency. If the significant "others" have not appreciated the seriousness of the situation, they should be so advised. Often during an emergency there should be someone with the suicidal person at all times until the crisis is passed. An interview with the closest other person gives the physician a chance to decide whether that person can be supportive or whether he is, in fact, dangerous to the suicidal person because of carelessness, indifference, or hostility. Some of the decisions made about suicidal persons are family decisions; for example, the decision to put them in a hospital. Sometimes patients say, "My husband isn't interested" or "My wife doesn't care to bother," but a telephone call will usually reveal that relatives are concerned and cooperative. One interesting point is that where there is one suicidal patient in a family, there is often another person who is near suicide.[10]

CONSTRUCTIVE ACTION. Suicidal patients are often overwhelmed by feelings of failure, paralysis, and immobility, relieved in some by sudden impulsive spasms of action. Often the self-injury is a desperate attempt to regain the ability to initiate acts. Wherever possible, the physician should direct the patient toward planned and organized actions of a limited scope, which the patient can be expected to negotiate with a degree of success—for example, going to the physician's office for consultations and tests and making telephone reports to the physician at a certain time of the day. The patient might be asked to call a certain friend or take a simple psychological test. Persons who are recovering from suicidal states should be cautioned against prematurely resuming positions of great responsibility in which initiative is required. More routine and limited tasks have a great therapeutic value, in that they take attention away from the patient's self-preoccupation, and tend to create a feeling of confidence when they are successfully completed.

CONSULTATION AND REFERRAL. Whenever possible, the physician should share some of the responsibility for the management of suicidal patients by discussing the situation with a colleague, associate, or consultant. The most serious suicidal crises are best treated in a hospital, preferably psychiatric. The decision for psychiatric hospitalization of a suicidal patient is a full-fledged medical emergency, since about 15 percent of suicides occur in persons who have

had a recent recommendation of hospitalization but have not followed the recommendation. In hospitals, the same principles of suicide prevention apply. Physicians should pay attention to nurse's notes and patients' communications as possible clues to suicide.

In most patients, however, suicidal potentiality is less immediately critical, and out-patient treatment can be considered. If the patient has a long-standing, chronic personality disorder, or if his behavior has been obviously psychotic or has indicated severe emotional disturbance, or he continues to be suicidal for several weeks, a consultation with a specialist in the field of emotional problems is recommended. Most often this would be a psychiatrist, but clinical psychologists and psychiatric social workers are helpful in certain types of cases. Community agencies, such as social work and family service agencies, are very useful for assistance with reality problems such as finances, jobs, supportive care, and home visits. Mental hygiene clinics or community-supported mental health centers are available in some places. In areas in which there are no community or private agencies for care and in which there may be no psychotherapists in private practice readily available, the physician will find the public health and mental health officer of the region able to offer considerable assistance and advice.[11]

After physicians, police officers deal most frequently with suicidal persons. Discussion and planning for suicidal emergencies between the police and the physicians of a community have proved beneficial for both professions and the public.[12] The legal aspects of detaining suicidal persons in hospitals for their own safety vary from state to state. In California several methods are provided, and physicians are encouraged to use their authority for this purpose.

Chapter 28
SUICIDE PREVENTION IN HOSPITALS
Robert E. Litman and Norman L. Farberow

*Hospital patients who are temporarily depressed or confused
present a special problem in identification, as well as in vigilance
on the part of the staff. The rationale for suicide prevention
is based upon the concepts of crisis, ambivalence, communication,
and identification, with action response. Here described
are ways in which these concepts can be applied to suicide
prevention in hospitals, with educational programs for the staff,
improvements in hospital design, and improved communication
between nursing staff and physicians.*

Because we tend to think of hospitals as preserving, prolonging,
and enhancing life, the suicide of a patient in a hospital comes as
a special shock. The suicide is not only a tragedy for the family
but is felt as a blow to the physicians, nursing staff, and hospital
administration. Often, there are accusations of negligence, and
consequent legal complications. In this article, we will report on
studies of suicides in hospitals and the circumstances under which
such suicides are most likely to occur. We will consider various
special problems associated with suicide in general medical-surgical
hospitals, convalescent nursing-hospitals, and psychiatric hospitals,
and we will offer some recommendations for suicide prevention in
each of these settings. Finally, we will discuss the contributions
hospitals can make toward preventing suicide beyond their walls.

The Rationale of Suicide Prevention

Can suicide be prevented? Case histories and clinical observations
by reliable authorities in many different countries inform us that
individual cases of suicide certainly can be prevented. On the other
hand, programs of organized community suicide prevention efforts
are in their infancy and are much more difficult to evaluate. Perhaps hospitals are a logical place in which to initiate and evaluate
a systematic suicide prevention program.

A rationale for suicide prevention is based upon the following
considerations: (1) Crisis: For most patients, the suicidal state

is limited in time duration. If suicidal people survive for a period of time, they usually readjust and are nonsuicidal. This is especially true of patients in general medical-surgical hospitals. (2) Ambivalence: In the great majority of cases, the self-destructive individual is struggling within himself. He has conflicting feelings about death and dying; often he is mixed up and confused. A suicidal action may constitute not only an effort to escape pain, atone for guilt, force a revenge, or make a cry for help but it may, in addition, denote a desire to be rescued, redeemed, and reborn. We should remember that it is almost impossible for the human mind to comprehend the finality and totality of death. (3) Communication: The suicidal individual retains the human tendency to communicate what is on his mind. He gives clues to suicide in the form of verbal comments, action communications, or syndromatic signs. (4) Action response: These clues to suicide can be the basis for special protective actions by persons in the hospital environment. Suicide generally occurs in a context of separation from other people, accompanied by aloneness, alienation, and withdrawal from human relationships. One of the most effective suicide prevention measures is to initiate and foster contact between the patient and other persons, giving him the feeling that others are interested and care what happens to him.

Occasionally, the ethical-philosophical question is raised: "Why should we make a special effort to prevent a person from committing suicide if that is what he wants?" We should note that this question has special pertinence with regard to patients in nursing-convalescent hospitals where all too often groups of aged, chronically ill, socially rejected persons are concentrated to await death. Generally, however, the most perceptive answer to the question "Why help them?" is to point out that the suicidal person has mixed feelings and not only wants to destroy his present image and situation but also wants to be rescued and rehabilitated into some different image and situation. We believe that suicide prevention is the established social policy of the community. Moreover, from a strictly legal point of view, the courts have increasingly tended to delineate suicide prevention as one of the responsibilities for the welfare of patients that hospitals must accept.

Some indication of the frequency of suicides in hospitals is given by the experience of Los Angeles County for years 1963 and 1964.

In those two years, there were a total of 2,284 suicides, of which forty-four occurred in hospitals: twenty suicides occurred in nursing-convalescent units, twelve suicides in general medical-surgical wards, and twelve were in psychiatric hospitals or psychiatric wards. Reviewing the cases revealed that the problems of suicide prevention are somewhat different in each type of hospital.

GENERAL MEDICAL-SURGICAL HOSPITALS. During a two-year period in Los Angeles, twelve patients on general medical-surgical wards committed suicide. When one considers that the average census of patients in general medical-surgical wards in Los Angeles County is over 20,000, one concludes that twelve suicides in two years represent a suicide rate not greatly above the rate for persons outside hospitals. The average 400-bed community medical-surgical hospital might expect no more than one suicide every five years. The occurrence of suicide with appreciably greater frequency than this should arouse self-criticism and self-scrutiny in a hospital administration. After any suicide in a hospital, there should be an investigation and a report to determine the causes and make recommendations for future prevention of a similar event.

Of the twelve suicides, eleven were men. The median age was 67 years, the median stay in the hospital from admission to suicide was three days. Ten of these patients jumped from a height to their deaths. (See Table I.) Most of the self-destructive acts were impulsive in that they had been planned for only a few minutes to a few hours. The patients had been hospitalized for a variety of physical illnesses. All of them were temporarily depressed or confused.

Cases 1 and 2 had been hospitalized several times previously and were both obviously depressed when they were rehospitalized. Both of these men were physicians. Because of their profession, the hospital staff did not view the depression as a danger signal.

Case 2 brought an overdose of sleeping pills into the hospital with him concealed in his toilet kit.

The other death by ingestion, Case 5, was a man with delirium tremens who suddenly snatched a bottle of oil of wintergreen from a shelf and drank it.

Case 3, a 65-year-old man, was admitted to the third floor of a community hospital for treatment of acute bronchitis. After three

days of treatment with antibiotics, his fever had disappeared, but he became confused and unreasonable. He demanded his immediate discharge on the grounds that something terrible was happening to his family, and he had to go home to take care of them. He was given more sedation. He insisted upon lying with his head at the foot of the bed. The charge nurse became alarmed and left the room to obtain restraining devices that could be used to hold the patient in bed. While she was gone he jumped out of the window.

Case 12 showed a similar confusion. A 50-year-old man became confused four days after gall bladder surgery and pulled his catheter out. He wandered around the ward explaining that he was looking for a basketball. He was given sedatives. He demanded a change in his room which was granted. While an attendant went back to his original room to get his clothes, the patient went out through the window.

Case 10 was one of typical depression. He was a man who lived

TABLE I—Suicides in Medical-Surgical Units
(Los Angeles 1963, 1964)

Case No.	Sex	Age	Method	Hosp. Days	Time	Diagnosis and Condition
1	M	68	Fall	1	8:00 A.M.	Pre-op bladder surgery—depressed
2	M	70	Ingest.	2	3:00 P.M.	Cerebral thrombosis—depressed
3	M	65	Fall	3	8:00 P.M.	Acute bronchitis—confused
4	M	44	Fall	3	5:30 P.M.	Acute hepatitis—confused
5	M	68	Ingest.	10	11:00 A.M.	Alcoholic psychosis—confused
6	M	66	Fall	2	12:30 P.M.	Acute alcoholism—depressed
7	M	81	Fall	8	8:15 P.M.	Cerebral thrombosis—depressed
8	F	27	Fall	6	2:00 P.M.	"Diagnostic studies"—panic
9	M	73	Fall	4	10:15 P.M.	Emphysema—depressed
10	M	41	Fall	1	9:00 A.M.	Chest pain—depressed
11	M	76	Fall	300	3:20 P.M.	Arteriosclerosis—depressed
12	M	50	Fall	4	4:15 P.M.	Post-op gall bladder—confused

Median Age: 67 years   11 Males   10 Falls
Median Hospital Stay: 3 days   1 Female   2 Ingestion
Median Time of Day: 3:20 P.M.

alone and had withdrawn from his friends and relatives. He was admitted to the hospital because of chest pains. That night he was sleepless, and he talked to the other patient in his room, expressing loneliness and hopelessness. After breakfast, he said goodbye to his neighbor and dived head-first through a window.

Only one of the twelve patients planned his suicide over a period of time and left a note. That was Case 11, who was also the only patient who had been in a hospital for a considerable period of time. In this respect, Case 11 resembled the typical patient of a nursing-convalescent hospital.

Apparently, one essential problem of suicide prevention in general medical-surgical wards is to prevent patients who are temporarily depressed or confused from falling from the third floor or above. Simple safety devices, which would limit the opening of windows, or modern safety screens on doors and windows would, we believe, prevent about 200 deaths by falls yearly. Screening devices for exposed stairwells are also recommended. Some attention should be paid to the frequent complaint of nurses that they have difficulty in communicating with the physicians in charge of cases. For example, nurses would note that a patient was confused and demanding to go home or threatening suicide or testing the strength of the screens. The physicians, however, were not responding to the implications of the nurses' observations but would merely order routine sedation for the patient. Hospitals might adopt a special signal-flag for nurses to place on charts of patients who might be suicidal. If doctors are not available, ward nurses should be able to communicate through the head nurse to obtain consultation. The consultant should recommend some clear, direct action.

It has been suggested that with elderly patients, some article from home be brought with them to the hospital to remind them of their usual identity and help prevent personal disorientation. This is a device that is used frequently with children. It has also been suggested that lights be left on at night. In this small series of twelve cases, suicide at night was not particularly noticeable. Neither was suicide during the changes of shifts of nurses and attendants noteworthy.

None of the twelve patients was in the hospital because of a suicide attempt. We conclude that suicide on general medical-surgical wards is rare. However, it must be added that suicide immedi-

ately after discharge from general medical-surgical hospitals is less rare. One of these twelve cases illustrates this dramatically:

Case 6 was a 66-year-old man who was admitted to a general medical-surgical hospital for acute alcoholism with mild delerium tremens. He responded well to supportive treatment, and his doctor discharged him two days later at 1:00 P.M. The patient complained that he was all alone in the world, and he said that he had no place to go. His pleas for sympathy were ignored. He then jumped from the third-floor fire escape of the hospital to his death in the alley below. The reaction of the doctor and hospital staff was anger, and a temporary rule was initiated prohibiting the admission of acute alcoholics. However, the relevant medical issue concerns to what extent the hospital should hold itself responsible for the after-care of discharged patients. In the same time period, in which there were only twelve suicides in general medical-surgical hospitals, there were more than 150 persons who committed suicide within two months after discharge from such hospitals. We believe that it is a fair question for the medical staff and administrators of medical-surgical hospitals to consider whether they are doing justice to their patients from the standpoint of follow-up and after-care.

CONVALESCENT-NURSING HOSPITALS. Unlike general medical-surgical hospitals, which emphasize rapid discharge, convalescent-nursing hospitals represent in general the end of the road. For suicide, the median age is 76 years, and the median hospital stay is measured in years. The primary diagnoses are tuberculosis, diabetes, cardiac disorders, and other chronic, serious diseases such as arteriosclerosis, multiple sclerosis, and cancer. Nurses and other patients noted severe depressions in most of these suicidal patients, the majority of whom communicated something about their suicidal intentions. A majority left notes. These patients seldom jumped from heights, possibly because nursing homes tend to be one-story structures. They committed suicide by the ingestion of pills that they had saved up or smuggled in, or by cutting themselves. Although for the most part they gave ample warning about what they were going to do, they were not closely supervised. Apparently, many professional caretakers still ignorantly believe in the myth that people who talk about suicide won't do it. Some informants, in

discussing these cases, raised the philosophical-ethical problem of why there should be any sanction against suicide in patients who were in their eighth decade of life, ill with incurable diseases, suffering from loneliness and abandonment, debility, and conscious of being unwanted and a drain on the resources of the family. In these patients the suicidal tendency did not take the form of a crisis. Many of them had made previous suicide attempts and were chronically suicidal.

It should be noted, however, that only a small minority of the patients in convalescent-nursing homes actually do commit suicide, although nearly all share, to some extent, the pattern of chronic illness, isolation, and a downhill course. The patients who committed suicide seemed to have been characterized by a special inability to adjust to their environment. While most patients made a reasonably satisfactory adjustment to the hospital, these patients constantly complained and made efforts to change things, often arousing some impatience and antagonism in the hospital staff. We do not know if it is feasible to change the whole approach of convalescent-nursing hospitals to their patients in order to inspire in them more of a feeling of belonging and of usefulness and meaning to their lives, but we recommend that in individual cases special efforts be made to make changes in the treatment plan when a given patient has made a suicide attempt or has expressed fairly constant dissatisfaction together with suicidal threats or ideas. As a minimum, we recommend a psychiatric consultation for such patients. At least then the suicide of such a patient should not come as a surprise, and the staff of the unit would not be left with a feeling of guilt over something therapeutic possibly being left undone.

SUICIDE IN PSYCHIATRIC HOSPITALS. Patients who commit suicide in psychiatric hospitals are much younger, with the median age of 44. Hanging is the most frequent method used. The length of time of hospitalization varies from one day to several years, with a median period of two to three weeks. Many of these patients had made previous suicide attempts. Even with psychiatric patients, suicide occurred relatively rarely within the walls of psychiatric hospitals—only twelve in two years in Los Angeles County. During the same period, there were three times as many suicides of psy-

chiatric patients who were being carried as patients of hospitals but were out of the hospital on trial visits at home or had run away.

The most serious crises, associated with the highest suicide potentialities, occur just before admission and immediately after discharge from psychiatric hospitals. In a recent analysis of suicides in Los Angeles, we observed that 15 percent of the people who committed suicide had received but not followed a recommendation for psychiatric hospitalization within a few weeks before their deaths. Seven percent of the suicides had been recently discharged from psychiatric units.

Why do people fail to accept a recommendation for psychiatric hospitalization which might save their lives? We find that there are still great resistances to psychiatric hospitalization, even though facilities are more readily available, therapy is more flexible, and often liberal insurance plans bear much of the cost. The patients and their families argue that hospitalization is inconvenient. For men, it means loss of earnings. They fear that the psychiatric label will make them unemployable. Women fear the separation from family and children. Generally, however, the symbolic attributes of hospitalization far outweigh the reality factors. People express shame and resentment about being categorized as psychiatric cases. Often they feel that by going to the hospital they are taking upon themselves a responsibility for what should be acknowledged as a family problem. Often the resistance to hospitalization is more of a family resistance than an individual resistance, and it can best be handled by family conferences in an attempt to obtain the cooperation of a number of the people who are concerned.

Another important barrier to appropriate psychiatric hospitalization stems from attitudes about hostility and rejection directed toward suicidal persons by physicians and their assistants. Doctors sometimes tease or belittle these patients and refuse to take them seriously. Sometimes a physician and his psychiatric consultant hesitate about hospitalization for someone in the community who is a leading financial, political, professional, or social figure whose image might be damaged by publicity about psychiatric illness. The outcome of such hesitation may be suicide. It is appropriate to consider sending such a notable person away to another community for hospital treatment.

A suicidal crisis may complicate office psychotherapy for many reasons. It may be due to an extraneous factor in the patient's life, such as the death of a loved one, or to some problem brought out in the therapy such as the need to separate from a parent, or it may involve some issue with the therapist; for example, his undesired vacation, or some subtle transference-countertransference tension that cannot be resolved. Often a crisis is signaled by a break in communication, by missed appointments and silence. In these situations, the hospital offers not only a sanctuary and refuge, but also a setting for continuing the therapy. Certain patients have a capacity for entering into a deeply regressive, symbiotic relationship with the persons who are meaningful in their lives, including their therapists. The effort to work through this kind of involvement frequently produces a deep depression that may alternate with acting-out behavior, and this can take the form of repeated suicide threats and suicide attempts. Such patients should often be hospitalized during a crucial part of the therapy. In the hospital they tend to stir up rivalries between members of the staff and exploit any difficulties in communications that exist. One of the advantages of the hospital is the easy availability of shared communication and formal and informal consultations.

Excessive use of sleeping pills is a problem with many suicidal patients. The hospital is the ideal place to control the sleeping-pill habit. Often the patient will plead that he should be the special exception to the hospital rule of decreasing medication, and his doctor will agree. At this point, consultation with the rest of the staff will tend to correct what may be an overprotective attitude on the part of the doctor.

Preparations for discharging a patient from a psychiatric hospital should include an evaluation of the suicidal potential. For this, the recorded observations of the nursing staff, who live with the patient around the clock, are invaluable. Certain clues may alert the responsible physicians. For example, some psychiatric patients are extremely overdependent on the hospital. When the possibility of discharge or home visit is mentioned, these patients become agitated and panicky. They commit suicide on trial visits home if insufficient attention is paid to their anxious states and the type of home environment to which they are being returned. Favorable

outcome after psychiatric hospitalization has been closely correlated with efforts to prepare the environment to accept the discharged patient. Often the accepting or rejecting attitudes of the
most significant other persons make the difference between life
and death.

Of hospital patients who will eventually commit suicide, about
one-half do so within three months after leaving. Depressive patients tend to have at least one recurrence of symptoms after
discharge. Since manic-depressives tend by character to have all-
or-nothing psychologic reactions, they feel the transient symptom
as a total crisis. "The treatment failed. I can't stand another depression now." So thinking, they take suicidal action. The nature
of depressive cycles should be explained to depressive patients, and
they should be warned that brief low moods are expected after
hospitalization and do not necessarily mean the start of a new depressive period. Patients should be encouraged to call their doctors
when mood swings occur. Regular outpatient, follow-up consultations for at least three months after hospitalization are recommended.

UNITED STATES VETERANS ADMINISTRATION HOSPITALS. Probably the
most extensive study of suicide prevention in hospitals has been
reported by Farberow, Shneidman, and co-workers, who examined
the charts of over 300 patients who committed suicide in Veterans
Administration hospitals over a period of nine years and compared
these charts with the files of persons who did not commit suicide.[1]
They recommended that suicide prevention training, like fire prevention training, should be part of the education of every person
who works in a hospital of any type. Such training would tend to
increase the sensitivity of the physician, nurse, psychologist, social
worker, attendant, and others to both the overt and subtle clues
that are often the precursors of suicidal behavior. They would establish a professional climate on each ward and within each hospital
that would permit easy communication from patient to aide, from
aide to nurse, and from nurse to physician, thus making the problem of suicide prevention everyone's problem and everyone's responsibility. They recommend the creation in each hospital of a
suicide prevention committee, which would take the responsibility
for continuing staff education and, in addition, would investigate

every case of suicide that might occur in the hospital. The committee would also make any recommendations for physical changes in the hospital plant that might be indicated.

They suggest that special procedures be established for discharging patients, especially those who at any time during their stay in the hospital aroused a suspicion of suicidal behavior. This would include investigation of the home environment and arrangements for follow-up and after-care, as a minimum. Finally, the possible use of psychological testing to pick up cases of covert suicidal potentiality was suggested.

In a special study of suicide in patients with chronic terminal illnesses, who might be found especially on convalescent hospital rolls or as repeated readmissions to general medical and surgical acute units, they repeatedly noted that the psychological status of the patient was most important. Such patients should never be debarred from human contacts, for example by transfer to a private room to await death. Continued interest by the physician and the staff, and continued communication to the staff about the patient, was emphasized. Every facility of the hospital should be mobilized to carry the patient through his last days. This includes attention to his physical comfort by judicious use of tranquilizing drugs, narcotics, analgesics, and sometimes the use of antidepressive medication. In addition, psychological support is essential, and the use of family, friends, volunteer workers, and the hospital staff for this purpose should never be neglected. "What must be done is to give such a person a reason to live until the moment of death."

In the case of one chronic illness—cancer—they found that the highest risk was associated with older men with cancer of the throat and larynx, and younger men with Hodgkins disease or leukemia. It was pointed out that suicide occurred in all stages of disease, including advanced terminal physical conditions. It occurred in cases in which there was relatively little pain or discomfort from the illness, as well as those in which there was much. Regardless of age or disease site, a suicidal potential was considered present if all, or most, of the following factors were present: (1) emotional stress; (2) severe depression and anxiety; (3) dejection, agitation or overdependency; (4) low tolerance for pain or discomfort; (5) excessive demanding and complaining behavior with strong need for attention and reassurance; (6) controlling and directing activ-

ity (for example, insistent requests for or refusals of treatment and medications) ; (7) relative alertness in orientation; (8) exhaustion of resources, physical and emotional, including lack of support and attention from family or hospital; (9) prior or present suicide attempts.

Especially observed was the predictive value of diagnosing the dependent-dissatisfied presuicidal chronic patient. This kind of patient makes increased demands for attention and reassurance—wanting to see the doctor, the nurse, the chaplain, asking for unnecessary physical examinations or dental work, requesting sedation, seclusion, therapy of various kinds, and the like. In many cases, the patients made excessively self-centered demands for attention that were simply impossible to satisfy. Statements, such as "Nothing is being done for me," "Other people don't like me— I should end it all," "There is no place for me anywhere," were further indications of intense dissatisfaction. This demanding, time-consuming, attention-getting behavior was often irritating and disturbing to the hospital staff and to other patients as well, and this patient was, on occasion, referred to as the hospital pest.

In handling this type of patient, it was suggested that hospital staff be alerted to the seriousness of such behavior from the standpoint of suicidal potentiality. Also suggested were new treatments or medications that often give this type of patient temporary relief and improvement; and sympathetic recognition by the hospital staff that the excessively complaining, demanding, depressed behavior of the dissatisfied patient is an expression of desperate, although excessive, need for care and support. Finally, nursing staff, which has the responsibility for the psychological support of patients in the hospitals, was especially commended. Often enough, in reviewing charts of persons who committed suicide, the medical notes were of virtually no help in revealing the character of the patient concerning the reasons for his death, whereas the nurses' notes contained many clues to the patient's personality and special problems.

Summary

The rationale for suicide prevention is based upon the concepts of crisis, ambivalence, communication, and action response. This paper describes how these concepts can be applied to suicide pre-

vention in hospitals. For general medical-surgical hospitals, an essential problem is to prevent patients who are temporarily depressed or confused from jumping from a height. A special suicide prevention committee that sponsors educational programs for the staff, reviews cases of suicide, considers improvements in the hospital design, and facilitates communication between nursing staff and physicians is recommended. Special clues to suicide in chronic patients and in psychiatric patients are described, together with measures for the psychological support and rehabilitation of such patients. Emphasis is placed on the need for follow-up and after-care programs for discharged suicidal patients.

Chapter 29
WHEN PATIENTS COMMIT SUICIDE
Robert E. Litman

Psychotherapists seem to react to the suicide of a patient
much as other human beings, according to interviews of more than
two hundred psychotherapists. The first reaction was often
one of pain and defense, and the second depended on their
special role in society. The intensity of their reactions varied
in accordance with the degree of relationship with the deceased,
as well as with their theories of therapy and personal
responsibility. Grief, guilt, depression, personal inadequacy,
and sómetimes anger were expressed, as well as the intention to
use this experience to become more sensitive as persons
and therapists.

Although the amount of information in this taboo area of psychology is limited, one knows enough to assume that attitudes toward death are complexly structured and ambivalent.[1] One might expect that therapists would express more philosophic attitudes when asked to consider the possibility of death as an abstraction. Yet the same persons might describe quite different personal emotional experiences after a direct encounter with death as an actual event.

Most psychotherapists contemplate the concept of death with fairly tranquil attitudes. Death is to be avoided or postponed but it is inevitable. Indeed, dying is a part of living. A number of philosophic-minded psychotherapists contend that the constant awareness of the possibility of death has a positive moral value in that it keeps one conscious of being vital and alive. May doubts "whether anyone takes his life with full seriousness until he realizes that it is entirely within his power to commit suicide."[2]

Suicide is a particularly tabooed form of death, condemned as a grave social wrong by the prevailing religious, legal, social, and medical ethics. Considered abstractly, for instance in an educational seminar, the suicide of one's own patient strikes most psychotherapists as an unfortunate event to be averted, if possible. On the other hand, overanxiety about the possibility of suicide could

seriously impair the therapist's effectiveness. Kubie has concluded, "We must ask whether we want to prevent every suicide if such an effort will render us therapeutically impotent?"[3]

A number of philosophic notions have been advanced that make it possible for therapists to consider the idea of patients' suicides with greater equanimity. Some are legalistic: "In a free society, a person must have the right to injure or kill himself."[4] Others are strategies that claim pragmatic success. One system of psychotherapy demands that the practitioner maintain rigid nondirectiveness and nonresponsibility.[5] Another recommends that he communicate his indifference to the patient's possible death.[6] As an extreme example, some therapists state that the essence of their therapy is the quasi-religious death and rebirth of the patient's soul. "If the soul insists on organic death through suicide, cannot this be considered an unavoidable necessity, a summons from God?"[7] In this schema, the psychotherapist has neither responsibility nor motivation toward suicide prevention.

In summary, most therapists regard suicidal potentiality as a disturbing element, complicating and sometimes restricting the therapeutic process, and requiring special care and consultation.[8] Some theories of psychotherapy contend that the practitioner has no responsibility for the suicide of a patient and should feel no concern or anxiety about it. A small minority of psychotherapists speculate that at times suicide is a justifiable or desirable goal of therapy.

What in fact are the psychologic reactions of psychotherapists after their patients commit suicide? No systematic investigation of this question has been published in the literature available to me. The present communication does not pretend to be conclusive or exhaustive, or to have solved such methodologic difficulties as sampling error, nonstandardized interviewing procedures, and incomplete data-processing.

The attitudes of psychotherapists toward the deaths of patients were not in themselves the direct objectives of a systematic research program. Rather, these observations about therapists are by-products of various clinical and research experiences. Several sources of data should be mentioned.

1. Because I am the chief psychiatrist of the Suicide Prevention

Center therapists seek me out for informal discussions of suicide incidents.[9]

2. Previous studies focused on the communication of suicidal intentions contain many clues to the attitudes of therapists receiving the communications.

3. My colleagues and I have investigated more than 1,000 suicides in collaboration with the Chief Medical Examiner and Coroner of Los Angeles County. The primary objectives of these investigations were to ascertain who commits suicide and under what circumstances. The method used was to interview the survivors of the individual and, in addition to his relatives, his friends, employers, physicians, and especially when available, psychotherapists in order to reconstruct the life situation and attitudes of the deceased as part of a "psychological autopsy."[10]

One series of fifty randomly selected and unequivocal cases of suicide was given a most thorough and time-consuming investigation. Ten of the subjects of this research were in treatment with a psychiatrist or clinical psychologist at the time of death. Four others had recently been terminated or discharged from treatment. Since this is not a statistical paper, I mention these numbers only as a reminder that the suicide of a patient while in treatment is not a rare event. The observations reported here are derived from interviews with more than 200 psychotherapists. Each was questioned shortly after a patient committed suicide.

There are barriers to communication about such an event. The question, "How do you feel about the death of your patient?" breaks taboos and intrudes into highly personal reactions. The inquiry can provoke anxiety in both the therapist-informant and the investigator. Naturally, the answers given vary greatly in candor and completeness.

A majority of therapists were interested and cooperative. Some welcomed an opportunity to review the suicide. Others, guarded and uncommunicative, stated, "I can't discuss it without written permission from the family." Initially, some practitioners were casual or flippant, others superscientific: "You can't do anything about suicide, why worry?" Or, "What's the correlation between suicide and hostility?" A patient and persistent interviewer could almost always obtain cooperation and elicit many of the therapists'

attitudes and reactions. Among a number of questions, the interviewer asked the following: "Is there anything you would have done differently?" "What can we learn from this?" "What effect did it have on you?"

According to my observations, therapists react to the death of a patient, personally, as human beings, in much the same way as do other people. They react, secondly, in accordance with their special role in society. Their theoretical, philosophic, and scientific attitudes serve a defensive and reparative function, being used to overcome the pain they feel as human beings and as therapists.

The personal reactions depend, of course, on how the therapist viewed his patient, how long and how closely they worked together, and the degree of his professional commitment to the other. This commitment can vary from none to almost total. As an example of none, a therapist refused to accept a referral when he realized that the patient was possibly suicidal. Later, when that patient committed suicide while seeing another therapist, the first therapist felt relieved and even elated over his decision. As an example of great commitment: One practitioner virtually adopted an intelligent and beautiful young woman, one of his psychology students, and when she committed suicide while in psychotherapy with him, he went through weeks of deep mourning and grief.

In recalling how they felt about the suicide of a patient, therapists have said that the first experience of this nature was the worst. One hears expressions such as "I could hardly believe it." "I was completely crushed." "It shook my confidence in what I thought I knew."

A number of younger therapists identified in themselves a strong emotional reaction after the death of an older patient who reminded them of a dead parent. Therapists who had struggled for a long period of time to help a patient overcome chronic suicidal tendencies often reacted to his death as a personal defeat, and experienced a period of hopelessness and depression. Therapists who had worked in partnership with another human being in intensive psychotherapy as a mutual relationship noted, in their own dreams or symptomatic actions, partial identifications with the deceased. For instance, a number of therapists reported having accidents in the week or two after the death of a patient by suicide.

As human beings, therapists felt a special sort of guilt that was

the exact replica of a type of guilt experienced by relatives of persons who have committed suicide. This guilt took the form of self-questioning: "Did I listen to him?" "Did I try hard enough to understand him?" "Was there something in me that didn't want to hear what he was saying?" At the professional level, too, the same questions arose but with less painful guilt and more sense of inadequacy, taking the form of obsessive thoughts. "How did I miss it?" "If only I had done something differently."

On a personal level, painful feelings were handled in several ways. Unlike families and relatives, therapists seldom mentioned religious attitudes as a consolation, but sometimes they would say, "Maybe it's just as well that he is dead. He suffered a great deal." Personal gestures were felt to be important. "I spent several hours with the bereaved spouse trying to help her with her feelings." In some instances, the therapist attended the funeral.

Some therapists were extremely angry at someone, usually the patient's spouse, occasionally a medical colleague or psychiatric supervisor, whom they held responsible for the death. Anger at the dead patient, expressed indirectly or by inference, was common. Overtly hostile statements about the deceased were rare.

First and foremost, the psychologic mechanisms that were universal in relatives and in therapists were denial and repression. Therapists manifested denial in many ways. Often they questioned that the death was a suicide. "Are you sure it wasn't a heart attack?" They forgot details of the history, or they unconsciously omitted or distorted relevant features of the case. A psychiatrist, who admitted to newspaper reporters that he had prescribed the sleeping pills with which a patient committed suicide had, in fact, not prescribed the pills. They had been obtained from other physicians.

The reactions of therapists as therapists emphasized fears concerning blame, responsibility, and inadequacy. These feelings were especially prominent if the deceased was a person of high social status or potentially great social value, such as a successful professional man, a young mother, or a college student. Therapists expressed fears of being sued, of being vilified in the press, of being investigated, and of losing professional standing. They were afraid that others among their patients would be adversely affected by the

news, or ask embarrassing questions, or that there might be reproaches from the relatives. Sometimes therapists felt marked and exposed.

In these circumstances, a supportive consultation with another professional person often proved to be of great psychologic benefit. A helpful maneuver, in trying to work through a painful reaction affecting the therapist's professional role, was to review the case and present it to a group of colleagues with the attitude: What can we learn from this? It is not surprising, however, that relatively few of these cases were written up in a formal way and published.

Many therapists have stated that the suicide of a patient in an institution, for instance a psychiatric hospital or clinic, is much easier to tolerate than one that occurs in the course of private practice. A death occurring within the purview of a well-defined social institution is easier to accept and view objectively. This is especially true if there was a spirit of mutual support, shared responsibility, and cooperative teamwork among the staff of the hospital or clinic. On the other hand, the suicide of a patient being treated in private practice provokes associations of the unusual, the unexpected, the uncanny. Therapists invariably felt better if they could say that they had explored every therapeutic avenue and possibility, and had discussed the case with colleagues and with consultants before the suicide. "I felt helpless." "I did everything I could." "I guess it was inevitable."

My colleagues and I have never interviewed a therapist who advanced the notion that the suicide of his patient was philosophically acceptable to him and congruent with his theoretical expectations regarding the methods and goals of therapy. The concept of an autonomous and insightful individual initiating an act of self-validation or self-fulfillment was not mentioned in these postmortem discussions. A number of therapists said that in the future they would do everything possible to avoid working with potentially suicidal patients. Many others expressed the view that episodes of anxiety about patients were inevitable hazards of the profession. They planned to continue to try to do their best for every patient and would regard the next one with suicidal tendencies as a special challenge. No change in their general attitudes toward suicide or toward death appeared to be indicated, they said, but they would try to use the experience of the death of a patient to enlarge their

own psychologic horizons, to become more sensitive as persons and therapists, and to improve their professional judgments and professional actions. This is an attitude I would endorse.

Let me close this report with a vignette from Sigmund Freud:

> In August, 1898, Freud was vacationing in Italy with his wife when a piece of bad news reached him. "A patient over whom I had taken a great deal of trouble had put an end to his life on account of an incurable sexual disorder. I know for certain that this melancholy event and everything related to it was not recalled to my conscious memory during my [subsequent] journey to Herzegovina." Two weeks later, however, during the next stage of his journey, Freud was astounded when he could not recall the name of a well-known artist whose fresco he wished to recommend. He tried to visualize the painting and the artist in question, and the inadequacy of his associations became a source of inner torment. The missing name, which finally came to him, was Signorelli. The essential blocking thought which accounted for its loss was the repressed news of the suicide, elements of which had become associated with the name in Freud's unconscious. His analysis of this incident is the first illustrative example in "The Psychopathology of Everyday Life."[11]

To us it seems quite natural, even inevitable, that a patient's suicide should disturb the analyst's unconscious. Many of the therapists we interviewed reported similar reactions. News of the death was received, and part of the painful emotion was repressed. Its return from the unconscious later was expressed in various symptomatic moods and actions. Finally, the associations were made conscious and the working through of the traumatic incident was manifested in a personal change, a professional broadening, and occasionally some scientific or philosophic contribution.

Summary

On the basis of information communicated by more than 200 psychotherapists, each of whom was interviewed shortly after one of his patients committed suicide, two types of reactions are reported. It is observed that therapists react to such deaths personally as human beings much as other people do, and also according to

their special role in society. Their theoretical, philosophic, and scientific attitudes have a defensive and reparative function and help them to overcome the pain they feel as human beings and therapists.

The reactions of the therapists as human beings varied in accordance with the specific feature and intensity of the relationship with the deceased. Therapists felt such emotions as grief, guilt, depression, personal inadequacy, and sometimes anger. Some of them noted partial identifications with dead patients in their own dreams or symptomatic actions. For example, accident-proneness often followed the death of a patient by suicide.

Denial was the most common defensive mechanism used by therapists (and by relatives and friends of the patient as well). A psychologic maneuver that was helpful in working through pain affecting the therapist's professional role was to review the case and present it to a group of colleagues with the object of learning from it. Many practitioners sought to use the experience to enlarge their own psychologic horizons, to become more sensitive as persons and therapists, and to improve their professional judgment and actions. Occasionally, the incident was worked through in the form of a scientific or philosophic contribution.

PART VII
FORENSIC AND
PROFESSIONAL ISSUES

Chapter 30
THE PSYCHOLOGICAL AUTOPSY
OF EQUIVOCAL DEATHS

Robert E. Litman, Theodore Curphey, Edwin S. Shneidman, Norman L. Farberow, and Norman Tabachnick

Suicide implies a direct connection between the deceased's intention,
his self-destructive action, and his subsequent death.
Uncertainty about the correct certification results when the
victim's intention is ambivalent, with coexisting wishes both
to live and to die, or when the self-destructive action is in
itself inconclusive, or when death follows the action after a
considerable delay. Investigations of 100 such cases are reported
with illustrative examples. The present classification of deaths
into natural, accident, suicide, and homicide, obscures the
fact that individuals may make a considerable contribution
toward their own deaths under circumstances not ordinarily
considered suicide.

In Los Angeles County, as in most other communities, both custom and statutory law require that the death certificate include a statement not only of the cause of death (e.g., bronchiogenic cancer, coronary artery thrombosis), but also the mode, that is, whether the death was natural, accident, suicide, or homicide. Problems of certification arise when, as might be expected, some cases fall into borderline areas. The term "equivocal suicides" describes cases in which suicide is a possibility but in which there could be more than one interpretation and, therefore, the decision is uncertain and doubtful. We are reporting some typical examples. The investigations tend to focus attention on the role played by the individual in his own demise, a subject that deserves more thought and more research.

The relative frequency of equivocal suicides may be estimated as follows. There are about 50,000 deaths yearly in Los Angeles, of which some 10,000 are referred to the medical examiner for special study. Approximately 1,000 of these are certified as suicides. About 100 cases a year are regarded as equivocal suicides.

Although relatively few in number, these cases often involve a

disproportionately large amount of individual distress and public concern. They tend to stir up a storm of family anxiety and neighborhood gossip. If the death was, in fact, accidental or natural, a decisive and accurate certification is necessary to dispel the lingering doubt in the community and the guilt in the survivors. Sizable insurance awards may depend upon the correct determination of the mode of death. If the death was a suicide, then a tactful and considerate investigation, together with an explanation to the survivors of what went wrong, may help them adjust to the loss, reorganize their lives, and carry on, often with heavy responsibilities. Above all, consideration for the importance of accurate public health records and the integrity of the medical examiner-coroner's office in fulfilling its quasi-judicial responsibilities demands that there be a very thorough and objective investigation of cases in which suicide is suspected or confirmed.

When suicide is the issue, diagnosis often requires a painstaking evaluative judgment of the deceased's "intention," which is a psychological phenomenon. Realizing this, Dr. Theodore Curphey, Chief Medical Examiner-Coroner for Los Angeles County, requested consultation from the staff of the Los Angeles Suicide Prevention Center.[1]

This report is based upon 100 consecutive cases of equivocal suicide selected by Dr. Curphey and referred for investigation in the latter half of 1959 and the first half of 1960.

In Table I, 100 equivocal suicides are classified according to the method involved in the death. The equal proportion of men and women in the total group is of interest, since no effort was made to select cases on the basis of sex. From the standpoint of sex distribution, equivocal suicides fall midway between unequivocal suicides (70% men) and suicide attempts (70% women). The modal age range was 40 to 50 and every decade but the first was represented. Fifty-five patients were eventually certified as suicide cases, forty-five as other than suicide.

The largest category of cases consists of deaths caused wholly or partially by barbiturate ingestion. There were fifty-five such cases, subdivided into three subcategories. There were seventeen cases in which the victim was known to be a chronic user of alcohol and the death occurred because of use of a combination of alcohol and barbiturates. The usual question asked was whether the bar-

TABLE I—One Hundred Equivocal Suicides

Method	Males	Females	Total	Certified as Suicide
Barbiturates involved	19	36	55	39
a. Barbituate and alcohol	8	9	17	7
b. Barbituates addicts	2	12	14	9
c. Barbiturate death (no addiction; no alcohol)	9	15	24	23
Gunshot wound	10	1	11	1
Carbon monoxide	4	3	7	4
Hanging	4	0	4	0
Drowning	3	1	4	1
Burning-Explosion	2	2	4	2
Train or car	3	1	4	2
Fell or jumped	2	0	2	1
Miscellaneous	3	6	9	5
Totals	50	50	100	55

biturate was added merely to supplement the effects of the alcohol in the usual activities of the alcoholic individual or whether the barbiturate was ingested for a specific lethal purpose.

Usually, when the former situation existed, the blood alcohol level was extremely high. We encountered readings of alcohol percentage in the blood of 0.36, 0.34, 0.32, 0.27, and many over 0.20 (the intoxication level is 0.15). Often, large amounts of alcohol occurred in combination with relatively low barbiturate levels insufficient in themselves to cause death, but the additive effects of alcohol plus barbiturates were responsible for fatalities that were accidental.

On the other hand, investigation sometimes uncovered a history of recent depressive episode or an important recent change in life situation, plus evidence that a large amount of barbiturate was ingested at one time, which generally pointed toward suicide occurring in an alcoholic.

The second subgroup of cases illustrates the problem more dramatically. These were cases in which the victim was a barbiturate addict in the physiological sense. There were fourteen such cases. For these persons, securing and maintaining a plentiful supply of barbiturates had become the most important thing in their lives. They purchased and stored sleeping pills by the hundreds, often from illegal sources. They took large amounts of barbiturates day and night and were unable to tolerate even a day without drugs. Such addicts frequently placed themselves in a rather deep stage of anesthesia almost every night. For such, a mild intercurrent in-

fection or merely twisting into an awkward position that cut off the airway might mean death—which was not intended for that particular time. Investigators found the premises untidy and disorganized, with pills all around. The barbiturate level was usually in the middle ranges.

In addition to the possibility of accident in the course of the barbiturate habit, it should be remembered that addicts are disturbed persons often on the edge of deliberate suicide. Clues toward suicide were present if all of the barbiturates were gone, if the blood barbiturate level was extremely high, and if there was a history of a recent disturbance in life pattern (e.g., arrest, loss of love relationship, physical illness). We have noted that people who committed suicide tended to get their pills from physicians, while people who died accidentally of drug addiction tended to obtain their pills by illegal means.

Finally, there was a subcategory of twenty-four persons who were not in the habit of taking either barbiturates or alcohol in large amounts. When such persons died of barbiturate poisoning, investigation usually revealed sufficient evidence to substantiate suicide.

Automatism

An additional possible syndrome of accidental barbiturate death has been brought to our attention many times by medical colleagues and by survivors of deceased persons. This is the hypothesis of "automatism." It is speculated that certain persons take a prescribed therapeutic dose of barbiturates, which causes them to enter a state of automatism, in which they ingest additionally a lethal quantity of barbiturates without awareness of their actions. We have been unable to confirm this hypothesis in these investigations. Similarly, our intensive studies of persons barely surviving the ingestion of large amounts of barbiturates have failed to turn up cases of automatism. The patients who described to us behavior that somewhat resembled automatism had ingested low to moderate, relatively nonlethal amounts of drugs.

This series included eleven gunshot deaths. As a general rule, it can be said that more than 95 percent of all self-deaths by gunshot wounds are suicides, but occasional equivocal cases on investigation turn out to be accidental. For example, there were three exhibitionistic "Russian roulette" cases that were actually accidents; these

men were performing what they considered a trick to impress other people, rather than gambling with death. One youth was practicing quick draws when he killed himself; three persons were cleaning their guns. In four of the eleven gunshot deaths the victims had a very high blood alcohol content. In two cases there was a possibility that the deaths were actually homicide, and these were quickly returned for further police investigation.

Investigation of the seven deaths by carbon monoxide poisoning illustrated the usefulness of reconstructing the person's habits. The problem was to decide whether the individual habitually exposed himself to the possibility of carbon monoxide poisoning by working on his car in a closed area or by sleeping in the car with the motor running. In several of these cases investigation revealed that these persons actually were in the habit, for various reasons, of enclosing themselves with the motor running. These cases were certified as accidents because, although these victims had taken the chance of being overcome by the carbon monoxide, they had no conscious or specific lethal intention at the time of the death, according to our inference.

Los Angeles heating and cooking gas is of low lethality, a fact not generally known. Typically, suicidal persons turn on the gas and wait to be overcome, but, after several hours, finding themselves still alive, they sometimes decide to smoke a cigarette while they wait. When the match is lit there is, of course, an explosion. In case of death from burns in these cases, we usually have recommended "suicide."

Most deaths by hanging are suicide, but the four cases in this series of investigations were accidents. They were typical of hanging accidents. There were two boys, ages 12 and 13, who were playing pranks to frighten or impress friends and families. There were two men, ages 18 and 21, who hanged themselves while masturbating in women's clothes, acting out erotic fantasies of being tied up and abused. Certain people seem to demand a degree of asphyxiation as part of their erotic need. In another case, a man who habitually inhaled chloroform while masturbating accidentally asphyxiated himself.

The data summarized in Table II are of special interest to physicians. It is evident that of 100 persons who died in unequivocal circumstances, those who were eventually certified as having com-

TABLE II—Previous Medical Attention

	Suicide Cases	Non-suicides	Total
No physician	11	23	34
Routine medical last year	5	9	14
Special medical treatment last 6 mo.	22	11	33
Had been referred in past for psychological or psychiatric evaluation or treatment	17	2	19
Totals	55	45	100

mitted suicide tended to have been much more closely associated with physicians than those who were certified as having died of accidental, natural, or undetermined causes. Only one-fifth of the suicide victims had no physician. A majority of the nonsuicides had none. Most of the suicide victims had seen physicians within the last six months of their lives. The opposite was true of the non-suicides. We do not consider these findings to be an artifact of the certifying procedure. Rather, they provide additional confirmation of the reports by Motto, Vail, and others that suicidal persons seek out physicians as potential rescuers.[2]

Comment

Examples of these investigations have been reported previously in detail.[3] After a review of the police report on the case, and the autopsy findings, members of the Suicide Prevention Center staff, acting as deputy coroners, interviewed survivors of the deceased: relatives, friends, employers, physicians, and others who could provide relevant information. We tried to reconstruct the victim's background, personal relationships, personality traits, and character, that his, his style of living. In addition, we obtained in great detail an account of the events immediately preceding the death. These data were then reviewed at a meeting of the full "death investigation team" in the coroner's office and a decision was then reached that was based on all of the information available for this "psychological autopsy."

The difficulties in deciding whether to certify cases as suicide or other modes stemmed from two distinct sources. First, there was often a lack of information about the victim, particularly information that could be used for a reliable inference concerning his psychological state. The routine police reports varied consider-

ably in completeness. If the possibility of homicide was obviously ruled out, the police often showed a relatively minor interest in the residual uncertainties about the cause and mode of death, which problems, of course, are more the coroner's concern. A number of police officers expressed feelings that these cases were best buried quickly and forgotten.

Information was usually sparse when there were particularly painful emotional states in the survivors of the victim. Our own team of investigators noted many times that the emotional reactions of an investigator, in response to the concern of the victim's family, could interfere with his objective judgment. Often, the inexperienced investigator of a case would identify strongly with the bereaved family and conclude in the face of obvious evidence that "this probably wasn't a suicide." Because of this, the case conference and review by others was essential.

Another difficulty in collecting data arose from the distortions of the informants. At times we encountered evasion, denial, concealment, and even direct suppression of evidence. For example, some relatives had deliberately destroyed suicide notes. Other evidences of emotional pressure were letters to the coroner protesting the possibility of certification of suicide, such protests even at times accompanied by petitions from a whole neighborhood. Insurance money was involved in fifteen of the 100 cases in this category.

It was necessary, and sometimes difficult, to explain to informants that suicide often occurs in responsible, religious, "successful" families. The fact that persons have plans for the next day or week, and tickets for vacations in resort areas, is not incompatible with simultaneous suicidal preoccupation and planning. In fact, the inescapable realization of his inability to enjoy a vacation may be the "last straw" for a depressed person. Our interviewers were professionally oriented and, when appropriate, would explain what we were doing, and why, to facilitate the cooperation of informants.

The interviews nearly always reduced guilt in the survivors and made it easier for them to accept the death of the victim. In fourteen of the cases the survivors had demonstrated great difficulty in accepting the idea of possible suicide and in twelve of these our intervention was felt as therapeutic. Persons who suspected that the coroner was giving the case insufficient attention were reas-

sured by our efforts. Interviews that had primarily an investigative purpose were therapeutic as well.

Even when the circumstances of the death and the character of the victim were clearly reported in excellent detail, a second major difficulty in certifying deaths arose out of the ambiguous and unclear aspects of the concept "suicide." Suicide implies a direct connection between the deceased's intention, his self-destructive action, and his subsequent death. Uncertainty about the correct certification resulted when the victim's intention was ambivalent, with coexisting wishes both to live and to die, or when the self-destructive action in itself was inconclusive, or when death followed the action after a considerable delay.

Suicidal actions take a great variety of forms and have different significance. Moreover, the reasons, motives, and psychological intentions of suicidal persons are quite complex. Briefly summarized, some of the prominent mental trends in suicidal persons are: (1) a wish for surcease, escape, rest; (2) anger, rage, revenge; (3) guilt, shame, atonement; (4) a wish to be rescued, reborn, start over; and (5) suicidal actions include an important communication or "appeal" element.[4] Destructive ideas or impulses that ordinarily are well controlled or mostly unconscious can be activated or released under the influence of emotional stress, physical exhaustion, or alcohol, conditions that favor suicidal behavior.

We have tried to classify deaths according to the self-destructive element, arranging them in a continuum in which the gradation corresponds to the clarity of the intention and the decisiveness of the lethal action. Cases of high lethality on this continuum were easy to certify as "unequivocal suicides." For example, one man wrote a long letter in which he described in detail his reasons for suicide and his planned method. He specified the exact clothes he would wear, the location, and a rather complicated technique. He then carried out his plan in every detail.

At the opposite end of the continuum, however, the line between suicide and other modes is indistinct. Here were persons who placed their lives in danger and risked death. They were confused or careless and self-negligent. Often, they had an obvious wish to be rescued or to derive some benefit or thrill from the danger situation. For example, certain alcoholics and addicts combine liquor and barbiturates in order to increase the desired effect.

In general, when someone died in a suicide attempt because an expected rescuer failed in the allotted role, we called it suicide.

Report of Cases

Case 1: A woman took a considerable quantity of barbiturate tablets at 4:30 P.M. and fell asleep on the kitchen floor in front of the refrigerator. She knew that every working day for the last three years her husband came home at 5 P.M. and went straight to the refrigerator for a beer. There was thus a strong possibility that she would be rescued. However, her husband was delayed and did not reach home until 7:30. Recommendation: suicide.

Case 2: A man ingested barbiturates and went to sleep in his car, which was parked in front of his estranged wife's house. A note to her was pinned on his chest indicating his expectation that she would notice him when she returned home from her date with another man. This possibility of his being rescued, however, was obliterated by a dense fog that descended around midnight. Recommendation: suicide.

In general, if the deceased was following his usual style of life during the period preceding death, suicide was less likely. If the death followed or resulted from a significant change in the patient's style of living, then suicide was more likely.

Case 3: The engineer of a train that killed a man at about 1 A.M. reported that it seemed to him that the victim had kneeled down on the tracks in an attitude of prayer, facing the train. Based on this, the death was tentatively classified as suicide. Further investigation revealed that this victim was a happy and contented alcoholic. On the night of his death he had followed his usual, nightly pattern of getting drunk on wine, purchased at a nearby liquor store, and stumbling homeward on a shortcut path that led across the railroad tracks. The blood alcohol level in the victim's body was extremely high. Recommendation: accident.

Case 4: Another man was killed when his car was struck by a train in the afternoon. Witnesses said that it seemed to them that he had stopped the car on the tracks and

waited for the train. Investigation revealed that this intersection was not on the patient's regular route home from his office. It turned out, moreover, that on this day he had not gone to his office at all, an omission that was very unusual for him. Then it was learned that he had been having marital difficulties and had consulted a physician for symptoms suggestive of depression. Recommendation: suicide.

Case 5: A married man stayed out late drinking with friends from work about once a month. To avoid his angry wife when he came home late at night, he habitually went to sleep in his car, parked in his garage, and in the winter he would sometimes run the motor of the car to keep warm. One morning he was found dead of carbon monoxide poisoning. Recommendation: accident.

Case 6: A physician was addicted to barbiturates. He frequently made himself deeply unconscious by taking large amounts of the drug and several times he fell asleep while smoking and set the bedclothes on fire. He died unexpectedly in one of these comas. Recommendation: accident.

In Cases 5 and 6 it might be argued that the victims had a strong, unconscious, self-destructive wish. This was obviously true. However, the crucial distinction was made that these men were following their usual pattern and had made no special, specific, unusual action tending toward their own death.

When people gamble with death, at what odds should the line be drawn to decide between suicide and accident? We believed that to take a needless chance of one in six for death was suicidal.

Case 7: A 30-year-old man wrote a note that said, "I am going to play Russian roulette again." The six-chambered revolver contained one fired bullet and five empty chambers. Although this gambler actually had had five chances in six to survive, we recommended certification as suicide.

By contrast, there were three cases of Russian roulette deaths in this series that did not conform to the classical model. These men did not consider themselves to be gambling with death. Each of them thought that he knew where the bullet was located (and was

in fatal error). Victim 1 had a large collection of revolvers and would demonstrate Russian roulette whenever a new, impressionable woman was invited to his house. He had several tricks that enabled him to determine when a single bullet in the cylinder was not in firing position. The second victim was a bully in a gang. He suggested Russian roulette to frighten a new initiate to the gang and prove the youth a coward. He indicated to other members of the gang that he knew where the bullet was located. The third so-called Russian roulette victim was a police officer who, it was discovered, actually had been attempting to convince a young woman acquaintance that the gun he carried was not dangerous. In all of these deaths the recommendation was accident.

Sometimes a delay of time between the self-destructive action and the death, or intervening events, clouded the direct sequence of cause and effect and created difficulties in certification.

> *Case 8:* When her husband threatened to divorce her, a woman ingested ant poison in front of him; her husband immediately took her to a hospital. After emergency treatment for arsenic poisoning she felt better and told the doctors that she did not really want to die. However, she developed severe kidney damage and died after two weeks of uremia and cerebral hemorrhage. After some consideration, the recommendation was suicide.

> *Case 9:* An alcoholic with cirrhosis of the liver was warned that alcohol would surely kill him. He continued to drink heavily and soon died. Traditionally, such deaths have been certified as natural. We could see no benefit in recommending a change in this tradition.

Conclusions

Studies of equivocal suicides point the way toward an answer to the vexing question raised by Dublin and others, that is, how accurate are suicide statistics?[5] Is there a valid basis for comparison of suicide rates between countries or even between counties? In this series, before a case was referred to the death investigation team, it was given a tentative certification by the medical examiner. After investigation the original certification was changed in nineteen cases. The revision was from accident to suicide in eleven cases

and from suicide to accident or natural death in eight cases. The investigations were of great help in confirming the original, tentative certifications as the final certifications in thirty-nine additional cases that might otherwise have been certified as "undetermined," and the investigations made some contribution toward confirmation in thirty-two other cases. The death investigation team made no contribution in ten cases, usually because it was impossible to interview any important survivors. We noted the possibility that significant numbers of suicide deaths are being misreported as accidental traffic fatalities.

From a practical viewpoint, these studies may be useful to certifying authorities and social statisticians by creating a model for comparison. As examples of such comparisons: One city had a suicide rate approximately one-third of that recorded for Los Angeles. A visit to that city revealed that the authorities certified cases as suicide only if there was a verifiable, handwritten suicide note. (In Los Angeles about one-fifth of the suicidal victims leave such notes.) In several communities approximately 50 percent of the self-inflicted deaths by gunshot were certified as suicide. By contrast, in Los Angeles more than 95 percent of the self-inflicted deaths by gunshot were certified as suicide. In some California counties approximately 40 percent of deaths in which barbiturates were found in the blood of the victims were certified as suicide. In Los Angeles 85 percent were suicides.

More importantly, these investigations lead to theoretical speculations of considerable interest. The present classification of deaths into natural, accident, suicide, and homicide is derived from ancient customs and legal procedures. The goal of this classification was to assign "responsibility" for the death in a moral and legal sense. If, instead, we consider as objectively as possible the role played by the individual himself in causing his own demise, we see that the individual plays a greater or lesser role in his own death in many situations that are not ordinarily considered suicide.[6] Further research in these areas has considerable importance for the future in the prevention of deaths, regardless of the label.

Chapter 31
SAMPLE PSYCHOLOGICAL AUTOPSIES
Edwin S. Shneidman and Norman L. Farberow

Various types of psychological autopsies conducted by the Los Angeles Suicide Prevention Center are illustrated by case examples. These include initially equivocal cases recommended to be certified as suicide, accident, probable suicide, suicide or accident undetermined, natural death, and even homicide. The therapeutic element for the bereaved survivor, in the work of the Death Investigation Team conducting the psychological autopsies, is emphasized.

This chapter is intended to illustrate various types of investigations, conducted by the Suicide Prevention Center, of equivocal cases in which suicide is a possible mode of death in the process of certification by the Los Angeles County Coroner's office. It is intended to present an abbreviated casebook of actual investigations by the SPC, which might serve as guidelines for persons who must decide certification as to mode of death.

The Los Angeles County Coroner Theodore J. Curphey, M.D., invited members of the SPC to assist him in equivocal cases of possible suicidal deaths by conducting psychological autopsies focused primarily on the *personality* elements associated with suicide, such as suicidal intention, subtle communications relating to suicidal intent, reactive or psychotic depression, and schizophrenia. The coroner named this group, when they worked in connection with his office, the Death Investigation Team. The approach of the team was to reconstruct the life style and personality of the deceased, mainly by interviewing the spouse, grown children, parents, physician, and others who knew him well. On the basis of these psychological data, and any other physical evidence of suicide, accident, homicide, or natural death that might be found, the Death Investigation Team attempted to make informed extrapolations over the last days of the victim's life and then to report these conclusions and recommendations to the coroner for final integration with his other findings.

The activities of the Death Investigation Team have raised some interesting questions concerning suicide statistics in general.[1]

Whereas mortality rates are probably extremely reliable (the operational definition of *dead* is fairly clear-cut and unambiguous) the instances of suicide, within any geographic area and for any given temporal interval, are not so reliably reported and are, in no small part, squarely dependent on the certifications as to mode of death made from case to case. These certifications are often influenced by social, religious, and sentimental factors. The activities of the Death Investigation Team in the Los Angeles County Coroner's office may result in raising or lowering the apparent suicide rate in Los Angeles County (either would be an artifact) ; at least, the veridical value of the statistics for "suicide" from that area should be increased.

It is not implied that every death should be certified as suicide, homicide, accident, *or* natural, even if one accepts this somewhat archaic classification. Dr. Curphey has stated that, so far as he is concerned, one of the characteristics of a scientifically operated coroner's office is its willingness to certify deaths as probable or undetermined (as, for example, suicide or accident, undetermined) in those cases where the facts neither warrant nor justify straightforward certification by one of the four usual modes. This concept is introduced to indicate that a legitimate outcome of an investigation by the Death Investigation Team is a firm recommendation, based on clearly inconclusive evidence, for an undetermined certification.

With these comments as preamble, some sample cases will be presented. These cases have been selected to illustrate each of the following general circumstances:[2] (1) a death recommended for certification as *suicide;* (2) a death that initially appeared suicidal but was recommended for certification as *accidental;* (3) a death recommended for certification as *probable suicide,* in which some psychic homicide played a role; (4) a death recommended for certification as *suicide or accident, undetermined;* (5) a death finally recommended for police investigation for *homicide;* (6) a death recommended for certification as a *natural death;* (7) a case of unequivocal suicide in which *therapeutic functions* for the bereaved were served.

The following case was recommended for certification as *suicide.*

A 33-year-old male of German descent, working as a butler for a well-to-do investment broker, was found

dead in his bathtub with his head under water. The bath-tub was filled to the brim. The police report stated that he had been in ill health for the preceding two months and that the day prior to his death he had told the cook where he worked that he did not feel well. A glass containing a yellow crystalline substance was found on top of the water closet next to the bathtub. Autopsy revealed a large quantity of water in his stomach and proximal small bowel, associated with marked pulmonary edema. The heart and aorta were essentially normal. Toxicological examination showed the absence of alcohol and the presence of 1.4 mg per 100 cc barbiturates in the blood. The residue in the glass was found to be pentobarbital.

With these facts, the preponderant opinion was that this was a suicide, but in light of the realistic possibility that this could have been an accident, it was felt that an investigation by the Death Investigation Team was indicated. Their study revealed many interesting facts. It was ascertained that the victim had been depressed for some time previous and had made a serious suicide attempt just two months before in the home of a nurse, where he had been staying. As a result of that attempt, he had been taken to a local hospital, where he had been comatose over twenty-four hours and where he had then spent eight days. On recovery he told his nurse friend that he had taken twenty-four Nembutal tablets.

His life history, as reconstructed from the informants, was most interesting. At the age of 15 he had entered a military academy in Germany; Hitler was then in power. He was trained as a fighter pilot and engaged in heavy fighting. While he was on a mission, his best friend had been killed. Upon his return, he requested his superior officer to send him again so that he could either avenge or join his friend. Upon denial, he threatened suicide and actually attempted it by shooting himself through the left chest. He survived this attempt and was hospitalized. Later, he was taken prisoner by the British and sent to Egypt in 1945. In 1946, he returned to Germany and fell in love with an airline stewardess, who was later killed in an airline crash. He then left Germany and went to Argentina, where he flew for Peron until the dictator was ousted. From there he went to Brazil and later to Venezuela, where he worked until the revolution oc-

curred and he lost everything he had. He finally made his way to the United States in 1956, and came to Los Angeles, where he worked until the time of his death.

In the course of gathering the foregoing information, members of the Death Investigation Team investigated the actual scene some days after his death. Because of the feelings of his employer, the victim's quarters had been left undisturbed during this time. The investigators, on checking the bathtub, found a wad of cloth stuffed in the safety, or overflow, drain, thus allowing the tub to be filled to the very top. Mindful of the victim's prior experience with barbituates, we reconstructed that he had taken this precaution to make certain of his death by drowning, if the barbiturates failed to kill him.

The most striking general principles to emerge from these investigations are (1) the importance of obtaining as complete a history of the past life of the victim as possible as a basis for making judgments about the victim's personality; and (2) the importance of examining, if possible, the actual site of death, inasmuch as such an examination may well yield significant evidence necessary for the proper decision.

The following case initially appeared suicidal but was recommended for certification as an *accident*.

In practically any coroner's office, a death that results from playing Russian roulette would automatically be certified as suicide. Indeed, there is now legal precedent for such certifications. Because of a special interest on the part of the Death Investigation Team in this type of death, this case was turned over to them by the coroner for investigation, with, as it turned out, extremely surprising results. On the basis of interviews it was ascertained that the victim, a 28-year-old male, was an Army veteran who had a collection of revolvers, which he kept in perfect operating condition. It was determined from his best friend that the victim's favorite activity at parties was to play Russian roulette (following the usual rules of the game by having one chamber of the cylinder loaded) and that he had done this literally dozens of times in the preceding few years. At this point, the Death Investigation Team wondered about the psychology of a

man who would behave in such a fashion: was he psychotic or was he intent on killing himself? Interviews with the widow clarified the situation: the victim had told her that there was no possibility of his hurting himself, as he always glanced at the gun to ascertain that the bullet was in a nonlethal position before he pulled the trigger. If the bullet was one notch to the left of the barrel, he would spin the cylinder again. There had been no suicidal ideation and no evidence of depression, psychosis, or morbid content of thought. What had happened? The Death Investigation Team knew that the death had occurred in someone else's home. Interviews developed the information that he shot himself with a revolver that was not his own but belonged to his host of the evening. What seemed most important was the fact that, whereas his collection consisted entirely of Smith & Wesson revolvers, he had killed himself with a Colt revolver. The actions of the two guns are different; that is, the cylinder of the Smith & Wesson revolves counterclockwise, while the cylinder of the Colt revolves clockwise. It was believed that the victim, checking and seeing the bullet one space to the right of the barrel, thought that he could not possibly kill himself, whereas in reality pulling the trigger put the bullet in the lethal position and he died immediately.

In the absence of any indication of suicidal affect or any indications of suicidal ideation, and with the additional information about the two types of revolvers, the Death Investigation Team recommended that this death be considered as accidental.

The following case was recommended for certification as *probable suicide,* in which some psychic homicide played a role.

The autopsy report concerning a 57-year-old female who was found dead in her home indicated that the cause of death was acute barbiturate poisoning. On the face of it, the mode of death appeared equivocal, and the case was referred by the coroner to the Death Investigation Team for investigation.

The victim's physician was contacted and he reported that she had been emotionally upset for several years. She felt her husband's personality had changed and that he was moody and was not spending time or doing things

with her. On two occasions she had been severely depressed but seemed to have come out of these moods fairly
quickly. Prescriptions from her physician made it possible
for her to have refills for tranquilizers and barbiturates
whenever she wished. The physician did not know how
long before the victim's death she had had the prescription refilled nor how many pills she actually had. It was
his impression that she was not a heavy drinker or an
alcoholic.

An appointment was made with the victim's husband.
He exhibited many feelings of remorse and guilt, with
much crying at times. He had a number of questions concerning the coroner's decision as to the cause of his wife's
death and how available this information would be to
the public and, particularly, to his neighbors. He felt
suicide was a stigma and hoped his wife's death would
be certified as the result of a heart attack, although it
was fairly clear that there was little rational cause for
him to entertain this hope.

The husband stated they had been married for twenty-
five years; there were no children. From the beginning
the marriage had many elements of discomfort in it as
a result of his wife's hysterical, excessive demands and
lack of consideration of their economic situation. After
about ten years of marriage, there was a period of separation by divorce, but they came together again and eventually remarried. He at first stated there had never been
any prior suicidal attempts or threats, but it later became
known that there actually had been many. These were
described of minimum lethality and had had a dramatic
quality to them. For example, she would put a little iodine
around her lips and say that she had swallowed some,
but when he took her to the hospital iodine was not found
in the stomach contents. On a number of such occasions,
he had responded with a good deal of anger to his wife's
suicidal attempts. Once she had threatened to kill herself
with a knife and he had given her a hunting knife, telling
her to use that since it was sharper.

The husband stated that during the previous six to
eight months he had made up his mind that his marriage
would never be successful. He had not communicated this
to his wife, because he did not intend to divorce her.

It was felt that the husband was a man who had very marked dependency needs that were not being met by his wife, and that he had reacted to these with a good deal of anger and rejection of her. The wife apparently needed the marriage very much, and she made the suicidal threats and attempts in an effort to bring her husband closer to her. On most occasions, such suicidal attempts or threats brought about a reconciliation. However, at this particular time, the possibility of reconciliation had lessened considerably because of the husband's decision. Whether this decision was based on something specific, such as an attraction to another woman, was impossible to tell. He denied this specifically, however, even without being asked.

At the time of the suicide, the husband, a salesman, had gone to a neighboring city to conduct some business. His usual practice was to call his wife and tell her the time he would be home for dinner. He tried but was unable to reach her until late. She was very angry when he arrived home and threatened to leave him. He told her to go ahead, and then he went out to a restaurant. Later he returned home and found his wife sleeping on the floor in the hall, "breathing heavy." Her clothing was not disarranged in any way, so he had given no thought to anything like violence being involved, and he supposed she had simply gone to sleep on the floor. He apparently made no attempt to arouse her except to place a pillow under her head to allow her to sleep more comfortably. He then left the house and went to a hotel. One significant fact the husband related was that the night before her death his wife had called her sister and brother-in-law and had made a will, leaving all her possessions to the sister.

The impression by the investigator was that this was a chronically depressed woman of hysterical type, anxious about the separation from her husband, and that the husband, for reasons unknown, had decided not to continue the marriage on an effective basis. What was considered pivotal was the denial by the husband to himself of his wife's desperate situation, which was probably symptomatic of their destructive symbiotic relationship. While unconscious death wishes on the part of the spouse might be inferred, what seemed clear was that the dyadic rela-

tionship was one that permitted the rejection of the victim by the potential rescuer. Thus, the victim's gamble with death was lost because the person who could have saved her did not permit himself to receive the intended communication.

The following case was recommended for certification as *suicide or accident, undetermined.*

The case is the death of a 45-year-old male, operating a small business involving the use and storage of lacquer thinner. At 3:30 A.M., witnesses saw the place of business on fire. The police and fire department reports noted that an explosion had taken place, the front windows of the shop having been blown out. The victim was found face down and showed extensive burns. A sample of blood showed 45 percent carbon monoxide and was negative for alcohol. The victim was in the habit of returning to his shop to work after hours. On this particular occasion he left for the shop around 2:00 A.M. His wife called a neighbor after he left, expressing concern about him, upon which the neighbor volunteered to drive to the place of business. When he did so, he found it on fire. Later information revealed that the victim was careless about smoking in the shop around the cans of explosive or inflammable material used in the course of his work. The arson experts who studied the scene and the evidence were unable to decide whether it was a set fire or an accidental explosion. Interestingly, the police officers of the Arson Squad were of the opinion that it was set with suicidal intent, and the captain from the Los Angeles Fire Department who was commanding officer at the scene disagreed that a flash exposion of this type could have been induced with suicidal intent.

This case with its voluminous records was turned over to the Death Investigation Team for investigation and opinion. A large array of friends and neighbors were interviewed about the victim's mental state and his work habits. The final report stated: "There are no indications of a previous life pattern consistent with suicide. However, it should be noted that the informants most likely to give information indicative of such a pattern were (as usual) defensive because in this case the widow informed

us that an insurance settlement hinges to some extent on the type of death certificate. . . . The reconstruction of the psychodynamics in this case appears to offer no sound basis for an opinion as to the mode of death."

In view of the general disagreement, therefore, the certification of the mode of death was recommended as accident or suicide, undetermined.

The coroner's comments to the SPC on this investigation touched on a special point:

> The insurance economics of this case are most interesting. The victim had fire insurance on his store. If his death were accidental, the insurance was collectible; if suicidal, it would be voided on the basis of the perpetration of a felony. His life insurance was even more interesting. He had taken out a policy three weeks before his death and had not yet paid the first premium. Because of the one-month grace period in premium payment, if his death was accidental, there was a question as to whether his survivors would recover from the insurance company without his having invested a penny of his own. This case illustrates the limitations at times faced in arriving at final certification, if such certification is to be based on the objective gathering of facts and not on impressions and preconceived opinions, as is often true when these problems are handled on the basis of superficial or incomplete evidence.

The following is an ambiguous case in which the final recommendation was that the police investigate for *homicide*.

It is an unfortunate fact that in the public mind the coroner's function is largely to ferret out undiscovered homicides (this misconception is fostered by mystery stories and TV programs). It is also true that often-times police personnel, in making an investigation of a death, will lose interest precipitously if it appears that the case cannot possibly involve homicide. So far as the coroner's office is concerned, cases of homicide actually make up the smallest percentage of his caseload but receive the greatest percentage of publicity.

The following case is one of the rare instances in which the certification lay between suicide and accident and was discussed

with the coroner with the recommendation that it be returned to the police department for further investigation as a *homicide*.

The deceased, a 55-year-old male who was found drowned in the bathtub of a downtown hotel, was fully clothed except for his shoes. Autopsy and post-mortem analyses revealed he died by drowning and that that there was neither ethanol nor barbiturate nor any other poison in his system. The story, as pieced together from his widow, two of his brothers-in-law, his attorney, a government employee who had been a friend of the victim, and an individual who had loaned the victim a considerable sum of money, was a complicated and confusing picture.

On the morning of his death the victim had been at a hearing at which he had been accused of having obtained over $200,000 from wealthy persons under false pretenses. His wife, who was his third wife, felt he was a wonderful, God-fearing, and religious man who would never do any wrong, even though she knew he had been in penitentiaries twice before. One brother-in-law, a professional man, thought that the victim was the world's worst scoundrel and in a two-hour interview openly expressed a great deal of hostility toward him, feeling he was capable of any kind of culpable behavior. The second brother-in-law, an equally eminent professional person, thought the victim was a pathological liar but was not angry at him and had been rather bemused by his behavior. The fourth informant, the victim's attorney, indicated that he thought the victim had a good chance of winning his case and that he had been in much tougher situations before, that the evidence had really disappeared, and the victim was never the kind of person, considering his character structure, who would ever think of suicide. The informant from the Corporate Commissioners Office said that office had been following the victim for many months and knew a great deal about him. He had indeed been in prison, had married other women, had swindled other persons, had pretended to be wealthy but was not, and had put on such a wonderful front that very responsible persons would trust him with great sums of money, never thinking to ask him for a receipt. The sixth person contacted was an individual who had lost a considerable sum of money to the

victim and characterized him as an extremely clever man. None of the informants, his widow included, felt that he was ever suicidal or depressed. All but the widow felt that he was a "cool customer" who could ride out any storm, especially when his chances of acquittal seemed quite good. The widow reported that he was to have met some persons from Kansas City in the hotel room to get back money that he claimed he had loaned them, in order to repay the local persons from whom he had taken money. The attorney also believed that he had met some persons in the hotel room. When the victim checked into the hotel, he had rented a safe-deposit box, which he might do in anticipation of receiving some money. In addition, it seemed difficult to understand his drowning himself, sober and undrugged, in a bathtub.

In the absence of any clear psychological or psychiatric features pointing to suicide, and in the presence of psychopathy, extremely large sums of money, mysterious going-on, and the like, it was deemed a logical possibility that foul play might have been involved. The case was recommended for further police action.

The following case was recommended for certification as a *natural death*.

A 55-year-old female died in the hospital as a result of severe bromide intoxication. The investigator reported that he interviewed the husband, who described his wife's illnesses, which had been considerable for the previous ten years. She had had, among other things, kidney stones and surgery for a kidney suspension, osteoporosis, stomach ulcers, and a sympathectomy. Reading backward chronologically from the time of her death, she had spent four days in a general hospital and eleven days immediately preceding in a sanitarium. She had been home for a month before that and, preceding that, had been in still another sanitarium for one month. In the three years preceding this, she had been hospitalized twelve separate times for her various medical and psychiatric illnesses. She had lost weight from 120 to 95 lbs., and she had begun to exhibit blackouts, which would occur at unpredictable intervals. In the last several months she had lost control of bladder and bowels and suffered continuously from severe pain.

During the last month of her life she drank Bromo Seltzer and gulped aspirin in excessive amounts. The husband could not say how much she had taken, but she apparently would frequently reorder bottles of Bromo Seltzer from the pharmacy as well as have him bring supplementary supplies from the grocery store. She was taken to a sanitarium with a tentative diagnosis of toxic (bromide) poisoning and, after eleven days, was transferred to a general hospital for more intensive medical care. She died after four days in the hospital.

It was learned that three years previously the victim had consumed an overdose of Seconal, estimated around ten or twelve. This is the only report of a prior attempt on her own life by the victim. She worked as a registered nurse, and the last place of employment was a sanitarium for alcoholics. The marriage of the couple occurred ten years previously and was the first marriage for both. There were no children. Much of their married life was filled with the illness of the victim. She was practically incapacitated much of the time, unable to keep house or to prepare meals.

The files of the local general hospital revealed that the victim had been a patient twice in the previous five years, the most recent admission being for a possible hyperparathyroidism and gastrointestinal bleeding. In addition, when she was discharged, the diagnoses of chronic brain syndrome and reactive depression were added. The history described inappropriate behavior, disorientation for time and place, confusion, and memory impairment. It also stated that she took many Seconal tablets when she could get hold of them. The previous hospitalization 5 years before was for similar complaints, with reports of delusional and hallucinatory experiences. An additional diagnosis of narcolepsy was noted at that time.

In summary, the victim was seen as someone who suffered primarily from severe bromide intoxication. Prior to this she had had a great variety of illnesses, which had required at least fourteen known hospitalizations within the preceding two years. Mentally and psychologically, from a pleasant, hard-working person she had developed into a person unable to care for herself, to think logically or appropriately, or to judge and direct her own actions ade-

quately. There were symptoms of blackouts, confusion, delusions, and hallucinations, indicating that mental control and judgment were rather seriously affected. The victim had attempted to control severe pain with almost uninhibited ingestion of analgesics. There may have been some inkling in the victim's mind that her use of medications was approaching excess, but it was impossible to evaluate the extent of the intention finally to terminate her troubles. Conversation with her physician indicated that she was barely rational and was a severe management problem during her last two weeks of life. In the light of the mental status of the victim and the lack of any substantial evidence of intention to end her own life, the certification of natural death was recommended.

The following is an unequivocal suicide case in which *therapeutic* functions for the bereaved were served.

The coroner serves several functions. Not only does he keep his fingers on the health pulse of the community (by knowing what persons are dying of), and not only is he in the position of unholding medical standards (for example, through his investigation of deaths under anesthetics), but among his other functions he also can act for the best mental health of survivors of deceased persons.

Since the Death Investigation Team began to work with the coroner's office, there have been a few instances where the coroner has asked members of the Death Investigation Team to see a bereaved person (where there was literally no question of the mode of death) with the advertent purpose of helping the emotional orientation of the surviving person.

> The victim in this case was a 40-year-old female who was found dead in her automobile in her garage with the door closed, the automobile engine having apparently operated until it ran out of gasoline. She was dead from carbon monoxide poisoning. It seemed to be a clear case of suicide. The husband, who appeared to be an intelligent and generally sophisticated man, came to the coroner's office not so much to urge a change in the certificate of the mode of death as apparently to ventilate his general distress and somehow to obtain some reassurance. At this point the coroner suggested that he be seen by a member of the Death Investigation Team. An appointment was made to interview him.

The husband was a 47-year-old, outgoing advertising executive, bluff, hearty, and gregarious. He had become successful by his own wit and effort. He now found himself in the position of not only having to integrate the loss of his wife, but in addition, to be solely responsible for his four young children. The greatest block, however, to his emotional well-being was the terrible sense of shame that his wife had committed suicide.

During the interview he expressed a great number of feelings: guilt, dependence, and even resentment and hostility toward his late wife. He seemed to imply, but did not directly state, that she had been emotionally distraught, if not mentally ill. It was an hour filled with a great amount of ventilation for him, in which he gained a few insights. At the end of the meeting he expressed the opinion that, in spite of the content of the discussion, the interview had been a rewarding experience for him. He expressed his gratitude and felt that it had been therapeutic to talk about some of his feelings.

During the interview he had casually mentioned the name of a physician. This physician was subsequently contacted by telephone and asked about the deceased. It was learned that the dead woman had been emotionally disturbed, in fact, acutely schizophrenic. In fact, the physician had administered electroshock treatment to her some months before because she had been hallucinatory and had had bizarre religious delusions. Further, she had not been making an entirely satisfactory adjustment after the shock treatment. The physician felt that the husband was blind to the wife's disturbances because of his affection for her. The doctor said that he had no doubt in his mind that the victim was psychotic at the time of her death. He also had no question that the death was a suicide not only because of the manner in which she had died but also because she had been psychotic and depressed.

Thus, in this case, which unequivocally was suicide, the Death Investigation Team still performed an important function by assuaging some of the feelings of distress in the surviving spouse. It needs only to be added that this same function has been served in several other cases.

Chapter 32
MEDICAL-LEGAL ASPECTS OF SUICIDE
Robert E. Litman

*Because society is tending to view suicide less as a sin or crime
and more as an unfortunate consequence of mental illness and social
isolation, there are significant changing legal aspects of suicide
and of their relationships to psychiatric practice. Social and
judical attitudes regarding suicide have been gradually turning
away from assessing guilt and enforcing punishment toward
protecting suicidal persons, when possible, and compensating the
victims of suicide deaths.*

For centuries, English law designated suicide as a special crime
punished by mutilation of the body, sanctions on the place and
manner of burial, forfeiture of property, and censure of the family.
It is questionable whether these laws were effective in preventing
suicide. Possibly they tended to decrease the frequency of nonlethal
suicide attempts. It became apparent that in order to bypass the
excessive penalties, self-deaths were often labeled something other
than suicide, and most suicide attempts were not reported. In Britain, the penal sanctions against suicide were gradually modified,
and by 1962 the last of them had been repealed.

It should be emphasized that suicide is not against the law in
most parts of the United States of America. According to written
reports from the Attorney General of each of the states (in 1964),
there are only nine states—Alabama, Kentucky, New Jersey, North
Carolina, North Dakota, Oklahoma, South Carolina, South Dakota,
and Washington—in which suicide is a crime. Since such punishments as mutilation of bodies or forfeiture of estates are repugnant
to the American spirit, no penality is provided for breaking the
law against suicide, but in these states suicide attempts are felonies
or misdemeanors and could result in jail sentences, although the
laws are seldom enforced. In recent times, two states (Nevada,
New York) repealed such laws, stating in effect that suicide is a
grave social wrong, but there is no way to punish it. Twenty-three
states have no penal statutes referring to suicide. Eighteen states—
Alaska, Arkansas, California, Florida, Kansas, Louisiana, Michigan, Massachusetts, Minnesota, Mississippi, Missouri, Montana,

Nevada, New Mexico, New York, Oregon, Wisconsin, and Wyoming—have no laws against suicide or suicide attempts but they specify that it is a felony to aid, advise, or encourage another person to commit suicide.

Prosecutions under these laws are infrequent. The following case indicates why:

> In May, 1963, in Los Angeles, two men, Valdez and Wilde, each ingested approximately fifty sleeping capsules as part of a suicide pact. Wilde died but Valdez recovered. He was found guilty of aiding in the suicide of another under Section 401 of the California Penal Code and was sentenced to a term in the state prison. Upon his release from prison in September, 1963, Valdez returned to the scene of the previous suicide pact and ingested 100 sleeping capsules, which killed him.

Society's condemnation of suicide persists as a function of the County Coroner, a time-honored institution of English law. This official certifies the mode of each death, and in effect assigns the legal blame for the death either to God (natural, accident) or to man (homicide, suicide). The relatives and friends of suicide victims feel themselves to be not only bereaved but stigmatized. They often attempt various orders of persuasion and coercion to influence the coroner against the certification of suicide. Evidently, certifying suicide is equivalent to a judicial verdict of "guilty." Often the coroner is perplexed because the statutory and customary definitions of "suicide" are ambiguous and even contradictory, leaving a broad borderline area between clear-cut suicide and the other modes of death in which fall many more or less equivocal deaths.[1] With no distinct guidelines as to what should be termed suicide, certifying practices vary widely. As a result, suicide statistics from different communities in the United States are not comparable. Moreover, the general uncertainty leads to many perplexing insurance contests in which the outcome is quite unpredictable. Some experts, notably Shneidman, feel that the present classification is anachronistic and should be discarded.[2]

Compensation for Suicide Death

Within the last ten years, there has been a dramatic reversal of judicial decisions on the question of compensation for suicide

death. This is most obvious in Workmen's Compensation rulings. In the case of an injured worker suffering pain with no response to medical treatment and the development of depression followed by suicide, the former judicial test was, "Did he know what he was doing?" If he did, the suicide was considered an independent intervening cause of death and there was no compensation.

Example: Roberts, an aircraft worker, injured his neck and back in September, 1955. Pain and disability continued despite medical treatment and he became increasingly depressed. Twenty months after the injury, he committed suicide by carbon monoxide fumes in his garage. Recovery was denied. According to the California court, "The decedent's actions . . . indicate that he was capable of planning the act with knowledge of its consequences. . . . We are not convinced that it was so irrational and that there was such a loss of mental control that the act was involuntary or that the decedent did not have the mental capacity to know what he was about when he planned to end his life."[3] This decision was in agreement with most precedents.

Two years later in the case of Burnight, a higher California Court took an entirely different stand: "It would not be realistic to require that in order for Workmen's Compensation to be paid in a suicide case, the employee must have been insane in the narrow sense of the word. . . . Where an employee receives an industrial injury and the resultant pain is such that he believes he cannot continue to stand it, where he becomes so depressed that he feels there is only one way out, where any condition results which causes him to feel that death will afford him his only relief, his act of suicide is one directly resulting from his injury, unless it appears that he could have resisted the impulse to so act. . . . In most Workmen's Compensation cases involving suicide, it is unrealistic to determine that suicide is an independent intervening cause, since a conscious volition to produce death does not necessarily make the suicide a seperate agency unconnected with the primary injury, nor an intentional or willful self-injury."[4]

This more generous line of reasoning has been followed by a number of courts in California and other states.[5] A similar change in the judicial viewpoint may be expected in civil cases of wrongful death by suicide following negligent injury, as in traffic accidents.[6]

Current legal reviews emphasize the importance of the psychiatric evidence in these cases.[7]

Psychiatric Responsibility and Liability

Meanwhile, the changing pattern of psychiatric practice has focused increased attention on the problem of suicide. With the extension of psychiatric services into new areas of the community,[8] the development of crisis therapy centers as part of mental health programs, and the emphasis on short-term hospitalization, open wards, and the earliest possible discharge for psychiatric patients, psychiatrists find themselves responsible for suicidal patients in settings that are deliberately designed to give the patients maximum freedom of action as part of the therapeutic milieu.[9]

The trend in psychiatry is to strip away the prisonlike features from the mental hospital, to abolish restraints, and encourage a maximum of patient self-responsibility. Most psychiatrists regard suicidal potentiality as a disturbing element complicating and sometimes restricting the therapeutic process and requiring special care and consultation. Among their other anxieties about the possibility of suicide in a patient, psychiatrists fear that they may be sued for malpractice.[10]

It is reassuring to learn that practicing psychiatrists have a relatively low rate of harrassment by malpractice litigation.[11] It is recognized that the psychiatrist has little control over the actions of outpatients, although he might be held liable for incorrectly or negligently prescribing drugs, these prescriptions being under the doctor's control.[12]

However, there has been a growing tendency for society and its courts to expect psychiatric institutions to prevent suicide if it can be done reasonably. In general medical and surgical hospitals and psychiatric hospitals, suicide is a rare event (about 12 a year in Los Angeles), accounting for only 1 percent of the total number of suicides. During the last two years in Los Angeles, about one-third of the suicides in hospitals have been followed by lawsuits.

In a recent comprehensive review, Perr stated the guiding legal principle, "The law demands reasonable care in foreseeable situations."[13] At present, however, the standards for reasonable psychiatric care with regard to suicide prevention are unclearly stated and inconsistently applied.[14]

According to Mills, "The first issue in any suicide liability case must be to determine whether or not the patient had presented sufficient evidence to warrant the conclusion that he or she was suicide-prone. The answer can be found only in the facts of each case, and it is upon these facts that expert judgment must be exercised to decide that some sort of protection was required. Obviously, some cases have been defended successfully at this point because their facts did not raise the degree of extra caution. However, other suits have been lost here, too, merely because the physicians did not take sufficient time or effort to evaluate their patients accurately. . . . The next issue deals with the manner by which these patients are protected against themselves. Of those suits resulting in verdicts adverse to psychiatrists and their institutions, this is the most common shortcoming. Somewhere along the evidentiary trail, an item of carelessness or inattention created the opportunity for death."[15]

Recent decisions illustrate these points: If the hospital had no way of knowing that the patients were suicidal, no negligence was found.[16] When the patient was given adequate diagnostic evaluation and treatment, no liability was held even when the patient eloped from the hospital and committed suicide[17] or took advantage of his open ward privileges to commit suicide in the hospital.[18]

Negligence was found when the psychiatric staff was aware of the patient's suicidal tendency and took measures to deal with it, but these measures were ineffective—for example, when a suicidal patient, placed in an isolation room, committed suicide by strangulation with the plastic tubing used for intravenous feeding,[19] or when the patient was put in a closed ward and hanged himself from a pipe.[20]

Standards of Psychiatric Care

A recent liability suit concerned Baker, who was admitted to a Veterans Administration Hospital in Iowa for psychiatric treatment after the attending physician and the wife advised the hospital that the patient had suicidal tendencies and had hidden a gun. The admitting physician decided he was not then suicidal and sent him to an open ward. After three days with free access to all areas, the patient jumped into a window well in a suicide attempt and sustained severe injuries. The plaintiff contended that the hospital

was negligent in failing to cover the window well and in failing to diagnose the patient as a sufficient suicidal risk to require more supervision.

The United States District Court ruled that the defendant hospital was not negligent in failing to close the window well and the doctor who diagnosed the patient was not negligent under the standard of care prevailing in the community in failing to find that the patient was a sufficient suicide risk to require closer supervision. The Court placed great emphasis on the practices generally prevailing in psychiatric institutions relative to the degree of care and supervision required by the patient's known physical and mental condition.[21]

In the very similar case of Lawrence, who in 1962 injured himself in a fall from a New York hospital ward, the Court of Claims gave the widow a sizable award.[22] Different standards of care may be applied to cases in the various states. The problems of suicide prevention in psychiatric hospitals have been reviewed in recent reports.[23]

Hospitals that maintain psychiatric units should formulate written administrative and professional policies relative to the care of psychiatric patients and should determine from time to time that these polices are in accord with the recommendations of the American Psychiatric Association and the Joint Commission on Accreditation of Hospitals and the established customs and practices of other hospitals in the general geographic vicinity relative to the confinement and treatment of suicidal patients. It is suggested that each hospital should have a suicide prevention committee that has the function of conducting on-going education of the hospital staff in suicide prevention and of reviewing the policies of the staff and of recommending changes in the physical construction of the hospital when indicated.

According to my observations in Los Angeles, some cases of questionable medical-psychiatric care occur under the following circumstances:

1. On the emergency admission service—occasionally physicians express contemptuous hostility against suicide attempters. "Next time make the cut over here so you'll get the artery." Sometimes a suicidal patient has been denied admission to a hospital with in-

sufficient examination and with inadequate records explaining the reasons for rejecting application for admission.

2. Premature discharge from the hospital—the possibility of negligence occurs when a patient is goaded into leaving the hospital prematurely "against medical advice." I doubt if the legalism of having a patient sign a paper would impress a court unless the physician made an honest attempt to persuade the patient to stay in the hospital.

3. Failure of staff communication—there is a serious question about how much alienation between the nursing staff and the ward physician can be permitted before neglect of the patient is obvious. For example, I have known of cases in which the discharge of a patient was made by a ward nurse without the knowledge of the psychiatrist who was in charge of the ward.

4. Failure to deal with the family—this may bring about a charge of negligence when the patient commits suicide. Relatives report instances in which the family has begged to be permitted to talk to the psychiatrist because they felt they had important information to contribute or they needed guidance in how to deal with the patient, and the psychiatrist refused to talk to them on the grounds that "psychiatrists don't talk to relatives." Can this be defended as the standard of psychiatric care?

5. Overly free prescription of potent drugs—this has led to claims against psychiatrists and may grow to be a formidable problem. Psychiatrists should be aware of the local standards for prescribing sleeping pills, especially to persons known to be careless and self-destructive in the use of such pills. When such requests are continuous, careful records should be kept, and consultation is advisable.

6. Insufficient consultation—our medical colleagues, when confronted by a special problem that may endanger the life of a patient, are accustomed to obtaining consultations. The result uniformly is an improvement of care for the patient plus a certain amount of protection for the physician in case the outcome is bad. Psychiatrists should be encouraged to use consultation more freely.

Psychiatrists are expected to evaluate the suicidal danger at certain transition points in the treatment of a patient: at admission, on discharge, when there is a major change in ward assignment,

when the family or nursing staff expresses concern about suicide possibility, when increasing amounts of dangerous drugs are requested, when there has been a suicide attempt. The evaluation and treatment plan should be recorded. Since not all suicides can be predicted or prevented, and since the standards of psychiatric care with regard to suicide prevention are unclearly stated and inconsistently applied, every psychiatrist should carry adequate malpractice insurance.

Chapter 33
POLICE ASPECTS OF SUICIDE
Robert E. Litman

*The police officer encounters suicide both after the commission of
the act and before, in cases of citizens who attempt or threaten
suicide. The police officer's responsibility to distressed persons in
crisis and to their families requires intensive indoctrination
in immediate suicide prevention techniques and in techniques for
cooperating with various individuals within the community,
including physicians, mental health workers, clergy, and the
judiciary.*

Among their many duties, police officers, from time to time, must
deal with suicidal persons under a variety of circumstances. What
are the responsibilities of police officers with regard to suicide?
Is suicide illegal? Who are the suicidal people? Why do they do
what they do? Are there symptoms by which they can be recognized
in advance? Are they sincere? Can suicide be prevented? What
is a community suicide prevention service? These are some of the
questions to be considered in this article.

Legal Aspects of Suicide
In the United States, there are approximately 20,000 suicide
deaths yearly. Each must have a conscientious police investigation.
Probably the police in this country respond to almost 200,000 calls
a year about persons who are threatening or attempting suicide.

The laws bearing on suicide are different in various countries
and in various states. Moreover, the legal aspects of suicide are
changing rapidly. The police officer should understand something
about the history of suicide and the law.

According to the law of old England, suicide was a special crime,
punishable by mutilation of the body, sanctions on the place and
manner of burial, forfeiture of the estate, and censure of the family.
It is questionable whether these laws were ever effective in preventing suicide or even in reducing the number of suicide attempts.
In practice, self-deaths were labeled something other than suicide
in order to bypass the excessive penalties, and suicide attempts

were not reported. In Britain, the penal sanctions against suicide were gradually rewritten, and in 1962 the last of them was repealed.

In the United States, as of January, 1964, according to written reports from the attorney general of each of the states, there are three main legal approaches to suicide. In nine states—Alabama, Kentucky, New Jersey, North Carolina, North Dakota, Oklahoma, South Carolina, South Dakota, and Washington—suicide is illegal. Since, however, such punishments as multilation of bodies or forfeiture of estates are repugnant to the American spirit, there is no legal penalty provided for breaking the law against suicide. In these states, suicide attempts are felonies or misdemeanors and could, in theory, result in jail sentences. In practice, the laws are seldom enforced. Eighteen states have no laws against suicide or suicide attempts, but they specify that it is a felony to aid, assist, encourage, or abet anyone else's suicide. These states are: Alaska, Arkansas, California, Florida, Kansas, Louisiana, Michigan, Massachusetts, Minnesota, Mississippi, Missouri, Montana, Nevada, New Mexico, New York, Oregon, Wisconsin, and Wyoming. Prosecutions under these laws are infrequent. Finally, in the twenty-three other states, there are no penal statutes referring to suicide.

That much of the old, moral stigma attached to suicide remains in our modern society becomes obvious to police officers during investigations of deaths that might be suicide. Friends and relatives may alter evidence that would tend to point toward suicide; suicide notes are sometimes concealed or destroyed; pressures are exerted on investigators and responsible officials to certify the case as accidental or natural. Although one cannot help feeling sympathy with the efforts of survivors to "clear the name" of the deceased from the implication of suicide, it is the police officer's duty conscientiously to report the evidence for and against suicide, which may then be reviewed and evaluated by impartial authorities.

In general, the more direct evidence that is included in the first police report the better. The following elements are recommended as essential: (1) description of the death: The appearance and location of the body should be described. Whenever possible, the method of death should be reconstructed by examining the surroundings. Firearms, pills, or other mechanisms suspected of playing a part in the suicide method should be booked as evidence. An

attempt should be made to discover how the weapon, drug, or mechanism was obtained. (2) Interview: Interviews should be obtained with persons discovering the body and with some informant who was on intimate terms with the victim. A report from some professional person trained in objective evaluation, such as a physician who knew the deceased, is especially valuable. It is important to try to reconstruct the last moments and hours of the victim's life. (3) Special information needed from informants: It can be extremely important to know something about the habits of the deceased, especially with regard to the method used for death. For example, if the lethal weapon was a gun, what were the victim's habits in handling firearms? If drug poisoning is suspected, how did the victim customarily use drugs? If death was from carbon monoxide in a garage, did the deceased have a history of running the motor of the car with the doors of the garage closed? It is important to ask about recent changes in the victim's life and in his personality. Was there any evidence of mental disturbance? Any recent visits to physicians, psychiatrists, ministers, or lawyers? Any recent arrests?

In reviewing police reports on suicides, I have noticed that many officers seem to lose interest in a case once it seems to be established that homicide is unlikely. The two most frequent omissions are failure to interview someone who knew the deceased person intimately and failure to interview someone, such as a physician, who had a professional knowledge of the deceased. Officers should check for barbiturate poisoning in all cases of bathtub and swimming pool drownings. One should be aware that accidental gunshot death is quite rare, whereas suicide gunshot death is frequent. Finally, in the case of automobile fatalities, we have become more and more suspicious that a sizable number of automobile traffic deaths are deliberate.

According to present-day popular and judicial attitudes, the police officer is concerned not with the apprehension, detention, and punishment of suicidal persons, but more with the prevention of damage to property and persons and with the assistance of people who have been injured. Local regulations usually provide that if there are reasonable grounds for believing that someone has been injured, a police officer is justified in forcibly entering a dwelling, although whenever practicable, he will attempt to have a member

of the family, a neighbor, or landlord accompany him into the home or apartment.

In most jurisdictions, the police officer is directed to place a person in protective custody when the officer has reasonable cause to believe that the person is mentally ill to the extent that he is likely to cause injury to himself or others and when he is in need of immediate care. Most police officers feel that they lack the special training needed to evaluate mental illness. Certainly, the policeman's task is eased if he has ready access to medical consultation. Since, however, medical consultation is often not immediately available, every police officer should have some background that enables him to use his judgment in evaluating a possibly suicidal person and then taking appropriate action.

Handling Suicidal Persons

Individuals have been known to commit suicide despite strong efforts to restrain them—for instance, in mental hospitals or in maximum security prisons. Such cases have led some police officers to say, "If a person really wants to commit suicide, there is nothing that can be done to stop him." This statement contains a particle of truth but is substantially in error. Although there are some extreme cases of individuals who will go to any length to achieve self-destruction, it is an error to assume that all suicides are committed by persons who are that wholehearted and persistent. Investigations of people who committed suicide have revealed that, for the most part, these people approached the idea of suicide gradually over a considerable period of time, in a very confused, mixed-up, contradictory frame of mind. While in part they wanted "out" because of frustration, anger, helplessness, guilt, fear, and other painful feelings, at the same time they had wishes to be rescued, saved, and to resume their lives. Often, the outcome as to whether a person lived or died seemed to depend on chance elements or upon the energy and alertness of possible rescuers.

These observations actually should come as no surprise. Experience tells us that we all have psychological conflicts, mixed feelings, and indecision about the important moves that we make in life, and surely the idea of self-death could be expected, in common sense, to create a maximum of psychological conflict and indecision. Also, it is an error to view all suicide attempts as failures

at self-murder. Actually, suicide attempts can be divided into three categories:

In the first category are those people who, in their own minds, have little intention of dying. They cut their wrists or ingest pills or crash cars in an effort to communicate something to somebody. Often, the content of the communication might be phrased, "I can't go on this way. Something's got to be done."

In the second group of suicide attempts, the main theme is that the person places his fate, whether he shall live or die, in the hands of chance or leaves it up to the actions of someone else. For example, a woman ingested an overdose of sleeping pills and left a note for her husband which said, "Wake me if you love me." He came home late, found her sleeping, read the note, and threw it into the wastepaper basket. He then went out to a bar. When he came back much later, she was dead. Many people recover from such an ordeal with a feeling of elation, "God must want me to live, since I have survived!" Often, suicide attempts achieve the goal of reawakening the interest of someone who has threatened to leave. "I never realized that she loved me that much."

Finally, there are suicide attempts that closely resemble committed suicides, in that the action that was taken could easily have been fatal and the person was saved only by fortune. It is interesting to find that the great majority of persons in this category, who were saved only by fortune, are extremely grateful for their good luck and do not go on to commit suicide. We sometimes observe, in the case of a slow-acting poison such as arsenic, someone who is doomed to die express the wish that the suicidal action had not been so "successful."

Sometimes, the communication that is expressed in a suicide attempt or suicide threat has a suggestion of blackmail, which often antagonizes the police officer who hears about it. For example, a man might say to his wife, "If you divorce me, I will kill myself," or a mother might say to her daughter, with whom she is living, "If you get married, I will kill myself." When I hear about such a problem, I always suggest that the person who is receiving this suicidal communication should discuss the matter with people who are important in his life: his doctor, clergyman, employer, friends, relatives, and the like. The effect of such a series of consultations is to distribute the responsibility for the final decision among a number

of people and remove the pressure of the blackmail threat. I seldom give direct advice to the caller to challenge the suicidal other, "Go ahead. I'm going to call your bluff." All too often such challenges have ended tragically, not only in suicide but sometimes in homicide.

Often, the police officer himself is confronted directly by a person who is making a suicidal threat. The classic example is the disturbed man or woman balancing on a ledge of a high building, while a crowd gathers below, shouting, "Jump! Jump!" But this same sort of confrontation occurs under less dramatic circumstances every day when someone barricades himself inside a bathroom with a gun, razor blade, or other weapon. It is extremely important for the police officer, especially the younger police officer, to know that he is not expected to be a "hero" and risk his own life under such circumstances. In general, any sudden, aggressive move by the police officer will only make things worse and add to the danger for all. The fact is that these potential victims are mentally ill. When dealing with mentally ill persons, the police officer should move slowly, cautiously, and thoughtfully. In these situations, talk can be more effective than action. Every effort should be made to engage the disturbed person in conversation and especially to find things to talk about in which the officer and the victim can be in agreement. One should try to find out from the potential suicide if there is anyone in the world whom he trusts, has confidence in, and would like to talk to. This person might be a spouse, some specific relative, a clergyman, a doctor, or some friend. Some people feel a reaction of trust and confidence when they see the police uniform. Other people are antagonized by this same image. The problem is to find the right person to whom the disturbed individual will respond favorably.

Recently, a disturbed and delinquent teen-age girl locked herself in the garage with her foster father's gun. Two police officers, who were summoned by the foster mother, hesitated, trying to decide what to do. She taunted them, called them cowards, and demanded that they break down the door. When they broke in, the girl shot herself and died. Then the foster mother sued the police, charging that they had caused the death. It would have been much better to have waited, for hours if need be, until someone could have been found who could talk to the girl.

Another case had a much better outcome. A mentally ill young woman stood on a ledge ten stories above the ground. She rejected the first attempts to talk to her. Then a policewoman arrived on the scene. She was told that a divorce had triggered the potential suicidal situation. The policewoman said to the disturbed girl, "We're both women. I understand your problem—come on in. Let's have a cup of hot coffee and talk it over." The woman on the ledge responded to this invitation and reentered the building.

According to the best recent estimates, based on surveys, life insurance statistics, and other analyses, there are now living in the United States approximately 3,000,000 people who made suicide attempts at some previous time in their lives. Of these, the great majority were suicidal during some previous crisis in their lives and made no second attempt, nor will they ever repeat. A minority of about 15 percent of these persons who made suicide attempts will go on later to repeat the suicidal action. Such repeaters should be referred for the evaluation of a specialist in mental illness.

The police officer should be especially alert for suicide under the following circumstances: (1) When a "respectable" citizen is arrested for an offense that he feels is shameful, such as child-molesting, homosexuality, embezzlement, or alcoholism. Such people should be watched closely during their first night in jail, since they may hang themselves. (2) The person who has made a suicide attempt and continues to be depressed. (3) The mentally ill person, often with a history of hospitalization in psychiatric facilities, who has talked of suicide. (4) Persons who have recently been rejected by sweethearts or spouses and are threatening suicide or homicide, or both. It is suggested that the police officer should secure a reasonably complete story about the problem and urge the family and friends of the suicidal person to make sure that he gets professional help. This will usually be from a family physician or a specialist psychiatrist, although it might be from a psychologist, social worker, minister, or admitting officer in a hospital.

Suicide Prevention Services

Organized antisuicide agencies are active in many communities. Their efforts are based upon three sets of observations: (1) Suicidal behavior tends to be associated with crises. These are life situations of special stress over a limited period of time. (2) People consider

suicide with great psychological ambivalence. They have mixed feelings about it. Wishes to die or be killed exist simultaneously with, and in conflict with, wishes to be rescued and survive. (3) Even in crises, people retain the human need to express themselves and communicate with others. The notion that suicide usually occurs suddenly, unpredictably, and inevitably has been contradicted by numerous investigations.

Viewed in retrospect, the typical suicide victim is seen as psychologically ill for a considerable period before his death. He is confused and in conflict with himself about dying. In his imagination, he struggles against his ideas of suicide, which represent in his mind such goals as escape, revenge, punishment and atonement, ecstasy, rescue, and rebirth. He tries to relieve his anxiety or painful depression by various trials and errors. When none of these actions succeeds in bringing relief, he returns repeatedly to the idea of suicide. He tends to signal his preoccupation with suicide to the people around him by his words and actions. Many suicidal communications can be interpreted as "cries for help." One aspect of suicide prevention, therefore, might be to arrange for appropriate rescuing responses to more or less disguised communications about suicide.

Most suicide prevention services share the concept of answering the suicidal person's "cry for help." An emergency telephone number is usually the nuclear element of the service and often constitutes the entire program. Emergency telephone services have been sponsored by a variety of organizations, including churches, religious orders, public health agencies, hospitals, clinics, mental health associations, medical societies, and police departments.

In giving emergency psychological first aid, the telephone therapist frequently accepts responsibility despite considerable handicaps. For instance, a limitation of the telephone call is that one is deprived of visual clues and most nonverbal communication. Obviously, the connection with the patient is extremely tenuous and can be broken off completely if the caller is affronted or startled. In answering a telephone call, the emergency therapist performs three functions which overlap. He tries to secure the line of communication; he evaluates the patient's condition, particularly the degree of danger; and, finally, he forms a treatment plan and begins

to act on it. While these three activities occur somewhat sequentially, they are also going on simultaneously. Thus, at all times during the telephone interview, with shifting emphasis as conditions permit, the interviewer is trying to establish, maintain, and solidify the relationship with the caller and, at the same time, evaluate his needs and strengths while trying to effect a therapeutic change.

In order to maintain, broaden, and solidify the telephone contact, the interviewer strives to find common ground where he and the patient agree. Usually, the starting point is that the patient has problems and needs help desperately. The interviewer wants to help him. Frequently, however, the caller is so ambivalent or so frightened that it takes quite a while to clarify a position on which he and the interviewer can agree. The interviewer-therapist uses the word "help" frequently and repeatedly in different contexts and offers optimistic ideas whenever he can, especially if he can elicit some agreement from the caller. Each time the caller and interviewer discover that they have another common bond, the communication line is strengthened. In addition to the usual therapeutic techniques of showing great interest in the caller, discerning his feelings, and responding appropriately, the therapist looks especially for emotional reactions with which he can sympathize. For example, anger at a spouse may be recognized or agreement with the caller's desire to "set the record straight" may be expressed.

Efforts are made to get the name, address, and telephone number of the caller, since the call may be cut off and one wishes to remain in communication. Many callers are ashamed of having to ask for help, and comments from intreviewers which indicate that the calls are expected, welcome, and familiar tend to put the person more at ease. Comments from the interviewer describing previous experiences which show that the interviewer has talked with persons in similar situations tend to increase the confidence of the caller. People calling the service feel a maximum of insecurity, confusion, guilt, fear, and suspicion. Our techniques must counter these emotions.

Trust is encouraged by straightforward, unevasive replies to questions. The interviewer should be ready to identify himself and his organization and give a clear, simple account of who the personnel are and what they are going to do and why. At times, it is

appropriate and reassuring to the caller for interviewers to take advantage of suicide prevention publicity and refer to articles that have appeared in popular magazines and newspapers.

To function well as a telephone therapist, the interviewer should have a talent for interpersonal communications, a willingness to become personally involved, and a need to rescue people in trouble. The danger of over-involvement with the patient is real but can be handled readily by consultation and supervision.

Turning now to the evaluation of the potentially suicidal caller, there are, of course, different degrees of suicidal danger. Some callers have motives quite remote from self-destruction: "I just called to find out what you have to do in this city to get your taxes reduced—commit suicide?" Sometimes, people on the waiting list for psychotherapy in clinics call, trying to get a referral for more immediate care. On the telephone at night, the more dramatic elements of a disturbed person's story tend to dominate the attention of the interviewer. To insure a more complete evaluation of the suicidal status of the caller, we devised a schedule focused around the "lethality" of the caller, which we ask our interviewers to complete as they talk with the patients. The schedule has been reported in other publications. It includes such factual items as sex and age; type of onset of the self-destructive behavior; method of possible self-injury; recent loss of loved persons; medical symptoms; constructive resources such as relatives, friends, and financial support; and certain judgmental, evaluative items such as the status of communication with the patient, the kinds of feelings expressed, the intuitive reaction of the interviewer, and the patient's general personality status and diagnostic impression.

The therapeutic plan and the therapeutic tactics depend upon the evaluation of the patient. Certain principles of emergency, supportive psychotherapy apply in nearly all cases. Most patients feel helpless and immobilized. Their view of the world is constricted. Self-esteem and self-confidence are low. Often, there is a profound loss of the usual feeling of identity. Various techniques are used to widen the patient's view of the world, reestablish his sense of self-identity, and encourage communication between him and the persons who could play a significant role in his life. History-taking is used not only to gain information about the potential strength and

resources of the patient but also to remind him of his past, present, and future—that is, to remind him of his identity.

Subtly and directly, we try to stimulate toward action. For example, we set up a series of return telephone calls back and forth which necessitate action on the part of the patient. Thus encouraged, most patients do call again. If they fail to call the next day, we call them. Whenever possible, we try to catalyze a reinvolvement between the patient and other people in his environment. Approximately 20 percent of the callers are evaluated as being in serious suicidal danger, and about half of these eventually are referred to a psychiatric hospital. Patients must be placed in the hospital not only to protect them against suicide, but also because that is where appropriate therapeutic modalities are located. Less than 5 percent of the calls represent actual physical emergencies, but these can be extremely dramatic. There may be a suicidal husband in the adjoining room with a newly purchased shotgun. Some callers have already taken a large dose of poison or lethal medication. One young woman called at midnight, refused to give her name, and said only that she had taken many pills. During the conversation she revealed that she could hear the ocean and was in a church. Then she collapsed. With those clues, the police were able to find her and take her to a hospital in time to save her life.

Special mention should be made of the antisuicide program sponsored by the Mental Health Committee of the Woman's Auxiliary of the American Medical Association, which has initiated more effective cooperation between physicians and police officers in many communities, as reported in *Today's Health* (1964). This group has organized workshops and conferences for police authorities and physicians. They highly recommend *The Cry for Help*, a training film about suicide, for police officers. This film can be borrowed from the National Medical Audio-Visual Facility, Atlanta 22, Georgia, or prints and discussion guides can be purchased from Norwood Studios, Inc., 926 New Jersey Avenue, N.W., Washington, D.C.

Since the suicide problems and the resources available for antisuicide work vary in different cities and states, the police, public health authorities, and responsible citizens of each community should be encouraged to approach the problem of suicide prevention

in their own community with originality and enthusiasm. Different problems will call for different types of solutions.

Summary

Suicide is a major public health problem. The police officer encounters suicide in several contexts. When a suicide death is suspected, there should be a complete and conscientious investigation. In responding to calls concerning persons who have attempted or threatened to commit suicide, the police officer has definite responsibilities and duties. Such persons should be given aid, assistance, and protection. Families, relatives, or friends should be notified of the situation. If mental illness is suspected, there should be an effort to secure examination by the proper authorities. On the other hand, if the suicidal person has placed himself in a situation of physical danger, an act of physical heroism which places the rescuing officer's life in danger is not recommended. Rather, efforts should be made to talk with the victim, obtain his trust, and find someone who can interest him in turning away from his hazardous position. Because of the complexity and variety of the problems, antisuicide efforts require the cooperation of various individuals and groups in the community, including physicians, the judiciary, mental health workers, the clergy, and many others, as well as the police.

Chapter 34
FREDERIC V. THE UNITED STATES

Action was brought against the United States under the Federal Tort Claims Act for the death of a patient who committed suicide by jumping from a window of a Veterans Administration hospital, on the grounds that the agents of the United States had been negligent in failing to detect the suicidal intention of the patient and in not removing him to a psychiatric ward or taking other measures for his security. The district court held that evidence was insufficient to establish that the United States was guilty of any actionable negligence in its treatment of the patient.

Margaret FREDERIC, Widow of Robert L. O'Donnell, Individually and on Behalf of Her Minor Children, Plaintiff,

v.

The UNITED STATES of America,
Defendant.
Civ. A. No. 13873.
United States District Court
E. D. Louisiana,
New Orleans Division.
Oct. 12, 1965.

Action was brought against the United States under the Federal Tort Claims Act for death of patient who committed suicide by jumping from window of Veterans' Hospital, on ground that agents of the United States were negligent in failing to detect suicidal intent of patient and in not removing him to psychiatric ward or taking other measures for his security. The District Court, Ainsworth, J., held that evidence was insufficient to establish that the United States was guilty of any actionable negligence in its treatment of the patient.

Judgment entered dismissing action.

1. Physicians and Surgeons
   14(4), 15(2)
   Generally, it is duty of physician under Louisiana law to exercise, not highest degree of skill and care possible, but degree of skill

ordinarily employed, under similar circumstances, by members of his profession in good standing in same community or locality, and to use reasonable care and diligence, along with his best judgment, in application of his skill to case.

2. Negligence 10
Foreseeability of harm is essential element to actionable negligence.

3. Hospitals 8
Evidence was insufficient to establish that United States was guilty of any actionable negligence in its treatment of patient, who committed suicide by jumping from window of Veterans' Hospital, and therefore United States was not liable for patient's death under Federal Tort Claims Act. 28 U.S.C. §§ 1346, 2671 et seq.

Duplantier & Kabacoff, Adrian G. Duplantier, James A. McPherson, New Orleans, La., for plaintiff.

Gene S. Palmisano, Asst. U. S. Atty., Eastern Dist. of Louisiana, for defendant.

AINSWORTH, District Judge:

This action was brought against the United States of America acting through the Veterans Administration by Mrs. Margaret Frederic, widow of Robert L. O'Donnell, individually and on behalf of her three minor children, under the Federal Tort Claims Act, 28 U.S.C. §§ 1346, 2671 et seq.

Damages are sought by plaintiff for the death of her husband, Robert L. O'Donnell, which occurred on October 16, 1962 when he committed suicide by jumping from a sixth-floor window of the Veterans Hospital at New Orleans, Louisiana, after having cut the window screen with a pocket knife in his possession. Plaintiff alleges negligence on the part of defendant and its agents in failing to detect suicidal intent of the deceased and in not removing him to the psychiatric ward or taking other measures for his security.

The hospital building is ten stories high; it is a general medical and surgical hospital for United States veterans and has a separate psychiatric service on the ninth floor, consisting of a closed or locked ward and an open ward. Both wards have strong protective screening on the windows, and each ward is normally occupied by ap-

proximately twenty patients who are either emotionally or mentally ill. The closed ward is used for patients who become violent or exhibit tendencies of harming themselves or others and is kept under constant supervision with a permanently assigned hospital staff. Patients in the open ward are subject to supervision and observation with a more or less permanently assigned staff; however, they enjoy the freedom of the various hospital facilities, such as the dining room and the canteen, and are allowed to come and go as they choose. Although these patients may be as ill as those in the locked ward, the aspect of their illness is different in that they do not exhibit traits of behavior or personality changes which would alert psychiatrists to the possibility that they were dangerous to themselves or to others. While the surveillance in the open psychiatric ward is not as rigid as that of the locked ward, it is greater than in the other medical or surgical wards.

The medical history of decedent shows that he suffered from ulcerative colitis. He had undergone surgery for this condition prior to being admitted to Veterans Hospital. On January 10, 1962 a colectomy and a revision of the patient's ileostomy were performed by Dr. Mohammad 'Atik, surgeon, at Veterans Administration Hospital, and the patient was discharged in February of 1962. He was again admitted on May 24, 1962 complaining of "vague abdominal pains, intermittent shortness of breath, swelling of the feet and ankles, dizzy spells, orthopnea and stiffness of the fingers." Various examinations and clinical tests were made. Dr. George A. Adcock, Jr. examined the patient and wrote the following order: "Consult psychiatry in the A. M. Forty-eight year old white male post-operative colectomy for ulcerative colitis. Has lost all interest in caring for self and exhibits marked intermittent periods of hostility and feelings of persecution. Would you evaluate? Thanks." The consultation was not had, however, as the patient left the hospital three days later against medical advice. A final summary of his May 1962 hospitalization by Dr. Adcock shows, ". . . The pt was gaining weight and said he was satisfied with the results; however, he appears slightly hostile to the examiner . . . He is very vague to answer questions and appears hostile and somewhat contradictory . . . The initial impression was anxiety reaction, possible underlying psychosis and post-operative status chronic ulcerative colitis . . . He was placed on placebos to determine if organic pain

was present. The placebos at times remarkably relieved the pain. The pt continued to be very careless with his ileostomy and refused to take proper care of it. On 5/27 the pt demanded to see the physician on call. When the physician had not appeared within two hours the pt obtained his clothes from home, dressed and stated he was leaving. He refused to discuss the situation with the physician on call or to accept any pain medication. He signed himself out AMA [against medical advice]." The patient was again admitted to the Veterans Hospital on October 3, 1962, complaining of mild pain and a discharge from his rectal stump. He was ambulatory and did not appear to be acutely ill. The admission history shows, "Neuropsychiatric Systems: Negative." Various tests were made in contemplation of possible additional surgery. On October 8, 1962 a routine psychiatric consultation was ordered by Dr. Atik and Dr. Richard S. Cohen, with the notation, "Psychiatric consult. Patient-ulcerative colitis. Past history psychosis. Please evaluate." The request was received by Dr. Richard Stone, staff psychiatrist, but the consultation was not made prior to Mr. O'Donnell's death. However, on October 13, 1962 the patient was presented by a senior medical student to Dr. Henry O. Colomb, psychiatrist and professor of psychiatry at L.S.U. Medical School, in connection with a demonstration form of clinical teaching. Student notes made as a result of this demonstration showed, "Patient presented this A.M. to Dr. Colomb. Diagnosis of anxiety with some degree of depression was arrived at." Three days later, on October 16, 1962, the patient jumped to his death from a bathroom window of the sixth floor of the hospital.

Numerous members of the Veterans Administration Hospital staff and other physicians who had occasion to have contact with the patient by means of examination or observation, including seven medical doctors, one of whom is a psychiatrist, Dr. Henry O. Colomb, testified. It was agreed generally that there are emotional components connected with the disease of ulcerative colitis, and it was the opinion of all seven doctors that the patient had no unusual symptoms, that essentially his emotional make-up was that of a normal patient, that the patient did exhibit signs of a slight depression but that depression is not uncommon, not only with patients suffering from ulcerative colitis, but with any patient contemplating possible surgery. None of these doctors considered

the patient to be a suicidal risk, and it was their unanimous opinion that there was no indication that would justify placing the patient in a neuropsychiatric ward. Dr. George A. Adcock, Jr. said that when he had made the notation in the clinical record on May 24, 1962 that the patient had lost all interest in caring for himself, he was referring specifically to the patient's gross neglect in taking care of his ileostomy, and that his purpose in ordering a routine psychiatric consultation was because of underlying psychological problems usually associated with the disease of ulcerative colitis. The purpose of the request by Dr. Atik for such a consultation was the same—the nature of the illness and because some of the patient's complaints were unfounded. Dr. Atik's request was a routine request, definitely not of an emergency nature as the patient did not impress him as being dangerous or self-destructive, and if he had been so impressed he would have immediately called in a psychiatrist. Requests for consultation at the Veterans Administration Hospital fall into three categories: routine, urgent and emergency. The requests for psychiatric consultations on both admissions were considered routine. Routine requests are answered anywhere from two to three days to as such as several weeks depending on the situation. In the absence of the two staff psychiatrists there are three consultants available for emergencies. Emergency requests are given immediate action. During the period of 1963 and 1964 the average length of time in which consultations in the psychiatric service were answered was 3.2 days, with a spread of from 1 to 12 days. A delay of eight days was not considered an unusual delay.

The nurses who attended Mr. O'Donnell in October of 1962 considered him to be a cooperative and quiet person, not a potential suicide victim, and not the type of patient who should have been in a psychiatric ward. There were never any prior attempts at suicide by Mr. O'Donnell, he had never threatened suicide, and had never mentioned the subject to anyone, including his wife and family. Mrs. O'Donnell and several relatives of the deceased noticed that his disposition was moody and depressed during his last hospitalization compared to his usual former happy and jovial disposition, but none of them were concerned to the extent that they reported their impression of the patient to the hospital staff.

Dr. William Sorum, a psychiatrist licensed to practice by the

State of Louisiana and a member of the American Board of Psychiatry, testified as an expert. He was of the opinion from reading the record that Mr. O'Donnell was depressed and disturbed. He considered certain signposts helpful in detecting suicidal tendencies. Some of these are previous attempts at suicide, a patient's conversation relating to suicide, changes in behavior pattern, a feeling of persecution, vagueness or impulsiveness in actions, depression, loss of weight or loss of appetite, early morning awakening, expressions of hopelessness and any changes in personal habits. He indicated, however, that no one of these symptoms alone would be indicative of suicidal intent. In retrospect he believed that the patient had suicidal tendencies "because he did take his own life." He further commented, "When you're sitting in this vantage point, you can look back and second-guess what could have been done to prevent this, but as to just what action I would have advocated prior to this suicide, I couldn't say at this time."[1]

Dr. Sorum testified that he was not in a position to say whether a delay of eight days between the time of a request and the psychiatric consultation would be an undue delay. In his experience consultations are delayed for various reasons. He felt, however, "in retrospect," the sooner the consultation occurred the better it would be for the patient.

There was nothing in Dr. Sorum's testimony to indicate that defendant had deviated from the standard of care required by the medical profession.

Dr. Edwin Shneidman, co-director and co-founder of the Suicide Prevention Center at Los Angeles, California, clinical professor of psychiatry (in psychology) of the University of Southern California School of Medicine, a diplomate in clinical psychology and a member of the Board of Directors and Vice President of the American Board of Examiners and Professional Psychologists, testified as an expert in the field of suicide prevention. Since 1958 he has been engaged in a special project of the Veterans Administration called the Center for the Study of Unpredicted Deaths, which Center serves all of the Veterans Hospitals in the United States. In connection with this project, all folders on patients who have committed suicide while hospitalized at Veterans Administration Hospitals, along with the next folder in numbered sequence, which is a record of a non-suicide (called a "control folder"), are sent to the central

research unit in Los Angeles, for the purpose of analysis and comparison of the two folders in an effort to ascertain the motivating factors of the suicide in question and to attempt to determine if there were any clues of contemplated suicide. The principal purpose of the study is to take a case of suicide out of the realm of unpredicted deaths into the realm of predictable suicides, the results of which are hoped to prevent suicide in many cases. The biggest problem encountered is sudden, unexpected deaths, where there has been no indication that it was about to occur. The procedure is to have an assistant present a case to a panel consisting of Dr. Shneidman, Dr. Farberow and other consultants, giving all pertinent details up to the last few entries in the chart. The panel discusses the case and each member indicates whether he is of the opinion that the case was a suicide or a control folder, and gives reasons for his opinion. A discussion of the clues used in arriving at each opinion is then had. When the procedure was first used in 1958, there was much disagreement in the results. However, through the years the clues or "distilled notions" have been refined and a disagreement is now a rare event.

At the request of the government, Dr. Shneidman reviewed the folder of Robert L. O'Donnell, after having been informed of the patient's suicide. He found evidence of perturbation and anxiety, considered normal concomitants of hospitalization. Had he used the "blind autopsy" procedure he would have assessed this case as non-suicidal. He found lacking the usual conscious or unconscious communication of intention by the patient. The only clues of any significance were not contained in the record but stated by the widow on the witness stand. He referred to the patient's holding on to her and squeezing her hand on the night before his death. However, even if that information had been in the record, in itself it would not have been of deep significance to Dr. Shneidman. When asked about the relationship between a condition of depression and suicide, he stated that depression has classically been related to suicide; if one were limited to one single symptom, the best answer to suicide would be depression, but most depressives are not suicidal and many suicidals are not depressives. It is an overlapping ellipsis, but the two terms are far from being synonymous. The same is true in regard to the relationship between psychotics and suicides. Most psychotics or over 99% of them do not commit suicide. On the

other hand, there is an overlap between psychosis and suicide. He detailed some of the signposts found in clinical records of patients who have committed suicide: Previous suicidal attempts, a continuous concern on the part of others of the generally downward course of the patient, a history of eating and sleeping disturbances and impulsive self-destructive behavior, which behavior might include happenings that wouldn't look like suicide intent, such as accidents, some sort of mutilation, and getting hurt in different ways if supported by other symptoms. It was Dr. Shneidman's opinion that the main thing missing from the O'Donnell record indicating suicidal tendencies was the wholeness of it and the fact that no one, relatives, doctors or hospital staff sensed that the patient was contemplating suicide. He concluded that the patient should not have been placed in a psychiatric ward; that no special action on the part of the Veterans Administration Hospital staff was called for; that removing the penknife from the patient or effecting other minimum security measures was not justified.

Dr. William C. Super, psychiatrist, Director of Psychiatry at Charity Hospital since 1955, a staff member of Tulane and L.S.U. Medical Schools and of DePaul Hospital, testified as an expert. He is certified by the American Board of Psychiatry and Neurology and is a fellow in the American Psychiatric Association. He has dealt with several thousand patients in which suicide has been a question. Some of the clues which he considers to evidence suicidal intent are diagnoses of a manic depressive, schizophrenic reaction with depression, alcoholism with depression, language of despondency or hopelessness, preoccupation with death, severe insomnia, lack of appetite, weight loss and previous attempts at suicide. He stated that the whole picture must be viewed for diagnostic purposes. It was his opinion that the evidence was insufficient to indicate Mr. O'Donnell was a suicidal risk or to warrant removing him to a locked ward. He also felt that inasmuch as Dr. Colomb, a qualified psychiatrist, saw the patient three days prior to his death and found nothing unusual except a mild depression, the Veterans Administration Hospital had the right to rely on his recommendations. He found that the treatment rendered the patient was equal to the standard of care in the community and that the staff acted according to ordinary medical practice.

Plaintiff alleges negligence in the failure of the hospital personnel

to detect Mr. O'Donnell's suicidal potential and to have taken necessary precautions which would have prevented his self-destruction. It is further contended that defendant was negligent in failing to provide the patient promptly with a psychiatric consultation, which failure contributed to his suicide.

[1] The question with which the court is concerned is whether or not defendant or its agent was guilty of negligence which proximately caused the death of plaintiff's husband, or did defendant fail to exercise the proper degree of care under the circumstances.[2] The standard of care required by the medical profession was announced by the Supreme Court of Louisiana in Meyer v. St. Paul-Mercury Indemnity Co., 225 La. 618, 73 So.2d 781 (1954), in which the court stated:

> "A physician, surgeon, or dentist, according to the jurisprudence of this court and of the Louisiana Courts of Appeal, is not required to exercise the highest degree of skill and care possible. As a general rule it is his duty to exercise the degree of skill ordinarily employed, under similar circumstances, by the members of his profession in good standing in the same community or locality, and to use reasonable care and diligence, along with his best judgment, in the application of his skill to the case."[3]

There is nothing in the record which shows a lack of care and diligence or error of judgment on the part of members of the Veterans Administration Hospital staff. The evidence is overwhelming that the accepted method of procedure was followed by the hospital in its care and treatment of the patient. The patient had not been admitted as a psychiatric patient, had not been classified or diagnosed as such, and there was no evidence that he was in need of such treatment. Therefore, it would have been unwarranted and unreasonable for the hospital to have placed the patient in a psychiatric ward or to have imposed the security measures customarily employed with patients who are violent or dangerous. Plaintiff's argument that Mr. O'Donnell should have been placed on a lower floor and deprived of his penknife is untenable, for even if these precautions had been taken, nothing would have prevented the patient from walking up to a higher floor or securing another instrument for cutting the screen; all of the patients, with the exception of those in the locked ward, had free access to higher floors and

to the canteen where such articles as razors or penknives could have been obtained. The only measure that could have possibly prevented suicide would have been placing the patient in the locked ward reserved for the violent or dangerous. There was no evidence to justify this precaution; to the contrary the testimony of all the doctors and members of the staff at the hospital was to the effect that there was no basis for removing the patient to a psychiatric ward.

It is suggested that there was a breach of duty in the failure of defendant to hold a psychiatric consultation more promptly. The request for this consultation was considered a normal routine request, not urgent, and certainly not an emergency calling for immediate action. The procedure of the staff in this respect was in conformity with the accepted standards of the community and elsewhere. Dr. Colomb, the psychiatrist who interviewed the patient, detected no symptoms that would have justified psychiatric treatment. The hospital staff was not negligent in relying on his observations.

[2] Foreseeability of harm is an essential element to actionable negligence. Brown v. Liberty Mutual Insurance Company, 234 La. 860, 101 So.2d 696 (1958). This element is completely lacking here. None of the witnesses suspected or had cause to suspect that the patient might commit suicide or that he was even contemplating such action.

[3] Plaintiff has therefore failed to prove that defendant was guilty of any actionable negligence in its treatment of decedent. Accordingly, judgment will be entered for the defendant, dismissing plaintiff's suit.

Chapter 35
SUICIDE AS A TABOO TOPIC
Edwin S. Shneidman

*Tabooed areas that, by definition, are socially disapproved of
and stigmatized present special problems to research investigators.
A discussion of different kinds of taboos is presented. Suicide,
because of the guilt and hostility it generates in survivors,
proves especially difficult to investigate at first hand. The taboos
surrounding suicide, related to religion, sin, hereafter, and
the usurpation of divine right, are beginning to lift just
enough to allow efforts at serious investigation and aid in
prevention of suicidal acts.*

The history of suicide reveals that it has been viewed with varying attitudes by society. Some primitive and some recent cultures
have accepted and approved of suicide. But by far the most prevalent attitude, especially in Occidental cultures, has been negative,
and suicidal behavior has been met with hostility, censure, and
condemnation. Suicide falls directly in the middle of a taboo area
and thus encounters all the blind prejudices and resistances that
encrust proscribed topics. As Glanville Williams remarks: ". . . It
raises the marital disputes of order and freedom, effort and indulgence, holiness and happiness, authority and conscience, which
have vexed philosophy for as long as these problems have been
thought of, and are unable to achieve any permanent solution."[1]

Taboos generaly involve various kinds of activities that are forbidden. For example, there are (1) things that one would not do
(the taboo is on the action) ; (2) things that one does with relative
impunity, if not enjoyment, but would not talk about having done
(the taboo is on the discussion) ; and (3) activities that one would
not even dare to do or even wish to think of (the taboo is on the
thought or label). Suicide seems to cut across all three kinds of
taboo; the prohibitions against suicide (and murder) may be found
more often in the first (action) and third (thought) kinds of taboo,
whereas the topics of heterosexuality and homosexuality may be
found more in the second (discussion) type of taboo.

There is a large number of taboo topics; yet, without indulging
in any competition as to which topic is *most* taboo, it can be said

that suicide shares taboos with each of the major areas in a kind of overlapping that is not necessarily reciprocal. For example, the overlap of the taboos of suicide with those relating to death, sex, and the hereafter may be presented briefly.

The relationships between death and suicide would appear obvious, but turn out to be, on examination, somewhat complicated. True, committing suicide involves death, but the act of committing suicide can also be conceived as a way of living (or nonliving).

Death is reified and reacted to in many ways. A recent Radcliffe dissertation has helpfully outlined some attitudes on the meaning of death.[2] She lists the following: death as *unreal* (". . . the difficulty or impossibility of accepting one's own death. Because we are reluctant to die, the concept of immortality always has been enticing to man . . .") ; death as *punishment* (". . . death as punishment for forbidden [tabooed] wishes . . .") ; death as *separation,* especially from the mother or parents; death as *reunion,* especially with the mother or the incestuous love object; and death as *lover.* (The literature on this last point is an extensive and fascinating one and is discussed by McClelland).[3] The reader will note the many and rather clear threads of taboo running through this tapestry of death. And suicide, with its dark motivations for immortality, punishment, and reunion, is spun from the same loom.

What are some of the relationships between suicide and sex? Over and above the notions that people seem to commit suicide over unrequited heterosexual love and that some adolescent transvestites as well as some homosexuals commit suicide—it has been reported that homosexuals are disproportionately represented in the suicide population, but we have never seen any good evidence of this—a most interesting concept is that, alluded to above, of death as symbolically sexual, as a lover. McClelland discusses the association of "death, seduction, and demonic power."[4] In women (men were not studied), excitement, sexual fantasies, and upsurge of libidinal energies were found to be associated with death, that is, expressed more often by women dying of cancer than by seriously ill, but not dying, counterparts. In this area, all the taboos about sex, death, and suicide are compounded.

A recent study of ours on suicide in patients with malignant neoplasms revealed additional relationships between suicide and death.[5] Cancer, as a fatal illness with death lurking in the shadows, arouses

feelings of disquiet and displeasure similar to those aroused by suicide. Suicide was viewed paradoxically when it occurred in such patients, often being seen as justifiable and reasonable. Many people, when asked under what conditions suicide would ever be justified, offer the presence of a serious terminal illness as just cause. Yet, even when it did occur among patients with cancer, the familiar feelings of guilt, shame, and embarrassment appeared, not only in members of the family, but also among the hospital staff. Why does a person at the threshold of death commit suicide? Perhaps the value of his life is lessened for the man who knows that he will not live much longer anyway and faces a foreshortened future filled with pain and suffering. The choice of suicide over an existence in which the life pattern has been totally disrupted, the body image attacked, the self-concept severely strained, and all familiar interpersonal relationships practically destroyed seems, on the face of it, understandable.

Yet the number of suicides that occur in cancer patients is only a small percentage of the total number of patients who contract the dread disease. Perhaps the question equally deserving to be asked is why so many cancer patients do *not* commit suicide. The strength of the taboos against suicide becomes even more remarkable when the attitudes of the physicians toward the dying patient are studied. Feifel, and Weisman and Hackett, have described some of the tendencies toward rejection and denial which appear in the physician when faced with the impending death of a patient.[6] Weisman and Hackett say: "The patient's capacity to face his own imminent death is often underestimated, while the doctor's capacity to face the patient's death is usually overestimated. . . . If the doctor can accept death as a fact of life and not as a failure of treatment, he can accept the reality of the dying patient."[7]

Suicide and the hereafter have an intimate, complicated relationship. Among the many notions, two facts can be stated: (1) some people believe in a hereafter, some do not, and some are not sure; (2) belief in a hereafter seems to inhibit suicide in some people and to facilitate it in others. This entire topic is not only a fascinating one, but one which is, to put it strongly, fundamental to more effective understanding of suicidal phenomena and ultimately basic to more effective treatment, control, and prevention of these behaviors.

Tabooed areas are, by definition, socially disapproved, stigmatized, and unpopular. Harold Hildreth, of the United States Public Health Service, has suggested that researches or investigations in taboo areas often have three common characteristics. First, they often deal with fundamental social problems—the types of things that people do not want to recognize or proper people do not want to get involved in. Second, there is some suspicion of investigators in such areas. There is a personal cost in an investigation in a generally taboo area, the least of which is the ubiquitous journalistic question, "How did you come to be interested in this topic?"—with the sly implication that it must be some grossly overdetermined interest or concern on the researcher's part. Third, there are common methodological problems in investigations in taboo areas; for example, the data are characteristically difficult to obtain, and there are pervasive questions of the reliability of the data, in that people tend to dissimulate and conceal.

From the research standpoint, these methodological issues are most important. They lead directly to the problem of the reliability of statistics of suicide. Much of the technical and popular literature on suicide is filled with figures, statistics, and norms comparing suicide rates of various races, regions, religions, nationalities, and so on. The question is important in both social and personality theory as to whether these differences do exist or what are the true statistics. It may be of interest to note that the word "statistic" is derived from the Latin *status,* which in the Middle Ages had come to mean a "state" in the political sense of the word. Statistics, therefore, was originally an inquiry into various conditions of the state and has been called "political arithmetic" and, later, "vital statistics." In these early labors, much attention was given to tables of mortality for the state, so that the present discussion of statistics on suicide is, in terms of the original sense of the word, particularly appropriate.

Statistics on suicide come from the individual certifications of individual deaths. These certifications are made by county coroners or medical examiners and are then compiled by state, region, and nation. Differing procedures, however, are followed in various countries, so that some certifications are made on the recommendation of the local or family physician only. Assuming an omniscient power privy to the real nature of each death, any departure from the tab-

ulations by such a power would represent a distortion in the statistics. These errors in statistics on suicide occur for one of the following reasons: (1) There are inadvertent errors of diagnosis (for example, calling a suicidal death an accidental death) where there are no taboos influencing the diagnostician. (2) There are deliberate or unconscious suppressions of the diagnosis for reasons related to taboo.

Coroners certify each death as homicide, natural, accident, or suicide. This is often difficult simply because the *mode* of death is not readily apparent. For example, a woman can be found dead, and the coroner's ancillary people—the toxicologist, the histologist, the biochemist, and so on—can tell him rather exactly what the distribution of a barely lethal dosage of barbiturate is among the organs in her body, but this may give little information as to whether the death was accidental or suicidal. The *sine qua non* of suicide is some lethal self-destructive intention, so what is missing from the coroner's information is the victim's motivation or intention; and these are psychological concepts. In Los Angeles County, staff of the Suicide Prevention Center have been deputized by Chief Medical Examiner-Coroner Theodore Curphey to serve as his "death investigation team." We do "psychological autopsies," interviewing, in cases of equivocal accident-suicide deaths, the relatives and friends of the deceased; reconstructing the life style of the victim; searching for undiagnosed depressions, psychoses, and personality changes; and keeping our ears attuned for coded messages of suicidal intent that may have been dropped by the victim into the matrix of communication. It may be added that these interviews with the survivors have a generally therapeutic effect, just in relieving some of their taboo feelings. As a result of these activities, two conclusions emerge.

1. The existing fourfold classification of deaths into homicide, accident, natural, and suicide is oversimplified and often leads to inaccuracy. It is too confusing, primarily because the psychological factors—the individual's intentions, his motivations, and his role in his own demise—are omitted. What is suggested is a psychologically oriented classification of death phenomena focused on the individual's role in his own demise.[8]

Thus it may well be that few of the statistics on suicide in the world can really be deemed reliable. Certifications of obviously

suicidal deaths as natural deaths or accidental deaths by physicians and coroners often occur in rural and urban areas throughout the world. "Suicide" is a dirty word. Indeed, some languages have no word for suicide. Mussolini made it illegal, and thus there are no statistics on suicide in Italy for part of that period. In one of our studies, we compared, using a blind-analysis approach, the psychological content of 948 suicide notes from Los Angeles County for the years 1956 through 1958 with a set of socioeconomic variables determined by the area in which the note-writer lived and found that the taboos relating to the method and meaning of suicide varied among the socioeconomic levels.[9] Conscientious coroners must be making arbitrary decisions daily concerning the mode of death which they put on the death certificate.

2. Relatively few individuals who kill themselves do so unambivalently. Granted that some suicidal behaviors have no lethal intention, we believe that most suicidal behavior involves a gamble with death, magical thinking, or dependence on the role of the significant other in a dyadic relationship and is acutely ambivalent.

The taboo nature of suicide apparently does not prevent its discussion. The taboo seems to accrue much more to the act than to the writing about the topic. The bibliography on suicide printed in *The Cry for Help* covering the years from 1897, the date of Durkheim's book, to 1957 contains about two thousand titles— although it is fair to state that most of the items are discursive, philosophic, anecdotal, or theoretical in nature, and few have scientific substance.[10]

The taboo that emerges in the hostility of society toward suicidal acts also seems to vary according to the type of act. There is a great onus attached to surviving spouse, parent, or child of a suicide. No other kind of death—whether by accident, cancer, or heart disease—creates such a backwash of guilt, remorse, and shame. Open hostility, on the other hand, is often reserved, not for the person who commits suicide, but for the person who, to use a word in an un-American way, "unsuccessfully" attempts it. We have heard reports of emergency hospital personnel saying: "Next time, really do a good job and don't bother us." It may well be that these feelings are directed toward the person for his daring to do the tabooed thing, to show disdain for society and its values and disregard of the religious strictures. In addition, some of this anger may be di-

rected toward the individual for his semantic usurpation, that is, his indulging in *nonlethal* "suicide" behavior.

One example illustrating most of the points mentioned above occurred when the Los Angeles medical examiner-coroner received petitions from the family and friends of a man who had obviously committed suicide indicating that the deceased was a fine citizen and a good husband and father; when the coroner did not change the certification of mode of death, the widow sued him. The judge ruled that the medical examiner-coroner, using his own judgment and the services of our group, had shown diligence and care, and the plaintiff's case was denied. At this point, the woman became assaultive and hysterical. Rarely was the taboo nature of suicide more dramatically portrayed.

Consider another illustration of the taboo nature of this topic. Some months ago, one of us had occasion to conduct a workshop on suicide prevention in a large city and was contacted by a member of a well-known religious group interested in suicide prevention. This member indicated that he was going to visit and counsel a young man who had recently attempted suicide and extended an invitation to accompany him. Four hours were spent in the home with the young man and his wife. One of several interesting developments was that the suicide attempt was never mentioned, although the topic of sex and specific sexual behaviors was unabashedly introduced by the clergyman and answered with seeming candor and lack of resentment by the young couple. The taboo word in that context was "suicide," although that was the *raison d'être* of the meeting. It might be added that we do things somewhat differently at the Suicide Prevention Center. There is the apocryphal story that, when Kinsey died, a publisher indicated to Kinsey's group that he would like to publish their materials because, as he said, for him, " 'Sex' was not a four-letter word." For us, using the same kind of arithmetic, "suicide" is not a four-letter word either.

A final example of the effect of taboos on suicide statistics can be given. The sheriff-coroner of a large city once showed us some data on suicide in his city that were remarkable, for he had noted only a dozen suicidal deaths annually for a city of over one-half million. We looked at his records with some interest and discovered that he was reporting as suicide only those deaths in which he

found a verified, holographic suicide note. In those cases in which the individual seemed to have killed himself but did not leave a note, the case was not reported as suicide, but as "self-inflicted violent deaths," and recorded as accident.

There seems to be some slight change toward the lifting of the taboo nature of suicide, just as there have been great changes in the taboo nature of sex. For example, the status of suicide as a crime has been changing. State after state has taken it off the statute books. In only nine states is suicide a crime. As recently as 1961, in California, suicide was not a compensable industrial injury case. Now, if the suicide was precipitated by pain or mental anguish derived from the industrial accident, it may be compensable.

Taboo is such a generally negative concept that it is appropriate to ask a perverse question, namely: Are there any positive aspects to taboo? Are any taboos worthwhile and effective? In some taboos, especially in the sexual area, their purpose is obviously to perpetuate some ideal that society deems worthwhile. However, in other areas, taboos seem to operate against the goals of society. Thus, our information does not lead us to believe that taboos against suicide lead to any decrease in suicide rate. Indeed, quite the contrary seems to be true. (It is important to report that, on the other side, our activity has not led us to believe that research and study of suicide increase the suicide rate.) It must not be assumed that it is our wish to lift all taboos. What so often happens, however, is that the taboos are directed not only against the act but against the investigation and investigators of the act as well. We are against suicide; we seek principles that can effect a reduction in the suicide rate. But, being against the phenomenon means that we must break through the barrier surrounding the taboo and attempt, contrary to the taboo, to promote investigation of the subject.

In addition, we can ask if there is anything positive for investigators in a taboo area. Though there is obvious onus attached to investigating taboo topics, there are subtle rewards as well. Whereas we are seen by some as brash, we are seen by others as courageous. The approbation of many comes out in their being pleased that we are working in this taboo topic. This helps in the current mitigation of the taboo indicated above. Our problem is how to explain to the psychological conservatives our radical challenging of some of the unconscious primitive roots of the society. Our in-

tuitive explanation is that we are living in a rapidly changing world and that, because of this, we must have the courage to investigate the magical, irrational, and overfeared inhabitants relegated to the cellar of our societal edifice.

Aside from the taboo nature of suicide, if we have learned anything from our decade of work on this topic, we have learned that, happily, most individuals who are acutely suicidal are so for only a relatively short period and that, even during the time they are suicidal, they are extremely ambivalent about living and dying. If there are techniques for identifying these individuals before rash acts are taken and if there are agencies, like the Suicide Prevention Center, in the community that can throw in every resource on the side of life and give the individual some temporary surcease or sanctuary, then after a short time most individuals can go on, voluntarily and willingly, to live useful and creative lives.

Chapter 36
SUGGESTIONS FOR REVISION OF THE DEATH CERTIFICATE
Edwin S. Shneidman

*The urgent need to explore and describe current practices of
reporting suicide under the present archaic Natural-Accident-
Suicide-Homicide (or NASH) classification of deaths suggests
priorities of investigation. Equivocal deaths may fall under any
of the NASH categories, usually between suicide and accident.
Several questions are implied: How do certifying officials
arrive at the decision to list a death as suicide? What are the
criteria for special procedures in an equivocal death? When
should behavioral and social scientists be involved in the total
investigational procedure of a death? How can the psychodynamics
of death and dying be introduced into the death certificate?
The concept of "subintentioned death"—a death in which the
decedent plays an unconscious role in hastening his own
demise—is central to this paper.*

It is platitudinous to say that death is inevitable and that in each
life potential actuality of death is an inexorable fact, but having
said this, there is nothing at all that now precludes asserting that
the ways of our speaking about death and the ways in which we
dimensionalize death are nothing more than man-made—mutable
and subject to change and clarification. Indeed, one major explicit
goal of this chapter is precisely that of reexamining (with an
eye toward improving) our current conceptualizations of death.

Changes in the conceptualizations of death are constantly occurring. Each generation becomes accustomed to its own notions
and thinks that these are universal and ubiquitous. In this connection, it is salutary to recall briefly that from the time of John
Graunt and his London Bills of Mortality in the seventeenth century, through the work of Cullen in the eighteenth century, and
William Farr in the nineteenth century, through the adoption of
the Bertillion International List of Causes of Death in 1893, up
through the International Conference for the 8th Revision of the
International Classification of Diseases in Geneva less than two
years ago, the classification of diseases and of causes of death have

been constantly changing in their scope and in their dimensions. As one examines these changes, it would appear that they can be characterized primarily by an attempt to include and to reflect recent knowledge and information, including that from the new specialties as they developed, for example, anesthesiology, pathology, bacteriology, immunology, advances in surgery, and so on.

Accurate or comprehensive statistics on completed suicides in the United States do not now exist. There is widespread confusion and considerable difference of interpretation as to how to classify deaths. For example, what is considered suicide in one locality is often viewed as accidental death in another. The factors that determine decisions of coroners and medical examiners must be made clearly visible as attempts are made to develop criteria for gathering vital baseline data in the area of suicide.

The present U. S. classification "suicide" is based on the Seventh Revision of the International Classification of Diseases and Causes of Death, 1955.[1] When the Seventh Revision was put into practice for the data year 1958, the death rate for suicides, for males and females and for most age groups, increased markedly over 1957. Here is the explanatory paragraph for this phenomenon from Mortality Trends in the U. S. 1954–1963:

> About 3.3 percent of the total suicide rate for 1958 as compared with that for 1957 resulted from the *transfer of a number of deaths from accidents to suicide.* In 1958 a change was made in the interpretation of injuries where there was some doubt as to whether they were accidentally inflicted or inflicted with suicidal intent. Beginning with the Seventh Revision for data year 1958 "self-inflicted" injuries with no specification as to whether or not they were inflicted with suicidal intent and deaths from injuries, whether or not self-inflcted, with an indication that it is not known whether they were inflicted accidentally or with suicidal intent, are classified as suicides. The change was made on the assumption that the majority of such deaths are properly classified as suicide *because of the reluctance of the certifier to designate a death as suicide unless evidence indicates suicidal intent beyond the shadow of a doubt.* The magnitude of the comparability ratios for suicide varied considerably with means of injury, from 1.02 for suicide by firearms and explosives to 1.55 for

suicide by jumping from high places.[2] (Emphasis supplied.)

It is seen that this redefinition led to an increase from one year
to the next of 55 percent for suicides by jumping from high places.
Even more interesting is the official observation that the death
certifier would be reluctant to check suicide "unless evidence indicates suicidal intent beyond the shadow of a doubt." This statement
is interesting because it focuses on the function of the certifier in
the process of generating mortality data. He must establish, by his
own rules or by adopting state rules, what constitutes conclusive
evidence of *intent,* a subjective concept referring to the goals-and-
means of the deceased.

Our Judeo-Christian ethos and the American legal code perceive
suicide as the most negative of all modes of death—as murder committed on the self. No detailed evidence to support this statement
will be presented here; however, some obvious indications may be
found in the American linguistic patterns (e. g., euphemisms,
taboos) and in legal rules protecting the dead person and survivors
from real or possibly anticipated social harm (hence the requirement of "beyond the shadow of a doubt" evidence). That variations
in social outlook will lead to incomparability and unreliability of
the eventually reported suicide statistics seems almost evident. A
more striking piece of evidence is found in the comparison of reported suicide rates for adjacent states of similar ethnic and occupational composition: (1) Idaho 10.9 versus Wyoming 20.2, per
100,000 population. (2) Mississippi 5.5 versus Arkansas 8.8, Alabama 8.8, Louisiana 8.4.[3]

There is an urgent need to explore and describe present practices
of reporting suicides and the degree of consistency or inconsistency
of such reporting in the United States. Until such information is
obtained, it will be impossible to interpret the available statistics.
The coroners and medical examiners are the keys to the meaningful
reporting of statistics on suicide.

It is believed that it is of the highest priority that an investigation be focused around the following specific questions directly
related to this problem:

1. Who, at present, are the certifying officials, or officers, or
agencies? Are these medical examiners, physicians in the com-

munity, sheriffs, coroners? How are they selected; how trained?

2. What are the present official criteria given to certifying officials in various jurisdictions to guide them in reporting a death as suicide?

3. What are the present actual practices of certifying officials in reporting suicidal deaths? To what extent are these practices consistent with or different from the official criteria?

4. By what actual processes do the certifying officials arrive at the decision to list a death as suicide?

5. How often are autopsies performed? Who determines when an autopsy is to be performed? Are the services of a toxicologist and biochemist available?

6. What percentage of deaths are seen as equivocal, or undetermined or as a combination of two or more modes, for example, accident-suicide, undetermined?

7. What are the criteria for special procedures in an equivocal death?

8. How much of the total investigation of a death is dependent upon the police reports? What is the relationship of the coroner's investigation to the local police department?

9. When, if ever, are behavioral or social scientists involved in the total investigatory procedure of a death?

10. What percentage of certifying officials in the United States are medically trained? Does medical training significantly influence the way in which deaths are reported?

From data dealing with these questions based on appropriate sampling from regions, and taking into account rural-urban differences, size of municipalities, and the like, an agency like the NIMH Center for Studies of Suicide Prevention could then address itself to a number of important general questions, including the following:[4]

1. What local, state, regional or other differences emerge in the practices of reporting suicidal deaths?

2. What are the general implications from the data for the veridicality of present suicidal statistics?

3. What suggestions for improvements in conceptualization, practice, training—all pointing toward more accurate and mean-

ingful reporting and understanding of data relating to self-destruction—can be made?

Surely "death" is one of those patently self-evident terms, the definition of which need not detain a thoughtful mind for even a moment. Every adult person knows instinctively what he means by it. The dictionary defines death as "the act, or event, or cause or occasion of dying; or of the end of life, or of cessation." Herman Melville, one of America's foremost authors, provided us with an operational definition of death as "the last scene of the last act of man's play."[5] But through these definitions there runs a serious confusion between the concept of death and the concept of dying. Further, there has been an unnecessary distinction between living and dying.

Living and dying have too often been seen erroneously as distinct, separate, almost dichotomous activities. To correct this view one can enunciate another view that might be called the psychodynamics of dying. One of its tenets is that, in all cases except those where an individual dies with precipitous suddenness, the interval over which he is said to be "dying" is a psychologically consistent extension of his styles of coping, defending, adjusting, interacting, and other modes of behavior that have characterized him most of his life.

The notable physician George Draper stated: "Each man dies in a notably personal way."[6] Dying behaviors do not exist in vacuo, but are an integral part of the life style of the individual. The "Psychological Autopsy"—named by the author and initiated by Dr. Theodore Curphey—which seeks to clarify the appropriate mode of death in equivocal or unclear cases of death by interviewing relatives and acquaintances of the deceased in order to reconstruct his life-death style, is theoretically based on this principle.

On the death certificate that has been used in the United States and in many European countries for much of this century, among other entries to be completed there is one that has to do with the cause of death. These causes are numerous and include such specifics as asphyxiation due to drowning, myocardial infarction, cerebral hemorrhage, poisoning, lobar pneumonia, and so on. More important to the present consideration is another entry that indirectly refers to *mode* of death.

In the current grossly inadequate classification of modes of death, four modes are indicated or implied. They are: natural, accident, suicide, and homicide, the initial letters of which, as a mnemonic convenience, spell N-A-S-H. It is immediately apparent that the cause of death does not always automatically indicate its mode. For example, one might die of asphyxiation due to drowning in a suicidal, accidental, or homicidal mode. But by far the greatest inadequacy of this traditional classification of modes of death lies in the fact that it emphasizes relatively adventitious and often trivial elements in the death of a human being. This is so because it omits entirely the psychological role of the individual in his own demise. The N-A-S-H classification is Cartesian and apsychological in its spirit.

The origin of this anachronistic N-A-S-H classification was in John Graunt's day in England when the Crown was interested in assigning guilt or blame. Natural and accidental deaths were by definition acts of nature or of God. The survivors could only be pitied, and the legitimate heirs should then come into their rightful fortunes. On the other hand, in homicidal deaths and suicidal deaths there was a culprit who must be identified and punished and in those cases the Crown got the goods. From the beginning—as today —the mode of death served quasi-legal functions with distinct monetary overtones. But the most serious indictment of this classification is that it leaves the individual out of his own dying and treats him as an empty Cartesian biological vessel.

In order to avoid the inadequacies of this conceptual morass, it has been proposed that all human deaths be classified among three types: intentioned, subintentioned, and unintentioned. An *intentioned* death is any death in which the decedent plays a direct, conscious role in effecting his own demise. An *unintentioned* death is any death in which the decedent plays no effective role in effecting his own demise—where death is due entirely to independent physical trauma from without, or to nonpsychologically laden biological failure from within. But most importantly—and what I believe to be characteristic of the vast majority of all deaths—*subintentioned* deaths are deaths in which the decedent plays some partial, covert, or unconscious role in hastening his own demise. The objective evidences of the presence of these roles lie in such be-

havioral manifestations as, for example, poor judgment, imprudence, excessive risk-taking, abuse of alcohol, misuse of drugs, neglect of self, self-destructive style of life, disregard of prescribed life-saving medical regimen, and so on, where the individual fosters, facilitates, exacerbates, or hastens the process of his dying.

That individuals may play a subintentioned or unconscious role in their own failures and act inimically to their own best welfare seem to be facts too well documented from psychoanalytic and general clinical practice to ignore. Often cessation is hastened by the individual's seeming carelessness, disregard, foolhardiness, forgetfulness, amnesia, lack of judgment, or other psychological mechanisms. This concept of subintentioned demise is similar, in some ways, to Karl Menninger's concepts of chronic, focal, and organic suicides, except that Menninger's ideas have to do with self-defeating ways of continuing to live, whereas the notion of subintentioned cessation is a description of a way of stopping the process of living. Included in this subintention category would be many patterns of mismanagement and brink-of-death living that result in cessation. In terms of the traditional classification of modes of death (natural, accident, suicide, and homicide), some instances of all four types can be subsumed under this category, depending on the particular details of each case. In relation to the term suicide, subintentioned cases may be said to have *permitted* suicide.

Confusion also colors and obfuscates our thinking in the field of suicide. Currently there is much overattention paid to the categories of attempted suicide, threatened suicide, committed suicide, and nonsuicidal states. These categories are confusing precisely because they do not tell us with what intensity the impulse was felt or the deed was done. One can attempt to attempt, attempt to commit, or attempt to feign, and so on. What is needed is a dimension that cuts across these labels and permits us to evaluate the individual's drive to self-imposed death. We call this dimension *lethality*. Lethality is defined as the probability of a specific individual's killing himself (i.e., ending up dead) in the immediate future (today, tomorrow, the next day—not next month). A measure of the lethality of any individual can be made at any given time. When we say that an individual is "suicidal" we mean to convey the idea that he is experiencing an acute exacerbation of his lethality; that is the operational

meaning of being suicidal. It has been proposed that all suicide attempts, suicide threats, and committed suicides be rated for their lethality. It may be seen immediately that a group in a room, a section of a city, a community, or a nation might be followed in terms of its changing ratings in lethaltiy. Or, to use a comparable concept, such a segment might be rated for its changing values of its bellicosity—its potential for overt hostile action, for example, a riot. The rule of thumb would be that beyond a certain point one must be wary of the danger of explosion into overt behavior.

What is suggested is that, *in addition* to the present N-A-S-H classification, each death certificate contain a new supplementary item that reflects the individual's lethality intent. This item might be labeled "Imputed Lethality"—recognizing its inferential character —and would consist of four terms, one of which would then be checked. The terms are: "High," "Medium," "Low," "Absent." They would be defined, as follows:

High—First Degree. The decedent definitely wanted to die; the decedent played a direct conscious role in his own death; the death was due primarily to the decedent's openly conscious wish or desire to be dead, or to his (her) actions in carrying out that wish (e. g., jumping rather than falling or being pushed from a high place; he shot himself to death; he deliberately interrupted or refused life-saving procedures or medical regimen).

Medium—Second Degree. The decedent played an important role in effecting or hastening his own death. Death was due in some part to actions of the decedent in which he played some partial, covert, or unconscious role in hastening his own demise. The evidences for this lie in the decedent's behaviors, such as his carelessness, foolhardiness, neglect of self, imprudence, poor judgment, gambling with death, disregard of prescribed life-saving medical regimen, active resignation to death, mismanagement of drugs, abuse of alcohol, "tempting fate," "asking for trouble," and the like, where the decedent himself seemed to have fostered, facilitated, or hastened the process of his dying, or the date of his death.

Low—Third Degree. The decedent played some small but not insignificant role in effecting or hastening his own demise. The same as *"Medium"* above, but to a much lesser degree.

Absent—No Lethal Intent. The decedent played no role in effecting his own death. The death was due entirely to assault from out-

side the body (in a situation where the decedent played no role in causing this to happen), or death was due entirely to failure within the body (in a decedent who unambivalently wished to continue to live).

The item on the certificate might look like this:

IMPUTED LETHALITY: (Check One)

☐ High   ☐ Medium   ☐ Low   ☐ Absent

(See Instructions)

The reasons for advocating the suggestion are as follows:

1. This classification is more meaningful. It permits reflection of the role, if any, the dead individual has played in his own dying, in effecting his death, in hastening his own death, the ways in which he might have participated in his own death, and the like.

2. It is more fair. At present, individuals of higher social status who commit suicide are more likely to be assigned the mode of accident or natural death than are individuals of lower social status who no less evidently commit suicide. If the term is to have any meaning at all, it should be fairly used across the board, measured by the individual's intention.

3. The lethality intention item provides an important source for biostatisticians, public health officials, and others to ascertain and to assess the role of the mental health in any community; that is, knowing the number of deaths in which individuals hastened their own demise can give a measure of the costly role of inimical mental health factors.

It might be protested, inasmuch as the assessments of these intention states involve the appraisal of *unconscious* factors, that some workers (especially lay coroners) cannot legitimately be expected to make the kinds of psychological judgments required for this type of classification. To this, one answer would be that medical examiners-coroners throughout the country are making judgments of precisely this nature every day of the week. In the situation of evaluating a possible suicide, the coroner often acts (sometimes without realizing it) as psychiatrist and psychologist, and as both judge and jury in a quasi-judicial way. This is because certification of death as suicide does, willy-nilly, imply some judgments or reconstruction of the victim's motivation or intention. Making these judgments—perhaps more coroners ought to use the category of

"undetermined"—is an inexorable part of a coroner's function. But it might be far better if these psychological dimensions were explicit, and an attempt, albeit crude, made to use them, than to have these psychological dimensions employed in an implicit and unverbalized (yet operating) manner. The dilemma is between the polarities of a present traditional, oversimplified classification, on the one hand, and a somewhat more complex, but more meaningful classification, on the other. The goal should be to try to combine greatest usefulness with maximum meaningfulness.

The issue can be simply put: What is required in order to clear up the current conceptual confusion is that, in addition to a certificate of *death* appropriately cites the *cause* of death, there be, figuratively speaking, a certificate of *dying*, which reflects the individual's *intention* vis-à-vis his own death—that is, it would indicate the extent, if any, to which that individual played a psychobiological role in hastening or effecting his own demise.

In the present scene there are four developments relating to the mode of death—each of which supplements the other—that can be distinguished:

1. The extension of interest in the veridicality and meaningfulness of public health and vital statistics, including the veridicality or meaningfulness of death statistics.

2. The creation and development of the concept of the psychological autopsy—a procedure designed to clarify the mode of death in equivocal cases of death.

3. The clear differentiation between *causes* of death and the *modes* of death, and a recognition that at present four modes of death are stated or implied, these being natural, accidental, suicidal, or homicidal, which has been designated as the N-A-S-H classification.

4. The critical reexamination of the meaningfulness of the modes themselves and a corresponding emphasis on the role of the decedent in his own demise—specifically, his intention vis-à-vis his death.

Thus in summary, the following points may be emphasized:

1. Causes: The classification of diseases and of causes of death have been rather well worked out and are consistent with contemporary knowledge. There is currently an accepted international classification which has wide acceptance.

2. Modes: The modes of death have not been stated explicitly and

have not been too well understood. In general, four currently recognized modes of death—natural, accidental, suicidal, and homicidal—suffer from the important deficiency of viewing man as a vessel of the fates and omitting entirely his role in his own demise.

3. Intent: The addition of the concept and the dimension of lethal intention serves, appropriately, to modernize the death certifiicate, just as in the past advances have been made from the teachings of bacteriology, surgery, anesthesiology, immunology, and the like. The time is now long overdue for the introduction of the psychodynamics of death into the death certificate. A single item on imputed lethal intent on the certificate—High, Medium, Low, Absent—would provide an appropriate reflection of the psychological state of the subject, and begin, at last, to reflect the teachings of twentieth-century psychology. In this way we might again permit the certification of death to reflect accurately our best current understanding of man.

PART VIII
BIOGRAPHY
AND LITERATURE

Chapter 37
SIGMUND FREUD ON SUICIDE
Robert E. Litman

The development of Freud's thoughts on suicide, taking into account his clinical experiences and his changing theoretical positions, is retraced, step by step, from 1881 to 1939.

> The fateful question for the human species seems to me to be whether and to what extent their cultural development will succeed in mastering the disturbance of their communal life by the human instinct of aggression and self-destruction.[1]

According to Sigmund Freud, commenting on man's fate in 1930 toward the end of his own long career, suicide and war are different aspects of a unitary problem. They are expressions in human beings of instinctual aggression and instinctual destruction that, in turn, are interchangeable elements of the death instinct. Furthermore, the process of civilization, which offers the only possibility of deferring the end of mankind by group violence, undermines the psychic health of the individual members of the group and threatens each of them with suicide.[2]

In this essay I will review the clinical experience and theoretical steps that led Freud to his various conclusions about suicide. My purpose is to abstract from the totality of Freud's writings his pertinent observations and to evaluate the contribution they make to the understanding of suicide and of suicide prevention in our own time, a full generation after Freud's death. The reader who follows me in this task will, I am afraid, encounter difficulties in his path from time to time, although I will try to mark the way as clearly as I can. Unfortunately, Freud never synthesized his views on suicide into an organized presentation. There is no paper on suicide comparable to Freud's dissertations on war.[3] His many clinical observations, inferences, and speculations, which illuminate multiple aspects of suicide, are scattered through numerous papers concerned primarily with other issues and other goals.

In its general outline this review will trace the theme of suicide in Freud's writings from 1881 to 1939, deviating from a strictly temporal progression at points for special topical development. The

first section deals with Freud's earlier observations, mostly personal and clinical. The second section is concerned with Freud's later contributions, mostly theoretical and speculative. Section Three includes my attempt at synthesis and evaluation. To avoid unnecessary complications, the source material will be limited to Freud's writings and to the biography of Freud by Ernest Jones.

Early Experiences: 1881-1910

It would be a mistake to assume that Freud's experience with suicide was only theoretical or philosophical. On the contrary, Freud had considerable clinical experience with suicidal patients. There are, for example, references to suicidal symptomatology in all of the case histories that Freud published except that of Little Hans, a five-year-old child.

Suicidal behavior was an important aspect of the symptoms of Josef Breuer's patient, Fraulein Anna O. Breuer discovered the cathartic method of treatment that constituted the beginning stage of the treatment approach and that Freud later developed into psychoanalysis. Anna O. at times displayed complete psychic dissociation with two entirely distinct states of consciousness and for a while spoke only in English. She became suicidal after the death of her father. On the doctor's recommendation, and against her will, she was transferred to a country house in the neighborhood of Vienna (in June, 1881), because of the danger of suicide. The move was followed by three days and nights completely without sleep or nourishment and by numerous attempts at suicide by smashing windows and by other methods. After this she grew quieter and even took chloral at night for sedation.[4]

Although Freud described this case several times, he did not refer particularly to the suicidal elements. Very early in his career as a psychoanalyst, however, Freud was aware of the importance of guilt over hostile impulses against parents causing symptoms, especially after the parents' death. In May, 1897, in a letter to Wilhelm Fliess, Freud wrote: "Hostile impulses against parents (a wish that they should die) are also an integral part of neuroses. . . . They are repressed at periods in which pity for one's parents is active—at times of their illness or death. One of the manifestations of grief is then to reproach oneself for their death. . . ."[5]

Possibly Freud's most intense personal experience with suicide occurred in August, 1898. "A patient over whom I had taken a great deal of trouble had put an end to his life on account of an incurable sexual disorder." The suicide of the patient, according to Freud, stirred up in Freud certain painful fantasies connected with death and sexuality, which he more or less successfully repressed. Several weeks later, still under the influence of these unconscious fantasies, Freud was unable to recall the name of Signorelli, creator of magnificent frescoes about the "Four Last Things": Death, Judgment, Hell, and Heaven. Freud tried to visualize the frescoes and the artist and felt the inadequacy of his associations as a source of inner torment. With great effort he reconstructed his conversation with a traveling companion immediately before the forgetting. The topic was foreign customs, the Turks, their confidence in doctors, their resignation to fate, even death. Freud had thought of telling an anecdote. "These Turks place a higher value on sexual enjoyment than on anything else, and in the event of sexual disorders, they are plunged in a despair which contrasts strangely with their resignation toward the threat of death." A patient (Freud's?) once said, "Herr (Signor), you must know that if *that* comes to an end, then life is of no value." Feeling suddenly uncomfortable, Freud suppressed the anecdote, deliberately diverted his own thoughts from death and sexuality, and changed the subject to the famous frescoes. But in his unconscious effort to continue to forget the suicide, Freud now forgot the painter's name, which joined the memory of the suicide in Freud's repressed unconscious, until someone else suggested the correct name. Freud recognized it instantly and used it to recall the repressed fantasies and reconstruct the mechanism of forgetting. Freud reported the episode immediately to his friend, Fliess,[6] and published an account of it several months later,[7] omitting in these first two reports, however, that the specific unpleasant news that precipitated the forgetting was a patient's suicide. Later, when Freud rewrote the material as the first example in his book *The Psychopathology of Everyday Life,* he included the fact of the suicide.[8]

Ernest Jones says of this incident, "As I hope to expound in a revised edition of Volume I of this biography, it was connected with a significant episode which must have played an important part in the inception of Freud's self-analysis."[9] Unfortunately, Jones

died before revising the biography. We are left with an intriguing biographical mystery and an important scientific problem. We ask, Who was this patient? What happened in the analysis? Did Freud describe fragments of the case, even heavily disguised, somewhere in his writings? Or was the history of the patient totally repressed from the memory of science? Why did Jones, who has so much to report about Freud's work and his patients, choose to postpone the illumination of the suicide incident? The important scientific problem is this: Is the taboo on suicide so intense that even psychoanalysts are reluctant to expose their case materials and personal experiences in this area? But here, and many times hereafter, I must restrict digressions or this essay would be a book.

Hopefully, other biographers will supply the missing episode that Jones omitted. My guess is that it related to Wilhelm Fliess, Freud's close friend during the 1890's. Freud began his self-analysis as a systematic project in July, 1897. Why exactly then? For approximately ten years he had been listening to patients, developing and improving his ability to interpret dreams and free associations, including his own. From this material he was being forced to draw some strange and disturbing inferences. Repeatedly and consistently, the stories from his patients forced him to conclude that sexual abuse by the fathers was responsible for the patients' illnesses. He was becoming convinced of the disagreeable reality of rivalry, death wishes, and incest in families. The death of his aged father (October 23, 1896) affected Freud deeply. "At a death the whole past stirs within one. I now feel as if I had been torn up by the roots."[10] Freud's dreams revealed hostility and guilt, as well as admiration, for his father. Apparently, some of Freud's unconscious reactions toward his father were transferred to Fliess. Freud found himself becoming irritable with his friend. Freud's dreams and associations connected Fliess with Italy, travel, and Italian art.[11]

Freud was moody, anxious, and depressed for several years after the death of his father. He worked his way back to health through his self-analysis and his writing. There is no evidence that Freud was suicidal during this period, although a possible guiding fantasy was that of death and rebirth. In a letter of June, 1897, he wrote, "I have been through some kind of neurotic experience, with odd states of mind not intelligible to consciousness—cloudy thoughts and veiled doubts, with barely here and there a ray of light. . . ."

Freud continued the letter with a paragraph describing a new case, a 19-year-old girl whose two older brothers shot themselves, and then concluded, "Otherwise I am empty and ask your indulgence. I believe I am in a cocoon, and heaven knows what sort of creature will emerge from it."[12] During this whole period, Freud was struggling most particularly with painful feelings of guilty rivalry with his father and with Fliess.

As far as I know, Freud's only overt suicide threats occurred during his long, passionate, and stormy engagement. In 1885, he wrote to his fiancée, Martha, whom he eventually married, his decision to commit suicide should he lose her. A friend was dying, and in this connection Freud wrote, "I have long since resolved on a decision (suicide), the thought of which is in no way painful, in the event of my losing you. That we should lose each other by parting is quite out of the question. . . . You have no idea how fond I am of you, and I hope I shall never have to show it."[13] So Freud could understand how someone, like the Turks of the censored anecdote, or his deceased patient, could turn to death when frustrated sexually. "One is very crazy when one is in love."[14] Many years later, Freud was to comment that the two situations of being most intensely in love and of suicide are similar, in that the ego is overwhelmed by the object.[15] In his early theory the claims of love (libido) and self-preservation were opposed, and he consistently maintained that to love is dangerous (acknowledging always that not to love poses an even greater peril). "We behave as if we were a kind of Asra who die when those they love die."[16] (The Asra were a fictitious tribe of Arabs who "die when they love.")

The histories reported by Freud's psychoanalytic patients contained numerous accounts of suicidal behavior. For example, the only sister of Freud's most celebrated patient, the Wolf Man (so called because of his childhood phobia of wolves) committed suicide by poisoning herself. The patient's strange lack of grief over the sister's death aroused Freud's special interest until the psychoanalysis clarified the complicated processes of displacement of the mourning reaction in this patient.[17] The dramatic case of Dr. Schreber's paranoia (1911) included descriptions of Schreber's longing for death. "He made repeated attempts at drowning himself in his bath and asked to be given the 'cyanide that was intended for him.'"[18]

The first of Freud's longer case reports (1905) described fragments of the analysis of an 18-year-old female hysteric whom he
called Dora. She pressured her parents into obtaining treatment
for her by writing a letter in which she took leave of them because
she could no longer endure her life and leaving the letter in a place
where they would be sure to find it. Just when Freud's hopes for a
successful treatment were highest, she unexpectedly broke it off.
Dora was not the first person in the family to talk of suicide. Her
father once told the story that he had been so unhappy at a certain
time that he made up his mind to go into the woods and kill himself, but Frau X., a friend, recognizing his state, had gone after
him and persuaded him by her entreaties to preserve his life for
the sake of his family. Dora did not believe the story. No doubt, she
said, the two of them had been seen together in the woods having
an affair, and so her father had invented this fairy tale of the suicide to account for the rendezvous. From this case we learn about
suicide as a communication, attention-getter, cry for help, method
of revenge, and as a partial identification, in this case with the
father. Also, obscurely, there is in Dora's behavior a deep theme
of sadism and aggression; possibly she is doing to others, including
Freud, what she believes others have done to her (stirred up false
hopes, lied to her, abandoned her cruelly).[19]

Additional insights appear in Freud's 1909 case history of a man
with severe obsessional neurosis, whom Freud sometimes called
"the man with the rats" because of one dramatic feature of the
neurosis, a special fantasy about rats. The patient's many obsessions
and compulsions included suicidal impulses and commands. In the
analysis numerous examples of these suicidal commands were identified as punishments for rage and jealousy toward rivals. Freud
said, "We find that impulses to suicide in a neurotic turn out regularly to be self-punishment for wishes for someone else's death."[20]
Freud was well aware that suicide is not a great danger in obsessive
neurotics. The patient said that he might actually have killed himself on several occasions except for consideration for the feelings
of his mother and sister. The same sister, incidentally, had told him
once when they were very young that if he died she would kill herself. He knew that his own death would pain his mother terribly
because a cousin had killed himself eighteen months before, on

account of an unhappy love affair, it was said, and the man's mother, the patient's aunt, was still miserable.[21]

In *The Psychopathology of Everyday Life,* Freud cited numerous clinical observations that convinced him of the important part played in mental life by an instinct for self-destruction.

> There is no need to think such self-destruction rare, for the trend to self-destruction is present to a certain degree in very many more human beings than those in whom it is carried out. Self-injuries are, as a rule, a compromise between this instinct and the forces that are still working against it, and even when suicide actually results the inclination to suicide will have been present for a long time before in less strength, or in the form of an unconscious and suppressed trend. . . . Even a *conscious* intention of committing suicide chooses its times, means, and opportunity; and it is quite in keeping with this that an *unconscious* intention should wait for a precipitating occasion, which can take over a part of the causation and by engaging the subject's defensive forces, can liberate the intention from their pressure.[22]

The clinical examples include an officer who had been deeply depressed by the death of his beloved mother. When forced to take part in a cavalry race, he fell and was severely injured. A man shot himself in the head "accidentally" after being humiliated by rejection from the army and being jilted by his girl friend. A woman injured herself out of guilt for an abortion. After the injury she felt sufficiently punished.[23]

Despite his many clinical observations concerning suicide, Freud was unable to organize them systematically into his psychoanalytic theory of instincts. On April 20 and 27, 1910, there was a discussion in the Vienna Psychoanalytical Society on the subject of suicide. On this occasion, Adler and Stekel talked at great length and in great detail, emphasizing the aggressive aspects of suicide. Freud, by contrast, said very little, contenting himself with these concluding remarks:

> I have an impression that in spite of all the valuable material that has been brought before us in this discussion, we have not reached a decision on the problem that in-

terests us. We are anxious, above all, to know how it becomes possible for the extraordinary powerful life instinct
to be overcome; whether this can only come about with the
help of a disappointed libido or whether the ego can re-
nounce its self-preservation for its own egoistic motives.
It may be that we have failed to answer this psychological
question because we have no adequate means of approaching it. We can, I think, only take as our starting point the
condition of melancholia which is so familiar to us clinically and a comparison between it and the affect of
mourning. The affective processes in melancholia, however, and the vicissitudes undergone by the libido in that
condition are totally unknown to us. Nor have we arrived
at a psychoanalytic understanding of the chronic affect
of mourning. Let us suspend our judgment until experience has solved this problem.[24]

Actually, in 1910, Freud knew a great deal about suicide. He had
identified many important clinical features: (1) guilt over death
wishes toward others, especially parents; (2) identification with
a suicidal parent; (3) loss of libidinal gratification, or more accurately, refusal to accept loss of libidinal gratification; (4) an act
of revenge, especially for loss of gratification; (5) an escape from
humiliation; (6) a communication, a cry for help; and (7) finally,
Freud recognized the intimate connection between death and
sexuality. Sadism and masochism were obviously the deepest roots
of suicide. Freud could not decide, however, where to assign such
overwhelming sadism and masochism in his theoretical framework.
According to Freud, human behaviors are derived ultimately from
needs to satisfy instinctual drives. In his early theory the basic,
conflicting instinctual drives were thought to be libido (sensuality,
sexuality) and self-preservation (hunger, aggressive mastery). How
could suicide satisfy the needs either of sexuality or self-preservation?

Theories and Speculations: 1911–1939
Eventually, Freud revised his theory of the instincts in order
to provide appropriate recognition of the importance of self-
destructiveness. In 1932, reviewing his life's work, Freud commented, "Sadism and masochism alike, but masochism quite especially, present a truly puzzling problem to the libido theory; and

it is only proper if what was a stumbling block for one theory should become the cornerstone of the theory replacing it."[25] More accurately, the new concept of a death instinct supplemented libido theory rather than replacing it.

In considering the totality of Freud's writings, one must view his various contributions against the background of the time in which the writing was done. Up until 1910, the formulations on suicide were in the framework of the libido theory. After 1920, they were in the framework of the death instinct theory. The articles written in 1914 and 1915 form a transition chapter.

In *Mourning and Melancholia* (written in 1915, published in 1917), Freud followed his own suggestion and took as his starting point a special type of patient, melancholics who express great guilt and self-reproach.

> We see how in him one part of the ego sets itself over and against the other, judges it critically and in a word takes it as its object. Our suspicion that the critical agency which is here split off from the ego might also show its independence in other circumstances will be confirmed by every other observation.[26]

How does this splitting-off occur? The explanation in terms of psychic energy (libido) is quite complicated. Energy withdrawn from a lost object of love is relocated in the ego and used to recreate the loved one as a permanent feature of the self, an *identification* of the ego with the abandoned object. "Thus, the shadow of the object fell upon the ego, and the latter could henceforth be judged by a special agency as though it were an object, the forsaken object."[27] "Shadow" objects existing as structures in the ego (identifications) obviously are not fully integrated into the total personality. A demarcation zone or fault line remains, along which ego-splitting occurs.

Also significant was Freud's speculation that certain ways of loving are less stable than others. Narcissistic love of another, for example, is especially vulnerable to disorganization and regression toward immature and primitive stages of the libido, especially sadism.

> It is this sadism alone that solves the riddle of the tendency to suicide which makes melancholia so interesting

and so dangerous. So immense is the ego's self love, which we have come to recognize as the primal state from which instinctual life proceeds, and so vast is the amount of narcissistic libido, which we see liberated in the fear that emerges at a threat to life, that we cannot conceive how that ego can consent to its own destruction. We have long known it is true that no neurotic harbors thoughts of suicide which he has not turned back upon himself from murderous impulses against others, but we have never been able to explain what interplay of forces can carry such a purpose through to execution. The analysis of melancholia now shows that the ego can kill itself only if, owing to the return of the object-cathexis, it can treat itself as an object—if it is able to direct against itself the hostility which relates to an object and which represents the ego's original reaction to objects in the external world. Thus, in regression from narcissistic object-choice, the object has, it is true, been gotten rid of, but it has nevertheless proved more powerful than the ego itself. In the two opposed situations of being most intensely in love, and of suicide, the ego is overwhelmed by the object, though in totally different ways.[28]

The above excerpt is quoted frequently in the literature concerned with suicide, most often with misplaced emphasis on the aspect of the original hostility and murderous impulses. In my opinion, the more important creative concepts are those of regression, disorganization, and ego-splitting, pathologic processes that allow a portion of the ego to initiate action disregarding the interests of the remainder. Moreover, the positive, didactic quality of the isolated paragraph quoted is misleading in that the impression is created that Freud was making assertions about all suicides, which was not his intention. The tenor of the article as a whole is modest and tentative; and in the first paragraph Freud specifically disclaims general validity for findings based on the analysis of a few specially selected melancholics.

Within a few years Freud had discovered that the process of establishing objects as identifications in the ego was very common. In fact, the ego is made up in large part of identifications. Freud did not carry the theory of identifications much farther, but a consistent development of his concept has led to our modern notion that

the original representation of most loved objects is split into several parts, good and bad, in both the ego and the superego. These multiple object-identifications, plus the need for establishing defenses and maintaining repressions, result in splits and fissures in every ego. In the 1920's, Freud developed a structural model (id, ego, superego) of mental activity and assigned various functions to the different parts of the model.[29] He stated that the very earliest identifications play a special role in the total self, in that they are more completely split off from the rest of the ego, and become the superego, which includes conscience and ideals, has the functions of loving, supporting, judging, and punishing the ego, and may become diseased on its own account. Concepts or images of suicide appear only in the ego and superego, since the id knows nothing of its own death. "In the unconscious everyone of us is convinced of his own immortality."[30] Indeed, even consciously, it is impossible to imagine our own death. "Whenever we attempt to do so we can perceive that we are in fact still present as spectators."[31]

Freud paid little attention to the role, as spectators, participants, rescuers, or betrayers, of others in a suicide. He recorded the observations but had no room for them in his theory. For example, he wrote briefly in 1921 about a young man who was tormenting his mistress. He was trying unconsciously to drive her to suicide in order to revenge himself on her for his own suicide attempt several years before in connection with a different woman.[32] In 1916, Freud discussed the characters of the play "Rosmersholm." In this drama a poor wife, Beata Rosmer, is psychologically poisoned by her rival, Rebecca Gamvik. The wife commits suicide as a reaction to abandonment by her husband and her own sense of worthlessness.[33] Suicide is not a direct theme of either of the papers, which are concerned respectively with telepathy and with guilt over success. Another literary analysis (1928) concerns the story of a mother who tries unsuccessfully to rescue a young gambler from suicide.[34]

The last of Freud's longer case reports, "The Psychogenesis of a Case of Homosexuality in a Woman," was published in 1920. Freud used it to develop further his views on homosexuality, female sexuality, and some technical aspects of psychoanalytic therapy. The patient was an 18-year-old girl, who was brought to Freud by her father about six months after she made a suicide attempt. What

disturbed the family was not so much the suicide attempt as the girl's homosexual attachment to a woman about ten years older. The woman had not greatly encouraged the girl, and when one day they were walking together and met the father who gave them a furious look, the woman told the girl now certainly they must separate. Immediately the girl rushed off and flung herself over a wall down the side of an embankment onto the suburban railway line, which ran close by. Although fortunately little permanent damage was done, the girl was in bed for some time, and Freud felt that the attempt was undoubtedly serious.

> After her recovery she found it easier to get her own way than before; the parents did not dare to oppose her with so much determination, and the lady, who up until then had received her advances coldly, was moved by such an unmistakable proof of serious passion and began to treat her in a more friendly way.[35]

It seemed to Freud that much of the girl's behavior was a reaction to the birth of her third brother, three years previously. It was after that event that she turned her love away from children toward older women. Concerning the suicide attempt, Freud said:

> The analysis was able to disclose a deeper interpretation beyond the one she gave (despair over loss of the lady). The attempted suicide was, as might have been expected, determined by two other motives beside the one she gave: It was the fulfillment of a punishment (self-punishment), and the fulfillment of a wish. As the latter it meant the attainment of the very wish which, when frustrated, had driven her into homosexuality—namely the wish to have a child by her father, for now she fell through her father's fault. From the point of view of self-punishment the girl's action shows us that she had developed in her unconscious strong death wishes against one or the other of her parents—perhaps against her father out of revenge for impeding her love, but more probably against her mother, too, when she was pregnant with the little brother. Analysis has explained the enigma of suicide in the following way: Probably no one finds the mental energy required to kill himself unless, in the first place in doing so, he is at the same time killing an object with

whom he has identified himself and, in the second place, is turning against himself a death wish which had been directed against someone else. Nor need the regular discovery of these unconscious death wishes in those who have attempted suicide surprise us (any more than it ought to make us think that it confirms our deductions), since the unconscious of all human beings is full enough of such death wishes against even those they love. Since the girl identified herself with her mother, who should have died at the birth of the child denied to herself, this punishment-fulfillment itself was once again a wish fulfillment. Finally, the discovery that several quite different motives, all of great strength, must have cooperated to make such a deed possible is only in accordance with what we should expect.[36]

In a footnote Freud noted "that the various methods of suicide can represent sexual wish fulfillments has long been known to all analysts. (To poison oneself = to become pregnant; to drown = to bear a child; to throw oneself from a height = to be delivered of a child.)"

The most significant of the ideas expressed above is the discovery that suicide is multiply determined by the interaction of several motives. The emphasis is on ego-splitting and identifications. The suicidal act is explained as a reenactment, by a split-off ego identification with mother, of the delivery of the brother. The murderous look the father gave the girl is mentioned. Allusion is made indirectly to the theme of death and rebirth (rescue). The effect of a suicidal act as a communication that changes the environment is recorded. Erotic and masochistic elements of the suicide attempt are specially noted. Death wishes are described as the source of the energy required for suicide, yet death wishes are not limited to suicides but are typical of all human beings.

Evidently, from Freud's later writings, the announcement of a solution of the enigma of suicide was premature. Many questions and uncertainties remained. For example: Was it true that in most suicides the ego murdered the object? Or more often did the incorporated object murder the ego? Freud continued to feel that his theoretical explanations were incomplete for several major clinical phenomena associated with self-destructiveness.

The most important of these for psychoanalysis is the "negative

therapeutic reaction."[37] Some neurotics inevitably respond to good news, congratulations, or progress in analysis by increased anxiety, depression, or self-injury.

> Judged by all their actions the instinct of self-preservation has been reversed. They seem to aim at nothing other than self-injury and self-destruction. It is possible, too, that the people who in fact do, in the end, commit suicide, belong to this group. It is to be assumed that in such people far-reaching diffusions of instinct have taken place, as a result of which there has been a liberation of excessive quantities of the destructive instincts directed inward. Patients of this kind are not able to tolerate recovery toward treatment and fight against it with all their strength. But we must confess that this is a case which we have not yet succeeded completely in explaining.[38]

Also unexplained was the problem of masochism. Why should many people require pain, punishment, humiliation, and degradation as prerequisites for sexual pleasure? In 1920 Freud proposed for speculative consideration that there might be an instinctual drive toward death.[39] His arguments were partly on clinical grounds (traumatic neuroses, repetitive actions) and partly biological and philosophical. Although at first the new ideas were advanced tentatively and cautiously, Freud soon came to accept them fully and with increasingly complete conviction.[40]

> After long hesitancies and vacillations we have decided to assume the existence of only two basic instincts, *Eros* and *the destructive instinct*. The aim of the first of these basic instincts is to establish even greater unities and to preserve them thus—in short, to bind together; the aim of the second is, on the contrary, to undo connections and so to destroy things. In the case of the destructive instinct, we may suppose that its final aim is to lead what is living into an inorganic state. For this reason we call it the *death instinct*. . . . In biological functions the two basic instincts operate against each other or combine with each other. Thus, the act of eating is a destruction of the object with the final aim of incorporating it, and the sexual act is an act of aggression with the purpose of the most intimate union. This concurrent and mutually opposing

action of the two basic instincts gives rise to the whole variegation of the phenomena of life. . . .[41]

The dangerous death instincts are dealt with in individuals in various ways; in part they are rendered harmless by being fused with erotic components; in part they are diverted toward the external world in the form of aggression and, to a large extent, they continue their internal work unhindered.

> When the superego is established, considerable amounts of the aggressive instincts are fixated in the interior of the ego and operate there self-destructively. This is one of the dangers to health by which human beings are faced on their path to cultural development. Holding back aggressiveness is, in general, unhealthy and leads to illness. . . .[42]

The death instinct concept was a major theoretical construction. It has, however, received relatively little acceptance among psychoanalysts. Why was Freud so convinced of its usefulness? Ernest Jones suggests that there were subjective motives and reports insightfully on Freud's intense, complicated, personal, daily fantasies about death.[43] However, Freud's own explanation is logically consistent. Freud said he accepted the death instinct theory because he needed it to explain masochism (and suicide). How then do suicide and masochism appear from this viewpoint?

> If we turn to melancholia first, we find that the excessively strong superego which has obtained a hold upon consciousness rages against the ego with merciless violence. . . . What is now holding sway in the superego is, as it were, a pure culture of the death instinct and in fact it often enough succeeds in driving the ego into death. . . .[44]

In melancholia the ego gives itself up because it feels itself hated and persecuted by the superego instead of loved. To the ego, therefore, living means the same as being loved by the superego so that the death by suicide symbolizes or reenacts a sort of abandonment of the ego by the superego. It is a similar situation to separation from the protecting mother.[45]

The original quantity of internalized death instinct is identical with masochism. The individual tries to externalize this energy as aggressiveness or sadism. Where there is a cultural suppression of the instincts, the destructive instinctual components are turned

back into his superego. Now we see a helpless, masochistic ego in relationship with a sadistic superego. The modality of the relationship is punishment. In order to provoke punishment the masochist must do what is inexpedient, must act against his own interests, must ruin his prospects, and perhaps destroy himself. But since there is always some fusion of the erotic and destructive instincts, there is always an obvious erotic component in masochism, so that even the subject's destruction of himself cannot take place without libidinal satisfaction.[46]

Due to the prolonged, extreme biological and social helplessness of the human infant, who cannot unaided satisfy his vital needs or regulate his own destructive instincts, each individual must incorporate controlling, coercing, and punishment components into his superego.[47] By this process the instincts are tamed and the child can participate in family life and education. By an anthropological analogy, Freud viewed civilization as a group superego development. In civilized man, extra aggression is channeled into the superego and turned against the ego. It is now felt as unconscious guilt, masochism, a need to be punished, or an obscure *malaise* and discontent. The price we pay for our own advance in civilization is a loss, to some degree, of the possibilities of happiness.[48] "We owe to that process [civilization] the best of what we have become, as well as a good part of what we suffer from."[49]

To Freud, suicide represented a symptom of what we suffer from, a product of man and his civilization, a consequence of mental trends that can be found to some degree in every human being.

Synthesis and Evaluation

Experience has confirmed Freud's statement that each suicide is multiply determined by the interaction of several motives. Suicide is by no means a homogeneous or unitary piece of human behavior. On the contrary, suicide comprises a variety of behaviors with many important aspects—historical, legal, social, and philosophical, as well as medical and psychological. The psychoanalytic explanations of the psychopathology of suicide are complex, multidimensional and, at some points, ambiguous and redundant.

There are, according to Freud, *general features* of the human condition, at least in Western civilization, that make each individual person somewhat vulnerable to suicide. These general features in-

clude: (1) the death instinct, with its clinical derivatives, the aggressive instinct directed outward and the destructive instinct directed inward; (2) the splitting of the ego; this is inevitable because of the extreme helplessness of the human ego in infancy when it is unable to master its own instincts and must conform to the parents or perish; and (3) the group institutions, family and civilization, which require guilty compliance from every member of the group.

The above general features only begin to account for any individual suicide. Individual suicides involve certain *specific suicide mechanisms.* All of them involve a breaking down of ego defenses and the release of increased destructive, instinctual energy. Examples are: (1) loss of love objects, especially those who have been loved in certain dangerous ways; (2) narcissistic injury, symbolically through failure or by direct physiological injury through fatigue or toxins; (3) overwhelming affect: rage, guilt, anxiety, or combinations; (4) extreme splitting of the ego with decathexis of most elements and a setting of one part against the rest; and (5) a special suicidal attitude and plan, often based on an identification with someone who was suicidal.

Finally, there are a great number of *specific predisposing conditions* that more or less favor suicide, although they are not precipitating mechanisms of suicide. These include: (1) a disorganized or disharmonious ego structure that splits up under relatively low conditions of stress; (2) a tendency of the libido to be fixated at pre-oedipal positions, especially strong tendencies toward sadism and masochism; (3) disease of the superego due to cruel parents, dead parents, parents who wished the person dead, or due to some constitutional inherited superego trait of excessive destructiveness; (4) strong attachment of the libido to death, dead loved ones, or a fantasy of being dead; (5) vivid erotic fantasies that symbolize and cover up death wishes, for example, the fantasy of bearing a child by father, symbolically actualized as a fall from a height; and (6) a chronically self-destructive living pattern, expressed, for example, as gambling addiction or homosexuality.

The following evaluative comments are based on my several years' experience as Chief Psychiatrist in a multidisciplinary project of research, training, and clinical service for suicide prevention. My experience is in agreement with Freud's general schematic

view. Deep down there is a suicidal trend in all of us. This self-destructiveness is tamed, controlled, and overcome through our healthy identifications, ego defenses, and our constructive habits of living and loving. When the ordinary defenses, controls, and ways of living and loving break down, the individual may easily be forced into a suicidal crisis. At such times he feels helpless, hopeless, and abandoned and may or may not be aware of a great deal of unexpressible, aggressive tension.

However verbalized, most of the therapeutic actions of therapists at the Suicide Prevention Center are aimed at reinforcing the ego defenses, renewing the feeling of hope, love, and trust, and providing emergency scaffolding to aid in the eventual repair and healing of the splits in the patient's ego. Direct psychological techniques for turning the aggression outward have not been particularly successful in our experience. Frequently, we try to deal with the emotional turmoil directly by drugs. Hopefully, we may eventually move into the future predicted by Freud: "The future may teach us to exercise a direct influence by means of peculiar, particular chemical substances on the amounts of energy and their distribution in the mental apparatus." He added, "It may be that there are other still undreamed of possibilities of therapy, but for the moment we have nothing better at our disposal than the technique of psychoanalysis. For that reason, despite its limitations, it should not be despised."[50]

In my opinion, we still have nothing better at our disposal than psychoanalysis or psychoanalytic psychotherapy as remedies for many of the chronic neurotic reactions and weaknesses that, if uncorrected, may eventually lead toward suicide but are not, in themselves, precipitating mechanisms of suicidal crises. The years have brought innovations, based directly or indirectly on psychoanalytic principles, that greatly expand our therapeutic range. These include various brief psychotherapy techniques, psychotherapy in groups, and environmental therapy in hospitals and clinics. All of these approaches, and others, are effective when they are employed at the suitable moment in the appropriate case.

Many of Freud's perceptive inferences have been explored and consolidated by later workers. For example, Freud often referred to certain dangerous ways of loving, in which the ego is "overwhelmed" by the object. Typically, the psychic representations of

the self and other are fused, and the other is experienced as essential for survival. Modern writers have termed these attachments "symbiotic," making explicit the analogy to the primitive dependent relationship between a baby (or fetus) and its mother. Freud's observation that symbiotic love is a potential precursor of suicide still holds true.

Freud's dictum that suicide starts with a death wish against others, which is then redirected toward an identification within the self, has been overly accentuated among some psychotherapists, in my opinion, and has become a cliché. Freud is quoted to support a relative overemphasis on aggression and guilt as components of suicide with underemphasis of the helplessness, dependency, and erotic elements. Often, however, the suicidal drama reproduces not so much guilt for the unconscious wish of the child to murder the parent, but rather a reaction of abandonment, on the part of the child to the parent's unconscious wish for the child's death. The mechanism of regression and the themes in suicide of helplessness, constriction, and paranoid distrust have made the deepest impression on me.

Freud pointed out that infantile helplessness is the essential circumstance that creates masochism, but Freud was accustomed to using his concept of the oedipal complex as his reference point for psychopathology. From that viewpoint, guilt over rivalry with parents, especially the father, looms large. At the Suicide Prevention Center, I am more accustomed to using the mother-child pre-oedipal relationship as a reference concept. Further research, hopefully, will clarify this issue.

It is remarkable that Freud said so little about the all-important attitude of the mother in instilling into a child the desire for life. It is remarkable because Freud was well aware of the influence of his own mother in instilling into him a feeling of confidence and zest for living.[51] Moreover, he had found in his patients and in himself, as a reason for continuing to live, the idea that his premature death would be painful to his mother. When Freud's mother died in 1930, age 95, Freud noticed in himself a feeling of liberation. "I was not allowed to die as long as she was alive and now I may."[52]

Freud's personal attitude toward death, according to the sharp eye of his biographer, Jones, was altogether a rich and complex one with many aspects. "In the world of reality he was an unusually

courageous man who faced misfortune, suffering, danger, and ultimately death itself with unflinching fortitude. But in fantasy there were other elements." There was at times a curious longing for death. "He once said he thought of it every day of his life, which is certainly unusual."[53]

In three essays on war and death, Freud expressed himself as a cautiously hopeful realist. Horrified and depressed by the cruelty, fraud, treachery, and barbarity of World War I, he tried to extract some value out of discarding his illusions about civilization and facing disagreeable truths (1915). "To tolerate life remains, after all, the first duty of all living beings. Illusion becomes valueless if it makes this harder for us." And, characteristically, he added, "If you want to endure life prepare yourself for death."[54] Freud described himself as a pacifist (1933). "We pacifists have a constitutional intolerance of war . . . whatever fosters the growth of civilization works at the same time against war."[55] Perhaps some of the psychotherapists whose work exposes them continuously to affects of violence, sadism, and death gain in confidence and flexibility by partially identifying with the complex personality of Freud.

Freud had a few recommendations for society. Possibly, he thought, there would be less suicide if society permitted more sexual and aggressive freedom to its members, though one could not be sure. He thought there was an advantage in providing at intervals opportunities for mass release from inhibitions as, for instance, in carnivals or the ancient Saturnalia. Certainly, Freud saw in our present civilization and its future extensions the only hope for mankind.

> Civilization is a process in the service of Eros, whose purpose is to combine single human individuals and after that families, then races, peoples and nations into one great unity, the unity of mankind. Why this has to happen, we do not know. The work of Eros is precisely this: These collections of men are to be libidinally bound to one another. Necessity alone, the advantages of work in common, will not hold them together, because man's natural aggressive instinct, the hostility of each against all and all against each, opposes this program of civilization. Now I think the meaning of the evolution of civil-

ization is no longer obscure to us. It must present the struggle between Eros and death, between the instinct of life and the instinct of destruction as it works itself out in the human species. This struggle is what all life essentially consists of, and the evolution of civilization may therefore be simply described as the struggle for life of the human species.[56]

This philosophy of joining together and of enjoying each other has, I believe, played a large part in the forming of the spirit of the Suicide Prevention Center. The group spirit has in turn supplied a great deal of the constructive energy required to continue effective work in an area so full of destructive attitudes and hazardous outcomes. The injurious effect on the suicidal person of separation and alienation from the other persons who have loved him was indicated by Freud but not emphasized. We find that in helping a suicidal individual through a crisis, therapists often enlist the cooperation of many people. The goal is to reduce the patient's withdrawal and self-preoccupation and involve him once again in the common interactions of the living.

In our day-to-day therapy of suicidal crises we pay little attention to theory, particularly such deep abstractions as the death instinct. In speculative moments, however, we wonder if perhaps Freud's ominous correlation of suicide and war may not have been a fateful forecast. What if nuclear war were to be precipitated not by accident or policy but by a suicidal individual willing to kill "the others" with him? We encounter potential destroyers of their worlds at our Center fairly often. We take care to leave a door open and not to box them in. In such emergencies, of course, we work, not from theory, but with intuition and judgment, seeking words, gestures, or actions that will relieve tension and establish communication. The key might be an understanding look, a shared feeling, or a cup of coffee.

Freud was well aware of the difference between philosophic speculations about the general causes of man's misery and the requirements of practical life to do something about it. In a letter to Einstein (1933) on the problem of preventing war, he commented, "The result, as you see, is not very fruitful when an unworldly theoretician is called in to advise on an urgent practical problem. It is a better plan to devote oneself in every particular case to

meeting the danger with whatever means lie at hand."[57] Freud applied the same advice to his own clinical endeavors. In 1926, discussing a young patient, Freud wrote, "What weighs on me in his case is my belief that unless the outcome is very good it will be very bad indeed; what I mean is that he would commit suicide without any hesitation. I shall therefore do all in my power to avert that eventuality."[58] That last could well be the motto of the Suicide Prevention Center.

Chapter 38
THE DEATHS OF HERMAN MELVILLE
Edwin S. Shneidman

*The participation of an individual, subintentionally, in his own
death—the man "who sought to run more than half way
to meet his doom"—is here analyzed as the brooding thread
running through much of the writing of Herman Melville. The
chapter and verse quotations from eleven of his books are
juxtaposed with the circumstances of his life, presenting a picture
of a death-intoxicated man whose deepest investment was
in his "postself."*

I feel that I have about as much right to be here in this select
company as has a copy of *The Refugee* or *Redburn: or the School-
master of a Morning* to be in a definitive edition of the *Complete
Writings*. For my intrusion, you must blame entirely my all-bestow-
ing benefactor, Professor Henry A. Murray, who, in a myriad of
wonderful and mysterious ways of which he alone in this world is
capable, led me to Melville and, of equal importance in the charting
of my own course, to an abiding and appropriate concern with the
dark as well as the light compass-headings of the human voyage.
And now my travels have brought me to this gam.

A gam, is it? I, who should be listening silently in the dark
corner of the cabin, have been, with Captain Murray's urgings,
emboldened to speak. In this trade-around of tales, the ship that I
report from is a curious composite of ill-fated craft: It has torn
timbers from the *Pequod*, rotted spars from the *San Dominick*,
broken planks from the *Parki*. I speak, of course, about the vessels
of death—and would include even fragments from one of Melville's
earliest published writings: "The Death Craft." In short, I am the
scrivener-mate from the ever-pressing *Thanatopsis*.

Surely, "death" is one of those patently self-evident terms, the
definition of which, it is felt, need not detain a thoughtful mind for
even a moment. Every adult person knows instinctively what he
means by it. The dictionary defines death as the act, or event, or
cause, or occasion of dying, or of the end of life, or of cessation.
In these terms, by "the death of Herman Melville" one could refer
only to a description or a discussion of what occurred to Melville

on September 21, 1891—or by legitimate extension, one might choose to include those events and factors that immediately preceded Melville's physical death, or which were causally related to it. But what can one possibly mean by the *deaths* of Herman Melville?

Melville, in *Pierre*, quoting the highest power, provided us with an operational definition of death as "the last scene of the last act of man's play." But perhaps there is more—"the little lower layer." The main issue for this paper is whether or not the *concept* of death need only be dichotomous—granting that the *event* of death involves a distinct irreversible physiological termination and psychological cessation of one's viable existence. Specifically, the question is whether or not it is possible for us to talk about such matters as death equivalents, substitutes for death, and especially partial deaths, such as deaths of aspects of the self.

On the Death Certificate that has been used in the United States and in many European countries for over the last half century, among other entries there is stated the *cause* of death and *mode* of death. Currently, in the handbook for all those countries that report to the United Nations there are listed some 130 causes of death. These include asphyxiation due to drowning, myocardial infarction, cerebral hemorrhage, among others. More importantly for our present consideration is that in addition to the cause of death, the mode of death is stated. In the current—and in my opinion, grossly inadequate—classification of modes of death, four modes are indicated. They are: natural, accident, suicide, and homicide, the initial letters of which, for your mnemonic convenience, spell N-A-S-H. Each one of us must end up in one of the barren conceptual crypts. It is immediately apparent that the cause of death does not always automatically indicate its mode. For example, one might die of asphyxiation due to drowning in a suicidal, accidental, or homicidal mode. But by far the greater inadequacy of this traditional classification of modes of death and in the concept of modes of death itself lies in the fact that it emphasizes relatively adventitious and often trivial elements in the death of a human being. This is so because it omits entirely the psychological role of the individual in his own demise. The N-A-S-H classification is Cartesian and apsychological in its spirit. For example, it is a relatively unimportant difference to me whether the light fixture above me falls and I am invaded by a lethal chandelier (accidental

mode), or someone about me coughs and I am invaded by a lethal virus (natural mode), or someone shoots a gun at me and I am invaded by a lethal bullet (homicidal mode), in light of the fact that I do not wish (intention) any of these to occur. To be blunt about it, my own overriding interest in my own Death Certificate, if by some illogical magic I could ever be permitted to see it, would be almost entirely in the date.

In order to avoid the inadequacies of this conceptual morass, I have proposed, at the Suicide Prevention Center in Los Angeles—an organization that I helped direct for a number of years before I was recently persuaded to move to the Nation's Capital by the promise of "an opportunity to paint on a broader canvas"—that all human deaths be classified among three types: intentioned, subintentioned, and unintentioned. An *intentioned* death is any death in which the decedent plays a direct, conscious role in effecting his own demise. An *unintentioned* death is any death—whatever its determined cause and apparent conventional mode—in which the decedent plays no effective role in effecting his own demise—where death is due entirely to independent physical trauma from without, or to nonpsychologically laden biological failure from within. But most importantly—and what I believe to be characteristic of the vast majority of all deaths—*subintentioned* deaths, in which the decedent plays some, partial, covert, or unconscious role in hastening his own demise. The objective evidences of the presence of these roles lie in such behavioral manifestations as, for example, poor judgment, imprudence, excessive risk-taking, abuse of alcohol, misuse of drugs, neglect of self, self-destructive style of life, disregard of prescribed life-saving medical regimen, and so on, where the individual himself fosters, facilitates, exacerbates, or hastens the process of his dying.

At the Suicide Prevention Center we have participated with the Chief Medical Examiner-Coroner of Los Angeles County in assessing the psychological role of the deceased individual in his own death, especially in puzzling or cryptic deaths or deaths that are equivocal as to mode of death. We do this by careful and selective interview of a number of his surviving relatives and acquaintances.[1] What might be of especial interest to members of the Melville Society is my own attempt to illustrate this procedure, which I have labeled the "psychological autopsy," by a detailed

analysis of the engimatic and equivocal death—was it accident or suicide or what?—of Captain Ahab. This analysis appeared in an essay entitled "Orientations toward Death" published in 1963 in the book, *The Study of Lives*—a volume written in honor of Dr. Murray by several of his colleagues and former students.[2]

It is important to note that the role of subintention is not at all limited to dying behaviors. Indeed, the main point of this presentation is to assert the importance of the role of the individual—his conscious and unconscious needs, conflicts, thrusts—not only in his dying (his death style), but also in his living (his life style), the latter consisting in part of the ways in which individuals (all too rarely nowadays) elevate, ennoble, expand, or actualize their lives, or, conversely, the ways in which they (all too often) diminish, narrow, attrit, or truncate aspects of their inner and outer lives, or what we can now explicitly refer to as the partial deaths of their psychic and social selves.

We can be sanguine that Melville would not have, in principle, resisted this concept of subintention, certainly not on the grounds of its involving unconscious motivation. Melville was a veritable cerebral-fluid brother of Freud. His *Moby Dick* and *Pierre*, to name two, rest, in no insignificant part, on the concept of subintentioned motivations. Consider, from *Moby Dick*, Melville's explanation of the aboundingly empathic response of Ahab's crew in terms of "their unconscious understandings," which Melville reified as "the subterranean miner that works in us all."

I now further buttress my position with a quotation from our President. Professor Murray, in his paper "Dead to the World: Or the Passions of Herman Melville," an address that he gave under the auspices of the Suicide Prevention Center in Los Angeles in October, 1963, aware of our studies attempting to relate the permanent cessation of suicide to the temporary interruption of sleep,[3] asked the following questions:

> Why not some other related condition such as a temporary or permanent cessation of a part of psychic life, the cessation of affect, feeling almost dead, for example; or the cessation of an orientation of conscious life, the cessation of social life, dead to the outer world; or the cessation of spiritual life, dead to the inner world, for example. . . .

It might be well to take account of different degrees or changes of degrees of life, near cessation, as good as dead; or trend toward cessation, dying.[4]

The concept of partial death—death of an aspect of the self—is now the pivotal and critical concept for our consideration. Its manifestations—and again I quote from my authority—are

> . . . as if the person's primal spring of vitality had dried up, or as if he were empty or hollow at the very core of his being. There is a striking absence of anything but the most perfunctory and superficial social interaction.

This is accompanied by withdrawal from his society, grave social refusal, or even where the fires of feeling are still burning, they burn without glow or warmth, or pleasure-giving purpose. It has to do with repudiation of one's society, of ostracizing people, cutting them dead; it also relates to society's repudiation and ostracism of the person. Thus there are deaths of aspects of the inner self, and deaths of aspects of the outer or social self. Buchanan's failure to find Melville in America—

> I sought everywhere for this Titan who was still living somewhere in New York, but no one seemed to know anything of the one great writer fit to stand shoulder-to-shoulder with Whitman on that continent. . . .

—is a poignant example of Melville's not being totally socially alive, a partial social death that lasted for some "forty torpid years."

This may be the point to supply a brief but clear example of an individual who participated, subintentionally, in his own fate—in this case a broken jaw, lucky for him, not lethal. I refer, of course, to Radney, the chief mate of the *Town-Ho,* "the infatuated man [who] sought to run more than half way to meet his doom"—an excellent example of the moiety of self-participation in the subintentioned act.

Parenthetically, we can note that Melville is filled with moieties, partials, and parts, especially of the human body. I quote a few from many:

Moby Dick: . . . some deep men . . . are left living on
with half a heart and half a lung. . . .

Benito Cereno: . . . His voice was like that of one with lungs half-gone—hoarsely suppressed, a husky whisper. No wonder that, as in this state he tottered about, his private servant apprehensively followed him.

Mardi: Now, which was Samoa? The dead arm swinging high as Haman? Or the living trunk below? . . . For myself, I ever regarded Samoa as but a large fragment of a man, not a man complete. And the action at Tenerife over, great Nelson himself—physiologically speaking—was but three quarters of a man.

Melville had an intimate association with the idea of partial death. About it, he might have said: "I am quick to perceive a horror and could still be social with it." It is debatable whether *Moby Dick* is as much about terminal death as it is about partial death, and especially about suicidal equivalents:

. . . whenever it is a damp, drizzly November in my soul . . . then I account it high time to get to sea as soon as I can. This is my substitute for pistol and ball. With a philosophical flourish, Cato throws himself upon the sword; I quietly take to the ship.

And again:

. . . to the death-longing eyes of such men, who still have left in them some interior compunctions against suicide, does the all-contributed and all-receptive ocean alluringly spread forth his whole plain of unimaginable, taking terrors, and wonderful, new-life adventures; and from the hearts of infinite Pacifics, the thousand mermaids sing to them—"Come hither, broken-hearted; here is another life without the guilt of intermediate death; here are wonders supernatural, without dying for them. Come hither! bury thyself in a life which, to your new equally abhorred and abhorring, landed world, is more oblivious than death. Come hither! put up *thy* gravestone, too, within the church-yard, and come hither, till we marry thee!"

Before we turn to Melville's further explications of these qualitative nuances of death in the human spirit (including his own), I shall, as background material, attempt to present some few quantitative evidences of the extent of Melville's interest in the topics of death. I must confess that I present these quantitative data with both serious misgivings and deep trepidations. To reduce the grand scope of Melville's poetic outpourings to chart and figures can only remind one of Whitman's poem, "When I heard the Learn'd Astronomer":

> When I heard the learn'd astronomer,
> When the proofs, the figures, were ranged in
>   columns before me,
> When I was shown the charts and diagrams, to
>   add, divide, and measure them,
> When I sitting heard the astronomer where he
>   lectured with much applause in
>   the lecture-room,
> How soon unaccountable I became tired and sick,
> Till rising and gliding out I wander'd off by
>   myself,
> In the mystical moist night-air, and from time
>   to time,
> Look'd up in perfect silence at the stars.

Each of eleven of Melville's books—*Typee, Omoo, Mardi, Redburn, White Jacket, Moby Dick, Pierre, Israel Potter, The Piazza Tales, Confidence Man,* and *Billy Budd*—was examined, and a notation was made for each of five types of death material.[5] A brief definition and some examples of these five death categories will now be given.

1. Any reference to the death of the chief protagonist, including his wishes about death, his ideation concerning death, threats of death to him (either by himself or by others), or actions that might result in his death

2. The actual death of specific characters other than the chief protagonists, either in an individual or a group, such as the entire crew of a ship

3. Any reference to death relating to other than the chief protagonists: threats of death, actions that might involve the character in destruction, death thoughts, and so on

4. Death in nature, and references to death in the environment; examples would be storms, violence, natural destruction; other examples would include references to the dark, hostile, destructive, death-dealing aspects of nature and of life in general

5. Discourse on death, including historic references to naval battles where death occurred; philosophic dissertations on death; metaphysical discussions of death.

The result of this study was the tabulation of 1,802 references to death. Table I and Figure I reflect these data from among the eleven books. In the Figure, the solid line represents the manner in which Melville distributed the totality of his eighteen hundred thoughts of death *among* these eleven works; the dotted line indicates the relative concentration per page of death talk *within* each of these eleven works. Of what Melville said about death, he seems to have said most of it—about 30 percent—in *Moby Dick,* and next most in *The Piazza Tales, Mardi,* and *Pierre*—14, 13, and 12 percent, respectively. The vast majority—70 percent—of Melville's death thoughts is contained in these four books.

TABLE I—Death in Melville

		Among All Books		Within Each Book		
		No. of Items[1]	Per-cent	No. of Pages[2]	% Thoughts per Page	Per-cent[3]
Typee	1846	92	5	340	27	6
Omoo	1847	52	3	375	14	3
Mardi	1849	243	13	769	32	7
Redburn	1849	89	5	403	22	5
White Jacket	1850	109	6	504	22	5
Moby Dick	1851	538	30	725	74	16
Pierre	1852	218	12	505	41	9
Israel Potter	1855	63	3	225	28	6
Piazza Tales	1856	246	14	271	91	20
Confidence Man	1857	49	3	336	15	3
Billy Budd	1891	103	6	114	90	20
		1802	100%	4567	456	100%

[1] For five death categories: Cessation of chief protagonist, death of anyone, death in nature, discussion of death, and general cessation.

[2] Constable Edition.

[3] Percentage of thoughts per page divided by 4.5—in order to reduce 456 to 100%.

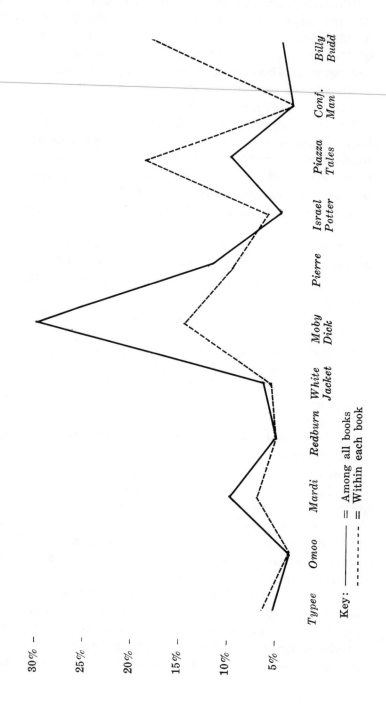

FIGURE I—Death in Melville

The dotted line in Figure 1, reflecting the concentration of death talk per page, was computed by comparing the number of death items per book with the number of pages in the Constable Edition of that book, and then reducing those ratios so that their sum was 100 percent. These data indicate that there was relatively more death talk per page in *The Piazza Tales* and *Billy Budd* than in any other books, and next highest concentration in *Moby Dick*.

The distribution of the five death categories among the eleven books is indicated in Table II. These data show us that most of the items (36 percent) were in the "Discourses on Death" category; least (7 percent) in the "Death in Nature" category. Among the interesting items contained within Table II is the fact that 45 percent of the death talk in *Pierre* relates to the death of the chief protagonist.

The quality of the references to death varies among the books: *Mardi* is more philosophic, reflecting a fantasied wish for idealization of society; *Moby Dick* is concerned more with actual death and symbolic substitutes for death as portrayed through the struggle of man with his internal and external environments; *Pierre* obsesses about death in the individual psyche, an introspective accounting of the psychodynamics of death; *The Piazza Tales* also deals with death in the environment, but the environment pitted against man; and in *Billy Budd* the emphasis is on the interplay of death-movements among the chief characters—Billy, Captain Vere, and Claggart.

In brief summary, we found some 1,800 death thoughts distributed among some 4,500 printed pages of Melville's writing, or about one death thought for every 2½ pages. The most death-laden book is *Moby Dick*, next *Mardi, Pierre*, and *The Piazza Tales;* the most death-concentrated books are *The Piazza Tales* (which followed *Moby Dick* by three years), and *Billy Budd* (which followed *Moby Dick* by almost forty years). Death remained in Melville's mind and flowed from his pen from *Mardi* on, that is, from the time that Melville was only thirty years old.

My saying "only thirty years old" would seem to indicate that some other standards or separate criteria are implied. And so they are. The main notion here is that of an appropriate time of life—an idea based in turn on the concept of stages or phases of life in the total human life cycle. The most famous explication of this

TABLE II—Analysis of Melville Death Items

	Typee	Omoo	Mardi	Red-burn	White Jacket	Moby Dick	Pierre	Israel Potter	Piazza Tales	Conf. Man	Billy Budd
Number of Items, 1802	92	52	243	89	109	538	218	63	246	49	103
Death Categories:											
A. Any reference to death of chief protagonist, including wishes, ideation, threats, etc.	18%	5%	10%	15%	12%	11%	45%	20%	26%	8%	33%
B. Actual death of specific characters other than chief protagonists.	3%	10%	10%	13%	8%	10%	11%	22%	18%	16%	27%
C. Death in nature; death in the environment.	11%	11%	8%	4%	5%	13%	4%	5%	8%	6%	1%
D. Discourses on death; discussion of death; historic references to death.	28%	31%	51%	37%	43%	26%	34%	32%	29%	57%	33%
E. Any reference to death relating to characters other than chief protagonists: wishes, thoughts, threats.	39%	43%	21%	30%	32%	39%	7%	21%	19%	12%	7%
	100%	100%	100%	100%	100%	100%	100%	100%	100%	100%	100%

notion is in Shakespeare's seven ages of man. In our own time, the psychoanalyst Erik Erikson has written about eight psychosocial stages in the human life cycle; Jung has discussed the two main ages of man; Gerald Heard has described his five ages of man; and Charlotte Buhler has delineated the several main stages in the human course of life, to name a few.

One main point that all these writers imply is that each major period of life is a special time—a time with its own modal special problems, conflicts, crises, ordeals, and mysteries. To give one example, adolescence—the teen years—is a time when the main problem is that of separation from the family and the movement into young adulthood, the latter movement carrying with it the problems of how to find and hold love, the role of romantic love and its relationship to sexuality, how to begin a career, and how to establish and support a family.

Building on these concepts, I have, elsewhere indicated that psychological crises can occur to a person *within* a period of his life (what I call *intra*temporal crises); in the interstices *between* periods of his life (*inter*temporal crises); or, occasionally, there are those crises that occur in individuals who are *out of phase* with what ought to be their own period of life (what I call *extra*temporal crises).[6] This group includes individuals who have "too early" savored experiences "beyond their years," and in this sense, are too old for their age (inappropriately precocious in life development); and, conversely, it includes individuals who are not "grown up emotionally," who are sheltered not only from experience, but from reflection (retarded in life's ways). These individuals are, in terms of their chronological age, out of tune with the modal psychological issues and conflicts that ought to be occupying their psyches. Experiences that come "too early" (like at too early an age having to be one's own parents, or having to integrate the impact of sexuality, or having to face annihilation) put one out of phase with one's own years. These individuals may be said to suffer from "information overload" or what might be called "stimulus inundation."

Listen to Melville in early out-of-phase *Redburn:*

> Talk not of the bitterness of middle-age and after life;
> a boy can feel all that, and much more, when upon his
> young soul the mildew has fallen; and the fruit, which

with others is only blasted after ripeness, with him is nipped in the first blossom and bud. And never again can such blights be made good; they strike in too deep, and leave such a scar that the air of Paradise might not erase it.

Again, from *Redburn:*

I had learned to think much and bitterly before my time; all my young mounting dreams of glory had left me; and at that early age, I was unambitious as a man of sixty. . . . Cold, bitter, cold as December, and bleak as its blasts, seemed the world then to me; there is no misanthrope like a boy disappointed; and such was I, with the warm soul of me flogged out by adversity.

Mostly, when Melville was producing these refractory images of his own inner life, his deeper concerns were about his own obsessing intoxication with the enigmatic and unanswerable issues that are more grim even than those of misery and death, namely, eternal and total cessation, naughtment, and annihilation.

And even more and still worse: Had Melville been able to postpone his invested concern with these depressing topics until a more proper time in his own life, he might have been a more measured and sanguine soul, but precocious psyche that he was, he encountered these core issues out of phase with his own life, too early, in his twenties and thirties, and then they could only be for him unconquerable phantoms and monsters, leviathans and krackens.

To answer a soul's need to deal with the issue of one's own annihilation before he is thirty-five is to tackle God's world in off-season, at hurricane time, and then one is faced only with the tortured choice of what nature of wreck will ensue—utter, partial, immobilizing, fatal—but not, alas, with the happier alternatives between wreck or safety, between escape or deep spiritual success, between destructive or positive affective transactions.

On the occasion of Dr. Murray's address in Los Angeles, he stated:

It occurred to me that a roughly analagous study might be made of the . . . cycle of affective transactions in the works of certain Romantic authors—authors whose credo en-

courages them to give vent in apt and telling words, to
emotions of all sorts. I need not tell you the name of my
first choice among eligible authors.

I have taken what I consider to be a reasonable calculated risk
and assumed that it could have been no other than Melville that he
had in mind. If this were so, what can we now say about Melville's
credo?

Melville's credo was to say Yes; Yes to his own sense of right;
Yes to his fealties to the depths of his own thought and inner
experience; but like any other brave man who feels overcome by
vastly superior forces, never to say Yes to the commands of others
or of fate or of nature to surrender. Melville had several mottoes,
for example: *Ego non baptizo te in nomine patris*—you know the
rest—but his credo seems to have been this: *better to be drowned
as a daring fool than be hanged as an uncommitted or timid coward.*
And this, as we shall see, was just a partial reflection of his great,
self-ennobling, courage-building, autonomous sense of pride. He
voices this credo over and over. But first, concerning his sense of
autonomy:

Moby Dick: I'd strike the sun if it insulted me.

I, myself, am a savage, owing no allegiance
but to the King of Cannibals; and ready any
moment to rebel against them.

. . . the queenly personality lives in me and
feels her royal rights. . . .

Here I am proud as Greek God. . . .

And in a letter to Hawthorne, April 16, 1851:

The man who, like Russia or the British Empire, declares
himself a sovereign nature (in himself) amid the powers
of heaven, hell, and earth. He may perish, but so long as
he exists, he insists upon treating with all Powers upon
an equal basis.

And now, to the core and substance of Melville's credo:

Moby Dick, about Bulkington:

Better it is to perish in that howling infinite than to be ingloriously dashed upon the
lee—even if that were safety.

Oh man! Admire and model thyself after the whale. Do thou too remain warm among ice. Do thou, too, live in this world without being of it. Retain, O man, in all seasons a temperature of thine own.

Pierre: For now am I hate-shod! On these I will skate to my acquittal! No longer do I hold terms with aught. World's bread of life, and world's breath of honour, both are snatched from me; but I defy all world's bread and breath. Here I step out before the drawn-up worlds in widest space and challenge one and all of them to battle.

Jimmy Rose: I still must meditate upon his strange example, whereof the marvel is, how after that gay, dashing, nobleman's career, he could be content to crawl through life, and peep about among the marbles and mahoganies for contumelious tea and toast, where once like a very Warwick he had feasted the huzzaing world with Burgundy and venison.

And from his letters:

June 1, 1851: *To Hawthorne:* All Fame is Patronage. Let me be infamous: there is no patronage in *that* . . . .

To the dogs with the head! I had rather be a fool with a heart, than Jupiter Olympus with his head. . . .

March 3, 1849: *To Duyckinck:* . . . then had I rather be a fool than a wise man. —I love all men who *dive.* Any fish can swim near the surface, but it takes a great whale to go down stairs five miles or more; & if he don't attain the bottom, why, all the lead in Galena can't fashion the plumet that will. . . .

Along with his many other ambiguities, Melville, with his great zest for life, was a death-intoxicated man. His concerns with

thoughts related to death and diminution appear through his works as a *Leitmotif,* subliminally haunting the reader with their baleful expressions of grandeur and woe. Nor are we surprised to find these thoughts in the man who asked so urgently about life's purposes and life's moralities.

What made this issue laden with even more than ordinary anguish was that, for Melville, death meant more than physical demise or even more—if one can imagine it—than psychological cessation; it meant complete, that is, eternal, annihilation. More than do or die; it was exult or never-have-been. The essence of his credo, from Melville's third book, *Mardi*—and one of my own favorite Melville passages—written when he was 29, reads as follows:

> Oh, reader, list! I've chartless voyaged. With compass and the lead, we had not found those Mardian Isles. Those who boldly launch, cast off all cables; and turning from the common breeze, that's fair for all, with their own breath, fill their own sails. Hug the shore, naught new is seen; and "Land ho!" at last was sung, when a new world was sought.

> That voyager steered his bark through seas, untracked before; ploughed his own path mid jeers; though with a heart that oft was heavy with the thought that he might only be too bold, and grope where land was none.

> So I.

> And though essaying but a sportive sail, I was driven from my course, by a blast resistless; and ill-provided, young, and bowed to the brunt of things before my prime, still fly before the gale;—hard have I striven to keep stout heart.

> And if it harder be, than e'er before, to find new climes, when now our seas have oft been circled by ten thousand prows—much more the glory!

> But this new world here sought, is stranger far than his, who stretched his vans from Palos. It is the world of mind; wherein the wanderer may gaze round, with more of wonder than Balboa's band roving through the golden Aztec glades.

But fiery yearnings their own phantom-future make, and deem it present. So, if after all these fearful, fainting trances, the verdict be, the golden haven was not gained; —yet, in bold quest thereof, better to sink in boundless deeps, than float on vulgar shoals; and give me, ye gods, an utter wreck, if wreck I do.

In any complete recitation of Melville's unusual combination of gifts, pressures, heritage, and inner thrusts, the role of his private sense of warranted and unwarranted overweening pride must be given the great emphasis it obviously merits. At the outset, we can, following Nietzsche, distinguish pride from vanity—where the former comes mostly from inner feelings and the latter from outside reinforcement and feedback, as in the case, for example, of poets. With Melville, it is pride, not vanity, that we mean.

It would appear that Melville's inner sense of pride stemmed largely from two main sources: Pride in his family and lineage; but mostly the pride that came from his recognition of his own active, first-rate, self-contained inner life, dealing creatively—and with a sure sense of its own extraordinary capacity—with core cultural and cosmic psychic issues. Melville not only had a self-sustained sense of being of somewhat noble birth, but he also had the feeling of being a more than somewhat gifted man.

His pride in his family is clearly indicated in his books; in *Moby Dick* he writes: "It touches one's sense of honor, particularly if you come of an old established family in the land, the Van Rensselaers, or Randolphs, or Hardicanutes." And it is explicitly stated in his letters, as, for example, his letter to his mother (May 5, 1870) and to his cousin (August 27, 1876).

As for his pride in himself, as early as 1839, when he was 19, Melville wrote in his *Fragments from a Writing Desk* about his own "mind endowed with rare powers"; all through his letters he writes either with the exaggerated modesty of a proud man or the proper self-respect of a proud man. For example, he writes to his father-in-law: "I hope the perusal of this little narrative of mine will offer you some entertainment." He describes himself in his letters as "conceited," "garrulous," filled with "selfishness" and "egotism." He was hungry to read the reviews and notices of his own works. He wrote to his brother to send him "every notice of any kind" and to John Murray to send him all the reviews of his

books. He had an enormous appetite for recognition and fame. Melville was obviously deeply wounded by the critics of *Mardi* and of *Moby Dick*. After the *New York Literary World's* review of *Moby Dick*, he canceled his subscription to that journal.

Now, if one believes in the power of the self-fulfilling prophecy, the role of pride can be a salutary one. It enhances one's self-confidence and increases his effectiveness, but the negative side of this coin is that it also makes him vulnerable. It is like an Achilles heel in an Olympic athlete.

The enemy of pride is criticism, rejection, verbal abuse. I need not take the time in this presentation to recite the criticisms that were leveled at the heart of Melville. The public, represented by the critics, liked his tobacco and wood-chopping works but railed and hooted when he wanted to say the things most meaningful to him. We all know his letter to Hawthorne in 1851:

> What I feel most moved to write, that is banned,—it will
> not pay. Yet, altogether, write the other way I cannot.

And, from *The Confidence Man*, the tale of Charlemont, a story of aristocratic pride—and its concomitant fear of dependency and vulnerability, the key lines of which are:

> When both glasses were filled, Charlemont took his, and
> lifting it, added lowly: "If ever, in days to come, you shall
> see ruin at hand, and, thinking you understand mankind,
> shall tremble for your pride; and, partly through love for
> the one and fear for the other, shall resolve to be before-
> hand with the world, and save it from a sin by prospec-
> tively taking that sin to yourself, then will you do as one I
> now dream of once did, and like him will you suffer. . . ."

In a situation where one has been verbally abused and behaviorally constrained, one can generally react in one of two global ways. He can protest and advance his best efforts and products, but if he takes this course he demonstrates how deeply he cares and how grieviously he has been hurt. This tack will make him more vulnerable, more pitiable, and often subject to more abuse. It is a course that runs directly counter to the instincts of a proud man. The other course is to be disdainful, ignoring one's critics as though they did not exist, as though they were dead, reducing them to the un-

important position of impotence by robbing them of their power to influence and especially of their power to hurt. But this maneuver, by its very nature, tragically can be executed only at the price of one's own total or partial self-ostracism and thus at the expense of the death of part of one's social and hence psychological self.

In Stedman's Introduction to the 1892 edition of *Typee*, we read a contemporary illustration of Melville's social death:

> Mr. Melville would have been more than mortal if he had been indifferent to his loss of popularity. Yet he seemed contented to preserve an entirely independent attitude, and to trust to the verdict of the future. The smallest amount of activity would have kept him before the public; but his reserve would not permit this. That he had faith in the eventual reinstatement of his reputation cannot be doubted. . . . Our author's tendency to philosophical discussion is strikingly set forth in a letter from Dr. Titus Munson Coan to the latter's mother, written while a student at Williams College. . . . The letter reads, in part: ". . . when I left him he was in full tide of discourse on all things sacred and profane. But he seems to put away the objective side of his life, and to shut himself up in this cold north as a cloistered thinker."

One human experience not inconsistent with pride is hate or hostile affect. Hostility can take many forms, including verbal criticism, verbal retaliation, physical abuse, and in its most extreme form, complete disregard of the other person—especially conscious disregard. There is great reciprocity in interpersonal or intergroup hostility and, as we know, great danger of escalation of this type of reciprocity. Some hostility is retaliatory, but much of hostility is anticipatory—to get one's blows in first. Melville had more than his fair share of hate—conscious and unconscious: against his parents—his mother and father for separate reasons—against society, and against Christendom—all the forces that he saw as wanting him to surrender and to acquiesce. Granted that his global hate was long repressed by his fear of retaliation; but who can gainsay his attacks on Christianity in *Omoo*, and on Western society in *Typee*.

We see this combination of pride, fear, and hate in Ahab's address to the Candles:

Oh! thou clear spirit of clear fire, whom on these seas I as
a Persian once did worship, till in the sacramental act so
burned by thee, that to this hour I bear the scar; I now
know thee, thou clear spirit, and I know now that thy
right worship is defiance. To neither love nor reverence
wilt thou be kind; and e'en for hate thou canst but kill;
and all are killed. No fearless fool now fronts thee. I own
thy speechless, placeless power; but to the last gasp of my
earthquake life will dispute its unconditional, unintegral
mastery in me. In the midst of the personified impersonal,
a personality stands here. Though but a point at best;
whencesoe'er I came; wheresoe'er I go; yet while I earthly
live, the queenly personality lives in me, and feels her
royal rights. But war is pain, and hate is woe. Come in
thy lowest form of love, and I will kneel and kiss thee;
but at thy highest, come as mere supernal power; and
though thou launchest navies of full-freighted worlds,
there's that in here that still remains indifferent. Oh, thou
clear spirit, of thy fire thou madest me, and like a true
child of fire, I breathe it back to thee.

Nor need we look too far, nor inappropriately exercise our imagination to divine Melville's attitudes about duplicity and criticism,
and especially about critics.

White Jacket: How were these officers to *gain glory?*
How but by a distinguished slaughter-
ing of their fellow-men? How were they
to be promoted? How but over the buried
heads of killed comrades and messmates?

White Jacket: Do you straighten yourself to think that
you have committed a murder, when a
chance falling stone has often done the
same? Is it a proud thing to topple down
six feet perpendicular of immortal man-
hood, though that loft living tower
needed perhaps thirty good growing
summers to bring it to maturity? Poor
savage! And you account it so glorious,
do you, to mutilate and destroy what
God himself was more than a quarter of
a century in building?

Moby Dick: There's a most doleful and most mocking funeral! The sea-vultures all in pious mourning, the air-sharks all punctiliously in black or speckled. In life but few of them would have helped the whale, I ween, if peradventure he had needed it; but upon the banquet of his funeral they most piously do pounce. Oh, horrible vulturism of earth! from which not the mightiest whale is free.

Encantadas: If some books are deemed most baneful and their sale forbid, how, then, with *deadlier* facts, not dreams of doting men? Those whom books will hurt will not be proof against events. Events, not books, should be forbid.

And from his letters:

April 23, 1848: *To Lemuel Shaw:* I see that *Mardi* has been cut into by the London Atheneum and also burnt by the common hangman in the Boston Post.

There is nothing in it, cried the dunce, when he threw down the 47th problem of the 1st book of Euclid—there's nothing in it. —This with the posed critic.

Dec. 13, 1850: *To Evert Duyckinck:* . . . I don't know but a book in a man's brain is better off than a book bound in calf—at any rate it is safer from criticism.

Jan. 18, 1886: *To John W. Henry Canoll:* For what can one do with the Press? Retaliate? Should it ever publish the rejoinder, they can.

Perhaps his penultimate comment, from *Moby Dick,* about the ravengers in life:

Sharks . . . like hungry dogs 'round a table where red meat is being carved.

And for pure, undiluted heart-breaking hate, no other passage in our literature is so concentrated as this one from *Moby Dick:*

All that most maddens and torments; all that stirs up the
lees of things; all truth with malice in it; all that cracks
the sinews and cakes the brain; all the subtle demonisms
of life and thought; all evil, to crazy Ahab, were visibly
personified, and made practically assailable in Moby Dick.
He piled upon the whale's white hump the sum of all the
general rage and hate felt by his whole race from Adam
down; and then, as if his chest had been a mortar, he
burst his hot heart's shell upon it.

For some, the often highly exciting and sometimes superb narrative novels—*Typee, Omoo, Redburn, White Jacket, Israel Potter*
—remain primarily as valued interstices between Melville's more
profound identity-seeking and death-focused labors, those works
that sprang out of his deeper shaping and crushing concerns, ce-
mented as they were to both his self and his *postself.*

The self or ego relates to the core of one's active functioning, his
cognitive and emotional masterings and maneuvers in the present
life; the *postself,* on the other hand, refers to the ways in which
one might live on, survive, or have some measure of impact or influence after the event of his own physical death—for example,
through one's children (in whom Melville did not before their deaths
seem to have that deep an investment, and in whom, after the premature deaths of his sons, he could not have any hope), or through
one's published works, in a selected few of which Melville most
was deeply invested.

Here are some samples of Melville's thoughts concerning the concept that I have labeled the postself:

> *Redburn:*   Peace to Lord Nelson where he sleeps in
> his mouldering mast! but rather would I
> be urned in the trunk of some green tree,
> and even in death have the vital sap cir-
> culating round me, giving of my dead
> body to the living foliage that shaded my
> peaceful tomb.
>
> . . . how much better would such stirring
> monuments be full of life and commotion,
> than hermit obelisks of Luxor, and idle
> towers of stone; which, useless to the
> world in themselves, vainly hope to eter-

nalize a name, by having it carved, solitary and alone, in their granite. Such monuments are cenotaphs indeed; founded far away from the true body of the fame of the hero; who, if he be truly a hero, must still be linked with the living interests of his race; for the true fame is something free, easy, social, and companionable. They are but tombstones that commemorate his death, but celebrate not his life. . . .

Moby Dick: It may seem strange that of all men sailors should be tinkering at their last wills and testaments. . . . After the ceremony was concluded upon the present occasion, I felt all the easier; a stone was rolled away from my heart. Besides, all the days I should now live would be as good as the days that Lazarus lived after his resurrection; a supplementary clean gain of so many months or weeks as the case might be. I survived myself. . . .

. . . I now leave my cetological System standing thus unfinished, even as the great Cathedral of Cologne was left, with the cranes still standing upon the top of the uncompleted tower. For small erections may be finished by their first architects; grand ones, true ones, ever leave the copestone to posterity. . . .

. . . immortality is but ubiquity in time. . . .

And from his letters:

April 5, 1849: *To Evert Duyckinck:* All ambitious authors should have ghosts capable of revisiting the world, to snuff up the steam of adulation, which begins to rise straightway as the Sexton throws his last shovelfull on him. —Down goes his body and up flies his name.

April 23, 1849:   *To Lemuel Shaw:* These attacks are matters of course, and are essential to the building up of any permanent reputation—if such should ever prove to be mine. . . .

June 1, 1851:   *To Hawthorne:* What "reputation" H.M. has is horrible. Think of it! To go down to posterity is bad enough, any way; but to go down as a "man who lived among the cannibals"! When I speak of posterity, in reference to myself, I only mean the babies who will probably be born in the moment immediately ensuing upon my giving up the ghost. I shall go down to some of them, in all likelihood.

Dec. 10, 1862:   *To Samuel Savage:* I once, like other spoonies, cherished a loose sort of notion that I did not care to live very long. But I will frankly own that I have now no serious, no insuperable objections to a respectable longevity. I don't like the idea of being left out night after night in a cold church-yard.

The concept of the postself is, of course, directly related to the notion of annihilation. To cease as though one had never been, to be "oblivionated," to accept defeat, to abandon any hope of love or fame, any hope of impact or memory-in-the-mind-of-another beyond one's death, to be obliterated, to be ostracized, to be muted, to be naughted, to be expunged from history's record—that is a fate literally far worse than death.

Not unexpectedly, Melville had a few things to say on these issues:

Lightning-Rod Man: Think of being a heap of charred offal, like a haltered horse burned in his stall; and all in one flash!

Israel Potter: Few things remain. . . . He was repulsed in efforts after a pension by certain caprices of law. His scars proved his only medals. He dictated a

little book, the records of his fortunes. But long ago it faded out
of print—himself out of being—his
name out of memory.

Redburn: But all is now lost; I know not who
he was; and this estimable author
must need share the oblivious fate of
all literary incognitos.

White Jacket: . . . it is a good joke, for instance,
and one often perpetrated on board
ship, to stand talking to a man in
a dark night-watch, and all the while
be cutting the buttons from his coat.
But once off, those buttons never
grow on again. There is no spontaneous vegetation in buttons.

Pierre: Unendurable grief of a man, when
Death itself gives the stab, and then
snatches all availments to solacement
away. For in the grave is no help, no
prayer thither may go, no forgiveness thence come; so that the penitent
whose sad victim lies in the ground,
for that useless penitent his doom is
eternal, and though it be Christmas-
day with all Christendom, with him
it is Hell-day and an eaten liver forever.

From his letter to Hawthorne, June 1, 1851:

Though I wrote the Gospels in this
Century, I should die in the gutter.

Implicit in the preceding is a broad hypothesis, the contents of
which run roughly as follows: that aspects of Melville's personality
are to be found distributed (in either a direct or a refractory way)
among his fictional characters; and further, there is implied a
refinement of this general notion in the specific subhypothesis that
proposes that within particular books there can be found a range
of characters some of whom reflect a particular segment or portion

of Melville's personality, and who, in their totality may yield the entire secret combination that unlocks the tantalizing safe. Related to this latter hypothesis is an article by the Italian critic Eugenio Montale (*Sewanee Review*, LXVIII, Summer 1960, 419–422), which mentioned, but certainly does not endorse—nor do I—the interpretation that the three principal characters of *Billy Budd* stand as different "narcissistic projections of the three ages of the author." More to the point and better documented: Professor Bezanson, in his "Introduction" and discussion of "The Characters" in the Hendricks House edition of *Clarel*, plausibly and convincingly advances the proposition that several of the main characters were intended to represent different aspects or potentialities of Melville's nature, and—what is especially relevant to our own present concerns—specifically that Mortmain embodied Melville's wish for self-annihilation. I quote, liberally, from Professor Bezanson: ". . . in the two decades after *Moby Dick*, Melville's descent into self had made him acquainted with an underworld of recalcitrant shades: the sense of defeat, willful isolation, unmanageable moods, fear of death, anxiety over his own physical and mental health. . . . These darker elements of Melville's sensibility are channeled into the striking series of monomaniacs who followed one another so ominously through the poem: . . . From his first appearance Mortmain is committed by name ('Death Hand') and symbol (his black skull cap) to *self-annihilation*. The roots of his personal malaise, running subtle and deep, have flowered into political, philosophic, and religious despair. . . . Consumed by psychic fury, driven to *intolerable introversion*, Mortmain has no strength left to hold back his own will to self-destruction."

I assume that every student of Melville is well acquainted with Professor Murray's explication of Melville's psychological positions over time in relation to his own annihilation. Quoting from Dr. Murray, they go something like this:[7]

In *Mardi* (1847), Melville's position was: "If I fail to reach my golden haven, may my annihilation be complete; all or nothing."

In *Moby Dick* (1851): "I foresee my annihilation, but against this verdict I shall hurl my everlasting protest."

In *Pierre* (1852): "I am confronted by annihilation, but I cannot make up my mind to it."

In 1856, in London, as recorded by Hawthorne: "I have pretty much made up my mind to be annihilated."

And in *Billy Budd* (1891) : "I accept my annihilation."

After Melville's early successes with *Typee* and *Omoo*, and the excitement of his being challenged for veracity and for his criticism of missionaries, but not for his style nor genre nor philosophic exploration, when he dared then to write his first real romance and turned, after the first one hundred pages of *Mardi,* to the infinite perspectives of his own ruminations and discovered, as consequence, that he was met with a grape-shot barrage of annihilating criticism, the issue for him was forever joined.

Thereafter, his most vital dialogue of the mind concerned itself with whether or not he could fully live, express himself openly, be printed publicly, be read widely, be adjudged fairly; or whether he would need to print himself privately, eschew critical support, retreat from public view, write to his own soul's need—all partial deaths of his talents, his energies, his natural desires, and his interplay with his own time.

Out of Melville's combination of his great sense of inner pride, his bravura inner life style, his imperious reaction to hostility and to criticism, his conscious and unconscious attrition of the social side of his literary life—out of all of these diverse elements grew his concern with death and annihilation and his enormous investment in his postself. In this sense, Melville wrote not so much for his own time as he did for any appropriate (that is, any appreciating) time to follow—for what Leyda has called a "posthumous celestial glory." Melville was partially dead during much of his own life, but he more than compensated for that lugubrious limitation by writing in such a way that he could realistically plan to live mostly after he had died. "On life and death this old man walked."

PART IX
BOOK REVIEWS

Chapter 39

A LOOK INTO THE DARK: A REVIEW OF JOOST A. M. MEERLOO'S SUICIDE AND MASS SUICIDE

[New York: Grune & Stratton, 1962]
Edwin S. Shneidman

Dear Reader: I am sitting here, pen in hand, not unaware that I have a pistol in my desk drawer, a bottle of Black Leaf-40 on the back porch shelf, at least 30 Doriden capsules in the medicine cabinet—my mind filled with suicidal thoughts. What occupies my mind are not, of course, thoughts of committing suicide, but rather reflections *about* suicide. There are so many unanswered key questions: What *are* suicidal phenomena? Why *do* people kill themselves? How *can* suicides be prevented? And so on. What has stimulated all this rumination is my having just finished reading Meerloo's *Suicide and Mass Suicide*. It didn't cheer me up, I can tell you. It's an interesting book though. The author, too, is apparently a very interesting person. In his book he tells about his surviving the concentration camps in spite of the Germans' attempts to kill him. He is very much alive today and very much lives in this book. This is a readable book filled with some gripping personal accounts, many psychoanalytically oriented assertions, and several thought-provoking reflections about one of the most—perhaps *the* most—frightening problems of our time. It is a book that each of us, were he to write it, would write in his own way.

"I like the essay form," says Meerloo in the very first sentence of his Foreword. "It liberates me from the limitations of scientific writings, I don't have to succumb to the scholar's compulsion to quote as many fellow professionals as possible . . . I can contradict myself and I can use emotional illogic just as frequently as scientific exactitude." He says it much more graciously and openly than most reviewers might dare.

Meerloo's main thesis in this book is "that there exists a very close relationship between personal suicidal feelings and the mass emotions in the world. Each individual, in the personal self-destructive feelings and habits of which he is usually unaware, contributes a grain of suicidal tendency to the collectivity. Moreover, because

one man's feelings of despair and final renunciation of life is often rooted in some infantile experience shared by all men, there can be a tremendous contagion between individual feelings and collective emotions."

Within the book there are various kinds of statements and beliefs. I often puzzled as to where he had obtained some of his facts and statistics—at variance with some of our information—but inasmuch as this was not the main burden of the book, I do not feel it important to stick on these points. The range of the nineteen brief chapters contains an intriguing array of exciting topics— "Man's Raving Frenzy as a Disguised Form of Suicide," "The Suicidal Population Explosion," and "Suicide, Menticide, and Psychic Homicide"—as the titles to chapters 12, 13, and 14, respectively, demonstrate.

Of particular interest to me was Meerloo's classifications of the various motivations for suicide. He indicates that he is "pleading here for an *infinite number* of motivations," but he actually presents two schemes. In relation to the first, he states that this scheme is based on a clinical analysis of more than 1,000 cases, and although this statement has a footnote subscript, I could find no further reference to these studies or these data. There are four categories in the first scheme: (1) suicides that "have no conscious motivation. These are usually impulsive suicides in mentally deranged and alcoholic individuals"; (2) suicides "committed by mentally unstable people who have a great variety of motivations, justifications and rationalizations of their act"; (3) individuals who "commit suicide on impulse during strong emotion . . . and are not psychotic"; and (4) individuals who "commit the act after quiet deliberation. . . ." His second classification of the various motivations of suicide include nine types, in which "the various categories overlap each other and our diagnostic labels are only shorthand for unique individual histories." The categories are: (1) suicide as the idea of magically being killed; (2) suicide as communication; (3) suicide as revenge; (4) suicide as magic murder and fantasy crime; (5) suicide as unconscious flight; (6) pathic (egoistic) suicide; (7) suicide as conscious flight (anomic suicide); (8) suicide as magic revival; and (9) altruistic suicide.

This second classification especially is of interest to all individuals who are concerned with suicidal behaviors. It may lead to con-

fusions, however, precisely in the overlapping of the several *kinds* of classifications contained within it. Among them are: (1) the role of the individual in his own demise; this is excellent in that no potentionally worthwhile or usable classification of suicidal phenomena can ignore this dimension; (2) the role of magical thinking, which appears in three of Meerloo's types, but which—if one accepts the concept at all—may run like a gossamer skein through all of them; (3) the role of communication, which is probably present in all suicidal behaviors, certainly all those in which there is a "significant other"; (4) the status of the individual vis-à-vis his society; in this connection it is refreshing to see reference to Durkheim's work in this volume; (5) the various roles of factors that are deemed to be conscious, unconscious, impulsive, deliberate, driven, and so forth. All these seem to be contained within Meerloo's suggested classification, but seem not to have been sorted and systematized as much as they might have been. But withal, Meerloo makes a laudable effort to step beyond the usual threaten-attempt-commit trichotomy (which seems to be so much in vogue today) and to eschew purely diagnostic labelings.

The very title of this book is a fair play on words: *Suicide and Mass Suicide*. Meerloo has a previous book called *Delusion and Mass Delusion*—as though the two were identical or, as least, similar. This thought raises some important issues not explicitly dealt with within the book itself. For example, if there is any meaning to the analogy or metaphor of suicide with mass suicide, can one also achieve any understanding of the threat of "international suicide" through the paradigm of tensions within a dyadic relationship? Specifically, would it be possible, from what we have learned about the reduction of tensions of two marital partners (who hate each other within the context of an inescapable marriage) to make suggestions that might be applied meaningfully to the stressful dyadic relationship of Aunt Vanya and Uncle Sam? Much has been learned by psychologists and psychiatrists from work in family therapy and from studies of stressful dyads on how to mollify interpersonal tension, suspiciousness, hostility, potentially destructive behavior, and these insights are being tapped by a number of psychologists interested in reducing international (potentially mass-suicidal) frictions. In this connection, the thoughts and con-

cerns and suggestions of Osgood, of Murray, of Ralph K. White, to mention a few, especially commend themselves.

It is evident throughout the book that the memories of the German crematoria are not—nor should they be—banked in Dr. Meerloo's breast. (The book is dedicated "To my brothers and sisters, who lost their lives on the altar of Hitler's destructive and suicidal delusions.") This book is, in some ways, one more opening of those satanic furnace doors, and in reading this book we are at times seared by the heat even if we are not continuously blinded by the light. Understandably a large part of the wisdom that Meerloo imparts seems to stem from his experiences with the dark side of life. Perhaps too much. And this very possibility raises one of the most interesting issues in this book. One of Meerloo's main themes, caught in the following passage, seems to be: "In a world where primitive drives are exalted into heroic ideals, man has to murder either himself or others. He kills something in himself by throwing himself into the turmoil of his instinctive drives. It may be called killing his ego or murdering his inner steering pilot." We are reminded of that remarkable scene in *Moby Dick,* in the chapter called "The Try Works" (Chapter 96), in which Ishmael, gazing into the awful "redness, the madness, the ghastliness" of the whale crematorium on board ship is induced to an "unnatural hallucination" that might have led to the destruction of his world, and unknowingly and confusedly becomes turned about, facing the stern, away from the guiding compass. "Uppermost was the impression, that whatever swift, rushing thing I stood on was not so much bound to any haven ahead as rushing from havens astern." The moral seems clear to Ishmael: It may well be (as Meerloo implies) that knowledge of darkness, along with knowledge of light, is an indispensable ingredient of the highest wisdom, *but* one must also beware of gazing into the Hells of the world too long lest one becomes turned about and lose his sight of the compass and his grip on the tiller.

Perhaps Melville wrote in an overall happier world—threatened only by mammoth intrapsychic conflicts—that did not know the crematorium and the bomb. Meerloo is not Melville (nobody is), but nonetheless, he reflects with a great deal of poignant confusion and poignant accuracy —with wisdom, deep intuition, and, at times, unabashed openness and self-confession—much of the suicidal agony of our age.

Chapter 40

A PUZZLE REMAINS PERPLEXING: A REVIEW OF HERBERT HENDIN'S SUICIDE AND SCANDINAVIA

[New York: Grune & Stratton, 1964]
Norman L. Farberow

The "Scandinavian suicide phenomenon" has been a perplexing problem to social scientists for many years. Why should Denmark and Sweden have such consistently high suicide rates (around 22 per 100,000), while Norway's rate on the other hand, has been consistently low (around 7.5 per 100,000)? The puzzle has been why countries, generally considered so similar in background, culture, and social systems should differ so markedly in this one respect? Other familiar measures of social tension, crime, delinquency, alcoholism, divorce, and the like do not show this wide discrepancy. The dissimilar Scandinavian rates for suicide also contrast with most other Occidental cultures, with the rates for the United States, Britain, France (averaging around 10 per 100,000), falling above Norway, but considerably lower than Denmark and Sweden.

The author of this book undertakes a twofold task—the exploration, evaluation, and description of the separate "psychosocial character" of each of the three Scandinavian countries; and an explanation, on the basis of each, of the differences in their suicide rates. Others who have attempted explanations in the past (not limited to social scientists) include one prominent official in the United States Government who not too long ago tried to relate the high suicide rate in Scandinavia (conveniently forgetting Norway) to the advanced social welfare program, implying that suicide was one of the major character defects that would accompany the provision by any government of important welfare services to its citizens. Hendin effectively counteracts such arguments by pointing out that Norway has had equally extensive social services for just as long, and that the Danish suicide rate has been high for over a hundred years, long before the welfare measures were put into effect. Sweden's high suicide rate, he states, might be better related

to the development of its industrial capitalism since the turn of the century.

The even older argument, "They keep better statistics than we do," is also readily met. This argument states that because the Danes and the Swedes do not have as strong taboos against suicide as the United States, it does not tend to be concealed when it occurs. As Dr. Hendin points out, the same prejudice against reporting suicide would also make it less likely to occur, thus probably canceling each other out in effect. Norway, too, has as much concern for accurate statistics as Denmark and Sweden.

Obviously, the explanation for the differences in suicide rates needs to be sought in other areas. The author of this concise book (seven chapters, including one each on the problem, the background, the psychodynamics of suicide, suicide in Denmark, Sweden, and Norway, and one on conclusions and applications) states that it must be sought in the "psychosocial character" of the people, which is formed by the culture and its institutions within which the individual grows. "Psychosocial character" can best be obtained by psychoanalytic interviewing techniques, with interest centered on predominant social attitudes and psychodynamic constellations, rather than on individual idiosyncrasies.

The premises are straightforward. First, patients and non-patients, suicidal and nonsuicidal, will reflect "pressures that are exerted on everyone in the society, whether he succumbs to them or not" (p. 3). The data obtained directly can then be verified or substantiated in the culture's pertinent literature, such as drama, cartoons, folklore, and women's magazine stories. While few will object to the above premise, many persons, however, especially psychologists and sociologists reared in the experimental tradition, will question the second premise, "that one can draw significant conclusions regarding the people in the three Scandinavian countries from a psychodynamic study of altogether less than 200 individuals" (p. 3). Considering the fact that there are approximately 4.7 million Danes, 7.5 million Swedes, and 3.6 million Norwegians, this means that, roughly each person included in the study represents samplewise almost 100,000 persons. While most will say this is a very small sample indeed from which to draw conclusions about the character of a nation, there will be others, it is certain, who will remind us that Freud and his followers provided us with some very

fundamental "truths" about man from their intensive studies of a few patients. The author has no doubts about his method. He gives an analogy that "If a psychoanalytically trained observer, with a frame of reference extending to society as well as the individual, sees in New York City (which, with its environs, has a population roughly equivalent to that of the three Scandinavian countries) only five Italian, five Irish and five Jewish patients, he can already begin to construct a picture of the difference in the family patterns, character and attitudes seen in people from these three backgrounds. By the time he sees a dozen of each group, distinctions will have become quite clear. . . . However, if he is concerned only with those features which characterize each group as a whole, a total of 50 subjects will probably suffice. More important than the number of people, is the method used for observing them" (pp. 3–4).

As Kardiner in his *Psychological Frontiers of Society* (1945) states, ". . . one biography in a culture will hardly suffice. We must have an adequate sampling of sex, age, and status differentiations, and no arbitrary number can be regarded as adequate" (p. 37). The reader will find few distinctions made between data obtained from patients, nonpatients, sex, age, status, or other pertinent features that might conceivably affect the conclusions. Does an intensive study of seventy-five suicidal patients and forty nonsuicidal patients controlled by a nonpatient group of six nurses in one country and twelve nurses in another country, plus an unspecified number of relatives of patients, give an adequate picture of the three nations? Could one, for example, determine the characteristics of the English nation by examining the prisoners (plus some of their jailors and relatives) in Old Bailey? Obviously, since crime or suicide encompasses a wide variety of persons, the sampling will have have to be carefully predetermined.

The author, through his psychoanalytic analysis of the literature, drama, and folklore of the three countries, obtains invaluable material referring to attitudes toward death, life, life after death, and suicide. However, the data he obtained indicate the current conceptions in the societies studied but do not tell us their genesis and development. The author is aware of this and states that such questions cannot be adequately answered without the research of a social historian. Yet it is the reviewer's conviction that it might be just this information that is most important in understanding

suicide. How did suicide become so acceptable as resolution to personal and social tension in Denmark and not in Norway? What fashioned a strong taboo in one country and a slight taboo in another? As pure speculation, for example, was there some factor in the early, predominantly fisherman culture of Norway that affected not only the quality of the mother-son and father-son relationships (emphasized in the book) but also fostered a sense of responsibility to others by keeping oneself alive in order to bring all on the boat back from the stormy sea? It might well be that such background relates to the incidence of suicide in a society as much as the hypothesis that one society teaches its children to be passive and dependent while the other emphasizes aggressiveness and independence.

Whether or not one accepts or rejects the author's method and procedures, the differences in character hypothesized between the countries are fascinating and challenging. They are phrased in psychodynamic terms and refer to dependency aspects, attitudes toward performance and accomplishment, handling of aggression and guilt feelings, relationships between the sexes, methods of discipline, and other dynamic features. The Danes are described as passive, oversensitive to abandonment, possessed of effective techniques for arousing guilt in others, inclined to suppress aggression, and to fantasying gratification after death. The Swedes (related to early separation of the child from mother) have strong performance expectation, and foster competitive drives along with strict control of aggression. They are contrasted with the Norwegians, who also foster independence, but permit emotionality, allow the expression of justifiable anger, make less demand for success, and have less need for self-punishment for failure. These psychosocial characteristics produce specific kinds of suicide, for Danish and for Norwegian males the "dependency loss" or "love" type, and for Sweden, the "performance" type of suicide. In addition, "moral" suicides, stemming from aggressive, antisocial behavior plus strong guilt feelings aroused by such behavior, are found in parts of rural Norway. Regardless of the problem involved in arriving at a comprehensive description of the national psychosocial character of a modern society, the clear delineation of these kinds of suicide patterns along with their variations among the sexes, are important contributions to the psychology of suicide.

While there may yet be a question whether the "Scandinavian suicide phenomenon" has been solved, it is certain that a vigorous, incisive attack has been made on this intriguing problem. A method has been championed and applied, and conclusions, worded forcefully and sharply and pulling no punches, have been unhesitatingly offered. This, despite the fact that the author both anticipated and received strong reactions to his formulations from the countries involved. Most important, he has provide hypotheses, clear, lucid, testable, verifiable hypotheses. Hopefully, social scientists of all disciplines will now want to apply their own methods and techniques in their own investigations. Whether such investigations will support or refute the author's findings, the importance of this book is indicated by the fact that it is certain to be both widely read and to become the focus of contention for many years to come.

Chapter 41

PIONEER IN SUICIDOLOGY: A REVIEW OF LOUIS I. DUBLIN'S SUICIDE: A SOCIOLOGICAL AND STATISTICAL STUDY

[New York: Ronald Press, 1963]

Edwin S. Shneidman

In the last half-century, the two American classics on suicide have been Karl Menninger's *Man Against Himself* (1938) and Louis Dublin's *To Be Or Not To Be* (1933), books widely apart in genre, each deserving its own wide reputation.

Menninger's book enunciates a theoretical position (largely relating to Eros and Thanatos) which, although not my particular choice in detail, is still widely current today. More than that, it introduced psychodynamic theory, specifically as related to inimical and self-destructive behaviors, to every literate person in the land.

Dublin's *To Be Or Not To Be* in 1933 was, for many of us, equivalent to the *Encyclopaedia Britannica* of Suicide, the one reliable source for background facts and figures. Logos, not Thanatos, was his totem. The updating of this book by Dublin is literally as welcome as a brand new encyclopaedic supplement would be to the proud owner of a 1933 edition. Dublin has done a marvelous piece of temporal refurbishment, bringing his work up-to-date, retaining what is meaningful from the past, and reflecting with solid scholarship what is useful in the current suicidal scene.

In comparison with his earlier book (*To Be Or Not To Be*), this new book—a rewriting too extensive to call it merely a revision—is shorter (and more pithy) and, at the same time, more wide-ranged and filled with deeper distillations of thought.

The book contains twenty-one chapters divided among five parts. These parts bear the following titles: "People Who Commit Suicide," "The Setting of Suicide," "The History of Suicide"—a book in itself—, "Psychological Aspects of Suicide" (including emotional factors in suicide and mental disease in suicide), and "Toward the Conquest of Suicide" (with a fine chapter describing current suicide prevention centers). And there are many bonuses in this book, even beyond the sociological and statistical presentations and summaries. For my part, I like Dr. Dublin best when he rumbles in

his wonderfully mature and moral way—commenting on trust and faith—as in the following passage:

> The positive message of religion to William James is the belief in the existence of an unseen order of some sort in which the riddles of the natural order may be explained. To paraphrase his thinking: The physical order of nature does not reveal any harmonious spiritual intent, and so we have a right to supplement what we see by an unseen spiritual order that we assume on trust. We cannot escape the conclusion that the science we know is but a drop, our ignorance is a sea; certainly the world of our present natural knowledge is enveloped in a larger world of some sort, of whose property we at present can frame no idea. It is a fact of human nature that man can live and die by the help of a sort of faith that goes without a single dogma or definition. If you destroy the assurance that there is some law and order in the universe beyond our comprehension all the light and radiance of existence are extinguished. Often the suicidal mood will then set in. Frequently faith is the only thing that makes life worth living; if you refuse to believe you may indeed be right, but at the same time you may perhaps irretrievably perish. If you surrender to the nightmare view of life and crown your unbelief by your own suicide you have indeed made a picture totally black. Your mistrust of life has removed whatever worth your own enduring experience might have given to it. Then his final challenge: "Be not afraid of life! Believe that life is worth living and your belief will help create the fact." No message could be nobler than these words of a great thinker and scientist! (Page 135.)

Dublin feels that we do not yet have enough facts—". . . we must await further accumulation and analysis of data"—for major theorizing about the etiological formulae of suicidal phenomena. That's an opinion, and he's more entitled to his opinion in this field than almost anybody. Even so, I would have been especially pleased (based on my own special interests in and approaches to suicidal phenomena) to have had Dr. Dublin's thoughts about the *definitions* and meanings of "suicide" and by his discussion of the problems involved in the certification of death and the *methodological* issues

imbedded in interpreting interclass, interstate, and international statistics.

My only other quibble, a minor one surely, is with the subtitle: It is anachronistic, specifically in the sense that Dublin's previous book on suicide, *To Be Or Not To Be,* was a sociological and statistical study, whereas this present volume is not only that but also a psychological, historical, and humanistic essay on self-destruction in man.

This book report may well be superfluous: an announcement of publication of this volume would probably have sufficed, in that every student of suicide will want to own it. What I can add to an announcement is my recommendation that all students of the human condition, especially of the maladaptive aspects of that condition, should treat themselves to a good taste of the stock and the broth contained within this meaty volume.

I thank Louis Dublin, the Grand Old Man of Suicidology, for this book because in it he has answered much of my cry for help and has given us all new clues to suicide.

Chapter 42
HOPE AS HELP: A REVIEW OF ARTHUR L. KOBLER AND EZRA STOTLAND'S THE END OF HOPE: A SOCIOLOGICAL THEORY OF SUICIDE

[New York: Free Press, 1964]

Norman L. Farberow

Seriously disturbed persons develop a wide variety of individual symptoms, but all cases usually demonstrate some general features. Among these are a deterioration of former defenses, a constrictive focus of both activity and fantasy to a central problem, and a loss of capacity for reality testing and, especially, a loss of judgment. In the distant past hospitals attended primarily to the behavioral end-result of these disturbances and treated people accordingly, that is, with custody, restraint, and "protection." Recognition has emerged only recently that such practices often resulted in the suppression of the individual and an end product of institutional cripples.

The period after the last World War saw many changes in the attitudes toward mental illness and there was a strong tendency to conceptualize emotional illness as interpersonal and reactive. Treatment methods were developed that stressed the environmental factors and situational field forces. The effects of the therapist, of the staff, and the entire hospital as a social field were studied for their contribution to the phenomena; and the open-door policy, the therapeutic community, and patient government have appeared as important procedures for patient care.

These changes have, of course, brought their problems with them. One of the most difficult of these has been the question of appropriate care for the patient who is dangerous to others or to himself, that is, the aggressive, assaultive, or the self-destructive patient. For these cases the hospital has had to walk the difficult path between providing nurturance, dependency, and protection at the same time that it attempted to foster self-sufficiency, independence, and self-respect.

In *The End of Hope,* the authors illustrate this problem of the

hospital in caring for the suicidal patient. Suicide behavior ranges over a wide continuum, from minimally dangerous to highly lethal potentiality. The hospital receives those patients who are more likely to be at the most serious end of the continuum. The hospital's responsibility to the suicidal patient is to help him to want once again to live and, at the same time, to keep him alive. The procedures followed in treating such patients have generally been characterized by the initiation of special precautions, such as placing the patient on "observation," or "suicidal" status, or "specialing" with around-the-clock nurse care. Inevitably, these have included both repressive and regressive measures, but the justification has always been that the patient needed to be protected from himself. Kobler and Stotland's account delves into the nature of this rationalization. Their history of the rise and fall of Crest Hospital emphasizes that it is not the restrictive features *per se* that are important, but rather the attitudes and feelings of the staff in interacting with the patients.

An "epidemic" of four committed suicides and one attempt occurred in Crest Hospital within a period of about six months. (One additional suicide case was not counted because the patient had been released from the hospital about a month.) The authors' thesis is that the hospital was undergoing changes and that, in the epidemic, "changes in directors and philosophy of treatment played a crucial part. Prior to the epidemic the hospital staff had suffered considerable loss of confidence. As time moved on the cumulative effect of the suicides and other facts caused a massive increase in anxiety and feeling of helplessness and a deterioration of therapeutic effectiveness. The hospital was a necessary, if not sufficient, part of the causal nexus which resulted in each suicide, and thus may be seen as the source of epidemiological nature of the groups of suicides" (p. 53).

Crest Hospital had taken great pride in its motto, "Psychological treatment for the psychologically ill." Therapy involved all of the ward staff in the treatment process; drugs, somatic methods, EST, or other shock methods were not ordinarily used. There were no suicidal deaths in the first nine years of the hospital's operation. (Two suicides during this period occurred a month after release and are not counted.) Two serious attempts occurred in the hospital and there were a number of minor suicidal acts. The authors'

histories of patients and hospital obtained from staff, families, patients, and others indicate that the hospital took these in stride. It showed concern and took precautions but did not "run scared." Patients were placed on suicidal precautions but there was no sudden clampdown, no retreat to rigid rule enforcement, and no fear that the patient would die by his own hand. Their point is that the staff felt confident and there was no marked reaction to the suicidal behavior.

However, with several rapid changes in directorship of the hospital, policies and procedures altered, the staff became confused, lost their feeling of confidence, and communicated to the patients their feelings that they had lost control. As the patients encountered increased feelings of helplessness from the staff, they in turn lost hope. The authors state, "For actual suicide to occur, a necessary (although not sufficient) aspect of the field is the response characterized by helplessness and hopelessness. The helpless-hopeless response is communicated through an implicit or explicit expectation that the troubled person will kill himself" (p. 252). The *expectation* of the staff that a patient would commit suicide became, for some patients, a demand that they kill themselves. The implicit point this reviewer would make explicit is that it is not just the expectation of suicide that is harmful, but rather it is the fear and apprehension that may accompany the expectation. People who serve in the helping professions must come to terms with the fact that death often lurks in the wings while they enact their roles. One must always be alert to the possibility of suicide in a patient, family, or friend, but this means neither preoccupation with nor denial of it. Frequently the fact that someone else realizes his desperation and is willing to protect him from himself is great relief to the suicidal person. However, if there is fear as the result of the awareness, or overreaction with helplessness or denial, or, at the other extreme, casual disregard and no concern, the person may well react to this communication with greater feelings of panic and consequent acting out.

The authors add in various places that other factors are contributory but their approach from "a field-theoretical, transactional point of view" emphasizes the role of the interacting others, in this case, the hospital staff. While overstated in the book, it is a point (of view) well worth making. The influence and significance of the

attitude of the resources, the potential rescuer of the suicidal person, needs to be overstated. More broadly, what the authors stress for their cases of severely psychiatrically ill, hospitalized suicidal patients is true also for patients physically ill, and for persons anywhere within the wide ranges of emotional illness. If the end of *End of Hope* succeeds in its message, more cries for help may be answered.

Chapter 43
TRAGEDY COMPOUNDED: A REVIEW OF D. J. WEST'S MURDER FOLLOWED BY SUICIDE
[Cambridge, Mass: Harvard University Press, 1966]
Edwin S. Shneidman

There are certain infrequent, unusual, and arcane events that, because of their unique dramatic and poignant nature, have a special lien on our interests and imagination, especially when they involve the heart-issues of life and death. *Murder Followed by Suicide,* a scholarly and lucidly written book, is of this genre. In format and style, it reminds one a great deal of the monograph by Stengel and Cook on *Attempted Suicide*[1] because it is filled with straightforwardly given data, tabular presentations, succinct case histories, and a common-sense organization of findings. The author, Assistant Director of Research at the Cambridge Institute of Criminology, has written other books, including *Psychical Research Today, Eleven Lourdes Miracles, The Habitual Prisoner,* and *Homosexuality.*

In England and Wales, as in Los Angeles County, murder-suicide is an infrequent event—one percent of all suicides in the former, and about one-half percent in the latter. But we are told in the book that in certain other locales (for example, New South Wales, Australia) 21 percent of the murderers kill themselves afterwards, while 42 percent of Danish killers commit suicide subsequently. The problems of the reliability and meaningfulness of the statistics relating to international comparisons of suicides are not at all resolved when homicides are also included in the data.

The book is essentially a report of seventy-eight unselected murder-suicides in England for the eight-year period 1954–1961. Techniques that remind one of "psychological autopsy," used by the Los Angeles Suicide Prevention Center staff, are reported. Many individuals and organizations were written to or interviewed in relation to this study; medical and psychiatric reports were sought and used whenever available. These seventy-eight cases were supplemented with data from an additional seventy cases for

the years 1946–1962. Furthermore—in a most appropriate application of the Canon of Difference—this sample of 148 murder-suicide cases was compared with an equal number of murder-only cases.

In this compact, succinct, and tightly organized volume, Dr. West directly or by inference raises many interesting questions. Mostly, he demonstrates again the complexity of self-destructive and other-destructive phenomena. The juxtaposition of murder and suicide permits us to see even more clearly that different homicide and suicide acts have: different phenomenological meanings, various affective components, a multitude of psychodynamic bases, a range of social milieu determinants, and varying roles of the victim in his own demise. The possible roles of the murder victim include (1) the victim's not knowing, not anticipating, or not wanting his demise; (2) his knowing of it, but not consenting; and (3) his consenting, joint planning, or even his active participation.

One wonders about the *unconscious* role of the victim in his own homicide and is reminded of the works of Wolfgang and Macdonald on the topic of victim-precipitated homicide.[2] Not unexpectedly, I am reminded of my own thoughts about subintentioned death.[3] A subintentioned death—as opposed to an intentioned or unintentioned death—is one in which the victim plays some unconscious, latent, covert, or partial role in hastening his own demise.

In this book Dr. West talks of three types of murder-suicides: those committed by the insane, by sane persons acting under stress, and by a small group of criminally motivated individuals. The questions of psychodynamics and diagnosis are moot ones and cannot be answered simply. Dr. West, like many people writing on these topics, tends to emphasize the psychodynamics of hostility and aggression. It may be that sometimes a murder-suicide represents the epitome of hate; but even some of the histories cited in this volume indicate that in some other cases these events reflect a greater concern with dependency and hopelessness and are, in some cases, a manifestation—albeit a tortured one—of compassion.

Chapter 44

CONCERN FOR SUICIDE—BEFORE AND AFTER: A REVIEW OF ERWIN STENGEL'S SUICIDE AND ATTEMPTED SUICIDE
[Baltimore: Penguin, 1965]
AND
JAMES HILLMAN'S SUICIDE AND THE SOUL
[New York: Harper & Row, 1965]
Robert E. Litman

Although the titles reflect a mutual interest in suicide, no two books could be more dissimilar in style and content than *Suicide and Attempted Suicide* by Erwin Stengel and *Suicide and the Soul* by James Hillman.

For readers who are interested in learning about suicide, *Suicide and Attempted Suicide* is a pocket-sized digest, assembled in 1963 by Professor Stengel, of the current scientific literature. His style is scholarly and scientific, with emphasis on the facts. He is a Vienna-trained neuropsychiatrist and psychoanalyst whose work has led him far into the field of social psychiatry. For Stengel, "the study of suicide illustrates that human action, however personal, is also interaction with other people and that the individual cannot be understood in isolation from his social matrix."

The book is a systematic and orderly review of the multiple aspects of suicide. It begins with definitions of suicide and reports the various factors that are positively and negatively correlated to the suicide rate. Then it discusses the various methods, warnings, notes, pacts, motives, causes, and fashions in suicide. Important psychiatric symptoms of depression, alcoholism, schizophrenia, and psychopathic personality are described. A good many statistical studies from various parts of the world are quoted. Since it is a small book (130 pages, pocket size), each section is quite abbreviated, even sketchy. Some of the chapters would benefit if the author added more of his personal point of view to integrate and illuminate collections of facts culled from the literature of different countries, especially since many of the statistics on suicide are unreliable and unexplainable.

Stengel is at his best when he discusses suicide attempts, an area in which he did a great deal of original research. He has demonstrated that suicide attempts should not be considered bungled suicides. Suicide attempts are made by a special population and have a special meaning and psychology of their own. It is most enlightening to view suicide attempts as social communications that have an appeal value and "release" an intense response from the environment, usually of a rescuing type. Thus suicide attempts are failures of adaptation; but also they are adaptive.

Professor Stengel is pessimistic about the possibilities of effective suicide prevention through individual psychotherapy. He sees suicide as a public health problem and reports favorably on telephone suicide prevention services in Europe and the United States, and on the International Association for Suicide Prevention. The book contains little case material and few specific recommendations as to how a therapist should handle a suicidal patient.

Because he feels that social isolation is the great common denominator in suicide, Professor Stengel suggests that the only effective suicide prevention would be primary prevention aimed at the suicideogenic factors in society, for example, the problems of old age, retirement, social maladjustment, and unemployment, as well as mental illness. "What is needed is a mobilization of the latent resources for helping and healing in our society. This may sound rather vague and even obscure, but the idea of employing the unused therapeutic potentialities of a community is not new. . . . We must match the scientific and technological revolution with as revolutionary a change in social living." The result would be a truly therapeutic community.

The book *Suicide and the Soul* is a passionate polemic directed against the very notion of a social matrix and the trend toward scientific studies of suicide. Unlike Stengel, who views death as a physical state and suicide as a behavioral event, James Hillman sees death as an experience, a transition from one reality into another reality, and suicide is only a symbol. Hillman's interest in suicide is to use it as a touchstone to illuminate what he considers to be the central issue in this generation, namely, the conflict between the soul and its enemies. Hillman, a relatively young American psychologist from New Jersey who is a leading lay analyst of

the Jung Institute in Zurich, speaks for the soul. All others, including medicine, theology, law, academic psychology, and the community, are the enemies of the soul.

For Hillman, the role of the psychoanalyst is to guide and assist the soul in its psychoanalytic task of consciously experiencing itself more clearly and completely. But what is the soul? "The soul is a deliberately ambiguous concept resisting all definition in the same manner as do all such symbols. . . . It has metaphysical and romantic overtones. It shares frontiers with religion." The purpose of the analyst is to understand and experience with the soul of his analysand. To Hillman, the whole idea of suicide prevention is antitherapeutic since the soul needs the death experience in order to undergo a radical change. "Usually the death experience is in the psychological mode, but for some, organic death through actual suicide may be the only mode through which the death experience is possible."

From the medical point of view, questions of the soul and its destiny are rather irrelevant when one is confronted with a corpse. No matter how committed an analyst might be to the soul, it would seem his work too is stopped by physical death. There is no psychotherapy with a corpse. To this argument, Hillman gives a radical answer: "We do not know if the soul dies." This reviewer cannot do justice to the ingenious argument by which the author explains the continuation of therapy after the physical death of the analysand.

The task Hillman sets for the psychotherapist with a suicidal patient is by no means easy. The analyst must work alone in secrecy and mystery, cut off completely from the help that might be offered by his colleagues, by the community, or the friends and family of the patient. Patient and therapist are closely united, and if the patient dies, the therapist must admit his complicity and in part he dies too. Yet Hillman offers his disciples an out from the fearful burden of responsibility. Could not the necessity for death come from the patient's soul? "If an analyst has permitted the death experience to the utmost and still the soul insists on organic death through suicide, cannot this too be considered an unavoidable necessity, a summons from God?"

Suicide and the Soul contains no case material. Obviously the author has used the concept of suicide to dramatize and forward

his own parochial philosophy of Jungian psychotherapy. Readers who favor writing aimed at their guts will enjoy this book as a wildly stimulating, infuriating, exciting protest against complacent mental health attitudes in an insane world. I feel that Hillman has enlarged my own philosophical horizon. But I do not believe it is possible to conduct psychotherapy in a social vacuum, and I question the value of such an ideal.

It is unfortunate that Hillman provides no clinical material as a medium for direct confrontation with opposing views. Philosophical polemics in themselves lead to no contact or progress. As Sigmund Freud put it, "The whale and the polar bear cannot wage war on each other, for since each is confined to his own element, they cannot meet." What is needed to provide a meeting ground for scientists, theorists, philosophers, and therapists who wish to discuss or argue suicide is publication of the essential material of clinical psychology: a collection of detailed case reports on the lives and deaths of a variety of intensively studied individuals who committed suicide.

NOTES

Chapter 1

1. F. BACON, *Novum Organum* (Aphorisms XXXVIII, XXXIX, XLII, and LIII).
2. E. DURKHEIM, *Suicide,* trans. J. A. SPAULDING and G. SIMPSON (New York: Free Press of Glencoe, 1951; original, 1897).
3. S. FREUD, "Mourning and Melancholia," in *Collected Papers,* Vol. IV (London: Hogarth Press, 1925); "The Psychogenesis of a Case of Homosexuality in a Woman" (1920), in J. STRACHEY (ed.), *The Standard Edition of the Complete Psychological Works of Sigmund Freud,* Vol. XVIII (London: Hogarth Press, 1955).
4. K. A. MENNINGER, *Man Against Himself* (New York: Harcourt, Brace and Company, 1938).
5. This important distinction was made by NORMAN L. FARBEROW, "Personality Patterns of Suicidal Mental Hospital Patients," *Genetic Psychology Monographs,* 42:3–79, 1950, and supported by A. ROSEN, W. HALES, and W. SIMON, "Classification of Suicidal Patients," *Journal of Consulting Psychology,* 18:359, 1954.
6. H. FEIFEL (ed.), *The Meaning of Death* (New York: McGraw-Hill Book Company, 1959).
7. G. DRAPER, C. W. DUPERTUIS, and J. L. CAUGHLEY, *Human Constitution in Clinical Medicine* (New York: Harper and Brothers, 1944).
8. See T. J. CURPHEY, "The Role of the Social Scientist in the Medicolegal Certification of Death from Suicide," in N. L. FARBEROW and E. S. SHNEIDMAN (eds.), *The Cry for Help* (New York: McGraw-Hill Book Company, 1961), and E. S. SHNEIDMAN and N. L. FARBEROW, "Sample Investigations of Equivocal Suicidal Deaths," in FARBEROW and SHNEIDMAN (eds.), *The Cry for Help.*
9. P. W. BRIDGMAN, *The Intelligent Individual and Society* (New York: The Macmillan Company, 1938).
10. C. S. PEIRCE, *Collected Papers of Charles Sanders Peirce,* Vol. IV, ed. C. HARTSHORNE and P. WEISS (Cambridge, Massachusetts: Harvard University Press, 1931–1958).

11. I am indebted to Professor Abraham Kaplan for this insight and information.

12. Miguel de Unamuno, who is probably as nonpsychoanalytical as it is possible for a cultivated twentieth-century human to be, agrees: "It is impossible for us, in effect, to conceive of ourselves as not existing, and no effort is capable of enabling consciousness to realize absolute unconsciousness, its own annihilation." MIGUEL DE UNAMUNO, *The Tragic Sense of Life*, trans. E. C. FLITCH (Gloucester, Massachusetts: Peter Smith, 1921).

13. The term "cessation" is used in this present sense by Bridgman on at least two occasions (*op. cit.*, pp. 169, 225).

14. I am indebted to James Diggory for suggesting this term to me.

15. "I know when one is dead and when one lives;/ She's as dead as earth. Lend me a looking-glass;/ If that her breath will mist or stain the stone,/ Why, then she lives." *King Lear*, V.iii. 260–263.

16. The cessation-states described herein are meant to describe only the *current status* (vis-à-vis cessation) of the individual. Thus, one would, in any complete description of an individual, need also a biphasic taxonomy that describes the relatively chronic, pervasive, characterological, "presuicidal" aspects of his psychological makeup.

17. This concept of the initiator was developed primarily by Calista V. Leonard of the staff of the VA Central Research Unit. CALISTA V. LEONARD, "A Theory of Suicide: The Implementor," unpublished paper, Veterans Administration Central Research Unit, 1962. See also the section on the unaccepting patient in N. L. FARBEROW, E. S. SHNEIDMAN, and C. V. LEONARD, *Suicide—Evaluation and Treatment of Suicidal Risk Among Schizophrenic Patients in Psychiatric Hospitals* (Washington, D.C.: Department of Medicine and Surgery, Veterans Administration, *Medical Bulletin 8*, 1962).

18. Three very different examples of Psyde-initiators—all eminent men—are contained in the writings of Wertenbaker, Leicester Hemingway, and Holten. It is of interest to contrast Ernest Hemingway's attitude toward his failing body with that of Dr. Hans Zinsser. L. T. WERTENBAKER, *Death of a Man* (New York: Random House, 1957); L. HEMINGWAY, *My Brother, Ernest Hem-*

ingway (New York: World Publishing Company, 1962); G. Holton, "Percy Williams Bridgman," *Bulletin of Atomic Scientists,* 17:22, 1962; H. ZINSSER, *As I Remember Him* (Boston, Massachusetts: Little, Brown and Company, 1940).

19. E. S. SHNEIDMAN and N. L. FARBEROW (eds.), *Clues to Suicide* (New York: McGraw-Hill Book Company, 1957).

20. J. A. GENGERELLI and F. J. KIRCHNER (eds.), *Psychological Factors in Human Cancer* (Berkeley and Los Angeles: University of California Press, 1953).

21. M. E. WOLFGANG, "Suicide by Means of Victim-Precipitated Homicide," *Journal of Clinical and Experimental Psychopathology,* 20:335, 1959.

22. J. M. A. WEISS, "The Gamble with Death in Attempted Suicide," *Psychiatry,* 20:17–25, 1957.

23. A. D. WEISMAN and T. P. HACKETT, "Predilection to Death: and Dying as a Psychiatric Problem," *Psychosomatic Medicine,* 23:232–256, 1961.

24. P. SCHILDER and D. WECHSLER, "The Attitudes of Children Toward Death," *Journal of General Psychology,* 45:406, 1934; and M. NAGY, "The Child's View of Death," in FEIFEL (ed.), *The Meaning of Death.*

25. For example, Swanberg says: "[William Randolph] Hearst . . . had a violent aversion for mortality, and there was an unwritten law never to mention death in his presence." W. A. SWANBERG, *Citizen Hearst* (New York: Charles Scribner's Sons, 1961).

26. At the Los Angeles Suicide Prevention Center, the staff has evolved procedures for assessing "suicidal potentiality." See R. E. LITMAN and N. L. FARBEROW, "Emergency Evaluation of Self-Destructive Potentiality," in FARBEROW and SHNEIDMAN (eds.), *The Cry for Help,* and N. D. TABACHNICK and N. L. FARBEROW, "The Assessment of Self-Destructive Potentiality," in FARBEROW and SHNEIDMAN (eds.), *The Cry for Help.*

27. The reader is referred to Henry A. Murray's masterful Psychological studies of Melville: "In Nomine Diaboli," in *Moby-Dick Centennial Essays* (Dallas, Texas: Southern Methodist University Press, 1953), pp. 3–29, originally published in *New England Quarterly,* 24:435–452, 1951; in MILTON R. STERN (ed.), *Discussions of Moby Dick* (Boston, Massachusetts: D.C. Heath and

Company, 1960), pp. 25–34; in RICHARD CHASE (ed.), *Melville: A Collection of Critical Essays* (Englewood Cliffs, New Jersey: Prentice-Hall, 1962), pp. 62–74; and his "Introduction to Melville's *Pierre: Or The Ambiguities* (New York: Hendricks House, 1949), pp. xiii–ciii.
28. WEISMAN and HACKETT, *op. cit.*, pp. 232–256.

Chapter 2

1. N. KLEITMAN, *Sleep and Wakefulness* (2nd ed.; Chicago, Illinois: University of Chicago Press, 1963); I. OSWALD, *Sleeping and Waking* (Amsterdam and New York: Elsevier, 1962); G. E. W. WOLSTENHOLME and M. O'CONNOR (eds.), *The Nature of Sleep* (Boston, Massachusetts: Little, Brown and Company, 1960); H. FEIFEL (ed.), *The Meaning of Death* (New York: McGraw-Hill Book Company, 1959); J. CHORON, *Death and Western Thought* (New York: Collier, 1963); J. CHORON, *Modern Man and Mortality* (New York: The Macmillan Company, 1964); and E. S. SHNEIDMAN, "Suicide: A Taboo Topic," in N. L. FARBEROW (ed.), *Taboo Topics* (New York: Atherton Press, 1963).
2. E. S. SHNEIDMAN and N. L. FARBEROW (eds.), *Clues to Suicide* (New York: McGraw-Hill Book Company, 1957); N. L. FARBEROW and E. S. SHNEIDMAN (eds.), *The Cry for Help* (New York: McGraw-Hill Book Company, 1961); and E. S. SHNEIDMAN, "Suicide: Some Classificatory Considerations," *Special Treatment Situations* (Des Plaines, Illinois: Forest Hospital Foundation, 1962).
3. E. S. SHNEIDMAN, "Orientations Toward Death: A Vital Aspect of the Study of Lives," in R. W. WHITE (ed.), *The Study of Lives* (New York: Atherton Press, 1963), and *International Journal of Psychiatry*, 2:167–200, 1966.
4. P. W. BRIDGMAN, *The Intelligent Individual and Society* (New York: The Macmillan Company, 1938), and *The Way Things Are* (Cambridge, Massachusetts: Harvard University Press, 1955).
5. SHNEIDMAN, "Orientations Toward Death."
6. W. JAMES, *Principles of Psychology* (New York: Holt, 1890; republished New York: Dover Publications, 1950).
7. KLEITMAN, *Sleep and Wakefulness.*
8. SHNEIDMAN and FARBEROW (eds.), *Clues to Suicide.*

9. J. M. A. WEISS "The Gamble With Death in Attempted Suicide," *Psychiatry*, 20:17–25, 1957.

10. H. A. MURRAY, "What Should Psychologists Do About Psychoanalysis?" *Journal of Abnormal and Social Psychology*, 35:150–175, 1940.

11. E. H. ERIKSON, *Childhood and Society* (New York: W. W. Norton and Company, 1950).

12. H. A. MURRAY, "In Nomine Diaboli," *New England Quarterly*, 24:435–452, 1951.

13. A practical extension of this belief is contained in the "Psychological Autopsies" that the staff of the Suicide Prevention Center conduct in connection with the Los Angeles County Coroner's Office in the certification of equivocal suicide-accident deaths. The basic assumption in this procedure is that the manner of dying is consonant with and part of manner of living. T. J. CURPHEY, "The Role of the Suicidal Scientist in the Medicolegal Certification of Death from Suicide," in FARBEROW and SHNEIDMAN (eds.), *The Cry for Help*; R. E. LITMAN, T. CURPHEY, E. S. SHNEIDMAN, N. L. FARBEROW, and N. TABACHNICK, "Investigations of Equivocal Suicides," *Journal of the American Medical Association*, 184:924–929, 1963; E. S. SHNEIDMAN and N. L. FARBEROW, "Sample Investigations of Equivocal Suicidal Deaths," in FARBEROW and SHNEIDMAN (eds.), *The Cry for Help*.

14. The following point must be strongly emphasized: A basic assumption in this entire scheme is that an individual's orientations toward his cessation are *biphasic*; that is, any adult, at any given moment, has (1) more-or-less long-range, relatively chronic, pervasive, habitual, characterological orientations toward cessation as an integral part of his total psychological make-up (reflecting his philosophy of life, need systems, aspirations, identification, conscious beliefs, etc.); and (2) is also capable of having acute, relatively short-lived, exacerbated, clinical sudden shifts of cessation-orientation. Indeed, this is what is usually meant when one says that an individual has become "suicidal." It is therefore crucial in any complete assessment of an individual's orientation toward cessation to know both his habitual and his at-that-moment orientations toward cessation. (Failure to do this is one reason why previous efforts to relate "suicidal state" with psychological test results have been barren.) In individuals in their "normal"

(i.e., usual for them) state, their habitual and their current orientations toward cessation will be the same. We have made the separate point that for most individuals their modal orientation toward their own cessation is not, as might appear on first thought, an unintentioned orientation, but rather that it is a subintentioned orientation. That is, for most of us, in order to "live" and to actualize ourselves we must move through the world in a way that constantly involves a certain amount of risk-taking, and it is only in times of great personal (intrapsychic) crisis that we shift from our habitual subintentioned orientation-toward-cessation to either an acutely intentioned (suicidal) position ("I'll kill myself") or a determined, cautious, frightened, resolute unintentioned position (*"They'll* have to kill me.").

15. H. A. MURRAY, "Studies of Stressful Interpersonal Disputations," *American Psychologist*, 18:28–36, 1963.

16. N. KLEITMAN, F. J. MULLIN, N. R. COOPERMAN, and S. TITELBAUM, *Sleep Characteristics* (Chicago, Illinois: University of Chicago Press, 1937); and H. M. HILDRETH, "A Battery of Feeling and Attitude Scales for Clinical Use," *Journal of Clinical Psychology*, 23:214–221, 1946.

17. E. S. SHNEIDMAN, "The Logic of Suicide," in SHNEIDMAN and FARBEROW (eds.), *Clues to Suicide*; "Psycho-logic: A Personality Approach to Patterns of Thinking," in J. KAGAN and G. LESSOR (eds.), *Contemporary Issues in Thematic Apperception Methods* (Springfield, Illinois: Charles C Thomas, 1961); "The Logic of El: A Psycho-logical Approach to the Analysis of Test Data," *Journal of Projective Techniques in Personality Assessment*, 25:390–403, 1961.

18. D. MCCLELLAND, "The Harlequin Complex," in R. W. WHITE (ed.), *The Study of Lives* (New York: Atherton Press, 1963).

19. One subject in our sleep study—a 50-year-old, college-educated man—spontaneously wrote the following: "To me at least, I have no significant attitude (or set of attitudes) toward the concept of SLEEP-PLUS-BED-PLUS-PRIVACY-PLUS-DARKNESS-PLUS etc., etc. (Mainly of course just SLEEP-PLUS-BED). Our language does not at the moment supply us with a portmanteau word to cover this concept. Categories such as 'escape from the work-a-day world' or 'temporary death' do not supply the meaning I have in mind. If I speak of SLEEP as a

refuge, which is the nearest one-word description of my attitude that I have come up with to date, I am not reifying SLEEP, but I come close to reifying the concept of SLEEP-PLUS-BED, and perhaps properly so, since BED at least is a *res*, and is a very important part of the concept. I look forward to sleep both as a period of oblivion and as a time for dreaming. I am quite serious when I say that to me SLEEP-PLUS-BED is a *wonderfully pleasant way to pass the time* (particularly during periods of depression), and that this is its main attraction to me . . . more so than *refuge*, or *return to the womb*, or *the protected place*, or *the private place*, although I give you all these labels as additional truths."

20. R. W. WHITE, "Sense of Interpersonal Competence," in R. W. WHITE (ed.), *The Study of Lives* (New York: Atherton Press, 1963).

21. BRIDGMAN, *The Way Things Are.*

22. Granted that a nonself can never experience anything, or that the self can never experience its nonself—although there are many instances in which an individual thinks that he can suffer termination and still not undergo cessation; that he can kill his body and, in some sense, survive, and even experience his own funeral—then the most pervasive philosophic confusions seem to be among the following three meanings of the "self": (1) I,— the living self experiencing itself, including the experience of being experienced by others; (2) the living self as he is experienced by others in *presence* of the I,—this is also an I, experience for the someone else; and (3) the experiencing on the part of the other of "I," in the *absence* of I. This absence can be in the physical absence of a now-alive person, or in relation to a once-alive but now-dead person, or in relation to a fictional, mythical, or apocryphal person. This event can have no possible meaning or impact on the individual—I,—unless it is translatable and translated into a behavior experience for him. (For example, consider the different meanings of the word "saw" from the point of view of the "individual" seen, in the sentence: When I was in Moscow recently I visited the Red Square and saw and had a conversation with Titov; I saw, from afar, Khrushchev reviewing the troops; then I went into the sarcophagus and I saw Lenin; but everywhere I saw Marx).

23. A further elaboration of the postego concept is the subject for a separate paper. In this setting, though, one frightening implication can be stated: that the great potential enormity of the super-bombs is not only that they are capable of killing every one who is alive, but by doing so they would murder every one who is dead; and not only might all present places be obliterated but all previous ages would be erased.

24. This concept of enforced continuation is reflected in the title of an animal study by Licklider and Bunch. J. R. LICKLIDER and M. E. BUNCH, "Effects of Enforced Wakefulness Upon the Growth and Mazelearning Performances of White Rats," *Journal of Comparative Psychology*, 39:339, 1946.

25. OSWALD, *op. cit.*

26. Lindemann's work on crisis theory (1944) and other work on reactions to major disaster are all relevant to this notion of metacrisis. In relation to disaster one can cite LIFTON's essays (1963) with its comprehensive bibliographic footnote on that topic, including references to BAKER and CHAPMAN'S *Man and Society in Disaster* and WOLFENSTEIN'S *Disaster*; E. LINDEMANN, "Symptomatology and Management of Acute Grief," *American Journal of Psychiatry*, 101:141–148, 1944; R. J. LIFTON, "Psychological Effects of the Atom Bomb in Hiroshima: The Theme of Death," *Daedalus*, 92:462–497, 1963.

27. Erikson provides us with a quotation that clarifies our notion of the metacrisis: "This is the truth behind Franklin D. Roosevelt's simple yet magic statement that we have nothing to fear but fear itself, a statement which for the sake of our argument must be paraphrased to read: We have nothing to fear but anxiety. For it is not the fear of a danger (which we might well be able to meet with judicious action), but the fear of the associated states of aimless anxiety which drives us into irrational action, irrational flight—or, indeed, irrational denial of danger." ERIKSON, *op. cit.*

Chapter 3

1. Appreciation is expressed to Professor Abraham Kaplan, Department of Philosophy, University of California at Los Angeles, for his logical and philosophical comments.

2. A. STORCH, *The Primitive Archaic Forms of Inner Experiences and Thought in Schizophrenia* (Washington, D.C.: Nervous and Mental Disease Publishing Company, 1924); E. VON DOMARUS, "The Specific Laws of Logic in Schizophrenia," in J. S. KASANIN (ed.), *Language and Thought in Schizophrenia* (Berkeley and Los Angeles: University of California Press, 1944); and S. ARIETI, *Interpretation of Schizophrenia* (New York: Robert Bruner, 1955).

3. These two syllogisms illustrate the process of identification in terms of the attributes of the predicate, but it can be pointed out that they can be seen in quite another way: that is, they also demonstrate straightforward Aristotelian reasoning if one only supplies the missing or suppressed premises. What these two syllogisms have in common is that the focus of attention is narrowed to only one attribute of the class. Consider: If Switzerland were the only class that loved freedom, and if I loved freedom, then I would indeed have to be Switzerland. Psychologically, this narrowing of focus may reflect the difficulty that the emotionally disturbed person has in grasping other than what is immediately before his mind.

4. It will be possible for the philosophically inclined reader to attribute existentialist implications to this point of view. As far as the authors are concerned, these are not necessarily implied. Nevertheless, it may be of interest to quote from Sartre, who states the following: "The lie is also a normal phenomenon of what Heidegger calls the '*Mitsein*' (a 'being-with' others in the world). It presupposes my existence, the existence of the *other*, my existence *for* the other, and the existence of the other *for* me. Thus there is no difficulty in holding that the liar must make the project of the lie in entire clarity and that he must possess a complete comprehension of the lie and of the truth which he is altering. It is sufficient that an opaqueness of principle hides his intentions from *the other*. It is sufficient that the other can take the lie for truth. By the lie, consciousness affirms that it exists by nature as hidden from the other; it utilizes for its own profit *the ontological duality of myself and myself in the eyes of others.*" (Last italics ours; J. P. SARTRE, "Self-Deception," in WALTER KAUFMAN, [ed.], *Existentialism from Dostoevsky to Sartre* [New York: World Publishing Company, 1956]).

5. R. S. WOODWORTH and S. B. SELLS, "An Atmosphere Effect in Formal Syllogistic Reasoning," *Journal of Experimental Psychology*, 18:451–460, 1935; and S. B. SELLS, "The Atmosphere Effect," *Archives of Psychology*, No. 200, 1936.

6. E. S. SHNEIDMAN and N. L. FARBEROW, "Comparison Between Genuine and Simulated Suicide Notes by Means of Mowrer's DRQ," *Journal of General Psychology*, 56:251–256, 1957.

7. O. H. MOWRER, *Psychotherapy: Theory and Research* (New York: The Ronald Press Company, 1953).

8. G. U. YULE and N. KENDALL, *An Introduction to the Theory of Statistics* (New York: Hafner, 1950).

9. This note is number 18-B of the total set of sixty-six notes.

Chapter 4

1. B. L. WHORF, *Language, Thought and Reality*, ed. J. B. CARROLL (New York: John Wiley and Sons, 1956); E. SAPIR, *Culture, Language and Personality*, ed. D. G. MANDELBAUM (Berkeley and Los Angeles: University of California Press, 1956); HAJIME NAKAMURA, *The Ways of Thinking of Eastern Peoples* (Tokyo: Japanese Government Printing Bureau, 1960; available from Charles E. Tuttle Company, Rutland, Vermont).

2. E. S. SHNEIDMAN, "The Logic of Suicide," in E. S. SHNEIDMAN and N. L. FARBEROW (eds.), *Clues to Suicide* (New York: McGraw-Hill Book Company, 1957); "Psycho-logic: A Personality Approach to Patterns of Thinking," in J. KAGAN and G. LESSOR (eds.), *Contemporary Issues in Thematic Apperception Methods* (Springfield, Illinois: Charles C Thomas, 1961).

3. E. S. SHNEIDMAN, "The Logic of Politics: An Analysis of the Kennedy-Nixon Debates," in L. ARONS and M. A. MAY (eds.), *Television and Human Behavior* (New York: Appleton-Century-Crofts, 1963).

4. E. VON DOMARUS, "The Specific Laws of Logic in Schizophrenia," in J. S. KASANIN (ed.), *Language and Thought in Schizophrenia* (Berkeley and Los Angeles: University of California Press, 1944).

5. S. ARIETI, *Interpretation of Schizophrenia* (New York: Robert Bruner, 1955).

6. E. S. SHNEIDMAN, "The Logic of Suicide"; "Psycho-logic"; "The

Logic of El: A Psycho-logical Approach to the Analysis of Test Data," *Journal of Projective Techniques in Personality Assessment*, 25:390–403, 1961; "The Logic of Politics."

7. E. S. SHNEIDMAN and P. G. TRIPODES, *Feasibility Study on Computerizing Logical Patterns* (China Lake, California: U.S. Naval Ordnance Test Station, 1967). ·

8. C. KLUCKHOHN, H. A. MURRAY, and D. SCHNEIDER, *Personality in Nature, Society and Culture* (2nd ed.; New York: Alfred Knopf, 1953).

Chapter 5

1. N. L. FARBEROW, "Personality Patterns of Suicidal Mental Hospital Patients," *Genetic Psychology Monographs*, 42:3–79, 1950; N. L. FARBEROW, "The Suicidal Crisis in Psychotherapy," in E. S. SHNEIDMAN and N. L. FARBEROW (eds.), *Clues to Suicide* (New York: McGraw-Hill Book Company, 1957); N. L. FARBEROW, "Suicide and Age," in SHNEIDMAN and FARBEROW (eds.), *Clues to Suicide;* N. L. FARBEROW and E. S. SHNEIDMAN, "A Study of Attempted, Threatened, and Completed Suicides," *Journal of Abnormal and Social Psychology*, 50:230, 1955; N. L. FARBEROW and E. S. SHNEIDMAN, "Suicide and the Police Officer," *Police*, 2:51–55, 1958; E. S. SHNEIDMAN, and N. L. FARBEROW, "Clues to Suicide," *Public Health Reports*, 71:109, 1956; E. S. SHNEIDMAN and N. L. FARBEROW, "Comparison Between Genuine and Simulated Suicide Notes by Means of Mowrer's DRQ," *Journal of General Psychology*, 56:251–256, 1957; E. S. SHNEIDMAN and N. L. FARBEROW, "TAT Heroes of Suicidal and Non-Suicidal Subjects," *Journal of Projective Techniques*, 22:211–218, 1958.

2. The godfather of the Los Angeles Suicide Prevention (and much of suicide prevention in this country) was the late Harold M. Hildreth, Ph.D., who guided and helped in more ways than we can acknowledge and who conceived of one comprehensive NIMH grant with several components: training, research, and clinical services. It was he who fostered and nourished our own visions for a research-oriented clinical and training Suicide Prevention Center. In 1962, we received from NIMH a seven-year project grant (MH-128). We have operated under the aegis of this grant, which is administered by the University of Southern California

School of Medicine, Dr. Roger Egeberg, Dean, and the Department of Psychiatry, Dr. Edward Stainbrook, Chairman.

3. AMERICAN PSYCHIATRIC ASSOCIATION. *The Development of Standards and Training Curriculum for Volunteer Service Coordinators* (Washington, D.C.: American Psychiatric Association, 1964); E. S. SHNEIDMAN and N. L. FARBEROW, "The Los Angeles Suicide Prevention Center: A Demonstration of Feasibilities," *American Journal of Public Health,* 55:21–26, 1965.

4. FARBEROW, "Personality Patterns of Suicidal Mental Hospital Patients"; N. L. FARBEROW and E. S. SHNEIDMAN (eds.), *The Cry for Help* (New York: McGraw-Hill Book Company, 1961); R. E. LITMAN, "Acutely Suicidal Patients: Management in General Medical Practice," *California Medicine,* 104:168, 1966; A. SCHRUT, "Suicidal Adolescents and Children," *Journal of American Medical Association,* 188:1103, 1964; E. S. SHNEIDMAN, "Preventing Suicide," *American Journal of Nursing,* 65:111–116, 1965; SHNEIDMAN and FARBEROW (eds.), *Clues to Suicide;* E. S. SHNEIDMAN, N. L. FARBEROW, and C. V. LEONARD, *Some Facts About Suicide* (Washington, D.C.: U.S. Government Printing Office, Public Health Service Publication No. 852, 1961); N. D. TABACHNICK, "Observations on Attempted Suicide," in SHNEIDMAN and FARBEROW (eds.) *Clues to Suicide.*

5. SCHRUT, *op. cit.*

6. FARBEROW, "Suicide and Age"; E. S. SHNEIDMAN, *Suicide and the Aged. Hearings Before the Subcommittee on Problems of the Aged and Aging, Committee on Labor and Public Welfare, Eighty-Sixth Congress* (Washington, D.C.: United States Government Printing Office, 1960), Part 4, pp. 970–980.

7. S. COHEN, C. V. LEONARD, N. L. FARBEROW, and E. S. SHNEIDMAN, "Tranquilizers and Suicide in the Schizophrenic Patient," *Archives of General Psychiatry,* 11:312–321, 1964; N. L. FARBEROW, E. S. SHNEIDMAN, and C. V. LEONARD, "Suicide Among Schizophrenic Hospital Patients," in FARBEROW and SHNEIDMAN (eds.), *The Cry for Help;* N. L. FARBEROW, E. S. SHNEIDMAN, and C. V. LEONARD, *Suicide—Evaluation and Treatment of Suicidal Risk Among Schizophrenic Patients in Psychiatric Hospitals* (Washington, D.C.: Department of Medicine and Surgery, Veterans Administration, *Medical Bulletin 8,* 1962).

8. N. L. FARBEROW, E. S. SHNEIDMAN, and C. V. LEONARD, *Suicide*

Among General Medical and Surgical Hospital Patients with Malignant Neoplasms (Washington, D.C.: Veterans Administration, *Medical Bulletin No. 9, 1963*).

9. N. L. FARBEROW, W. MCKELLIGOTT, S. COHEN, and A. DARBONNE, "Suicide Among Patients with Cardiorespiratory Illnesses," *Journal of the American Medical Association*, 195:422–428, 1966.

10. N. L. FARBEROW and T. L. MCEVOY, "Suicide Among Patients in General Medical and Surgical Hospitals with Diagnoses of Anxiety Reaction or Depressive Reaction," *Journal of Abnormal Psychology*, 71:287–299, 1966.

11. N. L. FARBEROW and R. PALMER, "The Nurse's Role in the Prevention of Suicide," *Nursing Forum*, 3:93, 1964.

12. LITMAN, *op. cit.*

13. E. S. SHNEIDMAN and N. L. FARBEROW, "A Sociopsychological Investigation of Suicide," in H. P. DAVID and J. C. BRENGELMANN (eds.), *Perspectives in Personality Research* (New York: Basic Books, 1960).

14. FARBEROW and SHNEIDMAN, "A Study of Attempted, Threatened, and Completed Suicides."

15. N. L. FARBEROW and E. S. SHNEIDMAN, "A Nisei Woman Attacks by Suicide," in G. SEWARD (ed.), *Clinical Studies in Culture Conflict* (New York: The Ronald Press Company, 1958).

16. N. D. TABACHNICK and D. J. KLUGMAN, "No Name: A Study of Anonymous Suicidal Telephone Calls," *Psychiatry*, 28:79, 1965.

17. S. EISENTHAL, N. L. FARBEROW, and E. S. SHNEIDMAN, "Follow-up of Neuro-psychiatric Hospital Patients Placed on Suicide Observation Status," *Public Health Reports*, 81:977–990, 1966.

18. FARBEROW and SHNEIDMAN, "Suicide and the Police Officer"; R. E. LITMAN, "Police Aspects of Suicide," *Police*, 10:14–18, 1966.

19. N. L. FARBEROW, E. S. SHNEIDMAN, and R. E. LITMAN, "The Suicidal Patient and the Physician," *Mind*, 1:69–74, 1963.

20. LITMAN, "Acutely Suicidal Patients."

21. FARBEROW and PALMER, "The Nurse's Role"; SHNEIDMAN, "Preventing Suicide."

22. S. M. HEILIG and D. J. KLUGMAN, "The Social Worker in a Suicide Prevention Center," in *National Conference on Social Welfare: Social Work Practice*, Vol. 2 (New York: Columbia University Press, 1963).

23. R. E. LITMAN, "Medical-Legal Aspects of Suicide," *Washburn Law Journal*, 6:395–401, 1967.

24. P. PRETZEL, *Suicide and Religion*, Claremont School of Theology, Th.D. Thesis, 1966; E. S. SHNEIDMAN, "The Clergy's Responsibility in Suicide Prevention," in *Preventive Mental Hygiene and the Clergy*, Alameda County Mental Health Service, 1960.

25. R. E. LITMAN, "Immobilization Response to Suicidal Behavior," *Journal of American Medical Association Archives of General Psychiatry*, 11:282–285, 1964.

26. TABACHNICK, "Observations on Attempted Suicide."

27. N. D. TABACHNICK, "Interpersonal Relations in Suicide Attempts," *Archives of General Psychiatry*, 4:16–21, 1961.

28. N. D. TABACHNICK, "Some Observations on Counter-Transference Crises in Suicidal Attempts," *Archives of General Psychiatry*, 4:572–578, 1961.

29. N. D. TABACHNICK, "Failure and Masochism," *American Journal of Psychotherapy*, 18:304, 1964.

30. R. E. LITMAN, "Suicide: A Clinical Manifestation of Acting Out," in L. E. ABT and S. L. WEISSMAN (eds.), *Acting Out* (New York: Grune and Stratton, 1965).

31. FARBEROW and SHNEIDMAN, *The Cry for Help*.

32. R. E. LITMAN, "Emergency Response to Potential Suicide," *Journal of Michigan Medical Society*, 62:68–72, 1963.

33. SHNEIDMAN and FARBEROW, "Comparison Between Genuine and Simulated Suicide Notes."

34. FARBEROW, "Personality Patterns"; SHNEIDMAN and FARBEROW, "TAT Heroes."

35. SHNEIDMAN and FARBEROW, "A Sociopsychological Investigation."

36. R. E. LITMAN, "When Patients Commit Suicide," *American Journal of Psychotherapy*, 19:570–576, 1965.

37. SHNEIDMAN and FARBEROW, *Clues to Suicide*.

38. E. S. SHNEIDMAN and N. L. FARBEROW, *Suicide Prevention Center* (Los Angeles: University of Southern California Press, 1961).

39. R. E. LITMAN, E. S. SHNEIDMAN, and N. L. FARBEROW, "Suicide Prevention Center," *American Journal of Psychiatry*, 117:1084–1087, 1961; and in J. H. MASSERMAN (ed.), *Current Psychiatric Therapies* (New York: Grune and Stratton, 1961).

40. SHNEIDMAN and FARBEROW, "The Los Angeles Suicide Prevention Center."

41. N. L. FARBEROW, R. E. LITMAN, E. S. SHNEIDMAN, S. M. HEILIG, C. I. WOLD, and J. KRAMER, "Suicide Prevention Around the Clock," *American Journal of Orthopsychiatry*, 36:551–558, 1966.

42. M. KAPHAN and R. E. LITMAN, "Telephone Appraisal of 100 Suicidal Emergencies," *American Journal of Psychotherapy*, 16: 591–599, 1962.

43. E. S. SHNEIDMAN and N. L. FARBEROW, *Suicide—The Problem and Its Magnitude* (Washington, D.C.: Department of Medicine and Surgery, Veterans Administration, *Medical Bulletin 7*, 1961).

44. E. S. SHNEIDMAN, "Suicidal Phenomena: Their Definition and Classification," in *International Encyclopedia of the Social Sciences* (New York: The Macmillan Company, 1968).

46. E. S. SHNEIDMAN and N. L. FARBEROW, "Suicide and Death," in H. FEIFEL (ed.), *The Meaning of Death* (New York: McGraw-Hill Book Company, 1959).

47. N. L. FARBEROW, "Therapy in the Suicidal Crisis," in E. S. SHNEIDMAN (ed.), *Essays in Self-Destruction* (New York: Science House, 1967).

48. N. D. TABACHNICK and N. L. FARBEROW, "The Assessment of Self-destructive Potentiality," in FARBEROW and SHNEIDMAN (eds.), *The Cry for Help*.

49. E. S. SHNEIDMAN, "Some Logical, Psychological, and Ecological Environments of Suicide," *California Health*, 17:193, 1960; E. S. SHNEIDMAN, "Psycho-logic: A Personality Approach to Patterns of Thinking," in J. KAGAN and G. LESSOR (eds.), *Contemporary Issues in Thematic Appreception Methods* (Springfield, Illinois: *Charles C Thomas*, 1961).

50. E. S. SHNEIDMAN, "Orientations Toward Death: A Vital Aspect of the Study of Lives," in R. W. WHITE (ed.), *The Study of Lives* (New York: Atherton Press, 1963), and *International Journal of Psychiatry*, 2:167–200, 1966.

51. N. D. TABACHNICK and R. E. LITMAN, "Character and Life Circumstances in Fatal Accident," *Psychoanalytic Forum*, 1:66, 1966.

52. E. S. SHNEIDMAN, "Suicide, Sleep, and Death: Some Possible Interrelations Among Cessation, Interruption and Continuation

Phenomena," *Journal of Consulting Psychology*, 28:95, 1964; E.
S. SHNEIDMAN, "Sleep and Self-Destruction: A Phenomenological
Study," in SHNEIDMAN (ed.), *Essays in Self-Destruction*.

53. R. E. LITMAN, "Sigmund Freud on Suicide," in SHNEIDMAN
(ed.), *Essays in Self-Destruction*.

54. FARBEROW, "Therapy in Suicidal Crisis"; N. L. FARBEROW (ed.),
Suicide and Its Prevention: Proceedings of the Fourth International Conference for Suicide Prevention (Los Angeles, California: Delmar Publishing Company, 1968); FARBEROW, LITMAN,
SHNEIDMAN, HEILIG, WOLD, and KRAMER, "Suicide Prevention
Around the Clock"; FARBEROW, SHNEIDMAN, and LITMAN, "The
Suicidal Patient and the Physician"; KAPHAN and LITMAN, "Telephone Appraisal"; LITMAN, "Emergency Response to Potential
Suicide"; LITMAN, "Immobilization Response"; LITMAN, "Suicide:
A Clinical Manifestation of Acting Out"; LITMAN, "When Patients
Commit Suicide"; LITMAN, "Acutely Suicidal Patients"; SCHRUT,
"Suicidal Adolescents"; SHNEIDMAN, "Preventing Suicide";
TABACHNICK, "Observations on Attempted Suicide"; TABACHNICK, "Interpersonal Relations"; TABACHNICK, "Some Observations on Counter-Transference Crises in Suicidal Attempts";
TABACHNICK, "Failure and Masochism"; TABACHNICK and
FARBEROW, "The Assessment of Self-Destructive Potentiality";
TABACHNICK and KLUGMAN, "No Name."

55. R. E. LITMAN, T. CURPHEY, E. S. SHNEIDMAN, N. L. FARBEROW,
and N. TABACHNICK, "Investigations of Equivocal Suicides,"
Journal of the American Medical Association, 184:924–929, 1963;
E. S. SHNEIDMAN and N. L. FARBEROW, "Sample Investigations of
Equivocal Suicidal Deaths," in FARBEROW and SHNEIDMAN (eds.),
The Cry for Help.

56. T. J. CURPHEY, "The Role of the Social Scientist in the Medicolegal Certification of Death from Suicide," in FARBEROW and
SHNEIDMAN (eds.), *The Cry for Help*; T. J. CURPHEY, "The Forensic Pathologist and the Multi-Disciplinary Approach to Death,"
in SHNEIDMAN (ed.), *Essays in Self-Destruction*.

57. S. M. HEILIG, N. L. FARBEROW, R. E. LITMAN, and E. S. SHNEIDMAN, "The Role of Non-Professional Volunteers in a Suicide
Prevention Center," *Community Mental Health Journal*, 4:287–
295, 1968.

58. FARBEROW, "Suicide and Its Prevention"; FARBEROW, LITMAN, SHNEIDMAN, HEILIG, WOLD, and KRAMER, "Suicide Prevention Around the Clock"; FARBEROW and PALMER, "The Nurse's Role"; HEILIG and KLUGMAN, "The Social Worker in a Suicide Prevention Center"; LITMAN, SHNEIDMAN, and FARBEROW, "Suicide Prevention Center"; Pretzel, *Suicide and Religion*; SHNEIDMAN, "The Clergy's Responsibility"; SHNEIDMAN and FARBEROW, *Suicide Prevention Center*.

59. K. BJERG, "The Suicidal Life-Space: Attempts at a Reconstruction," in SHNEIDMAN (ed.), *Essays in Self-Destruction*.

60. W. BREED, "Suicide and Loss in Social Interaction," in SHNEIDMAN (ed.), *Essays in Self-Destruction*.

61. J. CHORON, "Death as a Motive of Philosophic Thought," in SHNEIDMAN (ed.), *Essays in Self-Destruction*.

62. J. C. DIGGORY, "The Components of Personal Despair," in SHNEIDMAN (ed.), *Essays in Self-Destruction*.

63. H. GARFINKEL, "On Practical Sociological Reasoning: Some Features in the Work of the Los Angeles Suicide Prevention Center," in SHNEIDMAN (ed.), *Essays in Self-Destruction*.

64. G. HEARD, "Buddha and Self-Destruction," in SHNEIDMAN (ed.), *Essays in Self-Destruction*.

65. S. C. PEPPER, "Can a Philosophy Make One Philosophical?" in SHNEIDMAN (ed.), *Essays in Self-Destruction*.

66. H. SACKS, "The Search for Help: No One to Turn To," in SHNEIDMAN (ed.), *Essays in Self-Destruction*.

67. E. WHALLEY, "Values and Value-Conflict in Self-Destruction: Implications in the Work of C. W. Morris," in SHNEIDMAN (ed.), *Essays in Self-Destruction*.

68. SHNEIDMAN, *Essays in Self-Destruction*.

69. N. L. FARBEROW, "The Psychology of Suicide," in *International Encyclopedia of the Social Sciences* (New York: 1968); SHNEIDMAN, "Suicidal Phenomena."

70. SHNEIDMAN, "Orientations Toward Death."

71. N. L. FARBEROW (ed.), *Taboo Topics* (New York: Atherton Press, 1963).

72. E. S. SHNEIDMAN, "Suicide: A Taboo Topic," in FARBEROW (ed.), *Taboo Topics*.

Chapter 6

1. L. BELLAK (ed.), *Handbook of Community Psychiatry and Community Mental Health* (New York: Grune and Stratton, 1964).

2. *Ibid.*, p. 5.

3. MARJORIE FRANK, "Volunteers in Mental Hospitals," *Psychiatry Quarterly Supplement,* Part 1, 22:111–124, 1948; "Volunteer Work with Psychiatric Patients," *Mental Hygiene,* 33:353–365, 1949.

4. A. H. FECHNER and J. H. PARKE, "The Volunteer Worker and the Psychiatric Hospital," *American Journal of Psychiatry,* 107: 602–606, 1951.

5. RUTH EVANS, "Volunteers in Mental Hospitals," *Mental Hygiene,* 39:111–117, 1955.

6. J. N. HADDOCK and H. D. DUNDON, "Volunteer Work in a State Hospital by College Students," *Mental Hygiene,* 35:599–603, 1951.

7. D. T. LEE, "A New Dimension for Volunteers," *Mental Hygiene,* 46:273–282, 1962.

8. D. J. VAIL and MIRIAM KARLINS, "A Decade of Volunteer Services: History and Social Significance," *International Journal of Social Psychiatry,* 11:105–109, 1965.

9. *Ibid.*, p. 108.

10. CATHERINE A. MILLS, "Training of Volunteers," in *The Development of Standards and Training Curriculum for Volunteer Services Coordinators* (Washington, D.C.: American Psychiatric Association, 1964).

11. BELLAK, *op. cit.*

12. N. BECKENSTEIN, "The New State Hospital," in BELLAK (ed.), *Handbook of Community Psychiatry and Community Mental Health.*

13. J. BIERER, "The Mariborough Experiment," in BELLAK (ed.), *Handbook of Community Psychiatry and Community Mental Health.*

14. BELLAK, *op. cit.*, p. 281.

15. MAYA PINES, "The Coming Upheaval in Psychiatry," *Harper's Magazine,* October 1965, 54–60.

16. MARGARET RIOCH, CHARMIAN ELKES, and A. A. FLINT, "A Pilot Project in Training of Mental Health Counselors," *Public*

Health Service Publication No. 1254 (Washington, D.C.: U. S. Department of Health, Education and Welfare, undated).

17. MARGARET RIOCH, CHARMIAN ELKES, A. A. FLINT, BLANCHE S. USDAUSKY, RUTH G. NORMAN, and E. SILBER, "National Institute of Mental Health Pilot Study in Training Mental Health Counselors," *American Journal of Orthopsychiatry*, 33:678–689, 1963.

Chapter 7

1. E. DURKHEIM, *Suicide*, trans. J. A. SPAULDING and G. SIMPSON (New York: Free Press of Glencoe, 1951; original, 1897).
2. H. HENDIN, "Psychodynamic Motivational Factors in Suicide," *Psychiatric Quarterly*, 25:672–678, 1951.
3. G. U. YULE and N. KENDALL, *An Introduction to the Theory of Statistics* (New York: Hafner, 1950).
4. T. J. CURPHEY, "The Role of the Social Scientist in the Medicolegal Certification of Death from Suicide," in N. L. FARBEROW and E. S. SHNEIDMAN (eds.), *The Cry for Help* (New York: McGraw-Hill Book Company, 1961).
5. JEANNE L. BRAND, *Private Support for Mental Health: A Study of the Support, by Foundations and Other Private National Granting Agencies, for Mental Health and Related Disciplines* (Washington, D.C.: U.S. Government Printing Office), Public Health Service Publication No. 838, 35¢. This pamphlet gives the name, address, assets, types of support, and fields of interest in mental health for each of 142 foundations.

Chapter 8

1. L. I. DUBLIN, *Suicide: A Sociological and Statistical Study* (New York: Ronald Press, 1963).
2. E. ROBINS, J. GASSNER, J. KAYES, R. H. WILKINSON, JR., and G. E. MURPHY, "The Communication of Suicidal Intent: A Study of 134 Consecutive Cases of Successful (Completed) Suicides," *American Journal of Psychiatry*, 115:724–733, 1959; J. TUCKMAN, R. J. KLEINER, and M. LAVELL, "Emotional Content of Suicide Notes," *American Journal of Psychiatry*, 116:59–63, 1959; E. STENGEL and NANCY G. COOK, *Attempted Suicide: Its Social*

Significance and Effects, Maudsley Monograph No. 4 (London: Chapman and Hall, Ltd., 1958).

Chapter 9

1. O. H. MOWRER, *Psychotherapy: Theory and Research* (New York: The Ronald Press Company, 1953).
2. E. S. SHNEIDMAN and N. L. FARBEROW (eds.), *Clues to Suicide* (New York: McGraw-Hill Book Company, 1957).
3. We wish to thank the personnel of the Los Angeles County Coroner's Office, particularly Messrs. Ben Brown, Victor Wallage, Forrest A. Huntley, and the late William G. McFarlane.
4. The work of Gordon Allport on personal documents and of Berelson on content analysis in communication research are relevant here. G. A. ALLPORT, "The Use of Personal Documents in Psychological Science," *Social Science Research Council Bulletin*, No. 49, 1942; B. BERELSON, *Content Analysis in Communication Research* (Glencoe, Illinois: The Free Press, 1952).
5. G. U. YULE and N. KENDALL, *An Introduction to the Theory of Statistics* (New York: Hafner, 1950).
6. O. H. MOWRER, personal communication, 1954.
7. H. L. ANSBACHER, personal communication, 1956.

Chapter 10

1. The remainder of the notes were from non-Caucasian or foreign-born persons. Some notes by persons below age twenty were excluded because there were so few. Another group consisted of a number of notes randomly selected and held out for a cross-validation study.
2. K. A. MENNINGER, *Man Against Himself* (New York: Harcourt, Brace and Company, 1938).
3. G. U. YULE and N. KENDALL, *An Introduction to the Theory of Statistics* (New York: Hafner, 1950).

Chapter 11

1. J. D. HOLZBERG, E. R. CAHEN, and E. K. WILK, "Suicide: Psychological Study of Self-Destruction," *Journal of Projective Techniques*, 15:339–354, 1951.

2. S. S. TOMKINS, *The Thematic Apperception Test* (New York: Grune and Stratton, 1947).

3. E. M. RIZZO, "Un Caso di Tentato Suicidio; Narcoanalisi, Rorschach, TAT, Daseinanalyse" ("A Case of Attempted Suicide, Narcoanalysis, Rorschach Test, TAT, and Existential Analysis"), *Rassegno di Studi Psichiatrici,* 43:685–717, 1954.

4. T. C. KAHN, "A Comparison of the Clinical Data Yielded by a Test of Symbol Arrangement with Other Findings of Two Attempt Suicide Patients," *American Psychologist,* 7:532 (Abstract), 1952.

5. D. C. BROIDA, "An Investigation of Certain Psychodiagnostic Indications of Suicidal Tendencies and Depression in Mental Hospital Patients," *Psychiatric Quarterly,* 28:453–464, 1954. There is an interesting published exchange of notes in relation to Broida's study. In the TAT *Newsletter* Broida wrote: "I used only card 3BM of the Murray TAT to test the specific hypothesis that has been advanced by D. Rapaport (*Diagnostic Psychological Testing,* Volume II [page 422]) viz., that Card 3BM usually reveals preoccupation with and causes of depression and suicide. The study was undertaken to determine the incidence of suicidal and depressive themes on this particular card as produced by a group of known suicidal patients. For this purpose I obtained responses to the above card from twenty nonsuicidal patients, equated with the former group as to age, diagnostic classification, educational level, etc. . . . From a cursory analysis there appears to be no difference between the two groups in terms of frequency of themes involving suicide. I have not subjectively analyzed the themes for frequency or type of depressive ideation. Suicide is the essential theme in about three or four of the productions of the suicide group. Thus it appears that suicidal themes on the card might very well be an artifact of the stimulus value of the card *per se,* rather than a reflection of the needs and press or the dynamics of the individual." D. C. BROIDA, Letter in *TAT Newsletter,* 4:3–4, 1950; also printed in *Journal of Projective Techniques,* 14:205–206, 1950. To all this, Rapaport replied in a subsequent issue of the *TAT Newsletter* as follows:

"I think many of us will consider it a commonplace that a group of patients who later commit suicide, or patients who are rife with suicidal ideas, may give as many and no more outright

suicidal responses to a stimulus implying suicide as any other group of patients, or even normal persons. I believe that we generally assume that this happens because: (a) the fundamental impulses which underlie suicide are present—though in different constellations, and intensities—in all of us; (b) the controls prompting dissimulation, suppression, repression, denial, or reaction formation to such dynamic factors and corresponding ideas are also present in all of us. A second misunderstanding seems to lie in the conception of what constitutes 'revealing a preoccupation.' If somebody, for instance, blocks on the suicidal picture, that is, as revealing for the analysis of an individual case as a direct self-reference, and the both of them are far more revealing than a story with suicidal content—provided that the self-reference and the blocking (I could add here perceptual misrecognition, extreme elaboration of the story, etc., in other words, interpersonal deviations) are clearly inconsistent with the patient's handling of the rest of his own stories. . . . All we (i.e., Rapaport, Gill, and Schafer) meant when describing to what topic a card—in our experience—refers, was to point out what the examiner should look out for, where he should begin to make a hypothesis which he is to verify or falsify thereafter from the rest of the TAT protocol and the other available data." D. RAPAPORT, Letter in *TAT Newsletter*, 4:2, 1950. (Also printed in *Journal of Projective Techniques*, 14:472, 1950.)

6. H. B. CRASILNECK, "An Analysis of Differences Between Suicidal and Pseudo-Suicidal Patients through the Use of Projective Techniques," unpublished doctoral dissertation, University of Houston, 1954. There are two references to suicide using a technique closely related to the TAT, namely the Make-A-Picture-Story (MAPS) test. In the manual for the MAPS test there is a chapter on the suicidal male adult that reproduces one protocol of a 21-year-old serious suicidal threat, and Farberow, using the MAPS test in his research on thirty-two each hospitalized attempted suicides, threatened suicides, and psychiatric nonsuicidal (control) subjects, found interesting differences among the Threats, Attempts, and Controls and between the Serious (Attempts or Threats) and Nonserious cases. N. L. FARBEROW, "Personality Patterns of Suicidal Mental Hospital Patients," *Genetic Psychology Monographs*, 42:3-79, 1950.

7. TOMKINS, *op. cit.*

8. E. S. SHNEIDMAN (ed.), *Thematic Test Analysis* (New York: Grune and Stratton, 1951).

9. Paridiction involves correlation with *present* criteria, in the same sense as prediction and postdiction involve future and past criteria, respectively; E. S. SHNEIDMAN, "A Method for Educing the Present Correlates of Perception: An Introduction to the Method of Successive Covariation," *Journal of General Psychology*, 57:113–120, 1957.

10. I. FRIEDMAN, "Phenomenal, Ideal, and Projected Conceptions of Self," *Journal of Abnormal and Social Psychology*, 51:611–615, 1955; "Objectifying the Subjective: A Methodological Approach to the TAT," *Journal of Projective Techniques*, 21:243–247, 1957; "Characteristics of the TAT Heroes of Normal, Psychoneurotic, and Paranoid Schizophrenic Subjects," *Journal of Projective Techniques*, 21:372–376, 1957.

11. H. A. MURRAY, *Thematic Apperception Test Manual* (Cambridge, Massachusetts: Harvard University Press, 1943).

12. Of this number, six protocols were used solely in relation to a reliability substudy, reported under "Results," below.

13. FRIEDMAN, "Characteristics of the TAT Heroes."

14. E. S. SHNEIDMAN, "The Logic of Suicide," in E. S. SHNEIDMAN and N. L. FARBEROW (eds.), *Clues to Suicide* (New York: McGraw-Hill Book Company, 1957).

15. We are happy to extend our appreciation to Dr. Albert E. Ross, Dr. Harvey Ross, and Mr. Channing Orbach, clinical psychologists, who tested the attempted suicide subjects and obtained the TAT (and other test) protocols.

16. The other psychological tests are the Rorschach, Make-A-Picture-Story (MAPS) test, Sentence Completion form (devised by Carl H. Saxe), the Minnesota Multiphasic Personality Inventory (MMPI), and the authors' "Make Believe Situations Test." This last test consists of four questions in which the subject is asked (1) to indicate what he thinks he will be doing five years from now, (2) how he would describe himself if he were writing a novel about himself, (3) what suicide note he would write if he were going to take his own life (and were going to leave a note), and (4) what he would do if he had a million dollars. The most important question in this study, of course, relates

to the elicited or simulated suicide note, desired for comparison with several hundred genuine suicide notes we have collected. E. S. SHNEIDMAN and N. L. FARBEROW, "Comparison Between Genuine and Simulated Suicide Notes by Means of Mowrer's DRQ," *Journal of General Psychology*, 56:251–256, 1957; SHNEIDMAN, "The Logic of Suicide."

17. We are pleased to express our appreciation to Dr. Norman Tabachnick, psychiatrist, who obtained the anamnestic interview data from the attempted suicide subjects.

18. W. S. STEPHENSON, *The Study of Behavior* (Chicago, Illinois: University of Chicago Press, 1953).

19. The statistical procedures are essentially those of the Pearson correlation coefficient. One great advantage in using the Q-sort is that, of course, all the means and all the standard deviations are equal. In this case, N was 80, the mean was 4.0, and the standard deviation was 2.06. By reducing the formula for r, it gave us the following formula:

$$r_{xy} = \frac{\Sigma XY - 1280}{340}$$

The data were coded on IBM cards and the Correlations were run electronically.

20. We wish to take this opportunity to express our very deep appreciation to Dr. Ira Friedman, Psychologist at the Cleveland Psychiatric Institute and Hospital, for making available to us his Q-sort data for his forty-eight normal, neurotic, and psychotic nonsuicidal subjects that he had previously done, and for his vast labor and patience in doing the Q-sortings for the fifty-one subjects that we sent him in connection with this study.

21. FRIEDMAN, "Characteristics of the TAT Heroes."

22. A sample of a half dozen of Friedman's eighty Q-sort items can be given: (1) ambitious, (2) works hard to achieve a desired goal, (3) discouraged over lack of success, (4) capable, (5) believes in business before pleasure, (6) an independent person. A complete listing of the eighty items may be found in one of Friedman's reports (FRIEDMAN, "Objectifying the Subjective.")

23. Our appreciation is expressed to Dr. Joseph A. Gengerelli, Professor of Psychology, UCLA, for his help to us in thinking through the statistical procedures employed in this study. We

also wish to thank Mr. Al DeVries, UCLA Graduate Student in Psychology, for computing the statistical correlations.

24. These six subjects are described in greater detail in another publication, in which the B' Subjects are No.'s 206, 207, and 209, and C' Subjects are No.'s 210, 211, 212. K. B. LITTLE and E. S. SHNEIDMAN, "Congruencies Among Interpretations of Psychological Test and Anamnestic Data," *Psychological Monographs,* **73**: 1–42, 1959.

25. FRIEDMAN, "Characteristics of the TAT Heroes."

26. It should be indicated that a direct comparison between our within-group correlations and Friedman's within-group correlations may be handicapped inasmuch as in the present study each individual (within a specific group) was correlated with every other individual in that group, whereas Friedman's statistics (in which the Wilcoxon Matched-Pairs Signed-Ranks Method was used) are based on a sample of eight pairs of correlations within each group.

27. S. SIEGAL, *Nonparametric Statistics for the Behavioral Sciences* (New York: McGraw-Hill Book Company, 1956).

28. FRIEDMAN, "Characteristics of the TAT Heroes."

29. Again, it should be indicated that Friedman's between-groups correlations for each of his three comparisons were based on thirty-two pairs each, whereas in the present study the complete sample was statistically treated. E. g., in comparing Groups A and B (where each group had sixteen individuals) we computed 256 correlations. A total of 3,640 correlations were computed (by use of electronic equipment) to obtain the between-groups statistics.

30. J. P. GUILFORD, *Fundamental Statistics in Psychology and Education* (3rd ed.; New York: McGraw-Hill Book Company, 1956).

31. M. H. GORDON, E. H. LOVELAND, and E. E. CURETON, "An Extended Table for Chi-square for Two Degrees of Freedom for Use in Combined Probabilities from Independent Samples," *Psychometrika,* **17**:311–316, 1952.

32. It is interesting to compare the significant items listed in Table XV (characteristic of Groups A, B, E, and F) with those items that Friedman lists as more characteristic of his normals than neurotics, more characteristic of his neurotics than his normals, more characteristic of his normals than psychotics, and more

characteristic of his psychotics than the normals. It would appear that there is relatively little overlap between Friedman's findings and the present set of results.

33. It would appear that the most obvious differences occurred between the sortings for the heroes of *male vs. female* subjects, and, next in order, between the sortings for the heroes of *normal vs. disturbed* (but not necessarily suicidal) subjects.

34. LITTLE and SHNEIDMAN, "Congruencies Among Interpretations of Psychological Test and Anamnestic Data."

Chapter 12

1. N. L. FARBEROW, "The Psychology of Suicide," *International Encyclopedia of the Social Sciences* (New York, 1967) ; A. ROSEN, "Detection of Suicidal Patients: An Example of Some Limitations in the Prediction of Infrequent Events," *Journal of Consulting Psychology*, 18:397–403, 1954.

2. E. DURKHEIM, *Suicide*, trans. J. A. SPAULDING and G. SIMPSON (Glencoe, Illinois: The Free Press, 1951; original, 1897).

3. RUTH S. CAVAN, *Suicide* (Chicago, Illinois: University of Chicago Press, 1926).

4. C. F. SCHMID, "Suicide in Seattle, 1914–1925: An Ecological and Behavioristic Study," *University of Washington Publications in the Social Sciences* (Seattle: University of Washington Press, 1928) ; "Suicide in Seattle, Washington, and Pittsburgh, Pennsylvania: A Comparative Study," *University of Pittsburgh Bulletin*, 27:149–157, 1930; "Suicide in Minneapolis, Minnesota: 1928–1932," *American Journal of Sociology*, 39:30–48, 1933.

5. P. SAINSBURY, *Suicide in London: An Ecological Study* (New York: Basic Books, 1955).

6. P. M. YAP, *Suicide in Hong Kong* (London: Oxford University Press, 1958).

7. A. F. HENRY and J. F. SHORT, JR., *Suicide and Homicide* (Glencoe, Illinois: The Free Press, 1954).

8. L. I. DUBLIN and BESSIE BUNZEL, *To Be or Not to Be* (New York: Random House, 1933).

9. E. STENGEL and NANCY G. COOK, *Attempted Suicide: Its Social Significance and Effects*, Maudsley Monograph No. 4 (London: Chapman and Hall, Limited, 1958).

10. Los Angeles County has an area of 4,083 square miles and a fairly heterogeneous population of over five million persons. A comprehensive overview of the characteristics of the Los Angeles County population is presented in *Background for Planning* (Welfare Planning Council, 1955, No. 15).

11. T. L. DORPAT, H. S. RIPLEY, and R. LEIDIG, *A Study of Suicide in Seattle*; J. A. MOTTO and CLARA GREENE, "Suicide and the Medical Community," *American Medical Association Archives of Neurology and Psychiatry*, 80:776–781, 1958; E. ROBINS, J. GASSNER, J. KAYES, R. H. WILKINSON, JR., and G. E. MURPHY, "The Communication of Suicidal Intent: A Study of 134 Consecutive Cases of Successful (Completed) Suicides," *American Journal of Psychiatry*, 115:724–733, 1959; D. J. VAIL, "Suicide and Medical Responsibility," *American Journal of Psychiatry*, 15: 1005–1010, 1959.

12. The letter was sent out to physicians in May, 1958. The numbers and percentages of attempted suicide reported in this paper are proportionate (twelve-sixteenths) to estimate the data for the twelve months of 1957 in order to compare them with other data.

13. DUBLIN and BUNZEL, *op. cit.*

14. STENGEL and COOK, *op. cit.*

15. At the SPC, we make an effort to obtain such data by asking the person we are working with to duplicate his note or to write the note he would have written.

16. E. S. SHNEIDMAN and N. L. FARBEROW, "Comparison Between Genuine and Simulated Suicide Notes by Means of Mowrer's DRQ," *Journal of General Psychology*, 56:251-256, 1957; "A Sociopsychological Investigation of Suicide," in H. P. DAVID and J. C. BRENGELMANN (eds.), *Perspectives in Personality Research* (New York: Basic Books, 1960).

17. SHNEIDMAN and FARBEROW, "A Sociopsychological Investigation of Suicide."

18. In another publication, we compared for 1957 (1) the sociological data for each of these same nine area types with (2) suicidal information, that is, number of suicides, sex distribution, race, marital status, and the like for the area type and with (3) psychological information, or data concerning the emotions, quality of interpersonal relationships, and the like of persons

who committed suicide in each of the area types as obtained from an analysis of 948 *suicide notes* for the 3-year period, 1956–1958. The major finding of that study was that both sociological and psychological factors were important and necessary in understanding suicidal phenomena. In other words, *both* Durkheim and Freud were right; suicidal incidents can be understood best as events neither exclusively of the psyche nor exclusively of society but as an admixture of both, as sociopsychological phenomena.

19. *Background for Planning: Differentiating Communities in Los Angeles County* (Los Angeles: Welfare Planning Council, 1957); *Fact Sheets on 100 Study Areas, Los Angeles County, 1957* (Los Angeles: Welfare Planning Council, 1957).

Chapter 13

1. E. DURKHEIM, *Suicide*, trans. J. A. SPAULDING and G. SIMPSON (Glencoe, Illinois: The Free Press, 1951; original, 1897).

2. RUTH S. CAVAN, *Suicide* (Chicago, Illinois: University of Chicago Press, 1926).

3. C. F. SCHMID, "Suicide in Seattle, 1914–1925: An Ecological and Behavioristic Study," *University of Washington Publications in The Social Sciences* (Seattle: University of Washington Press, 1928); "Suicide in Minneapolis, Minnesota: 1928–1932," *American Journal of Sociology*, 39:30–48, 1933.

4. P. SAINSBURY, *Suicide in London: An Ecological Study* (New York: Basic Books, 1955).

5. L. I. DUBLIN and BESSIE BUNZEL, *To Be or Not to Be* (New York: Random House, 1933).

6. A. F. HENRY and J. F. SHORT, JR., *Suicide and Homicide* (Glencoe, Illinois: The Free Press, 1954).

7. The standard error of proportion was significant beyond the .01 level.

8. The chi square value was at the .05 level of significance.

9. The chi square value was at the .02 level of significance.

10. W. MORGENTHALER and M. STEINBERG, "Letzte Aufzeichnungen von Selbstmordern," *Beihefte zur Schweizerischen Zeitschrift für Psychologie und ihre Anwendungen*, No. 1, 1945.

11. E. S. SHNEIDMAN and N. L. FARBEROW, "Comparison Between

Genuine and Simulated Suicide Notes by Means of Mowrer's DRQ," *Journal of General Psychology,* 56:251–256, 1957.

12. J. TUCKMAN, R. J. KLEINER, and M. LAVELL, "Emotional Content of Suicide Notes," *American Journal of Psychiatry,* 116:59–63, 1959.

13. C. E. OSGOOD and EVELYN G. WALKER, "Motivation and Language Behavior: A Content Analysis of Suicide Notes," *Journal of Abnormal and Social Psychology,* 57:58–67, 1959.

14. Reference to the figures published by Guetzkow gives the least value that p—the probability that an item has been consistently categorized—might take 99 times out of 100 as .90; that is, the probability that an item has been incorrectly categorized would be as high as .10 only one time in one hundred. Such a figure may be considered as indicative of adequate reliability. H. GUETZKOW, "Unitizing and Categorizing Problems in Coding Qualitative Data," *Journal of Clinical Psychology,* 6:47–58, 1950.

15. E. S. SHNEIDMAN and N. L. FARBEROW (eds.), *Clues to Suicide* (New York: McGraw-Hill Book Company, 1957).

16. TUCKMAN, KLEINER, and LAVELL, *op. cit.*

17. The chi square for the differences among the nine Area Types for Reasons was significant at the .01 level of significance (indicating that these results could have occurred by chance only one time in 100) and the chi square for Affect was significant at the .05 level.

18. A. C. KINSEY, W. B. POMEROY, and C. E. MARTIN, *Sexual Behavior in the Human Male* (Philadelphia, Pennsylvania: Saunders, 1948); A. C. KINSEY, W. B. POMEROY, C. E. MARTIN, and P. H. GEBHARD, *Sexual Behavior in the Human Female* (Philadelphia, Pennsylvania: Saunders, 1953).

19. A. B. HOLLINGSHEAD and F. C. REDLICH, *Social Class and Mental Illness* (New York: John Wiley and Sons, 1958).

Chapter 14

1. E. S. SHNEIDMAN and N. L. FARBEROW (eds.), *Clues to Suicide* (New York: McGraw-Hill Book Company, 1957).

2. Since an understanding of the results of this study is not contingent upon a full understanding of the dictionary that was

used, a complete presentation of the tag categories will not be undertaken here.

3. For the most part, genuine notes were longer than simulated notes. Thus, even though more THINK sentences were retrieved from the genuine set, the percentage difference of such sentences remains in the simulated note writers' favor.

4. L. A. GOTTSCHALK and GOLDINE GLESER, "An Analysis of the Verbal Content of Suicide Notes," *British Journal of Medical Psychology*, 33:195–204, 1960.

Chapter 17

1. R. E. LITMAN, "Immobilization Response to Suicidal Behavior," *Journal of American Medical Association Archives of General Psychiatry*, 11:282–285, 1964.

2. R. E. LITMAN, E. S. SHNEIDMAN, and N. L. FARBEROW, "Suicide Prevention Center," *American Journal of Psychiatry*, 117:1084–1087, 1961, and in J. H. MASSERMAN (ed.), *Current Psychiatric Therapies* (New York: Grune and Stratton, 1961).

3. R. E. LITMAN, N. L. FARBEROW, E. S. SHNEIDMAN, S. M. HEILIG, and J. A. KRAMER, "Suicide Prevention Telephone Service," *Journal of American Medical Association*, 192:21–25, 1965.

4. R. E. LITMAN, T. CURPHEY, E. S. SHNEIDMAN, N. L. FARBEROW, and N. TABACHNICK, "Investigations of Equivocal Suicides," *Journal of American Medical Association*, 184:924–929, 1963.

5. L. BELLAK, "Acting-Out: Some Conceptual and Therapeutic Considerations," *American Journal of Psychotherapy*, 17:375–389, 1963.

6. From a prognostic standpoint, it would appear that the person who thinks through (or "rehearses") his intent in a "step-by-step" fashion is much more likely to act out than one who simply reflects on the possibility. This point needs further research.

7. This is particularly true if the loved person's death was by suicide.

8. One is reminded of Roger's keen observation that even a judgment of "good" can be threatening since it implies the power to make the judgment of "bad" at a later time.

9. A frequent phenomenon among individuals who feel an increased sense of "loss of reality" or "depersonalization"—the primary

purpose of the act being not to commit suicide, but to "snap back to reality."

Chapter 18

1. This bulletin is the second in a series of VA publications devoted to the topic of suicide prevention. The first bulletin (MB–7, Mar. 1, 1961), contained material on the definition of suicide, some statistics about suicide, some general suggestions for prevention, and some selected references.
2. Sincere appreciation is extended to Sidney Cohen, M.D., and Robert E. Litman, M.D., who served as consultants for this study and who contributed generously of their time and skill.
3. A comment about the word "schizophrenic" is in order. Ordinarily, the words "schizophrenic suicide" conjure up the image of a psychotic individual who might kill himself in response to a hallucinated command, a delusional thought, or a dereistic impulse. However, one of the findings to emerge from this study was that among the schizophrenic suicide group, the suicide occurred in almost all cases in which there was evidence of *improved* organization and control in the patient. This is contrary to the notion that suicide in schizophrenic patients represents the depth of psychoticlike behavior. The data from the present research indicate rather that the self-destruction was a somewhat organized and planned action by the patient in an apparent effort to extricate himself from what was for him an intolerable life situation from which he could see no other way out. These patients appeared to have their "reasons" for self-destruction (and often gave "hints" of their suicidal intentions), even though they were still clinically schizophrenic at the time. This finding has encouraging implications from the standpoint of identifying prodromal clues to suicide and for the control of suicidal behavior of the schizophrenic patient.

Chapter 19

1. Gratitude is expressed to Dr. Sidney Cohen, who served as consultant in this study.
2. Taken from data for 1959 reported by Biometrics Service of the VA.

Chapter 20

1. N. L. FARBEROW, "Personality Patterns of Suicidal Mental Hospital Patients," *Genetic Psychology Monographs,* 42:3–79, 1950; J. H. MASSERMAN, "A Note on the Dynamics of Suicide," *Diseases of the Nervous System,* 8:324–325, 1947; R. S. MINTZ, *Detection and Management of the Suicidal Patient* (Chicago, Illinois: Disease-a-Month Year Book, Medical Publishers, July 1961) ; E. A. SHIELDS, "Depression, Then Suicide," *American Journal of Nursing,* 46:677–679, 1946; E. STENGEL, "The Risk of Suicide in States of Depression," *Medical Practitioner,* 234:182–184, 1955.
2. N. L. FABBEROW and E. S. SHNEIDMAN; *Interim Unpublished Report No. 3* (Washington, D.C.: Veterans Administration Central Office, 1960).
3. All cases of suicide among patients in Veterans Administration Hospitals are reposited in the Central Research Unit for the Study of Unpredicted Death, Los Angeles.
4. FARBEROW, *op. cit.*
5. The help of Robert Jones, Ronald McDevitt, Dan Sapin, and Bruce Sutkus in preparing abstracts is acknowledged. Calista V. Leonard assisted in the early planning and organization of the study.
6. The "psychological autopsy" technique had been employed in other investigations by the Central Research Unit (schizophrenia, cancer, and respiratory studies) and had been described in detail elsewhere.
7. Dr. Anthony Brunse served as psychiatric consultant. His help is gratefully acknowledged.
8. One of these cases committed suicide sixty-five days after he was discharged from the hospital rolls. To be consistent with the design of the study, however, he is retained in the control population in the analyses.
9. Comparison of the anxiety suicides and the anxiety controls for age, using the Mann-Whitney U test, yielded a U value of 163, which is not significant at the .05 level of confidence. Comparing the depressive suicides and depressive controls for age, using a Mann-Whitney U test, a z score of .072 was obtained, which is associated with a probability level of .47, not significant. Comparisons were also made between all the anxiety cases versus all

the depressive cases. There was no significant difference between the median ages of these two groups.

10. S. COHEN, C. V. LEONARD, N. L. FARBEROW, and E. S. SHNEID-MAN, "Tranquilizers and Suicide in the Schizophrenic Patient," *Archives of General Psychiatry*, 11:312–321, 1964.

11. E. DURKHEIM, *Suicide*, trans. J. A. SPAULDING and G. SIMPSON (Glencoe, Illinois: The Free Press, 1951: original, 1897).

12. E. STENGEL and NANCY G. COOK, *Attempted Suicide: Its Social Significance and Effects*, Maudsley Monograph No. 4 (London: Chapman and Hall, Ltd., 1958).

13. S. EISENTHAL, N. L. FARBEROW, and E. S. SHNEIDMAN, "Follow-up of Neuro-psychiatric Hospital Patients Placed on Suicide Observation Status," *Public Health Reports*, 81:977–990, 1966; R. FOX, "Help for the Despairing," *Lancet*, 2:1102–1105, 1962.

14. N. L. FARBEROW, E. S. SHNEIDMAN, and C. V. LEONARD, *Suicide —Evaluation and Treatment of Suicidal Risk Among Schizophrenic Patients in Psychiatric Hospitals* (Washington, D.C.: Department of Medicine and Surgery, Veterans Administration, *Medical Bulletin 8*, 1962); *Suicide Among General Medical and Surgical Patients with Malignant Neoplasms* (Washington, D.C.: *Veterans Administration, Medical Bulletin 9*, 1963).

15. L. I. DUBLIN, *Suicide: A Sociological and Statistical Study* (New York: Ronald Press, 1963).

16. R. F. CHAPMAN, "Suicide During Psychiatric Hospitalization," *Bulletin Menninger Clinic*, 29:35–44, 1965; A. L. KOBLER and E. STOTLAND, *The End of Hope* (New York: Free Press of Glencoe, 1964).

17. N. S. KLINE, "Comprehensive Therapy of Depressions," *Journal of Neuropsychiatry*, Supplement No. 1, February, 1961.

Chapter 21

1. N. L. FARBEROW, E. S. SHNEIDMAN, and C. V. LEONARD, *Suicide— Evaluation and Treatment of Suicidal Risk Among Schizophrenic Patients in Psychiatric Hospitals* (Washington, D.C.: Department of Medicine and Surgery, Veterans Administration, *Medical Bulletin 8*, 1962); *Suicide Among General Medical and Surgical Hospital Patients with Malignant Neoplasms* (Washington, D.C.: Veterans Administration, *Medical Bulletin 9*, 1963).

2. B. B. BERLE, "Emotional Factors and Tuberculosis: A Critical Review of the Literature," *Psychosomatic Medicine,* 10:366–373, 1948; B. R. MERRILL, "Some Psychosomatic Aspects of Pulmonary Tuberculosis: A Review of the English Language Literature," *Journal of Nervous and Mental Disease,* 117:9–28, 1953; P. J. SPARER (ed.), *Personalitly, Stress and Tuberculosis* (New York: International Universities Press, 1956).

3. CLAIRE M. VERNIER, *et. al.,* "Psychosocial Study of the Patient with Pulmonary Tuberculosis: A Cooperative Research Project," *Psychology Monographs,* 75:32, 1961.

4. G. W. ALBEE, "Psychological Concomitants of Pulmonary Tuberculosis," *American Review of Tuberculosis,* 58:650–661, 1948.

5. N. G. HAWKINS, R. DAVIS, and T. H. HOLMES, "Evidence of Psychosocial Factors in the Development of Pulmonary Tuberculosis," *American Review of Tuberculosis and Pulmonary Diseases,* 75:768–780, 1957.

6. P. H. KNAPP and S. J. NEMETZ, "Acute Bronchial Asthma: I. Concomitant Depression and Excitement, and Varied Antecedent Patterns in 406 Attacks," *Psychosomatic Medicine,* 22:42–55, 1960.

7. B. KRAFT, F. W. COUNTRYMAN, and D. L. BLEMENTHAL, "Suicide by Asthma," *Annals on Allergy,* 17:394–398, 1959.

8. M. W. WEBB and A. H. LAWTON, "Basic Personality Traits Characteristic of Patients With Primary Obstructive Pulmonary Emphysema," *Journal of American Geriatric Society,* 9:590–610, 1961.

9. C. H. DUNCAN and I. P. STEVENSON, "Paroxysmal Arrhythmias: A Psychosomatic Study," *Geriatrics,* 5:259–267, 1950.

10. J. A. ARLOW, "Anxiety Patterns in Angina Pectoris," *Psychosomatic Medicine,* 14:461–468, 1952.

11. S. M. KAPLAN, "Psychological Aspects of Cardiac Disease: A Study of Patients Experiencing Mitral Commissurotomy," *Psychosomatic Medicine,* 18:221–233, 1956.

12. S. L. CLEVELAND and D. L. JOHNSON, "Personality Patterns in Young Males with Coronary Disease," *Psychosomatic Medicine,* 24:600–610, 1962.

13. FARBEROW, SHNEIDMAN, and LEONARD, *Suicide—Evaluation and Treatment of Suicidal Risk Among Schizophrenic Patients in*

Psychiatric Hospitals; Suicide Among General Medical and Surgical Hospital Patients with Malignant Neoplasms.

14. CLEVELAND and JOHNSON, *op. cit.*

15. R. H. DOVENMEUHLE and A. VERWOERDT, "Physical Illness and Depressive Symptomatology: I. Incidence of Depressive Symptoms in Hospitalized Cardiac Patients," *Journal of American Geriatric Society,* 10:932–947, 1962.

16. E. WEISS, *Emotional Factors in Cardiovascular Disease* (Springfield, Illinois: Charles C Thomas, 1951).

Chapter 22

1. H. MORSELLI, *Suicide: An Essay on Comparative Statistics* (New York: Appleton, 1897); E. DURKHEIM, *Suicide,* trans. J. A. SPAULDING and G. SIMPSON (Glencoe, Illinois: The Free Press 1951; original, 1897); M. HALBWACHS, *Les Causes du Suicide* (Paris: Alcan, 1930).

2. RUTH S. CAVAN, *Suicide* (Chicago, Illinois: University of Chicago Press, 1926); C. F. SCHMID and M. D. VAN ARSDOL, JR., "Completed and Attempted Suicides: A Comparative Analysis," *American Sociological Review,* 20:273–283, 1955; P. M. YAP, "Suicide in Hong Kong," *Journal of Mental Science,* 104:266–301, 1958.

3. S. FREUD, "Mourning and Melancholia," in *Collected Papers,* Vol. IV (London: Hogarth Press, 1925); K. A. MENNINGER, *Man Against Himself* (New York: Harcourt, Brace and Company, 1938); N. D. C. LEWIS, "Studies on Suicide. I. Preliminary Survey of Some Significant Aspects of Suicide," *Psychoanalytic Review,* 20:241–273, 1933; "Studies on Suicide. II. Some Comments on the Biological Aspects of Suicide," *Psychoanalytic Review,* 21:146–153, 1934; E. RINGEL, *Der Selbstmord* (Vienna: Maudrich, 1953); E. STENGEL and NANCY G. COOK, *Attempted Suicide: Its Social Signficance and Effects,* Maudsley Monograph No. 4 (London: Chapman and Hall, Ltd., 1958); E. S. SHNEIDMAN, "Orientations Toward Death: A Vital Aspect of the Study of Lives," in R. W. WHITE (ed.), *The Study of Lives* (New York: Atherton Press, 1963), and in *International Journal of Psychiatry,* 2:167–200, 1966; N. L. FARBEROW, "Personality Patterns of Suicidal Mental Hospital Patients," *Genetic Psychology Mono-*

graphs, 42:3–79, 1950; H. Hendin, "Attempted Suicide: A Psychiatric and Statistical Study," *Psychiatric Quarterly,* 24:39–46, 1950; "Psychodynamic Motivational Factors in Suicide," *Psychiatric Quarterly,* 25:672–678, 1951; "Suicide in Denmark," *Psychiatric Quarterly,* 34:443–460, 1960; V. W. JENSEN and T. A. PETTY, "The Fantasy of Being Rescued in Suicide," *Psychoanalytic Quarterly,* 27:327–339, 1958; M. KAPHAN and R. E. LITMAN, "Telephone Appraisal of 100 Suicidal Emergencies," *American Journal of Psychotherapy,* 16:591–599, 1962; C. NEURINGER, "Dichotomous Evaluations in Suicidal Individuals," *Journal of Consulting Psychology,* 25:455–449, 1961; E. S. SHNEIDMAN and N. L. FARBEROW (eds.), *Clues to Suicide* (New York: McGraw-Hill Book Company, 1957).

4. N. L. FARBEROW and E. S. SHNEIDMAN, "A Study of Attempted, Threatened, and Completed Suicides," *Journal of Abnormal and Social Psychology,* 50:230, 1955; N. L. FARBEROW and E. S. SHNEIDMAN (eds.), *The Cry for Help* (New York: McGraw-Hill Book Company, 1961); N. L. FARBEROW, E. S. SHNEIDMAN, and C. V. LEONARD, *Suicide—Evaluation and Treatment of Suicidal Risk Among Schizophrenic Patients in Psychiatric Hospitals* (Washington, D.C.: Department of Medicine and Surgery, Veterans Administration, *Medical Bulletin 8,* 1962); *Suicide Among General Medical and Surgical Hospital Patients with Malignant Neoplasms* (Washington, D.C.: Veterans Administration, *Medical Bulletin 9,* 1963); T. L. McEVOY, "A Comparison of Suicidal and Non-Suicidal Patients by Means of Thematic Apperception Test," unpublished doctoral dissertation, University of California, Los Angeles, 1963; C. E. OSGOOD and EVELYN G. WALKER, "Motivation and Language Behavior: A Content Analysis of Suicide Notes," *Journal of Abnormal and Social Psychology,* 57:58–67, 1959; SHNEIDMAN and FARBEROW (eds.), *Clues to Suicide;* E. S. SHNEIDMAN and N. L. FARBEROW, "Comparison Between Genuine and Simulated Suicide Notes by Means of Mowrer's DRQ," *Journal of General Psychology,* 56:251–256, 1957; E. S. SHNEIDMAN and N. L. FARBEROW, "A Sociopsychological Investigation of Suicide," in H. P. DAVID and J. C. BRENGELMANN (eds.), *Perspectives in Personality Research* (New York: Basic Books, 1960).

5. The authors wish to thank Gerald Blackstone, John Grdjan, George Jamieson, Ronald McDevitt, Theodore L. McEvoy, Michael

Mitchell, Michael Peck, Dan Sapin, and Bruce Sutkus for serving as abstractors.

6. The help of Leonard Staugus, Systems Development Corporation, Santa Monica, California, and the Western Research Support Center, Veterans Administration Hospital, Sepulveda, California, in carrying out many of the computations is gratefully acknowledged.

7. N. L. FARBEROW, E. S. SHNEIDMAN, and CALISTA V. LEONARD, *Suicide Among Schizophrenic Mental Hospital Patients* (Washington, D.C.: Veterans Administration, *Medical Bulletin 8, 1962*).

8. FARBEROW, SHNEIDMAN, and LEONARD, *Suicide Among General Medical and Surgical Hospital Patients with Malignant Neoplasms.*

9. N. L. FARBEROW, J. W. MCKELLIGOTT, S. COHEN, and A. DARBONNE, *Suicide Among Patients with Cardiorespiratory Illnesses* (Washington, D.C.: Veterans Administration, 1965; mimeographed report).

10. N. L. FARBEROW and T. L. MCEVOY, "Suicide Among Patients with Diagnosis of Anxiety and Depressive Reactions in General Medical and Surgical Hospitals," *Journal of Abnormal and Social Psychology,* (1965).

11. A. H. STANTON and M. S. SCHWARTZ, *The Mental Hospital* (New York: Basic Books, 1954).

12. HENRY A. MURRAY, in his essay "Dead to the World: The Passions of Herman Melville," in EDWIN S. SHNEIDMAN (ed.), *Essays in Self-Destruction* (New York: Science House, 1967), refers to this paper and summarizes and relates it to an analysis of Melville's works. Murray's essay illuminates this paper.

Chapter 25

1. N. L. FARBEROW and E. S. SHNEIDMAN (eds.), *The Cry For Help* (New York: McGraw-Hill Book Company, 1961); E. S. SHNEIDMAN and N. L. FARBEROW (eds.), *Clues to Suicide* (New York: McGraw-Hill Book Company, 1957).

2. R. E. LITMAN, "Emergency Response to Potential Suicide," *Journal of Michigan Medical Society,* 62:68–72, 1963.

3. N. L. FARBEROW, E. S. SHNEIDMAN, and C. V. LEONARD, *Suicide Among General Medical and Surgical Hospital Patients with*

Malignant Neoplasms (Washington, D.C.: Veterans Administration, *Medical Bulletin 9*, 1963).

4. N. L. FARBEROW, E. S. SHNEIDMAN, and C. V. LEONARD, *Suicide—Evaluation and Treatment of Suicidal Risk Among Schizophrenic Patients in Psychiatric Hospitals* (Washington, D.C.: Department of Medicine and Surgery, Veterans Administration, *Medical Bulletin 8*, 1962).

5. S. EISENTHAL, N. L. FARBEROW, and E. S. SHNEIDMAN, "Follow-up of Neuro-psychiatric Hospital Patients Placed on Suicide Observation Status," *Public Health Reports*, 81:977–990, 1966.

Chapter 26

1. E. S. SHNEIDMAN and N. L. FARBEROW (eds.), *Clues to Suicide* (New York: McGraw-Hill Book Company, 1957).

2. E. STENGEL, "Some Unexplored Aspects of Suicide and Attempted Suicide," *Journal of Comprehensive Psychiatry*, 1:71–80, 1960).

3. R. E. LITMAN, E. S. SHNEIDMAN, and N. L. FARBEROW, "Suicide Prevention Center," *American Journal of Psychiatry*, 117:1084–1087, 1961, and in J. H. MASSERMAN (ed.), *Current Psychiatric Therapies* (New York: Grune and Stratton, 1961).

4. E. ROBINS, J. GASSNER, J. KAYES, R. H. WILKINSON, JR., and G. E. MURPHY, "The Communication of Suicidal Intent: A Study of 134 Consecutive Cases of Successful (Completed) Suicides," *American Journal of Psychiatry*, 115:724–733, 1959.

5. J. A. MEERLOO, "Suicide, Menticide and Psychic Homicide," *Archives of Neurology and Psychiatry*, 81:360–362, 1959.

6. V. W. JENSEN and T. A. PETTY, "The Fantasy of Being Rescued in Suicide," *Psychoanalytic Quarterly*, 27:327–339, 1958.

7. N. D. TABACHNICK, "Some Observations on Counter-Transference Crises in Suicidal Attempts," *Archives of General Psychiatry*, 4:572–578, 1961.

8. A. BALINT, "Love for Mother and Mother Love," *International Journal of Psycho-Analysis*, 30:251–259, 1949; T. BENEDEK, "Toward a Biology of a Depressive Constellation," *Journal of the American Psychoanalytic Association*, 4:389–428, 1956; M. S. MAHLER, "On Sadness and Grief in Infancy and Childhood: Loss and Restoration of Symbiotic Love Object," in *Psychoanalytic*

Study of the Child (New York: International Universities Press, 1961).

9. G. H. POLLOCK, "On Symbiosis and Symbiotic Neurosis," *International Journal of Psycho-Analysis*, 45:1–30, 1964.

10. R. E. LITMAN, "Emergency Response to Potential Suicide," *Journal of Michigan Medical Society*, 62:68–72, 1963.

Chapter 27

1. F. B. ROGERS, "Extending the Horizons of Preventive Medicine," *Journal of American Medical Association*, 190:837–839, 1964.

2. R. E. LITMAN, E. S. SHNEIDMAN, and N. L. FARBEROW, "Suicide Prevention Center," *American Journal of Psychiatry*, 117:1084–1087, 1961, and in J. H. MASSERMAN (ed.), *Current Psychiatric Therapies* (New York: Grune and Stratton, 1961); R. E. LITMAN, T. CURPHEY, E. S. SHNEIDMAN, N. L. FARBEROW, and N. TABACHNICK, "Investigations of Equivocal Suicides," *Journal of the American Medical Association*, 184:924–929, 1963.

3. A. E. BENNETT, "Prevention of Suicide," *Postgraduate Medicine*, 32:160–164, 1962; R. S. MINTZ, *Detection and Management of the Suicidal Patient* (Chicago, Illinois: Disease-a-Month Year Book, Medical Publishers, July, 1961); J. A. MOTTO and CLARA GREENE, "Suicide and the Medical Community," *American Medical Association Archives of Neurology and Psychiatry*, 80:776–781, 1958; W. OFFENKRANTZ, "Depression and Suicide in General Medical Practice," *American Practitioner*, 13:427–430, 1962; E. ROBINS, G. E. MURPHY, R. H. WILKINSON, S. GASSUER, and J. KAYES, "Some Clinical Considerations in the Prevention of Suicide Based on a Study of 134 Successful Suicides," *American Journal of Public Health*, 49:888–899, 1959; D. J. VAIL, "Suicide and Medical Responsibility," *American Journal of Psychiatry*, 15:1005–1010, 1959.

4. E. S. SHNEIDMAN, "Preventing Suicide," *American Journal of Nursing*, 65:111–116, 1965; E. S. SHNEIDMAN and N. L. FARBEROW (eds.), *Clues to Suicide* (New York: McGraw-Hill Book Company, 1957).

5. N. L. FARBEROW and E. S. SHNEIDMAN (eds.), *The Cry for Help* (New York: McGraw-Hill Book Company, 1961).

6. N. S. KLINE, "The Practical Management of Depression," *Journal of American Medical Association*, **190**:732–740, 1964.

7. R. E. LITMAN, "Emergency Response to Potential Suicide," *Journal of Michigan Medical Society*, **62**:68–72, 1963.

8. KLINE, *op. cit.*

9. R. E. LITMAN, "Psychiatric Hospitals and Suicide Prevention Centers," *Comprehensive Psychiatry*, **6**:119–127, 1965.

10. R. E. LITMAN, "Immobilization Response to Suicidal Behavior," *Journal of American Medical Association Archives of General Psychiatry*, **11**:282–285, 1964.

11. N. L. FARBEROW, E. S. SHNEIDMAN, and R. E. LITMAN, "The Suicidal Patient and the Physician," *Mind*, **1**:69–74, 1963.

12. Editorial: "Bolstering the Will to Live," *Medicine at Work*, **4**:8–10, 1964.

Chapter 28

1. N. L. FARBEROW and T. L. McEVOY, "Suicide Among Patients in General Medical and Surgical Hospitals with Diagnoses of Anxiety Reaction or Depressive Reaction," *Journal of Abnormal Psychology*, **71**:287–299, 1966; N. L. FARBEROW, W. McKELLIGOTT, S. COHEN, and A. DARBONNE, "Suicide Among Patients with Cardiorespiratory Illness," *Journal of the American Medical Association*, **195**:422–428, 1966; N. L. FARBEROW, E. S. SHNEIDMAN, and C. V. LEONARD, *Suicide—Evaluation and Treatment of Suicidal Risk Among Schizophrenic Patients in Psychiatric Hospitals* (Washington, D.C.: Department of Medicine and Surgery, Veterans Administration, *Medical Bulletin 8*, 1962); *Suicide Among General Medical and Surgical Hospital Patients with Malignant Neoplasms* (Washington, D.C.: Veterans Administration, *Medical Bulletin 9*, 1963); N. L. FARBEROW, E. S. SHNEIDMAN, and C. NEURINGER, "Case History and Hospitalization Factors in Suicides of Neuropsychiatric Hospital Patients," *Journal of Nervous and Mental Disease*, **142**:32–44, 1966.

Chapter 29

1. H. FEIFEL (ed.), *The Meaning of Death* (New York: McGraw-Hill Book Company, 1959).

2. R. MAY, "Contributions of Existential Psychotherapy," in R. MAY, E. ANGEL, and H. F. ELLENBERGER (eds.), *Existence* (New York: Basic Books, 1958).

3. L. S. KUBIE, "Multiple Determinants to Suicide Attempts," *Journal of Nervous and Mental Disease*, 138:3–8, 1964.

4. T. S. SZASZ, *Law, Liberty, and Psychiatry* (New York: The Macmillan Company, 1963).

5. C. R. ROGERS, *Client-Centered Therapy* (Boston, Massachusetts: Houghton Mifflin, 1951).

6. B. P. KARON, "The Resolution of Acute Schizophrenic Reactions," *Psychotherapy: Theory, Research and Practice*, 1:27, 1963.

7. J. HILLMAN, *Suicide and the Soul* (New York: Harper and Row, 1964).

8. S. LESSE, "Editorial Comment," and S. Basescue, "The Threat of Suicide in Psychotherapy," *American Journal of Psychotherapy*, 19:99–105, 1965.

9. R. E. LITMAN, N. L. FARBEROW, E. S. SHNEIDMAN, S. M. HEILIG, and J. A. KRAMER, "Suicide Prevention Telephone Service," *Journal of American Medical Association*, 192:21–25, 1965.

10. R. E. LITMAN, T. CURPHEY, E. S. SHNEIDMAN, N. L. FARBEROW, and N. TABACHNICK, "Investigations of Equivocal Suicides," *Journal of the American Medical Association*, 184:924–929, 1963.

11. S. FREUD, "The Psychopathology of Everyday Life," in *Standard Edition*, Vol. VI (London: Hogarth Press, 1960).

Chapter 30

1. R. E. LITMAN, E. S. SHNEIDMAN, and N. L. FARBEROW, "Suicide Prevention Center," *American Journal of Psychiatry*, 117:1084–1087, 1961, and in J. H. MASSERMAN (ed.), *Current Psychiatric Therapies* (New York: Grune and Stratton, 1961); M. KAPHAN and R. E. LITMAN, "Telephone Appraisal of 100 Suicidal Emergencies," *American Journal of Psychotherapy*, 16:591–599, 1962; N. L. FARBEROW and E. S. SHNEIDMAN (eds.), *The Cry For Help* (New York: McGraw-Hill Book Company, 1961).

2. J. A. MOTTO and CLARA GREENE, "Suicide and the Medical Community," *American Medical Association Archives of Neurology and Psychiatry*, 80:776–781, 1958; D. J. VAIL, "Suicide and

Medical Responsibility," *American Journal of Psychiatry,* 15:1005–1010, 1959.

3. FARBEROW and SHNEIDMAN, *op. cit.*

4. K. A. MENNINGER, *Man Against Himself* (New York: Harcourt, Brace and Company, 1938) ; V. W. JENSEN and T. A. PETTY, "The Fantasy of Being Rescued in Suicide," *Psychoanalytic Quarterly,* 27:327–339, 1958; E. STENGEL, "Some Unexplored Aspects of Suicide and Attempted Suicide," *Journal of Comprehensive Psychiatry,* 1:71–80, 1960.

5. L. I. DUBLIN and BESSIE BUNZEL, *To Be or Not to Be* (New York: Random House, 1933).

6. E. S. SHNEIDMAN, "Orientations Toward Death: A Vital Aspect of the Study of Lives," in R. W. WHITE (ed.), *The Study of Lives* (New York: Atherton Press, 1963), and *International Journal of Psychiatry,* 2:167–200, 1966.

Chapter 31

1. It may be of interest to note that "the word 'statistic' is derived from the Latin *status,* which, in the Middle Ages, had come to mean a state in the political sense. 'Statistic,' therefore, originally denoted inquiries into the condition of the state." Until the eighteenth century, this discipline was called *political arithmetic;* later writers termed it *vital statistics.* In these early labors, much attention was given to tables of mortality for the state, so that a discussion of statistics on suicide is, in the original sense of the word, particularly appropriate. From WYNNARD HOOPER, "Statistics," *Encyclopaedia Britannica* (11th Edition, 1910), Vol. 25, pp. 806–811.

2. All names, dates, and places have, of course, been changed to protect the anonymity of the persons involved.

Chapter 32

1. R. E. LITMAN, T. CURPHEY, E. S. SHNEIDMAN, N. L. FARBEROW, and N. TABACHNICK, "Investigations of Equivocal Suicides," *Journal of the American Medical Association,* 184:924–929, 1963.

2. E. S. SHNEIDMAN, "Orientations Toward Death: A Vital Aspect of the Study of Lives," in R. W. WHITE (ed.), *The Study of Lives*

(New York: Atherton Press, 1963), and *International Journal of Psychiatry*, 2:167–200, 1966.

3. *Roberts v. I. A. C., Douglas Aircraft et al.*, Calif. Compensation Cases, Vol. 23, 188 (1958).

4. *Burnight v. I. A. C. et al.* (Civ. No. 19088, First District, Division One, June 17, 1960).

5. *Harper v. Industrial Commission*, 24 Ill. 2d 103, 180 N.E. 2d 480 (Supreme Court Ill., Jan. 23, 1962).

6. *Orcott v. Spokane County*, 58 Wash. 2d 846 364 P. 2d 1102 (Wash. Sept. 28, 1961); *Tate v. Canonica*, 180 Cal. App. 2d 898, 5 Cal. Rptr. 28 (1960).

7. P. R. RHEINGOLD, J. A. PAGE, and T. F. LAMBERT, *NACCA Law Journal*, 29:212–222, 1963, and 30:162–173, 1964.

8. R. E. LITMAN, "Psychiatric Hospitals and Suicide Prevention Centers," *Comprehensive Psychiatry*, 6:119–127, 1965.

9. P. M. MARGOLIS, G. G. MEYER, and J. C. LOUW, "Suicidal Precautions," *Archives of General Psychiatry*, 13:224–231, 1965.

10. R. E. LITMAN, "When Patients Commit Suicide," *American Journal of Psychotherapy*, 19:570–576, 1965.

11. W. A. BELLAMY, "Malpractice in Psychiatry," *Diseases of the Nervous System*, 26:312–320, 1965; D. H. Mills, "Medical Legal Exposures of Psychiatrists," *Southern California Psychiatric Society News*, 13:6, March, 1966.

12. H. A. DAVIDSON, *Forensic Psychiatry* (2d ed.; New York: Ronald Press Company, 1965).

13. I. N. PERR, "Liability of Hospital and Psychiatrist in Suicide," *American Journal of Psychiatry*, 122:631–638, 1965.

14. BELLAMY, *op. cit.*

15. MILLS, *op. cit.*

16. *Frederic v. United States*, 246 Federal Supplement 368 (D. La., 1965); *Lyle v. Johnson*, 126 So 2d 266 (Miss.) (1961); *Shockey v. Wash. Sanitarium*, 11 CCH Neg (2) 1302 (Md. 1961).

17. *Katz v. State of New York* (258 NYS 2d 912).

18. *Baker, et al. v. U. S. Dis. Court*, Southern District of Iowa, Davenport Division, Civ. No. 2-546, Feb. 13, 1964; RHEINGOLD, PAGE, and LAMBERT, *op. cit.*

19. *Kent v. Whitaker*, 364P. 2d 556 (Washington, Aug. 31, 1961).

20. *Szostak v. State of New York*, 247 N.Y.S. 2d 770 New York, Mar. 19, 1964.

21. *Baker, et al. v. U.S. Dis. Court.*

22. *Lawrence v. State of New York,* New York Court of Claims, Nos. 40715 and 43826. Cited in *Medical World News,* April 2, 1965.

23. LITMAN, "Psychiatric Hospitals and Suicide Prevention Centers"; MARGOLIS, MEYER, and LOUW, "Suicidal Precautions."

Chapter 33

1. M. BENSON, "Doctors' Wives Tackle Suicide Problem," *Today's Health,* 42:60–63, 1964.

2. L. I. DUBLIN, *Suicide: A Sociological and Statistical Study* (New York: Ronald Press, 1963).

3. N. L. FARBEROW and E. S. SHNEIDMAN (eds.), *The Cry for Help* (New York: McGraw-Hill Book Company, 1961).

4. N. L. FARBEROW and E. S. SHNEIDMAN, "Suicide and the Police Officer," *Police,* 2:51–55, 1958.

5. R. E. LITMAN, T. CURPHEY, E. S. SHNEIDMAN, N. L. FARBEROW, and N. TABACHNICK, "Investigations of Equivocal Suicides," *Journal of the American Medical Association,* 184:924–929, 1963.

6. R. E. LITMAN, N. L. FARBEROW, E. S. SHNEIDMAN, S. M. HEILIG, and J. A. KRAMER, "Suicide Prevention Telephone Service," *Journal of American Medical Association,* 192:21–25, 1965.

7. E. S. SHNEIDMAN and N. L. FARBEROW (eds.), *Clues to Suicide* (New York: McGraw-Hill Book Company, 1957).

Chapter 34

1. Taking the record in its entirety, Dr. Sorum felt that security measures were warranted, but when asked whether the ordinary standard of care would dictate that pending a psychiatric workup a weapon, such as a penknife, should be taken from the patient, he answered, "Oh, I would think so. However, we have used a lot of open ward care with certain types of patients, even if they have depression. I mean, sometimes we take what would be considered, I suppose, calculated risks, and I have at times ordered people to be allowed to retain certain things in their possession because it gives them a sense of identity, of being themselves."

2. According to the Federal Tort Claims Act, 28 U. S. c. § 1346 (b)

the law of the State where the alleged negligent act or omission occurred, that is, Louisiana, is the applicable law of the case.

3. This standard of professional care is the law of Louisiana. See *Fairley v. Douglas,* La.App., Orleans, 76 So.2d 576 (1955) ; *Norton v. Argonaut Insurance Company,* La.App., 1 Cir., 144 So2d 249 (1962) ; *Favalora v. Aetna Casualty & Surety Company,* La.App., 1 Cir., 144 So.2d 544 (1962) ; *George v. Travelers Insurance Company,* E.D.La., Baton Rouge Division, 215 F.Supp. 340 (1963) ; *Leavell v. Alton Ochsner Medical Foundation,* E.D.La., New Orleans Division, 201 F.Supp. 805 (1962). While there is no Louisiana case announcing the standard of care to be exercised in the treatment of a mental patient, other jurisdictions follow the same general standard of care as stated in *Meyer v. St. Paul–Mercury Indemnity Co.,* supra. See *White v. United States,* E.D.Va., 205 F.Supp. 662 (1962) ; *Baker v. United States,* 8 Cir., 1965, 343 F.2d 222, and *Mounds Park Hospital v. Von Eye,* 8 Cir., 1957, 245 F.2d 756.

Chapter 35

1. GLANVILLE WILLIAMS, *The Sanctity of Life and the Criminal Law* (New York: Alfred Knopf, 1957).
2. ELLEN S. GREENBERGER, "Fantasies of Women Confronting Death: A Study of Critically Ill Patients," unpublished dissertation, Radcliffe College, 1961.
3. D. MCCLELLAND, "The Harlequin Complex," in R. W. WHITE (ed.), *The Study of Lives* (New York: Atherton Press, 1963).
4. *Ibid.*
5. N. L. FARBEROW, E. S. SHNEIDMAN, and C. V. LEONARD, *Suicide Among General Medical and Surgical Hospital Patients with Malignant Neoplasms* (Washington, D.C.: Veterans Administration, *Medical Bulletin 9,* 1963).
6. A. D. WEISMAN and T. P. HACKETT, "The Dying Patient," *Forest Hospital Publications,* 1:16–21, 1962.
7. *Ibid.*
8. E. S. SHNEIDMAN, "Orientations Toward Death: A Vital Aspect of the Study of Lives," in R. W. WHITE (ed.), *The Study of Lives* (New York: Atherton Press, 1963), and *International Journal of Psychiatry,* 2:167–200, 1966.

9. E. S. SHNEIDMAN and N. L. FARBEROW, "A Sociopsychological Investigation of Suicide," in H. P. DAVID and J. C. BRENGELMANN (eds.), *Perspectives in Personality Research* (New York: Basic Books, 1960).

10. N. L. FARBEROW and E. S. SHNEIDMAN (eds.), *The Cry for Help* (New York: McGraw-Hill Book Company, 1961).

Chapter 36

1. *Manual of the International Statistical Classification of Diseases, Injuries and Causes of Death* (7th Rev., 1955; Geneva: World Health Organization, 1957).

2. *Mortality Trends in the United States, 1954–1963* (Washington, D.C.: U.S. Government Printing Office, 1965), PHS 1000, Series 20—No. 2, p. 53.

3. *Vital Statistics of the United States*, Volume II—*Mortality*, Part A (Washington, D.C.: U.S. Government Printing Office, 1965).

4. E. S. SHNEIDMAN, "Description of the NIMH Center for Studies in Suicide Prevention," *Bulletin of Suicidology*, July, 1967, pp. 2–7.

5. H. MELVILLE, *Pierre: Or the Ambiguities*, Book XIII, Part III (originally published in 1852; New York: Grove Press, 1965).

6. G. DRAPER, C. W. DUPERTUIS, and J. L. CAUGHLEY, *Human Constitution in Clinical Medicine* (New York: Harper and Brothers, 1944).

Chapter 37

1. S. FREUD, *Standard Edition of the Complete Psychological Works* (London: Hogarth Press, 1953–1965), Vol. 21, p. 145.

2. *Ibid.*, Vol. 22, pp. 110–111; Vol. 23, pp. 148–150.

3. *Ibid.*, Vol. 14, pp. 289–300; Vol. 22, pp. 213–215.

4. *Ibid.*, Vol. 2, p. 28.

5. S. FREUD, *The Origins of Psycho-Analysis* (New York: Basic Books, 1954), p. 207.

6. *Ibid.*, pp. 264–265.

7. FREUD, *Standard Edition*, Vol. 3, pp. 290–196.

8. *Ibid.*, Vol. 6, pp. 1–6.

9. E. JONES, *The Life and Work of Sigmund Freud* (New York: Basic Books, 1953–1957), Vol. 2, pp. 333–334.

10. FREUD, *The Origins*, pp. 170–171.

11. *Ibid.*, pp. 193–195.

12. *Ibid.*, p. 211.

13. JONES, *op. cit.*, Vol. 1, p. 122.

14. *Ibid.*

15. FREUD, *Standard Edition*, Vol. 14, pp. 247–252.

16. *Ibid.*, pp. 289–300.

17. *Ibid.*, Vol. 17, pp. 21–23.

18. *Ibid.*, Vol. 12, p. 14.

19. *Ibid.*, Vol. 7, pp. 3–122.

20. *Ibid.*, Vol. 10, pp. 153–318; Vol. 13, p. 154.

21. *Ibid.*, Vol. 10, pp. 153–318.

22. *Ibid.*, Vol. 6, pp. 178–185.

23. *Ibid.*

24. *Ibid.*, Vol. 11, p. 232.

25. *Ibid.*, Vol. 22, p. 104.

26. *Ibid.*, Vol. 14, pp. 247–252.

27. *Ibid.*

28. *Ibid.*

29. *Ibid.*, Vol. 19, pp. 3–66.

30. *Ibid.*, Vol. 14, pp. 289–300.

31. *Ibid.*

32. *Ibid.*, Vol. 18, pp. 191–192; Vol. 22, pp. 45–46.

33. *Ibid.*, Vol. 14, p. 325.

34. *Ibid.*, Vol. 21, pp. 191–194.

35. *Ibid.*, Vol. 18, pp. 147–172.

36. *Ibid.*

37. *Ibid.*, Vol. 19, p. 49.

38. *Ibid.*, Vol. 23, pp. 180–182.

39. *Ibid.*, Vol. 18, pp. 3–64.

40. JONES, *op. cit.*, Vol. 3, pp. 275–280.

41. FREUD, *Standard Edition*, Vol. 23, pp. 148–150.

42. *Ibid.*

43. JONES, *op. cit.*, Vol. 3, pp. 275–280.

44. FREUD, *Standard Edition*, Vol. 19, pp. 53–58.

45. *Ibid.*

46. *Ibid.*, Vol. 19, pp. 169–170.

47. *Ibid.*, Vol. 20, pp. 154–155.

48. *Ibid.*, Vol. 21, pp. 134–135.

49. *Ibid.*, Vol. 22, pp. 213–215.

50. *Ibid.*, Vol. 23, pp. 180–182.

51. JONES, *op. cit.*, Vol. 1, p. 5.

52. *Ibid.*, Vol. 1, p. 153.

53. *Ibid.*, Vol. 1, pp. 275–280.

54. FREUD, *Standard Edition*, Vol. 14, pp. 289–300.

55. *Ibid.*, Vol. 22, pp. 213–215.

56. *Ibid.*

57. *Ibid.*

58. S. FREUD, *Psychoanalysis and Faith* (New York: Basic Books, 1963), pp. 101–102.

Chapter 38

1. R. E. LITMAN, T. CURPHEY, E. S. SHNEIDMAN, N. L. FARBEROW, and N. TABACHNICK, "Investigations of Equivocal Suicides," *Journal of the American Medical Association*, 184:924–929, 1963.

2. E. S. SHNEIDMAN, "Orientations Toward Death; A Vital Aspect of the Study of Lives," in R. W. WHITE (ed.), *The Study of Lives* (New York: Atherton Press, 1963), and *International Journal of Psychiatry*, 2:167–200, 1966.

3. E. S. SHNEIDMAN, "Suicide, Sleep, and Death: Some Possible Interrelations Among Cessation, Interruption, and Continuation Phenomena," *Journal of Consulting Psychology*, 28:95, 1964.

4. H. A. MURRAY, "Dead to the World: The Passions of Herman Melville," in E. S. SHNEIDMAN (ed.), *Essays in Self-Destruction* (New York: Science House, 1967).

5. My great appreciation to Miss Jan Kramer of the Los Angeles Suicide Prevention Center for her enormous effort and help in this connection is here expressed.

6. E. S. SHNEIDMAN, "Sleep and Self-Destruction: A Phenomenological Study," in E. S. Shneidman (ed.), *Essays in Self-Destruction* (New York: Science House, 1967).

7. H. A. MURRAY, *Introduction to Herman Melville's* Pierre: Or the Ambiguities (New York: Hendricks House [Farrar Straus], 1949), pp. xiii-ciii.

Chapter 43

1. E. STENGEL and NANCY G. COOK, *Attempted Suicide: Its Social Significance and Effects*, Maudsley Monograph No. 4 (London: Chapman and Hall, Ltd., 1958).
2. M. E. WOLFGANG, *Patterns in Criminal Homicide* (Philadelphia: University of Pennsylvania Press, 1958); "Suicide by Means of Victim-Precipitated Homicide," *Journal of Clinical and Experimental Psychopathology*, 20:335, 1959; J. M. MACDONALD, *The Murderer and His Victim* (Springfield, Illinois: Charles C Thomas, 1961).
3. E. S. SHNEIDMAN, "Orientations Toward Death: A Vital Aspect of the Study of Lives," in R. W. WHITE (ed.), *The Study of Lives* (New York: Atherton Press, 1963), and *International Journal of Psychiatry*, 2:167–200, 1966.

BIBLIOGRAPHY

ALBEE, G. W. "Psychological Concomitants of Pulmonary Tuberculosis," *American Review of Tuberculosis,* 58:650–661, 1948.

ALLPORT, G. A. "The Use of Personal Documents in Psychological Science," *Social Science Research Council Bulletin,* No. 49, 1942.

AMERICAN PSYCHIATRIC ASSOCIATION. *The Development of Standards and Training Curriculum for Volunteer Service Coordinators.* Washington, D.C.: American Psychiatric Association, 1964.

ANSBACHER, H. L. Personal communication, 1956.

ARIETI, S. *Interpretation of Schizophrenia.* New York: Robert Bruner, 1955.

ARLOW, J. A. "Anxiety Patterns in Angina Pectoris," *Psychosomatic Medicine,* 14:461–468, 1952.

AUBERT, V., and H. WHITE. "Sleep: A Sociological Interpretation," *Acta Sociologica,* 4: Fasc. 2, 3, 46–54, and 1–16, 1959.

BACON, F. *Novum Organum* (Aphorisms XXXVIII, XXXIX, XLII and LIII).

Baker et al. v. U.S. Dis. Court, Southern District of Iowa, Davenport Division, Civ. No. 2–546, Feb. 13, 1964.

BALINT, A. "Love for Mother and Mother Love," *International Journal of Psychoanalysis,* 30:251–259, 1949.

BECKENSTEIN, N. "The New State Hospital," in L. BELLAK (ed.) *Handbook of Community Psychiatry and Community Mental Health.* New York: Grune and Stratton, 1964.

BELLAK, L. "Acting-Out: Some Conceptual and Therapeutic Considerations," *American Journal of Psychotherapy,* 17:375–389, 1963.

———— (ed.). *Handbook of Community Psychiatry and Community Mental Health.* New York: Grune and Stratton, 1964.

BELLAMY, W. A. "Malpractice in Psychiatry," *Diseases of the Nervous System,* 26:312–320, 1965.

BENEDEK, T. "Toward a Biology of a Depressive Constellation,"

Journal of the American Psychoanalytic Association, 4:389–428, 1956.

BENNETT, A. E. "Prevention of Suicide," *Postgraduate Medicine*, 32:160–164, 1962.

BENSON, M. "Doctors' Wives Tackle Suicide Problem," *Today's Health*, 42:60–63, 1964.

BERELSON, B. *Content Analysis in Communication Research*. Glencoe, Illinois: The Free Press, 1952.

BERLE, B. B. "Emotional Factors and Tuberculosis: A Critical Review of the Literature," *Psychosomatic Medicine*, 10:366–373, 1948.

BIERER, J. "The Marlborough Experiment," in L. BELLAK (ed.), *Handbook of Community Psychiatry and Community Mental Health*. New York: Grune and Stratton, 1964.

BJERG, K. "The Suicidal Life-Space: Attempts at a Reconstruction," in E. S. SHNEIDMAN (ed.), *Essays in Self-Destruction*. New York: Science House, 1967.

BRAND, JEANNE L. "Private Support for Mental Health: A Study of the Support, by Foundations and Other Private National Granting Agencies, for Mental Health and Related Disciplines," *Public Health Service Publication No. 838*, Washington, D. C.

BREED, W. "Suicide and Loss in Social Interaction," in E. S. SHNEIDMAN (ed.), *Essays in Self-Destruction*. New York: Science House, 1967.

BRIDGMAN, P. W. *The Intelligent Individual and Society*. New York: The Macmillan Company, 1938.

———. *The Way Things Are*. Cambridge, Massachusetts: Harvard University Press, 1955.

BROIDA, D. C. Letter in *TAT Newsletter*, 4:3–4, 1950. Also printed in *Journal of Projective Techniques*, 14:205–206, 1950.

———. "An Investigation of Certain Psychodiagnostic Indications of Suicidal Tendencies and Depression in Mental Hospital Patients," *Psychiatric Quarterly*, 28:453–464, 1954.

Burnight v. I.A.C. et al. (Civ. No. 19088, First District, Division One, June 17, 1960).

CAVAN, RUTH S. *Suicide*. Chicago, Illinois: University of Chicago Press, 1926.

CHAPMAN, R. F. "Suicide During Psychiatric Hospitalization," *Bulletin Menninger Clinic*, 29:35–44, 1965.

CHORON, J. *Death and Western Thought.* New York: Collier, 1963.

———. *Modern Man and Mortality.* New York: The Macmillan Company, 1964.

———. "Death as a Motive of Philosophic Thought," in E. S. SHNEIDMAN (ed.), *Essays in Self-Destruction.* New York: Science House, 1967.

CLEVELAND, S. L., and D. L. JOHNSON. "Personality Patterns in Young Males with Coronary Disease," *Psychosomatic Medicine,* 24:600–610, 1962.

COHEN, S., C. V. LEONARD, N. L. FARBEROW, and E. S. SHNEIDMAN. "Tranquilizers and Suicide in the Schizophrenic Patient," *Archives of General Psychiatry,* 11:312–321, 1964.

COPI, I. *Introduction to Logic.* New York: The Macmillan Company, 1953.

CRASILNECK, H. B. "An Analysis of Differences Between Suicidal and Pseudo-suicidal Patients through the Use of Projective Techniques." Unpublished doctoral dissertation, University of Houston, 1954.

CRONBACH, L. J. "Correlations Between Persons as a Research Tool," in O. H. MOWRER (ed.), *Psychotherapy: Theory and Research.* New York: Ronald Press, 1953.

CURPHEY, T. J. "The Role of the Social Scientist in the Medicolegal Certification of Death from Suicide," in N. L. FARBEROW and E. S. SHNEIDMAN (eds.), *The Cry for Help.* New York: McGraw-Hill Book Company, 1961.

———. "The Forensic Pathologist and the Multi-Disciplinary Approach to Death," in E. S. SHNEIDMAN (ed.), *Essays in Self-Destruction.* New York: Science House, 1967.

DAVIDSON, H. A. *Forensic Psychiatry.* Second Edition. New York: Ronald Press Company, 1965.

DAVIS, M. R., and W. H. GILMAN. *The Letters of Herman Melville.* New Haven: Yale University Press, 1960.

DIGGORY, J. C. "The Components of Personal Despair," in E. S. SHNEIDMAN (ed.), *Essays in Self-Destruction.* New York: Science House, 1967.

DORPAT, T. L., H. S. RIPLEY, and R. LEIDIG. "A Study of Suicide in Seattle."

DOVENMEUHLE, R. H., and A. VERWOERDT. "Physical Illness and Depressive Symptomatology: I. Incidence of Depressive Symp-

toms in Hospitalized Cardiac Patients," *Journal of American Geriatric Society,* 10:932–947, 1962.

———. "Physical Illness and Depressive Symptomatology: II. Factors of Length and Severity of Illness and Frequency of Hospitalization," *Journal of Gerontology,* 18:260–266, 1963.

DRAPER, G., C. W. DUPERTUIS, and J. L. CAUGHLEY. *Human Constitution in Clinical Medicine.* New York: Hoeber, 1944.

DUBLIN, L. I. *Suicide: A Sociological and Statistical Study.* New York: Ronald Press, 1963.

———, and BESSIE BUNZEL. *To Be or Not to Be.* New York: Random House, 1933.

DUNCAN, C. H., and I. P. STEVENSON, "Paroxysmal Arrhythmias: A Psychosomatic Study," *Geriatrics,* 5:259–267, 1950.

DURKHEIM, E. *Suicide.* Translated by J. A. SPAULDING and G. SIMPSON. Glencoe, Illinois: The Free Press, 1951. (Original 1897.)

Editorial: "Bolstering the Will to Live," *Medicine at Work,* 4:8–10, 1964.

EISENTHAL, S., N. L. FARBEROW, and E. S. SHNEIDMAN. "Follow-up of Neuro-psychiatric Hospital Patients Placed on Suicide Observation Status," *Public Health Reports,* 81:977–990, 1966.

ERIKSON, E. H. *Childhood and Society.* New York: W. W. Norton, 1950.

EVANS, RUTH. "Volunteers in Mental Hospitals," *Mental Hygiene,* 39:111–117, 1955.

FARBEROW, N. L. "Personality Patterns of Suicidal Mental Hospital Patients," *Genetic Psychology Monographs,* 42:3–79, 1950.

———. "The Suicidal Crisis in Psychotherapy," in E. S. SHNEIDMAN and N. L. FARBEROW (eds.), *Clues to Suicide.* New York: McGraw-Hill Book Company, 1957.

———. "Suicide and Age," in E. S. SHNEIDMAN and N. L. FARBEROW (eds.), *Clues to Suicide.* New York: McGraw-Hill Book Company, 1957.

——— (ed.). *Taboo Topics.* New York: Atherton, 1963.

———. "A Puzzle Remains Perplexing: A Review of Hendin's *Suicide and Scandanavia,*" *Contemporary Psychology,* 9:414–416, 1964.

———. "Hope as Help: A Review of Kobler and Stotland's *The End of Hope: A Sociological Theory of Suicide,*" *Contemporary Psychology,* 10:553–554, 1965.

————. "The Psychology of Suicide," in *International Encyclopedia of the Social Sciences*. New York: The Macmillan Company, 1968.

————. "Therapy in the Suicidal Crisis," in E. S. SHNEIDMAN (ed.), *Essays in Self-Destruction*. New York: Science House, 1967.

———— (ed.). *Suicide and Its Prevention: Proceedings of the Fourth International Conference for Suicide Prevention*. Los Angeles: Delmar Publishing Company, 1968.

————, S. M. HEILIG, and R. E. LITMAN. *Procedures and Techniques in Evaluation and Management of Suicidal Persons*. Los Angeles: Suicide Prevention Center, 1968.

FARBEROW, N. L., R. E. LITMAN, E. S. SHNEIDMAN, S. M. HEILIG, C. I. WOLD, and J. KRAMER. "Suicide Prevention Around the Clock," *American Journal of Orthopsychiatry*, 36:551–558, 1966.

FARBEROW, N. L., and T. L. McEVOY. "Suicide Among Patients in General Medical and Surgical Hospitals with Diagnoses of Anxiety Reaction or Depressive Reaction," *Journal of Abnormal Psychology*, 71:287–299, 1966.

FARBEROW, N. L., W. McKELLIGOTT, S. COHEN, and A. DARBONNE. "Suicide among Patients with Cardiorespiratory Illnesses," *Journal of the American Medical Association*, 195:422–428, 1966.

FARBEROW, N. L., and R. PALMER. "The Nurse's Role in the Prevention of Suicide," *Nursing Forum*, 3:93, 1964.

FARBEROW, N. L., and E. S. SHNEIDMAN. "A Study of Attempted, Threatened, and Completed Suicides," *Journal of Abnormal and Social Psychology*, 50, 230, 1955.

————. "A Nisei Woman Attacks by Suicide," in G. SEWARD (ed.), *Clinical Studies in Culture Conflict*. New York: Ronald Press, 1958.

————. "Suicide and the Police Officer," *Police*, 2:51–55, 1958.

————. *Interim Unpublished Report No. 3*. Washington, D.C.: Veterans Administration Central Office, 1960.

———— (eds.). *The Cry for Help*. New York: McGraw-Hill Book Company, 1961.

————, and C. V. LEONARD. "Suicide Among Schizophrenic Hospital Patients," in N. L. FARBEROW and E. S. SHNEIDMAN (eds.), *The Cry for Help*. New York: McGraw-Hill Book Company, 1961.

————. *Suicide—Evaluation and Treatment of Suicidal Risk Among Schizophrenic Patients in Psychiatric Hospitals*. Washington, D.

C.: Department of Medicine and Surgery, Veterans Administration, *Medical Bulletin 8*, 1962.

———. *Suicide Among General Medical and Surgical Hospital Patients with Malignant Neoplasms*. Washington, D.C.: Veterans Administration, *Medical Bulletin 9*, 1963.

FARBEROW, N. L., E. S. SHNEIDMAN, and R. E. LITMAN. "The Suicidal Patient and the Physician," *Mind*, 1:69–74, 1963.

FARBEROW, N. L., E. S. SHNEIDMAN, and C. NEURINGER. "Case History and Hospitalization Factors in Suicides of Neuropsychiatric Hospital Patients," *Journal of Nervous and Mental Disease*, 142:32–44, 1966.

FECHNER, A. H., and J. H. PARKE. "The Volunteer Worker and the Psychiatric Hospital," *American Journal of Psychiatry*, 107:602–606, 1951.

FEIFEL, H. (ed.). *The Meaning of Death*. New York: McGraw-Hill Book Company, 1959.

FOX, R. "Help for the Despairing," *Lancet*, 2:1102–1105, 1962.

FRANK, MARJORIE. "Volunteers in Mental Hospitals," *Psychiatric Quarterly Supplement*, Part 1, 22:111–124, 1948.

———. "Volunteer Work with Psychiatric Patients," *Mental Hygiene*, 33:353–365, 1949.

Frederic v. United States. 246 Federal Supplement 368 (D. La., 1965).

FREUD, S. "Mourning and Melancholia," in *Collected Papers*, Vol. IV. London: Hogarth Press, 1925.

———. "Thoughts for the Times on War and Death" (1915), in *Collected Papers*, Vol. IV. Translated by J. Riviere. London: Hogarth Press, 1925.

———. *The Origins of Psycho-Analysis*. New York: Basic Books, 1954.

———. *Standard Edition of the Complete Psychological Works*. London: Hogarth Press, 1953–1965.

———. "The Psychogenesis of a Case of Homosexuality in a Woman" (1920), in J. STRACHEY (ed.), *The Standard Edition of the Complete Psychological Works of Sigmund Freud*, Vol. XVIII. London: Hogarth Press, 1955.

———. "The Psychopathology of Everyday Life," in *Standard Edition*, Vol. VI. London: Hogarth Press, 1960.

———. *Psychoanalysis and Faith*. New York: Basic Books, 1963.

FRIEDMAN, I. "Phenomenal, Ideal, and Projected Conceptions of Self," *Journal of Abnormal and Social Psychology,* 51:611–615, 1955.

————. "Objectifying the Subjective: A Methodological Approach to the TAT," *Journal of Projective Techniques,* 21:243–247, 1957.

————. "Characteristics of the TAT Heroes of Normal, Psychoneurotic, and Paranoid Schizophrenic Subjects," *Journal of Projective Techniques,* 21:372–376, 1957.

GARFINKEL, H. "On Practical Sociological Reasoning: Some Features in the Work of the Los Angeles Suicide Prevention Center," in E. S. SHNEIDMAN (ed.), *Essays in Self-Destruction.* New York: Science House, 1967.

GENGERELLI, J. A., and F. J. KIRCHNER (eds.). *Psychological Factors in Human Cancer.* Berkeley and Los Angeles: University of California Press, 1953.

GORDON, M. H., E. H. LOVELAND, and E. E. CURETON. "An Extended Table for Chi-square for Two Degrees of Freedom for Use in Combined Probabilities from Independent Samples," *Psychometrika,* 17:311–316, 1952.

GOTTSCHALK, L. A., and GOLDINE GLESER. "An Analysis of the Verbal Content of Suicide Notes," *British Journal of Medical Psychology,* 33:195–204, 1960.

GREENBERGER, ELLEN S. "Fantasies of Women Confronting Death: A Study of Critically Ill Patients." Unpublished dissertation, Radcliffe College, 1961.

GUETZKOW, H. "Unitizing and Categorizing Problems in Coding Qualitative Data," *Journal of Clinical Psychology,* 6:47–58, 1950.

GUILFORD, J. P. *Fundamental Statistics in Psychology and Education.* Third Edition. New York: McGraw-Hill Book Company, 1956.

HADDOCK, J. N., and H. D. DUNDON, "Volunteer Work in a State Hospital by College Students," *Mental Hygiene,* 35:599–603, 1951.

HALBWACHS, M. *Les Causes du Suicide.* Paris: Alcan, 1930.

Harper v. Industrial Commission, 24 Ill. 2d 103, 180 N.E. 2d 480 (Supreme Court Ill, Jan. 23, 1962).

HAWKINS, N. G., R. DAVIS, and T. H. HOLMES. "Evidence of Psychosocial Factors in the Development of Pulmonary Tuberculosis," *American Review of Tuberculosis and Pulmonary Diseases,* 75:768–780, 1957.

HEARD, G. "Buddha and Self-Destruction," in E. S. Shneidman (ed.), *Essays in Self-Destruction*. New York: Science House, 1967.

HEILIG, S. M., N. L. FARBEROW, R. E. LITMAN, and E. S. SHNEIDMAN. The Role of Non-professional Volunteers in a Suicide Prevention Center," *Community Mental Health Journal*, 4:287–295, 1968.

HEILIG, S. M., and D. J. KLUGMAN. "The Social Worker in a Suicide Prevention Center," in *National Conference on Social Welfare: Social Work Practice*, Vol. 2. New York: Columbia University Press, 1963.

HEMINGWAY, L. *My Brother, Ernest Hemingway*. New York: World Publishing Co., 1962.

HENDIN, H. "Attempted Suicide: A Psychiatric and Statistical Study," *Psychiatric Quarterly*, 24:39–46, 1950.

———. "Psychodynamic Motivational Factors in Suicide," *Psychiatric Quarterly*, 25:672–678, 1951.

———. "Suicide in Denmark," *Psychiatric Quarterly*, 34:443–460, 1960.

HENRY, A. F., and J. F. SHORT, JR. *Suicide and Homicide*. Glencoe, Illinois: The Free Press, 1954.

HILDRETH, H. M. "A Battery of Feeling and Attitude Scales for Clinical Use," *Journal of Clinical Psychology*, 23:214–221, 1946.

HILLMAN, J. *Suicide and the Soul*. New York: Harper and Row, 1964.

HOLLINGSHEAD, A. B., and F. C. REDLICH. *Social Class and Mental Illness*. New York: John Wiley and Sons, 1958.

HOLTON, G. "Percy Williams Bridgman," *Bulletin of Atomic Scientists*, 17:22, 1962.

HOLZBERG, J. D., E. R. CAHEN, and E. K. WILK. "Suicide: Psychological Study of Self-Destruction," *Journal of Projective Techniques*, 15:339–354, 1951.

HOOPER, WYNNARD. "Statistics," *Encyclopaedia Britannica* (11th Edition, 1910), Vol. 25.

JAMES, W. *Principles of Psychology*. New York: Holt, 1890. Republished, New York: Dover, 1950.

JENSEN, V. W., and T. A. PETTY. "The Fantasy of Being Rescued in Suicide," *Psychoanalytic Quarterly*, 27:327–339, 1958.

JONES, E. *The Life and Work of Sigmund Freud*. New York: Basic Books, 1953–1957.

KAHN, T. C. "A Comparison of the Clinical Data Yielded by a Test

of Symbol Arrangement with other Findings of Two Attempt Suicide Patients," *American Psychologist* (abstract), 7:532, 1952.

KAPHAN, M., and R. E. LITMAN. "Telephone Appraisal of 100 Suicidal Emergencies," *American Journal of Psychotherapy*, 16: 591–599, 1962.

KAPLAN, S. M. "Psychological Aspects of Cardiac Disease: A Study of Patients Experiencing Mitral Commissurotomy," *Psychosomatic Medicine*, 18:221–233, 1956.

KARON, B. P. "The Resolution of Acute Schizophrenic Reactions," *Psychotherapy: Theory, Research and Practice*, 1:27, 1963.

Katz v. State of New York (258 NYS 2d 912).

Kent v. Whitaker, 364P. 2d 556 (Washington, Aug. 31, 1961).

KINSEY, A. C., W. B. POMEROY, and C. E. MARTIN. *Sexual Behavior in the Human Male*. Philadelphia: Saunders, 1948.

———, and P. H. GEBHARD. *Sexual Behavior in the Human Female*. Philadelphia: Saunders, 1953.

KLEITMAN, N. *Sleep and Wakefulness*. Second edition. Chicago, Illinois: University of Chicago Press, 1963.

———, F. J. MULLIN, N. R. COOPERMAN, and S. TITELBAUM. *Sleep Characteristics*. Chicago, Illinois: University of Chicago Press, 1937.

KLINE, N. S. "Comprehensive Therapy of Depressions," *Journal of Neuropsychiatry, Supplement No. 1*, February 1961.

———. "The Practical Management of Depression," *Journal of American Medical Association*, 190:732–740, 1964.

KLUCKHOHN, C., H. A. MURRAY, and D. SCHNEIDER. *Personality in Nature Society and Culture*. Second edition. New York: Alfred Knopf, 1953.

KNAPP, P. H., and S. J. NEMETZ. "Acute Bronchial Asthma: I. Concomitant Depression and Excitement, and Varied Antecedent Patterns in 406 Attacks," *Psychosomatic Medicine*, 22:42–55, 1960.

KOBLER, A. L., and E. STOTLAND. *The End of Hope*. New York: Free Press of Glencoe, 1964.

KRAFT, B., F. W. COUNTRYMAN, and D. L. BLEMENTHAL. "Suicide by Asthma," *Annals on Allergy*, 17:394–398, 1959.

KUBIE, L. S. "Multiple Determinants to Suicide Attempts," *Journal of Nervous and Mental Disease*, 138:3–8, 1964.

Lawrence v. State of New York, New York Court of Claims, Nos. 20715 and 43826. Cited in *Medical World News*, April 2, 1965.

LEE, D. T. "A New Dimension for Volunteers," *Mental Hygiene,* 46:273–282, 1962.

LEONARD, C. V. "A Theory of Suicide: The Implementor." Unpublished paper, Veterans Administration Central Research Unit, 1962.

LESSE, S. Editorial Comment, and S. Basescue. "The Threat of Suicide in Psychotherapy," *American Journal of Psychotherapy,* 19: 99–105, 1965.

LEVY, D. M. "The Act as a Unit," *Psychiatry,* 25:295-314, 1962.

LEWIS, N. D. C. "Studies on Suicide. I. Preliminary Survey of Some Significant Aspects of Suicide," *Psychoanalytic Review,* 20:241–273, 1933.

––––––. "Studies on Suicide. II. Some Comments on the Biological Aspects of Suicide," *Psychoanalytic Review,* 21:146–153, 1934.

LICKLIDER, J. R., and M. E. BUNCH. "Effects of Enforced Wakefulness Upon the Growth and Mazelearning Performances of White Rats," *Journal of Comparative Psychology,* 39:339, 1946.

LIFTON, R. J. "Psychological Effects of the Atomic Bomb in Hiroshima: The Theme of Death," *Daedalus,* 92:462–497, 1963.

LINDEMANN, E. "Symptomatology and Management of Acute Grief," *American Journal of Psychiatry,* 101:141–148, 1944.

LITMAN, R. E. "Some Aspects of the Treatment of the Potentially Suicidal Patient," in E. S. SHNEIDMAN and N. L. FARBEROW (eds.), *Clues to Suicide.* New York: McGraw-Hill Book Company, 1957.

––––––. "Emergency Response to Potential Suicide," *Journal of Michigan Medical Society,* 62:68–72, 1963.

––––––. "Immobilization Response to Suicidal Behavior," *Journal of American Medical Association Archives of General Psychiatry,* 11:282–285, 1964.

––––––. "Psychiatric Hospitals and Suicide Prevention Centers," *Comprehensive Psychiatry,* 6:119–127, 1965.

––––––. "Suicide: A Clinical Manifestation of Acting Out," in L. E. ABT and S. L. WEISSMAN (eds.), *Acting Out.* New York: Grune and Stratton, 1965.

––––––. "When Patients Commit Suicide," *American Journal of Psychotherapy,* 19:570–576, 1965.

––––––. "Acutely Suicidal Patients: Management in General Medical Practice," *California Medicine,* 104:168, 1966.

————. "Police Aspects of Suicide," *Police*, 10:14–18, 1966.

————. "Medical-Legal Aspects of Suicide," *Washburn Law Journal*, 6:395–401, 1967.

————. "Concern for Suicide, Before and After: A Review of Stengel's *Suicide and Attempted Suicide* and Hillman's *Suicide and the Soul*," *Contemporary Psychology*, 12:449–450, 1967.

————. "Sigmund Freud on Suicide," in E. S. SHNEIDMAN (ed.), *Essays in Self-Destruction*. New York: Science House, 1967.

————, T. CURPHEY, E. S. SHNEIDMAN, N. L. FARBEROW, and N. TABACHNICK. "Investigations of Equivocal Suicides," *Journal of the American Medical Association*, 184:924–929, 1963.

LITMAN, R. E., and N. L. FARBEROW. "Emergency Evaluation of Self-Destructive Potentiality," in N. L. FARBEROW and E. S. SHNEIDMAN (eds.), *The Cry for Help*. New York: McGraw-Hill Book Company, 1961.

————. "Suicide Prevention in Hospitals," *Zeitschrift für Präventiv Medizin*, 10:488–498, 1965.

————, E. S. SHNEIDMAN, S. M. HEILIG, and J. A. KRAMER. "Suicide Prevention Telephone Service," *Journal of American Medical Association*, 192:21–25, 1965.

LITMAN, R. E., E. S. SHNEIDMAN, and N. L. FARBEROW. "Suicide Prevention Center," *American Journal of Psychiatry*, 117:1084–1087, 1961; and in J. H. MASSERMAN (ed.), *Current Psychiatric Therapies*. New York: Grune and Stratton, 1961.

LITTLE, K. B., and E. S. SHNEIDMAN. "Congruencies Among Interpretations of Psychological Test and Anamnestic Data," *Psychological Monographs*, 73:1–42, 1959.

LITTLE, K. B., and C. L. WINDER. "A Scaled Thematic Test for Aggression Fantasy in Children." Unpublished manuscript.

MACDONALD, J. M. *The Murderer and His Victim*. Springfield, Illinois: Charles C Thomas, 1961.

MAHLER, M. S. "On Sadness and Grief in Infancy and Childhood: Loss and Restoration of Symbiotic Love Object," in *Psychoanalytic Study of the Child*. New York: International Universities Press, 1961.

Manual of the International Classification of Diseases, Injuries and Causes of Death. Seventh revision. Geneva: World Health Organization, 1957.

MARGOLIS, P. M., G. G. MEYER, and J. C. LOUW. "Suicidal Precautions," *Archives of General Psychiatry*, 13:224–231, 1965.

MASSERMAN, J. H. "A Note on the Dynamics of Suicide," *Diseases of the Nervous System*, 8:324–325, 1947.

MAY, R. "Contributions of Existential Psychotherapy," in R. MAY, E. ANGEL, and H. F. ELLENBERGER (eds.), *Existence*. New York: Basic Books, 1958.

MCCLELLAND, D. "The Harlequin Complex," in R. W. WHITE (ed.), *The Study of Lives*. New York: Atherton Press, 1963.

MCEVOY, T. L. "A Comparison of Suicidal and Non-suicidal Patients by Means of Thematic Apperception Test." Unpublished doctoral dissertation, University of California, Los Angeles, 1963.

MEADOWS, A., M. GREENBLATT, T. LEVINE, and H. C. SOLOMON. "The Discomfort-Relief Quotient as a Measure of Tension and Adjustment," *Journal of Abnormal and Social Psychology*, 47:658–666, 1952.

MEERLOO, J. A. "Suicide, Menticide and Psychic Homicide," *Archives of Neurology and Psychiatry*, 81:360–362, 1959.

MELVILLE, H. *Complete Writings*. London: Constable and Co., 1922–1924.

———. *Pierre: Or the Ambiguities*. Book XIII, Part III. Originally published in 1852. New York: Grove Press, 1965.

MENNINGER, K. A. *Man Against Himself*. New York: Harcourt, Brace and Company, 1938.

MERRILL, B. R. "Some Psychosomatic Aspects of Pulmonary Tuberculosis: A Review of the English Language Literature," *Journal of Nervous and Mental Disease*, 117:9–28, 1953.

MILLS, CATHERINE A. "Training of Volunteers," *The Development of Standards and Training Curriculum for Volunteer Services Coordinators*. Washington, D.C.: American Psychiatric Association, 1964.

MILLS, D. H. "Medical Legal Exposures of Psychiatrists," *Southern California Psychiatric Society News*, 13:6, 1966.

MINNIGERODE, MEADE. *Some Personal Letters of Herman Melville and a Bibliography*. New York: The Brick Row Book Shop, 1922.

MINTZ, R. S. *Detection and Management of the Suicidal Patient*. Chicago, Illinois: Disease-a-Month Year Book, Medical Publishers, July 1961.

MORGENTHALER, W., and M. STEINBERG. "Letzte Aufzeichnungen

von Selbstmordern," *Beihefte zur Schweizerischen Zeitschrift für Psychologie und ihre Anwendungen,* No. 1, 1945.

MORSELLI, H. *Suicide: An Essay on Comparative Statistics.* New York: Appleton, 1897.

Mortality Trends in the United States, 1954–1963. PHS Publication No. 1000, Series 20, No. 2. Washington, D.C.: U.S. Government Printing Office, 1965.

MOTTO, J. A., and CLARA GREENE. "Suicide and the Medical Community," *American Medical Association Archives of Neurology and Psychiatry,* 80:776–781, 1958.

MOWRER, O. H. *Psychotherapy: Theory and Research.* New York: Ronald Press, 1953.

———. Personal communication, 1954.

MURRAY, H. A. "What Should Psychologists Do About Psychoanalysis?" *Journal of Abnormal and Social Psychology,* 35:150–175, 1940.

———. *Thematic Apperception Test Manual.* Cambridge, Massachusetts: Harvard University Press, 1943.

———. "Introduction" to Herman Melville's *Pierre: Or the Ambiguities.* New York: Henricks House (Farrar Straus), 1949. Pp. xiii–ciii.

———. "In Nomine Diaboli," *New England Quarterly,* 24:435–452, 1951.

———. "Studies of Stressful Interpersonal Disputations," *American Psychologist,* 18:28–36, 1963.

———. "Dead to the World: The Passions of Herman Melville," in E. S. SHNEIDMAN (ed.), *Essays in Self-Destruction.* New York: Science House, 1967.

NAEGELE, K. "Sociological Observations on Everyday Life: First and Further Thoughts on Sleep." Unpublished manuscript, University of British Columbia, 1961.

NAGY, M. "The Child's View of Death," in H. FEIFEL (ed.), *The Meaning of Death.* New York: McGraw-Hill Book Company, 1959.

NAKAMURA, HAJIME. *The Ways of Thinking of Eastern Peoples.* Tokyo: Japanese Government Printing Bureau, 1960. (Available from Charles E. Tuttle Company, Rutland, Vermont.)

NEURINGER, C. "Dichotomous Evaluations in Suicidal Individuals," *Journal of Consulting Psychology,* 25:445–449, 1961.

OFFENKRANTZ, W. "Depression and Suicide in General Medical Practice," *American Practitioner*, 13:427–430, 1962.

OGILVIE, D., P. J. STONE, and E. S. SHNEIDMAN. "Some characteristics of Genuine versus Simulated Suicide Notes by Use of the General Inquirer," in P. J. STONE, D. C. DUNPHY, M. S. SMITH, and D. M. OGILVIE (eds.), *The General Inquirer: A Computer Approach to Content Analysis.* Cambridge, Massachusetts: Massachusetts Institute of Technology Press, 1966.

Orcott v. Spokane County, 58 Wash. 2d 846 364 P. 2d 1102 (Wash., Sept. 28, 1961).

OSGOOD, C. E., and EVELYN G. WALKER. "Motivation and Language Behavior: A Content Analysis of Suicide Notes," *Journal of Abnormal and Social Psychology*, 57:58–67, 1959.

OSWALD, I. *Sleeping and Waking.* Amsterdam and New York: Elsevier, 1962.

PEIRCE, C. S. *Collected Papers of Charles Sanders Peirce.* Vol. IV, ed. C. HARTSHORNE and P. WEISS. Cambridge, Massachusetts: Harvard University Press, 1931–1958.

PEPPER, S. C. "Can A Philosophy Make One Philosophical?" in E. S. SHNEIDMAN (ed.), *Essays in Self-Destruction.* New York: Science House, 1967.

PERR, I. N. "Liability of Hospital and Psychiatrist in Suicide," *American Journal of Psychiatry*, 122:631–638, 1965.

PINES, MAYA. "The Coming Upheaval in Psychiatry," *Harper's Magazine*, October 1965, pp. 54–60.

POLLOCK, G. H. "On Symbiosis and Symbiotic Neurosis," *International Journal of Psycho-Analysis*, 45:1–30, 1964.

PRETZEL, P. *Suicide and Religion.* Claremont School of Theology Th.D. thesis, 1966.

RAPAPORT, D. Letter in *TAT Newsletter*, 4:2, 1950. Also printed in *Journal of Projective Techniques*, 14:472, 1950.

RHEINGOLD, P. R., J. A. PAGE, and T. F. LAMBERT. *NACCA Law Journal*, 29:212–222, 1963, and 30:162–173, 1964.

RINGEL, E. *Der Selbstmord.* Vienna: Maudrich, 1953.

RIOCH, MARGARET, CHARMIAN ELKES, and A. A. FLINT. "A Pilot Project in Training of Mental Health Counselors." U.S. Department of Health, Education, and Welfare, *Public Health Service Publication No. 1254.*

———, BLANCHE S. USDAUSKY, RUTH G. NORMAN, and E. SILBER.

"National Institute of Mental Health Pilot Study in Training Mental Health Counselors," *American Journal of Orthopsychiatry*, 33:678–689, 1963.

RIZZO, E. M. "Un Caso di Tentato Suicidio; Narcoanalisi, Rorschach, TAT, Daseinanalyse" (A Case of Attempted Suicide, Narcoanalysis, Rorschach Test, TAT, and Existential Analysis), *Rassegno di Studi Psichiatrici*, 43:685–717, 1954.

Roberts v. I.A.C., Douglas Aircraft et al., Calif. Compensation Cases, Vol. 23, 188 (1958).

ROBINS, E., J. GASSNER, J. KAYES, R. H. WILKINSON, JR., and G. E. MURPHY. "The Communication of Suicidal Intent: A Study of 134 Consecutive Cases of Successful (Completed) Suicides," *American Journal of Psychiatry*, 115:724–733, 1959.

ROBINS, E., G. E. MURPHY, R. H. WILKINSON, S. GASSUER, and J. KAYES. "Some Clinical Considerations in the Prevention of Suicide Based on a Study of 134 Successful Suicides," *American Journal of Public Health*, 49:888–899, 1959.

ROGERS, C. R. *Client-Centered Therapy*. Boston, Massachusetts: Houghton Mifflin, 1951.

―――. "The Characteristics of a Helping Relationship," *Personnel Guidance Journal*, 6–16, 1958.

ROGERS, F. B. "Extending the Horizons of Preventive Medicine," *Journal of American Medical Association*, 190:837–839, 1964.

ROSEN, A. "Detection of Suicidal Patients: An Example of Some Limitations in the Prediction of Infrequent Events," *Journal of Consulting Psychology*, 18:397–403, 1954.

―――, W. M. HALES, and W. SIMON. "Classification of Suicidal Patients," *Journal of Consulting Psychology*, 18:359, 1954.

SACKS, H. "The Search for Help: No One to Turn To," in E. S. SHNEIDMAN (ed.), *Essays in Self-Destruction*. New York: Science House, 1967.

SAINSBURY, P. *Suicide in London: An Ecological Study*. New York: Basic Books, 1955.

SAPIR, E. *Culture, Language and Personality*, ed. D. G. MANDELBAUM. Berkeley and Los Angeles: University of California Press, 1956.

SARTRE, J. P. "Self-Deception," in WALTER KAUFMAN (ed.), *Existentialism from Dostoevsky to Sartre*. New York: World Publishing Company, 1956.

SCHILDER, P., and D. WECHSLER. "The Attitudes of Children Toward Death," *Journal of General Psychology*, 45:406, 1934.

SCHMID, C. F. "Suicide in Seattle, 1914–1925: An Ecological and Behavioristic Study," *University of Washington Publications in the Social Sciences*. Seattle: University of Washington Press, 1928.

————. "Suicide in Seattle, Washington, and Pittsburgh, Pennsylvania: A Comparative Study," *University of Pittsburgh Bulletin*, 27:149–157, 1930.

————. "Suicide in Minneapolis, Minnesota: 1928–1932," *American Journal of Sociology*, 39:30–48, 1933.

————, and M. D. VAN ARSDOL, JR. "Completed and Attempted Suicides: A Comparative Analysis," *American Sociological Review*, 20:273–283, 1955.

SCHRUT, A. "Suicidal Adolescents and Children," *Journal of American Medical Association*, 188:1103, 1964.

Schwartz v. U.S., 226 F Supp 84 (D.C., D of C, Jan. 27, 1964).

SELLS, S. B. "The Atmosphere Effect," *Archives of Psychology*, No. 200, 1936.

SHIELDS, E. A. "Depression, Then Suicide," *American Journal of Nursing*, 46:677–679, 1946.

SHNEIDMAN, E. S. (ed.). *Thematic Test Analysis*. New York: Grune and Stratton, 1951.

————. "Manual for the MAPS Test," *Projective Techniques Monograph*, 1:9–92, 1952.

————. "The Logic of Suicide," in E. S. SHNEIDMAN and N. L. FARBEROW (eds.), *Clues to Suicide*. New York: McGraw-Hill Book Company, 1957.

————. "A Method for Educing the Present Correlates of Perception: An Introduction to the Method of Successive Covariation," *Journal of General Psychology*, 57:113–120, 1957.

————. "Some Logical, Psychological, and Ecological Environments of Suicide," *California Health*, 17:193, 1960.

————. *Suicide and the Aged. Hearings before the Subcommittee on Problems of the Aged and Aging, Committee on Labor and Public Welfare, Eighty-Sixth Congress*. Part 4, 970–980. Washington, D.C.: U.S. Government Printing Office, 1960.

————. "The Clergy's Responsibility in Suicide Prevention," in

Preventive Mental Hygiene and the Clergy. Alameda County Mental Health Service, 1960.

―――. "Psycho-logic: A Personality Approach to Patterns of Thinking," in J. KAGAN and G. LESSOR (eds.), *Contemporary Issues in Thematic Apperception Methods.* Springfield, Illinois: Charles C Thomas, 1961.

―――. "The Logic of El: A Psycho-logical Approach to the Analysis of Test Data," *Journal of Projective Techniques in Personality Assessment,* 25:390–403, 1961.

―――. "Suicide: Some Classificatory Considerations," *Special Treatment Situations.* Des Plaines, Illinois: Forest Hospital Foundation, 1962.

―――. "Suicide: A Taboo Topic," in N. L. FARBEROW (ed.), *Taboo Topics.* New York: Atherton Press, 1963.

―――. "The Logic of Politics: An Analysis of the Kennedy-Nixon Debates," in L. ARONS and M. A. MAY (eds.), *Television and Human Behavior.* New York: Appleton-Century-Crofts, 1963.

―――. "Orientations Toward Death: A Vital Aspect of the Study of Lives," in R. W. WHITE (ed.), *The Study of Lives.* New York: Atherton, 1963, and *International Journal of Psychiatry,* 2:167–200, 1966.

―――. "A Look into the Dark: A Review of Meerloo's *Suicide and Mass Suicide,*" *Contemporary Psychology,* 8:177–180, 1963.

―――. "Pioneer in Suicidology: A Review of Dublin's *Suicide: A Sociological and Statistical Study,*" *Contemporary Psychology,* 9:370–371, 1964.

―――. "Suicide, Sleep, and Death: Some Possible Interrelations Among Cessation, Interruption and Continuation Phenomena," *Journal of Consulting Psychology,* 28:95, 1964.

―――. "Preventing Suicide," *American Journal of Nursing,* 65, 111–116, 1965.

―――. *The Logics of Communication: A Manual for Analysis.* China Lake, California: U.S. Naval Ordnance Test Station, 1966.

―――. "Tragedy Compounded: A Review of West's *Murder Followed by Suicide,*" *American Journal of Psychiatry,* 123:501–502, 1966.

――― (ed.). *Essays in Self-Destruction.* New York: Science House, 1967.

————. "Sleep and Self-Destruction: A Phenomenological Study," in E. S. SHNEIDMAN (ed.), *Essays in Self-Destruction.* New York: Science House, 1967.

————. "The Deaths of Herman Melville," in H. P. VINCENT (ed.), *Melville and Hawthorne in the Berkshires.* Kent, Ohio: Kent State University Press, 1967.

————. "Description of the NIMH Center for Studies of Suicide Prevention," *Bulletin of Suicidology,* July, 1967, pp. 2–7.

————. "Suicidal Phenomena: Their Definition and Classification," in *International Encyclopedia of the Social Sciences* (New York: The Macmillan Company, 1968).

————. "Orientations toward Cessation: A Re-examination of Current Modes of Death," *Journal of Forensic Sciences,* 13:33–45, 1968.

————. "Logical Content Analysis: An Explication of Styles of Concludifying," in GEORGE GERBNER *et al.* (eds.), *The Analysis of Communication Content.* New York: John Wiley and Sons, 1969.

————. "Psycho-logic: An Explication of Argument," in H. A. MURRAY (ed.), *Aspects of Personality* (in preparation).

————, and N. L. FARBEROW. "Clues to Suicide," *Public Health Reports,* 71:109, 1956.

———— (eds.) *Clues to Suicide.* New York: McGraw-Hill Book Company, 1957.

————. "Comparison Between Genuine and Simulated Suicide Notes by Means of Mowrer's DRQ," *Journal of General Psychology,* 56:251–256, 1957.

————. "TAT Heroes of Suicidal and Non-Suicidal Subjects," *Journal of Projective Techniques,* 22:211–218, 1958.

————. "Suicide and Death," in H. FEIFEL (ed.), *The Meaning of Death.* New York: McGraw-Hill Book Company, 1959.

————. "A Sociopsychological Investigation of Suicide," in H. P. DAVID and J. C. BRENGELMANN (eds.), *Perspectives in Personality Research.* New York: Basic Books, 1960.

————, and C. V. LEONARD. *Some Facts About Suicide.* Public Health Service Publication No. 852. Washington, D.C.: Government Printing Office, 1961.

SHNEIDMAN, E. S., and N. L. FARBEROW. *Suicide Prevention Center.* Los Angeles: University of Southern California Press, 1961.

————. "Sample Investigations of Equivocal Suicidal Deaths," in

N. L. FARBEROW and E. S. SHNEIDMAN (eds.), *The Cry for Help.* New York: McGraw-Hill Book Company, 1961.

———. *Suicide—The Problem and Its Magnitude.* Washington, D.C.: Department of Medicine and Surgery, Veterans Administration, *Medical Bulletin 7,* 1961.

———. "Statistical Comparisons between Attempted and Committed Suicides," in N. L. FARBEROW and E. S. SHNEIDMAN (eds.), *The Cry for Help.* New York: McGraw-Hill Book Company, 1961.

———. "The Los Angeles Suicide Prevention Center: A Demonstration of Feasibilities," *American Journal of Public Health,* 55: 21–26, 1965.

SHNEIDMAN, E. S., and P. MANDELKORN. "How to Prevent Suicide," *Public Affairs Pamphlet No. 406.* Washington, D.C.: Public Affairs Pamphlets, Inc., 1967.

SHNEIDMAN, E. S., and P. G. TRIPODES. *Feasibility Study on Computerizing Logical Patterns.* China Lake, California: U.S. Naval Ordnance Test Station, 1967.

Shockey v. Wash. Sanitarium, 11 CCH Neg (2) 1302 (Md. 1961).

SIEGEL, S. *Nonparametric Statistics for the Behavioral Sciences.* New York: McGraw-Hill Book Company, 1956.

SPARER, P. J. (ed.) *Personality, Stress and Tuberculosis.* New York: International University Press, 1956.

SPITZ, R. A. "The Derailment of Dialogue: Stimulus Overload, Action Cycles, and the Completion Gradient," *Journal of American Psychoanalytic Association,* 12:752–775, 1965.

STANTON, A. H., and M. S. SCHWARTZ. *The Mental Hospital.* New York: Basic Books, 1954.

STENGEL, E. "The Risk of Suicide in States of Depression," *Medical Practitioner,* 234:182–184, 1955.

———. "Some Unexplored Aspects of Suicide and Attempted Suicide," *Journal of Comprehensive Psychiatry,* 1:71–80, 1960.

———. *Suicide and Attempted Suicide.* Baltimore, Maryland: Penquin Books, 1964.

———, and NANCY G. COOK. *Attempted Suicide: Its Social Significance and Effects,* Maudsley Monograph No. 4. London: Chapman and Hall, Ltd., 1958.

STEPHENSON, W. S. *The Study of Behavior.* Chicago, Illinois: University of Chicago Press, 1953.

STORCH, A. *The Primitive Archaic Forms of Inner Experiences and Thought in Schizophrenia.* Washington, D.C.: Nervous and Mental Disease Publishing Co., 1924.

SWANBERG, W. A. *Citizen Hearst.* New York: Scribners, 1961.

SZASZ, T. S. *Law, Liberty, and Psychiatry.* New York: The Macmillan Company, 1963.

Szostak v. State of New York, 247 N.Y.S. 2d 770 New York, Mar. 19, 1964.

TABACHNICK, N. D. "Observations on Attempted Suicide," in E. S. SHNEIDMAN and N. L. FARBEROW (eds.), *Clues to Suicide.* New York: McGraw-Hill Book Company, 1957.

————. "Interpersonal Relations in Suicide Attempts," *Archives of General Psychiatry,* 4:16–21, 1961.

————. "Some Observations on Counter-Transference Crises in Suicidal Attempts," *Archives of General Psychiatry,* 4:572–578, 1961.

————. "Failure and Masochism," *American Journal of Psychotherapy,* 18:304, 1964.

————, and N. L. FARBEROW. "The Assessment of Self-destructive Potentiality," in N. L. FARBEROW and E. S. SHNEIDMAN (eds.), *The Cry for Help.* New York: McGraw-Hill Book Company, 1961.

TABACHNICK, N. D., and D. J. KLUGMAN. "No Name: A Study of Anonymous Suicidal Telephone Calls," *Psychiatry,* 28:79, 1965.

TABACHNICK, N. D., and R. E. LITMAN. "Character and Life Circumstances in Fatal Accident," *Psychoanalytic Forum,* 1:66, 1966.

Tate v. Canonica, 180 Cal. App. 2d 898, 5 Cal. Rptr. 28 (1960).

TOMKINS, S. S. *The Thematic Apperception Test.* New York: Grune and Stratton, 1947.

TRIPODES, P. G. *Reasoning Patterns in Suicide.* Los Angeles, California: Suicide Prevention Center, 1968.

TUCKMAN, J., R. J. KLEINER, and M. LAVELL. "Emotional Content of Suicide Notes," *American Journal of Psychiatry,* 116:59–63, 1959.

UNAMUNO, M. DE. *The Tragic Sense of Life.* Translated by E. C. FLITCH. Gloucester, Massachusetts: Peter Smith, 1921.

VAIL, D. J. "Suicide and Medical Responsibility," *American Journal of Psychiatry,* 15:1005–1010, 1959.

————, and MIRIAM KARLINS. "A Decade of Volunteer Services:

History and Social Significance," *International Journal of Social Psychiatry,* 11:105–109, 1965.

VERNIER, CLAIRE M., *et al.* "Psychosocial Study of the Patient with Pulmonary Tuberculosis: A Cooperative Research Project," *Psychology Monographs,* 75:32, 1961.

Vital Statistics of the United States, Vol. 2—Mortality. Part A. Washington, D.C.: U.S. Government Printing Office, 1965.

VON DOMARUS, E. "The Specific Laws of Logic in Schizophrenia," in J. S. KASANIN (ed.), *Language and Thought in Schizophrenia.* Berkeley and Los Angeles: University of California Press, 1944.

WEBB, M. W., and A. H. LAWTON. "Basic Personality Traits Characteristic of Patients With Primary Obstructive Pulmonary Emphysema," *Journal of American Geriatric Society,* 9:590–610, 1961.

WEISMAN, A. D., and T. P. HACKETT. "Predilection to Death: Death and Dying as a Psychiatric Problem," *Psychosomatic Medicine,* 23:232–256, 1961.

———. "The Dying Patient," *Forest Hospital Publications,* 1:16–21, 1962.

WEISS, E. *Emotional Factors in Cardiovascular Disease.* Springfield, Illinois: Charles C Thomas, 1951.

WEISS, J. M. A. "The Gamble with Death in Attempted Suicide," *Psychiatry,* 20:17–25, 1957.

WELFARE PLANNING COUNCIL. *Background for Planning.* Los Angeles, California: Welfare Planning Council, 1955, No. 15.

———. *Differentiating Communities in Los Angeles County.* Los Angeles, California: Welfare Planning Council, 1957.

———. *Fact Sheets on 100 Study Areas, Los Angeles County, 1957.* Los Angeles, California: Welfare Planning Council, 1957.

WERTENBAKER, L. T. *Death of a Man.* New York: Random House, 1957.

WHALLEY, E. "Values and Value-Conflict in Self-Destruction: Implications in the Work of C. W. Morris," in E. S. SHNEIDMAN (ed.), *Essays in Self-Destruction.* New York: Science House, 1967.

WHITE, R. W. "Sense of Interpersonal Competence," in R. W. WHITE (ed.), *The Study of Lives.* New York: Atherton Press, 1963.

WHORF, B. L. *Language, Thought and Reality,* ed. J. B. CARROLL. New York: John Wiley and Sons, 1956.

WILLIAMS, GLANVILLE. *The Sanctity of Life and the Criminal Law*. New York: Alfred Knopf, 1957.

WOLFGANG, M. E. *Patterns in Criminal Homicide*. Philadelphia: University of Pennsylvania Press, 1958.

————. "Suicide by Means of Victim-Precipitated Homicide," *Journal of Clinical and Experimental Psychopathology*, **20**:335, 1959.

WOLSTENHOLME, G. E. W., and M. O'CONNOR (eds.). *The Nature of Sleep*. Boston, Massachusetts: Little, Brown, 1960.

WOODWORTH, R. S., and S. B. SELLS. "An Atmosphere Effect in Formal Syllogistic Reasoning," *Journal of Experimental Psychology*, **18**:451–460, 1935.

YAP, P. M. *Suicide in Hong Kong*. London: Oxford University Press, 1958.

————. "Suicide in Hong Kong," *Journal of Mental Science*, **104**: 266–301, 1958.

YOLLES, S. F. *The Tragedy of Suicide in the United States*, Public Health Service Publication No. 1558. Washington, D.C.: Government Printing Office, 1966. Also in L. YOCHELSON (ed.). *Symposium on Suicide*. Washington, D.C.: George Washington University Press, 1967.

YULE, G. U., and N. KENDALL. *An Introduction to the Theory of Statistics*. New York: Hafner, 1950.

ZINSSER, H. *As I Remember Him*. Boston, Massachusetts: Little, Brown, 1940.

INDEX

DATE DUE

FEB 24 '88			
APR 13 '88			
DEC 14 '88			

DEMCO 38-297